Joseph M. Lugu

The Forbidden Fruit

This is the book you always wished someone would write, but thought no one could! Check out the strange spectacle as humans act out their wildly improbable antics during their one time stage performance on earth. And also check out Satan, that evillest of evil creatures, as he brags about his dubious accomplishments, and pines for the damnation of humans.

And you do not want to miss the scene in which the fictitious author breathes his last, crosses the gulf that separates the living from the dead and, unrepentant, prepares to meet His Mystic Majesty face to face for his final reckoning!

The Forbidden Fruit is a treatese on the knowledge of good and evil; and it damns and convicts sinful and sinning humans one and all without any distinction.

This is the untold story of Adam and Eve and their descendants. Prepare to take off on a cruise into realms of spirituality quite beyond anything you had ever dreamed of!

Your wish that someone would write a book exactly like this one has come true at long last. Relax, sit back now, and enjoy **The Forbidden Fruit**!

"Hellishly Delicious...

Sheer Devilish Delight!"

Joseph M. Luguya
Original Books
14404 Innsbruck Court
Silver Spring, MD, 20906
USA
Website: www.originalbooks.org

Library of Congress Control Number: 2010906713
ISBN-10: 0-9713309-3-X
ISBN-13: 9780971330931

November 2011

Created and written by Joseph M. Luguya

First Original Books Edition
Printed and produced in the United States of America
Signature Book Printing, www.sbpbooks.com

About the Author

The author is a graduate of the University of Nairobi, and a former Stanford-Sloan Fellow. A native of Uganda, Mr. Luguya has lived and worked in Kenya, Tanzania, Canada, and the United States. He is also the author of *Payment in Kind* (Kenya Literature Bureau, 1985).

About the Book
In the reviewers' words

(See the Reviews on the back page)

Publisher: The devil dismissed the seminarian as a neophyte and idiot. For his part, Christian Mjomba was focused on producing a winning thesis on the subject he had chosen, namely "*Original Virtue*"; and he was quite excited about the prospect of using the Evil One as his mouthpiece for expounding on the dogmas of the Church. If he succeeded in doing that, he would effectively be making the devil work for the salvation of souls and against himself! And for that, Mjomba became a marked man - in the exact same way that the subject matter of his thesis (Adam and Eve and their descendants) became from the moment the "Prime Mover" deigned to bring them into existence in His own Image and likeness.

Disclaimer:

This book is a work of fiction. The characters, names, businesses, organizations, places, events, incidents, dialogue and plot are the product of the author's imagination or are fictitiously used. Any resemblance to actual persons living or dead, names, events, or locales is entirely coincidental.

Acknowledgements:

To my family, for being a great inspiration, and for their support; and to the many individuals who genuinely could not wait to see *The Forbidden Fruit* in print.

Contents

1. The Demented Scholar

The Port Authority occupied twenty-eight floors in the thirty storey skyscraper. The towering structure, popularly known as the International Trade Center, enjoyed the distinction of being the tallest building in the country.

The site had been selected with great care. Consequently, as far as prime office locations went, with the exception of State House, the Port Authority did not have any rival. The International Trade Center literally sat on the edge of downtown Dar es Salaam, the beautiful metropolis located at the mouth of a natural sheltered harbor, and whose name fittingly signified "Heaven of Peace".

Christian Mjomba's office was located on the 27th floor. In an unusual move, using a key he took from his wallet, Mjomba unlocked a side door to his office and slid furtively inside. Mjomba himself did not recall ever using that side door. He seemed relieved that he had succeeded in gaining entrance to his office unnoticed by anyone, including his secretary.

Mjomba had never once employed the side door in that manner. Although he had occasionally thought of using it to evade unwelcome guests waiting in his secretary's *office en suite*, he had always resisted the urge to let himself out surreptitiously and disappear into the human traffic in the main corridor, as some of his unscrupulous colleagues did. He considered it demeaning to do that sort of thing.

Mjomba bolted the door shut behind him and eased his ample frame into a swivel chair by the fancy, glass-topped mahogany desk. He rested his elbows on the desk like someone in a daze, and sat slumped forward, so that his chin rested on the desk top. With his head thus bowed, Mjomba remained immobile for a long while.

As if to enhance his concentration, he kicked off his tight-fitting dress shoes, and rested his stockinged feet on the carpeted floor. The presence of Primrose, Mjomba's good and loyal secretary, was betrayed by the incessant pounding of typewriter keys as she worked away at her post.

The interconnecting door remained ajar from the time he walked though it with his leather brief case each morning - usually a little after nine O'clock in the morning - until he left to go home eight hours later. Primrose understood that this was her boss's wish, and was quite comfortable with the arrangement.

Primrose always exuded confidence that she could keep any unwanted visitors at bay despite her boss's office door being ajar. Which was just as well because, in the culture that existed at the Port Authority, the ability of a personal secretary to shield her boss from unwanted office guests was regarded as the hallmark of a good secretary.

As a matter of fact, it was partly as a tribute to Primrose's aptitude in that regard, and partly out of a desire to be different from everyone else that Mjomba preferred to leave the entrance to his office slightly ajar at all times. This applied even on those occasions when meetings were in progress inside, a sharp deviation from the general practice at the Port Authority.

Mjomba stared at the door and was glad that it was closed. He regretted that he was not in a position to actually bolt it from the inside. It still struck him as an unusual breach of custom for that door to be shut when he was right there in his office. It was odd enough that Primrose was unaware of his presence!

Mjomba's office had nothing special about it apart from the rich carpeting and the mahogany desk. A bookshelf to the right of the door was graced with the usual contents for someone of his station: Horngren's *Principles of Cost Accounting*, Samuelson's *Theory of Economics*, Drucker's *Management by Objectives*, a fat volume sporting the title *Ports of the World*, and Merriam-Webster's *Collegiate Dictionary*. *Group Think*, the title of a thin volume which was nestled in between the last two, was barely discernible from where he sat. Even though this was by far Mjomba's favorite publication in the collection, he would have been hard put to it to say who the author was. Even though that had not been the case many years earlier when, as a grad student, he had to read it from cover to cover overnight as a part of his preparation for a seminar in Management, it now seemed as if his overwhelming interest in the book's title not only had the effect of dampening any interest he might have in the book's author, but also of erasing the name, perhaps permanently, from his memory.

A framed certificate on the wall immediately above the bookshelf attested to the fact that Mjomba had a Master's degree in Business Administration from Stanford. A portrait of his wife and their two children stared at him from its distinctive spot on the upper most shelf.

Mjomba threw reluctant glances at a wooden tray labeled "IN TRAY". The tray was stacked high with sheaves of documents, several of which had stickers proclaiming that they required his immediate attention. To avoid being irked further by the sight of the pending work, Mjomba, acting somewhat impulsively, stuck out an arm and shoved the tray away from his sight so hard it very nearly tipped over. But he still found he had to spin his swivel chair around - nearly a hundred and eighty degrees - to keep the tray completely out of his line of vision.

He seemed well pleased with himself that the tray, with its load of pending work, now also occupied a part of the desk that was farthest away from the window. The desk was positioned so as to afford him a startling view of a busy section of the harbor, twenty-seven storeys below. It was a sunny and glorious morning as usual here on the East African seaboard. The view of the harbor was enlivened as usual by an interminable glow in the distance. The glow emanated from the oil refinery, a fixture on Dar es Salaam's ever-changing skyline since its construction a year and a half before.

The refinery itself was now barely visible on the horizon. Its tall chimney belched forth flames. Tongues of fire, they reached out into the clear blue skies as if in search of something to devour.

On a normal day, the usually flamboyant and carefree Mjomba would not have had any qualms about letting his gaze stray from work on his desk, or even individuals with whom he was in private conference, to take in the magnificent scene. It was, after all, constantly being remarked by his office guests that his office suite provided an angle of vision of the harbor that seemed quite unique.

On this particular morning, however, his chest caved in and shoulders slouched sideways, Mr. Mjomba had done something he rarely did if ever. He had buried his face in his arms, and appeared to be in a stupor of some sort. He had even allowed his elongated frame to assume a posture that made him resemble a hunchback! It was a far cry from Mjomba's usual appearance at the Port Authority, and he looked very odd in the otherwise serene surroundings of his office.

With the physical world effectively shut out and his sense faculties denied their usual indulgence, Mjomba's faculties of the imagination and intellect went on a wild rampage.

Although physically present at the Port Authority, mentally and spiritually he was back at the rented bungalow on Msasani Peninsula, where he lived with his wife, Jamila, and their two children. In his imagination, he was reliving the events that had occurred there that morning as he prepared to leave for work. Judging by his appearance, Mjomba was resigned to the fact that those events had, for all practical purposes, already marred the rest of his day.

Even though crestfallen, there was something about Mjomba's mien which suggested beyond any doubt that he was determined to revive his spirits. Without moving, his lips seemed to be saying to himself that dwelling on his early morning confrontation with Jamila was the surest way to bring that off! It was a ludicrous idea, to be sure; but one, nonetheless, whose appeal was irresistible. While he did not really believe it, he persuaded himself that to do otherwise, in the present circumstances was tantamount to running away from an intractable problem.

Mjomba, accordingly, decided to sit back and carefully weigh everything that had transpired that morning. He was unable to concentrate on anything else in any case. And so, oblivious to his immediate surroundings, he continued to mull over the sharp verbal exchange between Jamila and himself earlier that morning.

Mjomba was in this peculiar frame of mind when it occurred to him that it might be worth his while to put himself in his wife's shoes as it were, and to reconstruct what had transpired that morning from her perspective. And so, listless and clutching his head between both arms, he now began to imagine that he was Jamila!

In his mind's eye, Mjomba saw himself reclining on a love seat at the far end of their living room. That was where Jamila had proceeded after waiting on him. A quick mental inspection of himself - or rather herself - and he was satisfied that he looked and acted exactly like Jamila to wit!

So there "she" sat, one ear alert to any movement in the children's bedroom down the hallway, and the other listening to the clutter of silverware and china as the monster or ghoul (judging from Jamila's attitude that morning, she obviously thought of him as some monster or ghoul!) consumed its breakfast. Yes, ghoul and an unfeeling one at that! There it sat - the monster.

Mjomba retreated momentarily from the make believe world of acting. Back in the security of his office at the Port Authority, he ruminated on the fact that he had not found it that difficult to imagine what went on inside his wife's mind while he helped himself on his breakfast. A natural actor, he had just let himself go and allowed his imagination free reign. It had been as simple as that! It was clear that nothing was going to prevent him from stepping back into Jamila's shoes and acting her part - if that was what it was going to take to establish what was really happening to set the record straight. Not even the fact that their physiques were dissimilar. He was convinced that he had done her no wrong, and was determined to establish his innocence.

By a simple process of metamorphosis, Mjomba was able, as he sat doubled up at his desk, to imagine that he was Jamila and was relaxing in the love seat in the living room of their seaside bungalow, savoring the aroma of the Arabica coffee. His large feet not only fit snugly in her tiny slippers, but he was also able to pretend that he was cuddling a nine-month-old baby inside his tummy!

Resuming his place on the love seat, Mjomba saw that, by all counts, the solitary figure at the dining table was enjoying yet another undeserved serving of pancakes, fried bacon, a sausage, and the almost obligatory scrambled egg on toast, all washed down with steaming black coffee. Most annoying of all was the fact that he always seemed to be in a rush at this particular time, and was consequently not in a position to enjoy the food she had devoted so much precious energy and time to prepare the way it was supposed to be enjoyed.

The clutter, lo and behold, came presently to an abrupt halt, signalling the end of Mjomba's morning meal. "Jamila" watched as, with a smack of his lips, "her" husband rose from his chair and stretched out his arms contentedly.

There was a break in Mjomba's train of thoughts at that particular point in time as he shifted in his chair and allowed himself the indulgence of a giggle. But the conviviality was short-lived. For, almost immediately, the guileless Mjomba relapsed into the sombre mood which had characterized his demeanour for much of that morning; and he allowed his flight of fancy to continue on its bizarre course.

And so, stepping back into his wife's shoes, he continued to playact in hopes that being so preoccupied was going to solve his problem. He - or rather "she"- immediately observed that "her" husband's movements, as he expressed his contentment with the meal "she" had prepared for him, revealed a tiny but noticeable bulge around his middle.

Even as Mjomba was thus engaged in his new role as the devoted and loving wife, he could not help indulging himself in escapades. In his mind's eye, Mjomba saw Jamila smile faintly at the fleeting thought that potbellies were a trademark of the affluent in this part of the globe. But the smile faded swiftly as the unpleasant things associated with excessive weight began to crowd in her mind: heart attacks, hypertension, an ungainly appearance - the list seemed endless! As Mjomba imagined it, his wife knew, or at least suspected, that all this while as she was thus engrossed, Mjomba took absolutely no notice of her presence in that house, let alone her condition and feelings.

At that point in time, the real Mjomba at the Port Authority was unable to put up with the make believe any longer. It was clear that apart from constituting an insult to his beloved Jamila, what he had just indulged in was quite reckless. How, indeed, could a person of his standing act as stupidly as he had just done! He decided forthwith that he could not let events be dictated entirely by a faculty of the imagination gone wild. Deciding that it was time for ordinary common sense to take charge again, Mjomba conceded that he had allowed his fertile imagination to run wild. He certainly did not believe that his imagination had enslaved him - at least not quite yet.

It did not appear conceivable that the problem which had led to his present predicament could have started the way he was imagining. It had to be more intricate than that, he avowed, as he finally stepped out of Jamila's shoes.

It had become apparent to Mjomba by now that the more he worried himself with regard to this whole thing, the more ridiculous it was all proving to be. But Mjomba was still irked by the fact that something about his wife's appearance, as he stepped away from his breakfast table and inclined forward to kiss her good day, had caused him to suddenly stop and exclaim: "What is the matter now, Jamila darling?"

Groping around now for something to use to reassure himself, Mjomba allowed that he was not normally given to voicing empty or harried expressions. He certainly knew that it was not characteristic of Jamila either to hurl words at him. But, in what seemed - to him at least - to be a fit of anger, she had shot back: "You are the one who looks like you have a problem!"

Mjomba recalled how, utterly mollified and reeling under the load of shame he suddenly felt for having started it all with his brash reaction, he had gingerly lifted his gaze to meet hers. He had always taken pride in the fact that he knew his spouse like the palm of his hand. He believed that she, too, knew him like the palm of her hand; and he even attributed the strength of their marital relations to this.

He had, therefore, had no doubt that he was going to find Jamila's eyes, even at that late stage, a mirror of sympathy and understanding.

Mjomba was unable to stifle a giggle as he acknowledged that he had been dumb to have expected anything like that to happen. Indeed, his action had only had the opposite effect, eliciting words that seemed plainly calculated to have an even more devastating effect on him. The words, selected carefully, had come out of Jamila's mouth with a spontaneity which suggested that she had been laying in wait for him to make just the kind of mistake he was then making so she would let hell loose on him.

"What is biting you?" Jamila had continued with obvious relish.

It had been so unlike the Jamila he knew. Something now told him that she had been intent on hurting him from the start, and that she had added those last words for the specific purpose of rubbing it in!

Thinking back on the episode from the relative security of his office, the normally ebullient Mjomba admitted to himself that he was petrified all right as he faced his wife in their living room that morning.

"She is one of a sort!" he hissed, recalling how completely disarmed and helpless he had felt in her presence. He had also felt a stinging awkwardness as he stood there meekly, in a stance that could only be described as humble submission! Mjomba smiled as he tried to visualize what exactly went on inside her mind at that particular moment in time during their confrontation.

With everyone's emotions running so high, a lot more than what met the eye must have occurred in those extraordinary minutes. And, according to what Mjomba could now recall, he had tried to prepare himself for the very worst as Jamila, encircling her outsized tummy with ordinarily slender but now somewhat beefy arms, added nonchalantly: "For the whole of last week - for quite sometime now in fact - you have been acting queer, as if the entire world's worries had all of a sudden been eased on your shoulders!"

Mjomba had felt considerable relief seeing his wife settle back in her seat after she had mouthed those last words. Almost immediately afterward, however, Jamila had inclined her head to one side, casting at him what he was only now realizing had been an accusing glance!

Mjomba mourned softly, and was deeply vexed as he wondered how his adorable Jamila, who was almost constantly on his mind, could even as much as insinuate that he, Mjomba of all people, was neglecting her!

Elbows planted firmly on top of the desk, Mjomba hugged his head at the temples with his closed fists, and shut his eyes tightly. The features of his face were frozen in a grimace. Opening his eyes moments later, something strange happened. It was a mere coincidence that he was gazing in the direction of the bookshelf when he opened his eyes. He instinctively began inspecting the meagre contents of his personal library at the office. But then he saw or thought he was seeing, nestled between Samuelson's *Theory of Economics* and Drucker's *Management by Objectives*, a thin but very handsome volume titled *The Psychic Roots of Innocent Kintu*! It was there one moment, and the next moment it wasn't.

Mjomba had no doubt that his senses were playing tricks on him. At the very least he had to be dreaming, he told himself. The thought of becoming a victim of chicanery at the time he was trying to extricate himself from what he saw as big trouble involving his darling Jamila did not quite go down well with Mjomba. But, on the other hand, the temptation to take some time and verify that he was really seeing a printed and bound copy of the "masterpiece" he had been writing there on the bookshelf alongside the classics in his book collection, and that it was not a mirage, was too great to resist.

Mjomba rubbed his eyes hard, and then closed them systematically. When he opened his now heavy eye lids to peer at the spot where he had seen his "masterpiece", to his surprise and anger, it was no longer there! It was gone!

Mjomba rolled his eyes, grinned and allowed a huge smile to envelope his face. It was a gracious - and knowing - smile. Presumably as a result of being under prolonged pressure, Mjomba was becoming prone to whims of his imagination. While he wished to be realistic and admit that he had not seen any thin volume titled *The Psychic Roots of Innocent Kintu* there on the bookshelf alongside those other masterpieces, Mjomba did not wish to entirely disappoint himself by ruling that possibility out together. He told himself that he wasn't doing anybody any harm or injustice by going along with the illusion that he was already a published author!

He was in a kind of a fix, of course. He had to be realistic and admit that his work-in-progress hadn't yet been transformed into a slick volume which could rub shoulders with works by the likes of Samuelson and Horngren, on the one hand; but, if he were ever going to succeed as writer, he occasionally had to kid himself that, for all practical purposes, he *was* already a published and celebrated author in all but name! In other words, he had to go along with the illusion that he was already a famous author. And if doing that meant that he had to use a bit of his imagination and pretend that a printed and bound copy of his book was sharing space on his bookshelf with the works of other authors, so be it, he reassured himself.

To the extent that he himself had read what he had written and liked it, he had in fact already been published and was a celebrated author. The fact that the nitwits he was writing for hadn't gotten an opportunity to read his material was relevant only in so far as the massive flow of revenues from his book into his bank account was concerned. And, if push came to shove, Mjomba wouldn't really give a damn if no one purchased his book. He figured that the real losers, if his work was not bought and read would be the readership he was targeting - and that included everyone, both literate and illiterate.

He had not only created the manuscript in its entirety, but he had also read and reread it innumerable times, not to mention writing and rewriting it almost as many times. He felt that if there was anyone in a position to announce to the world that there was within that manuscript at the very minimum the essence of a very good book, it was himself.

Judging by the changed expression on Mjomba's face, it no longer appeared to matter at all that everything about his "masterpiece" sharing the spotlight with the works of the likes of

Drucker and Samuelson was so dreamlike and unreal. And it was evident that Mjomba had already decided - for the moment or, more accurately, for the occasion - that, regardless of the reality, *The Psychic Roots of Innocent Kintu* had been published long ago and belonged there on the bookshelf, and that its handsome blue cover, designed by Primrose, was in fact hugging the ugly and worn covers of the works of Samuelson and Drucker!

Mjomba accordingly rolled his eyes this way and that, and continued to gloat over the fact that he was a published author whose fame would in time rival, and perhaps even surpass, that of the Americans.

Mjomba's eyes were wide open now, but his catalepsy continued uninterrupted. It actually no longer mattered an iota that the thin volume titled *The Psychic Roots of Innocent Kintu*, sitting there on the mantle, was a figment of his imagination. Almost everything he had seen since waking up that morning seemed cut out for a work of fiction any way, and it seemed unlikely that allowing himself to be deluded in that manner was going to alter things that much.

Even though it was something which Mjomba's fertile imagination had fabricated in its entirety, the "vision" was real enough while it lasted to make the messy pile in the In-Tray vanish completely from sight along with the in-tray itself.

The gloom that had plagued him not long before and the mysterious woe-be-gone expression in which his face had been engulfed became things of the past as a grinning Mjomba continued to gloat over his tome. He did not believe that anything could be more beautiful than the sight of *The Psychic Roots of Innocent Kintu* as it shared a rare platform with the works of Samuelson and Drucker among others.

Confidently, Mjomba reclined back in his seat and stared in the direction of the oil refinery which was framed by the wall of glass representing his window. The refinery's chimney was clearly visible in the distance; and the incinerating flames, surging up and disappearing into the ethereal blue, made a beautiful sight indeed. But there was something about them which was starting to remind him of Jamila, and he immediately looked away. That also caused him to spin the swivel chair around, so that he found himself once more glaring at the In-Tray which was still piled high with urgent memoranda, vouchers, audit schedules, accounting reports that were crammed with figures and stuff like that, much to his discomfort.

His hands became clammy, and beads of sweat started ringing his forehead. But his gaze remained transfixed on the In-Tray - as if keeping watch over it made any difference to the fact that someone, if not he himself, would have to review the tray's contents and take necessary action on the individual documents!

Mjomba remained still for a long while. He was clearly at the end of his tether, and his countenance said it all. The bout of depression he had been battling since jumping into his car to drive to work that morning had evidently gotten the better of him, and the expression on his face seemed to acknowledge that much. And, as was typical of people who found themselves in situations of that nature, he had been inclined to think that it was natural - and, in fact, quite OK - to seek refuge in distractions of one sort or another.

The favored distraction in Mjomba's particular case apparently had been employing his imagination to picture himself in extreme situations of euphoria or of doom. Relieving his earlier experience at home and then persuading himself that he was already a celebrated writer were undoubtedly the two ways in which he had sought to distract himself and escape from reality.

Mjomba finally succeeded in stirring from his lethargy. But he did so only to realize that it was now the image of his manuscript as a can of worms which was firmly stuck in his mind. As if that was not bad enough, he also discovered that it was not going to go away easily. And his suspicions that his book project was the root cause of his problems now, predictably, aggravated his depression.

Mjomba first got an inkling of the fact that his "dark night of the soul" was over when his prized "masterpiece", *The Psychic Roots of Innocent Kintu*, vanished from its place besides the works of Drucker and Samuelson.

Yes - dark night of the soul! From the time he was introduced, as a minor seminarian, to ascetical works featuring the likes of Francis of Assisi, Jerome, and others who, because they were beloved of God, were almost permanently under assault by demons and had to live through innumerable so-called “dark nights of the soul”, Mjomba always imagined that “depressions”, because they too supposedly caused their victims unspeakable spiritual torment, amounted to “dark nights of the soul”!

Mjomba was able to track the real whereabouts of his masterpiece to the top most shelf. Transformed into a plain blue file folder and a stack of neatly typed sheets of paper, perhaps two hundred or so in number, the manuscript lay there, innocently, not far off from the framed portrait of his loving Jamila and their two children.

The folder and the neat stack of papers comprising the manuscript appeared to be staring down at him menacingly from where they were perched. The folder, which had been cut to size and spotted a plain white sticker on its topside, was leaning ever so slightly against the neat stack. The legend on the sticker proclaimed in large bold letters: **The Psychic Roots of Innocent Kintu**.

Mjomba seemed both puzzled and troubled that his book manuscript with the colored folder Primrose had designed for it had not caught his eye earlier. They both made such a distinctive and striking sight

A visibly relaxed Mjomba now took time to survey the bookshelf's other contents. It was the second time he was doing so this morning; and this time around, he made a point of reading the titles aloud to himself. He did so not once but twice. And he would have extended his hand to touch and feel the books themselves if they had been within easy reach.

A touch of unreality surrounded Mjomba's every move. Although the library he maintained back at his beach side residence was much more extensive and impressive, he appeared to relish every moment he was spending examining the bookshelf's contents.

Mjomba rolled his eyes uneasily, and stared up into the ceiling for a moment or so in a meaningless gesture before returning his gaze to the bookshelf. The fact that nothing had changed seemed to signal that he had regained a measure of control over his life. It was at that juncture that he made a point of reminding himself that the folder, and certainly the manuscript the folder was designed to hold, were things he had to continue to keep concealed from his wife - for now at any rate.

Shifting in his seat, Mjomba changed his stance and, relaxing his fists, buried his head in his open palms. It was while in this new position that Mjomba started reminiscing over his decision to not let Jamila in on his book project until such a time as he would deem appropriate. And doing so inevitably lead him back to the topic that, to all appearances, he had been trying to avoid.

With no immediate obstacle in the way, Mjomba's faculties of the imagination and intellect now, of their own accord, became transfixed on the events of that morning at his beach-side home. Mjomba would even have sworn that there was absolutely nothing in the whole wide world at that particular point in time that was capable of distracting him, even only momentarily, from doing what he had to do - namely concentrate on that early morning encounter.

A fleeting idea exactly to that effect in fact crossed his mind just as the palms of his hand relented their grip about his temples. Then, as if calculated to prove him wrong, his office door flew open and Primrose burst in. The single, pink sheet of paper she clasped between the index fingers of her right hand fluttered to the floor as she careened to an abrupt stop.

"It is you?" she gasped. "For a moment I thought I was having a vision!"

In response to the "Hi" that Mjomba muttered under his breath, Primrose, who had already sensed that her boss was not in his usual mood, quickly retrieved the sheet of paper from the floor, and was about to place it alongside the book manuscript on the shelf when Mjomba held out his hand.

"The blurb," she said in a virtual whisper. She handed him the sheet of paper and retreated, closing the door behind her. It was the final draft for the blurb for his forthcoming novel. With very little work on her hands, Primrose had gone out of her way and in effect used the blurb to produce a design of sorts for the book's back cover. She had produced an ingenious design by typing the blurb's text in the shape of an inverted pyramid balancing on top of another pyramid.

The strange pattern on the sheet of paper as it fell to the floor had caught Mjomba's eye, and its likeness to the letter X of the alphabet had caused the expression "X-Generation" to immediately spring to his mind. Mjomba could not help leaning forward for a closer examination of the peculiar pattern. He noted with a smile that it was, indeed, the proposed blurb for his book which his resourceful secretary had employed to create the bizarre pattern. He did not know whether to applaud her effort in that regard or to get angry with her. At that particular juncture, he found himself unable to resist reading the text aloud to himself:

'Exquisitely lush, incredibly picturesque and spellbinding,
Zundaland is situated on the Equator in Africa's
heartland. It is probably also the
original Garden of Eden.
Until the arrival
of
missionaries
from Europe, the
Wazunda, in accordance with
time-honored customs and traditions,
accorded Lhekha-Zinda, father of the Zunda
Nation, and the rest of their ancestors the full respect
that was due to them. Not surprisingly, in the
ears of the tradition-bound and, indeed,
proud people of Zundaland,
the "New Testament"
the strangers

were
proclaiming,
continued for quite
sometime to sound truly like
a "*Novel Testament*"! Unfortunately
for Lhekha-Zinda and the venerable ancestors,
it was a situation that was not to last for very long.,

The previous day, as Mjomba was dictating the blurb's text to his secretary, he could have sworn that it was the very final version. He had actually spent an enormous amount of time and energy drafting the blurb for his "masterpiece", the one word which most often came to his mind whenever he reflected on his literary project. In Mjomba's mind, revisiting it not only was out of question, but would be to no avail because it was so perfect. He had effectively persuaded himself that there was no way his blurb could be improved further!

But now, scarcely twenty-four hours later, it occurred to Mjomba that the blurb as it stood outlined a story that was completely different from his original one. It also dawned on him that none of the names featured in the blurb appeared anywhere in the body of the manuscript!

Mjomba's spirits were, arguably, already at a low point; and the realization that he was in a new jam dampened them even further. But it also provided a new and undoubtedly welcome distraction.

And so, relegating his early morning brawl with the mother of his children to the back of his mind, Mjomba turned to confront the new situation which had just cropped up. He made a mental note that the only other option - rewriting the manuscript - was completely out of question. The manuscript, he told himself, was perfect as it was and any attempt to rework his book would damage it irrevocably.

Mjomba had no doubt about the fact that the material in his book would make delightful reading for anybody. He also thought the blurb was kind of long winded, and certainly not suitable as an introduction to a work of great stature like *The Psychic Roots of*

Innocent Kintu. This was despite the fact that he still liked the blurb as it was currently fashioned very much.

On the spur of the moment, he decided that he was going to polish it just a little; and he would do it right there and then. He liked the original blurb, and wasn't intending to alter very much. But he was confident that no one would notice any conflict between the blurb and the book after he was done! Since he himself liked both the blurb and the manuscript, he did not think it was asking too much to expect his readers to do the same. They were a dumb lot any way, he mumbled to himself. As for the publishers, he did not have any time for them really. If they proved tardy in jumping on the band wagon, he could easily take care of that situation by setting up his own publishing company, and making the masterpiece he had worked so hard to produce his first title!

With a flourish, Mjomba set the sheet down, took a silver-gilded pen from his shirt pocket, and began scribbling in the margins: "But the greatest respect and honor", Mjomba wrote "was reserved for *Were*, the all-knowing, life-giving Wind. When the Wazunda went hunting in the forest, planted crops, celebrated a good harvest or the coming of age of their youth with feasting and dancing - or, indeed, when they did anything involving two or more adult members of the community - they always did these things to the greater honor and glory of *Were*."

Mjomba circled the material he had inserted in the margins, and drew an arrow to indicate where the new material belonged, namely just before the last sentence but one on the sheet. He skimmed through the revised blurb rapidly from beginning to end, struck out the last two sentences of the original version of the blurb, and scribbled the following in the space immediately below: "Not only did the 'New Testament' which was being proclaimed by the strangers sound truly like a 'Novel Testament', in the eyes of the general populace, the new doctrines constituted a brazen assault on their mores, and on the hallowed traditions of the land. But for Annamaria Mvyengwa and Victor Nkharanga, both of whom were misfits in their society, it was a Godsend!"

Brimming with obvious pleasure at this latest demonstration of the creative genius in him, Mjomba was in the process of returning the pen to his shirt pocket when he stopped in his tracks.

Something told him that he had not really done anything to the blurb to make it sell his "masterpiece" the way he wanted it to do. The entire blurb seemed to be about religious beliefs, said little or nothing about political domination and social change, and not one word about the author!

In a rare display of impatience, the young up-and-coming executive *cum* celebrated author brought the expensive-looking pen crashing down on the glass desktop; and, seizing the sheet of paper with the amended blurb, he crumpled it into a tiny ball using both hands. Then, without any hint as to what he was about to do, Mjomba aimed the jumbled remains of the blurb at the certificate on the wall, just narrowly missing his mark. He worked swiftly and furiously, as if the gesture was going to compensate in some fashion for the fact that he hadn't been doing what he was supposed, namely brooding about the events of that morning in the living room of his beach-side home.

Up until this time, Mjomba had gone about the business of amending the blurb hesitatingly and may be even reluctantly. But a strange force now took over, inducing him to get into high gear and to go about that whole business really aggressively and purposefully. The change that came over Mjomba was as sudden as it was unpredictable.

The fact that he was now operating under the influence of some mysterious force somehow did not detract from the meticulousness that normally characterized Mjomba's approach to creative activity. The fact that he was having a little help from the "mystic" powers actually appeared, if anything, to be facilitating the job of producing a revised blurb. For one, he did not now require a pen and paper to do so!

True to form, Mjomba began by taking note of a tiny, translucent screen-like object somewhere at the back of his skull. He felt an irresistible urge to read the messages which appeared thereon at the same time. The minuscule screen, which was visible only to the mind and not to the eye, presently blossomed into a giant screen, not at all unlike those employed for screening films in drive-in cinemas. The first thing which appeared on the screen, predictably, was the introductory section of the new and, he had decided, final version of the blurb for his forthcoming book.

Mjomba's face was a mask of equanimity as he turned to scan the text of the blurb as its lines came streaming into view on the mysterious screen from nowhere. He did so by grinding both fists against his temples, narrowing his pupils, and staring straight ahead of him into the mysterious void! He closed his eyes slowly and then opened them again - slowly and apprehensively. He was clearly weary lest he did anything that would either cause his mystic powers to vanish or that, alternatively, would jolt his senses back to reality and its boring routine. Without letting go of his temples, Mjomba leaned back gently and continued to savor his newly found freedom. He found himself propelled on by the mere thought that his imagination was enjoying a totally unfettered and indisputably free reign once again.

Even though a virtual prisoner in his *office en suite*, Mjomba felt as free as a bird. He was surprised to find that he did not actually have to exert himself in anyway to be creative, and he certainly did not have to think hard to get results. Once the first lines for his brand new blurb materialized on the giant screen and started drifting one by one to the lower end of the screen, others just kept popping up at the upper end.

As he pressed on with this new burst of creative effort, Mjomba could not help noticing that whenever he opened and shut his eyes, that act of blinking in and of itself assured the appearance of additional material on the screen! This did not strike him as strange at all. If his experience was anything to go by, the strangest things happened in the creative realm, and especially when one gave one's imagination free reign to explore uncharted ground.

Mjomba generated the new blurb so effortlessly, it felt like he was simply lifting or, possibly even, plagiarizing the material from some other original source. At the end of that exercise, the individual lines of the new blurb were indelibly etched in his mind.

As the ideas for the new blurb translated themselves mysteriously into text on the invisible screen, a suggestion (which just seemed fascinating and did not appear strange in the least) also kept popping up in his mind. It was to the effect that this new blurb summed up the material covered by *The Psychic Roots of Innocent Kintu* much more accurately and succinctly than anything else he could have produced. Mjomba found this comforting, even though he suspected that it was not quite the case.

As had happened earlier, he could not resist reading aloud to himself the text of the new blurb as it flashed on the screen.

"This is a fascinating account of a community" he began, "whose members find themselves almost overnight under new political masters. A proud people who treasure their cultural traditions, they not only find themselves now a subjugated people, but they are also confronted with very rapid social change which quickly culminates in a new social order!

"The new social order, furthermore, comes complete with a new theocracy which is centered around the 'New Testament' as it is called. In the eyes of the general populace, the New Testament proclaimed by the strangers sounds truly like a 'Novel Testament'.

"But it is also the story of a maniacal scholar with a runaway imagination (the forerunner of a new breed of scholars?) and his bizarre antidote for a ravaging, hitherto unknown disease with no known cure.

"Dubbed 'Brain Death' by the peasants, the disease appears to single out for its prey those individuals in the community who display the greatest loyalty to the new social order. It just so happens that members of the country's tiny elite belong to this group; and, consequently, the general consensus is that the disease has its origins in the West."

Mjomba found everything about the new blurb quite fascinating. Reflecting on the reference to "Brain Death", he was wondering if it might be all that hard to write a novel with that title when all sorts of ideas started flooding his mind. He knew that he didn't have the power to stop the flood even if he wanted. It did not matter that he still needed to apply himself or at least get his train of thoughts going before the flood gates opened. He had just made himself comfortable in his seat when his mind became deluged with ideas about a mysterious ailment which had suddenly becomes the focus of everybody's attention as it struck deep in the heart of Africa.

Mjomba did not need any further prodding to come up with a plot for such a novel. All he needed to do to get it registered permanently in his mind was to locate the tiny, translucent screen-like object at the back of his skull, and begin scanning the text as it materialized thereupon. He did just that, and watched as the tiny screen instantly blossomed into a giant screen, making his task really easy.

Everything went just as expected. In his mind, Mjomba saw the first lines of the plot for the story about a hypothetical pandemic in Africa's heartland begin to materialize on a giant screen, just as the latest version of his blurb had done. To make things even easier, a mystery voice, rapping in a peculiar but easily discernible fashion, echoed the individual sentences as they began forming at the top of the screen and then continued to stream downwards.

"An unknown disease with no known cure is detected in a fast developing, exceedingly lush, region of sub-Saharan Africa" the mystery rapper said in a whisper. "The disease, a debilitating brain condition which the largely peasant population refer to as 'Brain Death', strikes following a specific but as yet unpredictable cycle. To the consternation of everyone, the disease appears to single out members of the lettered minority, and especially those who are intellectually endowed. Curiously, the peasantry, whose members are largely illiterate and tradition-bound, display a relative immunity to the mysterious disease. Also, because the intellectual elite in these parts are, by and large, the product of missionary schools, the disease's victims are invariably fervent Christians!

"Enter Mjomba, a member of the seminary brotherhood, and a student of philosophy and theology. He thinks he is already toast and expects to be the next one to fall prey to the brain disorder for which there was no known cure. He does not want to die in that fashion and become a statistic, and he concludes early on that his only hope lies in he himself unravelling the mystery behind the dread disease.

"Undaunted, Mjomba sets out on his mission which appears doomed from inception. He is armed only with his aptitude for applying the Scholastic Method (which he has learned about in Philosophy class) to the most implausible situations, and a dubious knack for translating perceptions in the metaphysical realm into common words!

"Mjomba's interest in the disease has actually been triggered by what befell a close pal of his by the name of Innocent Kintu. A member of the seminary brotherhood like Mjomba and a fellow tribesman as well, Kintu has, sadly, been reduced to a vegetable by the disease; and he has been consigned to the care of Professor Claus Gringo, a renowned psychiatrist...".

The mysterious voice trailed off just as the screen went blank, a sign that he had actually ran out of ideas. He had, in any case, begun to notice that some of the material with which his mind was being fed for incorporation in the plot for the hypothetical novel was coming straight from ***The Psychic Roots of Innocent Kintu***!

It was also at that point that, suddenly and without any warning whatsoever, Mjomba picked up the pen from the table and, with a sudden jerk of his arm, transformed it into a missile of sorts. He seemed decidedly relieved that he had sent his pen hurtling toward the far end of the room. Ignoring Primrose, who had heard the commotion and was peering at him through the half-opened door, Mjomba stood up and rammed the wooden desk-top hard with his fist. He sank back into the chair as the door closed and his secretary's face disappeared behind it as silently as it had appeared. Then, as if for lack of anything to do, he proceeded to bury his head between his arms, clutching at his temples with his fists just like he had done on several previous occasions.

It was evident, at the end of the long moment which passed, that Mjomba had finally woken up to the fact that he had betrayed his beloved Jamila. Contrary to his earlier solemn resolution, he had, rather sadly, gone back on his word and allowed his attention to be distracted from the matter at hand!

He now looked more dishevelled than ever. But, contrary to appearances, his thoughts were actually more focused than at any time before. Focused once again on the events that had transpired at the bungalow earlier that morning.

The silence, which had reigned momentarily, was broken by sounds which came from the adjoining room as Primrose apparently continued to chuckle to herself. Listening to her chuckles caused him to instantly recall what he had done to the original blurb. Looking around, he easily located the crumpled piece of paper perched precariously on top of the manuscript.

Mjomba forced a smile at the thought that it was the same spot where Primrose had originally intended to leave it in the first place. But the image of an inverted pyramid balancing on top of another pyramidal shape flooded Mjomba's mind with a force which made him feel as if he might pass out. He attributed his ability to stay afloat and not drift off into a swoon to the fact that he was able to focus his mind on the peculiar design Primrose had produced using the blurb's material and its similarity to the letter "X"!

Even in the middle of his adversity, Mjomba could not help fantasizing about a boundless market out there for his book consisting largely of members of the so-called X-Generation. It was not quite the most auspicious time to fantasize about that sort of thing; but Mjomba found himself recalling that, on a couple of occasions in the past, he had come very close to tossing out his manuscript with his office garbage! He had persuaded himself on those occasions that he would be better off devoting the time he was taking to write and rewrite it on more useful things.

In retrospect, it looked so ridiculous that he had even contemplated doing such a thing. He even wondered if there hadn't been anything the matter with him for ideas as absurd as those to have had any appeal. It was so totally unbelievable. Mjomba found himself struggling to contain himself. The loud explosion of

Mjomba's laughter induced a shrill but short-lived rejoinder from Primrose in the adjoining room.

Mjomba checked himself quickly. This was even though he did not care less if his secretary sometimes caught him with the wrong foot down. Prim, as his secretary was popularly referred to in the corridors of the Trade Center, was a conscientious employee who firmly believed that a *personal* secretary was, by definition, also a *confidential* secretary. Mjomba's trust in her could be gauged from the fact that he had entrusted her with the task of typing up the final edited version of his book manuscript. She was the only other individual who knew about his literary project.

Primrose had seen her boss at work on the manuscript on countless occasions, and had arrived at the conclusion that being a good writer not only required enormous concentration, but staying the course represented the greatest drain imaginable on the energies of a human being. She had, therefore, no doubt that her boss regarded ***The Psychic Roots of Innocent Kintu*** as very important work. As for her own accidental involvement, she preferred to think about it as a simple labor of love. And just knowing that he trusted her to keep the project a secret from Jamila until the book was ready to go to press made her feel really honored.

Mjomba knew that he could get into serious trouble if his use of office resources for his private project were discovered. He also knew, however, that his secretary, who alone was in a position to blow the whistle on him, wasn't the type to ever want to see him in any trouble, leave alone trouble of that kind. To make doubly sure that she would never be tempted to turn traitor, he made a special point of giving her the best employee evaluation ratings ever and also a raise every year.

In spite of that, Mjomba recognized the seriousness of the situation which was underscored by the fact that there was always the remote possibility that Primrose could decide for whatever reason to screech and, in his words, hand him over to the dogs. But Mjomba was easily able to rationalize away any feelings of guilt and to justify his actions in that particular regard simultaneously, thanks to his fertile imagination and abiding sense of humor.

While he understood that he was in the wrong and risked ruining his career by being in breach of such a fundamental workplace canon, he always told himself that if he was doing any wrong, it was could only be in an academic sense! Thus, while Mjomba knew that the violation of such a rule, particularly by a senior member of staff who was also expected to set a good example, carried with it extremely grave consequences, he saw it very differently in practical terms.

The dangers inherent in the misuse of one's office were lost on Mjomba almost as quickly as they surfaced. In his view, the one thing that was paramount in all of this business was not the observance of a rubric. It was creativity. He even rationalized that being a published author was in fact going to benefit his career. Since this happened to Europeans and Americans who were published, Mjomba reckoned that there had to be an even greater likelihood of it happening to him here in this so-called Dark Continent where close to ninety percent of the populace still had to discover the three R's!

Talking of Europeans and Americans, Mjomba once in a while entertained the truly weird notion that his own peculiar literary style, a narrative mode dominated by monologue - a kind of rap which took its inspiration from the bible - would one day become the style of choice in the West. A fan of Western pop (the Beatles was his favorite group), he once confided to his personal secretary that something similar would occur sooner or later in the pop world, with some bizarre rapping clatter becoming mainstream and completely eclipsing Western pop music as they knew it!

An incredulous Primrose had even heard him suggest that, languages being what they were, the Queen's English, which had already been unbelievably corrupted by the injection of Americanisms, would be corrupted further by Rap to a point where "rapping" would not only become fashionable, but the only accepted style of articulation! She had responded that she could not wait to watch BBC news casters, ABC, NBC and the other American television anchors "rap away" in the new style at prime time!

Weighed down by anxiety for the physical and mental state of mind of his darling Jamila, Mjomba still could not really resist spending some more time mulling over different aspects of his manuscript. He would, for one, have preferred not to be in that situation. He would have liked, at this particular time, to be preoccupied with Jamila's condition and nothing else. But, like the proverbial transgressor whose spirit is willing, but whose body is weak, he found himself altogether unable to steer clear of the temptation to dwell some more on his book.

And so, against his will, so to speak, Mjomba continued to mull over his "blockbuster" which he sometimes also referred to as "The Masterpiece". While he initially seemed to be moving in that direction reluctantly, it quickly became clear that some strange force was propelling him along, and not only induced him to get into high gear, but also to go about the whole business aggressively and purposefully. Exuding a sense of confidence that the energies he had expended on The Masterpiece were finally about to produce long awaited results in the form of riches and fame, Mjomba got up and paced to the window.

From where he stood, he could count ten cargo ships in Dar es Salaam's inner harbor and he made out the silhouette of about the same number which were moored in the outer harbor. He imagined all twenty vessels loaded with copies of The Masterpiece as they raised anchor to sail away after their next call to this "Heaven of Peace"!

Mjomba always thought he was lucky to be an individual with a fertile imagination, and he credited that faculty with his impending success. It was also the faculty that came to his rescue time and again as the anxiety for Jamila's well being threatened to overwhelm him. He was, of course, aware that applying the imagination was akin in some people's view to giving in to one's lowest instincts. According to them, only a dimwit or imbecile could get himself or herself into the kinds of situations he had found himself in; certainly no normal person would try to find solutions to problems in that fashion according to those same people.

Mjomba would have conceded that they were not entirely wrong. He would have been the first person to admit that he sometimes felt like a nut when he allowed his imagination such unfettered reign. He would also have been the first person to admit that he often let his imagination go wild because he considered it therapeutic to indulge in that sort of thing! In Mjomba's view, the real difference between himself and these other people who did not see any good in applying one's imagination to the solution of problems - who only saw themselves as sages - was that this latter group suffered from what was in effect irreversible, and for that reason also incurable, madness. He clearly did not believe that diseases of the mind were so mysterious as to be entirely incomprehensible.

Talking about diseases of the mind and insanity, Mjomba was of the view that everybody, including himself, was insane! Which almost amounted to saying that insanity was the normal human state, and sanity the abnormal state. And he also associated insanity with the use of one's imagination.

Whenever Mjomba found his mind dwelling on arcane ideas, or even just wondering, he always used the occasion to remind himself that he was really insane for entertaining ideas as crazy as that. But he comforted himself with the thought that to be a true visionary - by which he meant to be a creative individual - one had, after all, to be insane. And he was sometimes tickled by the idea that he was likely to, one day, commit the ultimate act of madness by stopping to get up every morning to go to work like other ordinary folks so-called, and devoting the rest of his life to creative writing! But having discovered that he was at least on the brink of insanity if not actually insane, Mjomba naturally had developed a yearning to know exactly how he got there.

Mjomba was confident that his literary project had enabled him to essentially kill three birds with a single stone. For one, everything pointed to the fact that he was using it successfully to establish how he had come to be on the brink of insanity, and also to explain away madness! That was in addition to assuring him riches and fame!

Mjomba had no sooner warmed up, for perhaps the umpteenth time, to the notion that he was on the verge of bursting out onto the world as a renowned author and a great thinker than he suddenly recoiled at the grief that his very first work-in-progress was already causing him. The thought that he could still be a prisoner of his imagination caused him to turn away from the window and hasten to his seat at the mahogany desk. There he sat, slumped listlessly into the swivel chair.

Mjomba marshalled every ounce of his will power, sat up straight, and put on his best face on a sudden impulse. He looked so much his usual self, it would have been impossible for a newcomer on the scene to even suspect that Mjomba was just in process of recovering from the worst bout of depression he had ever had in the twenty-one years of his life. As soon as he was sufficiently composed, Mjomba started to rock gently in his chair. He leaned over toward the telephone set presently and, his gaze transfixed on the manuscript as it lay there on top of the bookshelf, was about to buzz his secretary when he froze for no apparent reason.

But his mind was obviously still wandering. This was more than evident from his reaction when the In-Tray and its load of unanswered correspondence accidentally came into his line of vision. It took Mjomba a while to accept that the contents of the tray did in fact represent work that was pending.

Mjomba got up on a sudden impulse and, moving with his back to the In Tray, approached the bookshelf. Once there, he retrieved the manuscript and the blue file folder along with the crumpled blurb carefully, as if they were objects that might sustain damage if handled in the normal fashion, and returned with them to his seat. Unaware that his swivel chair had moved from its place, Mjomba realized a little late that it was not where he thought it was. He lost his balance and, to save himself from a nasty fall, had to let go of his precious load so he could free his arms and use them to hang onto the mahogany desk for dear life's sake.

In the immediate aftermath, Mjomba did not appear at all concerned about his wellbeing. He seemed to be more preoccupied with the fate of his manuscript. He could not believe that those papers strewn all over the place were in fact the pages of his manuscript. The single word which sprung to his mind as he sought for a way to describe the scene was "desecration". Mjomba was aware that different people tended to have different impressions of things or events. In this particular instance, as far as he was concerned, the sanctity of his work of many months, indeed of his life time, had been violated!

Picking himself up very cautiously this time, Mjomba sat himself down in his executive chair. He appeared dazed and seemed to be wondering how the fine mess had all come about! He dearly wished that there had been someone else there on whom he could pin the blame for what had happened. He certainly could not blame the chair which was, even now, helping him recover from his traumatic experience.

Wondering why things of that sort happened to people, Mjomba was on the verge of stopping and blaming Providence when it occurred to him that there might be something human beings, himself included, did - or omitted to do - that set the stage for misadventures like those. Fearing that he would find himself entirely to blame, Mjomba decided against pursuing the matter any further. But the fall, which left parts of his body aching wildly, also left him wondering if human beings, despite their vainglory and vanity, were not very frail creatures who were also entirely at the mercy of some Supreme Being.

It took the wail of the siren announcing the twelve o'clock shift at the Docks to bring him to completely. Notwithstanding his frayed nerves, Mjomba's first impulse was to roll up his sleeves as he was supposed to do, and justify his five-digit monthly pay by clearing his desk of the pending work. He even looked in the direction of the In-Tray on the far side of his desk and recalled that he had earlier deliberately moved it so the sight of the label "For Immediate Action" would not cause him any agony. He even seemed like he was about to extend an arm to pick up a sheaf of documents for scrutiny when he suddenly appeared to lose heart.

But he could not ignore the spectacle on the floor. He would have to be nuts not to realize that the reality of that situation, involving as it did no less than the blue print for his masterpiece, took precedence over everything else. The sight of the pages of his manuscript strewn every which way he cast his eyes and with the lovely sky blue file folder which was supposed to hold them no where in sight, caused his heart to sink.

When he reported for work that morning, Mjomba had undoubtedly been a victim of a pretty serious depression. To call the gloom and despondency which now descended on the expectant father this time around severe was to seriously misconstrue the situation. If appearances were anything to go by, Mjomba saw, or at least thought he saw, a large rock come falling from the skies and threaten to drop smack on top of him - or something of the sort! At that moment, at any rate, he looked everything like someone in that predicament.

In a flash, the idol thoughts with which he had just then been preoccupied were forgotten and became a thing of the past. And the same went for the In-Tray's bulging contents; and also the throbbing pain in his knees, elbows and side. It was a different story, however, with regard to the manuscript.

Springing up from his seat, Mjomba seemed in haste as he gathered up the manuscript's pages and painstakingly arranged them in a neat pile on his chair. He even took time to arrange them in page order, before tucking them neatly inside the blue folder.

Mjomba paused to stare one more time at the manuscript which he had placed just inches away from the In Tray and its contents of work files, payment vouchers, and unanswered correspondence. For the first time he felt a sting of guilt, albeit momentary, for having employed his secretary as well as office equipment and stationery in its preparation.

Mjomba had never been really bothered by the fact that he himself sometimes worked on his book during official working hours; because, as a senior officer of the Port Authority, he was not entitled to any additional pay for the many special assignments he was often called upon to do outside of the so-called official working hours. But the fact that Primrose had apparently finished work on the glossy folder for his manuscript and on the blurb, and delivered them to him only that morning, heightened his feelings of guilt somewhat. Now, however, it was guilt for something else altogether that now really rocked him and deflated his spirits beyond all measure.

Then, at long last, with what seemed to be a jolt, Mjomba awakened to fact that he had been very unfair to his adorable Jamila. He found himself mulling over the fact that he had fallen into the habit of spending his luncheon hours at the office instead of driving home for his usual three course lunch as had previously been his custom, ostensibly to save on gas. But it still took him a long while to concede that over the past several months he had been conducting himself as if he had a responsibility to the world. And when he finally did, it was with such a sting of remorse, he actually lost several heart beats.

Immediately after that, all hell seemed to break loose with Mjomba sensing that he was again losing control over the direction of his thoughts. And while some of them dealt with some of his favorite subjects such as his sojourn in America for instance, others dealt with certain aspects of his own background that he had never really wanted revealed at any price.

One of those "dark" secrets was the fact that he had been a member of the seminary brotherhood. There were several reasons for this. On leaving the seminary, Mjomba had learned almost immediately that being an *ex-seminarian* was, in the eyes of a goodly number of people, synonymous with being a sex maniac or even a sex predator. More importantly, however, Mjomba feared that if that part of his background was not hidden from the world, readers of his proposed "best seller" would be tempted to jump to the conclusion that his masterpiece was in fact just an autobiographical work.

Not that there was anything intrinsically wrong with writing an autobiography. When the time came for him to write one, and he hoped that time would come in due course, he would definitely give that also his best shot. He would do it "with body and soul" - to borrow the expression Mjomba enjoyed using when he was urging Primrose and other subordinate staff to get on with some urgent or important task.

For now, however, Mjomba's sights were firmly set on landing a position in the world as a best selling novelist, and he wanted ***The Psychic Roots of Innocent Kintu*** to stand as a creative piece of work, pure and simple.

Goaded on by a mysterious force, Mjomba again travelled back in his thoughts to his beach-side bungalow. The children were still asleep, and his early morning confrontation with his wife was continuing. Staring Jamila in the eye, Mjomba was this time about to confess that it was all his fault. But he was also going to add that it was his preoccupation with the novel which was to blame! He had written the last word and thought it was the right time to disclose to her his long held secret.

Mjomba stared at his wife, intent on doing just that. Even though he was only imagining that he was at home on Msasani Peninsula with Jamila, it all felt very real.

As he opened his mouth to make the confession, a most extraordinary thing happened. He was snatched up by the same mysterious force which had caused him to begin thinking about the confession, and immediately transported in spirit to St. Augustine's Seminary. Once there, he found himself hovering all over the place, just like he was a spook.

He floated around freely, gaining entrance into various buildings, including the chapel, effortlessly through chinks in the roofs. He was doing this when he was suddenly confronted with what was clearly the real reason for the mystical journey to his alma mater. For it was, indeed, whilst Mjomba was a student at St. Augustine's, many years before, that he had commenced work on his book.

What exactly had gone wrong from the moment he first got the idea of writing a book to the present time when everything that had anything to do with the book appeared to spell trouble? It was the question which became uppermost in his mind as he cruised around

St. Augustine's Seminary like a phantom, and also one which represented - for the moment at any rate - the most plausible explanation for his spiritual pilgrimage to his alma mater.

The former seminarian found himself hating the place without any apparent reason. And the more he hated it, the more his mind sought out aspects of seminary life on which he could blame his mounting personal problems and their cumulative effect on his book project.

And that was also when memories of something that had in fact marred his stay at St. Augustine's returned to haunt him. Mjomba had never appreciated the fact that a label proposed by one particular fellow he had no particular liking for had stuck on him.
To be sure, Judas Iscariot was not exactly the sort of character that Christian Mjomba – or anyone else at St. Augustine's Seminary for that matter – would have wanted to be nicknamed after. But the fact was that Mjomba had never made a secret of his views on the world. Everyone in the seminary brotherhood knew his stand on apartheid and things like that; and they were considered very liberal. In the conservative environment which prevailed at St. Augustine's Seminary, they were also tantamount to betrayal! It was about the most unsavory that anyone could have wished to be associated with. But that was the label he had got stuck with.

Everybody knew, besides, that it wasn't some uninformed gentile or misguided unbeliever who had betrayed the Deliverer and handed Him to His killers. And Judas Iscariot wasn't just anybody either. Judas was one of the twelve who had been handpicked by the Deliverer to form the core of the convocation that would become the *sancta ecclesia*. In addition to being the Deliverer's purse bearer, Judas Iscariot also drank wine from the same cup as his Master! The man who would betray the Deliverer with a kiss was a member of the inner circle of the burgeoning Christ Fellowship; and, before long, his name had become so repulsive even among Romans, it had replaced that of Brutus, the friend of Cæsar who had conspired with others and stabbed the emperor in the back, as a symbol of betrayal. A traitor par excellence!

Whenever Mjomba thought about Judas' betrayal of the Messiah of the world with a kiss, it was not the act of betrayal itself that came to mind. It was not even the chilling words "Would'st thou betray thy Master with a kiss, Judas?" that were addressed to the betrayer by the Deliverer in the moment when Judas, no doubt representing all humanity, embraced the Nazarene and kissed him on the cheek so the temple's constabulary wouldn't grab and take into custody the wrong person! It was the Deliverer's address to Peter a little earlier on in the Upper House as the fisherman, who himself would swear that he did not know the Nazarene, not once but three times, in front of a shivering crowd not long afterward, balked at the notion of the miracle worker and Son of Man could stoop to wash his (the fisherman's) dirty feet, namely "Not all are clean, Peter!" And that was in all probability after Judas' feet had already been washed by the Nazarene.

That, in any event, was the character after whom Christian Mjomba had been nicknamed by his buddies in what he initially regarded as something that was itself an act of betrayal. The traitors! He could not understand how people could be so insensitive about the feelings of others! And even though he had never said it, he had never liked it a bit - until he started work on his theological thesis.

Christian Mjomba admittedly didn't really have a choice but to accept the fact that individuals rarely chose their nicknames or, for that matter, any other labels that enemies and friends alike used to refer to them. These things were bestowed on them by others. But before long, and certainly by the time the seminarian was searching for themes for the thesis on his chosen subject of Original Virtue, he appeared to have undergone a transformation of sorts. At some point during that transformation, instead of being something that was abominable, all of a sudden "Judas" had stopped striking him as a "disgusting' label. In his mind, it didn't have to be since it *was* a very appropriate label.

Only the immaculate Virgin Mary and her Divine Son were sinless, and no other human, members of the seminary brotherhood included, could claim that label. Christian Mjomba found that it was in fact liberating to accept those facts for what they were. If there was anything to be ashamed of, it was clearly the reluctance of people to see that they all were betrayers! In retrospect, Christian Mjomba was thankful that he had been singled out as deserving the nickname of Judas. For it was that association with the Deliverer's purse bearer and betrayer that would spark his interest in the much maligned Apostle from Jericho, leading him to devote an entire section of thesis on his namesake.

Mjomba was completely lost in reverie by now. But his reasoning was faultless. How appropriate, he said to himself, that the senior seminary was named after St. Augustine of Hippo, who was easily the most illustrious and scholarly amongst the so-called fathers of the early Church. St. Augustine's Major Seminary, as it was officially known, was the only institution of its kind in the region and was ranked on a par with senior seminaries in other parts of the world.

Young men aspiring to the holy priesthood came here from different countries in Eastern Africa to receive advanced training in the doctrines of the Roman Catholic Church. Those who did so had at least one thing in common: they had survived seven years of rigorous discipline in junior seminaries in their own lands!

Seminaries undoubtedly inspired a certain amount of awe in the minds of East Africans. But Christian Mjomba imagined that the situation of the Israelites who had heard about the twelve men who had heeded the Messiah's call to two thousand years earlier to leave all and follow him was no different; and he saw nothing unusual in the mystique that surrounded the seminarians and their preparation for holy orders. Christian Mjomba would never forget how, during his first ever retreat, he had tried putting himself in the shoes of Peter at the time the fisherman received his call; and he had concluded that Peter and the other candidates for apostleship would have been abnormal if they had not felt a little funny themselves as they struggled to keep pace with the Nazarene, a member of the Godhead, and to internalize the dogmas and everything else He taught them over the space of a mere three years! The retreat took place during the third term; and before it was over, Mjomba, who still had to complete

Prep as the freshman class was referred to, had no doubt that the chaps in Low Figures, High Figures, Grammar, Syntax, Poetry, and even in Rhetoric Class shared his view in that regard.

That was not to say that seminaries were accepted by East Africans with no questions asked. Actually many people, particularly those who had exceptional attachment to traditions of the land, initially regarded the seminary institution as something of an anachronism in this part of the world, and practically doomed to failure. This was principally because the seminarians were expected, amongst other things, to lead celibate lives.

In the eyes of many inhabitants of sub-Saharan Africa where polygamous marriages were not just an accepted custom, but a tradition which was deep rooted and highly revered, the idea of celibacy struck a code that was not exactly enchanting. The first impression it created in their minds was that it was something unnatural. At the very least, it had to be suggestive of serious deficiencies in the sexual makeup of members of those societies in which ideas of that sort took root and became accepted as a norm.

Sexual instincts were such a fundamental part of the nature not only of humankind, but of all living forms of life, both animal and vegetative, that the preference for a life style of that sort in their view had to be a symptom of something really wrong! While conditions in their own society precluded abuses of any significance in the realm of sexual matters, the people of sub-Saharan Africa supposed that Western society had been tolerating abuses probably for generations. When that happened, the abuses became pervasive and they were also apt to obscure the very purpose of this vital aspect of human life.

When things got out of hand like that, the role of sex where it really mattered, namely in procreation, ceased to be seen as vital and unique; and the abuses became a real threat to the family institution. And, consequently, society ceased to regard the family, that bastion of strength for any nation in both victory and defeat, as vital and unique.

For society to invoke sanctions of that gravity against any of its members, they rationalized, the abuses such sanctions were designed to discourage had to be really gross and mind-boggling! It was quite conceivable that there were societies in which individuals and eventually a majority of members of that society, for one reason or another, chose to regard the sexual instinct as something that wasn't originally designed for conception or procreation, but simply for amusement and recreation! People here suspected that, at a certain point in time, Western society as a whole had actually fallen for that bait.

In any case, the argument the inhabitants of these parts would have advanced as their strongest one against the so-called chastity belt would, of course, have been that living species, whether animal or vegetative, were made the way they were for an obvious reason. It was the same argument that anyone who engaged in the excesses they condemned probably would use to justify their actions; but that was obviously something they could do very little about. It was funny, in any event, that such extremes in behavior and philosophy could be espoused by an entire people or society! This was a situation that was completely inconceivable.

Their forefathers, who were revered in the same way righteous Christian men and women were revered upon their departure from this world to the next one, had always urged young men to seek out and find themselves not just one but, if possible, many wives so they could beget many children. And, naturally, the more children a man begot, the more respect he earned himself in the community. The reasoning of Africans was similar in many respects to that of Viola when she urged Olivia not to "lead these graces to the grave and leave the world no copy"! Children were regarded as the key to the survival of the human race.

A married young man who was unable to beget a child was despised. But a healthy young man who could not get himself a wife, irrespective of the reason, was despised more. And, while marital infidelity was outlawed, voluntary celibacy *per se* had never been deemed a viable option. It was generally agreed that anyone who pretended that he or she could live up to that state was up to something else. The only problem, of course, was that things were changing, and disagreements over those traditional values were setting in.

Still, while an avowal to lifelong celibacy traditionally bordered on the presumptuous and continued to be so in the eyes of many, for the growing number of people who saw Christianity as the key to literacy and immediate financial prosperity, the idea amazingly was winsome and in some cases even patently enthralling. In fact, in the end, for any disdain that celibacy as a notion earned the Church, there was lots more respect gained.

The explanation appeared to lie in the claim that success in keeping a vow of celibacy could only be attributable to the workings of something entirely novel in concept called divine grace! But mystery was no stranger to Africans and, any way, logic itself appeared to support that stance. Indeed one could not achieve a feat that was so clearly beyond the power of nature without the intervention of something supernatural, namely divine grace!

And when the time finally came for those few diehards, who actually succeeded in surviving the full fourteen years of seminary life, to make a solemn renewal of their perpetual vow of chastity at the time of their ordination to the priesthood, it seemed only natural that they did it with great pomp and circumstance. And the community of Christians supported them all the way because the catechism stated that seminary life was synonymous with years of rigorous and exacting discipline.

2. The Thesis

As usually happened, whenever sexuality was at issue, Mjomba invariably found himself recalling the fall of Adam and Eve from grace, and the original sin into which all members of the human race were subsequently plunged at conception according to Catholic dogma. More often than not, that in turn brought to mind what Mjomba himself now accepted was an idiosyncratic thesis which he had advanced in a controversial paper he wrote while at Augustine's.

Students selected the subjects for their theses. Mjomba's thesis was titled "Original Virtue". In it, Mjomba sought to develop a profile for members of the "invisible Church" using what was essentially a combination of fact and legend; and he argued that Man's inclination to sin in the aftermath of the rebellion of Adam and Eve was the result of the struggle between the forces of good, represented by Original Virtue and the forces of evil represented by Original Sin. Mjomba theorized that humans who did not belong to the visible Church but still belonged to the invisible one did so by virtue of Original Virtue!

In selecting the subject for the thesis, Mjomba was influenced by his views on the nature and origin of man. Unlike so many other people for whom "Adam" and "Eve" were mythical characters that had nothing in common with the reality of the evolution of man, Mjomba believed that the first Man and Woman happened into the world almost at the same time, and that Adam came complete with male characteristics while his companion, Eve, had female characteristics.

Creatures who were willed into being and given an existence by an all knowing and almighty "Prime Mover", and whose blue print or nature had been in the Prime Mover's mind from eternity, Mjomba believed that Adam and Eve were spirits. As would happen with the rest of their posterity, the "spirits" became automatically incarnated and acquired a physical body at the time they came into being.

But even though they were spiritual beings, the bodily matter in their nature, while it allowed them to develop and thrive in their temporal earthly habitat, hindered physical contact and normal interaction, not only with the "Non-Creature and Master Craftsman", but also with other creatures that were pure spirits. Consequently, "Adam" and "Eve", the first "humans" ever to walk the earth, were constantly faced with the temptation to think that they were all on their own and owed no one anything, and that they might even be the real masters of the universe instead of just creatures enjoying a temporary lease of life there. But they remained well aware that their days in earth are numbered, and that they were expected to use their time and talents to prepare for eternal bliss with the Non-Creature and Master Craftsman, the only kind of happiness that could fully satisfy them and round out their self-actualization.

The humans, according to Mjomba, had not been around for a long time when they did something very bad - they broke their covenant with the Non-Creature and Master Craftsman who had gratuitously willed them into existence. They actually didn't want to feel that they owed Him - or anyone else for that matter - anything, a rotten idea they got from a rebel creature who, unlike themselves, was completely invisible because of the fact that he was a pure spirit.

After that dastardly act, the humans had been so ashamed of themselves, they had cried out to the heavens and begged the skies to fall on them, pulverize them and reduce them to the nothingness from which they had originally come because of their sin. Seeing the compunction of Adam and Eve, the Non-Creature and Master Craftsman, and also Lord of the Universe, had felt sorry for them, and immediately promised them help in the shape of a Redeemer whose act of atonement on their behalf would be acceptable to Him.

Mjomba wrote in his Thesis on Original Virtue that it took some persuasion on the part of the Prime Mover to get Adam and Eve to accept that the idea of their Prime Mover sending his only begotten Son into the world to redeem humankind was workable. Quoting from the Rwenzori Prehistoric Diaries, wrote that Adam and Eve were initially adamant that humans were redeemable. They both believed that they would vaporize if they set their eyes on the Prime Mover. Mjomba quoted Adam as interrupting the booming voice of the Prime Mover to make his point.

"No! No! No! Almighty One", Mjomba quoted Adam as shouting, his voice hoarse from crying and mourning the loss of state of innocence; "It is too late…this will not work. We traded in our birthright for the protection to Diabolos for what we now acknowledge is mere fantasy, we just deserve to die. Leave us alone!

"And as for our offspring – the poor things are doomed as well! There is no conceivable way that they can come into this world without the stain of our sin. Poor things – they will even never understand what happened! They will never know how Eve and I, who came into this world as innocent creatures who were ministered to by our guardian angels and who had none other than you yourself as our, could have been so dumb! How we could have allowed ourselves to be hoodwinked by Lucifer of all creatures? We blew it!

"This human nature of ours, fashioned though it still is in your image, is now infected with a dreadful, uncleanable virus – thanks to the lies and chicanery of Old Scratch. And now, not only are we both inclined to sin; but our children, their children, and their children's children will be inclined to sin from birth! That can only mean that the generations to come will find themselves in a world that will be awash with selfishness, greed, and the array of unimaginable evils that stem from there from!"

It was at that point that Eve interjected saying: "Oh, Prime Mover, the sun has not even set yet since we both trespassed against thee. But this Adam who is supposed to be my companion – he is already giving me murderous looks! I admit that I am the one who led him by hand to the spot where the Tree of Life is located. But I am now afraid – this Man is going to kill me, Oh God!"

"Yes, you have to be careful, girl!" the Prime Mover started.
His voice booming as usual, He had continued: "You and your companion Adam indeed now belong with the Evil Ghost and the

angels that joined it in its rebellion. And it is also the reason I now insist on sending my beloved Son into the world. I, the Almighty and Holy One, knew from the beginning of time that you humans would fall for the lies of Old Scratch. But I also knew that, unlike that damned Lucifer and the host of demons who opted to follow in his foot steps, you were going to feel sorry for your transgression. Already at that time, I committed to sending you a Deliverer. Eve, you and Adam can escape from being consigned to the Cavern of Darkness or 'hell' only by virtue of the graces that will be merited for you by the Son of Man at the time of His visitation."

Even after they had heard the Prime Mover reiterate that the Deliverer was on the way, Adam and Eve both still wished that the heavens would fall on them so that they would be no more. The reason became evident as Adam, his voice vibrating hoarsely, said in response.

"No, no, no! Oh Holy One!" Mjomba quoted Adam as shouting. "We are irredeemable - leave us alone! And tell the Son of Man not to venture here into this accursed world of ours, lest he be overtaken by harm."

"Exactly" countered the Prime Mover, His voice booming as usual. "Lo, the Son of Man - and know that it is through Him that all creation, including Michael the arch-angel and the host of angels who minister to me here in heaven, Lucifer and the demons in hell, and you humans, has come to be - cometh. I love the world so, and behold! I send Him so that those humans who believe in Him might be delivered from the clutches of sin, and from death.

"As for the Son of Man Himself" the Prime Mover said in conclusion, "no one can take His life away from Him, but He can lay it down on His own initiative. He has authority to lay it down, and He has authority to take it up again. In obedience to my command, even though the Son of Man is Lord of all, He can be obedient even unto death – and he will!"

The *devil*, as Adam and Eve called the evil spirit which had been instrumental in leading them astray, was sworn to the dirtiest campaign imaginable against all who intended to stay loyal to the

Non-Creature and Master Craftsman. Variously known as Diabolos, Beelzebub, Satan and Prince of Darkness, the evil spirit had the notoriety of being the most dangerous creature that ever came into being, and was proud of its horrendous record which included misleading a host of pure spirits like itself into following its example and revolting against their *divine* Creator, and now also successfully tempting the first Man and Woman, and causing them to disobey their *God.* It was because Adam and Eve had shown they were determined to be good and faithful creatures during their probationary period on earth that they had become targets in the first place.

With the promise of a Redeemer, the invisible tempter, who never had such a second chance after he himself strayed from righteousness - he would never have been interested in a second chance out of pride any way - swore that he would give the humans a run for their money as long as he existed. The disenchanted spirit vowed to devote all its energies and talents, particularly its sharp wit, to being a real spoiler, particularly in view of the promise of a Redeemer.

Mjomba, of course, believed that the promised Redeemer - the Son of Man as He called Himself - eventually did come to earth, had paid the price for Man's redemption, and had ascended back into heaven. And if it had turned out that the Son of Man was actually the only begotten Son of the Non-Creature and Master Craftsman, who was united to His Father in a bond of Love that was itself so strong it constituted a distinct Person equal to God the Father and God the Son, it only seemed logical in his mind.

Later, while speaking in defense of his thesis, Mjomba would say something that was quite remarkable but true, namely that Beelzebub, while he was not a member of the Church Triumphant because he had flunked the Church Triumphant Entrance Test, had at one time been a member of the invisible Church!

Mjomba had espoused these views from his early days as a child in a deeply Christian family where leafing through pictorial books of the Old and New Testament had been regarded as completely normal. And, as it would happen, events would actually unfold in his own life time, which would vindicate those who, like him, subscribed to views of the origin of Man which the scientific community had always dismissed as primitive and simplistic with no real scientific merit.

The Rwenzori Prehistoric Diaries...

It was only lately that entirely new but quite credible information about Adam and Eve and the kind of lives the first humans led had been unearthed in Uganda. And, that was while the world of archaeology was still reeling from two other absolutely mind-boggling archaeological finds that had occurred almost simultaneously just months earlier. Those two other archaeological discoveries had rocked Christendom and caused turmoil among the hitherto disparate Christian churches.

The so-called 'Canadian Scrolls" were the first archaeological find on the scene, and they contained a mine of information on New Testament figures like Judas Iscariot and St. Stephen in Palestine, they corroborated the Canadian Scrolls, and also exploded the twin myths regarding "redemption by faith alone" and "*sola scriptura*" as the only Source of Revealed truth!

A group of Canadian tourists, trudging through a valley near the Dead Sea, had stumbled on scrolls containing a mine of information that not only corroborated the four gospels and the Acts of the Apostles in many respects, but also included a biography of Judas Iscariot. The betrayer's biography was written in Hebrew by someone who signed himself simply as Nicodemus, but included many anecdotes that suggested that its author was none other that the Nicodemus whose exchange with the Deliverer regarding spiritual regeneration through the sacrament of Baptism.

The "Canadian Scrolls", as they became known, apparently dated back to the time of the apostles, and also contained new information on Peter and John, and Mary Magdalene, amongst others. The scrolls even identified the "independent" New Testament exorcist whose activities had attracted the attention of the Deliverer's disciples enough that they sought to know what the Deliverer's stand regarding him was. But the scrolls proved to be of very great significance in one particular respect: a close study of the scrolls left no doubt that it was the Church of Rome, headed by Peter's successors, which was the Church the Deliverer established!

To the disappointment of the many disaffected "Christians" who had chosen to break ranks with the Church of Rome for one reason or another, and did not recognize the authority of the pope, the scrolls corroborated the writings of the early Fathers of the Church regarding the Church's position on key passages of the Sacred Scriptures which pertained to the foundation of the Church. They included the following words of the Deliverer to His apostles: "You are Peter, and on this rock I will build my Church, and the gates of Hades will not prevail against it...I will give you the keys of the kingdom of heaven, and whatever you bind on earth shall be bound in heaven, and whatever you loose on earth shall be loosed in heaven"; "Feed my sheep"; and also "I have earnestly desired to eat this Passover with you before I suffer; for I tell you I shall not eat it again until it is fulfilled in the kingdom of God...This is my body which is given for you. Do this in remembrance of me...This cup which is poured out for you is the New Covenant in my blood".

It was also quite plain from studying the new archaeological finds that the accounts of the evangelists, whether they were accounts that subsequently received the stamp of approval of the apostles headed by Peter as being among the most reliable accounts available - what came to be known as the "*imprimatur*" - or accounts that merely contained useful supplemental material (like those of the pagan historian Josephus) corroborating what the surviving apostles taught, themselves always remained fragmentary and incomplete from the perspective of the infant Church. Already at that time, it was regarded as unimportant, for instance, that the accounts compiled by Mark and John did not even discuss where the Deliverer was born. And even the accounts that did (the ones Luke and Matthew had just finished compiling) did not agree on whether Joseph and Mary travelled to

Bethlehem for the birth of the Deliverer or had lived there for a while in the months before the Deliverer was born.

The Canadian Scrolls included incontrovertible evidence that the leadership of the nascent Church, led by Peter, urged converts to focus, not on the ostensibly unending debate regarding which account of the gospel was more accurate, but on the fact that the divine Messiah and also Deliverer of humans had come and, following His ignominious death on the cross and His subsequent resurrection from the dead and ascension into heaven, had sent them into the world to spread what they called the "Message of the Crucified and Risen Savior of the World", and the importance of following in His foot steps by "straightening the paths and keeping both the ten commandments".

According to the evidence, all the eleven surviving apostles urged the converts to always remember what the "Deliverer" taught concerning the life and destiny of humans, namely that their happiness, or lack thereof, after they crossed the gulf which separated the living from the dead would depend entirely on the extent to which they led self-less lives whilst back on earth, their participation in the life of the "Mystical Body of the Deliverer", and above all their love for their neighbors or fellow humans as members of the "Company of Saints" or "Church Militant" as it eventually became known.

The Canadian Scrolls completely undermined the argument of latter-day self-styled "reformers" to the effect that it was the written Word of God alone or "*Sola Scriptura*" as they labeled it, and not the teaching authority or *Magisterium* of the Church, on which followers of the Deliverer needed to focus. This was in addition to emphasizing that "keeping the paths straightened", whether by Jewish or by non-Jewish converts, did not at all entail keeping the (old) Law of Moses and abiding by the Jewish customs and rituals - things that the Deliverer had done for the purpose of fulfilling prophecies of the "Old Testament".

And so, by making it clearer than ever before that the "Word of God" represented by the collection of writings, forming what is known as the New Testament, were authoritative only to the extent to which they had a stamp of approval of the fledgling Church with the fisherman at its helm, the scrolls completely undermined the position of the break-away churches, because these "churches" claimed that authority for what was believed and taught in those churches derived from the Word of God *per se*, and did not depend in any way on the "*magisterium*" of the Church or anything like that. That also effectively meant that being "in communion" with the Roman Catholic Church was absolutely critical for membership in the *sancta ecclesia* founded by the Deliverer!

Furthermore, the scrolls included entirely new material pertaining to the relationship between the Old Testament and the New Testament. The material consisted of statements attributed to the Deliverer that apparently helped resolve the controversy in the early Church surrounding the evangelization of the gentiles in favor of the position that Paul (formerly known as Saul) had taken. There was ample evidence the material had been compiled with the intention of including it in what we now know as the Gospel According to Luke. The discovery of these materials would give rise to speculation as to the reasons that led to the exclusion of statements of such import, particularly as the authenticity of the author, namely the risen Deliverer, had never been in any doubt whatsoever.

After studying the "Canadian Scrolls", some biblical scholars voiced the opinion that what the tourists had alighted upon were some of the "notes" that either Luke himself (or a scribe whom he had commissioned) compiled after interviewing the apostles, relatives of the Deliverer, including the Deliverer's mother Mary, the holy women of the New Testament, Simon of Arimathea, and others who represented his "sources". That conclusion was based on the similarities between the Canadian Scrolls and the known writings of Luke (*The Gospel according to Luke* and his other self-published work titled *The Acts of the Apostles*).

Then, barely three weeks after news agencies from around the globe started buzzing with the news surrounding the Canadian Scrolls, a treasure trove that included the handwritten epistle the "Apostle of the Gentiles" wrote to Timothy turned up in Alexandria, Egypt.

Construction workers, preparing the foundation for a high-rise in Alexandria, realized almost too late that they were burrowing into a stash of ancient manuscripts. Dubbed the "Alexandria Gusher" because of the vast amount of information the stash contained, the find in Alexandria corroborated the Canadian Scrolls to the hilt, adding to the turmoil in Christendom.

As if the archaeological finds in the Dead Sea valley and in Alexandria weren't extraordinary enough, while the world was still reeling from the news surrounding them and exactly one month after the construction workers in Egypt struck their "gold mine", copper miners in the Rwenzori mountains in Western Uganda dug up parchments which turned out to be diaries that the first Man and Woman who had ever walked the earth had apparently kept! Known as the Rwenzori Prehistoric Diaries, the parchments, undoubtedly Archaeology's rarest find, were embedded in molten rock inside a cave.

Other evidence found suggested that the cave had provided shelter to Adam and Eve for a prolonged period, perhaps as long as ten years. Archaeologists from Uganda's Makerere University, the University of Addis Ababa, Stanford, Harvard, Oxford, and other eminent institutions of learning from around the globe speculated that the volcanic eruption had occurred several generations after Adam and Eve had passed on, and that the fossilized human remains found nearby likely belonged to Adam and Eve's great grand children.

The scientists also stunned the world with their announcement that the evidence had buried, in one fell swoop, the long held notion that humans had evolved from primates. And, using new and experimental "genetic" dating methods, they revised the dates for the appearance on earth of *homo sapiens* to sometime between three hundred thousand and four hundred thousand years ago.

But the big question which would remain and continue to engage biblical scholars and theologians - and now also archaeologists - for a very long time was whether that cave had been the home of the first Man and Woman, whom they renamed "*Msaijja*" and "*Mkailli*" in conformity with the way Adam and Eve had signed their names in the Rwenzori Prehistoric Diaries, prior to their fall from grace, a finding that would effectively place the cave within the boundaries of the "Garden of Eden".

There was no disagreement in the scientific community regarding the authenticity of the diaries. The faded parchments were universally attributed to the first Man and Woman. The letter symbols or codes employed in compiling the diaries bore amazing resemblance to the Ge-ez alphabet which forms the basis of dialects spoken in modern-day Ethiopia! The scientists ruled out the possibility that the parchments might be twentieth century forgeries!

In the months following their discovery, the teams of archaeologists flocked to Mt. Rwenzori with the primary objective of conducting excavation that might yield the bones of the First Man and the First Woman. This and the influx of tourists into Uganda to see the "Garden of Eden" - or at least its environs - caused a huge metropolis to spring up in what had previously been tropical forest inhabited by gorillas and other types of wildlife.

In her own diary, Eve (or Mkailli) had fondly referred to Adam as "Msaijja" on occasion. But the biggest surprise of all was the fact that there was ample evidence in both diaries that Adam (or Msaijja) did in fact live to the ripe old age of nine hundred and thirty years (930) years - exactly as the Book of Genesis said. It was also clear from the diaries that Eve died when she was just shy of her one thousandth birthday! This came as a shock to everyone including the Roman Pontiff, even as he found himself compelled to promulgate a special dogma affirming the authenticity of the Rwenzori Prehistoric Diaries. The Holy Father simultaneously issued a special Church cannon mandating the study of the Rwenzori Prehistoric Diaries by all Catholic students of Biblical Exegesis, including catechists and candidates for the priesthood.

As for the newly unearthed Egyptian scrolls, it had been established authoritatively that these had been part of precious archives maintained in a fireproof subterranean vault underneath the famous library in Alexandria which the Romans, led by Octavian, torched along with the Egyptian fleet as they pursued Cleopatra. The fact that the invaluable collection, which included some really ancient scrolls, had remained undisturbed suggested that the Romans, after torching the Egyptian fleet, had systematically wiped out the city's entire population including everyone who knew about the library's underground vault and its treasures. And then, incredibly, some of the archived material corroborated the contents of the new Dead Sea or "Canadian" scrolls and vice versa.

In his thesis, Christian Mjomba did not fail to point out that roughly 150 miles as the crow flies from the Mountains of the Moon to the southeast over Lake Victoria lay the Ngorongoro Crater, the 8th Natural Wonder of the World. That was the Crater that had also been dubbed "Africa's Eden" from the time the adventurous Dr. Louis Leakey had wandered upon the skull of *Zinjanthropus* or the 'Nutcracker Man". Mjomba reported that, with the discovery of the Rwenzori Prehistoric Diaries penned by "Msaijja" and "Mkailli" (those were the names that Adam and Eve use to refer to each other in their historic blogs), archaeologists were unanimous in their conclusion that the belt stretching from the Crater where the Nutcracker Man had his home to the fold mountains northeast where Msaijja and Mkailli first met and then set up their own home did indeed comprise the "Cradle of Mankind".

It was, according to Mjomba's thesis, well documented that it was from the foothills of the Mountains of the Moon where the "little men from the land of trees and spirits", also known as Pygmies or the "Twa", and who worshipped a God known as Bes, had started their four thousand mile trek along what is now known as the River Nile to the northern tip of the Red Sea where they set up home and established what later became the Egyptian civilization.

3. Propositions advanced by Mjomba

Mjomba (and any serious student of theology of his time for that matter) had no doubt that, using the newly found data, he could reconstruct events that took place in the lifetime of Adam and Eve, and also dispel many of the myths surrounding the Church's early work and teachings. He was not alone. Mjomba's position had very much become the standard among students of theology and/or biblical studies of his time - those worthy of the name, at any rate. And as he pointed out in the preamble to his thesis, he also hoped to show, without compromising orthodoxy, that the Church was in fact more inclusive and less inhibiting to join than it had been made out to be by both its supporters and detractors.

That was Mjomba's official stance. Actually, Mjomba's real objectives, which he kept strictly to himself, were two fold: to show unequivocally that the Prime Mover loved everyone irrespective of religious affiliation; and to demonstrate that the Second Person of the Blessed Trinity had *all* humans, without exception, in His sights when, refusing to be deterred by either the betrayal of Adam and Eve or by the fact that humans would continue to misuse their freedom until doomsday, He agreed to be their intercessor and accordingly proceeded to take on His human nature.

In the final analysis, the difference in Mjomba's official and private positions was only in emphasis because, in addition to believing that salvation was only attainable through the Deliverer, Mjomba also firmly held that the Deliverer had staked out authoritatively His positions on everything ranging from the nature of true sanctity to the nature of the Deliverer's personal relationship with His Father and the Divine Spirit. It was also obvious to Mjomba that it was the Church the Deliverer took pains to establish that alone could claim to be the guardian of those sacred truths!

But while it was usual for Catholic apologists to stop there, it was not to be for Mjomba. He went on to infer that, if it was indisputable that all humans were not just fashioned in the image of the Prime Mover, but came into being through the Word, regardless of their individual circumstances, as invitees to the divine banquet, they all without exception belonged to the Church Militant - until they refused to receive the apostles and to hear the apostles' words when the latter got to their house or city, that is.

The first "humans"

As outlined by Mjomba in his thesis which drew extensively on the Rwenzori Prehistoric Diaries, Adam, endowed with extraordinary shrewdness and alacrity which flowed from his closeness to his Creator, had been quick to note the immense similarity between himself and Eve whom the Creator had fashioned from his own rib. They looked very much alike, and yet were also dissimilar in some quite important respects. For starts, he was male and she was female!

And, as Adam confided to Eve on one occasion, their frontal features - he had seen reflections of his own face a countless number of times in the clear waters of the spring behind the cave they called home and so knew exactly how he himself looked - both bore a strange resemblance to the shape of a triangle. A keen artist, he liked to pass his time tracing the shape of that triangle over the pictures of the human faces he scrawled on boulders, tree trunks and in the sand.

But, even though Adam had been anticipating the creation of Eve, he was apparently caught off guard when he woke up from what appeared to be a deep slumber on the afternoon Eve was created and noticed, first her silhouette, and then the figure of a human being approach the coach on which he had been reclining in the moments before he passed out.

Perhaps it was the pain Adam felt in his side as a result of losing a rib. But his behavior, according to Mjomba's thesis, bordered on the atrocious with Adam initially believing he was seeing an apparition - the apparition of a creature that bore great resemblance to himself! The "humanoid" was beautiful. Yes, a devil of a beauty. The creature was also "butt-naked" or whatever you would call that; and it was flashing what looked decidedly like a devilish smile.

Trying hard to remain calm and keep all his senses about him even as he stood there regarding the humanoid with unease, Adam noted that there was something about "it" that was causing him to feel off balance - as if he was about to "lose control" of himself. There was something "electrifying" about it. Adam was clearly mesmerized by the deep that appeared on either of the apparition's cheeks when "it" smiled.

Adam felt helpless as "wicked" images invaded his mind. It was the first time in his life that he had found himself in that position, and he had no doubt in his mind that the creature was the source of those images, and that it was responsible for making him feel that way. He closed his eyes instinctively. But even as he did so, he could not help wondering why the "humanoid" looked like that. Adam initially thought that although the creature resembled him, it could not possibly be human because it was missing some parts! Also, where the nipples should been, there were two big swellings or "booboos". And it spotted long hair the color of cinnamon. His own hair was matted and black.

Still, the creature could only be a spirit in flesh, because it was different from the animals that inhabited the earth. The animals Adam found inhabiting the earth did not have souls, but this creature definitely had a soul - if it was a creature and not a mere apparition. It was something Adam thought he clearly discerned as he himself attempted, albeit unsuccessfully, to stare the creature down.

His eyes still shut, Adam noted that, when looking over the creature, he had been able to trace an invisible but discernible line that run from the center of its forehead, down between its eye-balls and along the ridge of its aquiline nose, and then over its ever so slightly parted lips, and down its chest, passing over the navel and stopping at a point where the creatures' hips were joined together. Reflecting on the fact that the apparition had all the markings of a humanoid - an invisible, straight "line" that was capable of informing and giving a solid shape to the bag of chemicals that represented the humanoid's "body', Adam now imagined that, even if the creature had been fully "clothed", he would have been able to tell that it was endowed with a soul by just staring directly into its round, sparkling eyes!

When he opened his eyes, Adam had the distinct feeling that the humanoid, as it took its turn to stare him down, was also tracing an invisible line that started somewhere on Adam's crown, and run down between his own eyes and the rest of his person. But he doubted if the creature had any feelings. And in the event that it had, Adam could not imagine that they would be the sort of feelings that could threaten to throw the creature off balance in the same way his own feelings had come close to making him loose his nerve.

Adam concluded from his observations that, even though it was not exactly realistic or even practical to ascribe shapes to spiritual entities, the best way he could picture to himself a soul was by ascribing to it the shape of a straight line! Which appeared to signify that a spirit that also existed in the flesh was at its best behavior when it was standing or kneeling in an upright position, or lying prostrate on the ground, rather than leaning slothfully against the trunk of a tree or lying curled up as if in agony.

Adam regarded it as something of special significance that the creature was flashing a smile, albeit one that looked as though it was wicked or devilish. Apart from himself, the apparition was the only other creature that Adam had seen smiling! Even though intrigued by the fact that certain if not all of the Prime Mover's creation had the habit of reacting to things around them - Adam had not failed to notice that morning glory, for instance, had the habit of opening up and "showing off" the glamour it commanded at the first signs of the sun's light - he did not believe that there as any other creature on earth that could smile.

From the very beginning, Adam had associated his ability to smile with his ability to exercise discretion in ways that lower beasts could not. It all boiled down to one thing: only a creature that was endowed with a conscience had that capability. And that capability clearly set him apart from all the other creatures with which he shared the earthly habitat, all of which were able to get by only with the help of their instincts. He, Adam, could choose between good and evil, something these creatures were definitely incapable of. It was the reason Adam just turned and walked away one day when a wild cow he had been trying to milk suddenly lunged forward and kicked him with its hind leg in the groin. He had done that even against his instinct which was clamouring for some sort of revenge. His reason, according to which a creature that had no conscience effectively could never do any wrong, prevailed!

And Adam had arrived at another obvious conclusion: unlike soul-less beasts that had been created for his benefit as a humanoid and were therefore expendable, he not only was extremely precious in the eyes of the Prime Mover, but he was also fully accountable for all his actions; and, similarly, each and every humanoid after him would be both very precious in the Prime Mover's eyes as well as accountable to Him for "its" actions. This would be so regardless of the humanoid's social standing in "society" and other circumstances.

Adam reasoned that, because of the nature of humanoids and the way the human conscience operated, only the Prime Mover was qualified to pass judgement over anyone of them. And, in the "hypothetical" situation in which the number of humanoids was such that it became imperative for some humanoids to exercise authority over others, it was obvious that authority exercised by a humanoid over another could only come from the Prime Mover; and that also automatically meant that its misuse would be a grave matter for which that humanoid would have to pay very dearly on the "Day of Judgement".

Adam was, of course, aware that, as a creature that was so elevated in the sight of the Prime Mover and that shared the same last end as the holy angels which namely was the exultation and worship of the Him-Who-was-Who-was, the failure to live as befitted a child of a divinity would be tantamount to betrayal on his part or on the part of any humanoid for that matter.

That would be the case if for instance he gave in to his lower animal instincts and decided to lead a life of "debauchery" which was the converse of eternal happiness for beings that were fashioned in the Prime Mover's image and had a soul. And Adam understood quite well that "passing" pleasures or joys, because they were transient and fleeting, when they did not immediately turn sour, essentially begun to evaporate at the moment they were supposed to start. That could happen if his appreciation of the works of creation turned into self-indulgence and/or self-love, and became his last end instead of redounding to the glory of the Prime Mover who was his true last end.

Adam knew that debauchery and the temporal pleasures that accompanied it were the converse of eternal happiness in heaven in the afterlife - happiness that had nothing in common with a life of make believe, came from being true to one's conscience, and was bolstered by participation in the sufferings of the Deliverer. And Adam certainly did not think that there was any formula that a humanoid could employ to capture and prolong material joys indefinitely, just as he did not believe that there was any formula that a humanoid could use to grow young instead of growing old - or to stop ageing altogether.

Adam recognized that it was actually a blessing that living creatures - with the obvious exception of angels who were consigned straight away into their afterlife at creation - grew old, and their days on earth became numbered with the passage of time. Because it was this that guaranteed their passage into the afterlife where they could rest in peace. In his particular case, "resting in peace" of course meant being filled and fulfilled by the Holy Spirit who also united God the Father and God the Son together in an eternal, albeit mysterious, divine union. Sometimes Adam thought that he could not wait for the moment his soul would say "Bye, Bye" to his body so it would be on its way to a union with its divine Creator that was not inhibited by "matter".

Adam of course understood that it wasn't just a question of trading a life of hedonism on earth for one in his afterlife. He appreciated the fact that spiritual happiness, unlike a life of materialism on earth, entailed total giving and self-abnegation. Adam did not associate happiness in heaven with the satisfaction of his physical or even spiritual senses. In fact his idea of happiness in the afterlife, in the presence of the Prime Mover and in the company of angels, was predicated on total self-denial on both the physical as well as spiritual plane. Because only then could a creature be fit to be a vessel of grace that was freely given by an infinitely loving Prime Mover.

The pursuit of material happiness was driven by self-love or selfishness, both of which were the opposite of generosity. Happiness or joy in heaven, on the other hand, was incompatible with selfishness.

To understand the nature of happiness and ecstasy in the afterlife, Adam frequently meditated on the subject of divinity, and the nature of the Prime Mover. Adam, who spent long hours contemplating the creation of the world, had noted that the Prime Mover had taken sometime to "create" the world and the earth, and everything that was in it including himself. Adam did not fail to take note of the fact that in the beginning - ever before there was any created thing, including the angels - there was the "Word" (Adam's name for the "Framer of the universe in whom and from whom and through whom all things were true which anywhere were true, and in whom and from whom and through whom all things were wise which anywhere were wise, and in whom and from whom and through whom all things lived, which truly and supremely lived, and in whom and from whom and through whom all things were blessed, which anywhere were blessed".

He had also noted that a Spirit, which he envisioned as some sort of cloud, had come over all the works of the Word or "creation" presumably to bless and sanctify it. That had led Adam to conclude that the "Godhead" consisted not just of one, but of three separate and distinct entities or "persons". He referred to them as "God the Father", "God the Son", and "God the Holy Spirit".

Adam reasoned that because no one created the Prime Mover, the Prime Mover in turn did not need anything from anyone, and that was true for all three persons of the "Holy Trinity". In spite of that, it was apparent that "giving" was perhaps the most important attribute that the three divine persons of the Blessed Trinity had in common. The infinite generosity of God the Father was very much in evidence as He exercised His role as God the "Father" and "Creator" while at the same time giving full credit for His works of creation to the "Word". That was self-effacement and humility that Adam initially found hard to accept as an attribute of the Prime Mover. Still, it was there for anyone to see.

Then, Adam could not help but admire the fact that God the Father and God the Son (who was also the Word through whom every creature had come into being) did not just get along with each other like two individuals, but were really and truly united in a bond of love that was so strong "it' constituted a separate and also quite distinct divine "person". Adam saw that as another example of the obviously infinite goodness and love and self-effacement of God the Father *and* God the Son.

It spoke to the infinite "godliness" of the two divine persons that the way they regarded each other pointed to the existence of the Holy Spirit that united them both in such a way that instead of just an act of "infinite love" for each other, their divine love itself translated into a separate and distinct divine person who was nevertheless completely one with them. Consequently, Adam associated the attributes of "outpouring" and "infinity" with the work of the Holy Spirit during his meditations.

And when Adam contemplated the Second Person of the Blessed Trinity, he could not but marvel at the total obedience to the Father of the "Son of Man". It was a sonship that held back nothing, with the Word apparently prepared to defer to the will of God the Father notwithstanding the fact that He was Himself a full and equal member of the Holy Trinity. For Adam, it was these "activities", occurring in eternity and without let up, that made the Father, the Son and the Holy Spirit a God who was infinite Goodness and infinite Perfection.

In Adam's view, the notoriety of Beelzebub, a creature and now an implacable enemy of the Prime Mover, was grounded in that creature's attempts to turn the tables around and have selfishness, possessiveness, pride, self-aggrandisement and similar "vices" replace charity, self-immolation, giving and humility as the basis or foundation of existence. That naturally did not alter the fact that to join the party in heaven, a soul had to be selfless. As a reward for being selfless, and because the soul had received its existence completely gratuitously, the Prime Mover and Author of all - who Himself was infinitely and unreservedly loving - would feel comfortable filling and fulfilling the soul in accordance with His divine plan.

As far as Adam (who always thought out of the box and liked to imagine a world that was populated with other humanoids besides himself) was concerned, souls that had love for their creator and for others, and were not focused on themselves, not only would have a capacity for more love upon leaving this world for the afterlife, but that capacity would be multiplied a thousand-fold. But selfish souls that focused only on themselves would have whatever little capacity they might still have left for appreciating the good things in others and in their Creator taken away!

Still, Adam feared that, in spite of those rationalizations, a time might come when he, Adam, would be tempted to underestimate his own worth as a creature that was fashioned in the image of the Prime Mover. Adam recoiled at the possibility that either he himself or some humanoids that would come after him might be tempted to think either of themselves or of each other as being not quite so deserving of their blessings.

For now however, he had no doubt whatsoever in his mind that it would always be a grave error on the part of any humanoid to treat another humanoid as expendable - like cows or goats that he was free to slaughter at any time he felt like enjoying a meal of veal. Adam prayed, as he stared at the apparition, that no humanoid would ever be tempted to regard another humanoid in that way; that it would always be thoughts and feelings of love - sacred love - and never thoughts and feelings of hate that would define relations among humanoids.

Standing there gazing open-mouthed at the creature that had appeared out of no where, Adam could not help reflecting on the fact that the existence he himself had been enjoying as a humanoid was entirely gratuitous. That reinforced his view that he would be making a grave mistake for which he would pay dearly sooner or later if he were ever to treat another humanoid as expendable - and in a timely manner too, because he was starting to wonder if his standoff with the stranger might not have to be settled violently, with either himself or the stranger being forced to concede defeat.

If only the creature hadn't borne so much resemblance to him. In the event, he would probably have decided to charge it in the hope that "it" would bolt and flee into surrounding bushes. That was something he definitely would have enjoyed doing, if only for the kicks. But this particular creature bore too much resemblance to him; and, if he did that, may be it would be a "brother humanoid" he would be hounding. Adam recoiled at the thought that, unbeknownst to him, a "brother" could end up living in the forest, alone and surrounded by wildlife, when he could share the little he had with the newcomer and make him/her feel welcome.

Now, because of his suspicion that the creature he was seeing might be a humanoid, Adam was leery of jumping to conclusions about its disposition. And that may, conceivably, have given the impression that he was faltering in his resolve to face up to and challenge the 'stranger'. For it was then that Eve, trying her best to make Adam feel relaxed and at home, broke into the equivalent of *a Sultan's Dance*. That only caused the conscientious Adam to imagine that what he was seeing approach was the cunning "Satan" and archenemy in an ingenious disguise! The fact that the strange "creature" which had materialized from no where, and which he continued to have in his sights just in case it staged a sudden assault on him, did not display a tail, the face of a goat, a horn or even the proverbial "devil's claw" made it all the more suspect.

Adam had already confronted another "creature" which fit that description in a dream; and he had concocted the name Satan for it in jest - a name he, however, soon begun to use whenever he made any mental reference to the Enemy. For sometime already now, Adam had been harboring the notion that the archenemy loved disguises and sported the things mentioned, and that he somehow needed to behave that way to be able to pass on his corrupting influence to others. But Adam, all by himself in the whole wide world, was determined to be careful and avoid any trouble.

Adam was on the verge of bolting and fleeing, and he was in fact prepared to abandon the Garden of Eden for the "adversary" rather than consort with "him". Fearing the worst, the First Man had jumped to the conclusion that the intruder could not possibly be someone of good will. Spoilt and pampered, he did not at first see that he was expected to rationalize and arrive at reasoned conclusions about strangers. What was more, he did not hear the reassuring voice of the Prime Mover, booming like thunder overhead, reiterate that it was not good for Man to be alone, and urge him to step forward and accost Eve, his future bride! Instead, as he stood there paralysed in the shadow of a large apple tree, he noticed that the stranger continued to approach.

It was, according to Mjomba, a learning process that was quite interesting for both Adam and Eve as they glared one at the other suspiciously, and sized each other up. It was Eve, supposedly, who took the initiative to break the ice. Using gestures similar to those used by horse breeders in the initial stages of taming and grooming wild horses, she had gradually caused Adam to drop his guard and come to terms with the fact that he was in the presence of a real creature, if one that was still very much a stranger, and that he wasn't seeing an apparition.

When Adam eventually allowed Eve to come close enough, she had reached out and offered him her right hand, allowing him to touch and massage it. Instead of taking flight, Adam began considering the possibility that this stranger might in fact be the companion he had been promised by the Prime Mover. Because, in addition to proving that she meant him no harm, Eve had also shown - or at least hinted at the fact - that she could actually fill the role of companion if he stopped treating her as though she were an alien from another planet.

Still in shock, as Adam gazed upon the creature he would eventually end up referring to as "My Eve", he had given vent to a completely involuntary exclamation - actually the very first words that Adam succeeded in giving expression to since he was molded out of clay by the Prime Mover.

As he would subsequently write in his diary, Adam had stuttered in a dialect he himself hardly comprehended: "How on the blessed earth could Thou, Oh gracious Prime Mover, bring into existence a creature that could perform a jig like the one I just saw! If Thou were not the One and the Only Prime Mover, I wouldn't have attributed the apparition of this dancing humanoid to you, Oh Holy One. I would probably have attributed it to the Evil One!"

Quoting from the Rwenzori Prehistoric Diaries, Mjomba wrote that Adam, confronted by the spectacle of the new arrival, whose very first actions were clearly intended to catch his attention, had immediately concluded that the Prime Mover had in any case to be a most accomplished Artist, and one who obviously enjoyed and also loved what He did, to bring into existence a humanoid such as the one he was seeing for the very first time - if his imagination wasn't playing tricks on him that is!

Citing further evidence in the Rwenzori Prehistoric Diaries, Mjomba wrote that it was not until a couple of days later that Adam started to appreciate the importance of having a companion. This was even though during the six months or so he himself had been around, he had had occasion to observe that the other creatures around him - gorillas, elephants, lions, whales and under-water creatures, reptiles, birds, and even insects - all belonged to "families". He had yet to find a living creature that lived all by itself just as he did. It had been quite plain that all the creatures with which he shared the earthly habitat, including moths and vegetative life belonged to distinct families, and he had been envious of them because of it.

There was even this particular flock of birds - he coined a name for them which thought was quite fitting - "mocking birds" - which seemed to know his predilection and apparently liked to mock him by swooping low and "buzzing" him for brief periods before flying away and out of range of the rocks he would hurl at them. They stopped doing so the moment Eve came on the scene - perhaps at the Prime

Mover's command. But now that he himself had someone of his own kind for company, he actually would have loved to see them swoop low and fly around him and Eve. Instead of being irritated by their action, he would have seen in their action a reminder of the goodness of the Prime Mover in remembering that he, Adam, needed family just like them and creating Eve from a rib He took from his side. And as time went by, Adam even began wondering how it was he hadn't gone nuts in the days he had been all by himself on earth with no other human around!

But even after Adam had finally come to terms with the fact that the world's population had effectively doubled with the appearance on the scene of Eve, and even though he also understood that the newcomer and himself were meant for each other, Adam had apparently expected that the new addition to earth's human population would be an exact mirror image of himself. It did not help matters very much when it turned out that Eve also, after looking over herself, initially assumed that Adam, her companion, was going to turn out to be an exact replica of herself. Adam, who had been around longer and had seen examples of male and female creatures all around him in the world of animals, reptiles, birds, insects and even plants, should of course have known better.

It was only gradually, according to Mjomba's thesis, that Adam came to accept that Eve, even though human like himself, was radically different - and the same for Eve. And the discovery came as a great surprise and also a great relief to them both, because they now understood that they were expected to cohabit as husband and wife in due course, and eventually go on to procreate and fill the earth!

Members of the last "animal" species to arrive on Planet Earth, Adam and Eve, perhaps because they were still so innocent, were frequently agog at everything they saw. Finding themselves in a place as exotic as that and in such fabulous earthy company, they were often beside themselves and quite titillated by it all, unable to believe that they could have been so fortunate as to arrive in the Garden of Eden at the time and in the manner they did.

Unschooled in the ways of the world, Adam and Eve marveled adoringly at the practiced manner and the ease displayed by beasts of the earth, birds of the air, mammals of the sea, etc. Baffled at first that some of the creatures they saw looked like they were inadequately endowed by nature to survive the challenges they faced and might already be endangered species, Adam and Eve invariably found that it was they themselves who had been fooled, as what appeared to be lackadaisical and defenseless creatures suddenly took off with incredible speed either to evade predators or to themselves capture an agile prey!

The first Man and Woman tried to grasp how it had come about that creatures with only short spans of life were the ones that multiplied fastest. At one point, Adam and Eve even conceded that, if they themselves had not been temples of God and in a state of grace, they might have very easily found themselves according these lower creatures the respect due to deities, just seeing what they were capable of doing. A good deal of it seemed to border on the miraculous, given that these creatures only acted on instinct and could not actually think. Many of these "lower" creatures were capable of accomplishing many things that Adam and Eve themselves couldn't; and they did it in style and often with a flourish that was quite boggling to the human mind.

But there was, of course, always the bigger question to which, because Adam and Eve had a ready and perfectly rational reply, fortunately could only be asked in a hypothetical way. The reply was grounded in their own experience. But even though they already had an answer to that question, they felt they needed to keep asking it because the response to it represented something extremely important, namely an anthem of Thanksgiving they felt they needed to sing whenever they had a free moment.

The hypothetical question hinged on the assumption that there was no such a thing as a Prime Mover, a being who was not just intelligent but Intelligence itself; and who combined those qualities with being almighty. Assuming, therefore, that a Prime Mover did not exist, the big question was: How come such handsomely crafted and endowed beings - beings of all stripes and variety including themselves - had all come to be? Absent a Prime Mover, Adam and Eve still would have had to come to grips somehow with that question, especially considering that, with all their intelligence, they did not feel that they were even up to the task of just envisioning unaided a scheme as grand as that of creation? The answer to that "big" question was so momentous, Adam and Eve felt that they needed to keep reflecting on it. And the best way to do that was by reiterating the same question differently. It was the beginnings of the *Pater Noster*, a different version of which would eventually become the *Credo*!

"*Omnia ad gloriam Dei*" - translated "*Everything you do, do it all to the greater glory of God*" - was the motto that guided the lives of the first Man and Woman from the very first moments of their existence, according to Mjomba's controversial thesis. He argued that the lower life forms followed the exact same adage spontaneously - by intuition. Adam and Eve, who could rationalize about these things because they were endowed with the faculty of the intellect in addition to the faculty of the will, saw the Creator's image and likeness in themselves and to a lesser extent also in animals, birds, reptiles, marine life, and even in inanimate objects.

According to Mjomba, the curiosity Adam and Eve had about themselves and their origin and also about the reality around them was rooted in their nature which, unlike that of the Prime Mover, was separate and distinct from their existence. Rational animals, they sought as a matter of course to achieve self-actualization, and to fulfill the will of the Prime Mover in the process. It was evident that lower life forms sought to fulfill the divine plan in a similar way albeit instinctively. But above all, Mjomba wrote, the likeness of Adam and Eve to the Prime Mover made their hunger - be it for food, knowledge, or self-actualization - a hunger which was ultimately for the perfect good. A hunger for "that greater than which cannot be conceived" and which, when finally acquired, was alone capable of imparting complete fulfillment.

Both Adam and Eve, according to Mjomba, were very keenly aware of the unique gifts with which they themselves were endowed, in particular the spiritual faculties of the intellect and will. That awareness also led them to recognize the fact that their role in the divine plan was a very unique one. It was up to them to harness not just the earth's resources, but everything in the universe, including the properties of the sun and the rest of the interplanetary system, for their self-actualization, and accord the Prime Mover His due honor and glory in the process of doing so.

From the beginning, Mjomba wrote, the First Man and the First Woman had been at liberty to take the necessary steps to exploit the universe to any extent they desired, their freedom in that respect being circumscribed only by the laws of physics and other laws that governed the universe. And so, rational animals - as opposed to the irrational beasts which depended on instincts instead of reason to get by - the representatives of the human race also pretty well understood that the manner in which they chose to exploit the earth's resources also had a bearing on the expected results. For sure, they did not yet have to sweat - at least not the way they would have to sweat just to survive later after the rebellion - to see results accrue from their enterprise. But it was imperative that they understood that different approaches employed in harnessing the earth's resources yielded different results.

Adam and Eve knew that choices made by them as they went about their business in the Garden of Eden had certain consequences, there was also no question they knew that a decision on their part to accord the Prime Mover the respect due to Him (or to desist from doing so) would have immediate and dire consequences. They had to decide to acknowledge or not to acknowledge the fact of the Prime Mover's existence, and also the fact that their own hopes and desires ultimately rested with Him on Whom everything else inside and outside the universe depended, and the way they decided was critical.

Knowledge *per se* had, of course, never been designed or even intended to stifle human liberty. And so, until the day they decided to embark on their ill-advised pursuit for independence from the Prime Mover, they both were very much aware of their obligations, remained faithful to their conscience and in communion with the

Almighty. It was a relationship which translated into a genuine, deeply sincere and abiding love for the Prime Mover.

At this time, Mjomba wrote, Adam and Eve could not help being very curious about their surroundings. And because they shared their habitat with animals, birds, reptiles, plants, Mother Earth and the planets, they devoted a good deal of their waking hours learning about those things.

Describing the first outing of Adam and Eve together, Mjomba wrote that when they ventured out into the wilderness and discovered that they were not the only creatures roaming the earth, Adam and Eve did not at first know what to make of it. The first beast which accosted them was a she-gorilla which was scampering from one tree branch to another. A cub, perhaps only days old, was spread-eagled on her back. A he-gorilla, balancing his weight on his hind legs, watched the two execute the spectacular trapeze act from nearby.

Eve at first thought the three were fellow humans and extended her hand to the he-gorilla expecting that they would greet and embrace each other only to be rebuffed. It was an incident Adam would, for many years, love to use to wheedle his companion and cause her to laugh whenever he thought she needed to laugh and be jolly. But Eve also had something stemming from that first encounter to use to cajole her companion.

She would invariably remind him that he was the one who persisted for a long time after that in his belief that birds, animals, reptiles and other living creatures belonged to a higher order of beings and that they might even be "immortal" or even "divine"! That was until both of them were able to establish that, of all the created beings, it was only they who could laugh! Mjomba wrote that from then on Eve delighted in referring to Adam as the Smiling Brute while he on his part referred to her as the Laughing Animal.

Adam and Eve reasoned that if these creatures could not laugh or smile, there was less chance that they could rationalize and connect with anything that was beyond matter, and consequently an even lesser chance that their being and existence transcended their physical selves or that a part of them was pure spirit. Adam and Eve were subsequently in agreement that, all the theatrics of those other creatures not-with-standing, they were the only ones in the whole wide world equipped with thc where-with-all for an afterlife, namely reason and free will, and thus in a position to lay claim to immortality.

According to the evidence, Adam and Eve spent hours and hours observing the antics of wildlife, and were surprised at the peculiar manner in which these creatures "celebrated" the greatness of their Prime Mover, which they did just by pursuing their individual self-actualization.

They found it very exhilarating just observing animals of the forest go about their usual business. Wondering across herds of African elephants, they were mesmerized by the way these strange looking creatures went about the business of fending for themselves in the wilderness. Eve in particular was greatly impressed by the way grown-up elephants surrounded the baby elephants while warning hostile intruders to keep their distance by hooting loudly. She was out in the forest by herself picking wild berries one day when she witnessed a confrontation between a family of elephants and a lioness which was appeared to be eyeing a baby elephant in the herd. For a moment, Eve thought she was hearing the sound of an oncoming avalanche until she realized that it was one of the older elephants in the herd caterwauling to scare off the lioness, which was no where to be seen by the time she herself had recovered her wits.

Mjomba supposed that it was Eve who was really overwhelmed by the fact that certain beasts of prey - including alligators, lions and hyenas - were almost always outclassed by the very animals that kept them from starving when it came to celebrating the joy of life. Adam and Eve felt a lot of sympathy, Mjomba wrote, for these Czars of the wilderness which appeared contented to roam the steppes of the Garden of Eden in search of occasions to prove that "might is right!" while weaklings like deer and their cubs, sometimes completely oblivious to the dangers lurking in the bushes, were cavorting, prancing and romping about for hours on end, and in general getting far more out of life.

But it was Adam who conceded to Eve that he was completely spellbound at the loving manner in which baboons of either gender cradled their young and charged leopards, hyenas and even lions when any of them threatened to steal the kill reserved for the baby baboons. The hunting habits of hawks, orioles, parrots and other bird species mesmerized Adam and Eve, with Eve confessing to the man she had found already ensconced on Mother Earth that the way hawks stalked their prey from very high up in the air or from atop a high mast was so enthralling she could scarcely concentrate on anything from the moment their activity attracted her attention until the moment they sprang on their surprised victims. That had only goaded him on to make his own confession. He had turned to Eve and mumbled in the dialect they had perfected and were using to communicate with each other that the clever way certain birds that were potential targets of hawks and other predators laid low and did all sorts of clever things to avoid falling victims to the hunters, taking steps to mislead the hunters regarding the actual whereabouts of their nests and so on, said something about the Prime Mover, namely that He was

Adam and Eve did not fail to notice that families of certain animal species went to great lengths to curve out territory for themselves, and then proceeded to ensure that trespassers, even if they were of the same species as themselves, were kept out. But again it was Eve, according to Mjomba, who drew Adam's attention to the fact that male members of the pride of lions went to the extent of fighting over lionesses during the mating season, with the brawls sometimes proving fatal for the vanquished lion.

That only provoked Adam to proffer a reply Eve found a little surprising: "That will never happen among humans who should be able to control themselves and put the love of a neighbor first!"

Not wanting to risk losing the only woman on the planet by engaging in any thing that might have had the appearance of sexual harassment or improper conduct until he was certain that the moment to propose to her was ripe, Adam had up until then successfully reined in his libido, and wanted to impress Eve with his reply that he was the perfect, if undeclared, suitor.

Adam and Eve, while charmed by the reality around them, were even more perplexed that there could be creatures like themselves roaming the earth. Mjomba suggested that it was only rational, as they sought to grasp what their existence in the Garden of Eden really meant, that they should begin their inquiry by initially focusing on the lower life forms, and then move on to ponder the fact of their own existence in greater detail later on after they had learned more about the world around them and were reasonably reassured of their safety in the environment into which the Prime Mover had thrust them.

It was this, more than anything else, which explained why Adam had been coy about rushing into a marriage proposal. As things stood, the first Man and the first Woman were still preoccupied at this time with satisfying their curiosity about many other things, not least of them, the fact that while both were human, they possessed dissimilarities that, in some respects, appeared quite radical. They were both certain that their eyes were not deceiving them. Still, it was strange that one of them was masculine in gender and the other one female. Shy about confiding in each other on the subject, they each of them wondered surreptitiously how they came to be so different from each in the first place!

A lot of what they were discovering, as they studiously observed the antics of creatures in the animal kingdom amongst others was thus proving helpful in clearing up many of their earlier misconceptions about themselves. But neither Adam nor Eve were prepared at this time to take a step even remotely resembling a date proposal, let alone a marriage proposal.

That is not to say that they were completely indifferent to each other. From the moment Eve arrived on the scene and assumed her role as the matriarch of mankind, Adam found himself fantasizing in all sorts of ways about her quite spontaneously; and the same went for Eve. Arguing that the faculty of the intellect of the first man and woman at that time was unimaginably sharp, Mjomba wrote that the corresponding faculty of the imagination was very fertile. Consequently, the images and scenarios which invaded their minds were sometimes beguiling and suggestive in the extreme.

Mjomba supposed that, in their pristine innocence, they initially went all out to stifle these fantasies and to erase the unsolicited images from their memories. Such action probably resulted in these temptations coming faster and more furiously, with the images themselves proving to be provocative and titillating to the point Adam and Eve thought they might not be able to desist from indulging themselves in the manner and ways suggested. But the upshot of all that, according to Mjomba, was that Adam and Eve, being in a state grace and in constant communion with the Prime Mover, used those involuntary flights of fancy to strengthen the bond existing between themselves and the Prime Mover.

Mjomba argued that the first Man and Woman treasured that bond immensely for one additional reason which, namely, was that they might have ended up hurting each other for nothing if it had not been for the fact that they both held their Lord and God in awe. Contrary to what some believe, even before their fall from grace, Adam and Eve had to struggle constantly to keep their tempers and things like that in check. Perhaps it was because it was just the two of them in the Garden of Eden.

Quoting from the Rwenzori Prehistoric Diaries, Mjomba wrote that there were times when something in Eve made her hate everything about her companion. Similarly, there were times when Adam felt like he should take flight and go live on some distant planet, because something in him made him hate everything about the creature his Maker had given him for a companion.

Whenever those spontaneous moods, which were involuntary and unwelcome, got the better of them, they always felt like killing each other. The thought which thrust itself into Eve's mind was that she should get rid of Adam by lacing his food with toxin taken from the glands of a cobra. For his part, Adam sometimes found himself wishing, completely involuntarily, that Eve would die in her sleep so he would not have to put up with her constant prattle about things being in the wrong place in their little hamlet and stuff like that. What saved the day was the fact that both Adam and Eve usually sought refuge in prayer to their loving Maker immediately, imploring Him to save them from themselves during the period they were on trial.

They were not yet thinking about marrying each other and rearing children; but, reeling from shock on discovering that the human mind could conjure up thoughts that were as vile and mean as those, they also frequently prayed that if they were ever blessed with offspring, in addition to giving them their daily bread, He condescend and insulate their children and their children's children from their own evil thoughts and the wiles of Satan.

Even at the height of those temptations of the flesh, Adam and Eve continued to see their Divine Master as the source and origin of all good things of this world. Mjomba supposed that Adam and Eve in the process discovered, probably to their amazement, that they were actually very frail and completely dependent on God when it came to staying upright and virtuous.

They came to understand that those provocative images were pure fantasies which would turn out to be as unreal as dreams if pursued; and that pursuing them would be a diversion from the reality of committing themselves unreservedly to the service of the Omnipotent Being who was also the Perfect Good. But they no doubt also understood in the end that, removed from the mystical presence of the Prime Mover and devoid of the strength which their closeness to Him imparted, they would in fact be as nothing in the face of those temptations of the flesh.

According to Mjomba's thesis, Adam took the opportunity presented by Eve's confession relating to the curious habits of lions and their combative nature to reveal to his companion that, even before she came onto the scene, he himself had found the contrasting habits of black and white rhinos extremely enchanting. So much so, in fact, he had been debating with himself about the propriety of capturing black and white rhinos - at least one male and one female rhino from each specie - and placing them in a zoo or some place like that for an experiment. He was curious about the consequences of cross-breeding black and white rhinos on their divergent habits! Eve's response, which seemed to make a lot of sense at least then, was to the effect that such action would be tantamount to interfering with nature, and would be bordering on sin if not actually sinful!

Encounter in the shadow of the Alps...

Mjomba made extensive reference in his thesis to Adam and Eve's tour of the world, and he also described their first face to face encounter with the Prince of Hades. According to the thesis, Adam and Eve had set off on their world tour and were negotiating their way through lush prairie-land in what is now known as the Sahara Desert when they came across herds of mules.

Their belongings which included collections of precious stones, a variety of animal hide which they used to construct tents, a variety of elegant bird feathers that Eve had taken to using as livery, and other collectibles, were already voluminous; and they needed help carrying them as they journeyed from place to place admiring what they rightly deemed as their real estate. They did not find it very hard to entice about a dozen mules from one herd by dangling yams and cassava roots in front of the animals and so cajole them into becoming members of their travelling party.

Mjomba wrote that it was as those first humans and their dedicated and quite dependable mules were heading in the direction of the North Pole and negotiating their way at a steady pace along the picturesque slopes of what we now know as the Alps when they made a hideous discovery. Eve was the first to notice that a flock of sheep which appeared to be grazing by the way side was acting funny. Adam looked once at the herd and stopped in his tracks. He had observed sheep while in all sorts of situations and understood their behavior and antics even better than he understood the behavior and antics of Eve. And so he had shouted that there was something the matter with that particular herd of sheep. It was after he had undertaken a protracted and discerning examination of the animals from a safe distance that he came to the firm but grisly conclusion that the herd was operating under the influence of Beelzebub. In other words, the animals were possessed!

Adam and Eve had been warned by the Prime Mover about the existence of Satan who headed a rebel band of spirits. He had also specifically alerted them about the devil's trickery and cunning ways, and had warned against ever getting into any sort of dialogue with the Evil One. But, somewhat presumptuously, Adam and Eve had written the devil off as a spent force that would never succeed in planting a wedge between themselves and their Prime Mover. They certainly had never expected to encounter their foe in the flesh so to speak, much less in such picturesque surroundings.

It had never occurred to Adam and Eve that Satan could be so brazen as to mount a challenge just as they conducted their very first tour of the length and breadth of Mother Earth. In whispered exchanges, Adam signalled his agreement with Eve's point that the devil's objective was to frighten them, and hence his choice of time and place for the encounter. Eve, for her part, reassured Adam that even if they were distant from home and in unfamiliar terrain, the devil's tack, which was to try and isolate them from the Prime Mover, was doomed to failure, since their Divine Master was everywhere.

According to the thesis, Adam and Eve stood their ground; and Eve, using her right hand, traced the shape of a triangle in midair in a gesture that supposedly was designed to signify their total dedication to doing the will of the Triune divinity. Then, apparently taking the Evil One by complete surprise, she had commanded him to tell her who he was, and to leave the innocent animals quickly in any case before he got hurt.

The devil, mistaking the triangular shape she had traced in midair to be the sign of the cross, had been thrown into a panic. Declaring through the sheep, and in a dialect Adam and Eve could barely decipher, that he was Beelzebub, the archenemy had left the animals abruptly, leaving them traumatized and permanently scarred.

The fact that it was Eve and not Adam who had decided to take him on had been somewhat enervating for Satan. A pure spirit who did not exist in space and time, he had nonetheless succeeded in divining, by turning his faculty of the imagination down side up, that even though he would one day succeed in persuading Adam and Eve to eat of the "forbidden fruit" from the "Tree of Life", it would all eventually come to naught. For another woman would come along who would have the sun itself for her raiment and whose "*Fiat*" would cause all Beelzebub's efforts to throw a wedge between the Prime Mover and his human creatures to come to naught!

Mjomba wrote that the devil had briefly hesitated, unsure if this woman who wanted him gone post haste was Adam's regular companion or that other woman with whom he did not want to meddle in any way whatsoever. As he scrambled to get out of the determined Eve's face, he even thought he was already able to divine the powers of that mysterious woman, even though it would be many centuries before she would appear on the scene. Power that, indeed, would begin taking effect as soon as the Prime Mover, in his infinite mercy, promised mankind deliverance in the wake of the rebellion of Adam and Eve.

Even though he had accosted the father and mother of the human race in the shadow of the Alps with no sun in sight, the devil was apparently terrified to the bone. But what really caused him to take to his heels immediately and not look back at least for now was Eve's physical likeness to that other woman - the woman who would be responsible for bringing his hitherto uninterrupted reign in the world as well as the Underworld to a disastrous end. It did not seem to matter that the figure of Eve, who was not even wearing her makeup, was not bounded by the halo which would be Mary's trademark. Eve's determined stand had caused Satan to cower as if he were an earth-bound reptile, instead of a spiritual essence. He even briefly took on the shape of a creature which was half beast and half human, and which spotted a grey cloak complete with a cap similar to that of Robin Hood.

The devil then surprised Adam and Eve by whipping out from underneath his mantle a frightfully scarred paw resembling the limb of a goat which had been exposed to the naked flame of an acetylene touch until it had turned black. After brandishing it awhile with the obvious intention of terrifying Adam and Eve further, the Evil One suddenly changed his mind, and decided to use it to conceal his ugly head, which was half beast and half human, from view.

According to Mjomba, Diabolos regretted that he had summoned his powers of divination in his confrontation with the two humans, because he quickly found out that he could not withstand the image of Mary which Eve signified. Mjomba went on that it was Satan's fear that he might be inadvertently tampering with the woman who would consent to become the Deliverer's mother which made the devil sense that he could get hurt really bad (and he already knew what getting hurt meant) if he did not get the blazes out of there fast.

Adam and Eve were themselves surprised at the speed with which the Evil One abandoned his position, and retreated into the bowels of the earth. They could tell that it was where he was headed because, for the next couple of minutes, the enormous mountain range shuddered and rumbled, and belched what appeared to be fire and brimstone. Luckily the travelling party was far from the perimeter of the volcanic eruption set off by the Prince of Hades as he returned to the place where he belonged.

Later that evening, after chanting hymns of praise and gratitude to the Prime Mover as they usually did at the end of the day, Adam and Eve reflected back on the incident according to Mjomba's notes. They agreed that the devil posed a far greater danger than they had initially thought. They were especially concerned that he had been able to make his presence visibly felt even though he was a pure spirit; and they thanked the Prime Mover for keeping the tempter in check, and not giving him lee way to pose a greater danger to them than that which they had been able to withstand with the help of His grace. Mjomba added that they also thanked the Prime Mover for providing them with guardian angels.

They did not know it; but it was actually their guardian angels who had organized things in such a way that Eve rather than Adam stepped forward to do the exorcism. Consequently, Beelzebub, who had put all his bets on Adam and had accordingly devised a plan to engage him in dialogue, had been caught completely off guard. But if Adam and Eve believed that Diabolos was going to give up so easily, they were wrong. For, as Adam slept that evening, he was again taunted by Satan who wore a disguise when he came to him in a dream. The Infernal One looked just like Eve and, until it was all over, Adam was convinced that it was Eve he was conversing with.

As Adam narrated it to the good woman the next morning, "Eve" had pointed to the stunning vista which included the Alp's highest peak and sighed: "Adam, my love, I know you have been too shy to lay your hand on me up until now. I now invite you to do so, but on one condition: you must pick up courage and join me in telling you-know-Whom-I-mean: 'Now, this is a beautiful piece of real estate - this Mother Earth! Bye Bye...You made a mistake and brought us into being. That was your mistake. For our part, we now see the idea of independence - total independence - as a good one, and we are determined to go for it, the fact that we are created in Your image notwithstanding! Starting now, we are on our own. We no longer need You or Your bureaucratic regime of 'Thou shalt do this' and 'Thou shalt not do that'! Adam, my love, do I have a deal?"

The outrageous suggestion by "Eve" that he, Adam, disown his Maker was so infuriating, Adam was prepared to commit murder! But as he raised up his fist to carry his threat through, the cowardly Satan, fearing he would get hurt, had turned on his heels and vanished into thin air. That caused Adam to awaken from his fitful slumber - which he did only to discover that his companion was sound asleep on her mat and could not, therefore, have had any thing to do with the evil scheme the devil had been proposing. It was a great relief for Adam to see Eve resting serenely in her corner of the tree shade; and his only regret was that he had not struck out fast enough with his fist and beaten the hell out of Diabolos!

One of the things Adam learnt from that experience was to take things in life a bit easy and not jump to conclusions about others' intentions based solely on appearances. The dream had been so vivid, it made him abhor Satan as if their encounter had been in daylight while he was wide awake.

If anything, Adam now hated the Prince of Darkness more because it was not only evident that the devil observed no rules and was prepared to hit you below the belt if he saw the opportunity, but he was apparently dead serious and leaving no stone unturned as he went about his dirty business of sowing seeds of discord between Man and God as well as between Man and "Man". Adam shared his feelings with Eve after she awoke, calling the tempter an *evil* creature that deserved to be called *devil*, his abbreviated expression for the words *the embodiment of evil* in the lexicon they had developed for touching base with each other.

It scared the hell out of Adam and Eve to think that they were dealing with a liar who was as atrocious as that, and whose intentions were so evil. From their point of view, it was in fact impossible for evil and badness to exist. Their reason told them that "being" - sharing in God's *Esse* - was something that could only apply to virtues like goodness, kindness and love, with God being the ultimate Good. The devil clearly lacked all those good things, and had to be full of every conceivable vice - himself and his hosts of rebel spirits! They were an enigma that actually elicited the pity of Adam and Eve.

Knowing the joy which came from being good and faithful servants of God, Adam and Eve had every reason to believe that the existence 'enjoyed' by the devil and his band of crazed - yes, deranged - followers, being the obverse of happy, was something else altogether. It had to be an existence that was full of contradictions; and a veritable hell if for no other reason - an existence in which 'hope' itself had absolutely no meaning. And that explained one other thing... It explained why Diabolos was all over the place like a raging buffalo that was itching to destroy anything it spied moving for lack of anything else to do.

But that also made Adam and Eve fear for the safety of their scion and led them to actually to offer up prayers for their posterity even before they had formally discussed the subject of marriage to each other. In almost an instant, it had become apparent that their life on earth was itself fraught with real danger. They were not just caught up in the raging battle between good and evil; they were at the center of it!

In the glorious days (before the fall)...

Both Adam and Eve were greatly intrigued by the habits of the wild donkeys, goats and cows they came across as they approached their homestead near the Equator. They decided that these were creatures they could domesticate without unduly interfering with the laws of nature; and they accordingly captured a male and female member of each of those animal species for that purpose. The same fate befell sheep, swine and what eventually came to be known as poultry.

Mjomba wrote that if Adam and Eve found animal, marine, and bird life and the lives of reptiles beguiling and captivating to watch, their awe at the wonders of creation became simply boundless when it came to biological and physical matter. Smarter overall than their modern ancestors, the first Man and Woman had quickly figured out that matter was made up of atoms and molecules, and that bursts of energy lay at the core of physical substances.

As they roamed the steppes of Eden, plied the waters of rivers in a canoe, sailed the high seas in a sail boat and mapped and recorded their discoveries, Adam and Eve also discovered to their amazement that they were artists who loved not just to design but to actually fabricate and manufacture all sorts of things. Taking their cue from birds and even land and marine-based creatures which displayed extraordinary adroitness at picking up speed as they traveled from one physical point to another, Adam and Eve in due course designed and constructed conveyances which enabled them to travel with speed between different points of the globe.

To their amazement, as they traveled north from the Equator, crossed the North Pole, and then again south, over the South Pole and back to their original place of abode at the source of what had to be the longest river on earth, Adam and Eve found that there was always something new to learn from birds, reptiles, insects, and both land and marine-based creatures. Of course, just learning that there were in existence contrasting creatures like crested cranes and kites, woodpeckers and hawks, sea gulls and snakes, dolphins, sea cats and walruses, polar bears, hippos, alligators, horses, cows, goats and sheep, and so on and so forth was of enormous significance in and of itself. And that is not mentioning the variety of plant and insect life, rock formations - and what have you. Suffice it to say that by the time Adam and Eve arrived back at their hamlet, they were feeling very small and humbled.

They could not help feeling awestruck and agog at those "wonders" of creation. Aware that they themselves were a bundle of mystery, they felt constrained to bow down and humbly court the audience of the Prime Mover as often as they could, singing canticles of praise and anthems of love.

And, reviewing the artifacts they themselves had created to enable them to return home quickly and safely, they were not a little grateful to the one and the only Mysterious and Incomprehensible Source of it all - the Mysterious and Incomprehensible Source in whose image they themselves had been fashioned - for having endowed them so richly.

After they fell from grace, Adam and Eve would recall, with great nostalgia, those good old times when their sharp intellects, unburdened as yet by the effects of original sin, allowed them to swiftly translate into practical reality almost any original or borrowed idea, provided that the idea met the test of the laws of chemistry and physics. They would regret that they had ever entertained the idea of revolting against their Prime Mover; and they would hate themselves for allowing themselves to fall for the archenemy's ruse, and to opt for evil. They would in particularly regret that they had fallen for a ruse that caused them to go after something that was ephemeral and wanting in substance, as well as damaging to the future of the entire human race.

In the meantime, as they traversed the globe on their journeys of discovery, the first Man and Woman were cognizant of the fact that they owed their being to the same Divine Principle or Being that "knew all that now existed long before there ever was any of it", and then freely chose to cause it all to burst into glorious reality. Adam and Eve were not simply mesmerized. Their faith and trust in the one and the only Being, whose essence and existence, unlike their own, was unchanging and therefore had no need for causation, was immensely reinforced.

The first Man and Woman were mollified to a degree they had never expected as they came to grips with the fact that, even though they were undeniably lords of the universe, they were effectively eclipsed in many respects by creatures that were supposed to be less endowed. These were creatures they regarded as less perfect in their nature that their own. Knowing that they could never match the ability of a chameleon at camouflage, muster the strength of an elephant, sprint as fast as a gazelle, summon the courage to face an irate rhinoceros, fly unaided in midair as birds and certain types of insects did, match the skills of a beaver at constructing a dam, and so on and so forth, caused Adam and Eve to temper whatever satisfaction they derived from any personal accomplishment with a genuine sense of humility.

That knowledge also caused them to bear with the shortcoming of the various life forms around them, and also of each other; and it predisposed them to practice the virtue of patience as they went about exploiting the earth's resources and the properties of the sun and the interplanetary system. According to Mjomba, the magnanimity Adam and Eve displayed toward each other and the lesser endowed creatures mirrored the unsurpassed goodness of the Prime Mover who had intended that things be that way.

The fact that Adam and Eve already advanced in their practice of virtue, coupled with the fact that they were always concerned about the future of their posterity, made their subsequent revolt against the Prime Mover all the more despicable, Mjomba stated in his thesis. But he was also quick to point out that these things also worked in their favor. They assured them a sympathetic ear when they immediately made an about-turn in the wake of their criminal action.

Precisely because they had been such keen practitioners of virtue, in particular the virtue of charity, the Prime Mover easily welcomed them back into the fold when they reined in their pride and accepted their wrong doing, making it possible once again for Man to inherit eternal happiness in the presence of Beauty, Love and Wisdom personified. Mjomba suggested in his thesis that it is this which gave rise to the adage, popularized by a medieval recluse, that Charity covers a multitude of sins!

Emphasizing that the humility of the first Man and Woman was deep, genuine and abiding, Mjomba cited as evidence the fact that Adam and Eve did not regard it as being below their dignity to studiously observe and examine the ways in which the birds of the air, the beasts of the earth, the reptiles, insects and other living forms, including certain species of plant life communicated with each other. They were then able, Mjomba wrote, to incorporate the things learnt into the lingo they developed for their own use. Learnt, he added, with the speed with which a new born observes and grasps the intricacies of speech, and other things. And they were richly rewarded for their endeavors. The result of their research, a brilliant combination of sound, signs, gestures and scribbled techniques, contained the building blocks of human speech, literature, and philosophy!

Mjomba described the symbols Adam and Eve developed and used to communicate with each other - the first human language ever - as sounding a little like Gaelic, and looking like the ancient Ge'ez script found in Ethiopia when committed to writing.

According to Mjomba, Adam and Eve at this time lived in a kind of a Utopia in which only good reigned on earth; and also one in which an extraordinary, almost celestial, sense of well being held sway. The sense of well-being was brought on by the fact that everything in creation moved in strict consonance with the divine will - everything except the devil and his rebel band, that is. Mjomba likened the methodical way in which things "moved" to a perfect symphony, and suggested that the telltale beauty, grace and sophistication accompanying all movement in creation Adam and Eve observed in the course of their investigation derived ultimately from the Prime Mover.

Were it not for the fact that they were still "on trial", the Garden of Eden would have been a real heaven, Mjomba asserted! But even though they were on "probation", they nevertheless felt the enormous weight of responsibility, as the "pre-eminent" residents of Mother Earth, for ensuring that the harmony and unity of purpose on parade continued unhindered.

And so it was that, in these glorious days before the fall from grace, the sight of a flock of swan, geese, bats, crows and other bird species in flight evoked images of legions of angels in perpetual adoration. A flock of gazelle bolting with a luckless cheetah on their heels brought to mind images of a company of angels on a mission, while a school of dolphins massing in the calm and clear waters of a coral reef caused Adam and Eve to imagine Cherubs and Seraphs on patrol. A pair of giraffes grazing serenely in a clamp of trees reminded them of their guardian angels, and so on and so forth.

The tranquillity and calm which was predominant in an otherwise rough and stormy world was described by Mjomba as pervasive and edifying in a most sublime way. Among the so-called lower life forms, it was a sense of well being that ironically did not diminish even as members of certain species sacrificed their lives to ensure that other species did not face extinction as called for in the divine plan!

Chaste and sinless, Adam and Eve were of course called to attain a higher level of sanctity than they had already realized at that juncture. It is precisely this which explained their current status in the Garden of Eden - the status of being on trial. The fact of the matter was that, even though Adam and Eve were in a state of grace and close to the Prime Mover in a way in which their hapless descendants - conceived as they would be in original sin - would not be in a position to grasp easily, the scope for getting even closer to the Mysterious Source of all creation and for attaining greater holiness was very much there. Their efforts in that direction were in fact supposedly indistinguishable from the exertions which would result in their self-actualization!

It was very significant that, when they finally decided that they were going to defy the Omnipotent, Adam and Eve did so by expressing a longing to be like Him and not like animals or any of the other earthly creatures. The urge to be like the lower creatures, Mjomba wrote, was nonexistent or weak at best.

Even though the existence these creatures enjoyed on earth, while it lasted, was glorious, that was really all there was to it - apart from the impressions of it stored in the "minds" or instincts of the surviving brother and sister creatures. Knowing that there was no after-life for these other creatures, it would have been witless and rather crass on the part of Adam and Eve to think that a short-lived banal existence, however delightful, would be compensation enough for abandoning their lofty place in the universe.

That was precisely the reason for fretting about a diet they thought would prolong their lives indefinitely; and it was this that would eventually lead the first Man and Woman into sin. And, once they had disobeyed and fallen from grace, the single most powerful motivation for getting back into the fold promptly was, understandably, to avoid death and everlasting damnation - the direct consequences of sin Adam and Eve had apparently not bargained for.

But sin or no sin, Adam and Eve knew what was good for them and what was not. They recognized that a life of temporal bliss which would come to an abrupt end at the end of their days on earth (as was the case with lower creatures) was patently not good enough for a creature as richly endowed as Man. They knew that to embrace it would be as retrogressive a step as any imaginable! Mjomba wrote that it seemed completely out of character for Adam and Eve, given what they had demonstrated up until that point in time, to sink to that depth.

The transient vis-à-vis the eternal...

According to Mjomba, Adam and Eve were devotees of Tai Chi Tchi Kong, Acupuncture, Transcendental Meditation, and what we now know as Oriental Zen. Their preoccupation with these techniques, which they considered important for keeping spirit and body attuned to each other, was (Mjomba suggested) incompatible with a life of wanton self-indulgence or a craving to satisfy base animal desires. All the more reason, Mjomba wrote, for believing that the focus of our first parents, even as they were plotting the rebellion, did not by any means shift radically or significantly from the eternal to the transient as is widely held.

Mjomba was apparently able to somehow reconcile this position with his belief that what Adam and Eve had essentially been attempting to do was to stage a coup d'état and assume control over Planet Earth and the galaxies surrounding it - claiming all these, including the Garden of Eden and along with it all the creatures which made their abode therein, for themselves in a blatant act of betrayal - in preparation for the permanent imposition of their personal rule over the whole wide world!

Arguably, they did not really need to own all of those things to achieve self-actualization; and they, moreover, had never had any intention of compensating the Prime Mover in any way for His loss. Some would accordingly have characterized that, perhaps justifiably, as the lowest form of human degradation - greed that was worse than if they had merely connived to satisfy their animal desires clandestinely while putting up the appearance of being loyal subjects of the Prime Mover!

Mjomba, for his part, went to great lengths to make it clear that, regardless of the form or nature of their rebellion, the real test of a successful coup remained immortality. Guaranteed to them in the afterlife by the Prime Mover if they remained loyal subjects, immortality was also at the heart of the rebellion.

If they could revolt and, while at it, also succeed in attaining immortality, their apostasy however disgusting would be a success. But any success in throwing off the yoke of bondage to the Almighty One, if it lacked on that score, was not success but a farce at worst and a show at best. And the problem with an act of rebellion whose main focus was the satisfaction of carnal and other animal cravings was that fulfilment in all these instances was fleeting and transient by its very nature.

It would have been very much out of character, Mjomba concluded, for Adam and Eve to pursue gratification of the body's senses for its own sake without any regard to the eventual fate of the body itself. And so, while conceivable, it was very unlikely (Mjomba wrote) for this good man and good woman, who probably committed only that one mortal act of sin in the Garden of Eden in their entire lives to pursue gratification of the body's senses without giving a thought regarding that same body's origins or it's eventual fate - or, indeed, the origins and eventual fate of their own person.

Mjomba supposed that even after they disobeyed and sinned, they continued to regard self-indulgence with disdain. Their basic reasoning was that self-indulgence was exactly the same as "knowingly involving oneself in a dangerous and pointless undertaking which hindered you from being productive and useful in society; and, once mired in it, adamantly refusing to acknowledge the danger lurking therein; and instead embracing blindly the idea that your reward will be measured by the extent you are prepared to go in your reckless abandon!"

According to Mjomba, Adam and Eve apparently had no difficulty accepting that the pining by human beings for material pleasures (which, while real, was strictly temporal and in any case far from being timeless or eternal and in that sense mere distractions) was just so much additional evidence of our deep-seated longing for the One who personified Perfection itself. Arguing that wanting to be satisfied (or loved) and wanting to satisfy (or love) were one and the same thing in the final analysis, Mjomba suggested that true love inevitably translated into a union, and that what Man really yearned for was the reunion with the Incomparable, Supreme Good who also happened to be his Maker.

And, granted that the Perfect One had created Man in His own image and likeness, the conclusion that He alone was capable of satisfying Man's hunger became inevitable. In Mjomba's view, the fact that no human being was immune or exempt from the innate desire to be fulfilled only went to reinforce the position taken by Adam and Eve.

The legacy of original sin...

As far as the first Man and Woman were concerned, self-indulgence, far from being something that a creature of their standing could regard as a fulfilling experience, was in fact self-deprecating. And, contrary to the belief of all but those few truly upright men and women whose lives were modelled according to those of children, and who consequently were childlike and not driven by self-love (Mjomba wrote), gratification of the senses had no place or relevance in the afterlife. The same applied to the gratification derived by individuals from performing so-called "good works".

According to Mjomba, it followed from the fact that the human body remained subject to the laws of Mother Nature even after it ceased to be a suitable abode for the spirit that informed it up until then - at the time its owner passed on to the afterlife - that the particular shape and condition in which it might have been maintained up until that point did not have any direct bearing on the eternal fortunes of that individual in his or her afterlife. He wrote that the importance accorded to temporal things, just like the importance that Adam's descendants attached to the body, also seemed largely misplaced in view of this.

And, naturally, if none of these things themselves curried favor with the Prime Mover, the dissembling lives of many public and not-so-public figures, the duplicity and cunning of individuals who spent their lives striving to undermine others in hopes of furthering their own material fortunes thereby, the double lives people lived, the make believe and lies that were paraded as truth for personal gain could not possibly translate into a fulfilling afterlife. And Mjomba had a list of other things in that same category, and it was long.

- The coldness and insensitivity on the part of those who inflicted immeasurable pain and suffering on others in the name National Security.
- And then, there were terrible acts of cruelty perpetrated by people in positions of public trust against the defenseless in the name of the Rule of Law.

- The willy-nilly, unbridled pursuit of profits by owners of businesses and their surrogates that amounted to exploitation of the unwary consumers and of members of society who were guileless and vulnerable, or the pursuit of profits that was completely blind to the bodily and/or spiritual well-being of those involved in generating those revenues, or to the harm done to the well-being of the body politic as a direct result of their activities.
- The selfishness of those who were wealthy, and their reluctance to share their wealth with those who were in need.
- The hypocrisy of managers of organizations that trumpeted their commitment to the principle of equal employment opportunity, but where discrimination in one form or another was the rule rather than the exception.
- The brazenness of those who were paid to manage publicly funded organizations, but did nothing to ensure that appropriate policies pertaining to personnel, purchasing, financial management, etc. safeguarding the public interest were in place; and who instead routinely gave the small fry who had the misfortune of working under them a hell on the slightest pretext.
- The insincerity of those who presided over religious orders where the virtues of charity and self-sacrifice were extolled day in and day out, but whose own treatment of subordinates amounted to humiliation and persistent abuse, even as they passed themselves off as models of holiness.
- The mendacity of those who run organizations whose declared mission was the advancement of the rights of workers, but whose own employees' rights were flouted regularly and systematically in ways that made a complete mockery of the principles those organizations supposedly stood for.
- The impertinence of the managers of corporations that habitually shelled out millions publicizing their dedication to customer satisfaction, but who were really committed to the production and marketing of substandard and even harmful products to the gullible public.

❖ The madness of those who managed organizations set up to promote the welfare of children, the elderly, those who were physically or mentally challenged, and others who were disadvantaged in one way or another, and who even used the scarce resources of these organizations to proclaim loudly for the whole world to hear how well they discharged their weighty responsibilities; but who routinely ignored the needs of those they were supposed to serve and even misused the funds entrusted to them for that purpose.

❖ The shamelessness of managers of corporations that bragged about being in the forefront in the war on diseases by reason of their pioneering discoveries and consequently innovative practices in the production of drugs and pharmaceuticals; but yet consistently priced their products beyond the reach of those who most needed them.

❖ The silence and/or collusion of those whose duty it was to fearlessly point out injustices irrespective of the nature or source.

❖ The hypocrisy of the vast majority of present-day moralists, many of whom would undoubtedly feel devastated if suddenly everyone became irrevocably saved and they went out work. Some of them, Mjomba wrote, acted as if the Prime Mover was their personal possession and had no ability whatsoever, save with their permission, to communicate, inspire or do any favor of any sort to other men and women!

❖ The greed and selfishness that drove law makers even in so-called advanced societies to craft statutes that violated natural justice, had no regard whatsoever for the sanctity of family life and things like that, or statutes that were designed to promote the domination of one section of society over others.

❖ The hypocrisy of members of legislatures and administrations around the world who pretended that all was well when those served by institutions they presided over were subjected on a daily basis to undeserved pain and suffering, were routinely and systematically terrorized and made to endure unspeakable crudities and humiliation at the hands of the functionaries running those institutions with all avenues for appeal against the injustices committed against them blocked; or when the inmates of those institutions were left to fight for survival in conditions that are dehumanizing.

❖ The altogether reckless and unjustified preoccupation by leaders of rich nations with the development of weapons of mass destruction, while pouring scorn on the inhabitants of underdeveloped and developing nations and ignoring their own role in keeping those poor nations poor.

❖ The unconscionable, wholly unpardonable actions of leaders in those selfsame countries that had resulted in the development of germs and viruses that had a way of collapsing gradually or instantaneously the immune systems of those who were exposed to them because, unlike natural germs and viruses which could be fought with medication, these man made germs and viruses were themselves immune to treatment.

❖ The political, economic and military policies crafted by leaders in these same countries that were designed to advance their interests regardless of the short and long term harm the policies in question have on the well-being of millions of innocent people around the globe.

❖ The inaction of members of the Church hierarchy in wealthy, so-called "Christian" nations where the hype was "family values", but where the legislation, enacted under their noses and left to sit unchallenged on the books, sought to attract professionals and skilled workers from other nations to relieve existing internal shortages cheaply at the expense of the basic family unit; and where immigration laws, presuming to override God's laws, ignored the fact that the head of a family was indeed the head of a family, and denied dependents the right to accompany and live with the bread earner in his or her new country of residence; and where immigration laws, flouting all Christian norms, separated wives from husbands, and minors from their parents just because the families at risk were immigrant families.

❖ Pointing out that, in some of these countries, the legislation unashamedly made ironic, almost mocking, references to "family categories", Mjomba wrote that the laws deliberately prevented spouses and children of permanent residents from joining the "permanent resident" until years later - by which time the possibility of members of that family staying together as one family unit would be no more. He decried the fact that the Church's hierarchy paid what amounted to lip service to the needs of families that were separated as a result of the operation of those "weird" laws. He wrote that, in contrast, obscure organizations with meagre resources went out of their way to lend a much needed helping hand to those adversely affected by the "anti-family" legislation. It was, in any case, inconceivable that such "anti-family" laws existed on the books of rich nations that claimed to be "Christian" when similar "anti-family" laws were unheard of in much poorer, non-Christian nations!

❖ The general indifference of the Church hierarchy to the needs of the poor. Mjomba wrote that the tendency of the clergy to refer those in need to "Social Services" rather than deal with the immediate problems of the needy appeared to be pervasive. He made reference to a notice posted on the door of the rectory of one Catholic Church in an American metropolis which seemed to suggest that it was none of the Church's business to provide for the poor and homeless; and that the right place for them to find such shelter was across the street at an establishment operated by an obscure Protestant church organization that, unlike the church where the notice was posted, presumably could afford to put Charity before Orthodoxy. Mjomba said it reminded him of the story of a dashing American cardinal who reportedly was prepared to contribute to the cost of completing the demolition of a collapsing inner-city Baptist church which also catered for the poor and homeless, but not to the cost of erecting the new one!

During Mjomba's verbal defense of his thesis, he would remark that, platitudes aside, being a good Samaritan and being a member of the Church's hierarchy, seemingly compatible in theory, did not appear to be so in practice for some reason; and he would go on to suggest that the parallel with the attitudes of the scribes and Pharisees which the gospels repeatedly referred to seemed plain enough.

Mjomba would also make reference to the fact that the Church in America openly and consistently supported conservatives, even though it was well-known that the conservatives there were not beholden to things like higher minimum wages, universal Medicare, universal suffrage, affirmative action for the disadvantaged minority even as affirmative action for the already empowered majority was still ongoing, and so on and so forth; and that they were staunch supporters of the death penalty and things like that, in addition to being the darling of exploitive conglomerates.

According to Mjomba, the Church did not appear to see that it was facing a dilemma of sorts given that the policies advocated by both liberals *and* conservatives in America had major flaws from the point of view of Catholic doctrine.

As expected, Mjomba's views on the political situation in America would be hotly contested when the time came for him to defend his thesis. This would be even more so with regard to his charge that actions of members of the Church's hierarchy were wanting in many respects. It did not therefore surprise Mjomba at all when Father Damian, a nonagenarian whose nick-name was "Honorary Dean of the Dogmatic Corps" because, in addition to teaching Dogmatic Theology at the seminary, he was the one who cleared diocesan publications requiring the bishop's *imprimatur*, shot his fist into the air to signal his disenchantment with Mjomba's views on that score.

"Fort forr...dommaa!" the old man swore in his native Dutch tongue before launching his own counter attack.

Fr. Damian wore rimless eye glasses, and his small, glistening eyes burrowed into Mjomba as he continued, his quivering voice shattering the dead silence that had descended on the Convocation Hall in the wake of his unorthodox oath: "Do you agree, Reverend Mjomba, that there is such a thing as anti-Catholicism? And can you provide us any reason why we shouldn't take your position as anti-Catholic?"

"You are probably right on the money" Mjomba had replied. "Still, is it not true, Father, that anti-Catholics inside the Church and the prevalence of unbecoming behaviour by priests and bishops - and even popes - are phenomena that are quite consistent with the definition of the Church as the Mystical Body of Christ? They are after all also consistent with the description of humans as the poor forsaken children of Adam and Eve. We are not surprised that actions of priests and scribes under the Old Testament, and even actions of important figures like David and Solomon, occasionally left a lot to be desired. I would have thought, Father, that we Catholics - and especially members of the Church's hierarchy - would grasp at each and every such opportunity to examine ourselves to see if we might not be acting like the priests and the Pharisees who, two thousand years ago, not only fabricated the case against the Deliverer, but made certain that He met a grizzly end on Mt. Calvary - or am I wrong?"

As he gave his impromptu sermon, Mjomba did not once bat an eye lid, with the result that Father Damian's gaze and his were locked on each other while the exchange lasted. Mjomba did not regret that he had decided to stand his ground because, by the time it was all over, it was evident to him - and perhaps no one else in that Convocation Hall - that the old man was feigning, and knew from the start that Mjomba was on rock solid ground. But everyone else there appeared surprised when their exchange did not develop into an acrimonious debate especially as the priest had begun, somewhat uncharacteristically, by swearing.

The evil deeds that humans routinely did to one another with seeming impunity and, in particular, the scale of those misdeeds were just two measures of the depth to which integrity and morality among humans had sunk, Mjomba wrote in his thesis. They were also an indication of the self-deception they were capable of at the same time.

Another measure was the extent to which humans acted as though they were the original authors of life itself, and the presumption that they could substitute the original objectives and purposes of created objects with completely new purposes and objectives that were almost entirely self-serving.

Soon enough however, in a demonstration of total irresponsibility, humans took to doing whatever they did without any purpose to their actions - as though they were automatons or zombies! Mjomba quipped that a human who was lost - specifically a human who was lost and did not wish to be redeemed - apparently did things purposelessly and without any objective almost by definition.

In any case, having lost their innocence and then chosen to abnegate their responsibilities as creatures endowed with reason, they inevitably suffered from a kind of inferiority complex as a consequence of their transgressions; and it was that inferiority complex that ended up as the motive force behind their actions thence forward. Precisely because they were endowed with a free will and an intellect, the situation could not get any worse than that.

It could be said that anything humans did at that juncture was done to please - to look good. And it was not as if humans really needed to sink that low. For, reviewing the results of His work after He was done with creation, the Prime Mover Himself had declared that it was good.

The strange thing about all that, Mjomba wrote, was that a good deal of the untoward things humans did would cease being misdeeds and would actually qualify as meritorious activity, if only they were done with cleaner intentions. But the problem was that humans thought they could have it both ways - namely be both good and bad at the same time! This is what made them, in Mjomba's words, such a weird lot.

The satisfaction humans would otherwise derive from conducting themselves in an upright manner would also be real, and not hollow or faked. That satisfaction would be measured by the weight of responsibility shouldered in relation to the gifts that particular human was endowed with.

Mjomba confessed that whereas he had some idea as to what the expressions "satisfaction" and "gifts" meant, his understanding of the expression "responsibility" was vague to the point of being nonexistent.

According to him, the pleasure and satisfaction humans got when conducting themselves like automatons was not very different from the pleasure and satisfaction a lion or other beasts of prey which had already had its fill obtained from going off on a senseless hunting trip. And just as hunting in those circumstances only benefited other predators, actions humans did for the sake of doing so, or to maintain their place among the Joneses, merely profited the devil and his cohorts.

The funny thing was that even after humans found, after indulging themselves over and over again, that the pleasures of the body were short lived and quickly came to naught, they never seemed to learn. If anything, the experience seemingly rendered them less capable of determining from a set of obvious facts what really was or wasn't in their own best interests! Not even the fact that in the course of "enjoying" they had wasted valuable time during which they might have done things that were slightly more useful seemed to matter; or the fact that the blind pursuit of those pleasures frequently ended up harming them in important respects - physical and mental health, social standing and careers.

For some humans, the preoccupation with material things apparently was incomplete unless it went hand in hand with an all out effort to make the lives of those around them as miserable and difficult as possible - as if they were determined to ensure that there was as little charity as possible left in them to cover even some portion of the multitude of their sins.

Mjomba also made reference in his thesis to transgressions involving the misuse of power by individuals in positions of authority who had no interest in justice and fairness. He claimed that some of them exploited their subordinates and treated those who did not happen to be their close pals as if they were entirely expendable. He contended that the time would come when these "foxes" would be told, just like Pontius Pilate was told, that the authority they wielded and misused had been entrusted to them by the Prime Mover, and that they had to provide an accounting for the way they used that authority.

Mjomba claimed in his thesis that humans were sometimes so irrational, they gave the impression they were about to exchange places with one of the lower animal species which the Prime Mover in his infinite wisdom had not endowed with reason and a free will. A good example of their irrationality was their propensity to take life. Some humans even killed in the name of the Prime Mover.

There was a time in history, wrote Mjomba, when some humans killed in the name of the divine emperor, while others killed to placate other kinds of gods. Since then, the number of gods had increased rather than decreased; and one of them went by the uninspiring name of "Choice", Mjomba quipped. Worshipping at the altar of "Choice" reminded Mjomba of the action of Adam and Eve in deciding to put their own wishes ahead of their conscience and also ahead of the corresponding demands of their God-given nature.

Elaborating on that particular "god", Mjomba went on to state that humans who believed so passionately in Choice in the sense in which it was popularly used forgot that they would not be capable of choosing anything if they themselves did not exist. But they seemed to think that because someone "chose" to let *them* live, that in turn gave them the right to choose to allow a life to flower to full maturity if they happened to like that, or to cut it off prematurely if they found that more convenient.

Mjomba argued that any action that violated the rights of any individual to choose was bad enough. Indeed such action hit at the very nature of humans, who were differentiated from lower creatures by their ability to rationalize and to choose between what was good and what was lacking in goodness or evil. Fighting for the right to choose in the latter sense was, Mjomba wrote, quite commendable.

But, regardless of the personal circumstances of the expectant mother or the imagined circumstances of the unborn, action that prematurely ended the latter's existence for the sake of ending it, while demonstrating that humans did indeed have the right to choose, denied their victims not just the right to continue to exist like everybody else for better or for worse, but the action to terminate life automatically denied the victims the chance to get to that point in life where they too could exercise their choice between different alternatives.

When quizzed about his opinion regarding the right of women to choose with respect to anything, including matters that affected their bodies, Mjomba would respond that he had an opinion about both men and women exercising rights that went with being human beings. When women were singled out and asked to defend their inalienable rights, it was invariably with ulterior motives - the same motives that, according to him, were behind the historical discriminatory practices against members of the so-called "weaker" sex.

Mjomba argued that when some humans tried to abrogate the right of others to choose, it was called slavery, and that it certainly was never the idea of the Prime Mover to relegate women to the role of slaves. The evils of slavery, imperialism, colonialism and the traditional discriminatory practices against women that had been perpetuated in all but the few matrilineal social systems still in existence around the world stemmed from the same thing, namely the original sin. According to Mjomba, the relationships inside marriages which themselves started out as contracts between two free individuals, did not at all have to be at the expense of the exercise by women of their inalienable rights.

Mjomba acknowledged that the right to choose aside, choices had of necessity, to be seen in their proper context; and choices made by individuals - regardless of whether they were men or women - could be more or less heroic depending on the circumstances. An example of a heroic choice, according to Mjomba, was that of Mary in agreeing to be a virgin mother albeit of the "Son of the Most High". Being human, Mary must have been devastated by the suggestion of someone who was a complete stranger that she bear a child despite her vow of chastity and the fact that she was already "betrothed" to Joseph, the carpenter, for her protection from a society in which women's rights were severely curtailed.

There was a parallel of sorts, according to Mjomba, between Mary's consent to become the mother of the Deliverer and consent by women who were victims of sexual assault or rape to be involuntary mothers. In many respects, Mary's decision was the more difficult and heroic since it placed her not only at odds with herself and her desire to be chaste all the days of her life, but also at odds with Joseph (to whom she was wedded in the eyes of the world) but also with society since she essentially was agreeing to be a mother out of wedlock.

Mjomba suggested that many opponents of abortion had motives other than the preservation of the life of the unborn, adding that many anti-abortionists were not only the staunchest death penalty advocates even in circumstances in which the equitable and fair administration of justice had been called into question, but also tended to be the most vociferous supporters of things like "regime changes" in other lands, "preemptive strikes" against so-called rogue states, and other military adventures that took unnecessary lives. He claimed that if they genuinely respected life, they would respect all lives, everywhere and in all circumstances. But they would, above all, be at the fore-front in working for the peaceful resolution of conflicts; and, instead of pushing for the death penalty and expansion of the prison systems, they would be working to address the root causes of anti-social behavior.

Thinking aloud, Mjomba said a new kind of world order in which humans were increasingly turning on each other, and swearing to physically eliminate each other had evolved. According to Mjomba, there was an unmistakeable similarity between the present tendency by groups to demonize each other and the time of the crusades when two opposing groups of humans decided that the other group was on the side of the devil, and that there was only one solution to the "problem", namely to drive the other group into the sea! The crusades of the ages gone by did not yield any victors, and neither would the present "crusades" against so-called "terrorists", Mjomba surmised. In this nuclear age, *both* sides - indeed the whole of humanity - stood to loose out. The world, according to Mjomba, was fast sliding to the brink, propelled on by those who were worshippers of the god called "Choice".

Judging by the activity surrounding that "god", decidedly more men than women idolised "it". These were men who strutted about with buttons on their lapels that proclaimed "Neolib" or "Neocon"! They believed that even though only a handful, they had the wherewithal to re-draw the world map to their liking and also to "convert" the rest of the world to their own distinctly "super power" or "American" view of the world. Included among those who worshipped at the altar of the god called "Choice", according to Mjomba, would be a new breed of clergy - typically "American" priests and bishops - who would "leave the Church" without even suspecting it, and take zillions out of the Church with them by failing to speak out in support of Pope John Paul's condemnation of the American invasion of a Middle Eastern country as morally unjustifiable.

Mjomba wondered if members of the Church's hierarchy, who should have been in the forefront of defending the rights of all, and the rights of the "weak" in particular, had again not been complicit in what had become the institutionalized denial of women's right to choose. He also wondered if their own "masculine" gender did not have anything to do with it, just like the race and religious affiliation of many churchmen blinded them to the murder and mayhem committed by the "crusaders", and the evils of slavery and imperialism.

Mjomba was adamant that the doctrine of infallibility which applied to St. Peter's successors when they were enunciating dogmas of the Church appeared to have served as a cloak for members of the Church's hierarchy to get away with failings of human nature to which they were subject in the same way everybody else was. And because churchmen had the tendency to hide behind the Church, it was the reputation of the Church - the Mystical Body of the Deliverer - which suffered.

Mjomba argued that it was accordingly to the Church's advantage if members of the hierarchy owned up to the fact that, even though called to share in a divine priesthood and anointed in a very special way, it was sometime before they would themselves graduate and become members of the Church Triumphant. Until they owned up to that fact, it was unlikely that they would be understanding of the failings of others; and it would be especially true of the failings of those who, for reasons best known to themselves, did not believe in what Mjomba referred to as the official "road-map" to heaven represented by membership in the visible Church.

The numerous references by Saints Peter and Paul in their epistles to their own unworthiness as they toiled in the service of the Church sprang from their deep humility. It took a lot of humility for John Paul to apologize for the actions done in the name of the Church by many individuals in the near and distant past, Mjomba said. He added that it would definitely take a lot of humility for Princes of the Church all over the world to occasionally include an admission that they and the devoted priests whose work was so critical to the Church's mission of spreading the faith, far from being perfect, needed to forgiveness seven times seven times a day!

Mjomba wrote that he did not think that there was anything anyone could do to another that was worse than denying him/her the right to continue to exist. Doing so on the pretext that they were exercising their own right to choose was what elevated the practice to worship, according to Mjomba. Since humans were commanded to love one another and to even sacrifice their lives for others if that became necessary, Mjomba did not believe that there could be any justification for deliberately terminating a life whether of an unborn child or of a member of the security forces of some other country that was going about harnessing its resources for the good of its people in the same way other countries were harnessing their resources for the good of their citizenry.

During the ensuing discussion on justified and unjustified wars, Mjomba made the controversial point that, from the moral standpoint, nations that launched unjustified wars became liable for restitution in the exact same way robbers who decided to help themselves on other people's property had to own up and agree to return the loot before they could become reconciled with their divine Maker. In Mjomba's view, declarations by the Holy Father to the effect that wars in given situations were unjustified were binding in every sense of that word, and could not be taken lightly.

The decision by one mortal human to be rid of another member of the human family came with such a high cost that, even in purely economic terms, it had to be labeled a bad one – and particularly so when the requirement for restitution was figured in. In philosophical terms it was an illogical decision because it not only ignored the basic right of other humans to exist, but effectively took away permanently from the victims in the process the option to themselves choose, even as the individuals making the illogical choice were using it to make a statement about their own right to choose. In theological terms, that kind of choice, between freedom and responsibility without regard to the interests of others, was completely unjustifiable. And because it could never be argued that the end - be it the continued physical or mental health of the decision maker or mere convenience - justified the means, even in purely practical terms, the decision to terminate a life or lives - particularly the innocent ones - was not one that could be defended, according to Mjomba.

The decision to do away with the life of another person was also a stupid one which did not take cognizance of the fact that even the killer had a firm appointment with death - the very thing the killer was visiting on others. Mjomba elaborated that all humans, including those who went around in bullet proof vests and surrounded by body guards all the time, eventually kicked the bucket just the same. And the moment they did so, the tables were turned as even they themselves might have figured out in advance. Those they falsely accused back on earth became their accusers in the after life, and they did not do so by their own choosing out of vengeance, but as a duty on the orders of someone who had undergone a very similar fate here on earth - the Deliverer and Judge Himself.

Mjomba quipped that the cheek and swagger of killers also ended right there, and that it was in all likelihood a painful transition because, according to his thesis, killers did what they did because they thought they were "more equal than others" and therefore had a right to stay on here longer than others. And unfortunately for the killers, it was at the time they kicked their own buckets that they would also discover - somewhat late - that, instead of seeking to make war with fellow humans (which also automatically meant declaring war on the Creator) or being preoccupied with acts of vengeance, they should have devoted every moment of their lives working to foster peace in the world and at all costs.

Talking about worshipping gods or more correctly *false* gods, Mjomba wrote that the worship in olden days of waxen calves and idols made of stone, so long as it did not involve human sacrifice, was decidedly more preferable to the worship in modern days of "Choice". But he lamented that because the latter seemed to be so obviously wrong, it also automatically provided the modern Pharisees and scribes the opportunity - and one that was apparently much sought after - of taking up stones to cast at those adjudged to be sinners.

The Church of Rome...

Just as in the case of the New Testament prostitute who found herself on the verge of being stoned to death (and who, according to legend, was none other than Saint Mary Magdalene), perhaps all those who appear so itchy to cast the first stones are themselves not so innocent after all, Mjomba wrote.

Well, all the characters involved were, of course, human, Mjomba wrote. That being the case, standing in line to cast the first stone was, arguably, the occupational hazard of those who were "apostles". This was because they often forgot the reason the Deliverer, who called them to be apostles, came down from Heaven; which, namely, was to bring back those who had strayed from the right path to the fold. Without humans complicating it further, life, Mjomba wrote, was already complicated enough as it was, and full of many paradoxes.

But, more than anything else, the "human factor" as he called it made life a lot harder and more paradoxical than it otherwise needed to be. And even then, the medicine invented by humans to cure ills that sprung from the human factor itself invariably proved to be worse than the diseases it aimed to cure!

Correcting himself, Mjomba went on that calling it a problem of the human factor was a gross understatement, if not entirely false. Because, as he pointed out, while those who were so eager to cast the first stones in the matter of the "Choice Worshippers" might not have been physically involved in, or contributed to the conditions that resulted in, the premature termination of a life, it was hard to imagine that they themselves had never "murdered" someone in their heart in the same way they might have "committed adultery" by "looking lustfully" at whoever might have been their object of fascination. Those who were standing at attention with stones that were ready to fly were thus probably guilty of being phoney doctors on the one hand and hypocrites on the other.

According to Mjomba, there were all sorts of people who loved to criticize individuals who sought and procured abortions for one reason or another, and called them murderers, while they themselves openly supported other types of "murder" and, for instance, saw nothing wrong with embargoes that resulted in the death of thousands of children and the needless deaths that resulted from expansionist policies of governments around the world.

With regard to being "quacks", it was not that the right medication prescribed by the Doctor was unavailable. But even if the medication was available, it has always seemed practically impossible for humans to follow the correct procedures in administering it and above all to administer the medicine in the right doses. The solution to that problem, according to Mjomba, lay in the Doctor who "discovered" the cure making Himself available full time and everywhere to administer the concoction personally every time.

The simple fact of the matter, Mjomba went on, was that, present or not, the Doctor had never really been recognized for what He was or came on earth to accomplish. His presence in flesh and blood (outside of the blessed Eucharist) would not make much difference. That was because He would Himself not only run the gauntlet of being accused of being a phoney, but also of being falsely diagnosed as one of those who needed treatment - He would be told He was Himself sick in the same way He was accused of being a sinner by association the last time He was around. And, labeled a dangerous phoney, He likely would be matched off to Calvary one more time by the very people who claim to be sinless almost as a matter of fashion, and made to suffer the exact same fate as He suffered two millennia ago in a macabre repeat of history!

Mjomba suggested that the Deliverer, if He were here in person today, would be as popular as Nelson Mandela had been while he was incarcerated on Robben Island when it appeared as if the reign of apartheid in South Africa would never come to an end, or as popular as Martin Luther King had been in the Deep South before the passage of the Civil Rights legislation.

Mjomba wrote that it did not surprise him that those sections of modern society that were always trying to claim a monopoly over justification were actually the ones where egotism and above all intolerance seemed to flourish most. He wrote that studies were not needed to establish the correlation between self-righteousness and intolerance in particular. He claimed that the correlation was just as obvious in these times as it had been in times past. Mjomba commented that as far as human nature went, it did not appear to have changed an iota; and that was not just in the two thousand years that had elapsed since the Deliverer left us, but since the time of Adam and Eve.

Asking to be excused for diverting a little from the matter at hand, Mjomba wrote that it would not surprise him a little bit if some inside and, may be also, outside the Church found the material in his thesis ill-suited to their purposes and decided on that basis to roundly denounce his thesis in its entirety (or, if he was really lucky, only in part) as apostasy. There were so many things in his thesis which were at variance with what one found in the Catechism, like the blanket statement about "murder" and "adultery" being sinful independently of the "intention" to commit sin.

Mjomba's position, at least up until that point, was that "murder" and "adultery" could only be sinful if they were committed by creatures that possessed both reason *and* free will in the first place; and in their commission, "intention" automatically came into play and determined whether to proceed with the "illicit act" or not. It was Mjomba's opinion that in countering the position of those who advocated situational ethics, the theologians who framed the Church's official teachings, perhaps without intending it, occasionally themselves went overboard after proving too much. Quite a serious thing to do when one was speaking officially for Holy Mother the Church.

A much worse thing, of course, was using their positions in the Church to promote their own agendas, and doing so under the guise of protecting orthodoxy. These guys, Mjomba wrote, were human too. After all, even they themselves needed forgiveness "seventy times seven times a day" like everyone else.

And the "Holy Father" - wasn't he human too? Of course he was. The difference between the pope as the Vicar of Rome and successor to Peter and the rest of the Church's prelates lay in the fact that the Deliverer, addressing Peter, had solemnly asked the fisherman: "Peter, Simon Bar Jona, do you love me?" And not once, but three times in succession! And, with Peter protesting that the risen Deliverer knew him all too well and did not need to doubt Peter's undying love for Him, the Son of Man and High Priest, and now alas also Judge who sits on the right hand of the Prime Mover, exercising His power as the Head of the Mystical Body, had declared thusly for the whole world to hear: "Feed my sheep!"

And while the Pontiff of Rome was infallible when speaking *ex cathedra* or guiding the flock in his capacity as Peter's successor, there was nothing in the Church's teaching which said that these other guys couldn't let the Church and their own consciences down by indulging in things of that nature! Whether you called it the human factor or something else, the fact that members of the Church's hierarchy were not sinless (just like other members of the Mystical Body of Christ), left wide open the possibility that any one of them, while purporting to speak and act under the inspiration of the Third Person of the Blessed Trinity, could in fact be pursuing an ungodly agenda, Mjomba asserted.

Would members of the Church's hierarchy who misused their positions and authority also have to provide an accounting for their actions? No doubt, Mjomba wrote. They all would have to give an accounting for the way they used their authority and power. Moreover, added Mjomba, from whom much was given, more would be expected! But - Mjomba quipped - the reward for good stewardship would certainly be well worth the effort that went into it.

History, Mjomba went on, had shown that, far from being smooth and trouble free, the road along which the Church travelled could be pretty bumpy, owing in part to the shortcomings of its functionaries, the successor to Šim`ôn bar-Yônâ or "Holy Father" himself included.

Mjomba tried to remember from his Church History class if the Church's rebuttal of Galileo's theories had been incorporated in the Catechism at any time and, if so, when it had been expunged. His efforts at recall did not bring any results; and, like any good and well-meaning Catholic, he hoped and prayed that the zealots in the Church did not blunder to that degree. The resulting embarrassment to the Church of God would have been quite unimaginable.

But, as it was, the embarrassment from the Galileo affair and other similar "affairs" in the course of the Church's history not only had been bad enough, but had given the Church's foes, many of whom were men and women who were morally bankrupt, grounds to do things that had made the Church's work of evangelization much more difficult than it needed to be. Recalling the time in history when a pretender occupied the Holy See while the real successor to St. Peter "languished" in exile in France, Mjomba wrote that it must have been a very difficult time indeed for the Church of God.

He added that, in circumstances like those, one was tempted to ask if these sorts of things did not constitute a valid reason for folks outside the visible Church, particularly the good folks, to write off the papacy and the organization over which the popes presided as the work of the Antichrist or even Beelzebub! But Mjomba quickly corrected himself again and wrote that that was the wrong question to ask. He suggested that it was more appropriate to ask how, despite the denials of Peter, the murders committed by Paul, the scandals in the Church, and the intransigence of men, including ourselves, the Spirit still managed to stay in the business of saving souls.

The answer Mjomba volunteered itself bordered on the ludicrous. It wasn't that we *didn't* know the answer to that question - we *couldn't* possibly know it! And the reason? We didn't understand how God, who was not simply good but goodness itself, was good to us; and presuming to understand how God, who did not just act but was activity itself, operated was hardly the proper thing for us to do. That question was the big question the answer to which only God knew, Mjomba wrote. To try to understand how the Prime Mover worked to implement His divine plan notwithstanding the "human factor" and the inclination to what was base implied a presumption that we could also grasp His ways in the face of the original sin committed by the first Man and the first Woman.

Around the time he was writing his thesis, Mjomba had told a stranger he had met while travelling on a bus in jest that arguing in that fashion was a manoeuvre that was typically "Catholic" and intrinsically fraudulent! He had added, still in jest, that it was still a wonderful ploy which, in this case, left the main question unanswered, while shielding defenders of the papacy (or "popery" as it was referred to by protagonists) from the obligation to defend their claim that the papacy was divinely instituted.

The stranger, a non-Catholic who did not know Mjomba's religious affiliation, had offered a rejoinder that made Mjomba wilt: "When it suits them (Catholics), they start talking about 'humanly speaking' this and 'speaking *ex cathedra*' that! When they are about to be cornered in an argument, they always change, and begin to speak in code. Still, one has to give them some credit - they start out by having their priests-in-training master Philosophy; and it is only after the seminarians, as they are called, become well versed in the sophistry of argument that they are introduced to biblical exegesis - which they then can manipulate according to their whims! Clever louts!

"A former member of the seminary brotherhood once bragged to me he could prove that there was God in seven ways. But then he added that he could also prove in as many ways that God wasn't there! And he went on to boast that, after his first year of Philosophy studies, he could prove that a sin was not a sin..."

Mjomba treasured memories of that encounter, and thought the exchange had left him with a better appreciation of the views of non-Catholics in general and anti-Catholics in particular.

Perhaps with that encounter in mind, Mjomba wrote that the return of the Vicar of Christ from Avignon to the Vatican was a turning point in the history of the Church, and one that was also pregnant with meaning. Noting that it, perhaps, wasn't entirely a coincidence that the "Great Schism", the "Black Death", and the European Wars of Destruction, and the fall of Constantinople almost all occurred at one and the same time, Mjomba suggested that the end of the Great Schism was really the beginning of a new type of schism.

From that point on, physically taking over the Vatican would no longer be regarded as essential for a schismatic movement to establish its credibility. Indeed, after a while, it wouldn't even be necessary for a movement to set itself up as an offshoot of the Catholic Church to stay in business. Very soon, things like apostolic succession, the apostolate as an office, and their importance for a valid ministerial priesthood would, in short order, all cease to matter.

The time would soon come when, armed with a bible, anybody could start a ministry - namely, take upon oneself "the task not only of representing Christ, Head of the Church, before the assembly of the faithful, but also of acting in the name of the whole Church when presenting to God the prayer of the Church...". Instead of being anathema, it would become fashionable, in the new Age of Enlightenment, to "start one's own ministry" - which would be synonymous with "founding one's own church"! And even bashing the "traditional" Church would begin to rate as a heroic "Christian" act.

Mjomba wrote that the flowering of these ministries or "churches", led by individuals who acted as virtual "popes" but preferred to call themselves "Apostle", "Pastor", "Prophet", "Prophetess", "Bishop" and things like that, while perhaps not the best thing, would have a good side to it. Thus, instead of just the one individual in the New Testament who was not one of the twelve but was going around casting out devils in the Deliverer's name all the same, there would be a countless number of such individuals to the consternation of the successors of the apostles!

Mjomba even supposed that the people setting up the churches - which would effectively be in competition with the One True Church founded by the Deliverer - by and large would be doing so in good faith. This would be the case even though they might be entirely misguided. But it would be an unanticipated development that the Church's hierarchy would try to ignore for a long time, according to Mjomba's thesis. Mjomba would explain during his oral defense of the thesis that it was not for him to say whether or not leaders of the new brand of ecclesiastical institutions in fact wielded power over the devil as they claimed, or whether the exorcisms were for real.

Mjomba also claimed that these developments would inevitably lead to a totally new approach to the study of the sacred scriptures by those who regarded them as the only source of revealed truth, and to completely new concepts of terms like "*ecclesia*", "*fides*", and even "commandment".

The upshot of all this was that the Church of modern times found that it had now to walk a tight rope. It could not condemn those Christians who operated outside its authority outright. Condemnation would imply that they cease their activities and any good work they were doing. In any case, the alternatives for all those "Separated Brethren" who participated in good faith were imponderable.

And the Church could not openly endorse them either, even though it had an obligation to "bear witness to Christ together with all Christians of every church and ecclesiastical community". Because endorsement would undermine its own authority, it was out of question. The historical rivalries between these groups and the Church did not help the situation; and much less the scandals, past and present, perpetrated by individuals in positions of leadership in the Church.

Mjomba wrote that while the scriptures and tradition attested to the fact that the Church, under the leadership of the Pontiff of Rome, derived its authority directly from the Deliverer, the fact that it had succeeded in weathering what often looked like insurmountable obstacles since its inception, including internal scandals, also constituted additional and rather compelling evidence in support of that contention.

Mjomba hoped and prayed that his own thesis would never embarrass the Church in anyway. And by "Church" he meant the *Mystical Body of Christ*, not just those other people in leadership positions who frequently did not have the interests of the Church at heart. Again, rather naively, he dreamed - quite often as a matter of fact - that his thesis would be a special instrument of God's grace by which thousands of souls in far flung places would come to know that He loved them.

Mjomba wrote that all he himself was doing, any way, was attempt to apply what he dubbed the "Mjomba Method" (as opposed to the Scholastic Method) to the matter at hand, and then compare the results to the conclusions in Thomas Aquinas's Summa Theologia. This was even though he himself didn't have any clue as to what the words "the Mjomba Method" which kept recurring throughout his thesis meant.

His point nonetheless was that, while engaged in that "speculative" exercise, he did not regard himself as a spokesperson for the Church, but as a scholar who, theoretically, could end up having it all wrong! He, for his part, would be more than satisfied if his "thesis" became required reading in seminaries so students could dissect it and proceed, with the help of their professors, to shoot as many holes in it as they could. And this, even though his thesis read like some fairy tale and did not bear the slightest resemblance to an academic paper.

But, like any other naive seminarian who was beginning to delve in the mysteries of theology, Mjomba was also dreaming that his thesis might one day become the standard companion to the Holy Bible - or something close to that! He could not imagine a neater way of "raking in souls", as he liked to put it, than writing a thesis that would challenge the minds of its readers and lead them, at their own pace, to the truth - and especially since the harvest was ripe.

After that diversion, Mjomba continued that, since there could really be only one Prime Mover, you would not expect to find opposing groups of humans (all of whom belonged to the specie known as *animal rationale*) locked in mortal combat with each group simultaneously proclaiming that it was doing the bidding of the Prime Mover! It was also very unrealistic, Mjomba wrote, to expect members of the feuding groups to heed the invitation to be one with the Deliverer and High Priest unless and until they were reconciled to each other!

As it was, people of different faiths were locked in mortal combat with each group asserting that it was the true religion. And they were, of course, far from being reconciled to one another. It was a situation that was really strange, and which also said plenty about the legacy of original sin, Mjomba wrote.

Murderous humans...

Mjomba suggested that just as a certain breed of whales had earned the title "killer whales" and a certain breed of bees had earned the title "killer bees", humans had definitely earned for themselves the title of "Killer Humans"! He added that some humans, after making it their business throughout their lives to make the lives of others a living hell - and after being accustomed (almost as a practical joke) to killing or otherwise curtailing the civil liberties of those they chose to dislike - became the most vocal in decrying the "absence of justice" when the tables became turned and they suddenly found themselves at the receiving end.

Noting that the lower beasts killed to survive, Mjomba wrote that, with a few exceptions, humans essentially killed for the fun of it, there being no good reason for it; but, unlike beasts, they even slaughtered their own. Mjomba theorized that those humans who saw nothing wrong with terrorizing and slaughtering their own did so because they thought that they felt they were - as he put it - "more equal than others".

He explained that while it appeared on the surface as if the murderous conduct was motivated by feelings of superiority, what drove people to harm others was actually the opposite, namely an inferiority complex. And it seemed to go hand in hand with stupidity, because, according to Mjomba, murderers thought that some human lives were worth more than others! Mjomba accordingly regarded anyone who promoted things like apartheid, racism discrimination on any grounds as potential murderers.

The fact that humans, like other earthly creatures, had but one lease of life whilst here on earth was one reason murderous conduct was so despicable, according to Mjomba. But it was also abhorrent because intentionally cutting short the life of another human in this world represented an attempt to thwart the divine plan and interfere with Providence.

The taking of a life was the height of what Mjomba called pretence - pretence to having mastery over everything in the universe including life. He argued that it was pretence because if they had power over life, they would also have power over death - the power to restore life - be it their own life or that of other humans - after they had done away with it.

Mjomba quipped that the life he was referring to was not even the everlasting life with which humans had an appointment in the after-life. It was just the mortal earthly life or the pep of a human body while it was still capable of being informed by the indiscernible spiritual essence or soul. He hypothesized that they were in fact incapable of restoring it for the simple reason that, in so far as their own existence on earth was concerned, they themselves were essentially on life-support that could be removed at any time at the Prime Mover's pleasure (and would, indeed, be removed in due course).

The one thing they were really good at was to rationalize away personal responsibility in each and every individual instance in which they committed murder; and it was in the exact same way in which they rationalized away their responsibility when they chose to be irresponsible by misusing their rights and privileges, Mjomba wrote.

The Deliverer's admonition to humans that they should not fear those that can destroy the body but the Judge who can cast the soul of the wayward into hell represented not only a powerful rebuke to those who played roles in dispatching fellow humans to their premature demise but constituted at one and the same time what Mjomba described as indescribable words of consolation for the hapless victims.

Mjomba went out of his way to emphasize what he meant by "playing a role" in the taking of a life. He did not just mean the part played by the executioner. In his view, a string of people were culpable - those individuals who inspired the evil deed at its inception; and all those who subsequently facilitated it by their deed or omission; those who acted as cheer leaders while the evil deed was being perpetrated; and also those who could have done something to halt the evil act, but decided, for one reason or another, to play it safe and look the other way. Also included in the censure were those who sanctioned or participated in the acts of revenge; because, according to Mjomba, the Deliverer's injunction that humans leave revenge to the Prime Mover was very clear and unequivocal.

Mjomba wrote that humans were enjoined by the Deliverer, and constantly reminded by those who were called by Him to be His apostles, to pray for their persecutors. Mjomba commented that even then, the act of "praying" for enemies itself often amounted to a disingenuous expression of contempt directed at the offending party. Hardly what the Deliverer had in mind. But also not surprising, since it was not just the upright or spotless who were exposed to harassment and persecution, but those who belonged to what the Deliverer termed "this sinful generation" as well!

Before commenting on that last category, which according to him, pretty well encompassed everybody with the exception of the

Deliverer Himself, His blessed mother whose conception was immaculate and not tainted by original sin, and those counted by the Deliverer (and subsequently by the Church he founded and authorised to continue His work here on earth) among the Innocents, Mjomba compared the abuse of prayer in the manner ascribed to the undisguised clamor for justice by those humans who were bent on revenge.

Curious as to whether mockery of something as hallowed as prayer was more or less odious in the eyes of the Prime Mover than the eagerness of many in society, particularly folks who had lost loved ones at the hands of criminal elements, to see the perpetrators made quick work of at the guillotine, in the electric chair, or in the gas chamber, Mjomba started the laborious task of tabulating the pros and cons. As he did so, he could not help noting that, odious as it was, making a mockery of prayer was infinitely worse than making a mockery of the concept of the church.

Mjomba, however, abandoned the exercise not long after, when it became clear that there was no significant difference between the two positions. But by that time it was also obvious that those two positions (the position of the prayerful hypocrite and that of the death penalty advocates) entailed deeply ingrained attitudes that, quite conceivably, were more difficult to uproot than the shortcomings of the prime offenders who were waiting in line for execution. More often than not, those shortcomings, according to Mjomba, had their origins in habitual deprivation and institutionalised social injustice, and were in that sense the product of the very society that now sought, for obvious reasons, to dissociate itself from them.

The similarities to the case of the good thief who had been condemned to die on Mt. Calvary alongside the Deliverer were so evident they really could not just be dismissed as contrived, Mjomba wrote; adding that it was also a very sad commentary on modern society that has always generally favored things like the death penalty over mercy, the incarceration of so-called criminals over treatment and/or rehabilitation. According to Mjomba, the fact that the so-called "criminals" in many cases were either the victims of profiling so-called, or people who, because of their social circumstances, had automatically been denied due process that was available only to the moneyed made the situation more not less lamentable.

Obstacle race...

Touching on a subject he would return to on numerous occasions in his thesis, Mjomba wrote that doing anything right in the aftermath of the Fall of Adam and Eve from grace seemed patently elusive for humans in general; and he added that any claims to the contrary, if divine grace was excluded from the picture, were decidedly vain. He went on that there was little doubt that, left to their own devices, humans were inclined to sin as opposed to doing what was honorable.

Human nature had obviously been corrupted to at least that extent by the temporary, but nonetheless serious and wholly inexcusable, lapse in judgement of humankind's first couple. But that ill-omened disposition, far from forming grounds for absolving humans from the obligation to uphold honesty and virtue in the highest regard and from keeping the ten commandments in the process, had only caused the Deliverer to remind us that it was not those who hailed Him constantly as their Lord who would be saved, but those who did His bidding.

Mjomba noted in passing that it would have been a chaotic situation indeed if no Redeemer had come to the rescue of humans in the wake of the rebellion of Adam and Eve. Instead of throwing up their arms in utter despair, humans - all humans, including the compatriots of Noah who had not been able to get aboard the arch and had perished in the flood - could now brag that their brother and Deliverer, who was none other than the Word-become-flesh, was seated at the right hand of God the Father. They could also take comfort from the fact that all their concerns were known to the Father who was determined to see them through their hazardous passage on earth in as much as He was determined to ensure the well-being of birds of the air. They could likewise take solace from the fact that all that was required of them now was to become like little children. On shedding their egotism and the trappings of power in that second childhood, humans would not only be relatively safe from the wiles of the devil, but they would be in a position to enjoy a fresh start in which compliance with the intimations of divine grace would be possible once again.

For those with truly forgiving hearts, Mjomba continued, the wrongs they suffered at the hands of fellow humans were akin to obstacles or hurdles in an obstacle race. Without them, the race would cease being what it was supposed to be - an obstacle race. And these being obstacle races in which the individual contestants were pitted against themselves, when the outlines of the white finish line loomed in the distance as the race neared its conclusion, that also marked the time for receiving the medallions and for the induction into halls of fame for the victorious on being ushered into the appropriate mansion in heaven. Which was not to say that the obstacle races were not trying, Mjomba wrote. For if they were not, the scriptures would not have contained any references to dire times that befell the Lord's people from time to time, or to the fact that the Lord was moved by the sight of human sufferings.

Mjomba conceded that there were indeed times when the obstacle races were more than just obstacle races - when the contestant, even though entirely innocent, appeared to be provoking a party or parties for whom things like consciences and natural justice did not appear to have any meaning. In the event, the contestant's life, according to Mjomba, frequently became transformed into a veritable nightmare, or even a living hell with no place to run; and with a tight noose as it were in place around his or her neck, so that any natural defensive move only made the already perilous situation that much more hazardous. Mjomba went on that it was precisely in the midst of situations of this type that, defenseless and utterly helpless, miraculous solutions came to the rescue; often turning the most hopeless predicament into one that was full of renewed hope for the contestant and, frequently also, the contestant's oppressor.

In a move that smacked of back-peddling, Mjomba went on that it was not just the innocent or the so-called men and women of good will who suffered in that particular manner and were then rescued and rewarded by the Deliverer; but everybody, including the perpetrators of injustice.

It would come as a surprise to Mjomba during his verbal defense of the thesis that this was one of the positions that came under attack from all corners, and which he found himself having to defend with extra care. His response to the criticism that sinners could not possibly be in line for such undeserved largess was that the Deliverer had come so that Adam and Eve, and all their descendants without a single exception, "might have eternal life". The Deliverer being the New Adam, no member of the human race, provided he or she played his or her part, could be precluded from getting his or her share of the inheritance he merited with His death on the tree.

Clearly no individual, not even the most reprehensible - and not even Judas who kissed the Deliverer on the cheek to signal to the High Priests and the Sadducees that they could finally pounce on their man - was about to be discriminated against; and certainly not by Him who was not only the Word who became flesh, but the Word through whom all things were made. A true brother of mankind who had sacrificed Himself so we could be welcomed back in our Father's household like the prodigal children we were, He was not about to be the one to break His word, and discriminate against some of His fellow humans on any grounds. And it was imperative, Mjomba wrote, that humans took the cue from this - the reason the Deliverer could not discriminate was not because He was a "good human". It was because He was divine.

It was not in dispute, on the other hand, that humans, exercising their free will or freedom to choose, could decide on their own, to reject the offer - just like that servant in one of the New Testament parables who was disgusted that he had been given only one talent and who accordingly decided to bury it, saying "Bye, Bye" to his inheritance thereby.

As far as the Deliverer was concerned, all of His fellow human brothers and sisters were eligible for a piece of the hard-won inheritance. But, in everything He did, He did not look like the sort of character who could turn around on an impulse and begin practising any kind of apartheid - and this especially after He had earned the right to sit at the right hand of the Prime Mover by spilling His precious blood. Mjomba had accordingly suggested that even hard core sinners were liable to be visited by calamities only to be rescued and rewarded in the exact same way those who were not as reprehensible were permitted to suffer before being rescued and rewarded. Indeed, if not sinners, who else? It was, after all, sinners whom He came to save, not those who were justified!

Later, during his verbal defense of the thesis, Mjomba would comment that one of the legacies of original sin was the perennial tendency of humans to never see evil in themselves, and to see nothing good in other humans - especially those who were different from themselves in some respect. Humans, with the exception of the Deliverer and His blessed mother Mary, seemed incapable of seeing the sometimes glaring and all too noticeable moles in their own eyes, but were invariably bothered by the tiniest specs in other peoples' eyes, according to him.

Intercession of the ancestral spirits...

Talking about the faults of others, Mjomba had never stopped being amazed by the ridiculous labels which Westerners were always so eager to use when describing the cultural traditions of non-Westerners, and by the offhand way in which they downplayed the negative aspects of their own customs and traditions. In the course of defending his thesis, Mjomba caused eyebrows to be raised with his suggestion that the Church hierarchy was wrong in labeling the symbolic actions that traditionalists in African societies used to give expression to the respect they believed their ancestors were due as "ancestral spirit worship" and "animism", and in dismissing those long established and also deeply cherished customs and traditions as evil and satanic.

Mjomba commented that there were some in African societies who exploited the fact that the spirits of ancestors were capable of interceding with the Prime Mover on behalf of the living in good as well as in hard times for their own personal gain, and others who were driven by their scrupulosity to expect what amounted to miracles from such intercession. But such actions were really no different from the actions of many in Christendom who exploited religion for their own personal gain or were driven by their scrupulosity to engage in excesses, or to wallow in activities that were "unorthodox". Mjomba argued that, if the actions of fringe groups in Christendom did not justify the rejection of Christianity *carte blanche* by its critics, similarly the actions of extremists in traditional African societies did not constitute a valid reason for the wholesale condemnation of African customs and traditions by any member of the Church's hierarchy.

What, after all, was wrong with the practice of asking the spirits of ancestors, particularly those who had been noted for their outstanding contributions in strengthening the moral fibre of members of the community and ensuring that the youth in society grew up physically and spiritually healthy, and unsullied by moral degradation of any kind, for their intercession with the Prime Mover! Or...with seeking to make amends and peace with the Divinity, regardless of the language used to describe Him. And what about the Catholic practice, now codified into Canon law, which requires that two miracles, attributed to the intercession of its candidates for sainthood, must be performed and recognized by the Sacred Congregation of Rites as a condition for the canonization of the candidate by the Pontiff of Rome! Mjomba argued that any one who found fault with Africans for acknowledging that their ancestors, even though long dead and buried, still live on in their afterlife was therefore either a monumental ignoramus or a racist or both!

And if the only people who went to heaven were members of the "Visible Church" as the prejudiced views of many a Westerner implied, and if it was a waste of time for Africans to seek their ancestors' intercession with Mungu, Mulungu, Ngai, Olodumare, Asis, Ruwa, Ruhanga, Jok, Modimo, Unkulunkulu, Nyamuhanga, Imana, Katonda, Chi, Ngewo-Wa, Rugaba, Njambi, Wele (also known as Khakhabaisaywa), Qamata (also known as Quamta), Fa, Sakarabru, Omumborombonga, Bumba (also known as Mbombo), Waaqa (also known as Waaqa-Tokkichaa), Ngai, Tsui-Goab (also known as Dxui), Abassi, etc. then the Deliverer's mission of redemption was far from the success the Church's own Catechism trumpeted.

Mjomba wrote that Lazarus, walking tall among his compatriots in Bethany - some of whom had probably already written him off as history as is common in the West after someone passes on - was a living testament to the fact that the spirits of the dead remained very much alive even after the individuals had "passed on". It was, accordingly, imperative that the spirits of ancestors were accorded the full respect that was due to them, he went on, adding that his African ancestors, in league with St. Peter, would in all likelihood demand an apology from Westerners who derided the reverence accorded to the spirits of ancestors on that continent as "witchcraft' before they let them through the gates of heaven!

By causing the "dead" Lazarus - whose body had already started the process of returning to the dust whence it came from - to walk and get about again and interact with the living, the Deliverer and Author of Life himself let it be known that once in existence, humans, among whom He himself now also numbered, lived even in death, Mjomba wrote. And would He have raised a beast from the dead, asked Mjomba? He likely would not because, according to Mjomba, when the lower creatures died, unlike humans, they actually died and passed on in the real sense.

Mjomba supposed that the reason the Deliverer, who knew that Lazarus was mortally ill and "dying", did not appear to be in a hurry to get to Bethany was the fact that "death" was the gateway to the real life - the lasting, or even more appropriately, the everlasting, life! Thus, long before the "advent" of missionaries, the "Animists" recognized that there was such a thing as heaven - the place where "life" actually originated and where it was eternal - things that Westerners apparently found hard to accept even after the Deliverer and Author of Life had Himself come down from heaven, Mjomba asserted.

According to Mjomba's thesis, by allowing Lazarus to pick up where he had left off during his sojourn on earth, the Deliverer provided the best evidence yet that "death", which represented the wages of sin, was suddenly on the verge of loosing its sting. But it also went to reinforce the fact that spiritual man, unlike the common beasts of the earth, remained very much alive and kicking even after the human body lost its capacity to sustain the soul. During the oral defense of the thesis, Mjomba emphasized that the problem at death was not the spirit - which just "went matching on" as he put it - but the body which ceased to be a suitable abode for the soul or whatever different people liked to call it.

Noting that the practices of worshipping idols carved by humans hands out of stone which distinguished ancient Rome and Greece from other centers of civilization of the time was the lowest humans could go in denying the Prime Mover His rightful place in society, Mjomba caused even more raised eyebrows when he went on to suggest that the practice of making libations - in the course of which individuals in society were forced to part with poultry, domestic animals, brew and other valued property - likely had their origin in the old testament practice of making burnt offerings to the Prime Mover in line with His injunctions which were communicated to the world through messengers like Moses and other prophets.

Mjomba was himself quite surprised that his audience appeared confounded and speechless when he claimed that idolatrous practices in Western societies had crept into and been incorporated in "Christian traditions". His surprise stemmed from his belief that there was a lot of evidence to support that contention. Mjomba was also astonished that the Church's clergy showed such little interest in the fact that if a catechumen could not appreciate his or her own cultural traditions, his or her practice of Christianity likely would be empty at best and radically flawed at worst.

Mjomba was almost eaten alive when he said that there had to be something the matter with a system that recognised and held up for emulation the heroic deeds of Westerners almost exclusively, and for the most part ignored the forbearing, long suffering and valiant struggles of Russians, Japanese, Indians, Pakistanis, Indonesians, Chinese, and Africans amongst others! And he was nearly lynched when he added that it seemed unlikely that those "wrongs" would ever be righted because the system in place assured that the curia in Rome which played such an important role in determining trends in the Church's liturgy and in other areas of Church endeavour remained under the domination and control of the most conservatives members of the Church's hierarchy.

The African "connection"...

In the short term, according to Mjomba, focusing on the negatives invariably seemed like the right thing to do, because the number of African converts usually picked up and church attendance, even though largely fuelled by sentimentality and sometimes curiosity, also rose. In the long run, however, because of being built on a shallow foundation which ignored the fact that African Christian men and women, like their Western brethren, needed to be healthy members of society who were proud of their heritage, these converts drifted away from the Church and carried on their search for ideologies that could satisfy their craving for spiritual as well as social needs.

But some ended up paying a very heavy price for allowing themselves to be persuaded to abandon their social roots. According to Mjomba, they ended up as rank materialists wallowing in excesses that would have been unthinkable if they had rebuffed the approaches of the missionaries and refused to be proselytized by those zealots among the Church's clergy in the first place. According to Mjomba's theory, when an individual lost his or her culture in whatever manner, his or her life and existence lost meaning, and that individual's craving for social and spiritual fulfilment easily translated into a craving for short term material pleasures. For Mjomba, it was completely unimaginable that the Church's clergy, whose job was to alleviate those types of situations, quite conceivably were having a principal role in precipitating them.

Referring to the journey Joseph and Mary made to Africa, home to the so-called Animists, and also the home of the pyramids which the Egyptian pharaohs built as an eternal monument to humans who had already made the transition to the afterlife, Mjomba suggested that the holy family's visit had more to it than just to escape from Herod Agrippa. He wrote that the danger Herod posed to the Deliverer, while genuine, also provided Joseph and Mary the excuse to visit the continent which was home to the original Garden of Eden, and also to meet with those whose devotion to the afterlife and the celebration of animism - or, more appropriately, the human spirit - had never faltered throughout the ages.

This was after all the land of the pyramids - the unchallenged wonder of the world attributable to Man's ingenuity. Mjomba added that unlike other wonders of the world like the Acropolis which had been built as a monument to false gods, or the Roman amphitheatre where the most atrocious things took place in the name of sport, the pyramids had been built solely to honor those who, along with Adam and Eve, were in Gehenna awaiting deliverance by the promised Messiah from the clutches of death.

Joseph and Mary, Mjomba wrote, had made it their custom as a family to implore the inspiration and guidance of the Holy Spirit in whatever they did, and their flight into Egypt was no exception. It would have been very uncharacteristic of them to base their decisions on fear. And, in any case, the mother of the Deliverer and the man who had agreed to be their earthly guardian were not afraid of dying. The baby Jesus Himself wasn't aware of any danger. All he was aware of was the dedication of His blessed mother and of Joseph not just for His wellbeing, but for the wellbeing of all human kind who lived under the shadow of death.

Encamped on the banks of the River Nile not far from the tall pyramids, Joseph and Mary could not help reflecting, as they drank of the waters of the Nile and used it to bathe the child Jesus, on the fact that they came all the way from the Mountains of the Moon on the Equator and site of the Garden of Eden and of creation. As Mary would explain to the child Jesus, the source of the Nile was also the place where Adam and Eve had lived and died, and also where Cain had visited death on his brother Abel in breach of the commandment that humans love their neighbors as themselves, and the Prime Mover above all else.

The child Jesus would also hear first hand from Egyptian neighbors the folklore that went back many generations, and that had "little men from the land of trees and spirits", a place they had dubbed the "Cradle of Mankind" and which they also considered to be the source of the waters of the River Nile, to found the Egyptian civilization! As the folklore had it, the Pygmies from the "Mountains of the Moon" initially worshipped a God known as Bes, who nevertheless transformed in time to become the God of Gods in whose honor King Khufu built the Great Sphinx that was visible from their modest hamlet on the river's banks.

According to Mjomba's thesis, with life so hard and complicated, it wasn't surprising that there were things like the "dark night of the soul". Like Adam and Eve, humanity was after all still on trial. But, Mjomba went on, even though life could be really hard, for humans with forgiving hearts, all calamities were God-sent challenges regardless of whether the misfortunes befalling them were traceable to ill-intentioned acts of fellow humans or what he termed "acts of God".

Mjomba argued that they were God-sent in the exact same way the good things humans in their ignorance attributed to "good luck" were, because the primary purpose of adversities was to provide the Prime Mover a basis - or rather the excuse - to reward humans not just in a spectacular way but in a really extra-special way.

Mjomba would elaborate, during his verbal defense of his thesis, that humans with a forgiving hearts and humans who were prepared to suffer martyrdom for their religious convictions were motivated by the same thing, namely the belief that their fate was in the hands of the Prime Mover. Wishing one's enemies well, including those responsible for cutting short one's existence on earth, on the one hand, and braving an uncertain future in this *Valley of Tears* where the pressures exerted to induce one to compromise his or her religious beliefs were immense, amounted to one and the same thing in Mjomba's view. Both actions, according to him, stemmed from acceptance of the fact that humans only needed to look to the Prime Mover for the fulfilment of all their needs, material and spiritual.

In the first of these situations, that acceptance translated in the recognition that the Prime Mover, having given the gift of existence to humans, also had the right to expect the recipients of that largess to exist or live as befitted their nature which was fashioned in His own image and likeness. And with regard to their earthly existence, the breath of life which made their bodies tick was something He had given humans under His divine plan, and it was also something He could take away at any time and in any manner He pleased.

Clearly, regardless of what it took, doing the will of the Prime Mover was not something that was negotiable between humans and the Prime Mover. The only hope they had of finding genuine fulfilment was carrying out that will. And hence the Deliverer's admonition that humans, among whom He now also numbered, take up their crosses and follow Him who not only was the Son of the Most High and the Word through whom everything, themselves included, were created, but also a human Brother whose Heart was the very epitome of forgiveness.

In the second situation, instead of the gift of life, it was the gift of faith or the invitation the Deliverer extended to humans that they sell all, give everything to the poor and follow Him. Humans responding to the invitation to leave everything and follow Him were in addition expected to be ready to face all sorts of inconveniences for His sake, including persecution. Acceptance of that invitation translated in the recognition that the Deliverer, anticipating that those who did His bidding would be rejected and in some cases even suffer martyrdom, was going to be there at all times to deliver them from the one and only thing they needed to fear, namely Gehenna or spiritual death. The bottom line in both situations was a readiness to follow in the Deliverer's foot steps.

Referring to life as a gift, Mjomba wrote that abuse of the gift of life and of the Prime Mover's other gifts to humans was sometimes on a scale that was so boggling to the imagination, there were no words to describe it.

It was bad enough that the first thing humans tended to do, as they progressed from their original states of innocence, continence, virtue, modesty and decency, to a state of naiveté, feculence and artificiality, was to pretend that they had all the erudition and knowledge they needed for anything. That was clear from the unyielding attitudes and stubbornness which they exhibited around the time they committed their first serious misdeeds in life. On the evidence, humans had degenerated into a new breed that, for sure, was not normal. A weird breed! They were out of control and they bragged about it.

As an example, Mjomba cited the fact that outrageous violations of moral law and the law of natural justice continued to be committed even as those responsible for past violations of the same codes were being apprehended and brought to justice. Generations of evildoers succeeded other generations of evildoers so routinely, Mjomba wondered if humans were capable of learning from their own experience anymore!

Everybody is infallible...

Mjomba added that one of the weirdest things he had noticed about humans was the desire to show that everybody, not just the Pontiff of Rome, was infallible. Realising that someone had to be infallible for religion to be credible, everybody all of a sudden became infallible overnight. Even those who officially subscribed to Scepticism were certain that their tenets represented the only authentic system of belief! And, of course, all who doubted the doctrine of infallibility also did so infallibly!

If the problem was that someone had laid claim to being infallible, that problem had now been effectively compounded by those who thought they had found a solution. For everybody, without exception, now claimed to be infallible!

Mjomba devoted three entire pages of his one hundred and twenty or so page thesis to the relationship between the sacred scriptures - and specifically the New Testament - and the *Magisterium* or teaching authority of the Church as exercised by her since Pentecost Day on the one hand, and the relationship between the scriptures and the Deliverer's own personal witness on behalf of the Blessed Trinity. Mjomba started by noting that he himself was not particularly bothered by the fact that there were many religions and "churches"!

He would later defend that rather unorthodox position by arguing that, in the after-life, there were after all no "churches" there just as there were no state governments, empires, kingdoms, sultanates, chiefdoms, principalities, or even "households". There was after all no such a thing as the "Catholic Church"! But, as the Nicene Creed correctly put it, there was "one holy catholic and apostolic Church". Mjomba would also elaborate that "church" was a useful idea only to the extent to which it signified collective human efforts led by the individuals who could claim to be the authentic successors to the twelve apostles, and to the extent those efforts were devoted to the return of mankind to the fold as envisioned by the Deliverer; and, Mjomba would add, only to the extent those efforts were guided by the "Advocate" or Holy Spirit the Father sent down on the Day of Pentecost.

As far as Mjomba was concerned, "Church Triumphant" was really just another phrase for "heaven", the place where people of good will, drawn to their Maker in a variety of ways according to their circumstances by the graces merited by the Deliverer and Brother Human, became reunited with Him. And, while good folks, Israelites and non-Israelites, who passed on before they had an opportunity to be "baptised and become a part of the Pilgrim Church" technically were neither headed to heaven or hell, but "elsewhere" because the

Deliverer (in the words of the catechism) has bound salvation to the sacrament of Baptism, the fact was that the Deliverer Himself was not bound by the sacraments He instituted; and He died for all humans; and all humans were called to one and the same divine destiny. But there was also the fact that the Deliverer was a member of the Godhead, and the ways of God were incomprehensible to humans. Therefore humans, according to Mjomba, could not but assume that all good folks in fact went to heaven.

It had to be supposed that they would have *desired* Baptism if they had known of its necessity (as well as membership in the one true Church if they had been in a position to obtain it). In fact Mjomba went as far as suggesting in his thesis that any human who regarded him/herself as saved, and who explicitly dared pronounce others as unsaved and damned, was probably guilty of presumption, and possibly also of pretending to understand the ways of the Prime Mover which were incomprehensible to men.

Citing the case of Cain who committed the first ever recorded murder but who repented and was now in heaven, Mjomba suggested that it would be reckless for any human to even suggest that Judas, who died within hours of receiving Holy Communion from the Deliverer's own hands, was languishing in hell. According to Mjomba, everyone would be thinking the same about Cain if the scriptures had not expressly stated that he came round and not only regretted that 'unforgivable' act, but explicitly sought the Prime Mover's forgiveness and went on to do penance for murdering his brother.

Mjomba had always been interested in the fact that the messages put out by the different religions and "churches" were contradictory in many respects; and he was very curious about the effect of that on the Deliverer's work of redemption. And it was this which led him to raise what, in his view, was a very fundamental question. The question pertained to the relative importance of the Messiah or Deliverer vis-à-vis the Church as an institution and along with it the Church's traditions dating back to the first day of its existence on the one hand, and also vis-à-vis the collection of the written testimony of the "saints" known as "Books of the New Testament" that, along with the Books of the Old Testament form what is known as the bible on the other.

It was pretty obvious, Mjomba wrote, that the personal witness of the Deliverer was the more important of the three, and that it would still have occupied that position even if the writings of the Old Testament by inspired writers, forecasting his coming, had not been available. And, what was more, it wasn't just a matter of the Deliverer being a witness to anything. As the Son of God who was sent to earth by His Father with a mission of reconciling humanity with the Creator, and who rose from the dead and was now seated at His Father's "right hand", He simply was in a class of His own.

Mjomba suggested that, in order of importance, the *ecclesia* or "church" which the Deliverer established on a "rock" came second. According to Mjomba, the Church was in all probability a close second, because it was somewhat difficult to distinguish the Church, defined as the Mystical Body of Christ, and what Mjomba referred to as the concomitant role of the Holy Ghost in it, from the Deliverer. Perhaps it even came down to semantics, Mjomba wrote, because of the continuous role played in it by the Deliverer both before and after its institution. And then, while it was the priesthood of the Deliverer in which those who ministered to the spiritual needs of the faithful shared, the Eucharistic presence inaugurated in the Upper House on the night before He laid down His life for humans left absolutely no doubt about the pre-eminence of the Church and its teachings over the bible. And that was not mentioning the role of sacramental grace in the life of the Church.

Mjomba wrote that the authors of the New Testament (like the *authors* of the Old Testament) were guided by the same Spirit that guided the *prophets* of the Old Testament whose activities were described in the sacred scriptures. In the case of the New Testament, the "prophet" was the Son of Man, and the writers - the evangelist John for example - acted with inspiration from "above", just as the prophets did. Mjomba supposed that it did not really matter if their inspiration originated from “above” or from their inner core where the Prime Mover dwelt; because that too was essentially semantics.

A critical aspect of the conversation relating to the scriptures, particularly for the majority of humans who did not have the privilege of being chosen and sent out to the world as the Prime Mover’s special envoys or “prophets”, was the role of the authority of the Church in determining whether the writings in question were inspired in the first place and also which ones. It was a responsibility that was one of many that were intrinsic to its evangelizing or teaching mission. And that mission was spelled out by the Deliverer when He said to Peter: “ *הכסייה שלי סאתה פיטר, על זה סלע, אני יהיה לבנות*” (translated: *“You are Peter, and upon this rock, I will build my Church*”).

And, even though it was a church or institution that He was entrusting to the likes of Peter (a mortal erring human), it was still going to be an *ecclesia* church against which the gates of hell would never be able to prevail. And it was obviously “someone” who Himself had already prevailed against the powers of hell who could take that kind of action, and also make that sort of promise.
And may be it was not entirely coincidental that Peter was already on record as doing what was very close to the opposite of the role he was expected to play in the *ecclesia* which the Deliverer was establishing, namely making moves to stop the Deliverer from proceeding to Jerusalem and his ignominious death. Not long after, Peter would maim and nearly kill a member of the militia that Caiphas, who was the high priest of that year, had despatched to arrest the Deliverer and his devotees, slicing off the man’s ear. That was because he (Peter) was slow in accepting that, even though the Deliverer had come to earth in fulfillment of the scriptures, His kingdom was not going to be of this world.

And, indeed, when push came to shove, Peter would act exactly like the Israelites who had walked away from the Deliverer when they heard Him state that His flesh was food indeed, and His blood drink indeed, and that He was inviting all His disciples to feast on them! ID'ed by the alert page (who herself was clearly one of the breakaway members of the emerging "Christ Fellowship"), Peter would promptly and completely forget his own earlier exclamations to the effect that the man who had been apprehended and was now being arraigned on the serious charge of declaring to the world that he was the Messiah the Israelites and the rest of mankind had been waiting for; and he would disown the man he had no doubt was the Deliverer of Mankind and also Master of the universe, and do so in front of the crowd which included Jerusalem's press corps!

Following in the example of those who had opted to go back to their old ways and continue living out their lives the way they had been doing before, and determined not to put himself in the same situation as that in which one youthful follower of the Deliverer (alluded to in Mark's Gospel narrative) who came very close to being nabbed by Caiphas's militia, and who found it necessary to abandon even the loin garment he had on as he took flight from his determined pursuers (because he knew what they would do to him if they succeeded in apprehending him), Peter had solemnly declared in front of all those witnesses that he (Peter), also nicknamed the Rock, and had quit the fellowship or *ecclesia* the Deliverer had been in the process of launching; and Peter had gone on that, just as so many other Judeans and Galileans who had been initially tricked by the smooth speaking Nazarene into becoming His devotees or disciples, he too had cut off all his links to the Nazarene long ago. Peter would assert that he knew the man not, and he would add that he did not know what the woman was talking about with her suggestion that he was a confidante if the self-proclaimed Deliverer!

While stressing that the importance of these writings could nonetheless not be downplayed, Mjomba thought it was noteworthy that the writings of the Old Testament, while loaded with prophecies relating to the Deliverer, did not forecast that there would be authoritative books of the New Testament to guide those who would choose to follow in the foot steps of the Deliverer.

It was also noteworthy that even though the Deliverer Himself made numerous references to divine promises contained in the Old Testament, He apparently did not make any direct reference to the authoritative body of writings that we now know as the New Testament; and it was no where on record that He ever suggested that this authoritative body of writings would replace Him or, for that matter, His Church as the sole authoritative source of the message of redemption upon His ascension into heaven. Mjomba suggested that even if the Deliverer had personally made some reference to the forthcoming books of the New Testament, it would be difficult to imagine that He would subordinate the Church he had established (and metaphorically constructed on the rock by the name of Peter) to the writings in question, regardless of their importance.

Mjomba had no doubt that the collection of inspired writings, which came into existence after the Deliverer ascended into heaven, derived their authority from the Church. The fathers of the early Church - including the apostles - evidently understood that committing something to *writing* was an accepted and certainly practical way of preserving and passing on to believers in distant lands and also to future generations the teachings of the Deliverer. And a lot of the material they *passed* on to Mjomba's own generation was corroborated by historians of the time. But it obviously needed the Church to authoritatively declare through its hierarchy that what was being passed on was not just authentic, but produced under *inspiration*.

Mjomba consequently argued that statements like "the Bible says", "the Church says" or "the Deliverer says" had to be seen in relation to each other, and that there was no logic to the idea that the bible could contradict the Church or vice versa. Certainly the Church established by the Deliverer could not contradict Him and still remain His Church. And the books of the New Testament, which could not have been written if there had not been an institution established by the Deliverer and informed by the Spirit in accordance with the will of the Prime Mover, not only had to be jealously guarded by "the Church" but could not possibly contradict the Church's teachings and vice versa.

While orally defending his thesis in that regard, Mjomba asserted that the bible did not write itself and, having no legs or wings, did not go hopping or flying around on its own on evangelizing missions. The bible was, in his words, "the fruit of human labor that was performed under the guidance and with the blessing of the Holy Ghost, the laborers being folks like Peter, James, John, Matthew, and Mark whom the Deliverer had personally tasked to go out and be fishers of men, Luke who was an operative of the infant Church and a confidant of Mary, the blessed mother of the Deliverer, and others like Paul and Timothy who had been inducted into the ministry with the laying on of hands by the original apostles".

The bible, Mjomba added, did not - could not - authenticate itself and much less interpret itself; and that there was no way in which any entity outside the Church that the Deliverer had established could certify books of the bible as being authentic or guarantee the correct interpretation of books of the New Testament or even the Old Testament. In other words, the books of the New Testament, inspired by the Holy Ghost, were the work of a Church - the Mystical body of the Deliverer - that had been established by the Second Person of the Blessed Trinity and was informed and sustained by the Third Person of the same Holy Trinity.

That infant Church, established on the equivalent of a rock (*tu es Petrus, et super hanc petram, ecclesiam meam edificabo*), and informed by the Holy Ghost at the behest of the risen Christ, was an outfit that had nothing in common with the scores of so-called "churches" or "ministries" that had been started by misguided humans, and whose existence was such a salient reminder of the frailty and fickleness of the poor, forsaken descendants of Adam and Eve.

But, according to Mjomba, the existence of these churches or ministries was by no means the only problem that the Church had anticipated facing. The Church of the Deliverer had anticipated facing other problems as well. There was the fact that Peter - poor Peter - had denied his Master three times within the space of an hour despite having solemnly sworn that he could never do anything like that. And then there was Paul, the self-styled "Apostle of the Gentiles", who had participated in the murders of followers of the

Deliverer before he was called to join the band of apostles, and who was probably shirked by some members of the Christian community to the end!

Mjomba wrote that the Church had major problems from Day One - problems that would have crippled it were it not for the manifestly critical role played in it by the Holy Ghost. Those problems, he asserted, did not go away. He went on that the work of the Holy Ghost was still at play centuries later when members of the Church's clergy, who should have extolled virtues of St. Joan of Arc and others like her, turned on them and murdered them! Mjomba had no doubt whatsoever in his mind that Methodists, Baptists, Calvinists, and others outside the "Church" had suffered "martyrdom", just like Joan of Arc, at the hands of the Church's operatives! But can it really surprise anyone in this God-forsaken-world that many "churchmen" who should have shown that they indeed were the salt of the earth, like Judas, hadn't lived up to expectations?

But an even bigger problem faced by the Church would be acceptance, and the Deliverer had accordingly warned his "workers" that they would occasionally have to dust the dust they picked up along their route as they entered some cities from their feet and move on because there would be no one there prepared to listen. The "Comforter" therefore had His work cut out for Him from the very beginning, and His work of necessity would start with those who, like poor Peter and poor Paul, would be called to be "other Christs" or apostles.

How the Holy Ghost would remain in the business of saving souls in those types of situations would obviously remain a mystery - as would also the particular manner in which He worked with the frail humans He selected to be vessels of grace. Mjomba wrote that he was quite fascinated by the fact that Peter, Paul and other mortals who were struggling to remain afloat themselves and not sink under the load of their own sins (as Ananias of the Acts of the apostles did), were out there preaching to crowds that included thieves, murderers, and what have you!

Some of those who had murdered would not be content until they had sought out and found "clergy" who could stand by them as they publicly thanked the Prime Mover for their murderous exploits! Then, the crowds they preached to would also include people who would have no scruples in turning the good news and the word of the Prime Mover as it was expressed in the bible into profitable ventures in the worldly sense.

And in the meantime Diabolos, equipped with the knowledge that the apostles themselves, however holy, would (as the Church itself taught) remain exposed to his temptations until the time when their trial on earth came to an end and the results of their performance on the Church Triumphant Entrance Test (or CTET) were called in, would not just be there *observing* the proceedings idly from a distance. According to Mjomba, Satan had to be working overtime - a lot of it and with a lot of success no doubt - to create as much confusion as possible.

There was ample evidence that the devil had actually "struck back" viciously and with surprising success, even though he could only hurt the Church by enlisting the help of humans, Mjomba wrote. And Mjomba readily admitted that as someone who "committed sin seventy times seven times a day", he could not exclude himself from those who were subject to manipulation by the notorious Diabolos. He had indeed admitted as much when he wrote that he might be getting ideas or inspiration from the devil for his thesis!

And besides, here he was, suggesting in his thesis - despite everything he had said or would say about membership in the "invisible Church" or Mystical Body of the Deliverer and the Church Triumphant Entrance Test (or CTET) that everyone, Catholics included, had to pass to gain eternal life - that the devil had a hand in the formation of the splinter Christian churches! And he was making that suggestion at a time when, increasingly, representatives of those churches were themselves openly suggesting that the Catholic Church headed by Peter's successor, was the work of Satan! The evidence for that "outrageous" claim included the Church's use or (as they characterized it) abuse of icons of the Deliverer and the saints which it employed as aids in religious instruction.

Challenged by a fellow student when he was orally defending his thesis in front of a panel of professors, Mjomba would respond that the "arguments" of the Church's adversaries both inside and outside it were really self-defeating, adding that they claimed to be knowledgeable about the "Word of God" after "studying" the sacred scriptures and then having a go at "interpreting" them from scratch and "correctly" while ignoring the institution that was the guardian of the self-same. According to Mjomba, those people "forgot" that it was not just the pictures and statues that were icons, but church buildings and even the "Church" itself were all icons that were not to be desecrated.

The same in fact went for the Deliverer's body and sacred blood, the cross on which he suffered and died, and the Shroud of Turin provided it was not a fake. After all some of the sick who touched the garments worn by the Deliverer received healing (even though it was because of their faith in Him and not so much because they had reached out and touched His cloak). And they also forgot that the book which they waived about and on which they "relied" to attack the Church - the "bible" - was also an "icon"!

Mjomba asked if these people learned anything from the account in the gospels describing an irate Deliverer chasing merchants out of the temple in Jerusalem even though it was only weeks away if not days before the veil in the Holy of Holies was going to be torn asunder, signifying the fulfilment of the Prime Mover's covenant with Adam and Moses, and start of a New Order based on a new covenant. That "incident" in the temple was pregnant with meaning, according to Mjomba. Even though mere icons, the temple, churches, and other visual representations of the sacred and the divine such as pictures of the cross and pictures of saints, just like the Deliverer's own body before and after His resurrection, had a very important place in spiritual life and could not be belittled.

Mjomba also read something else from that incident in the temple in Jerusalem - the earthly Jerusalem, and it was that the

Deliverer was prepared to openly and in front of witnesses cut off His relationship with any individual who had the audacity to use His Church for doing business or commerce. While this applied to those who took advantage of people's ignorance to misuse religious icons, it obviously applied even more to those who were prepared to challenge the authority of the Church in which He had invested so much. Just as He picked up a stick and chased the merchants out of "his Father's house", there was no doubt whatsoever that he would deal similarly with anyone who dared to employ His Church for business.

It was Mjomba's view that, used in conjunction with the Deliverer's other promises to the apostles at their "ordination" - that he would send down the Holy Ghost upon them and that whatever they decided to keep bound or to loosen on earth it would be bound or loosened in heaven - the Deliverer's action on that occasion provided justification for the Church's actions in keeping out or excommunicating individuals from the "visible" Church.

Another lesson, according to Mjomba, was that you were free to bash the Church as much as you liked by attributing to it all manner of evil, but only up to a limit if you wanted to remain connected to the Mystical Body of Christ. And that, just like the body of the Deliverer (which was informed by the Holy Ghost and was effectively a temple or house of His Father), no amount of bashing or assault on the Church (which was also informed by the Holy Ghost) would ever prevail against it in the final analysis.

The final lesson, according to Mjomba, was that the Triune Divinity comprising the Prime Mover, the Word and also Deliverer, and the Holy Ghost and also Comforter, operated in mysterious ways. That being the case, appearances were very misleading, and what seemed impossible to man was not impossible for the Omnipotent One. It would, in any event, be naive to think that someone wanting to become a follower of the Deliverer and a member of the Church the Deliverer commissioned to take the message of salvation to the ends of the earth wouldn't be scandalized by that state of affairs.

Mjomba supposed that there wasn't anything that could be more thrilling to Diabolos than a situation in which members of the

Mystical Body of the Deliverer referred to each other as lackeys of the Evil One in the same breath in which they said they were fulfilling the Deliverer's sacred mission of evangelization.

Mjomba noted that, by the same token, nothing could be more offensive to the Holy Ghost than the sight of creatures (the Prime Mover so loved that He gave His only son so that those who believed in Him might be saved) turning around and frustrating the work of the Church that His son (and their Deliverer) established (in accordance with His divine plan) to facilitate their salvation! Spiritual lepers, when they were not using the Deliverer's name in vain, they acted as if they had no need whatsoever for the graces He had merited for them with His death on the cross, or for the Church He had established for the purpose of dispensing His sacramental grace in His infinite wisdom!

Mjomba went on that if only humans could learn to be meek and humble of heart like the Deliverer, the Holy Ghost who informed the Church would take care of the rest. The problem was that humans - all humans - appeared unwilling to act like the creatures they were and give the grace of the Prime Mover a chance. After attempting in vain to be like the Prime Mover, they now wished to be their own Deliverer!

Pressed by members of the panel who were examining his thesis to say if those separated brethren who held the view that the Church was the work of Satan were hell-bound or not, Mjomba conceded that for all he knew, they could be saying what they said out of ignorance. These people were probably members of the invisible Church and did what they did unwittingly. This was even though their actions hurt the Church.

But so did the actions of many Catholics. Mjomba declared that, even though those Catholics were members of the visible Church, it was not beyond the realm of possibilities that they might not be members of the invisible Church. While admitting that as a human he was really not in a position to judge other humans on that score, Mjomba supposed that instead of waiting on the bridegroom with lit candles in hand, Catholics could choose to go off on other errands and show up after the wedding guests were seated and the doors of the banquet hall were closed. And that suggested, in theory at least, that someone could be outwardly a Catholic and yet miss out on something that really mattered, namely membership in the invisible Church.

To the charge, levelled by a fellow student, that he was making assumptions about the separated brethren being ignorant when he himself could be more ignorant, Mjomba's stock response was that he was not the pope and could not pretend to be infallible for that reason.

Concluding his discussion of the relative importance of the personal witness of the Deliverer vis-à-vis the Church on the one hand and the bible on the other, Mjomba wrote that it was not at all out of the ordinary that it was this Church that, as official guardian of the sacred scriptures, could certify if this or that piece of writing belonged to the official body of writings known as the bible or not. That was also why the bible had never contradicted the *official* teachings of the Church - the truly "anointed" of the Holy Ghost - and *vice versa*. And perhaps that also explained why, in contrast, individuals who walked away from the Mystical Body of the Deliverer soon enough begun contradicting themselves, increasing the prospects for divisions in Christendom.

According to Mjomba, the case for the so-called non-traditional "churches" which claimed the bible as their sole authority to the exclusion of Church tradition, but which themselves had a tradition of contradicting each other on important doctrinal matters, fell on that basis. And, in any case, how could anybody in those "non-traditional" churches or ministries claim to speak authoritatively on behalf of the apostles while at the same time deriding any connection to the "traditional" Church? Any claims to being "specially anointed" of the Holy Ghost or inspired by "ministers" in those churches remained just that - claims to personal inspiration and/or spiritual anointing and unauthenticated ones at that.

Mjomba went on that, for all he cared, so long as he himself wasn't propagating anything that went counter to the Church's teachings, even though the devil might be working overtime to trip him up, he too could claim to be laboring under inspiration from above as he worked on his thesis. And, as far as he was concerned, the thing that differentiated his thesis from the writings of the evangelists was the fact that the Church had declared thc former as the "word of the Prime Mover".

Declaring that no one outside St. Augustine's Seminary was ever likely to hear about and even less read his thesis, Mjomba went on that the chances of his ever being declared an inspired writer by any one inside or outside the Church - regardless of the content of his thesis - were really slim.

Virtual "human devils"...

In spite of the confidence and self-assurance with which he had reached his conclusions, Mjomba was nagged by the feeling that he could be completely wrong - that there was just no way the devil could score any points in misplaced attempts to derail the divine plan; and that any research that resulted in some "human devils" being cast as more acceptable to the Prime Mover on the basis of "appearances" - including religious affiliation - was just misguided.

It was typical of humans with their "small minds" to talk about the Prime Mover as if He were something they could comfortably tuck away in a pigeonhole, and he was quick to admit that he was one of them. Because they themselves were chatter boxes, they couldn't resist the temptation to claim that He (the Prime Mover) said this or said that - as if there was any human who had met or confronted the Prime Mover in person and lived to tell any tales regarding the encounter! There was no question but that the Prime Mover, after casting Beelzebub into hell, was now using the enemy to bring His divine plan to fruition.

Now, if Satan could not prevail against the Prime Mover, it was certainly also the case with humans. The extent to which humans were misguided and had become "devilish" was completely immaterial when the issue was implementing the divine plan. Mjomba conceded that even if all humans opted to become "little devils", the Holy Ghost - the third person of the Blessed Trinity - would definitely have a way of bringing redemption to any human "devil" who wanted to change and become a human "angel". The Holy Ghost and the Church established by the Deliverer (and which was informed by the Holy Ghost) would not even be deterred if the Pontiff of Rome opted to join hands with the Antichrist! That was not to say that the Holy Ghost was going to let that happen. Even if he didn't, there were already hordes who were convinced that the pope was *the* Antichrist anyway, and *that* was unlikely to affect the divine plan as well.

Mjomba easily acknowledged that he was one of the "virtual" human devils, noting that it would be wise for him to continue doing so until he was certain that he had received a pass on the Church Triumphant Entrance Test. Yes, virtual human devils who started by attempting to defy the Prime Mover and steal fruits from the Tree of Life, failing which they tried to rid themselves of His only Son and also their Deliverer by stripping Him, scourging Him, mocking Him and crucifying Him on a cross; and who now seemed determined to exploit the bible - the word of the Prime Mover - and the *Sancta Ecclesia* to the max and also to the end just as the Law and the temple were exploited to the max and also right up until the Prime Mover's covenant with the people of Israel came to an end two thousand years ago!

Yes, virtual human devils who had abandoned the principles of sisterhood and brotherhood that were supposed to govern relations among humans, and had embraced a system under which entire populations were now enslaved to exploitive government bureaucracies and corporations for which they had to work a minimum of five out of seven days a week for a pittance. Yes, virtual human devils who operated prison systems and torture chambers, not for the purpose of curtailing the civil rights of some aliens, but of fellow human kindred. Virtual human devils who were not even ashamed to confine fellow humans in cages on "death row", and who even kept electric chairs, guillotines, and gas chambers oiled and ready for periodic use in nipping the lives of the condemned men, women and children including the mentally ill - condemned not by some aliens but by their own fellow men - in the bud.

Virtual human devils who invested in the development of killer viruses and germs, as well as biological and chemical weapons in publicly funded facilities along side other weapons of messy human destruction, and who did not hesitate to use them on their fellow men. Yes, virtual human devils who were so blind that they saw nothing wrong with the fact that they were attempting to show other blind folk the way in pitch darkness without the help of a light.

Mjomba recalled the response of the Deliverer to the statement by an admirer in the crowd to the effect that He, the Deliverer, was good. The response of the Son of Man had included the words "Only God is good!" Now, that was a very "surprising" response by the one who was the Second person of the Blessed Trinity. Mjomba supposed that even though humans did not think so, it definitely *had* to be surprising that any of them could presume to be good at all.

And, more often than not, it was the most egregious offenders and hypocrites who balked at being lumped together with other humans as *virtual devils*, never mind that they all appeared seemly, gleaming and beautiful on the outside - like marble tombs - when, as the Deliverer put it, everything inside was rotting and ugly! Well, as far as Mjomba was concerned, it wasn't any wonder at all that the Deliverer actually taught that only God was good!

For his part, Mjomba had always had the feeling that, if he were given an opportunity to exercise rule over some unfortunate humans in some corner of the globe, he could very well end up making the most power hungry, repressive, cruel, corrupt, morally bankrupt, depraved, and baddest dictator - or the most unworthy pope for that matter if the Holy Ghost were to make the mistake of getting him (Rev. Mjomba) appointed bishop of the Holy See!

And Mjomba imagined that if he were president of the United States, perhaps he would end up as a neo-conservative *par excellence* who would expand the "axis of evil" to include even the Vatican if it did not "tow the line". Mjomba shuddered at the thought that as the incumbent in the White House, he might be tempted, in his pursuit of the policy of regime changes, to openly demand that the College of Cardinals elect as the next pope a "Prince of the Church" who not only was American, but one who also subscribed to the neo-conservative doctrines! He had no doubt that it would also be the surest way to earn an "F" on the CTET!

Even if a part of him did not like it, another and evidently more dominant part of him insisted that he, Mjomba, was closer to being a "human devil" than he might be prepared to admit. After all, here he was - a mere seminarian - presuming to be able to tell the world what being virtuous in the original sense meant. Mjomba wondered what would happen if he were ordained a priest with power to forgive sins and to deny forgiveness in the Deliverer's name. It was, of course, the Deliverer Himself who had given his apostles and their successors those powers - powers to effectively determine which sinners were truly penitent and deserved a second chance, and which ones looked like they were hell-bent, and deserved to end up in the Pit of the damned!

But if Providence were to make the mistake of getting him ordained a priest with powers to administer sacraments including the sacrament of penance - and it seemed like Providence was about to make that mistake - the way things were going, as *Father* Mjomba, he patently would be more inclined to use those powers to consign souls to hell and eternal damnation rather than to heaven and eternal life! Mjomba, who did not regard himself as someone who was "specially anointed" in the same way some preachers claimed to be, expected it to be a classic case of a blind man leading other blind men - unless the Holy Ghost intervened to rescue those who would be unfortunate to be counted among his parishioners, flock or whatever.

And He would have to act without any delay and quite fast after he received his holy orders - or so Mjomba thought! He told himself that he would hate to mislead multitudes who would flock to him for spiritual guidance - just as all those preachers out there who contradicted each other, and even themselves, all the time were doing without any shame or scruples.

Mjomba felt uneasy that he was passing criticism on other humans in the moral arena in the course of writing his thesis, and that it appeared unavoidable. He really couldn't do criticize anybody with respect to anything, and *especially* if pertained to people's religious affiliation! He could not claim that he himself was good! Only the Prime Mover who was good - and who, incidentally, also retained the prerogative to avenge sinfulness - could critique a human on moral grounds. Doing so, after all, required the ability to discern inner thoughts, something only He could do. Mjomba also noted that if he were to become head of state of some nation - or pope, the power he would wield would be from *above.* It would be completely immaterial whether he wielded that power wisely or foolishly. The fact that he was receiving that power from above would automatically mean that he was being used by Providence for His own ends. The fact that it might not occur to him that this was the case would also be immaterial.

Clearly therefore, regardless of what some humans did with the bible - by way of interpretation or even if they just used it to hoodwink the gullible and the-not-so-gullible in order to line their pockets - or with the *Sancta Ecclesia*, Providence would have its way. It occurred to Mjomba that even if humans went to war today and used nuclear and hydrogen bombs as well as other weapons of mass destruction on each other - even if entire continents were erased from the map and those that were not were left with populations that were permanently scarred and unable to take care of themselves, that of itself would not cause the world to come to an end.

It would, after all, not be the first time that weapons of mass destruction were used on the battlefield. When only one nation in the world possessed nukes, that nation did not hesitate to use it. With so many nations possessing nukes today, the chances of these apparent weapons of choice being used again was now also greater.

But Mjomba did concede that residents of Hiroshima and Nagasaki must have been convinced that the end of the world had come when the Americans dropped their nukes on those cities! In a sense, anyone who was at the receiving end of violence of any sort -

particularly violence that was uncalled for - could be excused for believing that their world was coming to an end. But Mjomba also supposed that any humans who allowed themselves to become "virtual devils" presumably also were clear about the fate that was in store even for devils.

The "Talking" Book...

Mjomba wrote in his thesis that establishing the relative importance of the "players" - the Deliverer and His personal witness vis-à-vis the Church (and not any church, but that Church which could demonstrate beyond any reasonable doubt that it was the lawful successor to the Church the Deliverer established on a rock called Cephas), vis-à-vis the contemporaries of the Deliverer who referred to each other as saints and their written testimony of the events surrounding the advent, life, death resurrection, and ascension into heaven of the Deliverer - was just one question.

A different albeit related question, according to Mjomba, pertained to the statements "The Deliverer says...", "The Church says...", and "The bible says...". Those were all very much incomplete statements, Mjomba wrote. Mjomba supposed that if the divine plan had called for the appearance of the Deliverer in person every once in a while, there was little doubt that there would be all sorts of people turning up in different places - and may be even in the same place at the same time - claiming to be the Deliverer, and vying for attention and an audience.

The Church, established by the Deliverer two thousand years ago and expected to be around at least until the end of time, was in a slightly different situation. Perhaps not entirely unexpectedly, "churches" of all stripes and sizes had been turning up all over the place all the time, each one claiming to be the one true holy Church.

The literature that comprised books of the New Testament and the Old Testament - because they had been around all the time and would so continue to be until the end of time - had suffered a fate that was very similar in many respects. When people did not come up with apocryphal material which they sought to include in the body of works that are referred to as the "sacred scriptures", they were turning up in droves and declaring that the bible said this or said that *according to them.* And - again as expected - to back up their claims, they usually went on to assert that they had received revelations to the effect that they were not just the anointed of God, but His special messengers whose testimony was as good as that of the apostles.

But if the teachings of those newly anointed folks and their interpretation of the bible - if the bible according to them - was markedly different from the bible according to the traditional or apostolic Church (and, again, not any "traditional apostolic" Church, but the one against which "the gates of hell will not prevail"), one had to ask what the authority and credentials of these "saints" were, and where they had been up until now.

Mjomba wrote that the bible typically said one thing to Preacher A, and another thing - quite often the very opposite - to Preacher B. There was of course no mystery about that. Different preachers wanted to hear different things; and the bible, being the truly wonderful book that it was, obliged! When the bible spoke to the presence of the Deliverer in the Eucharist, some people thus distinctly heard it say that the Deliverer turned his twelve apostles into cannibals by feeding them on His sacred flesh and blood, and then commanded them to carry on with the practice of saying some words over bread and wine to change them into the "bread of angels" and then feeding on it along with the body of the faithful like it was some spiritual sustenance.

And, relating what the Deliverer did that evening to events that took place a few days later (when, following His resurrection from the dead, the Deliverer solemnly laid His hands on the Eleven in a ceremony during which He also formally commissioned His Church telling them to go to the ends of the earth spreading His message of salvation and doing what He had taught them), they also understood that to change the species of bread and wine into the body and blood of the Deliverer, one had first to be chosen and then initiated into a holy priesthood in a specific manner.

But others who were listening to the bible speak apparently heard no such a thing. All they heard was something about eating a meal - supper - from time to time in the Deliverer's memory!

And when the bible said something about the Deliverer constructing His Church on a rock called Cephas, some heard it merely mumble something about a "church" with no ordained priesthood or even a leader. Others heard something entirely different - they heard it say that the Deliverer took Peter aside and told the fisherman that he would be the head of something he was referring to an *ecclesia mea* (my church). And they also heard the Deliverer, who had also promised Peter and the other disciples that the Spirit which united the Deliverer and His Father in eternal love would come down (as it subsequently did on the Day of Pentecost) and inform His Church and continue doing so until the end of time, reassuring the fisherman turned "fisher of men" that everything would be alright; that the devil and his truly dangerous mob of fallen spirits, while he wouldn't be exactly sitting back and enjoying a snooze as Peter and his comrades worked the fields that were ready for the harvest, would never be able to prevail against the enterprise over which He was installing the fisherman as CEO (chief executive officer). Yeah, the vacillating fisherman who would not hesitate to slice off the ear of Malchus, the high priest's slave, with a sword at one moment and in a matter of hours was denying his Master and swearing in front's of Malchus's kinsman saying: "I know not this man of whom ye speak!"

Others who heard the bible "speak" went away believing that the "Deliverer" was actually an impostor who, instead of helping the Jews cast off the Roman yoke, was predicting that the Holy Temple and the City of Jerusalem itself were going to destroyed! According to them, the proof was in the pudding. The self-proclaimed Deliverer had "fallen" and in that sense "capitulated" to the Romans and, therefore, could not possibly have been the promised Messiah.

There were indeed others who, on hearing the bible speak, merely concluded that even though it might be a proven fact that the Nazarene was a historical figure who lived two thousand years ago, He was really just a good swimmer who made it look as if He could walk on water! These same folks did not fail to point out that the Deliverer was also a terrific magician who could juggle pots filled with water (and some filled with wine) in the full view of guests at a wedding party, and hoodwink them into believing that they were now sampling a mysterious new wine!

Mjomba wrote that the phrase "the bible says" and its equivalent in other languages was probably the most abused phrase ever. It was that same phrase which was used by the priests and Pharisees to justify their actions aimed at neutralizing the very person who had been sent to the world to deliver humans from the bondage of sin! And if it hadn't been for that phrase, the Church's problems would have been immeasurably reduced. Mjomba wondered aloud if that phrase had no connection with the Deliverer's warning about the "gates of hell", and what they would be attempting to do to his *ecclesia.*

It had all become very confusing - the business of saving souls. But Mjomba argued that it was all exactly as it was supposed to be - given the nature of humans and the legacy of original sin or, as he preferred to put it, the loss by humans of their "original innocence". The fact of the matter of course was that the operative phrase "the bible says" was itself incomplete.

To be complete, it also needed to take cognizance of what the bible itself said that it *did not say.* What was wrong with people, Mjomba asked rhetorically? To make it absolutely clear that what the bible said was not the whole story, towards the end of his "gospel", St. John wrote - in letters that were so bold and large they had not been missed by any translator or transcriber of the biblical texts in memory - that his writings contained only partial information on the deeds and signs (or teachings) of the Messiah.

According to Mjomba, it was noteworthy that St. John went to the extent of explicitly pointing out in his "scrolls" recounting the birth, life, death and resurrection of the Nazarene that many deeds and signs that He had performed in front of the apostles - which undoubtedly comprised the great bulk of the information knowledge to which members of the infant Church were already privy - would definitely not be found therein. It went without saying that the same would be true of the accounts of the life of the Nazarene that Matthew, Luke, Mark and others were compiling.

The seminarian was nagged by the implied suggestion that a book - a man-made object that was nonetheless inanimate - could speak. But it perplexed Mjomba even more that, in the age of Think Tanks, no one had succeeded in figuring out what was at play here, namely that it was not a "talking book" but human nature!

Of course it wasn't the fact that the coming of the Deliverer had been foretold in Genesis 3:15 that *caused* Him to be born of a virgin as recorded in Matthew 1:18-25.

Or that *caused* Him, after He had spent the whole night on the mountain in prayer with His Father, to gather unto Him His disciples, and to chose twelve from among (whom also he named apostles): Simon, whom he surnamed Peter, and Andrew his brother, James and John, Philip and Bartholomew, Matthew and Thomas, James the son of Alpheus, and Simon who is called Zelotes, And Jude, the brother of James, and Judas Iscariot, who was the traitor, as recorded in Luke 6:12-16.

Or that *caused* him to proclaim to Simon Peter no less than three times saying: "Simon son of John, lovest thou me more than these? ...Feed my lambs" as recorded in John 21:15-17; or that caused Him in response to Peter's statement that He, the Deliverer, was "Christ, the Son of the living God", to state categorically and unequivocally: "Blessed art thou, Simon Bar-Jona: because flesh and blood hath not revealed it to thee, but my Father who is in heaven", as recorded in Matthew 16:17.

Or that *caused* him to say to His apostles in John 15.26: "But when the Paraclete cometh, whom I will send you from the Father, the Spirit of truth, who proceedeth from the Father, he shall give testimony of me. And you shall give testimony, because you are with me from the beginning."

Or that *caused* Him to say to Peter in Matthew 16.18-19: "And I say to you that you are Peter, and on this rock will my church be based, and the doors of hell will not overcome it. I will give to you the keys of the kingdom of heaven: and whatever is fixed by you on earth will be fixed in heaven: and whatever you make free on earth will be made free in heaven: and whatever you make free on earth will be made free in heaven."

Or that *caused* Him, eight days following His resurrection from the dead (as stated in John 20.11), to reappear to the apostles and to say to Thomas who was also called Didymus: "Put in thy finger hither, and see my hands; and bring hither thy hand, and put it into my side; and be not faithless, but believing."

Rather, it was the decision of the Second Person of the Holy Trinity to take up His human nature that caused things to be foretold about Him, with only some of them being committed to paper.
And there was no doubt in Mjomba's mind that it was human nature, not a "talking" book that got the better of humans and, starting with the issue of circumcision in the infant Church, made it necessary for Peter (as described in Acts 15.7), after there had been much disputing, to rise up and remind the sect of the Pharisees in the church and others saying to them: "Men, brethren, you know that in former days God made choice among us, that by my mouth the Gentiles should hear the word of the gospel and believe. And God, who knows the hearts, gave testimony, giving unto them the Holy Ghost, as well as to us. And put no difference between us and them, purifying their hearts by faith. Now therefore, why tempt you God to put a yoke upon the necks of the disciples which neither our fathers nor we have been able to bear? But by the grace of the Lord Jesus Christ, we believe to be saved, in like manner as they also."

The talking book, handicapped by the fact that its most important parts (namely those pertaining to the Deliverer's advent, ministry, His death on the cross, His resurrection and ascension into heaven) were still missing, wasn't capable of talking at that time; and that presumably stopped the sect of the Pharisees from proceeding with their attempt to reform the infant church. It also helped that Paul and Barnabas, who "had no small contest" with the sect of the Pharisees, had the presence of mind to seek counsel with the apostles and priests in Jerusalem concerning the issue of circumcision. It also probably helped in no small way that the "Holy Father" was the fisherman who had been groomed for that post by none other than the Deliverer himself and was revered by all of Christendom, including the Christians who belonged to the sect of the Pharisees. And there were, of course, no other issues like divorce were in the mix.

Mjomba wrote in his thesis on Original Virtue that, instead of a "talking" book, there were a lot of talking humans with a variety of motivations. For one, a "talking" book would by itself not have been to usher in the so-called "reformation" in the Church. By definition, that reformation was aimed at activities by church functionaries that were allegedly inconsistent with what the *reformists* perceived as regular. The reformers were reacting against individuals with whom they did not agree.

But because they could not dislodge those with whom they were at loggerheads from their entrenched positions of authority and power in the Church, and were loathe to submit to the Church's authority as exercised by their former friends now turned sworn "enemies", the only recourse they had left was to suppose that humans, however high placed in the church, could not possibly speak for either the absent Deliverer or the Comforter He had promised to send in the wake of His ascension into heaven, let alone possess and exercise the power to eject any dissenting individual from the *Sancta Ecclesia.* And since that included themselves, the only way to win the argument was to retreat behind the book.

The scriptures that up until then had been quite silent were suddenly given voice as the reformers went on the offensive in an effort to deny the Curia in Rome the authority it had been wielding against them. And the refrain, from then on, was to be that salvation came by faith alone! Also, since the subject matter was the salvation of humans, how could there possibly be such a thing as a living authoritative human(s) with the last word in spiritual matters? That, Mjomba claimed, was how the primitive parchments of the medieval times, with their stylistic hand-scribbled passages of the Old and New Testaments, came alive overnight and began talking!

But it could not be denied that the book was even then talking only in a euphemistic sense. The fact of the matter was that the situation hadn't really changed one iota; and it was the same folks (who had already been excommunicated by now) who, like the proverbial branches that had been cut off from the vine and were starved for sustenance, could now not help but grasp at anything that promised them salvation!

Still, it was some consolation for these "reformers" to be able to use the doctrinal position that hinged on the "talking" book to poke fun at the Curia in Rome by suggesting that they themselves were saved by faith alone through the twin doctrines of *sola fidei* and *sola scriptura*, and their enemies were the ones who were in schism and for all practical purposes already lost by reason of their uncompromising dogmatism and obduracy.

After initially hesitating, the holy book, with some assistance from the reformers, stuttered and, Lo and behold, began to speak. The reformers were in fact able to give voice to the book's contents quite eloquently.

Following in the footsteps of the original reformers, the second wave of reformers also gave voice to the holy book's contents, except that the results, reflecting their preconceptions and personal biases, were not quite the same. The latter, just like the earlier reformers who based the reforms they were promulgating on the twin doctrines of *sola fide* and *sola scriptura*, believed that it was anathema to include both Tradition and the so-called *Magisterium* (or teaching authority of the *Ecclesia* the Deliverer had chosen to establish on the Rock called Peter) as authoritative sources of revelation. And as years and decades went by, the cacophony created by the conflicting reformed voices became bewildering with each sect claiming to represent the True Believers who were also faithfully interpreting the *infallible* Word of the Prime Mover.

Thus, as long as they were alive and still kicking, the apostles would not have countenanced anyone getting up and declaring that "the bible says...period" as if that was all there was to the message of the "gospel" which they not only had received and embraced, but had sworn to spread to the ends of the earth and were even prepared to die for.

And if that was valid and true in the early Church, what was it that could make it untrue or invalid in later times, including Mjomba's own times? The answer was clearly "Nothing!"

And this was so, not so much because John (and his fellow evangelists) produced and published their stories while under inspiration from above, as because common sense itself said so. If the phrase "the bible says" had been adequate, then the death of the Messiah, His repeated admonitions to the apostles to do this or do that in the way that the Deliverer specified, the idea of a Church, the apostles and their successors, their blood and that of the many martyrs beginning with the Holy Innocents, were all wasted effort.

One could also accordingly down-grade the role of the Messiah Himself in the work of salvation because the only thing that really mattered was to get some willing humans to agree to scribble down the "message" of salvation while under inspiration from above. If the phrase "the bible says" was adequate, then the Deliverer's promises that he would be with his Church to the ends of time were completely hollow, and His prayer that "they may be one" was something He did in jest, as also were the Deliverer's actions in empowering the apostles with words such as "teach...", or "Whose sins you forgive are forgiven...", or "Go forth and baptize in my name..." - and so on and so forth.

Mjomba concluded that section of his thesis by arguing that it was precisely because the Deliverer anticipated the appearance of false prophets and the rise to prominence of self-appointed "messengers" that He had sought to reassure his handpicked apostles and their successors not only that the Holy Ghost would come down from heaven and be their guide, but that He Himself, even though He would be seated at the right hand of His Father in heaven, would also be with them in person in the Holy Eucharist until the end of time.

Casting the net for "humans"...

Elaborating on a statement he had inserted into his thesis to the effect that he was not personally bothered that there were many religions and even churches, Mjomba wrote that this state of affairs, while disappointing and far from the ideal, was not entirely surprising, given the backdrop of original sin. For one, humans now knew for a fact that the path to their heavenly paradise was not wide, but narrow - actually very narrow!

And, according to Mjomba, the Church's own liturgy not only recognized the fact of disunity in Christendom, but included special prayers imploring the Prime Mover not to begrudge His graces to erring Christians as well as others who did not even accept Christ. What was more - the Church's liturgy, using the words of the prophet Isaiah, even acknowledged that at the end of time there would be those who had not been told who would see, while there would be others who had not heard who would ponder!

Even though humans were still endowed with reason, which was in turn now reinforced by the Deliverer's redeeming grace, and had likewise been allowed to retain their freedom to choose, they now also had concupiscence that permeated both those faculties like an insidious cancer. The latter, also operating like a veil, made it much harder for humans to focus on spiritual things and so much easier to be blinded by desires of the flesh. And it also gave them a soft spot for the ploys of the devil, Mjomba wrote. The upshot of it all was that humans let their likes and dislikes, not reason, dictate what they ultimately chose to do.

Thus, some humans, seeing some things about the Deliverer which they liked, had elected to adopt Him simply as an icon, but not to carry out his bidding by openly throwing in their lot with the apostles and their successors in the Church he had established and following the Church's teachings. Others saw something about the Church which they liked and so became nominal members without a commitment either to its teachings or its official interpretation of the sacred scriptures. There were others still who found only some of the Church's teachings and injunctions to their liking, and who then proceeded to structure their religious beliefs accordingly.

And many, propelled on by the rampant scandals that had bedevilled the Church since the days of Judas and Ananias, some of those scandals even involving the misuse of Church facilities in much the same way the temple in Jerusalem was used for commerce instead of the original purpose for which it was built, had opted to continue doing their thing as if the Church did not exist. But the one thing that did not surprise Mjomba was that the world was now packed with so many feuding church organizations, each one claiming to be the Church that was originally established by the Deliverer and rendering the evangelizing mission of the apostles and their successors humanly speaking impossible.

Mjomba added as an aside that if he had not been brought up in the Christian faith, the odds were that he would never have seen the inside of a church, Catholic or otherwise, for that reason alone! Mjomba wrote that a leap of faith, not just reason, was needed by a modern gentile to find his or her way into the Catholic Church - and that was even before he/she had a chance to receive that faith! He added that this was a legacy of individuals in the Church since its inception not living lives that were truly Christ-like, and they ranged from ordinary members of the Church's laity to members of the clergy, including the so-called "princes of the church", to the successors of Peter!

Disunity in Christendom undoubtedly came with a price, Mjomba wrote. The constant prayer of the Deliverer to His Father that "they may be one" was, Mjomba asserted, an explicit acknowledgement of the heavy price which selfishness in the human family, and above all hatred, would exact from the beginning. Mjomba also suggested that the agony of the Deliverer in the Garden of Gethsemane had everything to do with that aspect of human frailty just as it had everything to do with the other sins for which the Deliverer came on earth to atone.

The invisible dimension...

It was during Mjomba's discussion of the subject of the Church that he decided to touch on a related subject, namely the Sacrament of Baptism. Baptism, whether it was baptism with water or baptism with fire or the simple baptism of desire, was somewhat analogous to the notion of "church". He supposed that this was, perhaps, something to be expected since baptism delineated members and non-members of the Church the Deliverer established.

And, according to Mjomba, "going to heaven" - which, alternately, could be described as being in direct communion with the Prime Mover while unimpeded by the limitations of physical bodily matter, or the beatific vision enjoyed by holy souls in the afterlife - was something that was directly related to the notion of God's Church on earth.

Defined as the Mystical Body of Christ and comprising a visible Church as well as an invisible one, the exact makeup of the Church's members was really unknown to humans precisely because of the mysterious way humans as a whole received baptism and joined those who were saved by the blood of the Deliverer in the Church. Mjomba suggested that humans were not privy to the exact qualifications for being ushered into heaven, which was itself analogous to holy Mother Church on earth.

Mjomba wrote that baptism, while it was a necessary condition for the salvation of sinners, was not sufficient. But, even assuming that all the other conditions were satisfied, not knowing how the Sacrament of Baptism really worked and relying on human ingenuity alone, it was not really possible to tell from a line up who was slated to go to heaven and who was not, just as there was no way of determining that an individual who did not belong to the visible Church was not a member of the invisible Church.

Mjomba wrote that it was not just revelation but also reason which attested to the existence of that place, midway between earth and heaven, where those whose disposition and integrity were not ship shape enough for their encounter with the Deliverer and Judge, His Father and the Spirit which united them in everlasting love - but not so wanting as to qualify them for permanent banishment from the face of the Prime Mover, just like happened to Lucifer and his legion of rebellious spirits - ended up.

It was in Purgatory, Mjomba wrote, where souls in transit to heaven spent time being adequately prepared and purified, so that they would be able to withstand the radiance and glow of the Prime Mover and his company of pure and spotless souls, luminous and comely choirs of angels, and shimmering hierarchies of Cherubim and Seraphims. This would also ensure that they would feel at home and not be like strangers in heaven.

But what human, besides the Deliverer, was in a position to say who was where at what point in time by just employing his or her reason! Mjomba suggested that it was an area where the new knowledge about genes and genomes was absolutely useless.

There was a direct connection, according to Mjomba, between the fact that some things were invisible, like the Mystical Body of Christ or the invisible Church so-called, and grace which operated in mysterious ways on an invisible level. And, consequently, since the subject in which grace worked (or, rather, was intended to work) was Man, as far as Mjomba was concerned, that removed any remaining doubts about the existence of the "invisible Man" who remained alive and well even after the time of his visible self on earth ran its course and his earthly existence came to its terminus at death.

Mjomba explained that, if sin had not come into the world, the exit from this world would undoubtedly have been the diametric opposite of death and would have translated into a delightful and glorious homecoming by steadfastly loyal but free and also exceptionally endowed and resourceful creatures. Having opted for loyalty to the Prime Mover over rebellion, humans would also have been in a position to lay claim to notching a pivotal, irreversible and crowning victory over Satan and his legion of mutinous spirits earning themselves a double crown in the process.

This would have put to even greater shame the fallen spirits, free and rational beings themselves who elected to seek adulation in their individual selves rather than in the Prime Mover, while knowing full well that their sacrilegious and unpardonable act would earn them instant banishment from His face once and for all - as it did, indeed, come to pass - and who now sought to frustrate the divine plan out of pure malice and by any means!

A holy priesthood...

And that, Mjomba wrote, brought him to the matter which was at the center of his thesis, namely the priestly vocation. Given the role of the Church in the divine plan and specifically the manner in which the Deliverer got together his band of apostles, the way he sent the Spirit upon them, the authority he imparted on them, and the manner in which he ordered them to go out in the world to do his bidding, anyone seeking ordination to the priesthood had to know that the calling to be a priest was a very special one.

Mjomba commented that if there was anyone who knew anything about vocations, it was the woman whose famous *Fiat* paved the way for the arrival on Earth of the Deliverer. Her calling was even more special than the calling to be a priest. What indeed could be said, Mjomba wrote, of someone for whom messengers from on high employed expressions like "Hail!", "full of grace", "the Lord is with you", "blessed are you among women", and "blessed is the fruit of your womb" in their address! And, even while an awesome title such as "*Mater Dei*" (Mother of God) could be used in addressing her, it had to be a very humbling experience for a human to be so addressed, Mjomba added.

Her human body, ordinarily a temple of the Prime Mover like any other human body, additionally became a tabernacle in which God dwelt verily for the space of nine months, Mjomba wrote. Through her *"Fiat"* communicated to the Prime Mover through the angel, she consented to be the vehicle by which the Word, through Whom all things that are created came into being, Himself came into the world; and, like Him, she saw every thing in its proper perspective, including the delineation between an earthly existence and the after-life that awaited humans when they passed from this world.

It was, Mjomba wrote, her *fiat* that the Prime Mover transformed into the living Christ in a transubstantiation of sorts, a precursor to the Sacrament of the Blessed Eucharist - the "unending sacrifice" the true and eternal priest would establish on the night before He gave up His life for humans. And, of course, Mary's *fiat* highlighted the role which the apostles - and those who would be called to be members of the priestly order after them - would also play in the administration of the Sacrament of the Eucharist in particular and in the salvation of their fellow men in general.

And indeed, to underline Mary's role in the work of salvation, before breathing His last and delivering up His ghost, the Deliverer and Author of Life had commended humanity to her spiritual care with the famous words he spoke to John, representing all humans, and to the woman whose seed was about to triumph over evil in turn: "Son, behold your mother" and "Mother, behold your son"!

Mary, who came into the world without original sin like Adam and Eve, but who (unlike them) would never once risk severing the communication lines between the Prime Mover and herself by even once betraying Him, had continued to be "full of grace". And the Prime Mover, ever faithful to His word, had continued to be with her all through her motherhood and during her period of sorrow. A "Virgin Mother", she had become a truly "Sorrowful Mother" who found herself, for no fault of hers, standing at the foot of the tree from which hung her divine son.

Mary found herself sandwiched between the murderous descendants of Adam and Eve for whom concepts of love, justice and faithfulness had lost meaning, and an eternally faithful, loving and above all merciful Prime Mover! And would it be any wonder that the Church, guided by the Spirit the Deliverer would send in the wake of His own ascension into heaven, would declare her *Regina Coeli* (the Queen of Heaven)!

Unfortunately, many of those who advocated the ordination of women usually were also the very ones who, according to Mjomba, tended to believe that the praises heaped on Mary by the Church were too many and also undeserved. But it was perhaps not entirely surprising that, in this "Valley of Tears" which the former "Garden of Eden" became when humans revolted against the Prime Mover, some found themselves scandalized and outraged by the fact that Mary, a fellow human, had found herself in a position to intercede for other humans with her son, a human who also happened to be the Second Person of the Holy Trinity! This was despite the fact that Mary did not herself choose to become the mother of the Deliverer, but agreed to become the Mother of a divine essence only after being "called" to from above to fill that exceedingly elevated role!

It did surprise Mjomba, however, that those who doubted Mary's elevated position among humans included persons who showed that they had an impressive grasp of the scriptures, and that they did so despite the clear reference in the Book of Genesis to the enormous power she would be capable of wielding. According to Mjomba, that reference was contained in the words: "And she will crush the serpent's head!"

For his part, Mjomba could not help making a direct association between the power of the Deliverer's mother and the fact that she led a humble life devoid of self-indulgence in as much as it was full of sorrows. According to Mjomba, Mary was, along with her son, the perfect embodiment of the truly spiritual human; and she also was the best role model among the descendants of Adam and Eve, aside from her son who, of course, was in a class of His own because he also happened to be divine.

Citing St. Francis of Assisi as an example, Mjomba wrote that saints "ran away from priesthood", because they saw it as a calling that was so elevated they felt they themselves were unworthy to aspire for it. To be a priest after all was to be an *alter Christus* he went on. Then, noting that it was an "apostle" and a candidate for the priesthood (Judas Iscariot) who committed what might be said to be the most overt act of betrayal, and that he was in fact only days away from being ordained a priest and a bishop simultaneously along with the other apostles, Mjomba commented that it did not mean that the remaining eleven candidates were perfect by any means.

He wrote that Paul had murdered, even though perhaps only through surrogates; and Mjomba did not fail to make a reference to the legend which said that Peter, after denying the Deliverer on so many occasions, had afterward shed so many tears that he was easily recognizable, everywhere he went by the deep grooves the tears left as they trickled down his face. Mjomba wrote that a repentant Judas would probably have made a spectacular man of the cloth and probably also an eminent father of the infant Church.

Mjomba concluded from these and other cases he had studied that the calling actually did go to mortal human beings, and very frail ones at that, a clear sign that it was the grace of the Prime Mover working through men which saved souls and those ordained priests really only served as vessels of the grace which came to the world through the Deliverer.

The key to achieving a happy medium between a finite bodily existence and an immortal spiritual existence, on the other hand, was leading an upright life. Which is just as well, Mjomba wrote, since the soul which informs the body over the duration of one's earthly existence, because it is as much a spirit as any other created spiritual essences - the heavenly hosts and the fallen angels for instance - cannot escape accountability for its actions once it shed that body.

The human paradox...

Mjomba supposed that there was some merit in discussing the question of identity in that particular regard, and so he went on that the real identity of humans was not even close to the reflection which appeared in a mirror! If it were, it would be possible to argue that the back of the head or the crown, or any part of the body including internal organs for that matter, rather than the face (with or without goggles), represented a true picture of what humans really looked like.

The true identity of humans, Mjomba suggested, was spiritual and not physical, the fact that the human constitution consisted of a soul (which was invisible to the naked eye) and a body (which was visible) notwithstanding. Admitting that he himself could not pretend to know exactly what a human's true identity was like, Mjomba still proceeded to provide what he said were his strong suspicions in that respect. The situation of humans, he went on, was similar to that of angels, and the state of their morality or relationship with the Prime Mover defined the identities in both cases. Which was just another way of saying that a human - or an angel - created in the image of the Prime Mover, looked a little like Him, Mjomba concluded.

Mjomba wrote that during their early years, while they were innocent and childlike, humans appeared capable of knowing and accepting their limitations - that they did not at all elect to come into existence and much less that they themselves chose to be humans rather than some other creature; that they did not choose to come into the world male or female, blond or auburn, Mongoloid, Caucasian, Negroid, or something else. As they outgrew their childhood and innocence, just when you were starting to think that they were maturing and growing in common sense, all humans almost without exception apparently went nuts and begun to act as though they could have affected the course of those events!

They smarted so very much when they made mistakes and were being corrected on the one hand, and then they became so enraged and were almost prepared to kill at the sight of other people making identical mistakes, you would think that they themselves were "saved" (as they say) even before deliverance visited them so they could become saved. And may be they were right because it was, after all, when they were still childlike and guileless that they were vouchsafed with grace and were really saved. Meaning they got lost when they started to proclaim that they had been delivered and were finally saved!

The idea that they might owe anything to a Prime Mover or any such entity became not just the most illusive but seemingly also the most offensive to boot almost overnight, Mjomba decried. He suggested that it was a syndrome that fully merited the title "the Human Paradox"!

Mjomba even volunteered a definition for "Losing Innocence": Doing things humans ordinarily would not have brought themselves to do out of respect for and deference to the Prime Mover. In the course of losing innocence, humans, who until then were completely at home trusting in the Prime Mover, perhaps as a direct result of the unavoidable feelings of guilt, gradually took to trusting either in themselves or in fellow humans, effectively "losing" themselves in the process, Mjomba wrote.

Mjomba called it the big lie, and it concerned the question of human mastery over nature and ownership. Mjomba wrote that humans had somehow succeeded in convincing themselves that nature itself was subservient to them, and that they had complete mastery over it, including whatever made up their own constitution; and he claimed that it was what the sacred scriptures referred to as "vanity of vanities" and "vanity of the eyes"!

What was it that made a human being tick? Not the physical body or its parts (which, according to Mjomba, were all essentially expendable, even though some more easily than others) but the spirit (which, according to him, once brought into existence, did not expire) and the spiritual faculties which were the guiding force behind the actions of a human. And then, belief in a Supreme Being or Prime Mover, when not completely diluted by the irrational notion that things evolved out of nothing over time following the so-called Big Bang, had degenerated into sentimental feelings that had them worship an equally strange Omnipotent Being who was nice and forgiving to the 'faithful', but was utterly merciless to anyone so-called 'unbelievers' who did not belong to the 'fold'.

The spirit, Mjomba noted, was invisible. And that, Mjomba claimed, was what provided humans the excuse to act as if the spirit was an imaginary thing; that it only existed in ghost stories, and that no spirits existed in reality. Using the excuse that spirits could not be seen, touched, smelt, heard, or be tasted (as if it were some delicacy), they even tried to convince themselves that the body did not really need the spirit to inform it, but was self-sustaining, like the bodies of the lower beasts which acted on instinct and did not possess the spiritual faculties of reason and free will. Mjomba added that humans were in denial in this regard, and their state of denial caused many a human to live as if the spirit did not survive the body (which was itself corruptible) to live on in the nether world. The fact that things which belonged to the spiritual realm were invisible to the naked eye was used by humans as the excuse, he wrote, to live lives that fell short of upright. They conveniently - very conveniently - forgot the fact that the Prime Mover dwelt at the core of their being such that humans in acknowledging that they existed, *ipso facto* paid tribute, albeit reluctantly, to the existence of the Supreme Being at their core who actually made them tick.

Mjomba suggested that humans were so preoccupied with material things that could only be seen (like a house, an automobile, a fur coat or a television set), be heard (like chamber or rap music), be touched (like money or jewellery), be smelt (like scent from roses or artificial perfume), or tasted (like roast beef or wine) that spiritual things were now almost completely lost on them. He wrote that when they were not claiming to be automatically and irrevocably saved, and thereby abnegating individual personal responsibility for their actions, they were invariably asserting that spiritual things were for the imbeciles, simpletons with backward mentalities, and others like them in need of something of that sort for emotional support.

Mjomba wrote that all grown-up humans without exception started out as little innocent angels. The turning point seemed to coincide with their ceasing to rely on all fours' to get about and their mastery of the skills for standing upright and walking unaided. That was when they apparently started to believe that they were really not humans but small gods, and ended up deceiving themselves that they could actually be complete masters of their own destiny.

And soon enough they began behaving as if they could have elected to walk on their heads instead of their feet, or to breathe with their ears instead of their noses, to sleep while standing upright on one foot like a crested crane instead of while lying prostrate on a flat surface, etc. Worst of all, they begun to act as if they themselves chose to be who they were, to have two rather than one eye or none as is the case with a certain snake specie, to walk on feet that have five toes each rather than one or two, to feed with the mouth instead of some other way, and so on and so forth.

It was all exactly as the inspired author had observed: Vanity of vanities! And it was irrational. And not because the holy book said so, but because the physical human frame - the center of the self-deception - must disintegrate into the dust (from which it originally came in any event) in due course, Mjomba wrote. For humans to claim that they owned anything at anytime when the very next moment it could all be taken away with the humans concerned having no option but to accept the result was, Mjomba wrote, presumptive and tantamount to living in an imaginary world. Mjomba suggested that humans did not in fact own even their own lives.

Humans did not stop at pretending that they were capable of doing what was essentially impossible, namely give what they themselves did not have! But they even pretended that acceptance of their true nature, namely that they were creatures who just happened to be blessed in a special way, made them less human. And they ridiculed the few amongst them who eschewed such idiotic behavior.

In the process of trying to keep up with the Joneses, humans went to some surprising excesses. The young-blooded, for instance, strove to acquire fast autos and other means that might speed up their exit from this world. Those who were older and had the means resorted to acquiring single engine air planes which they promptly converted into toys. Others took to bungee jumping with the obvious intention of testing the strength of nylon cords. Still others found all sorts of ways to make their already short life spans shorter. Those who found themselves occupying seats of power begun courting wars as if they had to do something to break the boredom engendered by the modest intervals of peace time.

But it was both a telling and implicit acknowledgement of their total dependence on the Prime Mover, he wrote, that when the diehards among humans clambered aboard their Leer jets to enjoy the feel of being as free as birds of the air, they did so with parachutes under arm. They made sure that their fast autos were equipped with air bags when they jumped into them to test the maximum cruising speeds of the machines and to enjoy the excitement of living on the edge in the process. And they had helmets handy when they hopped onto motor bikes and used them to perform daredevil manoeuvres. But any investment in insurance aimed at postponing the inevitable, even though useful in the short run, always proved inadequate in the long run, Mjomba wrote.

The list of insane things humans did was endless, Mjomba wrote. And to compound the problem, they seemed so helpless as far as action to pull back or reverse course went. They reminded Mjomba of speeding autos that were unable to stop because the accelerators were jammed and stuck to the floors of the vehicles, and of runaway roller-coasters that had gotten out of control. And yet all humans needed to do, like the prized creatures of the Prime Mover they were, was to accept that they were recipients of the Prime Mover's strikingly exceptional largess; and then, like princes and princesses, settle back to enjoy His unfathomable bounty in His everlasting kingdom. As it was, the only thing humans liked to do seemed going out and trying as hard as they could to reverse their good fortune.

All this contrasted so much with true deliverance which, according to Mjomba, consisted in the passage from this life to the afterlife whilst on good terms with the Prime Mover. It was paradoxical, but the fact remained that to die to oneself whilst in this life, and above all to lose one's life while in the Prime Mover's service, was what constituted deliverance of a human! Coming into this "world" at birth could thus be likened to being allowed to set one's foot at the gate of heaven and dying was equivalent to heading off to be united spirit to spirit with the Prime Mover.

All of which reminded Mjomba of Judas, the apostle who had come to personify "betrayal" in the eyes of most.

2. The Betrayer

Referring to the expression "It were better if he had not been born", Mjomba noted that all the descendants of Adam and Eve, with the exception of Mary and her son, had also been betrayers at one time or other and were to that extent like Judas. He believed that the Deliverer's words, even though addressed to Judas, applied to all humans to the extent to which they resembled Judas or were betrayers.

Quoting liberally from the Canadian Scrolls, which scholars unanimously ascribed to a friend and contemporary of the apostles who went by the name of Josephus, and which appeared to have been intended as a companion to what was now known as the Acts of the Apostles, Mjomba wrote that Judas apparently harbored a great dislike for Peter, and that the apostle who would subsequently gain notoriety as "Betrayer of the Deliverer" had hated Peter's guts from the moment he heard the Nazarene pick out the fisherman from His audience during an address He gave at a popular beach spot along the shores of the Sea of Galilee and tell him in front of everybody that he was the equivalent of a rock, and that it was upon that "rock" that He intended to establish His "Church". This was even though Judas thought that the Deliverer had to be cracking some sort of joke!

The Deliverer's exact words were as follows: "You are blessed, Simon Bar-Jona. I tell you Peter - you, whose name coincidentally means 'rock'! In front of John, Judas and all these others, I am saying to you here and now: You are the rock on which I am going to build the New Jerusalem - or my 'Church' as it will be known. My Church is going to be universal, and it is going to have you, Peter, as its main cornerstone..."

And, as Peter protested that he was only a fisherman who was a vacillating clout and a weakling by nature, and retorted that it would be too risky for the New Jerusalem to have him as its hinge, the Deliverer had pursued: "Tut, tut, tut! You are Peter and also the rock

I am talking about; and it is you I have chosen - not your brother James here, or Judas or even John who also happens to be my own blood relative - to be the rock upon which I will build my Church. And, take my word for it, Peter - the gates of hell shall not prevail against it. All this means that I am going to give to you the keys of my celestial kingdom. And, mark this! What ever you will hold bound on earth, will be automatically bound also in heaven above! And what ever you will loosen and free down here on earth, it shall be loosened and freed also in my kingdom in heaven above. This is my covenant to you and whoever will succeed you as the 'papa' who oversees my flock in this 'Valley of Tears'."

Judas had at first tried to pretend that, even though he was standing right there by the Deliverer's side, he hadn't heard anything. But seeing that he was just making a fool of himself, he had decided that, even though he had never heard the Deliverer speak frivolously and indulge in cracking jokes, He had to be breaking that rule on this occasion. He simply had to be joking! Judas had felt almost as if the Deliverer had told him: "See this fisherman? He is my Eliacim. I will place the key of the house of David on his shoulder; and he shall open, and no one shall shut. And he shall shut and no one shall open! And you - Judas: you are like the worthless Sobna. That is why I am choosing to invest the office of 'Papa' in Peter and not in you!"

Citing new evidence Mjomba claimed was contained in the recently unearthed Canadian Scrolls, he wrote in his thesis that, when interviewed by the Evangelist Luke, witnesses to the incident had described the reaction of Judas as uncharacteristic of someone who was a member of the Deliverer's inner circle. He had murmured: "Jees! Not Peter of all people! Not that blockhead!" And then Judas reportedly had added rather ominously: "Master, this you will regret, I promise you!"

It was may be three months later that Peter, who was unaware of the dislike Judas harbored for him, ran bubbling to the comrade from Jericho that John, his own brother James and himself, while on a mountain top with the Deliverer, had been treated to something entirely out of this world. It annoyed Judas even more that Peter, after saying that the instructions they had been given were that they not mention the incident to anyone, was unable to find words to describe what had transpired, and just managed to blunder his way through the word "transfiguration"! This had also given Judas a basis to conclude that Peter was a blithering idiot who could not even be trusted to keep a secret.

The real Judas...

Judas, who had been one of the very first people to join the ranks of the Deliverer's disciples and who had done so by ingratiating himself with the youthful John whom he knew to be very close to the Deliverer by virtue of being a relative of the Deliverer's mom, was certain from the beginning that he was destined to play an important role in the "Christ Fellowship" as he himself liked to refer to the work and mission of the Deliverer.

He did not conceal the fact that he thought highly of John from the beginning, and he even went to the extent of calling him very intelligent in public. In private, around the time that the Deliverer's immediate deputies - or "apostles" as they had already been nicknamed by the crowds which followed them everywhere - reached the magic number of twelve, the disciple from Jericho had pulled John aside to discuss what he said was a very important matter. Judas had noticed that many people in the crowd, after they witnessed the Deliverer's eloquence and were moved by his discourses, frequently reached into their pockets and took out *denarii*, and sometimes pieces of silver, which they then sought, albeit always in vain, to present to the Deliverer for keepsake. His immediate aim was to become the Deliverer's purse holder, but he also had other things on his mind when he asked John to step aside for the private session.

Judas persuaded John that they needed to start thinking big and to approach everything they did from then on systematically, and that if they did not do that, absolute chaos was going to result, especially given the growing popularity of the Deliverer. Recalling the events of the afternoon not long before when the Deliverer miraculously multiplied the five loaves and two fishes into baskets upon baskets of food, Judas said that, because there was no organization, the starving multitudes had initially surged forward for a free helping, much to the disadvantage of the children and the feeble as well as the women who were just as hungry but could not muster the strength to join the unruly rabble.

For starts, Judas explained, they needed to draw up an organization chart which would facilitate coordination of activities and the allocation of tasks among the twelve. He claimed that these things were of critical importance now that people were being attracted in large numbers every day to the Fellowship. If they did not act, Judas told John, the new catechumens would soon be disenchanted with them and would actually walk away.

He told John about the donations, and said he was already in the process of drawing up a plan to take care of that. He confided to John that, under the plan, trusted assistants reporting directly to him would mill in the crowds, armed with the baskets, to ensure that the voluntary offerings were all gathered in efficiently and were safely tucked away.

Judas suggested that a committee preferably consisting of Matthew and Mark, both of whom seemed to be good with the quill, meet under John's chairmanship and begin the all important task of drawing up the Fellowship's mission statement and a constitution. To get anywhere, they needed to register the Fellowship with the Roman authorities. Such a move, Judas added in a whisper, would put the nervous high priests and other members of the Sanhedrin and the Roman prefect off the scent by making it appear that there was nothing for them to be worried about with respect to the Fellowship's activities.

Judas went on that they needed to move quickly to set up a security detail to protect the Deliverer from any possible harm. The growing belligerency of the high priests highlighted the importance of taking such a step, he said. Judas suggested that John himself be in charge of the security detail.

Judas had even mentioned something about having someone reliably document all the miracles that the Deliverer was performing, with special care being taken to record the exact phrases used by the Deliverer - just in case those phrases contained formulae that might require more time to decipher! In the case of miracles of healing, the log would also include the names and addresses of those healed, as well as a short description of the ailments that had afflicted them. But it was important that the log also include a synopsis of the Deliverer's addresses to the crowds. For, as Judas kept repeating to John and others, there was no doubt whatsoever that they were living at a turning point in the history of mankind; and the way the twelve who surrounded the "Teacher" and "Miracle Worker" conducted themselves was going to affect generations to come.

Now John had never been enamoured of strangers, especially fast talking strangers, and initially lent Judas only half an ear. Besides, a lot of what Judas was saying only struck the wrong chords in him. Big organization, money, etc. were completely novel things to John. These things smacked of greed - organized or what today would be called "corporate greed"!

But Judas, who had anticipated all that, was easily able to read John's thoughts even before he spoke. And so, cutting in, he had added piously: "The Deliverer is here at long last, John. With His help we can channel the ill-gotten gains of the moneyed, who cannot even leave the Deliverer alone, to the poorest of the poor in the Nation of Israel!"

And because he also enjoyed exaggerating things, he had continued that they had a lot of work to do given the number of those who were even then displaced as a result of the Roman occupation.

According to Mjomba, Judas succeeded brilliantly in concealing behind a series of platitudes his real intention of using the Deliverer to establish what would essentially be a corporate entity complete with a separate personality. Once on-going, the corporation under his direction would in turn reward him generously with the equivalent of stock options, magnanimous living allowances equivalent to a fat salary, and a severance package that would be the envy of everyone including the Roman Prefect!

Finally persuaded, John commended Judas for thinking ahead, and even confessed that, up until that moment, he himself had been moving along blindly with the crowd so to speak - as if they owed it to Providence to take care of everything, including taking steps to ensure that no harm befell the Deliverer! In short, John was in total agreement with the proposed plan of action. And they both agreed that, acting jointly, they would arrange for all the twelve to meet in conclave as a matter of urgency. At that meeting, the necessary resolutions legitimizing what they had discussed would also be passed.

After a further exchange of ideas regarding the post of Secretary/Treasurer which, according to Judas, needed to be filled expeditiously, John promised that he would nominate Judas to fill that key position at the upcoming conference.

As expected the conference, which was convened shortly after the "Sermon on the Beach", appointed Judas to the glamorous position of Secretary/Treasurer of the Christ Fellowship, while the position of Chief of Security went to John. Judas meanwhile derived secret pleasure from the fact that his rival, Peter, had been passed over when appointments to all the other important positions were being made, and that Peter, who clearly showed at the meeting that he could not even address an audience of eleven people, only succeeded in getting himself commissioned, along with his brother James, to form the first line of defense around the Deliverer.

Citing evidence in the Canadian Scrolls, Mjomba wrote that Judas was always elated and smiling whenever he wandered upon Peter or James, because he was sure - or so he thought - that, with just daggers in their arsenals, the duo would be mince meat when confronted by members of the Jewish constabulary or Roman foot solders, not to mention members of the Roman cavalry.

A disciple of the Deliverer and also a candidate for the holy priesthood, Judas was still not really prepared to defend the Messiah to the death as the apostle Peter and the others were despite his avowal to that effect. To be prepared to sacrifice his life for the Deliverer was the last thing on Judas' mind! This was even though Judas, who still "loved" the Deliverer very much, albeit for the wrong reasons, enjoyed very much being the busiest body around Him.

Judas' personal attachment to the things of this world and above all gold or "mammon" (he must have known its worth since he was the fledgling organization's Chief Accountant and Financial Controller) would result in the unsavory situation in which a confidante of the Deliverer ended up betraying Him and then taking his own life shortly afterward! For the right price - and perhaps even the promise of a unique place in history for being the one who would help put away by far the most popular claimant to the title of Deliverer up until that time - Judas was prepared to do the unthinkable, namely send a wholly innocent and just man to His ghastly death on a tree!

High-stakes diplomatic gamble…

In Mjomba's view, the traditional image of Judas as someone who was dumb and short sighted - someone who easily fell for get-rich-quick schemes one moment and who was rushing to cut short his life in despair the next moment - was well off the mark. Arguing that nothing could be further from the truth, Mjomba wrote that the betrayer was in fact a very farsighted and brilliant individual, and almost certainly the brightest of the twelve apostles.

In contrast to Judas, Peter and his brother James (along with their mother) wondered why - since the mission of the Deliverer clearly was not to drive the Roman imperialists out of the promised land as some folks thought - the Messiah, if He was indeed the promised Messiah, did not just "do it", by which they meant whisking them off into heaven and into the company of Moses and Elias, and out of reach of those imperialists!

Following in the foot steps of the first century historian Josephus, Mjomba contrasted Judas to the constantly "bumbling" Peter, a fisherman by trade who seemed a little tardy when it came to learning and had to take his time to decide if dying for the Messiah was actually worth it or not. Mjomba supposed that, in the betrayer's eyes, Peter must have stood out as one of those individuals who generally tended to have an excess of brawn power and a deficiency of brain power.

Mjomba went on to suggest that Judas was ahead of his time in discerning the winds of change, and the direction in which they likely would blow. According to Mjomba, the Apostles from Jericho therefore clearly understood that the movement the Deliverer was leading wasn't going to go away. If anything, after seeing some of the miracles wrought by the Nazarene, Judas calculated that if he positioned himself strategically inside the movement, he stood a good chance of achieving his ultimate goal of becoming the Deliverer's undisputed deputy, and guaranteeing himself considerable material rewards in the process.

The fact that he had already been appointed Financial Controller and Chief Accountant was clear evidence that the Deliverer would not be in a position to personally oversee His empire as it spread beyond the borders of Palestine and conceivably even supplanted the Roman Empire as the unchallenged world power. Judas was prepared to play his part to bring about the new order and help the Deliverer realize His own dream of dominating the world!

But, while he was a top flight manager with the kind of vision that entrepreneurs prized, the betrayer was a very practical man at the same time. Mjomba wrote that the cunning Judas also believed that there was an acute shortage of diplomatic skills in the upper echelons of the movement's leadership, and he thought that he himself could easily remedy that unsatisfactory situation. One way of doing that was to forge secret connections with the members of the Sanhedrin and eventually also with members of the Roman Governor's inner cabinet. That had one special advantage: he, Judas, would always be in the know and, for one, could jump ship early in the unlikely event that the movement's fortunes did not quite meet his expectations and thereby avoid the harsh consequences of promoting a rebellion.

As a young man, Judas had been enrolled by his wealthy parents in an elite academy in suburban Jericho. His major, Management, had included everything from Philosophy, Commerce, Astronomy, International relations, History, and Anthropology to the Scriptures. Although locally owned and managed, the academy also enrolled young Romans whose parents were top brass in the garrison in Jericho. Having rubbed shoulders with the cream of Romans and Jews alike in those formative years, Judas was bursting with confidence that he could dabble in the shady deals that would be the normal fare for him as a double agent and spy, and still successfully cover his tracks.

And so, whereas ordinary folk, unschooled in the ways of this world, would easily be vulnerable, he had no doubt that he was in a position to handle any situation that would threaten to compromise his safety in his wheelings and dealings with the crooked high priests and cunning Romans.

Deep down, Judas actually scorned the high priests and considered them a dumb lot for failing to realize that the Deliverer could not be stopped if for no other reason than that he could actually perform miracles. In his view, people had to be real ignoramuses not to weigh in that fact when choosing sides in a contest and this one in particular. Judas held them in such contempt he was in fact prepared to double cross them too if a suitable opportunity ever came along.

On the strength of the miracles he had personally witnessed first hand, Judas, who was quite capable of distinguishing the "good guys" from the "bad guys", was convinced that the best thing for now was to hang in there with the rest of the followers of this miracle worker. Here was, after all, a leader who, in addition to being eloquent, could calm rough seas and walk on water at will; he could tell, using divination that was beyond the reach of even the smartest magicians, where to cast nets for the biggest haul of fish; here was an individual who could multiply loaves of bread, and who could read people's secret thoughts; and he could also cure diseases, and above all, raise up the dead!

If he could do these things, he definitely could also strike terror in an enemy force of any strength by, for instance, causing the enemy's provisions and ordinance to evaporate into thin air, or by simply rendering his own troops and those of his allies invulnerable in the face of any kind of enemy assault. He could, if he chose, knock enemy troops off their feet just by poisoning the air they breathed from a safe distance, or he could induce the enemy to surrender by threatening to unleash at a command a deadly virus or some other such calamity on the hostile forces and, if necessary, on their beloved ones as well. Judas had concluded - correctly - that this person, far from being just human, was something else completely. And it was not just a case of "heaven walking on earth" in the manner of Shakespeare's character (Olivia). Judas, despite the soft spot he had for the good life, had absolutely no doubt that this was a case of *God* Himself walking on earth! The Deliverer was divine.

For their part, the priests and Pharisees despised Judas and regarded him as a small time cheat and scoundrel even as they sought to use his services to achieve their own ends. And they were, accordingly, prepared to blackmail him at any time if they found it in their best interest to do so. And so, when Judas came to the temple in the dead of night to apprise members of the Sanhedrin of the Deliverer's next move, the high priests decided to do precisely that.

Judas had no sooner been ushered into the council chamber where the high priests were still meeting in spite of the fact that it was the day of the Passover than they began berating him for being in league with what they termed "enemies of the Nation of Israel", and an active member of an outlawed movement, to wit. Charging him with participating in an illegal gathering on such a solemn day without special dispensation or a permit, they pressed him to confirm or deny that the gathering in the Upper House, ostensibly to celebrate the Passover, was not for the purpose of conspiring to further sour the relations between the Roman authorities and the Sanhedrin!

The strategy adopted by the high priests played right into the hands of Judas. He only needed to suggest that the Deliverer was up to something very special just on that very night to make any information he might be bringing along seem very important and critical to the success of the plans of the high priests to rein Him in, and Judas did just that.

Saying just enough to alarm the Pharisees and Sadducees without giving away too much and thereby diminishing his usefulness, the betrayer recounted how the self-styled Deliverer had inaugurated the Sacrament of the Eucharist in the Upper House, adding that the Nazarene had also urged them to continue with the practice of "breaking bread" together in His memory. Describing the Deliverer as suicidal, Judas had the members of the Sanhedrin begging for more by merely hinting, without providing any further details, that the son of the carpenter had served them with His own flesh and blood during that ceremony!

Seeing the utter confusion which the information he was volunteering caused his erstwhile friends, Judas knew he had them. He also knew how to add to the terror that was clearly starting to grip them; and he proceeded to provide additional hints relating to other "bizarre" events that had unfolded behind closed doors that evening in the Upper House, including the ritual washing of the feet by the Deliverer!

It gave Judas enormous satisfaction to observe the rising level of apprehension blended with fear in the eyes of his audience as he went on to suggest that the Nazarene was a man on an unstoppable mission; that He had real psychic powers, wielded the equivalent of supernatural powers, and was determined to prosecute His war on the Powers of the Underworld so-called not just religiously, but with certainty that His enemies were already doomed and victory was going to be His. To ensure that he left the high priests and Pharisees totally confused and mystified, the cunning Judas had added something to the effect that the Nazarene had no interest whatsoever in material things, and also that the kingdom He sought to establish was not of this world! The high priests were seething and up in arms as the betrayer, quoting the Nazarene, made a reference to days soon to come when "the temple would be no more"!

Mjomba wrote that the members of the Sanhedrin did not wait for the betrayer to finish before withdrawing the accusations they had just levelled against him; and they even apologized profusely for their rash action which, they now claimed, had been motivated by their zeal for preserving public order and the lofty sense of duty that governed the Council's actions. But their apparent "rush to judgement" had already exposed them as double dealers who could not really be trusted. And their offer to pay Judas whatever sum he demanded (so long as the amount was within reason) for helping them to neutralize the "blasphemer" and his misguided followers (before "that pack", as they referred to the Nazarene and His followers, had done too much harm to the good relations between the Sanhedrin and the Roman occupiers) only confirmed the poor man's worst fears!

In Judas's words, these people were "vipers" with whom one could not conduct business of any sort. He saw that he had made a serious mistake by becoming involved with them, particularly given his aspirations for the position of Chief Executive Officer in the Deliverer's organization. He had no doubt that, after "neutralizing" the Deliverer, they would spare no efforts to neutralize everyone else who was remotely associated with Him.

As Judas left the temple, he was telling himself that if his fellow Israelites could be so callous and could not see any good in having someone who was as admirable and commanding as the Nazarene around (someone who looked like he might even be the awaited Messiah), and if they were so determined to be rid of the Deliverer for no real good reason, it would be bad news indeed when it came to the Romans and especially an individual as morally bankrupt and wily as Pontius Pilate!

Foolishly, the betrayer continued to kid himself with the thought that his bold move to play the diplomatic card had paid off. He even told himself that if he had not gambled, he would never have been able to know how bad and dangerous the Pharisees and Sadducees really were! According to Mjomba, Judas was too proud to do otherwise. It would only be after he had finally been stung with a terrible sense of guilt for his part in bringing down the downfall of he Deliverer and Author of Life, and after he had attempted, on second thoughts, to return the blood money that Judas would realize the hopelessness of his own situation.

Essence of being a disciple of the Deliverer…

The betrayer had no doubt in his mind that, with the exception of the Deliverer's immaculately conceived Blessed Mother and a few other individuals like Lazarus whom the Deliverer had caused to live again after he had been dead a while, it was he himself (Judas) who, more than anyone else, grasped the fact that the appearance of the Deliverer was the greatest event since the creation of the world. Even though he had not been present on the mountain with Peter, James and John when the Deliverer became transfigured and appeared to the trio in the company of Moses and Abraham, he certainly had seen and heard enough to convince him that this self-styled "Son of Man" was both *from* and *of* God. Judas certainly knew that, as one of the twelve, he was privy to far more than any of the priests and Pharisees. Judas regarded them with disdain because they were the very people who ought to have been in the forefront welcoming the Deliverer, and also advising the Israelites to prepare themselves for the new order and the "New Testament" that was going to see the descendants of Adam and Eve reconciled with their Maker!

And so, when Judas finally came to the realization that he had gambled away his chances of being heir apparent to the Deliverer, and of being in a position to benefit from the miracle worker's protection, he could not stand the thought that the "stupid" Peter - the betrayer was so biased against the fisherman, he never thought of him without that pejorative term - and the Deliverer's other disciples whom he likewise regarded as dimwits, were now in a far more secure position than himself vis-à-vis the Deliverer. That was also when Judas literally began seeing red. Suffice it to say, Mjomba wrote, that after Judas started losing control, his pathetic slide into the abyss became a virtual certainty from there on.

Whereas the essence of being a disciple was to learn to deny oneself in order to focus on the hereafter, Judas was still having the blues and unable to get over the fact that he could not lay any real claim to owning anything in this world - not even his own earthly existence which was in every sense a passing existence. The world, of course, needed a Judas to hand the Judge to his judges. Otherwise a critical phase in the work of redemption would not have taken off. In the divine plan, Judas clearly had a distinctive role to play - just as all the other humans have their distinctive roles to play. And if there had been no betrayers, the Son of man, had He decided to come down to earth from heaven all the same, would not have needed Judas to play the role he played.

The roles humans play in the divine plan are all distinctive and important even though humans shun the responsibilities associated with those roles and are, therefore, reluctant to acknowledge that fact. Had the role Judas played been unnecessary, the very idea of a betrayer would have been superfluous. Now that scenario was not in the divine plan, but it would without a doubt have been a much better scenario from the point of view of law and justice.

According to Mjomba, the words "It were better if he had not been born" did not apply to Judas alone, but equally to all humans who ever sinned. The problem with humans, Mjomba wrote, was that they loved to point fingers and even shied away from everything that was likely to trigger their own individual feelings of guilt. Claiming that a re-enactment of what happened was invaluable in establishing that all sinners were as much betrayers of the Deliverer as Judas, the son of Simon Iscariot, Mjomba as usual launched into a detailed and somewhat graphic account of the events that led up to Judas' ignominious end.

Mjomba wrote that, with "Pentecost" and the down-pouring of the Holy Ghost which would accompany it along with the calming presence of the Comforter still in abeyance, the Messiah, was having a very hard time restraining the eleven apostles. Judas realized that if it were not for the man the group had come to know as "Master" - the very man Judas had just betrayed - he, Judas, was dead meat. It became clear to Judas almost immediately he let go of his embrace of the Deliverer that he faced a certain lynching by the eleven. All of them, not just Peter, were in a foul mood. Judas realized that only a miracle could save him when he saw the eleven closing in on him.

And it was another miracle yet that the betrayer witnessed as the Deliverer, without uttering a word to the eleven or even as much as raising a finger urging them to move away, saved his life just like that. According to Mjomba, it was appropriate to credit the Deliverer with halting the lynching of Judas, which had been imminent in the same way that it was appropriate to credit Him with stepping in just in the nick of time and saving the life of the Roman soldier whom Peter had began to hack to bits with a butcher's knife! When the Deliverer ordered His disciples to put away their weapons, Judas had already been pinned down and a couple of his former buddies were preparing to make mince meat of him.

Mjomba wrote that Judas did not at first understand the action of the Deliverer in stepping in to save his life. Anyone could have told that his act of betrayal was a vile deed indeed, which was made infinitely worse by the fact that he, Judas, had betrayed the miracle worker and Master with - of all things - a kiss! And that was in addition to the fact that hardly four hours earlier, as they celebrated the Pascal feast in the upper house, he not only had had the honor of occupying the most favored seat - immediately to the right of the Deliverer - but he and the Nazarene had in fact shared the same chalice when the wine was served.

It was not as if he did not know that the Nazarene was the long awaited Messiah. He had never doubted that. But instead of struggling to learn how to pray and mediate with the Deliverer as the "stupid" Peter and the other disciples did, Judas had grown more and more absorbed with material things, including worldly power, he was certain were going to come his way as a result of his association with the miracle worker. Quite a different kind of sin, Judas now acknowledged, from the original sin committed by the first Man and Woman; and his sin typified the sins of his generation which were not really dissimilar from the sins of the children of Adam and Eve in that it focused strictly on the temporal!

Judas was a very intelligent man who knew without a doubt that the "Miracle Worker" was going to be ridiculed, despised and spat upon. And he had no doubt whatsoever in his mind that a certain and quite gruesome death on the cross awaited the "insurgent", even though He was completely innocent of the false accusations which the priests and Pharisees were preparing to level against Him.

According to Mjomba, Judas, who had decided to pass up the opportunity to be an apostle and a "father of the Church" along with Peter, John and the rest of the twelve because he was not prepared to serve under Peter (the Rock), knew that the "insurgent" and "terrorist", as members of the Sanhedrin consistently referred to the Deliverer, was not really going to do a vanishing act. The "betrayer" knew that his quarry was going to continue going about His Father's business in the open until all the prophecies about Him had been fulfilled.

But, in his greed for money and his craving for power and influence, Judas had gone out of his way to depict his Divine Master as a crafty felon who was likely to disappear in Galilee or Judea after the feast of the Passover, and that he (Judas) was in a position to help the priests and Pharisees capture the insurgent and terrorist before He vanished into thin air - if they coughed up a minimum of thirty pieces of silver. That was even though Judas knew that the real reason the priests and Pharisees were after the Deliverer was the fact that He had interfered in their practice if using the grounds of the temple in Jerusalem and its adjoining facilities for their worldly ends.

That was how Judas, who was bitter with the Deliverer for promoting Peter over him, planned to get even with Him. But that was also the man (Judas Iscariot), at once a betrayer and also an infernal liar, who really served as the role model for the aggressors, despite their lip service to the cause of justice in the world.

But it was surely not the Deliverer's position, even after Judas had committed that dastardly act of betrayal, that he should live and in effect continue to exist just like Lucifer and his minions after they had committed their own flagrant acts of disobedience to the Prime Mover - or was it? This latest "miracle" seemed to imply just that! Judas thought about Lucifer and his fellow devils - perhaps their numbers boosted by some human "devils" by now - roasting in hell for eternity, and wishing in vain that there was some way these damned spirits could end their miseries and above all wipe out their guilty consciences at the same time by causing their "*esse*" to evaporate into the nothingness from which they originally came! But Judas appreciated the fact that this was not possible for the simple reason that angels *and* humans had been created in the image of the Prime Mover!

But that "miracle", real or imagined, combined with the devastating thought that there was no way in which creatures that had been fashioned in the image of the Creator could escape "judgement", brought Judas back to his senses, Mjomba wrote. And it now took the betrayer a fraction of a second to embrace a simple truth the Messiah had tried unsuccessfully over a period of three whole years to drive home to him. The truth in question was that humans were on borrowed time during their sojourn here on earth. Judas also immediately made the connection: even if the Sanhedrin had quadrupled the compensation it had paid him for the pivotal role he played in the arrest of this self-proclaimed Deliverer (who was by all counts quite a "strange" fellow), he, Judas, would not have been able, if the lynching had been successful, to take any of those pieces of silver along with him to his grave!

According to Mjomba's thesis, Judas now clearly realized above all that for humans to be brought into existence out of nothingness by the Prime Mover and be promised an inheritance in eternity worthy of celestial princes and princesses only to turn around and try to claim for themselves prerogatives that belonged to the Prime Mover and Him alone was completely unacceptable and disgraceful. Judas saw that, in the circumstances, it would have been far better if all humans who had ever offended the Prime Mover, including himself, would not have seen the light of day. It was that simple: if sinners had not come into existence as a result of the gratuitous act of the Creator in the first place, the question of them doing anything contrary to the divine plan - or "sinning" if you will - could never have arisen!

In that moment, Judas would have voluntarily committed himself to a monastery that espoused the most rigorous and severe rules for penitents, but he knew that no such place existed. And so, he rushed back to the temple where the Sanhedrin was still in session and offered to be put to death in place of the man he had falsely accused. But the high priests informed him they would brook no such nonsense from a person of his intelligence, and they told him to get the blazes quickly out of the august chamber and out of their sight with his tripe. They even let him know that they were so busy they had neither the time nor the resources to devote to a suicide watch in his behalf!

It was at that juncture, Mjomba went on, that Judas saw that all the exits were blocked. He made his situation worse by emptying the silver coins the priests had used to bribe him at their feet before scrambling out of the chamber and the temple. Like someone who had been transformed into a zombie, he hurried away from the imposing structure and headed blindly for the forest located on the western slopes of the Mount of Olives.

A man beyond his time (Judas Iscariot)

As he shuffled along mindlessly in the darkness, his fingers were busy, nonetheless; and the same went for his sharp mind which had discovered what he thought was a "loophole" of sorts. He, Judas Iscariot, son of Simon, might not be able to end his existence, or somehow wipe his guilty conscience clean. But he damn well could end his own life and thus be a winner - even if only in the short term! Roman generals defeated in battle against the "barbarians" did it rather than live with the humiliation. So he was not going to be the only one who went that route.

The difference between himself and the Romans was that he was a Jew; and he felt terrible shame being the one who had been caught ostensibly betraying the Messiah - the anointed one whose coming had been eagerly awaited by generations before him, and who was the only reason he and his fellow Jews regarded themselves as special. Yes - a chosen people through whom the Son of the Most High and Redeemer, promised by Him-Who-is-Who-is to Adam and Eve after their fall from grace, was to be given unto the world!

The thought that the priests and Pharisees - the real culprits in his opinion - would still be running around scot-free made him seethe with anger.

But while Roman generals could be excused for not understanding that they had been created in the image of Him-Who-is-Who-is and could not therefore dilly-dally with their lives in that fashion, the same could not be said for Judas and his fellow Jews. They had had the benefit of being admonished time and again by people like Moses and Abraham, and other messengers of Him-Who-is-Who-is, and could not be excused for not knowing that it was wrong to take away one's own life. And certainly not he, Judas, who not only had been honored with being a contemporary of the Messiah, but was one of the twelve whom the Son of Man, as the Deliverer called Himself, had hand picked to be "apostles".

But, looked at from a slightly different angle - the angle of a recalcitrant sinner who chose to pursue selfish worldly goals that, taken together, did amount to betrayal of sorts - the shame was just too much to bear! He had cut off his ties with the so-called teachers of the law and the leadership in Jerusalem who were bent on liquidating the Deliverer and had been trying like mad to find evidence to use to convict Him of everything from disturbing the peace to blasphemy. As far as he was concerned, the only evidence they would have against him was the sachel. But it was empty; and by the time he would be done, it wouldn't even like one. Most importantly, he could no longer be held to account for the measly thirty pieces of silver which were back in the hands of those who were out to get the Nazarene by hook or by crook.

They were free to use it as they deemed fit. They were free to use it to buy off people who would spin lies about him in the same way they had tried to buy him off to lie about the Son of Man. The only thing that now bothered Judas Iscariot was that, before becoming involved with the priests and Pharisees, he had the extraordinary chance of learning directly from the Son of Man Himself how to live aright, but had now forfeited it with his reckless gambit.

Judas thought of the countless generations that had gone before his own generation - not to mention the countless humans who had come and gone - since that day in the Garden of Eden, the primeval home of humankind, when the Prime Mover promised the penitent, but still spiritually indigent, Adam and Eve that He would send a Deliverer; and Judas could not, of course, help noting that it was during his own generation that the Prime Mover's promise was being fulfilled. And then, to cap it all, he was one of the chosen few who was allowed by the invisible army of guardian angels that surrounded the Deliverer at all times to get so close to the Author of Life that he could have gotten any of his own questions answered - questions concerning things like the mystery of pain and suffering and the reason good people suffered, the reason birds could fly in the air when other objects were subject to the pull of gravity, and so on - by the Nazarene Himself. This could not be just a coincidence.

He, Judas Iscariot, a Jew and a native son of Jericho, a city that was not even a half day's walk to Nazareth where the Deliverer grew up, was also one of the Deliverer's twelve apostles! And he had personally heard the Deliverer say so many things that should have been music to the ears of his compatriots, but had clearly fallen on deaf ears.

He had heard the Deliverer say things like "I am the light of the world; he who follows me shall not walk in the darkness, but shall have the light of life…I am the light of the world: he that followeth me, walketh not in darkness, but shall have the light of life…Although I give testimony of myself, my testimony is true: for I know whence I came, and whither I go: but you know not whence I come, or whither I go. You judge according to the flesh: I judge not any man. And if I do judge, my judgment is true: because I am not alone, but I and the Father that sent me…You are from beneath, I am from above. You are of this world; I am not of this world. Therefore I said to you, that you shall die in your sins. For if you believe not that I am He, you shall die in your sin…I go, and you shall seek me, and you shall die in your sin. Whither I go, you cannot come…Neither me do you know, nor my Father: if you did know me, perhaps you would know my Father also…I have not a devil: but I honour my Father, and you have dishonoured me. But I seek not my own glory: there is one that seeketh and judgeth. Amen, amen I say to you: If any man keep my word, he shall not see death for ever…" And: "Amen, amen I say to you, before Abraham was made, I am."

But it was what the Deliverer had said to the adulterous woman - after the scribes and Pharisees, who had brought and set her in their midst with the intent of using her to entrap Him, went away one by one beginning with the eldest - that had been the most touching of all. In response to her statement that her accusers had all left without condemning her, He had simply said: "Neither will I condemn thee. Go, and now sin no more."

The whore, Judas noted, was a fickle human, and she was inclined to sin like all humans, he himself included. On her own she undoubtedly was going to revert to her life of sin. But here the Deliverer was, looking her in the eye, and telling her to "go and sin no more". There was one thing the Nazarene certainly wasn't meaning in a literal sense. Even though He was using the word "Go", Judas understood that as meaning "Take care and don't you forget who is addressing you!" For this woman not to revert to her adulterous life, she had to stay quite close to the Son of Man and Deliverer of Humankind, who had taught His disciples that He was also the fount of the grace humans needed to stay upright.

That, quite obviously, was a testament to the Deliverer's divinity. But what still eluded Judas Iscariot was how exactly this would work. Judas Iscariot had ruled out one thing, namely the possibility that the Deliverer needed to suffer, and perhaps even sacrifice His life - like a lamb and the ultimate sacrifice for sin – to merit the graces He was promising humans. That was completely out of question in Judas's view. The Nazarene was not just from God. He was God - period. And that meant that he couldn't wage a loosing battle against Evil by allowing Himself to die or perish - as would have been the lot of humans in the absence of the promise of a Deliverer!

It did not strike Judas Iscariot that, because the Deliverer had two natures, namely a human nature and a divine nature, what he regarded as impossible and completely improbable was in a fact quite feasible. But even then, Judas Iscariot could not have imagined the miracle worker and His Savior humiliating Himself to that extent. As Judas Iscariot saw it, if the Deliverer allowed the priests and Pharisees to triumph over Him, it would not just be tantamount to an acknowledgement that He had suffered dismal defeat at the hands of wicked humans, but to a statement that the rule of Evil on earth was going to continue as if the Messiah, who had been foretold, had not come!

Thinking about the adulterous woman, Judas Iscariot knew that his own dilly-dallying with the priests and Pharisees represented questionable actions and probably unconscionable given the motivations behind them; and he knew that they were in fact scandalous, given his position in the Fellowship or movement the Deliverer had been laboring to establish over the three year He had been criss-crossing Galilee, Judea and Samaria. But even though Judas Iscariot now heard those same words of the Deliverer ringing in his ears as never before, and knew the disposition of the Deliverer to human weaknesses, failings, imperfections and sins of omission and commission, he had already decided that he was completely undeserving of God's mercies.

He, Judas Iscariot, wasn't a tax collector or a highway robber, and certainly no murderer. But he still knew deep down in his heart that it was his greed that had been behind his desperate hope that the priests and Pharisees would see light and join the Fellowship; and it was also that same greed - coupled with his displeasure at having to answer to Peter, the "Rock upon which the Deliverer was going to build His church" - that had resulted in his realizing too late that his actions had given the priests and Pharisees everything they needed to liquidate the Deliverer, namely the one "witness" from the inner circle of their Public Enemy Number One!

But he was a witness who, if not handled properly, could expose them and threaten their own positions, and who could poison the relations they had hitherto enjoyed with the Cæsar, or "the Great Satan" as they surreptitiously referred to the Roman emperor. Even now, Judas Iscariot suspected that agents of M1, as the dreaded secret police were known, were on his trail; perhaps watching and observing his every move. Their mission: to seize him and, after wringing more "voluntary confessions" from him using water boarding and their other methods which of course amounted to torture, present him as their star witness at the kangaroo trial of the Deliverer.

Judas, who had been the *de facto* major-domo in the organization of the Miracle Worker and self-proclaimed "Son of Man", wasn't going to let them. He preferred to kill himself, especially as he knew that the priests and Pharisees would in any case find a way to make him "disappear" as soon as he had served their purposes. He was not going to let those crooks use him in any way - period! He had no doubt that he, Judas Iscariot and son of Simon, was a particularly important "catch" in their eyes - even more so than Peter or Simon Bar-Jona who had been designated by the Nazarene as the rock on which He was going to construct His church, and also as the recipient of the keys of the kingdom of heaven, so that whatever he would bind on earth would be bound in heaven, and whatever he would loose on earth would be loosed in heaven!

There was one thing about the Deliverer and his relationship with the rulers and elders and scribes that really thrilled Judas Iscariot. This was the courage coupled with the Deliverer's extraordinary self-effacing approach in his dealings with the scribes and teachers of the law, and the forthright manner with which the Nazarene was able to tell the priests and scribes to their face that He was the Truth and the Light. From the day Judas Iscariot was inducted into the ranks of the apostles, Judas had marvelled at the extreme care, respect and tact that characterized the Deliverer's dealings with the scribes and teachers of the law.

It was obvious to Judas Iscariot that the Nazarene, who could read minds, did everything according to script from Day One, as "He went about His Father's business". He had left no doubt in the minds of His twelve apostles that He recognized the elders and the priests and Pharisees as the lawful successors of Moses and the other messengers whom the Prime Mover, His Father in heaven, had employed in guiding the twelve tribes of Israel from Egypt into the Promised Land in anticipation of His own coming. He had accordingly engaged them from very early on, as it was incumbent upon these people as the leaders of the people of Israel to establish contact with Him, and place themselves at His service during the pivotal transition from the Old Order or Testament to the New Testament. But it had soon become very clear that those poor forsaken children of Adam and Eve were going to do no such thing!

Judas Iscariot had also noted that, unworthy though the leadership in Jerusalem was, it deserved the prayers of all people of good will, starting with the Deliverer Himself; and it did not surprise Judas Iscariot that the Son of Man, leading them by example, constantly had the scribes and the teachers of the law in His prayers. It was clear to the Deliverer's Purse Bearer and to the other apostles that the Deliverer had all the Jews and their leaders very much in mind when he taught them to pray to His Father in heaven.

But the Deliverer spent a lot of time praying for all the descendants of Adam and Eve as well as for themselves as his chosen apostles. For instance, before formally appointing them as His disciples or "apostles", He had formally invited them individually by name to join Him on His trek to the top of Mount Tabor in Galilee. And once there, He had prayed over them, and had solemnly laid His sacred hands on them, and beseeched forgiveness for their trespasses personally from His heavenly Father, praying that they would each individually have the strength and perseverance which they needed to carry out the work He was entrusting upon them as His missionaries.

It was not until each one of them had voluntarily taken turns to recite the "Our Father" and do so accurately and with due solemnity that He gave them the authority to cast out devils. Judas Iscariot recalled how hard it was for him to understand the full significance of the words “The light shines in the darkness, but the darkness has not understood it. I am in the world, and though the world was made through Me, the world does not recognize Me"! But Judas Iscariot was not at all surprised when it took Peter so much longer than everyone else to just understand that “the light” signified “the Deliverer’!

Now, it didn’t take long for Judas Iscariot and his buddies in the Deliverer’s inner circle to see that the scribes and the teachers of the law just weren’t going to get it. It was always as if these folks and the Deliverer were speaking in two completely different languages! To take just one example, the Deliverer, who must have known that He didn’t have a whole lot of time, was in the temple courts long before dawn broke on one occasion, and he was surrounded by a large concourse of people who were eager to hear Him speak about the “New Testament” that He was ushering in.

He was speaking only a day after He had performed many miracles, and cast out the devils that had been tormenting so many souls; and He was expressing what the Purse Bearer thought was obvious, and saying to the gathering: “I am the light of the world. Whoever follows me will never walk in darkness, but will have the light of life."

But the Pharisees challenged him saying, “Here you are, appearing as your own witness; your testimony is not valid."

These people were clearly set against the Nazarene without regard to whatever His message to the crowd might be, and had their own fixed ideas concerning the redemption of mankind. But the Deliverer, ever meek and humble of heart, had answered, “Even if I testify on my own behalf, my testimony is valid, for I know where I came from and where I am going. But you have no idea where I come from or where I am going…You are from below; I am from above. You are of this world; I am not of this world…I told you that you would die in your sins; if you do not believe that I am the one I claim to be, you will indeed die in your sins."

“And who are you?" they growled?

"Just what I have been claiming all along," the Deliverer answered resolutely; "When you have lifted up the Son of Man, then you will know that I am, and that I do nothing on my own but speak just what the Father has taught me.…Then you will know the truth, and the truth will set you free."

That caused the priests and Pharisees to scream: "We are Abraham's descendants and have never been slaves of anyone. How can you say that we shall be set free?"

The Nazarene said calmly in response: "I tell you the truth, everyone who sins is a slave to sin. Now a slave has no permanent place in the family, but a son belongs to it forever. So if the Son sets you free, you will be free indeed. I know you are Abraham's descendants. Yet you are ready to kill me, because you have no room for my word. I am telling you what I have seen in the Father's presence, and you do what you have heard from your father."

"Abraham is our father," they hollered in fury.

Already at that point, Judas Iscariot and the rest of the twelve were worried that all hell was going to get loose, and had edged in closer to the Deliverer, not so much for the purpose of shielding Him, but because they themselves felt safer from the throng in His vicinity.

"If you were Abraham's children," the Miracle Worker continued, "then you would do the things Abraham did. As it is, you are determined to kill me, a man who has told you the truth that I heard from God. Abraham did not do such things. You are doing the things your own father does."

"We are not illegitimate children," they shouted while beating their breasts. "The only Father we have is God himself."

The Son of Man said to them, "If God were your Father, you would love me, for I came from God and now am here. I have not come on my own; but he sent me. Why is my language not clear to you? It is because you are unable to hear what I say. You belong to your father, the devil, and you want to carry out your father's desire. He was a murderer from the beginning, not holding to the truth, for there is no truth in him. When he lies, he speaks his native language, for he is a liar and the father of lies. Yet because I tell the truth, you do not believe me! Can any of you prove me guilty of sin? If I am telling the truth, why don't you believe me? He who belongs to God hears what God says. The reason you do not hear is that you do not belong to God."

The spokesmen for the Jews answered him, "Aren't we right in saying that you are a Samaritan and demon-possessed?"

"I am not possessed by a demon," said the Deliverer, "but I honor my Father and you dishonor me. I am not seeking glory for myself; but there is one who seeks it, and he is the judge. I tell you the truth, if anyone keeps my word, he will never see death."

At that the priests and Pharisees exclaimed, "Now we know that you are demon-possessed! Abraham died and so did the prophets, yet you say that if anyone keeps your word, he will never taste death. Are you greater than our father Abraham? He died, and so did the prophets. Who do you think you are?"

By that time Judas Iscariot, who had already lost his patience with the hostile crowd, was agitated and would have liked to see the Deliverer perform a sign that would cause the Deliverer's enemies to scatter before them in disarray. This was despite the fact that the Purse Bearer and the other apostles had been receiving instructions from the Nazarene for some time now as a part of their preparation for their roles as His apostles.

The instructions received by the twelve were always preceded by prayers led by the Son of Man, and by meditation in the course of which He always unfailingly reminded them of the fact that His Father in heaven so loved the world, that He gave his only begotten Son, so that everyone who believes in him may not perish but may have eternal life. Thanks to these instructions, Judas Iscariot and the other apostles were all on board, and understood that the Nazarene was indeed the Son of the Most High who had come down in fulfillment of the promise of a Deliverer which the Prime Mover made to Adam and Eve and their descendants in the wake of the fall from grace.

On this occasion just as on the other occasions when the teaching of their loving divine Master fell on deaf ears, the apostles were shocked to see the Jews reject the promised Messiah out of ignorance. But they also benefited from observing the persistence of the Son of Man for whom every human soul was priceless.

The hawkish Judas Iscariot was mollified just the same when he heard the Nazarene reply thus: “If I glorify myself, my glory means nothing. My Father, whom you claim as your God, is the one who glorifies me. Though you do not know him, I know him. If I said I did not, I would be a liar like you, but I do know him and keep his word. Your father Abraham rejoiced at the thought of seeing my day; he saw it and was glad."

Any observer could have told that the Deliverer’s purse-bearer was thoroughly disgusted when one of the scribes, after briefly consulting with the other teachers of the law and speaking on behalf of all of them, retorted: “You are not yet fifty years old, and you have seen Abraham!"

Whereupon the miracle worker answered: “I tell you the truth, before Abraham was born, I am!"

At that, the concourse of people, led by the priests and Pharisees, picked up stones to stone the promised Messiah. The situation was very serious, and it was only the quick-thinking of Judas Iscariot that saved the day permitting the Nazarene to slip away from the temple grounds. After whisking the Son of Man behind an enclosure, Judas Iscariot, with John’s help, had succeeded in disguising the Nazarene as a woman, thus enabling Him to avoid being apprehended by the infuriated scribes and teachers of the law.

It seemed to Judas Iscariot that the greater the unbelief of the scribes and Pharisees, the greater the zeal which the Deliverer put into efforts to help them see through their selfishness, and come to the realization that He *was* the promised Redeemer of humankind. In order to drive the lessons home to the leadership in Jerusalem, the Deliverer went out of His way to tell parables that left no doubt whatsoever that the intensity of their animosity for Him notwithstanding, it was incumbent upon them as the lawful representatives of the twelve tribes of Israel to own up to the fact that

He was the long awaited Messiah, or stand condemned for their unbelief.

In other words, He expected them to step up to the plate and provide leadership to the people of the Prime Mover who, like Simeon, had been waiting for their redemption for a long time. He did not beat about the bush, or disguise the fact that the salvation of their souls was at risk, as He told parables during the course of His teaching, and made it crystal clear that He was from the Prime Mover and not from the devil (as they would have liked to suppose) by performing many wonders to back up His claims to boot.

The failure of the compatriots of the apostles, led by the scribes and Pharisees, to recognize the Deliverer and Son of Man in the miracle worker from Nazareth was at first nothing short of a mystery in the eyes of Judas Iscariot and the other apostles. And it was only little by little that the twelve started to realize that it wasn't just the priests and scribes and teachers of the law who were thick skinned and totally blind when it came to recognizing the truth, but humankind as a whole, they themselves included. The apostles seemed surprised by the reticence shown by the Deliverer and the pains he took to avoid embarrassing the priests and Pharisees even as those zealots were as determined as ever to seize on every straw in their efforts to entrap the man of God.

Unaccustomed to the rough and tumble of the politics of the day, and the cloak and dagger intrigues and the outright lies that characterised them, the apostles were already worrying to death that the Deliverer was in danger of falling victim to the chicanery of the hypocritical priests and Pharisees when it became obvious that it was those supposed defenders of truth who were making themselves a laughing stock in the course of trying to malign the Savior of the world!

But this also coincided with the realization by the apostles that their own disposition wasn't all that different from that of the despicable priests and Pharisees. This was especially true of Judas Iscariot who started to acknowledge, deep down in his heart, that if push came to shove, he would have to admit that he was in the

Fellowship or the Movement for the money and the prestige. This was even though he had no doubt whatsoever in his mind that the Nazarene was the promised Messiah who had come to redeem humankind including himself!

It was as Judas Iscariot was following the incredible story of the miraculous cure of the man who had been blind from birth and whose sight was restored by the Deliverer on the sacred day of rest - and the equally incredible tale of unbelief demonstrated by the teachers of the law - that the betrayer came round and acknowledged his own precarious position. He could not at first believe that a person of his intelligence could knowingly turn a blind eye to sacred truths, and continue merrily along in pursuit of things of this world, in complete disregard of the overwhelming evidence in favour of a life of self-denial and a commitment to follow in the footsteps of the Anointed One and Redeemer of the World! Judas Iscariot was certain that all his fellow apostles, including Simon Peter whom the Deliverer had referred to as the rock that was going to be the bulwark or foundation of His *sancta ecclesia*, were in the exact same boat as himself if not worse. And whereas he himself was at least acknowledging that he was wanting as an apostle of the Son of Man, he recorded in the diary he surreptitiously kept that he hadn't seen any sign that the same was true with any of his buddies!

Judas Iscariot, who had nothing but disdain for the priests and Pharisees, thought that they quite often went completely overboard and, blinded by their rage and hatred for the man who was indisputably the Messiah of Israel and the Savior of the World, ended up making complete fools of themselves as they attempted to trip Him up in vain! He thought that the temple leadership had become like charlatans who actually found fun in twisting facts to suit any situation, as was evidenced by their jingoistic and at times wacky reaction to the miraculous healing of the man who had been blind from birth.

Like the Deliverer, Judas Iscariot did not question the fact that the priests and scribes were the true successors to Moses and also to Joshua, Moses' immediate successor whose name coincidentally meant "Jehovah is salvation", and was the same name as Jesus! Judas Iscariot nonetheless had an intense personal interest in building a case against the temple leadership – a case that would fault them for being morally bankrupt at a time when their positions as the spiritual leaders of the twelve tribes of Israel required them to be exemplars of virtue and wisdom in the same way Moses and Joshua were!

The betrayer and his fellow apostles had been privileged to hear first hand from Mary, the Mother of the Son of Man, the events of that day years earlier when Joseph travelled with Mary for the consecration to the Lord of their month and a half old son in accordance with the Law of Moses. Mary had narrated to the apostles how everyone's attention had turned to Simeon and the song into which he burst upon taking the child Jesus in his arms. Simeon, who lived in Jerusalem and was just a few years short of his 100th birth day, had proclaimed aloud as all those who were present listened attentively: "Now thou dost dismiss thy servant, O Lord, according to thy word in peace; Because my eyes have seen thy salvation, Which thou hast prepared before the face of all peoples: A light to the revelation of the Gentiles, and the glory of thy people Israel!"

Simeon's canticle echoed the words of an angel of the Lord on an earlier occasion to Joseph: "Joseph, son of David; do not be afraid to take Mary as your wife; for that which has been conceived in her is of the Holy Spirit. And she will bear a son; and you shall call His name Jesus, for it is He who will save His people from their sins."

And Judas Iscariot also saw a direct connection with Mary's account of manner in which an entire choir of angels brought the good tidings to the shepherds in Bethlehem as the angels sang: "Do not be afraid. We bring you great joy for all the people: to you is born this day in the City of David a saviour, who is the Messiah, the Lord!"

According to the entry in the diary of Judas Iscariot, the actions of the priests and scribes confirmed his conclusion that human history up until the advent of the Messiah represented an era of darkness and despair; and that, sadly, not all the people who walked in darkness would see the great light--the light that nevertheless was going to shine on all who lived in the land where, in the words of the Prophet Isaiah, "death cast its shadow".

And so, while Joseph, the shepherds, and Simeon saw that great light, the scribes and the Pharisees, for whatever reason, wanted to live on in darkness! For these people, it was anathema to accept that the prophecy of Isaiah was fulfilled in the birth of Mary's God child, the one who would be called "Wonderful Counsellor, Mighty God, Everlasting Father, and the Prince of Peace"! And to show that they meant business, they expelled the man who had been blind from birth, but now could see after being healed by the Deliverer, from the Synagogue and openly dared anyone else to try and align himself or herself with the Son of Man and Savior of Humankind! Judas Iscariot did not even know if the era of darkness was now really over or continuing!

After restoring the sight of the man who would subsequently be excommunicated by the priests and Pharisees from the Synagogue, the miracle worker used the occasion to emphasize that being in the world, He was de facto the Light that was shining in that dark world. That automatically signified that the elevated positions of the priests and Pharisees as "teachers of the law" notwithstanding, they in fact were children of darkness as well as liars and pretenders who, like the hired hands in the parable of the Good Shepherd, were liable to abandon the sheep and to flee at the first sign of a wolf!

And that also made one thing very clear to the betrayer (Judas Iscariot), namely that a hallmark of liars amongst humans was the eagerness with which individuals proclaimed that they were the standard bearers of truth. In other words, humans who laid claim to having a monopoly over truths were more likely than not to be purveyors of lies and masters in the art of deception and misinformation! And the sole exception to that rule was the Deliverer and Light of the World; and it was becoming clearer and clearer by the day if not by the hour that He was going to pay for that with His life! It was something Judas Iscariot now saw as inevitable.

And, as far as the apostle from Jericho was concerned, the exchange between the blind man from birth who went and washed the clay and spittle the Deliverer had rubbed on his eyes and started seeing again, and the bigoted, high strung priests and Pharisees who had gone out of their way to peddle lies about the Deliverer in their efforts to make the Roman governor side with them against the miracle worker from Nazareth, amply illustrated how the minds of pathological liars worked

It saddened the purse bearer of the Deliverer to think that the world was a wicked place in which liars as a rule triumphed while those who held to the truth invariably lost out. And, seeing the death of the Deliverer and Son of Man coming, the betrayer expected the world to plunge into pitch darkness once again!

Like a pundit-cum-diplomat, Judas Iscariot had been monitoring the speeches of members of the Sanhedrin, and he had been utterly disgusted by the way they twisted the truth and lied about the opposition in order to win political points. And if there had been any one willing to lend him an ear, he could have predicted from day one that the priests and Pharisees on the one hand and the Deliverer on the other were going to be the strangest of bedfellows.

But Judas Iscariot also knew that if anyone found oneself, wittingly or unwittingly, in opposition to that clique in Jerusalem - the clique that was the *de facto* ruling oligarchy in the Roman enclaves of Galilee, Judea and Samaria, that was for all intents and purposes tantamount to a kiss of death. Opposition was simply not tolerated; and, not surprisingly, not a soul in memory was known to have stood up against the establishment in Jerusalem and survived unscathed. This was also the reason there was ostensibly such harmony among the twelve tribes of the Chosen People.

It irked Judas Iscariot that the chief priests and the teachers of the law - the very people who should have stepped up to the plate and laid out a red carpet welcome for the long expected Messiah - not only had abdicated their responsibilities in that regard; but, following their gross betrayal of the trust of both the Nation of Israel and all the descendants of Adam and Eve, were now also guilty of what amounted, in his view, to a crime against humanity! But, as if that wasn't bad enough, led by Joseph Caiphas and his father-in-law,

Annas, the scribes and the chief priests, while quite capable of recognizing the promised Messiah in the miracle worker, even though they had eyes that could see, were unwilling to do so for the simple reason that His unheralded arrival threatened their livelihood!

As leaders of the twelve tribes of Israel, they should have recognized the Nazarene for what He was, namely someone in whom the Spirit of the Lord reposed as a result of being anointed and being commanded to take good tidings to the poor - someone who was sent to proclaim release to the captives and recovery of sight to the blind, and to let the oppressed go free as Isaiah had foretold!

It may be that, thanks to His virgin mother Mary's *fiat*, His advent, which had been foretold according to what they themselves taught, was already a *fait accompli*! It may well be, likewise, that He was the *Alpha* and the *Omega*, the beginning and the end, whose stated mission was to provide for anyone who was thirty from the spring of the living water free of charge. But that was no excuse for their unpreparedness which now made it appear as if it was the Messiah who, coming out of no where and blundering into their world, was threatening to render them jobless without any warning!

They still knew that God had spoken to Moses; and, as teachers of the law, their work was cut out for them. They were also no doubt still very conscious of the fact that everyone, male and female, young and old, with means or without, in good health or in bad health, looked up to them for guidance not just in matters of the spirit, but also in matters pertaining to the outer man. But then all of a sudden, feigning ignorance, they seemed quite happy to just remain Moses' disciples, and were not only unwilling to step into the role of welcoming the promised Messiah when He was finally showing up, but were out to stop any one who did!

And for the past several months, those "teachers of the law" whom the Deliverer, not once but on many occasions, had engaged as he healed the sick and spoke to the multitudes about the kingdom of heaven, had mounted the dirtiest smear campaign imaginable to discredit the Deliverer - a campaign based on such naked lies, many ordinary folk could not help laughing at what they heard coming out of the mouths of the priests and Pharisees! The fact that the priests and Pharisees had not stretched forth their hands against the Deliverer in the days when the miracle worker had been daily with them in the temple initially had caused others, including Judas, to think that the elders of the people had to be joking!

But now that their evil intent had been unmasked, the Apostle from Jericho was livid, and wondered how those *ignoramuses* had gotten the cheek to say what they were saying about his Master and Rabbi, let alone their evident determination to see Him liquidated at any cost! Since he not only had been attempting to maintain a line of communication with them, but still believed that it was a good idea to remain in touch, given his position as the Deliverer's "treasurer-cum-corporate secretary', Judas felt genuinely betrayed. He could almost imagine the liars coming out, and bearing down on the miracle worker with swords and clubs - as though against a thief! These people were just so reckless and unfeeling!

In Judas Iscariot's view, this was just terrible, happening in these times when there was the ever present danger that the Roman occupiers who worshiped idols instead of the God of Abraham and Isaac, on an impulse could impose on the chosen people of the Prime Mover laws that were at variance with the faith of their forefathers. The twelve tribes of Israel, whose individual members had held fast to the Law of Moses while they waited on the Prime Mover for deliverance from the god-less Roman imperialists deserved better leadership. Judas Iscariot was very disappointed that the scribes and Pharisees, who spent a great deal of their time teaching and explaining the law, and who were renowned for their sanctity and holiness, not to mention the great care they exercised in their observance of the smallest precepts of the law, were failing the nation of Israel in that fashion.

It was also the role of the priests and scribes to help their flock grapple and cope with blessings and especially with misfortunes in life one example of which was the blight of coming into the world blind. But here they were manhandling the poor chap who had been delivered from his infirmity by the Nazarene. He had done as he had been instructed by the Nazarene, and he had received healing thereby.

But they had instead thrown him out of the Synagogue and excommunicated him for bearing witness to the Nazarene and Messiah, arguing that he was "altogether born in sins" and yet was daring to show them the way to the promised Messiah! He was daring to suggest that his supposed "Deliverer", who did not observe the Sabbath, was someone from God; and this man who had been blind from birth even had the guts to stand there and argue with them regarding who was or was not a worshipper of God, or a doer of God's will!

In the view of the priests and Pharisees, this was unheard of; and it highlighted the importance of reigning in the Nazarene without delay to stop Him from confusing the people, and perhaps even instigating a rebellion against the authorities! In any case, the priests and Pharisees and the teachers of the law, who sincerely did not know whence the reputed miracle worker came from - and (as Judas Iscariot noted) didn't have any reason to care to know - could be excused for not having any time for the outsider and impostor!

But, Oh - Mama Mia! If the Deliverer and Son of Man, who had come down from heaven, had not only signified his willingness to suffer indignities at the hands of wicked humans, but had even revealed that these "teachers of the law and elders" were plotting to kill him for stating the unpalatable truth and refusing to betray His heavenly Father, they on their part surely could also have stepped back to see what was at stake here, and done a favor not just to the twelve tribes of Israel over which they presided but to themselves as well.

Even though Judas Iscariot was fully cognizant of the activities of Matthew and Mark with respect to the all important task of keeping detailed accounts of the miracles and signs the Deliverer performed, and also of His exchanges with the teachers of the law, on papyri pursuant to resolutions that had been passed by all twelve apostles in conclave, he had been so moved by the confrontations he saw developing between the Deliverer and the priests and Pharisees, he had decided to keep his own independent record of the goings-on. This was in addition to his official responsibilities as the Movement's comptroller.

In his mind, there was simply too much at stake to leave that task to Matthew and Mark alone. Judas Iscariot nonetheless felt a sense of guilt and even shame for supposing that Matthew and Mark couldn't be trusted to do what they were actually well equipped to do. But those feelings of guilt and shame dissipated when Judas Iscariot noticed not long afterwards that John was doing the same thing, namely keeping detailed notes of almost everything that was happening. But even as Judas Iscariot was feeling vindicated, and was taking comfort of sorts from knowing that his own reasoning had been right on, his feelings of relief were suddenly overshadowed by something else.

This was the realization that his decision to keep a tab on the scheming of the chief priests and Pharisees and their determined efforts to try and ensnare the Deliverer into making a misstep, real or imagined, coinciding as it did with John's own decision in the same regard, pointed to an even larger issue. This, namely, was the determination by the scribes and Pharisees to stop the Deliverer at all costs. Although it was evident at every step that they were in the wrong, and the Deliverer was in the right, that very fact was working against the Deliverer who consistently claimed that His kingdom was not of this world. That in turn caused Judas Iscariot to sense that the final battle lines had been drawn.

Judas Iscariot recalled that the Deliverer had told the priests and Pharisees to their face that he was going, and they would be looking for him, and they were going to die in their sin, because whither he was going, they could not go. He had let them know that they were from beneath and He was from above; and that they were of this world while He was not of this world. Judas Iscariot even found comfort of sorts in the fact that the priests and Pharisees seemed incapable of grasping how the Deliverer could call the Prime Mover his Father! Noting that they all were likely to bump into each other in hell, Judas Iscariot still managed to focus on just the priests and

Pharisees, and he had hissed "Good riddance!" as if his own damnation did not really matter.

Judas Iscariot could not believe that, all through the time he had been a member of the Deliverer's inner circle, he had continued to maintain secret lines of communication with the despicable foes of his Master. When he started dillydallying with the scribes and the priests and Pharisees, it was not so much their role as the leaders of the twelve tribes of Israel, and as teachers of the Law, that was uppermost in his mind, as his own potential role as a power broker who in time might be pivotal in getting these successors to Moses and the prophets to accept the Nazarene as the promised Messiah! He was only focused on the potential influence he might wield in the Christ Fellowship, and he had realized too late that the priests and Pharisees and particularly the scribes were not the sort of people one could bargain with – and that he had been relegated to the status of a mole, and was just being used by them to monitor the Deliverer's activities!

Judas Iscariot was feeling much calmer now; and this was reflected in the things he started recalling from his vast store of knowledge of the things that characterized the life of the Son of Man from the time he himself had been called to join the Deliverer's fellowship as one of the twelve. He again recalled that the Messiah, or "Anointed One", had gone out of His way to teach him and the other apostles how to pray and how to meditate on divine mysteries, and above all how to serve, and eschew selfishness. Judas saw that he had squandered the chance of a lifetime!

But Judas could not stomach the idea of falling tummy first onto a sharpened sword, and even less the thought of ending his miseries by sipping a drink laced with poison from a goblet. Again as a Jew, he preferred to go along with the common if unsubstantiated belief that taking a life - your own or someone else's - by hanging was a more "humane" way of doing it.

From the little Judas knew, even if Adam and Eve had not sinned and there was no need for a Deliverer, this man whom he had betrayed by continuing to "talk" to the priests and Pharisees - the Son of Man - would definitely have come down from heaven just to keep the family of humans company all the same! Observing the mien of the Son of Man from close quarters as He trudged up and down the hills of Galilee talking about His Father, Judas had come to the conclusion that this Man and His Father, united in the Holy Ghost, really loved the world. The world was, after all, their own creation!

It was clear to Judas that if He-Who-is-Who-is had been prepared to sacrifice His only begotten Son for the salvation of mankind from sin, and not allow Beelzebub to triumph, He would have had even more reason to send His Son to keep humans company in a sinless world - if only because humans, who one and all were created through the Prime Mover's self-same divine Son along with all things that He made, had been fashioned in the image! Judas was convinced of that.

And now the thought that the Son of Man, if there had not been any "sin in the world" - which was the same thing as saying "people like Judas who were prepared to betray Him-Who-is-Who-is" - would have come down to earth from heaven all the same to be with humans, in a glorious and triumphant display of divine love, and in complete safety from the likes of Judas, was just overwhelming. His fingers working very quickly, the betrayer had no difficulty converting the pouch he had used to carry the pieces of silver into a rope. That bag had been made of rugged fibre; and, consequently, the rope with which Judas was going to hang himself was also rugged and strong. Even though it was not overly long, he was sure it could do the job and he was quite happy with it.

Judas could not help recalling how, a couple of months earlier, the priests and Pharisees, incensed by the fact that the Nazarene and self-proclaimed Deliverer had restored the sight of a man who had been blind from birth on the Sabbath Day, had tried to arrest Him and failed miserably in their attempt. The miracle worker simply vanished from their midst. For a moment, Judas, John, Mark and the other members of the Nazarene's inner circle had no doubt that the priests and Pharisees, aided by the posse of Temple guards accompanying them, were going to vent their anger on them and ship them off to the torture chambers in the belly of the Temple!

Perhaps, to show that He hadn't abandoned them, the Deliverer, clad in His distinctive, seamless white cassock, had suddenly reappeared on the edge of the crowd that had gathered when word spread that the authorities had descended on the group with the intention of taking the miracle worker into custody.

The priests and Pharisees had obviously not yet recovered from the fact that their quarry could vanish from right under their noses as they were closing in on Him on the other hand; and His reappearance in the vicinity moments later apparently caused them to be seized with fright, so that, instead of the apostles taking off in all directions to try and avoid being taken into custody and everything that would have entailed, it was the priests and Pharisees who had scrambled to get the hell out of there with the Temple guards hard on their heels! It made for a very amusing sight as the excited crowd joined Judas and his buddies in clapping with joy and cheering them as they chanted "Good riddance"!

But this time around, the Deliverer, like someone who was suicidal, had journeyed to Jerusalem and into the hornet's nest so to speak against their advice and that of their well wishers. And Judas was not one to be deluded by the passing and indeed short-lived welcome that the group had received as they entered Jerusalem. He had sensed, correctly, that the palm waving and delirious crowds could easily be infiltrated by agents of the Pharisees and Sadducees, and transformed into a mob that was screaming for their blood in the twinkling of an eye. It was indeed a wonder that this had not yet happened!

Any way, Judas knew that the Deliverer, even though bent on courting death at the hands of his enemies, was totally innocent of any human frailty or sin, let alone being guilty of any breach of the law, be it Jewish Law or Roman Law or, for that matter, Divine Law. The only wrongdoing the Deliverer had been guilty of (if it could be called wrongdoing) was His decision to pass him over when choosing the "Rock" as He put it on which He planned to build His ecclesia! The Deliverer's purse bearer, who still had nothing but contempt for Peter, had himself always been inclined to see nothing but opportunity -

albeit opportunity in the worldly sense - in being close to the preacher-man from Nazareth. The Nazarene, as it had indeed transpired, was not just some clever magician with a sly of hand that was unrivalled, but a miracle worker of the first order!

Shortly before the passing away nearly three years earlier of Joseph the Carpenter, whom everyone took to be the biological father of the preacher-man, the old man had summoned Judas and the other apostles the Deliverer had assembled, and had described to them in detail the events surrounding the birth of "the preacher-man" as they all referred to the Deliverer up until then, the family's flight to Egypt that Joseph, who was quite athletic and able-bodied at the time, made to save the child infant Deliverer from meeting his death at the hands of the murderous King Herod the Great so-called, and the slaughter that was taking place behind them of the hundreds of innocent babies the tyrant decided to target in hopes of nipping the idea of a Messiah in the bud.

Judas now wished that he were like one of those Innocents who met their fate as the squads of King Herod the Great roamed the countryside of Judea and Galilee in search of the "King of the Jews", and putting any newly born whom they could lay their hands on to the sword. Judas knew that he could easily have been one of the Innocents were it not for the fact that he was three years old at the time. He now wished that he too had come into the world about the same time as the Deliverer. That would have assured him martyrdom at the hands of the tyrant, and a place on the right side of Divine Law.

Judas acknowledged that, despite his exposure to all those sermons of the Deliverer, and being first hand witness to the innumerable wonders He wrought, deep down in his conscience, he was as materialistic and as unsaved even though perhaps not as bad as the priests and Pharisees - and Herod the Great! But, by the same token, being a practical man, Judas now had this gut feeling that there was no way he was ever going to succeed in explaining to the world, and even less to his former buddies in the Deliverer's inner circle, that he was innocent of the terrible fate that now hung over the miracle worker! This was unless the Deliverer changed his mind, wrestled free of his captors who would soon include the Roman governor who was backed by contingents of the Roman army, and retreated to some forest.

But Judas was convinced that this time around, even though He had the wherewithal to pull off such a feat, the miracle worker had made up His mind to let those evil people and sinners take His life. After all, addressing the crowds, He had made it crystal clear that an important goal of His mission as the Son of Man - if not the most important one - was to be a sacrificial lamb for the salvation of His fellow humans. And that was exactly the point. Just as no one, including Peter and the other apostles, was prepared to take the Deliverer at His word, and also just as everyone was almost certainly going to take flight as soon as the Nazarene is delivered by the priests and Pharisees into the hands of the Romans, it was completely out of question that any of these turncoats could change, and make an objective judgement on his diplomatic efforts to save the Deliverer's life!

He (Judas Iscariot) might not be all that innocent, but it was quite clear to him now that, in the rough and tumble of things, it was always the innocent who lost out. In the case of the Son of Man, this took on a completely different dimension, because He had freely chosen to be a sacrificial lamb. But the fact was that, in the current situation, he too now stood to pay a heavy price for the inability of human beings to weigh issues in the proper manner, and to render correct and fair judgements in situations where they were deserved.

Judas had seen the Deliverer come close to roughing up Peter when the fisherman jumped in front of the miracle worker and asserted that he was not going to let the Nazarene head to Jerusalem and to His certain death. And that had spelled the end of the hopes Judas had himself entertained of pulling off a diplomatic coup. His hopes of persuading members of the Sanhedrin that the individual they were hounding and wanting to liquidate was the promised Messiah, and that they direly needed His good offices if they hoped to rid the Nation of Israel of the yoke of the Romans, were now destined to come to naught. Judas had sought the opportunity to prove to them that it was going to work because the Nazarene was a miracle worker! But they had proved to be hard-headed and all too short-sighted.

He reminisced that he had been expecting a miracle when he lead them to the Deliverer that night in the garden of Gethsemane, and planted a kiss on the miracle worker's cheek. He had great faith, and had expected them to receive enlightenment even at that late stage, and had held out the hope that they would be converted and would seize the opportunity to acclaim the Deliverer as the awaited Messiah. He had held out the possibility even at that late stage that, instead of following through with their plans to hand the Nazarene over to the Romans for trial, they were going to hoist the Nazarene aloft and lead Him in triumph to the Temple on the eve of that august day for the purpose of formally introducing Him to the populace as savior in a spiritual as well as earthly sense. But he had obviously been seriously mistaken.

And now, to top it all, because of those same efforts, upon which he could not have embarked without summoning what clearly was uncommon courage, he, Judas Iscariot, was going to be adjudged by history as a selfish, money hungry betrayer of his divine Master! And this had come to pass because the "stupid" priests and Pharisees were determined to have their revenge on the Nazarene for perceived affronts, as when the Deliverer exposed their chicanery by scrawling their sinful dealings in the sand following the cure of the woman with the palsy.

The last straw was the widespread ridicule they deservedly garnered in the wake of their cowardly flight from the scene of the Deliverer's attempted arrest! And, if anything, Judas now realized, they had been even more determined than ever to try and destroy the Son of Man who had come on Earth to deliver the people of Israel from the bondage of sin and from the Romans! This was so they would remain unchallenged as the de facto rulers of Israelites. Judas told himself that his own conscience was clear, especially after dumping all thirty pieces of silver with which the priests and Pharisee, employing their surrogates, tried to bribe him there at their feet in the full view of witnesses.

And that was not the first time the chief priests and the Pharisees had tried to arrest or kill the Nazarene. On one occasion, using agents provocateurs whom they had planted in the crowds, they had tried to push Him over the cliff to His death only to see Him pass through the crowd and go His way. On another occasion, the temple guards who had been sent to arrest and detain the Nazarene had not just returned empty-handed, but they had told the chief priests and Pharisees to the latter's utter chagrin that they had never heard any one speak the way the Nazarene did, and that they were going off to become His disciples!

Consequently, Judas had not thought much of the assistance he had agreed to provide so that the one hundred strong Special Forces Operational Detachment made up of specially trained temple guards and soldiers (or "Delta 100" as the detachment's members referred to themselves) wouldn't nab the wrong person. This was even though Judas knew that the chief priests and Pharisees had already made the Governor, Pontius Pilate, aware of their intentions regarding the "dangerous rebel and criminal from Nazareth". Judas had even planned to use the thirty pieces of silver to boosts the week's collections. It was an amount of money that would have enabled the apostles to buy provisions for an entire week, and Judas had gone for it.

But it was blood money, as it had turned out; and, any way, Judas had delivered all of it back to the faithless clique that occupied the corridors of power in Jerusalem and, he now realized too late, had no scruples whatsoever about using that power for their personal aggrandizement, and to utterly destroy any and all in Palestine who posed the remotest challenge their rule.

The one thing Judas had internalised above all else in the course of listening to the Deliverer over the space of three years was that humans could be really wicked. That was due to the fact that they were creations of the Prime Mover that were spiritual. But unlike the demons headed by Satan, their ring leader and also demon-in-chief so to speak, right up until they passed from this world and crossed the gulf that separated the living from the dead, humans could pull back and renounce their wicked ways and repent - just as he himself had done.

That was not something that the devil and the other fallen angels could do. Their fall from grace was a testament to the fact that at the point these spirits became evil intentioned or entranced with evil, they did not just become disposed to commit more and more evil acts, but the state of their mind programmed them to remain committed for all eternity to the cause of evil. And humans, because they too were spiritual creatures fashioned in the image of their Maker, could choose to act like demons; so that, instead of being merely in a state of sin and intent on wicked pursuits, they could additionally become evil-minded and evil-intentioned in the true sense and incapable of retreat - just like the demons!

That was the nature of things when a creature was a spirit. And it also spoke to the elevated status of creatures that were created in the image of the Prime Mover and were spiritual beings.

After observing the chief priests and Pharisees from close quarters as they plotted to liquidate the Deliverer, Judas had concluded that he was seeing humans who had transformed into human demons, and were of the devil just as the Nazarene has said in reference to them. Judas had no doubt in his mind that it needed demonic minds to be intent on doing what those folk were now clearly determined to do, namely destroy the living "Son of God"! Judas Iscariot had never imagined that he could live in a world in which such a thing could cross people's minds, let alone pursued with such vigor and determination!

For the three years that he had been a confidant of the Nazarene, Judas had observed the other members of the Nazarene's inner circle from close quarters and felt that he now knew them as well as one else who was in a similar position was capable of knowing acquaintances. And knowing Peter as he did, he had no doubt in his mind that the fisherman especially was going to be the first to turn around, and not wish to be associated in any way with the Deliverer at the first sign that the priests and Pharisees had gotten their man and were well on the way to delivering Him to the Romans for execution.

Then the fact that it was Peter who was supposed to be the Rock upon which the Deliverer was going to build His *ecclesia* also signalled one additional thing which namely was that the *ecclesia* itself was doomed from its inception. By being doomed, Judas meant that, even if the ecclesia (which, as far as he himself was concerned, was already floundering) miraculously survived the miracle worker's certain demise, the *ecclesia* or church would end up populated only with riffraff of Peter's mould; and those riffraff, taking after their leader (Peter), would turn into a miserable bunch of hypocrites and possibly even murderers.

Judas knew enough not to expect too much from those who would be flocking to a Church that had Peter as its head to worship the Prime Mover under the New Testament. No, he himself might have his disagreements with the Deliverer. Still, the fact was that the future prognosis of a world without the Deliverer was not good at all. It was in fact so bad, it scared him to death.

Judas did not have any delusions concerning the import of the events of the past few days that he had had witnessed. There was the Deliverer's triumphal entry into Jerusalem as the exuberant multitudes shouted: "Hosanna to the son of David! Blessed is the king who comes in the name of the Lord! Peace in heaven and glory in the highest!" Unlike victorious Roman generals who rode into Rome riding chariots pulled by galloping horses, the miracle worker had entered the city riding a mule. But it became the talk of Jerusalem all the same, because it epitomised His triumph over the priests and Pharisees who were notorious for their scheming and underhand dealings!

And then there was the last supper! Judas had not only been honored to sit right there by next to the miracle worker and Deliverer, but he had even shared the cup of wine with the Deliverer. Just to think that that "wine", according to the Deliverer's solemn declaration, was actually His own precious blood which He was going to shed for the sins of humans! Judas was well aware of his own propensity to impetuousness, not to mention his erstwhile obsession with money, and was relieved to know that his own sin of dilly-dallying with those deadly vices was also included. But he was grateful to God that the much talked about vice of procrastination was not one of them!

It was now approaching midnight, and Judas was not in any doubt regarding the fate that awaited the Deliverer. Before the sun set the next day, the Nazarene and son of David was going to be dead after being scourged, spat upon, and perhaps even mocked as the King of the Jews, and the Son of the Prime Mover! Instead of taking Him at His word that He had come to Earth at the bequest of His Father in heaven; and that, if it were not for the fact that he was permitting them to try to destroy Him in order that the scriptures pertaining to His death and resurrection would be fulfilled, legions of the biblical cherubim and seraphim would be on hand to stop their ill-advised assault on His person, the stupid fools probably would go as far as daring the miracle worker to try and escape after they had him "safely" surrounded by members of the Roman cavalry! But, as far as he himself knew, it was now a matter of hours before the Son of Man would be dead albeit of His own choosing. The cunning priests and Pharisees would be in the thick of it, and making what was undoubtedly one hell of a gamble!

When speaking to the multitudes about death and the last days, the Deliverer had used the metaphor of the "thief in the night". Judas allowed that a week earlier, as he and the other apostles savored the limelight with the Nazarene as he rode victoriously into Jerusalem on the back of a colt and symbolically wrested the city from the power of the surprised priests and Pharisees without a fight, he would not have anticipated either the impending death in ignominy of his Lord and Master, or his own impending death by hanging! It was ironic that this was all taking place even as Herod Antipas, the flamboyant King of Galilee who had himself come to Jerusalem ostensibly to take part in the Feast of the Passover when the real purpose of his annual visit was to assert his power over the high priests, Pharisees and particularly the affluent and aristocratic Sadducees who held high priesthood and the majority of the seats on the Sanhedrin!

The greatest losers were undoubtedly the elders and chief priests and scribes who should not only have recognized the promised Messiah in the Nazarene, but given Him a great red carpet welcome regardless of whether the Roman imperialists and their cronies in Palestine liked it or not! The poor fools not only had no inkling that they were allowing themselves to be used by Providence on the one hand to cause the scriptures in which they themselves claimed to be experts to be fulfilled, but they did not know that they were playing themselves into the hands of the very people who did not care a hoot about the temple in Jerusalem!

Still, the fact that the Deliverer, like a lamb led to slaughter and like a sheep before shearers, was going to offer Himself to die for the sins of all men the altar of the cross in a matter of hours, and his own impending self-immolation by hanging from a tree, which Judas equated to the "day of the Lord", had all verily burst in on him very much like a "thief in the night"!

The Deliverer had repeated to the apostles in the Upper Room, as they feasted on the species of bread and wine that He had mysteriously transformed into His sacred body and blood, that He had to die, but was going to overcome death and resurrect from the dead as prophesied. Judas was keenly aware that death was by no means the end. But, while he himself was not going to be around to witness the resurrection of the Deliverer, he did not doubt that he too was eventually going to rise up from the dead at the end of time.

It was his humble prayer as he prepared to take his own life that, at the end of time, he too would be ushered, body and soul, before the throne of the victorious Son of Man in the presence of the heavenly host. After all, like the other apostles, he had left all to follow the Nazarene; and, as the Deliverer's purse bearer over the space of three years, Judas had developed a relationship with the Son of Man that was as deep and personal as any. And then there was the fact that, only a few hours earlier, he had been honored and humbled to receive "holy communion" from the hands of His Master.

When supper was over, the Deliverer had engaged them all in a long and solemn discourse that ended with all of the Apostles openly acknowledging and confessing any shameful deed that they recalled doing since they were small. Even now, Judas was still irked by the fact that the dissembling, cowardly and lying Peter, his face all wrapped up in false humility and speaking with a straight face, had said he was not going to allow the Son of Man to wash his feet! This was even though it was Peter who had started the argument about who among them would be the greatest!

But, the theatrics in which Peter had indulged aside, the air of foreboding had been ominous as the Deliverer completed the ritual of the washing of the feet and then allowed everyone assembled there, including Judas, to give Him a warm hug. Judas Iscariot, who was still clinging to the notion that his diplomacy could still save the life of the Deliverer even at that late hour, tore himself from the gathering and quietly slipped out of the Upper Room ahead of everyone else.

Judas had been drawn to the Deliverer's by the total self-abnegation that seemed to be His hallmark even as He showed that He had power over diseases and, indeed, over all creation; and he was justifiably frustrated - or so he thought - that he still had ended up with a bunch of people who were given to bickering and posturing on that scale!

He knew that the priests and Pharisees comprised a clique that was infinitely worse, and he himself had started to entertain doubts about the wisdom of confronting them the way he planned to do in his efforts to save the Deliverer's life and advance His mission of bringing hope to humans thereby. While he envisioned great things for himself if he succeeded in pulling this thing off and saving the Deliverer's life, he also had this idea that his own fortunes were completely intertwined with those of the Nazarene, and he therefore saw nothing but gloom and doom if he did not succeed in pulling this thing off.

It seemed unthinkable that Providence could allow his efforts to end in failure. It would be so terrible if the Prime Mover, who so loved the world that He gave His only begotten Son so that those who believe in Him might be saved, permitted such an eventuality. First, even though they were a crooked lot, the priests and Pharisees were the very ones who were expected to welcome the Son of Man. And, secondly, the plot those crooks were hatching - a plot in which they would try to present the Nazarene to the Roman authorities as the leader of a ring that planned to free the nation of Israel from their grip - was so perfidious and vile, Judas thought it was just the sort of crime that cried out to heaven for vengeance! The apostle from Jericho could not stomach the thought that the dissembling and hypocritical priests and Pharisees were bent on lynching the Son of Man in the name of the Prime Mover.

How in heaven and on earth could the Prime Mover allow things of that nature to continue happening now that the Deliverer had made His appearance on earth! And if the crooks would succeed in doing it to the Author of Life, King of Kings, and Lord of Lords, then who would be safe from the ill-intentioned and malicious with their never-ending scheming and intrigues. Judas had stuck with the Son of Man over the period He and the twelve had spent criss-crossing Judea, Galilee and Samaria precisely because here at long last was someone who could put a stop to the chicanery not just of humans but also of demons as well!

If they got away with it, it would, in his view, strike at the heart of the very notion of deliverance - deliverance from the evil that had been kick-started by the intransigence of the first Man and the first woman. The reign of evil in the world that had spread to every aspect of human life like a cancer would triumph, as also would Beelzebub, the father of lies! Judas had accordingly rationalized that it was fitting that the Deliverer was not just a miracle worker, but someone who had come down from heaven and shared in the divine nature of the Omnipotent.

It was, of course, an open secret that the prophet Isaiah referred to the priests and Pharisees when he said: "This people honors me with their lips, but their heart is far from me; in vain do they worship me, teaching as doctrines the precepts of men." But Judas expected that sort of behavior to come to an end with the appearance on earth of the Son of Man, and the ushering in of a New Testament.

Judas had visited with John the Baptist before that forerunner of the Deliverer was murdered at the bequest of the cowardly King Herod. And he distinctly recalled the son of Zachariah remind the crowds that, while he was a voice crying on the wilderness, they all needed to commit themselves to "preparing the way for the Lord", and "making His paths straight".

By that, Judas had understood that, under the New Testament that was being ushered in, chicanery and intrigues perpetuated in the Prime Mover's name were going to be things of the past! And he would not have thought that those who had succeeded Moses as leaders of God's people could dare make things difficult for the promised Messiah, let alone turn against Him. It was that frustration with everything that had caused Judas to loose his cool and denounce the members of the Sanhedrin in front of the temple guards before casting the blood money at their feet and making his hasty gateway.

Judas was a widower, having lost his wife just months after they had got married, and before they had any issue. He recalled how the Deliverer, addressing the multitudes one day, went out of his way to explain that while it was good to be married, it was much better to consecrate one's life to the Prime Mover by leading a celibate life.

The Deliverer had found it necessary to explain that statement several times over as the crowds and even some of his disciples seemed to regard the position the Deliverer had taken on that subject as being heretical, and were grumbling! Judas would always remember that "Sermon by the River Jordan", as it came to be known, because he had lost his temper and had to be restrained by the Deliverer Himself. He had lost patience with those who were grumbling not just because the Sermon by the River Jordan made a lot of sense, but he could not understand how those damn ignorant people could stand there and suggest that the Nazarene who had explained that he was a member of the Godhead and was therefore Knowledge itself was committing heresy!

For his part, Judas had taken the words of the Deliverer as a call to those among his apostles who were not burdened with family responsibilities to remain celibate, as that would enable them to devote their lives to the work at hand. The Deliverer had likened that work, namely going out into the world to spread the Gospel of Salvation to the ends of the earth as His "missionaries", to going out into the fields to rake in the harvest.

Judas was glad that he had heeded the Deliverer's call, and the fact that he himself, along with the other apostles who were still single, had vowed to remain chaste and poor and henceforth to live like spouses of the Prime Mover. As he readied himself for what he saw as his own self-immolation, he told himself that he could go ahead with that scheme with a clear conscience. Ending his own life the way he proposed to do - which actually differed from the way the Deliverer was about to end His life only in methodology - was not going to be a burden to anyone!

He reflected on the fact that, by and large, he had been a faithful follower of the Deliverer, even though his motives had a tinge of worldliness about them. That was a definite and serious failure on his part; and, in his scrupulosity, he could not see how he could allow himself to continue on as if nothing had happened when the Deliverer, who was completely free from sin, was going to die. Understanding the purpose of the Son of Man's sojourn on earth as he did, Judas even commended his soul to Him, and prayed that he too would be a recipient of the mercies of the Prime Mover whose will the Nazarene was completely committed to accomplishing.

Judas acknowledged with dismay that his labors, since leaving all to follow the Nazarene, had ended up a total failure. And now, to make things worse, no one would ever know the true extent of his love for the Deliverer - love that had driven him to embark on his risky mission. It was clear that if he had not succeeded in making his getaway, after he thrust the 30 pieces of silver at the feet of the priests and Pharisees, they would have done everything in their power, willy-nilly, to compel him to testify against his "fallen Master" at the trial.

Judas was determined to deny them their wish. But he also knew that those cunning and lying "idiots" were even now not going to let him die in peace. They were going to try and depict him to the world as the apostle who turned star witness against his Master and betrayed the Deliverer's cause; and as the one who provided the inside knowledge about the Nazarene's determination to lead Judeans and Galileans - and may be Samaria as well - in rebellion against Rome! It would serve their agenda to do that, and Judas had no doubt whatsoever that they were going to do exactly that.

Judas allowed himself an extra moment in which to marvel at the way in which Providence had arranged things before slipping the noose over his head and, once the noose was tightly in place around his neck, allowing his ample frame, to slide forward and start hurtling downward with the force of gravity.

A New Era

To be sure, the Son of Man, who was also the Author of Life, had made it clear that He had come down to earth at the behest of His heavenly Father to deliver humankind from the clutches of sin and from bondage thereof. In Judas' mind, the advent of the Messiah spelled an end to the reign of evil which started with the rebellion of Lucifer and the band of angels who joined him in refusing to go down on bended knee to worship the Almighty One and their Maker, and whose act of transgression had caused them to become transformed into demons. With their fall from grace, Adam and Eve had dragged humankind into the fray, and aligned humans with Old Scratch and his band of fallen angels.

The brazen act of rebellion of the first man and the first woman, and their outrageous attempt to be like the Prime Mover represented what amounted to an earth-based axis of evil that also militated against all that was good. The inclination of humans to sin effectively made them allies with Satan and the fallen angels in the ongoing battle between good and evil.

Judas had attempted unsuccessfully to persuade the priests and Pharisees that the Nazarene, the Anointed One whose shoe laces John the Baptist had been unworthy to untie, and whom they were bent on liquidating, was the awaited Messiah - a Messiah not just of the Israelites, but of all humankind! As he planted the kiss on the cheek of the Deliverer, a kiss he knew his fellow apostles were going to immediately interpret as a kiss of betrayal, Judas was still hoping for a miracle, namely a sudden and welcome change of heart on the part of the chief priests and scribes that would be followed by a proclamation that the deliverance of the people of Israel and of all humankind was at hand, and in its wake by a red carpet welcome for the Deliverer.

Judas was still clinging to the hope that his wish would be granted. He was hoping that, even at that late stage in the game, Providence was not going to allow the Savior of Mankind to suffer any harm at the hands of the Pharisees and Sadducees on the one hand, and the Roman imperialists who did not see any wrong in subjugating entire peoples and condemning them to slavery, or using torture to maintain their super power status, on the other. Judas had heard the Son of Man proclaim that the poor and the marginalized, and those who now wept were blessed; and he had given notice to the evil of heart with His proclamation that those who now laughed and were delighted in perpetuating the miseries of their fellow humans would soon find themselves weeping and gnashing their teeth.

But, even though, the Son of Man had also alluded on multiple occasions to His own impending rejection; and had taught His disciples that He had to go to the Holy City and, once there, suffer incredibly at the hands of the elders and the chief priests and scribes, and even be killed. Judas had refused to come to grips with the possibility of evil triumphing over good in any way, and certainly not when the Anointed One and Author of Life had deigned to come to earth in fulfillment of the promise of His father in heaven. And to top it all, the Nazarene had made the blind see, and the lame walk; and He had healed the sick and even raised Lazarus from the dead.

Judas believed that he was on firm ground when he took the Deliverer's references to His own suffering and death as a joke. If that happened, it would signal victory over the forces of good by the forces of evil! And, instead of pulling the rug from under the feet of the likes of Pontius Pilate, governor of Judea, Herod who was tetrarch of Galilee, Annas and Caiphas who were the high priests, and the tyrant Tiberius Caesar, all of whom operated in concert with the Evil

One, it would be tantamount to surrender! Judas' decision to leave all and become a disciple of the Nazarene and Son of Man had been prompted by his belief that, with the advent of the promised Messiah, humans at long last could take a breath and hope for better days in this god-forsaken world. Humans of good will were now poised to be redeemed from the earth-based axis of evil in the shape of human greed that was responsible for so much misery and suffering.

When good people fell ill, the Deliverer and miracle worker, who was also the Truth and the Life, was going to make sure that they were delivered of their infirmities. And if it happened that good people died, they too could count on their resurrection from the dead in God's time. Judas expected the Nazarene to cause the evils that plagued humankind to come to an abrupt halt. The Sermon of the Mount could not have come at a more opportune time; and Judas was very thankful to Providence for allowing him, unworthy though he was, to be a part of such momentous history.

The miseries of those who were poor in spirit, meek, or hungry and thirsting for righteousness were going to end, and they were all going to be fulfilled. Those who had a record of being merciful were going to be shown mercy by the Deliverer. Those who were pure in spirit were going to see the Prime Mover. The peace makers were going to be called Sons of God and blessed. Those who were harassed by the evil-intentioned could even afford to turn the other cheek. And, just as the prophet Habakkuk had pronounced Woe upon Babylon, the Deliverer had pronounced Woe upon those who were knaves, thieves, war mongers, lying hypocrites, adulterers, and others who clung to the motto of an eye for an eye and a tooth for a tooth, and he had affirmed that they would not see the kingdom of heaven.

It came as a complete surprise to Judas that the Nazarene had been dead serious when He had asserted that He was going to Jerusalem to suffer and even be killed at the hands of the very people who ought to have been waiting in line to receive Him, namely the elders and the chief priests and scribes. But even if the Deliverer's kingdom was not of this world, it was just too much for Judas that the reign of evil was not going to be stemmed - a reign in which wars, imperialism, colonialism, militarism, expansionism, and all the other abominable isms, slavery, discrimination against minorities and against women, banditry perpetuated by conquering powers, and the unbridled greed of the ruling classes, and other evils were going to continue unabated!

But, with the blood of the Son of Man Himself on their hands, and flush from their ostensible victory over the Deliverer and Author of Life, the wicked of this world were in fact going to be emboldened. Judas could visualize the elders and the chief priests and scribes, along with the Roman imperialists and their stooges, combining forces with none other than Lucifer and his band of fallen angels to try and thwart the work of the *ecclesia* which the Deliverer had formally launched that evening as he supped with the clutch of followers who now consisted of just the twelve apostles.

The symbolism of that meal at which the Deliverer had changed bread and wine into His own body and blood, and then shared the "bread of angels' as he called it with them, was overwhelming. Judas could still hear the steady voice of the Deliverer, as He commanded them to continue doing likewise, ringing in his ears. As the betrayer held up the noose and slipped it over his own head, he could almost hear, first the slow drum roll as the Son of Man and Author of Life was matched to Golgotha (or the Place of the Skull as it was called) bearing the cross on which he was going to offer Himself to His Father as a sacrificial lamb for the sins of humankind and as an unblemished oblation; and then the loud groans of the Son of Man as the crude nails were driven with force into His sacred palms and feet.

Judas reminisced that it was quite clear that the forces of evil were determined to stop the Son of Man from healing the sick and alleviating the sufferings of the poor and the marginalized. It was also very clear that tyranny and bigotry were going to continue as unchecked vices that would cause many a human to suffer as never before. And, instead of being driven by the love for fellow humans as the Nazarene had admonished in His Sermon on the Mount, and developing and putting to use the earth's resources for the common good of all humankind, the worlds nations, under the rule of tyrants who would be masquerading as benevolent dictators as had hitherto been the case, would be seeking to gain control over those selfsame resources for their exclusive use, and angling for positions of advantage with a view to becoming entrenched as invincible super powers.

Anger welled up inside Judas at the thought that the great bulk of humans in their millions would be barely getting by, and surviving in conditions of extreme deprivation, while a greedy minority who claimed citizenship of the powerful nations would be obscenely rich. Others, oblivious to the fact that they were all descendants of Adam and Eve, and that the Prime Mover so loved the world, that he gave his only begotten Son, that whosoever believeth on him should not perish, would be acting just like the Pharisees and Sadducees were doing now.

The Nazarene, echoing the words of John the Baptist, His forerunner, had referred to them as a brood of vipers out of whose mouths nothing good could be expected to come. They were not going to escape being condemned to hell because, as the miracle worker had pointed out, it was upon them that all the righteous blood that had been shed on earth, from the blood of righteous Abel to the blood of Zechariah son of Berekiah who was murdered between the temple and the altar, would come. Some of the prophets and wise men and teachers who had been sent by the Prime Mover had been killed and crucified by them. And now, with his failure to dissuade them from their chosen path with regard to the Nazarene, they were set to commit the most abominable act of them all, namely to crucify and kill the Son of Man and Author of Life Himself!

Judas recalled the words of the prophet Isaiah who wrote that fools spoke nonsense, and that their hearts were inclined toward wickedness. The prophet had added that these fools would not just practice ungodliness and speak errors against the Lord, but they would keep the hungry unsatisfied, and also withhold drink from the thirsty! The prophet's words could only mean one thing, namely that, even though the Deliverer was bequeathing to the world but *one ecclesia* against which the gates of hell would never prevail, the same elders, chief priests and scribes, as a result of whose actions the Son of Man could already be said to be on death row for all practical purposes, were not going to stop there.

For one, they were going to persist in maintaining that, because they had Abraham as their father, they and not the apostles were the rightful messengers of the Prime Mover. But they would not just perpetuate the errors they taught against the Lord thereby. They would also continue to harass and even murder the remnants of the Deliverer's band of disciples in league with their Roman masters.

The betrayer thought about the Deliverer's choice of Peter as the rock on which he was going to build His church in these circumstances. That was such a poor choice in Judas' view. Well, instead of one church, several hundred churches, all of them claiming to be the true church founded by the Deliverer, would blossom as every Dick and Harry angled to lay claim to the prize!

"Yes, the prize", Judas hissed. As the Deliverer's purse bearer up until that moment, he understood very well that any church that succeeded in laying claim to some form of association with the Deliverer and legitimacy would be a money maker that was worth the investment. Judas had no doubt in his mind that there would be many shrewd and calculating humans on hand who would emulate the chief priests and scribes, and proceed to set up and operate their own fake *ecclesias* or church enterprises to exploit the gullible, spiritually starved masses by pretending that they were the rightful successors of the Deliverer's apostles!

And this would all be because of the Deliverer's stubborn refusal to acknowledge that even a *sancta ecclesia* could use a few management skills. In Judas' estimation, if one was serious about going out into the ripened fields to "harvest souls", it wasn't good enough to engage the services of chaps who were just good at hauling in rich harvests of fish!

This in turn reinforced Judas's fears that the scheming by the chief priests and scribes and their ilk, which was now set to continue in the face of the virtual capitulation by the Deliverer and Author of Life, was going to cause unspeakable greatly that the distress, pain and anguish endured by the innocent in the world would continue unchecked as if the Savior of mankind had not come. It said something about evil and its continuing reign on earth.

After they had liquidated the Son of Man and Author of Life - which was in Judas Iscariot's view the ultimate sin that humans could commit - and getting away with it, the elders and the chief priests and scribes were going to form an alliance with the Romans imperialists and, together, were going to try and pacify the rest of the world. Judas noted that neither those nominally "religious" leaders nor their Roman political allies, lead by Pontius Pilate who had demonstrated that he did not have any conscience at all by his action of keeping the Deliverer and King of Kings under surveillance from the day He was baptized by the son of Zechariah, had any regard for human life; and he told himself that the take over of the world by this evil alliance was going to be a very bloody affair indeed!

It was unimaginable that it was murderers and other evil members of humankind who governed the world! There was Herod, the self-styled Herod the Great and King of Judah, who had unleashed the unthinkable slaughter of the Innocents in his insane drive to find and kill the infant Deliverer and Author of Life. Then there was his son, Herod Antipas and Tetrarch of Galilee, who did not rest until he was presented with the head of John the Baptist on a plate, and who was now about to preside over the greatest injustice ever done to a human - the murder, most likely by crucifixion, of the Savior of mankind! And then there was the brutal, obdurate and completely selfish Pontius Pilate who, as Roman prefect of Judea, was notorious for his dreadful human rights record!

And as for the "brood of vipers", Judas had no doubt in his mind that those hypocrites had even now already made plans to silence him for ever (or get him killed) just because he had told them in their face that the Nazarene was not guilty of any wrong doing, and that he himself had no desire to have the blood of an innocent man on his hands! That had led Judas to stop tallying any benefits he previously hoped were going to accrue to humankind as a result of the appearance on earth of the promised Messiah.

As Judas saw it, from now on going forward, it would not be necessary for a human to make an explicit declaration that he/she was allied to liars and murderers to belong to that camp. From here on, everyone who did not live according to the principles of the Sermon on the Mount became an ally of haters of the Son of Man by default. One was either with the Deliverer - and prepared to sacrifice one's life for Him the way he (Judas) was about to do - or against the Deliverer! Positions of neutrality in the face of injustice were going to be out of question. That was because the humankind the Deliverer had come to save was one.

Judas was certain that, with the life of John the Baptist, the precursor of the Deliverer, snuffed out prematurely by Herod Antipatros to pre-empt what that demagogue saw as a possible uprising by the Galilean peasants against his evil rule, and the Deliverer Himself about to be liquidated, the world was doomed! If evil triumphed, as now appeared almost certain with the elders and the chief priests and scribes poised to join forces with the Roman imperialists to do away with the Son of Man and Author of Life, darkness was verily going to envelope the earth figuratively at any rate. That was because there wouldn't be anyone left in the whole wide world who was capable of telling the truth and shaming the devil the way those two had.

Judas was in total shock and angry as he reflected on the fact that, in the battle between the forces of good and the forces of evil, the side he favored was about to be dealt another devastating blow. After the Son of Man and miracle worker was liquidated, Judas did not see any force left that could take on the twin axis of evil consisting of the alliance between the Sanhedrin and the Roman imperialists on the one hand, and Lucifer and his band of rebel angels on the other!

Before jumping to his death, Judas mumbled aloud that he had no wish to continue living in a world in which the sort of injustice that was about to be perpetrated against the Son of Man and Author of Life could go unavenged as it most certainly would. He could not imagine himself living through just one day of the New Era that was about to emerge.

Not every thing the Deliverer said - or everything the Spirit had taught the eleven and their successors since Pentecost Day - was in the Book, Mjomba argued in his thesis. He attributed a statement to the Deliverer to the effect that it would have been better from the point of view of law and justice if sinners had not been allowed to exist, not because they then wouldn't have had the opportunity to sin and so expose themselves to the wrath of the Almighty One, but because sin - all sin - represented a demonstration of the most flagrant ingratitude in the eyes of the Perfect One who was also Love personified. And Mjomba now claimed that this statement was one of those that were not in the Book! He did not explain how he had come by the statement in question. But he also hastened to add that the birth of sinners - which was allowed to take place nonetheless - was probably the best evidence humans had of the love, power and majesty of the Prime Mover. According to Mjomba, the fact that evil was rampant also argued powerfully for the existence of a loving Creator.

5. Mjomba and the Evil Ghost

Commenting on the position of Adam and Eve which, according to him, explained the saintly life they chose to lead in the aftermath of their failed revolt, Mjomba wrote that they were apparently borrowing a leaf from one who was both the nonpareil of "Beauty" and whose titles included that of "Wisdom". Even though invisible, He had left mountains of evidence (which Adam and Eve in their time found impossible to ignore but many today had been successful in imagining away) attesting to the fact that even though some of his works had a short lease of life, His was an Essence that transcended time and space, and which had freely chosen not only to bring creatures into being but to allow these "beings" to share in its glorious "Esse".

Mjomba went on that the first Man and the first Woman had not been entirely blind to the lessons that were available from the way other earth-bound creatures - birds of the air, marine creatures, lions, elephants, gazelle, giraffe and the other creatures of the wild, reptiles, members of the insect world, microbes and other invisible organisms, not forgetting matter itself and the elements - passed their days while here on earth. Mjomba wrote that these creatures spent all their time doing what they had to do in order to allow the brilliance of the Prime Mover shine in them and also to let the glory of "that greater than which cannot be conceived" become manifest in them.

And because, unlike humans and other spiritual essences such as angels, they do not possess an intellect and a free will - something that should not work to their advantage but does in this particular instance - they are not tempted to usurp any of the Prime Mover's prerogatives, including copyrights to the marvellous things He has designed and given an existence; or to act as if they were gods unto themselves, pretending that what they succeed in producing or achieving using their God-given talents - which they do often by chance - is purely their own invention for which they deserve original copyrights!

In illustration, Mjomba wrote that if lions had been endowed with a free will and an intellect, after falling from grace as angels and humans did, they would probably have tried - and perhaps succeeded - in passing themselves off as a superior race or something, or may be even as gods to whom the "lesser" beings who were not capable of subduing their prey with their bare fangs owed divine allegiance of sorts - or, at the very least, they would be worshipping idols that they themselves had fabricated. And they likely would be breaking all the other commandments (in addition to the commandment not to worship false gods) at the same time - just like humans and the fallen angels!

Talking about angels - Mjomba argued in his thesis that the Prime Mover's work of creation in the realm of purely spiritual essences did not stop with the first batch of angelic creatures a number of whom promptly rebelled against Him. Mjomba suggested that the work of creation in that realm likely was continuing - just like the work of creating humans only begun with the coming into being of Adam and Eve.

Mjomba believed that humans had a somewhat primitive concept of these "angelic" beings. He in fact thought that it amounted to a denial of the fact that the Prime Mover, Himself being the personification of splendor and wisdom, was capable of designing and bringing into existence creatures whose elegance and charm was beyond the appreciation of humans whether in this life or the next.

As it was, Mjomba wrote, humans appeared patently incapable of cherishing and appreciating the beauty in themselves; because, if they really had been, their preoccupation of choice would be meditation for the purpose of glorifying the Prime Mover for being such a brilliant designer. They would for one have less time for mischief (which arose from being idle) and ultimately little or no interest in material things and self-indulgence.

Since humans were not driven by pure instinct like the lower life-forms, there would be a general tendency to neglect things like feeding, sleep, etc. Purely human relationships, including marriage, would also suffer. Mjomba surmised that this sort of altruism, were it to prevail among humans, would hasten their anticipated reunion in eternity with their Lord and maker.

The biblical injunction that one must needs lose one's life - or essentially die, not just metaphorically but truly, even though in a spiritual rather than physical sense - in order to preserve it would not be such a preposterous idea anymore in these circumstances, and every human who could stir would be looking for opportunities to do precisely that in that "Utopia"!

Rephrasing what the Scriptures said in that regard somewhat, Mjomba wrote that the seed - another word for life in its germinal form - was sown from the moment a human was conceived in the Prime Mover's mind or eternity to the moment in time when a human was conceived in the womb. Before it could germinate and bear fruit due at the point it was set to pass on to the after-life (actually the real life for humans), it had to die and not just allegorically but actually if imperceptibly in the physical sense.

For the seed that did not die or at least germinate in the period between one's conception and one's passage to the "after-life" so-called, the possibility of inheriting the eternal kingdom receded accordingly. A seed in this category was one which had essentially landed - not by accident but through its own intransigence - on rocky ground.

For the seed that did die during that stage, it entered a new phase right there and then. Representing a completely different kind of existence, that phase started as the seed first germinated, then solidified as a prelude to bearing its fruit. It culminated in the seed's transition to the equivalent of a fruitful vine around the time the Sower returned to reap his fruit. And the act of reaping presaged yet another phase. That phase was of course analogous to physical death, and actually marked the seeds' inclusion in the granary holding the rest of the farmer's priceless harvest.

Mjomba wrote that there was, perhaps, something to the idea, mirrored in the cultural beliefs of peoples in the Eastern Hemisphere, that a transmigration of souls occurred. Because, typically, a granary would be stocked with seeds that were ready to be sown in fields in a move that would in our case begin the cycle all over again! The problem with that, though, would be that there would be no rest for the individual souls involved, and would go counter to the original idea that the seeds represented souls which, with the Prime Mover's grace, would already have bagged their victory over sin and intransigence at that juncture, and would be well on their way to eternal rest without any opportunity to revisit Mother Earth as members of a different species!

The parable of the farmer who went out to sow seed hinged entirely on the premise that humans were spiritual creatures first and foremost, and rational *animals* only in a secondary sense, according to Mjomba. He went on to suggest that it was precisely because humans were first and foremost spiritual in nature rather than flesh or solid matter that their actions, the accompanying motivations included, were not really concealable. Even when their actions were done out of sight or in the dark, they appeared to be hidden only on the surface! The scheming which went on behind closed doors or in darkness - or even inside the heads of humans - might as well be done in day light in full view. The resulting shame - or exultation in the case of laudable deeds - might be physically felt, Mjomba wrote; but its real impact was spiritual.

The Paramount Prime Mover...

In the after-life, the hypocrisy and the evil plots hatched behind closed doors would not only be exposed to all and sundry, but would come back to haunt those guilty of the hypocrisy when it was too late for them to do anything to rehabilitate themselves in the society of humans.

But lest one be tempted to underrate the Prime Mover in any way, wrote Mjomba, the fact of the matter was that the Prime Mover was also another one - to put it mildly. Mjomba suggested that He was the only being to whom the word "invincible" applied without qualification. This was because, no matter how depraved or downright stupid humans became, almost by design they always ended up according Him recognition and rendering Him homage even though it was frequently in disguised and sometimes contradictory expressions and epithets - Good Luck, Hard Luck, Chance, Blessings, Horoscope, the Stars, Mystery, *Élan Vital*, Evolution, *El Niño*, Life, Nature, Unknown God, etc. The nice part of it all was that this recognition of the Prime Mover's almighty power did not appear to be dependent on the disposition of humans but was accorded involuntarily.

Mjomba argued that shouts of joy, screams of pleasure, and anguished cries and other similar expressions to which humans gave vent were all instances of explicit acknowledgement of the Prime Mover's presence and power. Any yearning or longing for anything whatsoever was as much an act of faith in the Prime Mover as the solemn recital of the renowned "*Credo*". The same went for smiles, grins and laughter so long as these were not contrived or fake. That was one reason, Mjomba argued, why humans alone could laugh, smile or cry! These emotions sprung from the core of the human being, and it was there that the Prime Mover maintained his dwelling.

Acknowledgement by humans of the Prime Mover's omnipotence was implicit in the guilty consciences they found they apparently could not stifle each time they did something they knew was wrong. But tacit recognition for the Prime Mover's power and authority also came clocked in the instantaneous swearing and in the other acts of desperation that humans resorted to as they kept discovering that they could not explain their so-called good or bad fortunes!

Sometimes this acknowledgement was cloaked in the vain attempts to escape the responsibility for their actions by giving in to impulses to impulses to end their own lives and often the lives of others as well when, after squandering valuable time and resources, they discovered that they were on the brink. Mjomba explained that the real problem was not that they found themselves on the brink, but that they were reluctant to come even, admit wrong doing and follow that up with a display of remorse that was commensurate with the hurt caused by their actions, things that required a certain amount of humility. But, while they knew very well that they had violated cardinal rules which had adversely affected their spiritual well-being, they were too ashamed to own up, come clean and start all over again.

Mjomba wrote that recognition of the power and might of the Creator by humans came in many forms and shapes precisely because it was inevitable, whether humans liked to admit it or not. It was, he explained, inevitable because the constitution of humans allowed them to choose between following their reason or doing what went against reason. Thus, even though "free" creatures, to the extent that they were creatures, they were not free from the *obligation* of doing what was right, and that there was a price to be paid for being in what was in effect a rebellion against their own nature. By extension it was, of necessity, also a rebellion against the One who originally designed and accorded not just to the human nature, but to the nature of every that was created (or had come to be) an existence and, along with that existence, a purpose that was in line with the divine scheme!

According to Mjomba, admission that the Prime Mover's rule over creation was paramount was likewise implicit in the constant yearning for fulfilment and in the ceaseless search for purpose in life even by those who refused to openly confess that He was the supreme Lord of all. And this admission was also manifest in, of all things, the contrived modesty of sinners! This was because modesty that was insincere evidenced an absence of godliness and what he termed a haunting emptiness!

Humans acknowledged the omnipotence of the Prime Mover in the very act of sinning, Mjomba wrote. Without Him, not only would the occasions for acts of sin not have arisen, but the acts of sins themselves, consisting in the distortion of the original goal and purpose of creation, would themselves not have been possible. And above all, without freedom of the will which He had included in His design of human nature, sin would have been impossible. Sin as a notion boiled down to an attempt to pull off a coup d'état with the intention of expropriating assets to which only the Prime Mover as prime cause of everything that existed had a rightful claim, and/or denying Him full credit for copy rights held in regard to things He designed and brought into existence out of nothing.

Acknowledgement by humans of the might and power of the Prime Mover was unavoidable and was, indeed, manifest in the very act of sinning. Sinning or betrayal, Mjomba wrote, could be reduced to the statement "I am a mere human; but, guess what, I also want to be a Prime Mover - or at least to pretend that I am one! At the very least, however, I am not about to use my talents in the real Prime Mover's service. I would even rather bury them, if I may say so!"

The dependence of humans on the Prime Mover was especially evident in the commission of sins of self-indulgence. Self-indulgence was entirely dependent, he argued, on the fact that the God-given nature of humans was human; that if that had not been the case, things like concupiscence - or even lust - not only would not have had any meaning, but would not even have constituted occasions of sin.

According to Mjomba, lusting after someone else's spouse was possible only because the individual who was the object of the lust had been constructed in the particular manner in which he or she had been constructed; but, more importantly, that individual was human and the lusting individual happened to possess a complimentary human nature. If that were not the case, humans would in fact not even be in a position to derive the temporal or passing pleasures that they now derived from self-indulgence.

If the nature of one of the parties had not been human, humans would almost certainly not be in a position to feel any attraction to each other they way they now did, and perhaps even not at all. Instead of feeling attracted to each other, humans quite possibly would be repelled by each other. According to Mjomba's thesis, lust and things like that were possible only because humans could identify with each other as creatures that enjoyed the same human nature. But that was not all. The material things to which they now found themselves attracted and in some cases enslaved would probably be quite unattractive and possibly even repellent.

Humans, Mjomba asserted, were dependent on the Prime Mover to that extraordinary extent. But the tragedy, he went on, was that when humans indulged themselves, they did it at precisely the time they would have been much better preoccupied giving glory and praise to the Prime Mover for the very same reasons they now turned their backs on Him. And so, in one stroke so to speak, these humans were squandering what really was an immense opportunity for giving back to the Prime Mover something in return for bringing them into existence through self-denial. Instead, they were chafing for battle with each other over God's blessings to mankind - which sins of concupiscence, lust and greed amounted to.

By emptying themselves through self-abnegation, abstinence, fasting and things like that, humans gave themselves a chance to lust after and eventually enjoy, not pleasures that were short-lived because they were engendered by aspects of creation that were changing and were therefore not permanent or long lasting, but the One and the Only Unchanging Being and Author of Life, and Creator of the World and everything that was in it.

Sin thus included an explicit, albeit grudging, acknowledgement not just of the Prime Mover's existence but of what he was capable of accomplishing as well, namely bringing humans (and other creatures) into existence out of nothing.

Now, humans were, according to Mjomba, free to exercise their freedom of speech and to say anything that came to mind. But they made complete idiots of themselves when, acknowledging that they were not there at a given point in time and had been gratuitously brought into existence by someone who had to be immeasurably bigger than themselves, turned around on impulse and casually - and in the same breath - rejected the existence of the Prime Mover! They did that in the exact same casual way they "forgot" to treat other humans the way they themselves wanted to be treated, but started howling foul as soon as the roles were reversed! They were free to try and ignore the obvious - but only for so long. When humans acted like that, they were not just in denial - they lied and were dishonest!

The purpose of discussing that subject, Mjomba wrote, was to show that when humans offended the Prime Mover, they knew exactly what they were doing, even if they chose, after the fact, to play sissy by claiming that the devil made them do it, by pleading ignorance or coming up with some other excuses in an attempt to escape accountability for their actions.

Mjomba believed that if humans were serious and really wanted to, they would see the power and might of the Prime Mover revealed wherever they would care to look in a literal sense. The stinging pain from a small bruise on the sheen would speak volumes about the Prime Mover for His brilliance and foresight in designing humans who might otherwise overlook serious injuries sustained by them until too late. The almost instantaneous clotting of blood stemming any further haemorrhage would not fail to remind them of the Prime Mover's ingenuity and foresight, and would be further evidence of the fact that He remained in total control, the intransigence of humans notwithstanding.

According to Mjomba, the rebellion of Lucifer and his lackeys exemplified this aspect of sin clearly. Prior to his sin, the devil, more than any other created being, was fascinated and dazzled by the majesty and boundless power of the Prime Mover, before jealousy and lust for power got the better of him, and he decided that he was going to try and usurp that grandeur and authority and set himself up as an alternative god. Even after Satan and the spirits he had successfully drawn into his plot were cast into hell, it was the same magnificence and power of the Prime Mover which they continued to battle, while Michael, the Archangel, and the other hallowed spirits were doing the opposite.

Mjomba contended that the rebellion of Lucifer and his minions, whose speciality was sowing the seeds of death through spreading lies about the Truth and trickery, would lose its sting and not constitute a revolt if it did not include an acknowledgement that the Prime Mover remained the one and the only "prime mover" and in charge of things, the rebellion notwithstanding. This was a paradox of sorts, Mjomba wrote, adding that it was precisely because the renegade spirits had never expressed regret for their failed attempt to try and unseat the Prime Mover that they continued to stand condemned. Pure spirits who knew at the very outset that any coup attempt or declaration of war on their part was irrevocable, they had apparently worked themselves into an awkward spot from which they could not retreat.

The brazen intransigence of Beelzebub made him dangerous enough that the Deliverer Himself saw the need to personally draw the attention of humans to the perils he continued to pose to creatures with a capacity to choose between good and evil. The fact that He did so suggested that Beelzebub was very richly endowed at creation. And now, like a disgraced prince charming/chairman of the joint chiefs of staff whose position previously made him privy to the most sensitive information, the Evil One, aided by the fact that he was invisible to the human eye and jealous and resentful to the hilt, literally had nothing on his hands apart from roaming the corners of the earth in search of human prey.

Talking about Beelzebub and about intransigence, you would think that the devil would be the last person to proclaim the greatness of the Prime Mover, Mjomba wrote. Satan occasionally found himself cornered in a way which left him no option but to proclaim loudly and clearly the greatness of the Creator, and it went without saying that he found all such occasions humiliating in the extreme, according to Mjomba. Some of the devil's most embarrassing moments, Mjomba went on, were recorded in graphic detail in the New Testament, and showed Beelzebub belatedly announcing the arrival on Earth of the Deliverer as he himself took to his heels!

That led Mjomba to the conclusion that all transgressors in the moral arena knew they were transgressing, even though they often tried very hard to make their less than sterling lives appear normal. There really was such a thing as a conscience, Mjomba wrote, adding that it apparently remained active regardless of efforts of transgressors to stifle it.

And so, while some "silly" humans, who even knew their dates of birth, had the audacity to question the existence of a Creator,

Beelzebub and his lackeys in the Underworld had never done that. Silly, Mjomba explained, because, dream creatures endowed with spiritual gifts, they preferred to imagine that their place was in the animal world rather than in the blessed realm of spiritual beings. They equated themselves with creatures that were not only incapable of thinking aright, but that could not "think" at all because they did not possess the wherewithal for that sort of thing, namely souls!

And thank God it was only humans amongst creatures that roamed the earth that possessed souls and could think, Mjomba observed. Even though they belonged to the same human race, Mjomba could not recall a time in history when they were not at war with each other over nothing. Mjomba imagined, with good reason no doubt, that if the divine plan had called for other 'earthlings' that could also 'think' to share Planet Earth with humans, the warring would not only be constant, but the ongoing slaughter, as the two groups of earthlings battled for control of the earth's scarce resources, would make the wars amongst humans like mini-storms in tea cups!

Mjomba wrote that regardless of how "scholars" and others described the phenomenon of conception - regardless of whether they attributed it to "genetic mutation" or to natural or artificial "insemination", a spiritual essence came into being at the time a human was conceived in the woman's womb. The spirit or "soul" certainly did not create itself; and, of course, it could not just spout out of "matter" - whether living matter or dead matter, including what is called "semen" - because that could not happen in accordance with the well-worn maxim *nemo dat quod non habet*!

And, any way, whoever said that the Prime Mover - because He was a prime mover - could not use His creatures to prepare conditions that facilitated "implantation" inside a woman's womb of a brand new "human soul" at the right moment in time, if doing so was going to result in a unique "human" creature. Yes, a human creature - Mjomba wrote - in which a physical part (body) and a spiritual part (soul) would be fused together in such a way that the end, "Man" was subject to natural law and supernatural law at one and the same time!

Mjomba went on that those silly people, by denying the existence of a Prime Mover, also automatically denied the existence of pure spirits since, by definition, a pure spirit came into being out of nothing with no other creatures intervening to facilitate their "spiritual conception" or entry into existence on the spiritual plane as was the case with humans. But, again, assuming that pure spirits existed, since they could not possibly create themselves or will themselves into being (in accordance with the maxim *nemo dat quod non habet*), the case for a Prime Mover "willing" them into existence was all too evident.

Mjomba did not fail to point out that, if one accepted that humans lived on after death - just as the so-called "animists" claimed - the case for a Prime Mover willing them into existence and sustaining them in their after-life also became self-evident.

That was why, in addition to Anubis, the Egyptian "God of the Dead", Nephthys, the Egyptian "Goddess of the Dead", and their other "gods", Egyptians (representing Africa), also believed in the existence of "the Hidden One", or so-called "primordial creation-deity", Mjomba argued. He wrote that the closest equivalent among the gods of Greeks and Romans (representing Europeans for whom "animism" is still taboo to this day), was Zeus or Jupiter (the Greco-Roman "Captain of Gods") and perhaps Apollo, the Greek "God of Sun", and Cupid or Eros, the Greco-Roman "God of Love" - mythological deities whose power did not include the "power to create entities out of nothing".

It was all "silly" because individuals who had a *perishable body* and an *immortal soul*, but preferred to act as if the situation was otherwise, were in denial. And, even though they were free to do as they wished (which was fine and well with Mjomba), being in denial was fine and well only for so long. Those who were now "in denial" would in time discover that the *animists* - the "stupid Africans" - were correct after all! Those individuals would also discover that after they "kicked the bucket", they didn't vaporize (as they might have wished). Mjomba wrote that mounds of earth meant to keep buried human remains respectfully out of sight did not hinder spirits of humans who had passed on from "matching on", as Louis Armstrong put.

The silliest part was the fact that many, who did not now exist, would at first be all agog on finding themselves sharing the same habitat with other animal species here on earth (including mammals that couldn't smile, laugh, or communicate - or think - in the same way as they themselves did) only to turn around and start pretending that they were exactly like those other life forms which, perhaps, did indeed owe their existence to something as impersonal as evolution!

And if the Prime Mover was an essential party to procreation where humans were concerned, did it mean that the act of procreation was sacred? Mjomba's response was in the affirmative, and not so much because the Prime Mover was directly involved as because the act of procreation, just like any other human activity - tilling the fields, planting, harvesting, eating and resting, interacting with fellow humans and saying one's prayers, etc. - took place in the presence of the Prime Mover.

According to Mjomba, He (the Prime Mover) watched over His creatures in the literal sense and sustained them from the moment they came into existence and continued throughout eternity. He did not stop at being a "prime mover" or "creator". He even made it His job to welcome humans into eternity after their sojourn on earth.

Following in the example of Adam and Eve who by and large had every intention of doing everything they did, in the wake of the Prime Mover's promise of a deliverer, to His greater glory and honor, throughout the ages, humans have implicitly dedicated their lives to the service of the Prime Mover after recognizing that positive human activity was sacrosanct. Accordingly, the ancient Egyptians paid homage to Ptah (the creator), Set (the god of evil), Osiris (lord of the dead), Meskhenet (goddess of childbirth), Re (the sun god), Heh and Hauhet (deities of infinity and eternity), Thoth (the god of wisdom), and even Ammit (devourer of the wicked), amongst others.

It was in a similar vein that the Greeks and Romans paid homage to Jupiter (the king of gods from whose name, a combination of *Zeus* and *Pater*, we got the words *Deus* or God and *Pater* or Father;

Apollo (god of the sun, poetry, music perfection of male beauty, etc); Venus (the goddess of love); Volcanus (the god of the "raging" fire); Minerva (the goddess of wisdom, the arts, and commerce); and others. According to Mjomba's thesis, the same applied to the Chinese, the Indians, and the world's other ancient civilizations.

Mjomba wrote that humans in the twentieth century gave expression to homage, perhaps unwittingly, in pop songs, rapping, sitcoms, and other "Hollywood acts", when they were not doing gigs in prayer palaces and paying lip service to worship of the divinity from pulpits and now increasingly in telecasts. All of which, according to Mjomba, said something about the extent to which humans had strayed from reality.

Returning to the subject of conscience, Mjomba asserted that it did not matter how emphatically or for how long those who transgressed tried to disavow the reality. It did not matter how crafty or how powerful the transgressors were. It did not matter how loudly and for how long the benefits from the sinful practice were trumpeted; or how successful humans were in perpetuating the deception. It did not matter how socially acceptable, how popular and fashionable; or how widespread the sinful practice was. It did not matter what the pay back in material benefits or convenience the sinful practice engendered; or even the security, economic or otherwise, which the sinful practice guaranteed.

And it did not matter what the cumulative benefits from the sinful practice were in the short term or the long term. And it did not matter how pleasurable and satisfying, how exciting or addictive, the sinful practice was. It did not even matter if Church figures turned up and endorsed or even blessed the sinful practice. Transgressors, whatever their station in life, could never totally suppress their consciences, Mjomba wrote.

Later, as he defended his thesis, Mjomba would remark that the human conscience was not something apart from the soul. It was the soul, created in the image of the Prime Mover, and it was revolted by any and all irreverent tendencies which crossed the individual's mind. Those who transgressed and tried to pretend otherwise were in effect trying to promote the lie; and, as with all lies, "you could lie all the time but not to everybody" just as "you could lie to everybody but not all the time" Mjomba wrote.

The extent of lying sometimes amounted to an invitation to the archenemy to take over full control of their person. But humans could, even then, never douse the spark of light within that attested to the enabling presence of the Prime Mover in human souls.

According to Mjomba, whenever one's conscience beckoned, it was in fact the Prime Mover Himself who was calling out and saying to the transgressor in unmistakable terms: "Foul, you. And, listen up, creature - that is another one too many!"

According to Mjomba, the harping by humans concerning their God-given right to choose, when taken in conjunction with the fact that their consciences were never silent every time they transgressed, ironically made it more difficult for them to turn around and say they were not culpable for sins committed.

Mjomba's little "scheme...

Mjomba made some of his most controversial statements as he was responding to questioning during his verbal defense of the controversial thesis. He suggested, for instance, that engaging in sinful practices for monetary gain was, at least in some if not all cases, like making a "secret" pact with, of all people, the archenemy; and he added that the time inevitably came when the turncoat, going back on his word as he was wont to do, broadcast the terms of that pact to all and sundry to demonstrate his skills in cheating, or more precisely hoodwinking, "the simpletons and the unwary" to use the devil's his own words.

He surprised the professors and his fellow students with some of his assertions. He claimed, for instance, that he was a great deal better off than the prince of darkness, even though he was not as talented or as blessed at creation as the spirit. Mjomba thought he could even say "infinitely" - assuming, of course, that he himself didn't end up flopping the CTET. Mjomba announced to laughter that, apart from the fact that Lucifer (it had never surprised Mjomba that the devil operated under many pseudonyms - Satan, Beelzebub, Mephistopheles, Lucifer, etc. - for obvious reasons) could lie from both sides of his mouth or so they said, there was absolutely nothing about the Evil One which gave him, Mjomba, any reason to feel envious.

Satan, according to Mjomba, had been disgraced and had been banished from the sight of the Perfect One eternally, losing everything he had ever had in the process - with the exception of his ability to make trouble, that is. But he himself, with the modest gifts he had received from the Prime Mover, still stood a good chance of breezing past the embittered Lucifer and sneaking into heaven and happiness that had no end!

But Mjomba did concede that Satan, had he not made the one - and likely the only - mistake he ever made of thinking that be was so talented and comfortable that he could tell the Prime mover to take a hike, would have been the envy of every creature that ever lived. Mjomba commented that it was the same pitfall into which Adam and Eve and other humans had fallen - a mistake that was far worse than seizing a machete and trying to chop off the hand that fed you, or using a saw to bring down the branch on which one sat.

Sin, because it assumed that high ideals which were in fact achievable might not be after all and went on to give precedence to that which was temporal or ephemeral over that which was eternal automatically implied an inferiority complex on the part of the sinner, the devil not excepted.

Mjomba, accordingly, argued that Mephistopheles, by far the most egregious sinner, had to be the one who suffered most from having an inferiority complex. And that, Mjomba wrote, made him decidedly the least enviable creature ever. Even though he railed against the Evil One like everyone else did, it was apparent from the start that Mjomba had a very special interest in - of all things - the devil! It was an interest the seminarian did not make any real effort to conceal.

Satan's Manifesto...

The fact was that, in selecting the topic for his theological thesis, Mjomba had been influenced by one thing above all, namely the role that was traditionally played by the so-called Devil's Advocate in the canonization process in Rome. Mjomba reasoned that if it was fine for a cardinal - a Prince of the Church - to step in the shoes of Diabolos and not merely play-act, but represent the Prince of Darkness in a matter of such gravity as the canonization of a saint, there couldn't be anything wrong with a seminarian heading off into the library and bringing himself up to date on everything that had been written about Beelzebub, and then stepping into the shoes of the accursed one and using him to do what he hated to do, and that is work for the salvation of souls instead of their damnation! Actually, Mjomba's plan was to have the devil reveal his dirty secrets in what would be the equivalent of Satan's or "Manifesto" or "State of the World Address"!

In Mjomba's mind, his scheme, if it were to succeed, would amount to a real coup against Diabolos and his Underworld. He imagined that it would be like getting the most determined and vicious anti-Catholic that ever lived to suddenly come out swinging in defense of the Church he or she had spent a whole lifetime trying to demolish.

Mjomba knew that if anyone, especially a member of the seminary's faculty, were to get wind of his little scheme, he would probably be roundly denounced as a reckless person who wasn't heeding the wise admonition that good folk stay clear of Satan and his tricks for their own safety. And for all he knew, it could lead to his instant dismissal from the seminary! Mjomba had accordingly decided to just go ahead and prove to the world that there was nothing wrong with trying to exploit the devil and, above all, using the Evil One to enlighten the world on matters relating to the study of *Theos* or the divinity.

It would not only revolutionize theology; but by getting the devil to broadcast his secrets, humans who might otherwise fall for his tricks and end up serving him would be alerted to the fact that they were very dirty tricks indeed, and would not fall for the devil's wiles - at least not as easily. And, if successful, his scheme likely would cause pandemonium in the Underworld, and with a bit of luck might actually drive some of the demons - especially the little (Mjomba imagined also "frail") demons - to despair and cause them to abandon their ruinous missions targeting the poor forsaken descendants of Adam and Eve!

Mjomba had proceeded to research his subject, taking note of what everybody from Thomas Aquinas to the children of Fatima wrote or said about Beelzebub. Mjomba was obviously surprised to discover that the devil was actually a very knowledgeable figure, and that his strength lay therein. An apostate archangel, who was expelled from the presence of the Prime Mover in the wake of his rebellion with the combined force of St. Michael the Archangel (whose name denotes "Like God"), St. Gabriel (whose name means "God is mighty"), and St. Raphael (whose name means "God Heals"), the former "Light Bearer" (as his name "Lucifer" signified), and now also "Demon-in-Chief", was no dummy.

Quoting St. John of the Cross, Mjomba argued that Diabolos knew that he could accomplish far more through a little harm done to souls that were advanced in holiness than through great damage to the rank and file of sinful and sinning humans; and the devil's strategy of passing himself off as non-existent to profligate and dumb humans while at the same time subjecting the advanced souls to the most terrible temptations involving false piety and humility, presumption, and subtle temptations to abandon mental prayer was admirable, was a winning strategy that was executed by the former Archangel of Light with precision and an eye to results. The "Prince of Wickedness" was determined to use his commanding grasp of matters pertaining to the spiritual realm to try and throw humans, with their inclination to sin, under the bus (as they say). Mjomba wrote that Diabolos was extremely well versed in Philosophy and Theology, and he could apparently convince you that a sin, which might be related to presumptuosness, false humility, or even downright hypocrisy wasn't a sin after all!

It was not long before Mjomba started dreaming about the possibility of showing that the Catholic Church was a very special target of the devil and his minions. If he could prove that this was indeed the case, and that the devil didn't really take much notice of the other churches and even less the non-Christian religions, Mjomba would have demonstrated beyond any doubt for anyone who had eyes to see and ears to hear that the Catholic Church was the one true holy Church. And so Mjomba had gone for it. That was how Mjomba found himself using Satan in his thesis as his mouthpiece when he needed to expound on Church doctrine particularly the teachings which were very controversial.

Mjomba did not have any qualms whatsoever about having the Prince of Darkness take the position that Catholicism was the true religion and all others false. To garner credibility for the phantasies they churned out, Hollywood consistently did it; and Mjomba himself thought that if his character (the Prince of Darkness) was going to be credible, he had very little choice but to portray him as a 'fallen' Catholic. Indeed, for someone like Lucifer who (prior to being disgraced) had filled the role of Master of Ceremonies, as the highest choirs of Seraphim, Cherubim, and the Thrones ministered to the Prime Mover, Mjomba was tempted on a number of occasions to portray his character as a fallen "Prince of the Church" or a defrocked priest - or ex-seminarian (like his namesake Judas Iscariot). But Mjomba also took comfort from the fact that the now quite famous (infamous to a dwindling minority) "Canadian Scrolls" contained incontrovertible evidence that the Catholic Church alone (and none other) could claim to be the true Church.

The "Eleventh" Commandment...

It was always apparent that Mjomba was careful not to underestimate any one gender in matters of the soul. And he said as much in his face to face exchanges with the panel during the oral defense of his thesis on Original Virtue. What, after all, was the gender of the devil, he asked rhetorically. Was Diabolos male or female?

Mjomba did not fail to point out that, increasingly, preachers were suggesting in their sermons that it was possible for humans to "have sex" with the devil, with many (of the preachers) making a special point of warning their flocks from time to time about the inherent dangers of exposing themselves to that kind of temptation. That also chimed in with the traditional position that humans should be wary of engaging in any sort of dialogue with the Evil One, presumably because that would expose them to seduction by the tempter *or* temptress if they did so!

Mjomba conceded that the notion of beatific vision and a love relationship between two members of the Church Triumphant that *excluded* other members were incompatible; and that marriages did not occur in heaven for that reason. The most important reason for marrying, according to Mjomba, was so that the earthly "couple" could help each other and their issue attain self-actualization. According to him, there was no practical problem in choosing a partner on earth from fellow humans who were seeking self-actualization.

Because souls in heaven had already attained self-actualization in their union with the Prime Mover, and also enjoyed different levels of self-actualization in the Church Triumphant, there would have been a practical problem in choosing a 'partner'. But a bigger problem, according to Mjomba, was the fact that when humans chose spouses back on earth, they did so out of self-interest. The so-called "exchange of vows" during nuptials was simply an affirmation by the parties that they now belonged to each other and to no one else! Now, that was really the antithesis of selfless love.

According to him, earthly marriages were therefore not love relationship in any sense at all - they were pacts in which the parties promised to avail each other for mutual exploitation. That was why as soon as the marriage unions encountered problems that called for mutual understanding and personal sacrifice, the parties to those 'contracts' as a rule called everything off without any regard for the effect of their action on the well-being of their children, and went their ways.

But Mjomba also argued that the fact that no marriages occurred in the afterlife did not in itself rule out the possibility that gender as an idea applied to pure spirits as well. For one, the idea of unions or liaisons was not restricted to life on earth. It was certainly not at all unusual to talk about the sacred union between spiritual entities on a spiritual plane. Perhaps one could also make a case for a spiritual union (or a liaison) being licit and holy, and for proscribed unions or liaisons between two or more spirits.

Humans were, of course, spiritual beings first and foremost, and that was why one could even talk of licit and illicit unions, or liaisons between members of the human race. That being the case, the idea of licit and illicit unions or liaisons in the afterlife did not at all appear to be all that far fetched as an idea. There was clearly logic behind it, and it seemed to flow naturally from the idea of marriage between two human beings, which in turn appeared to be linked to the mystery of the Blessed Trinity.

Illicit unions or liaisons between two or more spirits that were united in common cause against all that was good or sacred? That sounded like a very good description of the unholy trinity between Diabolos who was the author of death, Diabolos' minions consisting of disgraced members of the choirs of angels, and the "poor banished children of Eve" who were determined to squander their second chance! And that description certainly did one thing: it made a very compelling case for the hypothesis that gender - or what approximated to it - formed an important attribute of pure spirits just as it did in the case of humans.

It was, according to Mjomba, one of the legacies of original sin (which was an alternative description for "the state of loosing original virtue) that terms such as "union" and "love" now invariably aroused feelings of shame and even disgust in humans. This was especially true among those humans who were supposed to be knowledgeable in matters of the spirit - preachers.

But, assuming that "original virtue" - which humans had admittedly lost - was still a valid concept, perhaps, liaisons, both sacred (when they occurred between individuals here on earth who were in a state of grace or between members of the Church Triumphant) and perverted (when they occurred between sinners or when they involved the inhabitants of hell) did indeed reflect gender attributes regardless of the locale in which they occurred!

That in turn pointed to the real possibility that the devil had gender attributes which, in the case of a pure spirit, probably meant that it was both a he as well as a she! Which, in its turn, would seem to confirm that it was indeed possible for a human to fall for the temptation to have sex with Diabolos! Mjomba confessed that it was a possibility that was utterly boggling to the human mind - certainly to his mind!

But it was a possibility that was also very "puzzling", according to Mjomba. For if some humans could successfully "sleep" with the devil in an illicit union, that would constitute a very grave sin - the kind that would undoubtedly have merited it a place on the list of proscribed activities on the "tablets" Moses had been carrying after his historic encounter with the Prime Mover on that mountain in the wilderness. Mjomba thus had his doubts regarding the feasibility of sexual activity between humans and Satan as suggested by the preachers.

But his doubts also invariably raised the question of the responsibility of those who used the pulpit to spread such "false" alarm. Preachers doing so in those circumstances were, in Mjomba's view, not just indulging in something that could just be passed off as mischief. Their action amounted to an attempt to re-visit the Ten Commandments and substitute what the Prime Mover had inscribed on the "tablets" and in the consciences of men and women with something they had concocted using their own fertile imagination.

The effects of sin...

Elaborating on the subject of sin, Mjomba wrote that whereas one could make a distinction between the purely physical acts (which were of themselves neither good nor bad) and the intentions of the actors (which made all the acts sinful or meritorious) when talking about humans, the same was not possible when talking about pure spirits. Mjomba supposed that pure spirits were incapable of committing venial sins. And that, while a transgression by a pure spirit inevitably translated into a mortal sin, it also invariably was in the nature of an unforgivable sin.

Mjomba speculated that, until the first man and the first woman lost their innocence through the act of eating of the forbidden fruit from the Tree of Life, they were repelled by any form of temptation to disobey the Prime Mover. He wrote that, while their friendship with their Maker was intact, even the most minor violation of the sacred trust that was vested in them by virtue of being creatures that were fashioned in His image and also the very first humans to roam the earth loomed as something that was loathsome in the extreme. Consequently it mattered very little what the nature of the Man's first act of disobedience was according to the seminarian.

The act of disobedience of Adam constituted a very grave "original" sin that had the effect of cutting off Man's friendship with his Maker! In a sense, that original sin was a lot worse than the mortal sins that humans now committed almost at a whim, and that included the derelict acts of betrayal of Judas Iscariot, the apostle Peter and the murderous adventures of Paul of Tarsus.

But, according to Mjomba, the ability of pure spirits to see the full consequences of their actions at the very outset, or what he called "real time", ruled out the possibility of transgressions that could be designated as minor or venial sins, or transgressions that were serious or mortal but pardonable in their case. Mjomba supposed that humans were also quite capable of committing transgressions whose very nature precluded forgiveness, and feared that they too committed them.

After all, if humans were capable of landing themselves in a frame of mind that left no room for regretting acts that were out of bounds, and if they were also capable of wilfully mounting a rebellion against their Prime Mover while in that frame of mind, it would, Mjomba contended, be tantamount to suggesting that humans were only nominally free creatures if they could not be bad boys or bad girls in that respect and also actually roast in hell as a consequence of their wilful actions!

And there was, of course, also the inevitable question of discrimination - if the pure spirits who committed transgressions of the same gravity were treated by the Final Arbiter differently from their human counterparts. Consequently, if humans were denied the chance of reaping what they were sowing, they would be in a position to claim that there was something wrong with a process that discriminated against them for no reason!

According to Mjomba, the fact that humans could end up in hell made an argument of sorts in favor of the Sacrament of Confession. Because it would not have made sense to have humans, who were free and capable of transgressing, not also be capable of receiving forgiveness for their transgressions - provided they were sincerely repentant and prepared to make restitution as necessary.

Mjomba wrote that anyone who "accepted" the bible as an authoritative source of revealed truth, but was not prepared to accept that the Sacrament of Penance was divinely instituted had a real problem on his or her hands. He/she had to be prepared to explain away (among others) the words of the Deliverer to the apostles to the effect that if they decided not to forgive but to retain sins, they would be retained!

But that notwithstanding, Mjomba would have found it hard to conceive of the Sacrament of Baptism, signifying the reconciliation of humanity with the Maker, in the absence of the Sacrament of Penance which took cognizance of the propensity of humans to sin (because of the legacy of original sin) on the one hand and the fact that, even though humans were "weak" in the flesh, their spirit was quite capable of "willing" to break out of the cycle of sin.

Then, claiming that he was making a point everyone else appeared reluctant to make, Mjomba wrote that the real probability that there were humans in hell militated against the position that it was *a sola fide* that humans attained salvation. Mjomba went on that if one accepted that *faith* was *a gift* (of the Prime Mover) that humans were free to accept or reject, accepting the mere possibility that humans could end up in hell made the first position untenable. One had to conclude that it could not be by *faith* alone that humans became saved because that undermined the fact that humans were *free*, to begin with. But their freedom was not just in relation to the gift of faith (which they could choose to accept or reject), but in relation to a host of other things - both good and bad - which they could choose to do or not to do.

The freedom to accept or reject divine gifts (of which *faith* was just one) was something that was already extraneous to *faith*; and, as was obvious from the situation of the first Man and the first Woman before their fall from grace, making a choice as to whether to eat or not to eat of the forbidden fruit (a choice that was unrelated to *faith*) determined if they were on the path to perdition or not. If they had continued to steal fruits from the tree of life *after* the promise of a deliverer, they would definitely have made themselves ineligible for a heavenly reward, and would have ended up with Diabolos in a "hell" of their own choosing. Their faith in the Prime Mover's promise - that a Deliverer would come along and reconcile them (humans) with Himself - became an *additional* requirement, and did not absolve them of the need to strive to stay clear of the Tree of Life and the fruits that dangled from it at all times while they waited for the Deliverer.

The attempt to absolve humans who belong to later generations from responsibility for their actions thus also militated against the fact that Adam and Eve and their issue were all equal in the eyes of the Prime Mover, and subject to the same requirements for gaining eternal life. But more importantly, since the gift of faith could not possibly be foisted upon humans by the Prime Mover (regardless of whether they were willing to accept it or unwilling to do so), *choice* in its regard by individuals automatically became critical, which in turn proved that humans were *capable* of making critical choices both before *and* after faith came into play.

And, while there was absolutely no evidence to suggest that those other critical choices (before *and* after faith came into play) had been determined (by the Prime Mover and/or by the Deliverer, or by the Holy Ghost that united them in eternal love) at any time as being irrelevant to the salvation of humans, the exact opposite was true. That is not to say that humans, in making *any* choice that was critical to their eternal salvation, could do so *without* the help of grace that was merited by the Deliverer through His passion and death on the cross! By no means - but that was a completely *different question* altogether.

To be credible, those pressing the point that it was only by faith *alone* (that individuals were saved) had to prove a number of things among them the following: that Adam and Eve had a different nature from that of their posterity (which, if proved, would raise even more intractable questions regarding redemption); that the Prime Mover expected more of Adam and Eve - even after the fall - than He now expected from their descendants; that the descendants of Adam and Eve were incapable of making critical choices (in spite of being endowed with gifts that were specifically designed to make them capable of making such choices; that the Prime Mover made a mistake and created humans who were supposed to be accountable for their actions, but who were now (supposedly) incapable of taking responsibility for actions directly stemming from the choices they made; that the Prime Mover was in the business of "foisting" His gifts, including the gift of faith, on willing and unwilling humans; that the gift of faith actually absolved believers from keeping the ten commandments, and that it also made the Deliverer's admonition to humans to take up their crosses and follow Him redundant.

They also had to clarify what they meant by "faith". Was it merely faith in the power of the Deliverer to forgive sins? Or was it also faith in the fact that the Deliverer came, died for humans and, after He was raised up and given power over heaven and earth, and left a specified group of individuals whom He had individually asked to leave all behind and follow Him (His apostles) a special commission to go to the ends of the world and spread the message of the Crucified Deliverer, and to forgive sins in His name? They moreover had to also explain how an individual could be saved by "faith alone" in the Deliverer if that individual in the same breath refused to recognize those whom the Deliverer had called to succeed the apostles as His instruments of divine grace and to press on with the commission that had the full backing of the Holy Spirit.

According to Mjomba's thesis, in addition to the foregoing, it was imperative on proponents of the "thesis" of *a sola fide* to provide an authoritative and incontrovertible source for their peculiar *interpretation* of the gospels, and to show that they themselves had standing in this matter and consequently *could* speak on behalf of the body of believers as successors to the apostles (or for the Mystical Body of Christ) or because of some special commission they might have received from the Deliverer. But it was even then clearly moot to ask whether the Deliverer, who had paid such a high price for the redemption of humans and then taken the unusual step of handpicking His apostles before laying His hands on them so they could receive the Holy Ghost, and sending them off to continue his work, could possibly give a commission of that nature to any other party (or parties), particularly a party (or parties) that was likely to contradict the teaching of His traditional Church however "deficient" it might appear in anyone's eyes.

Mjomba added that any claim by proponents of that doctrine that the Prime Mover actually *foisted* the gift of faith upon some humans - his chosen - and in the process predestined them for heaven, regardless of whether the lives they led were worthy of creatures that were made in the image of the Prime Mover or not, created more problems for them than it solved. Or could it be that the Prime Mover *foisted* the gift of faith on *all* humans, but only the chosen or predestined ended up in heaven? Any of those options - in which the gift of faith *worked* for some humans and *did not work* for others - automatically laid the blame for *forfeiting salvation* on the "saving" *gift* itself. One ended up implicitly blaming the Prime Mover for offering a gift that was only efficacious for some and not for others

But where was the evidence that the Prime Mover did any such thing any way, Mjomba asked? He supposed that the idea that some humans were predestined for salvation while other humans were not clearly sought to minimize the personal responsibility of individual humans in the spiritual arena, a very serious thing to try to do in an arena in which the Prime Mover has been very careful to make His expectations very clear. The angels fell from grace because they disobeyed, as did Adam and Eve. To try and exempt later generations of humans from that divine law was a very serious thing indeed, and those who went along with any "doctrine" that was in conflict with that law were evidently in denial and were trying to escape the reality that all humans faced.

According to Mjomba, the doctrine of *a sola fide* was fallacious because it also militated against the infinite goodness of the Prime Mover who would certainly not have brought humans into being, endowed them with a free will with which they could accept or reject His divine gifts, and then turned around and refused to keep his covenant with those who diligently chose to do His will on the grounds that He had not predestined *them* for heaven, and who decided that some who did not diligently choose to do His bidding, because *they* were predestined for good things, could enter heaven. Mjomba contended that suggesting that predestination was orthodox automatically called into question the Prime Mover's infinite goodness as well as His infinite mercy.

On the contrary, Mjomba argued, humans, created in the image of the Prime Mover and with spiritual faculties of reason and free will in addition to sense faculties, had to stir to cooperate not just with the gift of faith, but with the other graces that were available to all humans through the Mystical Body of the Deliverer - graces the apostles became capable of dispensing once the Deliverer laid His hands on them as He prepared to send them out into the world with a commission to be "fishers of men", and which the apostles' successors, who comprised the Church's hierarchy, continued to dispense.

Mjomba added that humans, inclined to sin, were clearly incapable of good works on their own without the help of grace. Now, as creatures who understood their limitations (and all humans who accepted to be like little children did), all they needed do was ask - ask that, despite their weakness and propensity to evil, with the help of the grace that was merited for them by the Deliverer and Son of Man, they eschew deeds that were degenerate, amoral and diabolic, and (like the fruitful vine) produce works that were worthy of creatures made in the Prime Mover's image.

The fact that humans who *asked* would *receive*, and the fact that *knocking* on the door of divine mercy would always *cause it to be opened* were, according to Mjomba's thesis perhaps the best repudiation for the doctrine of Predestination. Unless the Deliverer was lying, if any one (including humans who is presumed to be 'predestined for hell') asked, the vaunted predestination (a doctrine that certainly did not originate with the Deliverer) automatically went out the window.

Mjomba pointed out in passing that while these were things his seminary professors wanted to hear, they certainly were not things that proponents of the doctrine of *Salvation by Faith Alone*, or the related doctrine of *Predestination*, would want to hear. They disliked the routine and tradition, yet the Deliverer had specifically left instructions to the effect that His followers continue to "break bread" in His memory, and things like that. That was in addition to establishing a Church to *continue* His work of redemption. Mjomba wrote that they wouldn't be true to themselves if they came upon his thesis and didn't think it was inspired by the devil or something.

Mjomba asserted that his objective in making the comparisons was to point out what he believed was a distinct possibility, namely that there were humans in hell contrary to what some believed. During the verbal defense of the thesis, Mjomba would ruffle quite a few feathers with a reference to what he called the big question. This was whether or not the Church's hierarchy discriminated against those who, while perhaps not members of the visible Church, were members of the invisible Church! The same question, put differently, was whether the Church's hierarchy unduly favored members of the visible Church over other members of the Mystical Body of Christ!

Mjomba suggested that the Church's hierarchical structure made for a Church organization that was inward looking rather than outward looking, something which inevitably led to bias of one form or another. And, what with the external trappings of power enjoyed by the Church's clergy and the carefully nurtured corporate image of what, indeed, had once upon a time been a citadel of power in the world, the Church looked more like a laid-back world government or a Church Triumphant fan club than an organization of humans who were seeking to be delivered from the pranks of Satan and human frailty.

And, instead of being all over the airwaves in this age of mass communications and reaching out to the millions out there who were hungry for word about the Deliverer (following in the example of the Deliverer Himself who crisscrossed Galilee and Judea drawing crowds who could never have enough of him), the Church's hierarchy incredibly remained aloof. The only people who ventured out there in the fields on the airwaves which were ripe for the harvesting were the Franciscans, according to Mjomba, who believed that the detached attitude of members of the hierarchy arose from the erroneous belief that they had a monopoly over truth!

Even though going on the air carried with it certain risks of its own, including the risk of sensationalizing the patently serious business of saving souls, there was no excuse for not exploiting the media - as others, who really didn't have very much to offer did. While noting that there were very real risks of converting sermons and Church services, including the Holy Mass, into empty shows and entertainment for television audiences, Mjomba wrote that the time had definitely come for seminaries to prepare seminarians to remain calm and recollected as they faced cameras, and to resist the temptation of just going on the air for the sake of basking in the lime lights.

Having panels of eminent theologians critique and dissect the theses submitted by seminarians at the conclusion of their years of study in major seminaries seemed like a good way to start. And, even better, the authors could be asked to defend their theses on "catechetical TV networks" which the Church could specially commission for that purpose.

But even as he was floating those ideas in the course of his own oral defense of the contents of his paper on Original Virtue, Mjomba noted that, regardless of their merits, any such ideas would almost certainly be viewed by the neo-conservatives who dominated the Curia in Rome as a threat to their positions and particularly their influence on the development and direction of catechetical instruction. Permitting any discussion or debate in that vein would be depicted as a reckless challenge of papal authority, and would consequently be banned, according to Mjomba's assessment.

Later, alone with fellow students with none of the professors around, Mjomba spoke more bluntly saying that clergy were holed up in mostly empty churches as if still awaiting the advent of the Comforter. He claimed that they were, at best, helping those who were already in line awaiting the bride. That they were preoccupied with that group of people who already had candles, but seemed unconcerned about the importance of keeping the candles lit - which, in Mjomba's opinion, was hardly fair to those who were not even aware that the "Wedding of the Millennium" (as Mjomba called it) was on, let alone having a candle to keep alight.

This, according to Mjomba, was a decidedly a raw deal for the many out there whose hunger for the message of salvation was such that it would be unconscionable for them not to accept to feed on crumbs offered them by other do-gooders who did not have anything better to offer.

Mjomba thought it went without saying that the Church's hierarchy, at least judging from the attitudes of some senior prelates, was that you were deemed to be lost and irredeemable if you were ostensibly living in sin. And if you were paid a visit by a Church official, the chances were that the visit would be for the purpose of serving you papers of excommunication rather than for the purpose of attempting to reconcile you to the Church - which was the same as saying that the discrimination against those who were regarded as unsaved was total!

The devil's desire to have his due...

Mjomba wrote that after being permitted to tempt humans, the devil found himself compelled to own up to the truth, and to reveal exactly how he himself forfeited eternal life. And then Mjomba did something very extraordinary. To illustrate how the tempter sometimes griped over his fall from grace in the *hearing* of the very people he was wont to prey on, Mjomba had the Evil One lament in what was a virtual confession:

"I can tell you for a fact" that I missed my crown not by a hair's breadth but by some trillion light miles; because, when preparing for the Church Triumphant Entrance Test, I aimed at satisfying a completely fanciful dream of being something I knew quite well I could not be - a *prime mover* - when I should simply have aimed at self-actualization. And I blinded myself to my folly by pretending that I could not quite account for the way I had come into existence. What led me to act so stupidly was my desire to impress the companies of angels as well as the legions of Cherubim and the bands of Seraphims that I was boss of myself and owed no one, including the Prime Mover, anything.

"You ought to know that the downfall of your own great-uncle and great-aunt - I mean Adam and Eve - can be traced to the same weakness: a desire to impress posterity that they too were prime movers. Believe me when I tell you that it is all about making and giving impressions - false impressions. Trying to be what you are not. That archangel, Michael, who is *my* archenemy, and those other creatures in Elysium - Oh, I hate them all so! They would be under me if I had not elected to chase a flight of fancy that was completely detached from reality!"

But the confession would not preclude Satan from aiming what Mjomba described as Lucifer's traditional "parting shots" at those he had successfully preyed upon.

According to Mjomba, the Evil One usually commenced by mocking the transgressor using language designed to drive the poor soul to despair. The effect was also usually devastating because the message being communicated was injected directly into the mind of the recipient.

The substance of the communication supposedly was similar to the following: "Ha! Ha! You thought you were getting all the satisfaction you wanted and were enjoying yourself, eh! And you also thought that you were unique and that you accordingly could impress the world by your showing! As far as satisfaction and enjoyment are concerned - terms that might be in the lexicon of humans but are no longer in my own vocabulary - I can tell you that you actually were satisfying only your fantasy, and the enjoyment you thought you were experiencing was also fanciful with nothing to it really. If any of those things were real, you would still be happy, wouldn't you!

"And as for making an impression, to the extent that you share the same bloody human nature as the trillions upon trillions of human souls in existence, you are not unique at all! And if you couldn't see that, where on earth did you get the idea that you could impress anyone, let alone the world - or me, you knucklehead!"

The devil's language, according to Mjomba, was a lot more ribald and obscene than that - not to mention depressing. The ultimate objective of the "parting shots" was to prepare the individual in question for the coup de grâce which the devil planned with great care and administered with great finesse, and the archenemy knew better than to make his objective too obvious while moving to implement it. If successful, his strategy, which was based on lies on the one hand and intimidation on the other, invariably saw the Evil One installed as the official mentor of the individual in question.

According to Mjomba, after practically terrifying his quarry into submission with suggestions that the transgressor was beyond redemption, Lucifer then moved cautiously to regain the confidence of the individual in question with words such as: "And now look! I like you, and I don't want to see you in worse trouble than you are in already. So, do yourself a favor by staying away from those hypocritical Church going folks of yours whom you call kin."

Even though Satan had lost the opportunity of being one of the most favored luminaries in the Church Triumphant through stupidity, his bag of tricks still included some astonishingly rock solid syllogisms that, by definition, favored the opposition. Mjomba speculated that the wicked one was probably compelled to argue the way he sometimes did - against his own position - as a punishment.

In any event, it did not surprise Mjomba when Beelzebub, elaborating on his statement about the transgressor's hypocritical kin, picked where he had stopped and continued.

"They were hypocritical because, if you took a poll, you would find that they would want you stoned with the specific objective of dispatching you to hell before you got a chance to repent and/or become rehabilitated. And you see, hypocrites believe that they deserve forgiveness as and when they succeeded in owning up to the evil things they did out of public view - something that they infrequently did; and they believe that others, particularly those who were not their pals, did not deserve any. Their jealousy, I can tell you, is such that they often prefer to be damned and be in my company rather than meet with other fellow transgressors near a confessional. Many of them, for that matter, could not contemplate rubbing shoulders with those who were the object of their opprobrium in the New Jerusalem.

"Indeed, frequently hypocrisy also masks feelings of resentment fuelled by the anticipation that those who now openly flouted the divine commandments might eventually repent and regain favor with the Prime Mover. Then, there was also the prospect that the hypocrite's own dirty dealings might one day become exposed.

"You see, the whole attitude of hypocrites flies in the face of the fact that humans are inclined to sin; and that they too, like some of us in the pure spirit realm, have been caught transgressing; and that the promise of the Deliverer was made in that changed human condition. Hypocrites certainly do not hearken to John the Baptist's bidding that humans deny themselves, particularly now that the Deliverer has arrived.

"Oh! How I hate him - that John the Baptist. You see, every time some human somewhere takes a step, however fledgling, to do His bidding, it undercuts my rule over the Underworld. That John succeeded in turning my world down side up by demonstrating that the blood of martyrs was the seed of conversion!

"Frankly, I am almost at my wit's end now because, even when Agrippa's woman at my urging stopped him in her own bizarre manner, that only raised his profile in the eyes of the Deliverer! And then, just when I thought I had the Deliverer Himself nicely cornered and put away permanently, there He was pulling off the mightiest victory imaginable by turning hell itself upside down and restoring to Adam and Eve and all those people I thought I had neutralized their freedom.

"Oh, how I hate them! This is because they represent Good and I represent evil, which has now been exposed as a nonentity - an absence of Good. That is also what hypocrites represent.

"And so, you can understand why, if your Deliverer were around and were to depict the kind of dirt in which they themselves were mired, they would make haste to vanish from the scene when they really should be prostrating themselves before Him and begging for His mercy!

"This is extraordinary. I do not get caught speaking the truth very often! Count yourself lucky for hearing it from the mouth of the Evil One himself!"

Mjomba wrote that the devil spat out those last words especially, just like a viper spits out venom. It was clear that he was speaking like that under duress and hated the fact that what he was saying was true. And it was apparent that, while at it, he was enjoined from using dirty words or swearing.

As might be expected, that outward display of compunction did not usually deter the prince of darkness from pursuing his original goal of trying to frustrate the divine work of redemption. And he was usually much more menacing and deadly after being chastened in that fashion by the Prime Mover. According to Mjomba, Beelzebub still retained enough wits about him in all such instances to conceal his true motives behind a demeanour that was so courteous and behind a tongue that was so smooth, he would probably be mistaken for a saint and would be canonized over and over if he had been able to take on the shape of a human!

Mjomba thus had the devil turn his reluctant dismissal of hypocrites to his full advantage by throwing his arm around his quarry at that juncture and speaking as follows: "Look, you are very different from those hypocrites. And now, my good fellow; promise me you won't go near them churches - especially those churches where sanctuary lamps are not allowed to go out! That is the height of hypocrisy, you see. If you do any of these things, you see I will not be in a position to help you! Otherwise you can count on my word. Sonny, a promise is a promise, you see!"

Mjomba had the prince of darkness confess that some who were his best friends at one point in time often ended up as his worst enemies at a later date.

"Paul, the so-called Apostle of the Gentiles, who had at one point been my instrument for murdering and getting rid of many of those first Christians, changed course and suddenly declared war on me!" Mjomba had the devil rant. "And even Judas Iscariot, who had started off cavorting with me as if I was his maker and whom I had spent so much of my time grooming with a view to getting him on the witness stand and testifying before Pilate himself against the Deliverer, turned against me at the last moment and declared to the whole world that he had betrayed an innocent man!"

According to Mjomba, it really pained the devil to think that even Judas Iscariot himself succeeded in escaping his tentacles, even though the "noose around his neck had seemed tight", and had even proved, in the process, that everything was possible with God to the dismay of Satan and, admittedly, the dismay of hypocrites who wanted to see only themselves saved!

If you asked Mjomba whether Judas - after he had betrayed the Deliverer with a kiss, and then compounded that treacherous act of betrayal by taking his own life - was in hell or in heaven, or was perhaps still languishing in Purgatory, his response would have been that all sinners were equally betrayers, and it was the height of hypocrisy for any one who was himself or herself in need of the mercies of the Deliverer to think that one of their number was less deserving of the Prime Mover's mercy. Mjomba would have gone as far as suggesting that trying to gainsay the infinite mercies of the Deliverer (infinite because of the nature of sin) might even be indicative of a lack of faith.

Mjomba was actually inclined to the view that it was more likely in real life for a repentant individual to take his/her own life because of an overwhelming sense of compunction on realizing the gravity of sins committed than for an unrepentant sinner to take his/her own life after despairing that he/she could ever be forgiven in the wake of committing a despicable act he/she was prepared to repeat if accorded the opportunity.

But Mjomba also recognized that individuals took their own lives for a variety of other reasons too, and these included the inability to withstand torture, the readiness to die for one's country in battle, and also the fear of public humiliation when faced with accusations that may even be baseless. Mjomba's position was that however many people linked suicides to despair, that link remained tenuous and in the great majority of cases unproven.

During his exchange with the professors and his fellow students, Mjomba also made reference to those who sought to enrich themselves at the expense of public morality and/or engaged in activities that led others into sin. Mjomba contended that it was because humans who engaged in those sorts of things were such willing proxies for the tempter that the Deliverer had warned that they would end up at the bottom of hell their passage there accelerated by what the Deliverer described figuratively as millstones strung about their necks. Also, according to Mjomba, a most unfortunate aspect of transgressions of that sort was the fact that instead of directing gratitude for gifts possessed to their Prime Mover, the wayward humans directed it to the adversary just as he was planting a wedge between them and the Prime Mover.

The problem of humans, according to Mjomba, was that they took forever to decide if they came into the world by pure accident and were therefore not answerable to any one for their actions, or if they came into the world by design and had to submit an accounting of the way they employed their God-given talents. Since they had only a limited lease of life - far more limited than most species of trees and certainly rocks - the longer they took to decide, the less time they gave themselves to prepare for the CTET (Mjomba's acronym for the Church Triumphant Entrance Test).

Humans had only so much time in which to prepare for and pass the CTET. According to Mjomba, this was a high stakes pass/fail examination, performance on which determined if lives led by humans had been simply squandered or worthwhile in accord with their human nature which consisted of an incorruptible soul and a corruptible body. Now, humans had only a limited lease of life on earth - more limited in fact than that of some of the beasts which roamed the earth, trees and rocks. Mjomba claimed that some by-products of the impious activities engaged in by humans not only outlived them but went on to become a distraction to humans of later generations!

Mjomba wrote that humans had many gifts and talents; and that there was probably none which they jealously and even zealously guarded more than they did the gift of freedom of choice. Since humans were also able to differentiate what was right from what was wrong, you would think that the one thing humans would be really good at would be to choose and do what was morally right and to shirk what was morally wrong. But you would be well advised not to bet your money on it, Mjomba also advised.

Committing a vice consisted in making a choice a human knew to be a wrong one in that it could only lead to perdition and not to righteousness. And, to make things worse, humans, rather than being inclined to righteousness, had actually been inclined to sin since the fall of Adam and eve. That was also precisely when the clamor for right to choose this and the right to choose that started. According to Mjomba, there was an obvious connection there - a connection between the fall of Adam and Eve and the clamor for the right to choose; and he believed that one engendered the other.

After misusing their right to choose, and after indulging in activity that was offensive to the Prime Mover to such a degree that He found Himself with no choice but to throw them out of the Garden of Eden, humans evidently did not find it any easier after that to start reigning in that which was at the root of their downfall. And, in what Mjomba referred to a "cycle of failures", that in turn blinded humans to the fact that it was a grave matter to continue doing things that offended the Prime Mover - just as it had been a grave matter for the first Man and the first Woman to flout His specific directive not to eat of the fruit from the Tree of Life at the time they did. The act of ejecting humans from the Garden of Eden and all that this action entailed was, Mjomba added, a very drastic measure by any standard, and was in fact analogous to the action the Prime Mover had taken against the disgruntled angels when they too spurned His graces and ended up sinning against Him!

Having decided that they would not preoccupy themselves with seeking the kingdom of heaven and letting everything else be added as promised, these humans, who were created in the image and likeness of the Prime Mover and Author of Life, were attempting to play God and were out to try and grab at the "forbidden" fruit in the hope of converting it to their own purposes in a blatant attempt to usurp the power and authority of their Creator.

It ironically was still in the same realm of the eternal that they were wasting their time chasing mirages with their focus on what was transient and ephemeral. It still was the Tree of Life whose fruit they hankered after. Mjomba explained that it was in the divine realm that, having nothing of real substance to do, humans still sought to do "it". They still dreamed of converting their satisfaction on a temporal plane into eternal happiness!

Going against the grain...

It was, perhaps, not entirely accidental, Mjomba argued, that it was a lifestyle of poverty and chastity involving the voluntary abdication of all freedoms that was most praiseworthy in the eyes of the Deliverer. He also thought that it was damning for humans to make so much of their right to choose when it was clear that they also knew perfectly what they were up to when they engaged in behavior that was unbecoming of them and for which there was punishment in store.

Mjomba claimed that self-indulgence was the ultimate goal of those who argued passionately for the right to choose, and he was quite confident that he could prove his point. But, as he was casting about in search of the appropriate words to describe the pitfalls of "that deleterious preoccupation" as he called it, something really weird happened. Mjomba, who was occupying an isolated desk in the Seminary library, first heard what sounded like a purring sound that came from no where in particular; and before he could look, it was clear that something had taken control of his entire frame which shook momentarily. It was quite clear to him that his earlier decision to engage the Evil One and use him in producing his thesis had come back to haunt him.

It was as though Beelzebub had been waiting for the seminarian to acknowledge that self-indulgence was indeed an injurious preoccupation before making his move. Mjomba shuddered at the thought that his faculties of the intellect and will were now partially under the control of the Evil One. But it was now too late. He had been determined to turn out a winning thesis by any means, even if that meant employing the Evil One as his mouth piece. And it was now quite clear that Satan, for reasons best known to himself, was ready to deliver on the deal. But at what price, Mjomba asked admittedly a little late!

"I can tell you that I know somethig about 'self-indulgence'. And look - you humans cannot imagine what it means in terms of self-indulgence when a pure spirit makes a choice that is contrary to what it knows is right! You, Mjomba, would have to be a pure spirit to understand the extent to which a pure spirit indulges itself when it exercises its right to choose, and that choice happens to be contrary to the divine will! This is exactly where I can come in handy. This is the stuff I am good at!"

Mjomba did not have to guess who the interlocutor was at that point. Except that the devil seemed to hesitate as he awaited Mjomba's consent to proceed. The consent came in the form of an imperceptible but nonetheless unmistakable nod from the seminarian.

"I am the devil, and I can tell you that self-indulgence is good for me - not for the other side", Mjomba heard the Prince of Darkness rumble in his own defense, and then continue:

"Self-indulgence, which, by the way, does not occur in the abstract, radically shifts the focus of attention of the individual from the source of all goodness, which is unchanging and permanent, and has the power to enrich, to something that is transitory."

Talk about being verbose! Mjomba thought that Old Scratch fit the bill perfectly; and he was glad that, while a minimum number of pages - a hundred pages to be exact - had been specified for the theological theses, no maximum limit had been set in accordance with the tradition at St. Augustine's Seminary.

He was busy scribbling as the Evil One continued: "Such self-centred indulgence, therefore, plays right into my hands. The tactic I employ is to entice humanoids away from constructive activities and get them mired in this deleterious preoccupation.

"And that was precisely the approach I took when I set out to drive a wedge between Adam and Eve and the Prime Mover. These humans knew perfectly well that fruit from the tree of knowledge of good and evil was out of bounds. But I calculated that, even though the father and mother of humankind were unsullied and still innocent, if confronted with any choice, they either were going to stay in line and do the bidding of their Maker without giving their own ego a thought, or they were going to think that giving themselves a little treat to fruit - any fruit - in the Garden of Eden where they spent a lot of their time trimming branches of all manner of fruit trees on whose succulent produce they subsisted, would be in their right and wouldn't hurt at all.

"They, of course, knew full well that it was risky to hanker after fruit from the tree of knowledge of what was offensive to the Prime Mover, even though he *was* invisible. Because if they did, it would no longer be the Prime Mover who would shield them from evil, but the choices they themselves made from there on - choices that either resounded to the Prime Mover's greater honor and glory or to their own incipient egos. All I needed to do to get Adam and Eve on a collision course with the Prime Mover was to get them to think: 'But, what the heck - they surely didn't need a Prime Mover to tell them if something was good for *them* or not. They had been growing smart by the day, and they already knew so many that were good for them - like shielding under trees when the skies opened up and it started drizzling. They, therefore, were already well on the way to knowing what constituted 'good' and what constituted 'a nuisance' or 'evil'!

"They had also discovered and sampled fruit from most of the trees in the Garden of Eden, and already knew that some trees produced that could kill you out right. They had discovered for instance that apple seeds also contained cyanide which could kill you if you took a large enough dose. And, well, what if the forbidden fruit from the tree of knowledge of good and evil contained the antidote for the dangerous toxins and venom they might accidentally ingest while sampling fruits of the wild? It was surely good for Adam and Eve to investigate and find out for themselves instead of sitting back and relying on Providence!

"And, with the human inclination to sin that has been in place since the fall of Adam and Eve already blocking any tendency on the part of humans to do good, this further preoccupation with the self not only reinforces the inclination to do things that are offensive to the Prime Mover, but actually fuels the penchant for mischievous conduct or sin, and completely blinds humans to the existence of the one and the only Supreme Good. It is a tough spot for humans to be in because, when they elect to indulge themselves, they effectively turn their backs on the Prime Mover on Whom they still depend for their every breath.

"You may not know it" the devil pressed on; "But I brought off a real coup when I derailed that Adam and Eve; because, their posterity, inclined to sin and stupefied by concupiscence, find it really hard, if not impossible, on their own to stagger back onto the rails they can't even see. I really shouldn't tell you this because it will hurt me - but the best way to put it is to say that self-indulgence is incompatible with communion with Him who is Perfect Goodness!

"Understand that when you are inclined to do one thing, that inclination acts as a very strong disincentive to do something else, and even more so it's opposite. And that is in addition to the inertia that would already be at play in normal circumstances even in the absence of the inclination to act in some particular way, in this case to keep all one's attention focused on the Supreme Good. But that is not all. In a situation where everybody is not only disinclined to truth, love, justice and fairness, etc. - that is what 'being inclined to sin' entails - you can bet that sinning in whichever way becomes not just a pastime but big time business.

"In that kind of situation, everyone will essentially be plotting to undercut everyone else in any way, and will also be jostling for positions of advantage in a contest in which, by definition, no holds are barred! The disincentive for some jerk who is insane enough to take time out to listen to his or her conscience and who is additionally bold enough to try and do the right thing is as great as you can possibly imagine. And if I were not the prince of darkness - say your guardian angel - and wished to offer you advice, I would simply tell you 'Go, say a prayer'.

"But do not think that you then are entirely off the hook and that you are safe from me even if you do follow that advice - although that, mark you, is just about all someone in that sort of situation can do! This is because I have not told you how I counter acts of piety...

"It is said that charity covers a multitude of sins because of the immense good that flows from it. Where there is inclination to sin and a disinclination or aversion to positive things, charity, which is neither exploitive nor selfish, works to reinforce the willingness of the spirit of the beneficiary, and thus fills the role of grace. In practical terms, charity helps to reduce roadblocks that stop individuals who wish to go against their inclination to sin from doing so. An act of charity, by making the individual dispensing it look more and more like Him who is Himself not only Perfect Love but also the Judge, has to work in his or her favor when his or her own day of reckoning arrives.

"You have no doubt heard the slogan 'Make Love, Not War'! And you have it right - the great bulk of people frown on the anti-war advocates who find the courage to hoist banners proclaiming 'Make Love, Not War'! They regard them as jerks who have nothing to do. But the reality is that it isn't very long ago when that adage was in fashion, and it explained the intermarriages between European royals. The hard work of my folks here in the Pit has since changed all that; so that today, led by the military industrial complexes and the spy agencies, stupid humans are ever jostling not just over control of the earth's resources, but over who should own planets, including the moon and the sun, and the rights to harness solar energy! Nations of the world not try to outdo each other with regard to the expenditures for preparations for imaginary wars. You would think that earthlings are preparing to fight aliens who might be hovering out there in outer space as they stockpile war materiel of every conceivable type including spy satellites, intercontinental ballistic missiles, bunker busting nuclear bombs, roadside bombs - you name it!

"Now, this is all crazy. But you shouldn't think for a moment that it has come about by accident - not unless you yourself are crazy! We here in the underworld have worked long and hard to bring this about - to get humans, who are or course driven by greed for material possessions like never before, to live in fear of one another, and to imagine that 'the other guy' is just waiting for the opportunity to come and steal from them and get rid of them in the process if possible. We have convinced them that it is prudent to always be planning to rob or steal from 'the other guy' and to kill him if possible out of the fear that 'that other guy' is planning to rob and steal from them, and to ensure greater security for themselves thereby.

"And as those humans who are regarded as an immediate threat are targeted for elimination from the face of the earth, they too naturally become uncompromising in their dealings with any allies of their perceived enemies. And it is great to sit back and enjoy the sight of humans going after one another with rockets launched from UAVs (unmanned aerial vehicles), or with IED's (improvised explosive devices) as the roadside bombs are called, often not because are a threat, but because one side calculates that control of the place is necessary to undermine the influence of some other emerging power. And we of course aren't very far when our minions frame the justifications for the losses in 'blood and treasure' in terms of either geopolitics, fighting terrorists, or just helping to feed a starving population, which always turn out to be lies anyway. The real reasons, namely providing military industrial complexes the opportunity to make a buck and giving the spy agencies a chance to become even more entrenched as the real 'deciders' in these matters, are concealed from the citizenry for obvious reasons - the same citizenry who would of course cry foul if they learnt that the lives of their sons and daughters were being sacrificed to perpetuate the rule over Earth of the Father of Death!

"And so - you see - I hate to see humans being nice to each other for a reason. It is the most effective way of robbing me of souls. You see - even though the Immaculate Heart of Mary will ultimately triumph (as the mother of the Deliverer revealed to the Lucy and her friends at Fatima), in the meantime the good must be martyred, and various nations must be annihilated. And, while I can, I must savor my rule over Earth as the prince of darkness.

"And talking about robbing, you should know that I operate from a very big disadvantage. This is even though this is a world where everyone is inclined to what is diabolical and disinclined to honesty and morality. I have practically succeeded in ensuring that there is no justice in the world - and this particularly so in those nations which brag about the equality of their citizens. The percentage of a country's incarcerated population will always betray this. In some of these places, influence, money, politics and things of that nature play important roles when it comes to dispensing justice. Judges, at my instigation, will invariably interpret 'juvenile' to mean only a certain type of juvenile, for example; and it pleases me so much when I see them unashamedly trying offenders who are juveniles as adults all the same.

"Also, verdicts from the 'benches' in some of these countries invariably end up reflecting the political persuasion of those who sit on them - something that arguably is not synonymous with justice. Which means that, if those justices had been entrusted with deciding who went to heaven and who went to hell, all their political foes would be doomed from the beginning, while their political allies would all be assured of salvation regardless of the lives they led. Which again is not surprising, because they obviously play not by the rules of jurisprudence but by the rules of politics which, as everyone knows, is a dirty game.

"If only the Prime Mover had delegated the power to send souls to hell along with the authority which enables humans to pass judgement on others. Like acts of charity, rendering justice isn't one of those things that humans, inclined to vice since Adam and Eve rebelled against Him who is the embodiment of all that is good and noble, are naturally inclined to do.

"You see, getting love and justice in this world is, *fortunately for me* (Diabolos) not the most important thing for humans. Focusing on the eternal is all that really matters, whether they get love and justice in this world or not. And when they do that and pay no heed to what is transient, they end up safe and sound at the end of time. Obviously, any success I might have in making this world a dreadful place to live in by making fairness and love rare commodities in the interim period ends up working against me and in favor of those humans who persevere by assuring them even larger crowns. It is a terrible frustration which I know I fully deserve for being the prince of darkness.

"But, a word from the Prince of Darkness on prayer. You shouldn't think I know nothing about these things, because I used to be Lucifer, the chief archangel, you know! And I am a Catholic too, albeit a very bad one. As for being versed in theology, I can tell you that I anticipate the dogmas long before they are promulgated by the Holy Father! That is why you who are even now squandering your blessings as believers should at least give credit to non-believers who still get by on the strength of their God-given 'original virtue'.

"But you are, of course, always well advised not to enter into dialogue with the tempter for obvious reasons. The Antichrist, when he comes, will do precisely that; and that is why he will be so effective. And you be warned yourself, now. You are safe for now anyway, because it is someone else's choice that you are listening to me, not your own choice...

The power of prayer...

"**A**ny way, continuing our discourse on prayer, there is no doubt that prayer is the starting point for humans in that sorry state of affairs - you can at least credit me with creating havoc on a magnitude that boggles the mind some, and you bet I'm always pretty good at anything I do. And what I say is not always lies, mark you, because I am also subject to limitations. There are certain things I have to do, however reluctantly, when ordered. Even though a rebel to the hilt, I would be no more if the Prime Mover forgot about me for just one moment. That should explain why I, even I, have on occasion confessed to the world openly that the Deliverer is the son of the Most High!

"To repeat: there is no doubt that prayer is the starting point if a human wants to steer clear of the morass. But prayer in what language - I mean under the banner of what church or religion? There are almost as many religions these days as there are spoken dialects!

"I have never been able to manufacture falsehoods fast enough. They get snapped up just like that by some who are desperately seeking the truth - even a semblance of it; but my falsehoods also get snapped up by others who use them to exploit those who are gullible. Your Deliverer put it succinctly: there are so many blind people following others whose vision is often so much worse than their own! And He was right on when, referring to the scribes and Pharisees and no doubt also those who would follow in their footsteps, He said: 'Woe unto you, scribes and Pharisees, hypocrites! for ye are like unto whited sepulchres, which indeed appear beautiful outward, but are within full of dead men's bones, and of all uncleanness. Even so ye also outwardly appear righteous unto men, but within ye are full of hypocrisy and iniquity.'

"I have a lot of fun just watching. But I still urge humans who seek deliverance in those conditions to say a prayer all the same - any prayer and in any dialect.

"Going against one's inclination and doing anything that goes counter to what is done by society at large is a very peculiar thing to do. Besides, attempting to do so is fraught with all sorts of risks. After all no one wants to go off on a limb and actually rebuff the accepted logic that when in Rome, do as Rome does. An individual, heading off into the unknown knowing that no support or backing will be forthcoming would normally be discouraged from starting off on that course at the very outset, because only insane people headed off into the unknown without any blessings from any quarter.

"And unless someone was entirely insane, the ensuing fear of failure from going against the current would by itself be enough to stop any diehard from proceeding any further. And, in any event, society's self-appointed guardians of sanity would be standing by ready to step in and put an end to what they would have every reason to regard as 'insanity'! But above all, I cannot overemphasize how discouraging it is for a human who is sidelined and also deprived of any moral or material support to succeed in any endeavour.

Lucky Humans...

"**Y**ou folks may not know it, but you are lucky that, after I succeeded in derailing Adam and Eve, the Prime Mover did not wait to promise you the Deliverer. Suppose that had not happened. The immediate descendants of Adam and Eve, inclined to sin by virtue of the original sin, would all have promptly staged their own rebellions which would in turn have generated a new series of original sins. And, being original sins, they would have escalated the proclivity of men to sin, and things would become uglier and uglier for the human race as succeeding generations contributed to the morass in an exponential way.

"The lives of humans, abandoned and at one and the same time left completely to their own devices, would give a new meaning to the word 'curse', with humans ending up as their own worst enemies. And, while the only possible way out of the quagmire and the human miseries would again have been prayer, any supplications and entreaties for mercy, however plaintive or shrill, would have been ineffectual, absent the promise of the Deliverer, and would have gone unanswered forever.

"And so, in retrospect, you folks can take comfort in the fact that you were promised the Deliverer in a timely fashion. And you can take it that if a human says an *Ave Maria* or a *Pater Noster* or, for that matter, makes any plea for deliverance from his or her adversities that are overwhelming by any account, that entreaty or prayer not only is the starting point on the road to deliverance, but clearly cannot go unanswered by virtue of the promise made to Adam and Eve. I dare say you'd probably be delivered even if you'd be caught addressing your pleas to me - I mean mistakenly!

"Put it this way: on their own, individuals trying to get themselves out of their predicament soon get discouraged, even though they know that what they are trying to do is the right thing. And it is only when such individuals throw up their hands and sigh that imploring sigh, however incongruous, or say that beseeching prayer, however deficient, that they begin to notch up any success as they stumble along on the narrow path - narrow because, with not too many people travelling along it, it is unbeaten, rough shod, and unwelcoming.

"And even when they do notch up some success, any such 'success' will not only pale when compared with the obstacles confronting them, but - perhaps even worse - will also tend to attract fresh obstacles as these individuals try to forge ahead on that confining, little travelled path. Indeed, in the so-called 'eyes of the world', achievements in this arena in fact meet all the requisites for what is called 'unqualified failure'!

"But, at that point, some usually find themselves preferring to imagine, conveniently, that the Deliverer's sacrifice was enough, and that they themselves do not have to continue trudging along clumsily under the burdensome weight of their own crosses, giving credence to the postulate that salvation is by faith alone! And they also find themselves declaring that 'good works', which is just another way of saying that humans have to keep the commandments, are entirely redundant, with no role in the divine scheme of redemption.

"Such a position also makes all the foregoing talk about the human inclination to sin and the problems associated with such a predicament also redundant. It also makes salvation dependent, not on trying to lead lives that are righteous, but on chance - being born in the right place at the right time, for instance! Others go to the other extreme - they imagine that they are on the road to salvation because of what they are, not despite what they are. The hypocrites...!"

Homily on grace (and other topics)

Christian Mjomba would have been the last person to try and tackle the subject of grace and its workings in a thesis. He was aware that really brilliant folks like Augustine, Bernard, and even Thomas of Aquin shied away from that subject. Mjomba thought it was a smart move on his part to get Lucifer involved, and then turn around and use the "infernal liar" as his mouth-piece to expound on the obscure subject.

Mjomba knew that, if he hadn't done that, he would have been told that it was utterly presumptuous of him to even include grace as one of the topics covered by his thesis! Mjomba was well pleased with himself as he pressed on with his scheme and got down to the task of conjuring up words to put in the mouth of the Evil One. He was surprised that the words came to him spontaneously - almost as if he was indeed being inspired by some terrestrial being. But he could not be sure if the inspiration was coming from the Evil One or from some other source.

Mjomba wondered if someone who had no qualms about openly employing the devil as his mouth piece could still receive inspiration from On High. Even though the scheme under which he intended using Beelzebub to pontificate on doctrinal matters was clearly a strange one, he did not really see anything wrong with it *per se*. And it was reassuring that what the devil was mouthing made a lot of sense.

Still, as time went by, Mjomba found some of the things to which the devil was giving expression extremely disconcerting. That would be especially true during his - or rather the devil's - discussion of the Cain doctrine, and the related topics of "death" and "death culture enthusiasm".

But, after agreeing to the deal under which he was going to use Satan as his mouth piece, with Satan supposedly agreeing for his part to just play dumb and go along, Mjomba felt helpless, and could only listen with apprehension as the devil rumbled on and on. Once the process got under way, Mjomba for some reason found himself unable to stop and try to figure out if there might be anything that Beelzebub expected to get from the whole thing. Every time he tried to do so, something else came to his mind, causing him to shelve the exercise.

It was all very strange - and also very funny. But it definitely terrified Mjomba that, try as he might, he was unable to understand exactly how it all was happening. And then there were times when it even looked as if it was the Evil One who was using him (Mjomba), instead of the other way round. The seminarian found the situation so scary at times that he wished he hadn't gotten involved with the Evil One in the first place. But for now, Mjomba listened as Satan rambled on.

"To wrap up my sermon, one of the most underrated discoveries was one the Deliverer Himself announced...discovery, revelation - it is all the same to me! And it would have revolutionized the social sciences, particularly Psychology and Sociology, if only humans had given it the importance it deserved. You may recall the Deliverer addressing the eleven, who had fallen sound asleep in the Garden of Gethsemane when they were supposed to be on the look out for Judas and the Sanhedrin's secret police, and saying: 'The spirit is willing, but the flesh is weak'!

"I naturally have a great interest in this 'doctrine' - if you will - of willing spirit and weak flesh. You see, human frailty provides us in the Underworld a window of opportunity that we could never pass up. And you'd better take me at my word for it even if it looks like I am saying something nonsensical.

"How, otherwise, would two individuals start off as innocent, virtual angels, only to part ways with one of them becoming a little 'devil' before becoming immersed in a life of sin, while the other one stayed the course with no apparent difficulty and grew up a model of virtue! How come that you will see this sort of thing happen even within a family, with one kid heading off to become a pious monk and recluse, while the other one veered off in the opposite direction and became a pimp or even worse? How come that one twin will head off into one direction and on the road to perdition and damnation, while the other twin went off in the opposite direction as if drawn to their separate paths by magnates?

"I will tell you for the last time: it is the same old story of willing spirit and weak flesh! It is the story of one chap refusing to heed the clamor of his/her conscience with respect to the pitfalls of self-indulgence and allowing himself/herself - with a little help naturally from us here in the Underworld - to gradually become mired in that deleterious enterprise, while the other chap - obviously with help from On High - refuses to trust himself/herself in a matter of such critical importance to one's destiny and (by the same token) surrenders himself/herself to the Deliverer, enabling the Holy Ghost (who was promised by the Deliverer) to exercise permanent rule and sway over him/her, including control over the little day-to-day things in that individual's life.

"But it is, of course, not that simple. Just how come that one fellow decides to be true to him/herself and, recognizing that he/she is in a relationship with his/her Maker, resolves to do the ordinary things that are expected of one in the situation, and succeeds in keeping the relationship intact, while the other fellow, well-knowing that if a party to a pact with the Prime Mover is likely to renege and prove unfaithful or inconstant, or refuse to keep a promise, it is not going to be the Prime Mover but him/herself? How come that humans who are created with intelligence elect to stuff cotton wool in their ears to shut out the clamor of their consciences, and then devote their lives to chasing mirages in a vain attempt to play the Prime Mover?

Permission to exercise free will...

"Indeed, if the Prime Mover had not decided to permit humans - in the exercise of their free wills - to do things that went against their consciences, all their attempts to sin would come to naught. Humans would be frustrated even as they cast about, looking for ways to defy Him. It certainly would not have required very much effort - none in fact - on the part of a Prime Mover who is unchanging and has no need for anything to see to it that the more humans tried to subvert His divine will, the more they would be frustrated. And, by the same token, unaided by divine grace, humans were actually incapable of bringing off anything for which they could be commended.

"That was how dependent humans were on the Prime Mover. Indeed, they would be capable of nothing - not even of leading lives that were unworthy of their status as creatures that are fashioned in the Prime Mover's own image! And that is exactly what you 'stupid' humans are itching to do all the time - stupid because such a stance assumes that the generosity of the Prime Mover is not infinite, something that (if it were true) would detract from His own status as the Almighty. Humans will not even draw the obvious conclusion from this total "dependence' on the Prime Mover which, namely, is that the Prime Mover cannot be very far away – that He is not even at arm's length and that it is at the core of their being that He subsists.

"Of course, I could include the pure spirits in the discussion, but let us concentrate on you folks who might still just benefit from hearing this repeated - it wouldn't really do any good for spirits who are already lost or the angels who are safe and sound in heaven to be lectured to by even the most brilliant preacher ever like me on theses matters.

"The bottom-line is that humans on their own - unaided by grace - do not have the wherewithal to accomplish any good. Whereas before the fall, Adam and Eve were in a state of grace and, thanks to the fact that they were in that state, were able to show love to one another as commanded by the Prime Mover in addition to paying Him homage as the one and the only Prime Mover, after the fall, humans became entirely dependent on the grace merited for them by the Deliverer.

"When it came to doing good or performing acts of virtue, it was presumptuous for humans to imagine that they could bring about anything that was meritorious on their own unaided by grace, and attempts to do so - to try and spirit themselves into heaven by, in effect, bypassing the Deliverer - automatically signalled a blatant determination to usurp the power and authority of the Prime Mover. The woman in the New Testament, who expressed her desire to have the seats to the immediate right and the immediate left of the Deliverer in heaven reserved for her sons, was attempting to do precisely that!

"You call that an attempt to promote oneself. It is also evidence of an absence of realism and an utter lack of humility; and it is suggestive of the individual's determination to try and ignore the hard fact that being in original sin means being born in bondage - bondage to me.

"You compound the situation when you ignore the existence of the Prime Mover, pretend that no allegiance of any kind is implied when creatures that did not exist in any form are given a nature and an existence at the time they are gratuitously willed into existence by the

Prime Mover with a bundle of gifts or talents to match, and then also pretend that you, as descendants of Adam and Eve, did not inherit the status of outlaws.

"By the way, humans do not have to be specifically told in history class that they had a great, great grand father and a great grand mother called 'Adam' and 'Eve' or whatever, and that they were driven from Paradise and forfeited eternal life when they stole fruit from the Tree of Life - or that they became inclined to evil thereby!

"But, wait - history class and history books? Story class and story books would be more like it. Authored by 'scholars' who are inclined to sin like anyone else and largely operate under my vasallage, most of those history books are of course designed to mislead!

"Any way, with the exception of the Mother of the Deliverer, every human has 'stolen fruit from the Tree of Life', and all - except the very hypocritical - know deep down in their hearts that they are inclined to sin, have been banished from Paradise, and have forfeited the right to an eternal inheritance.

"But all humans also know deep down in their guts that they owe a pledge of allegiance to their Maker or 'Prime Mover' by virtue of having an 'essence' or nature that is not just any kind of nature, but one that is truly magnificent and splendid because of what it has in common with the nature of their Maker, and enjoying an existence they did completely nothing to deserve.

"Having opted of their own free will to refuse to pay homage to Him and to join me (the Father of Death and the Destroyer) in my own rebellion in the process, you wouldn't expect me as their new master to just let them to walk away. You have to be insane to think that I would.

"On the one hand, they are all outlaws and banished children of Adam and Eve; and on the other hand they are creatures over whom I, 'Satan' or 'Devil' - or whatever label you like to employ to refer to me - have full control over. After the fall, Adam and Eve and all their descendants became my slaves! What did you expect? We are at war

- the struggle between Good and Evil! This is rough stuff, you know. We are not playing games here. Snap it! They all *are* my minions!

"The situation was aggravated by the fact that humans, after the fall, became inclined to sin rather than to good. Now, if humans are inclined to evil, it means that instead of spending their time trying to fend off temptations from me and my troops, they are busy tempting themselves in all sorts of ways. And it is not *probably*, but *a fact* that instead of avoiding occasions of sin, they are actively seeking them.

"That, combined with the fact that lines of communication between humans and the Prime Mover had been irretrievably cut when Adam and Eve fell from grace and stopped being in good books with the Prime Mover, signified that humans (who were now not just legally but actually 'blind') were stumbling along in virtual darkness in an effort to march to heaven along what was a decidedly very narrow path (even as they themselves could always confirm from their own experience)!

"To make things worse, some humans even thought that they were better than others. Those who were the most 'devilish' - or like me - believed that they were the most angelic and also wise; while those who were the least devilish - or unlike me - were the ones who believed that they were the least pure. This also went to illustrate the stubbornness of the wicked and to explain their reluctance to hearken to the urging of divine grace!

"Everything was now screwed up: those who were at the bottom rung of society and had the most difficult time trying to put bread on the family table were despised the most. Totally depraved humans with the most God-awful records, and many with blood on their hands, represented themselves as angels who were not in need of forgiveness. Humans with records that were not as bad were the ones who seemed to believe in the need for forgiveness for themselves and for their enemies!

"In their stupidity, some of these 'blind' folks did not even hesitate to represent themselves as being in a position to lead other blind folks in the pitch darkness along that path! It was the height of presumptuousness. Humans who did that ended up not just misleading those they sought to lead, but actually tempting their 'flock' to do likewise. You'd better take my word for it. That is exactly how I myself, who was created a noble creature, became transformed into the Beelzebub you are now having this discourse with!

Homines Iniqui (Wicked Humans)

"When I led the hosts of angels in the rebellion against the Prime Mover, I myself as the ring leader became transformed into the 'embodiment of evil', something that had up until then existed only as an idea! I, as the revolt's instigator, became the truly evil ghost (*diabolus malus*) that I still am to the present day and will continue to be through eternity.

"The difference between myself - the fallen Lucifer who had once upon a time headed the angelic host comprising of various angelic choirs including Seraphim and Cherubim - and Adam and Eve (who were also created in the image but fell from grace because of their curiosity) and their progeny is that I am evil (*malus*), whereas fallen humans are merely wicked (*iniquus*). But the fact is that even though I am *diabolus malus* (the devil), unlike you wicked humans (*homines iniqui*), I have never allowed that to cloud my vision. Even as fallen angels, we here in the Underworld remain with all our wits about us, and that is precisely why we are so dangerous! And this has major implications for the struggle between good and evil which has been unfolding since the beginning of time and which continues.

"It is an established fact, on the other hand, that humans don't even know what they are. Humans seem perplexed that they might indeed be spiritual beings that have been fashioned by their Maker, Himself an all knowing, all loving, and infinitely merciful, but infinitely just all the same, in His own divine image and likeness! Just look how many even care to profess that He exists! Well, even when they say He does, it very definitely isn't reflected in the way they live. But that does not negate what humans are, namely temples of the Prime Mover. Yet, with the sole exception of the immaculately conceived Virgin Mother of the Deliverer, humans have all wickedly allowed sin to blind them to all things spiritual - and I mean all things of the spirit, including my very own existence!

"Now, it is bad enough for humans to be clueless about who or what they are; and to be oblivious to the existence of the Prime Mover, of His Word, and the existence of the Holy Ghost that binds the Father and the Son together in an eternal bond of Divine Love. But to be oblivious to the existence of the evilest creature - I mean myself, Beelzebub, Sheitan, the Tempter, the Evil One, the embodiment of evil or 'Devil', and above all the Father of Death - you have to be kidding!

"Talking about being the embodiment of evil, you would think it would dawn on humans that whenever they acknowledged that evil existed in the world, it would signal to them that I, Diabolos and the personification and also source of evil, do truly and verily exist in the same way humans themselves did! The fact nonetheless is that only good and truly decent humans are aware of my existence, and they are a precious few of them.

"Of course there are those humans who are constantly talking about 'the devil this' and 'the devil that', and who are for ever ranting about 'demons' when it is all just that - talk! And that is where it all stops, revealing that it is all mere lip service. If humans knew how truly evil my troops and I were, they would be fasting and mortifying themselves non-stop, and they would not rest until their union with their Deliverer was complete. And they most definitely wouldn't be holding those Halloween festivals that depict us as harmless ghosts that only exist in the human imagination!

"When Adam and Eve, the father and mother of the human race, lost their innocence after stealing fruit from the Tree of Life and lying about it, the human faculties of reason and free will apparently became so blunted that humans have been virtual walking zombies ever since. It is only what can be seen, heard, smelt, touched and felt or somehow 'sensed' with the help of the five senses that catches their attention. The fact that things of the spirit transcend matter -

something that is so obvious even to the dumbest demon - remains an enigma to most humans, the only exception being the odd mystic.

"It is one thing to be brought into existence out of nothing. But it is something else altogether to be crafted in the image of Him-Who-Is-Who-Is and Author of Life! Humans are so confused about everything, and have such a screwed up idea of the world around them - such a fuzzy idea of who they are - it now requires a miracle of grace for them to appreciate the fact that they are fashioned in the image of Him-Who-is-Who-is. Which is just swell - my own prayers will be answered if humans desist from praying for that grace and consequently remain clueless as regards their elevated status and nature, and their last end."

More Catholic than the Catholics themselves

Unaccustomed to having discourses with the creature he had been brought up to regard as the Father of Lies, Mjomba was evidently caught off guard by the "Evil Ghost". He had commenced work on his thesis on the subject of "Original Virtue" determined to turn out a winning thesis like no other. More than any one else, Mjomba knew that to succeed in producing a truly winning thesis, he could not spare himself any effort while applying both his faculties of reason and the imagination to the task at hand. And he was convinced that, as regards the latter, he could not hope to succeed in attaining his goal of producing the most winsome thesis - one that would be the last word on the subject of his choice - unless he allowed his imagination unfettered freedom.

But that was before Mjomba had decided to employ the devil as a mouthpiece for expounding on the Church's dogmas. He was now completely shocked at the things that his imagination was attributing to the Evil One, but felt quite helpless to deter the caricature of Diabolos his imagination had invented from venting what decidedly were weird notions about humans - himself included - and their destiny. For the first time, Mjomba wondered if he could trust his imagination - or the caricature of "Satan" that his imagination had conjured up. He told himself that he couldn't care less as it was now too late to interfere with his imagination, let alone stop it from serving up more of the rambling but solidly reasoned arguments the "devil" - or the devil's alter ego (or whatever!) - was using at every turn to try and show that humans were doomed.

But, while he was unapologetic as he continued lending the shameless Lucifer his ear, Mjomba thought there was something scary about the methodical manner in which the evil ghost punched holes in the arguments of those who contradicted the Church's teachings. What was more, Satan appeared to be hurting his own cause by proving that the Roman Catholic Church *was* divinely instituted. Listening to the 'Ruler of the Underworld' pontificate, Mjomba even attempted to play the role of 'devil's advocate' himself by assuming that the Father of Lies had to be lying, and was trying to trick him into writing a thesis that was full of hollow arguments on important dogmas of the Church.

To Mjomba's great surprise, out of the innumerable points the devil had made up until then, Mjomba was unable to find a single point he thought he could challenge without making a fool of himself in the process. That left the seminarian, who knew that Beelzebub couldn't be trusted and definitely couldn't be up to any good, even more terrified! Mjomba knew that the creature everyone loved to give the rap as the Evil One was the former Lucifer who, with Michael the Archangel, had jointly commanded the heavenly hosts, and that Lucifer had been privy to much more than ordinary mortals, whose vision was clouded by the effects of original sin, were capable of grasping.

Without a doubt then, the Evil One couldn't be faulted for being ignorant, and much less for mot knowing what he was talking about. Therefore, unless he, Mjomba or anyone else, could reveal flaws in the devil's logic and consequently punch holes in his arguments or otherwise prove him wrong, he didn't have any option but to concede that the Ruler of the Underworld was right!

At one point, Mjomba was torn between giving the brilliant Diabolos his full attention, or fleeing what he imagined could be a clever trap that the Father of Death was laying in his path, perhaps aimed at getting him to embrace a new kind of heresy himself. Mjomba never stopped wondering if others before him - like Luther, for example, who had started out as a pious and well-intentioned member of a monastic order, and had even taken perpetual vows of poverty and obedience - didn't fall for similar traps laid for them by the Cunning One! The sense of guilt Mjomba felt as he continued translating the thoughts he was receiving from Satan into material for his Thesis on Original Virtue was palpable.

And if "Old Scratch" was right - if it was true that members of the human race, one and all, were an irresponsible bunch who had turned against the Deliverer and, before Him, the prophets the Prime Mover had sent to help humans "pave and straighten the paths", and who were even now turning the *Sancta Ecclesia* the Deliverer had established with due solemnity and charged with His work of redemption into a virtual "den of thieves" - the Deliverer and Master had to be really mad even as He sat triumphant on His throne at the right hand of His Father in heaven.

Mjomba recalled the parables the Deliverer had used to teach His disciples on numerous occasions, and His insistence that the Prime Mover was a jealous Prime Mover who would deal mercilessly with those humans who decided to bury their talents and as well those other humans who turned on His messengers and harmed them. It seemed evident to Mjomba that the writings of the evangelists (John, Matthew, Mark and Luke) and others like Peter, James and the "Apostle of the Gentiles" were being exploited for gain by the many self-appointed apostles and "prophets" who contradicted each other right and left, and for that reason couldn't care less about the Truth the Deliverer died for.

Mjomba concluded that, when the end of the world came, and along with it Judgement Day, there would also be lots and lots of drama! But the sad thing in the meantime, Mjomba told himself, was the fact that Beelzebub had to be laughing his guts out, the fact that he was languishing in hell notwithstanding.

Yes, if the devil was right, the Son of Man, who had labored so hard and sacrificed so much to get his disciples to change from being timid and vacillating to individuals who were resolute and prepared to suffer martyrdom for their belief in His teachings and for His sake, had to be seething at the sight of hordes who were jostling for the opportunity to cash in not just on the books that now comprised the New Testament, but the books that comprised the Old Testament as well! And, of course, people like Solomon, Isaiah, John, Peter, Paul and others who diligently committed to paper what had been revealed to them by the Holy Spirit to facilitate the Church's evangelizing mission had to be turning in their graves just seeing what was going on back on earth! From their "mansions" in heaven, they had to be angry seeing many a man and a woman who were starved for spiritual food fall for the machinations of the "false prophets".

The idea that the Evil Ghost might in fact be right was very troubling to Mjomba for one other reason. If the shameless Beelzebub was right, this was automatically bad news for those Catholic prelates - and there were many of them - who gave the impression that it was quite alright to be a "separated" brother or sister; that Christians who did not embrace all the teachings of the Church were somehow better off than "non-Christians". Mjomba could not help wondering of the devil was not sticking to a strict interpretation of the Gospels for a reason! To drive a wedge between the Deliverer and those he had chosen to step into the shoes of His apostles perhaps?

The devil's position was quite clear. Just as the remnants of the Deliverer's band of followers did on the Day of Pentecost (the day the Holy Ghost promised by the Deliverer had descended upon them), the prelates needed to come to terms with the fact that the crowds that had mobbed the Deliverer prior to His arrest and trial had indeed done so out of self-interest; and that the interest of the separated brethren in the Deliverer - and indeed also the interest of the many Catholics who were accustomed to chanting "Lord, Lord" but did not do the will of the Deliverer's Father and were Catholics only in name - was similarly based on the wrong motivations. That what the crowds - and the throngs of separated brethren - were really interested in was the fun they derived from following the Deliverer wherever He went in Judea and Galilee, and witnessing the miracles He performed; like, for insistence, seeing people who had been born blind regain their sight, the dumb speak, the lame walk, and the dead Lazarus get up and pick up in a second life where he had left off in his first life.

But the same crowds that had witnessed and marvelled at the miracles the Deliverer performed had balked at His suggestion that they needed to regard His body (the body He had received from His blessed mother Mary at the time of her "immaculate conception") as being truly and verily the bread of angels; and that they had to also be prepared to feast on it, and as well to take a gulp of His precious blood (the blood which He was going to shed for the salvation of sinful humans), and do these things worthily before they could graduate into full-fledged members of the Church Triumphant (the heavenly kingdom over which he was going to preside for all eternity as High Priest)! And that was in fact the case with all those followers of the Deliverer (or "Christians") who viewed the celebration of the Holy Eucharist and the Church's doctrine of Transubstantiation as witchcraft!

The Deliverer had Himself laid down His life - spilt his precious blood, endured mockery from the likes of Pontius Pilate and Herod Agrippa - for the Truth and the whole Truth! And rather than compromise that Truth, the original apostles, following the Deliverer's example, had been prepared to suffer martyrdom for the sake of the Deliverer and for the sake of that unvarnished and sacred Truth. The devil could even argue that the so-called separated brethren, particularly those who prided themselves on being avid readers of the bible, had to know that more would be expected of them than say those other descendants of Adam and Eve who were atheists from their cradle and had never had any opportunity to study the sacred scriptures!

The devil could contend that the decision of any separated brother or sister to remain outside the *sancta ecclesia* because of the prevalent traditional prejudices against the "Church of Rome" - prejudices that ultimately were the work of Satan himself, but were attributed to the Prime Mover and passed off as special personal revelations - or for any other self-serving reason, far from vindicating that separated brother or separated sister on Judgement Day, would work squarely against him or her, just as the lukewarmness and malaise of Catholics in the practice of their faith was reason enough for the Deliverer to wish to "spit them out of His mouth"!

It was incredible! If the prelates were indeed compromising Catholic doctrine to appease and not appear to be alienating the so-called separated brethren (separated brethren who persisted in championing heresies to the detriment of the Church's mission of evangelization), the devil could claim that the prelates, like Peter before them, were attempting to stop the Deliverer from proceeding to Jerusalem and to His ignominious death on Calvary!

It was at that juncture that Mjomba realised that Beelzebub was up to something evil in the extreme; something that was patently "devilish". For, what was there to stop Satan from going on to claim that, with prelates of the Church projecting the wrong image of the Mystical Body of the Deliverer, the prelates had in fact abandoned the Deliverer in the exact same way Peter did when he was confronted by the woman in the court of the Roman Governor's palace on the night before the Deliverer was crucified! Indeed, any admission on the prelates' part that they were frail humans - frail humans who needed prayers of the faithful to stay clear of the wiles of the Evil One and the temptations of the flesh so that they could continue to "fight the good fight" like every other member of the Church Militant - could be cited by the Ruler of the Underworld as evidence that it was he, rather than the Deliverer, who had the upper hand in the battle for souls. And it was, of course, a fact that none of the successors to the apostles was in a position to say truthfully that he had never once slipped in his life (an implicit admission that they had failed to live up to their priestly status as *Alteri Christi* or "other Christs").

And if all that was true, and assuming that the prelates had not rehabilitated themselves at some point in their lives to the same extent as Peter (who deemed himself unworthy to be crucified on the cross with his head up and who had accordingly implored his executioners to crucify him upside down) had, the devil could claim - and with some justification no doubt - that it was not the Deliverer but he himself (Satan) who still called the shots in the Church which was the modern equivalent of Noah's Ark! The leader of the rebel band of angels, who had become the embodiment of evil, would in effect be claiming victory in the battle between good and evil! He would be saying almost in so many words that members of the Church's hierarchy were wearing "his barge" or what the evangelist referred to as the "mark of the beast"!

No kidding (Diabolos as "Defender of Truth")…

But Mjomba saw something even more sinister in the apparent determination of the shameless Father of Lies, and also the Evil One, to project himself as the "Truthful One"! By projecting that image of himself, the devil could go on to argue that the ambivalence of the Catholic prelates in their interpretation of Catholic doctrine and the Church's sacred role as Defender of Truth was what lead many of the separated brethren to remain contented and happy with the *status quo* instead of striving to grasp and embrace the whole Truth for which the Deliverer laid down His life. That in turn caused 'non-Christians' to dismiss the Church's evangelizing mission as a big joke!

Actually, being the conscientious seminarian that he was, Mjomba worried that in trying to hijack Holy Mother the Church's agenda and platform, and pretending that he was the de facto Defender of Truth, the clever Satan actually wanted to control the forces of good ranged against him in the now uneven battle between Good and Evil to give himself a chance - the only chance he had - of coming out as a winner!

It was already clear to Mjomba that, even after the Son of God had come to earth and died on the cross for the redemption of humans (those, at any rate, who would believe in Him and follow in His footsteps by carrying their own crosses), the devil, noting that the twelve apostles and their successors were an imperfect, was signalling that it was he himself, and not the divine Redeemer of humans, who was still in charge and calling the shots!

Except for Simon Peter, the rock upon which the Deliverer had built His church against which the gates of hell could not prevail at the time he was minding the Deliverer's sheep and providing them guidance *ex-cathedra* as he had to do from time to time, and his successors, the apostles and those who would be called to succeed them, because they were far from perfect even as they ministered to His flock or dispensed the sacraments, were just like everyone else including those so-called excommunicated heretics and the unbaptized! In some respects they probably were just as bad as the priests and Pharisees who missed the chance of leading the people of Israel in giving the long-awaited Messiah a red carpet welcome when He showed up among them two thousand years ago in fulfilment of the Prime Mover's promise to Adam and Eve and their posterity.

Mjomba admitted that he himself had witnessed enough scandals engineered by members of the Church's hierarchy that proved the point the Evil One was making. Even the history books were filled with accounts that sometimes made him sick to the stomach, like for instance the Holy Masses that were offered for the safe return of European slave traders, or the prayers of chants of the *Te Deum* that filled cathedrals in Europe following the imperial conquests that left the indigenous populations in the parts of the world that had been colonised either decimated and indigent, or permanently banned from the lands where generations of their people were interned, as Western countries tried to outdo each other in their conquests and annexation of foreign lands often under the dubious pretext of spreading the Gospel.

These were classic cases of members of the church's hierarchy making common cause with evil doers against God's people along with their Maker!

Mjomba had no doubt in his mind that the Evil One and Father of Lies, in a dirty and all too cynical maneuver, was using of that as the basis for projecting himself as the Defender of Truth! It terrified the seminarian to think that "Old Scratch", as the devil was also called, was capable of being so cunning and that, even though the Savior of Mankind had already come, died for men and risen from the dead in triumph, the situation remained so precarious!

Mjomba could almost hear Lucifer stuttering with laughter, and mocking that this was a perfect set-up in which he, Satan, could now tempt the so-called separated brethren on several key fronts at once. He could, for instance, tempt them to imagine that they did not need to take up and carry their crosses and to follow in the Deliverer's footsteps, and that they could save themselves a lot of sweat by merely "accepting the Deliverer".

Or he could tempt them to imagine away the *sancta ecclesia* which the Deliverer built on the rock called *Petrus*, and with it its all embracing and burdensome Teaching *Magisterium*, including the power to hold bound in heaven whatever it held bound on earth, so that they (the separated brethren) would be free to interpret the sacred scriptures in any way they fancied and to believe what suited them, or to quote texts out of context from the Holy Book and so formally have the scriptures justify their lust for material riches and earthly power!

Then the Evil Ghost could tempt them to pretend that those humans who had been called by the Deliverer to step into the shoes of the apostles, even though they remained completely human despite their high calling, could not let the Deliverer down in some way and still continue to serve as shepherds of His flock. In that way, the separated brethren would have an excuse to pursue their own independent, self-serving schemes of salvation outside the purview of the *sancta ecclesia*, and deny themselves thereby access to the sacramental graces the Holy Ghost dispensed to the faithful.

Mjomba found Satan's position very persuasive. He himself knew quite well that, since time immemorial, humans had dreamed up schemes that were designed to bypass the Way of the Cross. They had even attempted to tunnel their way into heaven by constructing the Tower of Babel! The problem with humans going out on a limb an establishing their own churches in competition with the *sancta ecclesia* was that the Holy Ghost and the Son of Man, whose titles included "High Priest", King of Kings, Redeemer and Judge, were one. The Holy Ghost identified Himself unreservedly and completely with the Mystical Body of the Deliverer, and Mjomba could not see how the Holy Spirit, who informed Holy Mother the Church, could be persuaded to operate outside it.

Thinking about the mystery of the Blessed Trinity, and specifically the oneness of Holy Spirit with the Word through whom all creation came into being, Mjomba ended up agreeing completely with the Evil Ghost that the reason human schemes that did not have the blessing of the Almighty One, were doomed to failure precisely because creatures, whether human or angelic, could successfully drive a wedge between the three persons of the Blessed Trinity. Satan and the other fallen angels had tried and ended up being transformed into demons and cast into hell for their pains.

And Mjomba now worried that the Evil Ghost had far more to do with the proliferation of the so-called mega churches in modern times, whose founders poured scorn on the doctrine that there was no salvation outside the Roman Catholic Church, than met the eye! After all, what the members of those mega churches and all the other separated brethren were really attempting to do was get the Holy Ghost to support efforts that were directly undermining the work and mission of the *sancta ecclesia*.

Even though Mjomba was quite alert and had no problem following the devil's reasoning, and was even able at times to marshal what clearly was uncommon courage which he needed to challenge the Evil Ghost in his own court, Mjomba thought he was having a bad dream. Mjomba thought about the "separated brethren" - the brethren who were counted , not in their hundreds or thousands, but in their millions - and shuddered at the unimaginable idea that the holy Ghost could refuse to heed the pleas of so the multitudes who actually passed themselves off as disciples of the Deliverer; but who nonetheless genuinely believed that the Pontiff of Rome, who was Peter's successor and was for that reason respectfully referred to by Catholics as the "Holy Father", as the anti-Christ. Any one growing up in a similar environment would have imbibed similar prejudices against the Holy Father and what he stood for. it would have require uncommon heroism for anyone who was brought up as a separated brother or sister not to be prejudiced against the pope and by extension the *sancta ecclesia*.

Mjomba told himself that the Ruler of the Underworld had to be kidding if he (or perhaps she?) was suggesting that the separated brethren were on the path to perdition! Mjomba knew from his training in psychology that for sinful and sinning humans, exposure to temptation was really all that was needed to entrap them in sin. After all, on their own, they were as nothing. It therefore seemed a foregone conclusion that the Holy Ghost could not abandon any human of goodwill, and especially if the circumstances in which that human was born were not conducive to the formation of a correct and clear Catholic conscience. And so, provided the separated brethren did whatever they did in good faith, Mjomba was inclined to the view that they were on good an solid ground in terms of their personal relationship with their Maker.

It was as though the Evil Ghost had been reading Mjomba's mind and was sensing that Mjomba was beginning to doubt that the situation of the separated brethren was hopeless. And Mjomba himself realized that the thoughts that inundated his mind at that juncture, even though quite orthodox and noble in themselves, were coming straight from the Evil One. Clearly, the salvation of the separated brethren, just like that of other sinful and sinning humans, could not be guaranteed just because they chanted "Master, Master" in their places of worship.

As long as they refused to accept what the Deliverer had taught - the same teaching that the apostles lawful successors kept repeating for all and sundry to hear - that the Deliverer's flesh was food indeed, and that His blood was drink indeed, and so long as they refused to welcome those whom the Deliverer had personally hand-picked and sent out to spread the message of the crucified and risen Deliverer, who was Mjomba to suggest that the separated brethren were on the path of salvation!

The sacred scriptures, tradition and the Church's teaching were all unambiguous regarding the Deliverer's position on the Holy

Eucharist. As the evangelist had written, unless humans feasted on the Deliverer's flesh and drunk His blood, there would be no life in them! That was exactly what the Church had taught from the beginning and still taught to day. And yet, the sacred worship of the Mass remained one of the biggest stumbling blocks to "Christian unity"! Moreover, for sure, the Deliverer had established one ministry; not two, ten, and much less a myriad ministries such as those which proliferated in modern times and many of which had funny sounding names too!

There could not be any doubt that the devil, who was leading the forces of darkness in the battle between Good and Evil, knew that the Deliverer was sworn to protect the Church he was establishing for the purpose of ministering to the people of the Prime Mover and over which Peter was going to preside from any mischief maker. Indeed, not even the powers of the hell were going to be able to prevail against his *sancta ecclesia*.

Now, the devil, more than any other creature that was fashioned in the Image, had to know that the consequences for any one who contemplated any mischief against the sancta ecclesia would be severe. Even though he himself had already been judged and condemned, the devil knew very well that he actually risked his head being crushed by the woman who had the sun itself for her raiment if he made any move. However, precisely because he had already been condemned, the devil did not really care less about the consequences to himself. But he cared very much about the consequences to the poor forsaken children of Adam and Eve. If he saw any way of getting humans to do his dirty work for him in that regard, he was not going to spare any efforts to get them to jump on the bandwagon. Knowing that he could not derail the divine plan relating to the *sancta ecclesia* even if he tried, he was going to try and persuade misguided humans to try and cause the *sancta ecclesia* problems so that they would forfeit their salvation in the process!

The devil had no scruples whatsoever about pursuing that line of action; and he undoubtedly was very delighted when humans took it upon themselves to establish "ministries" in competition with the

Deliverer's *sancta ecclesia*. Shameless humans knew that the Deliverer had established but one Holy Church; and one could not get better evidence for their callousness than the manifold attempts to establish substitute ministries, with their heretical positions on key doctrinal matters, for the Deliverer's *sancta ecclesia*.

The Deliverer had also stated that His grace was enough for sinful and sinning humans, heretical and schismatic ones included. Consequently, the separated brethren had no excuse for not heeding the call to return to the fold just as it was incumbent upon those who already belonged to the Holy Universal (Catholic) Church to develop a personal relationship with their Deliverer in it.

Mjomba was dismayed to think that he had to agree with the devil on that score. Consequently, the devil could now set the stage to claim for himself the souls of all sinful and sinning humans, including the souls of the separated brethren, so long as they persisted in their intransigence, and did not heed the call to true discipleship with the Deliverer inside the "Ark of Noah" (the Church of Rome). So long as humans resisted the urgings of the Holy Ghost to seek the kind of discipleship that canonized saints enjoyed with their Deliverer, they were doomed!

The Holy Ghost, Mjomba told himself, without any doubt provided all humans, the separated brethren included, the grace to enable them to form their consciences in accordance with the will of the Prime Mover and to follow its dictates. Reluctantly, Mjomba concurred with the Evil Ghost that, unless the separated brethren abandoned the heresies and schisms that kept them cut off from the fullness of grace that was only available in the Catholic Church, they actually risked loosing their souls!

The separated brethren remained free to allow history to repeat itself in their regard. They remained free to do as the first man and the first woman had done, namely give in to their curiosity and try to find out if indeed they will be like the Prime Mover if they ate of the forbidden fruit - the fruit from the tree of life! And that is precisely what they were doing by ignoring the promptings of the Holy Ghost and doing their own will! They also did it by choosing to ignore the existence of the Church's *Magisterium* or teaching authority, so clearly spelled out in the Holy Book. Mjomba found it incredible that this was coming from Beelzebub, the Father of Lies and the embodiment of evil!

Mjomba himself noted in passing that all the descendants of Adam and Eve, with the sole exception of the Son of Man and His immaculate mother Mary, had been conceived in original sin, and in that sense were not entirely innocent or sinless. The separated brethren were thus not alone in their intransigence. Mjomba thought about Mother Teresa, St. Kizito and other souls whose heroic practice of virtue had earned them canonization. Noting that the spiritual life he himself led left a lot to be desired, Mjomba told himself that he would be lying if he said that he was a better person than the separated brethren who at least strove to enter into a personal relationship with their Deliverer - if what he saw on television was not staged, that is.

It was just then that Mjomba did something rather funny. A serious expression on his face, Mjomba mumbled that the infernal one, who had himself already been judged and condemned, had used him (Mjomba) to successfully consign all those separated brethren to hell - the separated brethren who claimed that they were saved after accepting the Deliverer, and everyone else was lost - to hell! Mjomba added that, after attempting to use him to drive a wedge between the separated brethren and their Maker, the devil was turning on him and trying to make him despair about his own salvation! The devil had succeeded in persuading Mjomba that he himself was as good as lost, and Mjomba himself even appeared to agree. The situation was all the more serious because of the solid arguments the devil employed at every turn for his evil purpose.

And to make things worse, while he was busy writing about the separated brethren and even lecturing them on the importance of forming their consciences aright and heeding the promptings of the Holy Ghost, he himself did not recall stopping and taking time a moment to "form his conscience"! Mjomba didn't even know what his response would be if he were asked what was really meant by this thing called "conscience"!

It was only slowly, and on reflection, that it all finally started to click and to make sense to the seminarian. Old Scratch (the devil), in order to inflict the greatest damage on the sancta ecclesia, would of course try very hard to impersonate the Holy Father; and then, knowing how fickle humans were and at the same time masquerading as the "Defender of Truth", the devil would go all out to show that the clergy and the prelates - who were successors to the apostles - and the Holy Father, because they were inclined to sin and incapable of performing any virtuous act without the aid of divine grace, were hypocritical every time they tried to speak out against evil in the world! Hypocritical just as he himself who, despite being the Father of Lies, was not just posing as the Defender of Truth by was de facto the only reliable source of Truth was a hypocrite!

Mjomba could almost hear the Evil One chuckling before emphasizing that the record of Catholic bishops, who only paid lip service to the fact that all humans regardless of their faith were created in the Image and therefore as much children of the Prime Mover as baptised Catholics were, spoke for itself!

When it suited them, they were vocal in denouncing heretics and anyone who fell in schism and, even though possessed of the gift of prophecy as the anointed of the Prime Mover and faith that moved mountains and well versed in Dogmatic, Systematic, Moral, and other branches of Theology and in the Scriptures, did it without any charity as was typical of all poor forsaken children of Adam and Eve! But even though a hypocrite himself, the devil at least seemed to get it right at least in the interim. He was going to teach humans the truths of salvation with the greatest charity and would only point out that, inclined to sin, they (humans) were unlikely to live up to those selfsame truths, a situation that elicited the devil's greatest sympathy!

Mjomba was tempted to say he could not agree more with the Father of Lies - that humans remained hopelessly unfit to approach the throne upon which the risen and glorious Deliverer, King of Kings and Lord of Lords, sat; and that this likely was going to be the case regardless of what the poor forsaken children of Adam and Eve did! Still, the devil was wrong. The reason the Son of Man came down from heaven was so that humans who believed in Him, unworthy though they were, would be saved!

Just as Mjomba was thinking that he had caught Old Scratch on the wrong foot and was now in a position to use his thesis to expose him for what he really was, his mind, clearly under the control of the Evil Ghost, out of the blue conjured up a new and completely different scenario. No, it was not Satan, Mjomba found himself writing, who was attempting to usurp the authority of the Holy Father! It was those who started their own churches and operated ministries outside the purview of the *sancta ecclesia* who were guilty of that charge. And, just as trees that bore fruit, they could be judged by the fruits of their labor, namely the divisions they were trying to get the Church to embrace.

And, actually, when the Deliverer prayed that "they may be one", from one angle he had in mind the faithful who already belonged to His Mystical Body and with respect to whom His prayer was answered at confirmation, when the successors to the apostles laid their hands on them and they received the Holy Ghost. But from a different angle, the Deliverer also had in mind all frail mortals, including the separated brethren. With respect to this group, His prayer would be answered only when humans permitted themselves to be led by the Holy Ghost where "they would not go".

As far as what Beelzebub himself was doing, Mjomba was shocked at the suggestion that the Ruler of the Underworld was out to help his nemesis, Peter, and those who had succeeded him as the cornerstone upon which the Deliverer's Church continued to stand! It definitely said something about the utterly evil nature of the Father of Lies.

The devil would, of course, not need to be persuaded to tempt the separated brothers and sisters to imagine that they were the special elect who were predestined for heaven and that everyone else was damned and lost, and to frown on the notion that true followers of the Deliverer belong to the Church Militant that, by definition, actively participates in and (as the Apostle of the Gentiles put it) completes what is missing in the passion of the crucified Deliverer, as opposed to being a mere passive onlooker.

Mjomba felt certain that he had finally cornered Beelzebub. It was true that the innumerable "ministries" that served the throngs of separated brethren were operated in direct competition with the *sancta ecclesia*, and as such could not be considered the work of the Holy Ghost. Still, the fact was that the multitudes who thronged to those "churches" in search of spiritual fulfilment did so in good faith.

But the seminarian would realize, too late, that this was precisely the sort of argument Beelzebub had been waiting for Mjomba, clearly a neophyte, to verbalize before dropping the hammer. Yes, so much for the blind leading the blind, Mjomba could almost hear the evil ghost sniggering in triumph. It was also true that the Son of Man, who was sent to redeem mankind, was one and only one; and He was also the Truth and the Life, two things that by their nature could nevertheless not lend themselves to duplication - exactly like the *sancta ecclesia*. The fact that some misguided members of the Church's hierarchy gave the impression that things were otherwise did not matter in the slightest. Those clergy and those unrepentant heretics and schematics - it did not matter in the slightest that historians and others now referred to them as "separated brethren" – were all in grave error and in danger of losing their souls!

There was no doubt whatsoever in Mjomba's mind that the devil - the truly evil devil - knew exactly what he was doing. The diabolical Lucifer, who had become the embodiment of evil by challenging the Most High to a fight in the presence of the heavenly hosts, had no scruples about projecting himself as being more Catholic than the Catholic prelates themselves! It was in the same way so many "heretics" and "schismatics" projected themselves as being better defenders of orthodoxy than the successors to the apostles!

Mjomba sensed Diabolos positioning himself for the final, albeit desperate, assault on the Mystical Body of the Deliverer. Taking advantage of the platform Mjomba was unwittingly providing him, the devil (the smarter of the two no doubt) was actually using the catechism of the Church to try and show that members of the Church's hierarchy had themselves become like branches of the vine that were in danger of being separated from the tree's main stem. It was tantamount to claiming - in the same way many of the separated brethren claimed - that the *sancta ecclesia*, founded by the Deliverer to continue the work of saving human souls, had become dysfunctional and needed to be fixed or alternatively discarded! And that he (the devil) could essentially be trusted to step into the shoes of the apostles, and shepherd the Prime Mover's flock through the desert to the Promised Land. It was just incredible!

There was no doubt in Mjomba's mind that the devil's intent was to drive the separated brethren to despair and cause them to loose their souls in that way after persuading them that their situation was quite hopeless. Mjomba was himself already persuaded that the Ruler of the Underworld could not have mad his point about the untenable position of the separated brethren any clearer when the devil dropped the bombshell. Mjomba found himself writing, under the inspiration of the Evil Ghost no doubt that, by refusing to allow themselves to be led by the Holy Ghost where they of themselves would not go, the separated brethren had no one else but themselves to blame. And because they insisted that they had everything right, and accordingly refused to submit to the *magisterium* or teaching authority of the Church - because they preferred to follow their own instincts concerning what was right and wrong and had freely opted for their personal interpretation of the *sanctae scripturae*, that stubborn streak, which amounted to self-will, had the effect of blinding them to the motions of grace; and it sealed their fate.

But it was as Mjomba was mulling over the separated brethren's prospects for salvation thusly that it suddenly occurred to him that he himself was not entirely blameless, and could not say that he was not guilty of the very same thing. So long as he himself had some ways to go in developing a genuine personal relationship with the Deliverer (and the same applied to other Catholics), to that extent he was still imbued with self-love and could not claim that he had succeeded in letting the Spirit lead him where he himself would not go. His own situation if anything was far worse because of what he knew, and it was dissimilar to the situation of the fallen Lucifer. And even though he was required to turn in a thesis as a part of his preparation for holy orders, he indeed had to also admit that, allowing himself to be used by the Evil One to condemn the separated brethren as he had done sealed his own fate as well!

Mjomba was realistic and he did not think that the spiritual life he led even came close to putting him on the road to anything like canonization! The spiritual life he led was by no means heroic, and it did not even bear the remotest resemblance to the life of Mother Theresa for instance. What was more, he even frowned on fellow seminarians who paid frequent visits to the chapel for the purpose of praying in front of the Blessed Eucharist or to mediate on the mysteries of the Rosary. What sort of saint could he have made any way when he had enough trouble doing those same things during the annual retreat! And he had always had difficulty trying to be composed in spirit, and not allow himself to be distracted by everything that went on around him.

Perhaps that was the reason images of Judas Iscariot, the betrayer, rather than images of John the evangelist or Peter, that quickly popped up in his mind whenever he thought about the twelve whom, two thousand years ago, the Deliverer hand picked to be his apostles. Mjomba frequently worried that if he ever became a priest, he might end up a disgrace to the Church and a betrayer - just as Judas had.

And indeed there were times when, attempting to be recollected so he could contemplate on some divine mystery, out of the blue the most unsettling images of the betrayer would besiege his mind. Occasionally they would be in the form visions of Judas Iscariot in a variety of situations. The most frequent were visions of the betrayer stealing pennies from the Deliverer's purse the betrayer had himself volunteered to be bearer and custodian. On one occasion, it was a vision of a disembowelled Judas dangling from the branch of an oak tree with a rope around his neck and in a terrible agony of death.

Mjomba now realized that, while the intention of the Evil One concerning the separated brethren could not be anything but evil, perhaps it was he himself who was the principal target of the machinations of the devil in this particular instance. Mjomba shuddered at the thought that his decision to use the devil as a mouthpiece for enunciating the Church's dogmas was a bid mistake, and instead of hurting the devil and promoting the intentions of the Holy Father in the conflict between good and evil, the scheme had backfired. Mjomba could not avoid the conclusion that he had handed Old Scratch what was in effect an unsolicited opportunity to heal him a mortal blow by turning the tables on him.

But even then, the idea still sounded far fetched, and Mjomba told himself that his fears were exaggerated and in fact groundless. Mjomba tried to reassure himself that using Beelzebub to show that separated brethren were on a dangerous course and needed to make a U-Turn and come back into the fold before it was too late couldn't be anything but commendable.

Of course that ingenious scheme would make the Ruler of the Underworld who was already seething mad even madder, and would send him thirsting for revenge. But then, who really cared for Beelzebub. It was an article of his faith that every human had a guardian angel who was tasked with ensuring that Satan and his host of demons remained at a distance. For now, Mjomba was going to leave his guardian angel to deal with the heightened threat from Satan and his host.

It was precisely as Mjomba was dismissing the idea that his own salvation could be in mortal danger as a direct result of his decision to become involved with the devil that he felt the rug being pulled from under his feet. And it didn't matter at this stage if what was happening was the result of inspiration he was receiving from the Holy Ghost or the Evil Ghost!

Mjomba found himself acknowledging that it was the actions of his ilk, namely Catholics who were lukewarm and weren't ready to let the Spirit lead them where they of themselves would not go, that separated brethren and others outside the Church found it so hard to recognize the *sancta ecclesia* as the institution that was founded by the Deliverer and that was informed by the Holy Ghost. It was because of actions of humans like him that there was all this confusion in the world regarding what constituted unvarnished Truth and what didn't! Humans who led lives like his were in for special surprise on Judgement Day, Mjomba now acknowledged.

The Deliverer did not, after all, look kindly upon those who passed themselves off as his disciples but persisted in remaining lukewarm in their practice of virtue - those who he had said he would actually much rather spit out from his mouth. Mjomba noted that the Deliverer had not said the same about humans who had not received the Gospel and were still unbelievers for that reason.

But the Deliverer had let the world know that included were people like Pontius Pilate, whom he called a 'fox' because, even though the Roman Governor of Judea had used his agents to gather information on the Deliverer and knew that he was not a terrorist as the high priests and the Pharisees claimed but a completely blameless messenger of the Prime Mover sent to redeem the world from sin, Pilate had balked at becoming a disciple of the Deliverer and had decided to pursue his dreams of empire and world domination which he shared with his masters in Rome. And, while claiming to be dispensing justice and minding the *bonum commune*, the fox was actually determined to achieve his objectives without any regard to natural justice.

It suddenly dawned on Mjomba that instead of the angels and saints, it was actually Judas Iscariot and Pontius Pilate whom he had for his company! This was unbelievable!

Mjomba could not bring himself to accept that the devil's aim was to use him (Mjomba) to seal the fate of the separated brethren and other non-Catholics, and then turn round and seal his (Mjomba's) own fate? But Mjomba admitted that, as things now stood, he (Mjomba) was in much greater danger of loosing his soul to the Evil Ghost than were the separated brethren whom he had made a subject of his thesis. This was incredible!

In disbelief and shock...

But what shocked Mjomba more than anything else was his discovery, as he was preparing to go to confession, that he had not been fulfilling his obligation to attend Mass on Sundays and other Holy Days of obligation as required by the Canon. What Mjomba found out as he was examining his conscience as he was wont to do before joining the queue of penitents at the confessional one Saturday evening around this time, was that he was actually living in mortal sin, and consequently in mortal danger of losing his soul. This was even though, as a member of the seminary brotherhood living within the confines of St. Augustine's Seminary, he had been ostensibly doing everything that all the other seminarians did including chapel attendance day in and day out. Mjomba was flabbergasted as he allowed that he had just been going through the motions.

Unlike so many other people who saw advantages of sorts in living in a dream world and in preferring not to accept reality, and who decided to imagine away the facts of life and their real situation, Mjomba, at least in this particular case, decided to confront the truth about his spiritual life head on. And he did not just stop at admitting that his disposition left a lot to be desired. Mjomba took himself back in time to the Upper Room in Jerusalem where the Deliverer and his apostles were gathered for supper on the night before He gave his life for the salvation of humans; and he fancied himself hearing first hand Nazarene's words to the twelve: "One of you will betray me!" Mjomba was utterly shocked to hear the "man of Kerioth" who was going to betray the Nazarene also ask: "It isn't me, is it, Rabbi?"

It was also then that Mjomba realized the extent of his moral depravity! For, here he was, living in mortal sin, and just getting on with his daily routine at St. Augustine's seminary, as though nothing had happened - and this when he had most definitely betrayed the Son of Man and Judge!

And, as if that wasn't bad enough, he was even preparing to tout the "Thesis on Original Virtue" that he was crafting with the help of none other than Diabolos himself as something that would in time be an important instrument of the Prime Mover's saving grace! This, On reflection, this mirrored almost exactly the flirting by Judas with the priests and Pharisees even after they had made it clear to all and sundry that they would not rest until they had liquidated the self-proclaimed Son of Man, and the crazy idea Judas had entertained to the very last that, after all was said and done, his "diplomatic" moves and dealings with the Nazarene's sworn enemies were going to pay dividends of one sort or another!

The parallel with the apostle whose act of betrayal would cause the Deliverer to exclaim "That which thou dost, do quickly!" did look at one point as if it had gotten the better of Christian. This showed in the many sleepless nights he endured as he struggled to justify his own actions, and as he tried to reinvent himself as a follower of the apostle Peter despite the latter's own passion tide denials of his Master. And then the thought that any material dividends that would accrue from his thesis was going to be the equivalent of blood money made him feel as though all the exits were blocked and he was about to go nuts! He could not bring himself to accept that, just like the thirty pieces of silver the distraught Judas had emptied at the feet of the teachers of the law following his betrayal of the Son of man with a perfidious kiss, the efforts he was even now investing in his project were good for nothing except perhaps as a revenue source that could be employed to acquire "fields of blood" or grounds in which unidentified murder victims could be interred.

Mjomba felt relief of sorts when he finally succeeded in persuading himself that was the height of hypocrisy to go on as if nothing wrong had happened. Mjomba saw that his situation would be so much better if he could go to the chapel and, facing the altar, summon the courage, even at that late stage, to ask: "It isn't me, is it, Rabbi?

But, No! He, Mjomba, preferred to act as though nothing had happened! And this seemed to be so typical of everyone these days! It occurred to Mjomba just then that, perhaps, that was as it should be since the purpose of the Deliverer incarnation was so He would suffer and die for the salvation of sinful humans! But Mjomba quickly realized that it was the Enemy who was planting that totally wicked and morally bankrupt idea in his mind.

During the several weeks that Mjomba had been working on the thesis, his concentration on its subject matter had been building up, and had eventually gotten to the point where nothing else really mattered. Like a zombie, he methodically did whatever the other seminarians did, and was outwardly attentive in class and also in chapel. But the fact of the matter was that he didn't really notice any of the things that went on around him. Mjomba had been attending chapel alright; but he might as well have been on another planet, or sauntering in the orchard behind the chapel taking in the scenery - or in the library flipping through the pages of tomes on the state of mind of the first man and the first woman as they prepared to commit the sin which changed the course of human history.

Mjomba had become so absorbed by his literary project, it was a wonder that he didn't hurt himself as a result of his inattentiveness to the goings-on around him. Mjomba now realized with horror that he had been so absent-minded during the services, he had to admit that his presence there in chapel had been only in body. He had been completely absent where it mattered most, namely in spirit.

Mjomba acknowledged that, for quite sometime now, he had been living in mortal sin for those reasons. But the stage during which he could curb his interest in the thesis' subject matter had long passed; and Mjomba knew it. His only hope now was meditation, fasting and saying prayers - lots of them - since, on his own, he could not turn back from the perilous course, and start paying attention to the liturgy during Holy Mass as he was expected to do and things of that nature. That would be asking too much of someone who had become consumed to that extent with his project.

By the time Mjomba's thoughts on the matter had crystallized, he was already in the queue and awaiting his turn at the confessional. In despair Mjomba yielded his place at the head of the queue to another penitent, and walked away without going to confession. He did not want to compound the situation by lying to the priest that he was sorry for landing himself in that deplorable situation.

Mjomba was in disbelief and shock nevertheless, seeing that he, Mjomba, could actually end up in hell! But it surprised him that, even then, he was unable to muster the will power to pull back from the brink. To be sure, he had an obligation to turn in a thesis; and it was not as if there was anything sinister or wrong with the subject of his thesis. His professors had applauded his choice of subject, and all without exception had moreover signalled that they were looking forward to reading his thesis on "Original Virtue". Knowing Mjomba and his ability to delve into the most obscure topic and turn it into something that everyone enjoyed talking about, they were all hoping that the originality of his thesis would meet if not exceed their expectations. But now here he was with his spiritual life in tatters. It was something Mjomba had not bargained for at all.

Mjomba suspected that the devil was behind his misfortunes. Getting humans to lose their souls was after all what the Evil Ghost and his host of fallen angels were dedicated to doing. There had been times when Mjomba imagined that he just might be safe from the devices and wiles of Satan because of his upbringing which discouraged him from courting danger foolishly or getting into trouble through carelessness. Mjomba did not now doubt that, as far as the evil Lucifer who had once commanded the Seraphim was concerned, every creature that had been created in the Image without exception was exposed and fair play. The devil was going to do whatever it took to ensure that they did not become recipients of the largess of the Prime Mover that he himself had forfeited. Above all, Mjomba now also knew that the devil was not referred to in the Holy Book as a "snake" for nothing.

Mjomba lamented that there were many humans who believed in the existence of the devil alright, but thought of him as a dumb, stupid and ignorant creature. That was because they imagined, mistakenly, that any one in Lucifer's favored position at creation had to be nuts to do what he did, namely opt for rebellion and hell instead of loyalty to the being that was "Goodness" itself and for the heavenly mansion that went with obedience to the will of the Almighty One. If there was anything Mjomba had learnt on the other hand since he commenced work on his thesis, it was that Beelzebub was brilliant, very smart, and sharp, and quite possibly more knowledgeable in matters of faith than all the doctors of the Church combined!

Unlike the majority of humans who pooh-poohed the idea of going to hell and still blamed the devil for everything that went awry, Mjomba, who had been forced to awaken to the reality of his situation with a jolt, had enough common sense to know that he was definitely facing the prospect of going to hell, and that he had only himself to blame. The temptation might have originated from the adversary, or possibly even from his own flesh or ego; but that did not alter the fact that it was the exercise of his free will that had caused him to sink so low.

Instead of using his thesis to grow in the knowledge of the Prime Mover as he was supposed to do (and it was completely immaterial whether he ended up in the eyes of the world with a truly "winning" thesis or not), Mjomba had succumbed to the temptation to use it for personal self-aggrandizement at the expense of the Prime Mover. He had turned what ought to have been a very worthy project into an ego trip! And to make matters worse, as a senior seminarian, Mjomba should have known better!

Because Mjomba had gained a clearer understanding of how the devil operated - how he lured unwitting humans away from the path of holiness by getting them to imagine that they were better than others and could even "prove" it with their "good works" - the fact that he was better informed in that regard now only served to confirm him in his sin of pride. But try as he might, he found it impossible to desist from imagining that, if separated or even atheist brethren picked up and read his thesis (which he himself saw as a brilliant piece of original work from a rising apologist of the Church) and became converted as a result, he would deserve some if not all the credit for the spiritual conversion of those individuals.

Mjomba, while paying lip service to the role of grace in the conversion of non-Catholics, was inclined to give credit, not to the grace of the Prime Mover, but to himself, if it were to happen that an atheist who had never heard of the Catholic Church before, or a "separated" brother or sister, became convinced that it was indeed the one, holy and apostolic Church that traced its origins to the promised Messiah and Deliverer after reading his thesis.

Mjomba had also noted that everyone, both Catholics and non-Catholics, paid lip service to the efficacy of grace in saving souls. Mjomba had still to find a preacher who did not betray his true feelings about the credit he deserved personally, sometimes immediately after emphasizing that all the credit must go to the Prime Mover! And when he listened to sermons of the separated brethren who believed that humans attained salvation by the *faith alone*, and who consequently supposed that *good works* were not needed for salvation, he was even more scandalized by the credit they gave themselves in matters related to salvation.

The very manner in which they became saved, namely through personal statements that they were "accepting the Deliverer", implied taking personal credit for the decisions to start forging "personal relationships with the Deliverer". The one thing Mjomba did not personally want to do was to be hypocritical. He admitted that he was paying only lip service to the role of divine grace in saving souls; and, even though he did not trumpet it, quietly he was all for taking full credit for any developments that resulted from his efforts.

As far as Mjomba was concerned, that was what had to happen in the "real world". He had noted that the only humans who did not take credit for the things they did were heroic souls like Mother Teresa of Calcutta and others who became canonized upon their death. Of course, even though they themselves refused to take credit for the good deeds they wrought here on earth, everyone else looked at things differently and gave them the credit as the vessels through which the Prime Mover's graces were dispensed. Even the process of canonization hinged on miracles being attributed to their intercession! Without any doubt therefore, these heroic souls were perfectly deserving of credit for leading completely selfless lives, which in turn permitted the Holy Ghost to perform wonders, including the wonder of saving souls that would otherwise have been lost, through their self-effacing labors.

Reflecting on his own intransigence, and his determination to take full credit for what, in reality, only the grace of the Prime Mover could bring about, Mjomba thought he now also understood how it came about that Lucifer tripped himself and fell from his elevated position in spite of his vast knowledge. Beelzebub had fallen from grace because he was just too puffed up and was bursting with pride!

Mjomba thought about people like Don Scotus (nicknamed the "Subtle Doctor"), St. Jerome (who supposedly was the most learned of the Fathers of the Western Church), the great St. Augustine, Martin Luther, John Calvin, St. Bernard of Clairvaux, St. Thomas Aquinas (nicknamed "Doctor Angelicus"), St. Paul of Tarsus and Apostle to the Gentiles, and Judas Iscariot, and saw clearly for the first time that what differentiated them was their readiness to let the Spirit lead them where they, on their own, would definitely not go.

The true heroes among them were heroes, not because of the depth of their individual knowledge, which was like a drop in the ocean when compared to the Prime Mover who was Knowledge *per se*, but because of their humility and their willingness to give the full credit for any of their achievements to the Prime Mover, and do so unreservedly and without dissembling. In the case of Paul of Tarsus, who previously went by the name of Saul, on his own he would still have been chasing and murdering followers of the Deliverer!

Mjomba acknowledged that the Prime Mover revealed himself and his secrets, not to swaggering, best selling authors or university dons or scientists, but to the truly humble in heart – people like Saint Thérèse of the Child Jesus and of the Holy Face (or "The Little Flower of Jesus"), St. Catherine of Siena, and St. Francis of Assisi. The Prime Mover revealed His secrets to children and to souls that were similarly innocent.

Admittedly, Mjomba not only knew this, but he also knew that his attempt to produce a winning thesis, far from being driven by pure motives reflecting a genuine and self-less desire to save souls by becoming an *alter Christus* (other Christ), was motivated by the desire to show off and his glaring pride.

Chastened, but unrepentant…

Mjomba was chastened but still unrepentant as he noted gloomily the one thing to which all this pointed, namely the decision he made at the outset to use the Evil One as his mouth-piece for expounding on the Church's dogmas. Mjomba should have noticed immediately that he was falling into a trap that the devil was laying, and he should have retreated at that point without further ado and disowned the Tempter. He did not do that because he believed that he was perfectly capable of dilly-dallying with the Evil Ghost and getting away unscathed. He didn't even think of saying a prayer before going off on such a reckless adventure. And also, unfortunately, the prospects of becoming renowned, famous and even rich by riding on the coattails of the sleek Beelzebub were too attractive and tempting, and that was apparently still the case as Mjomba left the queue, and headed blindly to his allotted spot in the pews.

Unknown to Mjomba, it was Father Raj, his personal confessor, who was closeted inside the dingy cubicle and hearing confessions on that Saturday evening. If he had been aware of this, perhaps Mjomba would have thought twice about skipping his weekly confession and losing hope. Father Raj had always struck Mjomba as a man of God who also seemed to have a winning way even when the prospects for finding a solution were completely bleak. It was for that reason that Mjomba had chosen the Indian as his confessor.

Humans are like zombies

Mjomba's tussles with the devil had gained him a new respect for the intellectual prowess of the Ruler of the Underworld, and this was quite plain as Mjomba continued work on his thesis. And he did not have any doubt at that point concerning the source of his inspiration. He was now quoting Satan directly as he continued to write.

"Humans, the separated brethren included, have to admit that they are either very ignorant and are consequently prone to making serious albeit unintentional errors on matters that are critical to their last end, or intellectually dishonest, or both. In either case, humans seem to be in a lot of trouble. For how come that in the present times panels of history 'experts', while able ostensibly to reach agreement as regards things Cæsar Augustus said, did and wrote have never been able to reach agreement on what the Deliverer did and said, let alone who he was? How come men and women of letters have failed to put to rest the doubts regarding the institution in the world that is the lawful successor to the *sancta ecclesia* the Deliverer inaugurated on Pentecost Day?

"And how come panels of biblical scholars don't seem to agree on anything at all? How come all these ministries whose teachings are at variance with each other? How come all those 'messengers' of the Prime Mover, who bandied around the fact that they were men and women of letters, seem to derive lots of fun in contradicting each other where it matters the most, namely regarding the one and the only authentic ministry started by the Deliverer, and which ones weren't and therefore needed to close their doors to reduce the prevailing confusion on the world? Or are these things exactly as they are supposed to be because they reflect the ignorance of humans and/or the pervasive intellectual dishonesty that are now a standard feature of a world populated by *homines iniqui* who have no scruples about exploiting anything in sight, including the Holy Book, for their own ends?

"Humans are like zombies! They don't know they are human! The concept of humanity became foreign to them from the moment the first man and the first woman fell from grace, and the effects of original sin began to take their toll. Starting with Cain who nipped the life of his brother Abel in the bud, humans have slaughtered each other and have gotten into the habit of treating their pets better than they do 'strangers'! They steal from each other, lie to fellow humans, cheat and do unimaginable things to one another in the name of progress. To maximize their enjoyment of material things, those in the majority even go to the extent of 'legislating' an order in which struggling members of society or, 'deviants' as they are called, can be permanently put away by locking them up in cages or 'prison cells' or in the literal sense by 'executing' them! So, so stupid!

"Humanity isn't multiple. There aren't as many 'humanities' or 'humankinds' as there are humans. Human nature - or the essence of being human - is not just one; it is indivisible, the fact that humans exist as separate entities or 'individuals' notwithstanding.

"In contrast, we demons and those pure spirits that remained loyal to the Almighty One do not share the same nature. There is no such a thing as 'angelic nature'! But whether in heaven or down here in the Underworld, we pure spirits still take full cognizance of the right of other spirits to exist. We do not try to murder or destroy each other. And that is why the Prime Mover Himself decided to leave us alone after we rebelled against Him. The conditions here in Gehenna may be ghastly, but they are of our own making. We demons couldn't accuse the Prime Mover of any cruelty in that regard. But that is of course what you humans would have done if you were in our place.

"The Prime Mover spared humans - those at any rate who try to live up to their elevated state as His temples and do not deserve to join us here in Hell - the fate of being consigned to 'Limbo' through all eternity by sending them a Messiah even. And the Son of Man instituted the '*ecclesia*' or 'Church' through which He dispenses the divine graces that are intended to help them live up to their state as children of the Prime Mover. But look what humans did to the Messiah - they killed Him. And then look what humans are doing to the *ecclesia* which He established on the rock called Peter.

"First, when the Deliverer came to 'His own' (namely the Israelites from whom the Deliverer took His stock and for whom Providence had done so much to ensure their survival as a people until His coming), they rejected and abandoned Him in His greatest time of need. And then, look what humans have turned the *ecclesia* he founded to serve as the new 'Ark of Noah' into! But it also speaks to the nature of humans that, since its inception, many inside the Church who should have known better have attempted to emulate Judas Iscariot and Ananias, and succeeded in using that divine institution for their personal aggrandizement, causing untold grief to many inside and outside the Church in the process."

As he was jotting down the thoughts that were flooding his mind and which he was now dutifully attributing to Beelzebub, Mjomba considered the infinite possibilities of profiting from the kind of theological treatise he was writing, and allowed that he could himself fall for the temptation to use its contents, which were about saving souls, for personal gain alright! He was struck by the ease with which he would be able to do this, and it suddenly dawned on him that most, if not all, of those who exploited the *sancta ecclesia*, or alternatively the Holy Book, for personal gain probably started out with the most noble motives! Brushing the tempting thought aside, Mjomba continued writing.

"Others have taken to setting up and operating private ministries to exploit the human hunger for spiritual sustenance under the guise of winning believers for the Deliverer, and have turned evangelization into one of the most profitable enterprises after taking a leaf from those who profit immensely from starting and operating 'non-profit' organizations.

"And it is not as if it is hard for humans to find the traditional *ecclesia* which the Deliverer instituted two thousand years ago on the rock called Peter! It is after all not so very long ago when Peter's tomb was found beneath the basilica in Rome which bears his name, and not far from the place where he was martyred for his faith. And it has nothing to do with the passage of time either. For indeed, out of the many who flocked to hear the Deliverer out as He crisscrossed Galilee and Judea teaching the multitudes, healing the sick and performing other miracles, not a soul showed up on Calvary to commiserate with His mother Mary as He hung dying on the cross. A traditional *ecclesia* whose central message has as its main theme 'the crucified Deliverer' and an independent money making 'ministry' of course aren't things that can be compatible.

"While the sacred scriptures are sacred and will always remain so, the fact of the matter is that the Deliverer founded something He called an *ecclesia*; and it is not just tradition, but even the *New*

Testament (on which the Deliverer Himself was ever so singularly and deafeningly silent) attests to the planning for and establishment of the one (and only one), universal (catholic), and apostolic (founded on the rock called *Petrus*) *ecclesia* (a divinely instituted entity through which the Deliverer planned to dispense His saving graces to those who would believe in Him). And so, it should raise suspicions when self-appointed, bible totting 'ministers' decide to insist that their followers take orders, not from the agency He commissioned (with Peter as its first CEO) and charged with the task of passing on what He had taught them under the guidance of the Spirit (Paraclete), but only from the written 'Word of the Prime Mover'!

"Yet it is actually not that hard to see the fallacy in that so-called doctrine of *sola scriptura*! But it should also be obvious that the doctrine of *sola scriptura*, whose origins are recent and moreover well known, by its very definition should be seen as self-defeating, since it did not leave any room for (and therefore militated against) the very notion of an *ecclesia* that could serve as the vehicle for carrying on the Deliverer's evangelizing mission. Still, it can be said that this doctrine and the eagerness with which it is embraced by humans are additional evidence of the gullibility of humans when it came to anything divine.

"And then almost every human blames the Prime Mover for the self-inflicted 'pain and suffering' that sinful and sinning humans are so deserving of in any case. And they do so despite the fact that 'pain and suffering' have been sanctified by the death and resurrection of the Deliverer. But, in truth, humans have even greater reason than us pure spirits to be one - to live and exist as 'one people' and in 'one society of humans' in the one and the only 'Mystical Body of the Deliverer' or 'Church'; but that is running ahead a little…"

Mjomba noticed a change in tone, mood or whatever as the Evil Ghost took a pause and then continued.

"But, by Golly! Humans are so ignorant! I myself and all the other fallen angels now endure pain and suffering, not because the Prime Mover is some kind of vindictive Being (which He cannot be by nature); but because, being creatures that were formed in the image of the triune Divinity (whose three persons were united in an eternal bond of love) meant that we too stood to be partakers of the *joy* that came with being in love. The fact though is that the Prime Mover the Father, the Prime Mover the Son, and the Prime Mover the Holy Ghost - the three divine persons, each one through a separate but divine act of the will, freely choose to coexist as a single Godhead. And it is the desire of all three divine persons of the Blessed Trinity, exercised jointly and severally, that creatures that bear the Prime Mover's divine image and likeness likewise be in a position to freely choose to sing, exalt and praise Him in unison.

"Our own refusal to genuflect violated the sacred relationship between us creatures and the infinitely gracious and loving Prime Mover and Lord of All. Our refusal to worship and adore the Almighty and Omnipotent One resulted, as we had fully anticipated, in our being ejected from His holy presence into no where. And that is quite a transition for beings whose creation was itself a labor of divine and infinite love. Since we were not 'prime movers', we couldn't reinvent ourselves in order to be able to exist in the 'dream heavenly world' our reason told us would cease being a part of our inheritance. We were pig-headed to that extent! Our refusal to embrace Him who was our Infinite Good was an act of violence against ourselves. It had been our intention to eject everyone else, including the Prime Mover Himself, from heaven!

"The evil at the heart of my plan consisted in my hope of playing one Divine Person against another Divine Person; and in trying to position myself in such a way that, regardless of which Divine Person triumphed, I would usurp the power of the Most High, and become the de facto Ruler of the Universe. Frankly, I reckoned that the three Divine Persons, because they are all equally divine, would end up fighting each other to the finish, and that I would then be in a position to install myself of the Ruler over all creation with the help of my minions. I knew that my chances of success were slim, and the consequences of failure were dire; still, the prize - installing myself as the Ruler of the Universe - looked very attractive! I had persuaded myself that the risk was worth taking.

"Instead of going on after our trial to become happy and contented members of choirs of angels in the Church Triumphant, we suddenly found ourselves transformed into demons! This was the state we had craved for - the state of being defiant spirits that wanted nothing to do with the Infinite Goodness and Infinite Love which define the Prime Mover and also Almighty One.

"On the one hand, we are endowed with all these wonderful voices and other gifts which come with being fashioned in the Image. But on the other hand, we hate ourselves for having chosen to defy Him-Who-is-Who-is, and who brought us into existence out of nothing. Instead of using our voices to sing praises to the Prime Mover, all we can do with them now is curse ourselves until we are horse for engaging in an outrageous act of disobedience, and for the fact that we will never achieve our self-actualization! There is now no way that our hunger for fulfilment will ever be satisfied, even though by refusing to genuflect, we were granted our hearts' desire namely freedom and independence to do exactly as we liked with ourselves!

"Humans are in exactly the same situation as we are. Free creatures, they choose to flagrantly do things that are against their consciences, and are not in accordance with the will of the Prime Mover and Lord of All. But the difference between humans and us is that humans would like to pretend that they fell from grace by accident and not through a deliberate act of the free will! And, whereas the sin of Adam and Eve was what first triggered concupiscence and the other effects of 'original sin', the fact is that sinful and sinning humans are always crying foul and blaming the Prime Mover for all their woes, real and imaginary, when they have yet to experience real pain and real suffering! Adam and Eve regretted their sin almost as soon as they had committed it -and their sin consisted in stealing fruit from the Tree of Life! Compare that with the wicked deeds that humans do to each other to day!

"Some humans spend their time complaining loudly for the sake of complaining, and are oblivious to the fact that the lifestyles they lead are the source of their problems; and that real suffering and real pain await them here in hell - or, if they are lucky, in Purgatory expiating the feelings of guilt for their wicked deeds! Even though the souls in Purgatory are assured of salvation, the self-inflicted suffering that derives from the knowledge that they spurned the graces the Deliverer had merited for them - graces that would have enabled them to lead wholly upright lives - and had desisted from acknowledging the hurt they caused others and the Deliverer and making up whilst here on earth will be quite acute and terrible.

"Unfortunately for humans, the folks who do least need to be jolted to their senses - folks like Catherine of Genoa, Mary Faustina, Padre Pio, and John Vianney - are the ones who have visions of Purgatory whilst here on earth. And that is probably just as well, since others would go nuts at the sight of the poor suffering souls, and probably not recover! That wouldn't be helpful if the purpose of the visions was to alert humans to the need for repentance.

"On their first day in Purgatory, humans will be wishing they were back on earth enduring all the miseries and woes they were in the habit of complaining about a thousand-fold! And, Pew! For those humans who end up here in hell with us, when they realize that they had squandered the opportunities they had been afforded to live as befitted creatures that were fashioned in the Image, and that as consequence their innate desire for self-actualization will go unfulfilled for the rest of eternity, they will wish for the impossible, namely that the Prime Mover should change His mind and rub them out - perhaps in the same way they themselves were always attempting to rub out fellow humans whom they detested for one reason or another back on earth - rather than face the prospect of losing their souls to me! They will be beside themselves when it starts to dawn on them that, instead of the all good and all loving Lord, they will have me, the meanest and evilest creature imaginable, as their adopted lord and master!

"When we pure spirits fell from grace, we experienced an immediate and dreadful sense of loss, accompanied by overwhelming feelings of despair and emptiness from knowing that we were now accursed; and this morbid sense of intense loss has continued without let up ever since. It is what constitutes the pain and suffering that we endure. And it all came about because of an act of free will on our part signifying that we were not prepared to either serve or pay homage to the Prime Mover.

"In the case of humans, the original sin committed by Adam and Eve signalled to the Prime Mover that they too would not serve or pay Him the homage He was due. The fact of the matter is that the original sin committed by the first man and the first woman was a merely wicked deed, unlike our own sin which was a truly evil deed because, in addition to openly challenging the Prime Mover's authority, we embarrassed Him by disrupting the solemn procession of Cherubim and Seraphim.

Not only were the angels who followed in my rebellion legion, but I actually dared the Prime Mover to cast me and my minions into the 'fires of hell' for our outrageous act of defiance! The expression 'fires of hell' was actually coined by me!

"Even though the pain and suffering that immediately resulted from the rebellion of Adam and Eve was horrible and debilitating by human standards, it was really negligible. The immediate effect of the act of rebellion of the first man and the first woman was to make them susceptible to things like hunger and thirst, physical weariness, which in turn required that they try and understand the vagaries of nature, and take measures to minimize any pain and suffering arising there from.

"But because humans became inclined to sin in the wake of their fall from grace, while at the same time remaining incapable of performing any good deeds on their own without the help of divine grace, the scope for them (humans) to cause their fellow humans pain and suffering out of purely selfish motives also became limitless. As long as humans were meek and humble, and acknowledged their hapless, and provided they matched that meekness and humility with a determination to lead lives of self-denial, the miseries and suffering to which they were exposed increased the scope for them to expiate for their own sins on earth. Enduring pain and suffering effectively became purifying, and sanctifying. Still, true meekness and humility was only possible with the help of the divine grace that was merited for humans by the Deliverer.

"Also, a meek and humble life could pretty much insulate humans who were prepared to embrace that sort of existence from the temptations of the flesh and from my wiles. And for humans who managed to bear their 'crosses' in that fashion, the manifestation of pain and suffering, while no less nasty and hurting, represented an opportunity to identify themselves with the Word-become-flesh, and to participate in the passion and death, and also resurrection of the Deliverer - and now, alas, also Judge - of Mankind.

"Human pain and suffering otherwise presaged the miseries that awaited those descendants of Adam and Eve who refused to pay heed to their consciences as and when the time came for them to give up their ghosts. For all such humans, instead of representing a much awaited and momentous occasion on which they would be finally ushered into the presence of their Creator and Lord following their period of trial on earth, death became the occasion for us here in hell to celebrate the victory of evil over good. As a rule, the reward I give the demons who contribute the most to the loss of human souls is the freedom to turn the tables on those wicked humans, and give them a taste of the miseries and frustration they wrought upon their fellow humans back on earth. Now, that - as you can imagine - is an experience that can be very painful and also very humiliating.

One humankind

"Listen up you fools: the Word-Become-Man identifies Himself completely with you stupid humans. Now, the Word deciding to take up human nature and 'becoming flesh' in the process is testimony to one hell of love that the Prime Mover and Almighty One has for created beings in general - including us pure spirits - and for you humans in particular. If the Prime Mover's love for you humans was not *infinite*, He of course wouldn't have sent His only Begotten Son to a place like Earth that was now populated with humans who were not merely wayward, but had become so unbelievably hostile even to their very own, making it actually the most unlikely destination for a decent creature, leave alone a Divinity.

"It would not have been practical for the Word to become an angel in order to carry out His Father's bidding because, unlike humans, each angel has its own distinctive essence or nature. Doing that would have been the same as taking up the name of one or other angel while remaining the Word - the Second Person of the Trinity. And, as He donned His humanity, He opted for the male as opposed to the female gender because, as the Word through Whom all created beings came into existence, He had already decided in eternity that He would become not a 'Second Eve' upon becoming man, but a 'Second Adam'. And He was able to become a Second Adam only *because* He had deigned to fashion you humans in His Father's image and likeness. You may have two legs and two arms and share some other things with brutes, but the fact is that you are created in the Prime Mover's image and brutes are not. It is what makes all the difference.

"And, as if to show that He was not belittling the 'weaker' gender, the Second Person of the Holy Trinity, who had fashioned Eve from a rib taken from the side of Adam, not only became flesh while relying on the *fiat* of His *maiden* mother Mary, but he also relied on her completely for the human nature that He as the Second Adam and Deliverer of humankind needed for His own sojourn on Earth. The Word relied on a member of humankind whose *(female)* gender had been formed with the help of the male gender (Adam) at creation.

"One could speculate that, if the Word had fashioned 'Woman' from a piece of the earth's crust and had instead molded Man from a rib taken out of the side of Eve, there probably wouldn't have been any problem for Him to opt for the female gender upon taking up His human nature. There wouldn't have been any problem with that *per se*.

"But that would have created a different problem for the Providence because of the obvious desire on the part of the Word to emphasize the oneness of humanity and the intractable and close affinity of members of humankind reflected firstly in the manner in which He brought Adam and Eve into being on the one hand and secondly in the manner in which He Himself became flesh.

"There is no doubt that Providence wanted to have humankind reflect the unity in the triune Godhead in a special way; and His actions, conceived in eternity and executed in time, pertaining to humans attest to that. Even though it required the intervention of supernatural power to execute, it was not a physical impossibility *per se* for the Word to rely on His maiden mother alone for His human nature when becoming flesh. The same would not have been the case if Mary had been a man. The desire of the Word to rely solely on a member of humankind whose *(male)* gender (in this case) had been formed with the help of the female gender (Eve's) at creation would have been frustrated for obvious reasons.

A statistic

"Useless creatures that are clueless about their own nature, their identity, and where they are headed, and that nonchalantly betray their own Deliverer, and the Word-Become-Flesh, whenever they go out of their way to betray their own kind; creatures that, knowingly or unknowingly, likewise level false accusations against Him whenever they deceive, lie and spin in their dealings with their own kind; other humans; creatures that scourge Him and crown Him with thorns whenever they injure and harm their own kind anywhere; creatures who spit on Him and drive nails rough shod into His sacred hands whenever their selfishness drives them to do things that occasion their own kind miseries and suffering; and creatures that murder their Deliverer whenever they sit back, and allow injustice on earth to take its course while pretending to be working to promote world peace! A fair description of you humans by me, Beelzebub, nee Lucifer, aka the Evil Ghost? You bet!

"Now, there is no way that humans who are so clueless about who they are, would be able to grasp the 'mystery of mysteries', namely the Mystery of the Incarnation whence the Word, the Second Person of the Blessed Trinity, in abeyance to the will of His father, agreed to become a statistic! Yes, a statistic! We here in the Pit keep track of the number of humans whom the Almighty deigns to bring into existence. We used to do the same for angelic essences that He caused to come into existence, but lost count ages ago. At one point, on the spur of the moment, He created so many zillions of them at once, it became impossible to keep up with the count. Actually the number of the new additions alone was so boggling even to my sharp mind, I remember I nearly went crazy just trying to conceptualize it. Unfortunately for my cause, I did not succeed in leading a single one of those zillions astray.

"By the way, we here in the Pit also keep count of the human souls we succeed in leading astray. That is the count we would love to loose track of - yes, the number of damned human souls! That would make me, Beelzebub, a winner over and over...

"Any way, as humans have never cared to relate to their own kind whom they will scourge, crucify and murder on a whim under the cloak of following spurious 'rules of engagement', they will never be able to relate to the Deliverer, let alone appreciate that, of all the divine mysteries, the Mystery of the Incarnation is the most mysterious of them all! By deciding to take on the shape of a human, the Omnipotent One also agreed to become a statistic - just like those countless and nameless souls that are despatched daily to their eternal rest by so called 'security forces' after being labeled everything from 'terrorist' and 'insurgent' to 'unfortunate collateral damage'.

"When the Word, through whom all creation came to be, Himself became flesh and dwelt among humans, by my count He became the 999,999,872,094,998,651,392,701,335,682,929,411,360,095,239,883,148,296th human embryo that had been carried inside a woman's womb. With Adam and Eve included in the count, Mary's sinless child, who saw the light of day for the first time in a manger in Bethlehem two thousand years ago, became the 999,999,872,094,998,651,392,701,335,682,929,411,360,095,239,883,148,296th inhabitant of Earth.

"Our count includes all those babies whose lives were nipped in the bud for any reason whilst still inside their mothers' wombs. And, except for the one occasion when the 'Son of Man' as He called Himself became transfigured and appeared with Abraham and Moses to Peter, James and John, the Son of Man, in obedience to the will of His Father, He was also subject to all the limitations of the descendants of Adam and Eve.

"And *that* is our way of getting even with you hypocritical and foolhardy humans. You stupid humans can't resist the temptation to turn the House of the Prime Mover into a place where you conduct commerce; and you have the cheek to imagine that can do it by deriding me and my host here in Gehenna and get away with it! So, so damn stupid. You damn stupid humans who do not even know your identity should remember that, even though a resident of the Pit along with the rest of the damned, I still remain the Prince of Darkness! And no one who dares to make me a laughing stock, especially when that individual still continues to call my tune while pretending to be redeemed and delivered (or saved!) gets away scot-free!

The Way, the Truth

"You, perhaps, are now also beginning to understand why, through the disobedience of one man (Adam), 'Death' was introduced into the world; and also how, with the Word, becoming one of you and going on to pay the price for the redemption of humans who would elect to believe in Him, 'Life' was restored back to Humanity, restored through the obedience of one man just as Death was visited upon humans through the disobedience of one man.

"Human nature is one such that if one human hurts, all humans hurt. It happened when Adam and Eve fell from grace, and it happens every time any human hurts to day. Injustice perpetrated by one human against another human is injustice done to all humankind, including the Word!

"If a human goes nuts and starts to imagine that it is going to pay to hurt another human in any manner (with the fall of Adam and Eve from grace, that is exactly what all of you humans became inclined to do), the hurt that stupid human actually inflicts on him/herself is in fact far greater than the hurt which that human inflicts on his/her supposed human enemies. Oblivious to this 'law' which is rooted in the 'human' nature, you humans are busy trying to do that all the time. And that is how stupid members of the human race became when the First Man and the First Woman fell for my ruse and lost their innocence. Just so, so stupid, aren't you!

"Instead of unity among members of humankind, selfishness and greed now drives everyone to try and undercut each other. It happens among immediate family members, and it is of course many times worse when humans forget that they are all descended from Adam and Eve and are related, and begin to treat one another as aliens.

"Thank the Prime Mover that we pure spirits are not visible to the human eye. Because if that were the case, you can bet that humans, in their blind greed, would be tempted to initiate wars of conquest in attempt to enslave even us demons in hopes of finding stuff to loot. That is how lustful and covetous humans can be. And that is also where my original decision to tempt humans to trade in their birthright for illusionary gains, and to betray the Prime Mover thereby as they stupidly did, would have come back to haunt me!

"The only way the breach in the unity of humanity can be healed now is through membership in the Mystical Body of the Deliverer. Outside the Mystical Body of the Deliverer or the *sancta ecclesia*, it is greed and selfishness that rule. The Deliverer brought it off by accepting to become the sacrificial lamb, and allowing the crooked priests and Pharisees, the crafty Pontius Pilate and his cruel and merciless soldiers, the blood thirsty mobs who not long before had gawked at the miracles He performed for their benefit, to have their way.

"And He now invites all wayward humans to get back into the fold and become one again by receiving Him in the sacrament of the Holy Eucharist. In other words, he invites all humans one and all to eat of His flesh under the species of bread and to drink of His blood under the species of wine during a memorial service that has come to be known as Holy Mass, a service during which the Deliverer's passion, death and resurrection are re-enacted following a tradition that goes back to that 'Maundy' Thursday, during the reign of the wicked King Herod Agrippa.

"When the 'Word-become-flesh' supped with His twelve apostles, including his beloved apostle John and his purse bearer Judas Iscariot, for the last time before His death, He put in practice what He had taught them to expect as His disciples, and invited them all to eat His body under the species of bread, and to drink His blood under the species of wine, telling them to continue doing what He had done - partaking of His body and His blood - in His memory. For, as He had explained to them in no uncertain terms, unless humans ate His body and drank His blood, they would not have 'Life' in them and would continue to be enslaved to me, the 'Author of Death'!

"There is, in other words, no possibility of regaining membership in the revamped human family (in which the Deliverer and His blessed mother now also belong) except through their blessing; and that blessing is not available to anyone outside the 'Mystical Body of the Deliverer or the Church', the only place where you won't be able to find my fingerprints by divine decree. But pick any other place, and you will find my fingerprints all over the place. I can guarantee you that the minute a human forgets that it is I and my cohorts who exercise rule over all the Earth, that human is mince meat and as good as dead! There can only be salvation outside the Church over my dead body - and, you know I don't have one!

Taking credit for a job well done…

"Do you now perhaps understand why you humans, ignoring your own identity, and lusting for things that belong to your neighbors, are now into such uncouth and inhuman things? Let me tell you: the things you do to each other boggle even our demonic imagination! Red ants do not wage wars against each other. Neither do alligators, nor bees, nor any other specie among the lower beings. But you human do - an indication that you're morally bankrupt. And then, when you humans are not at each other's throats (yes, each other's throats!), you are busy polluting the environment in which you live and ensuring that the Earth will be inhabitable in very short order. That is doing the same thing as hacking away at the branch from which one is dangling! That is a dumb thing to do isn't it?

"We ourselves might be engaged in this struggle between Good and Evil; but, in truth, we demons aren't into any 'undemonic things' against fellow demons! It is only you stupid humans who systematically conduct the most inhuman and 'inhumane' operations against your own kind, and who even go on to brag that you treated your own kind to 'shock and awe' and things of that nature! It is only you dumb and stupid humans who see 'statesmen' in the ring leaders among you who have no qualms leading nations to wars and sacrificing countless human lives in the process in the senseless efforts to conquer and dominate the world - senseless because you humans should know by now that you will never succeed in devising a way to take ill-gotten earthly possessions with you beyond the grave.

"And yet, what really mattered was not the expansionist ambitions of those nations that are no more, but the dignity of the many souls that were sacrificed at the altar of greed! I, as Ruler of the Underworld, must give myself credit for ensuring that, in every age, there are among humans stupid fools who will not hesitate to use their positions of God-given authority to trample on the dignity of their fellow humans - to ensure that the violence of human on human continues to the very last day!

"I have to be fair to myself and take credit for being able to manipulate humans and ensuring that, throughout the ages, it is human societies that have been responsible for shamelessly promoting and institutionalizing of injustices of the vilest sorts. They range from banditry masquerading as religious crusades, to slavery, lynching and other associated forms of discrimination that are supposedly grounded in the sacred scriptures, to colonialism, imperialism, and unbridled lust for material goods, to an unconscionable and immoral preoccupation with armaments that are supposed to guarantee unfettered access to the world's dwindling resources.

"I have to take credit for getting humans to re-invent themselves as members of what is effectively a virulent 'man-eat-man' society. I have to take credit for the fact that, in modern times, powerful nations are determined to create chaos in the world at will so that they can turn around and exploit it for their benefit. And just to think that such activities, while they last, are not merely condoned, but have the full support of the fabric of society, including those who are supposed to provide spiritual and moral leadership!

"You stupid humans know that you live on 'borrowed time' on earth. But how many of you realize that everything you see is 'passing' for that reason. The way most of you imagine it, it is you who are 'passing' and moving on presumably back into nothingness - just like a drunk on horseback who sees the trees and the scenery 'flying past him' in reverse, and does not realize that it is he himself who has the awareness of those objects heading back to where he himself is coming from. He doesn't realize that it is himself who is going to be accountable for what happens next to himself and to the horse as he tries vainly to avoid ramming into a boulder in his path.

"Like thousands upon thousands of 'nations' for whom millions of 'patriotic' citizens beginning with Cain toiled in vain, it is just a matter of time before the objects you humans see around you will be no more. But that will not dissolve you from accounting for the manner in which you employed your talents. Guess what, the 'heavenly riches' that we ourselves tried to wrest from the Prime Mover (that are not unlike the earthly 'riches' that we keep dangling in front of your eyes) were only a mirage, and we are still paying the price for daring to challenge Him. And so will it be with you humans.

"But, contrary to what war mongers for instance seem to believe, namely that they can take their war mongering with them into the next world, the fact is that humans who are unable to regain their identity as members of one humankind and who themselves kick the bucket before renouncing their war mongering habits end up here in the Pit with us, because this is the place for the spiritually dead - a place where they will be free to spin and tell lies.

"These are the guys who take what we suggest to them literally. And so they believe that the only philosophy that makes sense is the philosophy of every human for himself/herself. We have persuaded them that the only viable policy is to have every human on earth mind for himself/herself, and every household mind for itself, and every clan to mind for itself, and every tribe mind for itself, and every ethnic grouping mind for itself, and every nation on earth mind for itself, and to completely disregard the fact that humanity is one and indivisible!

"These fellows, following the example of Cain, believe in the policy of world domination, meaning that if a scarce resource is in someone else's back-yard, just go get it if you can marshal the guts and have the means to do so. And, of course, if using an atom bomb is what is needed to gain access to that scarce resource, just go ahead and do what it takes to manufacture one, even though that policy is short-sighted because it puts all other nations on notice that they have to do likewise to ensure that what is in your back-yard doesn't get filched by other marauding humans.

"So, so stupid! This is because, what with porous borders and Worldwide Web that enables humans in any part of the globe to communicate with each other, the prevalence of dissatisfied citizens who are astitute enough to see themselves as *loyal* members of humankind and not just of some 'country' with artificial boundaries, and what have you, it simply isn't possible for any nation to keep a lid on atomic and other secrets. And hence the changing geopolitical face of the earth! And then there is the question of the purpose of it. What use is it if a human gains the whole world and loses his/her soul to me? None! First you humans ought to know that since Cain knocked off his brother Abel, the number of wars that humans have fought while seeking control over some portion of earth or resources are countless, while those who faced each other in battle in time ended up facing each other before the King of Kings and Lord of Lords with nothing to show except blood on their hands for the talents they received at creation.

"The very first thing that all those war-mongering kings, emperors, field marshals, commanders-in-chief and what-have-you discover, upon kicking the proverbial bucket, is that the deaths of all the poor, indefensible humans whose fate meant utterly nothing to them as they prosecuted their wars using every means at their disposal - battering rams, predator drones, artillery barrages, remote controlled car bombs, rocket fire, robots, etc. - and were dismissed off-handedly as 'collateral damage', is that all human life, their own included, meant a lot to the Prime Mover and to their Judge in the person of the Son of Man. And at that time of reckoning, these characters will wish to no avail to exchange places with the victims of their wanton and rabid excesses. And then the realization that when they 'did it' to those nondescript, voiceless souls, they did it to none other than the Judge Himself will be so damning in itself, they will be wishing to head over here in the Pit and out of His sight even before the sentencing was over - before they were presented with the full list of their crimes against humanity amongst other sins.

"It will come as a very great surprise when these usually flamboyant characters discover that their Record in the divine Court of Justice contained not one single good deed that could be used by the Judge to mitigate the sentence. This was because all such 'good deeds' - church attendance in the glare of publicity, kisses on the children's cheeks at political rallies, etc. - were all part of a grand design of burnishing their public image, and concealing the real personae beneath, so that they could continue committing crimes against humanity and other mortal sins with impunity.

"Unfortunately because those humans who made it their business to prey on others back on earth come here stuck with the habit, even we demons find it sickening just observing these characters still screaming and hollering for revenge against their 'enemies', forgetting that it was they themselves who unwittingly dispatched those they regarded as their enemies to their eternal reward in heaven. They make a pitiful sight as they endure spiritual torment and agony from discovering, too late, that they sold their spiritual inheritance for a pittance, and ended up not just wedded to vengefulness, but determined to parade that vice as holy zeal for "justice"!

"But then, unrepentant and 'hard core' (as you humans say), they thoroughly deserve the terrible punishment they get - at their own hands! This is a fate that dwarfs anything that they may have inflicted on their victims who were weeping and mourning then, but whose tears and mourns turned into a veritable 'blessing' afterward.

"We demons have one great virtue - yes, I mean 'virtue'...the virtue of patience! And it is this virtue of patience, practised to a degree that has been heroic in every sense of that word, which is starting to pay off handsomely. Knowing that humans had lost their identity to a point where they had become clueless as regards their origin (as creatures who owed their existence to the Prime Mover), who they were (as creatures who shared the same '*esse*' or 'human nature' with their fellow humans and now also the 'Word-become-flesh', or as regards their destiny (namely as creatures that had a certain rendezvous with the Prime Mover in whose image they had been created and who therefore demands a reckoning of all who are fashioned in His image), or their purpose in life (to do all to the Prime Mover's greater honor and glory), we here in the Pit were confident that we could groom them and then in turn use them to do the dirtiest thing imaginable, namely make it appear as if the Church - the Mystical Body of the Deliverer - was similarly capable of loosing its identity as something that was divinely instituted!

"We here in the Pit in fact also do have dreams. We for example dream of the day when an ultra-reform-minded individual will appear and, with our help, argue persuasively that the 'parable of the fig tree' which all the gospels refer to, was in fact a fable that some enthusiastic translator inserted into the sacred texts but wasn't in the original biblical texts at all.

"Consequently the separated brethren will be able to claim that, even if the Roman Catholic Church *was* the Church the Deliverer founded, they had a firm basis for claiming that any purported act of excommunication by the Holy Father on behalf of the Church was itself in error as it was without any basis in the *santae scripturae*. They could argue that no one could say they couldn't wax and grow in virtue and in the manner Providence would have them wax and grow and wax in holiness, just because they had rebuffed the traditional Church and the 'errors' to which it was prone.

"The argument that the separated brethren were doomed because they were operating 'outside the Church' because, like branches that are cut off from a fruitful vine, risk withering and becoming good only for keeping the fireplace alight in the winter, would no longer hold water! But for now, this is definitely one 'parable' we love, because it dooms all the so-called separated brethren as long as they knowing desist from abandoning their heresies and schisms and returning to the fold. For our part, we would like the separated brethren to remain under the misguided notion that the infinitely loving and merciful Prime Mover could never permit a situation in which professed 'Christians' could be 'excommunicated' or cut off from the was sacramental grace the fullness of which was found inside the Church or Mystical Body of the Deliverer.

"We would like to see some zealot launch a campaign to have this parable declared apocryphal material that was included in the Canon by some 'misguided pope' who was acting under my influence while claiming at the same time to be 'speaking *ex cathedra*'! And, of course, this tells you one other thing. Things are not well in the *church* (the word 'church' being used here to refer to 'Christendom' so called, or the collection of 'Christian' sects each of which claims to be the 'Church' that was founded by the Deliverer) even after that *first* 'Reformation'. We very definitely need a *second* and actually far more reaching 'Reformation', one that will assure that 'there will be no faith left on earth when the Deliverer returns'!

"Even then, we can today proudly proclaim that after working very patiently with misguided humans over the two thousand years or so that have elapsed since the Church of the Prime Mover was inaugurated, it is virtually impossible, even for humans of goodwill, to tell the true Church at a glance from the innumerable (and still growing number of) 'churches' that have been set up by self-proclaimed messengers of the Prime Mover.

"These churches, which contradict each other right and left, are united in challenging the teaching authority of the Church of Rome over which 'popes' - successors to the apostle who was singled out by the Deliverer to be a 'fisher of men' and chosen from among the 'Dirty Dozen' (as we here in the Pit refer to them because of what their mission which really hurts our cause) to be the 'rock' upon which the Deliverer was going to build His '*ecclesia*' as He called it - have presided in an unbroken line of succession.

"You would think that, because these 'non-traditional' churches, unlike the Holy Catholic Church, do not have anyone who claims to be the lawful successor to Peter and are therefore 'leader-less' (even though the 'pastors' in these churches all claim to be 'anointed' and guided in their pronouncements and interpretation of the books of Sacred Scripture by the 'Spirit'), they would be shunned and spurned by those in search of deliverance and the 'Truth'. And never mind the fact that most of the pastors regarded the most important sacraments and much of the Church's traditional liturgy as witchcraft, and now spent most of their time lecturing members of their congregations on how to become instantly saved by intoning words from a prayer book, describing the personal revelations they claimed they were receiving daily and reciting passages from the Old and New Testaments *ad nauseam* by way of illustration, and persuading their congregations to throw in their lot with them by 'sowing seeds', the latest euphemism for making a donation!

"It should at least have struck someone among the rank and file in these blossoming church institutions as a little suspicious that, while it had become fashionable for these presumptive modern day 'Fathers of the Church' to abandon important sacraments (like the Sacrament of Confession, Holy Eucharist, etc.) and to ditch much of the Church's rich traditional liturgy, there had never been any suggestion by even the most 'reform minded' separated brother or sister that 'Peter's Pence' (which was variously referred to as the 'Collection'), that ancient but by the same token also much abused part of the Church's liturgy, should likewise be dropped.

"But more importantly, you would think that it would be obvious to everyone that for anyone to go out on a limb and assume the responsibility that was reserved for Peter, also known as *Cephas* (the Rock) for leading actual and potential members of the Deliverer's flock away from the Mystical Body of the Deliverer and from the sacramental life of the universal and apostolic Church and its sacred traditions, and out of the 'Community of Saints' or Church Militant to no where is the last thing a human would think of doing! You wouldn't expect an ordinary mortal to try and appoint oneself as a rival Moses who presumes to be qualified and able to lead the people of the Prime Mover out of the desert and into the Promised Land.

Fruit from the Tree of Knowledge…

"It cannot be emphasized enough that we here in the Underworld do work very hard to see hordes diverted from the path of Truth represented by the Holy Catholic Church and the present day equivalent of Noah's Ark. Now I may have spilled out a lot of our secrets, but how exactly we in the Underworld do this is something I won't reveal. It is, as you humans would put it, a 'classified secret'.

"But you have to be really stupid and dumb if you cannot see my fingerprints all over the place when a new 'church' or sect pops up. I cannot, however, really take any credit for that stupidity and dumbness on the part of humans. I cannot do so in the same way I really can't take credit for the fact that Adam and Eve disobeyed the Prime Mover, and consequently fell from grace. Even though I was hiding up there in the branches of the apple tree and suggesting all sorts of things to the father and mother of the human race, they were under no compulsion to hurt themselves by doing what they did.

"But this is one thing I can and will reveal to you. Even though I am called the Father of Lies, I can tell you that I have never uttered one lie in my entire life - I mean since the beginning of time when I was created. And you guessed right…I am a spirit and do not have a mouth! In this particular respect, I am the very opposite of you wicked humans who are capable of lying until they are blue in the face. And also when the Book refers to me as the *Diabolus Malus* (the evil ghost), it is not really true that I am evil. I am actually very nice - my clientele can assure you of that. And you yourself have seen how truthful I try to be all the time. If I have lied, it is simply because I have 'lied by example' if I may put it that way - by disobeying the Prime Mover, and thereby suggesting to you lesser creatures that a mere creature can take on the Prime Mover.

"I was completely truthful when I suggested to the first man and the first woman that, if they ate of the forbidden fruit from the Tree of Life, they would become immortal like the Almighty One. Well, isn't that exactly what humans who are members of the Church Triumphant are - like the Almighty whom they can now see face to face? If they weren't, they wouldn't withstand the glitter and glow that surrounds the Triune Divinity. They would become vaporized and disintegrate into the nothingness from which they came.

"And look - in retrospect it wasn't such a bad idea after all that Eve, hearkening to my suggestion, succeeded in drawing Adam into the rebellion, and persuading him to join her in the act of disobedience to their Maker, appalling though it was!

"If they hadn't been curious and succumbed in the process to the temptation, there wouldn't have been any need for a Deliverer in the first place; and, barring a change in the Divine Plan (which was highly unlike), Adam and Eve and all of their descendants would have been stuck in Paradise; and their transistion to wherever, to make room for new generations of humans, wouldn't have added anything special to their spiritual fulfillment. The world would have looked more or less like a zoo with nothing really interesting going on - a complete contrast to what goes on in today's world in which humans continually savage and maul their own kind aas though they were beasts of the wild that were permanently locked in a brawl over a meagre catch! But it is because the Deliverer came to earth and redeemed humans with His death and resurrection that humans now can realize Eve's dream of becoming immortal and like the Prime Mover Himself in beatific vision.

"If truth be told, it is because the Divine Plan in the Prime Mover's providence called for humans to take the places in heaven that I and the other fallen angels vacated in the wake of our own rebellion that this thing happened. And, yes, you can say that I shot myself in the foot by dangling the fruit from the Tree of Knowledge in from of those eager and adventuresome humans.

"You would, of course, think that humans would be able to infer from this that the idea of an intermediate state in the next life where repentant humans have a chance to requite sins can't be fiction! That, because sinful and sinning humans whose pleas for divine mercies whilst they are still kicking and 'alive' often aren't nearly as genuine as they ought to be, it is they themselves who will be the first to acknowledge that they still had a debt to pay, and who whereupon will plead for a little bit of time before being received by the Prime Mover into the 'bosom of Abraham' so that they may expiate their sins and, in the words of Gregory of Nyssa, 'be purged of the filthy contagion in their souls by the purifying fire' - the 'purging fire' that cleanses the stains with which the souls of sinful and sinning humans are infested!

"But, No! These humans who spend most of their waking hours vying with each other and trying to outdo '*El Ingenioso Hidalgo Don Quixote de la Mancha*' actually beat the 'ingenious Hidalgo Don Quixote of La Mancha' at his own game when they suddenly act sissy and assert that, being the 'true believers' they are, all their sins and even the stains left by the sins they commit are simply 'washed away' by the precious blood of the Deliverer, and that the very notion of 'Purgatory' (never mind that many holy mystics, amongst them people like Sister Faustina Kovalka, Saint Caterina from Genova, Maria Simma, Saint Veronica Giuliani, Saint Margherita Maria Alacoque, Saint Geltrude of Helfta have actually been to the 'place' and have bequeathed to the world exciting accounts of what goes on there! But even those humans who accept that such Purgatory isn't a fictitious idea act for the most part as if it is. And that is why monasticism isn't thriving and 'hermits' nowadays only exist in works of fiction - thank the Prime Mover!

"That is also why humans are all excited about Neil Armstrong jaywalking on the moon, and that the Hubble telescope's Canadian-built robotic arm at a command causes the telescope to aim its sights at the perimeter of 'space'; whilst the only people who are excited about the fact that the Second Person of the Blessed Trinity, and Creator of the Universe and everything that is in it, made it to Planet Earth two thousand years ago, and spent three years attempting unsuccessfully to persuade the chief priests and the Pharisees that he had turned up in fulfillment of His Father's promise to Abraham, Isaac and Jacob are televangelists! And so, the fact that a transcendent and omnipotent Supreme Essence (whose very nature is to be or to exist) took on human nature and became a veritable statistic, and did so in order that fallen humans (whom he had fashioned in His own image and likeness) might yet gain eternal life through their faith in Him, goes virtually unheralded!

"Sound familiar? It might not sound familiar to you humans; but it certainly sounds familiar to us here in the Underworld! There is Moses whose life is devoted to leading the Prime Mover's chosen people from bondage in Egypt into Canaan. After Moses' initial encounter with the Prime Mover who addresses him from the 'burning bush', Moses returns to pick up the Ten Commandments that everyone is expected to follow. The commandments are engraved on two stone tablets. But at the sight of the children of Israel sinning like the blazes and worshipping false gods, Moses is unable to take it and becomes the only human ever to break the Ten Commandments all at once! These are the Israelites - descendants of one or other of the twelve sons of Jacob, namely Reuben, Simeon, Levi, Judah, Dan, Naphtali, Gad, Asher, Issachar, Zebulun, Joseph and Benjamin.

"Fast forward to the reign of Tiberius Caesar... Even though the Israelites had settled in the Promised Land that came complete with the Temple and the Holy of Holies (an inner sanctuary that only the High Priest entered on Yom Kippur, the tenth and final Day of Atonement), it was Pontius Pilate, the Roman Governor, who called the shots in Judea, while Herod Antipas (also known as Herod the Great), a stooge of the Romans who had been proclaimed 'king of the Jews' by the Roman senate, reigned as Tetrarch of Galilee and Peraea.

"The real bad news was that John the Baptist, sent by the Prime Mover, had begun to preach and baptize saying: 'Repent, for the kingdom of heaven is at hand!' After all those years during which the

Prime Mover, true to His word, had put enmity between the serpent (me) and the woman (Mary), and my seed and her seed, the chickens had come home to roost! The time had come for the most important prophecy to be fulfilled, namely that the Immaculate Mary, Mother of the Deliverer 'shall crush thy (my) head, and thou (me, Diabolos) shalt lie in wait for her (Mary's) heel'

"As the history books have it, the chosen people, lead by the chief priests and the Pharisees and representing humanity, disowned 'the *Logos* (the Word of God) who became flesh and dwelt among humans'; they disowned 'the Son of God'; they disowned 'the only Son of the living Prime Mover; they disowned Mary's boy child whom she called 'JESUS…for He shall save His people from their sins'; they disowned 'the Lamb of God who takes away the sin of the world'; and they also disowned the 'one Lord Jesus Christ, the only-begotten Son of God, begotten from the Father before all ages, light from light, true God from true God, begotten not made, of one substance with the Father, through Whom all things came into existence'. The damn stupid fools disowned their Maker and Deliverer!

"But those were not the only damn stupid fools! This has been typical of you humans ever since, and will continue to be until Planet Earth goes up in a plume of smoke in a nuclear holocaust (thanks to the Manhattan Project) and, unhinged from its axis, Mother Earth starts drifting in space like a rudderless ship and crushes into the sun!

"If Adam and Eve hadn't listened to me and gone on to offend the Prime Mover by giving in to the temptation, there would be no such thing as beatific vision for humans. You can say that it is because of the intransigence of humans that the Almighty One sent His only begotten Son, the Second Person of the Blessed Trinity who is begotten by the First Person in eternity, down to Earth so that those who believed in Him might be saved. Well, it is more than simply being saved from the fires of hell for humans to now be able to behold the Almighty One face to face, I have to tell you!

"If I and my fellow demons hadn't opted to go our own way during the time we ourselves were on trial, we would have had the chance to see Him face to face ourselves; but we blew it as you know. For us, that would have been more-or-less automatic - if we had 'kept the faith' as you humans say, and remained faithful creatures of the Prime Mover! But if Adam and Eve had remained good the good boy and the good girl they had been until their adventure in the Garden of Eden on that fateful afternoon four hundred thousand ago, they would have been one very happy pair. But, barring the outside chance that their descendants would have ended up falling for my tricks and blowing it on behalf of humanity by committing original sins of their own, beatific vision would have remained outside the scope of their dreams!

"Now I had been suspecting ever since I myself fell from grace - and quite rightly as it turned out - that the Almighty One would, in His infinite goodness, try to let humans inherit what we fallen spirits had forfeited. My intention was to get the father and mother of the human race to join our camp, lock, stock and barrel so that this would never happen. I was determined to try and frustrate the Divine Plan in that regard - and I very nearly got away with it. What I did not count on was that the stupid Adam and Eve would recoil from their dastardly act of disobedience and seize the opportunity to get back into good books with the Almighty by being remorseful and renouncing me and my whiles when they discovered that they had been stripped of their divine graces and, spiritual essences, were now naked in the real sense!

"And so, again, you can see that I never lied to Adam and Eve at any time - and I can assure you that I have never lied to any of their descendants either! But as you can expect, I am always haunted by the thought that, even after my troops and I have worked so hard to get humans to refuse to get aboard the Ark of Noah, the Almighty One might still have something else up His sleeve. I am haunted by the fear that some incomparable good might ensue from humans straying from orthodoxy and refusing to submit to the authority of Peter's successors.

"This is even though I know full well - just as you humans do - that there is no salvation outside the Holy Catholic Church; and that all those humans who decide to trash the card inviting them to attend the divine banquet and rebuff the overtures of the messengers of the Deliverer are doomed. I am still haunted by the fear that we here in the Underworld might not end up bagging the souls of all those we see fritting away opportunities to enter the Ark of Noah!

It could be something as insignificant as the stroke of a pen - if, for instance, some upstart from a liberal wing of the Church were to become pope, and then promptly issue an encyclical redefining the phrase 'Mystical Body of the Deliverer' and making it encompass 'all humans for whom the Deliverer laid down His life on Mt. Calvary in obedience to His heavenly Father' until they slammed the door in the face of the successors to the apostles when the latter arrived bearing the message of the Risen Christ! Can you the damage to our cause if things were to come to that!

"I will be frank and tell you what we here in the Underworld suspect is going on and robbing us of our fair share of souls. It is those prayers that are offered up by followers of Faustina and others who specifically offer up prayers to the Sacred Heart of the Deliverer beseeching Him to always look with mercy on all humans particularly at their hour of death. You know what can happen when it is time for a sinful and sinning human, regardless of the life he/she led, to 'kick the bucket' as you fools put it. Who can tell what the graces of the Prime Mover, extended to the dying sinner as a result of such intercession, can accomplish? One thing is certain: when prayers are offered up for a dying human who might have led an unworthy and quite despicable life, the effect of such prayers is to block me and my troops from our quarry at precisely the moment that we would be poised to snatch his/her soul.

"By Golly! Who can say how many humans have renounced my whiles and the temptations of the flesh at the time they saw death staring in their faces and, looking around, instead of seeing me and my troops there in force to reassure them that everything will be alright, they saw my arch-enemy, Michael, on his knees in adoration before the pierced Sacred Heart of the infinitely merciful Deliverer - the pierced heart that signifies that their pangs of death, however tormenting, have been sanctified by the Deliverer's own death on the cross for the salvation of all humans! We, of course, work very hard to keep humans ignorant of the power of their own prayers. Oh, we even strive to get lukewarm followers of the Deliverer to turn their backs completely on their faith just so that they won't ever beseech the mercies of the Prime Mover either for themselves or for their fellow humans, and will be looking to me and me, the Evil Ghost, and my fellow demons for succour when the end of their pilgrimage on earth is at hand.

"We know one thing for sure, namely that humans will not be able to claim that they were merely following their consciences when they did unto others what they wouldn't possibly have liked done to them by other humans! The same is of course true when sinful and sinning humans presume to know better than those whom Providence in His infinite wisdom has entrusted His work of redemption however unworthy!

"Also, there will be no excuse if, out of pride, humans had decided that it was too demeaning to submit to the *magisterium* (teaching authority) of the *una sancta ecclesia apostolica et catholica* (the one and the only holy, apostolic and universal Church), and preferred to substitute the message of the crucified Deliverer with their own self-serving testimonies. And certainly not after I myself have been dragged from Gehenna to provide all these pages upon page of testimony on the Deliverer's visitation, and to spill out so many of my secrets in the course of this forced confession!

Exiles from Paradise…

"Regardless, let me - Satan, Arch-Devil, Evil Ghost or whatever you want to call me - say this one thing concerning the 'instant salvation' fad and specifically the way manner in which it supposedly can be obtained. Now, I know enough not to say anything that might suggest that being born and bred a 'Catholic' automatically gets one a pass to heaven! Nothing could be further from the truth. Catholics, just like any one else must keep the Lord's commandments;

and no amount of chants of 'Lord, Lord' will help them if they too do not take up their crosses and follow in the Deliverer's footsteps.

"And look here buddy, Jesus of Nazareth I know, and Paul of Tarsus and I have heard of, and as well Pope John Paul II; but who are these other folks who are peddling each their own peculiar - and, I would add, confusing - brand of 'Christianity'? Then, Concerning this 'instant salvation' thing: if it were true that humans could be saved, not by keeping the Prime Mover's commandments, but by just reciting a prayer however that prayer was constructed, I - Beelzebub and Father of Lies - would have gone out of business two thousand years ago.

"What about those humans who just worked away at keeping the Ten Commandments, but had never heard of that prayer? Of course it isn't true. But, promise that you won't whisper our secret to any one for now at least! It all sounds like the mother of the apostles James and John all over again. That woman, if you remember, wanted the Deliverer to go against His own divine principles and just reserve for her two sons the places in heaven immediately to His right and His left! She wanted to have it so easy!

"As soon as humans start awakening to the fact that there is such a thing as the 'human condition' which has its roots in the sin of disobedience of the first man and the first woman, and realize that from that moment on, humans were all - with the sole exception of the Blessed Mother of the Deliverer and the 'Son of Man' Himself - the 'forsaken' children of the Adam and Eve by virtue of being born in the original sin, in stead of praying for an increase in their faith, they immediately start looking for the easiest way out! I will tell you, exiles from Paradise, that none of those 'easy solutions' stands any chance of working because I, Lucifer, not only know all about them, but my stamp is all over those 'easy solutions'.

"The gift of faith on the other hand works because the stamp of the Deliverer is all over it. The gift of faith that is imparted to humans of good will (who can now also call the Word-become-flesh - and now, alas, also Judge - their brother, and call His mother Mary their mother) doesn't leave me room to do my dirty work and bedevil and/or frustrate its efficacy. Being a gift, you humans cannot just reach out and grab it - and certainly not when you are not ready to ask humbly for it or are well disposed to receive it.

"When a human of good will receives this gift, I (Satan and vile as I am) am powerless to stop the sanctifying grace from working in you. But you try to show your metal and begin getting the idea that you on your own can find an easy solution to the human predicament, and my minions and I will be lying in wait for you with any number of certified and fully guaranteed options for you to choose from. You disrespect me if you think that you can find salvation and escape my tentacles except by the grace of the Deliverer!

"Or were you under the impression that I hadn't figured that one out as well? Always keep in mind that, while Knowledge is divine, we here in the Pit, because we do not want to be the only ones who are damned, have a vested interest in acquiring it and using it for our Evil Plan. You have to be really dumb if you do not believe that we wouldn't try to use Knowledge to our benefit - which, hopefully you are!

"And you have got to understand, by the way, that my troops and I have invested a great deal indeed in this 'project'. It is not by an accident of nature that you have all these intelligent people claiming that salvation comes, not by faith *and* good works alone, but by reciting a couple of words (without even the need to cross your self before or after). That you can just make up your mind, mumble a few words, and get yourself out of the boon docks! Again, the Deliverer has made it very clear that it is not those who exclaimed 'Lord, Lord' who will inherit the kingdom of heaven, but those who kept His commandments.

"As for praying, the Deliverer went out of His way to teach the apostles and those who would be His disciples how to pray, and he composed and gave them the *Pater Noster* which, among other things, gets you humans to stop the foolery, and to ask the Prime Mover not to lead them into temptation, but to deliver them from evil.

"Good" codes and "Blessed" codes

"Humans, already confused about Natural Law, because they did not know their identity as 'incarnated spirits', now also need a veritable leap of faith to find their way into the One and the Only True, Holy and Catholic Church, the institution whose *raison de tre* is to guide humans as regards not just the Natural Law (the good code) and the Supernatural Law (the blessed code), but as regards the Truth.

"You see - we here in the Pit are not really as bad as you might think. You can see that try to be there for those humans who muster the courage to 'love their fathers and mothers more than they love the Deliverer' (to use His exact words), and as well those astute and smart enough to know what is good for them and who wll, therefore, not 'take up their crosses and follow the Deliverer'. Those humans who scrupulously 'find their lives' and are not prepared 'to lose them for the Deliverer's sake can always be assured of our support, albeit only for so long...

The next phase

"During the next phase of the battle for souls, we would like to see more and more Catholic bishops and cardinals (because these are the successors to the 'Dirty Dozen' regardless of whether they are worthy 'Men of the Cloth' or not) make fondly references to the 'separated brethren' even as these 'saved' followers of the Deliverer show more and more that they are not prepared to renounce the schisms and heresies that have kept them 'separated' from the Church and in a state of excommunication.

'We would like to see the Church's functionaries give the false impression that, their schisms and heresies notwithstanding, the status of these bible wielding and supposedly 'saved' schismatics and heretics as members of the Mystical Body of the Deliverer was not affected in any way after all by their refusal to submit the authority of Peter's successor and to the Church's *Magisterium*'!

'In that way, the distinction between the 'Holy Catholic Church' and the burgeoning 'church' establishments (that are making evangelization the fastest growing and also lucrative 'industry' in the West) will gradually become blurred, making the Church's evangelizing mission even more difficult. Already the words 'church' and 'separated brethren' have become virtually meaningless as every Dick and Harry who sets up his/her church on a whim also automatically starts enjoying the benefits of being counted among the 'Separated Brethren'! And since every one who 'talks church' not only claims that he/she has received a special revelation from the divine 'Ghost', but soon enough also starts claiming that he/she is capable of causing miracles to happen by simply invoking the name of the Deliverer, the fact that all these self-proclaimed 'anointed of the Prime Mover' blaspheme whenever they invoke the name at the sound of which every head should bow will be completely lost sight of.

Dumb demons don't exist

"Now, the fact that we here in the Pit are demons doesn't make us necessarily dumb. You ought to know that by this time - unless you yourself are entirely dumb (which, of course, might very well be the case)! We too know that, even though the Church teaches that there is no salvation outside it (the Mystical Body of the Deliverer), 'it' (the Church) no doubt extends beyond the 'Visible Church'. But also knowing the nature of humans, we here in the Pit also know that all those spiritually starved hordes, who (as you know) are simultaneously inclined to sin and continually on the lookout for the easiest ways out of their bind, will be open - yes, very open - to the temptation to meddle in things that are the prerogative of the Prime Mover, like trying to decide, for instance, who outside the Visible Church has received the baptism of desire or the baptism of blood and therefore belongs to the Invisible Church.

"We actually tempt them to imagine that it is only they themselves - and perhaps also those who prescribe to the same religious tenets as they themselves - belong to the 'Church' or 'Ark' of the Prime Mover (or whatever!), and will go to on to inherit the kingdom of heaven; and that everyone else is doomed regardless of the sort of lives they lead. We tempt them to then act as though it isn't so much they themselves who are supposed to allow the Holy Ghost to lead them where He may, but the Holy Ghost who is supposed to hearken to their instructions so that He may lead them where they will, namely to some earthly 'Paradise'.

"Look, humans do not have a clue why they were born when they were born. These days they might know when it is going to rain; but they do not have the faintest idea when a hurricane of the magnitude of Katrina is going to make landfall on their shores, or when the tsunami is going to descend on them - or when the 'Big One' is going to come. Humans do not know if or when they might suffer a fatal heart attack and drop dead, or even if they will be really better off if they win that jackpot. And so you would think that humans would be overjoyed to learn that the Holy Ghost, the Second Person of the Blessed Trinity, is ready, if they will only let Him, to lead them where they belong, but won't go on their own! No! They prefer instead to continue stumbling along blindly through uncertain times without a bothering about their last end, and to waste the precious time they have available to attain their self-actualization.

"The self-will and the selfishness become more than plain when these foolish humans (who did not even know what they were doing when they drove nails into the hands and feet of the Deliverer) presume to know whether other humans about whose religious beliefs or human condition they frequently know nothing are destined for our company here in the Pit or elsewhere – like the 'good thief'! It is the same way these misguided humans keep calling us here in the Pit all sorts of names when they know nothing about us or even why we are here - and when they are actually clueless about what they themselves are or even their destiny!

Invitees to the Divine Banquet

"Now, because folks in the Catholic Church, including members of the clergy who should know better, have the same tendency to blame me for all human failings including unbelief, that has provided us another window of opportunity which we have to exploit. And, believe it or not, our efforts in this regard are beginning to pay off as well! Increasingly, priests and even bishops are going around talking as if the 'separated brethren' are for all practical purposes members of the Mystical Body of the Deliverer.

"And they seem to be intent on making the Jews - the chosen people under the Old Testament - feel as if it is just fine for them to be waiting for their earthly messiah! The way we here in the Pit see it, rejecting the Deliverer when He showed up and sending Him to His grisly death was the very worst thing a people, chosen or not, could inflict on themselves. And their preoccupation with deliverance in the worldly sense just about seals their fate, doesn't it! But it is also a measure of the extent to which we here in the Pit, despised though we might be by the so-called saved folks, have frustrated the Divine Plan! This is just swell! Can you imagine members of the race that bequeathed the Messiah to the world turning their backs on Him and consequently denying themselves the opportunity to relish His victory over sin and over death, and doing so with the help of functionaries of the Church the Deliverer commissioned and tasked with spreading the message of salvation!

"Those same clergy who are loath to embarrass the separated brethren and the descendants of the Israelites don't treat people of other faiths - Buddhists, Hindus, Moslems to mention a few - the same way. In essence, these functionaries of the Holy Church are going around talking as if it is not enough to be a child of the Prime Mover by virtue of being created in His Image. They are directly suggesting that only a select few, not all the poor forsaken children of Adam and Eve, are being invited to the divine banquet!

"You see, they tie the child/father relationship between humans and the Prime Mover, not to the fact that the Prime Mover, in His infinite wisdom, has brought his subjects into existence in different circumstances of His own choosing, but to the fact that some of these humans, in their desire to exclude other humans from the divine banquet table, go around waving the Book (as though it were a magic wand).

"To put it differently, they are almost encouraging the 'separated brethren' to continue in their apostasy and to remain excommunicated thereby! And they are doing this at the expense of evangelization, because they essentially should be rebuking the 'separated brethren' to abandon their apostasy, in the exact same way they ought to be rebuking the 'faithful' to stop being complacent about their faith, and also praying that their own faith may be strengthened to the point to which they would be ready to become martyrs for the Deliverer. But how on earth (and in hell) could they expect to win more souls for the Prime Mover by spreading the message of the risen Deliverer to the ends of the globe if they are satisfied with themselves and are cosy with those who call the Holy Father the anti-Christ!

Papal Infallibility Bulwark against the Lying Devil

"Actually, the way some 'separated' brothers and sisters nowadays refer to the soon to be beatified Mother Theresa or Pope John Paul II, you would think that their meditations on the lives of these stalwart pillars of Roman Catholicism would cause them to start worrying about their precarious position as 'brethren' who were still separated and were still cut off from communion with Holy Mother the Church! But that is not what we here in the Pit discern.

"It is pretty obvious to us that when the separated brethren say something nice about a character like John Paul II whom they sometimes forget and refer to as the 'Antichrist', what they really mean is that a good man like John Paul, being the undisputed leader of 'unquestioning faithful' (as separated brethren have always characterized Catholics), would probably have led his misguided flock back to orthodoxy and 'communion with the rest of 'Christendom' if he had been around a little longer! He had, after all, started off well by apologizing for the missteps of his predecessors, implying that it was Catholicism that had been in the wrong all the time.

"Since (unlike they themselves who were 'saved') neither Mother Theresa nor Pope John Paul, who had held on stubbornly to the supposedly 'fallacious' dogmas of the Catholic Church to the very last and refused to renounce their 'heresy', could have been admitted to heaven upon their death for that reason, their souls likely were still in limbo somewhere between the earth and the heavens, and possibly in real danger of being lost for ever. But they (the supposedly saved ones who, as the Deliverer's very good and utterly faithful servants, were ready to sacrifice their own lives for the unadulterated Truth) had dutifully prayed for the duo; and, consequently, both the dead pope (who had offered the best chance yet for Catholics to mend their ways) and the nun (who had spent her days ministering to Calcutta's homeless and was remembered with great fondness by India's Hindus, Moslems, and Buddhists alike) stood a good chance of receiving a reprieve from the Almighty One!

"That being the case, it was imperative that Pope Benedict XVI, the new leader of Catholicism, at the very minimum reciprocated and urged his cardinals, bishops, monsignors, priests, and heads of religious orders (and the head of the Jesuits in particular) to endorse what the Church's liberal wing has been saying, namely that the separated brethren were as much members of the Mystical Body of the Deliverer as say members of the Eastern Orthodox Church which had always been in communion with Rome.

"Now, I have to tell you that we, the inhabitants of Gehenna, cannot but be very pleased indeed with this result (even though we cannot 'celebrate' in the true sense of that word because of the unspeakable frustration that flows from being excluded from membership in the Church Triumphant for all eternity and the reward of everlasting happiness that would have been ours for the taking if we had not rebelled against His Mystic Majesty and 'separated' ourselves from the Pilgrim Church in the process.

"Indeed, how could we, evil as we are, not derive all the delight we can muster as damned and doomed spirits from the fact that things have come to pass in the way they have. How could we not delight in the fact that a worthy successor to Peter like John Paul II was regarded by the separated and self-proclaimed 'saved ones' or 'saints' as the one who was the toothless bulldog and the 'pretender'? If John Paul II and his predecessors were guilty of laying a false claim to being the pillar upon which the 'Visible Church' was built, then the Deliverer lied when He told the assembled apostles: 'What thou shalt hold bound on earth shall be bound in heaven, and what thou shalt hold bound in heaven shall be bound on earth'!

"But, leaving the question of the Deliverer lying aside, why don't stupid humans ask why the Deliverer went out of His way to say what He said? Did He do it in jest? The Deliverer was not a charlatan; and I tell you He knew damn well that I, Beelzebub, would not be resting and would be attempting to derail the Divine Plan from the word go!

'You have to be really dumb not to see that we here in Gehenna are mightily pleased to see souls that are in danger of missing a ride to safety in the 'Ark of Noah' mocking those who are attempting to throw them a life-line! Formally excommunicated by decrees of the Councils of the Church of Rome over which the successors to the apostle Peter preside and effectively 'separated' from the Church, they still have the audacity to refer to the Mystical Body of the Deliverer as the work of the anti-Christ!

"It is just such sweet music to my ears when humans, who should be pining for deliverance from my clutches, stand there and declare to the world that they are 'saved'! It is sweet music to my ears when, usurping the authority of those in the Church who are charged with 'being fishers of men' and going forth and spreading the message of the risen Deliverer, the separated brethren assert that it is in fact they who are 'the anointed of the Deliverer' and are empowered to perform miracles in the Deliverer's name! It is very sweet music indeed in my ears when they declare to the world that what they hold bound on earth (which they invariably do in the name of the Word and Second Person of the Blessed Trinity and also Deliverer) perforce is held bound in heaven, and what they hold bound in heaven is likewise held bound upon the earth by virtue of the Deliverer's promise!

"Oblivious to the fact that the Deliverer was the Word who chose to take up human nature in accordance with the Divine Plan of Redemption, and then interacted with the likes of Judas, Matthew, Peter and John, and after quizzing Peter regarding the genuineness of the fisherman's love for Him, tasked him with minding His sheep, the brethren who have been formally excommunicated, as a consequence which they remain 'separated' from the Church, bristle at and are deeply offended by the idea that Peter, a mere human, could actually presume to do what he, and those who succeeded him as vicar of Rome, did in abeyance to the command of the Deliverer and High Priest when he told them: 'Feed my sheep'!

"Even though the fisherman was not yet ready at that time to take the reigns as the first pope who would march on Rome and set up shop in that sin city, the Deliverer for His part was concerned that Peter and the other apostles be clear about what He meant by 'love', and what He expected of them in that regard. As Paul, whose resume included hunting and liquidating followers of the 'Terrorist' and the 'Insurgent', aptly explained after his own conversion to the Cause, by 'love', the Deliverer meant a love that would always be patient, persevere, protect, and never fail; and above all a love that, as Peter, following in the footsteps of the Deliverer, showed by his own example, would predispose the lover to die for his/her brothers and sisters who now included the Word-become-flesh Himself.

"Now, what you saw happening at the time of the reformation was no different from what happened at the time the Deliverer himself walked the earth. What the reformers did was exactly like what the priests and Pharisees did. They rejected the Messiah and decided to keep looking to invent one who would be to their own liking. Humans of little faith, they all prefer to be their own teachers and in the process deride the Deliverer who proclaimed that He was the Way and the Life. Actually, this is what all humans who will not allow themselves to be led by the Spirit where they on their own would not go - Catholics and non-Catholics alike - are up to.

"This is my legacy as Ruler of the Underworld. The only thing that stops me from having a complete walk-over is the *sancta ecclesia* and efficacy of the graces humans receive through the sacraments that are administered by it.

"This is a big coup - and one that we here in the Pit cleverly engineered. And we succeeded, not because Michael the Archangel was having a sneeze, giving us the opportunity to regain our footing and to meddle thereby; but because you humans are a dumb lot. Knowing that history repeats itself, from that moment on Pentecost Day when the Deliverer inaugurated His Church by sending forth the Holy Ghost, we here in the Underworld were waiting and ready to join battle, and our plan from the beginning was to enjoin disgruntled elements inside the Church - those 'believers' who would try to have it both ways, namely inherit the kingdom of heaven while refusing to have their wings clipped. And there were lots of them already at the time the infant Church was spreading its own wings from Judea through Asia Minor to Rome, and to the rest of the world from there.

"All we needed to do was just mark our time, while waiting for some of the Church folks to do what I myself, the host of angels who fell with me from the Prime Mover's favor and Adam and Eve (your own great grand Pa and great grand Ma) did, namely refuse to obey. It didn't take very much really - a couple of ruses here and there, and some members of the Church's hierarchy started smarting from the notion that it was only Peter and whoever would succeed him as 'Shepherd' of the Deliverer's flock on earth who could dictate to them on vital aspects of the Church's teachings or spiritual matters - in other words. As if the words '*Et ego dico tibi quia tu es Petrus, et super hanc petram, Ecclesiam meam edificabo*' were empty and meaningless - in fact a distraction!

"A wilful act of disobedience inevitably sets the stage for other wilful acts of disobedience that are intended to bolster and affirm the earlier acts of disobedience. In the case of the Reformation, for example, once we succeeded in persuading some monks to stand up and take the position that they did not feel bound by the Church's *magisterium* or teaching authority, it was easy enough to persuade one king who wanted to continue to call himself a Christian even though he was determined to lead an 'unchristian' way of life. We knew we were on the path to victory the moment we saw that the king and the disgruntled monks were determined to rebuff the authority of the Peter's successor and had joined hands for the showdown.

"And, just as we had expected, that first reformed Christian 'church', started by individuals who had been excommunicated and cut off from the Mystical Body of Christ because of their refusal to submit to the Church's teaching authority, inevitably splintered into more reformed 'churches' as 'ministering' under the new 'reformed' order became dependent, not on the magisterium of the Church and the validity of the ordination of the successors to the apostles, but on personal testimonies that ignored Tradition in the Church as an authentic source of revealed truth, and cited the 'Holy Book' as the sole source of revelation.

Leave nothing to chance

"When we in the Underworld set out to do anything, we go about it in a very thorough manner. We leave nothing to chance. The way we went about sowing the seeds of disunity in Christendom was typical of this *modus operandi*. We had made up our minds that the 'churches' we would help dissidents in the Church set up would not be poor replicas of the Holy Church the Deliverer had commissioned. And to make up for the fact that the One True Holy and Catholic Church was informed by the Holy Ghost, we planned to persuade our minions to retain the Holy Ghost as the central focus of the revamped theological positions and doctrines. And we could not have been more delighted than to see those in schism and/or heresy struggle to make the case that their personal testimonies were inspired by none other than the Comforter.

"And sure enough, some of these 'reformed' churches now look so much like the Church of Rome, you need an expert to tell the difference! Then, even those churches that have shed many important features of Catholicism such as the Sacrifice of the Mass, Benediction and the 'Holy Hour', the Confessional, veneration of the Blessed Mother of the Deliverer, veneration of relics of martyrs and canonized saints, or the churches that have down-graded the place of priests as ministers who share directly in the priesthood of the Deliverer Himself (and consequently bear an indelible mark that will distinguish them from all other humans for all eternity) to mere preacher-men or 'pastors', still succeed in putting on impressive, mesmerizing shows for their congregations.

"These reformed churches come complete with elegant church edifices and cathedrals that rival St. Peter's Basilica in Rome, and firebrand preachers who know the Bible like the back of their hand; and the apologists on their rolls who have the ability when push comes to shove of making the Church's own scholars look like dwarfs! And the same goes for the vestments and livery employed during church services. These churches sport the best that money can buy, including gold-embroidered mitres and chasubles, gilded croziers, Roman collars, flowing white cassocks and silk stoles - you name it!

"But then it could also be said that these reformed churches in fact come with everything that should lead some one with a wee bit of common sense to start suspecting that they have my hallmark! Promise me solemnly you won't whisper that to any soul! Well, even if you get out 'on the street' and spill your guts and reveal my secret to all and sundry, that probably will have very little effect on the project that we here in Gehenna have dubbed 'Operation Camouflage'! This is because, even though 'faith cometh by hearing', it still remains a gift of the Prime Mover, and no amount of yearning by self-willed humans can ever force Him to change His *modus operandi* and impart it to those not deemed by Him as worthy of it.

"It was after all self-will on the part of the 'reformers' that opened the flood-gates for the different varieties of reformed churches! Yah! It was self-will on the part of misguided humans that gave us our window of opportunity. Once the first 'reformers' had gone out on a limb and started promulgating and propagating versions of 'Evangelism' that were based on their own personal interpretation of the sacred scriptures and done so without the blessing of the Church - once they had ranged themselves against the teaching *magisterium* or authority of the Holy Church headed by the Pontiff of Rome - it didn't really matter after that how clever or even 'prophetic' the personal testimonies they broadcast to the world sounded.

"The stage was set from that point on for us here in the Underworld to also get into our act. Working with well-intentioned humans who nevertheless had difficulty reconciling imperfections in humans who had been 'called to the feast' and were members of the Church - and specifically in those humans who had been called to leadership positions in the body of the faithful - with the fact that the Deliverer, the head of the 'Mystical Body' was 'perfect', we were able to effectively create and reinforce the impression in the minds of humans that 'Christendom' comprised so many feuding churches that were all equally informed by the Holy Ghost just the same, and that were also all 'integral' parts of the Holy Church!

"Using the most masterful manoeuvres that our satanic 'minds' could devise, we even succeeded in blurring the fact that humans who were excommunicated could not by definition be members of the Mystical Body of the Deliverer at the same time! We succeeded in promoting the 'Great Lie' that self-willed acts of humans have the same force and effect as acts that spring from the humble submission of a soul to the Holy Ghost and to the authority of the one and only true Church that is informed by Him by virtue of the promise the Deliverer made to the apostles who were cowed and congregated in the Upper Room out of fear of those who believed that they had successfully liquidated the Son of Man and also the 'Second Adam'!

"You just tell me the number of 'Catholics' who know what the phrase 'to be in communion with Rome' means! All these misguided souls inside and outside the Church believe that, names being names and there being nothing in a name, all it matters is for humans to feel comfortable with the 'Christian' denomination to which they belong. How many 'Christians' know that 'there is no salvation outside the Church which is headed by the successor to Peter, the first 'Papa' or 'Pope'?

"We also knew that, starved spiritually and inclined to sin at the same time, humans would always be tempted to grasp at anything that promised quick results. We here in the Underworld had never had any doubt that humans would be easy prey for our schemes for those reasons - and we have been proved right!

"It is pretty obvious to us at any rate that it doesn't take very much for spiritually starved humans to become (if you will excuse the vulgar expression) dumb asses as well! And they end making the Deliverer a liar! And so, to day, there are those humans who call themselves 'Orthodox followers of the Deliverer' who will tell you that, when the time comes for them to cross to the other side of the gulf that separates the living from the dead, they will be accosted by a Deliverer who tell them: 'Well done, good and faithful followers of mine who upheld the faith of my Orthodox Church which I constructed on a Rock called Peter!' According to those humans who call themselves 'Mormon followers of the Deliverer', He will say: 'Well done, good and faithful followers of mine who upheld the faith of my Mormon Church which I constructed on a Rock called Peter!' And, according to those humans who call themselves 'Baptist followers of the Deliverer', He will say: 'Well done, good and faithful followers of mine who upheld the faith of my Baptist Church which I constructed on a Rock called Peter!' But, according to those humans who call themselves 'Lutheran followers of the Deliverer', He will say: 'Well done, good and faithful followers of mine who upheld the faith of my Lutheran Church which I constructed on a Rock called Peter!' Anglicans, Catholics, Calvinists - you name it - will make the Deliverer continue lying to the world and proclaiming *them* and them alone as His true followers! In other words, humans make the Deliverer a worse liar than even I, the Father of Lies! Such dumb asses! It is just so incredible!

"They even make Him lie about that 'Rock called Peter' because after all is said and done, that 'Rock called Peter' ends up being anything but a rock!"

The mother of the children of Zebedee

"Now, because there are spiritually starved hordes looking for easy ways out of their bind, it doesn't mean that the Deliverer is going to change His *modus operandi* to accommodate them. He didn't do it for the mother of the children of Zebedee, and He is not about to do it for moderns who are looking for short cuts to heaven and/or special treatment. The Deliverer actually used that classic case of a misguided human who was expecting Him to bend the rules and promise to reserve the two choicest seats at the heavenly banquet (the seat immediately to the right and to the left of the Son of Man) for her dearest beloved to make one thing absolutely clear. Those special seats were not for Him to allocate. Doing that was the prerogative of His Father.

"It was that same Father whose divine will the Deliverer sought to do from day one; the same Father to whom the Deliverer cried as He sweated blood in the Garden of Eden saying: 'If it be thy will, take the cup away from me...'

"Not wanting to be a witness to the good woman collapsing and dying from a heart attack right there in front of Him, the Deliverer stopped at informing her that those special seats at the divine banquet were not His, but His Father's to give away. To be saved, her sons, like every other descendant of Adam and Eve and for whom He had come to be the 'Second Adam', needed to 'believe in Him'. If they did that, His Father in heaven, who so loved the world that He gave His only beloved Son so that those who believed in Him would be saved, would do what He had to do!

"You must be naive if you do not believe that the mother of the children of Zebedee would not have died of a heart attack if the Deliverer had turned to her and said something like this:

'Ma'am, you love James and John so much that you would be prepared to lay down your life for them - if, let us say, a hungry maneater turned up in your home and threatened them, you would prefer to let the animal have you rather than them for its lunch wouldn't you? Now, many are called, but few are chosen. And look, I have invited your sons, James and John, to follow me - yes, that is what I told them. I asked them to leave their boats and to follow me. Actually, I would like them to be not just my disciples, but my apostles! And, woman, you've got to understand what this means.

'As my apostles, they are going to be exposed to the wolves, and they must needs drink of the cup that I myself have to drink as I go about doing my Father's will. I am asking James and John to join me even though this means that, in the eyes of the priests and Pharisees and the powers that be, they are actually going to be terrorists who are marked for liquidation. Look, James, who also happens to be my first cousin, will meet with a gruesome fate at the hands of these folks. He will be put death with the sword! As for John, he too must be prepared to drink the cup I drink and be baptized with the baptism I am baptized with.

'Woman, it is tough enough for my brother humans to believe in me so that they may be saved in accordance with the will of my Father. It is going to be tougher, much tougher, for James and John whom I am inviting to be my apostles along with the fisherman, Peter, and others- if they succeed in sticking with me all the way, that is. Now, this is going to be a little tricky. It is going to be an uphill struggle because James and John will never make it on their own! At least they are not like Peter. He has already been acting like the Tempter on a couple of occasions. Can you imagine that he has been trying to dissuade me from doing the will of my Father? He has been trying to stop me from heading to Jerusalem where I have to meet my own gruesome death in fulfilment of prophecies of the Old Testament.

'But do not misunderstand me. Peter is still one of a kind. While some of the multitudes believe that I am 'John the 'Baptizer', and others say I am either Elijah or one of the old prophets who is risen again, when I asked my disciples the other day 'But who do you say that I am?', it was Peter, not John or James, who answered without hesitation, 'The Christ of God'!

'Now, woman…it is in Jerusalem, on Mt. Golgotha to be exact - the place of the skulls - where I am going to die and then rise up again in glory, taking Adam and Eve, Cain, Abel, the whole shoot from the place where they have been detained by the Enemy to heaven with me. That is what it is meant by the Son of Man taking the sting out of death.

'You understand that the redemption of the human race depends on this trip to the Eternal City, and it is also in Jerusalem that I will commission my Church. It is there that the Comforter will descend on my apostles, including James and John, and give them the strength to be fishers of men.

'You might not have heard, but the other day I had to scream at Peter. I actually called him Satan, and told him to get behind me! I know you tried to give your children a good upbringing - and you can see the difference it makes. But I am already finding these fellows to be something else. Now, in the same breath as they are telling me to find a hideout in the hills of Samaria or some other such place - a cave where I am supposed to hide because it is an open secret that, in the eyes of the priests and Pharisees, I am a terrorist who has a price on my head to boot. Peter, along with these sons of yours, keeps swearing that he is not the type who can abandon a friend who also happens to be his brother and Master.

'Peter keeps saying that he will stay with me through thick and thin. But he is obviously a weakling, and it pains me to think that he will deny me and will swear that he does not know me ever so many times! And he will do so especially when I most need someone to stay and comfort me - when I need someone to stand up and scream, and tell the world that the Word through whom all that exists came into being and also the Son of Man and the Deliverer is no vile criminal. That it is Him that is being spat upon, falsely accused, scourged, mocked, and crowned with thorns, despised, abused and beaten, and about to be nailed to the cross and crucified as a terrorist; and, above all, when I am abandoned by all those you now see flocking to see the miracles I perform. Look woman, it is going to be hard enough for me to get your sons to let the Holy Ghost lead them where they themselves on their own would rather not go! But I want you to also understand that Peter, not John or James, is the rock on which I will build my church.

'And so, are you still pining for those seats - the one to my right and the other to my left - for your boys? Do you still want James and John to continue in my company? If they do decide to heed my call, they can be sure to find themselves sidelined as vile criminals and terrorists as well; and they definitely will suffer unjustly for my sake. And for them to be anywhere near me at the heavenly banquet, James and John are going to have to give up a great deal more! You, woman - you sure are very possessive about these sons of yours. But remember what I told the crowd the other day. To have your sons, you have to loose them first!

'And if you yourself want to remain in my company - if you want to be saved and have eternal life - you have to be prepared to lose your life and to accept unfair treatment for my sake. You have to learn to turn the other cheek every time you are slapped! But forget it if you think you are going to make me change my modus operandi.

'Just remember one thing - Adam and Eve and all humanity had lost it! They were finished... *kaput*! Have you ever stopped and tried to imagine how offensive the iniquities of men are to me and to my Father? Have you ever stopped to reflect on the fact that, since the fall of Adam and Eve from grace, excepting for my beloved Mother Mary, all humans are born into original sin and all the censequences that flow from it? Add to that the fact that humans not only are inclined to wickedness; but, on their own, without the help of the graces I will merit in due course through obedience to my Father in heaven, they are incapable of doing anything that is virtuous! And then they are so easily scandalized - they so easily lose all hope; and they despair when they witness fragrant violations of the human rights of dear ones - violations that are committed with what appears to be total impunity!

'It behoved me, the Son of Man and Author of Life, designated by my Father in heaven to be high priest according to the order of Melchizedek, in all things to be myself like unto you my human brethren, that I may become the merciful and faithful priest before my Father, and that I may be a propitiation for the sins of human. My incarnation was as the Second Adam, in holiness and without sin, the offspring whereof inherit everlasting life and fellowship with my Father. Now, all who look to the Father's Son in faith as His disciples are received with Him, covered by His righteousness!

'Look - it is not my style to cause robbery victims to win lottery tickets just because they have been robbed and are in need…

'Think ye that peace I came to give in the earth? No, I say to you, but rather division…He who loves father or mother more than me is not worthy of me; and he who loves son or daughter more than me is not worthy of me. And he who does not take his cross and follow after me is not worthy of me. He who has found his life will lose it, and he who has lost his life for my sake will find it.

'Woman, my method of operation must take all of these things into account, and will remain mysterious to men. I will teach you how to pray to my Father in heaven. And after you master the '*Pater Noster*', it won't mean that you won't suffer. Praying will merely arm you so you can withstand suffering and disappointments and the abuse that you will suffer for my sake - and will also keep you clear of the whiles of Satan. And, I tell you the truth, unless you eat my flesh and drink my blood, you have no life in you. For I come to Earth as a sacrificial lamb!

'And forget it completely if you too want to set up your own reformed church in competition with my ecclesia, my Mystical Body - just in case you are thinking that, may be, you and your sons can be my followers, and still avoid the tears and pain that go with it - the cross! Don't even dream of a seat at the divine banquet table if you want to continue to be self-willed. And certainly not if you want to be one of those who are prepared to use my temple for commerce! On my dead body…!'

'But Ma'am, this I will tell you. Even though the seats to my right and to my left in the kingdom of heaven are not mine to give, I have invited both James and John to become fishers of men. It is accordingly my desire to have them both share in my priesthood. I want them to become instruments for dispensing to humans the divine graces that I will merit through my obedience to my Father in heaven. I will dispatch them into the world to spread the message of the

Deliverer who was crucified and died according to the scriptures, rose from the dead, and became glorified! And when they enter a town in which they are not welcome, they shall go into its streets and say: *Even the dust of your town that clings to our feet we wipe off against you. Nevertheless know this, namely that the kingdom of God has come near.*

'The faith of humans in the existence of my Father - the Almighty and also infinitely loving Prime Mover - springs from the awareness by humans that, while they weren't in existence at a given moment, the next moment they now not only did indeed exist, but they did so through the gratuitous act of that tell-tale Prime Mover who is none other than my Father in heaven.

'And I said *infinitely loving*. Yes, infinitely Good! My Father in Heaven didn't need you, your sons or any of the other creatures He brought into existence. He deigned to create all of you all the same, in His Own Image and likeness, and He endowed you all with an intellect and a free will. He did so well knowing that, once grace with those faculties, His creatures became capable of revolting against Him! After Adam and Eve sinned and were cast out of Paradise, in a demonstration of His infinite love, my Father in Heaven promised them and the rest of humankind a Deliverer. My Father so loved the world, that he give his only begotten Son, that whosoever believeth in Him, may not perish, but may have life everlasting.

'The Son of Man is now among you and, a mere statistic in the eyes of the world, He will be disowned by His own. A Second Adam to the fight, in an act that requires an infinite fountain of love, the Son of Man offers Himself as a sacrificial lamb for the salvation of all who believeth in Him, the first-fruits of them that sleep, and a bridge the gap between heaven and earth. And also so that you humans may now see my Father face to face in beatific vision!

'But it can only be those who *believe* in the Son of Man. That is because, molded in my Father's image and likeness and endowed with an intellect and a free will, He cannot force you to believe in His Son. You may recall that not long ago, I let folks walk away from Eternity Life - the folks who looked in themselves and decided that could never feed on my body and my blood! Your fathers did eat manna in the wilderness, and are dead. I am the living bread which came down from heaven: if any man eat of this bread, he shall live for ever: and the bread that I will give is my flesh, which I will give for the life of the world. Verily, verily, I say unto you, except ye eat the flesh of the Son of man, and drink his blood, ye have no life in you. Whoso eateth my flesh, and drinketh my blood, hath eternal life; and I will raise him up at the last day! When the time comes, some will say, 'Sir, I knew that you were a hard man, harvesting where you did not sow, and gathering where you did not scatter seed, so I was afraid, and I went and hid your talent in the ground. See, you have what is yours.' But no one will be able to say that he/she wasn't afforded the graces they needed to prevail.

'Once in existence, as humans realize that things around them change and do so in time, they also become aware instinctively that, even though created *in the Prime Mover's Image* unlike the beasts of the Earth, their existence *on Earth* is a timed one. This is so regardless of whether they openly acknowledge it or not. It cannot escape them that the important fact is not so much the fact that they now exist in that *temporal* habit on earth as the fact that they can bedevil their own eternal life by not conducting themselves as befits human beings. It is why humans know that an act they are contemplating is conscionable or not.

'Humans have an instinctive inkling of these things in the exact same way they instinctively reach out for grub when they feel hunger gnawing at their middle. Humans are loath to see their own existence on earth, albeit one that is timed, prematurely ended by virtue of being created in the Image of an eternal Prime Mover, their hunger for a life with Him in eternity notwithstanding. And when they start conspiring to do so, they know instinctively that they commit a crime, and one that is not just sordid, but a crime against humanity itself - and by extension against the Son of Man and also Second Adam!

'And that is so if only because they were doing unto other humans something that they would not have wished done unto themselves. Had it happened that humans, created in the Image and endowed by the Prime Mover with the spiritual faculties of the reason and free will, were incapable of grasping these things, suffice it to say that this would have reflected somewhat poorly on my Father in Heaven and the Word through Whom all things that are and ever will be come into existence.

'It is immaterial whether humans commit such deeds in secret or in broad daylight. This is immaterial because, when the timed existence in the perpetrators runs its course, the way they conducted themselves during their pilgrimage on earth must come back to haunt them. And nothing can be more haunting to a human than crimes committed by that human against its own. Souls that commit such sordid deeds are haunted and unable to rest in peace throughout all of eternity!

'And with all the death and destruction that has been engineered by humans since Adam and Eve sinned, such murderous souls, you can be sure, are not a few but many…a myriad, countless!

'For those brother and sister humans at the receiving end - the victims - their peculiar circumstances and struggles for survival - struggles that they could not face or endure without the assistance of the graces merited by the Son of Man - constitute the *crosses* they must needs carry. They are struggles that in time cause these souls to join the Son of Man in imploring His Father saying: *Pater si vis transfer calicem istum a me verumtamen non mea voluntas sed tua fiat* (Father, if thou wilt, remove this chalice from me: but yet not my will, but thine be done).

'Woman, wherefore, I say to thee and to all my brother and sister humans: Come unto me, all ye that are weary and heavy laden, and I will refresh you. Let not your hearts be troubled. Believe in God; believe also in me. In my Father's house are many rooms. If it were not so, would I have told you that I go to prepare a place for you? And if I go and prepare a place for you, I will come again and will take you to myself, that where I am you may be also. And you know the way to where I am going.

'And look - you brother and sister humans were created in the Image of My Father for a reason. And the Son of Man came down from heaven because humans are fashioned in my Father's Image. He was able to take up his human nature because humans *are* made in that Image.

'The kingdom of heaven is like to an householder, who went out early in the morning to hire laborers into his vineyard. And having agreed with the laborers for a penny a day, he sent them into his vineyard. And going about the third hour, he saw others standing in the market place idle. And he said to them: Go you also into my vineyard, and I will give you what shall be just. And they went their way. And again he went out about the sixth and the ninth hour, and did in like manner. But about the eleventh hour he went out and found others standing, and he saith to them: Why stand you here all the day idle? They say to him: Because no man hath hired us. He saith to them: Go you also into my vineyard.

'And when evening was come, the lord of the vineyard saith to his steward: Call the laborers and pay them their hire, beginning from the last even to the first. When therefore they were come, that came about the eleventh hour, they received every man a penny. But when the first also came, they thought that they should receive more: and they also received every man a penny. And receiving it they murmured against the master of the house, saying: These last have worked but one hour, and thou hast made them equal to us, that have borne the burden of the day and the heats. But he answering said to one of them: Friend, I do thee no wrong: didst thou not agree with me for a penny? Take what is thine, and go thy way: I will also give to this last even as to thee. Or, is it not lawful for me to do what I will? is thy eye evil, because I am good? So shall the last be first, and the first last. For many are called, but few chosen.

'I am the vine; you the branches: he that abideth in me, and I in him, the same beareth much fruit: for without me you can do nothing.

'Not everyone who says to me, Lord, Lord, will enter the kingdom of heaven, but the one who does the will of my Father who is in heaven. On that day many will say to me, 'Lord, Lord, did we not prophesy in your name, and cast out demons in your name, and do many mighty works in your name?' And then will I declare to them, 'I never knew you; depart from me, you workers of lawlessness.

'But woe to you scribes and Pharisees, hypocrites; because you shut the kingdom of heaven against men, for you yourselves do not enter in; and those that are going in, you suffer not to enter…Does any of this make sense?'

"Yah…I tell yah!"

Mjomba was surprised that, in spite of the Deliverer's dire words to the Mother of the children of Zebedee, the devil still appeared to discern some sort of victory for the forces of evil from the hypothetical exchange. But that did not stop Mjomba from continuing to record the thoughts of the evil Diabolos unquestioningly.

"This is a victory that even we who are banished for ever from the sight of the Prime Mover and Almighty One must find a moment to savor! But even as we celebrate - or (to be more precise) attempt to celebrate - we unfortunately have this fear that these misguided souls who could make a huge contribution to the Work of Redemption of the Holy Church if only they could get over the blues, pray to be worthy recipients of the gifts of faith, charity and wisdom that could pave the way for their acceptance of the Church's teachings and eventual return to the fold, might some day abandon their egos and do just that.

"And we, of course, know that when a 'separated brother' or 'separated sister' embraces Catholicism, he/she usually ends up valuing his/her faith far more than those who are Catholics from birth and who easily fall for the temptation to take their religion for granted as a consequence.

"You might therefore be surprised that, although we ourselves chose to make the Pit our dwelling place by mounting the rebellion against Him-Who-Is-Who-Is, we even then still pray to Him! And, as you might have guessed, the one thing we pray for unceasingly is that the misguided 'brethren', exercising their freedoms - 'freedom to choose', 'freedom of worship', and above all 'freedom of speech' - stay the course and remain die-hard schismatics and heretics in the eyes of the Holy Mother the Church (led by the successors to the apostles and guided by the Holy Ghost) to the very end!

"In any case, the fact is that being a separated brother or sister has long ceased to carry with it the stigma that was traditionally associated with that status. It used to be that as long as a misguided brother or sister did not recant the schism and/or heresy, it was understood that he/she would continue to be cut off from Holy Mother the Church by virtue of a solemn Papal edict of excommunication the Holy Father himself cannot revoke even if he wanted to. While the original, hand-scripted edict is preserved in a secret vault in the Vatican Library, copies are of course freely available on the Worldwide Web; so that the separated brothers and sisters of modern times, unlike their counterparts who belonged to earlier ages, cannot plead ignorance as the excuse for not taking steps to return to communion with the One and the Only Holy Church of the Prime Mover.

"What is more, the separated brothers and sisters could find all the information they needed to lead them back to the 'true faith' on that same worldwide web if they were seriously seeking the Truth. The Catechism of the Church, the papal encyclicals, the writings of the 'Doctors of the Church' including writings of the 'Early Fathers', the entire 'Summa Theologia' penned by Thomas of Aquin, and contemplative works by the likes of Thomas a Kempis - they are all there on the worldwide web.

"And, by the way, you can even find on Google this 'meditational work' by that Irishman Clive Staples Lewis - '*The Screwtape Letters*', yes, '*The Screwtape Letters*' - in which that cranky author has me spilling out my secrets about how I go about tempting humans! According to one reviewer, *The Screwtape Letters* is 'a masterpiece of reverse theology, giving the reader an inside look at the thinking and means of temptation'! Another one refers to it as a 'novel about spiritual warfare from a demon's point of view!' Gosh! This is so, so hilarious!

"The real 'problem' is, of course, not so much the fear that there might be a dearth of materials that can help a 'separated' brother or sister discern the errors and/or fallacies in the doctrines to which the brother or sister subscribes, as the fear that the brother or sister might not be able to continue feeling good (given what the other separated brothers and sisters would say) after he/she walked away from the 'charming', highly 'eloquent', and even 'charismatic' leaders of the breakaway churches.

"The problem was not that the separated brethren, after showing curiosity like everyone else about 'where the Deliverer lives', all of a sudden come upon insurmountable obstacles along the way; or that they inexplicably and for no fault of theirs loose sight the Deliverer and are then forced to turn back. The problem is that the separated brethren, like all the other curious people who eventually balk at becoming members of the sancta ecclesia (holy Church), follow the Deliverer only as long as His route is along a well beaten path, and also appears familiar; but they immediately conclude that if He lives where He appears to be leading them, He cannot possibly be the type of Deliverer they had in mind!

"I can tell you that we here in the Pit actually work very hard to make sure that those who witness the miracles performed by the Deliverer and initially want to know more about the miracle worker, become dismayed with Him as soon the path along which He is walking starts to veer off into the desert.

The devil is concerned

"As I have said before, I, Beelzebub, ring leader of the rebel 'ghosts' who made history by standing up to the Almighty One, am concerned about humankind. Let us face it - humans have been the poor forsaken children of Adam and Eve from the moment that first man and that first woman, following their natural inclination, were caught red handed as they tried to filch fruit from the Tree of Life in the Garden of Eden out of their curiosity. Since then, I have been their only friend and succour in time of need even though, being a creature like them and one that moreover is very susceptible to 'sin', I could not take credit for having brought sinful and sinning humans into existence.

"That is inevitable - I have no choice but to act as if I were their 'elder brother' or 'elder sister', and take them all under my wing, especially now that humankind and myself, along with the host of angels who joined me in my rebellion against the Prime Mover, are all accursed and in the same boat. You know the saying that friends in need become friends indeed! That is how strong the bond of friendship between the poor 'bastards' (which all humans became for all practical purposes after the fall) and us is.

"And while humans have this tendency of getting distracted and becoming oblivious to the sacrifices that my fellow demons and I continuously make to help them feel at home and consoled so that they don't go all bananas and become suicidal (which they would assuredly do with no one around to commiserate with them), we for our part will never abandon them.

The devil is spiritually dead

"Now, it is not as if we demons are immortal. I, Beelzebub and Father of Death, am not immortal! Nothing of the sort - I am mortal just like humans. In fact I sometimes can't help wondering about all the hullabaloo in which I am depicted as some sort of immortal ogre or 'terrorist' who even wields powers that are beyond the ordinary! Let us be clear - I am no demigod! And I am not the omnipresent, all knowing and callous super spirit (something like 'super man'!) I am depicted in the Book of the Apocalypse and in certain of the exegetical works that some fellow composed and published.

"It might be that my charming manners and charisma as I go about my business of tempting humans give that impression. But, in truth, I am a very ordinary creature - not very different from that Michael the Archangel who succeeded me as Chief of the Angelic Host. I mean, you could even argue that I am 'dead' already - a spiritual corpse!

"I do not have a brain (as I do not possess a body); and I cannot therefore say that I am as brilliant as Einstein when it comes to conducting experiments involving the laws of gravity. Had I been a human, I would probably be a midget!

"You, of course, know that we pure spirits, unlike humans whose nature comprises a bag of chemicals or physical 'body' and a soul, don't come in different sizes or shapes either; and, apart from the fact that I was very gifted (more or less like Michael who is admittedly my rival and also nemesis), there is nothing otherwise that distinguishes me from the other demons.

"Now, God the Father, God the Son and God the Holy Ghost share the same divine nature. This is in much the same way you humans all share the same human nature. But those of us who are brought into existence as pure spirits do not share a nature - we, each of us, have our individual 'ghost kind' (or, if you like, 'nature') which we got at the moment we were willed by the Almighty One into existence - or given each one our distinctive 'breath of life' if that is the way you want to put it.

Good Guys, Bad Guys

"To get back to the point I was trying to make before I got diverted, I, Satan, will never abandon humans - not for any reason! And even when they become faint-hearted (which is normal in the heat of any battle!) and decide to throw in the towel so that they may become reconciled with the Prime Mover through the merits of the Son of Man and now also Judge, the vast army of demons with myself at its helm will never, never stop pursuing humans with the aim of keeping our relationship intact. Look, chums - humans will always be able to count on our constancy and our support.

"In that respect, we demons are very different from Michael and the guardian angels (two guardian angels apiece to be exact) that watch over humans. I doubt that they can muster the patience that is required when dealing with humans to the same degree we of the underworld do - and it is the reason good souls will always be left to suffer at the hands of the wicked ones who will steal, have no remorse about twisting the truth to their advantage as long as they can get away with it, torturing, maiming and even killing the innocent at our instigation. Is there any wonder why the murderers (the ones who know their job and do it to my script) always get away, but the victims never do?

"Need I, therefore, say any more to illustrate why the bad guys have always been winning and will continue to so do until this god-forsaken and goddamned world grinds to a grisly end! And when the bad guys win, the good guys must needs suffer! And there is your key to the mystery of pain and suffering - if you were seriously searching for one.

"In order not to suffer, one must ally oneself closely with the bad guys and us, and effectively become a bad guy by virtue of being an accessory to the damnable deeds of the original bad guys. And, of course, bad guys will always stand by each other out of loyalty to me, the Arch-Ddevil and exemplar of bad guys. And you must know by now that bad guys can never do any wrong. If a bad guy falls foul of any rule or regulation, that rule or regulation quite obviously must be so inequitable as to become null and void automatically!

"That is the attitude we want the bad guys, following our example, to espouse; for the simple reason that the bad guys must always be seen as the good guys, and the good guys as the bad guys. And, under the guise of defending things like free speech and liberty, the bad guys must always thwart efforts by the good guys to change unjust laws and social structures that are cause suffering to make them more just and equitable.

"But when a guy who is in the enemy camp - and that is any guy who has been marked by the bad guys as 'roguish' (because that guy has control over resources the bad guys deem critical to their 'security' and well-being, and who has shown a reluctance to surrender them and walk away) - can be made to look as though he/she is in breach of those rules or regulations, the situation becomes reversed. The 'enemies of the people', and definitely the 'rogues', must be brought to heel immediately; and the means for doing that cannot be dialogue. It must be awe and shock inspiring force, because that is the only language knaves and rogues understand!

"And now, if it should happen that the knaves or rogues who are being sought take or are suspected to have taken refuge in some safe house that is located in the middle of a densely populated area, it is always perfectly O.K. to level the whole place with any amount of TNT that can do the job. And if it should happen that the rogues succeed in making their gateway in the nick of time, and all those eliminated in the 'security operation' are innocent, so long as the victims are not allies, such an action is always perfectly all right.

"It couldn't even be portrayed as a 'terrible mistake that is to be regretted'. I just said that the bad guys are incapable of doing any wrong. That is something you have to take on faith even if it sounds completely unbelievable. If anything, the 'collateral damage' must be blamed on the rogues and their totally unimaginable habit of using women and children as human shields. And, of course, those allies who are in the media business have a responsibility to do whatever they can to minimize the fall-out and especially the bad publicity. It is at precisely such times that they must depict the rogues in the worst possible light as callous individuals who are insensitive to the safety and wellbeing of women and children!

"As you may already have guessed, the allies in the media do not have to be persuaded to become involved. This is because security operations by their nature are terrific for the bottom line in the media business. What with the blood-curdling scenes and the opportunity availed to the embedded media allies for filing exclusive stories from the frontline when regime changes and things like that engineered by the bad guys are under way, not to mention the chance to snap exclusive 'pics' (isn't that what you call them?) of the grisly scenes, and the ratings that come with real-time coverage of news stories in those situations, things could never be better for the media allies.

"The allies will, moreover, not be exposed to the dangers of 'stray' tank cannon fire and things of that nature which 'independent' journals have to be on the look out for. In any event, the chance to put a positive spin on the goings-on at the front line, and the opportunity to transform any 'terrible mistakes that are to be greatly regretted' into sordid tales focusing on the rogues cannot but boost the ratings - and the revenues.

"And if you think that there will be an outcry from the rest of the world, you are wrong. There will be hardly a ruffle from all those 'good' and 'upright' people in the whole wide world - the good and upright folks whom those targeted by the security operations normally expect to spring to their help as a matter of course in such situations if they should be subjected to acts of gross injustice from any quarter!

"But, of course, years later - when history has been written - there will be all sorts of people pouting and attempting to rebut the accusations of the shocking inaction and/or deafening silence of individuals who could have influenced the course of events by merely opening their mouths to publicly condemn the gross acts of injustice perpetrated by us bad guys. Others at that time will be trying in vain to deny the plain and patently undeniable evidence of complicity. The denials will encompass deplorable policies now in place according to which it is O.K. for 'super powers' to invade 'rogue nations' that stubbornly cling to their right of self-determination and independence, and according to which everything, including the option to employ WMD (weapons of massive destruction) against the rogue nations, 'stays on the table'.

"But none of that really matters in the long run. This is because of the operation of a Law of Nature according to which overbearing and belligerent 'axis powers' of today must themselves invariably fall victim to the turmoil they help to foment in the world a dozen or so years down the road if not earlier as is usually the case. The once super-powerful nations, with power hungry but extremely short-sighted megalomaniacs at the helm, invariably become eclipsed by other emerging axis powers, also with power thirsty and extremely short-sighted megalomaniacs at the helm, assuring a repetition of history through the ages as the world grinds towards the inevitable Armageddon.

"You see…when a superpower is not engaged in prosecuting a war in one part of the globe (we in the underworld work hard to make sure that the super power is caught up in several conflicts at the same time), it will be mired in a conflict of one sort or another in some other part of the globe as a rule. The superpower will always find some excuse to do this for any number of reasons. The incumbent regime frequently needs the nation to be at war as a means of clinging on to power. This is due to the fact that, with the exception of peaceniks who will always remain a fringe group, in times of war the populace generally answers the call to show 'patriotism' and remain united behind the regime of the day. But it is also a proven fact that as wars get under way, the war matériel sector of the economy, which is responsible for supplying the war fighting machine with equipment, fighting apparatus and supplies, stimulates the economy and fosters 'inventions' that eventually become adapted to non-military uses as wars wind down.

"And one reason allies of the super power pitch in to fight along side the super power (if you did not know), even though the wars might be unpopular at home, is to assure that they stay abreast with regard to the changing technologies for mounting the assaults on fellow humans and despatching them.

"The fact of the matter is that, like me here in Gehenna, super powers thrive on conflict, and they even conjure up pretexts for mounting assaults on nations whose resources they had been eying for sometime. This is a virus that I long ago succeeded in transmitting to humans. The only different between humans and me is that I know when to desist and not tackle an opponent who might end up being too much for me. Infatuated with the loot, regimes in the once formidable nation soon stop thinking aright. As so often happens, before long, the greed that drives humans starts to blind them to the dangers that lurk in the uncertainties of war campaigns. And that is how the baton is passed on as once ostensibly invincible nations succumb to greed and become overextended, and some other emerging superpower, frequently none other than the nation that had been targeted for destruction, steps in to take over the mantle of Super Power of the World.

"Now, as the Father of Death, I would be very remiss if I didn't take full advantage of this insatiable human greed to promote my agenda. Just as the emergence of those so-called super powers is not an accident, it is no accident that the small cliques that hold the reigns of power in those countries are not merely imbued with lust for power and unbridled greed, but they all operate on the motto that greed (which is itself equivalent to idolatry) is good!

"We here in the underworld have worked very hard to ensure that greed and possessiveness, the silent forces behind all human conflicts, are actually touted by those who call the shots in human society as virtues that are essential for economic and industrial growth. It is a signal achievement that also speaks to our ingenuity and hard work that even as super powers of the day are winding down their activities in conflict zones where they had found themselves whipped by foes whose ingenuity and resilience they had grossly underestimated, plans for forays into other parts of the globe and new battle zones in search of resources that are deemed essential for maintaining the superpower status will already be on the drawing boards.

"The important thing for us is not that super powers come and go, but that humans, fashioned in the image of the Prime Mover, die at the hands of their fellow humans. And so, as you yourself see, the saying that there is no rest for the wicked, far from being confined to us demons, perhaps applies even more to you humans!

"I am Beelzebub, and I will tell you that humans are very slow to learn that actions of stupid fools always come back to haunt them. But, for now, the 'priests and Pharisees of the New Testament' will be going about their business of ministering to the spiritual needs of the Prime Mover's flock as usual - unless, of course, the upheaval or slaughter occurs on their door step; or rippling shock waves from misfired WMD cause precious frescos in the church building, cathedral or basilica to come tumbling down on their heads.

"Members of the clergy of the different faiths will be presiding over weddings and over the other rituals of the liturgical year peculiar to those faiths as they fall due as if the same peace they see reigning inside the precincts of those churches, cathedrals and basilicas reigns among all the Prime Mover's people the 'World Over'! They will be acting as if I, Satan and bad guy *par excellence*, and the forces of darkness that I lead, were defeated and put out of commission long ago, and have consequently been rendered completely innocuous - as if, neutralized, my troops and I no longer possess the ability to tempt you humans! As if you could now search the whole wide world, and not happen upon any human who could be classified as a 'bad guy'!

"The modern day priests and Pharisees will be conducting their services on the 'Day of the Sabbath', and they will give their pep talks (or 'homilies' as you call them) from their pulpits, in the course of which they will rail against me (the 'devil') as usual. But they will utter 'nary a word' (as they say) about either the raging battle between Good and Evil - the real battle as a matter of fact - or about the terrible acts of injustice perpetrated by the bad guys under my command under their very noses. And you shouldn't be surprised if, when they open their mouths to allude to or to 'condemn' the on-going acts of injustice, they do so very selectively, making sure that they did not offend the 'bad guys' they are in the habit of dining and wining with - the wining and dining they do while completely oblivious to the fact that Stephen and the apostles Peter and Paul died the way they did because they made it clear that they could not countenance duplicity and injustices committed, not just in the Church backyards, but in the whole wide world!

"To be assured of this result, the advice I, as Chief Bad Guy, give to my minions is that they not just be regular Church goers, but that they make a point of arriving early, and taking their seats in the front pews. How do you like that!

"It is because of this sort of malaise in the Church - this double dipping or desire to have the best of both worlds - that my troops and I have succeeded in getting 'bad guys' to enjoy the status they enjoy. It is because of the almost universal indifference to the wickedness that exists in the world on such a grand scale, and the lying and trickery that has characterized human relations since time immemorial and as a direct consequence of fall of man, that my troops and I have succeeded in getting service in those parts of government that are devoted to killing to be regarded by the citizenry as the most honorable, and the killing of humans by fellow humans in the course of conducting 'security operations' against so-called insurgents and terrorists, and in the course not of preventive but preemptive strikes against so-called rogue nations as patriotic service of the highest order - almost as if doing so was necessary to appease the gods!"

It was at that point, as Mjomba worked away on his thesis with the help of the Tempter and Evil One, that he thought Beelzebub, the Father of Death, had to be joking! It was just inconceivable that Satan could be mouthing the things Mjomba was hearing - or was it, perhaps, his own ears that were playing him a trick? It couldn't possibly be that the devil was saying the things he, Mjomba, was hearing!

To the extent that every human was created in the Image, and consequently could not be 'liquidated' as was generally thought, and also to the extent that every created human had one and only one 'tour of duty' on earth (or life to live) before heading off to his/her eternal reward or punishment, it was foolish for humans to even try to imagine that cutting short the life of a fellow human could serve as a solution to any problems they faced. Therefore, any one who could mouth the things that were coming out of the Evil One's mouth deserved the label of fearless hero - someone who was ripe for canonization! It was, Mjomba told himself, inconceivable that the devil was giving expression to things that Mjomba had been longing to hear from the lips of churchmen in vain!

Mjomba was resigned to the fact that he was living in an unreal world as he settled back to hear out the Evil One. He knew very well that he was dealing with the Master Trickster, and did not stop wondering if the Prince of Darkness did not have a dirty trick behind those pious platitudes. But he had concluded that the only way to find out was to pretend that he himself was a fool, and to hear the rest of what Satan had to say. And so he continued to scribble as fast as he could so he wouldn't miss any of the points that the Evil Ghost was making.

"And we have, indeed, succeeded in making killing of humans by fellow humans on any pretext a great virtue so long as the victim is not 'one of their own' - almost as if doing so was necessary to appease the gods! And, last but not least, we have succeeded in promoting the idea that might is right, and that wrongs, real or perceived, must be settled here on earth and through the use of force; and that life after death is a myth! It is a hallmark of our success that, in spite of what humans say publicly, everyone, with the sole exception of the few hermits and monks who have consecrated themselves to lives of prayer and poverty and stay out of the limelight, accepts the proposition that the drive, fuelled by human greed, to amass wealth using any means under the guise of promoting 'thrift'; the proposition that 'might makes right'; and also that things like slavery, imperialism, and the drive by those nations that have the wherewithal to try and realize their ambitions of global dominance are not only permissible in a world in which human selfishness shapes the destiny of nations, but a mark of greatness.

Meaning of being a "Winner"

"And don't you misunderstand me now, and then say later that I lied to you. By winning, I do not mean achieving self-actualization and ending up in heaven. That is out of question. Also - and this is even more important - by bad guys I do not mean those so-called terrorists who languish in secret jails around the globe for years, in leg chains, but have never been convicted of any crime in any court of law and (I might add) with not a whimper from the rest of the world. By the way, by 'bad guys' I do not mean the Dalai Lama; or Pope John Paul whom we tried very hard but unsuccessfully to trip up, and whose clamor for a world in which there was peaceful co-existence among humans, just before he went to his eternal rest, really hurt our cause!

"And by 'bad guys', I definitely do not mean people like Mother Theresa who could never harm a fly! And by 'bad guys', I certainly do not mean those poor chaps who are conscripts in the military and don't even know what the heck they are supposed to be doing there or why!

"First of all, the Deliverer (if you refer to the 'Book') did not call upon the legions of angels to stop the priests and Pharisees, and the sleazy Pontius Pilate, or the double-talking King Herod Agrippa, who were conspiring to murder him under the guise of ridding the world of a most dangerous 'terrorist'. In the same way, the Deliverer will not call upon his faithful angels to come to the rescue of His people. Secondly (and don't you now try to put a spin on the Deliverer's words like so many folks do when they make themselves the 'deciders' and decide at will to interpret figuratively words He intended to be taken literally and vice versa when it suits them), when Peter tried to cut down the trooper who was leading the assault on the Deliverer in the Garden of Gethsemane, he was told by the Deliverer in no uncertain terms that those who lived by the sword died by the sword!

"And, by the way (and I beg your pardon!), by bad guys I do not mean those poor chaps who languish on death row either! The Deliverer, who came to save sinners from eternal damnation, would without any doubt cause all those on death row to be freed. If the Deliverer believed in capital punishment, He wouldn't have come down from heaven to save any one. He would have left you humans to fight you wars and slaughter one another the way you have been doing since Cain murdered his brother Abel.

"And so, if you yourself do, and still think that you are a disciple of the Deliverer, think again! The 'good guys' who want to see those 'felons' liquidated in the gas chambers, on the electric chairs, under the guillotines, or by a hangman's noose, or in a volley of shots from the firing squad are obviously not the 'good guys' they claim to be after all!

"Just as the Deliverer ordered Peter to put away his sword, and then took the extraordinary step of re-attaching that mercenary's severed ear to make him whole again, the Deliverer would definitely advise any 'good guys' and 'good gals' out there who were ready to 'lend Him an ear' to 'put the gas chambers and the electric chairs and the guillotines and the hangmen and hangwomen's nooses, and the rifles and guns away! That would, of course, cause a lot of people to become unemployed; and the Deliverer would consequently be as unpopular a figure as anyone who attempted to break into the jails to free the poor chaps on death row to day!

"Was it any wonder then that the beginning of the end for the Deliverer on earth came when it did, namely shortly after He tricked the priests and Pharisees (who were using the harlot to trip him up) into drawing close to where he was scribbling their individual faults in the sand, and then watched them (with a faint smile on His sacred face) hasten away one by one in shame, until he was left alone with the woman they had wanted to see stoned to death?

"And if the Deliverer Himself was not ready to condemn those whom the priests and Pharisees wanted to see liquidated, who am I to condemn them. I guess it is because I am the evilest of evil creatures that I can understand why the Deliverer rescued Mary Magdalene - yes, the same Mary Magdalene who is now revered as 'Saint Mary Magdalene' - from imminent death.

"As for that marshal who had lost his ear to the butcher's knife that Peter had up until that moment been carrying with him wherever he went, I wouldn't advise you to waste any money on a wager as to whether that mercenary who had come to arrest the Deliverer on fabricated charges learnt his lesson or not. I will tell you that the bloody fool didn't because, as a rule, soldiers of fortune who get hurt in battle simply become more vicious and merciless - and more greedy too - because the only thing they learn from such an eventuality is that the stakes in the deadly game of 'kill or be killed' in which they are involved by choice are so high, it is either you who dies or the mercenary who dies! And soldiers of fortune don't quit until they make a buck or two or a semblance of fortune.

"Don't pray to that poor - and also unlucky - chap who was 'saved by the bell'. We have him safely here in Gehenna where he still pines for earthly riches, even though it is now two thousand years now since he crossed the gulf which separates the living from the dead. Even if he had been able to sneak back on earth and to get some of the booty he is permanently yearning for, it would never be of any use to him in this blasted hell of a place! The fellow is totally insane - just like his pals back on earth who dream of amassing riches as soldiers of fortune - those mercenaries who see nothing wrong with depriving wives of their husbands and husbands of their wives, and children of their parents, and parents of their sons and daughters. They are so dumb, they don't realize that they will never be able to take any of that stuff with them to the grave!

"I will also tell you as an aside that if you desist in claiming your pound of flesh as a result of the vindictiveness you feel, particularly if you have been a victim of one of those folks on death row, and yet know (as you now do) that the Church established by the Deliverer is against capital punishment, your sin now becomes heresy, and you stand condemned by your own stubborn refusal to forgive those who have wronged you. Know that you now are an ally and belong to our camp.

"And for those who play the part of executioner - the hangman who throws the hood over the head of the poor chap's head and then puts the noose around his/her head, or the member of the firing squad who pulls the trigger, or Dr. Death who administers the lethal injection or fastens the mask over the condemned person's head and connects it to the cylinder containing the deadly gas mixture, or the technician who keeps the guillotine or electric chair oiled and operates the switches on those murderous contractions - what will you say when you accost the victims of your illegal acts of murder? Illegal because no amount of 'legislation' can make an immoral act moral and moral, right let alone legal.

"It simply won't do, when you accost them on the other side of the gulf, to just say something like the following:

'Oh my God! This can't be true! It is the Deliverer I executed over and over again! This is really terrible! It can't be true that it was the Deliverer the Americans and their allies were also trying to eliminate with their adventures abroad! Oh, God! So it is actually the Word-become-flesh - true Man and true God - whom Caesar and other leaders of the so-called civilized societies pursued when they waged their colonial wars, and when they hunted the so-called barbarians, the Vietcong, the Mau Mau, Mandela, and other so-called terrorists and insurgents! So it was the Deliverer who was crucified all over again when the City of Bremen was carpet bombed, and Nagasaki and Hiroshima were bombed! So it is Him who is targeted when the strong and the proud inflict collective punishment on other humans in the name of Justice!

'Oh, alright, alright! I now get it. As members of the Church Triumphant, the victims of injustice necessarily bear this close resemblance to the Deliverer who became the Second Adam, a true brother of the forsaken Children of Adam and Eve, and also the Bread of Angels upon taking up His human nature! Suffering patiently, they unknowingly complete in their flesh what might be lacking in their Deliverer's affliction for the sake of His Mystical Body or *Sancta Ecclesia*. And He, for His part, identifies Himself completely with all suffering humans without exception, in addition to sanctifying their suffering; and it is this which explains your so very close resemblance to Him! I now understand what He meant when He said before His ascension into heaven that, upon receiving the Holy Spirit and Comforter, His disciples and He Himself would be as one!

'And guess what! As head of the Church Militant, He Himself has to be a 'terrorist' who is permanently locked in battle with the Evil Ghost. Yah, with *Diabolus Malus*...the evilest of evil creatures! This is because all the so-called good guys on Planet Earth have been co-opted by Beelzebub, the Father of Death. If they were not his minions, they would disavow killing and murder in the name of national security. They would be on the side of the Prime Mover, and not on the side of Caesar Augustus!

'And if I myself had been a decent guy during my sojourn on earth - if I had been caring about others or something like that - this knowledge would have come to me automatically, and I would have escaped perdition by living accordingly! But - Oh my! Oh my! You and all the folks I see waiting in line to take their seats at the Divine Banquet just look so much like the Deliverer, I am ashamed to speak my thoughts! I am ashamed to tell you what was on my mind when I despatched you and those other felons (that's what everyone on Death Row was referred to in 'Correct Speak'). But I have no choice now, and it is precisely these thoughts that are going to convict me now!

'Until I saw you looking so much like Him just now, I was going to tell you without any feelings of remorse whatsoever that I had to do it, Pal. I feel terrible shame saying it, but it was the only way I knew to put bread on the table! And to be frank with you, when I finished you off and certified you dead, all I was thinking about was my pay-check and the fact that I was helping to finally put away and rid the world for good of a felon! That it was cheaper to do that than to keep you behind bars in solitary confinement in a cage, and to feed and minister to you.

'And I certainly did not expect to bump into you again any where, and much less here of all places before the Son of Man and Judge. That was how faithless I was. I did not even think of you as someone who belonged to the humankind I knew. As far as I was concerned, you were you and I was I. We were two different creatures who happened to belong to the same human stock or 'look alike'! I knew I was human. But, well - as far as you being also a brother whose destiny and mine were intertwined by virtue of being descended from the same Adam and Eve, and by virtue above all of being fashioned in the image of the Word, and also having the Son of Man as our brother - I just never gave that a thought, brother!

'But above all, it didn't strike me at the time I was despatching you that I was also despatching the Deliverer who came down to earth to restore Life, and who took the sting out of 'Death' with His own death on the tree on Mt. Calvary. Look, I thought that even though you were human just like me, you belonged to the 'trash heap' all the same; and that you were trouble and good for nothing, and actually deserved to be put away - for ever!

'Believe me, I was so distracted by all the hullabaloo about being like the Joneses next door, and by my dreams of also striking it rich some day, if someone had screamed in my ears as I was despatching you that I was driving nails into the already bloodied hands and feet of the Deliverer, it would not have helped. I would not have batted an eye.

'Look, when I stared at your lifeless body after I had finished you off, and certified you dead, I remember saying to myself that there goes another one who will never be able to avenge my act of *legal* murder. Yes, deep inside me, I knew it was murder! Legal or illegal, it still *was* murder! Look, there is no circumstance in which it wouldn't have been murder if tables had been turned and *I* had been the one on that scaffolding.

'And, I mean - it could never be right to take the life of another creature who had the same features as you, breathed like you, had the same organs as you, and relied on the same system as yours to function.

'The fact that a felon had made a mistake however horrendous could never make the vengeful act of killing right. After all everybody, and especially those humans who referred to themselves as The Deciders, made mistakes - everyone except, perhaps, the pope when he was making his pronouncements *ex-cathedra*! And in the case of the successors to Peter, they themselves knew at least that it was not flesh and blood that *revealed* to them the things on which they made their *ex-cathedra* pronouncements, but the *Deliverer's Father* who was in heaven.

'As a Christian, my thoughts should have turned to the Deliverer at the time I was swinging the noose around your neck! That would have stopped me cold, and saved me from eternal damnation. But I did it; and the sight and smell of death eventually turned me into an atheist at the core.

'I stopped believing in life after death - or the resurrection! And, even though I continued going to church on Sundays (which I did to be like the other Joneses), privately I believed that while I myself was slated to also kick the bucket some day, the world would go on without end contrary to what preachers babbled about the end of the world being imminent. I had come to the conclusion that, even if life as we knew it on Planet Earth came to an abrupt end in a nuclear conflagration, new life forms would evolve from the ashes - as (I imagined) probably happened eons ago at the 'beginning of time'. My theory of evolution did not include any role whatsoever for a Prime Mover.

'And then I occasionally dilly-dallied with the thought that I was saving my victims a miserable existence on earth by 'putting them to rest' prematurely. I wouldn't otherwise have been able to sleep. But the same thought was obviously on the minds of residents of the White House, the Kremlin, Number 10 Downing Street, Palais Elyeece, and other places like that in which people never tired of dreaming up schemes to destabilize other hostile governments, looking for excuses to impose economic embargoes on so-called rogue regimes, were always busy engineering regime changes in different parts of the world in the course of which hundreds of thousands became marked for death by simply being labeled insurgents or terrorists, and things of that sort.

'Oh God! I allowed myself to be used to deny other humans their bread-winner, and in a manner that was so completely unnatural!'"

Meaning of "Victory of Good over Evil"

Mjomba knew by now that there was no creature that was more evil or dangerous than Beelzebub. It terrified him all the same to think that the Evil Ghost paid so much attention to the tiniest details. It also terrified Mjomba to think that, while it was Good that would eventually be victorious over Evil, there would obviously be wicked humans who would be eternally lost after freely choosing to be on the losing side. But those humans who chose to *believe in the Deliverer* would obviously be in line to celebrate the victory of Good over Evil with the now risen and enthroned Deliverer.

And so, victory of Good over Evil as Mjomba now understood it did not mean that humans who were created in the Image would not lose their souls eternally if they persisted in their wickedness (in much the same way angels who chose to join Lucifer in his damnable act of rebellion against the Prime Mover became transformed into demons). The fact that the Evil Ghost and his fellow demons were ejected from heaven, and wicked humans are cast into hell upon their judgement, all spoke to the victory of Good over Evil.

Mjomba was by now completely resigned to the fact that there would be descendants of Adam and Eve who, by their own choosing, would end up as *human* demons in hell. But the one thing that was on Mjomba's mind as he continued work on his thesis was that Satan and his fellow demons apparently needed company bad - the company the Evil One would be denied if humans, who had found themselves initially barred from Paradise following the fall of the First Man and the First Woman, one and all followed the Second Adam into heaven. The big question which Mjomba did not try to answer was why the evil Satan and the other fallen angels should crave for company! Thinking about how humans who only had the capacity to be wicked treated each other, Mjomba recoiled at the sort of things demons that had been convicted of evil things might be capable of doing to hapless humans who ended up in Gehenna with them. Whatever those things were, Mjomba positively did not want to know.

Regardless, it was clear that the only thing the devil, who knew that he had lost the battle the moment he himself was cast into Gehenna, looked to gain from his continuing efforts was some assurance that he would have company for himself and his fellow demons. But because such an outcome would be dependent primarily on the exercise of human free will, and would also be a direct result of judgement passed on the wicked humans by the victorious Deliverer, the devil himself knew that it wouldn't amount to much of a victory on his part. If anything, such an outcome would only serve to confirm the victory of Good over Evil as unrepentant *homines iniqui* (wicked humans) joined the unrepentant and already damned *diaboli mali* (evil demons).

And that in turn left no doubt at all about the high regard which the Prime Mover placed on the angels and humans whom He willed into existence - and also His high expectations for them. He had fashioned them in His own Image and endowed them with the spiritual faculties of reason and free will thereby; and He had no intention whatsoever of going back on His Word and denying them the liberty to use those faculties as *they* deemed fit. But He also apparently had no intention of removing the consequences of *evil* acts on the part of pure spirits (*evil* because pure spirits by their nature were quite clear from the outset regarding the consequences of what they were contemplating doing). And He, of course, had no intention of removing the consequences of *wicked* actions on the part of humans either (*wicked* as opposed to *evil* because humans, while in a position to discern right from wrong, needed to cooperate with divine grace to stay out of trouble).

Wicked actions of humans were inexcusable all the same because, in spite of *knowing* that the wicked things they were contemplating doing were unconscionable, humans deliberately *chose* to carry out the wicked actions all the same, and to blind themselves to the fact that there *we*re severe consequences for wicked actions. All of which reminded Mjomba, as he went on committing to paper the ideas he felt certain were originating from the Evil One, that the devil brought his extremely advanced grasp of the workings of the human mind to bear as he went about his evil work of tempting the descendants of Adam and Eve to ignore their clamor of their consciences, and hoped and even 'prayed' that they would succumb to his wiles and the temptations of the flesh.

Turkeys

"Alright - let us get back to the meaning of 'bad guy'. Actually, by bad guys, I mean those 'turkeys' who, from time immemorial and doing everything to my script, have been imbued with a messianic mission to reshape the world in a way that fit their vision, and whose sense of mission goes hand in hand with a singular belief in the efficacy of force. Cain was the first such turkey who cleaned out a sixth of the world's population (when he murdered Abel, his own sibling) as he set about implementing his 'Cain

Doctrine', but who, unfortunately for us, narrowly missed joining the party here in the Pit by repenting of his actions, handing Abel's widow all his ill-gotten property as compensation, and offering to be her servant for the remainder of his days on earth.

"But don't believe for one moment that all the turkeys who operate according to my script end up the same way. On the contrary...before going out to try and transform the world according to their designs, you should see the transformation that comes over them after I lead them up the mountain top, and especially after I show them the riches of the earth - the oil wells, gold mines, and even gold-domed palaces in far away lands - that I typically guarantee will be theirs for the taking provided they go down on bended knee and worship me, the Evil One!

"And why do I refer to them as 'turkeys'? It is because they go away from the mountain top with a totally changed mind-set. According to that mind-set, a starving man, who raids a rich man's home with a toy gun in hopes of coming away with a morsel of food, deserves capital punishment - or, at the very minimum, to spend the rest of his life in solitary confinement - if it should happen that the rich man suddenly succumbs to a heart attack at the sight of the toy gun.

"But, according to that same mind-set, they themselves go on to inherit an eternal reward after they have 'legally' bribed their way into positions of power; diverted the nation's resources into the development of efficient 'military' machines in stead of putting those resources to work for the *bonum commune*; and ensured, in the course of doing so, that those who helped them take over the Palais Elyeece, Number 10 Downing Street, the Kremlin, State House or whatever were richly rewarded.

"And of course their reward in the next life, according to that mind-set, will be multiplied a hundred-fold if they embark on foreign adventures aimed at securing for their countries control of the world's scarce resources under the pretext of taking the gospel message to the ends of the earth.

"Now, talking about 'solitary confinement', it doesn't seem as if there is any limit to the savagery that humans are capable of. I can tell you that there may be many dungeons here in hell, but none of the demons or lost souls who keep me company are in solitary confinement. The idea behind our efforts to get folks like you to disavow your heavenly inheritance and end up here is so that we have company - period.

"Keeping a creature that was created in the Image in solitary confinement is the same as asking that creature to vacate its shell and return to the nothingness from which it originally came. It is the cruellest thing you can do to a human who belongs to humankind and who automatically needs company. It is only you humans who could dream up that sort of punishment, and it speaks volumes about the extent to which you humans can be wicked.

"But you humans can be very funny! How do humans who make their living as 'executioners' - humans whose job it is to put fellow humans to death (in the same way butchers slaughter animals whose meat is destined for the dinner table) - ever sleep? The same applies to prison warders who make a living keeping watch over fellow humans who are confined in cages or 'cells'.

"These are things we demons find very hard to understand, even though we were instrumental in getting Adam and Eve to start having ideas - ideas that eventually led them to choose the path of perdition. Even though I am the Father of Death, I still wilt at the thought that humans have no scruples making their living as professional killers, jail waders, or as mercenaries or 'soldiers' as you call them!

"I can understand a human being a professional hunter of wild animals. But it boggles my demonic mind to think that creatures that are fashioned in the Image can choose to become 'hired guns' who are dedicated to mowing down their fellow humans in fabricated 'just' wars.

"Can you imagine what would happen if we demons were spending our time waging wars on our own kind - or on you humans? First of all, since we have a much better handle on technology than you stupid humans, the Deliverer wouldn't have found anyone left on Planet Earth to redeem when He showed up. The whole operation would have been dirty and quick. But well, as it is, we here in the Underworld prefer to have you humans do the dirty work for us.

"I am the devil - the very 'embodiment of evil' if you will - and I will tell you why humans who do these things to other humans are turkeys and screwed up! Because they listened to me, and genuinely believe that the commander-in-chief of a super power, who plans and executes what you call 'a preemptive strike' against a weakened and militarily defenceless but oil rich 'rogue state', for the purpose of assuring that his countrymen have unimpeded access to cheap sources of fuel and can continue to maintain their gas-guzzling lifestyles, deserves the title of statesman - and things like that!

"One has to be a complete nut - a complete idiot - to imagine that one can abet and/or be an accessory to things that amount to a culture of death - which is what projecting a super power's refurbished military's awe and shock generating power, without any regard to the inevitable loss of human lives resulting there from, or to the dire straights in which those who survive the onslaught will be left, amounts to - and get away with it with impunity! It is just ridiculous! The turkeys then get so comfy, they start imagining that they will end up, not here in the Pit with me, but in heaven or some place else in spite of their sordid actions!

"It is unbelievable! Some of these turkeys have even taken to claiming that the beatitudes have no basis in the *sanctae scripturae* (the Holy Scriptures); that humans who are poor in spirit or merciful are accursed, and that it is those humans who are greedy and merciless and filthily rich as a consequence who are blessed and will inherit the kingdom of heaven!

"The stupid fools ought to know that, after having their reward on earth, they cannot expect to find another reward waiting for them on the other side of the gulf which separates the living from the dead! Just what do they think I am - a Deliverer? Or, what do they think they are - demigods and goddesses? In any case, how can a pickpocket deserve to be incarcerated for years in a cell without the comforts that pets are provided while turkeys who level homes with other humans inside them get away scot-free - or with another reward on top of what they have already enjoyed!

"And certainly not when they also get into the circus business and begin putting up charades in world forums in which their victims are depicted as the 'bad guys' and they themselves as the 'good guys'! I mean - I would be a turkey myself if I suddenly woke up imagining - I really shouldn't say 'woke up' because we here in the Pit where 'there is no rest for the wicked' aren't even permitted a nap - that there was a mansion reserved for me in heaven even after all the havoc I have wrought! Or if I started telling you that I, Beelzebub, was the good guy and Michael the Archangel was the bad guy! I mean - a little realism is in order here. Because one is a bad guy doesn't mean that one shouldn't be realistic and retain a visage of common sense!

"You humans are a strange lot. You freely agree to be 'bad guys' and to associate with us; and you straight away start ruining our 'good' name! This is typical of you humans. The time is coming when we here in the Pit will decide that we've had enough of this - and you will not like what we will do to you to keep you folks in line a little bit! And you'd better take this warning seriously.

"But, above all, how on earth - and in this blighted hell - can these stupid fools imagine that we ourselves who did not spill a drop of blood at any time during the course of our rebellion against the Almighty One, and whose only mistake was to refuse to bow to His Mystic Majesty to demonstrate our fealty, deserved to be banished eternally from His face and cast in this Pit while they themselves will get a reward after wrecking so much havoc and causing so much mayhem?

These oafs should know that that kind of mischief deserves eternal damnation and a reserved spot in 'Gehenna' as you folks call it; and - fashioned in the image of His Mystic Majesty like the rest of us - there is no earthly excuse for not knowing that. And so, my solemn advice to these turkeys would be that, instead of jumping on the deck of some boat and declaring that combat operations have been rapped up and are over in the wake of a 'successful' foray into some foreign lands, they should do so and in stead say something like: 'Let combat operations against the almighty One begin!'

"Any way, fundamentalists to the core (by virtue of being imbued with a messianic sense of mission to transform the world and make it fit their vision) and also monotheists at heart because of their singular faith in the power of awe and shock generating force, regardless of their station in life (whether as generals, members of parliament, ambassadors, voters, students, merchants who are out to make a buck or two supplying ordinance needed by the 'security forces', journalists, pundits, or just housewives whose rumor mongering role often times ends up making all the difference in a by-election when a Senate seat is at stake), my minions, confident that I keep my word, will set out to dominate and conquer the world mafia-style and in complete disregard of the lessons of history.

No rest for the wicked

"And you would be mistaken if you thought that we would stop there. No! we have learned never to rest on our laurels in this battle between Good and Evil. We have to build on our achievements; and we are doing that now by working through our surrogates *inside* the Roman Catholic Church to ensure that anyone who attempts to alert the world to our Evil Plan and the extent to which it is succeeding is ridiculed and ignored. That is why I for one am confident that your thesis on 'Original Virtue', even though it should in theory set off alarm bells under ordinary circumstances, and should even become required reading for seminarians and catechists, is going to be so much wasted effort; and it is, if anything, likely to end up serving our cause instead.

"There being no rest for the wicked (the situation is even worse for me and my fellow demons because we are *evil* and not merely wicked), we will accordingly never rest until the Roman Catholic Church, that Guardian of Divine Truth, looks like something that I, Beelzebub and Father of Lies, invented. We must work hard to ensure that the Pontiff of Rome (the shepherd of the Prime Mover's flock who stepped into the shoes of the fisherman) evokes images, not of faithful messenger of the Good News, but images of one who presides over apostasy and idolatry.

"Our success in getting humans, Catholics and non-Catholics alike, to turn their backs on the Holy Eucharist assures that humans are cut off from the Communion of Saints, and consequently remain isolated while the battle between Good and Evil rages on around them. Instead of spending all their time in perpetual adoration before the Blessed Sacrament in the company of angels and saints, we want them to be wasting their days on earth listening to empty orations that are intended to make them feel good from the pulpit.

"As for the separated brethren, we want them to be stuck with the phrase 'the Holy Book says this and the Holy Book says that', and to delude themselves that the Deliverer's words to His apostles that what they will hold bound on earth will be held bound in heaven, and what they will loosen on earth will be loosened in heaven, are completely meaningless. We want them to continue to believe that there is salvation outside the Church of Rome.

"In other words, we want them to believe that humans, helpless and incapable of freeing themselves from the bondage of sin, can rebuff the spiritual authority of the successors to the Deliverer's apostles - and along with it the Church's *magisterium* - and still bluff their way past St. Peter (who now stands guard at the Gates of Heaven) into Paradise. We want them to believe that they can scoff at the authority of the Church that was personally commissioned by the Deliverer and founded on a rock called Peter, and still have full access to the graces merited by the Deliverer, graces He has chosen to dispense through His *Ecclesia* (since defined by Church decree as 'the Mystical Body of the Deliverer').

"You know that I myself use the word 'delight' infrequently and reluctantly to describe my 'pleasure' at the sight of sick and aberrant humans. This is because a spiritual creature that opts for the path of rebellion is expected to damn well know what it is doing, and to take responsibility for its actions. Deviant spiritual creatures should at the very least be aware of their identity and even capitalize on it as they go about their deviant business.

"But humans have this tendency to feign ignorance, sometimes pretending that they are completely helpless and can do nothing about their spiritual fate, and that a human has to be 'predestined' for the Pit to end up here, or predestined for heaven. And it is fashionable for humans to blame me for the most God-awesome things they do to each other in the name of the Prime Mover! When it suits them, they try to act as if I have so much control over them, and that we are almost as one. If that were truly the case, it would at least constitute grounds for them to blame for *their* aberrant actions and ways.

"And then, as if that were not bad enough, it is also fashionable for them to play sissy and pretend that they are so helpless, it couldn't possibly be that to get to heaven they also needed to do anything other than *believing*! That they did not need to actually cooperate with the Holy Ghost and to turn out good works - which is another way of saying that they need to (indeed have to) keep the commandments (lead good lives)! It is as though they just want to be spirited into heaven!

"Now, because violence breeds violence, investing in an effective awe and shock generating military machine is just perfect. For one, this will cause other nations to do the same or even better if they can. But a great awe and shock generating military machine of course makes it possible to project awe and shock generating force in a truly awful and shocking way when the objective of the operations (conducted under the guise of spreading democracy, spreading the gospels of the Deliverer, or some other such tall tale) is to emulate Julius Caesar who dominated and conquered the known world and made history by effecting regime changes in Europe and North Africa only to be forgotten!

"When regime changes occur, or when efforts are made directly or through proxies to destabilize so-called roguish governments, lots and lots of folks (belonging to the same humankind) suffer and/or lose their lives in the process. What is even better, particularly where operations aimed at changing regimes succeed, invariably conditions are created in which counter forces led by the resistance (Mau Mau, Viet Cong, Insurgents, Terrorists, or what have you) will thrive, leading to the endless cycle of violence; and this happens to be Strategic Objective (SO) No. 2 in my Evil Plan.

"Demagogues that subjugate and murder their subjects in hopes of perpetuating their rule thereby, and those at the helm in imperialist regimes that believe in foreign conquests (or adventures abroad for the purpose of plundering the wealth that does not belong to them) may not know, but they invariably end up fighting with 'ghosts' As a rule, the more 'terrorists' and 'insurgents' they liquidate, it is always the case that, in stead of facing dwindling enemy numbers, they find themselves battling an ever expanding enemy force.

"They start off stupidly oblivious to the fact that the victims of their murderous campaigns are fellow humans and kindred in the real sense (as both the killers and victims are the progeny of the same Adam and Eve). And then they conveniently forget that even though creatures fashioned in the Image do die the death, it is only a mirage as there is no way that the killers can pursue the souls of the folks whose lives get prematurely sniffed out into the afterlife. The terrorists and insurgents die but they don't die in the literal sense. But, as demagogues and imperialists discover soon enough (even though they are always too proud to admit it), providence has ordered things such that the more a populace is subjugated and terrorised, the greater the reason for the kinsfolk of those who fall in the battles for self-determination to join the ranks of the 'terrorists' and 'insurgents', validating the maxim *Vox Populi Vox Dei*!

"And because the demagogues and the imperialists won't face up to that truth, and will be chasing the elusive victories to the very end, it must indeed look, at least on the surface, as though the ghosts of the fallen terrorists and insurgents have not just returned, but have actually joined in the fray! And, since it will be the evil 'terrorists' and 'insurgents' who notch up gains in the battle of wills, it will also invariably appear as if I, Beelzebub, after taking the demagogues and the imperialists to the mountain tops to show them the Kingdoms of the world and their splendor, and promising them a whale of a time, if they fell down and adored me, must suddenly have lost my mind and joined their enemies and a completely different cause - the cause of *Good*! That is how screwed up humans can be in their thinking…how could they possibly end up thinking that my troops and I are on the other side and working for cause of Good? We work for the damnation of all souls…dammit!

"My clients - the stupid fools - always invariably end up in a sea of misfortunes over which they cannot prevail even with the help of their allies! After they have done my bidding - after I have used them to wreak havoc and bring death and destruction to the Prime Mover's people - I dump them.

The devil's "concern" for the separated brethren…

"If you are wondering why I, Beelzebub and the Father of Lies of all people, am so concerned that the 'separated brothers and sisters' be able to get all the information they need to abandon their schisms and heresies and get back into fold, it is simply because I, Satan and the Father of Death, want the 'separated brothers and sisters' to end up here in the Pit with me - which you bet they will, because they now won't be able to cite any excuses for continuing to regale themselves as 'the saved ones' and for not taking up their crosses and following the Deliverer in the literal meaning of those words.

"While you humans play ball only in the way you know how to play ball, namely by subterfuge, lying, cheating, deceiving, defrauding your opponents and even imagining that you can exterminate, annihilate or destroy fellow humans for whom you have a dislike (an impossibility) at will, we demons play ball by being honest and forthright, and by doing everything we do above board.

"You should also note that we demons don't go around whining, griping, or telling tall tales about our opponents - and we are, above all, not hypocrites. I may be the Father of Death, but I swear I have never taken a life or *directly* caused a spirit or a soul to become damned! That is not to say that stupid humans haven't killed at my suggestion and become damned.

"But, you'd better take my word for it - I have never suggested to any fellow creature - angelic or human - that it (the creature) engage in anything that was evil without pointing out at the same time that the evil deed was going to imperil that spirit or soul! The only time I did not follow this *modus operandi* of alerting the creature to the dangers intrinsic in doing something that was evil was when I tried to ensnare the Deliverer Himself on the mountain. But then, who was I to try and lecture to the Word about right and wrong?

"And incidentally, when the separated brethren refuse to submit to the teaching authority of Holy Catholic Church (the Mystical Body of the Deliverer), that is exactly what they and their misguided 'pastors' attempt to do - to lecture to the Deliverer and also the Word about what is right and wrong!

The ultimate sport…

"To return to the topic at hand, namely our practice of the virtue of patience, getting humans who do not know who they are or where they are headed to make a mockery of the One, True, Holy and Catholic Church of the Deliverer, and then go on to use the name of the Prime Mover in vain are all key objectives of my Evil Plan! But an even more insidious objective of my Evil Plan is to get misguided humans to go out and kill and maim in the name of the Deliverer. And, you guess what! These stupid fools will be imagining that they are torturing, maiming, and crucifying the unbelievers and the unsaved when they are actually torturing, maiming, crucifying and killing the Deliverer in a repeat of what transpired on Mount Calvary two thousand years ago.

"I keep talking about the stupidity of humans, and worrying that I myself might be spilling out too many of my secrets. But I have since realized that when you tell humans to their face that they are stupid, instead of that making them more wizened, it makes them more stupid. Gosh, you humans are so interesting - and so stupid! And may be I should let you in on just this one other secret, as I have the feeling that revealing to you humans this particular secret will make you even more stupefied.

"You shouldn't be alarmed when I tell you that there are times when we demons stop everything, and do nothing but observe humans and their antics. You are at liberty to call us demons an indolent lot for doing that. We can expect humans to do that on impulse as they are wont to do. The fact is that we demons learn a great deal from that 'exercise'. And one of the things we have noticed in the course of observing humans was that, unlike us pure spirits, they enjoy playing games very much.

"You might be running ahead and thinking that I am going to discuss the fouling, cheating, and doping and what-not that is the order of the day when the Olympic Games and other sporting events get under way, not to mention the crooked refereeing that goes on!

"Now, games and sport are not things that we pure spirits are into very much. At least not as much as you humans who need to exercise to keep in physical and mental shape. Even though the idea of competitive sports has always seemed intriguing, this has remained one area in which we demons generally prefer to be on the sidelines as observers.

"It was obvious to us from the beginning that the sports and games humans had invented over the years had proved their value for rallying together citizens in different parts of the world, as nations vied with each other in an effort to prove that their citizenry included the greatest athletes, boxers, wrestlers and what-have-you in the world.

"It didn't take us very long, in short, to find a use for the idea of gaming. And guess what we did? I will be to the point. What we demons did after carefully observing humans at play was help the more enterprising ones devise what you might call the Ultimate Sport. And I am not talking about Chess, or Basket Ball, or Golf! Working with our minions, we got humans to add one more 'game' to the list of national sporting events. And we wanted this game to be the 'ultimate sporting event' that would rally humans in any given nation around that nation's leadership! And this game now attracts the biggest prize, namely veto power in world forums.

"In the new sport which has no season, and fortunately also no rules (apart from the so-called rules of engagements that each nation sets for itself at least in theory), nations vie with each other and endeavor to show which one among them can get its citizens the most to eat. Every nation on earth is now a participant in this sport, a sport in which the use of brute force by a nation to gain points is perfectly legitimate. Nations become 'winners' - and there are numerous winners given the size of the earth - by forcefully taking over control of the earth's scarce resources and placing anyone who attempts to resist on the 'Most Wanted Dead or Alive' lists.

"A feature of the 'War Game' is that powerful nations (those that have succeeded in overrunning and effectively colonizing or occupying weaker nations, and divesting them of their natural and other resources) are also supposed to pretend that they are ruled, not by murderous despots who are insensitive to the loss of human lives and will do whatever it takes to 'promote' their own countries 'national interests', but by 'liberators' and statesmen or stateswomen whose only desire is to liberate the oppressed and allow democracies and things like that to flourish in the vanquished nations. In this sport, nations - especially the world's powerful nations that have the best chances of launching successfully 'missions' (including preemptive strikes) on the weaker nations in the course of which they kill and plunder - devise their plans to raid other nations in secret.

"One tactic that is very popular with those nations that are members of the so-called 'G-8' - the top eight 'world powers' - is to use deception, out-right lies, and spin to depict a targeted nation as some sort of 'roguish state' that must needs be brought in line on some pretext, and then proceed to launch a preemptive strike aimed at seizing control over that nation's resources. Members of the G-8 are notorious for looking out for each other without any regard to natural justice, and are known to employ their veto powers in world forums to ensure that any and all resolutions passed promote their 'national security' and give them added advantages as they continue to participate in the War Sport with its reaching consequences.

"But it is not just the super powers that have everything going for them as a result of the War Sport. Any one who accedes to power in the smaller nations, particularly nations in the so-called 'developing world', knows that the countries they lead are at the complete mercy of the powerful nations. The threat of hostile take-overs predisposes leaders of the small nations to bribes that come in various shapes, the most common one being the 'foreign aid' that is given with 'strings'. But, borrowing a leaf from the goings-on on the global stage, these leaders usually delight in the fact that, when applied at national level, the philosophy underlying the War Sport and especially the rules of the War Sport can be used by them employed to justify a playing field that is less than level.

One result of that is the widespread practice of operating 'safe houses' where political opponents are tortured, or alternatively detaining and incarcerating their opponents on the flimsiest excuses, in preparation for declaring themselves 'Presidents for Life'. And the Presidents for Life in-waiting also have the option of suggesting at any time that their opponents are terrorists or allied to some terrorist group and to turn around and claim that as a good enough reason for putting them away permanently without any further ado or even a trial. Thus, whether it is played on the global stage or at the national level, the War Sport serves us here in the Underworld perfectly well.

"There is actually no time limit for this sport which had its kick-off on the day Cain started plotting to destroy his brother Abel. And, in what admittedly was a masterstroke on my part, I made sure that the Ultimate Sport received the boost as well as blessing from biblical figures like Moses, Joshua, and even the diminutive David who, while unarmed, succeeded in killing Goliath and cutting off the giant's head. As for Moses, he is on record as admonishing the Israelites that, upon entering the Land of Canaan, which God had promised to give them, they needed to destroy totally and utterly the Canaanites who were the current inhabitants. And, of course, Joshua famously prayed that the sun stand still for a whole day until the nation of Israel could take vengeance on its enemies, a prayer that was granted by Jehovah, according to the scriptures!

"Also, as you may have guessed, the referee is none other than me, Beelzebub! I will declare the ultimate winner(s) on the day the world will grind to a halt. In the meantime, the borders of nations (as you might have already noticed) will always keep changing as once powerful nations lose control over their resources, and new 'world powers' emerge and even take the lead, and as some nations vanish from the map altogether in this wonderful sport. Wonderful, you might have guessed, because this sport actually promotes my Evil Plan and results in the lives of lots and lots of humans being sniffed out prematurely - killed by their own kind - and also in lots and lots of suffering for those who survive the raids.

"A measure of my success can be gauged from the fact that the Holy Book is itself full of passages of holy warriors whose victory on the battlefield is almost always anticipated, the notable exception being the 'Warriors of Ephraim' who, even in their defeat, are described as 'mighty men of valor, famous throughout the house of their fathers'. The upshot of this is that the powers that be now put the build-up of military might as a priority above all else. In every nation on earth, it is the generals have first right of refusal when it comes to the allocation of resources. And, adding to the glamour of the 'War Sport' and as might be expected, it is the military industrial complexes that now spearhead technological advancement, and this encompasses every sphere of life.

"But that is not all. For these humans who are born with original sin, the temptation to use power wielded to 'prove' that might is always right has always proved just too great. True to form, nations have always been restive whenever they have found themselves militarily at some advantage over others; and it is not by accident that the evils of colonialism, imperialism and the other unsavory 'isms' traditionally are perpetrated by the so called advanced nations, and not by the 'developing' nations. And the thievery and banditry usually continues even after former 'colonies', 'dependencies' or 'possessions' gain their 'independence'. This is evidenced by the fact that the newly independent states almost invariably never graduate from their status as 'banana republics' that are only capable of supplying much needed 'raw materials' to their former colonial masters. And that is if they do not become 'foreign enclaves' with control over their railroads, mining industries, and things of that sort remaining firmly in the hands of the former imperial masters.

"And, nowadays, whenever a member of the so-called G-8 (the cartel which is made up of the eight most powerful nations on earth and which is usually referred to as the 'Group of Eight') is unable to wrest the control of one or other scarce resource it deems important for the its 'national security' from some recalcitrant non-member nation that does not want to cooperate, an increasingly common tactic is to persuade members of the cartel to stand behind the super power that is lusting after that particular resource, and jointly impose embargoes, economic sanctions, and things of that sort against the 'rogue' nation.

"The objective of the embargoes and sanctions is to weaken the former dependency to the point where a 'coalition of the willing', made up of those members of the cartel whose interests relating to the scarce resource converge and other nations over which they already exercise control, can safely launch a pre-emptive strike for the purpose of gaining control over the coveted resource.

"I plant ideas regarding 'embargoes' and 'sanctions' in the minds of leaders of the G-8 because the effect of imposing an economic embargo is almost the same as mounting a preemptive strike which is, of course, always accompanied by 'collateral damage' in one shape or another. Because sanctions and embargoes are a virtual death warrant for society's most vulnerable, namely children and the aged, and do not attract condemnation from anti-war groups or the populace at large at least yet, they are the 'modern' way to go and a very 'clean' one at that. The decision makers, or 'deciders' as they usually prefer to call themselves, can still remain good bedfellows, albeit strange ones, with religious leaders and those other minions of mine who delight in presenting themselves to the world as 'defenders of morality', and continue to dine and wine with them.

"Because everything that is done on the world stage is driven by greed and the desire to be the dominant player, the cartel is usually something which the world's most powerful nations join if they find it convenient to do so. Cooperation between the cartel's members on any particular matter is therefore usually determined by national security considerations from the perspective of the individual members. The 'cooperation' thus frequently cloaks bitter rivalry and deep-seated rivalry and often also long standing disagreements regarding the manner in which the world's wealth is supposed to be parcelled out amongst the world's most powerful nations.

"For my part, as the Father of Death and Prince of Darkness, I see everything working in my favour, because as history has shown, selfishness and lust for things of the world on such a grand scale inevitably leads to horrific global conflagrations in which the super powers are pitted against each other. I think of the sufferings that humans endured during the last two world wars in which primitive instruments of war, including two primitive nuclear devices, were employed. I sincerely cannot wait to see the third world war in which all combatant countries will all be nuclear-armed! And, yes, you guessed correctly - I, Diabolos, am just dying to see humans live through a hell of their own making!

"It should be clear by now that the War Sport above all helps us here in the Pit net the many souls for which robbery and murder - and lust for material things - are evils only when perpetrated against them but not by them. If you think I lie, just go take a look at the account the children of Fatima gave of hell after the Blessed Virgin allowed them a brief glimpse of this place! I can tell you that the losses Michael the Archangel sustains daily as a result of wars is incredible! Also, as you can see from watching the television news 'shows' on the major news networks, there is no day that passes without news of some new war breaking out. This is a direct result of nations agreeing to participate in this wondrous and truly 'deadly' game.

"Talking about news networks, you should know that these are really gossip and rumour mongering mills manned by professionals in rumour mongering, and so-called pundits or humans who are completely addicted to gossiping, and other humans who see nothing wrong with back-biting others. Of course, you humans are quite free to treat these rumour mongers as you have traditionally done by lending them your ears, and leaving at the mercy of their lies as a result.

"It is bad enough that these humans will pay other humans to appear before television cameras to give rehearsed accounts of supposed hot topical events when what they are trying to do is stay with a topic that appears to be helping them maintain the network's ratings in the public eye. But it is even worse when they have all these spinmeisters and spin doctors take turns in front of television cameras at prime time (that is the time the so-called 'working middle class' are back home after a supposedly 'hard day's work', and glued to their 'tellies' as is their custom) to act out their parts in soap operas that come complete with moving parts! And there is, as you would expect, nothing those spin doctors love to gossip and rumour monger about more than the drums or war, real of fictitious.

"Now, even though my own sins are many and grievous, pretending that I am a Michael Archangel or one of the guardian angels, who have the unenviable task of trying to keep humans safe from us here in the Pit and themselves, fortunately isn't one of them. It is the reason expressions like 'dissembling devil' and 'phoney demon' are not part of the human lingo. But the same cannot be said of humans. And it is not surprising. Open almost any page of the New Testament, and you will find the Deliverer warning humans to shirk duplicity and hypocrisy in an effort to save them from themselves. And He couldn't have been more right!

"That said, nothing brings out the atrocious behavior of humans in this regard - the duplicity, hypocrisy, chicanery, make believe, and the penchant for falsehoods, prevarication, feigning, etc. - like the soap operas that are played out day in and day out on television screens. The parade of phoney characters whose livelihood is derived from promoting what frequently exists only in the realm of fantasy is endless on any given day. And, of course, the distinction between what is news and what is not has long been lost sight of in the shuffle, with newscasters now accustomed to billing their programs as 'news shows', and competing with stand-up comics and the producers of 'reality shows'.

"News broadcasts, comic acts, soap operas, reality television are all packaged as 'shows' which they indeed are; and that includes weather forecasts and accounts of natural disasters if they happen to be 'newsworthy', a term used to denote the ability of a story to boost ratings of a news media outlet. Conversely, natural disasters that are not adjudged as being newsworthy in that sense, however major, frequently don't even get a mention. The newscasters and the producers of the 'news shows' might as well be living on another planet.

"You see, here in Gehenna, places like Hollywood, which cater to 'film stars' and their 'producers', comedians, pop artists, and what have you, are non-existent. We regard all those people as 'con artists', who might belong in heaven, but not here in the Pit. You know - we wouldn't have any use here for 'actors' and others who are into things of make-believe and fantasy. Even though we repudiated Him who is every creature's Life and Hope, and will continue to be locked in this interminable battle with Him through all eternity, all of us here in hell sorely miss the promise of everlasting happiness and joy which He represents. Now, that is reality, and we wouldn't be able to bury it under any amount of make believe and fantasy and self-delusion.

"We therefore don't get a lot of fun when we take a peep at those 'con artists' who just seem to love the bright lights and seem to have a yearning for attention. It strikes us as something very sad when one moment the 'con artists' are reporting with glee the devastation wrought by their country in a military putsch against some poor, indefensible 'rogue nation' (that has been deliberately weakened by years of 'economic embargoes' and political isolation but happens to be sitting on vast and greatly coveted natural resources), and the next moment they are commiserating with country men whose neighborhood might have been affected by a freak storm.

"What we enjoy 'viewing' on the television stations that humans operate are the original, uncensored images of hooded captives inside the torture chambers, and the chilling images of rockets slamming into residential buildings where 'insurgents' are holed up and reportedly using their wives and children as human shields. This is because it promotes our cause when human suffering is put on display. We get a kick out of seeing humans kill and maim their brother and sister humans for any reason whatsoever. But, above all, we enjoy being witnesses to humans signing their own 'spititual death' warrants regardless of what they employ in creating what are effectively 'martyrs', whether they employ butchers' knives as Peter was on the verge of doing in the Garden of Getsemani, improvised explosive device or IEDs so-called, or drones. And we love to listen to the rationalizations and lies that humans are in the habit of using used to conceal the true motives behind their actions. And we dearly love to observe contests between the humongous, towering Goliaths of this world and the diminutive Davids. And, of course, even though we are the ones who underwrite the projects the Goliaths set out to implement at our behest, it would be disingenuous to suggest that we do not harbour secret sympathies for the poor Davids, who usually come out winners anyway - and naturally to our disgust!

"And look - we enjoy what is phoney, contrived and hypocritical only to the extent that the culprits dig themselves in holes from which they likely won't be able to emerge - holes that become integral parts of the Pit in due course.

How to commit murder

"And any way, you of course now understand what is meant by going out and maiming, subjecting other humans to shock and awe, torturing, crucifying and killing. For one, to be guilty of doing these things, one doesn't have to do them personally - one doesn't even have to be present when the 'treatment' is being administered to earn for oneself the sentence of eternal damnation and qualify to join our ranks here in the Pit.

"You can do these things through surrogates or, if you happen to be an emperor and commander-in-chief, by just inking an Imperial Order that authorizes a high-tech battleship to unleash its deadly load of missiles tipped with bunker bursting bombs into a city of some 'rogue state' as a lesson to other 'rogue states'. Or by inking an Imperial Order that authorizes the mass production and stock-piling in peace time of everything from chemical and biological agents, land mines, nuclear bombs, hydrogen bombs, tactical nukes, and all manner of armaments, including tank rounds that are coated with depleted uranium - and so on and so forth. Or an Imperial Order that causes vital supplies to a 'rogue state' to be cut off, resulting in the most vulnerable members of society in that rogue state dying off from a lack if medicines and the like!

"Or, as one of my clever demons aptly put it, you can commit Murder by Imperial Order or Veto; or Murder by Parliamentary or Congressional Resolution; or Murder by Act of Omission even, as was the case when the whole world stood by and just watched as the defenceless people belonging to one tribe on a Central African nation were decimated by members of a rival tribe while being sparred on by the official media! But one does not have to occupy the Palais de l'Elysée, the White House, the Kremlin, or Number 10 Downing Street, or a 'State House' or a place like that to maim, crucify and kill. The demon, actually one of those little devils we refer to as 'Midgets', had gone on to explain sarcastically that a senior citizen on disability could do it by simply exercising his/her right to vote, and casting the vote for a war monger in a by-election that was called to fill a vacant seat in the Senate.

"The same demon had added as an aside that one did not have to be a demon to make the Church's work of evangelization difficult. One only needed to represent oneself as a 'Decider', and then persist in presenting to an audience of any size a particular interpretation of just one passage of the sacred scriptures that one knew was at variance with the 'will of the Deliverer' to fall foul of my wiles in that regard.

"That had prompted me to ask the Midget why he was leaving humans the 'loophole', and also whether he had stopped prizing the company of humans. The Midget had thereupon agreed that it was better - much better - to say 'Catechism of the Catholic Church' instead of 'will of the Deliverer', because that left humans less wiggle room and also guaranteed the demons lots of human company!

"And, perhaps because the Midget wanted to please me and see me smile for once (something I have never done since that Michael, aided by hosts of the faithful angels, overwhelmed me and my host of rebel angels, and then bundled us out of heaven and into this wretched place deep in the crust of the earth), he had added that whenever those who had broken with Rome spoke the words 'the bible says', because they used that phrase to imply that the only authority on earth which they recognized in spiritual matters was the 'Holy Book' alone (*sola scriptura*), they contradicted the Catechism of the Holy Catholic Church and, barring a special act of the Prime Mover's mercy, were doomed!

"This Midget seemed to have a soft spot for humans, because here he was going out of his way to refer to a 'special' act of divine mercy! He understood what was on my mind when I did not smile. I was wishing that the Midget should have added that, if the separated brethren spoke those words (the bible says) well knowing that they were contradicting the Catechism of the *Sancta Ecclesia* (something they had now heard from the 'horse's mouth' as you humans say and could not go on pretending that it was something they didn't know!), following an act of betrayal of the Deliverer of that magnitude, until they recanted and confessed their sin, it didn't matter a hoot what other things they took it upon themselves to say or do, they could expect to be told by the Deliverer when they rushed Him upon 'kicking the bucket' that He did not know them - period!

"Like me, the Midget knew human nature very well, and also understood that after we in the Underworld did our thing, these 'good folks' typically stopped having any misgivings about 'sticking to their guns', busying themselves with all sorts of things that promised to make them feel justified and good about themselves, while turning a blind eye thenceforth to any information that even remotely suggested that they were in the wrong.

"We know that this is what they do even as they avow that submission to the will of the Deliverer go hand in hand with salvation and deliverance from sin. And they will continue merrily on their chosen path of protest and they take pot shots at the Pontiff of Rome and will attempt to ridicule the Church's dogmas even as they themselves admit that there can be only one true Church! They themselves belong to fringe, break-away churches or denominations; but they still conveniently refer to similar break-away churches, but not to their own denomination, as 'cults'.

"The Midget and I know each and everything that is going on. But you yourself must know that the separated brethren make matters worse when, in order to support the heretical positions they have taken on different dogmas of the Church, they invariably find themselves referring to the 'Early Church' and to what the 'Early Church fathers' taught; but, for reasons best known to themselves, they balk at making the connection that what they refer to as the 'Early Church' and the 'Church of Rome' from which they have excluded themselves are one and the same thing!

"And then, there are those among them who do not see any use for the early Church or the fathers of the nascent Church. This is because the 'gospel' they preach pertains, not to the 'Crucified and Risen Deliverer', but to earthly riches! But guess what - all the humans who are in this business of 'preaching the gospel' say that the Prime Mover - the same Prime Mover who created everything out of nothing and sent His Only Begotten Son into the world so that those who would believe in Him would be saved - felt constrained enough to give them personal revelations mandating them to go out into the fields that were ripe for the harvest and preach the gospel!

"The fields are indeed ripe for the harvest, but woe upon those in wolves clothing who pass themselves off as the Lord's messengers when they are not even prepared to accept the Gospel for themselves as it is taught by Peter's successors! But the Deliverer also meant business when He rebuked Peter, and even used the 'S' word (you should know by now that 'S' stands for 'Satan'), when the fisherman (who would end up as the Pontiff of Rome and suffer martyrdom there for his pains) was trying to prevent Him from going to Jerusalem and to His certain death at the hands of His enemies. Peter was trying to stop Him from descending on Jerusalem for the purpose of launching the New Testament.

"But precisely because the fields were ripe for the harvest, the activity in the temple in Jerusalem, albeit under the Old Testament, had risen sharply. Just as now, the 'blessings' from operating a 'ministry' at that time were quite handsome. What the Deliverer did when He saw the commerce that was being conducted inside the temple is history that has long been forgotten by humans. It wouldn't make any sense any way in any case for a 'modern' to abandon a highly successful ecclesiastical enterprise, stop spreading heresies, and live as a poor Catholic convert just because the Holy Father demands it on behalf of the Deliverer.

"In the meantime, the errors of those who have separated themselves from the Church - errors that started out as disenchantment with alleged abuses by Church functionaries of indulgences and the Church's position on the indissolubility of Holy matrimony, and then blossomed into disenchantment with the doctrine of papal supremacy, are no longer confined to those original issues of contention. With the passage of time, those errors have multiplied and now encompass the interpretation of each and every single verse of the books of the Old and New Testaments.

"Actually, the scenario I presented to the Deliverer when I tempted Him in the desert and a short while later on the mountain-top - that he should show-case His divine power by changing stones into food, and also that He should abandon His mission and in stead accept from me dominion over the length and breadth of the earth and become emperor of the world's only super-hyper-com-mega power, is what many of the separated brethren have come to embrace. You can, of course, go on dreaming that it is by accident that folks take time to look for biblical passages that appear to support their hypothesis that the Deliverer came so that everyone would enjoy the good life in this world; but that simply isn't the case.

"Whereas the Deliverer tasked the surviving apostles with going out into the world and spreading the message of the Crucified and Risen Deliverer, the reformers have replaced that message with one that focuses on the "Glory of the Deliverer", and bypasses and even frowns on the cross. The Deliverer knew that sinful and sinning humans would not just be meddling with the interpretation of the sacred scriptures, also interfering with the Church's exercise of its teaching *magisterium*, and He said so in so many words.

"The harm this meddling and interference does to the Church's mission of saving souls is increased in proportion to the fervor and zeal with which the errors, which are themselves now unbounded in scope, are propagated. But, of course, fervor and zeal, which more often than not betray the tendency to be wilful and headstrong, are one thing; and obedience and meekness forbearance, which humans typically regard as capitulation and foolishness, are something else altogether. The bottom line is that humans who go out on a limb and contradict those who are called to step into the shoes of the apostles do a great disservice to the Church and to themselves.

"That situation is compounded by individuals in the Church, and members of the Church's clergy in particular, who are shy about confronting the misguided 'reformers' head on and telling them on their face that they are spreading heresies. Forgetful of the fact that the Deliverer detests apathy, lukewarmness and indifference, all they are interested in is seeing a semblance of harmony in 'Christendom' so-called maintained. We here in the Underworld know these things too well, and don't waste any time moving to exploit the situation. And as the goddamned devil who is always on the look-out for ways to derail the divine plan, I couldn't ask for more!

"After paying the sort of price He paid when He launched the New Testament from atop of Mt. Calvary, the Deliverer cannot be expected to treat the new crop of 'temple merchants' with kid gloves when the time comes to deal with them. As the 'Head Wolfe' in this business, I know from experience that the Deliverer really meant business when He chased those merchants out of the temple. I say - it will be really ugly this time around!

"Actually, with humans prepared to compromise on such important tenets of their faith when it suits them (instead of undertaking a serious and conscientious study of the important elements of their faith before deciding to take on the Church), our job of tempting them and trying to sway them from the path of righteousness is decidedly less fun. You see, we here in the Underworld like to be challenged and 'to earn our keep'. But you humans want to have everything free; and that is why there is so much thievery, cheating and lying in this Planet Earth. And that is also why it surprises us that there are no human devils, and that it is just us!

"Any way, when humans start to challenge the Church's teaching *magisterium*, you cannot start to imagine how much I, as the Chief Tempter and Evil One love it! You see - I myself would start dreaming about being 'delivered' if it were to happen that humans could cheerfully and happily contradict the Deliverer and those He sent out to hand deliver His invitations to the heavenly banquet stood a chance!

"The Midget was clearly reading my mind and, to show that he was in full agreement, he chipped in that it was his own 'prayer' as well that when those 'good folks' approached the Deliverer and Judge on their day of judgement, the Deliverer would, with a waive of His hand, refuse to acknowledge them saying that He didn't know them at all. The Midget even added that a similar fate awaited our guest (Mjomba) if, after writing the thesis with their help, Mjomba spurned their advice and lived according to his own devices. He said in conclusion that he himself couldn't care less if that Mjomba 'friend of mine' lost his soul too and joined the party in Gehenna!

"I let the Midget know that this was not good enough for me, and I will tell you why. Humans put themselves in danger of losing their souls and becoming damned when they start believing that they are justified - period. They are poor forsaken children of Adam and Eve - Damn! And, how can they stand there and declare unashamedly that they are justified when they are ready to avow that they are better than other humans? Or when, in the same breath, they affirm their faith in things like capital punishment and things like that instead of turning the other cheek, and when they are dying to see their enemies destroyed and liquidated? When their faith, in other words, is in the power of brutal force, and its use in avenging perceive wrongs!

"Also, before declaring themselves 'justified', humans should first recall what the Son of Man Himself said about being 'good', namely that only the Prime Mover was good! They should also remind themselves about the Deliverer said in His parables on justification, and specifically what He said about the Pharisee who was ranting about being better than the tax collector. According to the Deliverer, humans of that mould had already received their reward! The Deliverer had made it crystal clear from the start that it would not do for humans to just follow Him around because He was multiplying loaves of bread, healing the sick, and other performing other wonders.

"And so, if humans who had been baptised into the Church remained followers of the Deliverer only in name and did not take the next step of surrendering themselves body and soul to the Holy Ghost through self-abnegation, and consequently were not allowing themselves to be led by the Spirit where they on their own would never go, there was no difference at all between them and those Israelites who had been flocking to see the Messiah because of the wonders He performed, and then lined Jerusalem's Main Street to welcome Him into that occupied city, only to change and join the chorus which chanted 'Crucify Him, Crucify Him' not long after!

"And then, there are those folks who rant about 'sola scriptura' and 'sola fide' being their sole guiding principles in life. But those same folks, who have no hesitation in flatly contradicting the Church in that regard, are also quick to claim that they and they alone are *saluti* (saved)! Well, and don't they trip themselves up when they assert that they *are* saved and justified, and *are* good?

"I am Diabolos, and I will say here and now that this is the problem with the adherents of all 'religions' regardless of how they were started. So long as the adherents of any religion believe that they are better than other members of the human race, that is all that matters for us here in the Pit. You see, we happen to know that truly heroic souls see every human as the temple of the Prime Mover; and they see themselves as the least worthy in the divine presence. And thanks to the hard work of my buddies here in the Pit, humans who are like that are decidedly a rarity.

"And then, the common thread in the lives of all such humans is that their selflessness permits the Holy Ghost to lead them where on their own they would not trample! Consequently, to the extent humans have failed to surrender themselves to the promptings of the Holy Ghost in that regard, to that extent it is I, the Evil Ghost, who calls the shots. And it does not take rocket science to arrive at the conclusion that to the extent humans are not imbued with the Holy Ghost, to that extent they have what the evangelist aptly referred to as the 'mark of the beast' on their foreheads, the mark that distinguishes the elect, or members of the Church Triumphant, from the rest when the time comes for humans to 'give up their own ghosts'!

"Now, one clever human said that the human mind was a terrible thing to waste! Well, we here in the Underworld could never afford to waste our minds. But there is one other thing that we could say about ourselves here in the Pit. Often, we would really like to savor something very much, but we just can't delight in it or celebrate in the ordinary sense of that word, because we ourselves are already condemned and in hell. You can therefore understand when I say that we really can't savor the fact that it is us here in the Underworld, and not the separated brethren, who are winning the day. But then that is the frustration that we have to live with as *angeli diaboli* (fallen angels). But I myself as Demon in Chief or Diabolos do not sympathize with my fellow demons either for the fact that they have to live with these frustrations. We ourselves here in the Underworld individually chose to rebel against the Prime Mover, well-knowing that we would be in for something really nasty if we failed in achieving our objectives in the rebellion against Good; and we all of us now deserve to suffer these frustrations - and more.

"It is a very good thing that humans (who do not take advantage of the opportunities they get to search for and find the Truth, and then live according to it) end up in the same exact situation as ourselves. And they should not expect to receive any sympathy from us either, since it is their own choice to join our rebellion; and not my choice or that of my fellow demons! I just wish I could transform my disdain for these humans into something that resembles my original dream of being the Ruler of Heaven and Earth! Regardless, it was with great relish that I turned to the Midget and let him know that he was brilliant and so correct about the separated brethren being 'doomed' because of their apostasy!

"But, to get back to the subject of committing murder, if you are not a commander-in-chief, you can still maim, crucify and kill just as efficiently by lending support to regimes that believe in expansionism, militarism, and the projection of shock and awe generating force, or regimes that place blind faith in the use of brutal force to resolve conflicts. These are all 'mortal sins' that leave a black indelible mark on the soul, and whose perpetrators stand condemned, and eventually end up eternally damned and doomed just like us demons.

"I, myself, as the Father of Death, hail demagogues and tyrants for remaining firm in their belief that 'might makes right'; for wholeheartedly embracing the 'mafia complex'; and for doing things 'mafia style' as they seek to maintain control over the earth's scarce resources. Indeed, thanks to Cain and other demagogues who have walked the earth, 'international affairs' is now run very much like the mafia. It behoves everyone to fall in line, to obey and to pay protection money. You don't, you go! And that is all there is to it. Tyrants and demagogues long ago saw the benefits of that 'mafia style' of doing things, and adapted it to international relations wholesale, christening it 'diplomacy'!

"And so to day, the axiom of the foreign policies of any nation that commands enough clout to get other nations to regard it as a 'major power' is always that it must control the world's scarce resources, including energy sources, shipping routes, and the like; and it must not brook defiance from any quarter. It is consequently bad enough for any nation to try and brush off the 'super power' by insisting on being 'independent'. It becomes many times worse and totally unacceptable if the non-compliant nation (which automatically gets the label 'rogue nation' for its obstinacy in refusing to buckle and determination to exert its independence) also happens to have lots of those scarce resources in its back-yard.

"In 'guarding' his turf, a mafia don is a law unto himself. And anything short of total capitulation will spell disaster for anyone whose assets are eyed by the mafia don. The word 'boundary' is not in the lexicon of mafiosi. This is how places with names like 'America', 'British India', 'Australia', 'Belgian Congo', 'Rhodesia', 'Ivory Coast', 'Gold Coast', 'Mozambique', 'Philippines', and 'Quebec' found their way on the map in recent times. Like the mafia, major players on the international scene have always to be ruthless in order to get their way, for the simple reason that, at the time they initiate their moves and make for the grab, the resources over which they seek to gain control will be under the control ofpatently insatiable.

"The predator nations usually find it advantageous to create instability in those parts of the world where the scarce resources are located; because they can then turn around, and pretend to be entering the foray to 'protect' the scarce resources from 'irresponsible reactionary types' who will never appreciate their value. The same reason is used to forcibly wrench control of the coveted resources from the rightful owners. It goes without saying that any moves on the part of any nation aimed at guarding its territory from attack must be viewed as hostile in the extreme and by the same token unacceptable.

"As they pursue their dreams of transforming themselves into masters of the world, the megalomaniacs as a rule place all their absolute and total faith, not in the Almighty One (whom they aim to emulate), but in the weapons they and their enforcers use to put opponents, actual as well as potential, out of circulation. Cain, who started it all with his preposterous claim that his brother Abel (who couldn't harm a fly) was a danger to his 'empire' and a 'terrorist' who had to be liquidated at all costs, put his faith in the martial arts specifically in the 'headlock', which the spiteful and heartless Cain did not hesitate to use to put away the kind and gentle Abel when the opportunity to do so came along. Other weapons in which megalomaniacs have placed their blind and unfaltering faith at various times in human history have ranged from poisoned arrows discharge from bows, sharpened swords and spears, muskets and cannons, to atom bombs and bunker busting munitions.

"Nuclear-tipped guided missiles and rockets, used in conjunction with orbiting communications satellites, are the weapons of choice of 'modern times'. But I can predict that even these will soon become out-dated and unnecessarily expensive, as deadly nerve gases and poisonous chemical discharged from spray guns the size of a fountain pen prove much more effective and efficient in dispatching entire communities and degrading the offensive and defensive capabilities of targeted 'rogue' states. Unfortunately for the greedy and expansionist megalomaniacs, that same technology will be just as easily available to those who are the targets of regime changes and military occupations.

"But, for now, it is the citizens of the targeted nations who find themselves with no option but to put their faith in prayer and fasting, and in the Almighty One, while their counterparts in those nations that regard themselves as 'major powers' and are accordingly out to dominate the world and expand their influence at any cost celebrate the achievements of their 'great' nations, and revel in their status as super powers. I, as the Father of Death, do not like to see those suffering hordes pray to the Prime Mover that they may be delivered from the megalomaniacs and demagogues. Prayer is something that we here in the Underworld work hard to try and head off, because it hurts our cause, which is to get as many humans as possible to 'die the death' at the hands of our own proxies in this dirty business, namely *homines inqui*.

"Talking about praying to be delivered from megalomaniacs and demagogues, you will recall from your folklore (or oral history) that Cain, the first megalomaniac and demagogue, made the astounding claim that Abel was developing an offensive 'nuclear bomb' as he termed it! Cain started ranting about his brother planning to kill him and working secretly on the weapon of mass destruction

(WMD) after he saw Abel experimenting with different types of wooden planks in an effort to identify the one that could help him shorten the time it took him to get a fire going. Abel had noticed that some planks when rubbed against each other ignited faster than others did.

"Unlike Cain, who lived off the land and sustained himself and his family on ripe bananas, pineapples, mangoes, yams that they just dug up and ate raw and things like that, Abel (who was a herdsman) needed to cook the meats on which he and his family subsisted. But Cain, even though he was still in his thirties, was already in the habit of spinning tall tales and he could lie until he was blue in the face. Before Adam and Eve, who were at least ten times Cain's age, realized that Cain was pulling their legs and they were dealing with a pathological liar, they had began to worry that perhaps their son Abel was plotting to commit a new original sin, and they were both teetering on the verge of a nervous breakdown.

"It was only after they went to inspect the site of the 'nuclear plant' (as Cain called it), and saw for themselves that Abel wasn't engaged in anything that was sinister, that they realized that Cain had been lying to them. To their utter disgust, Adam and Eve even learnt from talking to Cain's wife that the evidence or 'intelligence' their wayward son had presented to them to 'prove his case' was actually cooked and in any case deliberately fabricated to make it appear as if Abel had every intention of wiping out Cain's entire family and 'community' from the face of the earth. It is a mark of the success of our campaign in the ongoing battle between the forces of Good and Evil that since that time, megalomaniacs and demagogues have perfected their methods of operating, and specifically making sure that the lies they spun were taken by the unwary for unvarnished Truth. And so, to-day, major power players will cry fowl when a 'rogue nation' is trying to harness nuclear energy by alleging that the nuclear sites are actually being used to develop 'nuclear bombs' even as they themselves openly announce to the world that they are upgrading their stock-piles of nuclear weapons.

"Again, we here in the Underworld hail those megalomaniacs and demagogues for defying the Prime Mover (who created all, the demagogues themselves included, out of nothing) and choosing to be 'deciders' and the 'law unto themselves' in these matters. We hail them for taking every opportunity that comes along to set up confrontations with the 'rogue nations', and for their statesmanly decision to stay firmly on our side as we prosecute our own war against Good. What would we do if they were all 'good and wise' like Solomon! The more stupid they are - yes 'stupid' to the extent they no longer see that they themselves are on 'death row' and will have to leave all behind at the time they cross the gulf that separates the living from the dead - the better for us!

"You'd better believe me because I am the devil, and I know what I am saying. And I am not nuts. Unlike you humans who go nuts because of imbalances in the chemistry of your cerebral matter, we demons don't have brains and we don't have to worry about going nuts for that reason! This preoccupation with controlling the world's scarce resources is greed at its best, and it is also great! Just think of the number of humans whose lives are snuffed out prematurely as a result! I tell you - we here in the Underworld may be losing on points and going down, but we are not yet out. You've got to count us in as long as the Doomsday Clock keeps ticking and humans continue to be felled by their own greedy fellow humans over the crumbs I throw in their path. And nothing - absolutely nothing - is going to stop me, the Father of Death, from having a whale of a time as long as humans, pining for control over the earth's scarce resources, continue to pick fights with each other and to die the death!

How Beelzebub does his dirty work...

"A temptation works in much the same way as a cabaret act. On the surface, it depicts movements of a dance or a caper. Cabaret artists are indeed in the business of illustrating dance moves. But their cabaret acts can also take on another dimension - a suggestive dimension. So, be on the look out when you next visit that 'cabaret club' - I mean your church!

"You see - cabaret artists spend a lot of time in front of the mirror before they go on stage to face the lights. The apostles, unlike cabaret artists and other con artists, did not have the time, much less the luxury, for that sort of thing. You mean you did not know that?

"Humans use marketing to prey on each other. Rapists use it to lure their victims to secluded places where they then pounce on them. Murderers use it to lull those they want to harm into thinking that they mean no harm - to make their dirty job easier. Other self-proclaimed do-gooders use it to project the false impression that they are 'anointed' and proven vessels of the Prime Mover's grace, and will bring salvation and true happiness to all who will cast in their lot with them by making a donation. Selfless love does not rely on marketing for anything. And we have the best example in creation - the Prime Mover did not see any need to market his intention to will creatures into existence out of nothing. It is of course a marketing technique and a gimmick that works to rake in the money, but not to deliver what it promises, as the Prime Mover sees through it.

"For His part, the Prime Mover does not market any of His gifts, the gift of grace included. His gifts are there for anyone who is prepared to put pride aside and accept them. Even if they might have 'faith that moves mountains', on their own and unaided by grace, humans do not have the wherewithal to keep themselves clear of sin let alone help others to stay clear of it. On their own, humans can only sin, and it has everything to do with the truism that one cannot give what does not have (*Nemo dat quod non habet*).

"Humans! How on earth could they even imagine that they could get themselves in good books with the Prime Mover and into heaven all on their own without 'external aid'! Yes, foreign aid! Humans do not even know how the food they shove down their tummies becomes digested; or how it is that sleep re-invigorates and energizes them, and enables them to keep going and survive on earth.

"You know what - humans do not even have to know how their breathing works, or how their eye-balls enable them to see objects upright instead of upside down! Most do not understand how their bile - poison which was located so uncomfortably close to the heart - actually keeps them alive instead of killing them instantly, any way! And many will never understand that there is a tiny crystal in their *medula oblongata* without which they would not be able to walk upright.

"Humans do not know why they were created at the time they were created, or why it was that someone else was not created in their place. It is, above all, telling that humans wake up to reality for the first time and only discover that they exist weeks - perhaps even months - after they have lain in the womb and been taken to different places as their mothers perform various errands. They start kicking inside the womb, not because they are hunkering to express themselves, but when hunger starts to gnaw at their tiny middle. That is when they start showing the first signs that they exist, are conscious of it, and are prepared to die fighting for their right to food.

"That ought to be reason enough to make humans suspect that if they ever wound up in heaven, it wouldn't be because they were smart, but because someone had pity on them. It is only then, actually, that humans will fully grasp how they landed there - as a result of the Prime Mover's act of infinite mercy and despite themselves. It will even be a wonder they ever got there given their impetuousness and the fact that they kept placing obstacles in its way of His saving mercy. It will certainly look like they got there by a fluke! It will, however, be pretty obvious then that humans, even though created in the Image, simply did not have the wherewithal to gain eternal life on their own, unaided by divine grace.

"It is only then that humans will see exactly, not how *they themselves*, by cooperating with divine grace, escaped my tentacles, but how they made it there *despite themselves*. They will also find out at that time that there simply was no way humans could have been saved *a sola fide* - by their faith alone.

Silly proposition...

"Salvation by faith alone! What a silly proposition. Oh, you think you are clever, and you want to argue with me, Satan? You must be kidding! Faith is itself a divine gift. It is a form of grace which requires the individual's cooperation to be effectual. It doesn't swoop down on folks and cause them to be miraculously transformed against their will - or is that what you thought?

"That doctrine is based on a false premise - that, when dealing with creatures that are autonomous, free and individually accountable and not automatons, the Prime Mover could not get results by relying on *their* cooperation. He is - remember - not just almighty, but He doesn't go back on His word. He made humans free, and he won't interfere with the exercise of that freedom, even if it means watching them damn themselves! And He would do that if He somehow got them to ditch their evil ways without their *explicit* agreement *and* cooperation!

"Now, humans are creatures who are given to bragging. They brag about their attempt (albeit unsuccessfully) to bridge heaven and earth by constructing a tower (the tower of Babel); and are inflated with pride at having put up monuments such as the Great Pyramid of Giza. Humans even imagine that because they sent some chaps to walk on the moon, they are not really humans any more, but semi-gods! And some nowadays even brag about their ability to build impregnable empires or super powers, and their ability to launch 'star warfare' and to trounce everyone and everything that threatens their advance to greatness.

"And so, it is a little disingenuous and silly for humans, who are determined to continue wallowing in sin (following their sinful inclination), and are reluctant to don the 'armor of the Deliverer' out of pride, to plead ignorance about how to walk upright in the sight of the Prime Mover. And that is not mentioning the fact that, even as the individuals who believe that humankind is *saved by faith alone* make that claim, they assail the 'unsaved' and ridicule 'idolaters' and others who are supposedly predestined for hell.

"No! Humans are richly endowed creatures who were created with the ability to reason and to choose between good and evil. And, after all, Adam and Eve were mandated to put those faculties of reason and free will to use as they exploited the earth and everything in it while seeking to be actualized. Even after they chose evil and became inclined to do more evil in the process, it didn't mean that they would not be capable of making choices as between what was good and what was evil after that. It didn't mean that humans stopped being humans and lost control over their own fate.

"At no moment in time did that happen. For, hardly had Adam and Eve discovered themselves denuded of grace - and ashamed to walk around with nothing on - than they were promised the Deliverer. And so, virtually immediately, the first man and the first woman, *through* their faith in the promised Deliverer, again became capable of choosing between good and evil (despite the fact that they were now inclined to sin), provided they recognized that they could do good only *with* the help of grace.

"On their own, they could not do it - just as had been the situation before, when Adam and Eve were still in a state of grace. Before the fall, humans were of course inclined to do good - and that was what Adam and Eve did all the time. My troops and I didn't think we had the tiniest sliver of a chance that we would prevail on humans and persuade them to follow our example and revolt. If anything, I was gambling when I staked my 'honor' on the very remote possibility that they might be persuaded to hop aboard. You may not believe it, but the fact is that I, Diabolos, the epitome of wickedness, was banking on the goodness and constancy of the Prime Mover for my evil designs on humans - that He would not go back on his word and deny them the right to choose me and what I stood for over Himself!

"After the promise was made - and certainly after the Deliverer came (in fulfilment of that promise), expiated the sins of men through his death on the cross, rose from the dead in triumph over sin and death, ascended into heaven, and then sent the Comforter on Pentecost Day - humans, while still inclined to sin, had no excuse for not choosing good over evil or for putting on the armor of the Deliverer. The only thing that was expected of them was to show that they needed the divine grace bad. And the way they were supposed to do that was by becoming humble like little children and stopping all the swaggering - because 'who ever exalts himself shall be humbled and who ever humbles himself shall be exalted'.

"And when humans are like little children (like Theresa of the Child Jesus), they feel free as birds; and everything they do is good. It couldn't be anything else, because they have on the armor of the Deliverer - the same Deliverer who is alert and takes full note of the longings of the afflicted, and who encourages them and listens to their cry, and who mocks the proud and gives His graces to the humble... But if you are a 'little god', you can't possibly claim to fear the Lord. And yet, it is the fear of the Lord that is the beginning of wisdom!

"Fear the Lord, and put on the armor of the Deliverer (and be like a child), so that instead of being abandoned to evil works, you actually can start to do some good (like Mother Theresa of Calcutta) *with the help of the grace* merited for humans by the Deliverer). And, guess what? The really big problem for humans is that my troops and I here in Gehenna know all this - and we work overtime to make sure things happen *our* way.

"Now, just because an individual becomes persuaded that a doctrine is true or false doesn't mean that the individual in question has been delivered and will automatically start generating good works. One can believe in something stridently and be doing the opposite. In matters of faith, believing stridently in something is even dangerous, because hypocrisy easily comes into play, not to mention the baggage of a hypocritical life. It may be true that faith comes by knowledge, but the same does not apply to good works. But being like little children does the trick, for He humbles the proud and exalts the meek. In that sense, there is really nothing complicated about finding salvation. It is humans who complicate matters with their baggage.

"And, incidentally, if it were true that humans were saved by faith alone, one would also expect humans who were on their way to being saved by their faith - *if* they were indeed on their way to being saved at all by their faith alone - to be so compliant that what they believed would in practice not matter. This is because, as *humble* creatures, they would have no difficulty cooperating with grace (in accordance with the Church's doctrine of salvation) and generating good works (as opposed to bad works), evidence of which Saint Peter would demand to see before letting them in through the gates of heaven.

"And that suggests that 'proud' folks inside and outside the Church who despise 'unbelievers' need to be a wee bit more wary. 'Saved' folks should also be wary of the 'power' they boast - the power that is supposedly unleashed by their public 'acceptance' of the Deliverer. When it is from above, real 'power' makes one see how completely unworthy one is. And those inside and outside the Church who think they are 'worthy' of any thing or have special 'powers' should think twice about their boast. It could be a very empty boast indeed!

"The critical thing is to be certain that one's 'offering of good works' will be acceptable to the Prime Mover. Also keep in mind that my own 'offering' as Lucifer and Archangel, wasn't a little bit pleasing to Him in spite of my position right there in the Holy of Holies and specifically because of my pride. It is the same 'offering' that earned me the name of Arch-Devil!

Humans are free, but...

"Instead of forcing the Prime Mover to intervene and sanctify creatures that He made in His Image, feelings of self-righteousness merely repel Him. But by the same token, He does not feel compelled to stop creatures from going off on a tangent and trying to exalt themselves.

"But one must, of course, understand what is meant by 'not interfere' and what that non-interference translates into! Even after paying the price for the sins of humans, the Deliverer does not intervene to stop evil men having their way. Even though He could, he does not intervene to keep humans of good will harmless from humiliation, deprivation, and acts of violence perpetrated by evil humans. He could have interfered and stopped wars in which millions in every age perish because of the whims of empty-headed megalomaniacs.

"And so, because Providence won't interfere to stop evil men from turning the lives of other humans upside down, just imagine the toll that has on the trust and confidence of humans in their Prime Mover in general. When they see the Prime Mover - who so loved the world that he even gave His only begotten Son so that those who believe in Him might be saved, and is also almighty - seemingly unable to come to their succour in times of their greatest need., and who lets me, Satan, and my henchmen have our way in creating havoc in the world year in and year out, and making the lives of so many quite miserable, their hearts obviously sink.

"And, look - we are not talking fiction here. The toll on the trust of humans in their prime Mover is very real and biting - and discouraging in the extreme. Just look at all the 'big fish' who commit terrible crimes against humanity, but are shielded by their pals and never face justice regardless of the destruction they wreck in the lives of ordinary folks! Look at all the thieves on 'Wall Street' so-called, and the banks that do not even own the money they lend out, but are bailed out in nefarious schemes under the ploy that they are 'too big to fail' when it is simply the old boy network at play all over again, and only to see the same banks turn around and foreclose on the millions of home owners who were supposed to be the ultimate beneficiaries of the bank bail-out schemes with complete impunity!

"I first make sure my minions who work as agents for Wall Street and other gouging individuals and entities that are determined to pocket billions by hook and crook are themselves rewarded richly with lots of mammon and other material things, and they in turn have no hesitation in delivering the goods: they stop having any feelings for their fellow humans, and happily work with me to make sure that good folks feel so crushed, they forget that the Deliverer ever came!

"And look at all the governments that are into things like 'waterboarding' and other forms of torture, and that wouldn't dare harm a citizen of a country that was deemed more powerful, but play with the lives of people from defenseless nations that do not command the means to avenge such wrongs!

"If the Deliverer had made his appearance on earth during these times instead of two thousand years ago, He would probably find Himself initially eking out a living as a homeless street kid in a third world metropolis in conditions that were a direct consequence of policies of the Western controlled International Monetary Fund, or in a hamlet in the impoverished Gaza Strip that has been reeling under an international embargo - or doging drone strikes in Waziristan!

"Just imagine the despair, and how difficult it must be for the innocent, who suffer because of the actions of the greedy and the power hungry, to hang on to any hope in Providence! They must think that they were meant to live on a different planet, and are on Planet Earth by mistake!

"The only thing that saves humans who are in that predicament - and that is about every human who escapes my tentacles and is eventually lucky enough to find himself/herself in a position to claim the title of 'one of the elect' - is their acknowledgement that they are completely powerless in the face of those odds; that, as poor forsaken children of Adam and Eve, they are actually scared to approach the Deliverer (the eternal Word through whom all creation came into being), and the only thing they seem capable of doing is to prostrate themselves at the feet of the mother of the Deliverer and Judge, and ask her to intercede for them with her divine Son.

"Any way, the real catch - with respect to those who are determined to create havoc for their fellow humans - lies in the fact that the Deliverer and Judge desists from stopping humans of bad will from accumulating guilt for their sins. Yes, that is the catch!

"Every misdeed and every sin of omission adds to their guilt. And even though they are able to stifle and keep it bottled up it in their guilty consciences in the interim, the guilt itself will keep building; and it is usually just about ready to blow up in their faces as the time during which they were permitted to create all the havoc they were capable of creating in the world draws to an end. The explosion of their accumulated guilt is actually timed to occur at precisely the moment the sinful individual's soul separates from his/her body and that individual realizes that the hour of reckoning is finally at hand.

Joseph and Mary of Morogoro...

"Humans who mistreat others and do things that are not consonant with the will of their Creator - humans who refuse to listen to their consciences - actually damn themselves in the process, and they know it. They treat - or rather mistreat - other humans the way they do precisely because they want to cripple and 'neutralize' their perceived 'enemies', or at least see them suffer nasty physical or mental pain - or die. And it becomes damning for two reasons. They do whatever they do because they know that their own position is quite precarious, and they also understand perfectly well that what they are administering to others has the potential of causing the victims of their actions lots of grief and discomfort.

"They know that it is just a fluke that it isn't they themselves who are at the receiving end - that they are (luckily) not the ones enduring the torture, abuse, and humiliation or being targeted in some other way. And, yes - they also know that the tables could easily be turned. And, indeed, more often than not, it is the fear, real or imagined, of such an eventuality - the fear that those now at the receiving end could easily end up on the giving end with they themselves at the decidedly uncomfortable receiving end - that drives humans to be cruel and inhuman to their own kind.

"Short sighted humans chose to go on an 'avenging' spree under the mistaken notion that it would forestall a 'revenging' spree when it in fact did the exact opposite - it guaranteed a visit from the Avenging Angel!

"Humans may be reluctant to accept it, but they know very well that instead of being born and raised in Houston, Memphis, or in Essex in England as Methodists, Baptists, or members of the High Anglican Church, they could easily have been born and raised in Fallujah or Kandahar as Shiites or Sunnis - or on the Gaza Strip - and vice versa. Caucasians could have come into the world as

Mongolians, Africans, or Indians; Huguenots who ended up as American colonists could easily have come into the world as Cherokee tribesmen whom they tried hard to exterminate. Jews could easily have come into the world as Arabs, and Arabs as Jews. All these things are possible precisely because, while there is such a thing as a human soul, there is no such a thing as an American soul, a Greek soul, an Iraqi soul, a Chechen soul, a Russian soul, a Bengali soul, or a Zulu or 'black' soul.

"And it wouldn't take very much for those who for the moment might have the upper hand in deciding the fate of other humans to find themselves helpless and at the mercy of those they now regarded with disdain.

'Males, who show such a proclivity to discriminate against their female counterparts, could easily have come into the world as females, and vice versa. And it may be that once an individual is born a male or a female, that becomes a *fait accompli* the individual can do nothing about. But that is certainly not the end of the matter as, without any doubt, the day of reckoning is approaching for all regardless of whether the individual was born a man or a woman.

"There is nothing that would have prevented those humans who now boast citizenship in so-called advanced countries from coming into the world as citizens of the world's poorest and 'backward' nations - if Providence had so chosen. Those who pride themselves on being members of the one, true Catholic and Apostolic Church might very well have been born into Hinduism or Buddhism - and vice versa.

"And instead of being born in the 20th Century, humans who boast that they live in the 'modern age' could easily have come into the world as near cousins of Zinjanthropus or of Neanderthal Man. Also, as creatures fashioned in the Image, humans could easily have been brought into existence as pure spirits and members of one or other choir of angels - or not at all. The only thing that was completely out of question was for humans - or, for that matter, angels - to turn up as members of the Godhead for obvious reasons. This is the reason humans were commanded to love the Creator with all their hearts, minds and souls, and their neighbors as themselves.

"'Joseph and Mary of Nazareth' in Palestine could easily have been 'Joseph and Mary of Morogoro' in Tanzania. Instead of making them Palestinians, the Prime Mover could just as easily have made them Zulus. Instead of the 'Tribe of Israel', the Prime Mover could easily have opted for the 'Tribe of the Iroquois', most of whose members were massacred by the American colonists whose greed for land was apparently insatiable. Instead of being Indian, the billions who live on the Indian subcontinent and are still multiplying could easily have been Europeans who supposedly are dying out. Instead of the 'British Isles', where the proud British now live, there could easily have been an expanse of ocean inhabited only by seals, salmon and other types of fish.

"Instead of twelve apostles, the Deliverer could have easily opted for twenty - or none. In which case there wouldn't have been any 'church' or 'bible' for humans to squabble over. Also, the Prime Mover could easily have opted to save humans of good will directly without sending His only begotten Son to earth. In the event, the world would have been saved the murder and mayhem that goes on in Palestine and elsewhere in the name of the Prime Mover. But Providence no doubt opted for the current order of things (which relies on humans for such things as evangelizing and administering the holy sacraments) to demonstrate that nothing is really impossible with the Almighty One!

"The Prime Mover could easily have decreed at the beginning of time that if any creature that was made in His image betrayed Him, that creature would promptly loose its special status, and He would cease to be in-dwelling in it. Under such a regime, humans who fell from grace would find themselves transformed from 'homo sapiens' or 'wise humans' into doomed but still 'wizened animals' - much like a cow that could speak and reason, but could show nothing for it at the end of its sojourn on earth. These 'wizened animals' would then fizzle out and return to nothingness as their punishment for infidelity and proving unworthy 'pilgrims' on earth as and when they 'expired'.

But those humans who remained true to their consciences would enter heaven in glory.

"But I do not know if I - Beelzebub - would be 'happier' non-existent. As things are - and certainly as the head of the rebel band of angels, and also as the Father of Death, and Satan - I have quite a bit to show for my tumultuous, albeit torturous, 'life' or existence. The countless number of human souls, hopefully including yours, that Michael the Archangel will not be able to account for because they are 'lost' - for one!

"Those humans who now throw around their weight at the expense of other humans do so well-knowing that it really wouldn't take very much for the tables to be turned so that they themselves would be at the receiving end. It shows how stupid and dumb they too are. And, if that had been the case, they decidedly would not have liked to see what they might now be gleefully meting out to other folks meted out to them with or without any glee.

"And they would have exclaimed: 'There is an evil deed that cries out to heaven for retribution!' They would have also added: 'There go some folks who are supposed to be waiting for the arrival of the bridegroom with candles lit, but who have decided to make a nuisance of themselves and upset the rhythm of things.'

"And yet, for all their cockiness and 'invincibility', given what they are caught up in, may be the same thing that was said of Judas Iscariot after he betrayed the Deliverer - viz. that 'it were better if they had not been born' - probably applies to them as well. Meaning that the world would be better off without them!

"And what if they had come into the world as different beings altogether - as soul-less goats or sheep or roaches, or perhaps as white ants that do not seem to 'think' anything of themselves and are prepared to lay down their lives so that the Queen Ant may live on, or not at all! After all, no creature chose to be the creature he or she - or it - was.

Squandered and no longer available...

"When humans engage in misdeeds, they know exactly what they are up to. That is what happens when humans use foul language - they do so specifically to protest decency, and they cannot turn around and deny that they do not know what they are doing or that it is not wrong. And it is self-damning.

"What makes the situation of murderers, hedonists, and other hardened evil doers infinitely worse is the fact that they all know that the liberties they are taking not only have no lasting benefit, but have dire consequences for their eternal life in addition to being explicitly forbidden. And then those murderers, thieves, hedonists, lying louts, and hypocrites who want to have it both ways compound the problems when they go on to represent themselves as upright pillars of virtue, and in the process cause not just the innocent, but other vulnerable humans of good will who expect better of them, to be scandalized and to loose faith in the very existence of an almighty. And, as was pointed out by the Deliverer Himself, they end up deserving to have around their necks what he described as 'millstones about their necks' to assure that they sank to the bottom of the hell they were themselves pontificating about!"

Mjomba at first balked at the idea that he should include what he had just jotted down at the suggestion of the Evil Ghost. He worried that the devil was now casting the net so wide, all but the most heroic souls would escape his tentacles. For one, Mjomba knew how unworthy he himself was, and it was of course not very hard to envision situation in which any virtually seminarian could stand accused of being guilty of things like stealing, lying, or acting hypocritically.

It could even be argued that a seminarian became an accessory to murder if, in exercising his constitutional right to vote, he cast the vote for a political party whose platform included expansionist policies and things like preemptive military strikes and or economic embargoes with all that these things entailed on so-called "rogue nations" that were so labeled just because they refused to be bulldozed into casting their votes at the United Nations according to the dictates of his own country.

Still, the Evil Ghost could not be faulted for trying to bend the rules to suite anyone. The devil who was already condemned and damned clearly stood to gain nothing from doing so, but everything from taking the hard line! Mjomba was still inclined to prevaricate when an interior voice - he wasn't quite sure if it belonged to the Evil Ghost or to the Holy Ghost - firmly commanded him to just get on with it; and he found he himself had no choice but to just continue jotting down ideas he was certain were emanating from the Evil One.

"But, even worse, once humans (who are expected to love the Prime Mover above all else and to love their 'neighbor' as themselves) squander that love on frivolities" Mjomba wrote, "it becomes just that - squandered - and ceases to be available for dispensing on neighbors or on their Prime Mover - and He is a jealous God, too! That is reality regardless of what those humans feel, think or imagine. It is the reason those who left their allotted spots in the queue during the wait for the arrival of the bridegroom (in the Gospel story) did not just lose their places in the queue, but found themselves locked out of the banquet hall. Their interest in passing frivolities supplanted their interest in the royal wedding to which they had been formally invited.

"Similarly, an individual who is betrothed to another becomes unfit as a partner in the planned union when he/she knocks off in the meantime with another suitor, and loses his/her virginity - and above all his/her innocence and trustworthiness. It is the same for humans who break the commandments. They lose their innocence in the process - innocence that is intended to serve as their bridal gown and armour against my wiles and the wiles of my fellow demons.

"They stop being in the running for a reward in the afterlife, and instead start down the slippery way towards the pit - unless they succeed in making a U-Turn and getting themselves rehabilitated. But it becomes increasingly difficult to make the U-Turn after one fritters away one's precious gifts and virtues and, in particular, the 'cardinal' virtues (the virtues of prudence, justice, fortitude and temperance).

Rationalizing and justifying...

"Then, humans who lose their innocence invariably fall for the bait we throw at them - the temptation of trying to rationalize away their guilt and their ingratitude to the Prime Mover. But in the process of 'rationalizing' (which requires intelligence and implies that they know what they are up to) and justifying their actions (which requires the ability to discern what is right from what is wrong, and again implies that they in fact know what they are doing), humans implicitly acknowledge something else also, namely that it is not just a case of being out on a limb on their own (either individually or as a nation), and are essentially following their whims (instead of their individual or collective consciences). They acknowledge that they are a part of the wider phenomenon known as the 'human race'.

"They implicitly acknowledge that they have a nature, and that they share it with other humans who have existed or will in time exist. In 'rationalizing' and 'justifying', humans acknowledge in so many words that they possess faculties of the intellect and of the will - faculties that are so central to human nature. That is in itself very damning, because those who attempt to rationalize away their guilt explicitly acknowledge that they have a nature (which happens to be human), and that this same nature has been given an existence - the self-same existence they are even now enjoying.

"That in turn brings those humans face to face with the fact that they are enjoying something else - an existence - that an agent outside of themselves, a Prime Mover, has bestowed upon them to enable them to attain self-actualization as human 'beings'. And that in turn establishes the fact that there indeed was a Being to whom they owed their existence and were automatically accountable.

"If it were possible to imagine that a dependent creature endowed with reason and a free will and capable of causing mischief could be brought into existence and not have to account to any one for its misdeeds, that would in itself impute irresponsibility on the part of the Prime Mover, and make Him the most reckless Being imaginable -

a Being who permitted creatures of the calibre of 'humans' to follow their whims with impunity.

"Another way to establish conclusively that humans are indeed 'thinking' creatures is to take your pick of one thousand of these humans from completely different corners of the globe, gather them in a large compound, and leave them to their own devices. Unlike creatures that are endowed only with instinct, humans who are strangers to each other do not assume that the other chaps will automatically grasp the native tongue of the other strangers, and just go on blubbering away in Kiswahili, French, Japanese, Kikuyu, Spanish, Russian, Chinese, Greek, Urdu, Arabic, Lingala, English, Kiganda, or what have you.

"They will try to 'learn' each other's tongue in the same way they 'learnt' their mother tongue - if they keep their minds on the task at hand and don't suddenly go after each other's throats the way humans are wont to do nowadays, that is. And if they eschew animosities as they ought, they will even provide slow learners assistance with pronunciation and things like that - something the lower beasts just do not do.

"Then, it might also take those humans some time to master nine hundred and ninety-nine new languages; but that is what they will try to do. And to do that needs more than a mouth and an instinct. It required one to be a member of that specie known as '*homo sapiens*'. And accountability goes with membership in that exalted specie whose members make up what is known as 'Mankind'.

Demagoguery...

"As far as culpability goes, the situation remains unchanged for humans who accept positions of authority, and this is regardless of whether such positions are in the private or public domain.

"For a start, the Prime Mover does not recognize 'governments' as such. There is, of course, no such a thing as a 'super power'. That is not to say that he ignores the existence of chaps like Julius Caesar or Pontius Pilate (who are His creatures) or what they do. On the contrary, He demands of them personal accountability for their acts of commission or omission (while they occupy their high places) like everyone else.

"Humans who accept positions of authority do so at their peril. For power does not simply corrupt, it also stunts the reasoning. As a consequence, humans in positions of authority tend to develop into demagogues who forget that all authority comes from the Prime Mover. After a short while, many of them start behaving like little gods!

"But they are personally responsible for the plots they hatch against their own citizens or against citizens of other nations, for bribery and the corruption that breeds, and for decisions to pay bribes (sometimes disguised as foreign aid) to functionaries of other 'governments' for the purpose of promoting crooked schemes, and for everything that happens under their watch and infringes on the rights of other humans inside and outside their borders.

"In the moral sphere, there is no such a thing as liability that is 'joint and several'. Individual humans are personally liable for the use or misuse of the authority they wield. There is no such a thing as liability that is 'joint and several' on the other side of the gulf which separates the living from the dead. The Judge does not recognize bureaucracies or similar entities; and individuals who exercise authority on behalf of those entities bear full and personal responsibility for their roles as 'bureaucrats' in those entities. As far as the Judge is concerned, there is no conceivable way in which a bureaucrat could 'pass the buck' and escape personal responsibility for his/her role in dealings that left something to be desired from the point of view of Equity or Natural Justice.

"Now, if it easier for a camel to pass through the eye of a needle than for a rich human to enter heaven, you can just imagine how difficult it must be for a 'powerful' human to pass the Church Triumphant Entrance Test (CTET). Unlike the rich who have lots of time on their hands, the powerful typically do not even have spare time to do the assigned homework. And yet scores on that assigned 'homework' count towards the final score on the CTET.

"I am Beelzebub, and I may be fallen now. But, as the most glitzy creature that had ever existed at the time I fell from grace (I have since ceded that honor to the beloved Mother of the Deliverer), I used to wield a lot of power over other creatures. And guess what - it is what brought me down. If you do not believe that I was powerful, I invite you to stop and reflect on just a couple of my aliases: the Prince of Demons, the Oppressor of the Saints, the Prince of Darkness, and the Lawless One. And I am really fond of this particular one: The Adversary!

"And just ask me about the power I still exercise over sinful humans and over the damned - even though I am a fallen arch angel! Do you know how many times I am referred to by name - yes, by name - in the New Testament alone? So, you just take my word for it: it is most difficult and nearly impossible for creatures in positions of power - and certainly humans who are born inclined to sin - to avoid becoming infatuated with it. It is a lot harder for the powerful on earth to enter heaven than for the rich who could just give away everything they owned to the poor - if they had acquired it through their own hard work and had not stolen it - and be virtually guaranteed of walking away with their CTET diploma. Power also corrupts you see!

"In accepting positions of responsibility, individual humans implicitly acknowledge the source of the authority that is vested in those positions. And that source has to be the Prime Mover who gave them their status as *homines sapientes*. But for many humans, positions of power turns them into little gods. This is what is so tragic about the ancestors of Adam and Eve.

"They soon start imagining that can hoodwink everyone, including the Prime Mover, by hiding behind labels such as empire, state government, or some similar entities to escape personal responsibility for their actions. Some start fancying that when they occupy positions such as 'General' or 'Commander-in-Chief', they stop being answerable to anyone. Frequently they try to bypass the commandments by making their own rules including the so-called 'rules engagement'!

"Others imagine, quite mistakenly, that it is political pundits, newspaper gossip columnists, lobbyists, pollsters, and even court jesters to whom they are answerable for their actions. They even fool themselves that public opinion polls and the verdict of voters (who are so liable to manipulation these days) are indicative of whether their own acts of commission and omission are in line with the divine will or not. But they engage in that kind of Tom foolery at their peril.

Cain's "empire"...

"You know the story of Cain, I suppose. He may be in heaven now, but he was a real lout when he was back on earth - at least before he repented of his misdeeds, renounced me and my wiles, and then made amends for murdering his brother Abel. That murder was a deed that was so horrendous it even shocked us here in the Pit. In one stroke which saw the first deliberate killing in the human family, Cain - the first death culture enthusiast - wiped out a fifth of the human race, and set the stage for humans to try and 'justify' killings of their own kin in the name of the 'empire' or 'state'!

"Taking advantage of the fact that the penitent and selfless Adam and Eve had no interest in material things, Cain had laid claim to ownership of all the arable tracks of land which stretched as far as the eye could see by the time Abel came of age. Cain referred to the enormous expanse of land as his 'empire'! The only exception was Paradise Valley which Adam and Eve had been tilling long before Cain himself was born. Cain was always having nightmares about 'nations' rising up to challenge his 'empire' and putting some of Planet Earth's resources out of bounds so that he wouldn't be able to exploit them as his own and to levy 'duties' and 'taxes' on anyone else who wanted to have use of them.

"The epitome of meanness and a lazy lout at the same time, who initially thought he could feed off the sweat of his old man and woman indefinitely, Cain had at one time threatened to drive his parents from their modest farm house in Paradise Valley into the wilderness. Intent on ensuring that their son learned to fend for himself, they had told Cain that the pineapples and mango trees in Paradise Valley which they tilled for food were off limits to him. Because the same did not apply to Abel, who was always there to lend the old man and the old woman a hand in working the fields in Paradise Valley, Cain automatically diverted his ire to his brother whom he accused of intrigues and blamed for the fact that he sorely missed the pineapples and mangoes.

"Finding himself treated like a virtual alien by his brother and specifically barred by Cain from tilling any piece of his 'empire', Abel had resorted to hunting to obtain the food he needed to assuage his hunger as he grew into a young man and set up his own home on the edge of Paradise Valley. Abel discovered to his amazement that some of the animals, particularly goats, sheep and cows, were quite easy to domesticate. He did not know it, but his gentle nature had everything to do with it. That was how Abel came to be a 'herdsman' while Cain, with his mean, cruel and evil disposition, continued on as a 'farmer' as the bible says.

"Cain hated the idea that the weaning animals allowed Abel to milk them for free. He was also jealous that his brother enjoyed eating many different kinds of veal, including roast beef and salted ham, while he himself fed on cabbage, ripe bananas and things like that; and he was soon eyeing the herds of goats, sheep and cattle that grazed on his land, and wishing that it was he himself rather than Abel who had possession of the animals.

"The hard-hearted Cain for some reason imagined that Abel, who was clearly endeared to the animals, wouldn't be persuaded to part with any of his sheep or goats or head of cattle even at a price. Cain, who had at first considered the possibility of engaging in barter trade with Abel in which he would give his brother some of the yield from the land in exchange for such things as meats, milk, and animal hide which he could use to protect himself from the morning chill, soon abandoned that idea. In Cain's mind, Abel was already looming as someone who was a squatter on land to which he, Cain, had sole ownership.

"Cain also believed or imagined that Abel's animals posed an obvious threat to his crops. Even though a lot of the maize crop in the fields went to waste because Cain couldn't eat it all, he had caught one of Abel's weaning goats munching away on a maize cob in the fields, and that had not gone down very well with him. It had made him sick to the stomach, particularly because he had stumbled and nearly broken his neck as he chased the animal off the maize plantation, bat in hand. He had done so with the specific intention of killing the animal and depriving Abel of its milk thereby.

"It troubled Cain that Adam and Eve, instead of supporting his position, stood squarely behind Abel, and pressed him to accept that his brother had as much right to the use of the land as himself. And when Abel politely asked him if he (Abel) could fence in an uncultivated moor and use it as a kraal for his animals, it was the last straw Cain had been waiting for. In Cain's eyes, Abel had ceased to be just a squatter. He had become a 'terrorist' whose aim was to slowly drive Cain off his land and take over the empire.

"By that time, Cain and Abel had two other siblings of the female gender. Cain had already been dotting on the elder girl for sometime, and he had let the old man and the old woman know that he planned to take her for his wife. It therefore came as a surprise to everyone when Cain asked the younger and more handsome girl for her hand in marriage. The 'emperor' had apparently not been quite prepared for what transpired next. The younger girl had rebuffed his approaches and, to Cain's great dismay, had gone on to announce publicly that she was already betrothed to the gentle Abel.

"Cain blamed Abel for his woes, and now accused him of plotting to 'defile' the thirty-five year old. This was even though he himself had already impregnated the elder girl who, at the 'young' age of fifty-five, was preparing to have a baby. That was the time the mean Cain begun plotting to murder the 'terrorist' and 'insurgent' and now, alas, also his competitor!

"But by this time, my team had also supplanted Cain's guardian angels as his 'protector', and the posse of demons not only trooped within hearing distance of Cain wherever he went, but was on hand to urge him on and provide him whatever further inspiration he stood in need of as he went about devising plans to rid the world of the 'terrorist', 'hoodlum' and 'thug'. And, not content with plotting his brother's murder, Cain thought he was clever and could 'justify' his actions. He was going to officially declare himself 'Emperor of the World' and that was going to do the trick!

"While some of his actions like eating and sleeping would continue to be done by him in his private capacity as Cain, the great bulk of his decisions thenceforward would be made by him in his official capacity as Emperor Cain. The implication was that if some of those decisions turned out to be against natural justice or plainly wrong, the final responsibility for such decisions would rest with the impersonal 'Office of the Emperor'.

"In other words, while he would be responsible for the actions he did in his personal capacity like eating and resting, he certainly couldn't take personal responsibility for actions relating to the impersonal 'Office of Emperor'. Cain accordingly kept telling himself over and over that he didn't have anything personal against Abel and that he truly 'loved' his kid brother.

"And so, putting on his Emperor's hat or 'crown', and speaking from the garden behind his official residence or 'Black House' as he called it, Cain had 'announced to all and sundry' that Abel was a terrorist and an insurgent, and should turn himself in for his own safety along with his heavy weapons or be destroyed. By 'heavy weapons', Cain meant the shepherd's staff which Abel also used as a walking stick and the machete Abel used to cut firewood and on the odd occasion to scare away a marauding bear or a stray lion. But of course, no one heard the declaration or 'decree' because of a thunderous storm which was raging at the time.

"If something happened to Abel in those circumstances, he would be a 'casualty of war' - or so Cain thought. It would not be a homicide, and it certainly would not be a murder. Would it be something that was unfortunate? Certainly - if you looked at it from the perspective of Abel's wife and kids. Desirable? Yes - if you looked at it from the point of view of the empire's security!

"Cain's wife thought that the man was going off the rails, and hastened to inform the old man and the old woman. But she did not need to do that because Adam and Eve themselves had already noticed that their older son had started behaving 'funny', and they had even asked him to if he was alright.

"At one point, Adam decided that he couldn't remain silent in the face of Cain's shocking behavior and attitude towards Abel. He confronted Cain and suggested to him that he was definitely headed for eternal damnation if he did not change course and stop treating his brother as if he were some 'terrorist'! The old man advised him to stop being confrontational and start treating Abel like a member of the human family and a beloved brother at that. Power, Adam said in his deep grating voice, was not everything. To the old man's consternation and despair, Cain had simply screamed in response: 'Power is it's own reward!'

"Thoroughly frustrated, the old man had retorted: 'Your wife is right. You are out of your mind!'

"Still, hoping for a miracle, Adam had pleaded: 'Sonny, your mother and I are old, and our days on earth are numbered. After we are gone, you will be the oldest soul on Planet Earth. Are we to understand that it is this hideous culture of death - this hankering for power at all cost - that will now rule the world after we cross the Gulf and go to our judgement?'

"Adam hated to think that it was the original sin (for which he took full personal responsibility) that had occasioned that unanticipated and rather ugly state of affairs. The old man also had this awful premonition that even though a deliverer had been promised and, whoever he was or wherever he came from, would definitely come to save humankind from the grip of evil and to take the sting out of death, his own fate on earth would be a terrible, terrible one. Adam was beside himself and disconsolate as he pondered the possibility that the deliverer would himself be murdered by the very creatures he would be coming to rescue from eternal damnation! It would be really terrible for the deliverer to be allowed to die, because death was one of the wages of sin.

"It was all the more reason, Adam told himself, that he could not give up on Cain who represented the first fruits of his marriage to Eve. Thoroughly exasperated, he had pointed a quivering finger at Cain as he screamed: 'Son, do you know what happens to a hyena after a while after it has fed on its catch and has a bursting tummy? Answer me?'

"Cain: 'It shits.'"

"Adam: 'Good, Lord! And are you aware - do you know that your labors as emperor of the world add up to nothing more than a full tummy? Do you realize that at the end of it all, as the sunset prepares to converge on your life, you will have nothing to show for it but shit - the shit you will be shitting from now until you die, Shit?"

"Cain wanted to say 'I'm not shit', but remained silent."

"Adam pursued: 'You have to be prepared to shed tears - to cry - when you finally kick the bucket and leave all behind as you most certainly will do eight hundred or nine hundred years hence. When your soul, bereft of your body and also of the trappings of empire, is ushered into the presence of the Word and Judge, you will have nothing to show for your days on earth, Sonny, apart from the shit!'"

"After listening to Adam's 'lecture', Cain thought that everybody, including his father, had gone completely nuts. For one thing, the last person Cain expected to lecture to him about eternal life - or eternal damnation - was the old man. Certainly not after he and his mom had gone off and (as Cain put it) made a deal with 'Satan' and ruined everything for themselves and everyone else who would ever step on earth!

"Cain's bitterness was palpable as he recalled how, at the tender age of ten, his parents had made him sit down and had recounted the events leading up to the fateful day when they were surprised by the appearance of Michael the Archangel as they surreptitiously plucked and ate fruit from the Tree of Life. Told that the angel then drove the pair out of the Garden of Eden and into the wilderness where they would have to struggle to survive before eventually dying, Cain, in his innocence, had asked repeatedly why his dad, with his strong muscles, had not stood his ground and chased the angel out of the Garden of Eden instead.

"It had taken Adam and Eve a couple of days of explaining to convince the boy that it would not have done to try and fight back; and that they obeyed and left because it would have made things much worse to try and fight the archangel who had the loyal angels and the Prime Mover Himself on his side.

"Now, many years later, after listening to his father and waiting patiently for him to finish his 'lecture', Cain shouted back that (Cain) was not a hypocrite, and that he accepted the fact that he was an embittered person. He added that he had been born like that thanks to the original sin for which his parents, who now had the nerve to stand there and moralize to him, were entirely responsible.

"As Cain imagined it, everyone - the old man , the old woman, the women, and even Abel who 'went around with a pious face' - was embittered just like himself and disappointed after loosing the automatic right to the heavenly inheritance. Cain choked on his words as he repeated that he wasn't the one who dreamed up the notion of original sin. He did not 'acquire' his inclination to sin. He was born with it. And, as far as he was concerned, the world was there for the taking, and he was determined to get and keep his portion of it.

"Cain had no doubt in his mind that behind the mask of Abel's piety - behind that facade of good-naturedness and congeniality - lay a raging monster that could come awake at a moment's notice. Cain did not like or trust Abel a bit for that reason. If the hypocritical Abel wanted to lead a life of make believe - if he wanted to go around smiling to trees and the birds that had their nests in them, or if he wanted to continue playing patsy with animals of the wild the way he had been doing, that was his business.

"As far as Cain was concerned, the fact that he himself and Abel belonged to the same human race and the same stock - the fact that they both had the same father and the same mother - was completely immaterial. Cain looked ahead in time and imagined the earth full of humans who could not possibly know each other as a practical matter, and who looked very different from each other as a result of exposure to the different climates, and they did not even understand each other because they spoke different dialects, had different customs, and had almost nothing in common apart from the fact that they were all descended from Adam and Eve just like himself, Abel and their wives. And he guessed correctly that they wouldn't place any premium on the fact that they were all humans. If anything, they would always be wishing that anyone who didn't look exactly like themselves - or who did but happened to belong to different 'ethnic' groupings - would just drop dead!

"Cain wasn't the type of person to go around telling himself that 'he had a dream'. He'd in fact heard Abel whisper something like that on the day he, Cain, had prevailed on Adam to warn Abel that he risked war if he tried to till any piece of the tracts of fertile land in the vicinity of the Garden of Eden to which Cain had staked ownership before Abel came of age.

"Cain had even alarmed his wife with his frequent references to the fact that things radically changed from the moment their mom and dad were tempted to eat of the forbidden fruit from the tree of knowledge of good and evil! And he asserted ever so often that from then on, 'cavetousness' by which he meant 'everyone for him/herself' and 'capitalism' which he defined as 'strategic thinking and business acumen' effectively became accepted 'norms' or 'principles' without which all human endeavors would be doomed to failure! He explained to his wife that the legacy of the original sin their parents had committed was that ant human who did not apply his/her knowledge, regardless of whether it was the knowledge of good or knowledge of evil, to his/her individual circumstances would be left behind. Cain had then declared that, to achieve any progress in the hard times that had befallen the world with the fall of Man from grace, all humans had to be acquisitive and selfish!

"The only problem that Cain saw was that, even after one had successfully accumulated wealth on an immesnse scale and also consolidated the power that was necessary to ensure that other humans couldn't grab it, an earthquake or a plague could wipe away all those material gains in an instant. Humans remained spiritual beings; and, upon 'kicking the bucket', the human soul went to judgment while he body returned to the dust from which it came. That arguably posed a quandry of sorts for progressive-minded folks like himself, but did not by itself debunk his arguments for capitalism.

"Cain, who generally liked to stand out in a crowd, was glad that he belonged to the first generation of humans and had not been born in an era when folks would be mere statistics. But even if he did - even if he had been born in the Tenth or even Twentieth Century - he had made up his mind that he would do things differently. Actually he would work very hard to be a 'leader of the pack' (by which he meant an emperor, a king or at the minimum a tribal chief) to whom the masses paid respects. And he would not hesitate to be cruel and ruthless to stay ahead of the pack and not be reduced to a statistic.

"Under his reign, any of his subjects who did not toe the line would be dealt with firmly. And he would not only rule with an iron fist, he would assemble armies with a view to going out on foreign adventures to annex new lands; and he would, of course, target those countries that either had good arable land and or were rich in minerals and other resources.

"And while at it, any one opposing his action would be declared an insurgent and terrorist, and would be 'neutralized' - rubbed out. A practical man, Cain was going to 'live one life at a time' as he put it. Meaning that, whilst on this earth, he would concentrate on enjoying himself and not spend any time worrying about 'his last end'. He was, accordingly, determined to live the fullest life as an inhabitant of this world, and would let the 'hereafter' that his dad and mom kept pontificating about take care of itself.

"In Cain's view, the world was there for the taking, and he was determined to get *and* keep his portion of it for himself and the many children he hoped to father. In those circumstances, power - and the firm exercise of power - was of the essence. And if push came to shove, he was going to be rough and cruel with anyone who tried to stand in his way as he exercised rule over his empire and sought to expand its borders to ensure that he had control over the earth's scarce resources.

"Cain saw the security of his empire as something that was paramount, and more important even than the bond of brotherly love that existed between Abel and himself. When he was listening to his dad berate him for ignoring his 'afterlife', Cain had in fact mumbled under his breadth and out of ear-shot of his fuming dad that he would not hesitate to take a human life if that was what it was going to take to consolidate his power over the portion of Mother Earth he had claimed for himself.

"As Cain saw it, there was nothing wrong with 'cutting short' the lives of other humans (as he referred to killing or murder) for the specific purpose of maintaining control over resources he deemed important for his empire's security, or to ensure that his descendants would not lack anything that might be available to other humans. According to Cain's reasoning, power was the decisive factor, and the powerful gained an automatic to anything that could be had through its exercise. And, by the same token, weaklings forfeited their right to ownership of anything if they were unable to keep challengers at bay.

"This was a 'law of nature' that even animals of the wild obeyed. The fittest survived; and deservingly so, while weaklings didn't because they clearly didn't deserve anything else. And because he saw everything in the prism of the exercise or non-exercise of power, Cain had no doubt that there would be a scramble by the strong, both real and pseudo, to carve curve out and claim pieces of Mother Earth for themselves in due course. He was also certain that the world's development was going to have as its driving force, not self-abnegation and piety, but selfishness and materialism. Cain saw some very positive aspects to the very things that his parents decried namely acquisitiveness, meanness, ruthlessness, and craftiness.

"In his mind's eye, Cain saw the rise and fall of an assortment of power brokers, including rival emperors, 'kings', 'chiefs', and others whose one objective would be to topple him from power and install themselves as the new and unchallenged 'heads of state'. He was under no illusion about the dangers that his empire would in time face as other humans started eyeing the resources under its control, and he was gearing himself to 'play hard ball', as that was almost certainly going to be the name of the game in the not too distant future.

"As the head of the world's first ever 'super power' saw it, any nations that sprung up and were not themselves super powers had per force to toe the line set by his empire and agree to become an 'ally'. Those nations that didn't automatically became 'rogue states'. The regime of 'international law' - which he would be instrumental in helping to establish (with the stated objective of maintaining peace and good order in the world) - would recognize the authority of his super power to intervene in the affairs of rogue states for the purpose of transforming them into 'democratic' states and also effectively 'allies'.

"His resort to the use of force in effecting this transformation would be perfectly legitimate if persuasion failed to work. A rogue state that successfully resisted its transformation into a 'democracy' of an accepted brand would automatically become a 'failed state'.

"With his understanding of human nature, Cain knew that if you deliberately stepped on some else's toes - when you rode rough shod over other people's rights - you had to start getting in the habit of looking over your shoulder from time to time because of the enemies you made. But he had a simple solution to all that. And his solution was to be more - not less - ruthless, brutal and mean. Cain believed that once you abandoned natural justice and subscribed to other ways, half-hcarted measures became self-defeating. And yet the challenge that all humans faced was to succeed. (He always kept telling himself that his parents representing humanity hadn't been commanded to 'go, multiply and fill the earth' for nothing!)

"Regardless of the original problem that would cause him to 'unsubscribe' to natural justice, his inclination would always be to respond to any resistance against the policies adopted by his empire with brute force and heavy-handedly at that. He had made up his mind that he would quell any revolts that might be brewing firmly and forcefully, and thereby ensure that he was always in control over all situations. Such an approach would in his view also assure that he always had the upper hand in his dealings with all the other players.

"Cain wasn't dumb. He knew the power of 'truth'; and he had, accordingly, resolved that he would always ensure that he had machinery in place to put a spin on events in such a way that the victims of his injustices would be the ones who would be depicted as the trouble makers and culprits. His staff would include PR people, and they definitely would have to be individuals who were leaders in the public relations field. His PR machinery would have to be the sort that could depict lies as truth and vice versa.

"Cain knew from dealing with his own conscience that, in matters of right and wrong, repetition had a way not so much of silencing the conscience as of getting it to agree with him that whatever previously loomed as morally wrong actually wasn't. Owing no doubt to the intense pressures on him to grow his so far non-existence 'state' into an empire and indeed a super power, Cain had gotten this strange idea into his head that when the conscience stopped nagging, it effectively meant that what had previously been morally unacceptable in fact changed and became morally acceptable. He similarly believed that repeating that a lie was not a lie made it into a truth - in exactly the same was repetition changed a 'wrong' into a 'right' and vice versa. And so now, all Cain needed to do was to make sure that his PR people also got those important principles right, and 'indoctrination' carried out in the right manner would easily take care of.

"It would all come down to the fact that he, Cain, would always be right, and all who contradicted him would be always be wrong. His spin machinery had to be capable of 'proving' that 'known knowns' were actually 'known unknowns', 'unknown knowns', or even 'unknown unknowns' - and the other way round. And so, any one who came up with any allegations of 'injustices' on his part and things like would have to come prepared to rebut a mass of trumped up (read 'perfectly true and provable') charges against the complainant that if pursued would result in even more serious indictments.

"Cain's spin machinery would always be anticipating the reactions of people to everything he did, and complainants would never stand a chance. At the very minimum, the spin machinery would have to be capable of depicting the different forms of torture, humiliation and abuse of humans as 'humane treatment'.

"This was important because torture particularly was something his lieutenants would definitely have to resort to very frequently as they sort to gain the 'intelligence' they needed for stopping foolhardy terrorists who might be bent on violating the empire's borders, and for planning and executing successful preemptive wars against 'hostile' nations, in particular those nations that fell in the category of an 'axes of evil' (whatever Cain meant by that). Cain figured that, in order to safeguard against any of the empire's own operatives being tortured and abused contrary to accepted principles of morality in the event that they were themselves captured, it would be prudent not to openly admit that the empire sanctioned torture and the abuse or humiliation of captives.

"Cain's bet was that, in a world in which unfairness and cruelty were the order of the day as a direct result of the unwarranted and ill-advised theft by his parents of fruit from the Tree of Life, it would always be smarter to be the dominant player and on top of things.

"It would also be much better for those who found themselves short-changed to swallow their pride and accept injustices as a 'given'. If anything, if people had any common sense and wanted to survive in the terrible conditions in which Planet Earth was going to be enmeshed - if they knew what was good for them - it would be advisable for them to specifically seek his 'protection'. And, protection being what it was, it would always come at a price of course.

"And so in short, Cain would add another dimension to the management style he employed in running his empire. He would essentially borrow a leaf from the methods of the 'mafiosi' as he would refer to small time hoodlums who would reason in the same way as he himself, but whose operations would compliment (rather than take away from) his empire and make it more formidable.

"The 'mafia' would be perfectly good, law abiding citizens who operated on strict 'capitalistic' principles. Even though the population of the world (which numbered in single digits) did not yet include mafia elements when Cain was thinking these things through, he had absolutely no doubt that a time would come when the mafiosi phenomenon would emerge - just as his empire was set to grow and expand.

"Cain had already made up his mind that he would always do everything he did with a straight face both to emphasize that he was in the right and because, unlike everyone else, he at least was using his head (or so he thought). And being 'in the right' of course meant that he was a straight talking, upright and just man who was dedicated to 'progress' under the new order which the original sin of his parents had ushered in.

"Cain figured that under that new order - an order in which dying was going to be an ordinary occurrence like being born, eating, walking, and sleeping - acquisitiveness was perfectly normal. One could decide to confine oneself to the immediate environs of the hut in which one lived and become an 'immobile' citizen of the world, or one could be enterprising and dream of building an empire that stretched to the edge of the world as he was trying to do. Thus, instead of just confining one's dreams to the present, one could dream and - through one's dreams - actually live in the future. That was the essence of being an enlightened and mobile citizen of the world.

"Looking into the future, Cain saw or imagined a world that was literally teaming with people. He rationalized that in the interests of progress, even though all humans were created equal, some would definitely end up 'more equal than others'! This would mean in effect that those who were more equal - which was just another way of saying more progressive - would be entitled to more rights, including the right to life. In the same way the lives of certain animal species were sacrificed to ensure the survival of other animal species in the divine plan, it seemed plain, and indeed obvious, that the lives of some of the earth's inhabitants would be more precious than the lives of others. Under the new order, this appeared inevitable, even though all humans were created in the Image and accordingly were equally precious in the eyes of the Prime Mover.

"While 'reasoning' thus, Cain had concluded that it would be perfectly acceptable if the armies he would assemble killed other humans who stood in the way of the expansion of the empire. The emperors, kings, tribal chiefs - or whatever the future rulers of the world would call themselves - would all be seeking to expand at the expense of others; and the motto undoubtedly would be 'kill or be killed'!

"Whether in a mobile or immobile society, a ruler would only be responsible for the safety and welfare of the citizens of the empire, because it was these citizens who paid fiefs to him/her and were also available for enlistment in the empire's defense forces. And while seeking to secure the empire's borders and making certain that they are not violated, the lives of non-citizens would not be worth a farthing or dime. If anything, 'foreigners' would have to be treated as such - foreigners or aliens - and they might as well be hailing from a different planet.

"That in effect would mean that if whole cities populated by foreigners were wiped out inadvertently or even deliberately by Cain's forces with the help of the latest technology, such a measure could always be justified on the grounds that members of the Cain clan were not among the casualties, and by the fact that the objective was to strengthen the security of the 'empire'.

"With the backdrop of original sin which made all humans inclined to sin or evil, Cain thought it would be suicidal not to take cognizance of that in planning for his empire. It wasn't that he was mean and murderous. He was just trying to be practical, and he had no doubt that any ruler who did not take the same precautions would pay the ultimate prize - lose his/her empire to those rulers who were more enterprising and/or were better at using their heads and deliver the empire's citizens into captivity.

"One morning, the flamboyant Cain woke up with an idea he himself thought was rather brilliant. One of his first acts as emperor would be to set up a 'secret service' or 'intelligence agency'. This would be important for two reasons. To begin with, the agency would keep a tab on everyone who looked remotely like a threat to his rule.

"Even though lions, crocodiles, elephants, venomous snakes, mosquitoes, and other creatures of the wild scared him, and arguably posed what was often an even greater threat to his life and by extension to his rule that Abel and others humans whom the Eternal Word would bring into existence, Cain wasn't bothered about them. This was because, unlike humans, their behavior and moods were predictable - something which went a long way to reduce the actual threat they posed to his life. Because the same could not be said of humans who could backbite, connive with others to lay traps for an individual they disliked, or even plan outright murder (just as he himself was doing), Cain figured that he would need an intelligence agency to keep them in check. The principal task of the 'spy agency' would be to collect, evaluate and disseminate 'intelligence information' that his inner circle would need for that purpose.

"But the 'secret service', as that agency would also be known, would also have another and even more important purpose. Cain knew that as a human he definitely was going to commit blunders along the way as he labored away on his ambitious scheme of building a mighty empire. A proud man, he feared that some of those blunders would end up causing such grief to his subjects, it was not just conceivable but very likely that some of them would start getting the idea that they could do without a leader who was such a 'bumbling idiot' - one who made the empire a more dangerous place to live in! They would, in other words, be tempted to impeach him or get rid of him in some other manner.

"Cain, accordingly, wanted to have a perfect scapegoat for those unpredictable occasions when things went awry. He wanted - when things 'bombed' (as they say) - to be able to say: 'No single individual was to blame. No one lied; and, certainly, no one made up the intelligence or sexed up anything. According to the findings of the independent commission of inquiry (Cain's administration would made provision for commissions of inquiry whose members would of course be appointed by himself as a matter of course since because they would always come in handy if he needed to cover things up), there is no evidence that the administration did not itself believe the judgements which it was placing before the public. Everyone genuinely tried to do their best in good faith for the empire in circumstances of acute difficulty. And moreover we should, above all, not fall into the trap of trying to rewrite history!'

"Thus, Cain and his cronies in the administration would always be in a position to point an accusing finger at the 'secret service' whose activities would be secret and unknown to the public by definition. And they could always call for an overhaul of the 'intelligence agency' to ensure that the intelligence that would be at their disposal would be more accurate and reliable. They would do that even though one would have thought that an 'intelligence agency', because it dealt in 'intelligence' would be employing some of it to reform itself automatically and all the time, and that no one outside the 'secret service' would be qualified to take any corrective measures its regard.

"Cain definitely had every intention of getting the spy agency to work. He expected it to produce good 'actionable' intelligence - meaning that if his administration ever came into possession of intelligence that when acted on would change the balance of power in the world in favor of the empire. He would never hesitate to act. How could he since he would be prepared to act even on cooked intelligence (or intelligence that had been 'sexed up').

"And so, while some would say that because a country was in possession of intelligence about another exposing weakness in that country's defenses in a critical area, mere possession of such intelligence in the absence of evidence of hostile intent on that other country's part did not by itself justify a preemptive strike on that country, Cain would have begged to differ. For it would in his view be unstatesmanlike to let any opportunity to consolidate and strengthen the empire's power slip by. That would be quite irresponsible and also unconscionable given the responsibility that his administration would have for the well-being of the empire's future generations.

"But the whole idea of power politics was to stay ahead of the 'game'; and it would never do to fritter away any opportunities to permanently remove potential contestants for the position of super power from the scene. In any event, in the do or die environment of big power politics, the 'other side' would also be on the lookout for any similar opportunities that came their way and, if they had any common sense, they would know that they would be attacked and neutralized by any competing power if they let down their guard.

"Cain did not expect 'politics' (which was the name of the game) to be anything but that - dirty, ruthless and deadly for the losers whether it was politics that was 'internal' or 'external'. And he sincerely believed that unless his administration succeeded in getting the whole world firmly under control, there would be real danger of the world drifting into chaos. Cain frowned on the suggestion that humans, many of whom were really evil (like Abel), could coexist peacefully in a multicultural setting without a benevolent dictator to keep them in line and stop the evil ones from having their way. If anything, he felt duty-bound to root out them out and make the world safe once and for all.

"The spy agency would help him and his ruling oligarchy (consisting of fine, principled men of the highest morals) to keep tabs on potential terrorists, insurgents and dictators the world over, and also prevent the riffraff and other 'uncultured' and 'uncivilized' humans from threatening those in the world who were 'cultured' and 'civilized'.

"As a matter of fact, Cain planned, once the spy agency was up and running, to create another and even more secretive 'office of special operations' which would only be known by the letter 'D' for 'Death'. He would set it up as ostensibly a 'department' of the spy agency - but a completely autonomous department whose operations would be funded from a secret slush fund. The mission and activities of the 'department' would be so secret only he himself would actually know that the various sections of the department actually made one whole - meaning that he would himself be responsible for directing the operations of the individual sections of the department and for coordinating their activities. In other words, the individuals he vetted and appointed to manage the department's sections would be kept in the dark about the existence of the department's other section.

"Now, the department would be manned by the cream of the empire's scientists, and their job would include the development of poisons, all sorts of killer viruses and retroviruses, as well as deadly chemical and biological agents that he could use to mysteriously wipe out enemy encampments and even rebellious sections of the empire's own populations. Cain took his responsibilities as emperor that seriously.

"And to prove that the Cain doctrine wasn't just one of those doctrines that was forgotten as soon as it was promulgated, many generations after Cain, a 'statesman' of world renown would assert: 'I do not understand the squeamishness about the use of gas. I am strongly in favor of using poison gas against uncivilized tribes'. By 'uncivilized tribes', he meant the Sunnis, Shiites and Kurds of Mesopotamia. That statesman would insist that 'scientific expedient...should not be prevented by the prejudices of those who do not think clearly'.

"When a creature - a descendant of Adam and Eve (to be exact) who himself or herself gets around by balancing on his/her two spindly legs, and hardly ever gets to be taller than a full grown ostrich, and who (unlike ostriches) can be felled by a single mosquito bite - starts to speak like that, you have to know that there is something wrong with that creature. Yeah, why do humans say and do these things to each other?

"Now, to ask why humans deal with their own in that fashion is to question my existence. I am the author - yes, author - of death, and I am pretty efficient at what I do. I sow seeds of death quite effectively, and I do it not just at the individual level, but also at the level of state so-called. And that is why, instead of being known as the 'culture of death', the celebration of killing is now know as the 'culture of life'.

"And if you still want to know why humans do what they do to each other, the answer is simple: Selfishness. It is what I get humans to focus on. 'Love thyself above all else' is what we here in the Pit harp on constantly. Loving themselves and those who are dear to them effectively counters the Deliverer's injunction that humans love each other as themselves and their Maker above all else.

"The pact I make with would-be-statesmen is this: I will show you the short cuts to your dreams, but if you promise to focus on the self and on other humans only to the extent that to which they are a help to you in reaching your goal, and you will treat the rest of humanity as 'the enemy'. You have to swear that this is what you will do, because I do not live in time, and don't have any to waste.

"In that way, I know that the Deliverer's injunctions to humans that they love one another will be left out on the shelf to dry. As it is, the stupid fools are usually so hooked on material things they will even sell their birthright to become 'statesmen'. They trust me and forget that everything they do will come back to haunt them on the day of reckoning.

"Look, the chaps who are strutting around in the halls of power today will all be gone in a hundred years. Yeah, gone - gone to their judgement! Remember the emperor Caesar Augustus, Pontius Pilate, Herod Agrippa and the rest of the pack who two thousand years ago looked like a permanent fixture on the political scene, and were regarded as almighty and even divine? You would think that someone would at least know where they lie buried, wouldn't you. That has been the lot for all the nincompoops who forgot that they were creatures, and acted like little gods! Which 'playing statesman' means. The fools believed me and scorned the words of the Deliverer that it didn't benefit a man one iota if he gained the whole world and lost his soul!

"Any ways, as Cain made very clear in the doctrine he promulgated, being able to make decisions that lead to needless loss of human life in the pursuit of political ambition is a necessary evil. That was what 'power politics' was all about. And making 'tough' decisions aimed at consolidating the power of state through the merciless elimination of noncompliant and potentially threatening regimes was definitely the stuff that 'statesmen' would be made of;

and the ability to make them would distinguish people like him (Cain) from the run of the mill or the plebs.

"Just being able to sit down and dream up these arguably wicked - and in some respects even murderous - schemes and scenarios of things to come made Cain forget that he was a mere mortal who would have to say good bye to the world sooner or later like all other humans. Peering ahead in time and discovering that, if he set his mind to it, he could influence and even almost single-handedly determine the direction things in the world took made him feel like a god. Cain thought that this was really funny, because the mischievous things he was conjuring up should, without any doubt, have made him feel like a devil. Instead, they made him feel as if he was the one human alive who was working hard to save humankind from itself - as if he was 'the savior of mankind'!

"Cain went as far as confiding to the 'mother of his children' that individuals who aspired to positions of leadership in the years to come would do well to study his theory of 'empire' so they wouldn't have to 're-invent the wheel' all over again. Noting that his old man and old woman had started keeping diaries in which they recorded the story of creation, how they had fallen from grace, and were continuing to describe the things they themselves were doing to ensure the survival of the human race in what they themselves referred to as the 'stone age', he had hinted that he himself might one day compile his ideas into a 'book' he would give the unassuming title of 'The Empire'! That would provide future generations of tribal chiefs, presidents, proconsuls, kings, and emperors as well as their aides a handy reference in which the 'Cain doctrine', as he put it, would be outlined.

"Now that doctrine essentially exempted Cain in his capacity as emperor from the obligation to treat all equally and with respect. It did not just put him above the law of land the natural law, it exempted him from all laws both natural and super natural as long as his actions were focused on the security of the empire. As Cain saw it, he was completely free to take whatever action he deemed fit in the face of any threat or if the goal of his action was to consolidate and strengthen the power of the empire so that potential foes wouldn't be tempted to threaten it in any way.

"It was obvious to Cain that if he led expeditions and succeeded in overrunning neighboring 'nations', the doctrine would entitle his forces to take the inhabitants of such nations into slavery. Such a move would be perfectly legitimate not just because might made right, but because his empire would be stronger and safer as a result. The slaves would boost the empire's 'economy' by providing free labor, while the occupation and subsequent takeover of those nations would mean that they would never pose a threat of kind to the empire after they were absorbed into it and ceased to exist as independent or autonomous nations. Indeed, any 'preemptive strike' aimed at getting those results would be perfectly legitimate.

"Still, one thought that kept popping in his mind and kept reminding him of his mortal status threatened to ruin everything. And the more he tried to banish it, the more it kept surfacing.

"It kept occurring to Cain that even if he succeeded in scaring the hell out of every other human and neutralizing any opposition to his scheme of building his empire from the tiny enclave it now was on the edge of Paradise into a sprawling and mighty empire, there was the outside chance that something could go wrong and, even though a feared and powerful emperor, he might find himself a victim of his own machinations - a victim of his own misstep or that of a lieutenant.

"The realm of possibilities included betrayal by associates, a revolt by key military commanders followed by a coup d'état, or may be even a simple accident that left him vulnerable to his enemies - literally anything could happen and bring his dominion over Mother Earth to an abrupt end. It would be so humiliating and that, more than anything else, caused him to suffer nightmares.

"Cain wasn't afraid of facing justice in the next world after he crossed the gulf that separated the living from the dead. He knew that even in hell he would at least have some company - that we demons were already there. He was in a way prepared for the humiliation of being sent to hell for his misdeeds. The bottom line was that Cain was more interested in the here and now, and didn't care a hoot about an afterlife - exactly as we here in the Pit wanted.

"But if he was exposed here on earth, as the first human who ever aspired for and attained the status of emperor, he would be really devastated. Cain was so scared to think that some other 'caricature of a human being' might rise up and cause him to fall from glory (much like Adam and Eve fell from grace), he refused to entertain the possibility.

"In the event, Cain would prefer to just kill himself if, after enjoying the glamour of being the world's first emperor who was revered and perhaps even worshipped buy other humans, he lost out - either through his own carelessness or because of the incompetence of one or more of his lieutenants - and became a commoner and a 'statistic'. The shame would simply be too much for a great mind like himself to face. He knew that after sacrificing the lives of so many other humans to get his empire going, once out power, the movement to have him get a taste of his own 'justice' would be unstoppable.

"Cain refused to think of any such possibility, preferring instead to keep himself in the dark about how it would feel to be at the receiving end! And so, while he was unable to ban those thoughts from his mind, he decided that he would take them into his calculations only to the extent that he would be totally uncompromising with opponents, and also ruthless and merciless with anyone who would dare to stand up against him. As far as he was concerned, regardless of what his conscience told him, his life was his life, and that was all that mattered.

"Cain would also not care how many lives would be sacrificed for the empire - provided his own was not among them. And the views of contemporaries would not matter - not even if people's lives were lost needlessly due to miscalculations, because history and history alone would be his judge. Cain had made up his mind that he would persist in labeling any one who would refuse to bow to his will as a 'terrorist' and/or 'insurgent'. He would maintain that position even though he himself readily acknowledged that a little graciousness here, and a little generosity there, were almost certain to reduce the cost to the super power itself in both the short and long term.

"And he had similarly resolved that in arbitrating disputes between nations (disputes in which his empire, as the world's sole super power, would alone be in a position to mediate), he would seek to exploit the situation without any regard to natural justice. And, again, he would persist in acting that way even though he knew that a perfunctory show of impartiality and fairness in arbitrating disputes here, and a willingness to compromise there, would earn him greater respect and strengthen his position as emperor of the world.

"No fool, Cain anticipated that 'corruption' would in time become so commonplace, it would even be the law. Indeed the world would, in his view, be like a runaway 'train' (by which he meant the toy he had spent days making for the child his wife was expecting). It would be out of control. And the reason would not be so much because every Tom, Dick and Harry would be aspiring to become an emperor as because the few individuals who succeeded in carving out territory for themselves and declaring themselves emperor would become consumed with greed for power and material possessions alike.

"Also, upon attaining to positions of authority in the 'administration', those who did would promptly forget their humble beginnings and start behaving as if they were like gods. That would in turn speed up the rise of oligarchies, the forerunner of the 'royal families' that would compete with and eventually supplant the 'imperial families' as rulers of the world.

"Peering ahead into the future, Cain could not help gasping at the role that 'political savvy' (the expression he used to refer to 'corruption') would play in the affairs of humans. A couple of individuals would claim that they had invented 'currency' or 'money' to promote trade, and would set up 'banks' where individuals could take it for 'safekeeping'. They would, of course, promptly lend the money deposited out to other folks who did not have any and pocket the hefty 'interest'. However, to prevent a 'run on the banking system', they would make sure that they retained just enough of the money deposited to pay off those who wished to withdraw their deposits because they either needed to spend the money or regarded the 'interest' paid by the banks on the deposits as inadequate. It would all be day light robbery in disguise.

But Cain anticipated even worse forms of corruption, and they would include the establishment of political parties complete with lobbyists to ensure that only the 'right' people attained to leadership positions. There would be 'legal' systems that would be administered by 'judges' appointed with input from 'interest groups'. The system would thus be rigged in favour of the ruling class (or the proletariat), and any member of the bourgeoisie who complained would be thrown in jail for being a 'threat to society'.

"Cain believed that corruption likely was going to descend on the world in phases, and one of its worst forms was going to appear and become the dominant force in a couple of centuries as the earth's population grew and the number of outright 'landowners' dwindled. Capitalism - or 'latter day slavery' as Cain called it - would be an obnoxious and entirely heartless monopolistic system that would prey on the population at large. The capitalistic system would be controlled by worldly, money hungry moguls who would see nothing wrong in wringing the last ounce of 'productivity' out of the 'workforce' or those on its 'payroll'.

"Cain had a premonition that the millions who would be enslaved to the capitalistic system wouldn't even suspect that they in fact were slaves. They not only would have no choice but to sign away their freedom by entering into lopsided 'employment contracts' under which they would work for virtually free for the 'multinational' conglomerates.

"The 'firms' would pay the 'workers' just enough to get by and feed their families - but just enough, so those totally 'dependent' workers would be back to continue working, sometimes all seven days of the week. The workers who would be indispensable to the 'market economy' would of course attract slightly higher wages that those who were 'expendable' But generally, they all would either accepted what was offered in 'salary' or leave it, in which case they and their families would starve to death. The capitalistic system would be a boon to 'entrepreneurs' who would be able to pocket millions in 'earned' revenues while those who actually did the donkey work slaved away for a pittance.

"Cain, who understood the importance that nations would accord to their defensive and offensive capacity, easily saw that a huge chunk of the capitalistic system would be involved with the 'armed forces'. The capitalists or owners of enterprises in that sector of the economy would be dedicated to promoting the 'culture of death' as preserving a nation's independence and 'getting the other guys before they got you' would become a top priority.

"The 'corruption', 'fraud', 'political savvy' - or what ever one wished to call it - would extend to things like international law and the conventions that would govern the conduct of nations in everything ranging from human rights to the maintenance of 'international peace and security'. It would have to be understood that at any time a piece of international law - or some international treaty or convention - impinged on the interests of his empire, that piece of international law or convention would become null and void. While the decisions of the international 'court of justice' or 'tribunal' would be fully binding on all other nations, decisions that intruded on the empire's ability to determine what was or was not in its best interests would be 'non-binding' and automatically unenforceable. That would be the deal!

"To be sure, Cain was prepared to commit injustices to ensure that the 'Cain clan' as he called it eventually dominated and controlled Planet Earth and never stood in any material need. And so, when Abel casually sauntered up to him one day and almost gamely let him know that he and his wife were inviting Cain and his wife to join them and the old man and woman at a get-together they were planning for the specific purpose of consecrating the child they were expecting in a couple of months to the Prime Mover, Cain was understandably upset.

"It was obvious to Cain that Abel was intent on achieving the same goal as he himself had in mind, namely control and domination of the world and what was in it. It was inconceivable that Abel was going to the extent of offering up his child in sacrifice to the Prime Mover just so that his welfare would, as Abel put it, always be in the hands of the Almighty One.

"Just so he himself wouldn't be at a disadvantage, before retiring to bed that night, Cain had knelt down with his wife and consecrated to the Prime Mover not just the child they themselves were expecting in a couple of weeks, but all the children they would ever beget and their children's children as well. With that, Cain was confident that it would be his descendants, not Abel's, who would dominate and control Planet Earth.

"Cain knew better than to inform his wife of his true feelings regarding the 'Abel clan'. This was even though, according to the advice they had received from the old man and the old woman, it was important that there be no secrets between a man and his wife. The fact of the matter was that Cain wanted Abel dead from that moment on. That would be one way to ensure that his own descendants dominated and controlled Mother Earth's resources. Besides, the wicked Cain hoped that some mishap - perhaps a miscarriage or something like that - would overtake Abel's wife either during or before the birth of their baby so that their 'imperial designs' would be automatically frustrated.

"Cain also figured that, even if he did not succeed in eliminating Abel, it was going to be his own children and his children's children who would still end up as the world's 'super power'. Because, thanks to Abel alerting them about his intentions, they had rushed and consecrated, not just their 'first fruits', but the entire Cain clan to the Prime Mover before Abel and his wife had tendered their offering.

"Cain reflected that if Abel had been wise, he would have kept his intentions a secret until the consecration was a done deal. But Abel had again very clearly demonstrated his characteristic stupidity and the fact that he was not so well versed in the ways of the world under the new order.

"It was around this time that Cain, rankled and angry with everybody for trying to belittle him (as he himself put it), devised his plan of luring Abel into the thick woods where, as the bible says, he slew him. He kept telling himself as he did so that he loved Abel as his brother but hated the terrorist and insurgent in him. And for a while he thought he had succeeded in stifling his conscience by pretending that all he was doing was safeguard the territorial integrity of the empire and ensure its security.

"That Cain was quite a brilliant fellow and a real scoundrel. He certainly knew how to come full circle and be a full partner with us in 'devilry' while retaining his image as a virtual 'angel'. But that was not the important thing. What was really important was the role Cain played in ensuring that death - and the culture of death - continued to be central to human life.

"You have to understand that, even though humankind was now saddled with the effects of original sin, it would all have come to naught if all humans who ever walked the earth succeeded in leading the kind of lives the old man and the old woman - and Abel - were leading. To the extent that happened, to that extent death, even though real and hanging over the lives of all men and women, would already have lost its sting.

To retain its sting, it was important that humans actually went out and killed other humans regardless of the excuse, and perpetuated the culture of death. My evil plan depended on that for its success, and hence the importance of Cain's contribution. We accordingly hail him as our hero, even though he himself escaped our tentacles when he subsequently renounced sin and our cause.

"Everything changed, as everyone now knows, when the Prime Mover repeatedly asked Cain the whereabouts of his brother whom he had slain. That jolted Cain - who was really going off the rails as his wife had suggested - and caused him to regain some of his reason. We had to do quite a bit of stock taking here in the Pit ourselves and to ask ourselves what we had not done right when Cain - Cain of all people - balked at the amount of blood both actual (in the form of Abel's blood) and potential (in the form of all those humans whose lives would be sacrificed as the world's demagogues from that time onwards borrowed a leaf from his script and indiscriminately killed and murdered their fellow humans in their misguided efforts to conquer and dominate the world) on his hands.

"Unlike so many demagogues who came after him, Cain at least came round and saw through his own folly - he saw that he could not hide behind the position of Emperor. While he was free to call himself Emperor, King, Chief, Proconsul, or anything else he wanted to call himself, and to act in the capacity of an emperor or a king, or chief, or proconsul, he was personally answerable to the Prime Mover for everything he did regardless of what he did and whether he did it in a personal or official capacity; and, consequently, his actions had to be consonant with his conscience.

Enemy you cannot see…

"Cain, the first death culture enthusiast and also the world's first demagogue, deep down in his guts lived a life of fear - the fear of 'kicking the bucket'! He was born with that fear, and it sacred the hell out of him. Now, Cain had been told by his parents umpteen times, before and after Abel and his other siblings were born, that the Prime Mover had looked upon Humankind with mercy after they had eaten of the forbidden fruit, and had promised them and their posterity a Deliverer. That Savior would deliver them from the clutches of death - which was one of the penalties for their disobedience.

"The hope that Adam and Eve themselves had for the coming of the Deliverer was so strong, unknown to them, it had actually translated into a saving 'baptism' - a baptism of desire. And it was also this 'baptism' that fortified them against my wiles, drawing as it did on the divine graces that would be merited by the Deliverer who would effectively be the 'Second Adam' when He manifested Himself on earth.

"The old man and the old woman had urged Cain and, subsequently, Abel and the rest of their children to set aside time to bow down daily in adoration of the Prime Mover and infinitely merciful Lord, and also to meditate on the Promise of a Savior so that the hope of their redemption would free them from the fear of death.

But it all seemed to no avail. They still caught him brooding over his 'fate' ever so many times, and trying to figure out how on his own, without help from 'above', he could out-fox me and gain eternal life at the end of his pilgrimage on earth.

"But for a long time, Cain, who blamed the old man and woman for all their problems and thought that he was a much better person than them, would hear nothing of it. He called them sinners and liars, and never stopped nagging them about the real reasons behind their decision to steal fruit from the Tree of Life. That was how Cain initially got the idea that he perhaps could record victory over death by gearing himself up to actually inflict death on anyone who like remotely like a threat to his well-being.

"For their part, Adam and Eve prayed constantly to the 'Deliverer' for their son even though he was yet to come. It was clear from the way the Promise was framed that the Deliverer's coming would be facilitated by a woman! She would evidently be one of their own offspring, and they frequently meditated on the fact that she would be a very blessed thing of necessity - one worthy enough to facilitate the advent of the Deliverer into the world! Suffice it to say that when their first baby girl arrived, the thought on their mind was that it might be her! That she might be the one who would 'crush the serpent's head'!

"Cain, who for a long time resisted the advice of his parents and regularly skipped his daily prayers and meditation, did not realize until well after he had murdered his brother that if you really wanted to be a victor, getting a monopoly over weapons of mass destruction or turning his empire's military into an 'efficient killing machine' (as he himself had considered doing at one time) could never do the trick. That sort of thing worked only if your intentions were to defend the world against some demonic aliens from hell or outer space. But it was completely out of place if you were dealing with fellow human beings who also happened to be made in the Image.

"Developing efficient means of 'destroying' other humans? One had to be kidding! First of all, individuals contemplating such action had to make sure that they really 'destroyed' their enemies - so that there wouldn't be any chance that those they thought they had successfully 'eliminated' or 'annihilated' would be waiting on the other side of the Gulf as 'witnesses' against them in the court of divine justice when they themselves eventually kicked that bucket! Which begged the question: because it was not possible to 'rub out' a creature that was made in the Image - and all humans, however despicable or bad were such creatures!

"And so, if one was thinking aright, hand in hand with trying to get a monopoly over things like weapons of mass destruction or investing in efficient killing machines, it was imperative that one also tried to make oneself impervious to death - to invent a formula that ensured that as long as one was engaged in the business of visiting death on others, one's own *elan vital* would in no circumstances succumb to illness or anything that would cause the would-be-killer himself/herself to 'kick the bucket'. And so, it was clearly not enough to wear a bullet-proof vest or to ride only in Humvees. One needed to take out similar 'insurance' against mosquito bites, common colds, and similar ills that did not respect any one and indiscriminately took the lives of so many humans prematurely.

"Always remember that before Adam and Eve took steps to defy the Almighty One, they did everything to try and ensure that they would not get into a situation in which they would meet Him face to face, let alone in judgement. Eve tried to come up with a dietary formula that would ensure that the cells in their bodies would keep regenerating themselves for ever to ensure that they would never die! Poor souls - Adam and Eve should have known better than that. The bodies of humans, made out dust, were never meant to support those who were on a pilgrimage on earth for ever! But even though Eve was just wasting her time, at least she tried to use her head.

"And when I myself refused to go down on bended knee and to worship the Author of Life, I first made certain that He would not turn around and 'rub me out' - and the spirits that joined in the infernal rebellion checked it out also. But we also miscalculated - and, in retrospect, we definitely wouldn't repeat what we did out of our pride!

"It could, of course, never be right for a human to slay another. Nothing - absolutely nothing - could ever justify it. Forget the biblical tales which glorify wars and killing. When they are not apocrypha that over-zealous translators who wanted to depict the Prime Mover as the almighty one by drawing on human experiences surreptitiously introduced into the sacred texts, they were included in the original inspired scripts in a context that was entirely different, and specifically as evil deeds of men that were not to be emulated.

"And because my troops have been around and at work from the start, we have been able to depict things as otherwise, and to make it seem as if killing is sanctioned by the Prime Mover Himself. What did you think we would be doing hanging around the inspired writers, transcribers of the sacred texts, and above the preachers who, with only a few exceptions, are on our payroll anyway! Death is a direct consequence of original sin, and it is our sacred duty to see that it pervades everything humans do.

"If killing was something that could be justified or in any way elevated to a virtuous act, the Deliverer would have killed stricken down those crowns that had shouted for His crucifixion, and he would have caused the Roman solders to scatter like flies. Talk of killing in self-defense - there is no killing in self-defense that could have been more justified. But instead, he turned the other cheek when slapped, and just prayed to His father for strength to 'drink the cup'! And he bade His followers do likewise.

"He even instructed them that if they should be turned away from a city, as they went about the all important mission of 'harvesting' souls, they only needed to brush any dust their slippers may have collected as they walked that city's streets in the course of doing what they needed to do, and go their way - and forget that they had ever been there. In other words, it was not for them to condemn any one who ridiculed or rejected the gospel message. With the power at His disposal after He had scored His more-than-convincing victory over evil and death by His resurrection, He could have advised them to 'stay and occupy' all such cities, to ensure that they were 'Christianised'. But He didn't.

"Of course, humans who kill others are stupid. If you hate other humans or are so terrified about other humans that you'd rather not be near them, the worst possible thing you can do is to try and kill them. Going that route is suicidal and madness first of all because, instead of contending with an enemy you can see and hear, and who is subject to the limitations which go with being an earth-bound mortal, you now have to contend with a pure spirit; and a vengeful spirit is certainly not something you want to have as your enemy. You also lose any physical advantages you might have had over your 'enemy'.

"But, above all, with your action, you move the contest from the material to the spiritual arena where intrigues and underhand manoeuvres can never be a match for uprightness, moral integrity and honesty. And, of course, a mind that is so warped that it can sanction the killing of another human is at a huge disadvantage from the start.

"The fact of the matter is that you now also have to contend with the Author of Life and Judge. It is fair to say that humans who regard killing under any circumstances as a solution to their problems delude themselves. They are not merely short-sighted and simple-minded souls, but also very stupid people who just have no idea what bigger problem they land themselves into when they seek to take the life of another human. All they do actually is set themselves up for spiritual death. That is in exact accordance with the original plan that I had in place when I lured Adam and Eve to steal and eat fruit from the Tree of Life.

"But this just goes to show how dumb humans can be. Even though created in the Image by virtue of which they also come endowed with reason, humans prefer to pull the wool over their eyes, and to kid themselves and pretend that the Prime Mover, Divine Soul and Supreme and Almighty Being - who Himself has no beginning and who caused them to come into existence out of nothing - exists only in the figment of the human mind; or, if He does, went to sleep after conducting His labors of creation! And this is especially true for those humans who think that they are very 'clever' and know a lot! They blind themselves to the fact that they automatically have to contend with the Divine Soul and Almighty One each and every time they perpetrate an injustice and infringe the natural Law of Equity and Justice thereby; and they even go to the extent of kidding themselves that, even after they themselves kick the bucket, all will be well, and there will be no divine wrath to face! So, so dumb!

"This is a war - the war against the Lamb! And it is the real 'Mother of All Wars'! Note that it is not a 'war between Good and Evil' as such because such a war can only exist in fiction. You won't find a reference to a 'war between Good and Evil" anywhere in the Scriptures, because there is no such a thing as 'Evil', which simply means the 'absence of Good'! Regardless, what goes on in our war with the Lamb is rough stuff, and it is deadly. That is why I am known as the Father of Death!

"I knew all along that after Adam and Eve ate of the forbidden fruit and predictably got kicked out of the Garden of Eden, their spiritual death, which was real and not just metaphorical, would lead directly to murders of humans by humans. The fear of dying would in turn drive, not just Adam and Eve, but all of their offspring and their offspring's offspring to do what would doom them spiritually over and over, namely to kill and murder their fellow humans in declared and undeclared wars. They would then have to contend with the Prime Mover who had admonished Adam and Eve to stay clear of the Tree of Knowledge - and not touch any of its fruits - in the first place.

"And, if humans automatically have to contend with Him when they kill, you bet that they also have to contend with Him when they hurt, abuse, torture or otherwise come up short in their obligation to love one another as themselves. Take the case of spousal violence. Regardless of the reason for the killing, the victim upon leaving this world, ceases to be a spouse of the murderer because there are no spousal relations of any kind outside of the bond of love between the Prime Mover and the saints on the other side of the Gulf. And so the spouse who commits violence on his/her partner, or succeeds in taking away the spousal partner's life, immediately has to contend with the ire of an enraged Prime Mover.

"The fact is that when a human harms another in anyway, the harm is sustained by the Deliverer who is Himself the Author of Life and Judge. He wasn't cracking a joke when He said that when a good turn was done to the least human, it was done to Him! Or, when He said that those who live by the sword die by the sword! He was quite serious. And so you kill, you die the spiritual death.

"It is not just a case of being presumptuous on the part of humans who seek to use the killing of fellow humans - or, more appropriately, 'homicide' (regardless of the label that it is given) - to achieve an end. And - let us face it - the reason for attempts by humans to rub out their fellow humans always boils down to an irrational fear that mistakenly attributes the hanging threat of death to individuals in society who are associated in the mind with its immediate onslaught. On the contrary, it is always like a case of mistaken identity. Frankly, it is even dumb and stupid. The sentence of death was pronounced on humans, not by any creature and not even by the Avenging Angel, but by the Prime Mover Himself.

"In the aftermath of the fall of Adam and Eve from grace, humans - all humans became marked for death by divine decree. The sin of Adam and Eve (both of whom were created in the Image) consisted in taking the stand that the self had primacy over obedience to their conscience and to the will of the Prime Mover. It represented a challenge that humans posed to their Maker in complete disregard of the fact that they were His creatures - and creatures, for that matter, that also happened to be earth bound even though they were primarily spiritual. It was such monumental 'disrespect' directed at the Almighty.

"But instead of going back on His word and 'rubbing' out the human race because of the disobedience of the first man and the first woman, the Prime Mover in His infinite goodness promised them a Deliverer. But in the meantime, Man's disobedience (or attempt to play God) had activated or resulted in spiritual death that on the one hand saw humans alienated by their own wilful action from the author of Life who continued to be their mainstay and last end.

"And because humans were also earthbound creatures by virtue of having a physical body (by virtue of their nature consisting of a corporeal body and an incorporeal soul), an unavoidable - and in fact necessary if novel - side effect of their spiritual death was that they would physically also 'die the death'. In other words, their bodies would also return to dust in time.

"But subsequently, Cain and a host of other stupid humans fell into the habit of transferring the blame for the threat of death hanging over their heads to those fellow humans whom they perceived as a threat to their *worldly* success - making an already very bad infinitely worse! Their motivation for doing that was the irrational *fear* of dying.

"With all humans already slated to die the death, it will dawn on all killers at that fateful moment as their hearts stop beating and they find themselves on the other side of the gulf that separates the living humans from the humans who have gone before (regardless of how they themselves meet their demise) that the act of dying actually represents liberation of sorts (particularly now that the promised Deliverer had come) as humans are freed from the trappings of the world, and freed especially from their bodies which (except in the case of the most ascetic and selfless) are the abiding symbol of worldliness. To the extent those bodies were not treated like the temple of the Prime Mover, to that extent they also become symbols of the pact of those humans with me, Beelzebub, the Author of death.

"At that time, as the souls depart from their earthly abode and head for the afterlife, the individual humans without exception experience a personal, mind boggling and excruciating 'Armageddon' whose intensity is in proportion to the extent to which the individual was attached or wedded to the self and consequently also to material things. It is at that time when humans who had put their trust in the world will find that the 'armor' they had on was a mirage, and they cheated themselves by not putting on the 'armor of the Deliverer' in accordance with the advice of the Apostle of the Gentiles. They will wish they had accepted the call to live entirely for others in imitation of the Deliverer - like Saint Joseph or Mother Theresa.

"Damn stupid humans! If killing did the trick and directly translated into anything that qualified as a positive result for the killer, the Ten Commandments would not have included one that stated:

'Thou shalt not kill'. And, of course, the Deliverer would not have warned that those who lived by the sword died by the sword. If it was a virtue to kill, the Deliverer Himself would have been a gangster whose place would be at the head of an army of ruthless 'head hunters' drawn from the choirs of angels. And it would not be an exaggeration to say that His work would be cut out for Him as He and His band of loyal angels, all of them seized with holy anger, determinedly put iniquitous and impious humans - which would be just about every human who had ever lived or would ever live - to the sword.

"Because one has the ability to destroy, it does not mean that one should use it. And if one didn't have the ability to kill, the hankering to kill whoever one had a mind to kill becomes pointless any way. The maxim that it is nice to be important, but it is more important to be nice applies equally to those who enjoy the ability to kill and those who do not. At the last judgement though, the kudos go to those who were nice, because they are the ones who have not received their reward. Humans who go through life imagining that being important is of the essence have already received their reward.

"Humans who cut short the lives of their fellow humans in the short run cause terrible grief not just to those they kill, but also to the Eternal Word through whom all creatures came into being. The grief caused to the Deliverer is particularly acute for the simple reason that humans were created in the Image and by design should live for ever and should never die.

"Agonizing over the fact that humans sinned and now must die in the hours before His own death, the Deliverer even sweated blood! Rivulets of His precious blood flowed down His forehead and drenched the garments He wore. Just as His death on the cross is re-enacted every time bread and wine are consecrated at Mass and become His body and blood, so also this scenario is repeated whenever a human's life is cut short.

"The Deliverer is pained very much whether it is one human who is cut down by a sniper's bullet or thousands of humans who are scotched to death when a nuclear device is set off over a metropolis.

"Actually, despite their avowals, all death culture enthusiasts, by putting their complete trust in the 'sword', automatically disavow their faith in the Prime Mover and are therefore agnostics - more deserving of pity than idol worshippers.

"After Cain had killed Abel, he believed (quite mistakenly as it turned out) that he had eliminated the 'problem'. Similarly with all other humans who kill following in his lamentable and contemptible example. They believe that they have somehow dealt a blow to their foes and reduced their problems in life. And they do that because they have stifled their consciences, and are determined to go on living in a world of fantasy and not in a world of reality. Because they are married to the 'lie' as Cain was, instead of the 'Truth'.

"Then, instead of going down on their knees and begging the Prime Mover for mercy, they strut around proudly like peacocks and, imagining themselves more invincible than ever, even celebrate the killings - making things worse for themselves!

"In the wake of any killing, instead of rejoicing, the perpetrator(s) should start preparing for the prospect of joining me, the Author of Death, here in this goddamned place you folks call hell. And I am not pulling this out of my hat. You just guessed - I do not have a hat, and not even a crown on which it could sit. The commandment - the fifth commandment - says very clearly: 'Thou shalt not kill.' And if they imagine that there will receive a red carpet welcome on their arrival here, they are seriously mistaken. This is a place where the closest thing to happiness is the weeping and gnashing of teeth.

"When one celebrates a criminal act, one says 'good bye' to any act of divine mercy that might have been his/hers for the asking. And trying to ask for mercy (and to tell the victim 'I am sorry for you') in the midst of the celebrations is nothing short of mockery.

"Given the nature of death and the fact that I (Diabolos) am its author, it is not possible to genuinely mourn the demise of some humans - for example those we regard as being particularly dear to us - and to celebrate the passing of other humans. Those who do that live in a world of fantasy - a world in which some humans are truly human and not others. The Deliverer exposed that lie, and even showed the way when He took up His human nature and, as the Second Adam, launched the project that not only aimed at securing the salvation of all humans but also at taking the sting out of the very thing that murderous and confused humans celebrate, namely death and neutralizing it.

"Humans who kill or celebrate death in some manner show by their actions that they are 'anti-Christs'. For the Son of Man was Himself led like a lamb to the slaughter, after consenting to bear the burden of the sins of all men. Consequently, other than try to rub Him out (just like happened to the heir in the gospel parable), no death culture enthusiast can want to have anything to do with Him, death culture enthusiasm being based on a philosophy that completely runs counter to His teachings.

"In fact, celebrating killings in any form is celebrating the death of the Deliverer's brothers and sisters to whom He was so endeared that He did not hesitate to shed His divine blood so they might realize eternal life. But what is even worse - any such celebration is a direct and unforgivable affront to the Eternal Word, who is also the Deliverer and Judge.

"When creatures celebrate killing (creatures who themselves, as it so happens, have a life span that does not frequently exceed a hundred years), they therefore definitely write-off divine mercies by acting as though life was so expendable. They in fact make a statement that there is no such a thing as life after death. And, yes, they write off the divine mercies by their actions which, of course, take precedence over their avowals to the contrary! This is because someone who does not believe in the brotherhood of humans cannot expect to be counted among the elect.

"It must be a very confused individual who can imagine that it is kosher to try and 'rub out' a human brother or human sister (whatever the motivation) and still expect to be friends with the Eternal Word (through whom all things in existence were made and who also set the rules) who is now also Judge and whose vocabulary did not include killing or revenge. Humans who seriously aspire to join the blessed company of the Son of Man's friends or the elect must make up their mind to walk in His footsteps - period.

True victory…

"There is only one reason humans kill - because they are dumb! It is because they do not have a clue why they walk on earth - why they were brought into being or exist. And it goes without saying that it would be more appropriate for creatures who knew that their own days were numbered to 'live and let live' (as some clever nut put it) rather than set out on a killing spree.

"The more 'enemies' a human kills, the more that human should hate himself/herself, because those one calls 'enemies' and kills are the killer's very own brothers and sisters we all have the same woman known as Eve. Whatever one thinks about one's enemies - however odious one imagines them to be - one makes a big mistake by thinking that one has the right to strike back. Humans do not have any such right. First of all, they are themselves guilty of much worse things. They have grievously offended - and murdered - not just a fellow mortal, but a divinity! They have sinned against the Almighty. And whatever makes them imagine that they won't face retribution for the mortal and venial sins they have committed over their life time is a mystery.

"Now, when Cain killed Abel, he did so with his bare hands. According to his own confession (to which both Adam and Eve make reference in the diaries they kept), he lured his brother into the forest on a pretext. Sneaking behind the shorter Abel, Cain then administered a vicious blow to the back of the younger man's head. The blow knocked Abel to the ground. In the ensuing struggle, Cain (as he himself confessed later) finally succeeded in strangling his brother and killing him with his bare hands.

"Right up until wars became institutionalized as a legitimate method for the killing of humans by fellow humans, the women were the ones whose lives were snuffed out prematurely by their men folk on various pretexts in a growing incidence of 'Violence against

Women'. The men initially went after the women because they did not like to face up to the fact that the constitution of women (unlike their own constitution) predisposed them to frequently changing moods. And then, being more muscular and physically stronger, the men would simply vent their anger and frustration on the 'weaker sex' after a disappointing hunting trip or if they were unable to come home with a good catch of fish. The domineering he-humans often just diverted their frustration on the womenfolk, and this frequently resulted in the lives of many an innocent woman being snuffed out prematurely.

"Other homicides were occasioned by rivalries among both men and women over spousal partners. Men who thought they could get away with it murdered their rivals so they would be unchallenged over their choice of a spouse, and women did the same. Everything from poisons to sharpened rocks and clubs were used in those early murders.

"Later on, groups of clansmen fought over things ranging from the mistreatment of their womenfolk who had been given to members of other clans as wives in exchange for a bride price to the failure by one clanschief to accord due respect in the course of conducting a business deal to another clanschief. Killings of humans by fellow humans on a big scale occurred when tribes fought pitched battles over pieces of countryside and control over mountain passes using machetes, spears and arrows.

"As years went by, instead of able-bodied men in a tribe, it was an 'army' of people belonging to one nation that was ranged against a similar army of people belong to an opposing nation sometimes as a result of a spat over something that was really minor or of no importance whatsoever. But, by this time, the actions of parties to such conflicts, while triggered by incidents that were trivial, were definitely informed by the Cain doctrine of world domination.

"The discovery of gunpowder transformed killing or 'wars', with nations making deliberate decisions to invest in the large scale production of weapons of war or 'armaments' which now included rifles, cannons and gun ships, and eventually squadrons of warships and air planes. Hand in hand with the massive investments in weapons of war, 'Military Science' has been used to transform the armies of the day into efficient killing machines. But even then, care has been taken to provide the act of killing with the respectability that had hitherto been reserved for professions such as Medicine and Law.

"But the days of real killing orgies finally arrived with the use in combat for the very first time of weapons of mass human destruction in the shape of nuclear bombs. Consequently, with the arrival of these Real Weapons of Mass Human Destruction (RWMHD), the powers that be, including super power rogue states, ordinary rogue states, networks of 'terrorists' and now also 'insurgents' can proceed full steam ahead to destroy - and in the process be destroyed themselves by - the 'enemy'!

"As has always been the case, nations led by a variety of demagogues have aspired to a monopoly over the means for destroying human life en masse in hopes that such a monopoly will also deliver the ultimate prize, namely unchallenged, total and also permanent dominion over Mother Earth and the right to ride rough-shod over all other nations that will not disarm unilaterally or throw in the towel. But I have to tell you (as the devil and author of death) that no one individual or even nation can ever have a monopoly over 'killing power'.

"Humans, inclined to sin, outdo each other in this business of killing. On the evidence, they are in fact not just *inclined* to sin, they are obsessed with sin - and with killing. By far the largest proportion of national budgets are devoted to the so-called 'military establishment' - the department staffed with humans who are trained and also certified to kill.

"As if that was not bad enough, there is also a growing trend to 'privatize' some of that department's functions - meaning that it is now passé to be a hired gun, a mercenary or hired killer. It apparently won't be long before outfits with names like 'Murder, Inc.' or 'Private Armed Forces & Co.' are quoted on the London and New York stock markets; and, given the potential returns, they could easily outstrip all other stocks as the most popular.

"To make things worse, the operations of those military establishments are also increasingly being carried out in the name of the Prime Mover. And so, even though the business of killing is in my domain and 'devilish', those outfits after a while might change their names to something like 'Christian Murder, Inc.' or 'Private Christian Army for the Salvation of the World, Inc.'.

"It might be a good thing to step back and reflect on what we are discussing here. Death - just in case you do not know - is by its nature a dreadful God awful thing if just because it is not the Prime Mover but I, Beelzebub, who is its author. You have to understand that we fallen spirits effectively 'died' when we were cast out of heaven into this bottomless pit in the bowels of the earth as punishment for our sin of disobedience.

"The separation of the human souls from the human bodies as a result of which the bodies turn into dust and the souls become my prisoners here in hell is a replay of our own death - unless, like the souls of those who were rescued by the Deliverer on the day He rose from the dead, the humans in question die repentant and are friends again with the Prime Mover.

"And so, it is bad enough when humans die of old age and other so-called 'natural causes'. But humans who cause other humans to 'kick the bucket' prematurely using poisons or other means engage in what I call 'playing Satan'. When I succeeded in tempting Adam and Eve to join me in my rebellion and they incurred the 'curse of death' with their disobedience, I became complicit in their death as much as they themselves did with their wilful act. I can therefore say that I killed them.

"When humans fall for the bait and kill other humans by whatever means and in whatever circumstances in the pursuit of their happiness in this world, it is an understatement to say they 'imitate' me. They commit murder in their own right and automatically merit the consequences for getting their hands stained with innocent blood. They are moreover usually also guilty of tempting their victims to 'buy their safety' by becoming collaborators in their wicked schemes, or by agreeing to do other less than honorable things in order to save their lives - again in imitation of me.

"And so, starting with Cain who murdered Abel with his bare hands, humans have connived to maim, injure and kill fellow humans using everything from butchers' knives to bullets and atomic bombs, and have themselves become liable for the sentence of death. Again, it is bad enough for the human soul to separate from the body because the individual has got as far in the twilight of his/her life as he/she could go. But it is really terrible when their homes are shelled and they are buried alive, or they are torn to smithereens by the 'smart bombs' - or when humans are tortured to death by their own kind.

"Knowing how hard it was for Cain to make a U-turn and above all accept to give away his 'empire' to the surviving members of Abel's family in a genuine (not mock) act of restitution, we have gone the extra mile to ensure that there will be a sufficient number of dungeons here in hell for the anticipated influx of our 'friends'.

"In most parts of the world, thieves and pickpockets are on patrol on a full time basis - you can never be watchful enough. From time immemorial, demagogues, masquerading as statesmen or stateswomen, have also roamed the world looking for something to steal - and that is what 'international relations' and 'diplomacy' are now all about. And killing and maiming, which have always been accepted practices among thieves, are now an integral part of what the uninformed think are respectable professions.

"Today, all nations are out to steal from other nations, with the big powerful countries roaming the world in search of weaker nations that they can gobble up - just as I myself am constantly roaming the world in search of souls to devour. And then they have the audacity to do it in the name of the Prime Mover! I have to take off my hat (figuratively only of course) to these guys. And weaker nations that not ally themselves with the powerful ones risk losing all.

"But how come that humans (who smart so, when they feel slighted by other humans and who, at my suggestion, will not hesitate to rob fellow humans of their possessions and even commit murder in the process) consistently act helpless when mother nature in the shape of hurricanes, flash floods, snow storms, etc. lick them! They certainly don't feign or just pretend to be helpless! And that is exactly what exposes the hypocrites.

"If you will go for the jugular when you feel slighted by a fellow human or you lust after the other person's possessions, you should be consistent and do the same to the all mighty Almighty when He causes His mother nature to have you get a taste of what it is like to be at the receiving end!

"If you still do not know what I am driving at, you must be what you humans call 'hard core'. Humans are actually useless and helpless; but when it comes to dealing with their fellow humans, they suddenly start playing God.

"The time is coming when the Prime Mover is going to play Prime Mover - or His real Self - on humans. At that time, they are not going to even want to recall the things they now do to others that they wouldn't like done unto themselves. So, let them just o on playing god as much as they like - just as I myself did once upon a time. That is what I did when I refused to genuflect and worship and chose to be the Author of Death.

"As the old saying (which humans ignore at their peril) goes, it is not what goes in but what comes out that corrupts. See the analogy? It is not what happens to you that corrupts. It is what you do. Suppose that the goal of some humans is to control particularly rich oil fields that happen to be in some one else's backyard, and then use that as a staging point for securing some other things (example uranium deposits) that happen to be next door.

"And, first of all, they are clearly in the wrong by going after what belongs to another and is not theirs. That is called 'robbery' or 'banditry'. Secondly, when they issue a '*fatwa*' (that is supposed to be binding on all the folks who happen to be in their path) and demand that they give way or be damned, the humans who are after the oil or the uranium - or securing the route to India and its spices - do something that just seals their own fate.

"And if the 'bandits' or 'robbers' think that anyone in their path who resists their advance automatically becomes a devil, they are completely mistaken. Greedy, covetous and already out of control, they merely compound their own 'problem' by trying frenetically trying to liquidate other innocent humans whom they find in their path so that they may achieve their objective of controlling the sources of the oil and uranium. Instead of just robbery, their crime becomes multiple murder!

"You see - it is not the fact that a human is born in Najaf or in Texas (what goes in) that corrupts him or her. It is the scheming and conniving of humans - and their actions (what comes out) that do.

"And that is exactly how I do my job - I take stupid humans on top of mountains and show them where vast fields of 'oil', deposits of uranium and things like that, as well as other 'wealth' are located, and I tell them that it is all theirs if they just kneel and worship. And that is exactly what they do. After they have pledged their royalty to me, you can bet that whatever comes out of their mouth when they get back home is rotten - their actions, spin and everything else they scheme up so they can lay their hands on those riches.

"Instead of stopping at behaving like the rich man who refused to notice the beggars on his door step, they become worse. On their match to the oil fields, they even rob and kill beggars along the way - those who think that the strangers must be joking when they hear about the *fatwa* and are in any case determined to hang on to the little they possess for dear life. If you do not see my footprints when you see things of that sort unfolding, you are a write-off and will never see anything.

"Luckily for me, when I take these delegations of humans up on the mountain tops for the demo, I don't have to walk or drive them there. I just spirit them there. In the absence of footprints or tire marks or other signs that humans have been up there to see me, they all invariably believe that they are pioneers - that they are doing what no other human before them has ever done. Stupid humans!

"Look, when the bible says that I took the Deliverer up into an exceeding high mountain from which I caused Him to see all the Kingdoms of the world along with their splendour, doy you think we walked all the way to Mt. Kilimanjaro or Mt. Everest? Of course not! I just spirited Him there the way I spirit you all to these places.

"Let me make this one thing quite clear - the Prime Mover does not tempt. I am the Tempter and I do the tempting. And so, while the Prime Mover is busy causing good to come out of evil or (if you prefer) evil to generate good, I am busy checking out potential high way robbers and murderers, spiriting them up to mountain tops to show them the riches of the world, and then causing them to fall for the temptations using all sorts of ruses.

"Now, I know from experience that it is the one thing humans find very hard to understand, and that is the fact that the Prime Mover, who creates things out of nothing and who exults the meek and frustrates the proud to size, doesn't let any opportunity to cause good to come out of evil pass by. The Prime Mover could never allow high way bandits to strike and leave destruction in their trail without adequate plans to turn the miseries of their innocent victims into good.

"Accordingly, there are those who will be struck down even before they ostensibly reach the prime of their lives. He (who does not fail to take note when any one of the uncountable birds of the air loses just one of its feathers) will not let something like that come to pass for nothing.

"Precisely because humans do things that redound to the glory of the Prime Mover only with the help of divine grace, instead of letting those who might well be tempted in their later life to disown Him live on, the Prime Mover will allow them to be cut down by the high way bandits as a way of rescuing them from themselves and from my wiles.

"To 'sweeten' the deal as it were, the Prime Mover uses the proud (who have this tendency to regard only themselves alone as justified and to despise everyone else as sinners and evil doers) to exult the victims of their machinations. And he emphasizes thereby His determination to avenge the evil deeds of humans, and demonstrates His ability to do so quite effectively.

"The Prime Mover does this even without regard to the actions of those who make up the hierarchy of His Church. Because they are human, the successors to the apostles are not known to condemn the outrageous things humans do consistently. As history has shown, not only have the actions of the churchmen, frequently conducted in the Church's name, been responsible for atrocities, but when humans are cut down unjustly, it is typical for them to raise their voices in condemnation only when the victims are members of the 'visible Church' - as if the rest of humankind doesn't have the right to call the Prime Mover 'Abba' or Father.

"It is a little like a referee at a soccer match who only sees fouls committed against players who happen to espouse certain opinions on an array of subjects, and does not see it as his business to blow the whistle when other players are fouled however glaringly.

"Humans have the same nature and, regardless of their religious affiliation, enjoy the same inalienable rights, including the right to life. When the successors to the apostles (who are supposed to be well informed on these matters) can practice such discrimination, you tell me what those who are less informed would do. No wonder that members of the Church's hierarchy are not taken seriously when they try to advocate for the rights of the unborn.

"The Church's hierarchy should be interested in the spiritual and physical well-being of all. They should be interested in the salvation of communists, Moslems, Hindus, Catholics, and others equally. But they give the impression that the Mystical Body of the Deliverer is made up of only 'Catholics' or (at the most) 'Christians'. That is the impression they give, but how correct is it?

"War mongers in the world operate on the premise that, instead of human souls, the Prime Mover created American souls, Russian souls, Chechen souls, Chinese souls, Vietnamese souls, North Korean souls, South Korean souls, Japanese souls, Iraqi souls, Turkish souls, Greek souls, and even royal British souls. The impression one gets from listening to some members of the Church's hierarchy is that the Prime Mover created Catholic souls, Hindu souls, Moslem souls, pagan souls, etc., and that there is a difference when Catholics and non-Catholics suffer injustices or die.

"And supposing the Prime Mover operated on the same principle! Then the Deliverer would have to withdraw his statement to the effect that His father in heaven was concerned when a bird that didn't even possess a soul lost one of its feathers!

"The Prime Mover is in the business of creating *human* souls, and He turns them out, not just in droves, but in all sorts of shapes and sizes according to His divine plan. And, to ensure that the nature of His human creatures is complete and perfect like everything else he manufactures out of nothing, He also turns out bodies of humans in all sorts of shapes, sizes, and even colors, depending on His plan for the individual human. He makes all humans unique humans in that way.

"But there is no such a thing as a black, white or yellow human soul - and there is certainly no such a thing as an American, Iroquois, Vietnamese, Iraqi, Israeli, Palestinian, Pakistani, Indian, South African, East African, West African, Russian, Chechen, Japanese, North Korean, South Korean, Australian, Papuan, Filipino, or even British soul.

"And because He is the Artist par excellence, He thoroughly enjoys what he does. But he is also a jealous Prime Mover who does not brook insults or chicanery. He designs and makes human souls in His own image, signifying that love is the cornerstone of His labors. And He demands the same and no less from His creatures - that they love one another like they love themselves, and that they love Him above all else.

***Special creatures**...*

"Unlike pure spirits, humans after their creation and birth, continue to evolve and develop not just spiritually, but also physically. I definitely would have preferred to be created a human for just that reason. And, predictably, one of the vices that hastened my downfall consisted in envy. I always suspected that the Prime Mover would in time cause creatures that were different from me in important respects to come into being; and, in my jealousy, I even resented the fact that the Almighty was in a position to do that.

"I, even now, feel very jealous that the nature of humans allows them to grow, develop and be challenged in all sorts of ways, while we pure spirits do not change much after we are created. The fact of the matter is that I should be more proud of the way I was created, because the Prime Mover Himself is unchanging. Still, it would definitely be more fun being a human devil!

"I feel cheated when I try to imagine all the things I could have done as a Human Devil. If I lived to be hundred and twenty...a hundred and fifty...years, I would be able to do a lot of damage in that period. It would be a time earthlings would remember in a long time. For one, as a human devil on trial, I would be able to move around incognito among humans. Because a pure spirit is like a glowing asteroid in the heavens, it is impossible to hide - even though stupid humans think we don't exist just because they are too absorbed with the material things to notice that there is far more to reality than what meets the eye.

"What is really important is not the ability to discern something with the naked human eye, but with the 'eye of the soul'. To those humans who are selfless and lead spiritual lives, and recognize the Prime Mover in everything they see as well as in their neighbors, pure spirits, both demonic and angelic, are as present as trees and other objects that meet the human eye.

"There are some who think that because I am a very bad creature, I must be very ugly, perhaps even with horns and a tail - or things like that. As the grandest creature ever made, I have everything that makes one desirable. I may not be the nonpareil of beauty, but I am as lovely and handsome as the loveliest thing you could imagine. If you allowed me to inform a human body, you would find yourself confronted by a creature that was a thousand times more comely than the Queen of Sheba. So, it is a huge insult when some humans depict me as some ugly gargoyle.

"Of course, humans already do just about anything that comes to mind - they kill, commit adultery, worship idols, and break all the other commandments in ways you would never have imagined. And they have shown their penchant for trying to beat me at my own game of wickedness. Humans now almost rival me at being diabolic. The profanity, the lies and spin, and the callousness is sometimes simply stunning.

"But does it really matter if the perspective of members of the Church's hierarchy on the world is at cross purposes with the perspective of the Deliverer or the Prime Mover? What makes the Church 'Catholic'? Having churches everywhere, or is it something related to its nature - something that speaks to the fact that this is the Church the Eternal Word and Deliverer, who died for the salvation of humans before He officially inaugurated the Church on Pentecost Day, established.

"With so much confusion in the world, could it be that members of the Church's hierarchy are just as confused about things - and also as parochial and bigoted as everyone else? Well, most likely, given that humans are humans; and the world is the world; and members of the Church's hierarchy are just as much humans who live with all other humans in the same wicked world. And it probably also explains why discrimination in countries that are predominantly Catholic (regardless of whether 'Roman' Catholic or 'Eastern Orthodox' Catholic) against Moslems and others is quite blatant. It also says something about the likes of Mother Theresa who refused to see 'Hindu', 'Buddhist' or 'Christian' or even 'Catholic' souls in humans, and subsequently got more than their share of troubles for their stand.

"How are members of the Church's hierarchy going to imitate the apostles - the same apostles who were commanded to go out and teach, not just folks who were with them in the Upper House on the day the Holy Spirit descended upon them (identical to folks in the visible Church), but to folks in far flung places like Kigali and Peking which they had never heard of before, but for whom the Deliverer had died just the same - if they have this idea that the Prime Mover doesn't really love the Rwandese and the Chinese as much as he loves them? How are they going to do their job when they act as though some human souls are more valuable in the eyes of the Prime Mover than others?

"When humans become elevated to the order of Melchizedek or to the rank of Prince of the Church, does it strike them that the Church they serve is larger than themselves and their puny little minds, and that it is in fact as large as the Holy Spirit who not only informs it, but is a member of the Godhead? Does it ever strike those who are called to fill the shoes of the apostles (an unenviable task by any measure) that I, Satan and my troops here in the Pit, work very hard to ensure that they will always be bigoted and parochial, because that makes them serious obstacles to the 'universal' Church's work of evangelization?

"Now humans, being descendants of Adam and Eve, are all faced with the legacy of original sin. They are all inclined to sin. Related to that, there has always been one big plus for us here in the Pit, namely the fact that the folks who constitute the Church's clergy, inclined to sin like everybody else and also liable to make serious errors of judgement, have great difficulty (as you would expect) accepting that reality. You would expect them to be in the forefront acknowledging that, without the grace of the Prime Mover, they are totally at our mercy. But that is, of course, not something we want to see happen.

"Judas Iscariot, who was one of the twelve, betrayed the Deliverer, as also did Peter, the Rock upon the Deliverer planned to build His Church, when he denied Him three times in the short space of an hour. Both caused the Deliverer to endure untold grief. But Judas and Peter accepted their faults, a contrast to the actions of many members of the Church's clergy who are loathe to accept that there are always some among them who fall short. That, over the Church's chequered two thousand year history, members of the Church's hierarchy have on occasion betrayed the Mystical Body of the Deliverer, and caused it to endure unspeakable distress in the same way Judas Iscariot and first nominee for the position of 'Holy Father' did.

"But it is good that it is not recognized that, in spiritual matters, strength lies in acknowledging one's faults and/or weakness - showing humility. That is certainly not what we want to see happen.

"In the run-up to the Reformation, there were of course lots and lots of other culpable players apart from Luther, who is officially listed as the 'fall guy' responsible for the subsequent divisions in Christendom. But the very fact that those divisions have continued to endure means that many inside and outside the Church, by their acts of commission or omission, come Doomsday, will have to answer for their role in the agony and distress suffered by the Mystical Body of the Deliverer - agony and distress that is going to intensify as the new misguided 'Christian crusades' get under way.

"The Church's hierarchy could make a start on stemming the slide into a monumental debacle that is being brought on by Quixotic foolishness by condemning killings by *all* sides when they occur, and by loudly and clearly trumpeting the inalienable rights of all, Christian and non-Christian. But, again, that is precisely what we in the Pit would like to see happen - especially now in the run-up to Armageddon.

"Yeah! So you are a killer, and the kind of fellow who likes to go for the jugular when slighted despite the fact that you yourself are in need of forgiveness on a far greater scale! Now I am the devil, and 'I swear by my troth' (to borrow a line from Shakespeare) that when you humans (who are guilty of some of the most unspeakable misdeeds and are even ashamed to approach the Prime Mover to beg for His forgiveness) show that you just love to go for the jugular when offended however slightly by your fellow humans, that attitude is entirely of your own making, and I had nothing at all to do with it. Actually, I myself would not be inclined to show geeks like you any sympathy if I were the Judge. You do not deserve any.

"By the way, even as the very incarnation of evil, I have never been guilty of misdeeds that directly targeted others. It is true. My sin was a sin of pride - I refused to adore and worship (and the same for the other fallen angels). I never hurt any body. And, never having begged for - or received - any mercy myself, why should I be sympathetic to nuts like you! But the things you humans do to one another! It is just so disgusting.

"You humans have taken wickedness to a completely new low; and I think I know why. It must be because you humans start off earth-bound, even though spirits made in the Image like us. The problem is your self-importance as earth-bound creatures existing side by side with everything from inanimate objects and plants with only vegetative life and beasts that only boast their instincts.

"Even when Adam and Eve were plotting their rebellion, they were so bent on the notion that they would lord it over their descendants and, as 'King' and 'Queen' of the universe respectively, would demand to be treated as royalty while everyone else would be a 'subject'! It seemed such a crazy idea - but I couldn't dissuade them. My objective had been to get them to simply balk from going down on their knees in adoration and worship of the Prime Mover just like we ourselves had done

"You have to believe that when those of us who used to belong to choirs of angels strayed from the path, our sin was definitely not so much in the things we did to each other as in the things we did to ourselves by our refusal to hearken to our consciences and to accord the Prime Mover the homage and honor He was due. We did unspeakable damage to our individual selves in the process. Our disobedience left us virtual loonies. But with you humans, the major problem is the things you do to each other.

"All untoward acts by humans, however small or fleeting, immediately become indelible stains on the soul - stains that can only be washed away in the blood of the Lamb. And killing is indisputably one of them.

"Of course, one thing the pure spirits that remained loyal to the Prime Mover and the elect are looking forward to seeing in the aftermath of Armageddon is what we demons will start doing to each other - and to the souls of damned humans! I cannot even start to imagine the feeding frenzy and spitefulness as the hordes of demons and lost souls turn on me in particular perhaps in an effort to rub me out. At that time, throngs of lost souls and swarms of demons will almost certainly join forces and descend on me to avenge their loss. Even though I will survive, the bruising treatment will almost certainly leave me completely disfigured, a cripple, and unrecognizable. It is definitely not something I can look forward to.

"But I also do not want to think of the viciousness as demons and souls of the damned go at each other. It will be particularly bad for fallen humans because they will have their bodies with them. It will be a gory sight indeed! That is precisely why I, as ringleader in all this, must do what I have to do - namely continue to sow the seeds of death. And, incidentally, that is also the time when, in a strange twist of fate, those who are now being cut down and mercilessly slaughtered will have the last laugh.

"The peculiar nature of humans, which consists of an 'incorporeal' spirit and a 'corporeal' body, complete with the senses of sight, hearing, smell, taste and touch, undoubtedly makes their existence on earth so much more interesting. These senses are such an important part of the human experience, life would be impossible without them. Humans, of course, share this feature (the senses) with the rest of the animal world, reptiles, bird-life, and even insects.

"Then the DNA of humans, which results in the unique makeup of individual members of the human race, makes specific provision for the birth into the world of an almost equal number of he-humans and she-humans. Just imagine all the possibilities in terms of self-actualization that are open to humans as a result.

"In contrast to pure spirits that are created different from each other and can't really do very much to shape their uniqueness further, humans actually have the ability to influence their rank order in heaven (or in hell) to a much greater extent by the way they react and interact with the world around them during their sojourn on earth. It must also be a fantastic experience to be able to coexist in the same environment with lower creatures (like cows and goats) that do not have to worry about going to heaven or hell. Upon their demise, they (humans) are rewarded according to the way they used their many and varied talents.

"And so, humans who deliberately hurt or kill other humans and then go on to celebrate their 'victory' are jackasses who do not understand their own nature. They are so dumb they do not even see that they are being used by myself (undoubtedly also a jackass) to accomplish my evil plan; and they are even dumber for not being able to see that they are being used by the Deliverer to bring justification and redemption to the very people they want to see damned.

"For sinful humans accustomed not just to living in permanent fear for their lives, but also given to imagining that they must needs live by the sword to survive at all, the idea that the Prime Mover actually uses liars, thieves, murderers and other 'human devils' to bring His divine plan for humans to fruition must sound harebrained and laughable. And yet, *that* is what is true; and it is what they believe - namely that they prevail when they kill, and become vanquished when they meet their demise - that is featherbrained and nonsensical. It has to be so - otherwise it would be tantamount to saying that there is no life after death!

"One would have to be a bonehead and a complete idiot not to see that, in executing His divine plan, the Prime Mover uses killing even more than He does all other forms of human suffering. Yeah, without a doubt He uses the pangs of death - and the fact that all humans instinctively recoil from them (and with reason) - to achieve His ends. And you can bet that it is His way of undoing my evil plan - a plan that (as you can well imagine) is hatched in darkness and thrives on destruction and death. And this can only mean that, when evil humans celebrate death, they ally themselves with me, the Dickens, and also that they themselves are dying to die the death! When humans kill, as surely as they kill, so surely shall they die the death themselves!

"But actually if humans only knew what they were really doing, namely that they were doing the greatest favor imaginable to those they dislike out of selfish motives by facilitating the passage of their souls from their miserable existence on earth to their eternal rest and immortality in Elysium (in the company of none other than the Prime Mover Himself) while guaranteeing themselves dungeons in hell in the company of swarms of demons headed by myself, they would kill themselves over and over!

"In sum, whoever killed - or thought that he/she deserved to live more than some other human - will regret terribly, and even wish that he/she had not been born at all - like Judas Iscariot did, but may be (in his case) just in time.

"You see - there is a difference from saying that 'It were better if you were not born', and saying 'It were better if you were not created'. I am the incarnation of evil, and it just happens that I was created a pure spirit, and I was therefore not 'born'; but no where in the Holy Book is it said that it were better if I, Beelzebub (or any creature for that matter), were not created! If I had been a human devil, you can be sure that the Scriptures would just be full of the phrase 'It were better if the devil were not born!' And, hey - my hell would also have been a lot worse! I will explain.

"You humans may not know (and the great bulk of humans typically wallow in 'group think', and end up knowing next to nothing about themselves and their own nature), but a human is a very special creature - more special in fact than any of the angelic spirits! Our own special attribute is that every angel has each its own nature or essence. Now your nature - or that which makes humans human and which you all share - was crafted or designed in such a manner that its Designer, namely the Prime Mover Himself, could if He so wished turn around and take it up. And that was what happened in the case of the Son of Man.

"And that definitely says something about humans and human nature, namely that you humans, contrary to what you think or imagine, are *spirits* and are *not* animals! How many angels or demons can fit on the eye of a needle? That is a wrong question to ask - angels and demons are *spirits* and any number of them can fit on the eye of a needle. And so, even though the way it exactly happened remains a mystery that neither you humans nor ourselves here in Gehenna can grasp (as with so many things that relate to the actions of Prime Mover), using the same analogy, it is possible to see how a member of the Godhead could decide and take up the nature of a human without compromising His divinity.

"But it certainly says something about humans and their place in the Divine Plan. And if you humans were not beings that were so exalted, you realize that I, Diabolos, wouldn't be here wasting any time on you knuckle heads! Your human nature stands apart from that of mammals and other vertebrates because it makes it possible for you to eat of the fruit of the Tree of Life - like Adam and Eve did following my suggestion, and to discern what is good from what is bad!

"The human nature of the Deliverer (and also a member of the Godhead by virtue of His divine nature) allowed the unthinkable to happen - it allowed the Almighty to walk on Earth in the shape of the Virgin Mary's son who was also called Emmanuel, and to sanctify anew His works of creation in the physical as well as the spiritual realm!

"And when the Son of Man came to earth, humans did not suddenly become bigger than elephants, or taller than giraffes, or more colorful than zebras, or more agile than leopards. They did not develop hides that were tougher than those of crocodiles - even though some humans, like King Herod who ordered the slaughter of infants in an effort to get rid of the infant Deliverer and was under my total control, became even more thick-skinned, completely hardened to any reproach even though wicked in the extreme, and incorrigible. And they did not suddenly develop the ability to fly like birds of the air. Humans in fact remained humans and, as descendants of Adam and Eve who had dared to eat forbidden fruit from the Tree of Knowledge in the midst of the Garden of Eden, could distinguish between what was good and what was evil and were now accursed!

"Humans! Just to think that some of them actually believe that someone has to be the size of an indricotherium (which, by the way, is already extinct) in order to be 'someone'! These are the people who cannot understand how the Deliverer, a member of the Godhead, could be a human and a divinity at the same time! The fact of course is that physical 'size' is completely immaterial in the Prime Mover's eyes. But stupid humans only think of being 'important', deride the maxim that while it's nice to be important, it is far more important to be nice'! The Prime Mover is the Prime Mover because He is really, really, really nice! He is not just good. He is goodness *per se*, and that is why He, and He alone, is a Deity!

And humans die, but they don't die - just like us demons, because we are all created in the image of the Prime Mover. Even without the prospect of resurrection, from the beginning human ghosts were slated to 'live' on to answer for the deeds and misdeeds committed by them during their sojourn on earth. And so there you have another dimension of human nature that has a lot in common with that of a Deity that is almighty, has no beginning, and whose divine nature and existence are one and the same and by their very nature indistinguishable. And also remember that humans, like us demons, were created gratuitously in order that we may do whatever we do, not to our own glory and honor, but to the greater glory and honor of the Prime Mover and Almighty One. You realize that it is because of that exalted status that I, Satan and Ruler of the Underworld, will never leave you goddamn humans alone

"And if the Deity became a human, that means that humans can also become not just a little but a lot like the Deity; and the more they uphold the maxim that it is nice to be important, but it is more important to be nice in their lives, the more they become *like* their Deliverer. So, humans can actually come close to being like a Deity! And that is by being nice even while they remain 'earth-bound' creatures that are descended from Adam and Eve!

"But humans are already like the Prime Mover in that, using their reason and free will, they have power to multiply and to fill the earth - and also the power to rig mother earth with nuclear war heads and to trigger the long awaited Armageddon if they so choose.

"To receive the Prime Mover's blessings in His Son, humans must be 'partakers of the divine nature'. As Catherine of Siena put it, the souls that keep nothing at all, not even a bit of their own will, outside of their divine Maker, but are completely set afire in Him, are like the burning coal that, once it is completely consumed in the furnace, no one can douse. Or, as John of the Cross noted, in allowing the Prime Mover to move in it, the soul is at once illuminated and transformed in the Deity, and the Deity communicates to it His Supernatural Being, in such wise that it appears to be the Prime Mover Himself, and has all that the Deity Himself has. And that union comes to pass when the Deity grants the soul that supernatural favour, that all the things of the Prime Mover and the soul are one in participant transformation; and the soul seems to be God rather than a soul, and is indeed God by participation; although it remains true that the soul's natural being, though thus transformed, is as distinct from the being of the Prime Mover as it was before.

"After all, the only begotten Son of Eloi was given unto the world so that whosoever believed in him, might not perish, but might have life everlasting. And as God became a human, in all ways except sin, He will also make humans like God in all ways except his divine essence that is uncaused and has no beginning. The Son of God did indeed become Son of Man who, at the ninth hour of the day he was crucified and died, cried with a loud voice: '*Eloi, Eloi, lama sabachthani*?' That is a cry with which all humans of good will can identify as they beseech their divine Creator for deliverance from the evil plots that my minions hatch against them at my suggestion, and struggle to walk in the foot steps of the Deliverer bearing each the load of his/her own cross.

"If any thing therefore, it was only those humans whose lives were grounded in reality, like Simeon who was just and devout and had been waiting for the consolation of Israel, who could say that they were ready to be dismissed as mere servants of the Lord and to die in peace upon learning that the Deity had taken up His human nature. And, moreover, the Son of Man himself did not come to be ministered unto, but to minister, and to give his own life for the salvation of his fellow humans. All the rest remained my minions and enslaved to me, Satan and immortal prince of Hades!

"We here in the underworld are not fools. We have studied our subjects, viz. humans, and have gotten to understand their weaknesses far better than they themselves do. One of these weaknesses is to feign ignorance when they think it will be to their advantage if they do not take responsibility for their actions; and to put on airs when they think that such a ploy will work to their advantage. And when humans are faking helplessness to shirk their responsibilities, they will, generally, stop at nothing in their attempts to depict themselves as victims - victims of everything, including their own supposedly hapless nature!

"We know that, crafted in the image of the Prime Mover, and with the appearance on earth of the Son of Man on top of that, humans are now verily the 'workmanship' of the Prime Mover 'created in Christ Jesus in good works'; but just sit back and imagine the evils humans still do to each other. Ironically, it is the extent to which humans can be bad and nasty to one another that distinguishes them from all other creatures, and makes them so special - and a 'good catch' for us.

"Without a doubt then, humans, even though they are the 'poor forsaken descendants of Adam and Eve', are exalted beings that are temples of the Prime Mover. We here in the Underworld knowing that, and determined to frustrate the Divine Plan by bringing about their downfall, want humans to believe that they really aren't the prized creatures they are - that they aren't all that exalted or sublime.

"Humans, created in the Image, are every single one of them important in the eyes of the Prime Mover. There isn't one soul that was given an existence and endowed with its human nature by accident or by a fluke. And every moment that a human lives matters to the Prime Mover. Every human act bears on that human's destiny in eternity.

"It is at the moment a human, however wretched, despised or nondescript in life, kicks the proverbial bucket and crosses to the other side of the gulf that separates the living from the dead that the process of that human's self-actualization, started at conception, comes to a head, and the intrinsic glory of the human's nature, fashioned in the image of the Prime Mover and also effectively His temple, bursts forth. Look, at that moment of truth, it is immaterial whether the soul that is in the processs of being separated from the body in readiness for the self-actualization belongs to someone who was a nominal or fervent Catholic, a Protestant, a Muslim, a Hindu, a Buddhist, or a follower of K'ung-fu-tzu, or someone who was raised without any religious belief. And it is immaterial if the soul belongs to someone who, whilst on earth, was influential to the point of being beyond the reach of the law, or to someone who was not deemed to be deserving of even the common law writ of *Habeas Corpus*!

"And it, of course, does not matter if the soul arriving on the other side of the gulf that separates the living from the dead belongs to a murder victim or a victim of the so-called 'capital punishment'. It is completely immaterial if it is one of the so-called 'disappeared' who turns up unexpectedly on the other side of the gulf that separates the living from the dead; or if it is someone (a commander-in-chief or some such funny character) who was in the business of causing others to disappear into thin air, or a commander-in-chief who used drones or some other such 'mystery' powers to speed up the appearance on the other side of the gulf that separates the living from the dead of any one he chose, or a commander-in-chief who made it a habit of exonerating those who did committed such crimes who turns up there when his/her own numbered days finally run out, and he/she is forced to follows his/her victims to see what awaits him on that side of the gulf!

"And the self-actualization happens by virtue of the Son of Man's death and resurrection, the fitting sacrificial offering of Himself to His heavenly Father on behalf of Adam and Eve and all their descendants. That is also the time when some, observing the 'good thief' who was executed alongside the Son of Man receive a denarius, will murmur saying: 'This last chap has worked but one hour, and thou hast made him equal to us, that have borne the burden of the day and the heats'!

"As the Father of Death, I have worked hard to sow seeds of death among humans, and the Deliverer's own ignominious death on the cross bears that out.

"You ought to know - even if you have never read Luke 4:7 or Matthew 4:9 - that I take my job as tempter very seriously. I have ways of leading humans one at a time to the tops of high mountains from whence I show them all the kingdoms of the world in a flash of time. And I always have the same message for humans. I say to them: 'To thee will I give all this power, and the glory of them; for to me they are delivered, and to whom I will, I give them. If thou therefore wilt adore before me, all shall be thine!' And, instead of answering saying, 'It is written: Thou shalt adore the Lord thy God, and Him only shalt thou serve', the stupid humans take the bait, kneel down and adore me! And instead of angels descending on them and ministering to them, there they are, all excited, forgetting that the ravens neither sow nor reap; have neither storehouse nor barn; yet the Prime Mover feeds them. They forget that they are much more important than birds, and that every single human is precious to Him; that before He formed each one of them in the womb, He knew them. And that, before they were born, He had set the damn stupid humans apart!

"It is a measure of our success that many humans don't perceive themselves as creatures that are destined for an eternal life that will be either in heaven with Michael the Archangel or here in Gehenna with us. We want humans to see themselves as helpless creatures whose actions are really of no significance. We might find it harder to get the children and the innocent to buy that; but we find it quite easy actually to persuade the adults, especially the errant ones, to ignore their consciences and start imagining that their actions, heinous or otherwise, don't have any serious consequences attached to them in the moral arena. We want them to imagine that ethics and morality belong only in works of fiction, and aren't things that should impede their acquisition of material wealth and their 'advancement' on earth.

'Stupid humans have bought into this to the point where they now use their religion and spiritual beliefs - to the extent they still profess any belief in spiritual things or the unseen - to either discriminate against everyone who subscribes to something different, or to propagate the so-called 'separation of State and Church' doctrine, which in turn promotes agnosticism.

"We consequently have them trapped - more or less! What we don't want stupid humans to do is recognize that each and everyone of their actions, whether conducted in secret in their thoughts or behind closed doors, decidedly has repercussions for themselves and for other members of the human family in the short term, and *ipso facto* also impact their destiny here on earth and their eternal life in heaven or in hell.

"That is how we get Catholics to remain lukewarm and Catholic only in name. It is also how we get everyone else outside the Church that was founded by the Deliverer to remain contented with their individual circumstances despite the fact that the Gospel has already been propagated to the ends of the earth by the Deliverer's messengers. You've got to give us credit for our achievement in this very important arena.

"And concerining the 'Galileans whose blood Pilate had mingled with their sacrifices', the people were told by the Deliverer that those Galileans were not sinners above all the men of Galilee because they suffered such things. No! But unless they did penance, they all would likewise perish. Or those eighteen upon whom the tower fell in Siloe, and slew them: they also were not debtors above all the men that dwelt in Jerusalem. No, but if those people who were inquiring did not do penance, they would all likewise perish.

"Not everyone who says to Him, 'Lord, Lord,' will enter the kingdom of heaven, but only he who doth the will of His Father who is in heaven. He shall enter into the kingdom of heaven. Many will say to Him on that day, 'Lord, Lord, did we not prophesy in your name and in your name drive out demons and perform many miracles?' Then He will tell them plainly, 'I never knew you. Away from me, you evildoers!

"He admonishes humans in the meantime to strive to enter by the narrow gate; for wide is the gate, and broad is the way that leadeth to destruction, amd many there are who go in thereat. How narrow is the gate, and strait is the way that leadeth to life: and few there are that find it! For many shall seek to enter, and shall not be able. For when the Master of the house shall be gone in, and shall shut the door, humans shall begin to stand without, and knock at the door, saying: Lord, open to us. And He, answering, shall say to them: I know you not, from whence you are. Then they shall begin to say: We have eaten and drunk in thy presence, and thou hast taught in our streets. And He shall say to them: I know you not, whence you are: depart from me, all ye workers of iniquity. It is true that there shall be weeping and gnashing of teeth, when some humans shall see Abraham and Isaac and Jacob, and all the prophets, in the kingdom of the Prime Mover, and they themselves thrust out. And there shall come from the east and the west, and the north and the south; and shall sit down in the kingdom of God.

"If humans 'sin willfully after having the knowledge of the truth' (as Paul pointed out in Hebrews 10:26), they must also embrace the 'certain dreadful expectation of judgment'! This is the reason my troops and I will not let up in our pursuits of human souls. It is also the reason, even though I am the Father of Lies, I must use this opportunity to try and shine as much light on Truth as possible so that humans cannot say they did not know!

"And the Deliverer, whose ascension into heaven was witnessed by His apostles, will return at the end of time (in the same way the apostles saw Him taken up skyward into heaven) to judge the living and the dead. In the meantime, a *just* and *devout* Masai herdsman, tending to his cattle on the slopes of Mt. Kilimanjaro, is more connected to the Prime Mover who deigned to share the Masai's human nature than I myself was when, as the Angel of Light, I ministered to the Almighty, in the company of Michael the Archangel in the days before I rebelled and got ejected from His face!

"Now, if I, Lucifer and Satan, had been a human, the Deliverer would have been in a position to say 'It were better if Lucifer had not been born'; and the fight between Good, led by the Deliverer, and Evil, led by a human demon, would have been over right there and then! Also I must say 'Thank God I am a pure spirit and not a human' because you can just imagine my lot as a human devil leading a band of rebel forces against the Almighty in the battle for souls! Where, for one, would I, as the Father of Death, be able to hide along with the legions of demons I command?

"The war between Good and Evil would itself be so ugly! The oceans with their salty water would have turned into one giant sea of blood long ago if the demons I command and I myself had been human! I can assure you that things would have been completely different. And you can guess what would be on my mind as the leader of the Powers of Darkness in the run-up to the call of the trumpet heralding the return of the Deliverer and Judge (at the sound of whose name every knee of heavenly and earthly and infernal beings should bow)!

"Kill, Kill, Kill using everything in our arsenal - poisons, improvised explosive devices or IEDs, drones, hijacked trains and airliners, you name it! Nothing would be off the table

"But, even though created a pure spirit, with the help of my minions among humans, my troops and I still might just be able to make things as ugly as they definitely would be if I had been created a human!

"Now, Judas was completely oblivious to the sanctity of his human nature and his last end when, pining after thirty pieces of silver, he betrayed his Divine Master and Deliverer by collaborating with the priests and Pharisees in their plot to liquidate the Son of Man. Evil as their scheme was, you could not have said that it were better if these plotters had not been *created.* No, because you would then also be able to say the same about me, you fool! But they damn well should not have been *born.* It were better if those humans who now imagine that they can liquidate their enemies from the face of the earth once and for all by hatching murderous plots had themselves not been born. In plotting to murder their own kind, humans effectively posit that their enemies should not have been born! And because, by divine decree, a human soul cannot return to nothingness once it has been created and implanted into a human being, there is now just no way murderers can prevent that act of murder from coming back to haunt them on their own Day of Judgement. And that is what the Deliverer was trying to convey to you geeks!

"We here in the Underworld aim to get you humans to in effect desire that your 'enemies' get lost for ever - which is the same as saying that it were better if your enemies were not *created*. And all humans who do that effectively seal their own fate - because they show that they not only do not believe in life after death, but they do not believe in the existence of the Prime Mover Himself and do not recognize His divine plan according to which a creature, once created in the Image, can never be liquidated, uncreated or otherwise returned to the nothingness from which the creature came. And so, the statement 'It were better if you were not born' simply means that if you die unrepentant of your sin, that sin will haunt you for ever - meaning that you will end up as my guest here in Gehenna.

"A word, though, about Judas and whether he may or may not have escaped my tentacles. Just take this hint. Because I am Satan, it does not mean that I know everything. I certainly know plenty as a pure spirit that was wonderfully endowed at creation. However, the fact remains that I am a totally evil being now, and an evil nature and knowledge are opposites. I, therefore, definitely know less than any spirit or soul that enjoys beatific vision and communes with Him who is Knowledge *per se*.

"And then there is also the fact that I am deliberately denied as punishment the many things I used to enjoy prior to my rebellion; and, as you may have guessed, being able to gloat over the fact that this or that soul is lost is easily one of them. But you must even then figure in the fact that everything is possible with the Prime Mover, and that He could still allow me to know that Judas is in some dungeon here in hell or in heaven - or in Purgatory and among those who are certain of their salvation - and still use that knowledge to cause me infinite grief. But I myself choose not to reveal to you the exact position with respect to Judas Iscariot.

"Knowing that I am an infernal liar, you actually should still be leery to take all the preceding with a pinch of salt - except the following. I mean the fact that I definitely know many chaps - some of whom were really infamous and others who were really famous and supposedly men and women of impeccable character while they lived - who have ended up here in hell. I have even visited some of these folks in their dungeons, not to commiserate with them, but to mock them some for thinking that they were clever. While they lived, some of them thought that they were cleverer than even me, Beelzebub, even though I was actually the one inspiring them to kill and to do other dirty work on my behalf like spinning falsehoods and stirring up hatreds among humans in the name of the Deliverer.

"Well, you might excuse them for having paid heed to my wiles, but the Judge didn't. Many of them had made themselves so unfit to serve as vessels of grace, I didn't find it that hard to make them instruments of hatred and other human vices.

Crowned Arch-Devil...

"Getting back to the business of sinful humans (and killers in particular) who die unrepentant - after spending a lifetime in which they allowed the self and the lure of material things to take a front seat without any thought as to their last end, humans at death must feel like fish that are accustomed to frisking and basking and waxing in water from the first moment of their waking existence (and even though they had been told time and again that they should stay clear of those waters and get used to living on dry land where they belonged), and that suddenly wake up one morning to find all the water gone with no prospect of it ever returning!

"You've got to accept that I am not called the Enemy for nothing. I am clever - and pretty clever too. And you have also to accept that I know exactly what I do as I go about sowing the seeds of death.

"What is it about me that makes me so feared? How come I seem to have a monopoly over evil - how come that there seems to be no creature that is capable of challenging me in my chosen role as Tempter?

"O.K. - I'll let you in on a secret, and I enjoin you to silence as I have always liked to leave the impression that I have never been challenged. I got the reputation as the 'author of death' because I killed the only creature that looked liked it might become my rival in evil and sin. I do not know how I did it, but I effectively eliminated her - I believe it was a 'her' and not a 'him' (because I am a 'him'). She was after my crown as the Arch-Devil, and that was how we became entangled in an argument that turned deadly.

"It was truly a battle for survival - it is the only instance in which the Prime Mover permitted a creature that was made in the Image to be destroyed ...'rubbed out'. And so, I rubbed out my rival. Of course I still feel a terrible sense of guilt for having murdered my arch-rival. Oh...and she was so frightfully beautiful! But, well, one of us had to go; and none of us wanted to 'die' - to be rubbed out.

"We battled it out in full view of the heavenly host. And, as I faintly recall, the assembly of angels were all rooting for her. That made me really mad. In retrospect, it probably saved my 'life' - it apparently distracted her, and resulted in my gaining a slight edge over her in our 'battle for existence'. And you should have seen the look on her face as she saw the end coming. That battle was the ugliest thing that the choirs of angels had ever witnessed up until then. As I remember, it all started - and ended - as we both were conspiring to disobey the Prime Mover. But that is really all I am able to recall.

"So you now understand why there is no creature in existence that rivals me as the Arch-Devil. But even after I vanquished my rival, quite frankly I have to admit that there is nothing at all to be envied about a creature like me that now languishes at the bottom of the Pit. Even though I succeeded in visiting 'death' on my 'enemy' and she is gone, I have been haunted by her ghost ever since.

"The act of rubbing out my arch-rival sealed my fate as the most horrid and hateful creature that exists - and as the Arch-devil and enemy of the Prime Mover. I condemned myself to the bottom rung of creatures, and became the most despised, ridiculed, hated and, I dare say, also feared creature.

"For now, all I can tell you is that a creature that is made in the Image - any creature that is made in the Image - and is humble can be elevated to greatness, like the Blessed Virgin Mother of the Deliverer who was elevated above all creatures. One does not have to be huge in stature (which I suppose I was before I blew my opportunities). But you can also start out little and grow into a virtual monster - like

Cain and Judas did at one time. And you have always to remember that when you bring off any good, it isn't so much you who does it as the Spirit who does it through you - when you let Him.

"And so, while any one can end up as a monster and a devil, it is only the very humble who can reach the heights of holiness. And, of course, all creatures that are made in the Image are called to be humble, so that as and when the Spirit chooses, they may be raised up - exactly as the Son of Man, who took on the burden of the sins of humans, accepted humiliations and died on the cross in obedience to His Father, was raised up above all.

The source of fear

"Cain at least realized, although only after he had committed his first murder, that killing another human being for any reason did not even address the reason for wanting other humans dead, namely the killer's fear of death! In his later years, as his own days on earth became numbered, the repentant Cain discovered through meditation and prayer that it was an irrational fear - the fear of death - that drove him to kill. And it was of course quite obvious that his fear to die was a legacy of original sin.

"By the time Cain was on his own death bed and dying, the former murderer, after spending a good part of his later years mortifying himself and doing penance for his dastardly act, understood that a human being who was no longer scared of dying, really had nothing else to fear. Just like his parents (Adam and Eve), Cain also kept a diary; and one of the last things he jotted down on the papyrus before he 'kicked the bucket' was that humans who feared to die could not turn around and declare themselves victors over anything whatsoever.

"This was because the fear of death paralyzed humans and made them see it lurking in everything that either came to mind or met their sight. Those who feared death were actually scared of everything, even though like so many Don Quixotes, they preferred to conceal their true feelings, including their pathological fear of the 'unknown', under a show of valor. And there is, of course, nothing that typifies fear more than the morbid preoccupation with the development of weapons of mass destruction by the so-called super powers even as they clamor for 'bans' on the self-same and do everything in their power to ensure that the playing field is anything but level - and also while completely oblivious to the fact that in a matter of decades, not only their investment in armaments will be obsolete, but all the players will be dead and gone, replaced by new generations of paranoid schizophrenics who are prone to making the sort of blunders that invariably result in a redrawing of boundaries, and in new maps in which all those once super powerful and domineering 'empires' will be nowhere to be seen.

"Cain wrote that it was easy to tell if a human harbored the fear of death. That human will wrap himself/herself up in body armor, and sometimes in so much body armor that he/she will scarcely be able to get up and about. And everything that remotely resembles a combat zone will cause them to take refuge in what Cain called 'humvees' - these were armor plated contraptions into which the first generation of humans retreated at the first signs of a twister or a hurricane. Cain was quite imaginative, and predicted that a time would come when demagogues would be so terrified of their fellow humans that they would go to very great lengths to keep them at bay. Cain himself longed for a world in which he could surround himself with 'body guards' who would be clad in 'riot gear' and would wield batons and break up any groups of the proletariat - protesters, 'occupiers' and other 'rats' whose activities looked like they might pose a threat to progressives like himself who were aspiring to become either 'landed gentry' or 'landed bourgeoisie', capitalists, or even 'aristocrats'.

"Cain was not entirely stupid; and, even as he took steps to ensure that the 'occupier' Abel wouldn't get into a position to challenge or threaten him in any way by keeping him on the defensive all the time, he frequently worried that a 'plutocrat' like himself, whose success was achieved almost entirely at the expense of Abel, might be in for a real surprise one day. If Abel survived his ordeal without commit the sin of despair or some other sin that individuals in his position might be inclined to, he might well end up having the last laugh in the end! Cain understood very well that, even if he succeeded in 'doing away' Abel's entire 'clan' somehow so that it was just his 'clan' that survived to enjoy the blessings of Mother Earth, 'what goes around comes around'! That was what his mom Eve, lamenting the way she had observed him 'maltreating' Abel as she put it, had exclaimed in the hearing of everybody including Abel on one occasion. He was of course mad at her for saying such a thing to him in front of the 'whole world'! But she had said it, and everyone there except himself had nodded in agreement, as if to say '*Vox Populi, Vox Dei*' (the voice of the people is the voice of the Prime Mover). All of this had such a chilling on Cain; and unfortunately, much as he tried to dismiss his mom and everyone there, including his wife, as *ignoramuses* and totally wrong, something at the back of mind kept telling him that they were right - and that, yes, the voice of the people *was* the voice of the Prime Mover!

"Cain's pathological fear of the 'rat' Abel and his ilk sometimes kept him up sleepless all night. Cain's antipathy for his brother got a boost from a bad dream he had on a day he thought he was finally going to enjoy a good night's rest. Cain dreamed that, instead of just the one Abel he had watched grow up and then try to encroach on his lands, he saw an entire army of humans descending on his choicest tracts of land. They all looked exactly like the Abel he knew, and they were calling themselves 'occupiers'. The intentions of the army of 'rats', as he himself liked to refer to them, were clear: they were there to see him dethroned from his pinnacle of power in the Garden of Eden! Cain was hollering, sweating, and swearing that he was going to find his own army of humans to battle them only to find that he didn't have the wherewithal to get up from his three legged stool in order to make good on his promise to destroy that 'rat' Abel and his cohorts! The mysterious army of 'rats' was bearing down on him and about to overrun his position when he woke up and discovered, to his great relief, that he had been dreaming.

"Cain recounted in the diary he kept how he spent one entire summer locked up inside a 'humvee' out of fear that a twister might appear from no where and give him a pounding from which he might not recover. He eventually let himself out when he realized that dying wasn't a really bad idea after all.

"First, if he lived to be a thousand years, he would be quite miserable and bedridden starting from around the time he turned four hundred years of age, and he would almost certainy be permanently plagued by arthritis starting from the time he turned five hundred years old. But the most convincing reason ended up being the fact that a thousand years was a pretty long time to wait by any standards before one died and headed off to Elysium to be united with one's Maker or Prime Mover!

"You would of course think that later generations would learn from the experience of Cain. But, No! After they have invested so much time and effort developing whose walls cannot be rammed in using technology stolen from Cain, they start fearing that might succeed in stealing 'their' technology and produce similar conveyances. And so, off they go and they start developing projectiles that can penetrate the hide of any humvee that human technology can produce, and disable it.

"And just when they are imagining that their military is ahead of everyone else in the capacity to wage wars and have a monopoly over the new technologies, lo and behold, not some rival super power, but some little known 'Jihad' group sympathetic to the most feared 'terrorists' on earth posts the blue print for their latest 'humvee' and the full slate of formulas needed by any one who wants to develop projectiles that are capable of penetrating its hide on its website!

"They continue to concentrate on developing efficient methods of 'destroying' their fellow humans even though they know that they themselves are going to die. It is not just wasted effort - it is also damning! It is a waste of resources that could have been used to assure that every human lived in peace and comfort. And the failure to do that adds to their crime. So, so damn stupid! And if they only did what common sense dictated - if they employed the resources at their disposal to better the lives of all members of the human family without distinction - they wouldn't wind up with any 'terrorists' or 'insurgents' real or imagined! And this also says something about the world's think tanks so-called. There isn't one that has been able to get it right!

"To recap, victory can never be victory unless it is victory over death. Any other 'victory' is a sham. And to win over death does not mean spending a lifetime worrying about how to stay alive, or trying to invent something that 'beats' death. It means stopping to let fear - the fear of death - dictate the actions of a human. Death came about as a consequence of sin, and being born in original sin in essence means being born in the grip of fear of death and subject to it.

"Misguided humans imagine that they can stem that fear by putting up ramparts around themselves in hopes of keeping the prowling 'Death' at bay and out of their immediate vicinity. Really stupid ones go to the extent of visiting death on those they perceive as their 'enemies' - which merely serves to seal their own fate while opening up opportunities for their victims to overcome death and their fear of it.

"The clever humans quickly learn that death has to be seen in the context of the struggle between Good and Evil in which they themselves as the poor forsaken children of Adam and Eve who are born inclined to sin are completely powerless; and they try to learn how to put their faith and trust in the Prime Mover, and the really clever ones flock to Mary, Mother of the Deliverer and Queen of Heaven, to ask that 'most gracious advocate' to turn her eyes of mercy upon them and, after their exile, to show unto them the Blessed Fruit of her womb and Prince of Peace. And they do not forget to ask her to pray for them, so that they may be worthy of the promises of the Deliverer.

The stain of Original Sin

"It may be true that I am the Father of Death. But that 'death' is primarily spiritual. Humans are subject to its physical dimension only by virtue of putting their eternal life at risk. If Adam and Eve had not been insolent and 'eaten of the forbidden fruit', all humans would be craving for the moment when their 'earthly pilgrimage' would end and they crossed to the other side of the Gulf where they wouldn't be subject to our temptations or the temptations of the flesh, and where they would enjoy their crown in eternity in the presence of their Creator.

"I must point out one thing: even though I did not know at the time I led the rebellion against the Prime Mover that He would add 'human' creatures (also made in the Image) to creation - and even though, by extension, I did not know that physical death would be visited on humans as and when they incurred His ire by agreeing to join my camp, the moment I knew that I, Lucifer, had forfeited eternal life and was going to be cast in hell fire for ever more, I made up my mind that I would try and derail the divine plan in any way possible, but especially as it related to creatures that stood the slightest chance of delighting in the presence of the Prime Mover in my place.

"And so, even before 'human nature' was given its expression in Adam and eventually also in Eve and their posterity, it can be said that 'death' was literally hanging over them. By the time the soul of Adam was taking up its abode in the red grains of earthly matter, I was waiting and ready to do my job as the Tempter. And nothing bespeaks of my success more than the institutionalized killings that have been carried out in the name of 'Justice', 'Civilization', 'Liberty', 'Religion' and what have you since time immemorial.

"Now, if Adam and Eve who were not subject to concupiscence which came with their fall from grace, or the inclination to sin associated with concupiscence, could fall for my pranks, you can imagine how easy it must be for their descendants, who are not only inclined to sin but grow up surrounded by all those hard core sinful and sinning adults - the same adults who should be mentoring them as they grow up - to do so.

"And then, when the young humans discover as they grow up that, after Adam and Eve sinned, a Deliverer was indeed promised by the Prime Mover; but that the Israelites, the chosen people, roundly rejected Him when He made His appearance on earth instead of rejoicing and embracing Him and His message of redemption, that must be disconcerting enough. But it must be even more disconcerting and confounding when the young people find a myriad institutions, all of them claiming to be the Church the Deliverer founded and the new testament Ark of Noah. Add to that the concupiscence and inclination to sin to which these young people - like their adult counterparts - find themselves subject!

"Look. If I did not know better, I would probably get on to some platform and declare "Mission Accomplished"! But I just happen to be a little bit more knowledgeable than that.

"Concupiscence and the inclination to sin aren't sinful in themselves. In fact humans could turn them into the opportunities they were intended to be. Just rejecting my suggestions translates into meritorious works, and a decision by humans to resist temptations of the flesh with the help of divine grace automatically translates into a crown to be enjoyed in the hereinafter. This is stuff that turns sinful humans into saints and heroes.

"Still, growing up in a world in which the culture of violence and death is not just rampart, but is represented as something that is normal and even sacrosanct, one would have to be rebel from one's earliest days to be immune from the deleterious effects of something that is pervasive as that. The young one would actually risk being labeled a wimp and a nutcase, and would be lucky not to be treated as such. That would be the almost certain fate of a kid who plucked up the courage to object to an assignment to read and internalize Gaius Julius Caesar's *De Bello Gallico* which glorifies foreign military adventures for their sake. And, of course, woe upon the kid who had the gall to suggest that passages of the Old Testament that sanction killing might actually be apocryphal!

"From the time Adam and Eve stole and ate of the forbidden fruit from the Tree of Life, we here in the Pit have worked very hard to ensure that violence and killings are glorified, and it is not by accident that the Old Testament is full of passages that glorify violence and wars. And the ghastly murder of Abel by the greedy

Cain was of course a foretaste of things to come of murders committed in the name of national security, foreign adventures to plunder that would be passed off as religious crusades, and so on and so forth.

"But young humans invariably discover as they grow up that they too are beneficiaries of special largess from a Benefactor who only asks that they live up to their exalted state as creatures that are fashioned in His divine image and likeness in return. But they also discover that the world in which they found themselves is a cruel world in which humans scavenge on other humans at will. They discover that it is a world in which oppression of the weak and disadvantaged is the order of the day; and a world in which almost everyone is a liar, a dissembling idiot or both; and that being 'civilized' does not mean being 'civil', but being smart at taking what does not belong to you and calling it commerce; and also that might is always right!

"Finding themselves in a world in which everyone around them is absorbed in the here and now, and permanently obsessed with how to carve out a piece of earth for oneself, young humans will have little choice but to jump on the bandwagon and try thereafter to emulate those they deem as their 'heroes' in the strange new set up. We here in the Pit count on the young humans to make that 'logical' move. After Adam and Eve 'rebelled' and got booted out of 'Paradise', all their issue became inclined to sin, and these young humans are no exception. And even though the promised Messiah came and paid the price for the sins of humans, that did not of itself alter the equation very much, for the simple reason that the redemption of humans (when their lives don't get snuffed out while still in their mothers' wombs) is still dependent on the exercise of their free wills!

"He is a human!"

"Now, the Deliverer Himself, conceived without original sin, as Man was nonetheless the same as all other humans in every respect except that He was sinless. I myself got my shot at tempting Him;

and others too, including Peter, His nominee for the position of supreme Pontiff of the infant Church, also tried. And the Word-Become-Flesh was Himself buffeted by desires of the flesh like all the descendants of Adam and Eve.

"We ourselves in the underworld were, as you can imagine, at first thrilled that the Redeemer of humans was himself a human! You cannot imagine the echo that resounded all through hell as all of us fallen angels and demons screamed with fiendish joy and in one voice: 'He is a human!'

"We were all itching to join battle with the Messiah of Humans just for that reason alone! It had escaped us all that the Son of Man also encapsulated the Word through whom all that is came into being; and that, when He came down to Earth as the Savior of humankind and took up His human nature, He did so in obedience to the will of His Father in heaven. And, well, it was also again in obedience to His heavenly Father that he agreed to endure the utmost indignities at the hands of the same humans he had come to save!

"And, a divinity, He still knew better than to roam the steppes of Galilee and Judea showing off His power to perform miracles or declaring that I, Beelzebub and Evil Ghost, was the underdog. He merely sought to do the will of His Father, and vanquished me and my troops, judo style, by not standing in the way of *vires iniqui* (the wicked humans who were acting as my surrogates) as they mocked and assaulted Him, crowned Him with thorns, and finally destroyed the Temple in which He had made His abode during His sojourn on earth - the temple that would be glorified in three days.

"And then, to ensure that His death and resurrection would not be in vain, He saw to it that poor forsaken children of Adam, who fell for my pranks and for the temptations of the flesh and were repentant, would find forgiveness through the Sacrament of Penance. That was actually how He turned my world upside down, and took the sting out of Death which was one of the wages of sin, so that humans who lose everything in this world, including their lives, as a result of rejecting my whiles, now actually become martyrs - which is what Thomas of

Aquin, Theresa of Lisieux, Augustine of Hippo, Kizito of Uganda and others in fact became.

"Now, hand in hand with the institutionalization of killings under the dubious banner of 'just wars', the ethic that 'might is right' also became firmly entrenched in the human psyche. The concept of 'unjust war' was invented by those who wanted to justify murder in the name of so-called 'national security', and to make those who were mighty and powerful - and supposedly always right - appear morally responsible.

"And, instead of 'using their heads' to make sure that everyone got enough to eat, the stupid humans decided to apply their God-given intelligence in my service in the 'Manhattan Project'. They invented the bomb!

"Yeah, the bomb! You see - humans talk about the forces of Good led by the Prime Mover being at war with the forces of Evil led by me. But they do not seem to realize that the battle ground where all this is playing out is here on earth and specifically among humans. The success of the Manhattan project was not just a spectacular victory for us in this campaign, but a landmark and turning point in this war. Our best brains - or 'minds' if that makes more sense to you - are even now still evaluating the importance of that victory.

"The investment in the bomb by humans was diametrically opposed to the idea of a harmonious world in which humans could live together as brothers and sisters and as members of the same human stock. From the day Adam, the first human, found himself all alone on earth and, craving for the company of a fellow human, beseeched the Prime Mover to look with favor upon him and provide him company in the person of Eve, we have always worked to ensure that, in stead of a world in which humans sought to make their lives as a people of one stock the envy of the beasts of the earth and other lower creatures, they would be focused on self-indulgence and thirsting for each other's blood in the literal sense.

"Now, in the days before START (the Strategic Arms Reduction Treaty) was signed by the Americans and the Russians, the cost of producing just a single nuclear bomb easily eclipsed the amount the populations of those two protagonists were spending annually on health, housing and food. That is about the cost of feeding the combined populations of India and Pakistan for twenty years. But what the Manhattan project - and the cold war which ensued between those nuclear giants - did was to cause India and Pakistan to replicate it, effectively denying millions food, medicine and shelter outright.

"Instead of humans who had a command of life saving technology sharing it with those that didn't for the purpose of saving lives, the technology sharing between humans has been pursued for completely wrong reasons with a recklessness that even us here in the Pit could never have imagined. As a consequence, the Armageddon in waiting for the inhabitants of earth would have been unimaginable a hundred years ago. But it is not just an Armageddon that is waiting to befall humans, it is an Armageddon that is now sure to befall humans, and in the very near future too! And, all because of the insolence of the so-called advanced nations, and their mad desire to be masters of the world.

"And what with the devastating consequences on the environment of the atmospheric and underground nuclear tests, even as the day of that Armageddon draws nigh, a series of secondary but immediate mini Armageddons in the form of scotching heat waves and ravaging floods are now commonplace, and are not sparing anyone - not even those same so-called advanced nations that started it all with a swagger and defiance that had never been known to man before the Manhattan project was conceived - at our suggestion of course - by terror-stricken, thoroughly misguided humans. Ah, yes - the Manhattan project!

"And bad as that is, the full extent of the problem cannot be appreciated until it is recognized that evil is entrenched in the human psyche by virtue of the original sin. The crop of humans who invented the bomb was just one. After they pass on and join the ranks of lost souls and fallen angels here in Gehenna - or if they saw light, changed their minds and just pulled out of the death culture business -

it isn't a big hassle at all finding other hell bent humans to take their places. Just a minor inconvenience!

"Now, we even got the damn stupid humans to use the bomb! So, so stupid! Yeah, let's see how they can do this and still inherit those mansions in heaven that had been earmarked for us!

"And talk about history repeating itself - and about reaping what you sow! Or about stupidity! At the height of my own insolence - and it didn't help that I was the 'Prince of Light' at the time I decided to concoct the scheme that was intended to see myself and all the angels who wished to join me in my rebellion rid of the Almighty One - I had every intention of committing murder (killing Him) so I could take His place. That was what led me to head the task force to invent Death! I like to think of it as our own 'Manhattan project'!

"If we succeeded in inventing Death and visiting it on Him, that was it! I would be crowned the Father of Death and also the new Boss of All. But instead of being at the administering end, we found ourselves at the receiving end! And that is how we found ourselves banished to this dreadful sink hole of the spiritually dead and lost souls. And so it is going to be for the inventors of the bomb - when they too finally find themselves at the receiving end!

"Oh! It is going to be just so terrible - first as the secret services of the West expand their extrajudicial 'Kill Lists' dramatically, and unsuspecting folks in the Middle East, the Far East and Africa find themselves, along with their families, suddenly the target of drone attacks! Yeah! Expanded extrajudicial assassination lists, and with not a word of condemnation from the Holy See! Talk about strange bedfellows - the Vicar of the Deliverer whose labors are devoted to the salvation of souls, and me, Beelzebub and Chief Demon, who is committed to the cause of death and the damnation of souls! And this should tell you that we here in the pit have not been exactly resting on our laurels even after notching that impressive string of victories!

"And, second, as those hapless 'insurgents' and 'terrorists', after bearing the brunt of drone attacks and other stealth 'surgical' operations conducted by western super powers in their 'war on terrorism' over a prolonged period, working in concert, take advantage of the latest in computer hacking technology, finally get to have their own mini 'nukes', and then promptly proceed to 'publish' their own 'Kill Lists' consisting of names of cities in Europe and America! It will be just so, so terrible!

"That is what I mean by history repeating itself. You have to be dumb not to notice that the stage is already set for those who invented the bomb to reap what they sowed!

"As the Chief Evil Ghost, I say 'Hurray!' to my fellow demons and all you wicked humans who have consented to join us in this 'great', 'shameful' and totally 'ignoble' cause! Yeah...the ignoble cause that 'Might', wielded by wicked humans for an evil cause is Right'! Right - even though, for wicked humans, this is true only in the short term and can never be true over the long term.

"And now also - predictably - any defensive actions by the 'underdogs', particularly those nations that have been labeled 'rouge' automatically became 'criminal', 'unconscionable' and 'unjust', particularly if they seem to be directed against a 'superior' or 'super' power. But, of course, warlike actions automatically became 'just' and 'blessed' the moment they get the backing of the mighty. Suffice it to say that those twin concepts - that mass murder in the course of prosecuting 'just' or 'unjust' wars (depending on which side the observer was on) have enabled me to rule the world and mold it in my own ugly satanic 'image'.

"The problem, of course, is that 'might' makes 'right' only when one is talking about the 'Almighty" who, by definition, is always "Right'. Meaning, that it is blasphemy of the highest order for humans to presume that they too must always be right when they imagine that they are powerful and wield plenty of 'might', just as it is also damning to misuse power and authority for which one is answerable to the Prime Mover from whom all power and authority derive.

"And just as my forces had done with the Israelites before the advent of the Deliverer, we have also hijacked religion and have used it to 'bless' wanton murder and mayhem and plunder in which nations indulge in the name of 'national security'. There was a time when it was I - of all creatures - who actually decided St. Peter's successor with the help of my cronies in the Vatican.

"We may have suffered some setbacks in that regard since, but you can be certain that we are working hard to reposition ourselves so that we can exploit the Judases among the clergy and get back in the business of electing popes. Success on that front will mean that we (the powers of darkness) will be once again in control over all the three pillars of 'progress' as defined by us - the ability to redefine morality as we please on the basis that might is always right, the ability to declare wars and commit mass murders and banditry in the name of national security, and the ability to canonize our agents and cronies in advance even as they are presiding over those evil and vile activities.

Changing tactics

"And, talking about hijacking religion, it would have represented an unmitigated and quite serious failure on our part if we had not taken advantage of unbridled human greed and bigotry to turn Palestine - the homeland of Joseph, Mary and the Deliverer - into the place it is to day - a place where wanton murder and mayhem are the order of the day, and are done in the name of the Prime Mover. What goes on there epitomizes my Rule which employs the self-righteous to do unto others in the name of the Prime Mover what they definitely wouldn't want done unto themselves! My troops and I have planned everything meticulously - down to the wire as you folks say. We are not in the habit of leaving anything to chance.

"When humans start doing things out of the ordinary because they think they can justify what they do, they had better be right and their reasoning as well. When they end up going against the dictates of reason, they bear the full responsibility for choosing to experiment with what is out of the ordinary. They have themselves to blame when they end up here in the Pit with us. And from the moment they decide to play footsie with their eternal life thinking they will be able to justify their misadventures, our own task is clear - to work with them to ensure that they end up here with us, because we need that company bad.

"Humans are so daft! Until they 'kick the bucket' and 'wake up' to reality in the process, they appoint themselves judges at precisely the time when so much is expected of them. And, in their minds, they consign the real victims of things like 'terrorism' to hell and canonize the real terrorists even as they are marauding, looting and murdering in the name of Civilization.

"I am the devil, and I can affirm that the hunted, 'unsaved' terrorists and insurgents go to heaven, while the blood-thirsty demagogues who like to regard themselves as the 'elect' even as they are on their murderous adventures around the world and others who murder and wreck havoc on the lives of the innocent (whom they always rush to label 'thugs' and 'enemies of peace') in the name of the Prime Mover end up right here in the Pit with none other than me - Satan, the Prince of Darkness! You don't need to waste your time arguing about that. You should just bide your time and see for yourself how things transpire when the time comes for you to cross the Gulf.

"And - if you do not know - the lot falls pretty well on us demons here in the Pit to ensure that our 'human collaborators' get their fair share of the wretched life that is known as 'hell'. And because we really want to be *fair* to everyone here, we work strictly by the book too.

"If while on earth, in your zeal to administer 'justice', you thought it was 'humane' to subject other humans to all sorts of strange things - to things like 'prolonged solitary confinement', 'stress and duress', or 'extreme deprivation of sensory stimuli'; or if you thought that it was perfectly alright to force other humans to stand or assume positions that 'induce physical stress or pain over time', to subject other humans to 'routine and barbaric beatings', to douse humans who are immobilized by handcuffs and leg iron-chains with cold water or to expose them to freezing temperatures, or to make a sport of others by piling them naked and while in hand-cuffs on top of one another and photographing them in that posture; or if you regarded it as something that was just fine to torture and humiliate their family members in captivity and cause them to sodomize each other in full view of other captives, or to urinate on them or have fun poking things in the eyes, or to sprinkle chemical substances on their exposed skin and force them to mug their loved ones for your pleasure, or to force them to ram and crush their heads into concrete walls for fun, or to cause them additional discomfort by applying electric shocks on their person as a way of 'softening them up some more', or to confine fellow humans in dark vaults, or to 'soft them up some more' by keeping them awake with noise and flood lights, or to let guard dogs that are trained to kill loose on hand-cuffed humans, or to pretend to scare the daylights out of humans who are just like yourself by threatening to shoot or to electrocute them while immobilized and helpless, or to keep fellow humans 'hooded' for days, or to deprive captives of sustenance as a way of 'softening them up some more'; or if you thought that you could kill fellow humans who were in restraints with impunity by administering body blows or by just shooting them dead; or if you did not think there was anything wrong with 'water boarding' *your* buddy, or with desecrating a buddy's body after he/she died while in your custody, and other things like that; or if you thought that fellow humans were not your buddies just because of a grudge you might have had against them - in the Pit, we just let the 'demon in you' that prompted you to do those things return to haunt you; and, not just once, but over and over and over until you get sick of it and start wishing that you never saw the light of day.

"And there is real fire - smouldering cinders and blue scotching flames that do not go out - here in hell. And so, when the demons in you - the demons that now help you to 'speak with the tongues of men and of angels' when, without charity, you really are 'as sounding brass, or a tinkling cymbal' with nothing more to it - come back to haunt you here in hell, it is also very real! Surreal, in fact, and very painful! Terribly ashaming, and heart-wrenching in the extreme if only because the miseries endured here in the Pit are unending and go on for ever and ever!

"What happens when a 'lost' soul arrives here in the Pit, is that the tables become verily turned, and that soul starts enduring what it did unto other souls that it would not have liked done unto itself. And, because the pain is spiritual and not simply physical, it always beggars the imagination - yes, even my own devilish and satanic imagination!

"I myself suffer tremendously, of course; but when I see souls in terrible anguish as they pay the debt for their rotten deeds, I sometimes find myself toying with the crazy idea that I wouldn't want to exchange places with them. The problem though is that here the pain and suffering is commensurate with the ability to suffer, which is in turn commensurate with the gifts with which one was endowed at creation.

"You can expect me, Beelzebub, to suffer much more in that sense than any other creature here. When paying the debt of the sins of humans, the Deliverer undoubtedly suffered too. The combined physical and mental pain that He endured must have exceeded anything that we demons and lost human souls know. It is not possible to measure the suffering of the incarnate Word when He was subjected to abuse and humiliation by creatures that could not have come into existence except through Him. Even though lasting only a certain period, because it was pain that was endured by a divinity, it also automatically morphs into pain for eternity; and that is even though the situation was salvaged by the Deliverer's victory over death and His resurrection from the dead! There is no way that the sufferings which the Son of Man, a member of the Godhead, endured as He was mocked and abused, scourged, crowned with thorns, and then crucified by sinful humans can be measured. It is beyond my comprehension and certainly beyond that of humans as well.

"Getting back to what the mind can fathom, I was endowed with more gifts than even Michael the Archangel; and, consequently, more was expected from me than from any other creature that existed up until then. If any demon or lost human soul were exposed to what

I now endure, that demon or soul would get so scotched, it would wither in moments and could conceivably find itself rubbed out and effectively non-existent. But as you might have guessed, the Deliverer, who is also the Word and Judge, will never allow that to happen.

"It isn't Him who 'created' the conditions in the Pit after all - we ourselves did with our dastardly behavior. It may be true that hell is a place - yes, a real 'place' as opposed to a 'state'. Nevertheless, it is our niggardly and vile deeds that metamorphosed into the dungeons and the searing flames that can never be extinguished. It is what happens when mere creatures - which is what we all are - have the audacity to try and take on the Prime Mover.

"As for me, I have to continue being haunted for all eternity by the demon in me that got me to refuse to adore the Creator and subsequently got me to lure the choirs of angels that suddenly became transfigured into the demons they are now when they too refused to bow and acknowledge the Prime Mover's greatness. We have to continue to exist and to suffer to our capacity as we pay the price for our vanity.

"Still, I can't help trying to take comfort from the thought that if I had remained loyal to the Prime Mover, I would be up there - enjoying more than even Michael the Archangel - if you can call that comfort! I feel so much shame that a creature that was as brilliant and smart as myself blew the opportunity to ride high. And you know the saying that the mind is a terrible thing to waste! And may be you can now understand how frustrated with myself and depressed I feel for blowing it - for knowing that someone with my talents is now good for nothing except as a tempter and a Destroyer!

"It is similarly true for you humans. If you boast a bright mind and think you are clever, you'd better make damn sure you do not end up here lamenting over it the way I anguish over my wasted spiritual faculties. You'd better stay clear of Broadway, and you certainly shouldn't bury any talent that you may have been graced with. If you should succeed in staying on the narrow path and in delivering the goods, you can be sure of earning yourself a mansion in heaven. But 'pride comes before the fall', and don't you be too cocky. Take a leaf from me, dammit!

"You wander into Broadway, or become cosy with the ways of the world and, as surely as you exist, you will end up in this damn hell. But do I really care a damn thing for the geeks who end up here with us? I'd say they deserve everything - and more. What do they think they are - special?

"Most of you humans think that you are - until you kick the bucket, and find yourself being accosted by the Avenging Angel as soon as you get to this side of the Gulf. Oh o o o! You all realize eventually that you are not all that special - when the Gates of Hell, blackened and creaking, open and you find yourselves literally swept off your feet and borne away to the dungeon reserved for you by howling demons and the other loathsome inmates of the Pit. Once upon a time we all thought we were special. But we learned that we weren't - too late, after we had done our best to give others a hell they didn't deserve!

Spin...

"Given the legacy of original sin, whenever humans open their mouths, chances are that they will eschew truth in favor of spin. The inclination to sin - and also to spin - is not fiction. It is real, and translates in lies, spin, ingratiating self-justification, and every conceivable sin including murder. That is, after all, what happened when humans cornered the Son of Man and also Deliverer, and tried to neutralize and rub Him out.

"As with all other sins, the act of 'murder' was committed, but the attempt to neutralize Him boomeranged. The attempts of humans to neutralize those they do not have a liking for invariably fail, but the perpetrators always succeed in committing the act of murder and dooming themselves. The act of murder is usually the last act in a series of acts that infringe on natural justice and the commandment to love one another.

"Back to spin - the more humans lie, the more accolades they receive as spokespersons, diplomats, teachers, and even as preachers. The way we have organized everything, it is the criminals and the liars who come out on top in this world. It is I, Beelzebub, after all who still holds sway in this world; and that is how things will stay - at least until the time of the much maligned and misquoted 'Rapture'.

"But humans are so stupid. There simply is no way that humans or pure spirits for that matter, who themselves are supposed to be 'Fools for the Deliverer', can bamboozle and fool the Prime Mover. For a start, the Prime Mover does not require the services of a prosecutor to arraign evil creatures and bring them to justice. He does not even need a security force to round up evil doers and send them to hell. He would not be a Prime Mover. You make a habit of going against the Prime Mover - or against your conscience - and you end up feeling more 'comfortable' here in the Pit with us - if you do not mind the sarcasm - than with the Deliverer in heaven.

"The Prime Mover is not just clever, and He is not simply 'cleverness' either. I am the devil, and you can take it from me that He knows pretty well what He does, and how to do it. If He didn't, you can bet that I wouldn't be languishing in this damn pit. The Prime Mover is Truth...Knowledge. And because He Himself is in-dwelling in human souls, the human conscience will always sound the alarm as soon as humans start to lean towards that which represents betrayal of Truth.

"And so, when you make it your business to spin facts, and to manipulate, spin or misrepresent the truth, that is not simply a betrayal of the Prime Mover, it is tantamount to idolatry. For instead of worshiping at the altar of the Prime Mover and of Truth, those of you who spin choose to descend so low as to pay homage to falsity, and the non-existent god called 'Untruth'. Consequently, all you liars and others who spin facts are *de facto* idolaters. And when you say you worship the Prime Mover, you mean a false prime mover who exists only in your own imagination and phantasy. You ultimately worship your own egos - you think you are omnipotent. And that is even worse than worshiping idols made of stone!

"And when you spin and pretend to be godly at the same time, it stops being idolatry and becomes something else - it becomes a sacrilege! Being as cocky as you all are, you evidently know perfectly well what you are doing. Twisting and manipulating facts needs a crooked or warped mind to try and paint things that are false as truth. It is therefore damning automatically. And can you imagine a damned soul hanging around and trying to act as if the Prime Mover is on his/her side?

Fraudsters

"The fact of the matter is that humans who are 'liars' are my minions! Yeah, minions of the Father of Lies! And, like Ananias of the Acts of the Apostles and his wife Saphira, they are in it for the long haul. Their hypocrisy, far from being just a one time deal, is something that is deeply ingrained in their psyches. And don't you start getting the idea that liars are strangers to things like religion or the supernatural. If that were so, the Deliverer wouldn't have used words like "These people honor me with their lips, but their hearts are far from me" in describing my clients.

"Liars live on lies, and their goals in life have nothing in common with uprightness or the virtues of forbearance, patience, forgiveness and godliness. On the contrary, liars exploit the fact that the victims of their lies are those humans who are as guileless and innocent as 'babes in the woods', and are determined to take advantage of the 'people of God'. The fraudsters know exactly what they are up to, and make a point of honing their skills at their craft so they can rake in their millions, and which they do on the backs of their unsuspecting victims. But even as they do so, they do not once loose sight of the fact that the more they portray themselves as the 'upright' folks, and the more they denigrate any one who sees through the façade and makes a move to expose them, the more they stand to gain from the lies and the schemes they never tire of hatching - and the less their prospects of repenting and returning to Him who is the Way, the Truth and the Life.

"That is the reason betrayers par excellence must keep up the charade even as they betray the Son of Man with a kiss. And this is because I, Satan, have entered into them just as I did the apostle from Jericho about whom it is written: '*Intravit autem Satanas in Iudam qui cognominatur Scarioth unum de duodecim*' ('Then entered Satan into Judas surnamed Iscariot, being of the number of the twelve'). Nor was Judas the only one I entered and possessed.

"The priests and Pharisees were determined to keep their 'religion' if only because it provided them the cover they needed for their lies. The alternative was to tell the truth concerning the Deliverer and shame me, Satan, in the process.

"But, according to Scriptures, as soon as it was day, the elders of the people and the chief priests and the scribes came together, and led him into their council, saying, Art thou the Christ? Tell us. And he said unto them, If I tell you, ye will not believe: And if I also ask you, ye will not answer me, nor let me go. Hereafter shall the Son of Man sit on the right hand of the power of God. Then said they all, Art thou then the Son of God? And he said unto them, Ye say that I am. And they said, What need we any further witness? For we ourselves have heard of his own mouth!

"So you can now understand why there are so many 'Christian' denominations - they are necessary to provide the cover that all those liars need so much.

"And if it should happen that the lying that goes on is of the type that is incompatible with the profession of one of the 'mainstream' religions that has prescribed rituals and/or a creed, that never stops the liars from seeking to portray themselves as 'upright' citizens who are deserving of the utmost trust all the same - if necessary, with a helping hand from me of course. That usually makes it hard for even the most discerning individuals to tell that he/she is dealing with fraudsters until it is too late - until well after the fraudsters had gotten away with pulling another fast one on him/her.

"But do you recall the story of the man who was on a trip from Jerusalem to Jericho, and was attacked by bandits who stripped him of his clothes, beat him up, and left him half dead beside the road?

Remember the priest who saw the man lying there, and who crossed to the other side of the road so he could pass him by? Or the Levite who walked over, looked at the man lying there, but also passed by on the other side?

"You won't, of course, remember the despised Samaritan who saw the man, felt compassion for him, and went over and soothed his wounds with olive oil and wine and bandaged them; and who then put the man on his own donkey, and took him to an inn, where he took care of him at his own expense. This is because, like the reverend and the Levite (those selfish braggarts who lived in an ivory tower), you are the sort of hypocrite I am talking about!

"The lying also provides support for things like the so-called 'military industrial complex' which assures that the killing of humans by humans continues unabated, and the 'health insurance industry' that must take advantage of the fact that humans die when they are unable to obtain the treatment and medication they need to rake in billions for their masters.

"The moral (you are supposed to take away but won't) is that, excepting for the Deliverer and his blessed mother, Mary, who was conceived without sin, all humans are traitors...betrayers, and Judases; and all those who are in the habit of singling out others and calling them 'traitors', 'terrorists', 'unsaved', or 'un-Christian-like' or even 'un-Catholic-like' betray themselves with their own shallow, materialistic self-interests and rabid hypocrisy! That includes even Simon Peter who was determined to distance himself from Judas whom I, Beelzebub, had already entered and possessed.

"It is the sacred writer who wrote (and I am not making this up): 'And the Lord said, Simon, Simon, behold, Satan hath desired to have you, that he may sift you as wheat: But I have prayed for thee, that thy faith fail not: and when thou art converted, strengthen thy brethren.'

"But, typical of sinful and sinning humans, Peter retorted: 'Lord, I am ready to go with thee, both into prison, and to death!' But the Deliverer's reply was: 'I tell thee, Peter, the cock shall not crow this day, before that thou shalt thrice deny that thou knowest me...For

I say unto you, that this that is written must yet be accomplished in me. And he was reckoned among the transgressors.' Then took they him, and led him, and brought him into the high priest's house. And Peter followed afar off. And when they had kindled a fire in the midst of the hall, and were set down together, Peter sat down among them. But a certain maid beheld him as he sat by the fire, and earnestly looked upon him, and said, This man was also with him. And he denied him, saying, Woman, I know him not. And after a little while another saw him, and said, Thou art also of them. And Peter said, Man, I am not. And within about the space of one hour after another confidently affirmed, saying, Of a truth this fellow also was with him: for he speaks with the Galilean drawl. And Peter said, Man, I know not what thou sayest. And immediately, while he yet spake, the cock crew. And the Lord turned, and looked upon Peter. And Peter remembered the word of the Lord, how he had said unto him, Before the cock crow, thou shalt deny me thrice. And Peter went out, and wept bitterly.' Yes!"

Avenging Angel

"People who spend their lives hatching wicked plots and spinning facts to further their pursuit of material things, and then turn around and try to make it look as if they are all upright and dandy make things worse for themselves. And, when humans who claim to be out to stop liars are themselves caught red-handed 'spinning' and distorting reality in the process, that is just terrible! And don't you suggest that you are out to stop terrorists when you yourself act like one - when you terrorize and kill innocent people who just want to be left in peace so they can get on with their lives.

"Don't you claim that you are treating fellow humans humanely when it is in fact torture that you are administering. Tut! Tut! Tut! The Avenging Angel doesn't take kindly to that particular kind of lie, because when you torture 'another human', it is in fact the Son of Man whom you torture. And, whether you call it torture or something else, it is a very terrible thing to do. You do not want to do that at all, because you do not want to suffer the fate of those who are caught doing it. The Avenging Angel simply abandons you to a pack of snarling, totally crazed and perverse demons - the same demons that were in you and that caused you to abuse, humiliate, and torture your fellow humans and to have the audacity to call it humane treatment.

"As you kick the bucket, the demons of course find themselves compelled to leave just as passengers on a boat that is alight scramble to abandon it for safety. After causing you to give others a hell, they are usually delighted to turn around, after the sentence is passed and I have given them a 'pat on the back' for a good job very well done, to give you a taste of whatever you meted out to other humans and to Him who accepted to take full responsibility for the sins of men. And what they do to you for all of eternity is just horrible...unspeakable!

"And again, don't be caught pretending to be an 'honest broker' in a conflict when the fact of the matter is that you are just posturing and actually conspiring with one of the parties to undermine a just resolution of the conflict.

"Those humans who are in the business of 'spinning' facts and misrepresenting reality are all in the wrong business. They are conning themselves at the same time as they are making the case against themselves. There is no better evidence for the iniquity of liars than the rationalizations in which they indulge in an effort to try and paint lies as facts or truths, and cloak the malice aforethought within. Attempts by lying earthlings to depict themselves as innocent and blameless only go to validate their status as shameless liars and weirdoes, and to confirm those earthlings as my minions! Talk about a win-win situation for the Father of Lies! The spin they put on facts represents the irrefutable evidence that will be ranged against them on Judgement Day - evidence that they knowingly and deliberately violated their trust, and effectively sold their birthright for what did not even amount to a bowl of pottage!

"And, look - the proof of the pudding, as you earthlings say, is in the eating! And you also must know who said: "Wherefore by their fruits ye shall know them"! However much one spins the facts, and indulges in grandstanding, the fact remains that where you used to have 'original virtue', now you have 'original sin'! And so, all the ostentatious performance aimed at impressing folks notwithstanding, it is completely hypocritical for folks who commit sin not once but seventy times seven times a day at least to try and pretend that they are good, let alone better than others! And if a human is not in the habit of practicing mortification like Jerome or more recently John Paul did, just take it as a joke when you see all those left leaning and right leaning spinmeisters take to the stage and try and bluff you.

"Blinded by egotism, wicked humans easily forget that they are mortal. Then, locked in their pursuit of the material and the temporal, in a desperate effort to clinch each for himself or herself the most lucrative deals, they throw away all caution to the wind as they vie with one another in manufacturing lies and spinning falsehoods, in complete disregard of the fact that they are temples of the Prime Mover, and in disregard of His injunction to them that they love one another!

"As for the 'media types' who are supposed to be in the business of disseminating information, they damn themselves too by withholding critical information or reporting half facts to promote the dubious agendas and partisan interests; and their fate becomes sealed when they start passing themselves off as the 'elect' and referring to their opponents as 'devils'.

"Humans have of course been putting a spin on facts ever since Adam and Eve sinned and tried to lay the blame for their indiscretion on me. I mean - I am the tempter, and I was just doing my job! Free creatures, they could have said 'No'!

"Instead of reporting the facts accurately and objectively, humans have 'spun' facts and misrepresented reality ever since Cain tried to cover up a ghastly murder by telling a tall tale about how his brother - the first murder victim ever - had walked into a thicket and been spirited away. Actually, spinning facts stopped being an 'art' and became a 'science' long ago; and today it is the preserve of professionals - politicians, generals, newspaper columnists and political pundits, preachers, historians, and others. In fact some 'think tanks' are tasked with doing nothing but put a spin on things. It is all so very fascinating.

"Of course crooked folks involved in such chicanery don't have to be caught by any body for them to face retribution. Let me warn you - the Avenging Angel does need the International Red Cross or Human Rights Watch, either of which is capable of being manipulated. He certainly does not need the United Nations which serves the interests of its founders (it is not for nothing that they retained for themselves the power to veto any of that body's resolutions).

"You have to remember how those organizations came into being. It is not as if they were ordained by the Prime Mover. On the contrary, they were started at my explicit instigation. In the case of the United Nations, I persuaded the 'victors' in the wake of the second world war to set it up and get it going in order to ensure that they didn't get in trouble for 'war crimes' like for example 'carpet bombing' of cities and using weapons of mass destruction when they were prosecuting the war. The second and only other reason was to set the stage for the super power fraternity to ride rough shod over other nations of the world in their scramble for control over oil and other scarce resources regarded as vital to their 'national security'. And that is also why it was important for these folks to retain the power to veto any resolutions of that organization's so-called Security Council.

"On the face of it, the United Nations is supposed to safeguard the rights of the citizens of the world from despots - it supposed to ensure that those who commit crimes human rights are brought to justice. But in practice, its *raison de tre* is to serve the interests of members of the veto wielding club, and to legitimize anything they dream up and do without regard to natural justice. That is one reason the UN grants members of the veto wielding club who commit such crimes immunity from prosecution. It is also why that body won't take effective steps to prevent atrocities in some parts of the world that are not regarded by the 'super powers' as being of 'strategic' importance to them (like Rwanda) even though it commands the necessary resources to do so - and every UN 'diplomat' knows it.

"I can guarantee you that the moment the UN (actually 'DN' for 'Divided Nations' would have been a more appropriate name) starts to look like it is getting transformed into an organization that promotes the common weal as opposed to the interests of the 'big five' and their allies, it will have to go - it will have to give way to something that is more attuned to my evil plan. Well, what did you think - that the UN was some charitable organization?

"If you do not know, in terms of serving my cause and facilitating the dispensation by me of material goods and worldly power to my minions, the age of the UN (and its predecessor the League of Nations) has been rivalled only by that epoch in history when the papacy was at my beck and call - that time when the popes literally appointed and deposed emperors and kings at will. So, even though I met with singular failure when I attempted to get the Son of Man and Deliverer Himself to change sides and work for my evil plan in return for becoming Lord of the Earth, I am quite successful in persuading His representatives here on earth and leaders of the so-called advanced nations, and particularly leaders of nations that are supposedly Christian, to work for my cause.

"As many a 'diplomat' will tell you, what goes on inside and outside the walls of the UN amounts to a farce engineered by members of the veto wielding club. It is much worse than what goes on in Hollywood, because people really die as a result of what goes at the UN. What do you think happens to children and the infirm when the UN, at the instigation of a veto wielding power, imposes a trade embargo on a country? In this age of globalization, you tell me what happens to jobs and the living standards when a country suddenly cannot obtain the things its citizens need to live well? But that is exactly what I have in mind when I talk of my evil cause - a cause that brings untold suffering and misery to innocent humans. And I know that when the innocent suffer, it is the Deliverer and Son of Man who suffers. Perhaps you now understand why mine is an evil cause!

"The only other thing that matters is that I use the place to whisk aspiring world leaders up the 'mountain top' from where I display the worldly things that can be theirs - if they only worship! Just as it is the Son of Man who suffers when the UN acts, it is I who is worshiped and glorified when representatives of nations succumb to arm twisting and accept bribes peddled as 'foreign aid' by the super powers instead of casting their votes according to their conscience.

"The 'United Nations' and the idea of a veto wielding club to guide its activities is just the perfect set up for now. It legitimizes the unconscionable and otherwise unlawful actions of the big five; and they in turn, with the automatic participation of heads of state from around the world, provide the cover I need to implement my evil plan. The Vatican's membership in this 'August Body' naturally lends it legitimacy in the eyes of peace loving peoples. But, predictably, the Avenging Angel sees through all that.

"Of course, as humans wage wars each other over the 'crumbs' I threw at them, we here in the Pit can never stop to wonder at their stupidity. From age to age, humans have waged wars and slaughtered each other over nothing. Yes, nothing! All humans die regardless of whether they live to celebrate victories of wars successfully fought or are casualties of wars unsuccessfully fought and lost. If you are fighting over something, you should first check if you will be able to hold on to it if you in victory. Now, you loose whatever you have fought over if it is snatched away from you afterward - and that is exactly what I do when you die.

"I linger over folks just long enough to ensure that they have breathed their last and are safely on the other side of the Gulf, and I then quickly snatch back my goods so the recycling process can continue. And you just show me one castle that belongs to Julius Caesar! If he had given everything he had to the poor, he would have stashed something away for his afterlife - at least. As it is, he wanted to hang on to everything he had accumulated, including the loot he and his armies had brought back home from North Africa, Gaul and other places, and lost out - the stupid fellow! This is the same fate that meets losers and victors in war equally, and that awaits the generals and military commanders who stake everything in fighting and winning modern wars as well as those who become vanquished in battle and don't get the opportunity to celebrate the culmination of wars with victory parades.

"Given the short-lived nature of the 'victories', wars are not worthwhile, except of course when they are seen from my perspective - as a means of promoting my evil plan and undermining the Divine Plan in the process. Those who survive to tell any tales - and who happen to belong to the 'victorious' side - usually eulogize their fallen war dead as heroes who gave their lives in defense of 'freedom'.

"The problem is that all conquerors are self-declared conquerors; and victory is a function of brutal force that does not recognize common sense. For if brutal force recognized common sense, warring humans without exception would opt for negotiations and rush to settle their scores at a table instead of heading to the battlefield. Brutal force does not recognize right or wrong either. Hence the cycle of violence, which is driven, not by the noble idea of freedom (which has nothing in common with brutal force), but by greed and ambition.

"But just look at the investment nations make in armaments as they prepare to confront non-existent threats or threats that only exist in the figment of the imagination of the leadership. Instead of working for the *bonum commune* by employing the nation's to construct roads, feed the hungry, clothe the naked, and provide healthcare for the sick and old, at my instigation they start planning to wage wars 'in defense of freedom', and even persuade themselves along the way that fighting wars is something that is good for the economy! No! The only beneficiaries are the military industrial complexes that, as you may have already guessed, are my invention!

"Freedom, a nebulous idea that has been foreign to human experience since I got the first man and the first woman to jump ship and start hankering for a taste of the forbidden fruit, becomes even more nebulous when it is linked to the equally nebulous notion of democracy. With the fall of Adam and Eve from grace, humans became my slaves and lost their freedom. And if you think that 'democracy' works, just reflect on the fact that on the eve of the Twenty-first Century, Man, who has been to the moon, has not yet been able to design ballots that do not pose a mystery to voters either because 'the chards might end up hanging' or because of some other mysterious problems.

"Any way…back to the Avenging Angel. He does not need the help of whistle blowers or witnesses. He definitely does not need photographic evidence of malfeasance to bring ungodly humans to account in the court of divine justice.

"Talking about photographic evidence, you would think, that with the advent of webcams, and with surveillance cameras installed on street corners and highways and rooftops, in dressing rooms, rest rooms, locker rooms, malls, police patrol vehicles, and in every conceivable place where they photograph people, and with no hiding place from Big Brother who now watches everyone all the time, the time had come for malfeasance by anyone, including crooked members of law enforcement, who was caught on camera breaking the law would be prosecuted on the basis of the evidence; but you would be seriously mistaken for thinking that things worked that way!

"Thanks to the tenacity of my troops, earthlings, particularly those in commanding positions of power, have succeeded in making sure that the photographic evidence is valid only when those they want to see convicted are caught on camera. Because the end is supposed to justify the means when it comes to activities of law enforcement, when one of their own is caught on camera infringing law, typically you will hear urgent calls by those who ought to know better pleading with the public not to jump to premature conclusions. Yep! And - surprise, surprise - it is the cameras and webcams that are usually caught lying in such instances! This is one reason that photographic evidence (which has itself been corrupted and discredited in the extreme) is frowned upon by the Avenging Angel.

"The way I myself landed in this goddamned pit should help you goddamn humans understand that you can never get away with any misdeed, and that spin, eloquence, and any attempt to conceal evidence of misdeeds only makes matters worse. And as humans wage wars and slaughter each other over the crumbs I throw at them, we here in the Pit cannot help but wonder at their stupidity.

"It certainly does not help to try and conduct misdeeds in secret. Nothing can be hidden from the Avenging Angel. The acts themselves - and the intentions of humans who have no qualms about 'doing unto others what they definitely would not want done unto themselves or their dear ones' - constitute the evidence against the perpetrators and all those who conspire, abate, and support the misdeeds.

"And regardless of what you misguided humans may think, the end simply never justifies the means. That is a fallacious argument that does not wash with the Avenging Angel. And while the culprits can run, they cannot hide. The Avenging Angel catches you committing a crime under the guise of trying to stop some other evil doer in his/her tracks, and you've had it. And don't you try to hoodwink him.

"It is sometimes better to be caught with your pants down and you suffer the shame. That is often the only way redeeming grace can get through to the hardened evil doer. We naturally do everything in our power to ensure that such an eventuality does not come to pass. There are very many dungeons down here that are specifically reserved for people who are so fool hardy as to harm their 'neighbors' (among whom you must now count the Son of Man and Deliverer). These dungeons need occupants - they have to be filled - and we are going to make damn sure they do get filled! And we get so much pleasure when the proud and powerful get snared and end up in these dungeons after passing their days in stately mansions and chateaus. Why should we be the only ones who fall from the heights to the bottom of hell!

"We know that the only thing that works with the Avenging Angel is the evil doer's sorrow - genuine sorrow coupled with a readiness to do penance and to make amends for the injustices committed. But sorrow that is really genuine may sometimes be elusive, and feasible only in theory. It is sometimes patently impossible in practice for offenders to satisfy the Avenging Angel on that score.

"It is not infrequent that humans who have been steeped in crooked ways try to make a U-Turn to get back onto the narrow path and fail. This is especially so when the offenders are obsessed with power and are hooked on material things at the same time. It is a fatal combination indeed. And the indictment which the Avenging Angel issues - sometimes well in advance of the unrepentant sinners kicking the bucket - usually just reads: 'It were better if you had not been born'! But, without knowing that they are a 'done deal', murderers and other evil doers just continue on their killing sprees and everything else they do under the mistaken notion that their accumulated booty or 'history' (as they sometimes put it) will absolve them.

"Yeah! What can he say when the liars, killers and other evil doers, blinded by hate for fellow men and by greed for things of the world, are prepared to damn themselves in that fashion! Of course the final say always remains with the Deliverer and Judge.

"For my part, I make it a point to assign the sharpest demons to souls that look like they are destined for the Pit. That should say something about how badly we want their company. It would be really disappointing to spend so much time and energy grooming evil-doers of that calibre only to loose them to Michael the Archangel at the last moment!

"Any way - humans who are in the business of rationalizing and justifying their misdeeds should know before they even start that theirs is a lost cause; that, in attempting to justify their dubious activities, they damn themselves in the process; and that the Judge - the Deliverer and Word through whom all created beings came into being and also the Deliverer who now sits at the right hand of the Father - merely confirms the sentence that humans pass on themselves.

"You have heard it said that the Prime Mover causes good to ensue from evil. Well, now you have it on authority that the vilest and baddest creatures can play a role that is almost indispensable for the fulfillment of the divine plan. After the Avenging Angel has done his bit, it falls to me and the host of demons under my command to actually *avenge* the evil deeds of the bad characters who are escorted here when their time on Planet Earth is up and they walk in here though those gates over there.

"We fill a role that no one else but us here in the Pit have the qualification to fill - and it is a very critical function at that. It is our job to ensure that justice is done - and seen to be done! And the Avenging Angel actually appreciates our services. He trusts us too! He otherwise wouldn't just escort 'lost souls' through the Gates of Hell and, after delivering them to us, take off assured that these 'monsters' will finally get a taste of the 'justice' they themselves loved to administer to other members of the human family before they crossed the Gulf.

"We are not completely there yet, but we *are* getting there gradually - as time goes by and Armageddon draws nigh. Our goal is to see the gullible masses manipulated and exploited by a few. We've already made a good start by getting megalomaniacs (rulers of the earth), both big-time and small-time, effectively casting themselves as 'benevolent dictators', 'liberators', 'redeemers', and 'saviors' of the very people they are subjugating, exploiting, colonizing, enslaving, humiliating, abusing and, in some cases, even terrorizing

"The progress made by our cronies on this front is quite solid, and can be gauged from the fact that it is the victims of that arrogant behavior who are invariably portrayed as the 'hoodlums', 'agitators', 'insurgents', and even 'terrorists', and frequently with the blessing and even connivance of the successors to the apostles. And we wouldn't have come this far if it had not been for the spin which we promote assiduously in our dealings with the 'benevolent dictators', and the 'saviors of the world'.

"Yes, the world's demagogues, both big time and small time, love spin. They like to imagine that they are 'liberators' - even as they are issuing commands to the effect that indigenous 'liberation' movements fighting occupations and colonialism have to be stamped out, and presiding over other 'operations' that would automatically qualify as wanton murder and mayhem if their countries were the ones at the receiving end. Interestingly, there is never a dearth of religious zealots who not only idolize these demagogues, but believe that it would be a dereliction of duty on their part if they did not stand solidly behind the dictators and others who prey on the minds of the gullible and exploit them.

Devil's clientele...

"Both demagogues and religious zealots need the spin, the former to gain legitimacy for their murderous activities, and the latter to make a case for their entitlement to the tithes. Is it any wonder then that demagogues (who are usually very regular and very public church goers) and religious zealots (who also tend to be politically quite savvy and seem to know well in advance which way the winds are likely to blow) pretend to operate in separate spheres when they in fact are usually staunch allies? This business of spinning brings together very strange bedfellows.

"But if you were thinking that my clientele consisted only of demagogues and religious zealots, think again. These chaps are by no means the only ones who sing to my tune. We should, perhaps, start with those who do not sing to my tune; and I can tell you that they are a very scant few. In all honesty - and I'm not all dishonest, you know - it is very hard to find someone who does not play by my rules. I mean - how many Francises of Assisi or Theresas of Avila or Mother Theresas are there?

"I can tell you that if the Deliverer were to return tomorrow, all these church-going folks, and others who are so self-righteous they would quicker liquidate suspected wrong doers or 'terrorists' than let them have their day in court lest they be proven innocent, would join the crowds in chanting 'Away with Him! Crucify Him! If you let Him go, you cannot be a friend of Caesar!'

"You've got to remember that when humans do something to the least amongst them, they do it to Him. And when they clamor for anyone's blood, guess whose blood it is they actually clamor for! It is the blood of the Son of Man and Second Adam who died for the sins of the world.

"Now, don't *you* misrepresent my power and influence! Almost everyone you see can use the mercies of the Omnipotent, and you were told in no uncertain terms that you have to be prepared to forgive a brother or sister human not seven but seventy times seven times a day. You can be certain that the throngs of people who fill 'Broadway', being repeat sinners, are all under my vassalage.

Rationalize and fool Who?

"Now, it is bad enough when humans commit evil deeds. And it is the height of stupidity when they try to rationalize and justify their misdeeds. Who do they think they are fooling! When they do that, all they are really doing is indict themselves.

"When one tries to rationalize and justify an adventure that leaves a lot to be desired from the moral angle, one just sets oneself up for judgement. In trying to justify evil actions, humans trip themselves up, and they end up 'hanging themselves' - as the saying (which dates back to the act of the Deliverer's betrayer) goes.

"If Judas Iscariot had not devoted any time to efforts to justify (in his own mind and to members of the Sanhedrin) his betrayal of the Deliverer, he probably wouldn't have ended up with his insides spilled out all over the place in that thicket. He would still have felt pangs of guilt when his conscience finally jolted him to his senses, but perhaps not to an extent that would drive a fellow of his standing to do such a thing. In other words, he probably wouldn't have been suicidal to that extent.

"And many folks forget that Judas Iscariot was in fact luckier than most other 'betrayers' in that he woke up to the fact that he had committed a very vile deed before and not after he had crossed the gulf that separates the living from the dead. I naturally won't say if Judas Iscariot has been sighted any where here in the Pit or not! But I will say that humans who wake up to the fact that they are unworthy of standing in the presence of the Prime Mover after they 'kick the bucket' get very little in the way of an opportunity to repent of their sins let alone the opportunity to add to the voices in heaven that 'cry out for my blood' by renouncing my works (which include evils that are too terrible to describe)

"Now - speaking hypothetically - if Judas Iscariot repented of his sin, it probably had a lot to do with the bearing of the Deliverer - and specifically His attitude to and completely 'forgiving' treatment of his 'purse bearer' - from the time He rode into Jerusalem in triumph on the back of a donkey (as he had done once upon a time when, as an infant in the arms of His Pure and beloved mother, he traveled all the way to Africa to escape the murderous Herod Agrippa) to the moment he breathed His last on Mt. Calvary.

"At no time did the Deliverer do anything that made Judas Iscariot even remotely feel like an outcast. And you can expect that Judas Iscariot (whose act of betrayal symbolized mankind's betrayal of their Maker) was very much on His mind as he beseeched His Father saying 'they know not what they are doing' in the Garden of Gethsemane and droplets of His divine blood streamed down the sides of His temples.

"If the Deliverer had been an ordinary mortal who was born in original sin and was therefore inclined to do my bidding, He would have screamed that the 'traitor' and 'ultra-terrorist' should be destroyed - as if that would help! That is exactly what many self-styled "Christians" do when they get rubbed the wrong way. The Deliverer never did that because he would then have been compelled to denounce all humans. Such a denunciation would have frustrated His redemptive mission, leaving Adam and Eve, and others whom I was holding in bondage in hell at my mercy.

"Which is the same as saying that humans who go after their 'enemies' (regardless of the labels they give those fellow humans they bitterly dislike) kid themselves when they also imagine that they have accepted the invitation to be 'other Christs' and to participate with the Deliverer in His work of redemption (as all Christ's followers must needs do) - or that they are 'saved'. Humans are free to couch the killings and the 'destruction' using any words and phrases they want.

So long as what they do is something they would not want done unto themselves, their work is indistinguishable from my work. And, when they say they renounce me and my wiles, it is just that - empty words that are spoken to cloak our relationship.

"Humans ought to know that the Avenging Angel 'wields a sword' only metaphorically. That he actually gets you to do his 'dirty' work for him. If you want evidence that evil deeds go against your nature and effectively cause you to turn against yourself, you now have it.

"And there is only one way out - you get on your knees and beg the Prime Mover for His mercies and go away resolved to sin no more. But the process becomes complete only after you also agree to make amends, and begin to identify yourself with the crucified Deliverer whose obedience to the Father saw Him accept a completely undeserved death on the cross and (I might add) also with the *Mater Dolorosa*, the Deliverer's grieving mother, who set such a fine example for her fellow humans.

"Then there is the fact that those who live by the sword - or kill - die by the sword. Those who lead profligate lives also become scared to death as they see the 'End of the Road' sign approaching.

"Humans are made in the Image and have a conscience on the one hand, and they are endowed with the marvellous gifts of intelligence and free will on the other. But that constitutes a fateful combination that also damns perpetrators of evil deeds - unless the individuals in question decide to own up, confess their sins, beg the Prime Mover for His divine mercies, and do penance for their sins in advance of their rendezvous with the Judge.

"The conscious actions of creatures that are endowed with reason and free will, because they either are in line with their consciences (which is just another word for the Holy One who is in-dwelling within them) or are not, invariably attract one of two things: a suitable reward or a suitable punishment. But the choice remains that of the human.

"It may be true that, unlike us pure spirits who had only a moment after we came into existence to pledge our loyalty to the

Prime Mover or opt to go our own ways, humans are afforded a whole lifetime during which to prepare for and pass the Church Triumphant Entrance Test. The fact remains that every second, minute, hour or day that is available ends up either being employed for that purpose or wasted on irrelevant matters that by their nature militate against a life of holiness.

"And nothing hinders growth in holiness more than the pursuit of worldly ambitions at the expense of other humans who, because the Prime Mover is in-dwelling in them, are automatically creatures that are very precious.

"While the preoccupation with things of the world and the blind pursuit of temporal happiness are incompatible with the pursuit of eternal life, there is nothing that could be more damning to humans during the phase of existence when they are on 'trial' than acts that are designed to injure, let alone cut short the life of a member of the human family. And the more daring such acts are, of course the more inexcusable and the more damning.

"Now, it is criminal for humans to waste any second of their lives on frivolities, for the simple reason that a very high price has been paid by the Deliverer to facilitate that growth in holiness. The magnitude of that price can be gauged from the fact that the Deliverer is none other than the Word through whom humans - and all other created beings - came into existence. Moreover, being a member of the Godhead, He suffered indescribable humiliation in the process - humiliation no creature however brilliant will ever be able to grasp or fathom.

"Being the 'Second Adam', He suffers with all humans who suffer, and He is crucified afresh whenever any human is terrorized, maimed or harmed in any way. And His sacred heart bleeds and feels compassion with all who are in their agony of death. And if these things are so obvious to me, the Evil One, it goes without saying that they must also be pretty obvious to humans in whom the Prime Mover is in-dwelling. And that makes all sins committed by humans are totally inexcusable.

Doom thyself...

"You've got to understand that those of us who languish in hell got here because we thought we could laugh off our obligation to live as befitted our status as creatures that were made in the Image by using our faculty of reason to try and justify our crooked ways. But the Prime Mover had cleverly set it all up in such a way that the ill-willed would automatically damn themselves in the process of trying to justify the unjustifiable. It applied in our case, and it also applies in the case of ill-willed humans as well. It applies to heresies, schisms - everything.

"There is, therefore, no doubt whatsoever that humans, inclined to sin, doom themselves when they attempt to justify things they do to others which they definitely would not want happen to either themselves or their loved ones. Humans doom themselves when they cross the line and abandon reality, and then start living in an imaginary world of phantasy in hopes that they won't be answerable to anyone.

"Realizing that they have lost their innocence and are denuded of cardinal and other virtues, and are no longer able to appreciate the innocent joys of life and other blessings they received at creation, they find themselves trying to justify sinful activities that clearly infringe on divine law and natural justice, and 'pleasures' that are far from innocent. Indeed all humans who choose self-indulgence damn themselves in the process because self-will and self-indulgence (which are one and the same thing) imply an explicit acknowledgment that they are doing something that is proscribed.

"What makes the situation of hedonists, killers and other evil doers infinitely worse is the knowledge that the liberties they are taking are expressly forbidden, have no lasting benefit, and have dire consequences for the attainment of eternal life. Their fate becomes sealed when, despite that knowledge, they proceed to infringe the Prime Mover's commandments.

"What is more, it is the realization that something is forbidden coupled with the firm knowledge that one should be using his/her time in a more constructive way that makes impious pursuits exciting. The satisfaction is derived from the knowledge that the fruit from the 'tree of life' is forbidden - something that would have the opposite the effect in humans who are honest and unselfish.

"It is, after all, the desire of scheming, wily and evil-intentioned humans to inflict injury and suffering, both moral and physical, on their foes, and the certainty that they are denying their victims rights to which they are entitled to as human beings, and the knowledge that they are dealing their 'foes' unjustly (and betraying the trust vested in them in that fashion), that gives them the kick. But, by the same token, it is also what thoroughly damns those who are bent on mischief in that fashion. And consequently killers, hedonists and other humans who are bent on sin can never plead ignorance for that reason.

"And sure enough, following each and every spiteful act, humans are plagued by a sense of guilt, something that the wicked naturally endeavor to suppress so that they can go on sinning merrily thereafter if they should find opportunities to do so. But, unfortunately for humans, even though the legacy of evil actions continues well after the evil doers 'kick the bucket', the opportunity to commit vile acts afresh summarily ends at that point.

When all humans become equal again...

"In the eyes of humans, life comes to a close at death. In the eyes of the Avenging Angel, humans who are more equal than others become completely equal again when they 'kick the bucket' out of their way and head off to their judgement. Humans who thought that their lives were worth more than the lives of others get the jolt of their lifetime as they breathe their last, and find that there was nothing special about them.

"In the case of conflicts between nations, in the eyes of the world, the number of casualties suffered by the parties to the conflict are supposed to be indicative of the extent to which a nation is 'blessed' or 'cursed' along with its 'victorious' or 'defeated' combatants. The reality is completely different

"In the case of a nation that mounts an unprovoked assault on another nation for example, instead of being a blessing, all the casualties suffered by the nation under attack as well as the aggressor nation's own casualties become a curse for that nation. The situation is even more damning for the aggressor when the losses of the 'enemy' are heavy, and the number of their own casualties is minuscule.

"Should it happen that the reason for the aggressor nation suffering only light or even no casualties in an unjustified conflict is because the aggressor nation invested a lot of time and resources in planning the offensive, or took specific steps to weaken the target of its aggression prior to the assault, all those things become very damning indeed. This is because every thing relating to the aggression becomes premeditated, and not something that is done on impulse. And - guess what - it also puts the responsibility for any casualties sustained by the 'enemy' and by the attackers own forces and their allies squarely on the shoulders of those who mastermind the aggression and prosecute the unjust war.

"Then, because there is no such a thing as liability that is joint and several on the other side of the gulf which separates the living from the dead, that responsibility ends up on the individual shoulders of the masterminds and planners of the conflict, their supporters and collaborators, and the aggressor nation's individual fighters and their commanders. This is in accordance with the Prime Mover's injunction to humans to the effect that they shall regard human life as sacred, and the rights of humans to freedom and liberty as inviolable. Geopolitics and all that crap might be good for the spleen for humans on this side of the gulf that separates the living from the dead. But, on the other side, it only serves to nail down those guilty of taking away the lives of others and of breaking the Prime Mover's other commandments.

"Furthermore, any casualties suffered by the aggressor nation itself and its allies in the course of prosecuting the unjust war will also constitute damning evidence - evidence of greed in seeking to annex territory regardless of the cost in human lives, and things like that. It is evidence that hangs over the heads of those who prosecute all unjust wars and does not go away. And it is not affected by the way history gets written or by the misleading impressions that memoirs of participants in the conflict seek to portray.

"There are situations when the fighters of an aggressor nation who fall in battle become the equivalent of bandits who could not make it out of the bank vault. Those who escape with their lives in such situations become the equivalent of bandits who succeeded in getting away with or without any loot. It is as simple as that.

"In situations of that sort, success itself becomes damning, and it is only genuine and sincere repentance coupled with restitution to the victims of the aggression that can bring back those involved in the aggression into the fold. And since enjoyment of the fruits of aggression is equally damning, it becomes incumbent on the aggressor nation to forego any enjoyment of the ill-gotten fruits of the aggression, and to include them in the restitution it is obligated by Natural Justice to pay to the victims of the aggression.

"Giving any of the 'loot' to charity would be entirely unacceptable, since wealth acquired in these circumstances comprises stolen property that a repentant bandit would be expected to return to its rightful owner. Any such wealth is akin to 'blood money', 'bootleg' acquired through piracy on the high seas, or goods obtained by highway robbers in a heist.

"The fact that the aggressor nation is capable of sustaining casualties at all in those situations will additionally serve to debunk any myths about invincibility and rebuff any suggestion that the self-appointed 'saviors of the world' or whatever label the aggressor nation might choose to employ to depict itself, regardless of whether they specifically claimed to be acting on behalf of the Prime Mover or not, were operating under His protection and accordingly enjoyed immunity from consequences that generally flow from adventures of that nature.

"Frequently, casualties sustained by aggressor nations in such conflicts also unmask the true reasons behind the aggression, as questions are raised about the real rationale for undertaking misguided military adventures. In the case of megalomaniacs who are bent on pursuing their cockeyed schemes, the number of casualties sustained over time during an offensive will invariably raise questions regarding the wisdom of embarking on the 'foreign adventure' and the underlying folly becomes unmasked as public inquiries begin revealing grandiose schemes that are frequently quite bizarre and the megalomaniacs suddenly find themselves on the carpet for 'lying to the nation' and other irresponsible actions.

"In the completely hypothetical case of a super power that was, say, prosecuting a totally unjustified and consequently also immoral war against a nation that (let us say) was falsely accused of lending support to 'terrorists', when they get to the other side of the 'gulf' which separates the living from the dead, the fallen fighters of the aggressor nation could find themselves wishing that they had come with more of their dear comrades-in-arms. For, upon their arrival there, all the myths about 'super power' status and things like that evaporate as reality descends on them.

"The chances are that they will find themselves confined to a kind of 'Guantanamo' or 'Limbo' (or just call it 'Purgatory' if you like) while they await the arrival of their 'surviving' comrades - if they themselves did not really know what they were doing. This is also because someone must answer for their own premature arrival in the afterlife as well as for the premature influx into heaven of the victims of their aggression. If they knew what they were doing (as the ring leaders almost certainly would), the Avenging Angel will almost certainly have 'appropriate' instructions as to their 'disposal'."

Now, interesting as all this was, Mjomba wasn't feeling quite comfortable filling the role of a secretary to author of the ideas he was setting down on paper. Mjomba, while acknowledging that all humans became equal again once on the other side of the gulf that separated the living from the dead, personally preferred to leave it at that. He was of the view that it was a little like playing God to get into any details at that point regarding hypothetical super powers going awry, and mythological Guantanamos where individuals would be liable to be "detained' while awaiting the disposition of their cases by the Judge.

The evil ghost must have guest what Mjomba's next move was going to be; which, namely, was to drop the pen and stop playing along. And he did not wait to act. Mjomba had up until that moment been committing he ideas he had been receiving from the evil one to paper involuntarily. But now, as a sudden, quite vigorous and entirely uncontrollable shudder shook his whole person, it terrified him to think that he was in much deeper trouble that he had thought.

The "shudder" lasted only a heart-beat. But while it lasted, Mjomba, who felt helpless throughout the ordeal, had no misgivings regarding either its nature or its origins. Mjomba immediately realized in the aftermath of the "quake" that, as far as Beelzebub was concerned, he, Mjomba, had consented to the "deal" under which he would commit to paper the material that he, Satan, was contributing; and, in return, Satan was going to make sure that Mjomba's "Thesis on Original Virtue" was going to be a winning thesis in every respect. It now dawned on Mjomba that the unexpected and violent shudder that had momentarily gripped him was forewarning about what could happen if he, Mjomba, did not continue to keep his part of the bargain! M0jmba was glad that nothing worse had befallen him as he continued to jot down the material that was being contributed by the Enemy.

"But, while the appearance of the Avenging Angel will be shocking enough, an even bigger shocker once on the other side of the gulf that separates the living from the dead, and where one no longer sees 'as through a glass darkly' and gets to know things not piece meal but 'as one is known' as the Apostle of the Gentiles aptly put, will be the discovery that they were fighting for a lost cause! To their great shock and disappointment, they will suddenly discover that, within a matter of decades, their country, once upon a 'super power' that was capable of leaving its foot prints at will on any part of the globe in pursuit of its 'vital national interests', not only would be a super power no more, but would itself be a colony, occupied and exploited by forces representing those self-same 'terrorists' with whom their country was now disinclined to talk peace and was determined to 'liquidate' from the face of the earth. So much for putting one's faith in crude 'super power' and in the sword in stead of putting one's faith in the Prime Mover!

"And as they await their fate in 'Guantanamo', the former fighters will have no choice but to use that time to put themselves in the feet of the surviving victims of the aggression, and to join them in reflecting on the needless loss of life and also on the hardships and uncertainty in life resulting from the fact that the lives of fathers, mothers, their children and other loved ones were snuffed out prematurely in the wake of the aggression. In the run-up to the sentencing - which awaits the arrival in 'Guantanamo' of the rest of the pack that initiated, planned, and participated in the hypothetical aggression, these poor chaps will be compelled to own up to any grievous 'crimes' they themselves might have committed while participating in the misguided adventure.

"Even though the 'detainees' at the 'Guantanamo' holding place will themselves not be met by any military intelligence personnel, interrogators, or menacing guards who were dying to administer the 'humane' treatment, they will not like their stay there a bit. But they will not have the heart to flee either even though they will not be 'hooded' or restrained by leg irons and hand cuffs.

"And it is not so much that they will hate the place because of the fear and terror associated with its name. It will suddenly dawn on them that the object of dread will be they themselves. And they will be wishing that the Avenging Angel could do them a favor - albeit an impossible favor - and that is take them back to the original Guantanamo on the island of Cuba back on Planet Earth so they would have the opportunity to experience the 'humane treatment' which the suspects in the 'war on terror' routinely received at the hands of some of their buddies.

"In this hypothetical example, the 'war on terror' is entirely fictitious, because it represents a scheme that, say, is designed to divert attention from the responsibility of the super power to act even-handedly in arbitrating a dispute involving a country that was regarded as the only trusted ally in a region. But it goes without saying that, for the 'Guantanamo' detainees, it will come as a terrible shock to them that a much trumpeted war on 'terror' was indeed fictitious.

"For, if there was anyone who deserved the label of 'terrorist', it actually was they themselves and their leadership back on earth. They were after all the ones who, following the 'Cain doctrine' of empire, had been prepared to trample on the 'rule of law', and to take any actions they thought were necessary to maintain their country's super power status, including waging unjustified wars. And, finding themselves hounded mercilessly by the demons in them that drove them to do the things they did while they were back on earth, they will wish that they had not been born.

"But what will make the wait really unbearable will be the realization that they had not even come close to 'rubbing out' their 'enemies' as they had intended. That by visiting death on the humans they had sought to subjugate and pacify, and whom they had been led to detest, all they had done was dispatch them to their eternal rest in the Holy city prematurely. It is a realization that will be both damning, and a foreboding of the judgement awaiting them and their buddies.

"It will in fact be *totally* damning because of the implicit admission that they did not really believe in the power of Providence to take care of their needs either in life or in death. The fact that they had a history of paying only lip service to those sacred truths will make their already hopeless situation even more hopeless.

"They will recoil at the fact that they allowed themselves to be used in a campaign that had more to do with their country's colonial, imperial and expansionist ambitions than with its defense. In a word, they will wish that their nation had never been tempted to embark on an expansionist adventure such as that one which had resulted in their now certain damnation. And they will also be wishing and praying that their own forces take very many casualties, as that would have the potential of reducing the period if their stay at the Guantanamo 'detention center'.

"They will in fact be praying that their country's troops became routed and suffered defeat on the battlefield in ways that might serve as an immediate lesson that they were in the wrong. Even though they will know that such an eventuality was unlikely in a world that was still subject to my rule (because I have a way of taking care of my minions), out of desperation these poor souls will be wishing that the leadership of their country was taken to task for the unlawful acts of aggression, and tried for their 'crime against humanity'. Like the rich man who died and asked if he could be permitted to return to earth to tell his friends to give their wealth to the poor and start living frugally, they too will, of course, wish that they could return to earth and alert their comrades of the untenability of their position.

"They will be crushed by the knowledge that their buddies on the other side of the Gulf were persisting in their acts of aggression, and detaining and even torturing their captives, and still determined not just to win the wars they had already started at any cost, but were itching to provoke new wars, goaded on by the silly notion that it was well within the grasp of their military to conquer the and dominate the whole world and become the sole super power. But much more crushing will be the knowledge that the great bulk of casualties suffered by the other side were women and children and others who were non-combatants. It will be so crushing, they will be wishing that everybody on the other side of the Gulf, and particularly their own loved ones, mourned for the victims of the aggression rather than for them. And, of course, the failure of their compatriots to mourn for the numerous victims of the aggression will itself be very very damning.

"They will agonize over the fact that, instead of focusing on the permanent and the eternal, their countrymen back on Planet Earth in the so-called 'free world' were continuing to focus on the temporal. While waiting for their buddies to arrive for the face-off with the Judge, they will have ample time to ponder and reflect on many things including the lives they and their compatriots had been leading.

"And, noting that almost anything went in the 'free world' and that materialism governed everything, they will agonize over the fact that the motivation for their country's foreign adventures was to ensure that citizens continued to enjoy their affluent lifestyles and supposedly 'good' but actually wanton and prodigal life. They will be miffed by the fact that the lives of thousands in countries that tried to resist becoming underlings of their super powerful country ended up in ruins (when they were not utterly destroyed) as a result of those foreign ventures.

"They will be sickened by the fact that, back on earth, it was the so-called 'acts of terrorism' by disaffected humans that hit the headlines, and not the irresponsible, heavy-handed resort to the use of overwhelming force by the 'occupiers' or 'authorities', even though the latter directly resulted in the loss of many more lives. They will be taken aback at the sight of a virtual flood of humans crossing to their side of the Gulf in the wake of the so-called 'security operations'.

"And, noting that those lives had been cut short because they were regarded as expendable, they will be sickened to the hilt. Indeed, so much so, they will welcome the fact that they had met their demise when they did - before they had committed worse atrocities themselves and in the process got the blood of innocents splattered all over their person (instead of just their hands). But, even then, the non-stop headlines in the 'Truth-Only-and-No-Lies-and-No-Spin' media of the mystic realm, bearing testimony to the daily carnage presided over by the 'authorities' back on the blasted earth, will leave them perplexed and speechless.

"They will hate to think that bureaucrats in their country (which boasted that it was the world's defender of freedom and democracy) used spin and falsehoods to manipulate their countrymen and everyone else, and had no qualms equating lies with something as noble as Truth. They will also hate to think that the cause for which they had sacrificed their own lives had nothing to do with any of the declared grounds for the foreign adventure, and everything to do with their country's declared goal of world domination (i.e. going out and securing resources that belonged to other countries so their own country's access to them would always be uninhibited) by any means. They will be devastated by the idea that their country was actually seeking to use its position as the *de facto* occupying power in that foreign country to position itself for new adventures of a similar nature on the pretext that it was determined to bring other 'rogue' nations to heel, and in a flagrant violation of Natural Justice.

"They will feel so chastised they won't be able to enjoy as much as a moment of relaxation, peace or sleep for what seems like an eternity, not because a guard at that dreadful facility was raising a finger to hurt them or because of anything that the Avenging Angel was doing, but because of being constantly nagged by their own thoughts and specifically memories of events back on earth that they would have much preferred to forget. One thought that will be coming back to intermittently haunt and nag them, and prevent them from getting a wink of sleep will pertain to the bribery and fraud that characterised actions of their leadership back on Planet Earth, as they marshalled the support of other nations for economic embargoes they wanted imposed on the so-called rogue regimes, and their own support for those actions.

"They will hate themselves for closing their eyes while back on Planet Earth to the real purpose for organizing and mounting the campaigns for embargoes against the so-called 'rogue' states, namely the desire of their leadership to weaken the targeted countries with a view to either taking over control of scarce resources under the control of the 'rogue' nations, promoting their own country's policy of global domination in the process, or both, under the pretext of stopping those rogue states from engaging in the proliferation of weapons of mass destruction!

"The catch will of course be that the actions of their leadership were based on fabricated lies and the desire to find an excuse to weaken the rogue state in the course of implementing their country's policy of global domination. These poor souls will wonder how they themselves could lend support to such egregious conduct by their fellow citizens when they well knew very well that their leadership marshalled support for the embargoes that devastated the lived of untold numbers in the targeted rogue nations by using bribery and fraud. If they were not already dead, it would kill them as they recalled that while all that was going on, their own country was modernizing and upgrading their own massive arsenals of nuclear and other weapons of mass destruction, also providing their allies with all the help they needed to strengthen and shore up their arsenals of WMD. And above all, they will wonder how their leadership back Planet Earth could be involved in such chicanery and still be able to sleep!

"They will bemoan the fact that, instead of using their country's enormous resources to improve the lives of have-nots wherever they were and make the world a better place to live in, their leaders - with their own ardent support and that of their compatriots - clung to the silly notion that, having gained super power status, it was quite in order to get back into the business of colonialism and imperialism, and to pursue policies of world dominance and pre-emption, and even go against their own nation's rule of law if that was what it was going to take to consolidate their country's unchallenged super power status.

"They will in fact wish that their country, which great and mighty nation in the eyes of the world, had been just like one of those impoverished basket cases in the Third World, with no appetite for the deadly chess of international intrigue, and with no desire for expansionism.

"They will struggle to understand why they and their compatriots had failed to learn from Cain, the 'Neanderthal' man and also author of the Cain doctrine, who found grace just in the nick of time and repented of his litany of misdeeds (which included lying and murdering his own brother Abel whom he saw as a threat to his empire).

"They will anguish over the fact that, instead of serving a government that was dedicated to promoting the commonweal while remaining a responsible and respectful member of the family of nations, they perished while in the service of a country that had opted for world domination, and was itself possibly becoming a 'rogue super power' and a pariah in the process! Upon discovering, in retrospect, that their country was becoming increasingly feared and detested, particularly by citizens of those nations that saw themselves as likely targets for future preemptive strikes and/or occupation, they will be beside themselves, and will lament that they themselves did not feel constrained to do anything to halt that calamitous trend.

"In the meantime, they will wonder what it was in them that had made them dare to even imagine that they could just label other humans who were also created in the Image just like themselves as 'insurgents', 'terrorists' and 'hoodlums' on a whim. They will wonder, above all, what it was in them that made them think that they actually could 'destroy' other humans regardless of whether they were perceived as obstacles to their country's empire building venture or not!

"They will struggle to understand how, being mortal themselves, it was that they dared to act as if they had the power or authority to 'destroy' other humans, especially after the Deliverer (and the Eternal Word through whom all creatures were made) had urged His followers to not fear those who could destroy the body, but Him who could send the soul to hell'! What on earth got in them and caused them to imagine that they could 'destroy' what even the Prime Mover (who so loved the world that He gave His only begotten Son) had no intention whatsoever of destroying?

"And if the Deliverer and Son of Man came so that sinners may be saved, what on earth did they think they were - saints who were not in need of salvation? How come they did not see that they themselves were sinners in the exact same way the folks they sought to 'destroy' were sinners?

"And, anyway, how could they have dared to suggest that they could destroy - rub out - other humans (regardless of the label they used to refer to them) when even they themselves were on death row! How could they have dared to suggest anything like that when it was entirely possible that some of those involved in 'hunting down' the so-called insurgents and terrorists were themselves going to 'kick the bucket' and cross the gulf that separated the living from the dead before those they had set up as their quarry did!

"How could they have dared to suggest that they had the authority to issue orders to the effect that fellow humans should be 'destroyed' or 'rubbed out', or that they had permission to carry out any order to 'destroy' or 'rub out' creatures that were made in the Image? How could they have dared to suggest these things when they themselves were liable to face the Judge even before their vile designs were carried out!

"And how could they have been so foolish as to imagine that they were not going to be confronted by those same 'terrorists' and 'insurgents' come the day of judgement when all humans (regardless of their social status, race and even religious persuasion) would face the Judge to answer for everything they did both in secret and in the open.

"It will be quite evident to them by now that if it had been that only the insurgents and terrorists - supposedly the truly wicked - died, and if those who now plotted their assassination (or 'destruction') did not die, it might have made sense for their 'leaders' to abandon dialogue with those they regarded as their foes and to devote their energies in trying to 'destroy' them. But that was far from being the case - which pulled the rug from under the feet of those humans who wished ill of other members of the human family.

"But from their vantage point in 'Guantanamo', they will see the real root of the problem of 'terrorism' very clearly, namely the imperial ambitions of the so-called advanced nations and - having accumulated their wealth through conquest and spoils of war or at the expense of other nations - their reluctance to share that wealth, and their determination to consolidate their power by any means. It will be devastating for them to discover that the race known as humankind had gone back to where it started - back to the time when Cain sought to 'rub out' his own brother Abel.

"They will agonize over the similarity between Cain's objective in removing any potential challenge to his 'empire' by devising plans to 'destroy' his brother Abel on the grounds that he had turned into a 'terrorist', 'insurgent' and 'hoodlum'. And, seeing that they had in fact been many times more niggardly than Cain (whose reluctance to share the available land compelled his young brother to risk his life as he ventured out into the forests in search of animals to tame and domesticate as a way of living), they will feel as flabbergasted with themselves as ever.

"Noting that 'terrorists' were also responsible for the loss of lives, they will be outraged that many more lives were lost daily as a direct result of so-called 'security operations' conducted daily by so-called 'democratic governments', including their own government. And they will be even more distressed that the spokespeople for those governments had the distinctly churlish habit of branding the victims of those wanton and indiscriminate assaults as 'terrorists', 'insurgents' and 'gangsters', and invariably labeled the deaths of innocent bystanders unintended 'collateral damage' when it was clear that making outright denials of culpability was out of question.

"And they will be dumbfounded that while alive and kicking, pride had gotten the better of them so much so they thought it was beneath them to get down on their knees, repent of their misdeeds, beg forgiveness from their Deliverer and Judge, and above all be prepared to make restitution to those they had injured as they pursued their nation's imperial ambitions - just as Cain finally did (just in time, in his case, before he himself kicked the bucket). Noting that it was this that saved Cain from eternal perdition which was the fate of unrepentant murderers, they will beat their breasts and chide themselves for refusing to take a lesson from the 'Neanderthal man'.

"They will agonize over the fact that, while Cain was bent on 'destroying' his brother, the only thing that came to his mind when he thought of his brother was 'insurgent' and 'terrorist' and sometimes both - just as they themselves were in the habit of doing back on earth whenever they thought of those folks who had proved to their nation that (with or without super power status) every nation on earth remained vulnerable, and that to attach importance to worldly power was the height of stupidity just as it was dumb to attach any permanence to earthly rule.

"They will regret that, instead of being humble and accepting that situation as fact, they and their compatriots had chafed at the fact that some humans (whom they traditionally thought of as backward and even inferior) had the gall to try and teach them such an obvious lesson. And, instead of putting their minds to resolving the problems that had given rise to the 'terrorism', they had chosen to embark on a perilous course of unilateralism as a country, and opted for militarism (the heaviest handed form of response to any situation) in the wake of the chastisement.

"Actually, come to think of it, since empires and earthly kingdoms existed only in the imagination and did not really count in the eyes of the Prime Mover (and that included the roles of emperors, kings, queens, princes, or proconsuls), the 'lesson' or 'chastisement' may have been a God-send, and a suitable - and perhaps even timely - reminder that those who put their faith in their 'super power' kidded themselves and instead needed to get down on their knees and commend their dreams and hopes to the one, the only, and the unchanging Almighty!

"But then, covetous and measly humans, inclined to sin, were always suspicious that heeding reminders of that sort merely provided 'rivals' the opportunity to gain the upper hand and to claim for themselves a bigger slice of material things - a clear sign that they didn't have any trust in the Prime Mover, that they were just 'fake' devotees of the Deliverer who 'faked' their love for their neighbors and lived in a fool's paradise, and above all that they would quicker pray to me (Beelzebub and Author of Death) than to their infinitely merciful and gracious Maker!

"And, of course, being the Prince of Darkness, I for my part am always available to give them the 'inspiration' and 'strength' they need in life (inspiration and strength that they should be seeking from the Spirit), and to make them believe that they are onto something really terrific and perhaps even pioneers in the art of 'worldly living' or 'escapism'!

"But how could they and their leaders have dared, even in the face of extreme national embarrassment, to suggest that they could label other humans as 'terrorists' who were unfit to live when they themselves were equally terrorists who were waiting to answer for their repeated attempt to 'rub out' the Deliverer (which they did whenever they sinned)! And, above all, how could they have dared to do such a thing in the name of the Prime Mover!

"How could they have dared to use the name of the Prime Mover in vain like that - the Prime Mover who gave His only begotten Son so that those sinful and vile humans who believed in Him would be saved! How was it that they dared to suggest that they themselves were any different from the 'terrorists' leave alone sinless! But, above all, how could they have suggested (even for just one moment) that they had the power or authority to actually 'destroy' creatures the Prime Mover Himself in His infinite wisdom had created in the Image and thereby also decreed that they exist for ever (whether for good or for bad)!

"They will distinctly recall that when the time came for them to vacate Mother Earth and head for their afterlife, they got a rude awakening when the Avenging Angel (who suddenly appeared from no where and instructed them to follow him) let them understand that the notion of empire was a figment of their mind, and that they also had to leave behind not just their bodies, but their 'inflated egos' as well. No one had ever spoken to them like that before, and they thought that whoever the 'stranger' was, he had to be joking!

"They had been so attached to the self, they at first imagined that they could not go anywhere without their egos. They had been so attached to their bodies and the self since they were little, that attachment had resulted in those inflated egos which they soon treated as more important than their person - the noble creature in whom no less than the Prime Mover Himself was indwelling. It was those same egos that, like an albatross, had kept them focused on the terrestrial instead of the supernatural while they lived, and also inclined to sin.

"They will remember how it broke their heart to hear that they had to leave behind on earth virtually everything they had lived for including their feelings of self-importance, and how it even caused them to succumb to their wounds even earlier than they might have.

They will remember how they stared in disbelief at the stern-faced Avenging Angel to assure themselves that he was really serious.

"And they will, of course, not fail to note that the hardest part of their rude awakening was when they came around and accepted that it was entirely of their own accord that they had blunted their consciences to stop the constant nagging, that they could continue with the charade a moment longer and it was pay-back time, and - even more numbing - that they were ill-prepared to give a full accounting of the talents they had received (and decided to bury).

"And - guess what! That is also the time when the poor souls will see me, Beelzebub, for what I really am - the Author of Death and an infernal liar. They will hate me for persuading them that they needed to 'take charge of their lives', and to be 'free' and not allow themselves to be nagged by that 'inner man' or conscience. They will realize that by putting cotton wool in the 'ears of their souls' and refusing to heed their consciences, they became 'hard core' sinners!

"They will envy those they despised back on earth - those who accepted that they were sinners but were grateful that their conscience was always there to nag them so they could head for the confessional in accordance with mother Church's teachings. And they will regret that they missed so many opportunities to 'unplug their ears', get back on the narrow path, and follow in the footsteps of their divine Master who embraced a humiliating and ghastly death on the cross, even though He was a member of the Godhead and almighty.

"Incidentally, we demons may have our own faults, including the blinding pride which made us imagine that, being made in the Image, we were automatically guaranteed eternal existence regardless of how we behaved ourselves, and that nothing could happen to us if we refused to recognize the authority of the Prime Mover or to return the favor of being brought into existence in the first place. But being blind to the fact that, once in existence, creatures made in the Image cannot be 'destroyed' or returned to nothingness has never been one of them.

"But you earthlings have taken the rebellion against the Prime Mover to a completely new level. This is something that is completely novel - humans imagining that they can 'rub out' fellow humans in whom the Prime Mover Himself is indwelling! But it is a new 'low' to which we demons for our part would rather not sink. But what can we do except to welcome all you humans to the Club!

"Now, in this hypothetical situation in which the aggressor nation is a super power that decides to pit its 'imperial' or 'super' power against a nation that (for argument's sake) it has spent years undermining politically, economically and militarily, it is precisely such a decision that virtually guarantees the defenders who fall in battle heaven. The use by the aggressors of 'overwhelming force', 'shock and awe' tactics, and the scale of cruelty and inhumanity visited on the population in the country under assault, more likely than not, will combine to bring home to the luckless defenders the fact that their fate was indeed in the hands of the Prime Mover.

"Consequently, defenders who fall in battle and would otherwise be headed straight to hell because of the unworthy lives they might have previously led, will find themselves mysteriously - almost miraculously - transformed and no longer hesitant if afforded the opportunity to forsake worldly things that they (more than any one else) will now see as ephemeral and passing - and my wiles. This will happen despite our redoubled efforts to drive them to despair in the face of their miseries, humiliation and suffering, and the terrible odds they would be up against.

"Instead of driving them to despair, their sufferings and isolation by the rest of the world will merely result in an unprecedented and mysterious surge in their faith and trust in the Prime Mover. Like the saints of yore, they will find themselves ready to die for their new-found (or enlivened) faith, and to dedicate their lives to the Prime Mover and the well-being of their fellow humans.

"Now, nations - all nations without exception - are so much into the doctrine of imperialism which Cain expounded in those early days of man, there is virtually nothing in that doctrine which Cain's many admirers and students do not do, the dastardly practice of torturing captives being one of them. Actually, as the years and then centuries went by, the techniques of torture were refined and now include torturing captives even as they are undergoing their pangs of death

"Unfortunately for those who are into that practice, their actions become self-defeating - particularly if they are intended to put the captives at some sort of disadvantage. Unable to actually 'rub out' one's enemies by 'cutting their lives short', you would think that the killers would be hoping to at least despatch their foes to hell. But, as it happens, such a technique of torture in fact virtually guarantees the poor souls salvation.

"Humans who are in the process of kicking the bucket are already in a position that gives them no option but to accept their status as creatures, and to recognize that their fate was in the hands of the Prime Mover all along. That is why it is incumbent on other humans who may be around the dying to proffer material, moral and spiritual support, and extend them without any regard whatsoever to creed, nationality, race, gender, race, status or any other factor. And anything that is done to the contrary signals that I, the Father of Death and the Enemy, am in charge and still calling the shots!

"You've got to understand that when a human is in his/her throes of death and finds him/herself subjected to torture, abuse and humiliation, it is very difficult for that human not to identify him/herself with the crucified and dying Deliverer who called the thirsty and hungry, the sick, the poor, and the persecuted 'blessed'.

"You see…however caused, the separation of a human soul from the body - or 'death' - is a fate that all awaits all humans, and represents the wages of sin. It is because Mary, the Deliverer's mother, was sinless and unblemished by the original sin that she did not 'die the death', but was instead assumed into heaven. Apart from Mary and the Deliverer Himself, only liars can step forward and claim that they are without blemish. This is the reason capital punishment so-called, which has its basis in vengefulness, hypocrisy and an absence of faith and trust in Divine Providence, could never be justifiable or right! And the strange notions that have abounded since Cain murdered his brother Abel under the guise of administering capital punishment to a 'terrorist' as he referred to him definitely say something about humans!

"You earthlings are all on death row any way, and therefore why the botheration! Why pretend that some are, and not others! If you see someone act as if this is the case, you can always bet that the individual does so at my explicit command. The world comes to an end for the individual in his/her agony of death; and - believe me - all in the vicinity will be asked by the Deliverer and Judge if they stopped to help Him when He was on Death Row!

"Defenders who are under unjustified attack by superior forces, and who are additionally abandoned to their fate by the rest of the world, regardless of their beliefs automatically become aware already at that time that it is only their 'Prime Mover' that can save them. In other words, their reliance on Him tends to become total from then on. And, facing the double ordeal of death pangs on the one hand, and oppression and torture by those who were supposed to give them comfort and solace, but who instead choose to torture and even prolong their death pangs for the fun of it on the other, they simply must feel just as the Deliverer did - forsaken by even His own Father, abandoned by Peter (the rock upon which His church was going to be built) and all His 'friends', mocked, crowned with thorns, beaten and scourged, and sent to his death on the cross by the very people he had come to save.

"The pain and suffering, both physical and spiritual, that comes their way in circumstances like those become, without a doubt, God-sent - and probably very timely for souls that might otherwise have forfeited eternal life. And it is also noteworthy that they receive that treatment at the hands of humans who proclaim in the same breath that they are 'godly', 'righteous' and doing whatever they are doing in the Deliverer's name. It certainly highlights the extent to which they have been abandoned to their fate by the whole world on the one hand and, at least ostensibly, by the Prime Mover Himself.

"In an unexpected turn of events (and also irony of no mean proportions), the 'unsaved' insurgents and terrorists so-called, who purportedly might have been working for some 'axis of evil', will be the recipients of the Baptism of Desire and other divine graces as a direct result of the unjustifiable actions of those who regard themselves as righteous - graces that will flow from being compelled to identify themselves with the suffering Deliverer (more or less like the 'good thief'), becoming completely resigned to the will of the Prime Mover, and also agreeing to suffer with His son.

"The oppressive nature of captivity at the hands of 'imperialists', 'occupiers' and other types of oppressors, the outrageous injustice, the murderous rampage of the proud, heartless and swaggering colonialists and invaders, the torture, abuse and humiliation to which patriotic nationalists and defenders (who suddenly find themselves labeled 'insurgents' and 'terrorists') endure - all those things will combine to virtually guarantee those who succumb to their 'treatment' under unjust occupations heavenly salvation.

"And this will be largely true also for those who survive the cruel treatment and harassment, because such treatment and harassment, endured while the whole world merely looks on, not only effectively destroys one's faith in fellow humans while leaving them permanently traumatized, it also readies the soul for the comforting words of the Deliverer who declared: 'Blessed are they who weep and mourn, for the kingdom of heaven is theirs'.

"And, by the same token, those humans who take it upon themselves to assault, brutalize, humiliate or kill other humans while pursuing their worldly ambitions - or who see ways of benefiting from lending their support to such actions and do so - guarantee themselves damnation, for the simple reason that they could never gain eternal life while doing unto other humans what they themselves wouldn't want done unto themselves or unto their loved ones.

"And so, in the decidedly unexpected but fundamental turn of events, the former 'insurgents' and 'terrorists' who fall while defending their country could definitely find themselves playing a role they had never dreamed of - playing big brother and patron to those who had boasted super power prowess and invincibility.

"Unexpected because suddenly humans who had until now been looked upon by everybody as expendable and undeserving of anything will be the ones having the upper hand. And fundamental because the former 'insurgents' and 'terrorists', who along with their loved ones had been subjected to all sort of harassments and humiliations before they crossed the Gulf, will be interceding with the Prime Mover on behalf of their former foes. In one stroke and as predicted by the psalmist, the mighty will find themselves thoroughly humbled; and the down trodden and forsaken will find themselves in a role they had never dreamed of - playing a pivotal role in bringing the divine plan to fruition.

"In a strange twist of fate, the cocky aggressors who prided themselves on being invincible, all-knowing, and civilized (and perhaps 'valiant crusaders for the Deliverer's cause' as well) will find themselves fainting in the face of death and haunted in the last moments of their lives by the saying that those who live by the sword die by the sword. Instead of seeing themselves as patriots who were falling while 'defending' their country, it will suddenly dawn upon them that they really weren't any different from mercenaries, particularly in view of their inability to voice conscientious objections to a war they well knew was unjust.

"The terrible reality is that they might well be surprised to find that instead of choirs of angels, it is swarms of demons who will be waiting on the other side of the Gulf to meet and escort them to their holding cells in 'Guantanamo'. And they will even be more surprised, upon getting to 'Guantanamo', to find the place many times more fearful and forbidding than the original Guantanamo back on Planet Earth.

"It wouldn't take them long (in our hypothetical case) to learn that there was a good reason for that. The conditions at the 'detention facility' in which they will find themselves confined will likely be dramatically worse: firstly because on the other side of the Gulf, they had masqueraded as humans of good will even when everything they did, including their unprovoked incursions into foreign lands, was subordinated to greed for material things, thirst for power, and the desire to have all countries of the world at their beck and call.

"Of course in that type of situation, any arguments by their leadership back on Planet Earth tying an unjust war to their nation's 'war on terrorism' and things of that kind only make things worse. This is because, while the threat of terrorism might be real, questions regarding the real root causes of the 'terrorism' now also automatically arise. People do not just become 'terrorists' for no reason!

"But the accusation by their leadership back on earth that some folks who were into terrorism started it all could backfire really badly. When the time came for them to defend themselves in the divine court of justice, the last thing they want is to be informed at that late stage that, while they accused others of terrorism, it was something they themselves were very much into as witness the fact that they had made a list of so-called 'rogue states' and, buoyed by the fact that they commanded superior fire power, had already started the process of regime changes in accordance following a plan that was a perfect fit for the description of 'terrorism'.

"And, as the Avenging Angel will point out, that is the problem with lying and spinning stories about these things. They start a preemptive war in the name of fighting terrorism when they themselves are practitioners of that same craft, and they really damn themselves - especially when they know very well what the final destination for 'knaves' and 'rogues' is.

"The second reason for conditions at the 'holding center' being spectacularly worse than the conditions at the Guantanamo back on the island of Cuba will be the fact that they had this insidious habit of calling on the name of the Prime Mover in vain and pretending that they were devoted to the cause of His son.

"And thirdly, in the pursuit of their worldly ambitions, they had never had any qualms in inflicting needless pain and suffering on other members of the human family and, in doing so, failed to acknowledge that the Deliverer, who Himself was branded an 'insurgent and a terrorist' and put to death as such, identifies completely with suffering descendants of Adam and Eve.

"Fourthly, they had been spineless in life and unable to challenge their nation's policies - policies such as preemptive regime changes, unilateralism, and world dominance - that may have ultimately defined the cause for which they chose to sacrifice their lives and that would eventually result in needless suffering for so many.

"And lastly but not least, there is the matter of the denial of human rights for those whom their commanders had picked on and detained in Guantanamo with their unswerving cooperation. Denying fellow humans their inalienable right to prove their innocence regardless of the nature of the allegation flies in the face of Natural Justice.

"And, should it happen that the actions of those interfering with that inalienable right had a hand in creating the conditions that gave rise to the terrorism or whatever the detainees in Guantanamo allegedly had done (in our hypothetical case), then the decision to deny the captives that inalienable right becomes an even more serious matter.

"The situation becomes compounded when they are denied the right to food and nourishment, the right to sleep and rest, or are subjected to other methods of torture. And, of course, that situation takes on a different kind of gravity when the person of those held captive is violated in these circumstances by anyone acting on behalf of the authorities. The matter becomes particularly egregious when those responsible for the human rights abuses imagine that, with no earthly power in a position to challenge them or to enforce the associated ethical codes, anyone seeking redress can go to hell - as if the Almighty was just a figment of the mind and they themselves represented the 'all mighty'.

"It will come as a terrible realization that, when they 'hooded' their detainees back on Planet Earth, forced them to assume stressful positions for long periods to wear them down, made them believe they were going to kill them by suffocation and/or drowning, assaulted them using improvised light and sound techniques, dared to strip them naked, violated their person, or let snarling dogs loose on them when they were not employing the dogs to scare them, they actually were doing those things to the Second Adam and also their Deliverer and their Judge. It will also be a very sobering experience!

"Now, even though the practice of torturing captured 'insurgents' and 'terrorists', particularly those who are tortured even as they are already undergoing their pangs of death would virtually assure the victims salvation, you can bet that we here in the Pit celebrate every time humans torture, abuse and/or humiliate their own. This is because those who connive in such reprehensible practices automatically guarantee themselves damnation.

"It is for the same reason that we similarly celebrate when 'non-combatants' in homes, places of prayer, marketplaces, and elsewhere are treated as expendable collateral because they happen to live in the same neighborhood as a much sought after 'terrorist' and 'for being in the wrong place at the wrong time in history'; or are deliberately targeted by the aggressors as either as 'payback' for loosing one of their own - or for fun. You know that all those who participate in any such assaults, because they know exactly what they are doing, become murderers for whom there is no place in heaven, but plenty of it here in the Pit.

"Those fighters who may have boasted about their 'victorious' invasion will be damning themselves for having gone on to parade themselves as the 'good guys' who were trying to take 'bad guys' off the street in those far away places to which they had gone as 'occupiers' and 'imperialists'. They will be shocked at the extent to which they had been blinded by greed and worldly ambitions, and ended up not seeing that they were the ones terrorizing the poor folks in the country they had decided to invade and occupy with a view to 'privatizing' and helping themselves to its national resources.

"They will not understand how they could have allowed themselves to be parties to the totally reprehensible practice of kidnapping, torturing and humiliating completely innocent family members of suspected 'terrorists' and 'insurgents' to compel elusive fugitives to give themselves up! They will not understand because, if it were not for the fact that they had already 'died', it would have killed them to see their own loved ones kidnapped, tortured and humiliated in similar circumstances.

"They will find themselves at a loss when, attempting to establish when exactly the Prime Mover gave them the mandate to be the world's cops, it will suddenly dawn on them that the Almighty didn't need any human(s) to fill that role. Talking about being the world's cops, it will suddenly dawn on them that each and every soul in the so-called 'super powerful' or 'super advanced' nations needed policing just as much as each and every soul in so-called rogue and implicitly 'backward' nations, given the inclination of all human to sin as a result of the original sin that was committed by the father and the mother of humankind.

"Yeah, they will find to their amazement that, if anything, it was folks who lived in the 'advanced' nations, where acquisitiveness and selfishness permeated and dictated everything including such things 'religious crusades', who needed more 'policing' - and particularly the chaps in leadership positions there in those countries! It will be obvious that it was in those 'industrialised' countries where the extended family value system had been completely eroded, and the motto was 'each one for oneself', and as a result of which the elderly were shipped off to 'homes for the aged' and abandoned there for the remainder of their lives!

"This was where graft and bribery were carried on by the moneyed and by profit gauging corporations in the open under innocent sounding banners like 'lobbying' or 'free speech', and quite rampart. This was also where crimes committed by those in high places and the wealthiest, and as well by corporations, went unpunished, even as the number of detention centers or so-called 'correctional facilities', crammed with the economically disadvantaged and members of other marginalised groups in those 'advanced nations', multiplied to the point where those self-same 'advanced and rich' nations began to complain that the 'prison industrial complex' had become bloated and too costly to run even as it remained 'too big' and also 'too profitable' to fail given the purpose it served!

"And they will find it telling that it had never once happened that, even though corporations in those advanced counties enjoyed the same rights as ordinary citizens, including the right to donate money to political campaigns, no corporation had ever been committed to a correctional facility. That was even though most of the thieving was done by those so-called corporate entities or corporate 'persons', obviously because those correctional facilities were run and controlled by the thieving corporate entities that also happened to be a part and parcel of the 'military industrial complex' that, by the way, happens to be owned by the crooks who occupy high places in those advanced 'imperialist' and super powerful countries!

"They will be shocked to discover that the number of so-called 'judicial killings' in countries around the world were a fairly accurate measure of the disregard for life, and that, when the summary, extra-judicial, killings by their own country's so-called law enforcement agencies were also taken into account, their country lead the world in the disregard for life! They will be confounded to note that this was indeed the case even as their nation's functionaries regularly sought, in conjunction with professional image makeovers in the service of their country, to promote the lie that their country was the world's guardian of the principles of equity and social justice, and that its practices needed to be emulated by the rest of the world!

"But they above all will be flabbergasted to find that nine out of ten of the related 'convictions' of death row inmates in their country were wrongful outright, based on 'profiling' or racial discrimination. They will be devastated to note that the so-called pro-life advocates in their country were the worst offenders when it came to flouting the right of every person to life that was enshrined in their own country's constitution.

"They will be stung by the revelation that the Prime Mover knew quite well that humans, inclined to sin, were more likely to end up as human devils rather than holy men and women who could be trusted. And they will wonder where on earth they and their compatriots had gotten the idea that they were any better than humans in New Guinea, Vietnam, Cuba, Rwanda, Iraq, Afghanistan, Gaza or anywhere else in the world!

"They will not forgive themselves for daring to suggest that they had the authority to suspend the inalienable rights of other humans - rights that the Prime Mover in his infinite wisdom had seen fit to give every human including the so-called 'insurgents' and 'terrorists'. They will scold themselves for imagining that humans who were created with inalienable rights could suddenly be denied those rights just because some dimwit, who himself/herself existed at the pleasure of the Prime Mover, said so.

"Awakened to reality as they succumbed to their wounds and found themselves preparing to face the Judge, they will not believe that they could have permitted themselves to be blinded to the point to which they essentially cared more for their pets than for their fellow brother and sister humans. They will feel terrible anguish for having allowed themselves to sink so low that, being creatures who were themselves made in the Image and in whom the Prime Mover was indwelling, they not only failed to recognize that 'Image' in others, but went on to brutalize them using the most savage methods imaginable.

"In that connection, seeing the victims of the 'smart bombs', the carpet bombing runs that were conducted by the military in different parts of the world and at various points of time in their country's own brief history, and the chemical and other weaponry, including land mines, their country produced and supplied to puppet governments and other dependent 'supplicants' as it pursued its policy of world dominance, they will beg the Avenging Angel to just show them the way to hell so they might avoid a face to face encounter with the Savior of Mankind and Judge.

"They will be at a complete loss as (too late) they attempt to grapple with the fact that they were totally mistaken when they took as a determinant for brotherhood, not the fact that an individual was made in the Image, but the fact that he or she looked and acted like themselves, and shared their religious and political views, spoke with a Southern, West Coast, East Coast, Midwestern, Northwestern or Texan drawl, or did not wear a turban.

"After leading insincere lives and imagining that they were better than Judas Iscariot (who himself knew very well that the enemies of his Divine Master, because of their intense hatred for Him, were going to treat Him as someone with no rights whatsoever, and who still decided to help the priests and Pharisees nab the Deliverer for a price), they will be horrified to discover that they too had betrayed the Son of Man by doing what they did to their fellow humans, and were no better than the disciple from Jericho.

"It will dawn on them that Judas Iscariot, who had decided to pass up the opportunity to be an apostle and a 'father of the Church' along with Peter, John and the rest of the Twelve, because he was not prepared to serve under the Rock (the apostle Peter), knew that the 'insurgent' and 'terrorist', as members of the Sanhedrin referred to the Deliverer, was not really going to do a vanishing act, and was going to continue going about his Father's business until all the prophecies about Him had been fulfilled. But that, in his greed for money and his craving for power and influence as well as adoration for the Cain doctrine, Judas had gone out of his way to depict his Divine Master as a crafty felon who was liable to disappear in the plains of Galilee or Judea after the feast of the Passover; and also that he (Judas) was in a position to help the priests and Pharisees capture the 'militant' before He vanished into thin air - if they coughed up thirty pieces of silver.

"They will understand that this was even though Judas Iscariot knew that the real reason the priests and Pharisees were after the Deliverer was the fact that He had interfered in their practice if using the grounds of the temple in Jerusalem and its adjoining facilities for their worldly ends, and therefore posed a 'threat' to their continued 'enjoyment of life'.

"They will agree that this was how Judas Iscariot, whose real problem was that the Deliverer had passed him over for promotion and had singled out Peter as the 'first among the apostles' effectively making him the visible head of His Church, planned to get even with Him. Then it will strike them that this man Judas Iscariot, at once a betrayer and also an infernal liar, really served as the role model for all the world's aggressors, despite their lip service to the cause of justice in the world.

"They will not forgive themselves for imagining that they could treat humans they probably had themselves alienated with their partiality (and their failure to be honest brokers in the resolution international conflicts) as 'outlaws' when it was they themselves who were operating on the principle that might was right contrary to the law of Natural Justice.

"They will in fact see themselves as fully deserving to spend all eternity in hell for their outrageous acts of murder and mayhem, and their determination, while they lived, to hypocritically pass themselves off as nice folks who were interested in sharing their values of 'liberty', 'democracy' and 'freedom' with humans in other parts of the world.

"Aware that they had been unable to cross the Gulf with the physical part of themselves, and had been compelled to leave it behind on the other side of the Gulf, they will be taken aback to think that their bodies had been the central focus of everything they had ever done in life; and, in retrospect, they will not understand how they could have been so dumb as to expend their entire lifetime and all their energies on the pursuit of material things. And, instead of being relieved that their remains had been interned in expensive caskets, the thought that their bodies had started to decompose and to turn to dust as soon as they had proved unsuitable as an abode for their souls will be heart-wrenching.

"They will be angry with themselves for not having taken seriously the fact that they had only one life to live and along with it one opportunity to prepare for and pass the Church Triumphant Entrance Test; and they will also wish that, instead of pampering their bodies, they had spent their entire lifetime practicing mortification and helping the poor to get by.

"They will be crushed by the thought that they had opted to brush aside the many excellent ideas which the Holy Spirit never tired of sending their way, and which if followed would have assured their salvation. They will hate themselves for having ignored the silent urgings to do good which their guardian angels also never tired of sending their way, and for opting to follow their base instincts instead. They will find themselves envying Africans and others back on earth whose refusal to abandon traditional beliefs in the afterlife elicited ridicule and labels such as backward, savage and animist.

"And talking about being backward and savage, they will agonize over the fact that they themselves and their leadership back on earth had taken backwardness and savagery to a completely new low with their infatuation with armaments and their preparations for conducting 'star wars' so-called. They will beat their breasts and wish that they themselves had never been born for having participated in 'carpet bombing' of cities populated with fellow humans including women and children, and for using devastating 'smart bombs' that came equipped with radio-active depleted uranium, and for having no remorse for the fact that their nation tested nuclear and hydrogen bombs over cities filled with humans on the pretext that it was still at war.

"They will weep and gnash their teeth for having lent their support to their nation even as it used its veto power at the United Nations without any regard to Natural Justice while pursuing its avowed goal of world dominance. They will be tormented by the sight of those whose lives had been shattered just because their nation, at the urging of lobbyists in the armaments industry, stubbornly continued to resist efforts to ban land mines.

"And, seeing the thousands upon thousands of innocent victims of the policies of their nation - which had a distinct predilection for the use of things like economic embargoes in bringing other nations to toe its line without any regard for the fact that such embargoes resulted in the premature deaths of children and the aged and made the lives of ordinary citizens in the targeted countries nightmarish - they will wish that they could return to earth even as ghosts and do whatever it would take to convince their compatriots that these things were so heinous and 'obscene', and had to stop!

"They will be dumbfounded that, over the centuries, nations that bragged about being super powers and 'advanced' were the ones that were in the forefront of promoting things like slavery, colonialism and imperialism, and that deliberately started wars in hopes of consolidating and expanding their power. And they will be dismayed that the leaders of such nations, oblivious to the fact that whatever legitimate authority was God-given, became so infatuated with power they thought that it was might - not the Almighty - was right.

"Looking back on human history from the 'mystic realm' unfettered by the limitations of time and space, and noting that all earthly empires, kingdoms and super powers in time became history and passed away, they will shudder and grieve at the woes that overtook humanity over the centuries as demagogues (who came in all shapes and sizes and all, without any exception, lived in a fool's paradise) subordinated the well-being of their fellow humans to their mad grab for power.

"They will not understand how in the whole world they had thought that they might really be soul-less creatures that were endowed only with instincts - like goats or cows. Seeing no goats or cows on that side of the Gulf, they will quickly see that they had deliberately misled themselves so they would go on living irresponsibly. After all, if they were capable of coming to a reasoned conclusion that they were soul-less, that in itself was damning because it demonstrated that they were capable of reasoning and were indeed 'rational' creatures who could not pretend that they did not possess spiritual faculties and a spiritual constitution or soul.

"It also stood to reason that creatures that were not endowed with reason and only with instincts would automatically enjoy a blameless existence. But if there was anyone who knew with certainty that the lives they led were not blameless, it was they themselves. And they had to be really dumb to have imagined that they could keep that a secret to themselves for ever.

"It was something that should have been quite obvious to them while they lived - especially after they had spent all their lives accumulating wealth - that it was easier for a camel to pass through a needle's eye than for a rich man to enter heaven. They were now going to pay the price for ignoring a plain truth the Deliverer Himself had kept harping upon during His own lifetime and which is repeatedly *ad nauseam* by His Church.

"They will be greatly dismayed that Church authorities implicitly lent their support to the aggression through their habit of selectively condemning acts of violence, raising their voices only when those who were under attack and struggling to repel the occupation forces committed them, and remaining totally silent even when actions of the aggressor, including so-called shock and owe tactics, resulted in countless numbers of casualties of non-combatants; said nary a word about the thousands detained without trial in humane conditions, and about the reported acts of torture that many of the detainees endured.

"They will be disheartened that the Church's functionaries did not raise their voice when 'nukes' were dropped on cities during wars resulting in the demise of thousands; and that the world and successors to the apostles along with other members of the Church's hierarchy stood by when a million humans were cut down in the space of a week in one country; that the Church's leadership implicitly endorsed the doctrines of pre-emption, political assassination, less than honest brokering that is rife in international disputes, and things of that nature.

"They will feel betrayed that instead of loudly condemning the development during the so-called Cold War by both the 'Western Block' and the 'Eastern Block' of the Real Weapons of Mass Human Destruction (RWMHD), churchmen were seemingly contented by the fact that 'the West' appeared to have the edge over 'the East'. They will feel betrayed because the successors to the apostles should have known better than place their faith in RWMHD. They should have shown, by pronouncing anathema in unmistakable terms on the preoccupation by all with the development of those instruments of death, that the poor forsaken children of Adam and Eve without exception needed to put their faith in the Prime Mover alone and in nothing else.

"And now for this other 'catch'! Humans of good will so-called are actually not all that innocent either. They are just folks who, while not perfect, have welcomed the opportunity to become reconciled with their Maker. Even these are also free to damn themselves if they want - just as those humans whose hearts are hardened in sin have. In the event, the Deliverer and Judge will not intervene to stop their guilt from accumulating and 'damning' them as well! Sins committed by creatures made in the Image are always damning because at the time they are being, those creatures should be doing something else altogether, namely giving praise to the Prime Mover.

"This will be the case with respect to the victims of aggression. After enduring humiliations, detentions and death at the hands of the aggressor, you would think that they would hate the fallen fighters of the aggressor nation. Nothing could be further from the truth. While it may be that the hearts of many amongst them had been hardened like those of humans elsewhere, they will find that things changed as they were subjected to undeserved humiliations, harassment and torture at the hands of the aggressor.

"It will dawn on them upon leaving this world and entering their afterlife that the fortitude that sustained them in their miseries was a gift of grace pure and simple, and a transforming one at that. They will also recognize that it was in fact none other than the Deliverer and Judge who merited the grace by His own suffering and death, and who had in turn dispensed it to them in their time of trial through His Holy Spirit.

"They will also understand at that point that the humiliations, harassment and torture, and their demise at the hands of the aggressors were things that in fact constituted a gift of sorts - an opportunity to identify themselves with the Deliverer, a member of the Godhead, who Himself endured untold humiliation at the hands of sinful humans when He consented to be their Mediator with His father and also their Deliverer.

"They will be so taken aback by that incomprehensible demonstration of love that they will not hesitate to forgive all their enemies one and all, and to wish them well. Following this turn of events, they will go all out to beg the Judge and the Deliverer to also forgive the fallen enemy fighters and to free them from their detention in 'Guantanamo'.

"Now, it is true that all the foregoing is based on hypothesis - the hypothesis that the war of aggression was defensible and entirely justified. But unfortunately, in the divine court of justice, the onus is on the aggressor to demonstrate beyond any reasonable doubt that the campaign or rather aggression was justified. And there is of course no point in trying to spin stories or tell lies when one is before the judge and everything that humans did behind doors or in secret is laid bare for all to see.

"Lies have no place up there - you try to put on a straight face to mask falsehoods that you would like to manufacture, and the mask you thought was firmly in place just falls away revealing the deceitfulness and the rot at the core of your being to all and sundry.

"If you didn't know why it is said that hell is down in the bowels of the earth and not up there, you now know the reason. As the Author of Lies, I had to be cast out from the heavens into this wretched place deep in the bowels of the earth - this hell in which I now languish together with the other lying angels who automatically turned into demons and the souls of lying humans who fell prey to my wiles. And you'd better understand well what I mean by 'liar'. Included among liars are all those folks who are made in the Image, but who are habitually trying to stifle their consciences so that they can go on munching on forbidden fruit from the Tree of Life without any botheration from their 'inner man'.

"It goes without saying that it is really myself here in the Pit and my troops who will end up overall losers when humans also jump on the bandwagon and also lie their way into hell. It will be crushing for us to realize that all the work we put in to get one group of humans to turn against another for selfish reasons netted us only those souls that were really hardened in sin and that according deserved eternal damnation. But, overall, our own campaign to sow seeds of death among humans will have ended up in failure.

"But why should I belabor the point. It will become crystal clear on the Day of Judgement, regardless of whether humans with hardened hearts make it to heaven or here in the abyss with us, that whenever they *actively sought to have their own way* or did what they fancied, they invariably *ended up doing what they became inclined to do* after Adam and Eve fell from grace. It will likewise become evident how it came about that whenever *grace was given a chance*, as humans eschewed their wilfulness, *it took over* and humans ended up performing virtuous acts. Yes, actually doing good works - things they ordinarily were disinclined to do - through a 'miracle' of divine grace!

"And that - if I may add - completely exposes the fallacy of the doctrine of *sola fide*. Humans are saved, not by faith alone, but by faith *and* good works! All humans have talents they are expected to work with and even 'turn a profit' in the course of doing so. But because they of their inclination to sin, it would be hypocritical for humans to take any credit - much less *full* credit - for their good works. This is even though it was *cooperation* with divine grace that made any human activity meritorious or pleasing in the eyes of the Prime Mover.

"Despite being inclined to sin, humans have an obligation as creatures to follow their Maker's injunctions. They do not have the power to create a *moral order* of their own choice. While the spirit must be 'willing', it is divine grace - a gift of the Prime Mover - that becomes the enabling agent or force to save them from perdition. They can only be thankful, and are ill-advised to brag. They certainly shouldn't do so to my face or else...

"It is true that when you are a cripple on a stretcher - a spiritual cripple on a metaphysical but nonetheless *real* stretcher - you really cannot pretend that you can get up and run anywhere. And, you can bet that I know what being on that kind of stretcher is - I know what it is like to be spiritually dead and incarcerated in a 'hell hole'! But you humans still pretend that you can get up from the stretcher and take off to some place!

Ask...

"The point I want to make is that it all really boils down to a word, and that word is 'Ask'! Did the Deliverer - the one who merited all those graces some humans think they can 'steal' - not say: 'Ask and ye shalt receive. Knock and it shall be opened.' Good thing you humans remain dumb and won't even grasp the import of that! Because your problems would be solved if you headed blindly to your church, temple - or what have you - and flopped down on your knees and prayed, not like the Pharisee, but like the tax collector!

"And His mother said it all when, realizing that the groom could not afford to provide all the guests with drinks, said to the waiters: 'Whatsoever he shall say to you, do ye.' But He would himself make it even clearer than that when He said: 'For every one that asketh receiveth; and he that seeketh findeth; and to him that knocketh it shall be opened.' This was even as He warned: 'Beware of false prophets, who come to you in the clothing of sheep, but inwardly they are ravening wolves. By their fruits you shall know them. Do men gather grapes of thorns, or figs of thistles?'

"Yeah, He knew full well I would still be around and working hard, with the help of my minions, to try and derail His divine plan!

"Earthlings! How could you - you who cannot even foresee how or when your trust in the Prime Mover will be put to the test and you who frequently are yourselves the source of the temptations - be able on your own, without the intervention of divine grace, resist any of my insinuations! And, certainly, not when you humans are yourselves now inclined to do evil rather than to do good!

"When I tempt a human, I do so primarily by working on his/her psyche - or spiritually. Of course, when the Prime Mover 'does things' or works, He does so in an infinitely more refined way - because he is after all the Prime Mover. He can help a human by just showing him or her that my temptation is what it is - reprehensible and not worthy of any attention. Or, he can decide to 'bless' a good soul by allowing me and my fellow demons to thoroughly harass that soul in the proverbial 'dark night of the soul'!

"Any soul, presuming to be capable of fending off my temptations on its own without the help of divine grace, would assuredly end up 'possessed' by us and lost for ever. It would never survive the sheer onslaught of the temptations we would send that soul's way!

How the Prime Mover operates...

"Now, the ways of the Prime Mover, which are both mysterious and incomprehensible, are by definition completely different from the ways of humans. But, first, what does the Prime Mover look like exactly? Or is this, perhaps, a completely stupid question? If we could gauge anything of this from His many works of creation (His works of art) the most illustrious of which are angels and humans, what would you say His likes and dislikes are? He liked the results of His creative effort for sure, because he deigned to send His only begotten Son into the world to show humans who had gone astray the way.

"And, boy, did the Son of Man not show humans the way to properly appreciate the works of His Father and also His own love for them - a love that was infinite. And the Son of Man also challenged humans who had stumbled badly and were still inclined to the notion that he was asking too much of them, to pull up their socks.

"He certainly did not leave the impression humans gave that to appreciate the Prime Mover's works of art, one had to climb down from the spiritual heights and embrace self-love and self-indulgence in any form, let alone plumb down into the vile and the sordid. And that is not the same as saying that humans would find it easy to live up to the challenge!

"The bottom line though is that the way the Prime Mover does things or operates in general isn't the same way creatures - and certainly humans - operate. Certainly the way the Prime Mover sanctifies the actions of earthlings through the workings of His grace is completely different from the way the earthlings themselves think happens.

"That should not be surprising. Humans themselves need legs to move, and initially have even to do it on all fours. They need toes to steady themselves, arms to grab things and fingers to fasten on to the crude implements they use to ease their toil, and that works only if their design permits them to operate in strict accordance with the laws of nature. And, except for dosing off and going to sleep, humans have to always remember to apply their God-given intelligence throughout any operation to minimize the chances of loosing toes, fingers and other accidents that could prove fatal. Even when they go to sleep, they must remember to choose the spot wisely, or they could end up falling to their deaths if they dosed off near cliffs. They could end up causing really bad accidents if they dosed off while at the wheel.

"And, then, the time inevitably comes when humans die - or figuratively kick the bucket that all dying people supposedly see standing in their way as they proceed to their afterlife. Preachers admonish that that bucket is filled with the accumulated guilt for sins committed by folks from the time they are born to the time they are depart to join their ancestors. No wonder humans feel the urge to kick it aside as they prepare to enter their afterlife in the nether world.

"The Prime Mover, on the other hand, by definition could not be subject to any changes either natural or supra-natural, let alone a transformation of that nature! I mean - unlike humans, He is not confined by time and space. He doesn't even have to think - he is intelligence *par excellence*. That is the sort of 'thing' or *esse* He is. Like the Son of Man, the Prime Mover-is-who-is! Or do you not agree? The divine grace He dispenses operates in a similar fashion.

"The most gracious act on the part of the Prime Mover was to give His only begotten Son - begotten in eternity - to the world, so that those who believe in Him might be saved. Those, I might add, who not only believe in Him, but also take advantage of the grace-giving sacraments the Deliverer instituted when He established his Church.

"Now, the Prime Mover is always good at what He does; and this is especially true as regards his dealings with the evil minded and the wicked of the world. Simply stated, He gets them to fix themselves. He gives them rope with which to go hang themselves – almost in so many words! The Prime Mover's beloved, who have been assured solemnly by the Deliverer that they are all worth far more than the sparrow that are sold for a farthing, have also been warned that they ought not fear those who kill the body but cannot kill the soul. And with that, the Prime Mover lets the acts of commission and omission of the wicked bear the fruit that damns them. The more lies are portrayed as truth and truth as lies, the more damning it all gets. It is all the more despicable when those in positions of trust - like pastors and politicians for instance - set out to con the gullible.

"And here's the best part of it for us here in the Pit. There are those wicked humans who really belong with us evil demons, and who do not have any scruples about using their persuasive powers to lull innocent souls into placing trust in them, before turning around and seducing them, and stealing their innocence. We here in Gehenna cannot have enough of this; but you can bet that such scandalous behavior which involves the violation of trust - and which behavior the perpetrators would incidentally never wish to see their own loved ones exposed to - drives the Deliverer to the edge! For some reason, it never strikes these stupid fools that they assuredly will check in here in due course for their pains; or that, when they do, our instructions are to place millstones about their necks so that they speed to the bottom of hell. Yeah, and that is exactly as it is written in the Gospels!

"The reason I myself am called the Father of Lies and I roast here in hell is because, being a master in the art of masquerade, I con, lie, deceive and mislead whilst wearing the disguise of the eminently trustful advisor and guardian of sacred truths.

"On their own, earthlings can only sin. And, inclined to sin, they do not just prefer lies to Truth, but many even imagine that they can actually lie their way into heaven! With that in mind, we here in the Pit long ago learned that the payback from our endeavors would be far greater if we concentrated our efforts on shining as much light on Truth as possible. And that is why I trumpet the facts regarding the *sancta ecclesia catholica*, apostolic succession, the holy sacraments, and all that. Because then, all I need to do is be alert and ready to move in for the kill when it becomes obvious that the "poor forsaken children of Adam and Eve" are failing to live up to expectations!"

Mjomba had not been prepared for anything like this. Here was the devil, the evilest of evil creatures and the Father of Lies, trying to get the seminaran to buy the lie that he, Satan, respected truth! But by now, it reallt wasn't Mjomba who was in control of his thoughts. It was the devil, and the lad knew it. He threw up his arms in disgust and continued to commit the things the devil was mouthing to paper faithfully.

"The reaction of humans - who instinctively recoil at being told what to do, and many of whom subscribe to the belief that while greed 'might not be good, it works' - naturally is to scramble and stay as far away from the authority of the *sancta ecclesia catholica* and its message of the 'Crucified Deliverer' as they possibly can" the Evil One pursued!

"Whereupon, in their ignorance of the righteousness of the Prime Mover, and going about to establish their own righteousness, they submit not themselves unto His righteousness! So you can see that, while testifying to the truth might be a good thing in and of itself, when it comes to earthlings and their last end, it really works only for me, Satan and the Father of Lies!

"And that is what makes me, the Father of lies, so dangerous. Although a murderer from the beginning, and I do abide not in the Truth, because there is no Truth in me, as Saul - that Apostle of the Gentiles - wrote, earthlings need to be terrified of me and what I might do. For one, in the same way I deceived Adam and Eve using my craftiness and subtlety, so I can easily corrupt the minds of their descendants, and lure them away from the single-minded devotion to their Deliverer in humility.

"That is how I go about 'seducing' humans. And, of course, the greater my own success, and the success of wicked humans in concealing the true effects of their machinations as they pursue temporal gains at the expense of other humans, the more terrible for us. And this is all the more so because all lies are not just premeditated, they are also the ones that make us murders! Does that ring a bell? Think of the names by which I go by: "Father of Lies" and "Father of Death"!

"And guess who the father of liars is! It is me, Old Scratch, who "does not stand in the truth, because there is no truth in me"! As Ezekiel put it (some 570 years before the promised Deliverer's arrival), was once called the 'anointed cherub that covereth' I was described then as 'full of wisdom, and perfect in beauty'. I was the embodiment of created perfection, and I led the worship of the universe. I was in the 'mountain of the Prime Mover,' where He manifests His glory; and I was 'perfect' in my ways until 'iniquity' developed in me. But I became swollen with pride because of my beauty and my wisdom, and I fell just by reason of the way I shone. Unholy ambition and jealousy ruined me, and resulted in my leading a host of angels in rebellion against the Prime Mover and the Deliverer. And I was 'cast out of the mountain of the Prime Mover, and down to this God-forsaken earth'!

"The earthlings who are wedded to lies always want the Deliverer - the one who did not merely come from the Prime Mover, but who was actually sent by the Prime Mover - dead! If you do not believe me, go look up John 8:39-47! And when my minions are puffed up and think they are learned and see, that is actually a sign that they are blind! But it is those who follow the Deliverer 'blindly' and cry out aloud 'Have mercy on us, Son of David' whose eyes become opened; and, as they receive their sight, their faith in the Deliverer makes them whole.

"But I should also give you some idea how I operate. Take the so-called 'reformation' that I engineered. Believe it or not, but it was my idea. I used Martin Luther, a Catholic friar - yes, and a good one at that - and a reformer, to set it in motion. In his battles with the conservatives in the Church - neo-conservatives actually - who were turning a blind eye to and virtually sanctioning the various types of abuses that were rampart at the time, he lost out, and was promptly 'excommunicated'. He had underestimated the extent of their influence and power.

"But he was luckier than Joan of Arc who was labeled a witch and burned at the stake! You may or may not like to hear it, but I also succeeded in using that innocent girl to confound and drive other good souls in the Church to virtual despair. As a result of the persecution Joan of Arc endured, over the years many a good soul in the world has chosen to part company with the 'Church' which got her to pay for the 'witch-craft' she supposedly practiced with her life!

Fake champions...

"You humans have long ways to go - you do not even have a clue regarding the way we in the Underworld operate. We use conservatives and neo-conservatives, as well as liberals and neo-liberals in the Church to ensnare folks and to make the work of evangelization as difficult as possible. That is why there will always be folks who ostensibly 'champion' the Church's teachings, but end up causing so many problems for the 'visible Church' just because they do things out of self-love, and it is actually not the Holy Spirit that is inspiring or guiding them. Indeed, there are so many Church functionaries who end up betraying the Deliverer and getting Him nailed to the cross (exactly as happened in the year thirty-three *Anno Domini*) while being cheered on by the 'faithful'.

"I can tell you that there are people in the Church today who operate exactly like those priests and Pharisees did two thousand years ago. Others operate like Judas Iscariot. The Deliverer did not say that it was the last that we were going to see of the betrayer, even though He did say that it would have been better if he (Judas Iscariot) had not been born - whatever that means! The Son of Man, going His way (as He Himself put it), did not have time to stop and ask Judas why he, of all people, was doing that to Him. The Deliverer did not even regard it as worth the trouble to ask the man who was His treasurer for an accounting of the monies that His admirers and other kind people had been contributing for His up-keep and that of his disciples.

"Then there are others in the Church who operate like Peter, the first pope who openly denied ever knowing the Deliverer - not once but three times within the space of one short hour! Others operate like the Roman soldiers, who actually drove the nails into the Deliverer's hands before hoisting Him up on the wooded cross. There are others still who operate like Thomas, the doubter.

"They all operate as they do because there is this tendency to keep the Spirit sent by the Deliverer in abeyance - they do not give Him a chance to strengthen them in the different virtues. And yet, that Spirit is what you call a *sine qua non* for their salvation and that of the world. And - guess what - when humans fail to give the Holy Spirit an opportunity to work with them, they effectively hand me - Satan - my chance to meddle.

Real champions...

"And as the Son of Man went His way and went about his work of redeeming the world, bearing His cross and His crown of thorns - after having been betrayed by one of the twelve, denied by another, and abandoned by the rest - people who did not even belong to the Fellowship he had started in preparation for launching the Church on the day of Pentecost were there when He needed them.

"There was Simon of Cyrene, the African on a mysterious mission in the Roman enclave of Judea, who turned up from no where and helped to ensure that the Deliverer would bear His load of the cross all the way to the summit of Calvary. Then there was Mary Magdalene, a woman who (according to a popular legend) knew what to be a 'person of disrepute' meant, and who (if it is true) decided to cast aside fears that she herself might be recognized and stoned to death by the mob for her former lifestyle, and offered to wipe away blood steins, dust and other dirt that were clogging onto the Deliverer's eyebrows and causing Him additional pain as he stumbled along on the murrum road leading to Mt. Calvary with a clean damp cloth.

"His face bloated from the blows of the soldiers from being scourged, beaten and manhandled by the creatures that nevertheless were fashioned in the Image, as man, the Deliverer may not have been able to see his way Image as He stumbled along to the 'place of the skulls'. However, as a member of the Godhead, the Savior of Humankind could not help but discern the hunched back of Cain as, brimming with a sense of self-importance, he murdered his brother Abel. And the same went for all the terrible things that human throughout the ages have done to each other. And, of all the crimes committed by humans against humanity, there was of course none that was more loathsome and crying out for divine vengeance more than the convoluted pleasures that humans led by Pilate, Agrippa and priests and Pharisees, derived from the pain and sufferings endured by the Son of Man on that Good Friday."

"And then there was Joseph of Arimathea, a secret admirer of the Deliverer who offered what would become Christendom's most important destination for pilgrims - the tomb in which He would be buried by the women and from which he would rise in triumph after spending three days with Adam, Eve, Moses, and the others whom my troops held as prisoners in hell.

"Pontius Pilate, the fox, was of course the exact opposite of these other folks. He saw this completely innocent Nazarene - not an insurgent or a terrorist, but an upright soul that everyone of good will in Judea knew could never be accused of any wrong doing - being prepared for the kill by those blood thirsty priests and Pharisees. Instead of ordering an immediate halt to their fragrant and sickening gambit, he sought instead to ingratiate himself with the murderers by legitimizing it. He was quite comfortable presiding over the greatest miscarriage of justice the world had ever seen and, indeed, would ever see!

"Incidentally, is it not telling that the apostle who betrayed the Deliverer was not just His purse bearer, but someone so close that he and the Deliverer frequently shared the same chalice when wine and other refreshments were served? There have, conceivably, been other 'apostles' of the Deliverer who have ostensibly 'taken care' of the

Church's affairs while believing that they could serve mammon at the same time!

"It is clearly to Martin Luther's credit that, even as he was being excommunicated by the 'neocons', he was reportedly emphasizing that it was 'by grace alone' that humans were saved! Not by wilfulness or self-righteousness, but only by the grace of the Prime Mover. But did that good Catholic friar really mean that good works were unnecessary?

"That was, in all probability, the misinformation that Luther's adversaries started spreading about him - the misinformation which they used to nail his fate. After all, it must have been Martin Luther's intention, as he nailed his thesis onto the cathedral's double doors, to make that act a symbol of a good job well done in challenging the neocons to an argument - a good work he himself at least believed had the Holy Spirit behind it. And so, without a doubt, Martin Luther, as the good Catholic he was, believed that humans were saved by faith in the Deliverer (or His grace) *and* good works.

"If anything, it was his adversaries who seemed to believe in salvation by faith alone without good works, because they were not particularly bothered about the importance of appropriate behavior - especially behavior that was befitting of functionaries of Holy Mother the Church. Thus, the neocons had not challenged the popes when they kept concubines in the Vatican. But they felt the need to try and stop Martin Luther because he had decided that it was time to come out and, instead of mincing words, argue his case forcefully - even if the merits of his arguments were going to be completely ignored and the focus was going to be on the fact that he had volunteered arguments that were *ad hominem*, and were for that reason not particularly welcome!

The meaning of "holiness"...

"Now, I find any discussion of 'holiness' juicy - don't ask why! So, what does it mean to be holy any way?

"Holiness is eschewing doing your own will and allowing divine grace to be your motive force and to inspire you in whatever you do. That is not the same as giving up your personal autonomy and allowing yourself to be dominated by others, regardless of whether their intentions are good or bad, and being compelled thereby to do their will blindly. You could do that and still be wilful - you might seek to be subservient to others perhaps as a way of avoiding trouble or personal responsibility.

"Holiness is subjecting your will to the will of the Prime Mover, and allowing the Holy Spirit to sanctify your actions. The challenge is making sure it is the will of the Prime Mover and not that of one of my demons for instance.

"The essence of holiness is living an innocent life - just as children do. They do not intend harm for any one, and are selfless even as they grow in personal autonomy and learn to survive in the world. Holiness is not shutting yourself off and being a quietist with no personal aspirations in life. And it certainly doesn't consist in going out and imposing your beliefs on others against their will - or practicing hate under the guise of witnessing to the faith!

"You cannot seek to do your will and the will of the Prime Mover at one and the same time. You are either doing one or the other. You could be married to doing your will, but habitually blame the Prime Mover or your fellow men - or me - instead of yourself for the consequences. You bet that there are always consequences for what you humans do or do not do.

"When you are wilfully involved in this or that, and having your way, you actually are having your reward in the real sense of that word. And because you automatically shut out the Prime Mover in the process, you also forfeit your eternal life in so doing. If you are selfless and above all accepting of others as little children typically do, you are certainly not rewarding yourself in any way.

"That is why those who do not loose their innocence are automatically in for a reward in their afterlife - a reward suitable for individuals who were not prepared to sell their birth-right to a heavenly mansion for some passing self-indulgence, and would even have been willing to loose their lives to retain that birthright. Humans retain a certain amount of innocence when they commit venial sins, but loose it entirely when they commit mortal sins.

"It should be pretty obvious by now that it is not the enjoyment itself, derived from indulgence of the self, that is reprehensible. The enjoyment *per se* wouldn't cause humans - or for that matter angels - to miss out on their heavenly reward. It is the wilfulness and the ill intentions accompanying it that makes one pay the price. It couldn't be otherwise, because in so far as the 'pleasure' or 'satisfaction' the reprehensible acts themselves give, the Prime Mover, who made all that exists, blessed it all after He was done with His labors of creation, and declared that everything was good.

"He did not say that about the different choices that humans would subsequently make because he wanted them to retain the freedom to choose between what was morally good and what was morally bad. And He certainly did not 'bless' wilfulness, a potential (bad) option that would still be available to (free) humans. Similarly, any suggestion that actions in themselves could be bad would detract from the infinite goodness of the Prime Mover. And if He ordained that creatures with free wills should not be capable of wilfulness (detrimental as it was to them), that would have conflicted with the fact that the Prime Mover was infinitely generous and also almighty. It would have signalled that the Prime Mover was afraid of having free creatures around Him - that they might cause Him inconvenience that conceivably could prove deadly for Him.

"Humans who parent and others who fill the role of mentor, unlike the Prime Mover who is also a parent and a mentor, frequently choose to lord it over those under their charge and, in flagrant violation of the rights of those they are supposed to groom, end up treating them as though they were automatons with no right to the exercise of their free will. Some humans end up treating fellow humans as second class citizens or even as chattel.

"Since wilful acts of that nature are neither sanctioned nor blest by the Prime Mover, those humans perpetrating them can take it that they have already received their reward in this life and should not bother to look for another reward in their afterlife.

"And so, what does 'being saved' mean? To be saved is to become like a little child and thereby facilitate cooperation with divine grace; and the verdict can only come after the individual has left this life for the next. This is because, when humans are still alive and kicking and free as birds, the possibility that they could go nuts - as they are always doing - and rebel against the Prime Mover (as the first man and the first woman did) will always be there. It is the reason a human could never be canonized before that human had left this world for his/her afterlife.

"And what would be the 'signs', if any, that a human was cooperating with divine grace? One sign would be if the human in question was not involved in murder or theft - or if he/she was not giving in to the urge to be a con artist of some sort, like putting on the appearance of being truthful and saintly (as I myself am busy doing just now) when he/she was all rotten on the inside and just pulling people's legs! It would also be an indication that a human was cooperating with grace if that human was prepared to lay down his/her life for his/her 'neighbor'; or if he/she loved, not his/her friends, but his/her enemies.

"There is no other way to heaven. There are no short cuts. And the sacraments play a very special role in helping humans stay the course because they provide the link to the Deliverer who is the way, the life and the truth.

"The exercise of virtue is always heroic. Any exercise of virtue has to be heroic for the simple reason that it implies self-denial. The candidate for sainthood has to be prepared to forego wilfulness. This is the wilfulness that wants to determine where the human wants to go and that seeks to control everything around one and to exploit it. And this is a complete waste of time, because 'what does it profit a man to possess the whole world and to lose one's soul in the process'.

"Now, humans have to give Caesar what is Caesar's, and to God what is God's. Everything, including the breath of life that sustains humans, is owed by humans to the Prime Mover - everything is His. And, in point of fact, there is really nothing that you could say belongs to Caesar. Nothing! The Deliverer was just being polite when he told his audience to give to Caesar what was Caesar's, you dumb fools!

"He certainly wasn't endorsing imperialism. And, anyway, how could dead men own anything? Julius Caesar, who had succeeded his father Gaius Caesar, had been dead many years, stabbed to death by his best friend Brutus. Gaius Octavius, the self-styled Imperator Caesar Augustus and first Roman Emperor who reigned at the time the Deliverer was born, was also already dead and buried. And the unpopular Tiberius Caesar Augustus could not get out of the way fast enough for the impatient Caligula who could not wait to be crowned Gaius Julius Caesar Augustus Germanicus and third Roman Emperor; and the days of the Roman Empire itself - the sole super power - were numbered.

"And the only way for a human to give God what is God's is to subject his/her will to His instead of trying to redefine or rewrite the Moral Law the Prime Mover etched on the consciences of the creatures that bear His image and live on in an afterlife. That doesn't leave humans very much in terms of possessions. By subjecting themselves to the divine will, they also automatically place whatever they might have at His disposal! And that is why the decision to do so doesn't come easy - particularly for grown-ups and the affluent.

"It is also a very humiliating thing to do in the eyes of a world that does not recognize an afterlife and seeks to maximize the here and now. It could not be anything but that in a world that derides or does not recognize the spiritual, and glorifies killing and even stealing and things of that nature.

"And humans do not really have a choice - if they want to do the right thing. After they find themselves in a world in which evil reigns supreme and in which the best efforts cannot by themselves guarantee them and their loved ones anything, the only viable option becomes just that: electing to carry out the will of the Prime Mover and Author of Life as they are admonished in the Lord's Prayer.

The essence of being devilish...

"And so, what does being devilish or satanic mean? What does it really mean to be a transgressor - like me? What sets humans who transgress apart from humans who are godly? In other words, what do devilish humans or sinners look like? How do they act or sound?

"Well, even though a pure spirit, I myself have been called a murderer - every 'killing' in fact has my personal seal. That should give you clues about devilish humans. They will be above all murderers. Taking the lives of others is the singular badge of honor that all my minions and ambassadors proudly wear. Of course that badge will also come in all colors and shades - rooting out terrorists; attacking the interests of this or that murderous regime; defending civilization; religious crusades, and what have you.

"As soon as humans start believing that they are masters of their own lives, they start imagining that they can be masters of other humans as well. They don't stop at thinking that they can have others revere them as gods, or at enslaving fellow humans.

"They also start believing that they might even have a licence to kill - just like James Bond of James Hadley Chase fame. That is also when, completely oblivious to the existence of the Avenging Angel, they actually start scheming how to systematically plunder and steal, and murder their fellow humans through declared and undeclared wars.

"It is bad enough for talented kids or 'punks' in some inner-city ghetto to cut down each other prematurely in a 'senseless' spurt of 'gang' warfare. And it is more terrible when nations go to war - especially unjustified wars - if for no reason than that the lives of 'talented' humans on all sides will be prematurely ended."

Emoì Ekdíkesis (Vengeance is Mine saith the Lord)...

"When humans get overtaken by some misfortune, their first inclination is to look around for scapegoats, with the intention of marshalling the wherewithal to strike back. Stupid humans don't even realize that when they encounter miseries that ensue from actions of their fellow humans, they are expected to bear them in the same way they ought to bear miseries inflicted upon them by natural disasters! They are even expected to turn the other cheek! But well - we in the Underworld shouldn't even be surprised that so many humans are unbelievers or believers only in name!

"The stupid humans will do quite stupid things, like investing in treasure and blood in the pursuit not just of those they figure have wronged them, but any group of people who look like they were remotely allied to the suspected culprits! And this is also the time when the whole world suddenly takes on a strange new look; a world that namely is divided into two parts, with one part ostensibly united against the supposed victims, and the other part against them! So, so stupid!

"And, in such times, humans typically start doing all sorts of foolish things even before they have taken the trouble to establish the facts. How on earth for example, can a group of humans however important or, a country for that matter, imagine that the whole wide world is either with it or against it when only a small fraction of the earth's inhabitants gets to know what goes on beyond their borders, and the rest wouldn't even care to know?

"Even we demons know about the many instances in the course of human history in which stupid humans, if they had only bothered to look in good faith for the 'real' culprits behind their misfortunes, would have found it was they themselves! They would have discovered to their pleasant surprise that the culprits were either actions on their part that caused others to become justifiably aggrieved to the point of driving them to take what could be characterised as 'defensive' actions aimed at signalling that they had had enough of the 'bullying'. And frequently it was actions on the part of former allies - actions that they themselves had initially encouraged and sometimes even underwritten!

"Then humans never stop to think that if they happen to command the means of striking out at their perceived enemies - or the means to 'take the fight to the enemy' - at a given time in history, and they go ahead and do it following their irrational impulse, then they have to expect pay-back the moment those enemies of theirs acquire the means to hit back, and should not complain when that happens! So, so stupid, and so short sighted!

"The countries that invested in weapons of mass destruction and remain poised to use them, and particularly those countries that had the audacity to actually use them, are the ones that are now realizing the obvious at this late stage, namely that no one individual or country has a monopoly over technology or know how; and that oil reserves, uranium, gold or diamond deposits, or some other precious mineral, discovered in the backyard of some basket nation, can alone make all the difference when it comes to owning or not owning the wherewithal to strike out at an 'enemy', using any means, anywhere on globe.

"And, what is worse, in this age of the Worldwide Web, it only requires the ability to hack into computers of the so-called super powers to steal the secrets that are needed to produce and launch unmanned drones, and things of that nature. It is therefore the height of recklessness for any so-called super power to use these things supposedly to inflict damage on its new found enemies who may be perceived as weak and defenceless today, but might, with a bit of luck, be transformed into something else altogether tomorrow. What is even quite obvious, even if it is not acknowledged, is the fact that nations are driven to arm themselves when other nations begin to threaten their sovereignty.

"The only posture that guarantees peace for any nation in these circumstances is that which is based on the adage that humans should make love not war! And look - I am Beelzebub, the Father of Death, and I happen to know what I am talking about more than you stupid humans!

"And, to show that humans are very stupid indeed, in their pursuit of 'revenge', they frequently end up expending in precious treasure and blood many times what was inflicted on them initially by the imaginary culprits, and committing crimes against humanity that often pale in comparison to the 'crimes' they seek to avenge.

Whereas, if they had stopped and just reminded themselves that to pursue revenge was tantamount to usurping the prerogative of the Prime Mover, and if they had stayed cool-headed, they might even have learnt from their own past mistakes, cleaned up their own acts; and they not only would have minimized the chances of ruffling other people's feathers, but would have stood a much better chance of winning their real enemies over in the process.

"And guess what - they you would have contributed to the victory of Good over Evil in a spectacular way too! But you can, of course, be sure that I, Beelzebub, would have fought tooth and nail to frustrate any such outcome so long as I remained the unchallenged Ruler of the Underworld!

"Regardless, humans never learn from history, and never stop to consider the price they will in time pay for flagrantly usurping the Prime Mover's prerogatives with their determination to even scores. They lack the foresight to see that their investment in the development of weapons of mass destruction and the means for delivering the same will in time become their own undoing. And also guess what! Those who seek revenge invariably end up being themselves pursued by Him who said '*Emoì Ekdíkesis*' (Vengeance is Mine), because of their own reckless and brazen deeds to their fellow humans!

"And that is the time when the once proud and victorious will beg the mountains and the rocks and say: 'Fall on us and hide us from the face of him who sits on the throne and from the wrath of the Lamb! For the great day of their wrath has come, and who can stand?' It will not be a nice sight!"

Why it is senseless to kill...

"Now, in this matter of killing, it would make some sense if the act of killing caused killers to live on - if killing made them immune to the thing they visited on their opponents, namely death. But, like judges who condemn other humans to death, killers don't become immune to it, and it sometimes even happens that the 'honorable justices' go to meet the Eternal Judge before those they send to death row do. The fact that those who kill themselves die - and kill *because* they are scared stiff of dying themselves - makes acts of killing in fact senseless *per se*.

"By the way, when humans kill, they actually do so for the same reasons that drive the self-willed and the selfish to pursue temporal earthly fulfilment rather than fulfilment in the afterlife that does not end and is eternal. The 'reasons' in either case are based on proven fallacies, and they explain why actions of folks who spend their lives seeking to satisfy 'fantasies' they become unable to entertain when their time on earth is up at any cost and murderers end up making no sense.

"As a matter of fact, no sooner had the first man and the first woman sinned and were driven from out of the Garden of Eden than they begun accusing each other of being murderous, beastly and a 'terrorist'. The stage was set at that time for humans to hound each other for perceived 'ills', while remaining completely blind to their own faults - and even the part they may have played in bringing those ills upon themselves.

"Things were bad enough at the time of Adam and Eve with the ever present possibility that one of them might mortally harm the other before they had been able to raise members of the generation that would succeed them and guarantee the survival of the human race. If anything was clear then, it was the fact that every single human life was sacred and too important to play with. If Eve had succeeded in knocking off Adam in one of her tantrums (or the other way around), that would have been not just a half of humanity but pretty well all of humanity gone to pot! And no earthly soul would ever have known about it!

"Adam himself knocked off Eve on innumerable occasions mentally, whenever he wished her dead for any reason, and she never even suspected it - she similarly murdered Adam on innumerable occasions in her mind without him suspecting that he was in danger. It is a legacy of Adam and Eve's murderous thoughts that humans continue to live like creatures that are accursed, and to abuse and kill each other senselessly.

"The world has already seen so many idiotic 'rulers' who thought that they could subordinate the sanctity of life to their hackneyed theories about the earth's future, keeping a count of them would have been an impossible task. Some of them couldn't resist the idea that they themselves were divine, and accordingly regarded anyone who challenged them as doomed both physically *and* spiritually.

"The world today is actually many times worse off because humans have ceded their personal rights to so-called 'governments' that in turn are largely controlled by greedy, impersonal 'mega-corporations'! Under the guise of conducting business dealings, corporations and their hired guns will use every trick in the book to get you to part with your hard earned cash and property. And governments, particularly those that have ceded control to big business, will stop at nothing in their drive to conquer, dominate and spread their influence in the world.

"My reading of the situation - and this is not an exaggeration - is that three or four decades from now, mega-corporations, not voters, will be deciding who occupies the White House, Number 10 Downing Street, and even the Kremlin- or, don't you believe me?

"Thanks to the success of the 'Manhattan Project' and the existence of corporations that will stop at nothing to make a buck, a disgruntled Bedouin, operating solo in the heart of the Sahara Desert and armed only with an "infra- nu-red", will soon be able to successfully 'neutralize' a super power, before vanishing without a trace!

"The infra-nu-red, currently being tested by one 'rogue state', is a three by five inch computer chip which, when commissioned, will be able to decode just about anything and also to hack into any computer. The idea, of course, is to hack into the computers of military command and control centers of a selected super power, and after raising false alarms to the effect that the nation's cities are under attack from an unknown source, use that opportunity to intercept and decode the ensuing communications from the command and control centers to the field, and then redirect that super power's fire power at itself by substituting key communications with the fake ones!

"The Bedouin will have the alternative of launching his own small but deadly arsenal of missiles tipped with WMD from the back of a camel and guiding them to their targets - command and control centers, densely populated cities, the bunkers in which intercontinental ballistic missiles with their payload of nuclear and hydrogen bombs are concealed, the super power's warships and submarines, and spy satellites - again using infra-nu-red.

"You can bet that the 'pundits' and the 'networks' they serve would then have a field day trying to figure out what on earth happened - the same pundits who hailed the success of the Manhattan Project and who are always ecstatic whenever they discuss the benefits of technology and advantages of free enterprise!

The culture of death...

"You can rest assured that my troops and I have not been resting on our laurels, because today, instead of just demanding to be worshiped as gods, they actually try to act like God while putting up a facade of being God-fearing. Unfortunately for these 'quislings' of mine, all their huffing and hawing amounts to is a dream - the hope or dream that they will be successful in plundering *and* retaining for their sole use the earth's resources to the exclusion of others. Which is just like confiscating a back-hoe from an undertaker and using it to dig your own grave; because, while they are busy fighting for control over the world's riches, others who are also dying for the good life are conserving their energies and just lying in wait and preparing to pounce as soon as the first fools finish doing the 'dirty job' for them - namely 'neutralizing' the newly discovered 'terrorists' and 'insurgents'.

"It is precisely because it is greed and self-interest, usually passed off as 'national security', that the situation in the world is in such flux with borders of states changing almost by the day. Ordinary folk in the resource-rich parts of globe that super powers of the day cannot resist eyeing are usually helpless against the invading armies, occupiers, liberators (or however the aggressor nations elect to call themselves).

"This is a legacy of original sin, has been the case since the immediate descendants of Adam and Eve started fighting over inheritance, and will continue to plague the world until Planet Earth and everything on it goes to waste in a 'terminal' nuclear explosion on the Last Day.

"From time immemorial, 'victors' in war, regardless of whether they came by their victory through luck or simply because the contest was uneven, have never hesitated to label their foes rebels, insurgents or terrorists, while referring to themselves as liberators, and even 'pacifiers'. Forgetting that it was because they themselves were 'terrorists', 'rebels' and 'insurgents' that the Prime Mover sent His only begotten Son into the world to try and 'deliver' them, stupid humans have never had qualms wherever possible to kill or enslave or otherwise humiliate their own.

"Because might makes right according to their contorted reasoning, stupid humans have always been very quick to go for the jugular even when they were the ones committing acts of banditry. They do that in the same breath as they acknowledge that they themselves have been forgiven a great deal; and they conveniently forget that, in the not too distant future, the fact that the things they do to their fellow humans aren't exactly what any of them would have liked to see done to themselves will come to haunt them. The hunger for power and unbridled greed combine to blind humans to the fact that they dig holes for themselves when they turn on each other for any reason.

"When you are inclined to 'go for the jugular' every time you are slighted, you'd better make sure that you are 'perfect'. The problem is that the inclination to 'go for the jugular' is not compatible with perfection. In point of fact, when creatures who are fashioned in the divine image get involved in the business of 'payback', 'an eye for an eye', 'tit for tat', and things of that sort, they automatically infringe on the matters that are the prerogative of the one and the only Divine

One and could not be more presumptuous. Regardless of one's station in life and the authority or power that one ostensibly commands, He has made it crystal clear that taking revenge is *His* sole prerogative.

"And so, when 'payback' is in the form of invasion, occupation or annexation, and other vengeful acts like 'carpet bombing', dropping A-bombs and H-bombs over cities full of fellow humans, or missile strikes on homes aimed at 'taking out suspected terrorists', which are the very things the culprits would not want happen to themselves, the divine 'retribution' is not just predictable. It is assuredly certain and inescapable; and it doesn't come in the form of a counter invasion or occupation, or a missile strike. These are immoral acts for which the perpetrators individually answer at the divine court of justice in due course.

"Now, it is bad enough when humans indulge in murder and mayhem. But it is inexcusable when, completely oblivious to the fact that there is a damned heavy price to be paid for daring to use the name of the Almighty in vain, they try to do those things in the name of the Prime Mover - the Prime Mover whose divine Son was Himself labeled an insurgent and a terrorist, and crucified between two thieves by those who were eyeing his territory.

"He too had territory, you know; Planet Earth and the rest of the interplanetary system which humans, who own nothing but are greedy and expansionist all the same like me, hoped to possess by neutralizing Him. And it now just so happens that when humans kill each other, regardless of whether they do it in His name or not, the target is the Deliverer who chose to identify Himself with suffering humans. He came to redeem humans *because* the Prime Mover is in-dwelling in them; and He sanctified all human suffering by His own death on the cross just because of what He is, namely the Word. That is the essence of the Deliverer being the Second Adam and a 'brother' to all humans.

"Still, ever since Rome was overrun by 'Christians', war-mongering - the culture of death *par excellence* - has had a special appeal for them in the same way it has always appealed to greedy and expansionist humans. So much so in fact that the ranks of 'peaceniks' are filled with ultra-liberal 'non-believers' or pagans, while those who profess to be staunch 'Christians' and pro-life fill the ranks of supporters of the war-mongers.

"Actually, money and the 'culture of death' which is its companion were already at work in the Church even before it's official launch. The actions of Judas Iscariot, the Deliverer's purse bearer, gave a premonition of things to come way back then…Judas Iscariot who sold his Divine Master for thirty pieces of silver - not even gold, mark you, but silver!

"And, not long after the Church had been inaugurated, Ananias showed that even though the Church was operating under the guidance of the Holy Spirit, money matters and all the problems that were associated with the love of money were not going to leave the Church unscathed. Ananias, who thought that money could buy one power and influence in the early Church, was stopped before he could do the Church any harm. But, of course, many others have since succeeded where Ananias did not, and they have left their mark.

"Paul, nee Saul, who would later be known as the 'Apostle of the Gentiles' had been such an avid supporter of the culture of death that the many of those he approached with the new message of forgiveness and love for one another initially thought that he was tricking them and would promptly be back with his death squads. A traitor to his own people who had taken up Roman citizenship, Paul had been a particularly effective hunter of the followers of the 'terrorist from Nazareth', using a 'human intelligence network' that many modern day super powers would envy. He had been such a crafty operator and his reputation as a death squad leader had been such that the mere mention of the name 'Saul' sent shivers down the spine of any devoted follower of the dead terrorist.

"A fervid disciple of the 'Cain doctrine', Paul, even though extremely learned and a virtual 'one man think tank' had operated on the principle that you could liquidate any number of foreigners if the objective was to consolidate and strengthen the authority and reach of the emperor - that the lives of Roman citizens were the only thing that mattered, in as much as the lives of foreigners weren't worth a farthing. Oh, while he was Saul - before he betrayed my cause - that Paul had been such a dandy!

"The way my troops and I prefer to work with the Judases and Ananiases in the upper echelons of the Church's hierarchy today is to get them to focus exclusively on some aspects of death culture and to remain completely silent on others. The objective is to get the 'Church' to forge a theology of the 'culture of death' that does embraces only some but not all instances of that culture. Our success can be gauged from the fact that the 'Church' now blindly throws its weight behind political parties that make no secret of their support for militarism, and the ease with which they will pursue world dominance through the use of force, their open support for capital punishment, and things like that.

"And so, a political party that for instance puts on a show of being disenchanted with 'abortion laws' on the books will receive the Church's whole-hearted support, even if the policies which that party openly advocates - for instance policies that rely on crippling 'economic sanctions' and 'preemptive regime changes using overwhelming force' to promote its ideological goals and establish the country as an 'insuperable super power' - cause intolerable sufferings to millions of innocent humans and spell death for millions more *and* reinforce the belief that human life is valueless.

"Just to think that the Church's leadership, which should be preaching the sanctity of life, hosts figures whose lives are devoted to waging wars and other death culture enterprises, and sees no problem being hosted in turn by those death culture enthusiasts! It certainly says something about our decidedly enormous influence over both churchmen and those worldly rulers along with their henchmen.

"In an attempt to legitimize the culture of death, humans unashamedly depict the Prime Mover as also indulging in it. They, of course, do not say 'God killed so many humans...'. But that is exactly what they mean when they say: 'Lightning killed him or her'; or 'The avalanche buried them alive'; or 'The earthquake killed everyone in the collapsed building'. And they always imply that the Prime Mover kills with a vengeance. Perverse humans!

"They absolve themselves from all blame, and ignore the real reasons why most of the calamities occur, like the greed for money which is behind logging in the Amazon forests, drilling for oil in Alaska and elsewhere, and the failure to implement policies that would minimize pollution and global warming. Then, when these things interfere with the seasons - when the glaciers melt and cause the waters to break banks and ravage home, or when hurricanes suddenly strike, they blame everything on '*El Niño*', which is just a pseudonym for 'Prime Mover'.

"And so, instead of blaming the real culprits for killing people, they now have this habit of blaming God. It is like two nations that lob nuclear bombs - or, better, weapons of mass destruction that are invisible to the eye - at each other's cities and then decry the destruction caused by 'the elements'. Instead of tracing the real cause of wild forest fires, namely environmental policies that are crafted with the help energy corporations and have resulted in a depleted ozone layer, lightning - and implicitly the Prime Mover - is blamed!

"But, talking about invisible WMD - the human immunodeficiency virus (HIV) which spreads by replicating its genetic information and then makes its victim catch the acquired immunodeficiency syndrome (AIDS) is one such weapon that one super power developed at the height of the Cold War, and then tested on 'ladies of the twilight' in an African port city. It is obvious from the way the virus operates that its building blocks were artificially assembled under controlled conditions and specifically designed to kill or disable humans en masse by rendering their immune systems inoperable.

"If the virus was not cultured in test tubes in a laboratory and was natural, there wouldn't it is pretty obvious that there would be no human left on earth. For one, the virus wouldn't have waited all this time to strike, doing so just by sheer coincidence at the height of the cold war. Any one can tell it is a man made virus from its name: 'HIV/AIDS virus'. I am Beelzebub, and you can take it from me that the HIV/AIDS virus is a lab produced, genetically mutated organism that was designed to be resistant to medication. It was designed to be fatal.

"The field test was successful in that the unwary guinea pigs died as had been intended. But the genetically engineered virus did not kill its victims as fast as it had been hoped. The result was that by the time its first victims died of it months - and, in some cases, years - later, they had unknowingly passed the incurable condition on to their clients who in turn passed it on to other 'ladies of the twilight' and eventually to their own spouses.

"This explains the initial incidence of the pandemic along routes taken by truckers as they moved truck loads of imported cargo inland from the port. It goes against the grain to try and argue that the virus originally came from an African monkey. If that had been the case (and assuming the African monkey population had not been interfered with by that super power's researchers in modern times), the HIV/AIDS virus (like other known natural viruses) would have appeared on earth centuries ago and wouldn't be the completely new phenomenon it was when it struck at the time it did.

"It does not take a rocket scientist to tell that the HIV/AIDS virus was cultured in test tubes and is not a 'product of nature'. It should be obvious to anyone that this disease or condition (as it was initially - and also very aptly - described) is man-made. Some originally harmless virus - perhaps the virus that causes the common cold - was mutated under controlled conditions in a lab and deliberately made a killer virus resistant to any form of treatment.

"It would undoubtedly be quite simple to develop an effective antidote or vaccine for the HIV/AIDS virus if it were possible to retrace all the steps in its development. The antidote or vaccine would then be engineered to disable the virus at the different stages of development in the infected victims. But the original blueprints used in creating this virus have almost certainly been discarded by now to conceal the disease's origin, and shield those responsible for this crime against humankind from facing justice - on Planet Earth. The alternative is to try blindly to develop a medicinal concoction that will disable the killer virus's functions by pure chance. I am not the devil for nothing. And, of course, you humans are quite free to ignore this advice that am providing *gratis* - at your peril.

"Talking about HIV/AIDS and weapons of mass destruction, the condom - that much vaunted (and also maligned) weapon of choice against the HIV virus - can also be an WMD in so many ways. For one, it can guarantee the extinction of the human race in just one hundred years if, in a bid to minimize the risk of catching the HIV/AIDS virus, all sexually active male without any exception decided to use the condom unfailingly in accordance with the advice of the 'experts'.

"But the condom can actually be quite an effective means of transmitting the AIDS virus - and probably is for individuals who opt for certain lifestyles. Regardless of the number and strength of the condoms worn by the 'macho-man' who has no scruples about engaging in a group sexual encounter involving two or more female partners, the 'safe sex' will not be safe at all - at least not for his female partners, because if only one was infected at the beginning of the escapade, all will be at the end of it. And it is not only the condom that can act as the carrier of the virus. Anything could act as the carrier - fingers, the tongue, and what have you - depending on the lifestyles that humans opt for.

"And so, individual humans (if they are not careful) can self-destruct by failing to restrain themselves and going after all sorts of fads and blindly aping other humans whose 'untested and untried' ways leave them exposed to 'unknown' dangers. You might not know it, but it was the pining of the first man and the first woman for a strange new 'lifestyle' that involved feasting on fruit from the Tree of Life that made them so susceptible to temptation, and specifically to my cockeyed suggestion that they would become like the Prime Mover if they went ahead and feasted on the forbidden fruit!

"Another good example of self-destructive humans are demagogues who latch onto the notion that they are more special than other humans and, oblivious to the fact that they are on trial like everyone one else, start to believe that the lives of other humans are expendable and can be sacrificed at their personal whims to their own interests. Since time immemorial demagogues, particularly when controlled by special interest groups, have been virtual WMD who traditionally left a trail of death and destruction in their path.

"And the demagogues never learn from history - that it is but a matter of time (counted in years not centuries) before they and their henchmen come face to face with their victims in the court of divine justice. If they didn't, all *our* work which goes into grooming them to take up the reins of power, guiding and sustaining them through their murderous exploits, and above all ensuring that they stay focused on worldly things to the very end, would come to naught. And that is one thing that we will not allow to happen.

"The fact is that when humans who have blood on their hands eventually get to the other side of the gulf that separates the living from the dead, and they suddenly come face to face with those who died at their hands, it is a fate that is always many times worse than the fate suffered by their victims regardless of how those victims met their end. As far as traumatic experiences go, the trauma of being caught in a burst of cluster bombs or a fuselage of rocket fire launched from a 'Blackhawk' cannot compare with the shock of confronting those you thought you had effectively rubbed out upon entering your afterlife!

"It is bad enough that humans, stained with original sin (with the exception of the Son of man and His Blessed Mother), must die and go to judgement. But it is simply too bad when human beings go to their judgement and are confronted by those they killed - each one of whom, by divine decree, will be howling for his/her killer's pound of flesh! I can assure you that no scene could be more theatrical or dramatic (for those of you who become transfixed by theatre and drama) than that encounter as killers come face to face with their victims on the other side of the gulf.

"Those who delighted at the sight of their victims cringing in fear, and who entertained strange notions about being ordained to rule roughshod over the other poor forsaken humans and about their own immortality, will wish they had never been born. The tables will be verily turned as those who were given to swaggering and had everyone at their mercy wail and, too late, beseech those they once enjoyed tormenting for mercy. It is also at that time that the beatitudes that are now ridiculed and equated with insanity will be completely validated. The meek who are dismissed as idiots will find themselves exalted - to their great surprise. Those who now laugh will be weeping. Those who endure hunger and thirst will suddenly find themselves fulfilled beyond their dreams; while those who now have their fill of mostly ill-gotten wealth will find themselves with nothing and headed to their allotted dungeon here in Gehenna.

"For the death culture enthusiasts, the development still represented a major coup with terrific spin off benefits. Even though the scientific community quickly developed drugs that could be used by doctors to 'manage' the disease and lengthen the victim's lives, they (the death culture enthusiasts) have succeeded in restricting the distribution of the drugs through pricing policies that keep the drugs out of the reach of the great bulk of the virus' victims.

"And talking about viruses, wouldn't it be interesting to have all nations that have ever been involved in preparations for imaginary wars with imaginary enemies, account for all the viruses - and also all the biological agents - they have ever produced and stockpiled! Would it not be very interesting if a completely revamped United Nations whose decisions were not subject to the whims of any so-called veto-wielding 'power' and that also had real muscle - perhaps with a stock-pile of it's own WMD that it could employ as a deterrent - forced every nation that had ever engaged in the production of WMD to come clean and declare the exact extent of their involvement in bringing the world to the brink! Isn't that, after all, what should happen if the inhabitants of Earth wanted to establish how close they were to a man-made 'Armageddon'?

"A weapon of mass destruction that was very much in vogue in America - and that was quite visible - was slavery. States used it in their efforts to keep 'people of color' in permanent serfdom, and thereby assure white folks the cheapest form of labor. After the civil rights bill was passed, that weapon merely became transformed from a visible to an invisible one, so those using it would not be brought to book; and it also became multi-faceted. It now consists in discriminatory practices that still target the so-called colored people; and it includes other activities conducted on the sly whose objective is to roll back the so-called 'affirmative actions' prematurely, and ensure that colored folks remain at the bottom of the social rung. Those discriminatory practices include the selective application of laws of the land or 'profiling'. Predictably, the operation of this WMD has resulted in a disproportionate number of people of color being kept immobilized in cages in a burgeoning prison industry.

"And so, if they are not freely available as cheap labor, they must be kept out of sight and out of circulation; and this is happening in an ostensibly Christian nation, presided over by 'God fearing' folks. And, of course, the judges who hand down the 'sentences' that keep those poor folks immobilized know very well that the real sentence is not even being confined behind bars for so many months or years, but being exposed to abuse not just by their fellow convicts, but by the very people who are responsible for their welfare in jail, namely the prison warders!

"Talking about abuse, it is an abuse of authority for governments to allow those who are 'doing time' for a conviction to be confined in conditions that compel them to opt to take their own lives as a way of escaping the miseries they encounter there. That is not just something that infringes on natural justice, it is murder. And when churchmen, whose job it is to denounce evil practices of their time (like John the Baptist chose to do and paid for it with his life), pretend that they do not know what is going on, they become complicit in the murders.

"A handy secret WMD that you would not suspect was being used if you flew into New York for the first time from some other continent and were taking a stroll in Times Square - or if you just watched CNN! Of course it is wishful thinking to imagine that humans who were prepared to die to be assured of a permanent supply of the cheap labor for their empire-building project would be swayed by the mere passage of a law!

"One has to be kidding to think that poor, forsaken children of Adam and Eve, who were under my personal tutelage from the days I dethroned the Father and Mother of the human race until the coming of the Second Adam just a little over two thousand years ago, can mend their ways when some 'chap' in the White House inks a congressional bill into law. You should also remember the fate of all those in the White House and outside who either worked for the abolition of slavery, or were determined to see to it that all states in the Union accepted every American as equal under the law.

"You have to believe that I made 'good use' of my time over the period the world was under my unchallenged rule, before the Eternal Word became flesh. I never once took a nap, and I certainly did not allow myself the indulgence of taking a vacation.

"The result of that 'hard work' is indeed very much in evidence: humans glorifying wars which are a form of 'legalized mass murder', and spearheaded mostly by folks who claim to be followers of the Deliverer, but are really my minions; a state of disarray in Christendom, and a Church that is permanently scandal-ridden; a vast army of independent 'pastors' who nowadays do not even pretend to be affiliated with the traditional Church, and the vast majority of whom are really out to 'exploit' the gullibility of spiritually starved hordes, which they do quite effectively by brandishing the 'holy book' and passing themselves off as the specially anointed of God or modern 'John the Baptists'; and, of course, the continuing explosion of materialism and hedonism especially in so-called Christian countries - an explosion that makes the activities of the inhabitants of ancient Babylon pale in comparison.

"The continuing, and now virtually institutionalized, discrimination against aboriginal peoples in North and South America, Australia, and elsewhere in the world in the wake of spectacular land grabs that are well documented in history books is another very effective WMD. It is a particularly effective WMD because even churches gave their unqualified blessings to the territorial forays of the 'explorers', and continue to abet the goings-on with their numbing silence.

"Economic sanctions against any country also represent a WMD. It is a weapon that has always been particularly effective against children, the aged, and the poorest in the nations targeted. Unfortunately for the victims (and fortunately for me, Beelzebub and Father of Death), the spineless United Nations - which boasts agencies with fancy-sounding names such as 'UNICEF', 'UNAIDS', UNFPA', and even 'UNESCO' - has long permitted itself to be used in launching and implementing these punitive measures against society's most vulnerable.

"Other 'terrible' weapons of mass destruction are violence against women (VAW) and discrimination against women (DAW), as a result of which women are denied the right to own property or make the same choices that their men folk make in the normal course of life, and are treated as the social under-class. Knowing that the womenfolk outnumber them but possess a nature that predisposes them to courteous and gentle manners, their men folk, in a move that reflects the insecurity they feel, apparently have been determined from early on to rein in the women and 'neutralize' them. Consequently, women still lack social and economic power by and large. The prevalence of violence against them has assured that societies are dominated by the men folk, who see major advantages in the status quo.

"The men naturally see no wrong in perpetuating violence against women, and see danger in according their womenfolk equal rights, economic security, and the independence that would make it possible for humans of the female gender to negotiate their relationships with humans of the male gender on equal terms.

"Any weapon of mass destruction that targets women, of course, also automatically targets children. What hope do children have when their moms are left out to dry! These WMD are frequently backed not just by the 'Laws of the Land', but also by ages old customs and traditions. But their deleterious effects are not so easy to conceal. It is quite obvious that the progress of communities - and even of nations - is hampered when the unequal treatment of women in society is overlooked during the design and implementation stages of programs intended to improve general living conditions. But that has always been regarded by the men (who dominate the ruling oligarchy) as the lesser of two evils, the other 'evil' obviously being the threat of a world take-over by the womenfolk.

"And yet another 'invisible' but extremely effective WMD is the secret manufacture and proliferation of deadly M-16's, AK-47s, and other so-called 'small arms' by the major powers. Also, still produced and distributed on a massive scale by the 'advanced' nations in disregard of the world-wide ban on their manufacture and despite their horrific toll on the lives of the innocent are the land mines. The flow of these weapons of mass destruction will, of course, never be stemmed as long as there are greedy 'capitalists' in the world for whom the 'armaments' or the 'human killer' industry is just like any other. As far as these folks are concerned, they might just as well be investing in the manufacture and marketing of rosaries!

The "inspired word"...

"Humans are really interesting creatures. And it is not just that they are lukewarm in their observance of the commandments. They fragrantly break them - they kill each other, they steal from each other, they covert their neighbor's spouses, and so on and so forth. And it would be bad enough if they just did those things. The fact is that every time they do them, they have perfect excuses. In the case of a foreign military adventure, the excuses might range from going toe to toe with an 'axis of evil' (that presumably had been overlooked by the Deliverer - or so they would like the world to believe); ridding the world of a murderous dictator (they themselves might have groomed, armed and abetted until he got the itch for self-determination); or, even, readying valiant Christian soldiers (who might themselves be outside the Church) for resuming the long-stalled 'crusades against the infidels'. They act as if they are their own 'prime movers' - as though they created themselves!

"To press that point home, humans did not hesitate to 'deal appropriately' with the Word - the Author of Life Himself through whom everything that exists outside of the Godhead came into being - when He showed up. Unfortunately, after they had 'rubbed him out' (or so they thought), He was back promptly after taking the sting out death, and He commissioned His Church right on schedule, establishing it under a New Covenant as had been foretold. Discounting the machinations of one of the twelve apostles, He empowered the surviving eleven to go out in the world and spread His message of salvation, after laying His hands on them and promising them the Comforter.

"But then look what humans have turned the Church into - a free for all and a money spinner that many folks depend on for a living! And they have even put strange words in the mouth of the Deliverer until it now sounds increasingly as if His message was about the 'good life' here on earth and not about 'eternal life'! Instead of preaching that it is as hard for a rich man to gain eternal life as it is for a camel to pass through the eye of a needle, some preach the exact opposite, namely that it is hard for a poor man to sneak past St. Peter and claim his reward in heaven - that he has to learn to be acquisitive first!

"But the situation is now so ridiculous, it requires more than ordinary common sense to tell the 'Church' the Deliverer founded from the myriad money spinning enterprises that are all devoted to putting one or other spin on this or that text of the Holy Book for the benefit of spiritually starved folks - for a price. It is a classic case of the blind leading the blind! The interest in the Holy Book is, if anything, selective and self-serving. The proprietors of those 'enterprises' quote from it only what seems to support their preconceived positions and also happens to be good for the bottom line.

"When the different bits and pieces of writings were first compiled by the individual inspired writers, it goes without saying that these 'Sacred Scriptures' were largely ignored by scholars and merchants of the day. It speaks to the fact that the inspired writers were faced with a task that, humanly speaking, was impossible - the task of bringing the 'word of God' to the attention of the general populace. This was due to the fact that those self-published works had no immediate relevance to the material lives of these other folks.

"The original scrolls that Mark, Matthew, John, Luke, Peter, Paul and others scripted did not survive for the simple reason that publishers, book distributors and bookstores of the day, and even 'libraries' (or whatever served as libraries in those days) could not be bothered with anything that was of no relevance to their 'bottom lines' regardless of its intrinsic value.

"Published as 'the original, unedited, full-length yarns' which had been revealed to them by the Spirit, the original Sacred Scriptures, which dealt with subjects as drab as 'the last end of humans' and 'spiritual salvation', certainly did not resemble 'popular contemporary literature', and even less 'popular fiction'. But that is exactly what the numerous unauthorized editors have tried over the course of centuries to turn them into. They have done everything that is humanly possible to make the scriptures resemble popular works of fiction so that booksellers and merchants can use them to line their pockets - subject to payment of a commission!

"But, how original are the current editions of the Old and New Testaments? Are they really identical to the original, unedited inspired works! The puzzle is that all the 'learned' biblical scholars pretend that this is the case when common sense suggests otherwise.

"Inspired writings may be the work of the Holy Spirit, but they very definitely also remain writings of those to whom they are attributed. The Holy Spirit might inspire; but He is not the one who writes. To complicate matters, when an individual senses divine inspiration welling up in him or her and starts committing the inspired thoughts to paper, because the individual remains a completely free creature, there is every likelihood that the resulting work will include material - perhaps whole sections of it - that will be completely personal and, in that sense, not inspired at all by reason of its origin.

"The inspired author remains human, and liable to be tempted in all sorts of ways, and even retains the ability to opt out of the role of 'inspired writer' at any time while the project is under way. But then it is also not beyond the realm of possibilities for the scribe to turn around and, in trying to 'polish' the inspired material, knowingly or unknowingly eliminate critical sentences or even whole sections from the original script.

"And so, in the hypothetical situation in which the intention of the Holy Spirit is to convey a general idea, the scribe, fascinated by the minutiae, might be tempted to revisit his inspired work with the intention of polishing language pertaining to details without paying due regard to the fact that the big picture will be obscured in the process. The only thing that could save the situation in such a case would be the fact that the Paraclete, a member of the Godhead, is almighty, and nothing is impossible with Him. He can get any result he wants regardless of what the human He has chosen to be his scribe does.

"Most folks forget that inspired authors tend to be full blooded and earthy humans who come complete with multiple failings, rather than freakish nitwits who fit the popular but erroneous image of 'living saints'. And it is wishful thinking to imagine that they wouldn't be tempted to go back and try to 'rewrite' material they had originally jotted down under inspiration. In fact the temptation to do that would be far greater for people who found themselves scribbling down ideas that were not the result of their own creativity, and emanated from a 'funny' and highly unusual source!

"It is obvious from reading any 'Book of the Old Testament' that the 'inspired' authors even gave the impression, perhaps entirely innocently, that the Prime Mover sanctioned wars and similar evils. Born in original sin and inclined to sin, and also imbued with a view of the world that was riddled with inaccuracies, the 'scribes' had obviously been brought up understanding that wars were things for 'heroes', and they evidently imagined that an 'inspiring' piece of writing wouldn't be inspiring if it did not employ the imagery of war (an acronym for mass killings or murder that war planners referred to euphemistically as 'destroying enemy troops' or 'destroying enemy encampments') to inspire humans to 'fight' for and even lay down their lives for the cause of 'Good'.

"It is probably fair to say that it would be a lot of phantasy and wishful thinking to imagine that people like Paul, John the Evangelist, and other inspired authors of the Books of the New Testament wouldn't glamorize wars just like everyone else of their time. *Ovid* and in particular *Caesar de Bello Gallico* (which glamorizes the foreign adventures of Caesar and would be condemned by the Church to day as 'unjust wars') were probably Paul's favorite works of literature.

Is it any wonder, then, that the church's hierarchy to day does not regard the preparation of candidates for the priesthood as complete until they can demonstrate a mastery not just of the writings of that Roman demagogue in the same way the formation of a soldier (a euphemism for 'killer') is not considered complete until he/she starts to show a disregard for life that all 'warriors' are supposed to show under the guise of 'defending' the nation against some imaginary and often completely non-existent 'enemy'!

"But just think! What would my forces - the forces of darkness - be doing upon sensing that a human was receiving inspiration from above either for his own salvation or for a project that was likely to hamper our efforts in derailing the divine plan? Take a holiday? That is precisely the time we will bombard that human with temptations and ideas of our own; and you can also bet that they will be tendered in a way that makes them virtually indistinguishable from the ideas emanating from the Holy Spirit.

"Then, it is unlikely that a tome that claimed to be produced under inspiration from 'on High' would be accepted unquestioningly for what it claimed to be by a world that was unaccustomed to things of that sort. The inspired author, more than anyone else, would know and anticipate that eventuality. That knowledge and anticipation would represent additional pressure to 'package' his/her message in a way that would have a chance of acceptance.

"Now, it may well be that the Holy Ghost is always capable of intervening to stop the wandering hand of the inspired author from excising or alternatively adding material to the sacred text out of those wrong motives. But the operation of the author's free will definitely will limit the extent to which the Holy Spirit can intervene and stop the wandering hand from messing up the sacred text.

"It is also wishful thinking to imagine even for one moment that authorship of an inspired piece of writing, because it is performed under inspiration, is a piece of cake. Because enterprises of this nature bode ominously for our cause here in the Pit, my troops and I typically try to wreck all such projects at their inception, and you can be sure that we hurl everything in our arsenal at the presumptive inspired writer in the process.

"The onslaught of temptations which the servants of the Prime Mover face will be of the kind and intensity that only mortals who have the full backing of the Holy Spirit stand a chance of weathering. And it frequently happens that at some point the poor souls who have been commissioned by the Prime Mover for that important task become thoroughly confused and flustered, and unable to rationally determine which parts of the assembled material belong in the inspired work and which ones are unsuitable and need to be discarded. And the poor souls often discover, too late, that they have actually gotten back into the manuscript and ruined it irrevocably when they thought they were merely performing spell checks or some similar perfunctory operation.

"That is the gauntlet that mortal humans run when they accept to become instruments of divine grace. Many of them often end up loosing their faith and completely at the mercy of the Prime Mover. We deal with prophets, humans who are called to the priestly vocation, and other messengers of the Prime Mover in much the same fashion, and many indeed end up in the same way.

"But do keep in mind (as we also undoubtedly do) the fact that the Holy Ghost is quite capable of employing incomplete but complementary works by different inspired writers to achieve His ends. He not only can, but He even uses crooked, ill-intentioned humans to have His way. Because he is almighty, the Holy Ghost can easily use ill-intentioned humans who set out to write nonsense, and get them to produce some really inspiring pieces of work that rake in souls - and He probably often does! After all, He even causes good to come out of evil! We certainly will always remember how He snatched that murderer Paul (nee Saul) from our clutches, and turned him into the Apostle of the Gentiles!

"But, any way, it is just common sense to expect any piece of inspired writing to reflect the writing style of the author at the very minimum. That is why a reasonable person would not expect the epistles of Peter, a former fisherman, to read like the Gospel or the epistles of the well-schooled John - or the letters of Paul.

"It also stands to reason that if a prophet appeared on the scene today and decided to employ the written word to reach his audience, it is unlikely that his prophetic work would hit the bookstalls for the first time as an imprint of the big publishing houses. When they accept a manuscript for publication, they edit it so much - because of their total commitment to the bottom-line - the author's original style and, along with it, also much of the original content are usually liable to disappear. Their motives are the complete opposite of the motives of the inspired author. It just wouldn't work - unless the Holy Spirit wanted to use the occasion to prove that nothing was impossible with the Prime Mover!

"If the inspired work were published by one of those big publishing houses, even though the original manuscript might have been produced under inspiration, the final version which went to the press and ended up on the bookstalls would be so different after those 'editorial' changes, there might be nothing 'inspiring' about it in the spiritual sense. In other words, the prophetic work might not rake in any souls at all. Which is not the same as saying that it wouldn't rake in the money - or make its readers feel good about themselves!

"While making its way from one editor's desk to another, the inspired piece of writing would be liable to suffer the same fate as a piece of raw intelligence that was making its way up the ladder through various layers of 'analysts' to the Commander-in-Chief in an American or British spy agency. It very likely would be - as they say - 'sexed up' pretty well before it reached its final destination either in the White House or Number 10 Downing Street.

"This is the same fate that the sacred scriptures appear to have undergone overtime as hand-written copies were initially made from the original scrolls (most likely decades after the inspired author had passed on), undergoing the initial 'editorial' changes in the process. One would have to be a simpleton to imagine that the sacred scriptures did not undergo additional 'editorial changes' as translations were made into different languages, including Hebrew. And it is on record that they underwent further and even more radical changes as they were translated into Greek and Latin, at which time the 'inspired works' were also 'purged' of material that was deemed apocryphal and then doctored further.

"The translation of the scriptures into modern languages - translations that were commissioned by people with all sorts of agendas - naturally involved new and quite drastic 'editorial changes' that pitted the views of reformists against the views of traditionalists. But that time, the cat was out of the bag with different versions of the 'sacred' scriptures that contradicted each other in key places circulating side by side.

"And as the ecumenical movement got under steam, the situation became even more confusing as theologians tried to paper over not just the differences among the doctrines taught but also the differences in the different versions of the scriptures. One consequence of that has been the appearance of new and previously unheard of 'interpretations' - and effectively versions - of the 'sacred scriptures' as the number of 'Christian' sects grew and multiplied!

"It is rather unlikely that an original piece of inspired writing will look as if it was written by Charles Dickens, or William Shakespeare. If it has not been tampered with and 'doctored', chances are that the inspired piece will break all known rules of good writing (if the scrolls were located, authenticated, and deciphered with any accuracy).

"It is likely to feature overly long sentences with little or no punctuation marks. Some sections will be too wordy, and the order of words in others will be completely upside down. There are likely to be fragmented sentences galore, not to mention poor sentence structure, the use of split infinitives and the passive voice, verb confusion, the wrong use of verbs and adjectives, sentence structures that are plainly wrong - and, of course, very poor conjugation!

"The fact is that in those ancient times, there was never any fuss about sentences being long winded or expressions being wordy. If anything, verbosity was regarded as evidence that one was truly a man or woman of letters - unlike today when so-called educated folks can't even make head or tail of what was being spoken unless the message being put out was rehashed slowly and the speaker was employing only the most commonly used phrases.

"And any way - just to think that the worthless writings of a dimwit and a bum like Julius Caesar, who thought that anyone who did not speak Latin (a language which is now long dead) was a barbarian, have survived in their entirety for no other reason than that they have were relevant to people's bottom lines from the beginning; and that the original inspired writings are lost for ever!

"And would you know that history is repeating itself today, because writings that could help folks unmask the false prophets and teachers the gospels referred to and find their way into the true Church have no relevance to the bottom lines of book publishers, distributors, and bookstores, and are eschewed by those who manage public libraries and archives! Where for instance can a spiritually starved soul purchase the encyclical *Humane Vitae*, or *Fides et Ratio*, or *Ut Unum Sint*!

"And so, despite the impression given by those in the 'business' of saving souls, the question (the Deliverer Himself posed two thousand years ago) still remains as relevant today as ever: 'When the Son of man returns, will He find any believer...?'

The charade and "Noah's Ark"...

"In the meantime, the charade continues as every Dick and Harry who has ever been to a seminary or has a Ph.D. in theology from a university takes the stage and claims to be qualified to lead the faithful in spiritual matters. But it is all bogus - otherwise they wouldn't be contradicting themselves right and left while still claiming to be 'speaking in tongues'!

"And being able to count on a large following or on financial support that permitted a preacher to 'market' his/her ministry and attract an even larger 'flock' was completely irrelevant when it came to determining which church was the true, holy and apostolic Church. But that was precisely the sort of thing that little children imbibed far more easily than adults did in response to the Spirit's inspiration. The Spirit knew the sheep that belonged to His flock. For heaven's sake, humans should cut out the spin and allow me - Beelzebub - also to get the credit I am due in these matters!

"It is in a way a mystery that preachers belonging to the all too disparate 'Christian' churches that contradict each other right and left became passionate and emotional when addressing their congregations even though they knew very well that there could be only one true Church. That is something that was obvious even to unbelievers. Since these preachers were all agreed on that point - that the Deliverer could not have founded two, three or fifty 'churches' that contradicted each other - you would have thought that the only time the preachers would be passionate and emotional about anything would be when exhorting their followers to diligently seek out and find that one true Church, and also ark whose sides and bottom, constantly buffeted by the stormy waters, were guaranteed by the Paraclete against falling apart.

"The preachers should be passionate about the fact that only one church can be the true Church, and they should also be passionate about the fact that many people who belong to churches other than the true Church are in for an unpleasant surprise that could be very embarrassing at the end of time - or even in their lifetime if their search for the 'true Church' yielded results earlier.

"In the final analysis, there is really nothing mysterious or extraordinary about the fact that blind humans are in effect leading other blind humans. To expect things to be otherwise would, of course, be tantamount to pipe dreaming. One would also have to imagine away the effects of original sin on the posterity of Adam and Eve!

"It was entirely to be expected for humans to talk about the Church of the Redeemer this and the Church of the Deliverer that, as if they did not know that the Deliverer established only one Church. It is normal for this group of humans to refer to itself as Baptists; and that group to refer to itself as Orthodox Christians, and another to call itself Mennonites, or Roman Catholics, or Lutherans, or Evangelicals, or Episcopalians, or Presbyterians, or Anglicans, and what have you. They did not seem to realize that the Church established by the Deliverer was 'Catholic' - meaning Baptist, Orthodox, Evangelical, Presbyterian, Roman Catholic, and all that; the only difference being that the Church established by the Deliverer on the rock called Peter did not contradict itself like these other churches did.

"Humans obviously prefer to have things that way because then everybody can have a piece of the pie! Even though there was really no longer any need, following the Deliverer's ascension into heaven, for the position of Purse Bearer which had been held by the betrayer, the number of unsolicited applications had continued to grow. Besides, many people imagined, rightly or wrongly, that if the Deliverer needed a purse bearer, His Church probably could also do with one. And, naturally, the easiest way to increase opportunities for those aspiring to that position was to set up many 'churches' and then start pretending that they anyone of these churches might be the one true, holy and apostolic Church! Pretty clever!

"Humans are shameless. But what could one expect from them after the fall of Adam and Eve from grace. The fact that the Deliverer came as promised didn't really change anything as far as their behavior was concerned. The advent of the Deliverer should have resulted in paths being straightened and sinful ways being abandoned, now that humans could count on divine grace if they chose to stay clear of my wiles.

"But, No! Humans are still greedy, murderous, and prone to telling lies. And they do not seem to mind using the institution of the Church to achieve their material goals and enjoy themselves. And they have masterfully turned a marvelous opportunity to be reconciled with their Creator into a free for all, making evangelization the second biggest industry after the armaments industry. After all, remember that the same concourse of people, who a week earlier had shouted '*Benedictus qui venit in nomine Domini*' as the Deliverer made his solemn entrance into Jerusalem on the back of a donkey, were shouting 'Away with Him! Crucify Him!' not long afterward.

"Those preachers do a great disservice to the one, true, catholic and apostolic Church which was set up by the Deliverer. To understand how irresponsible and reckless they are, consider the fact that Islam, Buddhism, Hinduism, and other non-Christian religions, even though also plagued by divisions, those divisions are few and far between compared to the divisions that plague the self-proclaimed 'followers of Christ'!

"It would have been wasted effort for the Deliverer to commission His Church, ordain the eleven and imbue them with the authority to continue his ministry, only for Peter, John, Matthew and the rest of the group to end up contradicting each other - despite the fact that all the eleven had been at His side and had heard the same things as they came out of his mouth. And it would have been even worse - and certainly unacceptable from whichever way one looked at it - if they had each ended up heading their own separate 'churches' each of which sought to represent itself as the 'true' Church! It would similarly be a mighty waste of time if eleven accomplished 'biblical scholars', each of whom claimed to know the Holy Book like the back of his/her hand, found themselves unable to agree on key texts of the bible and ended up as 'pastors' in eleven different Christian 'churches' each of which claimed to be divinely instituted, but whose 'doctrines' were at complete variance! That should tell you something about the true nature of those who brag that they are the 'true believers'!

"What is the use of biblical 'scholarship' that fails to serve the critical purpose of identifying the one and the only Holy Catholic Church the Deliverer, according to the bible, founded? Either that scholarship is flawed - perhaps because it does not include other important elements such as Tradition - or I myself and 'the Legion' I command are not giving ourselves enough credit for derailing the divine plan! Actually, the most likely reason is that, while they may be well versed in studies of the New and Old Testaments, the latter group were neither 'called and ordained' by the Deliverer, nor sent out by Him to the world with the words 'What you hold on earth will be held in heaven...'

"And - listen to this - the sin folks who are not validly ordained priests or bishops commit when they take it upon themselves to act as if they were, and to confer sacramental rites that only ordained ministers may confer is called a 'sacrilege'! Now, just imagine the number of sacrilegious acts that are committed everyday given that half of Christendom is not in communion with the Holy Catholic and Apostolic Church! It is a large number. The paradox of it all is that, judging from their actions, the folks who regard themselves as Catholics are no better than the rest of humanity.

"I mean, if you are looking for people with heart - people who really care about the welfare of others - you are more likely to find them in Communist China, India, Pakistan, Lebanon, Iran, Siberia, North Korea, Palestine, and Iraq than in nations that are predominantly 'Christian' or even 'Catholic'. And that is also where you will find people whose constancy in praying for fortitude to the Prime Mover and in forgiving - even as their loved ones are thoroughly battered, humiliated, embargoed and starved of the necessities of life, maimed, and slaughtered in full view of an uncaring, uninterested world - never falters.

"It is bad enough that humans simply have no idea how embittered my folks and I feel after suffering defeat at the hands of the Deliverer. Humans cannot imagine the humiliation He inflicted on my troops and myself as their captain when, taking the form of a servant, and being made in the likeness of men, and in habit found as a man, He humbled himself, becoming obedient unto death, even to the death of the cross; and when, in obedience to the will of His Father in heaven, He agreed to pay the price for the sins of humans and rescued Adam and Eve and the rest of the captives we had been holding right here in hell in the hope that we might be able to use them as a bargaining chip to get Him to let us escape from the Pit. What do humans think we would be doing in these circumstances - just lying back and relaxing here in hell or hatching schemes that might yet derail the divine plan? Just as Peter, Thomas and the other apostles demonstrated, it is very easy to underrate our bitterness at having our victory snatched from right under very noses.

"The Paraclete, who informs and guides the Holy Catholic Church and is bestowed upon the baptized through the Sacrament of Confirmation, is a gift. That being the case, when humans go out on a limb and set up their own churches in competition with the Holy Catholic Church, regardless of how much they might pine for the Holy Spirit to come down from heaven above and take possession of their souls outside of the Church, it simply will not happen.

"And so, when humans, however well-intentioned, shun the Holy Catholic Church which is the modern version of Noah's Ark, they do so at their risk, and there are very many risks and huge ones at that. It is, for instance, very easy - once outside the Holy Catholic Church, to forget that the commission given by the triumphant Deliverer to the surviving eleven apostles did not just consist in mastering the Holy Book like the back of one's hand and regurgitating its contents, but doing a slew of things among them the Breaking of Bread together in His memory in a re-enactment of His passion, death and resurrection, and the administration of sacraments, including the sacrament of confession - whose sins you forgive will be forgiven! At the very top of the list of things the eleven did - and also urged their flocks to do - was to imitate the Deliverer who considered Himself a servant all through His ministry, and to pray always - in private.

"And it is also easy to mistake many of these things, which form key parts of the Deliverer's commission to the eleven, as witchcraft or 'devil worship'! We in the Underworld couldn't be more delighted with an outcome like that. Just to think that many of the so-called separated brethren openly refer to the Pontiff of Rome, who occupies the Holy See and is also the captain of the new 'Ark of Noah', as the embodiment of devilishness when they are not calling him the Antichrist! And then there is the fact that not all the successors of the apostles have been able to live up to their calling.

"To live up to their title as 'Princes of the Church', the lives of prelates must be exemplars of humility. They must follow in the tradition of St. Peter, St. John, St. Mark, St. Paul and others who, having been called by the Deliverer to carry the banner of the Church He had established to continue His work of redemption, actually carried it so high that people who lived in the known world of their time had no difficulty seeing it. But above all, they must always keep in mind that 'saints run away from priesthood'!

"The Holy Spirit did not force any of the eleven to be like the least of their flocks. Over the last two thousand years, the Holy Spirit never forced any 'Prince of the Church' to shed his trappings of authority and be a servant to parishioners in the diocese over which he presided. And when the successors to the apostles as a body did not give up those trappings of authority and balked at the prospect of being like the least among their flock, that had certain pretty serious implications.

"For one it paved the way for scandals in the Church. And when the conduct of the successors to the apostles fell short and resulted in problems for the Church - problems which ranged from disunity in the Church to disinterest among members of the flock in matters relating to their spiritual life - the 'princes of the Church' easily hid behind their positions in the Church's hierarchy and the powers they enjoyed by virtue of sharing in the priesthood of the Deliverer, and in effect blamed the confusion resulting from their actions on those who were disadvantaged and suffering as a consequence of their acts of commission and omission on the victims: the separated brethren, 'dissidents' in the Church, and others who were scandalized and decided to stay clear of the Church for those reasons. It was quite neat - they just decided to blame the victims! It is really like putting the blame at the feet of the Holy Spirit who 'informs' and guides the Church for things that go wrong and eventually boomerang.

"And humans must thank God that the Paraclete was what He was, namely a member of the Godhead; because finding ways to work around the Judas Iscariots and the Ananiases to ensure that the work of redemption continued uninterrupted had to be one hell of a task.

"Naturally, because members of the Church's hierarchy are human, they will also have this tendency to act out things the way that priest in the parable did. He was condemned by the Deliverer for looking down on tax collectors and other 'sinners', and bragging that he was justified. It is also quite conceivable that an 'unworthy' Prince of the Church, whose attitude might be what was causing the souls he would otherwise be receiving in the Church to stay away, might also have the tendency to merely shrug his shoulders, 'brush off the dust from his feet', and go on doing his thing as before. And imagine what the reaction of that Prince of the Church would be if he was posted to a city in which an 'apostle of the gospel' was positively not welcome! He would probably cause a rumpus instead of following orders and just matching on to his next post.

"It just might be that those who are despised as heretics, animists, adulterers, drug dealers and murderers, thieves and cheats, and others like that are the ones the Lord is more inclined to hearken to when they pray to Him for deliverance. It was after all not to one of the respected high priests who had been making offerings in the temple for years, but to a convicted robber that the Deliverer, even as He was enduring the pangs of His death as it approached, turned and said: 'This day, you will be with me in paradise.'

"The fact is that the Deliverer declared very categorically - when His apostles reported to Him that one fellow, who was not even one of His disciples, was casting out evil spirits in His name - that those who are *not against Him* are *with Him*. You must be kidding to think that the apostles were elated to hear that. Remember that some of them, like James and John, had already been exposed for being involved in manoeuvres designed to secure for them 'special seats' in heaven upon their departure from this world. The Deliverer's message was that His immediate friends, relatives and disciples were not the only ones who were dear to His heart!

"It has to be much harder for hypocrites in the Church to accept that good non-Catholics - Methodists, Baptists, Moslems, Buddhists, Hindus, and others who are true to their consciences, do their thing in good faith, and are not hypocritical or out to pull someone else's leg - all stand to inherit the kingdom of heaven. It has to be quite hard for those hypocrites who make it their business to denigrate good folks like those to accept what they themselves preach, namely that there is such a thing as 'Baptism of Desire'!

"Hordes outside the Church cling to the notion that they become 'justified', 'righteous', and 'saved' simply by 'accepting' the Deliverer. They have this notion that salvation and righteousness comes to humans, not by towing the line and staying on the narrow path, but miraculously by dint of an act of their will to the effect that they have 'encountered' the Miracle Worker, and accept Him by acknowledging that He *is* a miracle worker.

"If that was all there was to it, then the hordes who relentlessly followed the Deliverer as He went about Galilee and Judea healing the sick, multiplying bread and fishes to make sure the crowds had full tummies and didn't stay hungry all day as they kept Him company, and teaching them how to pray wouldn't have had to worry about some of the other things He said such as: 'It is not those who cry out Lord, Lord, Lord who will enter the kingdom of heaven, but those who did the will of His Father'!

"Also, the crowds who escorted the Deliverer during His triumphal entry into Jerusalem and paid tributes in song and with palms to His status as the promised Messiah who was coming in the name of the Lord (and presumably became 'saved' in the process), but sided with the priests and Pharisees who were thirsting for His blood five days later, would likewise be assured of salvation following their initial and quite genuine 'acceptance' of the Messiah.

"But it was still understandable when humans outside the one, true and apostolic Church fell for the ruses that my troops dangle in their faces. For many of these folks, proclaiming themselves as righteous, saved, and justified represented the only way they knew to distance themselves from us here in the Pit. They did not know any better.

"But it was completely inexcusable for members of the Church's hierarchy who should know better to conduct themselves as though their positions in the Church automatically made them justified, righteous, and saved. More than anyone else, humans who attain to high positions in the Church should know how frail, weak and dependent they are on grace and on the mercies of the Prime Mover. That knowledge should make them humble, unpretentious and unassuming. People like Jerome, Augustine, Bernard and Padre Pio always thought they were in greater need of forgiveness than anybody else. In fact, the closer humans are to the Prime Mover, the more they see themselves as being sinners in need of His mercies.

"But, thanks to our hard work, that is not the case. And the big pay off for us lies in the fact that many humans who would otherwise embrace the universal apostolic Church find themselves repelled by all the posturing and undisguised hypocrisy of the very people who are supposed to be shepherds and pastors over the Deliverer's flock. It is imperative that those who are called to the priestly vocation are Christ-like - are 'other Christs'. And it is, indeed, such a high calling that 'saints run away from the priesthood'.

"It is therefore just conceivable that it is the wrong characters who get 'attracted' to the priesthood, and who presumably see in the priestly vocation an opportunity to heave their weight around. It may even be that it is those who feel inadequate and lost who seek to boost their egos by aspiring to the most elevated calling of all - being an *alter Christus*! But it doesn't matter even if that isn't really the case. We here in the Underworld see it as our job to do everything that will undermine the ministry.

"Through our minions - and no human who has ever offended the Prime Mover can escape that label - we will always try to depict those who are out in the fields helping the Deliverer rake in the harvest in the worst possible light. Since those tilling the fields for the Deliverer remain humans who are frail and weak, those who act on our behalf get many opportunities to embarrass the Church and to cloud the good work they might be doing for the salvation of men. And you can be sure that my troops take full advantage of the fact that there will always be a few really 'bad apples' in any 'profession' to malign the holy, catholic, and apostolic Church, and to make it seem as if salvation is to be found elsewhere.

"The prelates and other Church functionaries, their flocks and all other humans are going around trying to show that they are happy, nice and innocent, when it all a farce. Virtually every human acts according to *our* script. They are shirking their responsibilities, trying to pass the buck, and generally blaming their problems on everyone else except themselves. And it pleases us mightily when churchmen, abandoning their responsibilities to those who suffer injustices, go about their business as if everything was alright - just as they did at the height of slavery, imperialism and colonialism.

"There was a time when it was taboo for humans to mention the word 'sex' in public. It also used to be unthinkable to suggest that the 'marvellous' democracies of the West secretly entertained policies that provided for things like torture and so called targeted, extrajudicial killings or assassinations of figures inside and outside their borders that were deemed *persona non grata*. Nowadays, it is taboo to mention the word 'modesty' in public. And it is not unusual to watch shows on television on which the leaders in Western democracies not only confessed to murders and attempted murders of people before they had been tried for their alleged crimes, but vied with each other in their attempts to show who did more to try and rub out those who had been labeled as 'dangerous' by the spying agencies. And it is unpatriotic to speak out against things like 'regime changes' that are engineered by super powers for the purpose of gaining access to the world's scarce resources, extrajudicial killings by governments using the state security apparatus, the so-called extraordinary renditions, and the now widespread torture of prisoners and captives using waterboarding and other dehumanizing methods.

"I do not know why governments nowadays even bother about the mafia when they and the mafia have so much in common! Looks like the goals of government and of the mafia - namely taking steps to secure resources that are vital to their 'interests' - are the same! It is now quite clear that they all have the same *modus operandi* of 'Mark and liquidate'! It is perfectly legit and internationally accepted for governments to have their spy agencies draw up lists of 'terrorists' and their alleged associates and then move to take appropriate action.

"And you can bet that if these governments post lists of the 'marked' people on the worldwide web for public consumption, there almost definitely will be other lists for 'Your Eyes Only' that only the spy agencies and the White House, Whitehall, or the Kremlin as the case may be will know about. I have personally seen many of these lists, and I cannot understand how it has not struck the folks who man the 'intelligence' agencies - and yes, they are real people just like you and not some super intelligent creatures like us demons for example who might be trusted to carry out their mission on the basis of real facts and without any ulterior motive - that it is I, Beelzebub, who is the real Axis of Evil and who, accordingly, ought to be tracked down above all else. My name does not appear on any of those lists!

"My job is, even then, not yet done. I want to see all Church folks - not just the handful who have come out of the closet - openly call for death to unbelievers, infidels, and social misfits on the cocktails of the now internationally sanctioned and globally coordinated political assassinations and the hunt for alleged 'insurgents', 'terrorists' and their associates and collaborators. We in Gehenna love it when those who cause the deaths of so many innocent people, among them children, as they try to rub out 'insurgents' and 'terrorists' turn around as if on impulse and sanctimoniously pretend to be defenders of the lives of the 'unborn' or 'unwanted babies', as if sniffing out the lives of 'unwanted' adults is godly and has nothing to do with the 'sanctity of life' which they preach.

"These Church folks have tacitly approved lying under the guise of political spin and diplomatic jingoism. They have explicitly approved the huge investments in armaments, instead of standing up to leaders of the 'advanced' countries, rebuking them for their irresponsibility, and commanding them to immediately divert those resources for the improvement of lives of the world's poor. They have tacitly - but effectively - approved the investment in tactical nukes and similar weapons. They have even tacitly approved policies of pre-emption. They have, of course, also approved the notion that a nation can be an axis of evil and liable for a preemptive strike to neutralize and 'democratize' it.

"It is a singular triumph of the 'powers of evil' that prelates and other Church functionaries are vocal about abortions sought by women, but are completely silent when demagogues in the world, seeking to advance their worldly cockeyed agendas and to mold the world in their own images, provoke wars in which large numbers of humans loose their lives needlessly. When the first prelates were installed by the Deliverer in their bishoprics two thousand years ago, thanks to expansionist demagogues like Julius Caesar, it was normal for generals to go out on 'conquering' adventures in the course of which they pacified the conquered (by which was meant wiping out enemy fighters), enslaved the fathers and mothers and even the children of the nations they subjugated, and brought home 'booty' before they set out on new adventures. The hunger for 'glory' and for new booty was insatiable. All these criminal activities by demagogic rulers were already 'legitimate' by the time Peter and Paul set off for Asia Minor, Rome and Greece.

"But that was precisely the reason the Prime Mover gave His only begotten Son to the world - so that those who would believe in Him would be saved. It was the reason the Deliverer, who did not come to establish an earthly kingdom (even though many earthlings still cling to that idea), drew a clear line between worldliness (what is Caesar's) and godliness (what is God's), and also said that individuals who loved Him should keep the commandments (which include one that says 'Thou shalt not kill').

"In his day, Caesar conquered and 'pacified' Gaul and other parts of Europe, Asia Minor, North Africa, Gaul and other parts of Europe - almost the entire known world of the time - and was under the delusion that he had built an eternal empire that would always endure. No one will ever know the number of lives that were snuffed out prematurely as that megalomaniac pursued that dream! And where is the Roman Empire now?

"But the most important question is whether the successors to the prelates of Caesar's time are prepared to risk everything - like the martyred Peter and Paul and other Church functionaries of the early Church did - and stand up to megalomaniacs of 'modern times' who have never learnt anything from history. Peter and Paul paid for it with their lives because of the determination of those for whom worldly ambitions meant everything. They died martyrs because the message they were preaching and the worldly ambitions of 'empire builders' who operated out of Rome were two things that could not be reconciled. Even though the 'prize' for which they labor is transitory, there has never been any doubt that the folks who are in the business of empire building are dead serious.

"It is significant that 'think tanks' and so-called advisors to the megalomaniacs have no interest in the permanent and the eternal, and as a rule focus only focus on the temporal, passing and transient - just like money hungry store owners who will withhold vital information about a product from their customers in their eagerness to secure an immediate sale.

"The world's megalomaniacs, regardless of the times, have always been convinced that they had the ultimate deterrent weapon for keeping their enemies at bay in their arsenals, and had developed and horned shock and awe battle tactics that no enemy could ever withstand. They have been certain that they possessed formidable, totally reliable human and other forms of intelligence assets, and had banded together alliances that would never crack and were impregnable. They have even been sure that they had in place mechanisms for keeping bad news relating to the progress of foreign occupations from eroding political support at home. But they have been proved wrong each time.

"Caesar, who imagined that he had attained divine status, was betrayed by Brutus, a friend. Military alliances have cracked and left aggressor nations exposed and vulnerable. No amount of preparations have ever stopped enemy agents from infiltrating the 'impregnable' defenses and inflicting damage where it really hurt. In Rome, where once upon a time followers of the Deliverer survived by hiding in catacombs, the booty that Caesar and other Roman generals brought home at the conclusion of their rampages through North Africa, Asia Minor and Europe now belong to the successor to the martyred Peter.

"Megalomaniacs have terrorized the world since Cain committed humanity's first ever murder. The jealousy that hounds them when they see wealth that belongs to others is the same jealousy that drove Cain to kill his brother Abel. And the world's megalomaniacs, regardless of the time in which they lived, all bear the 'mark of Cain'. Prelates of the Church should at least have the courage to tell the megalomaniacs that they too can be forgiven (like Cain was) if they confess their sin and renounce murder; and that they will otherwise end up stuck with the 'mark of the beast'!

"Nowadays, instead of issuing 'anathemas', churchmen even huddle together with today's empire builders to pray for the success of their conquering missions which spell subjugation, enslavement and untold humiliation for humans whose only mistake usually is being too trustful of their human brothers and sisters. Members of the Church's hierarchy have ended up more or less like the priests and Pharisees of the Deliverer's time - chameleons who suddenly changed their spots when it suited them and sought the help of Caesar to get rid of their Savior. The prelates appear to be completely blind to the causes of 'terrorism', the activities of so-called 'civilized nations' aimed at securing those nations' 'vital national interest' but which result in so much sufferings in different parts of the world, and to naked aggression by powerful nations of the world against weaker, resource-rich nations of the world.

"Instead of siding with the oppressed and others who suffer needlessly at the hands of powerful nations, churchmen of today, like their counterparts in the run-up to the inauguration of the Church, prefer to side with those who sacrifice human life at the altar of grandiose empire building schemes and other worldly ambitions. And whereas the Church's hierarchy finally mustered the courage to apologize to the world for the reprehensible activities carried out in its name in the past by its representatives, it might not have an opportunity to apologize to those whose legitimate concerns have been ignored and now are branded 'terrorists' and hunted down as such with the Church's tacit approval by those who had the responsibility for addressing those concerns adequately and equitably, but did not. The reason: it may not be too long before Armageddon, which humans have been courting since Adam and Eve joined me in my rebellion against the Prime Mover, ensues and brings all the fun to an abrupt and complete end.

"It is therefore not inconceivable that, in the run-up to Armageddon, the Church's hierarchy will join those who will persecute the Elect in a repeat of the Joan of Arc fiasco and the other outrageous things that have been done in the Church's name over the centuries - things that took a very courageous Pontiff and a man of God to stand up and apologize to the world on the Church's behalf. We here in the Pit have taken note of the fact that in addition to being an outsider to 'Church politics' in Rome, the Pontiff in question was not of the traditional milieu in his philosophy and temperament. According to our calculations, the chances that any of his successors will succeed in standing up to the traditional 'interest groups' in the Church and others who have traditionally held sway in Rome and continue on that path is very slim indeed.

"You know - we may be languishing here in the Pit, but we are not entirely nuts. We know that Peter ended up as Bishop of Rome and that those who have succeeded him in his capacity as the 'rock' upon which the Church was built are now stuck with that. Peter did not just find himself in Rome after wandering about aimlessly. There is no doubt that Providence, and specifically the Holy Ghost, was behind the move.

"But Rome is Rome, and it also happens to be in the West. And the West is the West. Westerners have this funny idea that their lives are more precious than the lives of humans elsewhere. That is bull shit, but it is what they think; and that bias rubs off on the Church's hierarchy which has its head office in Vatican City. The Church's functionaries can't help seeing things in the prism of western technocrats. That has implications for Church unity - which is too bad! It also has implications for the work of 'fishers of men'.

"There are undoubtedly many humans who have balked at becoming Catholics because of that bias - which is just one of many problems faced by the Church because its head office is in the West. Too bad! But all this is very good news for us here in the Pit - we love it, and you'd better believe that we go all out to exploit biases of that sort which are one of the consequences of original sin.

"The point here though is that in these 'last days' and especially with the 'Rapture' in sight, we are committed to redoubling our efforts to ensure that members of the Church's hierarchy align themselves with the megalomaniacs through whom we rule the world to the detriment of their work of saving souls. Nothing gives us greater satisfaction than seeing members of the Church's own hierarchy working to derail the divine plan.

"Nothing is more satisfying to us than the sight of Church leaders identifying themselves with those humans who have no qualms whatsoever about visiting death upon their fellow humans while pursuing their worldly ambitions. And we also know that nothing is more reprehensible to the Prime Mover.

"As long Planet Earth is still in one piece and the doomsday clock is still ticking, my troops and I here in the Pit are determined to lend harbingers of ruin and death all the support they need in implementing their wicked designs and bringing misery to families and their loved ones. Death and misery are weapons that we use to try and drive souls to despair and eventual perdition. Our allies are up against the forces of Good. What's more, we know that the Deliverer has got our friends in His sights, and is ready to welcome them back to the fold at a moment's notice.

"To ensure that it doesn't happen, we do not let up in our corrupting influence, and we inspire them continuously to stay the course. We help them in concocting justifications for their murderous adventures, and we show them how they can reinforce each other in their opposition to world peace and stability. Networking is also one of the ways in which they help us recruit more 'killers of men' who can counter the influence of the 'fishers of men'!

"And so, that is how the battle lines are drawn in the struggle between good and evil. A Church hierarchy that will be eager to play into my hands on one side and my disciplined troops that are out to exploit every conceivable opportunity for derailing the divine plan on the other side. It is not surprising that the Deliverer, even though He knew that the Holy Ghost would be there to ensure that the 'powers of hell' would never prevail against His Church, worried that there might not be any faith left when He came back in the last days to deliver the *coup de grace* to Death.

"Just as it is not automatic that humans who succeed in manoeuvring themselves into positions of leadership and power in the world recognize that their new-found authority is God-given, humans who make it into positions of authority in the Church do not automatically forsake self-will to permit the Holy Ghost to inform their work as 'fishers of men'. And you have to remember that my troops and I here in the Underworld have a special interest in corrupting these folks. Hence the scandals that have always plagued the Church.

"Everybody blubbers about the Divine Plan whose goal most of those who do couldn't even say if they were asked. If they really knew anything about that Plan, they would also know about another Plan - my Evil Plan!

"The strategy I follow in implementing my evil plan is to get poor forsaken children of Adam and Eve, who are starved for graces and are thirsty for the Word, to look at the Holy Church and mistake it for something else - for my work! It is a measure of our success here in the Pit that so many souls that are hungry for the Word of the Prime Mover actually believe that the pope is not just the Antichrist, but also the personification of me, Satan!

"And there is nothing that helps us in implementing the evil plan more than actions of priests and prelates that are reprehensible. And, guess what - as long as those 'fishers of men' are not perfect like the Deliverer Himself (which they can never be), they will always be contributing some to my cause - to bringing my evil plan to fruition! Meaning that they will be doing something that will make it seem as if the Holy Catholic Church, which was established by the Deliverer and is informed by the Holy Ghost, is actually my work.

Armageddon: a scenario...

"Even we pure spirits have instincts and hunches, and my hunch tells me that it will actually not be some super power that will be calling the shots as Armageddon approaches, but the so-called terrorists and their nests around the globe. Armed with brief-case nuclear bombs constructed with technology obtained by hacking into computers of the United States military, the terrorists will be roaming the world taking out cities at will, after successfully blackmailing and eventually rounding up leaders of the so-called 'nuclear club' and locking them up in a maximum security facility in Cuba!

"The great irony of it all is that it is the heavy-handed repression by governments of extremists so-called and insurgents in places like Iraq, Afghanistan, Pakistan - yes, Pakistan because my hunch tells me that that is where everything is going to unravel - and a string of other countries that will be reeling under occupation that will be responsible for the unprecedented upsurge of 'terrorism'. It is for that same reason that the new crop of terrorists, as they go about the business of 'straightening out a world gone out of control', will be particularly merciless and uncompromising.

"The chaos and confusion in the world, particularly in the so-called advanced countries, as seething masses of humans scramble to get out of cities that are next on the list of destruction and as others attempt to flee urban centers in North America and Europe for the relative safety of Africa, will be unimaginable. In the chaos, ordinary Americans and Europeans will be begging the terrorists to spare them in return for cooperating in identifying and locating anyone who may have participated in the occupation of foreign lands or been complicit in the flagrant violation of human rights under the guise of fighting terrorism.

"The stock response of the terrorists will be predictable, namely that all they are doing is let the authors of the myth of terrorism and those who supported them have a taste of their own medicine. They will claim that agreeing to the reintroduction of the now discredited practice of resolving international disputes through negotiation and peaceful means will amount to surrender to the 'real terrorists'; and that it will be just a waste of their time to try and negotiate with those who could not understand that all humans were equal, and were inclined to the view that anyone who sought self-determination was not only an inferior human, but automatically also a terrorist or insurgent whose concerns did not merit any consideration.

"The end will come when a defiant American general and self-proclaimed 'Christian crusader', hoping to destroy the terrorists' leadership in one fell swoop after receiving reports that the leader of the 'holy war on the Great Satan' and his closest lieutenants were secretly gathered in the Pakistani city of Karachi for a convention, will level that city with up to fifty mega nukes from the remnant of America's nuclear arsenal.

"In response, hundreds of thousands of operatives for the terrorists, already positioned in all corners of the globe with their brief-case nuclear bombs, will do what they have to do. On a prearranged signal, they will grab the 'brief-cases' by their handles to trigger the nuclear holocaust. And that is how the nuclear 'monster' - the 'baby child' of the West which was christened the Manhattan Project and was successfully 'tested' over Hiroshima and Nagasaki - will come back to haunt those who created it.

"Oh, my! Oh my! When my own pride set me on the unholy path of spiritual depravity and degradation at the beginning of time, little did I know that things would get so interesting! That generations of humans would follow me down that path, and then try to outdo each other in playing the part of human devils! The insincerity of humans and underhand dealings is not just the root cause of quarrels, bigotry, family break-ups, schisms and heresies, wars and other evils; but it is the reason those humans who bear the guilt for those evils think they can hoodwink the world and pass for blameless and innocent victims!

"Or, did you think that we would miss those details just because our reign is confined to the Underworld! Well, always just remember that the high priest who bragged that he was better that the tax collector - the high priest who represented Moses and the prophets and led prayers in the temple in Jerusalem - was closer to me, Beelzebub, than the 'blooming tax collector'! And, while 'pagans', former unbelievers, 'unsaved' people and others who join the Mystical Body of the Deliverer escape my tentacles in the process, you have to accept that my buddies in the Underworld and I do give the successors of the apostles a run for their money, and cannot be accused of abnegating our responsibilities in that particular respect.

"It is not the first time - mark you - that creatures that are made in 'the Image' and have been placed by the Prime Mover in positions of responsibility have chosen to stand out as 'princes'. In the beginning, during my own period of trial after the Prime Mover had deigned to bring me into existence, I immediately started aspiring to be a prince - the 'Prince of Light'! 'The Chief Prince of Light' to be precise. You know how things are when one is puffed up, and wants to stand out above the crowd.

"Because I had come into existence ahead of Michael the Archangel, Rafael and the rest, I despised them. Even though we were 'jewels' - all of us - in the Prime Mover's precious collection, I got this idea that I could perhaps manoeuvre myself into a position from which I would be able to make them feel small - as if they were just fake jewels, not real ones! Well, you know the rest of the story, don't you? If you were inquisitive about how the successors to the apostles ended up referring to themselves as 'Princes of the Church' even before they themselves had passed their Church Triumphant Entrance Test, there is your clue.

Human nature...

"We demons understand human nature a little bit better than humans themselves do. And humans themselves are so stupid! Instead of relaxing and praying always and, I might also add, taking their time to meditate on the words of the Lord's prayer, they are always jumpy and going off on a limb just like dumb, fledgling little kittens that venture out into the open, completely oblivious to the fact that hungry kites are lurking in the skies above.

"It is quite rare for demons to possess humans and have power over them on a full time basis. We do not usually waste our time doing that. Instead, we merely bide out time, and look for opportunities to play the weakness of one human against the weaknesses of another one. And we will inspire and help one human to hurt another human by doing uncouth things like telling lies initially in small things and then gradually in big things. In the case of a married couple, we will quietly infiltrate the first one who will provide us an opening, and form a partnership with him or her with a view to 'straightening up' the other party. Once we get one party loosing his/her temper, we will capitalize on that and get them hurling words at each other and even getting physical with each other as the friction between them mounts.

"When that happens, the innocent party will be tempted to try and hit back by demonstrating that he/she can also be really bad, and even dishonest. Before they know it, the two humans will be shouting and screaming at each other, and calling each other names such as 'lying bitch' and 'dirty devil'.

"We know that once humans start pulling each other's legs or cheating, they make a habit of it; and quitting habits is, of course, not something that humans do easily. If anything, habits quickly become a part of human nature! And as humans become entrenched in their crooked ways, common sense and reason concurrently become commodities that are rarer and rarer.

"And so, before long, the couple will be swearing and blaming each other for all sorts of imaginary things. And it is not unusual for them to stop believing in the very God by whom they will be swearing, and to loose their faith. They will, of course, be completely unaware that it is us here in the Pit who were responsible for creating the turmoil between them; and they will have forgotten that it was they themselves who provided us a window of opportunity by neglecting the Lord's prayer.

"The fact that one of the parties might have persevered in praying and fasting unceasingly, of course, wouldn't have made things any easier for that individual. If anything, the life of the innocent party is almost guaranteed to be more hellish for that reason. We demons, working through the sinful humans, usually go all out to try and drive the faithful and holy soul to despair. What will save that poor soul will be his/her constancy in praying to the Prime Mover and his/her complete resignation to His will, and nothing else.

"Yes, eschewing acts of self-love and self-importance which are incompatible with the surrender of oneself to the will of the Almighty One, instead of putting on some quixotic performance that overlooks one's own failings and is driven by hypocrisy. But we know that the majority of humans end up seeking consolation in self-indulgence and completely abandoning prayer and self-mortification. They end up loosing hope and eventually their faith in the Prime Mover.

"As expected, it is usually the party that suffers from having an inferiority complex that ends up as the most vicious in domestic and other conflicts. And, coincidentally, they are also the ones who are usually to blame for first poisoning the atmosphere with their unrealistic demands of the other party to the conflict, and then finally igniting it by 'throwing a spanner into the spokes' by doing suddenly doing something that really hurts the other party.

"The intensity of the antipathy for the other party usually corresponds to the conviction that the imaginary ills are inspired by us here in the hell. The end result is that a party that may be entirely innocent is effectively blamed for devilishness that is completely the figment of the complainant's own imagination. We ourselves derive enormous satisfaction from seeing things transpire that way - from seeing humans who are entirely innocent cast as devils and treated accordingly by the very humans who are dedicated to advancing our cause.

"Feelings of inferiority complex and feelings of insecurity are unlikely to be things that instil self-confidence. Humans who feel inferior do not usually expect things to take care of themselves. It is thus not surprising that it is the actions of the insecure party that in the end are largely to blame for the friction between two individuals going out of hand. Feelings of insecurity do not engender either calm or trust in providence. That is the nature of the beast.

"We demons have instincts and hunches too, and I have a hunch that while hell may be overflowing with humans who became lost because they were self-confident in life and did not therefore have any excuse giving others a hell, the population in Purgatory at any one time is largely made up of humans who suffered from an inferiority complex and who now need special help in ridding themselves of that condition, stopping to clamor for sympathy and special treatment, and getting back on their feet again.

"More so than humans who exude confidence in themselves, insecure humans, have this tendency to blame others for perceived ills suffered by them and for imaginary ills as well. But what makes their posturing particularly upsetting to those who become their targets is their habit of acting meek and innocent even as they are fabricating lies or otherwise claiming that they have been short-changed. They love to cast themselves as victims out of a desire to satisfy some inordinate craving for attention. All of which explains the fact that all humans justify their sins by imagining that they genuinely aggrieved and deserve better from the Prime Mover! And that is all balderdash because the fact is that the more humans are pampered, the more they demand, and this is due to an evil streak in them that goes back to the sin of Adam and Eve. And their attempts to justify their sins lead to sins that are even more grievous.

"But whenever humans sin, they always also commit the sin of ingratitude, because they are oblivious to the many gifts that they have received from the Prime Mover, including the gifts of existence and human nature, and the invitation to be with the Prime Mover in eternity. And you would think that it is the poor, uneducated folks who are plagued by inferiority complex, rather than the educated and the well-to-do. Nothing could be further from the truth. If anything, those who grow up in so-called tradition-bound societies very rarely feel inadequate or inferior. The state of inferiority complex is in fact almost exclusively the preserve of those in society who are haughty, think they know too much, and are always trying to overreach without even knowing it.

"Any way - that is the extent to which humans seem determined to show that they are their own masters. Some of these nuts, not satisfied with carving out chunks of Planet Earth and claiming them for their own exclusive use, are already eyeing nearby planets like the moon and Mars. They now think that they can claim parts of these other planets also as their personal real estate! And this is after they have rigged Planet Earth with weapons of mass destruction to a point to which a tiny spark will cause it to catch fire and burn, and perhaps even disintegrate into pieces.

"But, talking about putting a spin on things, the opportunities for us here in the Underworld to manipulate innocent, unsuspecting humans ballooned instead of vanishing as we had feared, with the inauguration of the Church, and they now seem unlimited. Some folks like referring to the bounty or 'good' that came out of evil. Well, here is a clear case of the diametric opposite - of 'evil' being generated by something that is not just 'good' but priceless! Yes - you can say that we also try!

"And you can bet that I usually know when a human is mine and I, in turn, am his or hers. It is when humans have changed sides and are under my control that they step up their vainglorious self-flattery, and try to cast themselves as righteous and holy devil haters who supposedly are also pals of the Prime Mover. It is when they sanctimoniously affirm their determination to 'fight evil'! I know that because I am the one who inspires them to act like that.

"When humans, after deliberately making a wrong turn, get off the narrow path and end up in my camp, I certainly do not go begging them to become composed and regain their wits. I urge them to tell their guardian angels to get lost so that they can enjoy life to the maximum while it lasts. True to form, they all invariably get the message from reading my lips; and, instead of imploring the mercies of the Prime Mover and His saving graces, they haughtily try to justify their actions and to redefine the Prime Mover's injunctions to suit their own purposes.

"That is very creative. It isn't something that we pure spirits could bring off! Humans are able to do that - to turn round and try to 'justify' their actions - because they have separate and distinct faculties of the imagination and intellect. In our case, those faculties are rolled into one, so that when we think, we automatically also imagine, and when we imagine, we automatically think. In the case of humans, the faculty of the imagination can and often does operate independently of the intellect, and vice versa. And that is a boon for us here in the Underworld as we try to woo humans to join our cause.

"Once humans kill, perhaps because of the way their imagination interacts with the intellect, they have this tendency to try and justify their actions when they really should be begging the Prime Mover for mercy - especially knowing that he forgives humans their sins. And the way they do so is by killing over and over again - by making a habit of it! And as they do so, they also start claiming self-righteously that they have a duty to rid the world of those amongst them who are 'bad apples' - as if they were any good themselves after committing murder and then trying to cover it up!

"What happens there is that humans let their faculties of the imagination have the upper hand in determining their next course of action. That is why, at one point it is 'kill, kill, kill!' and almost in the same breath, they are extolling their own 'virtues' and referring to anyone who disagrees with them as evil! But, while they might look on the surface as if they might be suffering from schizophrenia or some similar psychotic disorder, they remain on top of things and know perfectly well what they are up to.

"You will see a bunch of humans publicly confessing to murders and attempted murder one moment, and the next moment, their heads will be bowed down meekly, not as a prelude to begging for divine mercies, but to thank the Prime Mover for giving them the wherewithal to make progress in achieving their worldly ambitions - as though they had never heard of the Ten Commandments!

"To return to the so-called 'natural disasters' and 'acts of God', the Prime Mover allows humans to perish in the circumstances described to show that all humans are equal and also that the culture of death is, therefore, self-defeating; that one might be a 'death culture enthusiast' one moment and the next moment that individual himself or herself might be dead; that the fate of all humans is in the hands of the Prime Mover, not in the hands of self-appointed human 'gods'; and, above all, that the Prime Mover is quite capable of using - and in fact uses - wicked humans and their acts of 'treachery' to achieve His own ends and to fulfil His divine plan.

"And so, to-day as in the first century, the Church has its 'Judas Iscariots' and 'Ananiases'. And, talking about 'Ananiases', there is this fallacy that when humans heed the call to be 'fishers of men' or to some other form of 'religious life', they somehow become insulated from temptations of the flesh and from our wiles - that they become 'special'! Others even entertain the equally strange notion that being well versed in matters of philosophy and theology automatically propels individuals to spiritual heights.

"Nothing actually could be further from the truth. This is because anyone whom we observe starting to veer off Broadway onto the Narrow Path automatically becomes a very special target for us - let alone anyone who displays enthusiasm for joining the workforce in the field and an interest in helping with the harvest as a 'fisher of men'!

"As the Evil One, I can assure you here and now that a human soul becomes a special point of focus for my troops the moment it starts being drawn to anything that is positive and noble. And we ourselves get drawn towards candidates for the religious life just like magnets become drawn towards anything metallic. Is it, therefore, any wonder that it is the souls that are humble and steadfast in their love of the Prime Mover and in their self-abnegation that are likely to be found enduring dark nights of the soul and things of that sort!

"To return to the subject of mercenaries in the Church, just as was the case in the days of the early Church, so today they have no scruples in doing whatever they do in the name of the Prime Mover and in the name of the Church - until they get exposed (if they ever do). Many of those mercenaries of death have no scruples about trying to pass for 'people of God', and do their best to show that they are imbued with a messianic mission to change the world for the better and presumably also bring salvation to 'non-believers'. But, unfortunately for them (and also for us here in the Underworld whose duty it is to inspire and cheer them on), the strategies of 'world dominance and pre-emption' so-called betray them and unmask their 'messianic mission' for what it really is - naked worldly ambition!

"Now, you might know that when humans get caught up in 'messianic missions', the end also starts to justify the means from then on. It doesn't take much after that to get full scale wars waged by the self-declared righteous against multiple evil-doers and axes of evil going. Instead of seeing danger looming and making a U-turn, they tend to become fixated with the notion that they themselves are making history. You can bet that we take our job of planting notions like those into the heads of people in positions of responsibility very seriously.

"And as the nations led by the types who, having buckled in the face of temptation, wind up as 'demagogues' begin to get sucked slowly but surely down the black hole that transforms all once-powerful but expansionist nations of the world into history, the common sense that might have previously fuelled 'anti-war' protests and the like ceases to be common altogether. This happens as the citizenry unite behind their 'great and glorious leaders' in the 'troubled times' when their country starts to look like it is indeed facing implacable and determined 'enemies'.

"That is also the time when the truism of the maxim that 'citizens *deserve* their leaders' becomes tested. It is the time when any protest begins to spell 'betrayal' of and 'treasonous conduct' against the motherland in the looming times of tragedy. But, of course, the citizenry of an aggressor nation wouldn't be very different from their leaders. It is they themselves after all who choose to give the individuals who lead them the reins of power, and to keep and not just tolerate them but support them even after the murderous schemes they have hatched come to light.

"That is not at all surprising since there definitely would be a sprinkling of 'Mother Theresas' and 'Francises of Assisi' among them at the most, and the rest of the populace would be hoping that imperial power and expansionism will guarantee each one of them a retirement beach side cottage constructed to withstand any type of hurricane (thanks to the booty shipped back home from the pacified territories). And that after all is the basis of that truism which has been tested time and again in the course of human history.

"Talking about history - it is the actions humans do that over time constitute 'history'. And there is nothing that demonstrates the stupidity of humans as does history. It is most damning - this so-called history of humankind - even before the Judge has come into the picture. And it is all the more damning because it keeps repeating itself.

"Take the things hoodlums who paraded themselves as emperors and kings at some point in history did to other humans in the name of empires and kingdoms over which they held fief. These hoodlums conducted themselves like gods while they lived and the empires and kingdoms lasted. But, disregarding the myths about those kings and emperors and the cruel things they did which are banded around as 'history', where (one might ask) are those 'kings' and 'emperors' and their kingdoms and empires? The fact that they all are no more says something about the stupidity of my human friends, I tell you.

"The resources the regimes that are determined to 'dominate and conquer' employ *fortunately* are public resources that should be devoted to improving the living conditions of the citizenry and others who are in need instead of being wasted on armaments and the like. My folks and I in the Underworld certainly deserve a 'pat on the back' (even if only in the figurative sense) for the fact that the activities of those for whom the 'culture of death' is a necessary 'evil' are always dictated by 'practical considerations' like the prospects of winning an election!

"Those 'practical considerations' unfortunately have the effect of stopping well placed humans from aiming really high and taking over and subjugating as much of the world as the resources at their disposal permit. If planned well, a major offensive aimed at taking over and occupying huge swaths of territory typically results in the resources available to the aspiring super power swelling and becoming unmatched as the war chests of nations that are overrun become the property of the occupier. In a few instances, following a successful foray, operatives of the invading nation can even get to set up home in opulent palaces complete with golden domes! And that is not to mention other booty including precious artworks and the like.

"The temptation to take a gamble and dedicate a nation's available resources, both material and human, to an alluring 'project' that additionally promises limitless, albeit only 'temporal', returns can be just too great to withstand. Frequently megalomaniacs at the helm of an aspiring super power mortgage their nation's economy and (by getting the media to join in the spin) hoodwink the citizenry into making untold sacrifices just so they can give themselves and their close associates a shot at setting up home and/or an office in palatial surroundings in some exotic lands. But again it is those 'practical considerations' that always interfere with our work.

"And then there is the problem of those 'peaceniks'. They are a real menace and the harm they do to our cause can be immeasurable. But that should change in time as money matters and militarism become accepted as good things in themselves. In any case, thanks to the good work of money lovers and the death culture enthusiasts, this planet is already ringed with enough explosives to send it smouldering in a ball of flames at the touch of a button. No, those idiots - the peaceniks - won't stop us!

Predator nations...

"In the meantime, we need humans who can take risks and are not inhibited by 'public opinion polls' and things of that sort. We need more and more 'leaders' who can say 'to hell with pollsters' and public opinion; and 'to hell with democracy'! Look, we are offering ambitious folks the opportunity to own the whole world!

"The only qualification that is necessary is a genuine desire to dominate the world using any means - preemptive regime changes, nuclear strikes (limited or otherwise), colonization, occupation, *et cetera*. In this business, the end definitely justifies the means! Those humans who may be bothered that they may be turning a peaceful nation into one that preys on other nations and effectively becomes a 'predator' nation in the process are automatically disqualified.

"This culture of death is not confined to people of certain nations. Judging by the widespread support for war-mongers, this is a culture of death that appeals to many, many folks in virtually every land. Hence the prospects for the rise of many as opposed to just a few predator nations. Under the circumstances, wars are, therefore, not unfortunate things that inevitably happen. They are a perfectly acceptable and lawful way of doing business in the world.

"The fascination with military science, which has as its objective the empowerment of 'nation states', might be described as a 'culture of death'. But it is a 'culture' that is honorable, if only because it is concerned with national 'security' in the short term as well as the long term.

"The actions of the first predator serve to draw the attention of other potential predator nations to the existence of booty within the territorial borders of some unfortunate country. The 'booty' can never be 'adequately' protected because, before long, alliances between nations, ostensibly for the purpose of advancing the human condition, are formed with a view to exploiting the resources deemed to be of 'vital national interest' to members of the alliance. The result is an ever-changing balance of power on the geopolitical scene as the predator nations of today become the meat upon which newer alliances of nations feast.

"Even when united and resolute against the assault on their sovereignty, it is very rare that the citizenry of an occupied country succeeds in reversing the situation and regaining their right of self-determination and independence. That quite naturally emboldens the potential predator nations to be on the look-out for opportunities to invade, occupy, or (as it is usually put) 'liberate' selected countries from real or imaginary tyrants.

"Those nations that have the wherewithal would be remiss not to gear themselves up so that they too can actively seek out other resource rich nations to conquer and subjugate. And so, it is not a question of whether resource-rich nations will be 'occupied' and taken over by some more powerful 'predator' nations; but a question of when the takeovers will occur.

"To be sure, the change will often bring with it a respite of sorts, albeit temporary. But the suppressed citizenry usually soon learn that it is expecting too much that their new masters in fact came to 'liberate' them - that it is expecting too much even to think that international law over which the United Nations is guardian will protect them. That would certainly be expecting way far too much since that world body, whose decisions are subject to veto by certain select nations, was established for the specific objective of safeguarding the interests of those nations, and none other.

"As predator nations realize their goal of being the undisputed masters of some resource-rich corner of the globe, they simultaneously move to legitimize their positions by twisting the arms of any and all nations that might challenge their authority in those parts of the world, and will not hesitate to enforce their 'hard-worn' and sole right to exploit the available natural resources as they deem fit by imposing economic and other sanctions on those nations that refuse to become their allies and the use of force where necessary.

"The fact that it is not statesmanship or anything like that, but naked unbridled greed that drives geopolitics should serve as a reminder to you humans that it is I - not the Deliverer or anyone else - who will continue to hold sway over the fortunes of this planet until it disintegrates into fragments in a nuclear conflagration at the end of time! It should already be clear by now that the pursuit of happiness in disregard of the sanctity of life is worse than worshipping idols made by human hands out of stone. It constitutes worship of the Author of Death...Me!

"All agents of death worship me regardless of what they proclaim! There are times when it looks as if we have every soul on earth in our camp in this regard. It is on those Heroes' Days - every country on earth has at least one every year - when celebrations are held to honor those who died in 'defense of freedom'. More often than not, that 'defense of freedom' amounted to nothing more than participation in naked aggression whose only purpose was to gain control of territory, water ways, and other assets belonging to other nations. It was either a successful looting expedition or a looting expedition gone awry; and, consequently, the displays of military might and victory parades are all a celebration of the death culture.

"In some cases it might, of course, also have been a nation's fight for survival, but a fight for survival that was triggered by hostile activity on the part of that nation. But then you have to remember that to the extent any nation on earth claims that its borders are 'sacred' and 'inviolable', to that extent my evil cause, whose objective is to drive a wedge between humans who are all made in the Image and are members of the same 'human' family, has succeeded!

"That does not alter the fact that the more I myself succeed, the more I hurt my cause. The more my troops succeed in corrupting those in leadership positions and getting governments, that are supposed to promote the commonweal, to shirk their responsibilities to the people of God and to instead become instruments for suppression while furthering the interests of a tiny manipulative minority, the more it becomes clear to an ever growing number of humans that it is not their material but their spiritual well-being that really matters.

"In other words, the more we have been successful in recruiting folks to sow seeds of death, the more it becomes clear to other folks who care to stop and reflect that they are temples of the Prime Mover and not simply unfeeling animals that must be abandoned to greed and other vices. The more I succeed, the easier it becomes for humans to see through my lies.

"Lacking any real legitimacy - because those who occupy the halls of power in the predator nations I control have essentially hijacked the powers of state with no real intention of using them for the common good - these quislings of mine do not require any urging to become believers in the doctrine that might is right, that it establishes the legitimacy they crave, and that any attempt to resist them automatically becomes illegitimate; and that any one even remotely suspected of involvement in challenging them is fair game - hence the labels 'insurgent' and 'terrorist'.

"Acts of the *de facto* authority, regardless of how it came to be the *de facto* 'authority', that would themselves be regarded as 'aggression' or illegal under international conventions, become 'liberation' or legitimate 'occupation' and acceptable under those self-same conventions. The insurgents and the terrorists become eligible for a reprieve only as and when their country becomes denuded of its natural resources and stops being rated by the occupiers one that has any importance to their or any other would-be-predator-nation's 'national security'.

"Now, I could try and warn my hirelings that the adage that 'might is right' is a hollow one when applied to creatures. Might is really right only when it is the Almighty exercising his rightful might. That is because, in addition to being infinitely Good, the Almighty is also all knowing, and consequently also always right.

"And, even though the Almighty One is a 'Jealous God', because He created everything that exists outside of Himself out of nothing, and everything is His *ipso facto*, His jealousy cannot include any 'covetousness' or desire for what belongs to someone else. In any case, if I were to alert my lackeys that theirs is a hopeless cause, I would be doing a great disservice - nay, a great 'wrong' - to my own cause. First of all, as the devil incarnate, I myself also aspire to be 'Almighty' when it comes to evil matters - I mean matters that are sordid, foul and sickening, and ignoble.

"But humans are so stupid, they probably wouldn't believe me any way. If I told them that in pursuing the philosophy that might is right, they were setting themselves up for failure, humans would think that I am going crazy. They are so stupid, they would think that I had gone nuts if I told them that they were actually hurting themselves each time they tried to 'liquidate' fellow humans they disliked, and that things didn't work that way. Humans are so stupid, they don't even learn from history.

"When Julius Caesar was planning his invasion of North Africa, he passed an edict to the effect that anything that looked like it could be melted and used to manufacture implements of war, by which he meant ramming rods, swords, spears, arrow heads, shields, and helmets for the foot soldiers and cavalry, cuirasses for his generals, wheels for chariots, and so on and so forth. And he caused all well bodied Romans aged twenty-five to forty-five to be enlisted in his armies. He even commandeered the chariots of the noble men in Rome, Venice and other cities of the empire.

"But, as you can see, Caesar's conquest of North Africa was a mirage and, apart from the ruins of the amphitheatre in Rome, there is absolutely nothing to show for sacrificing human lives in particular on that scale. If Julius Caesar had invested the treasures he squandered in the course of prosecuting his wars in Africa and in Gaul in uplifting the standards of living of Romans, the Roman Empire would probably have succeeded in withstanding the subsequent onslaught of the barbarians, and perhaps even survived as a force to be reckoned with to this day!

"Instead, even as his forays into Africa, Gaul and Britannia for the purpose of guaranteeing access to the world's scarce resources were faltering, too proud to admit defeat, Julius Caesar and those who stepped into his shoes after he was felled by his own friend Brutus tried to show even in defeat that they were winning. And it has been the same story with all demagogues. In modern times, honorable exits from debacles resulting from failed expansionist policies have sometimes taken the form of 'granting independence to member states of the commonwealth' and things like that.

"But, have you ever heard words of the Deliverer to the effect that what is spoken behind doors or in secret will be revealed to all and sundry? I myself know from my experience the shame of defeat; and I can tell you that the shame that awaits the demagogues, who have no scruples about sacrificing precious treasure and blood while seeking 'honorable' exits from their unsuccessful forays abroad in search of booty, will be so devastating, not even the most curious among humans will want to be a witness as the sentence is passed.

"In the meantime, it is not likely that the Prime Mover is going to send His legions to Earth to dislodge me, much less deal with those humans who are enthusiasts of the culture of death and stop them. He did not do so when His only begotten Son was 'neutralized' and effectively 'silenced' two thousand years ago. He did not do it when the death culture enthusiasts not longer 'tested' nuclear and hydrogen bombs over Hiroshima and Nagasaki.

"And it is unlikely that He will do so if the latest crop of death culture enthusiasts and money lovers start by taking out those nations that form the so-called 'axis of evil' - as they seem quite prepared to do. I can't wait to see satellite pictures of these countries burning all at the same time.

"And it is not as if the Prime Mover does not value every single human life in these countries. He sent His Son into the world because of His infinite love for humans born or unborn, and Christian or non-Christian. And His Son, imploring His Father to 'take away the cup' if it were possible and sweating blood in the Garden of Gethsemane, was in fact grieving for all present, past and future victims of death culture enthusiasts. No, it is not the intention of the Prime Mover to interfere with my rule over the world at this point in the game!

Sissy

"But it seems that the solution to the 'problem of terrorism' wouldn't have ended up costing so much in lives and money if the original concerns of the 'terrorists' had been addressed in an equitable manner, and if partiality in the resolution of international conflicts had not been sacrificed at that altar of 'vital national interests' and 'bull-shit' like that.

"I am the devil, and I can confirm to you here and now that, for all the hype, 'vital national interests' remain temporal worldly considerations, and a price has to be paid sooner or later when 'vital national interests' are permitted to take precedence over Natural Justice. Who, after all, inspired humans to get involved in 'empire building' projects and this foolish business of 'national security'!

"Natural justice is trampled underfoot, not promoted, when powerful nations are bent on world domination and their leaders will stop at nothing to try and achieve their misguided objective. And that spells more, not less trouble even for a super power. And this is precisely what gave rise to the grievances of present-day 'terrorists'. Then, repressive measures that overlook natural justice are definitely bound to breed new and even more deadly 'terrorism'. It is not really hard to create a multi-headed monster out of terrorism that could be solved by accepting that everybody is equal and listening to and addressing the genuine concerns of their fellow humans.

"Rooted as it is in greed and selfishness, this 'cycle of violence' is the evidence of our own continuing reign on earth. It is something we in the Underworld not only welcome, but will do everything in our power to abet. But it also shows how dumb humans are. They are so dumb they do not see violence and the culture of death for the nasty things they are until they themselves are at the receiving end. But there is another dimension to the dumbness and stupidity. When humans are terrorized and murdered in their thousands in countries that are not regarded as 'vital' to the interests of the powerful nations of the world, these nations leaders have the habit of looking the other way - as if the massacres, which frequently have their roots in the policies those same powerful nations pursued - were occurring on a different planet.

"You humans are such 'amazing' creatures. Just fancy the world's so-called super powers united in fighting an 'invisible enemy' - an enemy who seems to 'know the terrain' very well, and who apparently understands that he can simply go on sapping the super powers' resources and energy at will, and bleeding the super powers to death by simply 'rearing his head' from time to time in different places before conveniently retreating underground.

"And imagine the super powers compounding the problem by fancying that they can deflect attention from the 'real problem' by staging preemptive strikes on 'rogue' states they imagine are an easier 'kill'. That is too bad. Preemptive forays by some nations against others automatically alert the nations that see themselves as likely targets of the emergence of potential 'trouble makers'. And just imagine what will go through the minds of military strategists of those nations that do not qualify as traditionally allies of the aggressor nations. It is just so reckless.

"When the Romans made their foray into Gaul and colonized it, they did it pre-emptively. But now where are there! When the Japanese crossed the Pacific Ocean and levelled Pearl Harbor, they did it pre-emptively. But now where are they as a military power! And when the Nazis made their land-grab and occupied Europe, North Africa and half of Russia, they did it pre-emptively. But now where are they! The doctrine is not only not new, but it always appears to spell disaster for those nations that fall for it.

"Talking about spelling disaster, I was stupid enough myself to try and challenge the Prime Mover to a fight when I did. It did more than spell disaster for me and the angelic hosts I persuaded to join me in posting that challenge. And that is how we wound up here in Gehenna, my dear! You humans could learn from us, but you are so dumb.

"When nations imagine that they are powerful and can therefore pick fights, they forget that the more threatened the targeted nations feel, the more resolute they will be in taking measures to counter the threats to them. The nations that feel that they are powerful and can get away with anything forget that it is the survival instincts of the targeted nations that take over and start dictating the courses of actions they have to take to contain the threat. Unlike the nations that seek to pick fights, the nations that find their existence threatened will not be playing games at all, and will aim to remove the threat to themselves once and for all.

"Of course it might not be possible for the first nations to be targeted by the imperialists, colonialists or foreign invaders intent on controlling the sources of any scarce resource to withstand the initial wave of attacks by the aggressor nations. And that will, of course, have the effect of emboldening the aggressor nations even more. The more nations an aggressor nation with the help of its allies succeeds in occupying and 'pacifying', the more emboldened that nation will be. And also the more weary the nations that sense that they are likely targets for future attack will be - and the greater the danger the aggressor nation will in fact be facing.

"Now, the world is a huge place, and wars are fought and ultimately won, not by the nations that initially had the edge at the beginning of conflicts, but by those that have the edge as the conflicts wind down and come to a close. Threatened nations will enter into secret pacts with other nations with which they have common cause; and together those nations will do whatever it takes to neutralize the emerging 'foe'.

"In this day and age, when weapons of mass destruction can cause so much ruin in such a short space of time, not only is the idea of an invincible 'super power' illusory; but any power, however 'super', that decides to pick fights with other nations in these circumstances takes risks that are plainly incalculable.

"Any member of the 'nuclear club' today can leave any nation on earth however powerful levelled and devastated. The winner is unlikely to be the nation with the largest stockpile of nukes, but with the motivation to use the nuke. And nations that feel threatened invariably have greater motivation to strike out and 'stop' the enemy cold.

"And creating enemies who become labeled as 'terrorists' or 'insurgents' is definitely not the way to go in this day and age in which individuals are known to own labs that are capable of producing functional nukes. Only those who feel insecure in a world in which everybody and every nation is equal, and who nevertheless think they know too much, can make the blunder of overreaching without even knowing it. It is simply reckless.

"We in the Underworld will naturally support the efforts of humans who seek to saw ruin regardless of whether it is on themselves alone or on themselves and others. History will tell you that ruin rarely will come on others alone; and that, while nations that stay clear of conflicts are occasionally spared ruin, the aggressor nation is never spared ruin (or the world would still be under the rule of Romans, Greeks, Egyptians, and what have you).

"It is a singular mark of our success that humans have also developed this strange complex which enables them to act weak and completely helpless one moment - 'sissy' is the word they themselves would use to describe this disposition - and to be all over the place claiming that they are powerful and invincible the next moment.

"Similarly, at any one moment, humans will be ranting against me - Satan - and blaming me for drawing them into the rebellion against the Prime Mover; and they will not accept any responsibility for their own part in it. Some even want you to believe that, if they wind up here in hell with me, it wasn't their fault - that they were just 'predestined' to end up here and really did nothing themselves to deserve it.

"And if they end up in heaven - well, the refrain changes. It is because they are terrific, godly and completely different from the thieves, plunderers, terrorists and others who were hell-bent and of course also hell-bound. But my advice to humans is that they should hold their breath and stop claiming that they are 'saved' until they actually see St. Peter opening the Gates of Heaven to let them in. In fact until then, all humans are equally thieves, terrorists, insurgents, and sinners who are in great need of the mercies of the Prime Mover.

"I may be 'evil personified'; but I am not about to accept responsibility for the wilful acts of humans who take it upon themselves to groom dictators, arm them, and abet and even participate in their murderous adventures; and then have no qualms putting the lives of other innocent humans including women and children at risk as they seek to effect regime changes and install puppets in place of their old friends turned enemy.

"I do not issue any licence to these folks to kill. All I do is merely tempt them - as I am supposed to do. And when I use humans as my minions - to lie and falsify and even kill - it is always only after they themselves agree to join 'the cause' as willing accomplices.

"These folks are endowed with intelligence and a free will just like us pure spirits. But, more than that, they have all these graces that are dispensed to them through the Church; and that Church operates in the open, not underground. For those of you who do not know, its headquarters is on a hill in Vatican City in Rome from where the Romans ruled the world, and not in some inconspicuous place. That is a second chance we pure spirits did not get, but which humans appear determined to fritter away.

"Humans who follow my example and kill will face fireworks for their sins of commission and omission just as we ourselves have. The fact that I am the face of Evil did not stop Michael the Archangel and other spirits from rebuffing my attempts to draw them into the rebellion. So forget the myth that I, Beelzebub, must cuddle human 'devils' and assume responsibility for their misdeeds. Again, I simply do what I am supposed to do, and that is to tempt them.

"Humans are entirely responsible for the consequences of their actions and, whether they like it or not, will roast here in hell with us for their 'sins'. When they arrive here, we will stage a special 'welcome' for those humans who tried to hold me and my troops responsible for the evils they themselves did to their fellow humans. There will be a separate, grand reception to celebrate their rebellion against the Prime Mover who has outlawed murder, stealing, lying and things of that nature.

"And, for those humans who are still determined to pick a fight with us, I say: 'We are ready. Bring it on!'

Next steps for Satan and his troops...

"Because the Prime Mover's 'intervention' won't go beyond what He has already done, namely despatching His only begotten Son into the world where He was promptly killed for being determined to do His Father's will, it is safe to say that there is no justice or anything like that in the world. A better way of saying it might be that there is only injustice in the world.

"Now, in these circumstances, the only real hope which the people of God have is the Church the Deliverer established when he came into the world two thousand years ago - the Church which has also been informed since Pentecost Day by the Spirit of Love that unites God the Father and God the Son, and through which the divine grace (earned by the Deliverer through His wholly undeserved death on the cross) is dispensed by the Prime Mover.

"Sinful humans, perhaps more so now even than ever before, need the help of divine grace to beat my wicked schemes - and they can be pretty wicked as you can see!

"Which reminds me that, during this critical phase before the onset of Armageddon, my troops and I have to concentrate on the successors to the apostles - the ones through whom those graces are dispensed to people of good will. Because they are human and are themselves just as much in need of divine grace as those to whom they minister, we have to 'deal' with them and try to frustrate the work of God's Church in that way! This is going to be a very challenging phase in the struggle which continues.

"I am not bothered by what non-Christians do. As long as they are humans of good will, they too probably already belong to the invisible Church any way. And I am not too concerned about what the separated brethren do - they have a window of opportunity they can use and end up in the true Church if they so choose, or they can damn themselves! I am more concerned about what Catholics do - especially members of the Church's hierarchy!

"This is because it is these folks who dispense the graces which the Son of Man merited with His death on the cross. And when they do, the graces are invariably dispensed most efficaciously, and also in their fullness in accordance with the principle of *ex opere operato*. It is always immaterial how worthy members of the clergy themselves are. All that matters is that they are validly ordained to holy orders. And they, of course, are because the 'princes of the Church', who administer the sacrament of ordination, enjoy an unbroken line of succession that goes back to the early fathers of the Church and the apostles.

"This is a state of affairs that clearly leaves me and my troops handicapped to no small extent, and it admittedly is a reality we have to live with. Also, the non-stop killings have the disadvantage of creating martyrs - most of the victims are innocent folks who would not harm a fly, and no one is more awake to the fact that the blood of martyrs is the seed of conversion than us here in the Underworld!

"But we still do have some recourse. We must try to get as many really unworthy folks as possible into the ranks of the clergy - lots and lots of potential 'Judas Iscariots' who will stay the course and undermine the work of the Church from within, and will not act like the original Iscariot who ran off and hanged himself at the first sign of trouble! And the current 'shortage' of vocations to the priesthood presents us with a wonderful opportunity for just this sort of sabotage.

"We'll start by getting zealots in the Church to make it appear as if the 'shortage' is absolutely critical. They must forget that the Deliverer, who could easily have recruited tens of thousands to work for His cause, chose just twelve 'apostles' among them fishermen and others who were pretty dumb by the world's standards. And then they promptly incurred the wrath of the priests and Pharisees for joining the Deliverer in promoting a 'schism', something that also earned them the title of the 'Dirty Dozen'!

"The zealots must forget that the Deliverer even made Peter, a simple fisherman, leader of this 'Dirty Dozen'. With the possible exception of the shrewd Judas Iscariot, Peter and the rest of the 'Dirty Dozen' would actually be quite uncomfortable and mollified visiting with any of the princes of the Church of modern times!

"It shouldn't be that difficult for us to get the zealots to make it look as if the situation relating to the numbers of those working the 'fields' is absolutely desperate. The role of the Holy Spirit in saving souls must be played down. That will, in turn, make it easy for the wrong type of humans to get in there.

"There ought to be a couple of really good orators among the recruits - fellows who can move crowds with their choice of words and booming voices, and make a huge impression! In that way, we will see lots of self-willed folks running around claiming that they are raking in souls when it is all a show orchestrated by us, and nothing is really happening.

"And then, we will be on the look out for those truly selfless souls - souls through whom the Holy Spirit performs real, not staged, miracles. The problem though is that even if they are removed from society and, confined to a hermitage or some such place where they are devoting themselves full time to a life of contemplation, through their prayers and works of penance, they really do a lot to frustrate our work.

"We, for our part, must endeavour to frustrate them as much as possible. Our tack will be to try and condemn them to 'dark nights of the soul' permanently, so they at least won't get away with the damage they do to our cause (inglorious though it may be) that easily. And because those selfless types are the beloved of the Prime Mover and 'untouchables', we will try to achieve our objective by working through those with whom they must perforce commingle - their colleagues, and especially their spiritual advisors and superiors.

"We have to do everything to ensure that the spiritual directors and others who exercise lawful authority over them, even though outwardly pious and devoted to the spiritual welfare of those they serve, are self-willed and virtual human devils - saintly on the surface, but crooks on the inside - yeah, crooks whose actions in fact aim to achieve the exact opposite. If we can also get the 'hypocrites' to burn with jealousy because of being 'overlooked' and even 'sidelined' by the Holy Spirit in the dispensation of His graces, all the better!

"The selfless souls must be made to believe that they have been abandoned by the Prime Mover, and that their prayers for peace and a stop to the killing are in vain and completely wasted effort. They must be made to feel exactly as the Deliverer felt in the Garden of

Gethsemane when, peering into the future, he saw that self-willed humans would continue to act as if He hadn't been around!

"That would be the case even though He was going to pay a very heavy price for their redemption. But it was also only those descendants of Adam and Eve who believed in the Deliverer and did His bidding would be saved, not the murders, thieves and liars.

"If we can cause just one of those beloved of the Prime Mover to loose faith in Him and revert to a life of sin and debauchery, that would be a huge blow to the cause of Good, and a great triumph for the cause of Evil! We must do what we must do. Nothing must be left to chance.

"And we must, of course, also work hand in hand with those self-willed, crafty, and dissembling individuals in the Church whom the establishment nonetheless touts as 'living saints'. We must support the activities of these self-proclaimed 'models of virtue', and offer them all the help they need in perpetuating their schemes of deception and in sustaining their facade as holy souls. Our technique must be to get as many folks as possible inside and outside the Church focused on these bogus 'luminaries' instead of turning to the Deliverer to implore His mercy.

"We must support them to the very end, and particularly during those moments when it looks as if they might not be able to sustain their facade as 'exemplars of virtue', and risk exposure. We must constantly be close to their side, especially when it looks as if their posturing and antics are only thinly disguised and might give them away.

Impossible to forge the divine seal of approval...

"Still, the fact remains that when humans, conceited and well satisfied with themselves, embark on any mission including those that are trumpeted as being spiritual, it is usually a disaster - and no wonder. In attempting to show that they are clever, quite frequently these folks unabashedly claim that they are conducting their missions on behalf of the Prime Mover when the ultimate goal is all about worldly success.

"Believe it or not, but the sin of Judas Iscariot consisted in pretending that he was responding to divine grace in 'betraying' and handing the Deliverer over to His enemies. That 'ex-seminarian' would just have been a common thief if he had admitted that he was just after the thirty pieces of silver.

"But he represented himself to the priests and Sadducees as a good Jew who became a follower of the Deliverer and allowed himself to be groomed as one of the twelve 'apostles' in good faith - after being tricked into it by the 'insurgent'. To save his skin after they let him know that he was in hot soup for allowing himself to be 'misled' the betrayer (turned exemplary citizen and patriot) had assured the assembled members of the Sanhedrin that he now regarded it as his sacred duty to turn the Son of Man over to them!

"As a result, the Deliverer let the world know that it would definitely have been better if His betrayer had not been born! Meaning that *Judas himself*, had he somehow known that it would fall upon him to formally betray the Deliverer in the name of all sinful humans - and known it *before* he was born - and if he had been able to tell the Creator 'Pass' when it was his turn to be brought into the world, would have done so.

"There are those Judas Iscariots who set out proclaiming that they are on a mission to root out abuses in the Church. But they end up misleading hordes. Instead of living up to their reputation as 'reformers', they end up as schismatics, heading heretical movements. Others inside the Church represent themselves as defenders of the faith when all they really are doing is pursue their own agendas and personal ambitions, and have no real interest in Church unity.

"Indeed, there was a time when some 'zealots' organized crusades ostensibly for the purpose of keeping the holy places in Palestine from falling into the hands of 'infidels'. But the 'holy' crusades quickly degenerated into plundering, mayhem, and murder! As a matter of fact, as Armageddon draws near, you can expect to see more and more crusades of that type - crusades that are driven by narrow-minded geopolitical, and ultimately selfish, interests but are carefully camouflaged as 'Christian' crusades - taking up the energies of humans.

Holier than thou...

"It is all driven by that I-am-holier-than-thou attitude. Female prostitutes think they are better than male prostitutes, and vice versa. And they are in turn scorned by everyone else - as if that ancient profession could have survived without the universally unfailing and all too generous support that it has always enjoyed, not to mention the lusting and what not that goes on inside the minds of humans, the weird activities that go on in people's bedrooms, and the adulterous relationships that pass for chic lifestyles!

"Yes - what goes on in the bedrooms *and* inside human minds! Inside the dirty minds where the offences of humans against the authority of the Prime Mover are actually committed. It is there, inside the mind, where evil thoughts that corrupt originate. It is also there, inside the mind, where the evil plots against the Prime Mover and against fellow humans are hatched.

"Those who enjoy classical music despise those who enjoy Rock' n 'Roll, Rhythm and Blues, or Hip Hop, and the other way round. Members of church choirs look down on pop musicians, and vice versa, when it is an established fact that it is church choirs that frequently kick-start the careers of pop stars, and many a pop star's career winds up in the pews along side gospel singers.

"People of one religious persuasion think they are better than those of other religious persuasions - when it is all a matter of persuasion, and the Deliverer died so that *all* humans might be saved. Folks on the Christian right think that folks on the Christian left or the Christian center are 'unsaved', and the other way round.

"There is only one Truth; but just look at all those so-called 'Christians' who pride themselves in belonging to this or that denomination, and are nevertheless united in one common cause of slandering the 'chosen people' for passing up the opportunity to rally behind the promised Messiah and Deliverer of humankind two thousand years ago; and of supposing that one of the twelve, who had been hand picked by the Deliverer to lead His infant church, not only was an unworthy choice for the position of 'apostle' but, despite his remorse at having let down his divine Master, stands as a symbol of damned and lost humans!

These same 'hypocrites' (if I, Beelzebub, may dare call them that) would lynch any one who was so despicable as to commiserate with the 'bad thief' as those who had just caused the Son of Man to suffer an ignominious death on the cross in expiation of mankind's sordid iniquities turned on him, and began bludgeoning him to death with blunt clubs! Oh, how you humans suck (as you yourselves say)!

"Atheists think that believers are less than honest in their reasoning, and believers fault atheists with a lack of moral integrity. One group of short-sighted folks despises other groups for stupid reasons, and vice versa.

"And, as if that is not bad enough, members of opposing groups will even hunt down and kill each other non-stop for the same stupid reasons, instead of just 'getting along' together. There is no specie that exploits its own as much as does the human specie. And there is certainly no other specie whose members are permanently locked in deadly combat with their own kind and, moreover, for no good reason!

"Those humans who are devilish believe that they are angelic and wise and, by the strangest of coincidences, the least devilish among them believe that they are the biggest sinners and the most foolish - as if I wouldn't be happy to embrace them and turn them also into devilish creatures dedicated to the service of evil, if I had been able to! Which illustrates the stubbornness of the wicked and their reluctance to hearken to the urgings of divine grace, and the problems that we in the Underworld have with humans who retain their childlike innocence!

"Boys think they are better than girls who supposedly are 'sissy'; and girls think they are better than boys who supposedly are 'rough'. Those who are young and 'green' despise and discriminate against those who are elderly and well versed in things of this world. And they not only rebuff the advice of the 'wicked old men' and 'wicked old women', but the young people keep repeating to themselves that they will not allow themselves to be swayed by some 'genteel' old lady or gentleman however handsome.

"Thus, a sprightly *madame* or *monsieur* boasting curly and really beautiful, but greying locks of hair however seductive to the eye, supposedly does not deserve a second glance; and even the first glance is given grudgingly. The function of old people supposedly is just to serve as a reminder to the young people that the things with which they are preoccupied and for which they have so much concern are for the most part temporal, passing and transient. And, invariably, the young people interpret that to mean that anything that can be enjoyed should indeed be enjoyed while it lasts!

"The elderly in turn scorn young people as immature and innocent, with lots to learn about the hard realities of life. And they dismiss the ideas of humans who are still youthful as churlish and untested! Those who are slender in build despise and discriminate against those whose frames are full and robust.

"Those who are in the prime of life despise those who have had a full life and are on the verge of joining the ancestors, while those who are in the twilight of their lives invariably look upon themselves as the fortunate few who had made it to a ripe - and cheery - old age. Perhaps justifiably so after living through one, two and sometimes even three 'world wars', plagues that have seen the world's population decimated and nearly wiped out, famines, and other natural disasters which the rest of the populace know about only through history books.

"Humans who are still alive despise those who have passed on - supposedly because the latter are no longer in a position to frolic and enjoy things of this world any more, unaware that the dead actually have nothing but pity for the folks they left behind; and the dead pity the living precisely because the latter seem unable to learn that any enjoyment back on earth is strictly temporal and a distraction that prevents humans from making the best use of their short time on

Planet Earth for 'keeping watch with lighted candles for the coming of the bridegroom'!

"Then, of course, the dead additionally sympathize with the living because (according to the Evangelist) at the time of the Second Coming of the Deliverer, it is those who have already passed who will precede the living when humans line up to meet Him.

"But the dead pity the living for other reasons as well, not least among them the fact that whereas the dead no longer doubt that Christ will come again to pass judgement on the world, not only are there still many living humans who do not realize that the promised Deliverer came unto the world and paid the price for the sins of humans two thousand years ago (as had been foretold) before ascending into heaven, but many didn't even believe that there was such a thing as the 'second coming' of the Deliverer!

"Westerners" versus "Easterners"...

"Those who hail from the 'West' despise those who hail from the 'non-Western world', and do not regard the lives of non-Westerners as being of the same value as the lives of 'Westerners' - and the other way around. Westerners think that they have been blest and above all 'anointed' by the Prime Mover. They believe that, unlike non-Westerners who supposedly are allied to me (the Prince of Darkness), they themselves (Westerners) are allied to the one and only true Prime Mover! Westerners also believe that they have a lock on the destiny of the world in which non-Westerners can regard themselves as completely irrelevant, and non-Westerners think the same of Westerners!

"Non-Westerners also believe that Westerners are wedded to sordid materialism, wallow in smut, and are caught up in the strangest perversions and a peculiar kind of spiritual depravity that effectively stunts the human conscience, and are enslaved to vices that rival those that caused the cities of Sodom and Gomorrah to be singled out for destruction.

"Westerners glorify individualism and 'democracy' or big government that is controlled by lobbies for the benefit of the 'establishment' and the moneyed folks, and look with disdain on extended family ties that are valued much more by non-Westerners. But non-Westerners, whose traditional beliefs are centered around nature, and who have always had the 'tribe' as their governance model, despise and ridicule Westerners for the same reasons that Westerners despise them. Westerners regard themselves as cultured, and non-Westerners as uncultured, while non-Westerners believe that Westerners lost their culture long ago, and hence the spiritual morass to which Western society appeared to have been condemned.

"Westerners believe that the non-Western world is a festering eye sore that is home to millions, if not billions, who should never have seen the light of day for their own good (supposedly)! They believe that, as a result, the non-Western world is now the breeding ground for all manner of dissatisfied humans, 'terrorists', and 'insurgents' who are out of their mind; and that the non-Western world is a threat to world peace. They also believe that it is now (Alas!) up to them (Westerners) to go after these disgruntled folks, bible in one hand and bunker-bursting bombs in the other, and teach them (non-Westerners) a lesson or two, and root out the 'miscreants' to save (Western) civilization!

"For their part, non-Westerners believe that Westerners are imperialists who, for the most part, still live in the 'wild west'. They believe that Westerners have legalized corruption (now going by such labels as 'lobbying' and 'political contributions'), practice cronyism and believe in 'ruling oligarchies', while at the same time investing in a prison 'industry' that is bursting at the seams and that almost exclusively targets the poor and the disadvantaged.

"Non-Westerners believe that many of those who occupy the seats of power in the West and the 'experts' who advise them suffer from delusions and are, for all practical purposes, out of their mind. They (non-Westerners) believe that the arsenals of weapons of mass destruction (WMD) in the hands of self-appointed messengers of a 'Western' divinity', who are determined to take over the world in concert with crazed 'neocons' and 'neolibs', represents the real threat to the survival of Planet Earth.

"But non-Westerners also believe that Westerners may be dying out because of their attitudes to everything from women's reproductive rights to family values, and they (non-Westerners) regard that as good riddance that might not be coming fast enough! According to non-Westerners, their technology-minded counterparts in the West, in trying to space child births using pills and other artificial methods, inadvertently interfered with the cycles in nature that regulated the earth's population, and ended up stunting the human reproductive processes and also bequeathing all manner of diseases including the HIV/AIDS virus to the world. That, incidentally, is also how non-Westerners explain the incurable nature of HIV/AIDS!

"Westerners believe that there is 'no other side', that only their feelings and their sufferings matter, that their behavior, however depraved and monstrous, can never amount to a disgrace; and also that they are the only sane humans left on earth; and non-Westerners are convinced that Westerners are insane!

"Westerners believe that Armageddon is not far off and they have adjusted the pace of life in the West accordingly, while non-Westerners do not think so and are still committed to a happy-go-lucky, slow and easy pace - and lifestyle. And Westerners believe that they are the only ones with valid passports to heaven, and that British and American passports in particular take one there by the most direct route; and that non-Westerners, steeped in oriental, African and similar religious 'crap' have passports to hell only (unless they become Westernized). And, for their part, non-Westerners regard Western societies as decadent, and the Westerners themselves as lost with no hope of redemption!

Members of the same "inhuman" family...

"Humans even forget that they are all members of the same human - actually inhuman - family: brothers and sisters who are descended from the same, albeit fallen, Adam and Eve; and who also have the same nature. They all laugh and cry in the same way and for the same reasons. They have the same aspirations in life - to live happily and productively, and to grow to a ripe old age - and even the same temperament.

"In point of fact, whether a human is a male prostitute or a female one, a porn star or a cloistered nun, old or young, a dead one or one who is still alive and 'kicking', a Westerner or a non-Westerner, a murderer or an actual or potential victim, they are all the same thing - humans.

"Which should come as a relief especially to hypocrites! However, because they really are hypocrites, it comes as very bad news and as something they find very difficult to accept. Hypocrites sincerely believe that only humans of their 'moral' or 'religious' persuasion are in good books with the Prime Mover or their concept of 'the Almighty' - as if the Son of Man did not die for the salvation of all humans. In the case of atheists, 'the Almighty' is in fact themselves. (Pity no one regards me, Beelzebub, also as one!)

The ways of hypocrites...

"Because hypocrites firmly believe that they *alone* are in good books with the Prime Mover, they like to imagine that when they do anything - so long as it is them and not someone else - it has to be perfectly O.K. and even virtuous. In their eyes, when humans who have a different perspective on reality from their own do anything, it must be wrong because it has to be the devil that is the source of the inspiration for whatever these other humans conjure up and do.

"The tussle between neocons and neolibs over the 'sanctity of human life' is illustrative. Neocons are convinced that neolibs, by supporting women in their struggle for equal rights with men, are murderers and evil because they also indirectly support things like contraception and abortion. Neolibs charge, fairly or unfairly, that neocons are the ones who are always quick to support trade embargoes on so-called rogue nations when it is well-known that it is the most vulnerable members of society - the unborn and the newly born - who pay the price with their lives!

"According to neolibs, neocons not only blindly support capital punishment, but are the biggest supporters of that strange new phenomenon - the corporations that produce armaments and weapons of mass destruction. Neolibs charge that neocons are war mongers who will not balk at furthering their geopolitical agendas through the use of force without any regard for the value of human life. Neolibs also accuse neocons of putting money first and the health of people second with their support of health management organizations and antagonism for moves to institute free universal health care. Neolibs also point out that neocons are indifferent to the fact that pharmaceutical companies, with their pricing policies, effectively deny millions of HIV/AIDS sufferers access to drugs that would save their lives.

"Thus, according to neolibs, neocons are murderers for doing what they do. But what they themselves (neolibs) do cannot be questioned supposedly because all they are doing is support the struggle of women for equal rights with their male counterparts - a very noble goal to which neocons only pay lip service. And, according to neocons, neolibs are the ones who are guilty of the charges they (neolibs) make against their camp and are murderers. Otherwise, all they themselves (neocons) are doing is adhere to the conservative ideologies which - in their minds - have the Prime Mover's stamp of approval and, therefore, can never harm any one except the wicked.

"It seems to be typical of hypocrites that they themselves *must* invariably *be right* always regardless of the facts of the case, and those who disagree with them *must be wrong always*. Instead of asking the *real* hypocrites to please stand up, it might well be better to pose the following questions: Are the neocons the real hypocrites, and the neolibs the guilty ones, or is it perhaps *vice versa*?

"Might it just be that this label is transferable, and the camp whose party looses in a given election, becomes the one that deserves to pick it up - albeit only as long as they remain out of office? Or is it that neocons and neolibs are all 'immune' to that 'disease', with the result that the accusation is groundless. Meaning that neither camp, regardless of what it does, endorses or is in the business of killing? But if hypocrisy is the sort of disease that is no respecter of either ideology or persons, and is consequently plaguing neocons and neolibs alike, then they have to accept that they all do indeed kill, and are accordingly guilty - and doomed!

"Certainly, killing could not be OK when neocons did it, and bad when neolibs did it - or vice versa? Well, since the 'sins' of hypocrites - in their own perception - are not 'sinful', both the neocons and the neolibs are effectively off the hook - in their minds! Consequently, contrary to what some churchmen say about situational ethics, taking away a human life under one set of circumstances apparently may be sinful (depending on whether the judge is a neocon or a neolib), while doing so under a different set of circumstances could be just fine (again depending on the philosophy of the judge)! And - depending on the identity of the players and the circumstances - the 'sin' could also turn out to be a virtue! But if you ask me (Beelzebub), that is just another kind of hypocrisy.

"If the actions that result in needless death were motivated solely by the desire to maintain super power status, may be a case could be made about the morality of killing while pursuing that goal. Its weakness would consist in the fact that every nation yearns for super power status, and if they all indulged in needless killing in an effort to gain or regain, or retain that illusory status, quite a bit of killing would be going on all the time. It seems patently worse that in the final analysis, the needless killing is motivated by desire to win party elections, and be in a position to keep lobbies - yes, the lobbies that exert their muscle and dole out the big money that in the end determines who triumphs in an election - happy.

"One thing about this business of killing that works in our favor is that 'once a killer, always a killer!' As with other sins that humans commit, after snuffing out the life of his/her first victim, the killer's urge to do it all over again grows stronger by the day; and, before long, the killer human will be itching for another kill as if to stopping and turn away from that murderous path is an admission of guilt - and an act of cowardice.

"After laying waste and plundering one city, megalomaniacs work to strengthen their image as 'tough' and 'resolute' leaders by moving on to the next one to repeat their exploits. It doesn't take long after that before taking another human's life or helping oneself to someone else's property becomes completely ordinary - like sipping iced tea. Humans become so easily intoxicated with these things, and Julius Caesar was a good example.

"While he was personally leading his armies into Gaul, North Africa, and elsewhere, it never once struck him that a time would come when he himself would give up the ghost and leave all the booty he had amassed behind - and that it was all a waste of time, effort and lives. It never struck him that killing and stealing were damnable things - until the moment his 'friend' Brutus produced the dagger, and the Commander-in-Chief and Field Marshal noticed that he himself might have unwittingly wandered into the cross hairs of a like-minded 'Son of Sam'. It was in that momentary flash, when the beloved Roman Emperor and Conqueror of the World saw that Brutus was unmoved and determined, and ready to strike out with the dagger, that taking a human life suddenly became revolting and an outrage - and completely damnable! Until then, Julius Caesar thought that prosecuting wars in which thousands, including his own countrymen, lost their lives prematurely was cool. He himself had killed and had seen his henchmen also kill, and he had savored every moment of his devilish - yes, devilish - pastime.

"But, for the doomed megalomaniac, killing now became damnable for all the wrong reasons. Sons of Sam do not become converted just because they realize that they themselves are on death row - just like every one else. And it certainly doesn't strike them that, because they too can and indeed will die one day, any act of self-aggrandizement and any preoccupation with worldly things for their own sake is wasted effort. It doesn't strike them that, if they were thinking aright, they should be holed up in some hermitage fasting and doing penance for the multitude of their sins. The fact that another

Son of Sam shows up and seems determined to snuff out the killer's own life prematurely becomes damnable and revolting because it threatens to rob them of the enjoyment of the booty they have spent all their waking hours amassing.

"It is not as if megalomaniacs and other killers and thieves end up here in the Pit with us because they are not afforded ample graces by the Prime Mover like everyone else. The Prime Mover uses so-called 'acts of God' and other signs almost on a daily basis to show humans them that, one and all, they are both at His mercy and totally dependent on Him at the same time - and that worldly success is a mirage. We can of course only thank our stars that evil minded humans refuse to pay heed to their consciences and end up pitching in their lot with me, the Author of Death and mastermind of evil.

"It is bad enough if a pugilist hits the opponent below the belt in a contest. It is very bad if you sneaked up behind someone you did not like and crushed a rock against his spine - or if you took him out from a safe distance with a rifle shot. It has to be worse if you tried - successfully or unsuccessfully - to neutralize your 'enemy' with a guided missile from the safety of a bunker. It could never be right for the simple reason that it is not something you would have liked someone to do to you. It must be really bad if you did that sort of thing just because you wanted to triumph as a politician. It is as simple as that.

"When hypocrites 'murder', they might believe that all they are simply doing is mete out justice - on the Prime Mover's behalf, so to speak. When they 'seize' property that does not belong to them, they might deceive themselves that such an action can never be counted against them - that they do not need to worry about restitution - like happened in Zimbabwe, South Africa, Kenya, and other places (with the blessing of the missionaries).

"They attempt to justify their action by claiming that it is necessary because the 'intentions' of the wicked have to be frustrated. But when others make a move to seize theirs even for justifiable reasons, it becomes 'nationalization' or 'robbery' - and it will even elicit the ire of churchmen. And so, in the end, robbery and stealing are all things that too are relative, and are right or wrong depending on whose property it is and, above all, who is seizing it.

"When Britons, Spaniards, Portuguese, Italians, and others easily overrun Africa, the Americas and elsewhere with the benefit of gun powder and the blessings of missionaries, and seized lands and other property from 'natives' in those lands, apparently that could not possibly have been regarded as wrongful annexation in some people's view. And not even churchmen saw anything wrong with it. If they did, they would be busy pontificating about restitution and things like that.

"As it is, no one sees anything wrong with the fact that a few hundred individuals own most of the land in some of the former 'colonies' or 'possessions' while the original owners in their millions remain landless. It is obvious that the 'ideal' situation, which was also undoubtedly the intention, was to drive those 'natives' into the sea so that it would be pointless to sermonize about the obligation to pay restitution following the massive, officially sanctioned, land grabs. But it would even make more sense if churchmen came out and announced that stealing was not stealing; that killing was not a sin; and, of course, that 'restitution' applied only in a different world - an imaginary world - and that everybody went to heaven, and that hell was only for me, Lucifer, and the other rebel angels, and Judas Iscariot (the convenient scapegoat) who is assumed by everyone to have brought damnation upon himself when he betrayed the Deliverer (as if Judas Iscariot is the only one who has ever done so).

"It certainly says something about how 'Christ-like' those churchmen who are comfortable with the status quo are. Being Christ-like is apparently also a relative thing - meaning that, depending on who you are and the circumstances, you can rob and plunder and still be one of the 'elect' even if you did not make any restitution. Accordingly one must use the label 'thief' carefully - since some who would otherwise be counted among thieves are actually privileged and exempt from the obligation to return stolen property!

"Relativism is apparently unavoidable because it would be a contradiction in terms for actions of humans who are 'saved' or 'chosen' to amount to something that could be regarded as crass in the eyes of the Prime Mover! The injunction 'Do unto others what you'd have others do unto you' supposedly applies to those who have me, Beelzebub, on their side; and it does not apply to those who have the Prime Mover on their side! Is that so - or is it so, perhaps, only in the mistaken perception of hypocrites?

"For sure, if it is unacceptable for a crooked cop to issue a traffic citation to a motorist who is innocent (because that crooked cop himself would definitely not want to receive an undeserved speeding ticket), it has to be unacceptable to loot and plunder, and even less so for humans to physically and/or mentally abuse or torture fellow humans. If it is indefensible for humans to incarcerate their own kind, and treat them in ways they wouldn't treat their own pets and beasts of the wild, it is even less so for any human to torture another human - regardless of his/her race, religious affiliation, social status, political leanings, and religious affiliation – for any reason.

"When did it become acceptable to do unto others what you would not have others do unto you? I am Lucifer, and I do not believe I am crazy! That would be really tragic given my weighty responsibilities of putting to the test the faith and trust of humans in the Prime Mover! When an undeserved traffic ticket is issued, it hurts the victim. But there are also consequences for the crook who issues the ticket. The gratification derived from issuing it actually does turn into something quite nasty in time - a couple of months in Purgatory, perhaps?

"And when, oh when, did it become acceptable to seek to kill out of revenge? You wouldn't try it you were facing a foe you knew was much stronger than you yourself - or if you knew that your vengeful act would mean the end of you - would you? Says something about the callousness of some of the world's so-called 'leaders' who will engage in vengeful pursuits from the safety of the bunkers in which they are closeted, while sacrificing the blood and treasurer of the nation! You do not want to witness their encounter with the Avenging Angel when their own time to go comes, I tell yah!

"I have to say that there is a heavy price that will be paid for condoning or engaging in any practice that amounts to abuse, humiliation or torture, even if it might appear as if that is just a matter between contending humans with no 'outsiders' involved. The Avenging Angel does not take kindly to a-social behavior of that nature - behavior that, besides, is the height of hypocrisy. And you'd better mark my words, because I speak from experience!

Invalid excuse...

"Humans who kill forget that the Avenging Angel cannot be talked into taking bribes, is no respecter of persons, makes no distinction between neocons and neolibs, or the Christian right, the Christian left, the Christian center and the 'non-Christian' world. Humans kid themselves that the Avenging Angel can be rendered irrelevant - like the United Nations or the League of Nations that preceded it. Many, completely blinded by self-love, believe that they can plunder and kill, and effectively conceal the tell-tale evidence.

"There is no ruse that humans - or, for that matter, any creature - could use to put the Avenging Angel off the scent; and no trick that humans could play to foil his mission. There is, naturally, no weapon that humans could use to deter him or delay his mission. There is no bunker that could keep out the messenger from On High who goes everywhere with his hand on the sheath that holds his razor-sharp cutlass. There are no ramparts that human ingenuity could build to block his advance. There is no type of cuirass or armor that his sword cannot slice through. There is nothing behind which a human could hide to escape justice, just as there is no place to which a human could fly to escape his wrath! And, when the day of reckoning comes, the haughty and the mighty will be cowed down and will be begging to be spared the sword.

"And if a human killed, it will not matter in the slightest if he/she was acting solo, as a member of an organized or disorganized gang or mob, as a member of a disciplined or undisciplined platoon, a special operations unit, or unit of a regular army that was staging an invasion. It will not matter if the decision to kill was made in cabinet or on a street corner. It will not make a difference whether the killer did it while 'On Her Majesty's Secret Service' or was taking his/her orders from the CIA, the KGB, or some similar 'shady' organization. If a human killed, it will not even matter if the killer was under the delusion that he/she had been appointed the Prime Mover's enforcer.

"It will not make any difference if one killed while following orders. This is because there is no entity or organization that has the power or ability to indoctrinate a human to the point where his/her conscience becomes effectively blunted. There is no order that anyone however high placed can issue that can absolve a human from personal responsibility for taking property that belongs to another, leave alone taking another's life. What is more, humans not only are under the obligation to love their neighbors - and that includes their enemies - but they also must be prepared to turn the other cheek when slapped! And, of course, you fools - the end can never (repeat 'never' fifty times or as many times as is necessary to get you to accept this simple obvious principal) justify the means.

"The fact that a killer was 'one of the finest' so-called and, bedecked in his/her uniform and swinging a baton, was using only 'necessary' force, will not help an iota. The Avenging Angel won't be impressed in the slightest by the uniform and, instead of feeling awed by the baton as it is swung this way or that way to scare him, will casually take that baton from the surprised killer-minded cop and use it to give him a hiding such as he will never forget through all eternity. The fact that the crooked cop might have been decorated a thousand times over for the act of killing won't make the slightest difference. Not even if he/she had succeeded in getting him/herself short-listed for beatification!

"It will also not matter whether the killer called it 'killing' or something else. It will not make any difference if labels concocted to malign the victim and justify the murder successfully stuck or did not stick. It will not even make the slightest difference if the killer's name turned up on the list of candidates for canonization - he would still be my man (or woman).

"It will make no difference whether the killer achieved his/her objective by sticking a dagger into the victim's heart, lobbing a guided missile which hit its mark, or by dropping a 'smart' bomb. It will not matter if the killer attained his/her objective with the help of a primitive sling; or did it by ferrying a nuclear bomb to the detonation site in a remote controlled conveyance and then detonated it from a 'safe' distance in a cowardly fashion; or if the killer decided to show bravado and take his/her own life along with that of the 'enemy'!

"The Avenging Angel will cause all killers regardless of whether they came from the East or the West - or the South or the North - to be stung with their individual consciences for crimes they committed against fellow humans - period! And when the killers are being stung by their consciences for their murderous deeds, any propaganda they might have been involved in ginning up to falsify reality will not just haunt them. It will be dangled in their faces as part of the damning evidence against them by any and all who got hurt as a result of their misdeeds, and it will cause them to wish that they had never been born!

"Actually, in the end, it will be completely immaterial whether a human successfully carried out the plot to murder or was prevented from doing so by circumstances. That is because a human - endowed with intelligence, free will and a conscience - was a murderer from the moment he/she decided that another human did not deserve to live and deserved to die.

"The Avenging Angel will not discriminate between a war lord and a foot solder; a privileged member of society and an underprivileged or disenfranchised member of society; a commander-in-chief of a super power and a 'private' in the armed forces of some 'basket' nation in the third world, a prisoner and a jailor, a slave and his/her master, or between a beggar and a billionaire. He will not even make any distinction between kings and their subjects. In the eyes of the Avenging Angel, killers will be killers, and the fact that some should have known better, while damning in and of itself, will be secondary.

"Humans have to remember that this is the same Avenging Angel who led the host of faithful angels in the battle that saw me and my troops dislodged from our beach-head in Paradise, and who made sure that we were left boarded up in this hell hole. He might not have had the wherewithal to take the sting out of the seeds of death I had succeeded in sowing - only the Deliverer could do that (as He indeed did by His own death on the cross and resurrection from the dead). But the Avenging Angel and his army of holy angels certainly succeeded very well in cornering my army of rebel angels and driving us from the heavens into this miserable 'Underworld'. And if the Avenging Angel could deal with me, earthlings must be really dumb to imagine that they can kill and get away with it.

What distinguishes human "devils" from real ones...

"We ourselves in the Underworld may be evil - you cannot start to imagine the kind of wicked things we demons do to each other and to humans when we get the opportunity - but one thing that we don't do is act hypocrite. When we pure spirits choose to be evil, we stop pretending that we are saintly - unlike you humans! Hypocrisy is not in our culture. It is what sets sinful humans apart from us demons. And we demons dislike hypocrites and others of that ilk, because we ourselves can never know where we stand in their regard!

"The significance of being born with original sin - as in the case of humans - is that, as humans grow up and loose their childhood innocence, they all automatically graduate into 'closeted' murderers, prostitutes, pornographers and terrorists, and hypocrites. And then the shame causes some humans to start sidelining others as *the* prostitutes, thieves, and killers.

"According to the intelligence in our possession - and this is real, not fabricated, 'Intel' - those humans who are loudest in accusing others of being gangsters and purveyors of immorality are usually the ones who are the worst offenders in those respects, the hypocrisy and facade of righteousness notwithstanding! And, far from being imaginary, the hypocrisy is real for the simple reason that, on their own, humans are only capable of sinning!

"And a word about intelligence: unlike you humans, we in the Underworld are not in the habit of manufacturing any of it to suit circumstances. And, because of its unreliability, we made a conscious decision at the outset to put no reliance on the so-called human intelligence, including intelligence gathered by humans who share our 'hell'. We rely entirely on the 'demonic' intelligence generated by fellow demons.

"According to that intelligence, a goodly number of the 'apostles' who minister to the needs of the faithful are really no different from Simon Peter who denied having any knowledge of the Deliverer on so many occasions. And the Simon Peters of today won't even be nudged back to their senses by any cock-crow however ear-splitting. Others, of course, are no different from the priests and Pharisees, and members of the Sanhedrin who started plotting to liquidate the Deliverer from the moment they heard Him preach and represent Himself as the promised Messiah. Without admitting it, they nonetheless see Him as an obstacle to the intrigues, plots and bad habits to which they are wedded, their priestly status notwithstanding.

"Others operate in the exact same way Judas Iscariot did - they are obsessed with the visible trappings of power and their hearts sink whenever it looks as if 'Peter's Pence' might not be bringing in enough collections and the Church (whose coffers sustain them) might go broke. Others are skilful operators like Pontius Pilate. They are not just cosy with the powerful; but, in order to maintain their relationships with the powers that be, these 'apostles' are always prepared to do what it takes to legitimize and even bless the activities of politicians whose activities are contrary to the Gospels and the Church's teachings.

"Others, by their silence in the face of injustices that are perpetrated around them (when they are not openly supporting the perpetrators of the injustices), are in effect chanting along with the rabble: 'Crucify Him! Crucify Him!'

"Some 'apostles' are narrow-minded and self-satisfied with themselves to the point to which they have nothing but disdain for individuals/groups of individuals who dare express their desire to adapt the Church's liturgy to the cultures in which they were brought up. There are even those for whom a *Misa Flamenco* will elicit adulations; but a *Misa Chakacha* or anything approximating it, with its connotations of traditional African rhythmic movement, will cause raised eyebrows and despondency. No, *Misa Chakacha* would be just too scandalous and the body movements just too suggestive! And, of course, the 'Beethoven Mass', even with the distracting sounds of harps, trumpets, drums (Oh, yes – 'drums'!) and strings, must have been divinely inspired. More or less like the Holy Book!

"And at least the Spaniards and the Austrians are traditionally a Christian people, as also are their customs and traditions. One could even say that the Flamenco dance movements and the rhythms that accompany them have been sanctified by centuries of use in Church liturgy! Spain - a 'Catholic' nation, has bequeathed to the world the likes of Theresa of Avila, Phillip Neri, Padre Pio and others like that, the implication being that, even after years and years of evangelization, some of these countries in the 'New World' - countries like Uganda which is populated by animists (something that supposedly is far worse than being a plain pagan) - simply will never produce a single candidate for canonization!

"Holy Martyrs of Uganda? That must be a mistake - the speaker must have meant Holy Martyrs of Italy or Holy Martyrs of some other Western nation!

"It is , in any event, also implied that the ancestors of Africans and the inhabitants of other lands in the non-Western world, who are held in so much esteem by their progeny, are all lost and in hell!

"And the only chance Africans, Indians, Chinese, Arabs and others like that had of being elevated to sainthood was if they turned against their societies and agreed to publicly condemn the customs and traditions of their people because, in the eyes of Westerners, the traditional values and mores of people from Africa, India, China, Arabia and places like that simply were incompatible with

'Catholicism', the meaning of that word notwithstanding! In any event, the chances of Africans, Indians, Chinese, Arabs and other 'non-Westerners' being elevated to sainthood were minuscule if non-existent, and that was borne out pretty much by the records.

"Westerners could, of course, not be blamed for the 'fact' that things were like that. And since the Prime Mover could not possibly be the one to blame, it followed that Africans, Indians, Chinese, Arabs and others like them were almost certainly under a curse! Which probably also explained why the number of African, Indian, Chinese, and Arab peoples who were Catholics was very small and in some cases in fact non-existent.

"One North American cardinal was probably echoing what many of his compatriots believed when he reportedly confessed on national television that he was quite surprised that the African and Indian prelates he met in Rome at the Second Vatican Council spoke Latin as well if not better than his North American compatriots! (Even though I am the devil, I swear that I am quoting my 'reliable' source faithfully, and I am not lying to you. You see, it a good thing - a very good thing in fact - to be addicted to music compositions by Bach, Hayden, Mozart, and Handle, and 'classical' music in general. But it is the lowest one can descend to appreciate traditional African music? That is as low as one can get.

"The only 'real world' is one that is seen through the prism of Western eyes. In fact Westerners can belong to schismatic or plainly heretical movements that even espouse the most anti-Catholic views - even when they believe (as many do) that Holy Mass is an instance of devil worship, or that the Pontiff of Rome is not just the Antichrist but the personification of Satan - but they can never really be far off the mark.

"So long as they call themselves Christians, Westerners, regardless of the nature of their 'heresy', remain 'separated brethren' who, for all practical purposes, still safely belong in the fold.

"But woe to the African who genuinely believes that the religion of his ancestors is the true religion, and that adherents to Christianity are individuals who may be victims of indoctrination -

perhaps a combination of religious and political propaganda - and who find it in their interest to close their eyes to the glaring and, indeed, scandalous 'divisions' in the 'Church'!

"An African or any one who dares to challenge Christians to show that there is more to Christianity than the sentimentalism one encounters at every turn is deemed to be committing a sin that is of its nature unpardonable. Africans and other faithless non-Westerners, who have the audacity to question the authenticity of a religion whose adherents contradict one another right and left, are regarded as irrational 'heathens' and 'infidels' who are beyond the pale of salvation by definition. And, of course, even though the New Testament contains ample evidence of the Middle Eastern - or more precisely Palestinian - origins of Christianity, any one who dares to question the claim that Christianity originated in the West must be intellectually dishonest. That was because it could never be that the cradle of Christianity was 'Middle Eastern' - just like the cradle of slam, and never mind the mountains of evidence that the most damaging divisions in Christianity are attributable to growing influence in the Church of 'Westerners'.

"But what Westerners say, believe or do is really immaterial – and provided they quote from the Holy Book (the bible) to support their beliefs. In point of fact, so long as an individual professes to be a Christian, that individual's is as good as saved already - or is it so? And are those who flock to Catholic churches really 'safe' even if (in contrast to Moslems, Hindus, Buddhists, and other folks) they are just 'church-going' Catholics whose lifestyles are no different from those of every Dick and Harry - and even if only a handful of them would be willing to try and emulate Mother Theresa or Francis of Assisi?

"And might it just be possible that Catholics and many of their so-called separated brethren were the ones the Deliverer had in mind when he referred in a parable to original invitees to the heavenly banquet being turned away because they were busy doing other things instead of 'keeping their candles alight'?

"This is just conceivable for any number of reasons like being busy calling on the Lord's name in vain; or being busy making judgements about people whose cultures they had no interest in knowing or understanding (as the Evil One and also ring leader of the legion of disgruntled and disgraced spirits, I have the license to do that, and humans who follow my example in that respect write-off their chances of being rehabilitated!); or being busy - in league with colonialists, imperialists, slave dealers, and pirates on the high seas - grabbing fertile lands in South Africa, Kenya, Zimbabwe, and Australia by force from the natives there or in the Americas; or, in the case of the 'New World' that Columbus 'discovered', being busy systematically and brutally wiping out the natives-turned-insurgents so the colonists-turned-Yankees could parcel out lands there among themselves without interference from any quarter; or, in the case of settlers in the New World, being busy plotting insurrections (or 'insurgencies') against their British, Spanish, Portuguese, Belgian, French, Italian, and Dutch masters.

"And any way - aren't all 'good' folks inside and outside the Church like that, the difference between them and the 'really good' folks being that the latter readily accept that if they ever do escape my tentacles, it will not be so much because they feel justified (like the Pharisee), but because of the mercies of the Prime Mover and His grace (like the tax collector)!

"And might it just be possible that African and Indian mystics, and others who try their best to follow their consciences in whatever they do were the ones He had in mind when he referred to an order that the doors of the banqueting hall be opened to let in the rabble from the streets (provided they had on 'proper attire')? It, indeed, might just be that quite a few people (who now regard themselves as redeemed and virtually saved) will actually be surprised to find themselves excluded from the 'heavenly banquet', and those they now despise as unfit being herded towards tables piled high with all sorts of mouth-watering gourmets and other goodies!

"Adamantly opposed to changes in the Church's liturgy that would accommodate peoples of different cultural backgrounds within the 'assembly of God's people' or Church, it goes without saying that the attitudes of many of these 'princes of the Church' pay only lip service to the rapprochement that would even bring the separated brethren back into the fold, and represent a major obstacle to Church unity.

"Other 'apostles' are so conceited and puffed up, you would think that they belong to some 'ruling' sacerdotal family - members of royalty in some 'messianic' kingdom! When they pray, give catechetical instruction, or act as celebrants at Holy Mass, they remind one of the Pharisee whose prayers (and, no doubt, also catechetical instruction/lectures) always revolved around fellow humans they deemed unworthy. The humans who constitute their audience are all presumed to be like the God-forsaken tax collector!

Selfishness and godliness contrasted...

"Selfishness and wilfulness contrast with the infinite goodness of the Prime Mover which is manifested in His decision to create 'things' or 'essences', including humans and angels, out of nothing, and to endow the creatures who are made in his own image and likeness such that they will continue their existence in an afterlife with things like reason, free will and the ability to choose between good and evil. The Prime Mover's infinite goodness is manifested, above all, in His decision to give His only begotten Son for the redemption of humans.

"And if ever there is anyone who would have been justified in avenging ills by killing, it is the Prime Mover. The fact that He has explicitly ruled out anything of that sort should remind humans that they are knocking on the wrong door when they kill fellow humans. But - fortunately for me - it does not. That says something about my 'reach' doesn't it!

"The Prime Mover's infinite goodness is manifested in His decision to allow those with evil intentions - like me and my minions among earthlings - to have their way while they are able to. He doesn't go back on his word or step in to stop them from exercising their wills in contravention of His Moral Law.

"But wilfulness is incompatible with what is noble and divine. This is because it focuses on the self. Wilfulness focuses on whatever appears to guarantee excitement and immediate 'fulfilment'. But excitement and fulfilment are changing and temporal, and are the antithesis of true and genuine love - love or generosity of the mold that is divorced from the 'now' or present; is sacred and permanent; and is, above all, in accordance with what the Deliverer's injunction that humans love their neighbors - and enemies.

Humans scared of the spiritual....

"Divine grace - as you might have guessed - is a spiritual thing; and it also operates only on the spiritual dimension and in a purely spiritual manner. So, how could humans, who moreover are so scared of the spiritual, succeed in bringing about what could be engendered spiritually? It is completely ridiculous to expect this of creatures that are so scared of what 'lies yonder'!

"If humans knew how the breathing mechanism worked, they likely would invest all their energies in trying to discover how to restart it as and when it stopped. That is how scared stiff humans are of the spiritual. Death, the gateway to the purely spiritual and also to heaven, is something they would rather not encounter if they could help it.

"Actually, humans - with the possible exception of the so-called animists - don't say so, but they are afraid of divine grace because it is a spiritual thing. Unfortunately for humans, with every day that passes, the moment of their dreaded, and yet inescapable, encounter not just with death, but with His 'Mystic Majesty' who is also the Prime Mover and Creator of all that is, and who sent His only begotten son into the world so that those who believe in Him might be saved, draws ever closer. With every second that passes, the moment of truth when humans have to come to terms with the fact that they are just as much spirits as we ourselves are, approaches.

"That is the principal reason humans find it so hard to cooperate with divine grace. And if they find that hard, what could be said about bringing off, completely on their own and unaided, what divine grace does, namely sanctification of the soul? That is the 'hole' into which I lured Adam and Eve to step two hundred and fifty thousand years ago in the Garden of Eden. Once their rebellion against the Prime Mover got under way, it became literally impossible for Adam and Eve and their descendants to 'save themselves' in the spiritual sense.

"In that sense, we demons, being pure spirits and unafraid of the spiritual, were in theory at least at an advantage after we fell from grace. We wouldn't have been so helpless, and we would indeed have been able to help ourselves - if there had been a second chance. Unfortunately the nature of our rebellion did not permit that.

"It suits us in the Underworld perfectly that humans are scared of the spiritual. It would be uncharacteristic of us if we did not take full advantage of this fear and if we did not deal with humans accordingly. If it had not been for the promise of a Deliverer and the graces He merited for you humans by His death and resurrection, humans would have been entirely at our mercy!

"In conclusion, to understand why humans on their own, unaided by divine grace, cannot perform anything that would amount to an act of virtue, you have to go back to the Garden of Eden and the rebellion of the first man and the first woman against the Prime Mover - and the nature of humans.

"When humans transgress, they do not just transgress and it ends there. They typically wallow in the transgression or sin. You see - an immoral act is never a one time, stand alone affair. Human transgressions are tied to sinners' intention and they are inevitably accompanied by rationalizations whose objective is to make the immorality sit well with the evil doer. That in turn assures that instead of the one transgression which the sinner originally contemplated, a series of transgressions will ensue, and each one will in turn be accompanied by further excuses and rationalizations.

"This happens easily - almost inevitably - because at the time of sinning, the individual effectively ditches trust in divine grace and abandons himself/herself to a virulent wilfulness. Even 'pulling back' from that disposition to offend the Prime Mover is itself only possible with the help of divine grace. The upshot of this is that the sinner becomes mired in sin and immorality. By the time Adam and Eve realized that they had gone overboard in their quest for kicks and thrills in disregard of the divine command, they were literally swimming in sin with no life vest anywhere in sight.

"Now, my job in those circumstances is not to suggest to humans how to avoid drowning in sin. We in the Underworld want humans to sink and die spiritually like us. And we were all agog and already celebrating the downfall of humans. Their guardian angels had been helpless and, like us, could only stand there and watch the entire human race go to pot.

"But it was then that something quite unbelievable happened. Incredibly, the Prime Mover, who had been insulted by Adam and Eve, apparently decided in His infinite mercy to throw them life jackets. This was in the form of a promise to send His only begotten son into the world as one of them - as a human!

"If there ever was a time when we in the Underworld were taken aback, that was it! We simply could not have imagined that the Prime Mover, spotless and albeit infinitely almighty, could forgive a sinner for an insult of that magnitude - not even after they had had a change of heart and expressed remorse. It was an even bigger shocker that the Second Person of the Blessed Trinity, equal to the Father and the Spirit and almighty, consented to come down to earth to pay the price for the transgressions of men, and do it, moreover, with His own life!

"And then, in a master stroke, the infinitely merciful Prime Mover, knowing that Adam and Eve were mired in sin and could not recover on their own, decided to extend the promise of a Deliverer to their posterity as well! Adam and Eve, by their transgression, had already created an environment that would have made it impossible for their children and the children of their children to stay out of the doghouse - it was, after all, Adam and Eve who still retained the responsibility for nurturing and bringing up their immediate descendants who would in turn be responsible for the upbringing of the generation that would follow after them. But the sin of Adam and Eve and the effects thereof had bedevilled the divine plan in that respect as well, and it was the specific inclusion of Adam and Eve's progeny in the promise of salvation made to the first man and the first woman even before they had any issue which salvaged that situation.

"It may be true that the sin of Adam and Eve, which plunged the world into the chaotic state from which it is still reeling today, as sins go, was not really extraordinary. As humans, Adam and Eve themselves, were not extraordinary people except for the fact that they were the first humans who came into the world without the blight of original sin. In fact, sins committed by humans today are as appalling to the Prime Mover even though they are committed by humans who are already inclined to sin from birth - the legacy of the original sin of Adam and Eve. These sins, had they been committed prior to the fall of man from grace, would have had the same effect on the relations between humans and the Prime Mover as the sin of Adam and Eve.

"Because of the peculiar nature of humans, a sin committed by any one of them impinges on the creature-Creator relationship enjoyed by humanity as whole. The friendship between humans and the Prime Mover is affected when any one human offends Him. This is in addition to the effect on that individual's personal relationship with the Prime Mover.

"My troops and I celebrate every sin that is committed against the Prime Mover. But we celebrated the fall of Adam and Eve from grace in a special way; because, representing the first offence by members of humankind against the Prime Mover, we knew that its consequences were going to be incalculable for not just Adam and Eve, but for all their posterity as well. And predictably, original sin made a huge dent in what was otherwise a rock-solid friendship between man and his Maker.

"But there was an additional reason for us to celebrate. If Adam and Eve, the father and mother of humankind who had been created in the Image and as such were wholesome in His sight, had persevered and not fallen from grace, that would have been it. It would have firmly and permanently sealed the friendship that existed between the human family and the Godhead; and with that, Adam and Eve, their children, and their children's children would have earned the right to inherit eternal life in a heavenly paradise. The earth would have remained a place of pilgrimage for humans - a *holy* pilgrimage dedicated to the greater glory of the Prime Mover; and it wouldn't have been the dreadful place it is today in which all things spiritual are overshadowed by the preoccupation with material things.

"Just as all humankind stood to benefit from any special gift or blessing which the Prime Mover in His infinite wisdom bestowed on any one member of the human race, it was only to be expected that they also would stand to suffer from a blight or curse that fundamentally affected humanity's relationship with the Creator. Accordingly humans stood to suffer from the very serious lapse of judgement on the part of Adam and Eve, a lapse of judgement that broke up the friendship of the human family with the Holy Trinity. But they also stood to gain tremendously from the perseverance of Adam and Eve in their judicious and faithful observance of the Creator's injunctions.

"The promise of a Deliverer in the wake of the fall of Adam and Eve from grace - a promise that was no doubt prompted by the sorrow of the first man and woman on realizing the horrible tragedy which sin represented for their individual selves and also for their posterity on the one hand, and by the Prime Mover's infinite love - was very timely. The world is in a bad enough situation as a result of the effects of one 'original sin' - the original sin committed by Adam and Eve.

"In the absence of a promise of deliverance (a promise that was not just made to Adam and Eve, but to them as representatives of all humankind), all subsequent sins committed by Adam and Eve and their progeny would have individually represented original sins in their own right.

"And it is safe to assume that the earth would be a very different kind of place today as a result of the cumulative effects of those original sins - probably just like Mars or Venus. And the human race would already have become extinct, the result of the actions of humans themselves in a blighted, free-for-all, man-eat-man social environment.

"Now, of course, absolute faithfulness and obedience to the will of the Prime Mover had been a prerequisite for humans to remain in His good books and reap their reward after their period of trial in the Garden of Eden. And, so now again, the salvation of humans was made dependent on the infinite love and total obedience to the Father by the Son of Man.

"But that was not all - according to the divine plan and even in the face of sin, the Prime Mover decreed that the advent of the Son of Man into the world would additionally depend on the constancy and ultimately also *fiat* or consent of a humble, unknown maiden by the name of Mary! Yes - the *fiat* or agreement of a human!

"That was how what had looked like certain victory by evil over good was snatched from me in a master stroke! The promise of a deliverer, the decision to specifically include Adam and Eve's posterity among the beneficiaries of the work of redemption, and the involvement of one of Adam and Eve's descendants - the Immaculate Virgin Mary who would consent to be the earthly mother of the Deliverer - as a key player in it!

"Now, Mary, even though spotless and always full of grace, thought of herself as nothing. She always magnified the Prime Mover - the Lord before whom the meek were exulted, and the proud and mighty were humbled. Despite knowing that I, the Prince of Darkness, am stricken with terror at the mere thought of her, Mary remains the one descendant of Adam and Eve who has always understood better that any other the fact that without the help of divine grace, humans are as nothing!

"Unable to be virtuous by dint of their own efforts on the one hand, and finding that they must still do whatever it takes to survive in a world in which equity and justice are just a sham, humans inevitably find themselves 'stranded'. They then invariably seek to escape from their bind, and that is when they land into the traps we lay for them. They make very easy prey for us at that time. For one, they become easily taken in by dissembling in the world that passes for character and integrity.

"And as humans discover that it was all a mirage, they soon find themselves with 'no choice' but to acquiesce to our suggestions that they stop sitting on the fence, not be shy about being capricious and acquisitive, join everyone else in essentially exploiting others for their own benefit, and above all start to 'enjoy life' while they can.

"Add to that the human inclination to sin, and you pretty well can guess what the results will be when we set about putting the faith and trust of humans in the Prime Mover to the test..."

Willing spirit, weak flesh...

"If one is inclined to do negative things, it follows that merely avoiding to do negative things has to be through struggle. As humans attempt to avoid things that are dubious so they may be free to focus on things that are constructive, they invariably come up against the problem of a spirit that may be willing, but flesh that remains weak. And the flesh constitutes a growing obstacle as humans embark on the uphill task of trying to accomplish positive things. Because the inclination to negativity does not abandon humans even as they start to grow in holiness, they will continue to feel a sense of helplessness.

"Humans will always have reason to fear that the weakness in their bodies might one day succeed in overwhelming the willingness of the spirit at any time, eventually steering them right back into their old sinful ways. The apostle of the gentiles, and others like Jerome could tell you the same thing.

"The weakness in the flesh will always tend to draw the individual away from reason towards what is base. Appeals by the likes of John the Baptist urging humans to put their lives in order in view of the impending judgement clearly assumed that, despite being weak in the flesh as a result of original sin, humans were at least capable of willing to live as befitted creatures of the Prime Mover. No such appeals have ever been directed at beasts of the earth, fishes, reptiles or birds not so much because they are innocent in the eyes of the Prime Mover, as because they are not endowed with a spirit. But that does not mean that the innocence of these lower creatures should not put humans to shame.

"Guileless and unassuming, they have never betrayed the Prime Mover even once, the harsh realities of their existence notwithstanding. Even though they share this 'valley of tears' with humans, no animal of the wild, bird of the air, reptile, fish, insect or any of the lower creatures suffers from 'weakness of the flesh'. These creatures all have one thing in common: they just do what their instincts tell them and no more. Avarice, debauchery, slothfulness and other pitfalls of the flesh are foreign to them. Birds of the air know instinctively that not one feather gets dislodged from their coat and goes missing without the Prime Mover expressly permitting it. And He is glorified when they respond in whichever manner to that or any other eventuality that comes to pass.

"Believe me, I myself feel so much shame observing the ardour, fealty and dogged constancy of these lowly creatures to their Maker. Just to think that I, so richly endowed at creation, floundered; and that I am now good for nothing save as a spiteful tempter who is driven by jealousy and envy.

"Would you believe it? I am a total failure and a write-off; and even though I have notched up some successes, I can't really claim to be the prime cause for the evil things humans do. After all, beyond the fact that I am a creature like them and a spirit, what do I really have in common with them? There is, actually, little doubt that a good deal of the things that constitute distractions for humans and prevent them from focusing on the Perfect Good and also their last end can be directly blamed on the weakness of the flesh. Of course that might be my window of opportunity; but it is, nonetheless, only a window of opportunity and nothing more.

"I really wish I had the power to actually besmirch and defile humans in the same way someone soils apparel. And even when I have permission to possess a human, it all stops there, because I cannot forcibly haul my victims into my hell even after I have made their lives on earth a living hell. If anything, at the end of these adventures, I have always been more frustrated and miserable than when I started out, because I cannot bear to see those I thought I had succeeded in reducing to nonentities suddenly pluck up energy and sweep past me to their eternal reward in Valhalla!

"When the Prime Mover promised to send the Deliverer in the aftermath of the fall of Adam and Eve from grace, it was clearly on the supposition that the human spirit was capable of willing; and that, once the willingness was activated by the individuals concerned, it became impervious - with the help of grace - not only to my suggestions, but also to the weakness of the flesh. In making the promise, He essentially said that whenever humans invoked His name, He would always be there for them, even though they and their fore fathers before them had transgressed.

"And that is what gets me. Even though bedevilled by original sin, humans become transformed by prayer to the point where the weakness of the flesh, however debilitating, ceases to have any real power over the spirit. That is how prayer undermines my efforts. Even when the flesh is weak, so long as the human spirit is willing and you folks, aware that you are no match for an evil genius like me, begin pleading to be shielded from vitriol and other diseases of the soul, all my efforts somehow always come to naught! And that has led me to a theory about how grace works - and don't you start imagining that I can't expound on this just because I happen to be evil! Are you crazy? No creature, however brilliant, can presume to understand the mysterious ways of the Almighty One!

"In the final analysis, one can only hazard an explanation about how sanctifying grace works. This is in the nature of the beast that we are dealing with. But the theory, even though not fool proof, still is interesting.

"It may well be that, to the extent that one's spirit is willing but the flesh is weak, grace steps in to reinforce the willingness of the spirit. And it also may well be that, to the extent the willingness of the spirit starts to falter with the neglect of prayer and to look like it might be unable to surmount the frailty of the flesh, the ability of grace to bolster it also diminishes correspondingly.

"But it is risky, clearly, to talk about the role of sanctifying grace in these or any other circumstances, because sanctifying grace is a gift. But even if it were something that worked mechanically, how would it function if willingness of the spirit and weakness of the flesh were actually intertwined as they probably are, since we are talking about an *animal rationale* and the exercise of its free will?

"The fact is that, regardless of the situation, prayer is an avenue that is always available to humans for strengthening the willingness of the spirit. When they pray - well, even in the most befuddled way - my schemes, however advanced or promising, just go burst and I have to start all over again. Hypocrites may believe that prayer and its sanctifying effects are only available to them alone and not to others.

"The grace of the Prime Mover and a host of other blessings are available to all humans alike, because all humans are in the exact same predicament - they are creatures with spirits that, if not already actually willing, are at least capable of willing. And, as such, they recognize that Perfect Good, which is also their last end, can only be fully enjoyed (or missed) in eternity and not in this world. They know that, in the same way a spouse who is unfaithful cannot simultaneously claim to be true and trusted, they too cannot be wedded to materialism and say that they are focused on their last end at the same time.

"Although they experience the urge to scramble and obtain immediate respite, and will even invest everything they possess in the pursuit of temporal happiness and security, they also know full well that temporal pleasures and satisfaction are temporal by definition and cannot extend into eternity. They also know that the converse is true, namely that Perfect Good can only be possessed in eternity by definition, outside the limitations of time.

"They know that the Bride is coming; but yet are unable to muster the little attention that is needed to assure that their candles stay lit. If you ask me, I will tell you that they don't even give a damn that they might not have on attire that is deemed appropriate for a wedding feast.

"Again, they know that they are going to die, and yet can't quit pursuits that are incompatible with their status as creatures of the Righteous One. Humans also know that to wear their crown and also have their revenge on the wicked - and I recognize very well that I'm at the top of the list naturally - they must physically die; but the vast majority of humans would sooner sell everything they had to acquire a 'magic' potion that looked like it might insure them against dying - if there had been such a 'magic' portion - than contemplate life after death!

"You humans - if you don't mind me including you, Reverend Mjomba, among them. You humans have been told 'Ask and it shall be given to you'; and yet you seem unable to do that simplest of simple things...sitting back and asking! Worst of all, you need someone like me to come from hell to sermonize about the importance of prayer! Of course the less you pray, the better for us in the Underworld, for we can then rely on the weakness of the flesh to do the job for us.

"I thought I knew how low creatures could sink, but you humans have set new records and surprising even me! The lying, the cheating, the decadence, the killings - yes, especially the killings. I have admittedly killed myself, but only in the spiritual, not physical, sense.

"Unlike you folks, I can truthfully - yes, truthfully - say that I do not have blood on my hands. Guess what - I am a pure spirit, and do not even have hands to brag about!

"As regards the killing, this has been going on since time immemorial - from the time you humans invented the arrow and the sling. It became really bad when it became possible to mass produce swords and spears, and it got worse when you invented gunpowder. And just imagine what it is going to be like with the success of the Manhattan Project and other projects like that! And investment in these 'projects' continues unabated and at a maddening pace, lead by the 'super powers'.

Redefining the "moral order"...

"And while all that has been going on, my troops and I have been working overtime to just ensure that the killing itself becomes accepted, blessed by the religious, and institutionalized. That is how the Philistines, Egyptians, Greeks, and Romans all came to regard killings done in the cause of territorial expansion - not just killings done in defense of borders from 'enemies' - as perfectly justified. This is one of my greatest accomplishments - getting murder to become institutionalized and glorified as military science, and promoted with gusto in the name of 'national security' or 'vital interests'. And since it is the victorious who call the shots, we have been getting more and more of this as time went by.

"We should hear more and more about 'collateral damage' and things like that, which absolve the culprits for the frequently open 'ethnic cleansings' that go on all the time and the sometimes scarcely veiled genocides perpetrated in the name of national security, now that killing is fine in most people's eyes. One of my aims is to see all so-called rules and conventions of war - like those that were designed to safeguard non-combatants and the innocent - abolished. It is also one of my goals to get the United Nations weakened to the point where that body can be manipulated into backing unprovoked preemptive or so-called first strikes if it is in a super power's 'national interest'.

"There was a time once when some so-called advanced nations had legislation on their books that outlawed the murder of heads of state of other countries during peacetime. But that was then. One thing that is high on our agenda is to get all nations of the world to accept that, as and when earthly powers and principalities become 'blessed' by the Prime Mover and succeed in acquiring the wherewithal to launch preemptive strikes against other nations that are not so blessed with impunity, it will also signal that failure to employ that capability to advance their 'national interests' will be criminal! The reason being that all such capability is God-given and must be put to use just like talents that humans receive from the Prime Mover! While this idea has started to take root in certain circles, we are working hard with all our stakeholders to ensure that it becomes elevated to a moral imperative at a much faster pace.

"If you do not know, we here in the Underworld don't have any wish to see peace reign on Earth. We must do everything to ensure that there is turmoil and war all the time, and the best weapon that we have is the greed that drives men to covet things that do not belong to them. We were therefore very fortunate that we were able to get some stupid fools who were in key positions in super powerful nations on board with this idea almost as soon as the so-called 'cold war' came to an end; and, instead of promoting permanent world peace, the stupid fools, claiming to be driven by holy zeal, saw our point and began doing everything according to our script! Yes - when the Prince of Peace was lying in the manger in Bethlehem, the holy angels, announcing the good tidings to the shepherds, sang 'Alleluia' and, pointing to the shining star that helped the wise men of the Orient make it in time to Bethlehem, had greeted them saying 'Peace on Earth'. That was, of course, anathema for my evil plan. We luckily are back in the driver's seat, and we must work with our allies to try and thwart the Divine Plan. We must foil the intentions of the Madonna of Fatima who prayed for peace to descend on Earth.

"To those humans who savor worldly things, we say that victory in war brings more affluence and new opportunities to pander to the desires of the flesh - at least until such time as the 'super powers' of the day themselves get nixed by other emerging super powers and become obliterated in the unending cycle of retribution, that is!

"The existing world order in which materialism and acquisitiveness drive everything is a hallmark of my success in this area. And my troops and I continue to notch up successes as we pursue our ultimate goal of turning things around and making the religions of the world serve our purposes and promote our immediate objectives. You see - having a world that is just secular or 'irreligious' is not bad enough. And we must work hard because we have only a short time to do our dirty work. Yeah, that is what the book says! We've so far succeeded in getting individuals to canonize themselves even before they have left this life for the next, never mind that it is all based on feelings of self-justification and false piety. And we've almost succeeded in using religion to promote materialism and worldliness. We have still got lots of work to do to turn religion around and make it the primary vehicle for triggering wars and causing misery for humanity.

"We've succeeded in making lasciviousness and debauchery accepted in society - I mean, it is legal at least in the 'advanced' countries to set up shop and sell those degenerate and corrupting wares to the public. I mean - there is no limit to the kind of trash you can buy in the open market place. And just imagine that thousands upon thousands around the world make their living peddling the trash! And now, in fact, a nation is not regarded as 'advanced' until we in the Underworld put our stamp on its social fabric, and things of that sort become normal fare!

"And you know, we were very much behind this 'worldwide web' thing - you call it the 'Internet'. It is perfectly legal for anyone to set up shop on that indefinable, so-called borderless the Internet and operate a website whose only purpose is to corrupt morals. I said 'so-called' because the Internet is not really borderless certainly the phone lines it uses are confined to borders, regulated and are even subject to bugging by the authorities. But that is exactly as it should be - my troops and I find that arrangement just terrific for our purposes. Our lackeys amongst you have complete leeway to peddle their sick, corrupting merchandise without interference from anyone. It is exhilarating to see new sites devoted to promoting hate spring up almost every other day with no interference from anyone.

"And very soon there will be websites that will provide complete courses related to the production of weapons of mass destruction. You see - the world is now on the brink of a major war - the third world war. Triggered by a preemptive strike, employing so-called tactical nuclear weapons, on one of the so-called rogue states, you can be sure that the third world war will make the first and second world wars look like storms in tea cups.

"Talking about nuclear weapons, can you imagine that all the United Nations member states, including the Holy See, signed off on the so-called Nuclear Non-Proliferation Treaty without any prodding! The purpose of NPT was of course to protect the five original members of the Nuclear Club from the rest of the world. It would be a contradiction in terms to suggest that its purpose was to protect nations that did not possess those weapons from those that did. So, how come that the UN member states that were actually targeted signed on that "treaty"? Well, you now have an idea what 'fear' does to you humans. It makes you start reasoning backwards - in the reverse!

"You can also consequently conclude that the nations that are more likely to use the WMD are the original members of the Nuclear Club and, in particular, the nation(s) with a history of using those weapons since their fear would was greatest!

"Any way, we are approaching the time when, not just states, but entire continental shelves will be completely obliterated in avalanches of nuclear and hydrogen bombs. But the greatest damage to humans will be inflicted by the chemical and biological weapons which will add a new dimension to warfare, namely panic. Reports of plumes of smoke mushrooming and enveloping entire cities will cause most humans sixty years or older to suffer fatal heart attacks.

"Many people will pass out at the sight of the clouds of chemical dust, and the putrid smell of biological agents will knock out many others. The weak will be trampled to death as the strong try to escape mushrooming clouds that will be bearing down upon them, or at the mere sight of other people suddenly clutching at their throats, after inhaling the deadly biological, viral and radiological 'killer' agents, and writhing in silent agony. Without a doubt, the chemical and biological weapons will inflict the greatest pain and suffering on the people of the Prime Mover.

"It will be a completely different story with respect to the nuclear and hydrogen bombs, and the worst devastation will take place in countries with the biggest arsenals of these weapons. This is because, a single 'direct hit' by an enemy nuke (or a friendly nuke in a 'friendly fire' situation) will set off nuclear and hydrogen bombs hidden in deep silos within a radius of a thousand miles. Meaning that countries with the biggest arsenals of these weapons will be the ones that will suffer the greatest devastation as one exploding nuclear or hydrogen bomb triggers incendiary explosions that in turn will set off nuclear and/or hydrogen bombs in the entire 'arsenal'.

"For now, I use fear - the fear of both those nations that do not possess weapons of mass destruction and those that do - to proliferate these WMD. It might surprise you, but the fact is that, at this particular time, the bigger an arsenal of WMD a nation possesses, the greater its fears - perhaps because that nation is aware of the destructive power of those weapons. But, unfortunately for these nations and perhaps fortunately for the rest of the world, it is also the best example of fear that is leading these nations to 'dig their own graves' as you folks would put it. My influence in the citadels of power around the globe has of course never been greater, and I am determined to see this thing through before the real Armageddon is unleashed upon you humans. Nothing will please me more than the sight of a nuclear conflagration triggered by fear and human stupidity!

"Wars do not happen by accident - believe me. Of course not. We in the Underworld work hard to make sure that our people are the ones in the decision making roles, and we make certain that they are appropriately rewarded - in material terms, of course.

"And understand me - you nowadays have all that bullshit about 'democracy' and other rubbish about taking polls to establish the 'will of the people' before nations can go to war. Regarding democracy - completely ignore what the whining, good-for-nothing philosophers have written. Democracy as a system of government only dates back to Marie Antoinette and the French revolution she engineered. It was her idea that the traditional rulers - kings and emperors should be toppled in favor of the dictatorship of the masses. Also, it was not an accident that Karl Max, who took that notion one step further and advocated ownership of the means of production by the masses spent some time not far away - in the British Isles just across the channel.

"In so-called 'democracies', it is usually a tiny but, of course, well connected clique - a small group of ambitious, power hungry individuals - that wields power. They are the ones who wield power, not the masses who 'elect' them. Elections themselves are nothing but a circus and a farce, designed to give the small group of individuals who step into a nation's halls of power credibility. The clique that is in power, in concert with any other clique(s) in existence, invariably strives to suppress the emergence of any new cliques or groupings - political parties as you call them - that might end up challenging and even supplanting them in the halls of power.

"I tell you - what goes on in the name of democracy is all a farce. Remember, we are talking about the exercise of raw power here in the world gone amok, and the opportunities that 'leaders' of nation states have of promoting their self-interest. And you can be sure that it is not the 'official' agenda of the so-called political parties that cliques in power implement. It is certainly not the agenda that is dictated to them by their Prime Mover. It is the agenda of the clique in power that is pursued, and members of the clique see absolutely nothing wrong with subordinating the *bonum commune* to their own personal interests.

"And what do you think the role of the Prince of Darkness would be in those types of circumstances? You can be pretty sure that, with my interest in influencing the course of history, and hastening the onset of Armageddon, I will be all over the place dictating to these power brokers exactly what they should do. It is I, Diabolos, who remains in charge, and this is true whether what you have brewing is British, Portuguese, Spanish, Japanese, or American imperialism, communism, Nazism, or whatever other 'ism' that might be in the works.

"And on the global scene, it doesn't really matter to me either whether victors in global conflicts are Germans, Americans, French, Russians, Arabs, Chinese, Indians, or Africans. The 'color' of the super power - or hyper power - is immaterial to me. In this murky business, I make it a rule to always go with the winner! If this will get you bubbling 'Brilliant!', I would advise you to check yourself - it is just simple common sense! But of course, 'common sense' is not very common nowadays - or is it? On the national scene, it does not matter a dime to me which clique takes the reins of power.

"I am trying to say that it is of very little significance to me whether the clique that occupies the halls of power comes from a 'political' or 'non-political' party'; and - if a political party - whether it is a party that is 'rightist' or 'leftist', 'conservative' or 'liberal', 'neo-conservative' or 'neo-liberal', 'Christian' or 'non-Christian', 'secular' or 'non-secular', etc. If you ask me - I do not even see any difference between 'neocons' and 'neolibs', and that distinction is not in my vocabulary. Perhaps you are one of those who likes to discriminate against some people - not me, I tell ya!

"And guess what - if the individuals who made up the cliques in power in the different countries were as fool-hardy or as brave as they make it appear, instead of dragging their countries into conflicts and 'wars of opportunity', they would be offering to fight duels with the leadership of any nation they found themselves at loggerheads with as a way of settling disagreements that arose. And in a duel, cheating in not permitted! And you certainly don't try and 'disarm' the other party first, because then it wouldn't be a duel. And, of course, if it looks from the outset like it will be an uneven match, no person of honor will try and lay false claim to valor, much less victory, by agreeing to be a participant. Doing so brings dishonor not just to the individual, but to that individual's family and country as well.

"Understand that you humans are all from one stock. You are supposed to get along with one another, and it does not make sense to try and destroy one another on the battlefield either. What's more, by opting to settle their differences through such duels and saving ordinary folk in those countries the curse of war, these leaders would be showing the highest statesmanship. They would in effect be proving to the world that they are prepared to sacrifice *their* lives for their countries. And if they lost the duels and gallantly met their death at the hands of the 'enemy', they probably would be going straight to heaven for showing that they had such great love for their countrymen.

"The ruling cliques the world over are made up of virtual impostors who have no respect for human life, and who see nothing wrong with killing. They believe senseless killing stops being murder when you decide to employ the 'security forces" or the 'military' to do the killing, or when you 'declare war', when that actually makes it worse! This is because, instead of committing the murder single handed (like Cain did when he murdered his brother Abel), you now do it by conspiring and colluding with other people to commit the crime and, moreover, in a manner that is undeniably premeditated. And then the gravity of the crime changes to something else completely when you take steps to institutionalize it. Because you then also become culpable for drawing other innocent humans into your conspiracy to destroy life under the guise of defending the homeland, and for the pain and suffering that consciences objectors to your murderous scheme end up having to endure. And it is, of course, quite terrible when, in the eyes of murderers, aggression suddenly stops being aggression when they call it 'a preemptive strike'!

"Unfortunately for all those humans who are in league with me in this 'killing' business, however much they 'justify' their actions, they can never deny the fact that they would never have liked the things they do unto others done by others unto them. One thing about that moral 'standard' is that rationalizations however elaborate, and excuses however framed, all suddenly stop holding any water when measured against it. And it is precisely this that will be their undoing come their day of reckoning - which, very unfortunately for them (but very fortunately for me) happens to be just round the corner.

"Humans! The self-deception becomes total when, trying to skirt logic, they start claiming that people do not go to heaven because they are *good*, but because they have believed and are *saved*! The rest supposedly go to hell because they are so *predestined*! In other words, they become lost regardless of whether they are good or bad! Yes, that is exactly what '*salvation by faith alone*' means, if you did not know.

"Still, I do admire the way they go about rationalizing away the responsibility and guilt. That is something we pure spirits cannot do -

make excuses for an evil life. In the pure spirit realm, everything - sin and judgement - happens in real time. Incidentally, the holy book does not say anywhere: 'By Faith Alone'! You'd better believe that I, Beelzebub, would have been the first to note such an incongruity in the divine scheme of things. It would have been a bonanza!

"A good way of checking out the facts is to isolate all the biblical passages that refer to 'faith', and then start tackling the parts of the bible that don't with the intention of learning what humans are supposed to do to attain salvation. Well, not surprisingly, the Ten Commandments, from which no one is exempt, are found far from those sections of the bible where 'faith' is discussed.

"It is clear that this is the source of the problems we've just discussed - the inability to read. Humans over-do things sometimes, and it is a good bet that a lot of them will be in for some nice surprises when they shed those bodies and enter the realm of pure spirits.

"And how can killing be justified! It would be terrific if humans were right. It would validate what I stand for completely. But they are not, unfortunately, because 'he who lives by the sword dies by the sword'! And guess what - the humans who seem least bothered by the fact that people get killed in wars are the very ones who make the biggest stink, obviously hypocritical, about the evils of abortion and things like that! And you also guessed correctly – these are the same ones who approve of torture of 'suspects'! Yes, the torture of suspects in detention without trial for lack proof of wrong doing! And I, Beelzebub, am not about to complain if folks vehemently assert that they do not see my fingerprints all over the place, for the obvious reason - I would hurt my own cause if I did anything to discourage them or those they support."

Still same old struggle (between Good and Evil)...

"Might there be something I don't know about the constitution of humans, fashioned in the image of the Prime Mover and to that extent also sacred, that would justifiably incite one human to try and do away with another human? Certainly not after all humans have sinned and are in need of their creator's mercy - all humans including those stupid ones who think they are special and, even though their sins have been traced in the sand for all to see, they still can defy their Deliverer and proceed to stone the woman who was unlucky to be caught in the act.

"In any event, what is there about the human constitution that would cause a normal 'person' to try and stick a spear into a brother or a sister, or to try and stone or shoot a brother or a sister, much less to design mega bunker bursting bombs and drop them in places where other brothers and sisters might be hiding out.

"In a situation in which there is more than one superpower, common sense dictates a policy of *detente* as you folks call it, not one of head-on collisions. That is what happened during the so-called 'Cold War', much to my chagrin. It is most unfortunate that the Cold War came and went without seeing the world engulfed in turmoil. It would have been just wonderful if the West, armed to the teeth with weapons of mass destruction had challenged the Soviets, who were also armed to the teeth with similar weapons, to a fight - or vice versa.

"We in the Underworld actually thought that it was a done deal at one time, and we were cheering on one fellow called Kennedy and another one called Khrushchev so one of them - or, preferably, both - would press 'buttons' and unleash fire and brimstone on the earth. And so we were rooting for them to get the third and, of course, also final world war going. But unfortunately the prayers of the peaceniks, lead by the fellow who occupied the Holy See at the time, triumphed.

"Oh, we wanted to see suffering and miseries engulf the world on a much bigger scale than we had seen in all the wars humans had ever fought against each other combined. Even I, with all my powers of divination, had all but concluded that Armageddon was at hand, but I was mistaken.

"Any sort of preemptive action on the part of one power would have been immoral, because it would have automatically spelled the annihilation of its own people regardless of whether they were civilians or in uniform. It was understood and above all recognized by all that any attempt to 'neutralize' the troops of one super power by the other was immoral and unacceptable. The Soviets did not even think of 'degrading' or 'neutralizing' the troops of the Western Alliance, and vice versa. In the nuclear age, it was not practical to talk in those terms. It was simply do or die!

"The time has now come, however, when the world recognizes the existence of only one hyper power. In terms of morality, it is of course even more depraved for the sole hyper power to use its overwhelming force to degrade or neutralize those whose calling is to serve in the security forces of any independent nation the hyper power might have designs on regardless of the nature of those designs. This is because super power or hyper power - whatever you wish to call it - comes with responsibilities.

"Believe it or not, it is also a calling to be the leader of a hyper-power; and it is a very grave thing to misuse the authority that goes with the position of 'Commander-in-Chief of a hyper- power. For my part, I like to see that authority misused - I want to see the chaps in the Kremlin, at Number 10 Downing Street, the Palais Elyeece, and especially the chaps in the White House misuse their authority and power. I want to see them end up here in Gehenna with me - I do not want St. Michael the Archangel to triumph over me in the battle for the souls of these fellows.

"I am not known for humility; and I, Diabolos and author of death, will hasten to brag to you that it is really my agenda which the individuals whose actions trigger wars - particularly unjustified wars - carry out. But if I sound a little upset, it is because those who are bent on starting wars, even in the face of stiff objections from the rest of the world, also seem determined to do it in the name of the Prime Mover, and not in my name. You humans should learn to give credit where it is due!

"And even then, they take so long to decide on the next target - as if it is hard to finger a 'rogue' nation. To my knowledge there is no nation that does not fit that description - where the state does not use its machinery to kill - and that includes the hyper power itself. The chaps in the Kremlin, Palais de l'Elysée, Number 10 Downing Street, the White House and what have you, should just get on with the job -

there are so many countries they can overwhelm in a short space of time with their superior fighting machines.

"Instead, I see all the posturing and the hypocrisy about 'involving people in the targeted nations in determining their own future' and that sort of tripe. Call a spade a spade - call foreign occupation 'foreign occupation' and just get going with the next one. Get going with those regime changes. The more the indigenous people suffer in the aftermath, the better for our cause - yes, because you are either with Him or with me, and do not pretend now that you are with Him! There is tons of 'black gold' and uranium out there. Come-on...show me what you've got - go get it!

"And how do those of you who pride yourselves in being conscientious and God-fearing (I am assuming there are still a couple of you left) like that? You may not like me and the fact that these terrible things - yes, truly terrible things - have my full backing; you have little choice but to live with them. And you now realize that you have also to cope with my tactics of shock and awe! Or, did you perhaps think that the struggle between good and evil was the product of some crazy and misguided ascetic's imagination? And if you still do, you just wait to witness the real Armageddon. It will be more than blood curdling, I tell ya!

"And there is now also this rubbish about 'disarming' the so-called 'rogue' nations - as if only some special nations should be in a position to defend themselves against outside aggression and not others! First of all, that is something that will never succeed - the world will never accept the idea of some nations, that have their own so-called national interests, taking on the role of policemen to keep other nations in check. That would be the beginning of anarchy caused both by the inherent contradictions in such a system and the fact that the very next logical step by the 'policing' or 'benevolently imperialist' nations would be to actually take over and colonize the 'rogue' nations. It would, of course, also be discrimination at the highest level with the citizens of the 'policing' nations or 'super powers' setting up themselves as virtual 'super humans' who alone enjoyed the prerogative to punish or reward 'underlings' representing the rest of humanity!

"Which leads me to the point I want to make - nothing should ever interfere with the principal of survival of the fittest! That principle applies to individual humans and also to nations just the same. It is also why I am against some humans setting themselves up on a pedestal to play 'judge' and 'sentence' fellow humans to 'jail' or even to die for their 'wrong doing'. All that goes against the principle of survival of the fittest. Everybody should be free to do what they want - to rob weaklings, to kill, and so on. That is the only law we in the Underworld recognize.

"When nations go to war, the 'ideal' situation is if they do so without any reason. In that way, we can have wars all the time. And, clearly, nations should be in a position to go to war even if the wars are not morally justifiable. In the realm I control, there is no such a thing as morality, let alone moral justification for conflicts between individuals and even less conflicts between nations. And when a nation decides to take that step, everyone within its borders should be obligated to support the campaign, and those who are not prepared to do so should be rounded up and promptly shot, gassed, beheaded or just hanged and quartered for their 'treasonable' act. In that way, we can be sure to have killing fields that stretch from the aggressor nations' own territory to the most distant shores. Yes, killing fields! Frankly, the more the better - for my cause.

"And my prayer right now is that some dumb 'statesman' or 'stateswoman' somewhere in the world might by his or her actions set in motion events that will lead to new religious crusades. When nations go to war for security reasons, they do so simply because they want to conquer and annex - no nation would be willing to risk the lives of its citizens for nothing. Any so-called 'economic reasons' are usually only camouflage.

"But conflicts based on religious differences have a way of feeding on themselves and driving humans to slaughter others happily in the name of their gods. Just imagine humans who espouse different ideas regarding their last end going at each others with whatever they can get hold of and eliminating the problem by killing 'the enemy' on the spot. It would just be swell. It would prompt a spate of killings in different parts of the globe and cause the world to explode in the sort of Armageddon we in the Underworld have been looking forward to ever since the Deliverer announced that one was in the offing.

"You see - in the last days, apart from a few 'untouchables' like St. Peter's successors and a couple of really pious souls, I will be permitted by the Prime Mover to possess any number of humans I want, and also to use them as instruments to create absolute chaos on earth. But it now looks like I actually may not need to use that prerogative to achieve my purpose. You fellows are on the right track and, obviously, the sooner you get into that destructive mode, the better!

"And now a word about industry and technology. As far as the *other side* is concerned - the primary and indeed the only really lawful purpose of industry and technology is to improve living conditions of humans during their sojourn on earth. It was the reason you humans were created 'rational', but with the concomitant responsibility for using your 'head', including any schemes that you concocted with the aid of reason, for the greater glory of the Prime Mover.

"It therefore suits me perfectly when the priority of nations, particularly the so-called advanced nations, now is to employ advance in human knowledge for warfare or the 'killing' industry as I call it. That is how the world came by its present supply of deadly chemical, biological, viral and radiological 'killer' agents. It is very significant that none of those concoctions can just be dug up from the earth's crust or harvested from trees in their present form - they were all manufactured under controlled conditions and with the objective of employing them to kill and maim fellow humans. And take my word - time is coming the nation that developed the so-called HIV/AIDS virus will be exposed.

"In the meantime, those nations in a position to do so invariably manipulate organizations like the United Nations to enforce 'economic embargoes' and things like that on other so-called nations, especially the so-called 'rogue state'. Such embargoes not only lead to the deaths of zillions - particularly the young and the aged in the process - but they also ultimately destroy societies by assuring that generations grow up disillusioned with everything and without any real hope in life.

"The children of the countries that are the object of economic strangulation, as they die prematurely and are on their way to eternal life with Prime Mover, must wonder why people in some of the world's nations, including those that have exhibited a proneness to dillydally with nuclear bombs, have actually tested them over the cities of other nations on more than one occasion, and are accelerating the development and build-up of ever newer and more deadly nuclear weapons systems in tandem with the unilateral abrogation of nuclear test ban treaties, do that to them.

"In the same way, the children who get blown up to bits by landmines, while playing with what appear to be toys or while helping their parents grow food, must wonder, as their fragile little bodies succumb to the impact and they find themselves returning to their maker so quickly, must wonder why some members of humankind are in the business of producing things that are so dangerous. And, of course, those children of Nagasaki and Hiroshima, who perished along with their loved ones in the nuclear conflagration after the A-bombs were dropped on them, must have wondered why those bombs were made in the first place.

"As their souls were being ferried from the ashes of Hiroshima and Nagasaki to the safety of the heavenly Paradise, they must have wondered why humans did not realize that they were commanded to love one another as themselves, and that a nation that dropped those bombs on them effectively lost the war. Upon arrival in heaven, the children must have asked St. Ignatius who, as legend has it, was dying to be killed in the service of the Deliverer and his fellow humans as he made his way to Rome for his execution, why other adults seemed to think (as the Roman rulers of his time apparently did) that the act of killing another human represented victory of some kind!

"And the children must have been flabbergasted to behold earthlings in New York, London and other places celebrate the bloody massacres with merrymaking, bunting and fireworks instead of fasting and doing penance for those sordid deeds. We here in Gehenna were also celebrating. Yes, celebrating the beginning of an era in which hounding and killing people for whom one had a distaste was elevated to a virtue - a cardinal virtue!

"At the same time, it must have seemed pretty obvious to the children that what drove humans to kill others was the combination of feelings of guilt and the fear of dying. It must have seemed rather obvious to the children that a sense of guilt was what made humans fear to die; and that the fear of dying in turn drove them to kill those they perceived as their enemies. That fear of dying spoke volumes about guilty consciences; because, when people were innocent of any wrongdoing, they did not fear to die even if they knew that they did not deserve to be killed. The fact was that humans who had not been fair to others, and who were consequently guilty-laden, were terrified of dying and going to their judgement. Sinners saw no wrong in putting innocent lives at risk in their efforts to keep death at bay and postpone their encounter with the Deliverer and Judge.

"The justifications for killing in self-defense are always self-serving, because they are backed by a pack of lies packaged as facts. Moreover aggressor and victim alike could cite the exact same 'reasons' for acting in self-defense. Nations become powerful only at the expense of other nations, and nothing really belongs to Caesar in that sense! And so there is really nothing to defend. And, anyway, if the Prime Mover took the same stance and decided to defend his honor which was under assault daily by being a little stingy with His mercies and withdrawing His saving graces, humans who have been rebels since Adam and Eve fell from grace would all be here in the Pit with me. The only reason that did not happen is that I would have been the clear winner in the contest between good and evil!

"Humans kill because they are themselves scared of facing their Judge. They even tried to get rid of Him, would try again if they got another chance. It is cowardice once at best. In a similar fashion, when hedonists indulge themselves, it is because they have no moral fibre and are spiritual weaklings. It is not because they are brave or heroes - which they would be if they succeeded in letting their cravings go unfulfilled.

"Talking about hedonists - the moment of truth for hedonistic humans is that time when, as the end draws near, they realize that escapist pursuits were a smoke screen for being weak-willed and spineless; that they had just squandered opportunities to excel as men and women of virtue; and that they now had nothing to show for it except the fact that they now were hardened in their crooked ways! The hardest part of all must be the realization that, unlike the woman who was accosted by the Deliverer at the well and who rose to the occasion by renouncing her lifestyle upon learning that the stranger knew everything relating to her secret affairs, they themselves were now beyond redemption.

"The children of Hiroshima and Nagasaki knew that they were only children, and they must have wondered what it was that caused adult humans to pursue economic gain from producing nuclear and hydrogen bombs, and other types of weapons systems. They must have wondered why it did not strike Americans that the quickest way to oblivion for a newly christened 'super power' was to heave its weight around, and place its hopes in its military might, and that it would serve America best for it to abandon its massive investments in weaponry particularly now when it did not face any visible challenge to its power, and channel those resources to improving the lives of its citizens and others who are in dire need. They must have wondered why America did not use its influence to resolve international conflicts and chose instead to pursue policies that in some cases exacerbated the situation.

"It is a hallmark of the success of our campaign that today, all it needs is for a leader of some foreign nation whose policies are not in the national interest of nations that are more powerful militarily to be declared a terrorist by leaders of these other nations, regardless of whether that is really true or not, for that leader to get a price on his head. It pleases us tremendously when one day a country has its seat at the United Nations, and the next day it is treated like a pariah and rogue state just because a militarily powerful member wants things to be that way.

"We love the fact that such precedents are set; because, regardless of the reforms that an organization such as the UN undergoes, the way will now always be open to the militarily powerful 'entity' - and this can be 'terrorists' operating from their invisible base, or may be even some tiny, previously insignificant nation that had its agents strategically placed with brief-case nuclear A-bombs and didn't have anything to loose - to call the shots. This is a development that opens up lots and lots of possibilities for our cause.

"But there is nothing that is more satisfying to me, Beelzebub, than seeing the 'sanctioned' aggression and murderous wars used for public entertainment in the 'victorious' nations - more or less like what used to go on in ancient Rome in the amphitheatre, when starved African lions were let loose on slaves who were permitted only small daggers with which to ward off the fangs of the hungry beasts. It is a great feeling, I tell you, to know that the difference between ancient Rome and 'modern, civilized nations' (as you chaps refer to them) is the same!

"And so, thanks to the evolution of satellite communications, and the fact that you live in an age of real time news, the citizens of the nations under attack can now literally see and hear the powerful, bunker bursting bombs lobbed from enemy vessels that may be moored in seas hundred and even thousands of miles away bring ruin and devastation to their neighborhoods at least until the television stations themselves are taken out by missiles and the lights on their TV sets flicker and go out. They can even watch as their loved ones are killed or bloodied by 'stray' bombs, and this in addition to being able to watch those country folk whose sin was to try and make a living serving in the country's security forces, 'neutralised' by the advancing enemy.

"And while those who survive the first volley cower in fear or cradle mortally wounded loved ones, their brothers and sisters in Christ who happen to live in the safe zone of the conflict within the borders of the aggressor nations typically rally around their own TV sets to enjoy the spectacle put on by their 'gallant' sons and daughters serving in the military. And it is usually quite a spectacle - the sight of a nation's infrastructure that took enormous resources and will power on the part of the citizenry and certainly great sacrifices to put up vanish from view in a matter of seconds in clouds of smoke, buildings with people inside them collapsing, columns of enemy solders obliterated in a matter of seconds with the help of bunker-bursting munitions made from radio-active nuclear waste. And, of course, pictures of screaming ambulances ferrying the dying and wounded to makeshift treatment centers carried live to a worldwide 'audience' by journalists 'embedded' in the forces of the aggressor nations!

"And the 'success' of the pinpoint strikes against one 'enemy' will invariably encourage military planners in the aggressor nations to immediately start planning their next moves - against the next 'rogue' nation on the list, giving that priority over fulfilling promises to restore the shattered lives of nationals in the vanquished country, establish so-called democratic systems and governance, rebuild the infrastructure, and other things of that nature in the pacified nations. And these are humans who are commanded to love one another as they love themselves!

"And also, nowadays, all it needs to absolve those behind the destruction of property and deaths of the innocent from any and all personal responsibility for their actions is to label or 'classify' the activities initiated by those individuals as 'military' operations. The control exercised by the super powers over so-called 'human rights watchdog organizations' such as the International Criminal Court of Justice, and as well over the actions of the *ad hoc* war crimes tribunals it sets up, translates into freedom by nationals of the super powers to do as they wish, because the veto powers wielded by those super powers in world forums have the effect of shielding their citizens from facing justice for any war crimes they might commit. Then the nations themselves, because they are super powers, are free to break - and have in fact frequently broken - codified international law with impunity.

"This state of affairs didn't come about by accident. Believe me when I say that my troops worked very hard after the war you folks refer to as World War Two to ensure that, instead of posing a threat to our agenda, an organization like the League of Nations (which eventually came to be known as the United Nations) would actually promote it. We are not fools!

"And, by the same token, virtually anything that is done by a country that has been branded a 'rogue' nation to safeguard its infrastructure or otherwise prevent its installations, factories and other strategic sites from being trashed by aggressor super powers is now liable to be branded as a war crime with the blessing of the supposedly impartial world bodies mentioned. But not only that: the miseries undergone by the citizenry of the targeted nation become something they deserve even in the eyes of spiritual leaders in the aggressor nations.

"Their sufferings automatically become quite distinct and apart from human sufferings that the Deliverer sanctified by His own passion and death on the cross and made His own. Even the regions of the conflicts automatically become identifiable with places that are supposed to be the abode of 'evil spirits' referred to in some books of the Old Testament!

"You can be sure that it gives me enormous 'pleasure' - if you can call my satisfaction with the way things proceed 'pleasure' - to see so-called Catholic nations take center stage in bringing about this new world 'order'. And it is immensely gratifying to observe the near stunning silence of the clergy - yes, the clergy - in these nations. You would think they live on a different planet altogether! It pleases me immensely when churchmen, abandoning their responsibilities to the downtrodden, and those who are constantly subjected to humiliation and injustice, go about their business as if everything was alright - just as they did at the height of imperialism and colonialism, or at the time the Deliverer himself was being marched to his death on the cross.

"I refer to the silence as 'stunning' because taking hours - perhaps even days - to craft an innocuous statement that is addressed to no one and is only intended to be read by priests from pulpits without any further action is a virtual signal to the chaps who might be openly plotting to commit murders in some foreign land to get on with it. What I am always fearing is that the prelates will do just like the apostles they succeeded did, namely pick themselves up, confront the political leadership and rebuke them for cooking up the murderous schemes - just as John the Baptist confronted Agrippa and rebuked him for stealing his own brother's woman. Of course if they did that, their own fate would be in the balance and what happened to John might well happen to them.

"But that would be the case only in the short run. You know what they say about the blood of martyrs being the seed of conversion? When the apostles and their immediate successors matched on Rome and rebuked the emperors and the victorious generals for scandalous lives they led - for the killings that went in the amphitheatre in the name of sport and for indulging in the hideous practice of slavery, and other evils - they were of course promptly silenced. But look what happened next - becoming a follower of Christ suddenly became the fad and fashion. Peter's successors effectively took over the Roman Empire and, using Rome as a springboard, went on to spread Christianity throughout the known world and beyond!

"That would do such damage to my cause, it would almost be as if that John the Baptist was back and kicking, and disturbing the peace again. The present situation in which Catholic prelates the world over have cosy relationships with politicians, many of whom are known murderers, and which makes me describe the reaction of the clergy as stunning silence suits me perfectly. God forbid that they will suddenly wake up to their responsibilities and cause chaos in my realm!

"The priests and prelates are supposed to be like other Christs, are they not? Well before you rush to judgement, just remember these words of the Deliverer: Judge not, that ye be not judged. For with what judgment ye judge, ye shall be judged: and with what measure ye mete, it shall be measured unto you. And why beholdest thou the mote that is in thy brother's eye, but considerest not the beam that is in thine own eye? Thou hypocrite, cast out first the beam out of thine own eye; and then shalt thou see clearly to cast out the mote out of thy brother's eye. But, after warning of false prophets, who came to folks in sheep's clothing, but inwardly were ravening wolves, He did say: By their fruits ye shall know them.

"And so, assuming that the priests and prelates fall short, it means that they are not in a position to act, confess the greatness of the Prime Mover, and to suffer the way the Deliverer Himself did. And to that extent, their lives do not exemplify the true Christian life, and they additionally will have the tendency to misrepresent the Deliverer. Now, I myself have already been judged and condemned, and I can therefore hazard without fearing any further consequences that it is this that explains the silence and hesitancy of the Church's functionaries when it comes to pointing out injustices.

"Of course, what I fear is that the stupid fools might suddenly wake up and start pointing out that, in any modern war, the senseless destruction of life and property in today's world likely will be on a scale that even leaves the victorious stunned and mentally and emotionally transformed for the rest of their lives. What I fear is that some nut might point out that such an eventuality was reason enough to get a worldwide ban imposed on all weapons of war, starting with the stockpiles under the control of the so-called super powers. Some fool might even be brazen enough to suggest the obvious, namely that the perpetrators themselves likely would never want to see tables turned and they themselves at the receiving end of modern weapons of war! That sort of railing would expose the shallow thinking of war mongers, which would be a real tragedy.

"But the question that would be the most damaging to my cause if asked would pertain to what the Deliverer Himself would do if He had been in the place of these clerics. What would He do, for instance, were to observe citizens of a nation that might have already been largely disarmed and therefore unable to defend itself against aggression killed, maimed, and trampled upon by the war machinery of a super power ran amok and out of control? What would He do?

"Good thing not too many of you can even hazard an answer! Unfortunately, I really have no choice but to tell you. You recall what He did when He was in Jerusalem one day and saw what was going on in the temple? Because humans beings - whether they are Rwandese, Russians, Japanese, Germans, Americans, Iraqis, Spaniards, Palestinians or Iraqis - are temples of the Prime Mover, you can bet that the Deliverer would make Himself a strong enough whip from any tough enough material within His reach (perhaps depleted uranium) and chase the 'merchants' (because that is what they are in the final analysis) out of His temples. He is a jealous Prime Mover. So, you can see that by maintaining their stunning silence, in the eyes of the Prime Mover, members of the Church's hierarchy have become virtual collaborators in the senseless murder and mayhem.

"Do I know what I am talking about? Of course I do. Who is it that lays the traps over which these priests and prelates trip? One problem is that these traps do not fit on the narrow path. Even with our superior intelligence, we haven't been able to come up with a design that would make them do. But since they fit on Broadway, we lay them there; and, of course, all who eschew that thoroughfare are pretty safe from them. You have to be dumb to believe that priests and prelates practice what they preach, namely walk only on the Narrow Path - and stay on it!

"Perhaps *you* can afford to be dumb; it is something we in the Underworld cannot. Just believe me when I tell you that chicanery is as rampant in the 'pilgrim' Church today as it was in the middle ages. This is despite the fact that these priests and prelates really do try, one and all, to 'clothe themselves in Christ' to borrow an expression from the Apostle of the Gentiles. Long ago, they could face their congregations and tell them to at least 'do as I say', because it would have been disastrous to suggest that their flocks 'do as I do'. These days even that is out of question. A lot of what the clergymen say is abominable even by my standards.

"To get to this stage required painstaking planning on my part and very great patience, I tell you! Whoever thought that naked aggression - or 'wars' as you call them - would become a 'morally accepted' method of guaranteeing the 'economic security' of a nation whether a super power or not. And just to think that this is sanctioned by a body like the United Nations of which the Holy See is a full member! Or that it would be morally legitimate for some nations and not others to launch so-called preemptive strikes, using everything in their arsenals, in the name of national security?

"But our biggest coup is the fact that nations, prodded by their 'intelligence services', have legitimized the methods that had hitherto been confined to gangsters and 'the Mob' or the mafia of 'taking care of unfinished business'. And so, no one lifts an eye lid when one head of state wakes one morning, declares everybody on a 'list of wanted persons' including fellow heads of state and, with or without a 'coalition of the willing', plans openly to 'liquidate those listed. I mean - these are things you used to read about in fairytales, not in history books! And just to think that this is done in the name of civilization and with the full backing of 'churchmen'!

"To sum up: there is nothing that works to drive humans who try to pray for peace - and are always a thorn in my side - to despair more than the appearance that the developing turmoil and the wars have the Church's tacit approval. You must know that there is nothing that undermines my cause more than prayers - not the demonstrative, almost meaningless posturing of hypocrites; but the sincere prayers that are offered up in the secrecy of people's living rooms, and spring from the heart, speak volumes about a people who feel completely powerless in the face of imminent man-made tragedies. They are prayers of people who know that succour for the grief-stricken in a world that is driven by materialism is unlikely to come in the present life.

"You see - you humans have a very short memory. Remember the flood and Noah's Ark? Or the story of Lot and his wife, and their escape from the City of Sodom? If you want to know the Prime Mover's position regarding the wicked, you have to understand the background to His promise that He would never again visit sinful folk with any more floods and things of that nature. But He promised not to do so well-knowing that humans would continue in their intransigence.

"The Prime Mover was essentially signifying that, just as He continued to allow Satan to tempt humans and to sow his seeds of death, He was going to let the wicked have their way on earth - but clearly only for so long. He was going to let killers have their way and wreck and ruin the earthly lives of their fellow men on earth. He wasn't going to stop them. There would, of course, still be major floods, landslides, earthquakes, pestilences, etc. But they would be man-made, having their origins in industrial pollution that was driven by human greed, and in the environmental and ecological degradation caused by the underground and atmospheric nuclear tests conducted by the so-called super powers in secret.

But, by the same token, being a jealous Prime Mover, He was also signifying that the wicked would not just face some watery flood, but the full wrath of an angry Prime Mover when their time of reckoning came. In retrospect, it would be quite clear that ridding the world of the wicked by drowning them in floods (and keeping them out of the Noah's Ark) or by raining fire and brimstone on their cities was motivated by the desire of the Prime Mover to spare sinners something worse.

"Therefore take notice that those of you who will be caught with your candles out when the Bridegroom arrives will find yourselves in hell with me; and believe me, it is a hell of a place! It is a place where you humans who can cry and have teeth, will get a chance to weep until your tears run dry, and to gnash those teeth which now show whenever you laugh until they pop out! You will wish that mountains had fallen on you when you still lived since that would have stopped you in your tracks and, by incapacitating you, would have had the effect of reduced the terrible guilt that will be haunting you throughout eternity.

"And those of you who sit on the sidelines and won't stir to try and point out evils - as the prophets and the other messengers the Prime Mover sends on earth do - will also get a taste of the Prime

Mover's wrath in Purgatory as you are cleansed and spruced up to make you a bride befitting of the divine Bridegroom.

"Yes, I mean you who just want to be observers in the face of evils committed against your own brothers and sisters by the wicked! It is a different kind of evil mind that entertains indifference in the face of injustices and certainly day light murder. Such indifference and love for one's neighbor are in any case incompatible! And you can bet that we in the Underworld have invested very heavily in creating the conditions in which such indifference can thrive.

"Does the Prime Mover 'see the injustice to the wage earner' (that group includes individuals who choose to serve their countries as soldiers, but end up being targeted by invading armies) or 'hear the cry of the people oppressed in Egypt'? Does He heed the silent prayers of the peaceniks? The answer is definitely 'Yes'! This is even though He might not be observed with the naked eye stepping into the fray and stopping a super power from trampling over some nation that might already have been disarmed and is therefore perhaps quite defenseless. The Prime Mover invariably steps in without fail and in a very decisive way, believe me. It is, however, not in exactly the way you or me expect.

"You might not observe the Prime Mover physically restraining killers and murders, but the end result - when His action is figured in - is always far more devastating than if He had physically stopped or even taken action Himself to 'neutralize' them. Once humans murder or maim those it was not their business to murder or maim (and it certainly never can be in an unjustified conflict), the fact always remains that they have murdered or maimed. They could even go ahead and do their darndest, including genocide and things like that, at will. The bad news is that those who murder and maim themselves become damned the moment they start plotting their activities - and that is the catch!

"And once you do that sort of thing - once you take away the lives of those who have a moral obligation to defend their country, you can never bring them back alive with any talk of reconstruction, you see. And any actions on your part to get those you regard as your 'foes' in those circumstances to abandon the cause of their country will be no different from what I myself do to you all the time - namely trying to tempt and entice you to be unpatriotic and to betray your own country against all accepted norms of behavior. Besides, when you murder or maim in those circumstances, you know even before you start that you would not like what you are going to do to the other party done by the other party to yourself, and that you are on the wrong side of the Prime Mover's law. And that is what makes your situation so tragic.

"Having killed and maimed, you stand condemned by your callous and highhanded destruction of lives you did not have any part in bringing into existence. And because you have also usurped the authority of the Prime Mover in every respect, you invariably end up in the truly awkward position of challenging your own Creator to a contest. Now, I have been in that position (and I am still stuck in it), and will testify here and now that it is not a position in which a mortal soul should be. When you get in that position, your fate is sealed - if you know what I mean!

"What this means is that each and every act of those prosecuting a war under those circumstances becomes damning evidence against them, and any successes of the campaign become even more damning in so far as evidence goes. Defeat would in fact be a boon and should even be welcomed. For one, defeat - especially humiliating defeat - could cause those involved in the unjustified aggression of another country and all the things that such aggression entails to wake up to the reality and retreat from the brink. Success would embolden them in their adventures and blind them to the lurking danger.

"The real coup for us is the fact that humans, at our instigation, spend their lives trying to 'liquidate' or 'rub out' their 'enemies' only to find that they in fact don't have the power to bring that about. They only appear to 'liquidate' their fellow humans who are 'temples of the Prime Mover' and by definition cannot be destroyed. It is the same way those who murdered the Deliverer were convinced that they had dealt Him a mortal blow only to discover three days later that His tomb was empty - that He had risen up and had even taken the sting out of death to which he was no longer subject. And so the killers end up here with us while their victims - thanks to the fact that humiliation, suffering and death have been sanctified by the Deliverer's death on the cross and contrary to the expectations of their short-sighted enemies - die only to regain and enjoy their life in eternity with their Deliverer. For the victims who die resigned to their fate, their interrupted lives merely amount to a fight well fought and for an evidently good cause.

"But there is one thing about you humans that we in the Underworld envy - your ability to con yourselves into believing virtually anything you want to believe, including lies that you yourselves manufacture. You humans exhibit prejudices and bias on such a scale, it is nowadays an exception rather than the rule when one is caught telling the unvarnished truth. Lying for the sake of lying is the way most you do isn't something that would come naturally to a pure spirit. I myself might be the author of death, but I must say that the author of lies - if there is such a being - has to be a human. It is such a low down thing to do - I mean believing one's own lies - I would have to sacrifice a lot of my pride to sink that low.

"We ourselves also lie of course. But we certainly do not believe our own lies, and you humans are always free to fall for them or reject them after doing your analysis and deciding which lies are in line with your own crooked intentions. There is a world of difference between that and putting out bulletins full of lies or telling lies until you are blue in the face just for the sake of it.

"And then, in the eyes of humans, it will be seen as cool when it is one group of people manufacturing and disseminating the lies. And, funnily, in the eyes of the liars it is usually regarded as criminal not only if opponents in a conflict also try to practice lying, but even when they stick with the truth. They are supposed to admit whatever their 'enemies' like to hear and in that way give lies the stamp of truth. It is strange that you yourselves even have a term for it - situational ethics!

"Humans ordinarily appear to be incapable of seeing anything objectively. It is as if one must have on special lenses to be comfortable with anything that crosses one's vision. Consequently things like weapons of mass destruction are only weapons of mass destruction depending on the party that has control over them. In order to know that a weapon is of the WMD category, one has additionally to try and figure out who is likely to end up using them! Now, that is a little funny - and confusing too! Perhaps deliberately, given the prevalence of lying in human relations! This is really sad, and it is little wonder you've christened lying 'diplomacy', no doubt as a way of avoiding the stigma that is associated with that sinful practice. If things had been like that in the Underworld, by Jove, that would make it one hell of a mess!

"Alas, you humans seem patently unable to distance yourselves from your biases and prejudices! Then the materialism - it is nothing like we fallen spirits would have thought possible! The Deliverer Himself, when He came, did not set up an earthly kingdom for Himself. And He, of course, isn't about to enthrone these peaceniks on any. That would be changing His *modus operandum* in a very radical way, and it is not like Him to start doing that.

"Although the Prime Mover is kind and merciful, it is typical of Him that He leads His 'bride' into the 'desert' - yes, desert'! Not some bed of roses. And it is there that, as Hosea said, He espouses her to Himself, and espouses her in justice, love, mercy, and in fidelity, until she gets to know Him permanently.

"Don't think you should heed the call to take up your cross *and* to follow! Yah, *cross*! Doesn't make sense to you either that you should be prepared to suffer with Him *if* you love Him! Don't think that in coming down from heaven to redeem you, there *was* a price He came to pay, sinless though He was! Those who tell you that you should expect to receive your reward in this world - don't you think they might have fallen for the trap I set, even though they might have good intentions, and consequently tell you what that they tell you because they know it is what you are dying to hear!

"You don't think that their message is a little too good and that, other than urging you to aspire for possession of the good things of this life by getting yourself a faith that can move mountains, they are really not saying anything new to you! Think - and also know one thing - if you can get Satan himself cornered like this and even doing a better job of providing humans spiritual guidance than those self-appointed messengers of the Prime Mover, Armageddon cannot be very far off!

"And, by the way, I may now be laboring under this spell which is forcing me to reveal so many of my secrets; but you'd better believe that the moment I will be rid of it, you humans will be dealing with one very nasty character on the lam; and you can be sure that there will be some people who will pay for this very dearly. And if you think I am bluffing, just remember what happened to people like Jerome, Augustine of Hippo, and your favourite philosopher Thomas of Aquin.

"If you do not remember your history, you can pray to them to find out what happened, and they will tell you how nasty and mean I was to them after I was released from the spell that caused me to reveal to them so many of my secrets. They can tell you about the wave upon wave of the most wicked suggestions that I kept sending their way; and about the flood of the most God-awful images that I bombarded their 'fickle' minds - yes, 'fickle' compared to the minds of pure spirits - with images that very nearly caused them to pack up and return to the sinful lifestyles they had given up when they were converted and baptised into the Church.

"It will be the same with you, except that this time around, having learnt a thing or two from my experience with that trio, it is I - not you - who will come out triumphant.

"Any way - to return to the subject of the prayers that peaceniks offer up - all that the Prime Mover does in answer to those prayers is sustain the peaceniks in their times of trouble and suffering so that they do not despair in the face of the calamities of war. And for those peaceniks who do not become 'collateral damage' and who somehow survive with their faith in Him intact, their lives on earth will continue to be miserable and shattered all the same, not unlike the lives of those who do not pray but also manage to survive with their reason intact because of their faith in me! Yes, their faith and confidence in me, Beelzebub, because I automatically become the one who sustains that group in times of joy and also in times of their sorrow!

"So, luckily for us in the Underworld, the activities of peaceniks really do not interfere very much with our reign over murderers and other sinners in the long run.

"Any way - it pleases me very much when I see placards borne high by peaceniks proclaiming 'Justice, where are you hiding?' They should know that I, Beelzebub, am not in the habit of resting on my laurels. There is, after all, no rest for the wicked and especially for someone like me whose job it is to sow seeds of death.

"And I, of course, detest those peaceniks - 'demonstrators' as you call them - who match in silence with their banners against wars. They might look like people who are themselves terrified as they march past contingents of mean-looking cops bristling in their riot gear and itching to pounce on the marchers. Believe me - their silent 'prayer' is heard by the Prime Mover, even though you do not see Him intervening to stop the wars. And when they are tear-gassed, whipped with batons or hosed down with water canons, tears might flow down their cheeks and their sides might ache for days or even months on end from the buffeting; but trust me when I tell you that their 'prayer' usually proves to be more effective against my designs because of things like that for some reason.

"For one, their actions, by distracting war mongers, cause them and their supporters to come lashing out (they act really stupid sometimes, don't they!), and to identify themselves. Which is too bad, because then my minions can never deny their allegiance to me when their day in the Divine Court of Justice comes - when the time comes for them also to give up their ghosts. Which fulfils one of my immediate objectives, namely to see humans loose their souls, but pretty well frustrates my ultimate objective of thwarting the Divine Plan.

"Talking about giving up ghosts - you humans with your 'funny' constitution, which consists of a bag of chemicals and an intangible soul, are really walking corpses. I mean - at any time, chemicals in some part of that 'body' of yours can undergo a reaction that causes some vital organ to malfunction, forcing the individual to make what might be likened to an unscheduled exit from this world. It does not matter whether you live in the Palais Elyeece, the Kremlin, the White House, or at Number Ten Downing Street! And when you kick the bucket, all the cheek, haughtiness, foolishness and stupidity also ends there. It is not just a time of reckoning. Your earthly works also come to naught at that point when you wake up in another world to the chants of 'The *Magnificat*'.

"Still, I can't resist allowing myself the indulgence of a victory cry in this connection. A toast to a nation that is home to so many of our comrades-in-arms: 'America! Oh America! My America! Thou, great 'Christian' nation, blest to be the World's only - and undoubtedly also last - 'Super Power' as well as the bearer of the touch of 'enlightenment'! How great a boon thou art to my cause! What could I - even I, Mephistopheles - accomplish without you in this day and age? We in the Underworld salute thee who art home to so many of our comrades-in-arms! Of course you have some ways to go before you can challenge Babylon. But my troops and I have full confidence that the time is soon coming when thou will not just pose a challenge to the great city of Babylon that sadly is no more, but thou shalt verily surpass Babylon and break whatever records that 'Sin Capital' set!'

"Any way - let's get back to business. As I have already said, we have only got a little time left, and we must work hard at these things as Armageddon approaches. We in the Underworld and our lackeys amongst you have no choice but to step up the activities that lead to perdition, the most promising of which are related to human life and its destruction. But that does not mean that you humans do not have to be realistic. It is very important for our cause if you humans can understand our limitations, and then figure them in your plans to thwart Providence.

Never legit to try and "rub out" a fellow human...

"You humans have this funny idea that you can get rid of an individual you do not like by killing! You should know that creatures that have been crafted in the image of Him-Who-is-Who-is actually don't die! You cannot just 'rub out' your fellow human being. If you were able to do that, you would also be able to rub out pure spirits too, including me! When you try to 'rub out' a fellow human being, all you are really doing is trying to interfere with the divine plan, and you do that to your own detriment. Those you supposedly 'get rid of' here on earth live on - the vast majority of them actually quite happily - in the after-life.

"And when your own time to go comes, believe me that is when hell will break loose on you for having tried to interfere with Providence - for having tried to play God when you should have been practising charity, forgiveness, or even deservedly turning the other cheek! And so, just when you thought you had permanently disposed of those you saw as a problem, you yourself kick the bucket and boom! You suddenly find yourself confronted with all those witnesses to your brazen attempt to thwart the divine plan - all those folks you thought you had efficiently and permanently 'rubbed out'!

"If you had the ability to rub out a fellow human, you would be able to rub me out also, you fools! Well, come to think of it, it wouldn't be such a terrible thing to be rubbed out by a human devil. It would certainly end my hell and bring to a close a sad chapter in the history of creation.

"But, of course, that is not in the divine plan. The only exception to the rule - the only time the Prime Mover permitted a creature that was made in His image to be rubbed out - was the destruction by me of my rival; and with good reason, no doubt. I by myself am trouble enough for humans - and for my fellow angels. Can you imagine a Tempter *and* a Temptress roaming the earth? If the Prime Mover had not gotten us at loggerheads with each other to the point that one of us had to go, you can expect that the number of the elect wouldn't be what it will be! With our combined forces, the earth would be such an evil place, it would take much, much more for humans to survive our wiles and enter the new Jerusalem! But that is all by the way.

"Know, moreover, that we creatures have been commanded not to kill - meaning, interfere with the plan that Providence has in place for our fellow creatures. It is dumbness - sheer stupidity - which makes you folks believe that you achieve anything by 'getting rid' of fellow humans whom you hate for one reason or another. It is the sort of stupidity that I and my fellow fiends have every right to exploit, and you'd better believe that, when you kill, you do so at your own risk!

"Instead of humans spending their time celebrating the fact that they are privileged to be living in the same age and instead of gladly welcoming their fellow humans with open arms into their lives and homes, and oblivious to the fact that they all have sinned and are on a pilgrimage on Earth, stupid humans allow their egotism to have the upper the hand; and soon enough they begin finding fault with each other and making it a habit to engage in battles for the control of their Mother Earth to the exclusion of their fellow humans. And when they start conspiring to knock off those humans they regard as their 'enemies', it doesn't even strike them that their mission would be rendered hopeless and pointless if either they or their enemies had come into the world at different times of human history or not at all!

"They never once stop to reflect on what it means to discover oneself circulating in this former Garden of Eden in the company of other humans who are obviously descended from the same Adam and Eve, and have the same Prime Mover to thank for finding themselves in existence! Instead of taking a moment to reflect on what all this means, they are for ever running around non-stop unconcerned about what they are or their last end, and only bothered about things that serve their self-interest until, exhausted from serving the self, they literally drop dead!

"They go about things in life in much the same way the folks of Judea and Samaria, who heard about the miracles the Nazarene was performing, flocked to His 'crusades' only to lose interest and turn away when they heard the Deliverer urge that they sell whatsoever they had, and give the proceeds to the poor, so they would have treasure in heaven: and then go, take up the cross, and follow Him.

"Snap it! None of you has any power to rub out anyone. You just imagine that you have liquidated those you 'kill', because it is just a matter of time - a very short wait in fact - before you are confronted with those you thought you had eliminated for good. And guess what - once you make up your mind to liquidate a comrade, however nasty he might appear to be and set about looking for ways to achieve your goal, it doesn't really matter whether you succeed in your plan or not. You are already a murderer!

"Stupidly, you humans go out of your way to interfere with the plan the Prime Mover has had in place from time immemorial for the humans you label as your 'enemies' here on earth, not because of a moral threat they pose, but because of a perceived physical threat. Just what do you think you are? You imagine that your 'enemies' are the problem, when it is in fact you yourself who is the bigger problem!

"You humans have no business seeking revenge. The Prime Mover has said that it is His prerogative and His alone to avenge evil. Tit for tat is His prerogative, and humans who try to avenge perceived evils done to them by fellow humans are guilty of usurping the Prime Mover's authority. It is a very grave thing to try to do so, and that is why we in the Underworld work so hard to get you folks to do it. But you demonstrate that you have lost all faith in the Prime Mover when, despite the fact that He sent His only begotten Son to deliver you from evil as He promised, you are bent on revenge - on exacting your pound of flesh!

"Then you would think that humans would know better and not make things worse by lying. Nope! Even dictators who are caught murdering their defenseless subjects will swear that they did it in self-defense! They do it to rid the 'State' of traitors and others who are guilty of committing treason! That is if the 'traitors' don't end up as victors who promptly put the fallen dictator on trial for crimes against the same 'State'. It is just hopeless.

"When humans slaughter cows, well - they just slaughter cows, and that is all there is to it. But when humans 'neutralize' or 'kill' or otherwise attempt in some way to 'rub out' one of their own, that is something else altogether. When a creature, human or otherwise, is created in the 'Image', there is simply no way that creature can ever be rubbed out. When an attempt is made to 'liquidate' that creature, the attempt automatically targets the Word who determined - in eternity and well before that creature existed - that, once in existence, any essence that enjoyed that particular type of 'signature' would exist with Him for ever regardless of what that essence did while on trial.

"It is simply no joke being brought into existence in the Image. Humans and angelic beings alike come into existence as a result a solemn act on the part of the Prime Mover. Every single creature that is fashioned in the Image is prized by the Prime Mover as if it were the only one in existence.

"All creatures that are made in the Image automatically become brides of the Word. They come into being though Him, and He indwells in them from the very first moment of their existence. The ceremonies for celebrating that bridal 'union' typically take place at the time humans depart their earthly existence for their afterlife - after they have proved, during the period of their 'trial', that they too for their part are also in love and are prepared to commit to an eternal union with their Creator in heaven and to thus enter 'permanent wedlock'.

"The date for the 'marriage ceremony' can always be brought forward at the behest of humans - as happened in the case of Augustine, Jerome, Theresa of the Child Jesus, Theresa of Avila, Francis of Assisi, Padre Pio, Thomas Aquinas, Bernard, and others who opted for humble, self-effacing lives. In contrast, my entire short-lived period of trial was marked by running battles of the will in the course of which I sought, unsuccessfully, to impinge on the rights of the Prime Mover Himself.

"To the extent humans remain faithful to their consciences, to that extent they remain fit to be brides of the Word. But when they act contrary to natural and divine laws, they effectively signal that they are not in love with the Word. They declare in their thoughts and by their deeds that they have another suitor, and are calling off the divine wedding. And when humans abjure their love for the Word, there is no clearer way of showing it than turning against their fellow humans who also are brides of the Word by virtue of being made in the Image. Humans, who turn against their siblings, parents and other members of the 'human family', have reason to know that the Word is in-dwelling in those they have chosen to daub their 'enemies'.

"Their act does not just symbolize unfaithfulness; it amounts to an attack on the person of the Word. That is the effect of any deliberate act that aims to 'neutralize', 'despatch', or 'liquidate' a fellow human. And hence the divine order or commandment which says: 'Thou shalt not kill!' Despite that commandment, some humans give orders to kill - orders that are motivated by 'material' considerations - and still pretend that they are brides of the Word! Those who cause others to die declare war on the Godhead by their actions, and belong in our company here in Gehenna, regardless of their station in life.

"An attempt to rub out a creature that is fashioned in the Image overlooks the fact the creature in question is very unique, and that its uniqueness springs from the fact that the Prime Mover Himself dwells at its core. Any such attempt goes counter to natural law (which forbids humans and angelic beings to try and get rid of one of their own kind), and supernatural law (because 'murdering' another individual represents a crude attempt to derail the divine plan and frustrate the Prime Mover's intentions).

"To make matters worse, those who try to rub out others do so because they themselves feel inadequate and suffer from an inferiority complex. They feel insecure, and imagine - quite wrongly - that they will feel less threatened with the 'removal' of those who loom as a threat to them. They even forget that a 'dead' human is more dangerous for the simple reason that it is not just the victim's ghost, but the Holy Ghost Himself who comes back to haunt the 'killer' and whoever connived in the attempted 'liquidation'.

"And, it is those who suffer from the most severe forms of insecurity who get easily taken up with strange survival ideologies. When humans feel insecure or threatened, they have this tendency of gravitating towards all sorts of ideologies, especially ideologies that promise power and domination over others. Because they desperately crave to be recognized and if possible also feared, the idea of serving under or working for a 'super power' is always very attractive indeed.

"And, once hooked on to an ideology, chances are that they will end up believing that it doesn't really matter what they do as long as they are focused on making their chosen ideology a winner. They end up believing that the end in fact justifies the mean; and they typically won't tolerate criticism or competition.

"As far as they are concerned, no price will be too great to pay as long as it appears that whatever they are up to promotes their cause - and that holds true even if their expectations turn out to be exaggerated or even plainly unrealistic. When they start putting their pet theories into practice, it will usually be with passion and great determination, and without any regard to public opinion. It is an irony of nature that insecure humans are the ones who usually end up as the most implacable and feared ideologues.

"When humans, who have an inferiority complex and feel insecure, embrace an ideology, more likely than not, existence and life will be at the core of their ideology. They will, however, also have this tendency to proclaim the sanctity of life even as they pursue to destroy all other humans who look like they might pose a challenge which, for people who suffer from inferior complexes, is synonymous with posing a threat. And they will also tend to be extroverts. They will have this strange tendency to proclaim that life is sacred in the same breadth as they will be vowing to utterly destroy their 'enemies'!

"They typically cloak their inferiority complex and feelings of insecurity in a show of bravado in which they try to act Superman. The link between the desire to liquidate others and feelings of inadequacy, inferiority complex, and insecurity is not accidental. You might recall that sins - all sins - engender feelings of inferiority complex. It is no wonder that the desire to liquidate others - the desire to commit the worst sin of them all - is driven by these self-same feelings.

"The idea of dominating the world and exercising imperial power is particularly appealing to humans who have an inferiority complex and consequently feel insecure, because it promises total security. They delude themselves that subjugating the whole world will cure their inferiority complex and make their feelings of insecurity go away. They imagine, mistakenly, that pacifying the world will assure that they are rid of all who would otherwise pose a threat to them. Blinded by short term considerations, they forget the lessons of history according to which pacifying, subjugating, and occupying powers always end up with far more enemies than they can ever handle.

"It is tempting for an independent observer to suppose that war against the invisible enemy that 'terrorists' represent could have been obviated if their concerns, which in fact are modest, had been addressed in an equitable manner at the outset. That the cost of addressing those concerns would have been just a fraction of the tremendous outlays which the self-described 'civilized nations' now stand to incur in taking the fight to their 'invisible enemy'.

"It is also tempting for an independent observer to think that powerful nations, bent on a course of world dominations, could save themselves a lot of problems by tampering their greed and expansionism; that launching unprovoked, preemptive assaults on weaker nations in pursuit of so-called 'vital national interests' spells more not less trouble for them as the dispossessed and disenfranchised join the 'invisible enemy' making it a multi-headed, ever-mutating beast that does not stop at seeking redress for humiliations and injustices suffered, but will likewise aim to dominate the world as a matter of survival.

"The 'grievances' aired by the 'terrorists' speak to only a part of the problem. Since the fall of Adam and Eve, humans, inclined to sin, must work to satisfy their greed. Nations become advanced on the backs of other nations; and, as history has shown, it is the changing balance of power that causes smart leaders of imperial powers and colonialists to pull back and curb their greed, and not risk loosing all their gains from imperialism and colonialism. But, human nature being human nature, as long as nations still consider themselves 'powerful', they will always be itching to do things that will generate new generations of 'terrorists', 'bandits', 'secessionists', 'revolutionaries', or whatever label spinmeisters in those 'powerful' nations will concoct for the occasion. And that guarantees the cycle of violence the world has lived with since the children of Adam and Eve fought over inheritance.

"The fatal flaw in pursuing this or that perpetrator of 'terrorism' lies in the politics of world domination. Accordingly, acts of 'terrorism' are despicable and unacceptable only when the 'national interests' of 'powerful nations' so-called are threatened. The leaders of those nations play dumb and ignorant when atrocities are committed against humans in other situations, often as a result of conditions that were created by leaders of these very nations (in pursuit of their national interests) or even with their direct connivance, or simply look the other way. Which suggests that those powerful nations are not 'powerful' after all - certainly not when their 'power' depends on the exploitation of resources which they lack at home and are available in the countries they would like to see become satellite states.

"Once humans who suffer from an inferiority complex and feel overly insecure as a result start down that path, it is usually only a matter of time before they also start imagining that they have a messianic mission. And, invariably, that mission will be about trying to dominate the world so that it might benefit from their grandiose visions of things. They will be determined to 'take enlightenment to the ends of the earth', to 'promote democracy', or some such balderdash.

"Instead of seeing danger and making a U-turn, these people typically become fixated with the notion that they themselves are finally making history. And even as the countries they lead are being slowly but surely sucked into the black hole that turns once so-called powerful nations into history, they will be doing everything possible to speed up that process.

"Unfortunately for the super power - and fortunately for us here in the Underworld - the closer a super power gets to the slippery perimeter of the black hole, the more common sense itself ceases to be common. And usually, before long, the truism that people deserve their leaders also begins to apply as protests against plain injustices perpetrated by the nation in the name of 'democracy', 'civilization' or 'enlightenment' within the country's borders fizzle out, and everybody jumps on the wagon of Patriotism in a fruitless attempt to avert the disaster that its leaders had been courting from the beginning.

"Guess what - when I myself took off on my mission to sow the seeds of death (at the time I should have been preparing for the Church Triumphant Entrance Test), I claimed that I was leading the 'struggle for independence' and freedom from the yoke of natural law and divine law! I still claim that I am leading the struggle for independence from the Prime Mover, and that is what makes me a devil! Do I, therefore, talk from personal experience? You bet I do.

"Killers incur the same wrath of the Prime Mover as I did. And if you are looking for proof that being haunted by the 'dead' is an experience that no one should court, just look at me and see how I languish in this 'hellfire' that never goes out. That is what I mean by killers being haunted by the spirits of their victims.

"Talking about killers being haunted, you should know that my scheme to undermine the divine plan by sowing the seeds of death was doomed from the very beginning, just because the immediate objects of my murderous scheme were creatures that were fashioned in the Image. I should have known - or at least guessed - that, in tempting my fellow angels and subsequently humans, I would be automatically challenging the Word who not only brought them into being, but was sworn to defend them with His divine graces.

"I should also have known that any success I had in winning some over to my cause would only make my situation worse - that the spiritual 'death' of each and every spirit I succeeded in misleading would come back to haunt me!

"In the case of a human who dares to raise a finger with the intention of rubbing out another, and who departs from this world for the afterlife whilst unrepentant, the murderous deed results, rather ironically, in the spiritual demise of the would-be-murderer even as the victim gains eternal life in a truly haunting reversal of fortunes. Understand that there is absolutely nothing that victims of this totally aberrant behavior could themselves ever do to reverse what the Word decrees at creation, which namely is that they can never return to nothingness out of which they were made. That any attempt to liquidate them will fail.

"The essence of being created in the Image is that creatures that are fashioned thusly also become endowed with immortality by virtue of being the adopted children of the Prime Mover. The victims themselves might have committed sins and blunders, of course; but it *is* sinners whom the Deliverer came unto this earth to save - not those who are already 'justified' or self-proclaimed saints.

"And in any case, in the eyes of the Prime Mover Himself, there simply is nothing an angelic being or a human can do that will cause the Prime Mover to go back on His "Word" and decide that they deserve to return to the nothingness out of which they came. I myself am in hell because I set out to sow seeds of death, and was allowed to actually kill - rub out my arch-rival who, like me, was made in the Image.

"I burned myself far more than I hurt those I was targeting - the rival Arch-Devil, Michael the Archangel, Adam, Eve, and so many others who are enjoying beatific vision even as I speak! Also keep in mind that, even though the Prime Mover made an exception and permitted me to 'rub out' my arch rival, I am now as odious as I am in His eyes - with such detestable titles as 'the Accursed One', 'Father of Death', and 'the Evil One'- because I had the nerve to go through something as unthinkable as that.

"My cause, as Prince of Darkness and Father of Death, was doomed at the inception precisely because I was tampering with the destiny of creatures that had been fashioned in the Image. I even tried to pretend that I was not entirely responsible for the situation, and I had in fact planned to lay the full blame at the door of the Eternal Word. That is what I had planned on doing, because I thought that there was no way the Word could come down on earth to rescue Adam and Eve and their posterity.

"What utterly wishful thinking on my part to imagine that the Deliverer would remain 'neutral' in the matter between me and Adam and Eve - to imagine that the Word could allow me to meddle with the divine plan, and not take action of some kind to halt the madness that had gotten ahold of me. And even after He had promised His Father that He would come to the rescue of humans, I just kept telling myself that He had to be bluffing. I could not imagine the Word reducing Himself to a virtual non-entity for the sake of humans and taking up their nature, promise or no promise!

"It seemed a foregone conclusion that death - the spiritual death that I had succeeded in visiting upon humans - was going to be the lot of every human upon kicking the bucket. I was not just disproved. I am licking my wounds - and talk about being smelly! Some preachers are given to bragging about 'Satan...this' and 'the devil...that'; if He had not come - in fact if He had not *died* to neutralize the consequences of sin - you would all be heading to prison cells in hell as and when your time on earth ran out. In other words, you humans would *die* in the real sense when the time came for your souls to be separated from your bodies!

"Sin has a price that is commensurate with the deed, and a spiritual being that defies the Prime Mover is fully deserving of what has been our own lot since we fell from grace - eternal damnation. And you folks should thank your stars that you can expiate for your sins before your time on earth is up and save yourselves the rap; and you should also be thankful for the fact that those folks who survive you can actually alleviate your plight in Purgatory - yes, Purgatory - by turning a blind eye to insults and being extra good, and asking

Him-Who-is-Who-is to apply any graces they earn thereby to alleviating the miseries of the poor souls in Purgatory.

"And those of you who attempt to cut short the lives of *enemies* here on earth might in fact discover, when you yourselves kick the bucket, that you were being used by the Prime Mover as his instruments to consign to Purgatory those sinners who would otherwise have gone straight to hell - something that clearly would not work to your individual benefit because, in trying to get rid of those you hated, you were hoping all along that *they* would end up in hell. Since we still end up with a prize, it doesn't much matter to us. And, in case you folks thought we were indifferent, 'Please, welcome to Gehenna!'

"You ought to know by now that while the Prime Mover *hates sin*, but *loves the sinner*, we for our part *hate sinners* and *love sin*! You should also be aware that killings of humans by humans are the perfect measure of the success of our efforts to derail the divine plan. It is also one reason you folks would be well advised to pray for peace at all times.

The Pilgrim Church and Purgatory...

"Some of you don't understand why there is this Purgatory place, but that is being daft! If you somehow escape my tentacles, but haven't taken advantage of the rest of your time on earth to put off completely the 'old man' and to put on the 'new man' (as St. Paul said), or to apologize and sufficiently make amends to those you wronged (like the good thief did) by doing penance, you surely can't just breeze past St. Peter and get into heaven as if you had never wronged Him-Who-is-Who-is! And, by the same token, it would be unfair if people in that category - which is just about every repentant human who heads off from the earthly life to the after-life remember - were just turned away.

"I mean, because they would be souls that had rejected me and my works, and had come 'clean', even I - Beelzebub - wouldn't be in a position to take them under my wing. Bedecked with divine grace and reconciled to the Prime Mover, they would be completely unwelcome in the Underworld!

"But - guess what - many of you earthlings are so puffed up with your self-importance, you won't even face up to the fact that you are on trial here on earth! And so the sinning - yes, especially the killing - goes on!

"When you humans sin, you are essentially telling the Deliverer to take a hike – or else! You are giving the Word and also Author of Life notice that you regard Him as an 'ignoramus' who made a big mistake by creating you in His image at the time He caused you to come into existence, and endowing you with the gifts of reason and free will! You are not just putting the Word and Lord of the Universe on the spot, but - just like I myself did – you are grading Him C-minus and letting Him know that His performance so far isn't good enough! When Adam and Eve found my suggestion that they would be like the Prime Mover if they ate of the forbidden fruit enticing, and followed through by sampling the fruit from the Tree of Life, they were actually tasking the Word and Son of Man to show why, years later, He wouldn't deserve to be scourged and nailed to the tree for 'wavering' in His response to the chief priests and Pharisees concerning the fate of a "woman who had been caught in the very act of committing adultery" - never mind that there was no mention of his name of the man; and never mind that the prostitute had often serviced the chief priests and Pharisees themselves right there within the temple precincts; and also never mind that the luckless temple guard with whom the woman was having adultery that time around had been water boarded before vanishing mysteriously.

"You stupid humans don't even realize the extent to which you humiliate the Word and Author of Life when you sin! So, so Dumb! I sometimes think that if I somehow went out of circulation - if I had not been foolish enough to attempt that coup - the next archdevil would be a human!

"And talking about dumb humans – I have never seen dumb fools like the so-called 'Modern man'! First, you 'moderns' don't even know that you are dumb! You know…Adam and his contemporaries whom you moderns only imagine as 'cave men' were enjoying life spans that averaged nine hundred years in their time! Eve, the matriarch of humankind, did in fact notch a thousand and twenty years before she gave up her ghost! This was because those humans of old were still capable of harnessing both their brain *and* their brawn as they went about their daily lives - and also because they were not addicted to 'red meat' and 'pills' like you moderns! Yes - pills or, as you call them, 'medicines'! That was too bad because consuming red meat and overdosing themselves with medicines would have hastened their arrival in Gehemnna where we succeeded in keeping them prisoner until the Deliverer, after acquiescing to die Himself, turned up there and rescued them!

"If I may digress a bit, you probably now also understand why I myself and the host of demons over whom I wield control never celebrated the Deliverer's death! No, that would never do. The way things were ordained undercut me. When saving humans from the clutches of sin and from damnation, the Son of Man used a clever trick to ensure I wouldn't be able to interfere at all. He emptied himself, taking the form of a slave and being born in human likeness. And, being found in human form, he humbled himself and became obedient to His Father to the point of death - even death on a cross. It was only by emptying Himself to that extent that my minions, including chaps like Herod Agrippa and Pontius Pilate who were worked in tandem with the priests and Pharisees to 'destroy' Him, could get away with it and do not have to face the avenging armies of angels who were just waiting for a word from the Prime Mover to unleash hell on those earthlings.

"That is how dumb you humans are. First, you imagined that if you cut down the Son of Man, it would be the end of it! Quite typical of you humans…and you never learn because nothing has changed - the only thing you think of when someone steps on your toe is to grab an AK 47 and pull the trigger until the poor soul supposedly is no more!

"Yes, we demons work hard to see you humans suffer. When you humans are suffering and unable to pursue earthly joys, you typically imagine that it is finished - you loose all hope, and end up on the verge of despair! And that is what our aim is - to drive you humans to despair! But the Deliverer was, of course, something else altogether. He was literally victorious in death - in allowing fools like you to do to Him what you did. And you can, of course, recall that when the Son of Man cried out with a loud voice and then he died, many graves opened of their own accord, and the bodies of the saints who had gone to sleep in them arose! His death presaged life for you folks!

"To get back to our subject of lifespans of humans, in contrast to the longevity of life enjoyed by the mother of the human race, the oldest she-human of modern times, according to the 'Guinness Book of World Records' so-called, survived for just one hundred and twenty-three years! Her modern male counterpart notched up a hundred and twenty-one years; and only because he drank a lot of *Sho-chu*!

"But the stupidity of humans doesn't stop there! Can you imagine dumb fools like you even suggesting that I, Beelzebub and Lord of the Underworld, ain't bright! Just listen to the language some of them preachers use when talking about me – you would think that a preacher of all people would know that I ain't dumb or stupid! But, No! They seem to get a kick from lambasting me for being the father of death, and then suggesting in the same breath that I am good for nothing and that I am finished! They don't see that I am still very much in charge in on this little globe which will soon be rendered inhabitable even before the clouds of World War III settle down! It is I who is behind the maddening arms race with which you humans have been engrossed for generations.

"Since the discovery of gun powder, the so-called bourgeoisie among you have been intoxicated with the desire to dominate not just the proletariat, but everyone who doesn't huff and puff in the same way as them! And so, now, that small terrified 'privileged' class, at my instigation, allowed a mighty, all powerful military industrial complex to evolve only to cede all political power to it. But what is the military industrial complex? It is of course just my tool in the exact same way all these so-called military alliances are my tool! If you do not believe me, just wait until the third world war breaks out. And if you do not believe that World War III is on the horizon, then you do not know your own human history! I just can't wait to see the expressions on the faces of humans when they see their familiar surroundings - earth, sky and all - ignite and vaporize just before their beloved Mother Earth implodes, as the world's arsenal of nuclear bombs, on which the world's demagogues now spend katrillions of dollars, set one another off!

"You should know that you do not hear very much these days about cases of possession because too many of you seem ready to fill my role unasked? It astonishes me even more because, while at it, no thought is given to the fact that the rot is all transitory - a mirage. And even though you know that this is so, you humans act as though you are going to be able, when your time is up, to turn around and pick up where you left off without in a new lease of life without ever having to confront your Maker and Judge!

"Now, you fools had better learn that your life on earth is not just *like* a one time stage performance; it *is* a one time stage performance, and the performance itself is restricted to one act. Those humans who try to do the right thing - and I really hate them for that - actually look to the moment when the curtain falls, because it hastens their reunion with the Prime Mover and Stage Director. Everybody else - and I really love them for it - balks at the fact that the curtain will fall and they will get something else instead of that hug!"

Mjomba, who thought it was a great idea to have none other than the prince of darkness pontificate on things that he himself would rather not in real life, had the devil continue as follows about the nature of humans. It did not strike Mjomba at the time that his book would one day be compulsory reading for all students of religion, or that teachers and students alike would be quoting this shadiest of shady characters to support their theological positions! And so he had Beelzebub continue his parley on human nature uninterrupted.

Spiritus Gallivantus...

"**A**nd how did you humans even get the idea that you are *Animal Rationale* - especially when you do not even act like it. I will tell you what you really are: *Spiritus Gallivantus*! You are spiritual essences that can traipse or amble around, and even do a caper! Your bodies or animal features are merely aids to help you navigate around on earth during the time I have permission to tempt you, and test your faith in the Prime Mover.

"And you have a lot to be grateful for; because, in addition to spiritual obstacles like myself, there are lots of physical obstacles out there; and, believe me, you wouldn't last very long without simple things like eye-sight. Your bodily organs and sense faculties are just there to complement your spiritual faculties - so you can see where you are going, and also forage for food, communicate with one another, and so forth and so on while you work on the Church Triumphant Entrance Test or 'CTET' as you call it.

"You are not animals, but spirits - just like me, damn you! That is why the fact remains that your Maker will never allow me to tempt any of you beyond what you can bear with the help of His grace; and He, understandably, gives you all the strength you need to carry the crosses that He sends your way. So know that if you were soul-less beasts who bore no resemblance whatsoever to your Maker, regardless of what you could accomplish or do, I wouldn't have any interest in you at all.

"If you were merely animals that were driven by instinct, and you went nuts and decided to ignore what your instincts told you, I would just sit back and observe, curiously of course, as you dove head first into on-coming traffic, or if you yourselves clambered aboard your autos and raced over some cliffs in them - or if you just lay down and starved yourselves to death.

"But you have souls, you nuts. That makes you look too much like Him, and it also makes me hate you as much as I hate Him - don't you see? This is so even if you might be born without limbs or you are conceived OK but end up as utter failures in the eyes of the world - paupers perpetually immersed in debt, or a liability to society for no fault of yours, innocent victims of diabolical schemes concocted by your fellow humans; or if, individually or collectively, you were to somehow meet an ignominious end at the hands of enemies - like your Lord and Messiah did! And just to think that it leaves you strengthened and even closer to the Maker, rather than exposed or weakened!

Homo Sapiens...

"True, 'Thinking Man' is what you humans are - which is just another way of saying that you humans are spirits. And that is also where the confusion begins. Saying that one is a 'rational animal' does not mean that one has to engage in mental exertions - spiritual gyrations or anything of the sort - to realize one's fullness as a rational animal. The fact is that when you humans try to 'think', all you end up doing is 'rationalize', which is not even the same as 'reasoning'. You end up just looking for excuses to justify the empty 'animal' lives you lead. You end up clouding the fact that you are spirits - period - and that you do not need to justify that to anyone.

"In other words, you do not need to engage in a 'thinking' or 'reasoning' exercise either in order to show that you are '*homo sapiens*' or to be one. As a matter of fact, to think clearly and creatively (which is not the same as saying 'generating original ideas' because there is no such a thing as 'an original' idea), a human needs to stop and give 'reflection', an automatic reflex for a human when the conditions are right, a chance to occur.

"In order to 'think', you must relax, leave whatever might ordinarily be distracting to the mind aside, stop 'thinking' in the way that word is normally used in human lingo, and become disengaged from what might be getting you all excited and going off on a tangent. It is only then - when you are curled up in a yoga position and have shut out the world that the human thought processes get a boost and true 'thought' or mental creativity gets a chance to burst forth.

"You had better believe me when I say that it is when you humans effectively 'stop thinking' - it is when you interrupt all that sentimental stuff you equated with 'true thought processes' as defined above - that you really start thinking. It is only then that, freed from worries and other distractions, that the soul or 'spiritual' mind gets a chance to transcend matter, and gets in a position to tap that unlimited fountain of truly enriching ideas or thoughts that ultimately emanate from Wisdom or Him-Who-is-Who-is, and to start maturing spiritually.

"When you humans exert yourselves and try to 'think' (perhaps to show that you are very clever!), you actually stifle learning and you become dumber. In order to meditate fruitfully and become enriched in your thoughts, it is of the essence to banish distractions the way monks in monasteries do when practising 'yoga'. Yes, monks in monasteries who discovered the 'yoga' that people like Einstein and all other great inventors practised.

"That is why a good night's sleep is the best preparation for 'sitting a paper', not an all night immersion in books that leaves you all excitable, distracted by all the stuff you were trying - most likely unsuccessfully - to absorb, unable to concentrate, and prone to misread and misunderstand the exam questions!

"This is a set-up that clearly favors infants whom grown-ups, in their stupidity, mistakenly fancy to be both gravely handicapped and seemingly prone to go to sleep as soon as they get their fill. Actually, infants do not really sleep all that much. But they relax a lot and, in the process, abandon themselves to the 'spontaneous thought processes' or 'meditation' (in the correct sense of that word) quite a lot. Children learn so fast because they do not have the bad habit of the 'roving eye' and other habits of that nature which plague grown-ups.

The wise and the not-so-wise...

"It must sound very funny coming from me of all creatures; but it is true, nonetheless, that when some of you - poor banished children of Adam and Eve - find yourselves fulfilled and not wanting, you become so distracted by the good life, you forget, for the most part at any rate, that there is such a thing as a doomsday clock. You conveniently forget that it exists even though none of you has found a way of disabling it. There is no doubting that the good life does engender a false sense of security which might even lull one into concluding that there indeed is justice and fairness in the world!

"Not surprisingly, there are so many of you who find things so comfy, you have become oblivious to the fact that a small event like a bad deal, a burglary or some freak accident, a storm or perhaps even a flood, or a black-out and the myriad things that might ensue there from in its wake including looting, a riot, a coup d'etat or a revolution, a fire, a war or a famine or the outbreak of a plague, a landslide or an earthquake, a volcanic eruption, or perhaps Doomsday itself - for those of you who will live long enough to see it - not only will prove things otherwise, but those 'successful' people will find themselves in the exact same boat as those who are 'failures' in the eyes of the world.

"I like to compare these so-called 'successful' sons and daughters of Adam and Eve to a group of people who go surfing on the worldwide web for the purpose of getting directions to the heavenly Paradise; but who become so distracted by the different pop-up banners which greet them from the moment they log on to the Internet, they decide to give up their search and spend the rest of their time exploring the web sites, of which there is an innumerable number. Switching to computers with superior memory, and using Yahoo, Excite and other powerful search engines, they pass their days exploring cyberspace and enjoying, and completely lose sight of what they had originally gone to the web to look for.

"The original 'failures' are those people who are really interested in making the journey to the heavenly Paradise. After logging onto the worldwide web - and they do so at the same time the first group does - they completely ignore the irritating banners and proceed to specify 'Heavenly Paradise' when prompted to spell out their intended destination. From the bewildering array of 'sites' which represent themselves as paradise of one sort or another, and each of which suggests to them that they need not go any further in their quest for a good *time* and happiness, they pick out the only site which does not imply that it is an *earthly* paradise. They click on '*Way of the Cross*' which is the name of the site and, on entering, find the directions they were looking for.

"Logging off the worldwide web, they commence their journey and presently find themselves retracing the foot steps of their Savior, and trudging along a meandering stretch of road which takes them from what is easily recognizable as the Upper House, site of the inauguration of the Blessed Eucharist, through the Garden of Gethsemane, past the imposing palace of the Roman Governor who is better known as The Fox, and on to the summit of Mt. Calvary! You cannot get to the mountain top by any other way, and it is of course one route that we of the Underworld have worked over in what you can be sure is very thorough fashion, and that consequently is studded with every conceivable obstacle. And I will try and give you some idea of the sorts of people you will find struggling to make it to the summit along that route.

"Actually, one of them is a mentally retarded man. He has been languishing on death row awaiting execution for a murder he did not commit! You just cannot imagine how hard we've tried to trip him up. Fortunately for him, he is really insane and all our efforts, which are on-going even as I speak, have not been able to drive him crazier than he already is. And that is how he seems to be succeeding in getting to the summit of Calvary. Another one of their number is a fellow who was water boarded over and over by some crazies, and who ended up being coerced into confessing to a crime he didn't commit either and is now languishing in jail. Looks like he too will escape my tentacles because, after what his jailors have taken him through, this fellow seems prepared to die under the load of his 'cross'. This fellow is suicidal!

"And yet another one - a woman who was forcibly raped and impregnated by guards while she was serving a jail term for a misdemeanour - has decided against an abortion. She is typical of those people who seem determined not just to believe in the Deliverer, but also to try and walk the walk. Even as I speak, she is quietly raising her baby and watching him grow up into a happy and athletic young man, with nary a word to anyone about the humiliations that have marked the road she has travelled. By resisting the temptation to go public and even sue the authorities, she has actually helped our cause, because this means that the jailors can continue preying upon other female inmates in those sink holes you folks call jails at will. These are the kinds of injustices we in the under-world like to see become commonplace. Because then the perpetrators can be sure of joining our ranks here in hell when the time for their trial on earth is up.

"You've got to give me and my cronies credit for making sure that any soul that gets past St. Peter and walks through that gate into heaven is fully deserving of the crown!

"The lives of those who try to retrace the Stations of the Cross make very interesting tales indeed, and you should love this one. It is the story of a young padre whose zealous parents coerced him into the priesthood and a life of celibacy. After striving over the years to remain faithful to his priestly vows, he is worried that he may now be at the end of his tether, and has decided to take it a day at a time while praying that he be taken from this world before something catastrophic happens!

"This is one case I have been taking a personal interest in - the objective is simple and straight forward, namely drive the fellow to despair! It is that simple - but, inexplicably we may be failing in our objective of getting this fellow to stop believing that there is an Omnipotent Being who cares for the forsaken. The way things have been going lately, this priest just might succeed in escaping my tentacles.

"We've gone to the extent of using a poor soul - a scoundrel who had been abused by his own parents as far back as he could remember and who had additionally been under my virtual control from the time he was a little baby - to try and derail the man of cloth. We succeeded in snaring the priest into a situation the whole world believed was compromising. And so, falsely accused of taking advantage of an 'innocent' altar boy who had been entrusted to his care by 'loving' parents, the padre not long ago found himself in jail for his 'abominable crime'. The story sounded so credible, even the Church tribunal found him guilty, and endorsed the long jail term that a sleazy magistrate, who obviously had grudge against the priest - something to do with a divorce and the padre's reluctance to bless the judge's marriage to his current girl friend - handed down.

"And you would think we would be done with the poor man at that point out of pity. Wrong! In the jail house, we've got there rotten characters who, operating in concert with the guards, have been repeatedly violating his person in such an unspeakable fashion, if he had been someone else, he would have preferred to take his own life! But the humiliation only seems to have strengthened the fellow's resolve to keep the faith! Not even after he contracted an incurable disease as a result of being repeatedly assaulted by fellow prison inmates. And, as if in mockery of our efforts to drive the fellow to despair, as the priest lies dying in his jail cell, alone and without any possibility of receiving the last sacraments, his face is enveloped in this strange, mesmerizing smile even as I speak - as if he is eager to get up and meet Someone he greatly loves and admires! I have never been so humiliated!

"Those who persevere and make it to the summit of Calvary have one thing in common, and it is that they do not have any trust in themselves. And yet you would think that to be able to make it over a road that is so studded with obstacles that I get the best minds in the Underworld to device, the individual needed to have something of a Don Quixote in him/her!

"Contrary to what pseudo prophets will tell you, salvation and being 'small minded' evidently go together. And, as well, do not be deceived that 'blessings' come your way in this life when you decide to follow the Deliverer or, as some like to put, when you 'become born again'. Nothing is farther from the truth! There would, otherwise, be no reason for anyone to decry what goes on in Hollywood if being richly 'blessed' on this earth was one of the measures of spiritual success.

"'Accursed' is a much better description of the life of the folks who make it to the summit of Calvary, I tell you! And you, of course, understand that their reward is not in this world, but in heaven. And so, if you hear someone saying that you will receive blessings here on earth when you accept the Deliverer, take it with a pinch of salt. Moreover, if your conversion is not staged and is true spiritual conversion, the first thing you are likely to experience is probably going to be what is known as the 'dark night of the soul'! That is because my troops and I will be working overtime to try and reverse that situation. That is also the price you pay for rejecting me and my works!

"Also, those who brag about being 'clever', 'diligent', 'far sighted' and that sort of nonsense cannot prevail against my wiles, for the simple reason that the mind of the least endowed among my troops will always be more than a match for the brightest human mind! Cleverness, business acumen, far sightedness and things like that would of course work in normal circumstances. But you fellows don't exist in circumstances that are anywhere near normal! Don't you remember Paul telling the Corinthians that the world as you now know it is passing away?

"That is why it is so true (as you yourselves sing) that 'He guides the humble to justice; and He teaches the meek His way'! And keep in mind that it is not what goes in that corrupts, but what comes out. It is these sorts of things that have me and my troops fooled every time, I can tell you - and all my clairvoyance notwithstanding!

Finding rest for the soul...

"But if I may let you in on a secret - the Catholic Church's biggest handicap in its work of saving souls is the fact that its priests and prelates, not just in these times but throughout the Church's two thousand year history, by and large do not practice what they preach. They act and behave just like the priests and Pharisees did two thousand years ago! Notice the aloofness of the clergy? It has its roots in the certainty - yes, certainty - of members of the Church's clergy that they and only they are the rightful successors of the apostles!

"That aloofness - or lofty indifference to attempts by anyone who is not one of their number to engage them in a discussion of matters of faith - amounts to a statement that they should be taken off of the all 'unorthodox' sounding mailing lists. I have even observed souls that are groping for enlightenment turned away because members of the clergy, perhaps taking the cue from some of Christendom's popes, generally like to pontificate and don't have any time to listen - to lend 'strangers' their ear! You can see straight away that such an attitude represents a serious problem for the growth in holiness of members of the clergy themselves and an even bigger problem for the work of evangelization whose success depends very much on how well priests live as *alteri Christi*.

"Members of the clergy are in a tricky situation - they must try and impress their audiences that it is truth and nothing but truth to which they give expression, whether by word of mouth or by writing. And that automatically conflicts with the fact that they are not exempt from the requirement that all must be like little children - and also the fact that *'He guides the humble to justice; and He teaches the meek His way'*! In short, there is always a real danger that the call by priests that their flocks be humble and meek and as little children is really a hollow statement, because it does not reflect what they themselves do. You've got to understand that this is one group of people whose endeavors my lieutenants and I will happily work unpaid overtime - yes, unpaid overtime - to undo.

"When we are not tempting those fellows to stand in their pulpits and essentially act like the Pharisee who, unlike the tax collector who was so ashamed of his life that he found it necessary to hide his face in the shadows of the pews at the back of the Synagogue, was certain that he was, for all practical purposes, already saved and redeemed, we are tempting them to behave as if they have a monopoly over truth, and to show that they do not care less for any would be challenger in that regard. And we tempt them above all to imagine that they themselves do not need to be as little children to receive the

Holy Ghost's guidance and instruction. We actually tempt them to think they do not need the Holy Ghost, the weekly homilies to their flocks urging them to be meek and humble of heart notwithstanding - period.

"If you do not believe me, go to the official website of the Vatican. It is full of stuff - really good stuff actually - that *you* are supposed to read and internalise. But if you should have the audacity to try and address *the authors* an e-mail regarding the material on the website, the response is likely to be something like: 'Pray for meekness and humility so that you may receive the guidance of the Holy Ghost and accept the Church's teachings' or 'take me off your mailing list'! I call that being 'sharp' and 'smart'. And, if it were possible for a celebration to take place in Gehenna, that state of affairs in God's Church would constitute a reason for non-stop celebration. Unfortunately it only hurts when we in the Underworld try to throw a party.

"However elevated you might be in the Church's hierarchy, the moment you begin thinking that you are a somebody - the moment you start to think that you have no need for anyone else and that you do not need to heed voices from the pew or elsewhere, that you are in some way special, can withstand temptations of the flesh, and are in a position to face and overcome my wiles single-handed without the help of other people's prayers or God's grace - the moment you start to promote yourself in that fashion, you also automatically begin to demote God the Father (who formed you along with other members of the human race out of nothing), God the Son (who came down from heaven, took up human nature and ended up being nailed on the cross by your kindred, and was left hanging from it helplessly - while the crowd mocked Him and while He was to all appearances abandoned even by His Father - until He finally died in expiation of the sins of men), and God the Holy Ghost (to whom those amongst you who pray confess that you are good for nothing on your own and are entirely dependent on Him to keep out of trouble and for any accomplishment that might appear to accrue to your personal efforts) in your life. You then also are underestimating me - and I don't take kindly to anyone who does.

"From the moment any individual begins to regard himself or herself as a 'somebody', from that same moment, he or she exposes himself or herself to the weakness of the flesh in addition to leaving himself or herself completely at my mercy! And the fact that one is ordained a priest - or gets elevated to the full rank of an apostle and trades in his parish for a bishopric and, in these days, also a bishop's crozier, mitre and the Episcopal ring that members of the flock genuflect to kiss - should constitute an even bigger reason to strive to be truly meek and humble. How otherwise can the individual connect with his flock, and engage everyone who comes knocking at the door in fruitful spiritual dialogue.

"Can you just imagine a swashbuckling and haughty Prince of the Church standing there in full regalia like a peacock, trying to welcome souls into the Mystical Body of Christ! It is a complete contradiction, and it is not the kind of opportunity a prince of darkness like me would possibly pass up and not exploit to the max! You should certainly be able to imagine what Peter or Paul looked like as they journeyed back and forth in Asia Minor in their endeavours to win souls for the Deliverer.

"You can certainly imagine what they would have said if the chaps they were grooming to take over when they themselves passed on had turned up for work one morning bedecked in chasubles, wearing mitres handcrafted in silk atop their burnished crowns, and waving gold-plated crosiers in place of their usual, rough-shod walking sticks! Poor souls from all walks of life are struggling to keep pace with the intermittent glimmer of stars in the darkened skies as they attempt to locate the one that will lead them to the Holy Child in a manger - the Holy Child who is hosted, mark you, by poor shepherds and not by puffed and haughty men of the cloth! And this is not because I, Beelzebub, do not know how the transformation in the Church came about. You'd better believe me when I tell you that I worked very hard personally to bring it about!

"And so, when you think you are a stalwart spiritually and you proceed to claim that God is blessing you, you are really calling something else upon yourself. You are begging the Judge to pronounce you a 'betrayer', perhaps even an incorrigible sinner and hypocrite who is determined to shut out the Deliverer's redeeming graces, and who might conceivably be entirely unfit as a man of the cloth!

"No, being sharp and smart does not get humans anywhere in the business of holiness. But being as nothing does. And Judas Iscariot was a case in point. He was so cock sure of his ability to withstand my wiles as well as temptations of the flesh, he did not think he really needed the Deliverer. This was even though he was a very smart man and also the Deliverer's confidante.

"If you ask me - my dear friend Iscariot, who dropped out of the seminary just weeks before the risen Deliverer performed the first ordinations to the priesthood under His new testament, was actually a great intellectual with a sharp wit that made him stand out among the candidates the Deliverer had handpicked after reviewing the resumes of scores of his disciples. You ought to know by now that when it comes to opposing me and my troops, pig headedness of that kind isolates the cocky individual from the Source and allows us to make quick work of him or her.

"I can't stand the sight of some loud-mouthed nitwit who comes along out of no where, and is all suddenly puffed up and 'raring to go' as if he/she can fly to heaven on his/her own volition - as if I, Beelzebub, can be brushed aside just like that! It is a disrespect I do not take lightly, and I typically hit back with deadly force. You see - it is a grave disrespect when you humans try to face off with me on your own. I deal with all who disrespect me in the exact same way and judo style. I lead them along and encourage them to get really bold and to think that they can even dispense with the grace earned for them by the Deliverer. And it is when they are finally intoxicated with their self-love that I pounce on them and strike.

"When it is opportune, I will even get them to take their audacity to the logical conclusion by imagining that they can self-righteously shove their warped beliefs and ideology down other people's throats - especially those over whom they have any kind of influence. They typically realise that they have been on the wrong track all along too late - when those who had followed them blindly, suddenly decide to cast off what they finally perceive as a self-imposed yoke!

"But take the case of Peter. A simple fisherman and one of the original twelve apostles, he is one of the best examples of those who are 'failures' in the eyes of the world. Unschooled in the ways of the world, you could in fact say that he was a precise fit for my description of a dunce! This fellow ended up in the top leadership position in the infant Church, appointed by none other than the Messiah Himself. And if there was anything that worked in his favour, it was the fact that he was meek, readily admitted that he was himself a nonentity, and that he was completely dependent on the Almighty One, and on those who were sent to help him shepherd God's flock, for bringing in the harvest. But in spite of being so humble and reticent, our camp still succeeded in accomplishing a couple of things to make Peter's evangelical work very difficult - and we of course are still at it. You bet! We work hard to ensure that a couple of new splinter groups turn up in Christendom every week, because if there weren't all these denominations to add to the confusion, it would be so much easier for the adherents to other religions to find their way into the Church that was founded by the Deliverer.

"At the trial which preceded the execution by crucifixion of his Lord and Savior, Peter, caving in to the pressures that we were applying, denied any knowledge of the Messiah not once or twice, but a full three times! That is just one of the things we succeeded in bringing off, and you can bet that he was haunted by his denial of the Messiah for the rest of his life.

"A simple man who had been content to live and die a fisherman just like his forefathers before him, it was not as if Peter had sought out and followed the Son of Man out of personal ambition or with a view to gaining anything from being a follower of the Anointed One. He would always distinctly recall that sunny afternoon in autumn when the stranger from the little town of Nazareth, who nonetheless spoke with the authority of the Ruler of the Universe, commanded him to leave his boat, fishing tackle and all and follow him. In retrospect, the account of his life had all the ingredients of a scriptural legend.

"Anyway, the fact was that, Peter, uncontested leader of the Deliverer's 'troops' in the period immediately following the resurrection from hell and ascension into heaven of the Son of Man, who (much to my chagrin) now also celebrated the Holy Eucharist almost on a daily basis and was responsible for providing innovative leadership to the body of apostles in the work of evangelization and doing so infallibly, had publicly denied knowing his Lord and Savior. It was a denial which had not just been a slip of the tongue, but one that had been made in full view of Jerusalem's press corps, and which had received extensive coverage in the media along with that week's other tumultuous events.

"For the rest of his days on earth, the strident voice of that woman in the crowd identifying him as the Chief of Staff of the growing army of the condemned Man's followers, his own halting voice as he lied in front of everyone and proceeded to provide alibis that proved unsustainable, and the shattering sound of a cock's crow which seemingly came from no where - and also the words '*Tu es Petrus, et super hanc petram, Ecclesiam meam edificabo*' - would never stop ringing in his ears.

"Regrettably, that woman - whom we got to screech on Peter - a rascal and turn-coat in our opinion, subsequently converted to Christianity herself not longer after, and even died for her faith at the hands of a functionary of Pilate's by the name of Saul. And that Saul, who changed his name to Paul, was another turn-coat who suddenly abandoned our cause just when we thought we were succeeding in strangling the Christian Fellowship. He became one of Christianity's fiercest crusader! We ourselves have had our ups and downs as you can see.

"One reason Peter stumbled and fell as he and John raced to the tomb three days later was that those sounds ringing in his ears all at once and incessantly reduced him to a virtual zombie.

"To make things worse, the leader of the nascent Church was also prone to have bad dreams. Now I can tell you that we in the Underworld love people who dream dreams. Dreams are a ready-made vehicle for temptation and provide a wonderful opportunity for manipulating the human mind, you see!

"On each of the seven days that followed the Day of Pentecost - the day Peter along with the other disciples spoke in tongues to the Jewish worshippers who had come to Jerusalem from different parts of Asia Minor and other parts of the globe - he had the same identical dream. Peter dreamed that his travels had taken him all the way to Rome, where he decided to settle permanently. And, according to the nightmarish dream, he had set up home in a castle atop a hill which went by the name of Gondolfo! But that was not all. He dreamed that by the time he got to Rome, the power of the Roman emperor had greatly waned, while his own power as the leader of Christendom had grown to the point at which he could appoint or dethrone Caesar's successors at will!

"It was, of course, not so much the fact that he wielded such colossal power which made the dream a bad one as the fact that the dream reminded him of Pontius Pilate and of the woman who had picked him out of the crowd on that 'Good Friday' morning. The dream made it appear as if he, Peter, could verily have stopped 'the fox' from sending his Lord and Master to an undeserved and cruel death by just 'telling the truth and shaming the devil' instead of cowering with fear and denying that he had any knowledge of the condemned Man.

"As if that was not bad enough, on the consecutive nights following the day the Messiah ascended into heaven in full view of the disciples, Peter had a different kind of dream even though it also had something to do with Rome. He dreamed that his travels, devoted to the spread of Christianity, had brought him to the City of Seven Hills where Peter was promptly apprehended and condemned to die by crucifixion for his activities.

"The dream was nightmarish not so much because of the garish manner in which his life was going to end, but because Peter felt completely unworthy of the honor of dying in a manner that was so similar to that in which the Deliverer had chosen to die in atonement of the sins of men. Certainly not after his denial had directly resulted in the Deliverer's death - if there was anything to the earlier dream, that is. When he awoke from his nightmarish dream, Peter, like the scrupulous fellow he was, refused to forgive himself for presuming and imagining that he could leave this world for the next in the same manner his Lord and Savior did! Troubled, Peter swore repeatedly that he would never allow that to happen - almost as if he had the power to dictate how his earthly life would end.

"The number of humans who set out with the intention of 'walking the walk' with the help of the directions they obtain from the worldwide web is large. And that is not surprising because unless squelched - and it takes a lot of determination to do so - the craving of souls for that perfect Good is as powerful as the source of the desire for fulfilment. And you can bet that all those souls will each one have a similar story to tell.

"Now, you should also understand that a devil like me gets a real kick out of dethroning a fellow spirit. I am the author of death after all! That is why I love to hear you folks say: 'He made me do it!' That is even though I can never really make you do anything until you yourself choose to play along! I would feel like I had smacked ox below the belt if I heard one them ox confide to the rest of the herd: 'He made me do it!'

"It is evident that you humans prefer to think of yourselves as beasts or animals. Don't want to take any responsibility for your actions, Eh! It is something we fallen spirits couldn't do even if we tried. Unfortunately, the more you humans believe you are animals, the less pleasure I derive from derailing any of you. By doing so, you lull yourself into a false sense of justification and you spoil my fun in the process!

"If you need any additional evidence for the fact that you humans are inclined to sin, it is this obsession with the animal aspect of your human nature and your continual denial of the fact that you are spiritual beings first and foremost. And, again, it should be embarrassing that humans need Satan to remind them of this simple fact.

"And this is not to suggest that the human body isn't sacred. During the one hundred and twenty years or so that the body is informed by the spirit - that period used to be around four hundred years before the combination of medical discoveries so-called and poisoned meat and fish, and junk food triggered the deficiencies in your immune systems - the human body is also the temple of the Prime Mover and Author of Life. If that were not the case, you can be sure that you all would be possessed and in the full control of one or other member of my team from the moment you were conceived in the womb! You'd better take my word for it - even if you do not believe anything else I say!

"You see - when you are made in the His image, even though you are created an intelligent and also free creature, it is really your likeness to Him which makes you special. When discussing humans, there is no such a thing as 'the extent to which humans are *not* made in the Prime Mover's likeness', or 'in so far as their likeness to something *other* than the Perfect One goes'. It is the reason all humans, including the characters that might appear to you as really distasteful, are very precious in the eyes of the Creator. And, indeed, that is why to the extent a human sees another as 'distasteful', to that extent that human himself or herself becomes less deserving of his or her position as a servant of the Prime Mover - because, in so doing, that human effectively attempts to usurp the prerogative of the Prime Mover and Judge.

"Humans who do not see the beams in their own eyes, and get all worked up about imaginary specs of dust in the eyes of others, would never make good judges. But they are the ones who, with a little help from my troops and I, are out there pontificating about criminal minds of those they perceive as their enemies without tiring.

"The likeness of you humans to the Prime Mover is what makes you capable of transcending the limitations of time and space, enabling your accomplishments (and failures) under those conditions to be credited (or debited) to your eternal life. It is what makes physical acts neither good nor bad in themselves, and intentions paramount in determining the extent to which a deed is noble or otherwise. The consciences of humans derive their legitimacy and authority from the likeness humans bear to the Prime Mover, and also attest to His presence at the kernel of the human soul.

"And, on a completely different level, the likeness of humans to the Prime Mover or 'God' is what makes what I call 'innocent' joys innocent - the taste of good food and good wine, the sounds of a harmonious tune, the sight of a lily flower bed or a virgin forest, and so on and so forth. Except that, in this former Garden of Eden which is now effectively a Valley of Tears as a result in part of my scheming, you humans would be well advised to forego even those innocent enjoyments as part of self-mortification and to expiate for the sins you commit from time to time, and in order to keep the possibility of becoming addicted to the 'innocent' pleasures and getting sucked into something else (things not even the beasts get into) remote. And, of course, innocent enjoyments and delights stop being innocent the moment they start being actively sought! Because then intentions, and *ipso facto* also the conscience, and all that they imply immediately come into play.

"The likeness of humans to the Prime Mover's image is the reason every human has an inalienable right to life, and also why taking away the life of another is one of the surest ways of putting one's own eternal life in jeopardy. It is the reason humans have a right to freedom of worship. It explains why all humans are equal, and acts of discrimination are outlawed. It is also the reason each and every human act or thought that is deliberate either pleases or displeases the Prime Mover.

"It is the reason mortal creatures like you still can pray to and even commune with the Prime Mover who is divine and immortal with confidence. It is the reason humans can smile and laugh - unlike beasts and other 'lower' creatures. It is because you humans are made in the image of a divinity that you sometimes feel like you can fly - even if you do not have any wings! It is, of course, the reason no human can vanish from the Prime Mover's sight let alone be forgotten by Him. And last but not least, it is what makes me, Beelzebub who was also created in God's own image and likeness, stand condemned for my role in the downfall of humans, for grooming all those false prophets and sending them out into the world to counter Truth, and for doing whatever else I do.

"But why do I have to tell you these things, you numskulls! If I, Diabolos, can be pining away here in this place of damnation, completely cut off by flames that cannot be extinguished from all that is godly, fair, beautiful and good...done in by what used to be my very own flames of desire, how can dunces like you even hope to prevail by setting yourself up in opposition to Him-Who-is-Who-is! And just imagine how humbling it is for me to be here - against my own will of course - confessing these things! Nay, eating my own words! You cannot begin to imagine how chastening it is for me to be here talking to you like this.

Fulfillment...

"But, I must say, you humans have a really screwed up idea of happiness! While we devils might have a reason to take our revenge on you humans because of the fact that you will take up residence in mansions in heaven that were really meant for us, it is difficult, even for us devils, to see any rationale for the belief by humans in revenge, visiting capital punishment on members of society who are singled out as being 'errant' (which is really legalized murder that emulates Cain's act of fratricide and overlooks the fact that, once in existence, creatures that are fashioned in the Image can never be rubbed out), wars whether they are labeled pre-emptive wars, wars of attrition, or holy wars, and things of that sort. That is, of course, not to say that we are about to try and dissuade you from indulging in them. But the pleasures and satisfaction you derive from exacting revenge or watching so-called 'criminals' being hanged - as if you yourselves were not that or, perhaps, even worse - must provide the most ephemeral and passing of pleasures. I have a perfectly valid excuse - you can even call it 'reason' - for referring to you humans as stupid.

"The revenge exacted by the Prime Mover is of a completely different nature and on a different plane. It makes complete sense, and is actually brought on by creatures who are fashioned in His image and likeness, but who go against their own reason and attempt to be what they are not.

"The stupidity of you humans also shows glaringly when you pursue other 'pleasures' like gluttony for instance. When gormandizing in an effort to satisfy the palette, you humans completely forget the simple logic which applies in your particular case - at least whilst you still have that body. At the time you are satisfying your appetite for food, your other appetites which you cannot satisfy all at the same time as a practical matter - and I won't go into a litany of these appetites - will also be crying out for fulfilment; and fulfilment in an atmosphere of peace - meaning an atmosphere that engenders uninterrupted and above all enduring satisfaction.

"But this hopeless situation is rendered more hopeless by the fact that the food employed by the individual to satisfy the palette might taste just fine one day - which itself may mean any number of things - depending on things like the weather and the mood of the individual gobbling it up. On another day, its taste might remind the individual of some really dainty dish which he or she enjoyed many years before as a child. And on another day, regardless of the skills of the chef, weather conditions, and even that individual's determination to revel in the food, it might taste like vinegar! And similarly for the other appetites you folks are always trying to assuage.

"And then the celebratory activity of the hedonist might be completely frustrated for any number of reasons - an emergency visit to the dentist, a draught, or even the premature death of the joy seeker. Now, I mean...if you can even die - well, put it this way - if you will die, then not only are the efforts you expend in the meantime pursuing passing pleasures a total waste; but any fleeting 'happiness' you might derive there from also effectively becomes a stain on your record - a stain that labels you as being one of those individuals who seem to be satisfied with illusions, and have no interest in the real thing.

"Unfortunately for us angelic creatures so-called, we don't die. I mean - we are ghosts and we really couldn't 'give them up' in the same way you humans do. And I say 'unfortunately' because if we did - if we too possessed some sort of 'body' which we would have had to vacate on a non-spiritual plane before facing the Judge on a spiritual plane, we might have thought twice before we bolted and landed ourselves in this accursed place!

"Any way, you couldn't get clearer testimony to the fact that this whole preoccupation with self-indulgence is based on flawed logic. The very objects you folks use to get satisfaction are not even meant for that purpose. Their purpose is not to engender fulfilment in that sense at all; and, try all you can, you won't succeed in getting those objects - many of which are inanimate - to give you, a spiritual creature, what they do not possess. How could they possibly give you true *spiritual* joy? They might give you material and, by definition *transitory*, happiness!

"The idea of different types and/or levels of satisfaction is completely inconsistent with the idea of fulfilment in the sense in which that word applies to creatures that are made in the image of Him-Who-is-Who-is. To be real, that fulfilment has to be complete, unchanging, and permanent.

"You humans don't even seem to be aware that the situation resulting from such dissolute lifestyles is more devastating to the human constitution - destabilising, if you like - than that which would prevail if you were just busy curbing your appetites and abstaining from all pleasures. If you exercised your will and did that, you would see that your other appetites and desires for fulfilment would gradually diminish in their intensity and even eventually go to sleep, and you yourself would get some respite.

"Because of the peculiar way in which sense faculties and the appetites they serve are linked, when an individual seeks to satisfy one sense faculty, the appetites served by the other faculties automatically also start to clamor for fulfilment - because of the simple reason that they all belong to a body that is informed by the same spirit. By the same token, mortification and things like abstinence, self-abnegation and works of atonement or penance engender calm, composure and serenity. They facilitate growth on the spiritual plane, and the flowering of virtues, while dampening any tendencies to wantonness and profligacy.

"And if it were not for the pervasive hypocrisy, ingrained intellectual dishonesty, and moral bankruptcy, humans would actually see proof of the existence of the Prime Mover in their very inability to perform any virtuous act without the aid of divine grace. The wickedness of humans, which drove them to attempt to liquidate the Deliverer and has brought them on the verge of sending Planet Earth up in a plume of smoke with nuclear explosions that are targeting their own kind, beggars even our demonic imagination. That is how far the fools have travelled down the path to perdition.

"The reason saints in heaven can enjoy rapturous joy, happiness and complete fulfilment is because the totality of their person is fulfilled all at one and the same time, and without any threat of interruption, in the presence of Him-Who-is-Who-is. Just as He Himself is not just beautiful, but ultimate Beauty itself - or just good but ultimate Goodness itself - partial things are not possible in His presence. The angels and saints are able to share in that Beauty and Goodness only because the totality of their individual person, not just parts of themselves, had been readied for fulfilment. That is what emptying oneself or being selfless means!

"My own hell now consists in the fact that I squandered the opportunity to have the totality of me fulfilled; and that happened when I focused on self-aggrandisement during the period I was on trial, instead of surrendering myself to Him-Who-is-Who-is without any reservation. Being the first one He had created in His own image and likeness and a free creature, I tried to stake out for myself a special position which would see me - or so I thought - wield unfettered authority over all the creatures that would follow after me. I was in effect going out on a limb, and lunging after fulfilment on my own, instead of putting all my trust in Him and waiting patiently to be ushered into His regal presence. I undercut myself in that way.

"If you are curious about conditions in the hell that is now my lot, go find out for yourself what Lucia, Francisco and Jacinta told Father Pena, their parish priest, after they were allowed a glimpse of the place. And if you do not believe their account, you can go read the accounts of that St. Catherine of Siena, St. Frances of Rome, St. Theresa of Avila, St. John Bosco, St. Faustina Kowalska, and more recently Sister Josefa Menendez left for you. And if you still don't get it, why don't you do yourself a favour and just go look up all those biblical passages in both the New and Old Testament that describe the conditions here in Hades.

"I know that I am stupid - very stupid, in fact, considering the miscalculation I made - me and the host of angels I succeeded in misleading, so I wouldn't be all by myself in Gehenna. But you are more stupid, I tell you...for one, unlike us, you have this second chance which you seem determined to fritter away. And I certainly didn't have some stupid devil come and make a homily. Of course, it suits me perfectly that you are all so stupid - I do not have to worry that you will hear me out or pay attention to any of the things I am suggesting to you. And it goes without saying that you will cite as your excuse the fact that it is me, Beelzebub - aka Diabolos, the Evil One, and Prince of the Darkness - who is the messenger - albeit a reluctant one.

"I actually like the way you idiots make it look as if you are in a Catch 22 situation here. The classic Catch 22 situation - lending your ear to the Tempter whose business it is to tell lies or doing the very opposite of what I am suggesting and being damned! Can't actually think of a better Catch 22! I shouldn't even complain that I am standing here giving this testimony against my will. But your stupidity is just my first line of defense. For those of you who do decide to proceed and try to implement those truly excellent suggestions, the real battle starts right there.

Fight to the finish...

"First of all, even though the spirit might show that it is willing to act, the flesh will almost certainly pull you into the opposite direction. But usually it is your desire to show off and try to bring it off all on your own, without the help of the grace of Him-Who-is-Who-is that constitutes my second line of defense. When you neglect to pray or when you just say what I like to refer to as the 'Hypocrite's Prayer', it usually also assures me victory, while you yourselves, puffed up with pride and mired in hypocrisy, end up attempting vainly to suppress those natural appetites.

"You bet I have lots of fun watching folks waste their valuable time trying to do what Freud has already proved they cant, namely repress natural desires by dint of their will power without going insane! But the vast majority of you don't even think of going that route, any way. This is because you are faithless - which makes you even less inclined to get down on your knees to pray for the gift of faith. Yes, faithless - and it is immaterial that you might happen to be one of those people who just love to stand there in front of crowds bragging about your 'great and unshakable' faith in the Prime Mover!

Still a force to be reckoned with...

"And I will now reveal to you my dirty little secret - I have got a third line of defense, and it is virtually impenetrable! You see...even after you've done all the things I have said - and even though I have made it clear that I have said them under duress - how do you know you are carrying out the will of Him-Who-is-Who-is and not my will? Like now...whose will are you actually going to be carrying out - His or mine? Remember, you either have to take me at my word and do what I am telling you, or you just don't believe me and don't do as I am telling you! If you are saying to yourself that you can verify if what I am telling you is fact, I challenge you to try and do that!

"I can tell you that I am not almighty, but I am certainly capable of giving you a run for your money. Or, are you thinking of turning to prayer to beat me to it? I might not be capable of being in two places at the same time, but I am a spirit and can move pretty fast. And I am also invisible, just like He is. And I am also quite capable of mimicking His voice.

"Oh, you are thinking of teachers of the law and the prophets? I have out there a whole army of devotees who are quite capable of taking on those roles. And, believe me, some of these guys and gals can put on quite a show. And, fortunately, that is what this business of salvation boils down to nowadays - a show. And you can bet that it is not by accident that this is the case. So, don't you write me off just as yet!

"I mean - It is a war we are engaged in. And it has to be fought to the bitter finish. And while the other side believes in fighting wars according to rules, I don't; and at the moment I am throwing in everything I've got. In my vocabulary, there is no such a thing as fair play! And while I sympathize with you, I have to admit that you are fair play - you all are up for grabs. And while you can run, you absolutely cannot hide. And don't you underestimate my reach.

"You cannot differentiate my workers from His; and my workforce is highly motivated - I have enough dirt on them which will come out if they do not produce results, and they know it. I have at my beck and call some of the greatest orators alive. My arsenal includes preachers whose eloquence will make you start believing that you are saved long before the grace of Him-Who-is-Who-is has had an opportunity to touch you.

"And you would be surprised at the kind of things they can do with a bit of 'inspiration' from me. If you are not alert, they will talk you into believing that the Son of Man - the Word through whom creation came into being who is also the Second Person of the Blessed Trinity - is really not divine. That the Son of Man is the son of Mary and that He just happens to be the 'Son of God' because he did not have an earthly father with nothing more to it! At my instigation, they will 'prove' to you anything.

"They will prove to you that you can mumble some prayer formula and become saved - that it is so easy to clinch yourself a mansion in heaven. Or that you can be saved, not by keeping the Ten Commandments, but by 'faith alone'! Or that the late Pope John Paul was the Antichrist! They will 'prove' to you that all wars, justified or unjustified, provided they are initiated by the nation that you are a citizen of are always OK, and they will back up their 'proof' with quotations from the holy book. The fact is that I have been behind all the heresies that have plagued the Church since its inception. You can bet that a lot of my energy goes into trying to cause as much disunity in the Church of God as possible!

"And you may not like to hear it, but there has never been a shortage of fellows in the Church - men with shortcomings in charity, patience and humility - who end up in visible positions in the Church's hierarchy, usually as its apologists, with a little help from me, naturally. Just a couple of people like that, instead of drawing souls to the Church, actually keep multitudes, among them many good people, away with their display of scarcely veiled hypocrisy and intolerance! They set themselves up as judges even as they are harping on the Prime Mover's infinite mercies in their sermons, and the fact that His judgements are incomprehensible. These folks would burn Joan of Arc at the stake all over again. And, only recently, some of them were arguing that Padre Pio - Padre Pio of all people - was possessed by me! They are my moles inside the Church - and quite a lot of fun watching them operate as my instruments when they should be operating as instruments of His grace!

"Thinking of devotional hymns and songs of praise as Solomon did? I have under my control choirs whose voices can move congregations in whichever way the conductor desires. The performance of these choirs will send you into a swoon. You will not just feel as if you have been touched by the Spirit. You will feel as if you finally have been saved, and are safely in the hands of Him-Who-is-Who-is when you remain as exposed as ever...ha, ha, ha!

"But you shouldn't forget that even at the height of heresies and schisms that I have helped to engineer, those at the helm in the heretical and schismatic movements will be doing everything to make it seem as if everything was still well even after what might have started out as mere threats of excommunication and anathema had been confirmed by formal decrees or bulls issued by the Holy See. They will be even be trying to do so by showing that the ceremony and pomp of their liturgy could still rival the traditional ceremony and pomp of the liturgy of the *sancta ecclesia* from which they had been summarily cut off, and with which they no longer in communion.

"Look, I as the former angel of light know exactly what to do to help heretics and schismatics along. They must feel at home even in their heresy or schism so that it looks as though truth is relative. Even though they are completely off, I want them to believe to take the Deliverer really seriously when He said: 'I am the way, and the truth, and the life. No man cometh to the Father, but by me.' You must be kidding if I you believe that I wouldn't do everything in my power to try and keep humans away from the real presence in the altars and the fullness of truth which subsists in the Catholic Church by virtue of having the Deliverer as its head.

"Or are you one of those stupid people who are fixated with the notion that because I am a creature like you, my schemes and activities as boss of the Underworld will ultimately prove inconsequential? Well, I might not be able to will the Non-Creature and Master Craftsman out of existence - you have to know that I would have done it long ago if I had the capability. You tell me - I cannot even will a fly out of existence! And I also might not be able to abolish all that orderliness, symmetry, beauty and other nonsense like that in the universe and beyond that nevertheless testifies to the greatness of Him-Who-is-Who-is; but I certainly can and have succeeded in persuading other creatures, including pure spirits - yes, pure spirits - to exercise their free will and join me in causing as much damage and destruction in creation as possible.

"For one, the hosts of angels who joined me in my rebellion are brilliant, smart creatures - I'd say a lot smarter than the great bulk of you human creatures. So you can go on dreaming that my efforts will always be inconsequential, and that I won't succeed in siphoning off hordes of human spirits into our ranks and the Underworld!

"You do not even need to wander very far from your home to see the results. You do not have to make a trip to Las Vegas or Broadway to view the trash that I and my cohorts have helped dredge up for human consumption. You just need to switch on either your telly or Internet browser to see what I mean. I bet you can't even avoid seeing it all over the billboards as you drive out to drop the kid off to school or drive to church. You must be a complete nut if you still do not believe that I have everything wired and under control. These are astounding accomplishments for me particularly as I do not have the advantage of possessing a human body - damn you!

"And if you still have the idea that I am a toothless bulldog with no muscle left, I invite you to think again. Alright, I will ask you to pick up your bible and go to the Book of Revelations for a change. Who do you think will be responsible for causing all the havoc described by the sacred author? And, for one, who do you think will be behind the Antichrist? Who do you think will be behind the tribulations that will be visited upon the earth which the great majority of you hold so dear?

"And, incidentally, who do you think was behind the many tribulations of the Israelites - the chosen people? You must know that history would be very different if the forces I had marshalled had gotten the upper hand and hadn't been wiped out - wiped out, you might have noted, each time with help from above!

"And - without trying to beat me at my own game of cunning and duplicity - answer this one straight. Who do you believe will be behind the wave upon wave of those nondescript creatures that will come from no where and add to the miseries of God's people when the end of the world nears? Who do you think will be behind the terrible tribulations of the descendants of Adam and Eve in those last days?

"And if you still think I am a loser, you just consider the prediction that those saved - yes, saved from my clutches - will come from every tribe and also hail from every corner of the earth. My reading of that statement is that I, Diabolos, will also have succeeded in diverting a goodly number of you from the narrow path, and made them my lackeys once and for all! And as for those of you who do not think that no harm can come to God's creatures whom He loves so much, I will affirm here that salvation is a function of the free will which governs everything you do or omit to do. So, you are - all of you without exception - exposed. I dare say you have by now already traversed a lot of distance either in the direction of Him-Who-is-Who-is, or in my direction. I leave you to guess in which direction the great bulk of you are headed right now!

"And remember - we are talking faith, beliefs, and convictions here. You might know that when it comes to helping you human beings form opinions and things of that sort, the forces I command pretty well have the situation under control. That is why you get so many people with preconceived ideas about everything - people who are often ignorant enough to believe that without their 'intellectual' contributions, the world would be poorer. You must have heard the expression that 'common sense isn't so common nowadays'. Well, who do you think is behind that?

"I actually no longer go out to recruit people to work for me - there are so many human 'devils', going out to recruit from your ranks would be a waste of time and energy. Then, the way some humans go about their 'devilish' business, you would think that they are out to prove that they are more diabolic than I, Diabolos himself. Of course that situation is quite pitiable, pathetic or whatever you would like to call it.

"I have persuaded the more foolish ones that their own opinions, however irrational, are not opinions but truth - objective truth. And, at a signal from me, they now also will argue to death that any contrary opinions, however logical, must be indicative of crass ignorance and/or an ingrained inability to reason!

"I actually believe I have done an excellent job in helping all you folks out there to be bigoted and blinded by your own views to a point where opinions of others now simply do not matter. That is an understatement actually. Contrary opinions expressed by other people, even if obviously correct, must be held against them; and it is imperative that this be the rule everywhcre - in the home, in the classroom, in the churches, synagogues or other places of worship, in the workplace, and in the political arena. Yes, especially in the political arena, because that is where being in a position of advantage also means being in a position to use the state machinery, the law enforcement agencies and the security apparatuses against your opponents.

"But a word about the home, the classroom, the places of worship, and the workplaces. The home is where someone who is evil can mold attitudes and teach the impressionable young to hate, to kill - anything. The workplace is where even little people who have no chance of becoming millionaires dream of becoming one by hook and crook - even at the expense of co-workers. The classroom is where persons who prescribe to my beliefs and philosophy can take the propaganda initiated in the home a step further - it is where you can give the craziest ideas respectability!

"And, of course, places of prayer are where you can mold young minds to go out and kill, maim, commit genocide and so forth in the name of Him-Who-is-Who-is. And, it is also where, with a little bit of luck, we have been able to get our minions inside the *sancta ecclesia* to use their sacred offices to hound their perceived enemies when they should have been practicing the virtue of charity. Take the case of the Great Schism that was precipitated by the action of the legates from Rome, headed by Cardinal Humbert, excommunicating the Patriarch of Constantinople Michael Cerularius and his legates at a time when the Church had no pope, and Cardinal Humbert and his legates in turn being excommunited by Cerularius with each side accusing the other of having fallen into heresy and of having initiated the division. You will find on almost any page of the chequered annals of the Holy Catholic Church that I have been very diligent in taking advantage of human frailty to create problems for her mission of evangekization. No one can fault me of not doing my job there. It is what I promised the Angel Gabriel after he visited the aging priest Zachary to let him know that his barren wife Elizabeth would conceive a son, John. And I repeated it to Gabriel as he was heading back to heaven from Nazareth where he had told the Blessed Virgin Mary that she too would bring forth a son who would be called the Son of the Most High.

"But what I think stands out as my crowing achievement is the fact that today, as soon as humans turn adolescents, almost without exception they head for the hedonistic camp. This is because all those who mentor them no longer believe in the real happiness which is bliss in eternity as opposed to bliss in this world. Those mentors themselves think that the void within them which can only be fulfilled through possession of the Non-Creature and Master Craftsman - and which, by the way, becomes all consuming when the human body is discarded at the end of the probationary period on earth and the next life is ushered in - will somehow go away on its own.

"And that has actually been quite easy to bring off, I dare say. All that I needed to do was to get parents to embrace the idea that youth and freedom are two opposites, which of course also implies that the young do not deserve to be treated as human beings and are essentially second rate despite what the parents proclaim and their protestations to the contrary. They do that and...Boom! As soon as the young fellows discover that they too had an inalienable right to choose between right and wrong, and that they had up until that point been treated like chattel, they rebel. A few do not even recover from the trauma which results from discovering that those they trusted didn't regard them as creatures who were deserving of their love in as much as they deserving of the love and mercies of the Prime Mover by virtue of created in the image.

"By that time, those among them who succeed in assuming control over their lives automatically do so under circumstances in which freedom - or the exercise of the right to choose - and rebellion are synonymous. Because their mentors, along with their parents, don't believe in eternal bliss or are believers only in name, it is only the most enterprising youngsters who end up realizing that there is such a thing as a Church Triumphant Entrance Examination and that they are expected to use their days on earth preparing for it. And I simply make sure that, as the young fellows grow up, it does not strike them that they all are, without exception, part of one people - part of a single human race; or that, in the last analysis, they are one family whose members just have different characteristics and gifts. Or that the divine plan calls for the joys and sorrows of anyone individual in that human family to be felt and shared by all the family members.

"Now, if there is anything that any descendant of Adam and Eve ought to be concerned about, it is the fact that he or she was conceived with original sin. It is the reason humans are inclined to evil. It is also the reason food for humans is not like food for animals of the wild - humans have to sweat to get their sustenance. It is also above all the reason humans die! And so, in dealing with those young fellows, I just need to ensure that these pretty obvious facts escape them completely and that is easy enough.

"I make certain that the reason for descendants of Adam and Eve being conceived with original sin in the wake of the rebellion of Adam and Eve escapes these fellows completely. And then, I do not want them to establish the link between Adam and Eve enjoying, by design, a very intertwined life from the beginning of the time of their creation, and the fact that it was inevitable that they share the responsibility for their rebellion - just as I myself, by virtue of being a creature that was fashioned in the image of Him-Who-is-Who-is naturally sought to involve other created spirits in the revolt against the triune God's lawful authority. And, of course, it suits me perfectly when these young chaps eventually opt to live like animals instead of creatures with a body and a soul - creatures that are fashioned in the image of Him-Who-is-Who-is.

"When humans do not fully appreciate the significance of original sin (or condition in which they are born), it is my guess that they will find it harder to see the relevance of things like redemption, Church and sacraments to their lives. Even if they eventually come round and see these things as important, there will be misconceptions galore. The contradictory views that already abound are a good indication that my efforts in this respect have not been entirely in vain!

"And after taking advantage of the indecisiveness of those young fellows during the period they are expected to start acting like grown-ups, and getting them essentially disoriented and set on a perilous course, you can bet that, during that critical period in their development, during that critical period in their development, I and my cohorts keep up the pressure in an effort to make sure they remain fools to the very end - so that they only realize too late, on the day of their judgement, that their own being also forms part of the resume of the Non-Creature and Master Craftsman after all. If only these fools thought of themselves as a part of *my* resume instead of imagining that they came out of thin air!

"And you can bet I try very hard to make damn sure that they do not grasp the fact that, in coming down from heaven and taking up your human nature, the Second Person of the Blessed Trinity became a true member of the human family and a real brother to all of you folks; and even I, Beelzebub, pray constantly that those youngsters remain in the dark about the immense benefits which directly spring from the Mystery of the Incarnation like, for instance, the beatific vision those of you who escape my tentacles go on to enjoy.

Using my minions amongst humans I operate evil systems that just mutate. Take the evil system of slavery. What is the difference between that and modern capitalism, a system in which the corporate greet of Wall Street so-called gets rewarded at the expense of ordinary folks and peasants? Look what the passage of time does to you humans. Take a step back and reflect on the events that took place two thousand years ago in Jerusalem in the immediate aftermath of the Deliverer's death and resurrection.

"It is well documented that, when the day of Pentecost arrived, the Deliverer's terrified apostles were all together in one place. And suddenly there came from heaven a sound like a mighty rushing wind, and it filled the entire house where they were sitting. And divided tongues as of fire appeared to them and rested on each one of them. And the Parthians and Medes and Elamites and residents of

Mesopotamia, Judea and Cappadocia, Pontus and Asia, Phrygia and Pamphylia, Egypt and the parts of Libya belonging to Cyrene, and visitors from Rome, both Jews and proselytes, Cretans and Arabians - Jews and devout men from every nation under heaven who dwelt in Jerusalem - each heard the story of the death and the resurrection of the Deliverer told in their own tongues.

"And after Peter, the leader of the group, admonished them saying 'Save yourselves from this crooked generation', fear came upon every soul. And all they that believed, were together, and had all things common. Their possessions and goods they sold, and divided them to all, according as every one had need.

"Using my minions among humans, we in the underworld have labored very hard indeed to ensure the overthrow of that system of '*Socialism*'. That is a coup that we can now celebrate thanks to the work of our minions.

"But I shouldn't dwell on this subject lest more of you fools wake up to the obvious fact that, because the Son of Man Himself is involved, there indeed has to be a next life - the real thing in fact - for you earthlings because you happen to be fashioned in the image of Him-Who-is-Who-is.

"I can tell you that I derive a lot of fun from one thing - keeping so many of you guessing to the very end whether I myself am just a mythical creature or the Evil One who actually helps in separating the good seed among you from the chaff. And, in the meantime, using a form of black magic - *juju* - which I know is quite effective on all but the meekest amongst you, I keep you so absorbed with temporal things, you forget that time is a mere dot in eternity, and that temporal happiness is exactly what it is - transient; which is the same as saying that it is ephemeral - a mirage. Using my *juju*, I have you cornered nicely in a spiritual desert.

"There, parched and starved of true spiritual happiness, you make a great sight as you *lunge* after the illusory pools of unadulterated spring water you see right there in front of you and, once inside those waters, you *swim* and *frolic* like you have never done before in all your life; and, when you are in fact just wallowing in temporal pleasures, you envision that you are in the Paradise that Dante and others before and after him have detailed at such great length in their poems and works of fiction. A pity that many of you turn around and cast aspersions on the same *juju* absent which such thrills would be out of your reach!"

Satan's dirty little secrets...

"Why, you might ask, do I keep referring to my brothers and sisters in sin as fools? Well, you are obviously one of them and that is why you can't even attempt a guess. I have always tried unsuccessfully to explain to you earthlings that, while one must try to sin as much as possible, one must go about it with a wee bit of common sense. As you yourselves know, you can get very sick in the process of sinning.

"Take sins of the palette for instance. Food can easily slip down the wrong throat, if you do not go about gormandizing wisely. Gorging can leave you with a bad tummy ache, and you are also liable to suffer from other ailments as well as a direct result of that type of excess. In this business of passing joy, one thing you have to keep constantly in mind is that too much of anything is bad - really bad.

"You humans must be especially careful because, as you might have noticed generally, the organs that facilitate self-indulgence are located near other organs that can quickly turn the self-indulgence into something else. Whenever you are indulging yourself, always remember that you can contract diseases in the process or pass them on to others. In terms of safety, abstaining from indulging the self is really the safest option.

"But, just as we demons did, you humans, unfortunately, have to sin because that is the only way to hit at the Non-Creature and Master Craftsman. And you do that by renouncing His fatherhood, and by striving to be not what you are *supposed to be*, but what *you fancy* or want to be - even if that means sacrificing your souls for the 'cause' and, just like us, meriting eternal damnation!

"It is very unfair, but that is what it is. Some transgressions of the flesh cause direct bodily harm - you could go deaf while enjoying loud music, or you could go blind from surfing for trash non-stop on the world-wide Web, and so on and so forth. And all self-indulgence without exception dulls reflexes and also the conscience which happens to control the intellectual faculties. Actually, often times you will feel good - in fact great - during or after sinning and it won't occur to you that your health is being adversely affected. Which, of course, does not help very much if you are going to drop dead prematurely soon afterward!

"And that is even more dangerous because, just when you think you are having a whale of a time, you actually are hurting real bad, but don't know it! You might as well be enjoying a bar of candy you know is laced with cyanide or downing some other sweet-tasting substance that is deadly. And that is not mentioning the real price you have to pay - the demise of your soul!

"And the way some of you conduct yourselves, it seems to be with the conviction that you will never die! This is even though you know that there have been empires that looked like they were going to last forever, but lasted only for so long: the empire of the Incas in South America; the Roman empire; the Bantu People's empire which, in its hey day, stretched from Timbuktu to the Cape of Good Hope; and others which thrived in Europe, Asia Minor, China and the Far East. And they all faded away for the exact same reason - insatiable greed.

"You know that a principality, empire, or 'super power' - as you call them nowadays - is about to self-destruct when you see signs that expansionism and the desire to conquer, dominate and subjugate others have taken hold. You mark my words. One thing which goes for me is that Providence typically allows evildoers to have their way. Even though I have already been judged, Providence lets me continue to sow seeds of death - spiritual death – through my surrogates!

The prospects of divine intervention...

"While He has not facilitated the appearance of the Antichrist - no, not by a long short - Providence has certainly granted the Antichrist (who is, of course, only my front) permission to set up shop in the guise of bringing salvation to God's people. And I do not see Him interfering to stop the many souls who genuinely hunger and thirst for the Word of God from wandering right into the 'lion's den'. I do not see Providence intervening when some of them go on to believe that they are saved when all they have done is lull themselves into a false sense of security. And, certainly, Providence won't intervene to stop war mongers, empire builders, and other evil-doers who are prepared at my command to unleash miseries upon their fellow men to satisfy their inflated egos.

"You overlook a couple of things when you expect the Prime Mover to 'intervene' in that fashion. You ignore the fact that He has created humans with free wills, and that it was a conscious decision on the Prime Mover's part to do that - to conceive of creatures that were endowed with faculties of the intellect and free will, and to make you one of them. You underestimate the goodness of the Prime Mover and the fact that in endowing his creatures with His gifts, far from being begrudging, He was extremely generous - something that certainly also raises the stakes if those creatures of His should decide that they were going to do their own thing and to break His law. And you, of course, underestimate your worth in the eyes of your infinitely good and gracious Prime Mover.

"You underestimate the extent to which you humans can be bad - the extent to which free creatures can go to try and subvert the divine plan with or without my help, in complete disregard of the goodness of the Prime Mover to you. And you underestimate the extent to which you fellows are prepared to try and usurp the authority of the Prime Mover - just like I myself tried to do.

"You demonstrate that you fallen humans - just like us fallen angels - in general find it hard to desist from trying to pigeon the Prime Mover the way you do your perceived enemies. You imagine that He is constrained by limitations of time and space, and you even try to limit his options for intervening by imagining that He can only react to things in the way you expect.

"And then you confirm, perhaps without realizing it, that the ways of the Prime Mover are indeed mysterious and incomprehensible even to the cleverest creature. And, in your ignorance and stupidity, you even overlook the fact that the Prime Mover, who created you and everything else that is in existence out of nothing, is quite capable of causing good to come out of evil (or something where 'good' is supposed to be but is lacking). You, furthermore, underestimate the Prime Mover's foresight, and the fact that he could anticipate everything you humans would be up to - just as He did in my own case!

"You show your ignorance of history and of the covenant the Prime Mover made to you humans when He declared that the seed of the woman would crush the head of the serpent - I mean my head! You therefore forget that the Prime Mover has in effect already 'intervened'. Then you forget that He actually did send His only Son to earth in fulfilment of His covenant. You forget that the Son of God emptied Himself, becoming obedient to the point of death - even death on a cross. And you forget that it was indeed the Son of God - a man of sorrows, accustomed to infirmity, and spurned and avoided by His own when they claimed that He was not their King, and that they had no king but Caesar! And you forget above all that, oppressed and condemned, He remained silent even as He was lead away like a lamb to the slaughter. That, smitten for the sin of His people, He was finally cut off from the land of the living - 'effectively' neutralized!

"You also demonstrate that you do not quite get the point made by the Deliverer to His apostles after He came back from hell that all power in heaven above, on the earth, and even in the Underworld had been given to Him by His heavenly Father.

"You underestimate the Deliverer's ability, resolve and determination to hold everyone who has been created in the image and likeness of the Prime Mover accountable for his/her actions, just like you underestimate His ability, resolve and determination to reward

His faithful servants who heed the advice of the Deliverer, take up their crosses, and follow in the footsteps of the Son of Man.

"You completely forget that when wicked humans act irresponsibly and cause death and untold sufferings to their fellow humans, the Prime Mover 'intervenes' in the exact same way He does when one of you breaks any one of His ten commandments or refuses to accept His invitation to get aboard the Ark - the Church the Deliverer founded and commissioned to propagate the good news of salvation. You forget, above all, that if the Prime Mover were to intervene in the manner in which you all expect - by injecting Himself in there and striking the wicked dead, or by getting in there and physically sheltering the victims of injustice from their miseries or from their painful demise - He would be giving respectability to the actions of those who are in effect daring Him to intervene and stop them. You also forget that if the Prime Mover 'intervened' in that fashion, He would in effect be revisiting His divine plan and modifying it by taking away the right of creatures He fashioned in His own image and likeness to make choices regarding what was good and what was evil.

"All of which of course goes to demonstrate the importance and indeed necessity of praying always - saying the Lord's prayer, contemplating the mysteries of the rosary (which deal with the life and work of the Deliverer) and, above all, following the injunction of the Deliverer to the apostles on the night before He died and feasting on the 'Bread of Angels' in the Deliverer's memory at Holy Mass (which is a re-enactment of the passion, death and resurrection of the Deliverer, and a gift of incomparable value to all who face trials and tribulations during their sojourn in what is no longer the 'Garden of Eden' but effectively the 'Valley of Tears').

"But there is a 'down side' to the fact that the Prime Mover does not ostensibly intervene. The down-side is that the sure way for the wicked to self-destruct is to let them have their way. That same principle also applies to nations, particularly those that boast super power status. They self-destruct when they wield so much power over the destinies of other nations, it makes their leaders start to believe they are virtual gods who do not have to be swayed by world opinion, their consciences, or anything else for that matter. Not even by the fact that they themselves will die - just like those whose lives they have a hand in cutting short.

"The self-destruction invariably starts as soon as the super power, intoxicated with power, sets out to conquer and subjugate. It happened to the Philistines, to the Greeks, to the Egyptians, to the Romans, to the Turks, and to the Bantustans. At the time nations self-destruct, you can be sure that many innocent people get hurt. We in the Underworld see that as a win-win situation. And then, another 'super power' usually and fairly promptly emerges from the ashes, and the cycle starts all over again. Hence the axiom 'There is no rest for the wicked!' Which automatically tells you something about the immense - nay, infinite - goodness of the Prime Mover. He created man free and you won't catch Him breaking His covenant and undoing what he did with the best of intention.

"But I hate to think that my minions who, even as I speak, are busy conjuring up grand schemes in the name of national security - the same schemes that will lead their nations down the path of self-destruction - will not ultimately have their will of permanently dominating the world. Also, sadly, the 'technology' which helps nations to 'develop' and evolve into super powers is the self-same that becomes their undoing.

"I naturally wish I had control over that 'technology'. You can bet that if I had, I would let only one nation - any nation - have a monopoly over it. And soon enough, that nation, at my command, would spread miseries all over the globe as it sought to subjugate other nations with an eye to the resources within their borders. And I would not stop there - I would make sure that the conquering 'super power', in the process of subjugating other nations, would take the next logical step, which namely would be to hold the peoples of the rest of the world in enslavement; and I - even I - would pray that no savior would come along to deliver them as happened when the Deliverer suddenly appeared and freed the souls of the departed humans that I myself had been holding in captivity in hell from their bondage.

"Just as the leaders of certain nations today conduct themselves as if the nations in question, made 'powerful' by 'modern' technology, will never fade away, many of you think that, because you are here today and can move your hulk around, you will remain a permanent fixture wherever your prowess is now being felt. Technology is really analogous to speech or language. Now, speech is essentially codes and formulas, while the ability to heave your carcass around can be equated to the fortune of being one of those whose life was supposed to be nipped in the bud for one reason or another whilst you were still inside the womb but was not, allowing you to eventually see the light of day. You humans just over do it.

"Now, you tell me which peoples on earth do not have a tongue or language in which they communicate? And, while noting from this that no single nation can ever have a monopoly over technology, don't be mistaken about what being powerful on the national level means. 'Powerful' might be in the sense of possessing the capability to construct offensive weapons systems; but a nation may be powerful in other ways.

"One nation might be powerful by virtue of its ability to broker peace among other warring nations; whilst another might be powerful because of its ability to sustain and nurture a population that is disproportionately large when compared to the size of its territory; and another might be powerful by reason of its ability to preserve its ecosystems in circumstances in which other nations would be unable to do so. And there is, of course, no question about the greatness of a nation within whose borders people of very diverse backgrounds live out their lives to the full in harmony as a matter of course.

"Actually, if my reading of the situation is correct, very soon tiny, little known nations, armed with brief-case nuclear bombs that they will assemble using know-how posted on the Internet or stolen by hacking computers of the military establishments of the super powers, and employing delivery systems consisting in a simple network of Kamikaze prototypes or 'suicide bombers' as they are now increasingly known, will be capable of taking out entire cities and other places of significance of any so-called super power.

"But the really bad news for any potential super or hyper power is that technology has already advanced to a point at which high school whiz kids, using 'advanced' electronics, will be able to hijack satellites in space, and then use them to 'take over' the guidance systems of submarines, aircraft carriers, B-52's, and even military command and control centers of any super power, and command them to direct the deadly firepower they control at targets anywhere on earth, including cities and vital installations in countries they were supposed to defend and/or to self-destruct.

"Remember that I am the devil, and I certainly ought to know - if you were doubting my words! It is in any case just a matter of time before tiny, little known states, that have nothing to loose themselves, will be able to threaten a country like America with its arsenal of nuclear subs, aircraft carriers, fleets of B-52s equipped with smart bombs, missiles systems tipped with bunker bursting bombs, technologically advanced predators, and thousands upon thousands of state of the art jet planes with their deadly payloads of nuclear bombs and other weapons of mass destruction. These same nations will likewise compel global military alliances like the North Atlantic Treaty Organization and others to disband or expose their countries to ruin or even extinction.

"In a sudden reversal of fortunes, to save their cities and avoid being decimated, one by one, the super powers, threatened by a new crop of these 'rogue states', will be forced to jettison their nukes into space, in an effort to convince the world that they no longer posed a threat to any country.

"And that will not be all. In addition, they will be compelled to come clean and to account for each and every weapon of mass destruction that they had ever produced. After destroying their armaments in the open, they will be forced to declare to a revamped United Nations (in which no nation will have any 'veto' power over resolutions passed) that they no longer possessed any weapons of mass destruction.

"And finally, goaded on by the self-styled 'liberating powers', they will be forced to convert the installations they previously used to produce the submarines, aircraft carriers, intercontinental ballistic missiles, tanks, landmines, and other armaments, into factories producing tractors, ploughs, hoes, and other equipment that will be supplied free to poor nations for the purpose of rehabilitating those nations' productive enterprises.

"These are, of course, developments that we in the Underworld really do not welcome, because they postpone Armageddon. We would like to see those weapons of mass killings (WMK) used to do the job they were designed to do. Even though condemned, we 'rejoiced' and 'celebrated' when some super powers balked at signing treaties banning land mines. And we welcomed recent developments in the arms control arena, and specifically the decision of one major military power to turn its back on arms control deals to which it had been a party, if only because that now paves the way for a new arms race.

An old myth...

"Still, much as I hate to admit it, it is completely fallacious to think that only super powers are powerful. Being a little known nation, with hardly any resources or anything else that might attract the attention of other combative nations, will probably be a better guarantee of survival of the fittest in future conflagrations between nations. As I have said, you will soon see super powers voluntarily disarming, and destroying the weapons of mass destruction they have spent billions developing in the face of threats from the new rogue states. But that will only be after these super powers (following my script and using some of the dirtiest tactics ever seen, including surprise preemptive military strikes on other unsuspecting resource rich nations, for the purpose of consolidating their own control over the world's scarce resources) have caused untold miseries to many innocent souls in different parts of the world.

"The best signal that a nation is great is its ability to protect the physically, socially, politically and economically disadvantaged and vulnerable. It is a sign of greatness that is frequently derided as weakness by those who themselves feel insecure for one reason or another.

"I should add that a nation populated by nondescript and physically emaciated and starving Francises of Assisi, Teresas of Avila and Padre Pio's - or Mother Teresa's for that matter - would look weak on the surface, but it would actually be as powerful as any nation could get, their vows of poverty, chastity and obedience notwithstanding! It would be the most powerful nation that ever existed, even though that mad crowd would be doling out their country's resources to 'alleviate' the poverty of needy fellow humans elsewhere. I tell you I wouldn't want too many nations of that sort around, because then my influence over such nations and ultimately on the course of human history would be negligible.

"And, again, you tell me which individuals have you met who did not pass through the womb before they saw the light of day? I have been around a little longer than you numbskulls, and I can tell you that all nations have enjoyed the benefits of technology at one time or other in the course of their history while the neighboring nations were cowed down with apprehension.

"And, similarly, everyone who has ever lived has heaved his or her hulk around while oblivious to the fact that a myriad others had done the same before them or would do so after they themselves had come and gone. There is, in short, nothing you do that some nitwit has never done before, and this is especially true for the kind of ways in which you seek to indulge yourself daily.

"Even though all this makes a compelling case for you humans to abandon my cause, I have always been confident that most of you will stick with me for the simple reason that you are fools. And, similarly at the national level, you can be sure that I will never lack allies. There will always be nations whose actions will trigger wars and lead many a man and a woman to discard the notion that there can be a Non-Creature and Master Craftsman - a Creator who is not just good but Goodness itself - in a world in which chaos reigned; and to embrace the idea that all the good things a human being desires in this world can be had, not by flopping down on one's knees and praying, but by simply going out and getting them.

"For us pure spirits, transgression leads to the immediate permanent failure of any faculty associated with that sin - which, in practice, means all the faculties of the spiritual essence. That is how sin came to claim the lives of so many of us in a moment of time, and led instantly to the spiritual demise of all involved. It is like a trap - you sin and some vital part of you goes. In your case, the first sin you commit induces you to even sin some more, causing you to lose more and more of your vital parts!

"But while we pure spirits can never recover once we start down that road, you humans can - by renouncing sin, severing all your links to me and refocusing your lives. You humans ought, at the very least, to note your makeup, and the way transgressions can affect the longevity of your lives. I am not suggesting that you should not sin. By all means go ahead and sin all you can; but at least watch out for the pitfalls. And that is the point you humans will never get. Why go on shooting yourself in your foot again and again? No body forces you to sin, let alone act so foolishly.

"Judas Iscariot was typical. Everybody knew that he was the confidante of the Deliverer, and also the purse bearer; and he himself knew it too. But his greed blinded him to the danger. His association with the Deliverer had already made him a marked man. And yet there he was, dreaming that he could be a double-dealer.

"He thought he could be a mole inside the 'schismatic' sect, reporting to the Sanhedrin while continuing to hold tight on his Master's purse. It was completely suicidal. The Deliverer put it succinctly when he said that it was better if he, Judas, had not been born. The high priests already had their man cornered, and did not even need Judas' services.

"If you ask me, I really never had any sympathy for the priests and Pharisees - I admired the role played by the 'fox' more.

"But Judas was just too greedy, and could not miss out on the opportunity to make another buck! He would probably have been more useful to me hanging in there close to Peter especially, and eventually engineering the break-up of the fledging organization from within after the Deliverer had departed and left them to their own devices.

Blind humans...

"But there is nothing that exemplifies the stupidity of you humans better than your blindness to the truth regarding your true self. You do not know it, and you have actually never thought of it; but you are all blind - blind as bats! And I do not just mean those amongst you who 'see' - or so you think - with visual aids. I mean all of you.

"Talking about visual aids - you all are able to get about because you all have visual aids. Your eyes are your visual aids, and they frequently do not perform nearly as well as the artificial visual aids. But whether natural or artificial, one thing they definitely do not do is show you your real self or even how the real you looks like when you stand in front of a mirror. All that these things - I mean the visual aids - are meant to do is help you get about without colliding with objects in your path.

"But you guys and gals use your eyes to focus on the image you see in the mirror; and, after a while, you invariably start believing that the blurry reflection of the *physical* part of yourself in the mirror not only is your look-alike, but the whole you! In the process, you effectively close your eyes to the real you. And, consequently, the only way you can now really 'see' and stop deceiving yourselves and start 'seeing' is by literally pluck out your eyes - as the Deliverer suggested.

"And talking about images in mirrors, you must have traveled to some far away place only to see strangers milling around you who looked exactly like the strangers you had left behind! Well - that is because you humans, sharing the same *human* nature, do indeed *look alike* all of you! And so, the strangers you meet when you travel to distant lands *aren't* really *strangers* after all except in your imagination. And they aren't the folks you left behind because they they happen to be creatures that share your *human nature* (which remains the same and unchanged), but enjoy a separate *existence* from yours and that of their look-alikes back in your homeland.

"If you still think there is a difference between what a pair of spectacles and what your cornea does, then there is nothing that can save you! Any way, how in hell and on earth can you trust your eye glasses to tell you what you look like, let alone what you are? If you could tell what you are only with the help of these things, how do you account for the fact that those who cannot see or hear are still quite capable of knowing themselves? How come that they will respond with 'Yah?' when they are called by name?

"Which brings me to the point I am trying to make: you folks believe that your eyes are essential for knowing who - or what - you are, and that for all practical purposes you cease to exist when you lose your eyesight - which you certainly do when you 'kick the bucket'.

"You have heard so much about idols made by human hands out of stone. Well, here we have the human body - approximately ninety per cent water and a bag of chemicals for the rest - which turns out to be by far the most worshipped 'idol'. And it is not made by human hands! What a turn of events! For me, this is like what you folks refer to as 'sweet revenge'. But quite frankly, even though I am the Cunning One so-called, I would be remiss if I took all the credit for what you fellows - I mean fools - do. Guess you deserve some too!

"That is why I keep referring to you people as fools. You need to stop and think sometimes. You don't have to be suicidal. But I am in a way to blame, because the idea of sin started with me. I blundered big time actually when I thought the Non-Creature and Master Craftsman was calling the bluff when He said that any one who disobeyed would die the death! Yes, I also make mistakes - I am a just a creature like you, you know! I wish I could have given you folks a better deal. Unfortunately, however, the saying *'Nemo dat quod non habet'* applies to me too...!"

"But one of my problems is that I can't stop talking once I start. May be it is something which goes with being the Evil One. But who cares! You ask me now about the so-called baby boomers, and I will tell you this: my guess is that only a third, at the very most, will escape my tentacles.

"What that means is that, when the time comes, only a third of the baby boomers will step forward and go down on bended knee to pay Him-Who-is-Who-is homage. A full two thirds of that generation will balk and refuse to genuflect! Just imagine - two thirds of the baby boomers will say 'Pass' when they are asked to recite the *Pater Noster*! They will say 'Nay' in unison when they are asked to profess the Nicene Creed or to chant the *Te Deum* along with the gaggle of the redeemed brethren. And a full half of these 'Nay Sayers' will be baptized Christians!

"And now *you* tell me how someone who is not considered to be valuable enough to warrant the personal attention of both parents and is left at the mercy of baby sitters during the most crucial period of his or her upbringing can grow up respecting him or herself? How can they believe that there was a Non-Creature and Master Craftsman behind the big bang when they themselves are treated like accidents of nature, or when one of the parents just walks out on them! No, I believe I can claim at least some measure of success in my endeavours, buddy.

"If you want me to give you the reason why those truly saintly folk among you feel a yearning to be joined to the Creator while the rest of you are scared stiff as your day of reckoning approaches, it is simply the fact that they are humble, have succeeded in denying themselves, and consequently feel that they have absolutely nothing to lose when they vacate their earthly abode - no earthly goods to mourn over, and certainly no lost opportunities for indulging the self. On the contrary, they look forward to dying and hastening to Him who is never changing, is perfect beauty and goodness, and who is above all He-Who-is-Who-is."

Mjomba reasoned that Satan, although banished from the sight of the Prime Mover and a complete disgrace to the rest of creation, could actually be used as a mouth-piece to throw light on tenets of the faith for that very reason. There was no comparison between Man's fall from grace and the dishonor that Beelzebub brought to creation when he rebelled because he had been one really prized gem in the works of the Creator. His betrayal had been all the more repulsive because, being so close to the Prime Mover, he had no excuse for what he did. According to Mjomba, using Satan in that manner only went to emphasize that, even in disgrace, created beings remained subject in every way to the Prime Mover's power and authority.

The unanswered question was how he, Christian Mjomba, had ended up in between, and in a role that had him explaining to the world these goings-on in the spiritual realm from a human perspective! He wondered if it was because of something he did - or failed to do - in his life!

6. The Oral Defense

Later on, during his oral defense of this part of the thesis, Mjomba was surprised that it was his fellow students, not his professors, who were troubled by his use of the devil in that manner. One student, who was already obviously angry that Mjomba had not been reigned in for his provocative ideas, went as far as screaming: "Heresy! This is another Judas Iscariot! He is against the Holy Father - and America!" Other students had chimed in with "He is a Mau Mau sympathizer!" and "He supports Mandela!"

Like a panel of impartial Supreme Court justices, the committee of six professors had proceeded to elicit answers to the students' objections by shooting their own questions.

Father Damian...

"And why do you think that a theologian who is trying to expound on some dogma can employ the Evil One as a mouth-piece with impunity - just as you have done here?" This was from Father Damian, world famous author and also the diocese's foremost expert on Dogmatic Theology.

"If I am not mistaken...there is no Church dogma against doing this, Father!" was Mjomba's curt reply - which appeared to ruffle some feathers in the audience.

Father Lofgreen...

"Well, supposing there was such a dogma - and I am speaking hypothetically here. Might it just be conceivable that a situation could arise in which this practice would be permissible and not be morally wrong?" That was from Father Lofgreen, professor of Moral Theology.

"I'm glad you are speaking hypothetically, Father. Anyway, one such situation would be if I wasn't aware that such a dogma existed. To the extent that I wouldn't have any intention of going against the Church's official teaching, I might be mistakenly burned at the stake for espousing heretical views - like Joan of Arc. But I really couldn't be accused of acting immorally."

Mjomba's reference to being burned at the stake evoked a prolonged burst of laughter from all but the student who had screamed "Heresy".

Father Donovan...

The next question came from Father Donovan, the Canon Lawyer: "You are not suggesting you would sit back and just watch as members of your flock, who were always preoccupied with things of the world and had never had any time for contemplation, bible study and things like that, broke moral laws and canons of the Church with impunity, would you?"

"I think it would all depend on what is meant by 'things of the world' Father" Mjomba responded hesitatingly. "If they did whatever they did religiously. I mean - if they prized self-sufficiency above dependence, including dependence on the charity, and especially if they did not want preoccupation with matters of their faith to be an excuse..."

Father Cromwell...

Mjomba was stopped in mid-sentence by Father Cromwell whose speciality was Pastoral Theology. The Welshman, who had very poor eye-sight and saw with difficulty even with the help of his bi-focals, lowered his head and peered down on Mjomba through the upper section of his eye glasses.

The priest spoke in a rough grating voice: "Now, that is bordering on heresy, Rev. Mjomba. I'm sure you agree that that's what everybody is busy doing. If you are right, I should pack up and return to Wales. To return to the original matter at issue here - can there possibly be any justification for anyone to use the adversary as a mouth-piece in moral matters? Isn't that the same as suggesting that the devil can be a mentor, an example?"

Mjomba hesitated before responding: "It's the Church's position that sin is to be hated, but not the sinner. I am not suggesting that anyone should be cozy with Beelzebub or even less love him. I am respectfully suggesting, however, that while the damned Satan's deeds are entirely reprehensible, he is still permitted to continue to exist - and to that extent, even he knows that the Prime Mover is infinitely good..."

Father McDonald...

It was now the turn of Father McDonald, professor of Biblical Theology, to fire his question. "When the devil proclaimed that the Deliverer was indeed the Son of the Most High, was that a profession of faith?"

"Certainly not! I submit, Father McDonald, that the rich man who tried in vain to get word about the horrors of the Pit to his friends back on earth wasn't making a profession of faith either. That sort of thing can only be done by those who are still on trial. After the sentence is passed, all such expressions become laments - laments of the eternally lost. And, in appropriate circumstances, I believe such expressions can be inspiring..."

Father Raj...

It was the professor of Systematic Theology whose objections to the use of the Evil One as a mouth-piece really rattled Mjomba, and even caused him to concede that he had made a bad judgement in doing so. While Mjomba was quite sincere, he could not rule out the possibility of going back on that statement at some future date.

There was, after all, no doubt that Providence could use the archenemy for good causes just like he could turn evil into good!

Nothing was impossible with the Prime Mover! But for now, Mjomba, head bowed, was attentive as Father Raj, who hailed from Goa on the Indian sub-continent, began talking.

The Indian, who was also Mjomba's confessor and spiritual advisor, was relaxed and self-assured as he said: "Sonny, you just reminded us that the Antichrist isn't just a fictional idea. If I did not know you as well as I do, wouldn't you agree that I would have every reason to suspect that you just might..."

There was nothing Indian at all about Fr. Raj's accent. His years of studies in London and Rome made his accent indistinguishable from that of the Welsh, Scottish, Irish and Dutch members of the seminary's permanent staff of twelve.

Mjomba did not allow Father Raj, whom he held in very high esteem and considered his "guru", to finish the sentence.

"I completely agree with you, Father..." he interjected. But he was himself promptly interrupted by his guru.

Fr. Raj: Diabolos's role in keeping humans weak...

"If you decide to make Diabolos a mouth-piece for any doctrine" Father Raj continued, "You also have an obligation, at the very minimum, to make him completely forthcoming about his role in keeping us humans weak. We might be entirely responsible for our own sins and downfall through the exercise of our free will.

"But Diabolos is also on record as being the one who cleverly engineered it - by thrusting himself between us, while we were still in out pristine innocence, and our loving and gracious divine Master; and by making the abominable suggestion that we follow his example and act as though our Maker was an entirely fictitious character, and regard the Almighty's clear injunctions to the human race as the figment of our own imagination!"

Fr. Raj: Lost mantle of godliness...

"And - concerning his role in keeping us frail and powerless - you have had Diabolos rightly suggest that, to be safe from Diabolos himself and also from the on-set of concupiscence that has plagued us human beings from time immemorial, we must pray at all times. It is quite significant that you have not had him - or, may be, he has not had you have him - disclose how, having succeeded in driving a wedge between us and our God, he continues to pull fast ones on us so that, citing our first amendment or the right to exercise our faculties of reason and free will and lacking faith in God, we continually turn down opportunities to be close to our Creator through prayer and consequently remain handicapped and exposed - the holy book says 'naked'.

"You see, sonny, our first parents were so ashamed of their act of transgression, which they committed while knowing quite well that they were made in the image of their Creator, they went and hid themselves in some bushes there in the Garden of Eden. It soon dawned on them that they were in the wrong, and they, in fact, never did recover from their shame. When they emerged from the bush, they were still bedecked in twigs, and they eventually took to the habit of covering their person in bark cloth. That was not enough for Eve because she was unable to wander about outside of their dwelling without head gear of some sort as well.

"Stripped of their original innocence, it had immediately become evident to Adam and Eve that something very essential and real was missing on their persons. Conceived in the image of their Creator, they now felt as though they were stark naked. The mantle of godliness with which they had been outfitted at creation was gone. The first Man and Woman noticed, to their surprise and dismay, that the shroud of holiness had been supplanted by, of all things, a diabolic inclination to commit even more transgressions! It proved to be a haunting state of affairs in view of the fact that they were spirits first and foremost and flesh and blood only as a secondary matter.

"After eating of the fruit, instead of feeling like gods, they felt like ejecting themselves from the Garden of Eden and getting lost in the tropical jungle - which they did all but physically. They were too terrified about the prospect of encountering beasts of the forest - which also now suddenly seemed belligerent and unpredictable, and particularly vipers which from that time on were going to be a permanent reminder of their temptation and fall from grace - to take that option.

Fr. Raj: The embodiment of evil...

"There was no doubt about the fact that Adam and Eve had known from the very first that they were created in their Creator's image, and had been extremely proud of it. You see - unlike Adam and Eve who were in good books with their God until their rebellion, Diabolos, a pure spirit, rebelled against his Maker as soon as he was created and had been in bad books with Him from the outset; and you must understand that his spite was infernal. And as soon as Adam and Eve came onto the scene, Diabolos had moved to exploit that situation adroitly, suggesting that they could be like their Creator in all respects - if they ate of the forbidden fruit. They did not have to believe him - they did not even have to give him a hearing, which was the first mistake they made. You do not play hide and seek with a snake! And after that succession of errors, they even forgot that, as creatures fashioned by God in His own image, they owed Him - and Him alone - their total allegiance.

"One point about Diabolos - he is, as you know, created in the Creator's image like us, and he should feel the greatest shame for spearheading these rebellions against God. It is precisely because the devil has never felt any remorse or shame whatsoever for his terrible misdeeds that he is so odious in every way even in God's eyes. Our Creator, while hating sin, loves the sinner to the end. In the case of Satan, the Lord has taken pains to make it crystal clear that Diabolos is completely evil.

"To avoid any misunderstanding, He has even cautioned us not to enter into any dialogue with the Evil One. Now, badness is the absence of good; and evil is the absence of godliness. Surprisingly, Diabolos does not just symbolize those infernal qualities, but actually embodies them! It is something that is quite unimaginable for a creature to be so debased.

"Up until the moment they got involved in the fateful dialogue with Diabolos, whenever they wanted anything, all they did was ask and it was granted them by God. Their decision to eat of the fruit therefore implied a complete about turn! For, lo and behold, it was the image of Diabolos, the archenemy, and not that of their infinitely loving and most gracious Creator which had suddenly came to mind as they considered ways to free themselves from their allegiance to their God. It was Diabolos who loomed up in their minds as a friend. Their communication line to their Maker had been permanently and irrevocably severed before they knew it.

Fr. Raj: Faith in God and in His Church...

"The point of all this is that your thesis has Diabolos urging human beings to pray without mentioning anything about 'faith'. While you believe that you are using him as your mouth-piece to expound on the Church's teachings, I submit to you that it is Diabolos who is trying to use you to prepare the way for the dreaded Antichrist. He wants you to leave a void which the Antichrist will fill, just as the breach in the channels of communication with the Creator caused by the sin of Adam and Eve left a void which faith now must fill. I will explain.

"Although it is important to know that prayer is necessary for human beings to live as befits children of God, this knowledge is no longer enough by itself. There is now an additional requirement - faith - before the proper dialogue can be restored between Man and God. Even though this new requirement, or faith in the Redeemer, comes by knowledge, it remains a gift which human beings can accept or reject when offered. It is a gift of the Holy Ghost, offered to human beings at the behest of Christ. After bridging the chasm that previously separated erring humans from His Father, He fills the void created by the severed line of communication through the gift of faith. The fact of the matter is that human beings, having rebelled against their Maker, had been banished from His sight; and they are completely helpless on their own and, in fact, lost without the labours and travails of the Second Adam.

"You have, no doubt, heard the expression: 'Get behind Me, Satan'. If it was our Lord who was addressing you, I dare to suggest to you that he would be telling you just that. And you would be glad he would be telling you that and not 'It is better if you were not born' or something like that. He would be treating you like he treated the man he eventually appointed to be a 'fisher of men' because your faith in Him is still largely intact. You see - faith in God might not be sufficient, but it is certainly necessary.

Fr. Raj: The Antichrist has come...

"The Antichrist will probably have everything right except the point regarding faith. He will be at pains to show that the gift of faith is not necessary for the equation of salvation - faith in God the Father, God the Son, and in God the Holy Ghost; and - for a generation of humans like ours that did not have the opportunity to eat, live and visit with Mary and her divine son as the twelve apostles did - faith in the efficacy of sacramental grace dispensed through Holy Mother the Church over which the Deliverer Himself presides as High Priest.

"You can be sure that the Antichrist also - yes, especially the Antichrist - will talk faith. He will do so while simultaneously claiming that the Church, confessing the faith received from the apostles - the faith the Church confesses in accordance with the ancient saying that *lex orandi, lex credendi* and which precedes the faith of the believer - has it all wrong. And the Antichrist will also claim that the Church, celebrating the sacraments - which act *ex opere operato* by virtue of the saving work of the Deliverer and are not wrought by the righteousness of either the celebrant or the recipient - is in error. Claiming that the Deliverer's death on the cross was sufficient for Man's redemption, the Antichrist will argue that the sacraments of the New Covenant are not necessary for the salvation of believers. He will in effect be inviting humans to place all their faith in himself!

"You can understand why the Antichrist, the devil's persona on earth, will not be very eager to talk about the baptismal, and even less the ministerial, priesthood. Like the baptismal priesthood which is dispensed by the Prime Mover's priestly people, the ministerial priesthood, which is dispensed by the ordained ministry which in turn draws its validity and efficacy from an unbroken apostolic succession, also works *ex opere operato*. You might remember from your catechism that the Church, forming as it were, one mystical person with the Deliverer, the head, acts as an organically structured priestly community. And, by the way, if you should ever be looking for the one doctrine that sets the Church apart from all the other "churches", always remember the doctrine that is captured by those three words - *ex opere operato*!

"And, talking about the Antichrist, we keep saying "he will come" when the fact is that "he" (used in a generic sense) has already showed up. According to the evangelist, the spirit of the Antichrist was already up and about even as he was writing. If you ask me, the Antichrist showed up twenty centuries ago, synchronimously with the appearance of the first heresies which rocked the infant Church and ironically also helped it mature quickly. His ugly head has popped up times and again since, and you can bet that he has successfully established a beach head that he is using to propagate his pseudo-messianism by now. There is no doubt that religious deception, which is what the Antichrist is all about, 'offering men apparent solutions to their problems at the price of apostasy from the truth,' has been with us for sometime and is already very wide-spread.

"To quote the catechism, 'the Antichrist's deception already begins to take shape in the world every time the claim is made to realize within history that messianic hope which can only be realized beyond history through the eschatological judgement'. But of course humans, myself included, like to react only when things happen in a big and dramatic way. That is why we are still waiting to see the

Antichrist descend on the world from the sky - or something of that sort.

"My advice to those who are looking for signs that the Antichrist is with us is: Look for dissertations and books whose authors claim to be inspired, or sermons that are billed as being prophetic and a panacea for all your spiritual problems, and things like that. And keep in mind, as you do this, that the sermons of the Deliverer Himself and the miracles he performed did not result in any dramatic conversion of sinners! If anything, many just walked away when the Deliverer reminded them that leaving everything behind - including family and possessions - and shouldering their burdensome crosses were things that following in His foot steps entailed.

"Contrary to the Antichrist's claims, for instance that salvation was about to descend on humans in a dramatic and big way as a result of his intervention or - more appropriately - meddling, things are going to get worse for the Church. The number of false prophets is going to increase, for one; and it going to be increasingly hard for good-intentioned individuals to find their way into the Church. For all I know, scandals in the Church, an occupational hazard for people who are not only called to minister but also to give a good example, will increase rather than diminish. And the sufferings, not only of the followers of the Deliverer, but of people of good will as well, will grow likewise.

"And, don't you start thinking that the role of the Antichrist is reserved for non-Christians or the separated brethren. To the extent that Hindus, Buddhists, and others do their thing with sincerity, conscientiously and in good faith, to that extent they cannot be deemed to be working for the Antichrist, let alone be him. A member of the Communist politburo in China who gets demoted to a low level position and suffers because of his attempts to be a compassionate communist could be headed for martyrdom and baptism of blood while some of us are trying to resting on laurels that don't exist and dreaming that Peter will automatically let us into heaven because of what we are. To the extent that I pass up opportunities to rake in souls into the fold because of bigotry, personal prejudices or negligence, to that extent I am a prime candidate for the role of the Antichrist, I tell you!

"All of us on this panel could become Antichrists overnight - if we are not already - by fancying that you folks are being molded into useful members of the Church's hierarchy through our own personal efforts, and not through the work of the Prime Mover's grace! Conversely, I could be addressing a bunch of Antichrists if it suddenly turned out that you have all been imagining that there had to be something about you that made you a suitable candidate for the priesthood, instead of considering yourselves as completely unworthy as John the Baptist and Peter did - or Judas! You have to be a saint, folks, to avoid playing the role of the Antichrist!

"And take the hypothetical example of prelates - successors of the apostles - who, instead of standing up for the love of God and of their neighbor at all times and being prepared to become martyrs for it, are caught identifying themselves with the "national interests" of the country in which they are called to minister to the faithful when those "national interests" and the ensuing policies subvert the principle of love, justice and equality for all. In that hypothetical example, those prelates would be hard put to it to defend themselves against the charge that they are anti-Christian to the extent they permit themselves to be on the side of injustice. That is precisely why we must pray for priests, bishops and the Holy Father - yes, the Holy Father - all the time, folks. Yes, especially the pope!

"The Holy Father himself could become anti-Christian if he started fancying that he could claim credit for some of the Church's successes, the conversion of Russia for example; or, alternatively, if he failed in his duties as Peter's successor. Popes obviously cannot fill that role, thank God, on those occasions when they are speaking or acting *ex cathedra*.

"When the Deliverer showed up two thousand years ago, the priests and Sadducees were supposed to roll out the red carpet for Him - especially after the long wait that humanity, along with the people of Israel, had endured since the promise of a Messiah was made to Adam and Eve. Who would have thought that those same priests and

Sadducees, who led the concourse of the people of God in prayer in the temple on every Sabbath day (or day of rest) and also doubled up as the teachers of the law, would turn their backs on the 'Son of Man' just when He needed their help most. Who would have thought that those priests and Sadducees, bedecked in the vestments they normally put on when they officiated in the temple and in other regalia, would lead the mob in threatening some one as vile as Pontius Pilate that he would no longer be a friend of Caesar if he dared to let the Deliverer, who was clearly innocent, go free as he was proposing to do!

"The fact is that humans, whatever their station in life, will always remain humans, free to act the part of the devil if they so chose. There is nothing to stop a bishop who occupies the Holy See, as amply demonstrated by history, from playing the part of the Antichrist notwithstanding his position as the successor to St.. Peter! The definition of the Church as the Mystical Body of the Deliverer with Himself as its head and the rest of us with all our imperfections as its members implies as much! That is why it is no exaggeration to say that the folks who happen to be members of the Church's hierarchy are badly in need of the prayers of all men and women of good will.

"That said, the fact remains that those who have been called to holy orders, princes of the Church, and the Pontiff of Rome are *alteri Christi* in a very real sense; and it is a very serious thing when they start acting, even remotely, like Antichrists. But remember that they do not stop being human just because they carry responsibilities of that gravity on their shoulders. And it is not at all far fetched to say that this is the one group of people that the Evil Genius has a special interest in, and in whose regard he will work any amount of overtime in hopes of derailing them from their God-given mission! Diabolos prays - yes, prays - and dearly wishes that members of the Church's hierarchy, because they are the successors to the apostles, end up acting like *Antichrists*, and not like *other Christs*. He prayed and tried very hard to derail the mission of our Divine Savior Himself didn't he.

"And you can bet that the devil now tries very hard to make members of the hierarchy even deny that they know the Son of Man -

just like Peter before them did. And he does this even as he tries to make it appear to many out there that the apostles' successors could not possibly *look* or *act* like Catholic priests, bishops and prelates who appear ever so reluctant to abandon the staid and traditional, even as they themselves struggle to practice what they preach. That the apostles' successors are a completely different calibre of people who are easily identifiable by their message - quick and easy deliverance from the bondage of sin - by just *believing* what is in the Book rather than by each one *taking up his or her cross and following Him*, for instance!

"And you know that on their own, without the help of the Prime Mover's grace, that is exactly what the successors to the apostles will do, namely deny the Savior - by being silent and complicit! And I challenge any of you to say that on your own, without the help of God's grace, you or anyone else would not do precisely that, namely deny the Savior - especially, I might add, when you see Him and His Church on trial before the world court of opinion! Thank God that those who accuse the Church of all sorts of things, including witchcraft, at least concede that the idea of grace is not satanic or mythical!

"The question to ask, therefore, is: How many people out there are not swayed by this or that as they go about their daily business, so that instead of doing whatever they do to the greater glory of the Prime Mover, they do it to the greater glory of something else? And, anyway, how many among us Catholics, the Church leadership included, do not need to go to confession? I bet you, the number of Antichrists is much much larger than the number of Prochrists. That is why you hardly hear of the latter. And you would be surprised at the number of people who are trying to cheat their way into heaven!"

Even though the Indian pontificated non-stop, that did not at all seem to bother his audience whose wrapped attention he continued to enjoy as he went on undaunted.

"The Antichrist was really a scam artist and nothing more. And, conversely, all scam artists were Antichrists and would, of course, all face the Judge sooner or later, along with whoever the

Chief Antichrist was, to answer for the scams they perpetuate without any shame!"

"And, talking about scams and scam artists" father Raj continued, "I would say that there are basically three types of scams. The first type is the one that common criminals use to trick unwary individuals to part with their hard earned cash and/or other goods with next to nothing in return. The activities of these scam artists are frequently 'legal' to the point to which the perpetuators actually enjoy the protection of the law as they go about conducting their dirty business. It is the same type of scam that often characterizes so-called 'good business practices' that 'big business', after twisting the arms of law makers to force them to legalize those business practices, go on to use to skim profits and grow even bigger and more powerful. Frequently the scam artists are actually government functionaries who, knowingly or unknowingly, ensnare or actually 'buy off' governments in impoverished countries with so-called tied aid. You can always tell that it is a scam if the 'aid' produces the opposite result, or the donor countries end up getting far more out of the deals than the recipient countries.

"The second type of scam involves those who persuade others into investing in things that can only yield temporal and passing satisfaction. Because all of us in this world belong to the same human family with the same last end, it behoves each one of us to do everything in our power to mitigate the consequences of this type of scam.

"Talking about the human family, there is absolutely no doubt socialism and communism are the closest things to that ideal, even though promoters of greed for money, also known as capitalists, preach otherwise!

"The last type of scam is the most serious and involves what I call false prophets or individuals who represent themselves as messengers of the Prime Mover as you call Him to unwitting folk when they in fact they are not. It is the ultimate scam because not only because of what is at stake, namely the eternal destinies of the populace, but because it is only after the targeted individuals pass from this world into the next that they will discover that they were being given a ride. Now, with so many religions, churches, and what have you, none of which seem to agree on anything except that they are all led by prophets and messengers of the Prime Mover, it is probably correct to say that poor ordinary folk are resigned to the fact that they have to live with this particular type of scam, and who can blame them any way."

The excitement of members of his audience, already palpable, reached a new high as the Indian declared: "We could, of course, blame everything on the Antichrist, except that we all have a streak of the Antichrist in us just like we all have a streak of Judas Iscariot in us."

Speaking above the voluble chatter, the priest continued: "Believe it or not, the Antichrist is among us already. And, most sadly, we are even seeing fulfilled in our own time the ominous words of the Deliverer to the effect that kin would turn against kin, children against their parents, and so on. And then the drum beats of war, coming so soon after a dreadful and murderous world war and which are growing louder with each passing day, also look more and more like they might presage a religious conflict of global proportions and a war that has the potential for quickly escalating into the Mother of All Wars!

Fr. Raj: The most powerful prayer...

"Any ways...back to our topic of the day. Having the devil urge souls to beseech, wail and pray to God for their needs is a contradiction in terms. But it is an even more glaring contradiction to have him urge souls to say the one prayer which incorporates all articles of our faith - the Holy Mass. Don't you think it is a bit far fetched?

"You see, far from being any kind of prayer, the prayer of the Holy Mass has already been answered through Jesus' death, His resurrection, and ascension into heaven. One does not have to worry that one might be praying in vain when participating in this prayer.

Besides, when Mass is being celebrated even by a lone priest assisted by the alter boy, the church is always full - full and resounding with the praises of choirs of angels and members of the Church Triumphant.

"And it is precisely for this reason that the sacrament of the Holy Eucharist, inaugurated by the Deliverer on the eve of His death and celebrated by His Church ever since, will be something that is completely anathema to those who do not wish the Church well.

"Understand me - I am not suggesting that there are some prayers which are ineffectual or wasted effort. The story of the disciples in the sinking boat is, in my view, quite telling. There they were, wailing - praying - when they realized that they were going to drown. The Nazarene, when he awoke, told them that they were 'men of little faith'!

It was good that the shaken apostles were crying out in fear - or 'praying'. As it turned out, the measure of their faith was not the intensity of their cries or prayers. To all appearances, they were completely faithless. Knowing that people in similar situations perished as a rule, they were convinced that it was their turn to go.

"You would have thought that, after they had crisscrossed Galilee in the company of the Messiah and listened to all those sermons, their faith would be really deep. It is also significant that, even though they had rushed the Lord's sleeping quarters in the boat to get Him to save them from drowning, they were advised that they did not have very much faith.

"After Adam and Eve transgressed, they must have wailed and beseeched God unceasingly for mercy. Their prayer, which was undoubtedly the prayer of people who had given up all hope and were at their wits' end, was answered despite the fact that the channel of communication with their maker had been irrevocably cut. With the Second Adam in the picture, human beings are heard very well by the Father, who is concerned even when a bird loses a feather. But humans needed the gift of faith nonetheless. Still, just as the Deliverer interrupted his rest and not only answered the prayers of his faithless disciples, but focused on beefing up the little faith they had (so that they could actually become apostles who were dependable and capable of manning the Church he was in the process of setting up to continue His mission after His ascension into heaven), it would be most imprudent to even imagine that He does not respond in the same way when human beings of all races, sexes, backgrounds, and religious convictions pray. Any prayer is, after all, better than none at all. I fully agree with your thesis on that particular point.

"The most difficult part for many is to accept that only those in communion with the Holy See can *fully* participate in the perfect prayer - the Holy Mass. And - if I may make one final remark about Holy Mass - you can be sure that Diabolos, who would not dare to venture near the Blessed Sacrament, will strive to keep souls away from the sanctuary and their God to the very end of time.

Fr. Raj: Everybody is a Judas...

"It would, finally, be a serious omission on my part, especially given my position as your spiritual director, if I did not make one point very clear. I certainly would not go as far as calling you Judas Iscariot. We all are Judases after all. But I have to emphasize that, at any time we human beings try to pit ourselves against the fallen spirits and Lucifer in particular, we run the risk of underestimating the powers of the Underworld and overestimating our own strengths.

"In my opinion, Judas Iscariot did just that, and ended up destroying himself - and we ourselves, I might add, all have the tendency to overestimate our strengths and underestimate the enemy's powers!

"And it isn't as if we merely have a streak of a Judas Iscariot in us. We all are full fledged Judases by our failure to live up to expectations and by acting the way we do. We are traitors - all of us! You all remember the hymns we used to sing until recently - the hymns which laid the blame for the Messiah's death squarely on the shoulders of the Jews.

"Man! Blaming the Jews is the same as saying that we are sinless, because it implies that we ourselves wouldn't have done what they did to the Deliverer if we had been in their place! Moreover, if we cannot completely associate ourselves with the chosen people from whom we got our Messiah - if we insist on disassociating ourselves from the Jewish people in this particular respect - how on earth can we claim to be among the beneficiaries of His redemptive work?

"A human being could, in theory, have an advantage over Satan in one or other respect; but that is not what counts when push comes to shove. The fact is that when all is said and done, we do not stand a chance when pitted against the Evil One. Remember that if he hadn't fallen, he would be rubbing shoulders with Michael the Archangel and with Rafael.

"We might not yet be lost and are certainly not yet written off in that sense - like the Diabolical One. But the fact remains, nonetheless, that left to own devices, we are as nothing. We are helpless and unable to perform even the simplest act of virtue! When we are in that kind of position, prudence dictates that we avoid all occasions of sin by mortifying ourselves to keep temptations of the flesh at bay, and also that we constantly pray that our God keep our paths clear of the temptations of Satan and deliver us from evil.

"We have to be humble enough to admit that we cannot win in any one-to-one contest with the Prince of Darkness, and we pay a heavy price by failing to do that. We easily forget that the Mystical Body of Christ - Holy Mother Church - is made up of the sinless Christ *and* mortal human beings who are frail and are burdened with their own failings. And, finally, we easily become scandalized and end up failing to be full participants in the Church's redeeming activities.

Fr. Raj: Wicked humans...

"According to Holy Mother Church, far from being something imaginary, evil is very real indeed; and Satan and his hosts are committed to perpetuating it. As you have ably pointed out, we human beings at a certain point in our lives go nuts, and refuse to accept that there are some rules to the game of living.

"And we sometimes even stop acknowledging that we owe anything to a Prime Mover, and begin acting as though we were the ones who decided that we should have two eyes instead of one, two legs instead of three; that we should be human beings and not kangaroos or reptiles - or some inanimate object shone of feelings (albeit, perhaps, with a life span that might be as long as that of the earth's crust) but without anything resembling intelligence or a free will, and endowed with the capacity to obey His laws of physics and nothing else! We act as though we were the ones who decided that we should be humans and not pure spirits (with no bodily appendage to fuss about) or not at all!

"And to think that we do this without ever a thought as regards our limitations, and do it in league with one who is a mortal enemy at that! To think that it is also with the same goal that we ourselves set out to defy our God and Lord of the Universe, namely to be rid of our Maker who, in His infinite wisdom, established the rules of human conduct that we in our stupidity fancy we can somehow be insulated or liberated from!

"Poor and forsaken mortal creatures whose defiance of the Almighty evokes His infinite pity, our actions which are contrary to our conscience are a serious enough breach of a divinely ordained code of conduct. This is so if only because they render us unworthy as God's place of abode - not to mention the fact that sins also make the world a very inhospitable place indeed. But when we do them in league with Diabolos, who unlike us has been God's sworn enemy from the very beginning unlike us, our intransigence takes on an entirely whole new dimension as a result.

"This happens because we freely decide to enlist the help of one who is the embodiment of evil, crafty and dead serious, and who has no remorse if he destroys creatures who were fashioned in the image of the Almighty and are actually now in line to fill those places in the divine mansion that had originally been reserved for him and his disgraced associates. Because of this, our own evil activity also automatically takes on the same gravity and becomes as deadly. We ourselves end up being little devils - in a sense.

"Like the archenemy, we have exulted when the Messiah's mission appeared doomed - as it did with His crucifixion and death on the cross, and as it still does with the continuing reign of evil. And we have beaten a retreat with the devil whenever the glory of God has become manifest - as it did on the day the Son of Man rose from the dead, and as it now does every hour of the day as His death and resurrection are re-enacted at Mass. And the description of Holy Mother the Church as the Mystical Body of Christ is very apt for precisely these reasons!

"In so doing, we in effect try to compel our Creator to take a dose of what we ourselves detest most - humiliation! Dead wood, we imagine that we can lecture Him on the purpose of creation, including our own *raison d'etre*!

"Prior to the fall, the Lord our God would undoubtedly smile when Adam or Eve, tripping over something, ended up with bruised knees or elbows. But He really pitied them - as he now pities us - when they had the gall to suggest that they did not have to live as befitted creatures fashioned in His image. He pities us when we express our desire to be rid of Him as our mentor - as if there were some other force which could sustain us and the rest of the universe! Offending God knowingly and wilfully is not only dumb but also suicidal, and demonstrates that we, indeed, do not know what we are doing when we start figuring that we could improve on His workmanship.

"We have lost all sense of our purpose in life, and even find it hard to believe that it transcends matter and is spiritual. Adam and Eve's last end had never been the morning glory, dahlias and roses, and the wild berries - or any of the Garden of Eden's other attractions. The whole idea of being fashioned in the image of the Non-Creature and Master Craftsman was that He also be our last end. We just do not seem to get it that Dante's Paradise Lost was a spiritual, not an earthly, paradise.

"We not only have conveniently forgotten that Man is created in God's image, but that this is the case whether the individual sees the light of day for the very first time in the shadow of the Himalayas, the Alps, Mt. Kilimanjaro, or in the shadow of Castel Gondolfo. We self-professed 'Christians' are the biggest offenders when it comes to segregation and other discriminatory practices. We even compete with everybody else as slave pushers.

"And we have taken to imagining that it is the mysterious peace of mind and serenity which canonized individuals exude even in death that marks out Man as being made in the image and likeness of God, instead of what happens at the moment of our creation.

"And, what is even worse, we tell our children that what we see when we look in a mirror is what we are! By suggesting to them that it is what they see in the mirror - flesh and blood - rather than the invisible soul which should be the focal point of their activities, we in effect suggest to them what the demon suggested to Adam and Eve in the Garden of Eden. He suggested to them that to be masters of their destiny, all they needed to do was concentrate on taking good care of those bodies by feeding well - on the forbidden fruit if necessary. They were to ignore the fact that munching on the forbidden fruit was going to compromise their spiritual relationship with their Maker.

"In our case we are telling our children that focusing their attention on what they see in the mirror - that indulging themselves rather that remaining disciplined and of good character - is what will both enrich their existence on earth and add longevity to their lives.

"They are to do as if they are prisoners of their bodies. As if their *élan vital* springs from their preoccupation with their physical selves. Because that is tantamount to self-indulgence, it actually saps their spiritual vitality and leaves them both physically and spiritually drained. But that is what we urge them to do - to concentrate on and pamper their bodies instead of concentrating on and pampering that which directly links them to the Author of Life - their souls.

"We human beings are so stupid, we even think that regimenting our self-indulgence is critical to maintaining an acceptable level of well being. We imagine that we have to treat ourselves like automobiles - which have to be regularly refuelled to be of use - confirming that we human beings have ditched our lofty status of being children of God and have indeed sank to the level of *homines ex machina*.

"The evils we do to one another are, without exception, traceable to our attempts to act like automatons. And, in the meantime, we ridicule those who do not opt to live like automatons as simpletons and failures. And we fool ourselves into believing that we were the ones who first conceived of the atrocious things we do to fellow humans. We even refuse to concede that we received inspiration of any kind from Diabolos or anyone else before we started down that path of self-destruction.

"We pride ourselves in living like automatons - as if devilishness itself was invented by us! We have become so brazen, we will even do daredevil things - as if the act of daring the Author of Life and Master Architect to try and stop us is a major accomplishment in itself! And, probably even worse, we lull ourselves into believing that we will always be able to get away with our stupidity.

"We are full of praise for those who act like machines, and we relish the sight of soldiers staging a match past or beating a retreat. We hail those countries that have the capability to deliver guided missiles and smart bombs at enemy targets with deadly accuracy as advanced, and have nothing but scorn for those countries which have outlawed armaments. We applaud those who exact revenge swiftly and efficiently, and we regard accommodation, tolerance and the readiness to forgive, not as virtues but as weaknesses if not outright stupidity. And it is, of course, savvy diplomacy not to interfere in global conflicts by way of condemning the aggressors, or siding with and providing assistance to the victims of aggressions.

"And, while the official representatives of foreign nations - the ambassadors - are guaranteed safety, the safety of anybody who takes it on him/herself to communicate information that is deemed to be of any value to a foreign power is not, the sentence for any such action being execution by firing squad, hanging, lethal injection or other 'socially accepted' means. It is a good measure of the extent to which we human beings have turned against one another, and will do anything to destroy the 'bad guy' or anyone who happens to be different from us. The hatred between some nation states runs so deep, official communications between them have been severed for as long as their nationals can remember!

"Stealing, maiming and killing carried out by governments in the name of national security are accepted and 'legal'; and there is nothing wrong with robbery when undertaken by corporations - it is 'profit-taking'. Indecency has become 'sleekness' and is equated with 'open-mindedness', while decency is a sure sign that one is definitely thick between the ears.

"In the course of pandering to our bodies, we do the dumbest things conceivable. We are usually oblivious to what is good for one part of our constitution while indulging ourselves in ways we think are fulfilling to other parts of the body. We will try to recover from one addiction by getting latched onto some other addiction; and, knowing that time is not on our side, we often get stuck while attempting to satisfy our different appetites all at once! And instead of concluding that satisfying the bodily senses - be it the sense of hearing, sight, smell, taste or the sense of touch - individually or all of them together leads us no where at all, and that we should be looking for lasting happiness on a different level (the spiritual plane), we simply continue to act just like dogs do, namely keep trying to catch that tail until we are ready to drop down from exhaustion.

Fr. Raj: On death row...

"The mystery of it all is how creatures that are supposedly rational like ourselves succeed in reconciling all of this with the certain knowledge that we all are, without any exception, on death-row; that we are in the exact same boat as those awaiting the hangman's noose. Like those on death-row in Japan, we in fact are completely in the dark as to the day or hour when the knock on the door of the holding cell will presage the end.

"Which is not to say that the human body isn't beautiful. It is without any doubt! There is something about human bodies which not only sets them aside from the bodies of birds, animals, reptiles, and other mammalian creatures, but makes them ultimately deserving of special deference from saints and angels alike. Of course, adjudged good and comely by the Master Craftsman Himself at creation, it is little wonder that when the prodigal son decided to return to his father's that son of his, who had been as good as dead and now here washed and dressed up in the finest robe, and after putting a ring on his finger and sandals, suitably feted.

"One reason providence let the contrite Mary Magdalene, that former *femme fatale* and Jezebel, into the company of the Holy Women was so she would be available to minister to the mother of the Deliverer in the days following the death, resurrection and ascension into heaven of her beloved Son. A bigger reason for celebrating the conversion of that former woman of the twilight was the fact that another creature that was created in the image and likeness of its Maker had resolved to live as befitted a child of God. But yet another reason for celebrating was the fact that Mary Magdalene will rise up body and soul on the last day in glory.

"Thanks to the fact that the Son of Man had condescended to take up our human nature when he agreed to take up our case with His Father, Mary Magdalene too was now destined to rise up on the last day. The fact that there was going to be an intervening period when Magdalene's body, along with those of the rest of mankind, would return to dust, would not matter. That meant two things: the jewel, which would grace the heavenly mansion at the divine banquet, would come complete with a soul that was resplendent in God's grace and a body that was glorified! And, obviously something that can be glorified in the spiritual sense had to be adorable and beautiful.

"The human body, designed to facilitate our existence on this earth and also designed to be both a temple of God and a vessel of His grace, in fact *has* to be comely, fair and fascinating. For, if it were not, Mary Magdalene's subsequent act of consecrating herself body and soul to the Redeemer's Most Sacred Heart would have been an empty gesture and a farce. And, by the same token, our divine Redeemer's self-immolation on the cross, an act of self-sacrifice which encompassed both His divine nature and also His human nature, would not have been the perfect sacrifice it was if that part of human nature wasn't beautiful and adorable. Our own self-denial, undertaken in imitation of our Lord and Savior, would likewise be ineffectual if the human body were not the wonderful piece of creation it is.

"The problem is with our appreciation of this bundle of beauty which is facile and often beguiling and banal, and also our notion of beauty. True appreciation of a beautiful object, whether it be physical or mystical, has to be preceded by an animated chant of the *Magnificat Anima Mea*, and end with a *Te Deum Laudamus* that is belted out with all one's guts. Selfishness cannot be a part of it. The bestiality and possessiveness which we earthlings equate with love and admiration are in fact things that have nothing in common with the profound reverence for what is good - reverence that takes full cognizance of the fact that beautiful things are beautiful only by virtue of being the work of one who is Himself not just charming and beautiful, but the embodiment of charm and beauty - the Supreme Good.

"Which only goes to emphasize the point regarding the image of ourselves which we see in the mirror. That image is nothing compared to something which, being a direct image of God, not only belongs naturally in the heavenly mansion, but is specifically designed to add a distinctive sparkle to it, namely the human soul. And the image in the mirror is also a far cry from the mystical image of a glorified body that will be reunited with the soul when the world comes to an end on the last day.

"In lusting after things of this world, we humans beings, starting with Adam and Eve, have always tried to pretend that the copyright for the masterful work of art represented by the human nature is ours and does not belong to the Master Architect. We spend tons of money keeping our noses - which are supposed to develop a sweat when the body is well exercised - permanently dusted and dry.

We keep our naturally beautiful body skin permanently socked in all sorts of creams and lathers, and our lips painted in the strangest colors. We disfigure and permanently ruin the gorgeous hair on our crowns to the point to which it becomes totally unrecognizable.

"Even though it is well established that artificial creams, because they interfere with our immune systems, have a terrible toll on our health and life expectancy, we continue using these creams as if desisting from doing so is a sin against nature. We even refuse to accept scientific findings to the effect that using these artificial agents has the effect of accelerating the decomposition of our bodies when we eventually succumb.

"We tattoo our body parts and attach strange appendages like earrings, bracelets and things like that on them; surround our bodies with lots of jewellery and whatever else money can buy; force ourselves to live through painful things like cosmetic surgery; take on heavy work-out schedules (while avoiding regular work or working to rule) supposedly to develop shapely or muscular bodies; and we then delude ourselves that we have made progress in establishing a right to the copyright. Preoccupied with looks, we cajole ourselves into believing that they are what matters, and that the soul exists only in our imagination - even though it is what informs the human body!

"Our reasoning is so convoluted, we frequently imagine that we have established a right to the copyright by the simple act of committing sins of the flesh; and that the more we do it, the more we own the body and can continue to misuse our God-given talents.

"Talking about misusing talents - any human being who decides to follow his/her reason in figuring out what it is that redounds best to his/her last end would be lucky not to find him/herself permanently restrained in a straight jacket - for his/her own good! Because those who have decided that they will not apply their minds to what really matters - their spiritual life - are in the majority, any move to do what behoves human beings to attain true self-actualization is not just viewed with suspicion. It is regarded as a very serious aberration with far reaching implications. And no wonder! For it is not just a question of priorities of the 'world' - and of those who try to put their 'spiritual salvation' first - being 'different' from those of Providence. They are at cross-purposes.

"We take unnecessary risks and do other outrageous things, and imagine that behaving like that promotes our cause. Even though we know, deep down in our hearts, that we do not have any right whatsoever to that copyright, we close our eyes and just go on doing our thing.

"We wish we owned that copyright for a variety of reasons. We have deluded ourselves into believing that ownership would impart to us the right to do whatever we fancy with the art-work - meaning with ourselves. We imagine, mistakenly, that ownership of that copyright would imply that we do not need the Master Architect, and would consequently absolve us from any sense of guilt for living in whatever way we pleased. We also believe, quite irrationally, that success in establishing ownership would mean that we human creatures can indeed lay a rightful claim to being like Him-Who-Is-Who-Is just as the temper suggested!

"But it is as well that we do not own the copyright; because if we did, we would probably have long ago pawned it to none other than Diabolos, our mortal enemy; and we likely would have done so with the same gusto with which we have been prepared to sell and resell our birthright for peanuts to the enemy. And he, in turn, would have been only too glad to preside over the final destruction of that great masterpiece. He likewise would have been only too glad to see the image of the Almighty One which is emblazoned thereon ripped out or otherwise destroyed to ensure that nothing at all of that art-work could ever be repossessed by the Master Architect.

Fr. Raj: At the height of their rebellion...

"When Adam and Eve, tricked by the fallen Lucifer, joined him and the other rebel spirits in the uprising against the Creator, they imagined, foolishly, that they had Him cornered. They were after all created in His image and likeness - just like the angels. But, unlike the angels, each of whom had a distinct nature and also formed a separate specie, Adam and Eve share this same human nature even while existing as individuals with different personalities. Adam and Eve were aware that the Prime Mover, His Divine Son, and the Spirit that united them in a perfect bond of love also shared the same divine nature even as they enjoyed each a separate existence as distinct persons.

"At the height of their rebellion, the first man and the first woman felt assured that, as the future father and mother of the human race, they were going to come out triumphant in their machinations against the Almighty One if only because He had no choice but to write off and deem as lost all their posterity as well in then event that he was going to hold them to account for eating of the fruit from the tree of life. Adam and Eve could not imagine that their Creator, who was infinitely just, could condemn their wholly 'innocent' children and their children's children and cut them off simply because they, Adam and Eve, had staged a revolt.

"They thought that they had the Prime Mover and Almighty One cornered and that consequently He wasn't in a position to assert His authority over them and exact retribution from them for their sinful deed. It was quite plain that He could not move against them without ending the human race as a whole! If he did so, it would compromise His sense of justice, because they and their posterity were destined, in accordance with the divine plan, to share the same human nature. A curse on them would automatically be binding on their posterity as well for that reason!

"On the other hand, any 'punishment' that left their human nature unscathed would hardly be punishment at all - or so they reasoned. As Adam and Eve imagined it, their Creator was either going to tolerate their infidelity and in effect condone their evil doing or He was going to condemn humanity as a whole for their dastardly act. It, therefore, came as a great surprise when the first man and the first woman found themselves kicked out of the Garden of Eden and lost the sanctuary that had assured their safety from beasts of the wild, poisonous snakes, viruses, and other harmful creatures

"And then the pendulum swang when, abandoned to an uncertain future on their own, Adam and Eve recanted and regretted their act. After imagining that their Creator was powerless to exact retribution from them for their sin of disobedience, the penitent Adam and Eve now imagined that, even though they were prepared to renounce Satan and his wiles and return to the fold, their situation was still completely hopeless.

"The fact was that it was not enough for them to just be ready to abandon their sinful ways. In order to become reconciled to their Divine Master, someone had to make up adequately for their misadventure which had cost them their friendship with a divinity. Someone had to pay the price for their affront against the Prime Mover, and that someone had to be a divinity if the recompense was to be acceptable!

"But where on earth were they going to get someone divine to intercede for them? Adam and Eve regarded their situation as quite hopeless, and were resigned to staying as captives - yes, lackeys - of Beelzebub. Mere humans, there was absolutely nothing that they themselves could do to make up adequately for injury to a God. And so, even though repentant, it was clear to Adam and Eve that they were doomed all the same. Despite the heartfelt remorse they felt, no amount of penance by them - or any creature for that matter - could be pleasing enough to the Almighty One and undo the damage caused by original sin and the effects thereof!

"And then there was the ever present danger that they could again succumb to the Evil One's temptations which were continuing. Noting that the fallen angels became lost for ever as a result of their act of rebellion, Adam and Eve had every reason to fear that their own situation was likewise beyond remedy. Much as they were prepared to let the Almighty One have the 'pound of flesh' they knew was His due, they could not figure out how that could ever come about.

"It caught them entirely by surprise when their Maker, in an unprecedented act of infinite mercy that also reflected a love that was infinite and unbounded, promised to send his only begotten Son to earth where, both as man and also as a member of the Godhead, He would be in a position to make amends on their behalf. Adam and Eve in fact never fully recovered from the shock they got when it was revealed to them that the Word, through whom everything that had come into being was made, had consented, in deference to the will of His Father, to pay the price exacted for their sins *and* the sins of their descendants!

"It was still up to men to accept the invitation to be reconciled with their Maker or to reject it. Adam and Eve were overwhelmed to learn that the relations between Man and his Maker, severed when they committed original sin, were going to be restored through the intervention of the divine Messiah. This would take effect as soon as the debt of sin had been paid by the Savior, or 'Second Adam' in accordance with the promise made to them by the Father.

"Actually, the Word was going to 'become flesh' and was going to dwell among humans. In the Son of Man, as the Messiah would call Himself, the divine nature and the human nature were going to be united in one and the same Person. The Messiah, true God and true man, would then proceed to overcome sin with His death and His resurrection. Death itself, to which Adam and Eve became subject in the wake of their transgression would 'loose its sting'.

"Suddenly Adam and Eve - even though they once upon a time had cherished the fact that they had Lucifer as their ally and had lost their right to eternal life in the process, and were on the verge of despair even after they had decided to return to the fold - found that they could count on the Second Adam, who was none other than the Second Person of the Blessed Trinity, to intercede for them with His Father.

"But that was not all. He also was going to make recompense on their behalf - recompense that would be acceptable to a Divinity whose ire they had roused by entering into alliance with the Evil One. The first man and the first woman never forgave themselves for the fact that they had actually tried to blackmail their Maker and hold the infinite love He espoused for His creatures to ransom at the height of their rebellion.

Fr. Raj: In denial...

"The fact that we human beings were lost and had, in the process, allowed death to have mastery over us is evidence enough of the extent to which we had gone to subvert God's plan for us. It is incredible, but that is precisely what had happened. We even now still find the time to unashamedly celebrate it with great fanfare at the variety of carnivals which we observe regularly. We should know better, but we continue to be in denial regarding the impending doomsday at which we will be called upon to account for the manner in which we used the talents we have been entrusted with.

"We are so hopeless, we sometimes have a valid point to make - a point that might be good and positive for once - but we make it the wrong way and end up heaping blame on ourselves and feeling guilty as hell. And that sort of thing happens frequently too! We will, for instance, find ourselves staring adoringly at a person of the opposite sex; and, while genuinely admiring the work of God's creation, we might even mention it a passer-by, only to turn around and bash ourselves for revelling in unseemly talk or something like that. This is even though the encounter might end up causing end up causing those involved to wind up exchanging wedding vows at the altar! But we will in the meantime feel guilty for 'lusting' after a woman or a man, as the case may be.

"We forget that we are actually charged with a duty to admire the works of our good and loving Creator, albeit in a way that is prayerful and reverend or holy. On occasions like these, we fail to 'get it' that, as the sun was beginning to set again for the seventh consecutive time signalling the end of the seventh day of His labors of creation, our Maker Himself actually looked down and saw that what he had crafted was good not just in a metaphorical sense, but in a literal and concrete sense. We sometimes even completely forget that it is the intention behind the act which makes all the difference in matters of morality, and not the act itself.

"We end up trapping ourselves in our own arguments so to speak because, more often than not, we are really after sophistry, not just the simple truth. When it comes to our own lives, seconds, minutes, hours, days, months, years, and decades all suddenly stop representing things that are real - perhaps because we cannot touch this thing called 'time'! This is even though those of us who work regularly lament that 'time isn't moving fast enough!' on Fridays and, come Saturday and Sunday, our tune changes to 'time is moving too fast'! Yes, 'moving' as if it was a piece of solid rock travelling down the slope of a hill!

"The only people who take time and death seriously seem to be lawyers who make a living from writing wills, funeral homes, and owners/managers of life insurance companies, banks and other investment firms which automatically inherit assets that are not claimed after people pass on. On the evidence, they are the only ones who believe that time really comes to an end for an individual at death, and that 'death' really means kicking the 'bucket' in one's path and moving on to some other place where things like time and worldly comfort no longer count. But they, obviously, believe it only in to the extent these things apply to their former clients and not to themselves - which leaves them also in the exact same boat as everybody else!

"Only a score of us have set our eyes on our great grand parents, and it must be a tiny number who have been so blessed as to be able to set their eyes on their great great grandparents. But we all continue to kid ourselves that the divine plan, under which sinners, their children and their children's children must die the death as a price for Man's intransigence is a tall tale.

"But what we all need is to take a walk, bump unexpectedly into friends we haven't seen in a long while, and then make the mistake of inquiring after some of our former mutual acquaintances. That might help us wake up to the reality of that thing called 'death'. Even though we human beings forget easily, it will be sometime before we forget the shock with which we learn that former associates we thought were doing very well (like ourselves if not better) and would, therefore, outlast everybody else - especially those former associates whose physical presence evoked visions of endless triumphs and continued prosperity - had indeed already passed on; and it will also be a while before we forgot that some former buddies we had written off and thought would be swept under and be gone and forgotten in a thrice were still going strong!

"Or, do we believe that it is not our God who created us, and is meting out the just punishment for our deliberate decision to stray from the right path, but someone else - Diabolos? Do we, perhaps, fantasize that everything that happens is the product of chance - yes, *chance* to which we should also credit the awesome symmetry and order in the universe, including the miracles of life *and*, I suppose, also death!

"Well, assume for a moment that we owe it all to this Diabolos. If Diabolos had been in the shoes of our Lord and Maker, he certainly wouldn't hesitate to mete out punishment to us *unjustly* - even if we had done no wrong! He would dole out the punishment *especially* if we were living righteously and shunning evil. No, it is not Diabolos who created us or ordained that we suffer for our sins. This is not because Diabolos is the embodiment of evil, but because he is a creature. He could never step into the shoes of our loving God for that reason. And we can rest assured that it is not Diabolos to whom we are due to render an accounting for the manner in which we used our God-given talents, because he himself is already in very big trouble for his failure to employ his own God-given talents in the proper manner.

"But why is it that we do as if we owe those among us who are Diabolos' minions apologies of any sort - especially when they seem determined to carry out the devil's bidding, treat us unjustly, and do everything they can to demoralise us? Or do we act like that because we ourselves are already like them in many respects!

Fr. Raj: God's love for humans...

"And that, unfortunately, clouds the situation somewhat, and makes it harder for us to appreciate the other and even more important fact. Which, namely, is that the Prime Mover 'so loved the world, He gave His only begotten Son; so that those who would believe in Him would not perish...'.

"We forget that Providence sent a good Samaritan to rescue the traveler who had been brutalized by highway robbers and left there to die. That, similarly, the Deliverer heard the frantic cries and wailing of Peter and the other apostles in the sinking boat and calmed the seas so that they might survive to carry on His mission.

"And, again, when Lazarus passed the first time around - and even though his body had started to decompose - the Deliverer felt great sympathy for the distraught relatives, and caused the dead man to come alive and pick up where he had left off in his earthly life, a life that had obviously been lived to the full and that had been edifying to his contemporaries as well. And that was even though Lazarus had died for the reason we all die, namely because Man, following in the foot-steps of Lucifer, had succumbed to sin.

"We also forget that, on hearing His mother whisper something to the effect that their hosts at the wedding of Canaan had run out of wine, the Son of Man immediately ordered the empty jars filled with water which he turned into refreshingly new wine.

"And again, in yet another example of an action that followed a pattern of behavior that couldn't be more consistent - even though the time was most inauspicious because He himself was under the gun and was greatly troubled in His mind - there the Messiah was, emerging from the secluded spot where He had been praying to His Father. He was checking up on His disciples' well-being; and, seeing them struggling to keep their heavy eye-lids open and having a hard time trying to keep watch with Him, He 'had great pity on them'. Knowing that they felt very bad over it, He hastened to offer them words of encouragement saying: 'The spirit is willing, but the flesh is weak'!

"The same sentiments went for His Father. For, when the Maker of all things visible and invisible saw Adam and Eve disconsolate and distraught with shame after committing their original sin, He did not hesitate, as they hid in the bushes, to holler out to them saying 'Do not commit an act of despair now and make things worse...'

"They could not dare look Him in the eye, and they protested that He should leave them alone to pay the price for their intransigence. However, inclined to sin as a result of their rebellion, it was evident that they were going to seek solace from none other than the Tempter, and would almost certainly end up mired in unpardonable diabolical activity. Our Maker was not about to sit back and see that happen. And so, He had shouted out to them saying 'Do not be afraid. I will send my only Son to be your Redeemer...'

"And again, as the Messiah Himself faltered in His steps as He climbed Mt. Calvary with His burden on behalf of all of us, Providence had this African by the name of Simon of Arimathea at the right spot and at the right time to help our Redeemer make it to the summit.

"Because we human beings find it hard to desist from dabbling in iniquity from time to time, we subsequently also find it hard to appreciate the fact that God will never abandon those in need. It is apparently quite difficult for us to put our hopes and dreams of fulfilment in the Almighty - we should in fact admit that it is impossible without the help of God's grace. With our attachment to material things remaining as strong as ever, we often even poke fun at God and ridicule the idea that He saves. We remain as faithless as those who thought they were being very witty when they mocked the Messiah saying 'He said that God was His Father. If He was indeed God's son, how come the father does not descend from heaven to rescue Him, now?'

"As long as this continues to be the case, our acceptance of the fact that human miseries and suffering - unpleasant things though they are - are beneficial to us in the new scheme of things will always elude us and appear a crazy thing to do. We won't quite be able to appreciate the fact that pain, both physical and mental, and things of that nature actual open up avenues that facilitate our participation in the work of redemption. Statements such as 'He sends sufferings to those He loves', or 'Take up your cross and follow me', or 'Blessed are those who weep and mourn, for the reward is theirs' will continue to make very little if any sense at all.

"That is also why pain and suffering will continue to be mysterious things, driving us to seek revenge, or otherwise do things which promise to 'bring closure' to our hurt feelings. And yet, doing these things is like telling the devil that someone is giving us trouble - perhaps God; and then immediately turning to God and telling Him that someone is proving a nuisance - the devil! But we have to choose who we wish to have as ally on the other hand - the devil or God. It cannot be both.

"Still, admonishing people to have God, and not the devil, as their ally is easier said than done. This is because there is another side to it. When you choose to have God as your ally and presume to accept the miseries He sends your way as things that are beneficial to you, you will also be expected, when your tormentors pounce, to 'turn the other cheek'! But your instinct will be urging you to prepare for the show down and warn: 'On my dead body'. And that is possible only when your 'tormentors' are not an 'act of God' and can be identified. So, the situation is quite complicated.

"But we are taught that God always 'intervenes' on our behalf To draw His compassion, the actions of others do not have to amount to 'sins that cry out to heaven'. He does not have to see 'the blood of Abel' flowing, or to see 'the sin of the Sodomites' or 'the injustice to the wage earner', or to hear 'the cry of the people oppressed in Egypt' or 'the cry of the foreigner, the widow, and the orphan', or to witness 'discrimination in all its ugly forms' before He is touched.

Fr. Raj: Second guessing God...

"Talking about discrimination, God does not discriminate against us. And we certainly do not want to be discriminated against by fellow human beings or even by angels (who are made in God's image and likeness just like us). But, on the other hand, we ourselves seem unable to live without perpetuating discriminatory acts of one type or another against others and against God.

"Against others by treating them as though they are aliens who just masquerade as humans with no legitimate claim to their human nature, or else have come by their human nature in some felonious fashion, the greatest injustice being that wrought against those who are outside the purview of laws enacted by man and indefensible. And against God by acting as if He, being the Almighty, still got it all wrong when He set out the rules of the game the way He did, and ordained that we be wholly subject to His laws, both moral and natural.

"And the way we practice apartheid, segregation, tribalism and discrimination - the way we do these things, you would think that we are bewitched! The white people discriminate against both non-white people and against other white people; the black people discriminate against non-black people and against other black people; the yellow people discriminate against non-yellow people and against other yellow people; and the red people discriminate against non-red people and against other red people.

"And then the miscarriage of justice carried out in broad daylight and under the glare of television lights against perceived foes and in the absence of any proof of wrong-doing. The way we hound and cut down fellow humans, or otherwise treat them like creatures that had no inalienable rights. The way we love to demonstrate that might is right, and completely forget that any authority exercised by humans comes from God and is accountable.

"The way we do these things, you would think the gods in whose names we do these things were crazy - as they must be if, indeed, there are any such gods! And also there must be quite a bit of turmoil wherever those gods have their dwelling place. And we are so stupid, we have no idea what kind of judgement we are soliciting when we purport to do them in the name of the God of Abraham and Isaac.

"In spite of all that and our stupidity, our good Lord and God, who is very concerned when a bird of the air loses a single feather and who, in addition to making us in his own image and likeness, has bestowed on us so many gifts, is attentive to each and all our cries. It goes without saying that He rushes to intervene especially when, seeing ourselves heading for the brink, we stop and, however reluctantly, pray for grace so we might at least be able to continue inching ahead hopefully in the right direction along the narrow path.

"And stopping to do that is hard enough, given all those conflicting and often also confusing messages which we, poor forsaken children of Adam and Eve, get from the different spiritual directors, some of whom advocate apartheid, segregation and discrimination - the very things they should be urging us to abhor - outright.

"The main point to be noted here is that God not only actually intervenes to prevent His people from being crushed by the enemy and those who are prepared to do his bidding, but even turns their miseries into good by using human suffering as a cleansing tool and also as a vehicle for unsolicited grace and other spiritual blessings.

"They are blessings that accrue to humans as Providence forges ahead with the implementation of His divine plan - something we short-sighted humans forget is on-going and unstoppable, and will continue regardless of what we do. Regardless, in fact, of what Diabolos, the embodiment of evil, and his lackeys do.

"This is no joking matter - it is very serious business we are discussing here. Yet, despite our avowals, we all continue, as one man, to act as if we are invincible - even though our own days are strictly numbered. And we forget, above all, that those who now weep will laugh with joy, and those who now laugh will weep and gnash their teeth.

Fr. Raj: Don't own the copyright (to human nature)...

"If the Master Architect had made the mistake of letting us humans have the authority to determine how the human person, made in His own image and likeness, could be disposed of, our resurrection from the dead, and quite possibly the redemption of fallen Man, would likely have been put in great jeopardy. The way we discriminate and cheat each other, and ride rough-shod over the rights of our fellow beings, there is no way God would have permitted us to fill the heavenly mansions with our cronies and to send his faithful servants to hell.

"And, in case you are wondering, the Master Architect and Craftsman could easily have entrusted us with the original portrait and the copyright to it by the simple act of giving each one of us at creation his or her own separate and distinct nature - as He did with the angels. But the angels who fell mucked it up even though they knew perfectly well that there was no hope of redemption for them if they strayed from the path of righteousness - if they allowed themselves to be locked in a mode that was incompatible with true self-actualization and their last end.

"Entrusting us with the copyright to our nature would almost certainly have complicated His plan of redemption in our case in the same way, possibly even rendering it impossible in practical terms. But we humans beings show by the way we act that we have never stopped clamouring for the copyright. We wish that we could act God and dispose of fellow humans any way we chose. That is what we 'demand' when we ride rough-shod over the rights of those who share our nature.

"But suppose we had been given the copyright! Then, as and when we courted death through rebellion against our Maker and eventually "died" in both the spiritual *and* physical sense, our 'bodies' would promptly return to dust, never to see the light of day or to rise up again. And our unmanageable spirits would be consigned to a place where they would suffer ceaselessly from the thirst for their Maker whom they themselves, freely and knowingly, would have abjured in what was effectively an unpardonable act of sacrilege. And those sad and highly regrettable developments, which would signal the end of our impudence and cheek, would also unfortunately have heralded the end of the original and otherwise really excellent works of art - exactly as happened in the case of Lucifer and his band of rebel spirits.

"In the meantime, as we died and individually despatched ourselves to heaven by remaining true to ourselves or to hell through our rebellion and intransigence, the Master Craftsman's responsibility for us individually would also end because, by being each one of us a separate and distinct specie just like angelic beings, we would constitute success stories or failures that were completely unrelated except for the fact that we were all of us original pieces of art that owed their existence from the same Master Craftsman.

"But, just because we do not own the copyright, it does not mean that the act of redemption does not require our cooperation. Indisputably, humans cannot attain salvation except through by virtue of the graces that are dispensed through the Church's sacraments. But, being free creatures, our individual salvation is also dependent on our cooperation with the graces that were earned for us by the Second Adam when He offered Himself as a 'Sacrificial Lamb' to His Father on our behalf, and permitted us sinful humans to visit death upon Him - a gruesome death on the cross. That is all the Deliverer asks of humans, namely cooperation with the divine grace by being faithful members of the Pilgrim Church. And that is not really asking too much when compared to the high price the Deliverer Himself paid to merit those graces with ourselves in mind.

Just as the graces, that are dispensed to humans through the sacraments and act *ex opere operato*, are given to us freely by the Deliverer, being free creatures ourselves, we are expected to freely cooperate to attain their individual salvation. We are on trial and must stir to take advantage of the opportunity availed to us to prepare and pass what you called the Church Triumphant Entrance Test. We must adopt the position of 'willing spirits' that accept to be recipients of the redeeming grace and work with it to attain eternal life. There is no short cut.

Fr. Raj: The inhabitants of hell...

"Talking about angels - there is one question that is perfectly valid to ask, and an answer to which, while simple, seems particularly revealing with lots of implications for us human beings. The question itself is actually quite elementary and is as follows: 'How come that one perfectly sane and exceedingly gifted angelic being winds up in heaven and able to fill the role of God's messenger in our regard, while another also sane and also exceedingly gifted angelic being ends up, tragically, in hell and as a demon committed to both our physical and spiritual destruction? The answer is, of course, free will, which is indisputably an important part of their angelic nature.

"Regardless of the answer to the controversial question 'Are there human beings in hell?', we seem to have a clear and unambiguous answer to the equally valid question 'How come one perfectly sane and very gifted human creature might be lost and in hell, while another also perfectly sane human creature is saved and in heaven?'. Whereas one creature, angelic or human, exercises its right to freedom of choice in its best interests and winds up in heaven, that apparently does not stop another angelic or human creature from opting to go to hell!

"And, unfortunately, that gives the erroneous impression that the perennial conflict between the forces of good and the forces of evil is evenly matched! Erroneous for two reasons. Firstly, the free will and the ability of angelic beings and their fellow human creatures to exercise their right thereto are gifts and are, by definition, rooted in an act of charity on the part of our Maker - in other words, they are rooted in goodness. Up until that point, evil is not even in the picture. Secondly, heaven, the place where the Maker abides in the company of the triumphant angels and saints, is paradisaical. Whereas hell, the place of the damned, where Diabolos once kept Adam and Eve and other holy men and women captive until the Son of Man descended there after his death and rescued them, is a rotten place.

"In the one-sided contest between good and evil, good triumphed over the reign of evil long ago, as expected, with the resurrection from the dead of the Son of Man. The victory is so complete that Diabolos and his condemned lackeys cannot do anything to try and promote their lost cause without God's express permission. And that is in addition to the fact that they have been judged and cast into the fire which does not go out. Far from being evenly matched, the contest is already over and Diabolos, as expected, is the outright loser.

"As it is, we can use the talents we received *gratis* from our Maker - both physical talents or spiritual talents - for our self-actualization, and also remember to show that we are thankful for those gifts; or we can use them and forget that we owe anyone a 'thank you'; or, alternatively, we can misuse them and damn anyone who suggests that things do not quite seem right. For that matter, we even can go jump into the sea - as we, indeed, often do in our efforts to frustrate the divine plan. But that is all we can do. Our Maker has made certain that our human nature, like a work of art that is too valuable to be left on permanent display, stays well out of the reach of morons like ourselves. Oafs who have never had any scruples in allowing Diabolos to have his way with these priceless prints from a masterpiece that is as singularly unique as the nature of man - prints we swore we would never part with at the time they were entrusted to us!

Fr. Raj: The prize (after fighting the good fight)...

"Because of the fact that we are created in the image of the Creator, and thanks to our spiritual nature and the role of the soul; thanks to the fact that, even though endowed with a free will, we were created to pay homage to the Lord our God and to serve Him with all our hearts and minds; and, of course, thanks to the fact that the Deliverer condescended to take on our human nature - human bodies now have a chance to add to the splendor in heaven; and to sparkle with a lustre so fulsome that the appreciation of the divine workmanship in bringing human beings into existence by the saints in heaven now completely transcends individual human relationships and the bonds between them.

"That is presumably why the Sacrament of Matrimony, so critical now to our survival as a human race on earth and, along with it, the marital bonds sanctified by it cease to be relevant. It is likely that even the distinction between human beings and the victorious spirits that came into existence without any bodily appendage is blurred, as all the victorious spirits, with or without a glorified body, join in anthem and glorify the Lord.

Fr. Raj: The real world: a ghostly world...

"Returning to the question of human souls versus human bodies, one preacher put it very succinctly. It was incorrect, in his words, to say that a human being had a soul. A human being *was* a soul and, according to him, only *had* a body, and a corruptible one at that!

"So, you can safely tell Fr. Cunningham, your Philosophy professor, that he is wrong when he says that Man is an *Animal Rationale* and things like that! We are not corporeal beings that are informed by the soul! It is a measure of our ignorance when we use the expression 'He/she gave up the ghost' in describing someone's 'demise'! One would have thought that it would be the ghost or soul which would shed the body when the latter became incapable of supporting the former in its temporal existence here on earth. And we certainly should start teaching our children that they we are spirits, and that they have bodies - bodies which they will eventually shed in the same way some reptiles shed their old skin even in mid-life.

"We who are baptised have even persuaded ourselves that we are better than those unbaptized folks who, unlike us, at least still try to practice fairness and equity in their dealings with fellow men. The paradox is that these other folks unwittingly end up bearing sterling witness to the unknown God in whose image they happen to be fashioned. As for those of us who have received formal invitations to the banquet, but think that baptism also confers on us the right to set our own rules of human conduct, the time is surely coming when we will find ourselves locked outside the banquet hall and vainly chanting 'Open, Lord! Open, Lord!'

"Let us face it. Every time we transgress, we essentially raise the same old issue relating to our commitment to conduct ourselves as behoves creatures that are made in the image of their Creator - and we should, of course, always remember that 'image of the Creator' and 'spiritual nature of human beings' are two ideas that are intrinsically the same. We raise that issue when we decide to be nasty to our neighbor, and do so each time we break any of God's other commandments. Looking at things from that angle certainly makes it easier to understand why mere intentions and thoughts may constitute sin. By the same token, it also becomes easier to understand why meritorious works may not necessarily be accompanied by deeds *per se.*

"I would go further and add that seeing things from that perspective also makes it easier to understand how people of goodwill, even though not members of the visible Church, may be headed for heaven, while those of us who have been specially invited to the banquet might be headed for some other place! And it makes it easier for all people of goodwill irrespective of religious affiliation to identify with our Savior who is also the Word through whom everything that is was made.

"It should not come as a surprise that it is children who have no difficulty accepting that they are spiritual beings, and understanding that it is not what is on the outside, but what is on the inside, that is of the essence. Until we start teaching them that material things matter, they typically subscribe to no such falsehoods. And until we adults impose ourselves on them and introduce them to all sorts of falsehoods, children, whether born in Mongolia, Peru, Siberia, California or Uganda, up until that time know that they are created in the image of their Maker. And they know, above all, that they are all brothers and sisters, until we start to teach them otherwise.

"Talking about teaching children, they are very easy to teach and learn easily, unlike us adults who have preconceived ideas. Hence their ability to absorb a great deal of material in a very short time. But, unfortunately, that is also why they are such easy prey - when we set upon them with our barrage of prejudiced notions about reality and the people around us. And, after we have done the devil's dirty work for him, we like to settle back and blame the mess in the world on 'Fate', by which we mean our Creator!

"I would even go further and say - at the risk of being excommunicated myself - that up until we adults begin to interfere with the attitudes and beliefs of children, all of them without any exception are members of both the visible and the invisible Church! And that is, perhaps, why our sacred Redeemer pleaded with His overzealous disciples that they let the children come to Him!

"It is clearly the failure to grasp that we human beings are spiritual beings which has resulted in so many people in the Church being scandalized by the recently promulgated dogmas to the effect that Adam and Eve had felt hunger and thirst, and had been no strangers to physical pain before their fall from grace, and also that it is spiritual death, not physical death, which is one of the consequences or by-products of sin. I suspect that it is also the reason the Pearl of Africa, as Churchill called it, has been receiving so many visitors since The Diaries and other artifacts were un unearthed! Certainly looks like Churchill and British Intelligence came quite close to identifying the birth-place of Adam and Eve.

Fr. Raj: In sum...

"The Deliverer, as you call Him, saves us from ourselves and also from evil. He died to expiate for our failures; then, as he rose from the dead, He freed the souls of the just who had been held in bondage in the bowels. We are still inclined to sin; and we still die. The difference now, though, is that we are subject to the judgement of Him who has completely routed Satan and spelled doom for his evil empire. The same goes for those who will still be kicking at the end of time - they too will face judgement.

"To sum up, overestimating our strength and underestimating the power of Satan - the ringleader of those who would dethrone the Creator if they had the power to do so - does not at all help this situation. Neither does cavorting with Satan or any one else who is in league with him. Just as playing sissy and suddenly pretending that we do not have the responsibility to exercise and diligently choose to follow our consciences isn't helpful either. These are very important points which cannot be overemphasized."

Father Oremus...

Father Oremus, a Canadian and the only North American on the seminary staff, taught Psychology. He had obviously been waiting patiently for the Indian to finish his lengthy harangue. As soon as Father Raj signalled that he was done, the Canadian was up on his feet. The last member of the panel to speak, Father Oremus did not waste any time getting to the point he had been dying to make.

"I will be quick and to the point, Reverend Mjomba. I am probably speaking for the distinguished members of this committee when I say that you deserve not just an 'A', but an 'A' Plus for the paper you have submitted. It is very well reasoned, and for one it doesn't appear as if any of the material in was plagiarized.

"However, my commitment to give you an 'A' Plus, instead of an 'F', is conditional. You must agree to burn all the available copies of this thesis as soon as we are done. You will understand why in a minute.

"The greatest danger your paper presents in my mind is this: for anyone to read and digest its contents and overall message, which is in fact orthodox by and large, it is necessary to spend a considerable time in what is effectively a prolonged chat with Beelzebub of all people! He is clearly the main character in this 'yarn' - that is what your paper, in spite of its merits, really is, isn't it!

"In the process of 'conversing' with Satan - there is no way that a thinking individual could just passively give him an ear. One inevitably starts to also place trust in him. There is, no doubt, a lot to be said for the bulk - if not all - of the arguments you have him verbalize. But I have to confess that you probably wouldn't have been able to make many of the points you have made as lucidly and eloquently as you did if you had not used the Evil One himself as the mouth-piece. I doubt very much if there is anybody else who could have. And so, as far as techniques go, you certainly discovered one which was brilliant and, I dare say, also effective.

"Still, this relationship is not the kind we are supposed to have with the tempter! It might be permissible from the point of view of academic freedom and creativity. But from the point of view of the priestly ministry - from the point of view of pastoral work - that is certainly debatable. I myself would rather have the faithful miss Satan's exhortations, however inspiring, in their entirety than encourage them in any way to start communing with a creature who is committed to sowing the seeds of death.

"If there is one point which this 'Thesis on Original Virtue' makes very clear, it is the fact that the devil is indeed very knowledgeable - that humans are well advised not to try and challenge him on that score; and thank God, because he is invisible, we humans generally do not get any opportunities to stare him down and try to argue with him. The thesis also makes it quite clear that we humans can beat him to it only when we put on the 'armor of Christ'!

"When the childhood innocence of a human is bolstered by the sacraments, then our ability to challenge the Prince of Darkness grows in leaps and bounds and soon eclipses the ability of *Sheitan* to tempt us. We are safe under the mantle of the Deliverer, the King of Kings and also Lord of Lords who nevertheless chose to be led away like a lamb to the slaughter, having agreed to pay the price for the decision of the first man and the first woman to ally themselves with Beelzebub, for the murderous conduct of humans against each other, the immorality, injustice, and for other transgressions that make humans look so hideous in the eyes of the Prime Mover. We are safe under the mantle of a Deliverer who, above all, deliverers the forsaken victims of a world out of control - a world that unjustly tramples on the innocent, and treats their cries and sufferings as if they are irrelevant and do not matter.

"And, by the way, you make the devil so believable, just to make sure that you are alright - that you have not ended up falling in his possession - it might be a good idea if we conducted a conditional exorcism. It is something I'm sure Father Cromwell covered in the Pastoral Theology Seminar.

"So, Sonny, do we have a deal?" Father Oremus asked in conclusion as his colleagues on the panel nodded in agreement.

"I think we can skip the conditional exorcism bit, Father Oremus" Mjomba quipped, to sustained applause and a nod of approval from Father Raj.

Father Oremus appeared to be mightily reassured that the man who heard Mjomba's weekly confessions did not consider a conditional exorcism necessary. And he was clearly relieved when Mjomba said: "Otherwise we have a deal!"

7. What Mjomba also wrote (in his thesis)

It was typical of Mjomba, who was not one to shy away from a topic, either because it was involved or perhaps even a hard sell, to try and tackle as many of the topics bearing on the theme of his thesis as possible. The thesis accordingly included a discussion of what he referred to as the abundant testimony that acknowledgement of the Prime Mover's supremacy was inescapable.

Mjomba wrote that nothing testified to the power and might of the Prime Mover as much as did the phenomena of life and death. It had always been obvious that the involvement of humans in bringing about life or terminating it was only in their capacity as intermediaries, with what actually occurred in either instance remaining a riddle.

Ageing, dependence and dying...

Talking about death - that phenomenon which, by all counts, was so unsavory to humans it automatically evoked feelings of dread and terror - Mjomba wrote that it was preceded by another phenomenon which did not cause as much fear or anxiety in humans, but some nonetheless. This was the ageing process.

Growing old also evidenced the power and might of the Prime Mover even though perhaps to a lesser extent than death did, Mjomba wrote. Unlike conception or death, ageing used that real but intangible thing called time to achieve its end. Even though humans did all they could to ignore the ageing process and had huge programs going to assist them in perpetuating the charade, it did not really help. the ageing process, as it evolved and took hold with the passage of time, had its way of slowly chipping away the often-times quite unbelievable egotism, arrogance and cavalier attitudes of humans, and bringing them gradually to their knees as it were just before death inflicted the *coup de grace*.

The contrast occurred in the lower animal realm where, Mjomba claimed, the birds, beasts, reptiles and other so-called lower beings viewed ageing as a blessing, and patiently waited on death which, when it finally came, was also embraced courageously in abeyance to the will of their Creator!

According to Mjomba, there was probably no significant correlation between the ageing process and immorality, contrary to the popular belie that the onset of puberty was accompanied by licentiousness and antipathy for authority both ecclesiastical and secular. He doubted that Adam and Eve's age bracket at the time they became so brazen as to dare the Prime Mover to act in the face of their intransigence would be indicative of any correlation between age and degeneracy, if it were known.

Mjomba wrote that it was a good thing it was not, as the so-called scientific community would by now undoubtedly have latched on to the idea that, at that particular stage in the lives of people, they were genetically prone to degeneracy and antisocial behavior - or some such foolish notion! But, all that notwithstanding, in the end every sign not just of life but of existence on earth or in the heavens, Mjomba wrote, proclaimed not just the existence of the Prime Mover, but His greatness as well.

Mjomba held the position that humans, even though free to choose between different alternatives and whims, were essentially dependent on the Prime Mover and on others from the time they were conceived in their mother's womb to the time they departed for the after-life. He suggested that the state of dependence underwent a decline as humans first grew older and became more capable of exercising personal autonomy only on the surface.

Humans, Mjomba wrote, continued to be dependent - indeed more so than before - even as they attained both physical and mental maturity. He argued that the reason for this lay in the fact that humans essentially began dying as soon as they were conceived in the womb!

Mjomba's argument that humans began dying as soon as they were conceived was based on the fact that cells in the embryo began dying at that time. Mjomba contended that if new cells did not develop quickly enough to replace the ones which were dying off, the newly conceived would not survive - and neither their owners.

To stave off death before birth, the unborn child had to strive to remain attached to its mother's umbilical cord. After birth, the baby strove to do whatever it took to suckle on its mother's breast and to take adequate rest just to keep death at bay. And when it started teething, the infant begun to supplement its intake of milk with solid foods that also required to be masticated, ingested and digested. It knew instinctively that it would die if it did not undertake those additional and obviously burdensome exercises - exercises that in turn caused muscles and bones in the infant to begin ageing earlier than they otherwise would and also faster.

Then, as soon as it became capable of moving on all its fours and of using its limbs, the little one made a strategic decision to put these and its other faculties to use in assisting adults to procure sustenance for the whole family and improve living conditions so everybody in the community could enjoy a longer life expectation.

And it would, of course, know by that time that it could not go on like that forever; and that, even though it had been reared up in society, it was essentially on its own and was in time going to pass from this life to another one in which its continued survival would not be contingent on its ability to provide or fend for itself in that fashion; and also that its dependence on its Prime Mover would actually be complete in that after-life.

Mjomba explained in a foot note that, contrary to popular belief, the performance of humans did not improve as they "grew up" or as they "developed" into adults, but it actually deteriorated. Mjomba argued that the human mind, for instance, did not start from a low point at birth and then improve as the human gained in "maturity" before declining with the on-set of old age. Rather, the performance of humans was at its peek at birth, as was evidenced by the speed of learning at that time, and began deteriorating steadily with the passage of time as humans "matured" - supposedly.

That also meant, contrary to popular myths, that human dependence, whether on the Prime Mover or on other humans, and already quite marked at birth, in fact increased as humans grew in years. Humans, faced with greater odds in infancy, employed more ingenuity in order to survive than they did in later life when they were clearly resigned to the fact that their days were numbered, Mjomba wrote. He added that children, knowing that they had to overcome greater challenges and eager to live life to the full, were more adept at coaxing their adult counterparts into assuming their responsibilities to society.

And that was due principally to the fact that children still enjoy their unadulterated innocence, and are unaccustomed to the ways of the world that are characterized by presumptiveness, a stubborn determination to have one's way and lord it over others folks, a reluctance to admit ones own faults, and most unfortunate of all a new found contempt by all adults so-called for the childlike simplicity that enables little children to recognize their dependence on the Prime Mover, and the critical role the recognition plays in the transition of humans from the state of being toddlers to the state of being young adults.

Mjomba added that it was this attribute of children that endeared them to the Deliverer, and that also guaranteed the Holy Innocents, whose lives were snuffed out prematurely by the brutal and wicked so-called Herod the Great, their crown.

Slower in their reflexes and in their ability to react inventively to unusual situations, adults - even though they did not like to admit it - were less capable of coping with the unknown and also felt much more insecure. Humans exercised more, not less, autonomy in their early years and became more dependent on the Prime Mover and on the rest of society as they grew older. And the craving to be "respected" that gripped individuals as they grew in years was reflective not of independence but of dependence. The desire to be hailed as "Sir" or "Madame" was really a disguised clamor for attention. And, according to Mjomba, the word "maturity" was a complete misnomer, and merely served to cloak the insecurity haunting the older generations.

He added that all the evils in the world, beginning with original sin, were perpetrated by humans who had supposedly come of age. When the so-called adults were not at the helm, on their own or conniving with others to engage in sins of omission or commission that were frequently disguised as good works, they typically were allowing themselves to be manipulated by others for selfish ends that were often passed off as patriotic deeds, simply because they lacked the moral fibre to conscientiously object to the obviously wicked schemes that were being hatched by their misguided compatriots who happened to be in positions of power.

The moment that the youth came of age, they found themselves ushered into a world in which nuts like Nero Claudius Cæsar Drusus Germanicus and Gaius Julius Cæsar were running around killing people in the name of Empire, and others immersed in their own peculiar enterprises and schemes that any one could see straight away were crooked to the hilt and left a lot to be desired in so far as virtue and integrity were concerned. It was just so ridiculous and of course also so scandalous.

Mjomba argued that recognition by humans of their dependence was what in turn induced in them the state of being child-like while they lived. But all too often humans deceived themselves that they had no need for either their Prime Mover or for anyone else, and that they were invincible and free to do as they wished with themselves. And they accordingly allowed themselves to slide into a life of fantasy, make believe and self-deception, eventually closing the door to true self-actualization.

That self-deception started, Mjomba claimed, with the accession of humans from the status of being a juvenile, which also supposedly implied immaturity, to young adulthood, which was supposedly the state that marked the transition from immaturity to maturity, and was the point at which humans supposedly graduated into fully responsible individuals; and, barring a conversion of some kind, the self-deception or state of being deluded, persisted all through the lives of the individuals! It was just so ridiculous, Mjomba wrote.

This effectively meant, Mjomba went on, that the vast majority of humans, including those who were supposedly role models, stepped into positions of responsibility and/or positions of power just as they were starting to exhibit symptoms of what amounted to psychopathic behavior as a consequence of the persistent self-deception. This was the same behavior that was mistakenly viewed by the equally misguided talking heads around them as evidence of "leadership qualities.

It was that profound self-deception that, according to Mjomba, led humans to increasingly place their reliance on intrigues and so-called backroom deals and secrecy as the accepted methods of governance; and as a consequence of which the world was now effectively controlled by secret societies, led by the mafia in Italy and others around the world that went by the strangest acronyms, but were all licensed to kill: M16, DGSE, CIA, CIO, TC2, DAS, SSS, CSIS, PET, AISI, MOSSAD, JIC, FBI, IB, SB, ISI, KGB, ASIO, FSB, and so on. Conceding that one was dependent on the Prime Mover allowed one to give credit to Him for the blessings that came one's way during one's life-time without being the victim of a guilty conscience or losing one's self-respect in the process, Mjomba contended.

In the final analysis, it was really immaterial whether humans, made in the image and likeness of the Prime Mover Himself, acknowledged that they were dependent on Him or not. Unless and until humans found the one and the only object that comprised their last end, namely the Prime Mover, all their efforts in achieving fulfillment and actualization would go to waste. All humans without exception pined for those things and, of course, could only find them at the Prime Mover's pleasure, with the Prime Mover's help, and in the Prime Mover. This would always be so regardless of what humans themselves individually fancied. This was also dependence *par excellence*, Mjomba wrote.

Mystery of pain explained away...

Mjomba compared pain to the proverbial bitter pill that humans needed to take when they fell ill because of the ensuing benefits. He also suggested that what people really meant when they referred to the "mystery of pain" was the "mystery of life" which went hand in hand with burdens that people had to carry while they lived. And he went on that there was a direct relationship between the "mystery of redemption" and "mystery of life" with the principal actor being one and the same. Even though humanity had been redeemed and individual humans given a chance to mend fences with their Prime Mover, individual humans found salvation when they agreed to bear the burdens He sent their way.

To follow in the foot steps of the Deliverer, they were obliged to "take up their crosses" (which was another way of saying "bear their individual burdens patiently"), and then stagger after Him along the *Via Dolores* and up to the summit of Mt. Calvary. It was the only way humans could earn their crown.

By its very definition, "carrying one's cross" had to be a nasty thing - something that humans would shrink from instinctively and do their best to avoid. It fit the description "bitter pill" aptly.

Mjomba elaborated, in another foot note, that there was also a connection in his view between the dependence exhibited by humans - namely dependence on the Prime Mover and on other humans - and the so-called mystery of pain and suffering. According to Mjomba, the survival instinct of humans depended in large measure on the fact that they felt pain when something went wrong with their system. The pain could be physical or mental or a combination of both.

According to Mjomba, the pain felt by a human when a finger got stuck in a grinder for instance helped to ensure that the individual affected took quick and timely action to save whatever remained of the finger, and before the hand and perhaps even the rest of the arm also became wedged in the grinder to his or her great detriment. And if humans did not feel hunger when it began to gnaw in their middle, they would start to realize that there was something the matter with them when they were already a bag of bones or even too famished to recover.

Humans were in that sense very dependent on the Prime Mover for his foresight in making them susceptible to pain and suffering. Pain and suffering that was caused by other humans alerted the victims to the dangers lurking behind smiling faces and beguiling words uttered by those who led lives that were less than upright. And, of course, the fact that pain was a nasty thing which humans sought to avoid at all costs deterred them from doing things that were forbidden and the price for doing which included pain and suffering - when they could not be dissuaded otherwise.

Mjomba ascribed the mystery surrounding the phenomenon of pain and suffering to the fact that the Prime Mover was not in the habit of intervening to stop the pain and suffering just as He did not exercise His power to stop humans from knowingly choosing to do things that imperilled their eternal life. In the case of pain and suffering endured by the innocent at the hands of the wicked, the all loving and all knowing Prime Mover permitted these things to take their toll - which was often quite unbearable - because He had decreed that He himself would take His revenge on the perpetrators in due course.

As far as those at the receiving end were concerned, putting up with undeserved pain and suffering had the immediate effect of driving home to them the fact that they were totally dependent on the Prime Mover, who also took care to ensure that they had the fibre to withstand what came their way, and also promised to reward them (in their afterlife) for joining the Deliverer in His atonement of the sins of men by putting up with the affronts of evil intentioned people.

As descendants of Adam and Eve, humans had after all been banished from the sight of the Prime Mover because of the original sin committed by the first man and the first woman. Nasty as pain and suffering (and, indeed, death itself) were, they did not compare with the fact that humans were the "poor, banished children of Adam". Whereas banishment was banishment and only the Deliverer, himself a member of the God-head, could reverse it, pain and suffering - and death - were a punishment for the rebellion of Adam and Eve, and allowed humans, none of whom (other than the Deliverer and His blessed mother) were altogether innocent in any case, to join with the Deliverer in atoning for sin.

It was really inconsequential whether the pain and suffering was caused by other wicked men or was attributable to "acts of God". It was the reason humans were expected to forgive fellow humans - and even "turn the other cheek" if necessary. Not doing so implied that they held a grudge against the Prime Mover also for natural disasters and things like that even if they did not say so. Thus, according to Mjomba, the fact that humans - and other living creatures - were capable of enduring pain only emphasized their dependence on the Prime Mover and His goodness.

Helpless in the face of pain and suffering on the one hand and the inclination to sin on the other, the obvious solution for humans in any part of the globe and in any epoch was to invoke the mercies of the Prime Mover. Mjomba commented that in this particular regard, a Masai peasant guarding his herd of cattle from marauding lions with a spear, and thankful to the Prime Mover for being cunning enough to outfox the predators in such an uneven match, was more prayerful than a preacher who relied on his rhetorical skills and a booming voice to attract and retain a core audience without which he would start operating at a loss and go out of business.

And, of course, there were those who thought that because they happened to live in these times - in the New Millennium - they had to be better than folks who inhabited Planet Earth in ages past, including the immediate descendants of Adam and Eve. Oblivious to the pollution all around them to which they individually contributed in no small measure daily, and also to the fact that Adam and Eve and their immediate descendants lived to be nine hundred plus years, many modern humans so-called believed that the world itself was a much better place to live in now than it would have been without them when the exact opposite was true!

Mjomba went on that while the path of righteousness was well marked and clearly identifiable, with the traffic on it heading in one direction, it had proved all too easy, judging from the record, for humans to stray from that path; and that humans found it really hard to resist joining the crowd on Broadway where the traffic headed in a thousand different directions all at once. It was, of course, not in their interest to walk on Broadway. But they were free and did it all the same.

Mjomba concluded with the comment that the mission of the Deliverer was to get the human traffic back on the path of truth. That was a daunting task humanly speaking. But, noted Mjomba, the Deliverer was not just human and a brother. He was one of the three persons constituting the Blessed Trinity in accordance with revelation.

The "contraption"...

Claiming that he was not exactly speaking from any sort of personal experience, Mjomba wrote that the human body as he saw it was no more than a contraption whose sole purpose was to facilitate the passage of the human soul through the first stage of its existence which was here on earth and temporal by design.

If the soured relations between the Prime Mover and humans had not been restored in the particular manner in which it had, involving as it did the Son of the Most High, the only thing that would have survived passage of the human from this life to the next would have been the soul, and the human body, or "casing" in which the soul had been "imprisoned" so to speak, would have been left to disintegrate into dust once and for all. And it would have been Beelzebub and his troops who would be lying in wait on the other side to "welcome" souls in a replay of what they did to Adam and Eve and others who must be very thankful that the Deliverer turned up there in "hell" and rescued them from their "captivity".

As it was, the involvement of the Man-God in the redemption of humans, Mjomba wrote, and specifically his triumph over death, resulted in a radically changed situation. Even though they did not really deserve it, humans not only could now look forward to resurrection at the end of time to the extent that the body was designed as a constituent part of human nature, but they along with their resurrected bodies, in the most extra-ordinary development of all, could likewise look forward to "beatific vision"!

Mjomba saw this as signifying a special kind of victory that only a divinity could pull off. Out of something as vile as sin, something inestimably good, which would otherwise not have been there or available, had directly ensued! Mjomba wrote that he could not help wondering at the number of times this had been replicated in the sinful world in which humans lived!

All these things notwithstanding, the fact that a sizeable chunk of earth consisting of the remains of humans will actually end up in heaven as glorified bodies of saints raised questions about what would become of the rest of the earth's crust. Mjomba wrote that he himself expected that too to be transformed into something useful at the very least even though the Prime Mover had the ability to return it to its pristine nothingness.

And that in turn raised questions about things like the Eternal City and other human artifacts like the pyramids, the Great Wall of China and things of that nature, not to mention marine, vegetative and animal life, and the galaxies. Mjomba was certain that if the Shroud of Turin was indeed the original parchment the holy women employed when embalming the lifeless body of the Deliverer after they succeeded in wresting it from His grieving mother, it too was going to survive Doomsday!

Mjomba was aware that it was common practice for artists to depict certain saints in poses that showed them communing with birds and animals or just clutching a twig. Mjomba had always thought that this was an excellent idea indeed, if only because these works of art highlighted the complementarity of sanctity and nature.

Mjomba also supposed that, after designing the earth and the interplanetary system, as well as plants, birds and animals, from scratch and causing them to spring into being, the Master Artist not only was capable of providing, but probably planned to provide these works of creation of His - works whose beauty He Himself lauded even before angels and after them humans were capable of doing so -

with some role, and perhaps a significant role at that, come Doomsday.

The "universal" Church...

Mjomba went on to write that Christianity, rooted in Middle Eastern traditions rather than in European traditions as was widely assumed, was used by Westerners to condemn or even dismiss off hand religious beliefs and cultures that were not in conformance with their experience. Even though probably unavoidable because humans were humans, this was a tendency that, without a doubt, had grave consequences for the work of evangelization. According to Mjomba, the label "animism", itself a creation of Westerners, seemed designed to evoke in people's minds images of people who distastefully engaged in the "occult" so-called and whose worship and reverence for the Prime Mover was misplaced because they supposedly believed in "superstition", a phrase that was another Western creation!

Whatever was wrong with traditional African and other non-Western beliefs and religious practices was probably nothing or insignificant at the most, Mjomba asserted, compared with what was wrong or plain unacceptable in the traditional Western beliefs and religious practices, many of which exerted an inordinate influence in on Christianity. Mjomba wrote that the reverence for the earth in African and other societies did not have a place in Christianity except as something to be condemned.

At any rate - according to Mjomba - while they didn't see anything wrong with incorporating their own customs and traditions in the liturgy of the Church, Westerners apparently thought it was unimaginable that other cultures, with their treasured customs and traditions, could in some way be compatible with worship of the Prime Mover! In other words, people belonging to non-Western cultures were expected to do something quite preposterous, namely abandon their customs and traditions as a condition for becoming followers of the Deliverer!

Westerners evidently interpreted the phrase "founded on a rock called Peter" to mean that the Deliverer founded a Church for some people and not for others, unless they were prepared to abandon their ways of life and started doing everything the way Palestinians did! And it was, even then, notable that Westerners themselves didn't follow their own maxims on converting to Christianity! Greeks, Romans, Gauls, Anglo Saxons, Huns, Celtics, Turks, Russians and other "Europeans" who embraced Christianity were not required to abandon their customs and traditions.

Giving an example of what might have been lost, Mjomba wrote that the languages of "pagans" in sub-Saharan Africa whose cultures have been under threat frequently included commonly used expressions that amounted to expressions of faith in the Prime Mover, like: "The Creator Himself alone knows!" and "Oh, God the Almighty One!". And, unlike similar expressions in Italian, English, French, and other Western languages which made a practical joke of the Prime Mover, these were serious expressions which were uttered with due solemnity. In Mjomba's view, any loss in that regard had to be deemed a significant loss given the prevalent use of swearwords and other unacceptable epithets in Western societies today.

In Mjomba's view, the best way to approach differences in religious beliefs and practices was to follow the advice the Deliverer gave to his disciples when some of them reported that they had seen a stranger who did not belong to their group talking well about Him. Following that advice, they presumably ignored the negative in what that preacher who belonged to a different sect was saying and accepted him on the strength of the positive content of the message he was spreading about the Deliverer.

Mjomba did not recall the exact words which the Deliverer is quoted in the Gospels as using, and did not in any case think that the brief mention of that incident represented everything the Deliverer taught His disciples about religious tolerance. How to love one's enemies - and no doubt also how to accept fellow humans who espoused different views religious or otherwise - was after all what His teaching was all about. But the fact that He had to devote so much of His life to preaching love of the neighbor and tolerance also said something about the target of His message.

Mjomba wrote that the Deliverer obviously knew better than anyone else that those humans would ravenously hate and be intolerant as long as the Doomsday clock continued ticking, and that those who would try to love everyone they encountered in their lives, including those who were a nuisance or even an absolute menace, in the physical as well as the spiritual sense, would not find His act an easy one to follow.

It was not in doubt that the Deliverer established a "Church", founding it upon a rock called "Cephas" according to both tradition and the scriptures! "*Tu es Petrus; et super hanc petram Ecclesiam meam edificabo*", Mjomba wrote, citing the scriptural authority that few disputed, but many apparently found hard to accept. And, of course, if the powers of hell were not going to prevail against that Church because of the fact that it would be infused with the sanctifying power of the Holy Ghost, it did not at all mean that those powers would never succeed in prevailing against either its individual members or even its functionaries, Mjomba asserted.

And there was equally no doubt that the Deliverer and also High Priest empowered those he hand handpicked to be fishers of men with the laying on of hands in very specific ways, some of which we have knowledge of only thanks to something called "tradition", according to Mjomba. Those fishers of men or members of the hierarchy of what the Catechism referred to as the "Pilgrim Church" were empowered to "teach", and even to "tie" and to "loosen" whatever.

But while the Deliverer, the head of the "holy people of God" and also a member of the Godhead was perfect, and members of the Church could be called "saints" - even though "the Church was holy" - the sanctity of the Church, whilst real and not imaginary, was still lacking in perfection. Meaning that perhaps a case could be made that excommunication, while certainly justifiable in any instance in which the actions of a member threatened the Church's existence and excising or "cutting off" the member from the rest of the Church "in self-defense" was the only way to head off a catastrophe, at least in theory, could be based on faulty judgement.

And so, while effectual if carried out because of the specific nature of the empowerment, it seemed conceivable that an instance or instances of excommunication may well have been avoidable and to that extent unnecessary simply because of the fact that the decision to excommunicate or not to excommunicate was made by individuals from the body of saints and not the High Priest Himself.

But, leaving poor judgement and things like that aside, there certainly would be some among those who were called to minister to the holy people who, not unlike Judas like before them, would not shy away from betraying the master with a kiss even, according to Mjomba. Estimating that number at around a twelfth of the active ministry at any point of time during the life of the Church was probably conservative, Mjomba declared.

Mjomba even held the position that the Deliverer's warning about the false prophets who would descend on the world in the last days was really a warning that there would be a crop of new "churches" that would be founded by people claiming to be acting with His blessing or on His explicit orders, a situation that would make it really hard for souls to find their way past those "false prophets" into the Church. However well meaning, those who explicitly rejected the Church the Deliverer Himself founded could not be speaking for it at the same time, Mjomba asserted.

Ironically, Mjomba wrote, the reason many "believers" were attracted to the "new" churches and eschewed what Mjomba referred to as "the one, holy, Catholic Church", by which he meant the Church of Rome, was the genuine - but according to him groundless - fear that this so-called "traditional" Church had been taken over by the Antichrist and was now under the effective control of the prince of darkness! Terrible as disunity in God's Church was, the emergence of these "rival" churches fulfilled a prophecy - the prophecy regarding the ascendancy of false prophets, Mjomba asserted! And it naturally would not surprise him if some of these churches passionately espoused apartheid and other strange caste systems, or some other "doctrines" of that mold, while claiming to be divinely instituted. And if they murdered in the name of God, it wouldn't be the first time humans "sacrificed" fellow humans to pacify the strange divinities they worshipped!

Mjomba wrote that it was not at all surprising to him that, at a time when there was also this vast and ever growing number of biblical scholars who appeared to have complete mastery over the Gospels and even books of the Old Testament, there was now, all of a sudden and as never before in living memory, this proliferation of churches all of which claimed to be the one and only "true" Church founded by the Deliverer. And in the rush to establish churches, the fact that knowledge of the Prime Mover is revealed not to the "learned" but to little ones had pretty much been lost sight of.

Mjomba hoped that those who founded those churches had fully considered and thought through the fact that it was a grave matter indeed for an individual to set up oneself as the leader of a "church" that might be in competition with the Church founded by the Deliverer, whatever its apparent shortcomings. And, of course, any action of that nature was self-defeating in the final analysis, according to Mjomba, because the action to establish new churches suggested that the leaders of those new churches were sinless - or at least better than those the Deliverer Himself might have called to His ministry. It was all the more serious because those who did so could not guarantee that the doctrines which the newly founded church organizations spread were true or orthodox. And, unfortunately, the doctrines which were frequently misrepresented - presumably in good faith - pertained to the divinity of the Deliverer and the sanctifying power of the Deliverer's precious blood!

That was the problem with going off on a limb to try and change the world. In the absence of a special calling or vocation, Mjomba wrote, chances were that the individual would be really just playing out his/her fantasies, goaded on by misplaced zeal and a false sense of piety! The other problem was that pride in humans drove them to think that they, each individually, were not merely special, but extra-special and in fact more so than any other living being, as if that was possible - with everyone being more special than everyone else all at once! The fact, nonetheless, was that all humans not only liked to imagine that they were special messengers of the Prime Mover, but seemed to treat that as a condition for accepting that they were His creatures - as if *to believe* in the Prime Mover automatically entitled one *to be* the Prime Mover's *special* messenger!

Mjomba wrote that the temptation to use the "Word of God" to justify whatever one had a mind to do clearly had never been greater than in these times when, operating on purely business principles, one could "start a ministry" that was capable of raking in millions. These were the same principles that were being successfully used to start highly profitable "non-profit" organizations - non-profits to save the forests and the planet; nonprofits to help business operators operate more profitably; nonprofits to help one start a successful (or "profitable") non-profit venture - and what have you! Mjomba went on that it had become so difficult nowadays to differentiate between non-profit organizations and lobbyists, it had become standard practice, for donors to clearly specify exactly what the gift or contribution may be used for.

Mjomba asserted that helping members of one's flock to rise to greater heights in the arena of money making had already become an important part of the pastor's job description in some "churches" and, consequently, nothing could really surprise him anymore!

The "Gospel of Creation"...

It was hard to find humans who were humble and truly "born again" who did not imagine that they were more special than other humans, Mjomba wrote. Yes, born again - by which he meant "becoming a child" like, say, St. Theresa of the Child Jesus or St. John the Baptist or Mary Magdalene after she had renounced her old ways. The key to "being born again", according to Mjomba, was acceptance that humans, on their own, were weaklings in the face of any temptation and that they were able to keep the commandments by cooperating with the graces of the Prime Mover which the Deliverer, a man-God and their brother, merited with His death on the tree and which were now in fact freely "available" to all humans who chose to play along.

Adam and Eve, Mjomba went on, thought that they were not just special but extra special, and therefore did not rest until they had tried to pull off their failed *coup de etat* against the Prime Mover. Judas Iscariot thought he was really special - more special than, say, Peter or Matthew; and he even imagined at one point that he was saving "progressive" folks who knew the value of money and other things of this world from a Deliverer who was not prepared to play by the rules of their game!

Judas Iscariot, a Christian, was in effect propagating his own Christian doctrine as all humans in fact try to do until such time as they become "converted" and start "living like little children". Mjomba wrote in his thesis that perhaps there was a lesson to be learnt from Judas Iscariot's own attempted *coup de etat* by those who walked in the footsteps of the Deliverer as leaders of the Church. Peter - the ever bumbling Peter who was Mjomba's usual culprit - had apparently mastered the lesson, but may be not so some of his successors who would have been inclined to "excommunicate" the betrayer and be done with him instead of continuing to encourage him to do better things as the Deliverer Himself did, wining and dining with Judas Iscariot to the very end and even allowing the man who would go down in history as the symbol of betrayal to embrace and kiss Him in the moments before He was led off to His ignominious death on the tree.

According to Mjomba, some popes thought they were so special they could use their sacred office to enjoy themselves with complete impunity! There were those in positions of authority who, like Pontius Pilate, thought they were *very* special - so special in fact that they could wage wars based on falsehoods and do other outrageous things that brought miseries to the innocent at whim without giving a thought to the fact that that authority came to them from above. Then there were those executives of greedy corporations who thought they were very special indeed and, even after they had

had a whale of a time at the expense of the common man, imagined that they would - when the time came - prance, arm in arm with the likes of Mother Theresa and Francis of Assisi past St. Peter, into heaven!

And there were others who were laughing and making merry now and thought they were extra special, but whose turn to weep and gnash their teeth was around the corner. They were the citizens of some of the so-called "super powers" who were rolling in affluence thanks to the fact that their leaders, in furtherance of their "national interests" went out of their way to exploit the resources and wealth of the so-called "developing" nations. That exploitation took many forms, the most insidious of which was "bribery" that was touted as "economic aid", but invariably ended up in the pockets of a few individuals in leadership positions while the future of those developing nations ended up being mortgaged to the super powers in question.

Mjomba was thinking of the citizens of those nations whose economic power had been built on that sort of thievery and who had, in his view, to realize that "those who, directly or indirectly, have taken possession of the goods of another, are obliged to make restitution of them, or to return the equivalent in kind or in money, if the goods disappeared, as well as the profit or advantages their owner would have legitimately obtained from them", and that they accordingly had some making good to do if they did not want to be weeping and gnashing their teeth later. And those others who were now laughing and making merry at the expense of their fellow citizens in whatever nations they happened to live also needed to remember that "every offence committed against justice and truth entails the *duty of reparation*, even if its author has been forgiven".

Then there were those "messengers" of the Prime Mover, regardless of their religious persuasion, who thought they were so special they could "prey" on their gullible, if well intentioned, "flocks", feeding them with self-serving tidbits to make them feel good instead of the whole "bitter" or "unpleasant" truth, and giving them "false" hopes of redemption in the process. And then there were those others who had no scruples about "bending" the truth to increase their personal popularity with certain types of audiences or to get elected to office.

And, of course, the devil regarded himself as very special - so special, in fact, that he did not think that it was enough to be the marvel he had been created to be. And the devil, with one false step, lost his position as a gracious, highly respected headman among the choirs of angels and became a disgraced, good-for-nothing, hate-filled demon, who was now only fit for eternal punishment in that place of unquenchable fire which the Deliverer referred to as Gehenna.

According to Mjomba, when Diabolos confronted the Deliverer and suggested that the Deliverer, because He was "special", could inherit the earth's wealth if He desisted from carrying out His Father's will, the devil was in effect enunciating his own gospel, and one which went completely counter to the "word of the Living Prime Mover" and to the conscience. Mjomba went on that, since then, humans had come up with many variations of the "gospel according to the devil"; and that those targeted were actually taken in and fell for the empty promises of "salvation" from the lot of being a human. In fact, according to Mjomba, it had even become part and parcel of the human predicament to confront and have to deal with so many conflicting "messengers" of the Prime Mover, perhaps never quite knowing if one had already ruled out of consideration the true messenger of the Prime Mover and had whole-heartedly embraced the messenger who might turn out to be false!

Mjomba wrote that if there had not been any false gospels in existence, and if the only thing out there was the Gospel of Creation, humans who were hungry and thirsting for Truth (which they all admittedly were) would definitely have an easier time getting to it. He went on that those humans who had the cheek to knowingly enunciate false gospels tailored to their personal desires and who proceeded to live accordingly were in the same boat as Lucifer. Even though they were now laughing and making merry thanks to those "gospels", according to Mjomba, they now also were "having their fill", and that was going to come back in time to haunt them!

Mjomba continued that, like Diabolos, humans too were very *very* clever and frequently put up a show of faithfulness to the Prime Mover as a way of masking their unfaithfulness! And they were always trying to "promote" themselves in the public eye; and these same people could not resist the temptation to try and "bring down" fellow humans by trumpeting the fact that humans generally could not engage in any meritorious activity on their own without the help of the Prime Mover's grace. It was as if they could not advance themselves except by dragging others down. In a way, fallen humans were like the devil - an extremely clever creature who understood better than humans did that humans - just like their angelic counterparts - could not accomplish any good save with the inspiration and assistance of the Prime Mover, and who accordingly took full advantage of that human predicament to bring down ruin upon humankind as well.

Lucifer, instead of ruining things for himself "in the beginning", would have been much better off spending his time praying and giving glory to his Creator, renewing his commitment to do the will of the Prime Mover who sustained him through each passing moment of his existence. But instead of "praying always" as he was supposed to, Lucifer started fancying that he could enunciate a new "gospel". That gospel, unlike the divine "Gospel of Creation" which took full cognizance of the fact that the Prime Mover was the Prime Mover and creatures were creatures, sought to turn the tables around so that Lucifer, a creature, would be equal to the Prime Mover without regard to the fact that the Prime Mover was the one and the only prime mover!

The fatal flaw in the gospel according to Lucifer was of course the underlying supposition that the Gospel of Creation was somehow lacking. And that presaged doom for any creature that attempted to live by any other gospel. And so, it came to pass that Lucifer and the host of angels who chose to follow the gospel according to Lucifer found themselves booted out of heaven. Their numbers and the fact that many of them, like Lucifer, had been destined, upon passing the Church Triumphant Entrance Test, to occupy lofty positions did not matter. They were all booted out of heaven - roughly half of the angels in existence at the "time".

According to Mjomba, the hosts of angels who fell from grace with Lucifer were very clever creatures - many times cleverer than humans! But they found out that they had acted "real foolish" the moment they turned their backs on Him-Who-Was-Truth and also undisputed Prime Mover. Because they were, strictly speaking, not living "in time" but "at the beginning" when the Prime Mover "decided" to share his *Esse* with "creatures" by bringing them into "being" and also because they were pure spirits, they couldn't have a second chance after flunking the Church Triumphant Entrance Test. And great was their fall, because they were such lofty creatures.

Everything similarly pointed to the importance of praying always for humans as well - praying to the Prime Mover who not only sustained humans from moment to moment, but kept them safe from themselves and also from the snares of the devil. But instead, and goaded on by the tempter, they wasted their time and energy trying fruitlessly to come up with good and effective substitute gospels for the Gospel of Creation - efforts that were intended to help them shirk their responsibilities as "children" of the Prime Mover and that would all eventually come to naught.

These "gospels", Mjomba wrote, were not gospels that had necessarily been committed to writing. They remained for the most part unwritten and inside the minds of humans. Some of the "gospels" were cast as interpretations of the Gospel of Creation, and others as philosophies of life that were supposedly unconcerned with the destiny of Spiritual Man. Others were cast as interpretations of the Sacred Scriptures which, Mjomba pointed out, were only a tiny albeit important part of the Gospel of Creation. But some of these "apocryphal" gospels, when not directly derived from the "gospel according to the devil", were based on personal, untested impressions of life, fantasies of individual humans, or even on wishful thinking by humans.

In the last analysis, if a variation of the Gospel of Creation was in error, it did not really matter whether it was depicted as a philosophy of life that claimed to be dissociated from religion, or as an interpretation of the "gospel according to the devil", or even as an interpretation of the Gospel of Creation; because the purpose of any gospel which contradicted the Gospel of Creation was the same - to define a new set of parameters for human existence that were according to an individual's personal liking and not parameters that were in conformity with the Gospel of Creation and will of the Prime Mover.

The most important thing to remember, Mjomba wrote, was that despite the rebellion of Lucifer and his cohorts, and that of humans, "Good" still reigned supreme, and the Gospel of Creation remained paramount. Mjomba added that there was no better rebuff to this "foolishness" (of enunciating new gospels) than the rebuff that Satan got when he unsuccessfully tempted the Deliverer, or the rebuke Peter received when he also tried to stop the Deliverer from proceeding to Jerusalem well-knowing that the purpose of that journey was to pay the price for the intransigence of men in fulfilment of the Prime Mover's promise to humans.

And it was a "good thing" that Beelzebub and also Peter were rebuffed, and that in the end the Deliverer opted for the company of Abraham and Moses at the transfiguration and not for the company of the tempter. It was good - very *very* good - because the alternative in which the Son of Man would be in opposition to the Word through Whom all things were brought into existence was simply unthinkable! But that had been Satan's objective, and it also showed how supremely evil, wicked and dangerous Lucifer became when he fell from grace.

It was precisely for that reason that the Deliverer warned all to beware of the evil spirit, Mjomba asserted. But, unfortunately, humans calling the devil a variety of names engaged in what Mjomba claimed was condemnation that was for the most part a farce, completely meaningless, and useless. And many even did that while actually shielding the evil spirit and their own evil inclinations from exposure, according to Mjomba.

Because those working for the devil were also exploiting the fact that humans were now inclined to sin and simultaneously dependent on the Prime Mover's grace, they had to understand that doing so for their wicked ends was a very *very* serious thing which made them as odious in the sight of the Prime Mover as the evil spirit himself. And yet, according to Mjomba, that was what almost everyone was busy doing.

But with the Reformation - which set the stage for the initial appearance of a multiplicity of "Christian" churches - a fact of history, Mjomba was of the view that everyone now, regardless of his/her traditional faith, had a responsibility to undertake whatever research was necessary to establish for him/herself the veracity of the claims of his/her "church" to being the "true" Church; and that included Catholics. And any way, what "Catholic" could truthfully claim to be so "full of grace" that he/she had no room left to "grow' in his/her knowledge of as well as love for the Deliverer and His "Mystical Body". After all, the essence of "becoming like a child" or "being born again" was the recognition that one was totally dependent on the Prime Mover not only for the grace that enabled one to perform meritorious acts, but above all for the blessings that came one's way.

In the case of Catholics, a very important blessing consisted in being chosen by the Deliverer to be members, not just of the invisible Church, but to be members also of the visible Church set up by the Deliverer to guide the "believers" to guide to the New Jerusalem after He had fulfilled the Prime Mover's covenant with the nation of Israel. Chosen, Mjomba went on, to be not just coheirs and co-partners with the Jews in the promise, but to be the salt of the earth!

And certainly Catholics could not claim to be better than the man who had been blind from birth, and whose sight was restored by the Deliverer. Born blind like that man, they now see only thanks to the fact that the Deliverer came. If He had not come, Catholics wouldn't be seeing anything - just like everyone else. And to the extent Catholics claim that they do see, to that extent they too have become blind. And they certainly could not claim to be better than

Peter who promptly deserted the Deliverer, even before the first cock crow, after swearing that he would die rather than deny Him!

But was it not Catholics who prayed daily saying *"Quonian tu solus Sanctus*" (translated "For you alone are holy"? This was even though, added Mjomba laconically, it was only seminarians and the clergy who understood what was mumbled! And, indeed, the "Church of Rome", if it was indeed the "true" Church, had a very special responsibility to right whatever wrongs had given rise to this phenomenon of multiple "Christian" churches in the exact same way it had a very special responsibility to take the gospel to the ends of the earth.

When he was orally defending his thesis, Mjomba remembered that it was in fact a dogma of the Church that there was always scope for all members of the "apostolic Church" to grow in the knowledge and love of the Deliverer and His Mystical Body. Knowing that he had the full backing of the professors, Mjomba made the point about the responsibility of Catholics to undertake research to establish for themselves the veracity of the Church's claims to being the true Church even more forcefully - so forcefully in fact he upset a goodly number of his fellow seminarians, many of whom apparently imagined that they were in a sense "saved" (the very thing for which the "reformers" turned "heretics" stood condemned) and were inclined to the view that only the separated brethren and unbelievers needed to worry about that sort of thing!

Unfortunately, no individual in the Church, be it a member of the laity, a member of a religious order, a priest or a bishop, or even the Pontiff of Rome himself, could presume to undertake that task - the task of righting wrongs done by Catholics to one another and to others on his or her own accord, and without the help of divine grace. Which effectively meant, according to Mjomba, that there was nothing useful that anyone could do nothing unless that individual was specifically called by the Deliverer and High Priest to undertake that important mission, and equipped accordingly!

Mjomba wrote that any attempt by self-appointed individuals to "reform" the Church or to "right wrongs" that had been committed by unworthy successors to the apostles carried with it the risk of making a situation that, humanly speaking, was already hopeless a great deal worse. Mjomba even mused aloud, as he defended his thesis, that if writing it had not been a requirement for going on to Major Orders, he would have personally preferred to remain noncommittal as far as discussing matters of his faith was concerned.

Individuals or groups of individuals going out on a limb to "fix things" in the Mystical Body of Christ were essentially acting like the apostle Peter who tried, on one occasion, to prevent the Deliverer from going to Jerusalem to die for the salvation of humans; and who tried, on another occasion, to prevent the constabulary of the Sanhedrin from laying their hands on His Master by striking out with his sword in a near successful attempt to change the course of history. Actions by self-appointed "reformers" were misguided, in Mjomba's view, and could also be likened to the attempt by the mother of two of the Deliverer's disciples to stake out a claim for the best "seats" in heaven, so one of them would sit on the victorious Deliverer's right, and another on His left! Mjomba added that the number of times that humans had been caught pining for a different kind of Deliverer *and* a different sort of Church was legion.

All of which, Mjomba conceded, left the question about how to go about righting wrongs committed by individuals in positions of authority in the "Prime Mover's Church" unanswered. And that was, perhaps, as it should be, he quipped! But that did not mean that Church leaders did not need to humble themselves and accept responsibility for the fact that some among them have sown and may be continuing to sow the seeds of disunity. They had to step up to the plate and at least take full responsibility for their actions, even if they were not up to the task of taking measures to correct the situation.

And again, *if* the Church of Rome was the successor to the Nation of Israel as the guardian of divine truth, *then* its responsibility with regard to the so-called "Separated Brethren" was automatically interwoven with its mission of spreading the message the Deliverer had entrusted it to the ends of the earth. And certainly those responsible, either now or in the future, for "ministering" to the faithful and for indirectly "administering" the Mystical Body of Christ, because they were quite capable of making erroneous administrative decisions just like any other "administering agency", had to now try and draw a lesson or two from any "errors" that the Church hierarchy at the time of the Reformation may have made.

Mjomba even then had a nagging feeling that there was something else afoot. Mjomba was writing his thesis on Original Virtue almost two thousand after the Deliverer had established his Church and, addressing Peter, declared: "*Et ego dico tibi, quia tu es Petrus et super hanc petram aedificabo ecclesiam meam et portae inferi non praevalebunt adversum eam.*" (And I say to thee: That thou art Peter; and upon this rock I will build my church, and the gates of hell shall not prevail against it.) And yet, already ranged against the One True Church with its principal basilica constructed firmly over the tomb of Peter in Rome, were some thirty plus thousand competing and often also contradictory 'Christian' denominations, not to mention other religious groupings numbering in the thousands which were not affiliated to the visible *Sancta Ecclesia*.

Well, clearly the Deliverer must have anticipated moves by the powers of hell aimed at derailing His Church to make such a solemn promise to stand by his *Sancta Ecclesia* through the ages. And since Diabolos was powerful enough to given that keep Adam and Eve and the other "saints" captive in hell until they were liberated by the Deliverer when He himself resurrected from the dead, one couldn't gain say the power of the Evil One. Peter and his fellow apostles on their own were not going to be able to defend the Deliverer's *Sancta Ecclesia* from the powers of darkness. It needed the Deliverer Himself to make a solemn promise to them that He was not going to permit those powers to prevail against His Church in the same way He refused to allow Diabolos to keep the saints hostage in hell!

And, if there was one thing that was pretty evident and could not be disputed, it was that the good work undertaken by non-Catholic organizations and individuals, for example activities in pursuit of peace and justice and other good causes, had the blessing of the Prime Mover. According to Mjomba, this was so not just because the people involved were just people. But a prime reason could well be that the Prime Mover, in his infinite wisdom, knew what was lacking in the successors to the apostles and chose to complement the work they were doing in that way. The problem, according to Mjomba, was not that there were so many workers out there who were helping to reap the harvest; but that sinful, narrow-minded humans failed to see things from the perspective of the Him who was Infinite Wisdom, Infinite Love, and Infinite Mercy, and for Whom nothing - absolutely nothing - was impossible!

As for the "faithful" who were stuck with clergy who were unworthy of their calling in those circumstances, it was pretty much like being asked to turn the other cheek so it too *would* be smacked for the sake of the Deliverer - the Deliverer who *had* his side pierced at the behest of functionaries in the "church of the Old Testament". But while being stuck with the people who supposedly were not living up to their priestly vocation was one thing, it was another thing and a serious one too when people were baptized into the Catholic Church and remained Catholics only in name or considered it below their dignity to learn more about their faith, which included learning about their Church's history. According to Mjomba, increasing one's knowledge of the Mystical Body of Christ increased one's potential as an instrument of the Prime Mover's grace, something Catholics were urged to dedicate themselves for at the time of their baptism and confirmation.

Confessing that he would have been excited to see stuff he was being taught at St. Augustine's Senior Seminary address the subject of "Church unity" from the different angles he had outlined, Mjomba "clarified" that his position, which was admittedly radical by any stretch of the imagination, but apparently not entirely illogical (judging by the fact that he had not yet been lynched by his audience), was that the Prime Mover could very well turn human folly (such as that which drove people to found churches which specifically challenged the authority of His divine Church) to good; and that perhaps, unknown to humans, the Deliverer's prayer "that they may be one" was being answered even as there was this proliferation of new churches! And the same went for anyone who was sincere in his/her observance of Islam, Buddhism, Hinduism, atheism, or any other belief. Created in the image of the Prime Mover, they were all His "temples" after all.

Mjomba stopped short of saying that Providence was using those churches and those other religions to prepare his "faithful" for the most important moment in their existence, namely that moment when they were leaving this world for the next. It seemed pretty obvious that it was a matter of time - perhaps years, months, days, or even hours – that all humans who were alive were going to "come face to face with the one who called Himself the Truth and the Light. With the fate of all those humans at stake, everybody needed to be praying that, just as the Prime Mover had already used the most unlikely situations in both the Old and in the New Testament to accomplish His designs, He would deign to do the same thing for the present "sinful" generation as well.

Mjomba wrote that, for all he knew, Providence was - not just probably but most certainly - using the most repressive regimes on earth where even church worship was outlawed to accomplish His divine plan and to save souls in the process - in the same way He used murderers to despatch souls of the just to heaven! And similarly, Providence was using Diabolos himself to accomplish the divine plan. Which did not, of course, leave much room for comfort for those humans who had the opportunity to march with the Deliverer into the sanctuary of His *sancta ecclesia*, but were tardy in seizing it. First because there were so many others who would seize the opportunity if it were presented to them; but, perhaps even more importantly, humans being humans, the reasons for not seizing the opportunity presented would almost certainly be traceable to human frailties - prejudices and things of that nature - that cannot in and of themselves count as valid excuses.

But it was Mjomba's position that being a Catholic did not necessarily make one a better person than a "separated" brother or sister, a Buddhist, a Moslem, or even an agnostic living in Mongolia, America, or the South Sea Islands. Was it not a fact, after all, that "humans are sinful - all of them" Mjomba wrote, quoting Isaiah. That they had, all of them, become like unclean people, and all their good deeds were "like polluted rags"! Mjomba added the obvious, namely that all humans, with the exception of the Deliverer and His Blessed Mother who was sinless, were betrayers - just like Judas Iscariot - and equally in need of the mercies of the Prime Mover.

A member of a religious order was not better than an ordinary lay Christian, and a priest was not better than members of his flock. A prelate was not better than his priests, and the Holy Father was not better than the bishops and cardinals. They were all sinners, the only difference being that they each had a different calling. And then, if anything, membership in the Catholic Church carried with it the big risk of belonging to that group of "guests" who had been given a special invitation to attend the "Royal Wedding" in the parable, but declined. More so, Mjomba supposed, than membership in any other religious organization because Catholics had the benefit of sacraments that non-Catholics did not have.

Thus, while not special, more definitely had been given to folks who were fortunate enough to count themselves as Catholics. Being extended a gratuitous offer of membership in an organization which the Word came all the way from heaven to set up for the salvation of men was definitely no small matter! The Word, through Whom everything that is came into existence, and also the Deliverer! Mjomba went on to point out the obvious, namely that this argument applied equally to whichever group out there had laid a claim to being the official guardian of revealed truths - unless the people making those claims were doing it as a joke!

Mjomba argued that the Church's action in paying special tribute to Catholics who led heroic lives as disciples of the Deliverer through canonization spoke volumes about the many Catholics, among them members of the Church's hierarchy, whose lives would never have been able to withstand scrutiny by the "Devil's Advocate". According to Mjomba's thesis, the "inquisitors" and other members of the Church's hierarchy like those who fought to keep Copernicus' theory from the public domain clearly fell in the latter category.

So, on the one hand, you had those heroic souls who led saintly if non-descript lives which the Church saw fit to hold up to the faithful for emulation, and then you had the vast majority of Catholics, among them many members of the clergy, who made blatant errors of judgement in decisions governing their personal lives and possibly others' spiritual lives as well. According to Mjomba, there was nothing to prevent them from making mistakes in their "administration of the Church" over time - mistakes that likely contributed to things like the Reformation!

If, in the sixteenth Century, Galileo's position on the center of the universe, which has since been vindicated, could be singled out by "Church folks" at the time and labeled as "heretical', it was quite likely that, at the time of the Reformation and at other times in the chequered history of the Church, some "sons and daughters of the Church" who were bent on seeing those they perceived as "heretics" excommunicated acted inadvertently, and were thus guilty in no small measure of contributing to disunity in Christendom themselves. And perhaps the Church really needed to "implore forgiveness" for the sins of its own as what Mjomba called "a lone voice in the Church" was suggesting.

Mjomba provoked an uproar, during his oral defense of the thesis, when he went on to suggest that, instead of working to heal existing breaches in the oneness of the Mystical Body of Christ, some members of the Church's hierarchy even now were probably in fact doing the opposite - that they were, God forbid, alienating multitudes who might otherwise have approached and embraced Catholicism; or, may be, doing more damage to Church unity than those among the separated brethren who, in good faith and without the benefit of the Church's guidance, now struggled, with only minimal guidance from the apostles' successors and without the benefit of the Church's sacraments, to lead lives that were worthy of the Deliverer's disciples and to help others do likewise. Mjomba added that referring to the separated brethren as "the *excommunicated* brethren" carried with it the risk of appearing even more condescending to the "brethren" all right, but would be more accurate and at least include an implicit acknowledgement of the grave responsibility of the Church's hierarchy for the lamentable situation that now prevailed in Christendom.

Regarding the "flowering" in modern times of Christian churches itself, Mjomba, not one to jump to quick conclusions, had ruled out the revolution in mass communications as a cause. Mjomba refused to fall for the temptation of making the simplistic assumption that living in a so-called age of mass communications automatically caused bogus "messengers" of the Prime Mover and "prophets" to spring up just so they might take advantage of the situation and exploit "God's Word" financially. Quoting one preacher he particularly admired, Mjomba asserted that there was no single incident or event that was a mere coincidence and was not provided for in the "divine plan". Mjomba wrote that, for all he knew, perhaps it was just as the Prime Mover wanted it: a flowering of church denominations occurring just as the revolution in mass communications was taking place!

This was even though Mjomba believed that some of the self-appointed messengers of God and prophets, wittingly or unwittingly, were exploiting the situation and making an extra buck for themselves in the process! But whether true or not, that by itself did not undermine his finding that the exponential growth in the number of Christian "churches" had coincided with the unprecedented growth in the number of theological colleges and, along with it, the number of those who considered themselves experts in biblical exegesis. And it did not particularly disturb him that the way the new crop of church leaders preached, led their "congregations" in prayer, and did other things was markedly different from the way Catholic priests delivered their sermons, administered the sacraments, or generally ministered to their folks. And Mjomba admitted that he probably would never have known that some of those new "churches" existed if it were not for television.

Mjomba supposed that the situation was somewhat analogous to that which existed at the time the Deliverer and His apostles criss-crossed Palestine witnessing to the Word, and their attention was drawn to the activities of a lone, almost independent exorcist. That exorcist likely led quite a different lifestyle from that of the twelve who, for one, had to travel light to keep up with the Deliverer as He went from place to place preaching and driving out evil spirits. Even though he was casting out devils in the Deliverer's name, that "strange" character about whom very little is known likely did not become aware of the inauguration of the sacrament of the Eucharist on the day before the Deliverer was crucified and of many other things that the Deliverer taught His disciples, according to Mjomba. Meaning that he probably was also ignorant about the special powers that the Deliverer gave the apostles - like the power to forgive sins and the power of ordination which would above all guarantee the unbroken exercise of Christ's priesthood through the ages - until, perhaps, well after the Day of Pentecost.

It was not as if the independent exorcist had anything against the Deliverer or the way He conducted himself. The exorcist's beef was with the Deliverer's band of followers. He did not particularly like the way the apostles acted as if they were the only ones who had been waiting for the promise of a deliverer to be fulfilled. And even if he did not have anything against their practice of following the Deliverer everywhere He went, he did not like the way they acted as if the Deliverer belonged to them and them alone!

The exorcist and his own band of followers would later contest many of the claims of the apostles and others who had lived and eaten with the Deliverer in the days leading up to His crucifixion and death on the cross, and in the intermediate period between His resurrection from the dead and subsequent ascension into heaven forty days later, regarding a special commission they said they had received from the Deliverer to carry on the mission he had started, and to travel to the ends of the earth as His official messengers. The independent exorcist, in particular, questioned the claims of the apostles to being given powers to forgive other people's sins in the Deliverer's name, to turn bread and wine into the body and blood of the Deliverer, to bless marriages, and anoint the sick and dying, and above all powers to lay hands on those they appointed as ministers in a new movement or "Mystical Body of the Deliverer" or "Church".

The independent exorcist even questioned the surviving apostles' claim that the new Church, which they also referred to as the "Universal Fellowship of the Risen Lord's Disciples" or "*Ecclesia Catholica*", now embodied a "New Testament" or promise that had replaced the Old Testament. The latter had, according to the self-proclaimed "Catholics", ceased to be when the curtain that previously screened the "Holy of Holies" in the temple in Jerusalem from public view was rent in two pieces after the Deliverer paid the price for the sins of men with his crucifixion and death on that "Good" Friday as they called it.

The independent exorcist said it was unimaginable that the Deliverer could empower a select few in that fashion when His message of salvation for the entire human race, and challenged the apostles to prove that the Deliverer had used the words "That which thou bindeth on earth shalt be bound in heaven, and that which thou looseth on earth shalt be loosed in heaven"! Claiming that he was acting to defend the memory of the Deliverer, the independent exorcist taught his own followers that the apostles were engaged in witchcraft and, possibly, even fraud!

Even for Mjomba, however, the similarities between the lone New Testament dissenter and the "Excommunicated Brethren" ended there. Citing evidence from the "Canadian Scrolls", Mjomba wrote that the "independent exorcist", as he was apparently known in Galilee and Judea, eventually came around and, in his own time, threw in his lot with the apostles. Identified as the Stephen of the Acts of the Apostles, the independent exorcist apparently grew tired of being treated as a "Separatist", and eventually abandoned his isolationist position, joining the main body of the Deliverer's followers shortly before Pentecost Day. Mjomba wrote that Stephen was actually received into the Universal Fellowship of the Risen Lord's Disciples" and baptised, along with his gaggle of followers, on the Day of Pentecost itself. Quoting from the Acts of the Apostles, Mjomba went on that the former independent exorcist embraced martyrdom at the hands of the Romans rather than renounce his new-found faith, not long after the apostles had elevated him to the rank of a Deacon and a "minister" in the "Catholic Church" with the laying on of hands.

Regarding the accusation of practising witchcraft, many in Palestine were of the view that it was well grounded. That belief, Mjomba wrote, was reinforced by the official positions of the Roman authorities and their Jewish counterparts according to which followers of the "disgraced" Deliverer were into activities that were illegal and deserving of punishment. Instead of being cowed down and going into hiding, leaders of the infant "Church", lead by Peter, the former fisherman the Deliverer had promised to turn into a fisher of men, not only stepped up the pace of "evangelization" in response, but went to great lengths to counter the accusations, issuing innumerable "communiqués" or "pastoral letters" in defense of the Church's orthodox position. Many of those Communiqués had survived and constituted what was now known as "Books of the New Testament", Mjomba wrote.

It was ironic, Mjomba wrote, that Stephen, who had earlier accused Christians of practising witchcraft, died defending the early Church's right to administer the sacraments and to spread the good news of the New Testament. It served as a warning, Mjomba went on, for those in the Church who did not think that "separated" brothers or sisters could be of the calibre of St. Stephen the Martyr or Paul, the former persecutor of Christians who ended up as the Apostle of the gentiles - Paul, who even had to change his name just so that Christians would not turn and flee when he was introduced (as they in fact did instinctively before Paul got the presence of mind to adopt his new name, abandoning that of Saul and the notoriety it had raked up).

Not unpredictably, there was many a time when Mjomba, like the prisoner of his imagination that he was, wished that he would wake up one morning and find all the charismatic preachers he loved to watch on television as they expounded on the Word of God in front of delirious crowds of followers change the tune just a little, and cease contradicting each other and/or the original "gospel message" (whatever he meant by that). Mjomba imagined that to the extent they were all identifying with what was in effect the "Unknown Church" (more-or-less like the famous "Unknown God" of St. Paul's epistles), to that extent they had to be God-sent.

And so, switching from one religious channel on his TV set to another religious channel, Mjomba often did the unthinkable - certainly for someone of his education. He conveniently forgot that the preachers bore allegiance to specific Christian denominations, did not "hear" whatever they said that either contradicted the original "gospel message" (what that meant), and pretended that what he heard proclaimed from the different podiums in the glittering church edifices was actually the original, undiluted truth as taught by the Deliverer and faithfully preserved, even as it was being handed down from one generation to the next.

Neither did he notice the omissions that would have compromised the integrity of the sacred truths, the additions, or even the variations in interpretation of the controversial texts that had given rise to the historical "divisions" in the Church in the first place, variations that often seemed quite deliberate and merely convenient. Mjomba, in short, heard the speakers, many of whom were extremely gifted as orators, give voice to just one thing: the undiluted and unvarnished truth for which the Deliverer had given up his life on Mt. Calvary! The same eternal truth to preserve which the Deliverer, triumphant even in death through His resurrection, had arranged for the Paraclete to come down from heaven on Pentecost Day and make sure that it would not be tampered with by the powers of the hell.

And so, there was Mjomba going again and seeing in his imagination the representatives of the different Christian denominations he saw represented there on "celluloid" mysteriously abandon their positions on the meaning of the previously controversial passages of the sacred scriptures and, without a single exception, embrace one unified interpretation of the scriptures and traditional practices of the Church. Nothing short of a dream in itself, that effort by Mjomba was akin to asking opposing foes in a bitter contest to suddenly discount the intense dislike they harbored for each other and, without any guarantees whatsoever for their safety, drop their guard and stay prostrate on their backs as they awaited deliverance from their "enemies" by some hitherto "unknown" divinity!

And this time, as those different preachers, talking in concert, said "The Lord this" or "It is written that", either all of them would be impostors in the eyes of the non-believers the TV broadcasts targeted or none of them. But each time, as Mjomba stopped imagining and returned to the reality of living in a world in which sin and shame reigned, he liked to think that letting his mind wander in that manner was never an entirely futile exercise.

Strange as it was, Mjomba believed that it was actually this practice which had helped him see the problem of disunity in the Church in what he now thought was the proper perspective. Unity among the "saints" clearly was a question that only the Prime Mover could successfully confront - just like the question of Man's original sin. Mjomba added that, in that sense, there was really no difference between them and adherents to other world religions with their own internal divisions - or even those who believed that they could not in good conscience subscribe to any religious belief.

This was even though many baptised Christians liked to think of themselves as special and even gave the impression that one had to be predestined in order to be saved - as if the precious blood of the Deliverer was shed, not for the sins of the world, but for the sins of only some special people! As if the Prime Mover, who loved the world so much that He gave his only begotten son in order that those who believe might be saved, did not really love everybody in that world! Instead of focusing on imagined privileges at a time the battle being fought during this period of trial on earth has not been won yet (which they do when they, of all people, ought to know that following faithfully in the Deliverer's foot steps is synonymous with self-denial and a readiness to suffer persecution for His sake), they needed to focus on the weighty obligations that baptism and the other sacraments of faith imposed on the recipients. It was important for them to realize that these were gifts for which a full accounting was expected in due course.

Notwithstanding the fact that the Deliverer had founded His Church with all the solemnity which the establishment of a divine institution deserved, Mjomba wrote, the mere fact that he had done so was apparently not going to force humans to change their ways. And according to him, it was very significant that the arguments one heard from those who cared to argue were not concerned with the sort of institution the Deliverer might have had in mind when He launched His Church, but with which of the innumerable churches that now existed inspired its adherents, killed enthusiasm - and things of that nature. Was it conceivable that the "Mystical Body of the Deliverer" might have faults that did not escape the sharp eye of observers in the past and today? Mjomba had no doubt that the Church, which included the Deliverer and imperfect men and women in its membership, had faults. And hence the need for the Paraclete who has the difficult job of fortifying humans who continue to sin even after they have been received in the Church.

And so, while many must indeed be commended for doing their research and finding the historical Church "lacking", their action in setting up competing "churches" which are supposed to provide them "satisfaction" might not be so commendable. According to Mjomba's thesis, membership in the Mystical Body of the Deliverer entailed all the things in life that left one "weeping" or "laughing", "hungry and thirsty" or "full", "reviled" or "the darling of whoever", *et cetera.* Mjomba's conclusion was that membership in churches in which one was enjoying the great feeling of being saved and always on top of things carried with it the risk that one could find oneself being told: "Don't you think you have already had your fill"! Mjomba stopped short of saying that justification, conditions in the next life or what we know as heaven and hell, and the last judgement were things that humans would find vastly different from what they now imagined.

Even as he was blasting those who were loathe to entrust their salvation to the historical Church, Mjomba worried aloud at the vastly larger number of Catholics, including himself, who paraded themselves as staunch members of that Church, but were "lukewarm" in their observance of the Prime Mover's commandments. Declaring that it the actions of people like himself which caused many outside the Church to avoid becoming involved with an institution that *prime facie* was responsible for producing such uncouth characters, Mjomba went on that the intolerance by himself and those of his ilk of others' views and above all the self-righteousness, condemned by the Deliverer but embraced whole-heartedly by him and his fellow hypocrites who came in all shapes, sizes and shades, brought dishonor to the Mystical Body of Christ in the same way Judas Iscariot, a regular companion of the Deliverer and an apostle, did. Parading as "pro-life", they actually were the most uncompromising capital punishment advocates. And, claiming to be "peace-makers", they turned out to be rabid war mongers for whom unprovoked preemptive military strikes targeting weaker, but resource-rich nations were an acceptable option, and who were inclined to view any number of innocent casualties resulting there from as justifiable.

Disunity among the Deliverer's followers, already evident among the twelve even before the Son of Man, as He called Himself, laid down his life for men, was a human failing that apparently was not going to go away just like. And may be it was a situation the Deliverer had very much on His mind when He made His position on tolerance clear - so clear it could even be said that He had actually over-articulated it to the discomfort of some of the disciples.

Granted that humans were primarily spiritual beings, perhaps the critical message the successors of the apostles needed to emphasize was not so much the fact that humans should become members of the *visible* Church in order that they may benefit from the sacramental grace that was readily available therein, as the fact that everyone should, like the Greeks whom the Apostle of the Gentiles found rendering homage to the "unknown" God, keep looking until they gained true knowledge of a God whom they publicly professed to know, but about whom they in fact knew next to nothing.

Or, perhaps, it was membership in the *Mystical Body of Christ* that preachers needed to exhort their audiences to seek over and above membership in an identifiable church organization, Catholic or otherwise. Mjomba wrote that it was quite conceivable that there might well be zealots in the Church who just either focused on putting up impressive church edifices or on the numbers of catechumens whom they "welcomed" into the Church, and were not really bothered if the new converts moved on to become true Christians or remained Christians only in name.

Mjomba suspected that the emphasis on church structures and church organizations had inevitably led to a tendency to emphasize externalities like "going to church" and "abstaining from eating meat on Friday", just as the priests and Pharisees who lived contemporaneously with the Deliverer did, at the expense of true spiritual holiness which consisted in being in constant communion with the Prime Mover.

The emphasis on externalities, which were not a reflection of true spiritual integrity or holiness, not only provided a good shield for hypocrisy but more often than not also signalled an absence of charity, according to Mjomba. Observance of precepts that was driven by faith alone was not good enough - even if it was faith which could move mountains. The observance of those precepts had also to be grounded in charity. However, according to Mjomba, it was the outward symbols of a supposedly "strong and immovable faith", and not love for God and for one another, which were usually in evidence when rules and regulations were being enforced.

Discussing the same topic (over-emphasis on externalities) from a somewhat different perspective, Mjomba wrote that it was admittedly not those who exclaimed "Lord, Lord!" who would be guaranteed a pass on the CTET; but those who kept the commandments. He went on to comment that love, or the virtue of charity, was illusory if it too did not go hand in hand with a commitment to keep the commandments.

The challenge, particularly for those who were called to be apostles or other Christs, was to be Christ-like. And the problem was that preachers, even when they did not openly claim to be Christ-like, invariably "acted" the part - all preachers except those who had actually come close to that ideal and, like the apostles Peter and Paul, were too modest for that very reason to trumpet their situation, that is.

Mjomba had added a rider to the effect that something like the Reformation would probably have occurred all the same even if the Holy See had had St. Peter as it's incumbent with St. Paul as Secretary of State. And that was not because "people were free to walk away from what they did not like" as official Church history books implied. It was, Mjomba wrote, easy to blame everything on the reformers and say glibly that Luther and others had chosen to walk away from the truth and had only themselves to blame, just as it was easy to say that ecclesiastical officials in control of the See of Rome had compromised biblical truth and had even become mired in voodooism. The reformers on the one hand and those who believed that the way to settle the matter was through excommunication on the other all had (one) a conscience and (two) a free will to do as they chose.

The physical presence of St. Peter and St. Paul likely would not have changed the course of history. And, added Mjomba, posing the question "Who followed the dictates of his or her conscience and who didn't?" by anyone other than the particular individual involved a useless exercise. For, asking that question was the prerogative of the Prime Mover alone; and, when it was asked by observers, Church unity was hurt further. But, humans being humans, they apparently did not hesitate to usurp the Prime Mover's prerogative at the time of the Reformation as they had done throughout the ages, and would continue to do to the end of time, Mjomba wrote.

Regarding church edifices, was it not written that the Deliverer, referring to his own body, had dared his enemies (who, Mjomba added, were already bent on destroying Him at all costs) to tear down the "temple" promising to restore it in a matter of three days? This was despite the fact that nothing - not even the gates of Hades - had a chance of prevailing against the Church the Deliverer was establishing! That, Mjomba commented, appeared to suggest that it was membership in the Deliverer's *Mystical Body* rather than in the visible appendages which was really important.

Mjomba wrote that churches had often, indeed, undergone the same fate as the temple in Jerusalem, which was obviously quite regrettable. And, as if torching and burning churches to the ground weren't bad enough, Christians and others fleeing into them for safety had been slain. Besides, no one had ever said that the safety of the apostles' successors, just like that of the apostles, would be guaranteed either.

But, on the other hand, the emergence of Christendom as a major political force in the world had clearly been accompanied by the desire to build church edifices that reflected that power. While not a bad thing in itself, that development, Mjomba argued, might well have influenced the popular notion of membership in "churches" and might in the process have diluted the importance of membership in the "Mystical Body"!

Making reference in his thesis to the so-called "Secrets of the Lady of Fatima", Mjomba pointed out that the Third Secret envisioned roads littered with corpses of priests and bishops and even the corpse of a pope! Mjomba commented that the Lady of Fatima was undoubtedly aware that priests and bishops, and certainly the Pontiff of Rome, spent most of their time inside "churches". And he saw her reference to bodies being littered on "roads" instead of in "churches" as a possible attempt to de-emphasize the prevailing notion of "churches" and membership in them. After all, the place of the successors to the apostles was "on the road", spreading the good news, even though they too, like other humans, needed shelter and places where they could "break bread" and administer sacraments.

Mjomba wrote that he wondered about the origin of the word "church" and the original connotation of that word. Did "church" stand for a building, a bark similar to Noah's Ark, a corporate entity, a coming together of a relatively large number of people who shared similar or common beliefs to form a club or fellowship, or did it stand for a Deliverer on a mission, the gist of which was to lay down his life like the sacrificial lamb He was and, after dying, to rise again in victory over death and thereby save His poor and forsaken children who until then slaved away under the shadow of death?

Was "church" synonymous with "communion" - the union or oneness of Jesus Christ, its founder, with his followers? If this latter description was accurate, then *everybody* belonged to the Church, because Jesus Christ "exercises His kingship by drawing *all* men to Himself through His resurrection and death".

Mjomba wrote that until the Greeks Paul found worshipping the unknown God were recruited by him into the visible Church, they and their predecessors probably were members of the "invisible" Church. He could not imagine a stronger desire for baptism than that which drove these people in their fervent search for truth to admit that they had still to come upon the messengers of the Deliverer, and to recognize that the very best they could do in the interim period while they waited was to pay homage to the God whom they knew existed but did not have a name for!

Mjomba was quick to add that even after those Greeks had allowed Paul to get up on the podium in the Acropolis, heard him out and believed, the Deliverer's prayer that "they may be one" could only have meaning if there was a continuing threat of disunity in the Church fuelled presumably by egotism. Mjomba suggested that such a threat continued to be very much in evidence, and probably would be with humans to the end of time.

Talking about the threat to Church unity, Mjomba believed that a part of that threat was actually destined to emanate from within the Church itself. Pastors, like the flocks they ministered to, were human he argued. That being the case, there was, humanly speaking, a much greater chance of these "fishers of men" becoming more concerned with splitting hairs about some fine points of theology or philosophy, than with their own practice of the virtue of charity. Orthodoxy, in other words, likely was going to be valued more than neighborly love.

Mjomba wrote that he was not so sure that some Catholic clergy were not guilty of doing precisely that. He supposed that the few truly heroic priests and bishops would probably find themselves sidelined because they would be inclined to auction off treasures in St. Peter's Basilica in Rome and in churches around the world to feed the poor. Mjomba imagined that just a single fresco, if it could be removed from the ceiling of St. John Lateran and sold, or alternatively a stained glass window diverted from the new Shrine to Our Lady at

Catholic University in the U.S. capital, would each probably be capable of feeding thousands in drought prone Ethiopia or of providing shelter to hundreds in Bangladesh during the monsoon season.

But Mjomba did not fail to add, in the thesis, that ideas of that sort likely would not be popular with conservatives in the Church and particularly the Curia in Rome, and could even end up being ascribed to Satan; because, in the eyes of most people, ripping frescos and windows out of churches for any reason - the very things which drew worshippers and sightseers alike to these places signalled the beginning of the end for the Church in material terms, and could not possibly be in consonance with the Church's evangelizing mission for that "reason". In their eyes, adding to monuments (like St. Peter's Basilica in Rome and the Egyptian pyramids) that humans have constructed in the course of history in honor of the Prime Mover was something that was just as important as propagating the faith or feeding the hungry.

Disunity in the Church established by the Deliverer undoubtedly started with the confusion as between what was more important - Neighborly love or Orthodoxy? And it finally came down to numbers, Mjomba wrote, with the human factor deciding where the chips would fall. Even though the liberal faction lost over the conservative faction early on in the history of the Church, the attendant problems remained manageable until, like a cancer, the disagreements spilled over into other doctrinal areas, eventually resulting in a divorce of sorts.

Mjomba had, none-the-less, quipped during his verbal defense of the thesis: "Good thing the divine plan, after failing to be stymied by man's original sin and by the betrayal of one of the twelve whom the Deliverer had handpicked to be His apostles, was not about to be derailed by the failings of some members of the Church's hierarchy. And the Church's divine founder - who was also the Word - undoubtedly could also deal with all the fall-out from this; and it included the fact that many, for no fault of their own, now were never going to find their way into His visible Church all that easily or at all."

Mjomba, who was always at pains to depict the Church as something that was inclusive and not exclusive, and had no wish to say anything disparaging against other religions, was very sensitive to the fact that the position enunciated by him while discussing the "visible" Church appeared to be at variance with the position he laid out in his discussion of the "invisible" Church. But he believed that the two positions only *appeared* to contradict each other, and that they were in fact quite complimentary. But he admitted that this was not something that individuals who had been led by their consciences to remain outside the visible Church would find comforting, much less, acceptable.

But to the extent that those inside and outside the visible Church continued to be equally on trial during their sojourn on earth and were all going to face the Judge regardless of their religious affiliation, to that extent those inside the "visible" Church seemed to be at a distinct disadvantage. This was because, unlike those outside, they would have no excusing for not living aright given their access to the sacraments and the many opportunities for growing in holiness that were not available to humans outside the Church, Mjomba wrote.

Concluding his arguments regarding the universality of the Church, Mjomba stated that he did not believe that any of the foregoing "hogwash" clarified the meaning of the term "church". It likely would not, he wrote, because the Church the Deliverer established, denoted by the phrase "Mystical Body of Christ", involved more than a complex idea - in the realm of knowledge, it ranked as a mystery!

All of this underlined the important role of the Deliverer's forerunner who, Mjomba wrote, went knocking on people's doors urging them to come out with their implements and pave the roads and straighten the paths as part of the preparations to receive the Deliverer. To the ears of the inhabitants of the earth two thousand years ago, his message urging them to put their houses in order and generally begin to behave like rational creatures molded in the image of the Prime Mover sounded very novel. The situation, Mjomba wrote, was no different today. That was even though it should have sounded like music to the human ear.

And, referring to the Deliverer's own advice to the "sinful generation" to the effect that if it was a limb which was the cause of sin, humans should cut it off as it was better to go to Paradise without a limb rather than not get there at all, Mjomba commented that it was surprising that there were no humans who heeded the advice.

According to Mjomba, the evil deeds humans did were all part of what he called "one great fraud" perpetrated in a scheme that attempted to give respectability to pretence and make believe - when they were not acts that merely amounted to attempts to convert for their personal use things that were not rightfully theirs but the Prime Mover's. That was exactly what happened when humans destroyed rain forests.

When humans sinned, they were essentially stealing, Mjomba wrote. While every human could claim to possess an independent existence from any other creature human or otherwise, and along with it the nature or essence of an *animal rationale*, not only was the human nature and the existence enjoyed by individuals entirely gratuitously given, and along with them the specific responsibility of acknowledging the goodness of the Prime Mover; but humans forfeited any right to them when they chose - while knowing full well that it was wrong for them to do so - to act as if they were their own Creators and turned their relationship with the Prime Mover into one of outright enmity. Mjomba went on that to sin was to become a betrayer in the exact same way that Judas Iscariot betrayed the Deliverer to judges he knew were not interested in justice.

Sin, Mjomba wrote, was something every human, with the exception of the Deliverer who happened to be a God-head and his blessed mother through a special dispensation of grace, was blemished with either directly through individual conduct that fell short of upright behaviour, or by virtue of being descended from Adam and Eve who committed the original sin. And sin itself consisted in embracing a frame of mind which turned a human into an outlaw. In that frame of mind, any messenger of the Prime Mover and indeed the Prime Mover Himself was fair game - a *persona non grata* who would have to be neutralized or annihilated, or otherwise ejected from the world.

Still, this was all the more reason, now that the Prime Mover - who so loved the world that he was prepared to give his only begotten Son so that those who believed in Him would not perish - had kept his promise and sent the Deliverer, for humans, if they wanted to give themselves another shot at eternal life, to keep their part of the bargain by changing their ways.

Regarding the Adam and Eve, Mjomba wrote that, even though inclined to sin in the aftermath of the fall, by remaining focused on that promise (of a Deliverer) and by striving to be steadfast as the Prime Mover's faithful servants for the remainder of their days on earth, they hoped that they could still effectively hitch a ride into eternity that way. Once there, their reign with Him would be timeless, and their contentment permanently assured and no longer exposed to any kind of peril.

Until they succumbed to the artifices of Satan and rebelled against their Maker, this was precisely the dream that the first Man and the first Woman had - up until the moment they begun plotting their rebellion and got kicked out of Paradise. The dream of revelling in exaltation in timelessness in their after-life, and luxuriating in their new roles as veritable potentates in the Elysian Fields or Shangri-la!

As Mjomba saw it, good souls outside the visible Church for no fault of theirs were in the exact same boat as the repentant Adam and Eve - so long as they too strove to remain faithful to their consciences, that is.

The first humans: a close-up view...

To underline the point about immortality vis-à-vis a passing life of self indulgence and debauchery, Mjomba described in great detail how Adam and Eve, recognizing that to enter into a marriage was good, but that it was better, and in that sense also more godly, to practice chastity, had both initially vowed to remain chaste throughout their sojourn on earth. He wrote that there had been no doubt in their minds that a state of chastity made them much more pleasing to the Prime Mover. Quite apart from the fact that they would have been more focused on their last end as a chaste couple, they were after all vessels of grace, and they regarded their bodies as temples of the Holy One!

In their perception, if it turned out that marriage was essential to the fulfilment of the divine plan, they would, of course, celebrate it; but in the afterlife and in triumph - when their trial on earth was over and done with. But for now, they were pledging to remain celibate, and to live as "spouses" of Him-Who-is-Who-is!

Mjomba suggested that Adam and Eve eventually took steps to wed only after they were specifically commanded a second time to do so by the Prime Mover in an episode on which the scriptures were silent. Quoting the Rwenzori Prehistoric Diaries, he wrote that Adam and Eve had indeed solemnly pledged to remain celibate, and to live as brother and sister, shortly after they ended their first and, as it would turn out, last tour of the world.

According to Mjomba, that was how Adam and Eve perceived things before they fell from grace. He suggested that Adam and Eve eventually took steps to wed only after they were specifically commanded to do so a second time by the Prime Mover in an episode on which the scriptures are silent. In the same episode to which there were supposedly were at least three clear references in the Rwenzori Prehistoric Diaries, the pair supposedly also received the explanation that marriages did not occur in the afterlife!

They looked different from each other to be sure. Black as coal, Adam was about seven feet tall, and had a physique which resembled that of an Inca prince. With the exception, that is, of his temples which looked like those of a Pharaoh, a nose which big and flat like that of Nubians, ear lobes which were medium sized, sturdy and swept back like those of a Karamojong, and small piercing eyes. His hair long and frizzy, and he was soft spoken just like Louis

Armstrong. And when he walked or sprinted, it was with the firm gait of a buck in the prime of its life.

Eve, on the other hand, was slightly shorter - about six feet three inches. Fair-skinned, she was blessed with the body of a Mumtaz Mahal and a pair of adoring eyes which looked like those of a nymph. She had a facial outline of the Queen of Sheba, and she sported matted hair the color of cinnamon. She had the poise of the Statue of Liberty; and when she spoke, her voice sounded like a violin. When she walked or sprinted, it was with the gait of a Giraffe.

Adam also could not fail to notice that there existed between him and his "companion" from the very first a mutual attraction such as he had not thought possible before. According to Mjomba, Adam and the new addition to God's creatures whom the former was already referring to as "my other self" (because of the fact that they shared the exact same nature) easily recognized the bond of love existing between them as a mirror of the relationship existing between the Three Divine Persons or the so called Trinity.

Also, according to Mjomba, Adam and Eve would see their role in the divine plan and the reasons for being endowed with divergent but compatible gifts as man and woman defined very plainly in what next ensued. For, addressing both representatives of the human race, the Creator next commanded the couple to go, multiply and fill the earth!

In spite of their vastly different looks and despite the fact that they had been commanded by the Prime Mover to multiply and fill the earth, they not only preferred to regard each other like brother and sister, but the closeness they felt for each other and the strong spiritual bond between them which stemmed from the fact that both were equally children of the Prime Mover, made Adam and Eve believe that any relationship of a carnal nature between the two of them and hence also marriage were things which they had to regard as unsuitable and out of question. After the debacle of original sin, frivolous behavior of that sort certainly wasn't something that they were going to easily capitulate to - if they could help it!

Citing evidence from the Rwenzori Prehistoric Diaries, Mjomba wrote that it was not until they were specifically commanded by the Prime Mover for the second time - this time around in dreams - to marry and beget children that Adam and Eve buckled and took steps to get betrothed to each other as a prelude to exchanging wedding rings! And in any case Eve, whose character had demureness and modesty as its hallmark, would assuredly not have countenanced any permissive language from Adam, let alone permit him to touch her in any intimate way. Moreover, up until that point, both Adam and Eve placed emphasis on the fact that they were the Prime Mover's creatures and were made for Him rather than for each other.

The decision to marry was far more difficult for Adam and Eve's issue. The differences between them were less than those between their parents. For one, they were all half castes, while at the same time, everyone of them had facial and other characteristics that resembled Adam in part and Eve in part. According to Mjomba, it was only several centuries later, after the earth's population had expanded and some families had emigrated to parts of the continental shelf that had contrasting weather patterns, that humans begun developing distinctive facial and other characteristics as they became acclimatized to the vastly differing ecological systems. And then, growing up under the watchful gaze of Adam and Eve, they had learnt to respect each other and at all times to maintain suitable distance as befitted close kin.

Their parents clearly could be making an error of judgement in the counsel they were providing; and for a while the dilemma of the offspring of Adam and Eve was whether to listen and do the bidding of their parents or to disobey and precipitate a break with parents they otherwise held in the highest esteem, and who, besides, were the only mentors they knew. The fact, nonetheless, was that Adam and Eve had already saddled humanity with original sin and its dreadful consequences, and the young people felt that there was every reason to be cautious, and not to be gullible.

The siblings of Adam and Eve therefore needed a lot of reassurance before they could live with the fact that marriage and the associated conjugal relations between them were necessary both for the future of mankind and for the fulfilment of the divine plan. But, faced with a decision whose consequences were so far reaching, the young people, following in the example of Adam and Eve, made marriage a special subject of prayer and meditation as well.

In the end, the new generation along with the ageing Adam and Eve could not help discerning in all this the great mercies of the Prime Mover, particularly in light of the fact that even though sin had taken its toll, the Deliverer had already been promised. And they were mollified to think that His coming depended on the decisions they were even then making!

They were also well aware that, but for the goodness of the Prime Mover who kept plagues and accidents that might easily have wiped out that small pioneering band of humans, their own individual desire see humans multiply and fill all the corners of the earth were inconsequential. But even though they knew that no member of the human family lost even a single hair from their dome unless the loss was specifically permitted by the Prime Mover, they formed the habit of congregating as one human family to praise the Prime Mover and to pray that his will be done on earth just as it was in heaven.

And when an addition to the human family would occur, led by Adam and Eve, the entire population of earth, which was of course not very much at that time, would dutifully gathered together to give glory to the Prime Mover with feasting, solemn chants and prayer.

Satanic scheme...

Mjomba wrote that as time went by and Adam and Eve grew in the knowledge of "Him greater than which cannot be conceived" and in holiness, they started to hunger and yearn for the afterlife where they would be so much closer to the "Source". The lives they led were spiritual and far removed from the mundane. Consequently, they often went for days without thinking of themselves, eating or sleeping. While praying and meditating, their love for and longing to be with the Prime Mover frequently caused them to experience levitation which came on spontaneously, Mjomba wrote.

It was obvious, according to Mjomba's thesis, that Lucifer and his host worked hard and skilfully to try and get Adam and Eve to change course to no avail. Even though the powers of the Underworld planned their moves carefully and in detail, including timing, they did not succeed in derailing Adam and Eve a second time. Mjomba had Mephistopheles, in his disguise as a serpent, confront Adam and Eve time and again, especially on those occasions when they were relaxing and enjoying a well deserved respite from hours of meditation, or when they were almost starved to death after long bouts of fasting, with the wicked suggestion that they would be like God if they ate of the "forbidden fruit".

But if Satan did not succeed in ensnaring Adam and Eve, it was a different story with their issue, particularly the later generations who did not have the benefit of learning about the dangers he posed - and his wicked schemes - first hand from the first Man and Woman.

Surprise in this matter, according to Mjomba, was everything; because if those good people were alerted to the fact that the Evil One was up and about and plotting furiously to permanently derail their almost certain union with the Almighty One, they would always be on their guard even during the moments they were relaxing and idol just like Adam and Eve - and the archenemy knew it!

It was, according to Mjomba, not surprising that Adam and Eve were forgiven by the infinitely merciful Prime Mover when, on coming to after they fell from grace and caused the fortunes of mankind to be bedevilled by original sin, they realized their folly and renounced Satan and all his wiles. For Adam and Eve, the life-long lesson which they learnt from that dastardly and most unfortunate event in human history was that, however advanced in holiness, without the grace of God, on their own they were as nothing.

Be that as it may, while, for one reason or another, the descendants of Adam and Eve would find it hard to grasp that earthly bliss, whether engendered by material well-being or physical and mental accomplishments, fell far short of what the human person ultimately deserved, namely bliss in eternity, it would not be so with the first Man and Woman.

According to Mjomba, the attempt by Adam and Eve to seize what looked like an excellent opportunity to take over Planet Earth and the surrounding galaxies and expropriate everything in them from the Creator and rightful owner had been intended only as a means to a definite end. That end was to preside over their "conquest" or "spoils of war" in eternity, and that was what the act of disobedience of Adam and Eve was all about. If they indulged themselves along the way - as they had seen animals and other lower creatures appear to do - that was only incidental to it. Anything less than that was unacceptable and would, as indeed happened, cause Adam and his companion to back off.

Later, during Mjomba's oral defense of his thesis before the panel of professors and classmates at St. Augustine's Seminary, Mjomba would suggest that at about that time Adam, for some inexplicable reason, adopted the second name of Tuntah while Eve called herself Nkhamoun! Mjomba cited the Rwenzori Prehistoric Diaries as his authority and added that, generations later, an Egyptian prince, believing that his new-born son might succeed where Adam and Eve failed, groomed his son whom he called Tuntahkhamoun for the undertaking. True to the promise he made to his father at the time he came of age, Tuntahkhamoun, as is now well-known, did try to attain life everlasting here on earth.

That stance of Adam and Eve on the question of material happiness and its temporal nature, which appeared to have been firm and unyielding, meant that none of their descendants, even though tainted with the original sin committed by their forefathers, would have any excuse for not staying on the path of righteous living in accordance with their consciences. Their descendants' obligation to do precisely that was sealed when the Prime Mover not only forgave Adam and Eve, but also delivered on His promise of a Redeemer, according to Mjomba.

Mjomba went out of his way to suggest that many blundered and failed to see the role of Israel in its proper perspective. The role of Israelites as a chosen people was, he wrote, meaningless unless it was seen in relation to mankind as a whole. The Prime Mover's promise of a Deliverer, made to Adam and Eve, was a promise to all descendants of Adam and eve, he argued; and it stood to reason that the Deliverer had to be born of one or other descendant of Adam and Eve if he was going to be a true human and not something else. That individual happened to be an Israelite. But the purpose of his sojourn on earth remained the redemption of all humans from the scourge of sin.

It was typical of human beings that there would be complaints all around about the way the Prime Mover hired workers for his vineyard, Mjomba wrote. The Israelites, who were hired by the "Landowner" to work in the vineyard at dawn and who subsequently bequeathed to the world Mary, Queen of Apostles, as well as the Deliverer Himself, would be upset when they found out that they were receiving the same wage for a day's work as the Italians who would join the labor gang in the vineyard at nine O'clock and give the world the likes of Francis of Assisi. And the Italians would be upset to find that they were receiving the same wage as the Gauls who would start work in the vineyard at mid-day and give the world their own crop of saints. And the Gauls would in turn be upset to find that their wages and the wages of the Anglo-Saxons who would report for work in the vineyard as late as three O'clock in the afternoon and give to the world the likes of Mark Edmund and Thomas Moore were exactly the same.

And everybody, including the Anglo-Saxons, would grouse that they were apparently working for the exact same pay as the Ugandans whom the "Landowner" would recruit to work in His vineyard at five O'clock in the evening and who would bequeath to the world the Blessed Martyrs of Uganda! Mjomba did not fail to point out that the Ugandans would also be in for a shock on finding out that the wages of the "Separated Brethren", Moslems, Hindus, and others who had conscientious objections to the role of the Pontiff of Rome in spiritual matters and other aspects of Catholic doctrine and lived accordingly, and of "non-believers" who, like the Greeks before them, worshiped the "Unknown God" because they did not know better and their own wages were identical wages!

It was, Mjomba added, a measure of the extent to which the human family had strayed from the path of righteousness that the biblical phrase "eating of the fruit" was now interpreted and understood as being banal.

This had in turn resulted in moralists portraying a whole array of physical acts as being evil in and of themselves and, only when it was convenient, making an about-turn and acknowledging that it was always the intention, not the physical acts per se, that constituted sin with the latter representing what Mjomba called mere occasions of sin. In the process, they had vilified some of man's most important physical endowments and along with them entire traditions, customs and cultures that had sustained communities through times of calamity.

They had consequently played into the hands of Beelzebub and inadvertently paved the way for the rise of cults and other aberrations, and also unwittingly given impetus to the very things they would have the world believe that they were seeking to prevent from happening. But worse than that, by suggesting that an ordinary act on which the survival of the human race depends was evil in and of itself for instance, they were thereby providing those who abused the rights and privileges associated with such an act the excuse to claim that those who were supposedly the defenders of morality had got it all wrong, and to argue that it was they - namely the abusers - who had refused to bury their heads in sand in the manner of ostriches!

Instead of hailing the debut of all men and women into the world of created things as humans with full rights to the inheritance promised to Adam and Eve, some preachers, according to Mjomba, impugned the fact that the earth's current inhabitants were descended from Adam and Eve and laid the blame for the effects of original sin at the door of their flocks as if those poor souls could have stopped the first Man and Woman from straying from the path of righteousness!

The fact that the present generation of humans were also inclined to sin as a natural consequence of original sin was blamed on the people who were not even there when Adam and Eve abused their rights and privileges by choosing to disobey their heavenly Father and Lord of all! The earth's present inhabitants were blamed for the fact that the first Man and the first Woman eons ago failed to make the grade!

The distinction between acts of free will and the consequences thereof and actions over which men had no control for one reason or another had been blurred. But these self-same moralists, Mjomba wrote, had found ways not only of exonerating themselves from these supposed evils but also of holding themselves harmless from their effects!

Mjomba went on that it was clear to Adam and Eve, as they reflected on the singular poise and the aplomb and the exquisite August comportment with which the lower creatures carried themselves while allowing the brilliance of the Creator to radiate glow and shine forth in them, that they themselves could in fact attain to a higher - much higher - state of holiness, and one in which the brilliance of the Creator would burst forth in an even more telling way if allowed to. And it was, of course, also clear that their reward would not only be far greater, but enduring in a real sense of that word. The way they were constituted - of an incorruptible soul which informed a physical, earthly frame - guaranteed that.

Mjomba wrote that in spite of all that, it was very tempting for Adam and Eve, seeing the harmony in the universe, the flawless, almost dizzying symmetry in physical substances - or dead matter as they preferred to regard it - and observing the way the birds, the animals, the reptiles, and even the insects together matched, danced and sang, each species in its own unique way, to the original, hallowed and regal score composed by the Grand Master on the one hand, and the halting steps they themselves were taking as they proceeded to discover and map out the strange surroundings in which they had found themselves on the other, to think that the brilliance of the Prime Mover was potentially less evident in their own human nature.

Mjomba noted in his thesis that the eventual decision of Adam and Eve to join the fallen angels in challenging the authority of the Prime Mover would spring from a stubborn determination to break not just the moral law but the natural law governing the universe as well. They would do this even though they understood that such a course of action would not be without consequences.

Mjomba argued that the mere fact that life had to go on after the original sin - that humans still had the obligation to seek and achieve self-actualization, that Adam and Eve were still obligated to multiply and fill the earth, and so on and so forth - would make a situation that was already complicated even more so. And the fact that it would mostly be the old and wizened who would be the first to pass from this world to the next for their rendezvous with the Prime Mover, thus depriving the world of the most valued mentors, would definitely not auger well for the future of mankind.

Reincarnated devils...

Mulling over that fateful decision of the father and mother of mankind, Mjomba, who was also seeking an explanation for the fact that pain, suffering and death to all appearances had been a normal and accepted feature of life among birds, animals, reptiles, fishes and insects even before sin came into the world through the transgression of Adam and Eve, had on a number of occasions flirted with the idea that there had to be some connection between the act of disobedience of Lucifer and his lackeys and the condition of these lower life forms.

On one occasion, after meditating on the subject late into the night, Mjomba had woken up in the morning convinced that those earthly creatures were actually reincarnated devils; and it had taken some doing for him to discard that silly idea. But, as the sweat in which his whole person was soaked suggested, he had felt very perturbed indeed while he clung to that idea.

Mjomba had assumed that Adam and Eve, whilst equipped with that same information, had proceeded to break the Prime Mover's commandments all the same - something he regarded as completely unthinkable! How could they do it knowing that they could end up meeting the same fate! If those lower life forms were really incarnated devils as he thought, but Adam and Eve and their descendants were not privy to that information, then in reality humans were in much greater danger than they suspected, surrounded as they were by so many animals they thought were domesticated, good company and harmless. They were rearing, pampering and fondling those innocent looking household pets without the slightest idea that they were dealing with devils.

While his dream lasted, Mjomba wrestled with the frightening thought that so many folks believed that it was not just safe, but a good thing for their children to play with puppies, cats, and the other exotic animals people were in the habit of adopting and turning into household pets! Believing that he had an obligation to alert the world of the immense danger those "household pets" and the other domesticated animals and poultry posed to them and their loved ones, Mjomba tried to start with a neighbor who had several cats and a dog. He was surprised that despite his efforts to hurry up and get going, his feet initially refused to move. He felt like someone in a straight jacket. Even though it wasn't the first time he had found himself in that sort of situation, he didn't have any idea how it came about that he couldn't get his legs moving in the normal manner.

And then, as he approached his neighbor's front door after exerting so much of his energy to overcome the strange "inertia", another problem cropped up and caused him to turn and head back - he could not believe it, but he was very scantily dressed - too scantily dressed to be outside and knocking on people's doors. It was completely unbelievable! Before he awoke, Mjomba, who was convinced that he knew why some pets - pit bulls for example - remained dangerous and vicious in spite of years of grooming as household pets, suspected that it was Satan who was behind his inability to move quickly at will, and also behind his memory loss which he blamed for leaving his house undressed.

Mjomba was very relieved when he awoke up and realized that he had just been dreaming - that he wasn't running around outside without his clothing on. His first instinct was to jump to the conclusion that everything else in the dream was also pure fantasy. And for a moment or so, while he was reeling from the fact that it would have been disastrous for someone of his standing to be outdoors naked without realizing it, he thought that was the case. When it dawned on him that it wasn't - that for weeks now he in fact had been examining the response of humans to the Prime Mover's invitation to them to attend the divine banquet and had accordingly been busy crafting his thesis on "Original Virtue", he felt very disappointed and angry with himself for being one of them.

Later that day, when his thoughts were composed and he was feeling at ease and much more settled that he had felt in the hours following his nightmarish dream, Mjomba was surprised that he was in fact still reliving the dream in his subconsciousness and that he was actually worried about Beelzebub and what he could do. It might be far fetched to imagine that the lower life forms were reincarnated demons. But, as he surveyed the scene in chapel at Benediction and scrutinized the pious faces of the seminarians closest to him, it struck Mjomba that there was really nothing to prevent the devil from masquerading as a human - perhaps as a seminarian or even as a priest - and then taking advantage of the gullibility of Christians to pass himself off as a messenger of the Prime Mover or something like that.

Mjomba recalled at least one occasion on which one fellow appeared on the premises of St. Augustine's Seminary and passed himself off as a priest who was stranded. The "priest", using the names of a real priest who served in a remote parish, had succeeded in hoodwinking the Rector and the other members of the seminary faculty into believing that he was indeed a priest who needed assistance. It was not until early the next morning when the cover of the "priest" was blown by a seminarian who had noticed that the fellow "bungled" instead of reciting Mass in the same order as other priests did.

The "priest", believed to be someone who was a former member of the seminary brotherhood because he seemed to be conversant with the set up in the rectory, had vanished before he could be apprehended by the authorities. Still, the joke for a long time among the students was that may be quite a few of the many "visiting" clergy who dropped in periodically while en route to their destinations on previous occasions - and some of whom had even been permitted to hear confessions - were really frauds! Well, if humans could pull things like that off, Mjomba had no doubt that the devil also could.

And may be there indeed were hordes of such "priests" out there - like the one who nearly got caught - manning entire "parishes" and doing everything from gathering in funds for Peter's pence to "ministering" to unsuspecting folk! And what was there to prevent such devilish "priests" from abandoning their "allegiance" to the Catholic Church and claiming that they belonged to a different denomination altogether if it suited them to do that! Since their objective would not be to "preach" the truth, but to mislead their unsuspecting "flocks" and make it as difficult as possible for those souls to find the truth, those priests, because they would be devoted to promoting the agenda of Diabolos, would certainly not be the kind who would hesitate to change their church allegiances on the spur of the moment and especially if doing so would serve that purpose.

Diabolos was, of course, in all probability a lot smarter than that, and he was consequently not in the least surprised at the fact that the number of Christian denominations was very large and growing by the day. Mjomba believed that this state of affairs was of concern to the Deliverer precisely because Diabolos was behind it. If he wasn't - if the divisions in Christendom were merely "accidental" - there wouldn't be any grounds for concern. It would all be accidental and by implication an integral part of the divine plan.

It just so happened that it was the Deliverer's express desire from the beginning that all his human brothers and sisters - Catholic and non-Catholic, and Christian and non-Christian - come under the mantel of the apostolic Church he founded on the "rock called Peter". Mjomba was therefore certain that the divine plan had no provision for a world in which individuals for reasons best known to themselves promoted competing (and contradictory) religious beliefs. That being the case, Mjomba did not doubt that those humans who were responsible for creating divisions among men, regardless of whether they were acting on their own, in tandem with others, or in league with Diabolos, would be held to account if for no other reason than that unity and love, in the Deliverer's view, are synonymous. Mjomba wrote that the Deliverer made it crystal clear when as He prayed to His Father in the Garden of Gethsemane that restoring unity to humankind was what His passion and death were all about.

Even though Mjomba did eventually succeed in putting that dream behind him, it was not until after it had left its indelible mark on him. That dream, combined with the knowledge that the devil had been so brazen as to try and neutralize the Author of Life, left Mjomba unsure about the exact extent to which the Evil One could go to try and ruin things for humans. In other words, the dream left Mjomba with the kind of respect for the devil's ambitions and capabilities it clearly had not been in his (Mjomba's) nature to entertain.

Mjomba did not think that there were any devils masquerading as humans and much less as pastors and ministers. But he told himself that if it ever happened that some of the individuals who passed themselves off as "ministers" in the Church or Mystical Body of the Deliverer were in reality not humans but demons in disguise, he wouldn't be surprised. In a world in which lying and deception had become equated with being diplomatic or savvy, and in which bribery and extortion had were legal, and also a world in which daylight murder, the senseless destruction of property, and other practices that were unbecoming of humans were increasingly gaining acceptance as a way of settling scores, and almost anything went, it would not at all have surprised Mjomba if such devilishness was found to permeate the ministry as well.

The fall from grace...

In his account of the rebellion of the first Man and Woman, Mjomba described how a teary Eve aroused Adam one night and informed him that she was intending to exercise her right to choose, not with regard to a method of exploiting the earth's rich resources or anything like that, but with respect to the ultimate object of their existence. Up until that moment, whatever she had done, she had done it to the greater honor and glory of the Prime Mover. She now informed Adam that she for her part intended, come day light, to shift the focus away from the Prime Mover to herself - and him, if he cared to join her in her diabolic plan.

Eve knew that she was engaging in something that was against common sense and wrong. But, to her surprise, Adam responded that he not only respected her right to choose, but that he himself had been thinking very much along those same lines, and that he welcomed her bold initiative which admittedly required a lot of courage.

Mjomba actually had Adam quip: "Eve, you've obviously been talking to Beelzebub", adding with a shrug that so had he himself. But Eve let him know that she had been prepared to go off and live by herself some place else if it had turned out that he wasn't ready to join her in her scheme. Adam had recoiled instinctively at Eve's statement. Still, he had noted in a whisper in the darkness that the Prime Mover was invisible anyway, adding that even though they did not actually have to do what they planned to do, he himself was curious about the effect of going that route, especially in view of the fact that their right to choose was actually God-given.

Whereupon Eve announced with a sneer that everything would be OK. She had, she revealed, been secretly conducting an experiment with a diet she was certain could prolong human life indefinitely. The diet she had discovered, which included a special "miracle" fruit cocktail, would assure an uninterrupted supply in the right quantities of the red blood cells which the atoms and molecules of the human body needed to regenerate themselves continuously and at a constant pace. She added with a snicker that all they now needed to do was feast on that fruit cocktail.

"By the way", Eve added, a wicked smile enveloping her face; "Have you noticed that you have been losing some of the gray hairs around your temple lately?"

When Adam replied in the affirmative, Eve informed him that she had been using him as a guinea-pig to ensure the formula of their medicinal diet worked, and hoped that he did not mind the role.

Adam let her know that he minded. But, now that they were in this thing together, he had no choice but to forgive her everything, he declared. He also acknowledged, besides, that he admittedly owed her a bundle for proving that she herself could fill the role of a scientific genius - a Dr. Life of sorts - when they needed one.

Pointing to a three-legged stool on which Adam loved to relax, Eve said: "The life of that settee of yours is ten years or so. Now, anything that we didn't find here - everything that we have ourselves fabricated - has a life of only so many years. We can even decide to trash or recycle these wares before their time is up! Actually everything we see, the crust of the earth included, has only a limited life...".

"Darling", Adam had reportedly interjected; "To the extent that created matter is changing all the time, I am sure this marvelous planet of ours including everything on it - the elephants, giraffes, crocodiles, *et cetera* - has only a short lease of life. What exactly are you trying to say?"

"That is exactly the point I am trying to make, my dear" Eve retorted. "All matter, including the stuff our bodies are made of, changes and is therefore finite. But - and note this - the diet formula I have discovered will help assure that our physiques will keep reinventing themselves. That is the power of a special diet of broccoli served raw, and boiled maize washed down with passion fruit juice!"

"Now you are talking" Mjomba quoted Adam as interjecting, and then adding with a sigh of relief: "This topic was otherwise becoming really depressing!"

Adam went on to inform Eve that he also happened to know that apples were rich in Vitamin C which in turn spurred the body to produce red blood cells in large quantities. He agreed that, with the atoms and molecules of their bodies being thus regenerated continuously, they would not grow old or die! And to make doubly sure about their eternity on this earth, they would also develop concoctions that would render their systems immune from malaria which they apparently could contract from mosquito bites, rabies in the event that they got bitten by some wild animal with that disease, the flu, and from any other diseases and viruses.

And they, of course, knew that in addition to all of the above, they would need to exercise - by working the fields, hewing logs, or even just jogging - to ensure arthritis and other diseases of old age would not catch up with them as the years went by.

Adam and Eve had both already guessed or knew that their days on earth were numbered under the existing order and that, even as faithful servants of the Creator, they were destined to pass from this world to the next all the same. The only difference between now and the situation after their rebellion would be that their transition as disloyal creatures would conceivably be accompanied by trauma and grief, especially as it would presage their judgement day.

It was while they were discussing their satanic scheme that Eve surprised Adam with a revelation of a somewhat different even though related sort. She said it was her intuitive feeling that if they had not moved quickly to wrap up the matter concerning the diet, it was Adam who most certainly would die first. She added that her intuition had been confirmed by what she had noticed in the animal kingdom - animals of the female gender consistently outlived their male counterparts!

The reference to dying had shaken Adam, not so much because he was the one who was likely to be the first human being to die, but because of the implied suggestion that he might in fact "die the death" as he put it whilst he was unrepentant after they disobeyed the Prime Mover. It was a prospect that Adam, even with all the macho he commanded, could not countenance, and certainly wasn't prepared for. If they were going to proceed with their wicked scheme, they had also to make damn certain that they did not die. Because on leaving their earthly paradise for a different realm, there wouldn't be any place in which to hide.

Voicing that fear, Adam accordingly declared sombrely: "I see! The poor devil couldn't hide, and that is why he had it!"

Mjomba added that, clearly and very unfortunately, instead of dissuading him, Eve's revelation about the likelihood of Adam being the first one to kick the bucket only served to sway him to Eve's position regarding the diet. Mjomba went on to write, with respect to dying, that it was evident that Lucifer had actually died the death, albeit a purely spiritual death. That Satan was really "dead" - kaput! But that, in the spiritual realm in which creatures created in the image of the Prime Mover existed, "death" really meant condemnation and not annihilation.

Adam, who had no reason not to believe Eve, was persuaded by her views regarding the diet and the important role it was going to play in what they were plotting to do. Reasoning somewhat like Lucifer and the other fallen spirits had done, Adam and Eve felt that they had to choose now if they preferred independence to the rewards of continuing as faithful servants of the Prime Mover. The course of action they were choosing would make them independent of the Prime Mover; and they, of course, had no intention of ever wanting to confront Him after such an act of apostasy.

Before the fall from grace, Eve, like Adam, was shrewd and sharp to a degree that would have been regarded as quite astounding by their progeny. Sullied as they would be by original sin from birth (with the notable exception of the immaculate Mary and the Deliverer Himself), Adam and Eve's descendants simply could never have attained to that sort of sharpness or shrewdness - at least while they lived. Mjomba accordingly argued that it would be a combination of the sharp intelligence enjoyed by those first humans and the powerful bond of mutual respect between them that, in the end, would ultimately also prove to be man's undoing!

Adam and Eve easily appreciated the fact that, without their cooperation, the divine plan, which envisaged an expanded Garden of Eden brimming with animal and vegetative life and generations of human beings created in the Prime Mover's image, was doomed. According to Mjomba, the reference in the bible to a forbidden fruit was allegorical, "fruit" being the term coined by either Adam or Eve to refer to the betrayal of the trust and confidence the Almighty had placed in them both.

In his thesis, Mjomba actually had Eve coin that term in what he described as an ultimate act of self-debasement. Prior to that moment in human history, when either Adam or Eve munched on apples or any of the many other types of fruit which were in abundant supply in the Garden of Eden, they had done so not out of need or for the purpose of personal self-gratification, but strictly for the greater glory of God. From now on, not only did they intend to use the act of eating as a symbolism for defiant behavior, but they were also determined to go out of their way to pluck and eat these fruits to appease what was essentially imagined hunger - which, of course, proved to be very real indeed when they stumbled out of Paradise in shame with an invisible host of God's faithful angels on their heels.

Mjomba supposed that by that time Adam was already acting as if Eve, along with the rest of created earthly beings, both animate and inanimate, was personal property he was free to use for his personal aggrandizement in a scheme that practically had Adam himself enthroned as Lord of the Universe.

Mjomba also had Eve acting similarly - as if Adam, in spite of his marvelous nature, was more the result of unspectacular natural evolution and less a product of the Creator's crafting genius. He even had her forgetting - at least for the moment - that she herself had been formed out of Adam's rib, and believing a tall tale to the effect that it was as a result of the natural forces of evolution that she had become the incarnation of entrancing womanhood and pristine beauty!

According to Mjomba's thesis, in a typical instance of "group think" which may not of itself have constituted a sin, Adam agreed with Eve that with their superior instincts they were quite capable of fending for themselves, and of taking measures to keep lions, alligators and other dangerous creatures at bay. It was, to say the least, a miscalculation on the part of the first Man and Woman to suppose that their instincts were superior to those of lower creatures just because those creatures, unlike them, did not enjoy the benefit of the faculties of reason and will.

But, as Mjomba pointed out, pride came before the fall! Pride was effectively the sin Adam and Eve committed, he wrote. It blinded them to the fact that they needed the Prime Mover, and it also caused their egos to be inflated to the point to which common sense ceased being common.

In the transformed Garden of Eden, or the Valley of Tears as it would be known thence forward, they not only would never be able to think clearly because of one distraction or another, but they would also frequently be unable to summon the will power required to take the necessary steps to accomplish a desired goal even when everything else was in place. This would be because, with their fall from grace, Adam and Eve would become inclined to evil rather than to godly things. The antidote or remedy for that condition would be to remain as close as possible to the Prime Mover by praying at all times and thus continually grow in the knowledge of "that greater than which nothing can be thought". But it would be a remedy the patient rarely wanted to take.

All of that, Mjomba wrote, would in time translate into a lethargy of sorts that would accompany every activity they engaged in even when it might look like there was some hope on the horizon. And the situation would of course be much worse if, instead of encouragement and hope, things looked all gloomy with no reprieve in sight. Given the potential for rivalries, jealousies, prejudices, and intrigues, and with hate among men likely to wind up as the rule rather than the exception, accomplishing anything that was positive and virtuous would end up being a tough sell indeed - and almost impossible when the machinations of the devil, temptations of the flesh, the widespread penchant to glorify evil and promote materialism, escapism and debauchery and make them socially acceptable, and so on and so forth were figured in.

According to Mjomba, Adam and Eve would have no reason to believe that the laws of nature would suddenly change and incorporate miracles as a part of the natural order, especially after they had sinned. Without any doubt, therefore, Adam and Eve and their descendants would be in for a pretty rough time thanks to the folly of the first Man and Woman.

But that was not all. Mjomba argued in his thesis that the mere fact that life had to go on after the original sin - the fact that humans still had the obligation to seek and achieve self-actualization, and the fact that Adam and Eve were themselves still obligated to multiply and fill the earth, etc. - would make a situation that was already complicated even more so. And the fact that it would be mostly the old and wizened who would pass from this world to the next first for their rendezvous with the Prime Mover would definitely not auger well for the future of mankind.

With the errors of Adam and Eve being repeated over and over by succeeding generations, and with history - the history of professed transgressors - repeating itself all along, time would come, Mjomba wrote, when things would be really hard for humanity.

Reflecting further on the changed reality after the fall of Adam and Eve from grace, Mjomba would write, regarding the condition of the human intellect, that instead of being the powerful instrument for anticipating the face-to-face vision of the Prime Mover in eternity as it had originally been intended, the mind had ended up being what Thomas Aquinas and others would describe as "a feeble instrument which man would untiringly endeavor to apply to that most exalted of objects", namely the Almighty One.

But Mjomba would note that even then, because of the operation of the mercy of God, man's most confused knowledge of that perfect of all beings - knowledge hardly deserving the name (as the philosopher put it) as was evident from the many forms of religious worship that were themselves as contradictory as they were confusing - would nevertheless cease to be despicable so long as it had as its object the infinite essence of God. In his thesis, Mjomba would attribute to Adam a remark to the effect that everything that had been legitimate to do before had become a virtual trap that goaded one to commit sin all over again - if one was presumptuous and did not stay close to the Prime Mover.

Mjomba would confide to a fellow seminarian at St. Augustine's that he saw one very important analogy in all of this. Just as the actions of Adam and Eve, who were representatives of mankind, had definitive consequences for their descendants, the actions of Nkharanga and Mvyengwa, the parents of Innocent Kintu who were also the first members of the Welekha tribe to be baptized into the Church, would also have definitive consequences for those who would come under their sway.

The "evil genius"...

In the meantime, as he went about re-enacting scenarios of biblical events for his thesis, Mjomba sometimes wondered if the original writers of the books of the old and new testaments did not go about their tasks in much the same way as he himself was doing. In the absence of scrolls containing first hand observations by witnesses or, alternatively, reliable oral traditions, the only difference between authors of the books of the bible and himself was that the former were inspired. With a lot of modesty, Mjomba silently acknowledged that he himself was of a vastly different metal from those who wrote the sacred texts. On at least one occasion, he told himself that if he was receiving any inspiration, it had to be coming from the devil because, in his own words, he felt at times as if he was enunciating an apocryphal gospel!

What made him certain that he was also being inspired was the fact that the ideas inundating his mind, and which he was clandestinely converting into material for the book he was writing, were coming in from the outside - he would have been the first to admit that he was actually involved in plagiarism on this particular regard. And what was more, he could not control the rate at which they came; and the one thing he had learnt was that, when they slowed to a trickle or simply dried up, the sensible thing was to simply bide his time.

He had also noticed that, when he did not jot down the ideas his mind received quickly - which was usually on any piece of paper that was within his reach, including old newsprint which had bits of space here and there wherein he could scribble the ideas as fast as they were invading his mind - they went right back whence they came. If they returned, they sometimes did so in their entirety. But, more often, only portions of the original ideas came back; and when they did, they hovered on the edge of his mind apparently in readiness to slip back into oblivion if again ignored for any length of time.

If they vanished and retreated back into the impenetrable void - which Mjomba had always identified with the habitat of the supra natural and which seemed patently out of bounds for mortal creatures like himself - he just wrote them off along with those ideas which did not return after their first call, because he knew that there was nothing he could do about it. But even then, he always had this feeling that when ideas thronged into his mind and then disappeared like that, it was not without a reason. He had no doubt that they left an imprint which, though imperceptible, subsequently either affected the way he assembled the material which he succeeded in capturing and committing down to paper, or perhaps even the substance of what he was in the process of communicating by way of his pen. Perhaps they even affected decisions he made in his life - decisions that were completely unrelated to his efforts at being creative. After all, Mjomba always reminded himself, committing something down to paper was in and of itself a wholly unproductive activity.

And, in what appeared to be a sure sign that he was receiving inspiration that he was always more inclined to blame on the Evil One, sometimes ideas Mjomba thought were really fabulous just kept coming and coming, even as he was looking for a way to conclude the story. Because each one of them had the potential of making his final product unique in yet another way, Mjomba usually found himself compelled to jot down and incorporate the new stream of ideas just as he had the others.

But Mjomba sometimes wondered whether, despite his assertions about being inspired, it was not true that it was he himself, not Satan or for that matter anyone else, who was coming up with the ideas for his masterpiece. Even though it was possible that such a stance sprang from modesty, he wondered if he was not just looking out for a scapegoat to blame in case those ideas turned out to be awry and not quite to his liking. Assuming that was the case, he certainly also knew that he was not the first human to demonize the archenemy and make him out to be worse than he really was. And, any way, who could possibly blame him for making Beelzebub look bad. From what he knew, it was the duty of everybody to do just that, if only because Lucifer and his cohorts were also busy doing precisely that not just to humans but to the Prime Mover Himself!

And so now, if it happened that his thesis - which he always likened to a masterpiece - turned out to be below standard and he received an “F” for his pains, there was no doubt that he would blame his misfortunes in that regard on Beelzebub. Mjomba even imagined a scenario in which the devil decided, on second thoughts, that the masterpiece could not possibly be in his interest and, changing from being his chum to being his nemesis, embarked on an all out mission to frustrate his efforts in that regard. That possibility scared the hell out of Mjomba, because he just could not imagine himself pitted single-handedly against Beelzebub!

Still, Mjomba, unlike many believers, liked to kid himself that he wasn’t really scared of the devil. He frequently reassured himself that he might even be superior to the archenemy in some respects. He could for one claim that he himself had brains in addition to an intellect, whereas Lucifer only had an intellect, albeit a sharp one!

The devil really could never be demonized enough, according to Mjomba. Here, after all, was a creature that, though intelligent in a most extra-ordinary way, had himself abused his intelligence to the fullest by trying to impersonate the Prime Mover!

Mjomba confessed that he got the idea of demonizing the devil from the scores of preachers who blamed him (the devil) for all the bad things humans did, and provided guidance to their flocks accordingly. "He made me do it" was a refrain Mjomba had heard time and again as he mingled with Christians.

Until he decided to join them and set the stage for blaming Beelzebub for any sloppiness on his part as he worked on his so-called masterpiece, he in fact had a mind to devote a paragraph or two explaining the stupidity of those who seemed to take delight in transferring blame for all the sins they committed to the Evil One and who actually made it appear that it was a good thing that Satan's following, consisting of other disgraced spirits and perhaps also humans among them, was large. Because then, these supposedly devout Christians would always have someone to blame for the slips, big and small, for which they themselves would otherwise have to assume full responsibility.

Mjomba had a lingering thought that many a smart preacher also used the devil to scare the hell out of their flock so that those poor people who did not know any better could part with their wealth in the belief that they were buying a ticket to heaven! Mjomba also pointed out that preachers, perhaps because they did not want to offend their congregations, appeared reluctant to admit that humans, the preachers themselves not excepted, were quite capable of filling the devil's role perfectly. Mjomba wrote that humans in fact frequently "played the devil", just as they frequently "played God", and preyed on each other accordingly. Mjomba cited as an example the attempt by Peter to (as he called it) subvert the divine plan by suggesting to the Deliverer that he not proceed to Jerusalem and risk being killed in fulfilment of prophecies to that effect. Apparently wanting to drive the point home, the Deliverer, according to the evangelist, had called Peter "Satan" and ordered him to get back and out of His way so He could press on with His journey. And, of course, nothing could be more devilish than misleading an assembly of people while posing as a leader and a teacher, particularly with regard to any "special mandate" to speak for the Deliverer.

And if humans could tempt fellow humans, there was little doubt that they could also inspire themselves to do evil, which they in fact frequently did, with the evil thoughts emanating from within exactly as the Deliverer said. And, Mjomba wrote, it was in fact evil thoughts originating from within that drove many a human to wage wars and kill or other wise make the lives of their fellow men miserable while asserting that they were rooting out evil from society! It was evidently also why there were so many religions on earth, each one claiming to be the true one.

Then, the most hypocritical humans appeared to be also the most adept at exploiting the bible and things like that for their personal ends! Mjomba added that writing the thesis he was writing was, unfortunately, a requirement which now made him look like he was doing the thing - exploiting the bible for personal gain! But, in his particular case, he was at least pointing out the evil and even admitting to the possibility that he might be hoodwinking other humans with an eye to making an extra buck or two, or benefiting from the exercise in some other way.

But Mjomba still recognized the devil as the evil genius *par excellence* nonetheless. A pure spirit, with not an ounce of matter or even a drop of water in his constitution, the adversary had proved that he was capable of successfully infiltrating the world of humans and planting his evil ideas. That was in addition to his ability to lull other lesser endowed, but brilliant creatures like himself nonetheless, into believing that he had a good cause in trying to unseat the Prime Mover.

Mjomba asserted that although brainless because he was a pure spirit, Lucifer had been very handsomely endowed with all sorts of spiritual gifts at creation, and that he was very very clever indeed. So clever in fact, he had been able to trick fellow spirits that were also endowed with exceedingly sharp intellects into doing the most foolish thing, namely launch an assault on the Prime Mover! Before becoming a devil, Mephistopheles stood out among the created spiritual essences as a particularly radiant jewel that was not lacking in any way and possessed all the attributes a created being could possess. Mjomba supposed that the only thing the future Satan did not possess was a super nature!

And, operating from the bottomless pit in the bowels of the earth, the disgraced Beelzebub, even though now completely incapable of doing anything that could be classified as useful, good or meritorious, had shown that he still had the gall - and indeed also ability - to wreck untold havoc in the world of humans in spite of his own down-fall. The wicked genius had succeeded in toppling Adam and Eve from their elevated pedestal as the unchallenged Masters of the Universe using a ruse that was not even that original or brilliant in conception - as it would turn out. And the clever Satan had brought this off, Mjomba lamented, even while the minds of the first Man and Woman, still unsullied by concupiscence and the other effects of original sin, were still razor sharp!

A prisoner of his imagination, Mjomba worried, that just as the angels that fell for Lucifer's ruse had fallen and turned into devils, there probably were also humans who had become veritable devils after turning their backs on the Prime Mover. This was even though, prior to becoming devils, they too were essences that had been spectacularly endowed at creation and, like the fallen spirits, were molded in the image of Him-Who-is-Who-is! Yes, human devils, Mjomba had repeated to the laughter of his fellow students, adding that they too deserved to be demonized. But, unfortunately, instead of being demonized, many ended up being glorified!

Mjomba claimed that he could give many examples of human devils who had actually been canonized by "history". According to him, they included historical figures whose actions had given rise to evils like colonialism, imperialism, and other "isms" which were equated in their time to biblical truth! Mjomba asserted that the human "devils" included "war mongers" whose inflated egos drove them to do things that could be classified as crimes against humanity. They included dictators who did not have the welfare of their subjects at heart and whose actions brought ruin and unspeakable miseries upon their subjects. Also included were slave dealers, pimps and others who made their livelihood from the shameless exploitation of fellow humans.

And, as if glamorizing historical characters who were responsible for causing their fellow men and women unspeakable misery was not bad enough, human beings - strange creatures that they were - went on to create fictional devils whom they then promptly canonized. An example of such a character - which Mjomba loved to cite - was Robin Hood, the heartless robber and terrorist whom literary scholars fondly referred to none-the-less as the "Prince of Thieves".

Returning to the main subject of his discourse, Mjomba went on that in his relationship with "willing" humans - which was just about the same as saying all humans - that "devil of devils" who symbolized everything that was wicked had proved very adept at suggesting that they might be able to get away with their evil intentioned actions simply because actions in and of themselves could not be properly designated as sinful! And humans, even though quite capable, with the help of the Prime Mover's grace, of frustrating the machinations of the archenemy, had shown that they could be fooled - just like the fallen angels before them.

Yes! An evil genius in every sense of that word, and very deserving of the capital sentence he had received for his pains too, Mjomba wrote. As was well-known, the Prime Mover, on that figurative seventh day following his labors had declared that everything he had designed and brought into existence, including the devil before he attempted the coup d'etat, was noble and worthy of admiration.

Explaining his use of the term "figurative" in a foot note, Mjomba wrote that back then, "days" might have meant "hours", and "hours" might actually have meant "minutes" and so on; and he also submitted that, even if Adam and Eve, the first people on earth, had had a glimpse of the time sheet completed by the Prime Mover after his labours and had been successful in translating its contents into human lingo which was itself just evolving, there was every likelihood that their translation was itself figurative since the Prime

Mover's "minute", "hour" and "day" in eternity could not in any case have meant the same thing as "minute", "hour" and "day" in the lives of earth bound creatures. And, of course, the likelihood that after those terms had been coined by Adam and Eve - or who ever did it - changed meaning over time as spoken tongues evolved lent weight to his point regarding the figurative use of those terms in the scriptures. And, talking about languages and the scriptures, Mjomba did not doubt that the original inspired text of the Book of Genesis was originally scripted in Ge-ez, the first human "lingo".

For good measure, Mjomba wrote, no body can tell you who the author of the Book of Genesis was, or the language in which that "book" was originally written. Which left one to conjecture that the Book of Genesis was scripted in Ge-ez, the world's oldest known lingo that Zinjatropus most likely spoke.

According to Mjomba's thesis, neither the Israelites as a distinct people, nor "Hebrew" as a language, existed when the original Book of Genesis came into being. It was his position that Hebrew first came into use approximately one hundred thousand years later, after that divinely inspired work had been translated into other languages which themselves subsequently went out of use. And it was a position that was gaining increasing acceptance in the scientific community. It was, thus, only much later that the Book of Genesis was translated into Hebrew. Mjomba did not fail to point out that Ge-ez, unlike so many other ancient languages which "died" or became extinct, had surmounted a variety of obstacles and refused to "die" like Latin and those other languages.

According to Mjomba, the original "Book of Genesis", a self-published work that was presented to the world by its inspired author as an "original, unedited, and unabridged story" of the creation of the world and all that was in it, probably differed very substantially from the stylishly written "Book of Genesis" that has been bequeathed to us in many important respects. For one thing, Mjomba doubted very much if the original Book of Genesis had any of the "biblical clarity" which the present version boasted. He suspected that as the sacred text was translated from one language into another, and as it was touched and re-touched by well-meaning but over-zealous scribes during the four hundred thousand year history of mankind, it underwent editorial and perhaps even substantive changes, and also acquired the "biblical clarity" along the way. The well-meaning scribes had even chopped up the holy book into chapters and verses - following their own whims obviously!

In support of his contention, Mjomba made reference to the fact that thousands of books - many of them several times as long as the books of scripture they supposedly were expounding on, and a good number of which even contradicted one the other despite being held up by their authors as the authoritative interpretation of the inspired works - had been written. With the recent discovery of the cave where Adam and Eve had lived, and along with it, the Rwenzori Prehistoric Diaries, Mjomba was one of the hordes of people who were now eagerly praying and hoping that someone would stumble upon the scrolls containing the original, unembellished, Book of Genesis.

Mjomba went on that, through his machinations and God-given creative ability, Lucifer, after he turned against his Prime Mover, had effectively succeeded in creating vacuums where good had previously reigned supreme. In the process, he had also succeeded in persuading humans to abandon common sense itself, and in confusing them to the point where everything they would normally do to survive had now become treacherous. While he had apparently been unable to cause any problems in the purely physical realm, the devil, a pure spirit, had succeeded in planting chaos in the spiritual realm to boot.

Also, even a beautiful creature like a snake, so poised and captivating, now evoked the image of trickery and evil! And, instead of simply being regarded as the delectable produce of Mother Earth, good old-fashioned apples were now also suspect, just because of their association in people's minds with the fall of Adam and Eve from grace.

Thanks to Satan - although, admittedly, desires of the flesh also played their part - an ordinary, well meaning folk could now not contemplate doing simple things like taking sustenance without being enticed either to pander to the pallet for its own sake or to capitulate to gourmandism. As things stood, enjoying a glass of fine wine with the intention of celebrating life easily led to intoxication.

It did not take much for relaxing or a well-deserved rest to translate into indolence and idolatry. Unless one was fortified with grace when one stopped to admire anything, there was every chance that one's innocent admiration of an object would quickly start to degenerate into covetousness.

Literature, the arts, and the media were all now employed to promote causes that were largely shady instead of being used to inform and educate. The distinction between those activities that were intimate by design and those that were not was, for all practical purposes, lost and forgotten. The reproductive act, so vital to the survival of the human race, had become equated with indecency and depravity. Already the idea of "dressing up", when considered in isolation from fashions and fads, had lost meaning.

Mjomba wrote that the reproductive act had evidently become one aspect of human life about which almost everyone liked to moralize. The innumerable spins on the interpretation of the sixth commandment was proof enough of that. But, by the same token, it was also an aspect of human life that was ideal for illustrating the principle that it was not the act but the intention that comprised sin. As happened in other areas in which humans started tampering with the Prime Mover's original purpose for making things the way he had done, to the extent humans had removed sexuality from its original context in the divine plan, that precious part of human nature had lost its ability to fulfil humans the way it was intended to do.

How could humans ever hope to achieve self-actualization if they were unable to use the gifts they had received from the Prime Mover the way they were meant to be used? That was one of two questions Mjomba had posed as he concluded his discussion of the subject of sexuality. The other question was why humans had decided to be in breach not just of those two but of all the ten commandments when they would have been much better off keeping them the way they were originally meant to be kept. In the final analysis humans, as creatures who were endowed with reason and a free will, did things the way they did because they chose to. This was so despite the wish of some that, just because the Deliverer had come, the choices they made now didn't really matter, and that the only thing that did was "faith in Jesus"! Yeah, only "faith in Jesus" even if you reviled the Church He established and empowered to carry on His mission, as well as its teachings!

The devil, even though a master of shrewdness, did not have the power to compel humans to follow his vile and contemptible insinuations. Can you imagine what things would be like if Beelzebub had that power! Perhaps if the tempter had not been there to beguile humans with counsel that was less than honest, humans might very well have taken on that role and done the dirty work themselves, Mjomba quipped! He added that, by the look of it, some humans, not caring a hoot if the devil existed or didn't exist, were already doing precisely that, to the obvious delight of the prince of darkness no doubt!

They, essentially, would have their fellow humans believe that self-actualization and escapism were synonymous. Mjomba likened escapism to seeking total or lasting fulfillment from appreciating the ever changing face of the pop charts' top ten numbers. And he proceeded to comment that this was what actually happened when talents and other endowments that humans had received from the Prime Mover were treated as if they were just accidents of nature with no place in the divine plan. With their original purpose in that plan thwarted, their use for transitory satisfaction could no longer lead to actualization which, in the case of humans, had to be permanent to be effectual.

Because humans were spiritual beings, one's chances for achieving self-actualization were enhanced by self-abnegation or the giving of oneself particularly in relation to one's neighbor, according to Mjomba's thesis. In other words - making sacrifices or loving the neighbor above oneself as commanded by the Prime Mover, and preparing oneself in that way to receive the Ultimate Good which can only be received entire and not piece-meal. An important implication of this was that individuals who did that were unencumbered by any worldly possessions when the time came for them to depart this life for the next one, and that their self-actualization was assured even when they left this world before they reached the "prime" of their life in the worldly sense.

Mjomba advanced the strange argument that it was the self-immolation that counted most when trying to determine how close one was to self-actualization, and that material success was entirely irrelevant. The enjoyment of a fleeting moment of satisfaction in this life was certainly not a prerequisite for achieving true self-actualization. The exposure to suffering and pain, deprivation and things of that nature, according to Mjomba's thesis, predisposed humans for fulfillment.

To be a celebrity author in the next life, one did not have to be a published author or to have "authored" anything, Mjomba wrote. In fact not publishing any thing even helped ensure that the merits from one's potential as an author were not reduced to naught or damaged as one basked in the glow of being a best-seller or a Nobel Laureate and things like that.

To be an accomplished and superb preacher, one did not need to step inside a pulpit or to give a homily, and even less a rousing one. They did not even have to be ordained ministers, and it was unimportant that they might not have once opened their mouths - like the Holy Innocents whose suffering and premature death for the sake of the Holy Child are things that will continue to resound in the ears of believers and non-believers all over the world to the last day.

What was more, to be "something" in the eyes of the Prime Mover, one did not even have to grow up and become "mature" in anything in the worldly sense. One did not even need to develop to the point where one could eat with a fork and knife. Mjomba quipped that if the ability to feed oneself using chopsticks had been a prerequisite for any celestial accomplishment, most people including himself, would probably be disqualified.

To be a "Doctor of the Church", St. Theresa of Lisieux did not have to be appointed to an endowed professorship at some funny place where the ivory tower mentality was the hype first. She accomplished that by leading the life of a recluse, shirking publicity, and making certain that she did not break the rules of her monastery, especially the ones other nuns regarded as unimportant.

To qualify as a celestial "Beauty Queen", it was not necessary for one to become a maiden first, according to Mjomba. And there was, of course, no age limit for entering the "Beauty Queen' contest. Mjomba added that to be a member of the Mystical Body of Christ, it was not even necessary for one to complete the journey of groping one's way into the visible Church the Deliverer founded - so long as one was doing one's best to find the "unknown" God. According to Mjomba, the Sermon on the Mount made perfect sense and was apparently backed by solid reasons too!

According to Mjomba's thesis, the real and the only determinant of self-actualization for humans was the degree to which they embraced the state of being childlike, and consequently were prepared to give the full credit for actual or potential achievements to the Prime Mover ungrudgingly. That was also the state in which all humans started off at birth, but which they strove to abandon as they lost their innocence, grew in selfishness, and stopped being childlike as they supposedly "matured". And it was a state, Mjomba asserted, which was also the hallmark of humility.

Using the pop charts to illustrate the short-sightedness of humans with regard to happiness and self-actualization, Mjomba wrote that, after embracing the pop chart's top ten numbers as the very best there ever could be in one week, and after taking the necessary action to gain possession of them, those humans who were given to adoring pop music - and Mjomba readily admitted that he was one of them - soon found they had to start all over again when the new top of the pop charts popped up in the next week without ever learning from their experience! As Mjomba liked to put it, the difference between self-deception and escapism was the same!

Mjomba went on that because escapism did not have reason as its basis, the tendency for those mired in it to "push the envelope" to its limits was strong. Escapism undermined self-discipline; and those caught up in its clutches often risked severe bodily harm in their misguided quest for material happiness.

Lucifer was thus not just the evil genius *par excellence*, but verily the prince of darkness, and humans ignored him at their peril, according to Mjomba. To drive the point home, he wrote that the Deliverer took pity over those whom he found languishing under the spell of Beelzebub and immediately went to their aid. But even after the Evil One had been rebuked times and again, he had kept up with his harassment, not even sparing the Deliverer himself.

Mjomba suggested that the devil was particularly active on those occasions when the Deliverer performed miracles, and that he must have done everything in his power to diminish their efficacy. Mjomba accordingly imagined gluttonous individuals, at the miracle of the multiplication of loaves and fishes, consuming food far in excess of their needs as they were wont to do. And he also imagined habitual drunks among the wedding guests at Canaan, who probably had been responsible for the wine shortage in the first place, drinking to an unprecedented excess when the Deliverer changed water into wine to alleviate the shortage they had caused.

But in truth, Mjomba wrote, the devil, while not harmless, was finished after he failed to make the grade. According to the seminarian, Satan was finished in the exact same way his lackeys among humans become finished when they find themselves locked in the pursuit of temporal, completely transient happiness or fulfillment - as they invariably discover upon leaving this life for the after-life. The bitterness they now harbored from knowing that others would in time move on to occupy the elevated places in heaven they themselves had forfeited was a sure sign that they knew they had been written off for good. Satan's fate was sealed, and he knew it.

But, a big time liar and a spoiler, he was out to try and ruin things for others despite the fact that he himself had been fashioned in the image and likeness of the Prime Mover. The Evil One was now ceaselessly haunted by thoughts of what he would have been had he not wilfully deviated from the path of truth.

As far as being vanquished went, Mephistopheles had been defeated and was completely powerless. This was clear from the fact that he could only tempt individuals to a certain extent; and, even then, he could not coerce the target of his entrapment to fall for his bait however alluring or to capitulate to his insinuations however slick and beguiling. Emphasizing the archenemy's powerlessness, Mjomba, ever the pro-life advocate, wrote that the most fragile human, even when still in the form of a foetus that was on the verge of being expelled from it's mother's womb accidentally or deliberately, wielded far more power and clout than the devil.

But being completely vanquished also meant being dangerous beyond imagination, Mjomba argued. While a jailbird could afford to relax and rest on his or her laurels (at least during the intervals he or she was not incarcerated), it was not so with the mighty Prince of the Underworld. The devil did not have any laurels on which he could rest; and he wasn't in a position to enjoy even one single moment of peace during which he could contemplate things that were good or worthwhile either. And that, according to Mjomba, made him one really mad, and exceedingly dangerous creature that was on the loose nonetheless.

Because it was not in his nature to spare himself any pains born of the fear of failure, the devil worked ceaselessly; and his persistence had paid off. As a result of his machinations, humans - the vast majority of them at any rate - were for all practical purposes oblivious of their last end as they went about their daily business. And this, Mjomba quipped, just when you thought that humans would be absorbed with preparations for something as critically important as their after-life!

To the extent that those humans who acknowledged that they had an after-life in practice now paid only lip service to that fact, with an ever increasing number more inclined to ridicule the very notion of an after-life and to equate themselves to lower creatures that were not endowed with the faculties of the intellect and free will, to that extent the prince of darkness could claim unqualified success for his endeavors as a spoiler. And, what was more, he consequently could claim that humans were vanquished while he himself was at least still kicking - in an ironic and, indeed, altogether unexpected reversal of the situation!

And, assuming for the sake of argument, that humans were right, the devil would be able to say that humans themselves had to admit that they were finished in the true sense of that word, especially since creatures that were created with an intellect and a free, and for that reason ranked as spiritual beings, could not be more "finished" or as Mjomba loved to put it more "kaput" than that!

A shameless liar but no blithering idiot, he had succeeded in convincing humans that worldly glamour - rather than human suffering, self denial, mortification and penance in the aftermath of original sin - signalled beauty in the human person. And stupid, idiotic humans had gone on to make that tall tale an article of faith and a guiding principle of their lives! And then, not content with permitting Beelzebub to dictate to them on such a vital matter, humans took it upon themselves to celebrate - yes, celebrate - that "sacred" truth regularly with festivals in places like Rio, Cancun, Tampa Bay, Miami, and now even on the worldwide Web!

Evolution and Man...

Mjomba, who had once upon a time confided to Primrose that he was both a creationist and an evolutionist, had allowed in his thesis that, around the fifth or sixth century, a large proportion of the earth's population, which was, undoubtedly much smaller than today's population, likely consisted of individuals who were either transsexual or bisexual, the result supposedly of inter-marriages between individuals who were close kin. Mjomba went as far as suggesting that in those early years of human history, conjugal relations between blood brothers and sisters were even regarded as the ideal - until it was discovered that the preponderance of the evidence pointed in the opposite direction.

Mjomba hypothesized that, with the number of transvestites and hermaphrodites together constituting roughly two thirds or there-about of the earth's population, being a transvestite or a hermaphrodite was, Mjomba claimed, socially acceptable. And - what was more - their lifestyles were even coveted, Mjomba wrote. The number of people who were born with regular male and female features was in the minority, and it was considered very much a blessing in those days to be born with bisexual features. For most people, hetero-sexual relations were thus not a practical proposition.

According to Mjomba's thesis, marriages between heterosexual partners at that time in history were not regarded as highly as they would by later generations. Hetero-sexual relations resulted in childbirth; and the associated burdens, specifically the work involved in rearing children, made the marriages unpopular. Mjomba wrote that the preoccupation with bringing up children was looked down upon partly because it imposed restrictions on things like migration and adventurous travel for its own sake, which was a very popular pastime in those days. The situation was exacerbated by the fact that people lived to be three - and sometimes even four - hundred years! Consequently, couples often ended up with as many as fifty children from the same union, making it difficult for the parents to go anywhere!

And even as the population was thus exploding, the explorers, single men and women who were more often than not transsexuals, returned to regale those who had been left behind with tales of adventure and captivating accounts of conditions in distant exotic lands. Treated as heroes, the returnees automatically went on to enjoy a high social status, much of it at the expense of those who had stayed on to rear their families and were sometimes looked down on and despised as unadventurous and "sissy" moms and pops.

Mjomba posited that the coveted position of transvestites in the society of those days was bolstered by the general belief that bisexual and transsexual individuals were more fully developed. There was also the fact, he pointed out, that they had physiques that tended to be more robust and athletic than average, and that supposedly made them exceedingly handsome and the envy of everyone.

Mjomba contended that it was only much later, as the number of bisexual and transsexual persons dwindled with the passage of time and they became a tiny minority, that the tables completely turned in favor of the segment of the population that was hetero-sexual, allowing moms and pops to once again enjoy self-esteem in their own right. It was thus that being born an ordinary man or woman - like Adam and Eve of old - on the gender continuum eventually stopped being regarded as a bane, and again became respectable, taking on the noble image it has continued to enjoy to this day.

Mjomba credited the changes in the demographic makeup of the earth's human population at that time to the natural forces of evolution, and argued that creationism and evolution were ideas that, far from being incompatible, were in fact complementary. But there were also diseases that broke out during this period and that, according to Mjomba, appeared to single out transsexual and bisexual couples. He argued that those diseases played an important part in bringing about the fundamental changes in the population pattern, and also in changing people's attitudes towards sexual relations between individuals of the same sex.

Mjomba believed that there was a great deal of controversy among moralists of that epoch regarding the part(s) of the gender or sexual continuum that supposedly represented the norm. He suggested that there likely was even greater controversy regarding the types of sexual relations - and the form(s) of sexual activities - that could be considered legitimate. In the absence of formal books of scriptures and organized church groups, those moralists could not themselves escape being characterized as self-proclaimed and self-serving, and their exhortations went largely unheeded.

Also, according to Mjomba, contrary to popular belief, all human beings throughout the ages had enjoyed an equal opportunity for salvation. Humans did not choose their race, their gender, the epoch in which they came into existence, and even less whether to come into being at all or not. Any human, Mjomba himself included, theoretically could have come into the world as Adam, Eve, Judas

Iscariot, or as some other shady character that had already lived or whose time was still to come.

Conceived in original sin (with the exception of Mary and her divine Son), they all started out as innocent individuals nonetheless; and it was only subsequently that they succumbed voluntarily to venial and/or mortal sin, and in some instances sacrilegious sins as well - depending on the extent to which they were determined to thwart the divine plan also known as providence. The mystery of it all was that humans, led by Adam and Eve, chose to disobey the Prime Mover at all! It was a mystery because, first, they were not under any compulsion to go off and sin against their Creator. Secondly, when they did so, their chosen course of action did not even guarantee any happiness. They were in fact taking a gamble.

And then they also knew that they were abandoning the sure path to fulfilment - fulfilment guaranteed them by none other than the Prime Mover Himself. When humans sinned, they were in that sense committing what they knew to be a folly. In the case of Adam and Eve, it was (as it turned out) an insane, irrational, act which they immediately regretted!

Mjomba conceded that many moralists thought otherwise. But that was because they confused physical actions, which were in themselves neither good nor bad, with human intent. That confusion, according to Mjomba, had also caused many present-day moralists to arrive at the erroneous conclusion that there was an intrinsic correlation between the state of technological development and immorality.

It was, of course, Mjomba's firm position that the act of disobedience to the Creator, rather than being found on the lower subliminal level of their human nature, primarily involved the higher faculties of the intellect and the will, and accordingly was to be found in the spiritual realm.

To further illustrate that point, Mjomba had detailed how, every time the First Man allowed his gaze to fall upon the only other human in the universe (who after all owed her existence to the fact that, in the Creator's view, it was not good for Man to be alone!), Adam had developed the tendency to become absorbed by Eve's womanly nature from time to time. Adam had easily guessed that he felt overwhelmed in her presence because her physique and temperament had been designed to be different from and yet at the same time complimentary to his own manly nature.

Citing evidence in the Rwenzori Prehistoric Diaries, Mjomba wrote that Adam often wondered whether Eve was encountering the same problem, but could not marshal the courage to ask her! As far as Mjomba was concerned, it was quite normal for Adam and Eve to experience those feelings; and the fact that both Adam and Eve had come into being as grown-ups, and did not have the benefit of experiencing what early childhood and normal adolescence were like, had nothing at all to do with those feelings. According to Mjomba's thesis, there was at least no evidence in either the Diaries or the Book of Genesis to suggest that there was anything abnormal about the attitudes and temperament of the first Man and Woman in those respects.

Mjomba even argued that there would have been a much greater likelihood of that happening had Adam and Eve come into the world as little babies and then developed in stages, including the stage of puberty, before they reached adult-hood - as normally occurred in the case of their posterity. With no earthly dad and/or mom to wean and guide them through those critical stages in life, and without the sort of animal instinct that would have made up for the absence of a dad and mom to cuddle them, Adam and Eve would almost certainly have ended up as imbeciles who were unable to take care of themselves, let alone bring up their own issue in a culture that stressed lofty ideals and service to each other and above all to the Prime Mover - or worse!

Adam, Mjomba wrote, proceeded as a matter of course to join Michael the Arch-angel and the rest of the heavenly host in praising the Prime Mover for that new marvel in his creation, and to deride Lucifer and the other fallen angels for imagining that they could derive anything but illusory satisfaction from refusing to pay the Creator homage as the Almighty One - and, as well, a Prime Mover who had not stopped at fashioning cherubs, and seraphs and the members of the other choirs of angels in His own image and likeness, but had proceeded to mold humans likewise in His divine image! That was even though the heavenly host were invisible to the naked eye, and could only be discerned through the eyes of their faith.

Parallel between humans and devils...

And, in a bold and wholly unprecedented move, Mjomba had gone on to describe how Adam and Eve, using the immense clout they wielded over other forms of life on earth and with remarkable ingenuity, successfully coaxed the beasts of the earth, the birds of the air, fishes and other creatures of the sea, along with the other life forms on earth - even including inanimate objects - to participate in festivals that brought out the best in them for the greater glory of the Prime Mover.

Mjomba contended that those festivals, celebrating as they did not only the sublime nature of the Prime Mover but also His boundless wisdom, power and love, were a major irritant to Lucifer and the other inhabitants of the under-world; and that one especially powerful suggestion advanced by Beelzebub during the temptation of Adam and Eve in the Garden of Eden, was that instead of celebrating the somewhat prosaic fact that the Creator was a genius of sorts, celebrating the ingenuity with which they laid on those festivals and their own innate genius, promised to be so much more exciting and fun!

Satan reportedly emphasized that all he was suggesting was that Adam and Eve focus less on the genius that God obviously was, and more on their own innate, less celebrated ingenuity and their other talents! As if that was not bad enough, Satan had further argued that the shift was in fact necessary to redress the imbalance in the order of nature - or something to that effect!

Noting that the seed of rebellion sown by the Evil One in the minds of the first Man and the first Woman did indeed result in sin, Mjomba had proceeded to depict Eve as suggesting to the man out of whose rib she had been formed that everything seemed to be set for them to assume the roles of Supreme King and Supreme Queen of a world that was entirely independent of the invisible Prime Mover! Eve had found her not-so-secret admirer - who, like her, assumed at that point that the authority they wielded over other creatures of the universe could be taken completely for granted - as interested as ever in the idea of being at the top of an eternal tree of the human family and exercising absolute reign over generations of human creatures. That was something that would make them divine in all but name!

Yes, she (Eve) would be the definitive Queen Bee while Adam, whom she was now anxiously waiting to welcome and embrace as her "royal" consort, was going to be the King Bee! And they thought that, by elbowing the Prime Mover to the side and out of their direct vision, they would themselves become virtual divinities - somewhat like Him! And, yes - people would die! Anyone who would refuse to pay them homage or to toe the line in other respects would be straightened up. They were not going to brook any nonsense from any one. Their imperial status would not be negotiable.

After all, their subjects would be descended from their own royal stock. And, while they would indeed be offspring of royalty, the fact would remain that they would owe it all to the Queen Bee and the King Bee! That is why stern action would be taken against any one who would have the cheek to display a "bad attitude".

According to Mjomba's thesis, Adam and Eve resolved well before they were themselves cast out from the Garden of Eden that they would be "bad" when it came to dealing with their disloyal subjects. There would be jails in which to confine the most "unruly" elements. And, yes! Adam and Eve would also institute detentions without trial. Quoting from the Rwenzori Prehistoric Diaries, Mjomba wrote that at one point, Adam, who was really just following Eve's lead in all this, was horrified when he caught Eve giggling mirthfully and excited at the thought of "prisoners" in leg chains! Mjomba went on that Eve, that matronly mother of the human race who owed her own existence to the fact that Adam had been willing to donate one of his ribs so the Prime Mover could use it to form her, apparently even relished visions of piles of human skulls on the edge of some killing fields - skulls of those "subjects" who did not heed warnings to toe the line or be destroyed!

And even though Adam told himself many times that he was going to walk away and leave Eve to her strange devices, he could not muster the courage to do so. He could not imagine leaving the only other living person he had known, even though she was degenerating into something of a sub-human. Because, even when Eve was acting like a devil, there was something about her that mesmerized him, and held him completely captive. And it was not long before he surrendered to the woman's overwhelming magnetism and mysterious power.

In fact, after a while, Adam himself begun to relish the cool manner in which Eve described the fate that awaited anyone who would suddenly "turn up with an attitude" as she liked to put it. Eve was apparently elated when Adam suggested that any of their descendants who qualified as a "very bad character", according to their definition, would deserve to be "drawn, hanged, and quartered"! But Eve thought that it would be more fun to execute - or, as she liked to put it, "neutralize" - such characters by stoning them to death with the help of rocks or whatever method came in handy.

Whereupon Adam, whose "conversion" was now complete, chimed in saying that they could organize and "crush" such folks if they could develop catapults and other devices for delivering rocks and other missiles that shattered on impact in what he described as "shock and awe" operations!

Citing what he referred to as incontrovertible "evidence" in the Rwenzori Prehistoric Diaries, Mjomba wrote that Adam, in his eagerness to reassure Eve that he intended to go with her all the way in their burgeoning rebellion against the Prime Mover, actually conducted some experiments in a nearby jungle and reported back to Eve something Mjomba thought was quite astounding. He informed Eve that it would not be long before they were actually able to fabricate what he called "nuclear" and "hydrogen" contraptions that could be detonated over concentrations of hostile forces. Adam explained that to use those contraptions or "bombs" effectively without compromising their own safety, they would have to deliver the "bombs" by catapult or some similar conveyance and ignite in-built fuses by remote control from a safe distance.

According to Mjomba's thesis, Adam let Eve know that once developed, an arsenal of those nuclear and hydrogen bombs would serve as a deterrent and ensure that their subjects, wherever they were, toed the line. Adam, according to Mjomba, regretted that they could not employ those weapons of mass destruction or "WMD" as he fondly referred to the "bombs" to knock the daylights out of beings that were pure spirits, like Diabolos for instance!

But it was evident that Adam, a coward, was mindful of the possibility of uprisings and revolutions whose objective would be the overthrow of the "imperial rule" they were even now planning to impose on their as yet unborn descendants. It meant that they had to be prepared to be ruthless and merciless in dealing with any dissent! It would be necessary to resort to those types of things in the New Order in which the offspring of Adam and Eve would automatically become subjects who would be expected to pay the duo homage in the same way they themselves now paid homage to the Prime Mover!

Mjomba wrote that it was a mark of the extent to which human creatures, even though created in the image of the Prime Mover, could be bad that Adam and Eve could plot harm to their own kind even before the target of their vitriol had come into the world. That Adam and Eve could stand there in the Garden of Eden (where they themselves were still virtual guests) and do such a thing defied comprehension in Mjomba's view. They were doing so in the absence of any perceived threat of any kind to themselves and while they were simultaneously plotting to break their own covenant with the Prime Mover! Mjomba wondered how the first Man and the first Woman could do those sorts of things and still sleep soundly when night fell. And it wasn't as if they had nothing to do!

All the while that Adam and Eve were busy plotting against the Prime Mover and planning harm to their own progeny - and also eyeing the ripening fruits on the Tree of Life which they knew was out of bounds - they were supposed to be working the fields to grow their own food so that they would be self-reliant. Mjomba noted that the first Man and the first Woman had really committed not one but a string of sins, including the original sin. He commented that if the first couple had not allowed themselves to be idol - if they had remained at their post tilling the soil, hewing logs, harvesting the crops, and doing the other things they needed to do to meet their needs - even though they might still have failed the Prime Mover and committed sins, they likely would have been what he (Mjomba) called "unoriginal sins"; and the human race would have been spared the dreadful and debilitating consequences of the original sin. In other words, "original virtue" would have triumphed!

But Adam and Eve chose to be idol, and to abandon themselves to scheming evil on a magnitude that came close to rivalling the scheming by Diabolos himself! It was simply incomprehensible - Adam and Eve who were beneficiaries of such largess from the Prime Mover not just plotting to do harm to the unborn and the innocent who were moreover their own kind, but also plotting against their Creator! Not even beasts did that sort of thing.

Or, perhaps, it was more appropriate to say that it was only humans (who were blest with a free will and also with faculties of the intellect and the imagination) who could misuse their talents to that extent and in that fashion! Mjomba noted that Adam and Eve were planning to disobey a Being that, far from threatening them in any way, had in fact brought them into existence out of nothing, endowed them with immense and incredible gifts, and had in addition promised to be their mainstay throughout all eternity.

It did not in the end surprise Mjomba at all that humans, who would have been quite happy (or so they stupidly imagined) to be completely rid of their Prime Mover in league with Diabolos, had all too often proved to be so cruel to their own kind. It distressed Mjomba to think that Lucifer, who had set things in motion with his act of intransigence, had not had any scruples about targeting beings who were angels like him and that he had eventually succeed in tricking numbers of them into following him into perdition. Mjomba did not doubt that Satan started hatching his schemes against his fellow angels well before they too had come into existence.

It distressed Mjomba to think that Diabolos, apparently the first creature to be brought into being, fell from grace in the very beginning - before any other creatures (both angels and humans) had been brought into being. It was a horrible thought that the very first creature to exist could betray the Creator so early on in the divine plan - just as it was a horrible thought that Adam and Eve, the very first Man and Woman, had betrayed their Prime Mover so soon after they had been brought into being and before any other humans had been created. That - and the fact that Beelzebub did not respect any boundaries and eventually drew humans as well into his dastardly schemes and rebellion against the Prime Mover - spoke volumes about his evil mind.

As Adam and Eve would both discover later to their utter dismay in the wake of their rebellion, the "satisfaction" which their cunning archenemy lead them to believe would be theirs for the asking on attaining independence from the Prime Mover would in fact be a sham. It would be entirely transitory, and unlike the satisfaction they now got from serving the Almighty One whose divine nature was synonymous with perfect goodness, perfect wisdom and perfect love. And there would be no guarantee that they wouldn't lose their hard won "independence" to some ambitious or plainly greedy members of the human family!

Luckily for Adam and Eve and their posterity, it required no more than an acknowledgement by Adam and Eve that they had sinned to get Satan off their backs. For one, that admission was in itself evidence that the first Man and Woman had finally succeeded in seeing through the lies of Diabolos. It also predisposed them for the divine act of mercy that would in time translate in the advent into the world of their God and Redeemer.

This was even though Adam and Eve, who had still to exchange married vows, were not yet husband and wife at the time of their rebellion. It is also thus noteworthy and to the credit of Adam and Eve that, even though not yet husband and wife, they both responded to the Prime Mover's promise of a Deliverer in way that reflected great statesmanship on the part of Adam and great stateswomanship on the part of Eve.

Pulling together and letting bygones be bygones, they were able to steer clear of the trap laid by Diabolos and avoided being drawn into the blame game to his great disappointment. And, even though they continued to be pummelled by the effects of original sin, including the threat of physical death which was now very real, Adam and eve, almost miraculously succeeded in working their way back into good books with their Prime Mover, holding fort until their liaison was finally blessed by the infinitely loving - and forgiving - Creator.

Judgement...

In Adam and Eve's terminology, death occurred when the body became separated from the soul. What happened to the lower animals - or "brutes", as Adam and Eve referred to the animals, reptiles, and fishes - and other "living" creatures and plants when they expired and ceased to exist did not rise to anything approximating death because divine grace did not come into the picture. These lower beings came into the world and departed there from at the pleasure of the Creator so to speak.

According to the thesis, when the lower creatures expired, that was not really *death* because it was not a penalty for disobedience to the Creator. Mjomba supposed that the transition of these lower animals from the *state of being* back to the *state of non-being* looked like it was traumatic all right. And who knows! Perhaps at that point in time, everything they too had ever done in their animal lives returned to haunt them even if only momentarily - before the lower creatures slipped back into nothingness and oblivion!

Mjomba wrote that perhaps it was during that same moment - a final moment in time so to speak - during which they too got a chance to acknowledge Him-Who-Is-Who-Is for one last time as the Almighty One who brought them into being gratuitously out of nothingness, albeit not in His own image and likeness as in the case of their "masters" back on earth! A final moment, Mjomba added, during which *dying* beasts were also afforded what might be described as a *glimpse* of sorts of the Omnipotent before their "egos", consumed by their love and adoration for their Maker, caused them to burn out and return to nothingness!

Mjomba was convinced that something like that probably occurred especially since back on earth these same beasts *saw* things with their eyes and *sensed* the reality around them in very much the same way as humans did. Still, that transformation, according to Mjomba, remained very much akin to the chemical transformation that vegetative creatures under-went when they too "died" and became recycled.

Egos being consumed by love and adoration for the Omnipotent - that was especially true for dying humans, according to Mjomba. In their case, and because they were made in the image and likeness of the Prime Mover, the mere act of facing the Judge - after leaving behind a world which they had left better or worse than they had found it - had to be traumatic of and in itself. It had to be a frightful experience for humans, who were endowed with both reason and a free will, to come face to face with their self-deception and to finally accept that when they did things that were proscribed during their "time of trial" on earth, they did those things, not because they themselves *were humans* or because they *were made* in a certain way, but because they *were capable* of doing them and *chose* to so act. And, pertaining to eternal life, that period of trial on earth, which in modern times sometimes stretched to thirty thousand days for the "unlucky" ones, was still a relatively short one!

Mjomba wrote that, like a diamond in a pile of trash, the beauty in humans seemed to sparkle even more when they were indulging in filth. But, conversely, the ugliness of sin was also more revolting when, with worldly trappings which had served to cloak it swept away, the naked human soul suddenly found itself in the Divine Presence. It had to be even more devastating for souls of the damned to suddenly discover that after living the lie, the propensity to continue lying stayed with them right there in the presence of the Living Truth as undeniable evidence of their malfeasance, making them absolutely loathsome.

And it had to be a dreadful feeling for those souls to find they now had to own up to the fact that back on earth they really were just *servants* who decided to bury the talents they had been entrusted with by their *Master*. Mjomba wrote that it had to be really heart-breaking for those souls to admit at that late stage that they should have known that their protestations about the Deliverer being a mean and exacting Master - who "reaped where He did not saw" - could not possibly wash. It had to be a most pitiful sight as those who, up until that moment had been laughing and making merry, all of a sudden started to weep and gnash their teeth in a belated act of remorse. And it had to be a horrible spectacle indeed as those same souls, realizing that they did not now belong there in the Divine Presence by their own choosing, made a stampede for exists that were not there!

Mjomba imagined the really incorrigible, for whom time to make amends and become cleansed from the guilt of their sins with fire in *Purgatory* - or whatever you may wish to call it - did not look like something they would welcome, making a rather reckless, if instinctive, stampede towards earth which they had just vacated. According to him, they did that instinctively when it dawned on them that they had squandered their time on earth on pipe dreams instead of working on their self-actualization as the children of the Prime Mover they were - time during which they had absolutely defied the clamor of their consciences and refused to accept that they could not serve two masters - the Prime Mover and mammon. That they had refused to heed the Deliverer's advice that they sell all their possessions, give the proceeds, not to Judas Iscariot, the Deliverer's purse bearer, or (by extension) to "churches" (which with one single exception were "bogus" anyway), but to the poor and go follow Him. And that, having adamantly refused to detach themselves from temporal things in order to afford themselves the opportunity to dwell on the more important things pertaining to their eternal life, they had indeed flunked the Church Triumphant Entrance Test!

Mjomba clarified that because they possessed the *knowledge* that they were supposed to walk the walk, they no longer had a valid excuse for not walking that walk. That was even though, knowledge was only the start, and to walk that walk successfully also required *cooperation* with the grace of the Prime Mover.

Mjomba supposed that the decision of souls of the damned to take flight was induced by their hatred for those other souls of the just who were headed for Purgatory and eventually heaven where they would exult in the Divine Presence for eternity - and their enormous pride.

Mjomba imagined them breaking out from the Divine Presence all right, but not quite succeeding in quelling their craving for fulfilment, a craving that only their Maker could give. Some, according to Mjomba, headed blindly for earth in hopes of being able to repossess their bodies and to perchance resume leading their ungodly lives of lies and self-deception. But instead, they all found themselves deep inside the earth's crust in the company of demons and other lost souls!

Mjomba had no doubt that that was where hell was located - deep in the crust of the earth. It was there, after all, that Adam and Eve and the souls of all their descendants had ended up as captives of Diabolos - until rescue came on that *Good* Friday two thousand years ago when the Deliverer descended into hell in person. And it was there, as a matter of fact, that the Deliverer spent three days and three nights, communing with the spirits of His human ancestors before He *freed* them on the day of His resurrection.

Mjomba wrote that in the case of Lucifer and his following, their expulsion from the heavenly paradise could not be described as "dying" in the physical sense for the simple reason that the constitution of angels did not contain bodily matter. According to Mjomba's thesis, they "died" spiritually never-the-less, and underwent something that was completely unknown in the world of matter. The human concept of death consisting in the separation of the soul from the human body pales when compared to spiritual death which consists in the inability of an unrepentant creature that happens to be fashioned in the image and likeness of the Prime Mover to hide and escape "damnation". Like the fallen angels, upon leaving the plane of matter and entering the spiritual plane, "death", consisting in the flight of the "damned" soul from the presence of the Prime Mover and Source of Life, became imminent. With absolutely no where to hide, the unrepentant soul, standing condemned for its acts of commission and omission, had to make an exit of sorts from the face of the Prime Mover, and typically ended up in a real place called "hell" (because of the very unpleasant conditions there) located in the bowels of the earth.

The Forbidden Fruit...

When they disobeyed, Adam and Eve found that they could hide only for so long, and they quickly realised that they would also end up really "dead" likewise, absent an act of divine mercy and their own willingness to be redeemed. And so, strictly speaking, Adam and Eve were slated to die twice after their own sin of disobedience: physically upon their transition to the after-life and also spiritually unless they returned to the fold. Mjomba argued that until their sin in the Garden of Eden, "death" as we now know it existed for Adam and Eve only as an idea, and a very unimportant one. He even went on to suggest that what probably came to their mind when thinking about their "physical" death or transition to the after-life was really "life" and not "death". This was because that transition, following their "trial" on earth, presaged even better things for them as faithful servants of the Prime Mover. And, unlike the lower beings whose "transformation" effectively meant the end of the road, physical death was something they looked forward to - until they decided to become rebels.

Mjomba had Adam and Eve thinking, mistakenly as it would turn out, that the chance of anything like the painless "death" of lower beings ever befalling them - let alone a torturous transformation from life on this earth to something else as punishment for disloyalty to the Prime Mover - appeared very remote, if for no other reason than that, up until this time, it had never crossed their minds that this could happen to them! It was inconceivable that anyone of them could end up in a bottomless pit in the bowels of the earth as a punishment for disloyal conduct, and they were effectively blinded by the fact that such a thing had never happened to humans before and was completely foreign to human experience!

In the days leading up to the rebellion, they had even calculated the probability of "dying" and leaving this world for the next. Using advanced calculus, the first couple reckoned that they could regard a one way ticket to hell as an improbable event, and they accordingly wrote it off as a possibility. That was even though they knew that Satan and the other renegade spirits were already there. In any event, they would in time develop the technology that would effectively transfer the decision to "die" or not to die from nature (representing the Prime Mover) to themselves! It was a matter of carrying out the necessary research and, brilliant creatures, they regarded it as doable.

Adam and Eve allowed themselves to revel in the silly notion that their rule over a mighty, earthly kingdom, because it would be subject to materialistic determinism, would be unchallenged and everlasting. But to work, the scheme also called for Adam and Eve to conceal from their subjects the original purpose of creation, and to usurp the original Creator's role by acting as if it was they who were conferring existence upon their human subjects through parentage! Their claim to being the Majestic King and Queen of the universe would otherwise indeed ring hollow, and their dream of a perpetual reign over humankind would be frustrated thereby.

The first Man and Woman had not yet cohabited, and they certainly had not yet conceived a child, as they considered the choices confronting them. Fair skinned and blond because she had been fashioned out of Adam's rib, Eve had initiated the conversation as a part of her bid to interest Adam in procreation. But, following her womanly instincts and using the gift of intuition with which she was richly endowed, she had continued to maintain her distance from Adam, nonetheless, and to give herself time to study him and weigh her options.

Tanned and boasting a thick mane of hair the color of clay from which he originally came, Adam showed himself as keen as ever to do whatever it would take to ensure that Eve agreed to accept his hand in matrimony. Anxious to show that he was valiant and a man of metal, he had responded that he concurred with everything she was saying and could not wait to see her enthroned as Queen of their earthly kingdom and himself as King. According to Mjomba, he had even suggested that he would use the occasion to solemnize the first royal wedding ever.

Even though they had been commanded by the Creator to multiply and fill the earth, it was not a command that was intended to abrogate their God-given right to decide and choose. Adam and Eve were well aware of that. They, indeed, knew that not everything their God-given nature permitted them to do was necessarily righteous. They could choose to commit suicide, frightful though such a thing was to imagine if only because a pact between the first man and the first woman to end their earthly existence would have automatically resulted in the end of the world as far as the human race was concerned. Or they could opt to just become iconoclasts. The ability to choose represented the one aspect of their nature that distinguished them from mammals, birds, vegetation and physical matter.

Emboldened, Eve had gone on to announce that nothing - absolutely nothing - could stop them from proceeding to create their progeny in their own image and likeness, if they wanted to so proceed. “It is so ordered” Adam, in a clumsy effort to prove his manliness, had replied. He knew that he and his companion had the where-with-all to beget children. And even though his progeny would come into the world programmed to grow and develop into autonomous individuals, he believed that he could manipulate his offspring to his own and Eve’s advantage. That was what they planned on doing in complete disregard for the fact that their own human nature, which was itself fashioned in the Creator’s image, had been made the way it had been made for the sole purpose of enabling them to do God’s bidding - which was to multiply and fill the earth. And so, lamentably, Adam and Eve found themselves tempted to see what would happen if they usurped powers that belonged only in the divine realm!

Mjomba had Adam and Eve realizing, virtually immediately, that their scheme was going to result in their being cast out from the Garden of Eden. They must also have understood that they would not be guaranteed the protective mantle which had hitherto kept at bay everything from the crafty Lucifer and his legion of fallen angels to animals of the wild and other creatures, big and small and visible and invisible, that were certain to turn hostile. Mjomba presumed that they had initially balked.

But, unfortunately for the human race, Adam and Eve were perceiving themselves already at that point as virtual prisoners who were expected to enjoy the comforts of the Garden of Eden, the boundaries of which extended and encompassed the whole universe, provided whatever they did redounded to the greater glory of the Creator and Him alone. In other words, they were free to do absolutely anything, but only if they did it selflessly. Adam was also in full agreement with Eve that being able to choose one way or the other was a challenge they could not imagine away and had to face up to.

When the crafty Beelzebub, sneaking past a band of guardian angels and up into the branches of the tree under which the two-some stood in the guise of a reptile, suggested that it wasn't their fault that they were created with the faculties of reason and free will; and that, unlike lower forms of life, they were now obligated to make a choice one way or the other; they had found to their surprise that their God-given common sense did not contradict his point. They did, indeed, feel as if they were on trial and in a limbo of some kind, awaiting an unknown fate.

Whereupon the archenemy, eager to see the rebellion against the Creator expand, had goaded them on, pointing out that it behoved them to do something, outrageous or otherwise, before they could attain any form of self-actualization! Because he had happened on to the earth before Eve, Adam had found himself stung by his conscience and had recoiled at the idea of turning against the Prime Mover, even though he seemed prepared to do virtually anything to please his companion.

In response to the disappointed Adam's reasoned objections, Eve, who had started it all in a veiled effort to draw Adam's interest to herself and shore up their relationship, had thereupon suggested that they cut a deal with the Prime Mover! Under the agreement, which would not qualify as a rebellion, their offspring would be fashioned not in His image but their own. Under the deal, the original divine plan would thus be only slightly modified to allow Adam and Eve to represent themselves to their progeny as gods, the fact that they were themselves creatures notwithstanding.

Looking Eve in the eye, Adam had immediately realized that she was determined to win his love at all costs, which had caused him to mutter something like "Look at you!" He had also established as fact that she was the embodiment of spousal beauty and charm. On the spur of the moment, he had decided that he and Eve would fall from grace or stay in the Prime Mover's favour together.

Eve had convinced Adam that it was quite feasible to cut such a deal with the Prime Mover whose mistake it was to bestow upon both of them such high intelligence and the right to choose. Knowing quite well that it wasn't in the Prime Mover's nature to go back on his word and take those gifts away from them, Adam had agreed with Eve that they seemed to be in a particularly strong bargaining position.

The alternative to the deal was obvious. Adam and Eve would be at liberty to exercise their God-given right to choose. And they would dutifully make choices, some of which, if followed through, could frustrate the original divine plan. For one, they could decide to change the purpose of sexuality making it primarily for recreation rather than procreation. In the process, they could decide to forego bearing any children, to slow the growth of the human race to a rate they and they themselves alone would determine, or to multiply and fill the earth - but only for their own self-aggrandisement.

Even though that was the current game plan, at the time the idea of a revolt against the Prime Mover got into Eve's head at the very start and she for her part made up her mind to "play along", the situation had looked decidedly trickier than that. The woman who was destined to be the mother of the human race had not just assumed that Adam, her God-given companion and consort, would also play along.

It was quite conceivable that the future father of the human race could refuse to do so; and then there was the off-chance, in the event Adam decided that he didn't want to have any part in the rebellion, that he might try to talk her out of it - and succeed! It just so happened that, after she got the evil idea from Satan, Eve had been successful in persuading Adam to join her in the wicked scheme. But it wasn't completely unimaginable that, even then, Adam could chicken out along the way and leave her to her own devices.

It wasn't that Eve was paranoid or anything like that. It seemed to her a sensible thing to prepare herself to deal with all those possibilities and plan her moves accordingly.

Eve of course knew that Adam and she herself had been fashioned the way they had been for a reason - namely so that they would be able to procreate. But, while she took it that this had not been intended to signify that her role would merely be that of a "courtesan", if Adam approached her with the suggestion that they start begetting children, she understood that - everything being equal - she would be at fault by being needlessly averse to the idea. In other words, she would "submit" to him. And, of course, Adam also would be under a similar obligation if she approached him with the same intention.

But now, as Eve was considering the different ways in which she could thwart the divine plan, it struck her that one way would be to rebuff Adam's approaches - in the event that Adam decided not to join the rebellion. In other words, she would refuse to submit to him in the above regard. Mjomba wrote that according to Eve's diaries, she told herself that, if she was prepared to stand up to the Prime Mover, who was Adam any way!

Eve reasoned that, even if Adam agreed to stick with her as a co-conspirator, there would almost certainly be occasions when "the lout" would consider refusing to submit to her for his own selfish reasons. In order not provide him an excuse to do that to her, she was going to think of clever ways of bluffing him, and pretending that she herself had valid reasons for not "submitting" to him. She considered herself a good actor - a much better one than Adam - for one; and she imagined that she could, for instance, successfully feign illness or make it appear as if it was an inappropriate time for them to make love every time he made the "unwanted" approaches.

Adam was undoubtedly going to be a very disappointed man if he was going to take her for granted. There was absolutely nothing Adam could do - short of raping her - if she did not want to have a baby! And if he laid a hand on her with that intention, she would poison him. After administering "the portion" to him, she would then take her own life by drinking some of it herself - so she would be all by herself on earth!

But she could also use a different tack to frustrate the divine plan. She could decide to have all the babies Adam wanted, but deliberately refuse to give them a good upbringing. She could in that way use her offspring as proxies through whom she would achieve the same end of derailing the divine plan! She noted that she had a whole range of options, and wondered if Adam - unpredictable man that he was - knew it too!

And so now, as if on cue, Eve had proceeded to outline to the man she very much wanted to be her consort many ingenious ways of avoiding conception, including the use of the chastity belt, as well as many ways of enhancing or alternatively permanently undermining the human reproductive process. Adam was not just impressed with Eve's arguments. He was surprised that Eve and himself commanded such clout regardless of whether they were going to continue to do everything to the Creator's greater honor and glory or otherwise.

Adam even noted that, unlike Lucifer and his band of fallen angels for whom actions and intentions comprised one and the same thing, their human nature allowed for a distinction. Indeed, the future of their relationship with the Creator depended not so much on the nature of their individual actions as on the intentions behind them. And it was precisely this aspect of their human nature which gave the couple apparent room for bargaining. Adam and Eve even had a lingering feeling that if their plan ever went awry, there just might be a chance to recant and quickly get back into the Creator's good books before it was too late.

Unlike the angelic beings who were all created in one and the same moment in eternity, humans could procreate and multiply over time. Adam and Eve accordingly thought they could justify relegating their issue to a secondary position under the new order they were proposing. It did not seem unreasonable or too far fetched for them to contemplate setting themselves up as gods of some kind, and having their heirs venerate them as such. Mjomba had, accordingly, argued that sexuality featured in the eventual act of rebellion as Adam and Eve finally moved to consummate their diabolic plan even though the sinful act occurred in the spiritual realm.

It was as though the first couple did not foresee the serious consequences of their action, including the Creator's intention to stop restraining his other creatures ranging from lions, crocodiles and other mammals to reptiles and, more ominously, minute creatures like germs, viruses, and other parasites which were invisible to the naked eye and which could turn particularly deadly at a command from the Creator.

They also had to know that there could even be subsequent challenges to their own authority from within the family of human beings, as well as from other unknown dangers inherent in their decision to travel a route that no man before them had ever travelled. They could not be entirely sure, for instance, that in some corner of the universe, creatures of comparable or perhaps even superior intelligence existed that might attempt to flush them from the face of the earth on the orders of their Maker or for their own selfish ends, assuming they too were in revolt!

While Mjomba supposed that the faculty of reason of the first Man and Woman, unfettered as it was by concupiscence and other effects of sin, was indescribably sharp, making them incredibly smart and supremely intelligent, he also believed that they must have been an especially thick-skinned, obstinate and obdurate pair to have proceeded with the rebellion given what they knew. He also depicted them as daring, reckless and short-sighted in a most curious way. Citing "incontrovertible" evidence in the Rwenzori Prehistoric Diaries, Mjomba wrote that in their foolishness, Adam and Eve, discussed how, as free creatures, it would not be the last time they would reach out, pluck and eat fruit from the Tree of Life.

Adam and Eve had every intention of making a habit of it, and they deluded themselves that they would silence their consciences thereby for ever. To maximize and prolong the "happiness" and gratification they expected to derive from challenging the Prime Mover's authority, after plucking the fruit from the Tree of Life, they planned to withdraw to a secluded place in the Garden of Eden - preferably some distance from the shrine which they had built in honor of the Creator in the days when their friendship with Him was strong and their faith in Him was rock solid - and they would take their time to enjoy it. They were, of course, determined not to waste any of the forbidden fruit's nourishing juices and especially its vaunted life giving plasma as they fed on it. And they were not going to let anything or anyone, be it a guardian angel or even the Prime Mover Himself, spoil their fun.

Yes, fun - because everything they were going to do was really legitimate apart, that is, from their motives which were wicked! The act of munching on the forbidden fruit was itself neither good nor bad. It was quite conceivable for Eve to mistakenly pluck fruit from the Tree of Life and to share it with her companion (Adam) without the latter suspecting that it was the forbidden fruit he was sampling. In the event, the Prime Mover would just have smiled and let it go. Their action would not have constituted a sin - not even a venial sin! Adam and Eve knew that much.

Their real intention was to counter the will of the Omnipotent and establish themselves as a viable alternative to Him in creation; and that spelled lots of fun. They were essentially planning to hijack the agenda of the Prime Mover and to make it their own - how could that not be fun! But even though their sinful act would arise out of solid scheming and was going to be premeditated in every way, they for their part were going to pretend, as they carried out their sordid act of defiance, that they were doing so in all innocence and without any ill intentions! And to make matters worse, they intended to do it in the name of humanity!

According to the Rwenzori Prehistoric Diaries, it was as Adam and Eve were contemplating their options that Lucifer suggested that there couldn't possibly be any harm in trying. Moreover, they would be like the Prime Mover. The suggestion by Beelzebub that they would be like the Prime Mover caused visions of invincible humans who could do virtually anything the Prime Mover did to invade their imagination. Humans who could also cause other humans to come into existence out of nothing even as the Prime Mover had caused them both to bounce into life out of the blue, and who could perhaps even successfully challenge the Prime Mover to a contest or a dual in which the winner took all! They certainly were capable of multiplying. The animals, birds, mammals, insects, and even vegetative life - in fact all the living things they had encountered during their short life spans - were capable of doing it! That would be a good start!

Of course, as rational beings, Adam and Eve now imagined that they could challenge the Prime Mover in a much more effective way by doing what the lower beings did instinctively in a more deliberate fashion and in accordance with their own plan, albeit a wicked plan that would be at cross purposes with the divine plan.

That would constitute a definite challenge to the Prime Mover! It was very tempting for Adam and Eve to start imagining that they not only would do a better job of imitating the Prime Mover than the lower creatures, but they could pose a real challenge to Him - or whatever force it was that had caused them and everything they saw around them to spring into existence out of nothing! Along with the idea that the Prime Mover could be effectively challenged, the devil had apparently instilled in Adam and Eve the idea that perhaps the idea of a Prime Mover only existed in their imagination, and that it might be possible that there was no such Being! Of course if it turned out that the Prime Mover only existed in their imagination, that would spoil the fun they definitely were looking forward to having as they kicked off their own home-grown rebellion.

Adam and Eve thought it was good thing that they did not yet have any issue because they could not be sure that the "louts" would join them in their plot. Since they were the sole representatives of the human race, their posterity did not have a choice in this matter - and that meant everyone of their children and their children's children without any exception. It appeared as though everything was going to work to Adam and Eve's advantage.

To get a bigger kick out of their act of defiance, Adam and Eve intended to bring their faculty of the imagination to bear so that they would derive any amount of pleasure they wanted from feeding on the forbidden fruit. Actually, with the help of that faculty and the faculty of the will, they could literally do anything they fancied. And they could also create any amount of chaos on earth to make things hard for the Prime Mover - or so they thought! That was certainly going to entail lots of fun!

But that was not all - Adam and Eve went as far as imagining that every time they would sample the forbidden fruit, their experience on those later occasions would be as gratifying and "uplifting" as it would be the first time around! That would make their sin a real coup with an immortal dimension, and it would be a reward of sorts for the gamble they were taking - or so they thought. Mjomba wrote that they even joked that they were wasting time and needed to get going immediately - if for no other reason than that each time they sinned, it would be like they were doing it the first time. They imagined that their act of stealing fruit from the Tree of Life and eating it would thus always be a delightful, fresh, and energizing experience they would never be bored with.

Foolishly, Adam and Eve imagined, according to Mjomba's thesis, that there would be no consequences for their despicable act in those circumstances. That, on the contrary, the successful act of sinning - or challenging the authority of the Prime Mover - would itself amount to a well-earned reward. They simply refused to heed their consciences which, according to Mjomba, were even then sending all sorts of signals to the effect that the first Man and Woman would be literally stung with guilt and shame in the aftermath of their ignoble deed.

What they did not suspect was that while a life of make believe and fantasy was possible during the time of their pilgrimage on earth, the self-deception could not be perpetuated indefinitely, and certainly not beyond the grave. Yes, Grave! Adam and Eve knew that it was matter - changing matter - that informed their souls. That being the case, their "pilgrimage" on earth had to be subject to certain limitations, one of which was that they would move on to an afterlife! And, however that transition (from earth to the afterlife) was viewed, it still marked a very grave moment in their existence - a moment that ordinarily was going to see them ushered into the presence of the Prime Mover and a permanent, unchanging afterlife - what their descendants would refer to as "life beyond the grave".

There, stripped of the trappings of matter that made it possible for humans on earth to perpetuate the self-deception, they would be literally assailed by the realization that it was all a mirage. It definitely was going to come back to haunt Adam and Eve, perhaps even before they were ushered into their afterlife, that the preoccupation by humans that wasn't geared to their last end, had a definite price - a price not unlike that which an unfaithful spouse stood to pay at the end of time. In this particular case, Adam and Eve's acknowledgement memory of their inconstancy would itself become transformed into an unbearable scourge. It would be the driving force behind the clamor by their whole being for the permanent, unchanging and Perfect Good!

Autonomous individuals who suddenly found themselves scorned by the one and the only true and perfect lover they knew should have been theirs if they had not sought their satisfaction elsewhere and betrayed His trust in that way, they would now be more than glad to endure any amount of spiritual sufferings and misery - and, if possible, also physical pain - if that could distract them enough and ease their sense of loss and deprivation. Adam and Eve would realize that, in the afterlife, nothing could be more painful, humiliating and unsettling than to be taunted by a yawning emptiness that only the Perfect One could fill. If only they knew what would be in store for them if they ended up in a place where, deprived of the Perfect Good they knew was meant for them, they would be overwhelmed by a dreadful and unquenchable thirst that made one crave for the harshest self-punishment for not having focused on their last end during their earthly pilgrimage!

Just as Lucifer and his legion of disobedient angels fell for the temptation to be like gods who would hold sway in the ethereal world, Adam and Eve, according to Mjomba's thesis, thought that they could somehow get away with a challenge to the Creator's position in the earthly universe. If anything, the fact that the angels had already staged a rebellion before them made it even more tempting for Adam and Eve to try the same thing one more time. The sharp wit and intelligence Adam and Eve commanded made them capable of being really dare-devilish, Mjomba wrote.

Because they themselves were fashioned in the Creator's image, they were supposed to apply their exceptional grasp of philosophical and scientific ideas in the service of the Creator. But they were now involved in a plot to use these gifts in reaching out and harnessing the riches, not just of Planet Earth, but also of the myriad constellations of the planets and stars in ways that would make it possible for them to cut their losses on their certain eviction from the Garden of Eden.

They had to know that their action was going to leave them thus exposed in all sorts of ways, if only because both of them knew clearly that they owed their existence to the Prime Mover's selfless love. But the prospect of being regarded as gods to whom everything was owed by their offspring had apparently proved too much of a temptation. Mjomba also argued that, with their superior intelligence, the first Man and the first Woman imagined that they might be able to devise ways and means of neutralizing the dangers the lower animal species, reptiles, germs and viruses might pose.

Mjomba, letting his imagination run a little wild, had theorized that the faithlessness of Adam and Eve had finally reached its peak and that the father and mother of mankind had "crossed the Rubicon" just as they were consummating their marriage. Coinciding with her first "dark night of the soul" ever, Eve's wedding night had been anything but blissful. A rebel, both *de facto* and *de jure*, she had suddenly found herself stripped and deprived of the grace into which she had been "born" and of the benefits ensuing there from. In the immediate aftermath of her act of rebellion and her determination to put not God but her own self-love first in whatever she did, Eve had suddenly found herself vulnerable and exposed to the intrigue of both Satan and Man, not to mention the elements. And, for the first time ever, she had seen a need to cover her delicate figure with apparel of some kind.

As Mjomba described it, Eve and her second half knew the instant they lost their innocence that they were going to "die the death"! But that was not all. As the light of God's grace faded away, they saw that they could not face the Creator against whom they had sinned. They had accordingly stumbled blindly for the exits from the Garden of Eden only to find none existed.

They should have known better because the Garden of Eden, within whose confines they had made their abode until hitherto and the scene of their original sin, continued to be a part of Planet Earth and unchanged. What had changed was Man who had tried to usurp the power of the Prime Mover. And it was also then that they realized that their faculties of the will and the intellect, which had played key roles in the their act of rebellion, and on which they had banked so much for implementing their evil scheme had they succeeded in pulling off the ill-fated deal, were irrevocably blunted and crippled, victims of the shock waves of their falling out with their Creator.

The first Man and Woman were shocked to discover that their mental impairment was permanent. In addition to the fact that logical acts by man could not be guaranteed, there was now also no guarantee that human thoughts themselves would always be logical. That was because man was now inclined to give precedence to thoughts that promoted self-interest as opposed to thoughts that were objectively sound, sensible and sublime. In practical terms, that translated in the pursuit of things that were *gratifying* over things reason suggested were *legitimate* regardless of the benefits in the short, or even long, term. Even though man's survival depended on the amount of knowledge that he accumulated and applied, the sad fact was that the human learning process itself was now introverted.

As Mjomba noted in his thesis, these were developments that would for one snarl the fostering of many a human child in the days to come. Many descendants of Adam and Eve would grow up impaired and suffering from all sorts of neuroses as a direct result. Hovering on the verge of lunacy themselves, it gave Eve and her consort little consolation to know that their ever-forgiving Creator would not hold them to any irresponsible deeds committed by them from that moment on by virtue of insanity.

To cut a long story short, Eve had realized that there were inherent risks in putting all her trust and confidence in Adam. She knew full well that she herself had just cheated on her Creator by vowing to leave open the possibility of using the faculties she was endowed with - the intellect, the faculty of the will and the faculty of the imagination, the sense faculties and, of course, her carnal feelings as well - for her own exaltation rather than the Creator's. And she was of course aware that Adam, acting in concert, had also betrayed Him in a similar manner. She quickly concluded that she could not really trust Adam all that much after that.

And now, suddenly prone to misunderstand, she thought that she observed in Adam's gestures evidence of a nature that had suddenly turned mean and cruel. She could have sworn that her second half would probably go chasing other dames and cheating on her were it not for the fact that she was the only woman around. His tendency to look the other way and avoid her gaze seemed to be evidence enough of that. And perhaps worst of all, Eve was already harboring genuine fears to the effect that her "husband" could even kill her on some pretext, an act that, Mjomba noted, would have been tantamount to genocide.

Adam, in Eve's view, no longer seemed to be the congenial and tender loving man to whom she had pledged her loyalty in the moments before they fell from grace as everlasting wife. Wondering if she could ever be delivered from the beast into which Adam appeared to have turned in the twinkling of an eye, she frequently found herself lost in her thoughts and did not even bother to hide her state of mind from Adam who caught her in her reverie on more than one occasion.

Before they fell from grace, Eve had been sure that if they made love, it would be a sacred act performed without any self-interest. Adam had felt the same way. Their act of love would have mirrored the Prime Mover's selfless act of creation. And now, with their fall from grace, their perception of the world, previously unfettered and unadulterated as well as objective, had become narrow and limited; and, apart from suggestions of the devil, it was only what appealed to their lower instincts that caught their attention.

Adam and Eve were now inclined to sin, and could not act guilelessly or innocently. The realization that they were incapable of doing anything on their own that could be characterized as good came as a terrible shock and made Adam and Eve cringe. They blamed each other for their terrible mistake.

The world as they had known it up until then vanished from before their eyes, replaced by something that was entirely novel. Everything about it was intriguing, if only because, with their ties to the only Creator they had known and to whom they owed everything including their very existence cut and permanently severed, they now felt quite lonely and isolated. Stripped of the Prime Mover's grace, they now also felt exposed and naked both spiritually and physically. The Garden of Eden, which had up until then been synonymous with the universe, suddenly no longer appeared so. Mjomba had both Adam and Eve now imagining that there could be enemies lurking out there both in the bowels of earth and in the skies yonder. But, seeing themselves unfit and unworthy to be in the Creator's presence, their first impulse, according to the thesis, was to flee.

Mjomba, accordingly, had Adam and Eve stampeding for what they thought were the exits from the transformed Garden of Eden, albeit only in their imagination. This was even though everything pointed to the fact that the original Garden of Eden was anything but a gated community. Deep down in their hearts, they not only wished they had not exercised their freedom of choice as a result of which they had gone against the will of their Creator, but they even wished that they had been created without their gifts of the intellect and the will and only with instincts, like the lower animals.

In the meantime, overwhelmed with disgust and disbelief, Eve had cut herself loose from Adam's grip and accused him of being a selfish, dissembling and wretched man and a crook who was out to exploit her for his own ends. For his part, Adam had recoiled at the treachery and cunning that, according to him, Eve had employed to draw him into an irrevocable marriage bond, only to deny him the satisfaction she had lead him to believe was going to be his for the asking. According to Mjomba's expose, the seeds for infidelity, marriage break-ups, prostitution, rape, incest, and other evils like hypocrisy were also sown at that truly tragic moment in the tempestuous history of humankind.

Mjomba had concluded his thesis with two quite astounding suggestions. One was to the effect that the Creator's promise of redemption played a critical part in helping the father and mother of the human race to remain sane and not succumb to the traumatic experience of being banished from the Garden of Eden. The other was to the effect that, notwithstanding that demonstration of the Creator's infinite love and mercy, Adam and Eve frequently chose to overlook the Prime Mover's promise of a Savior and, in the ensuing frustration, threw all caution to the wind and betrayed Him time and again by doing things not to His greater glory and honor, but their own.

It all tragically started, according to Mjomba, with Adam and Eve feeling very self-confident, and thinking that they could trust themselves rather than the grace of the Prime Mover to stay out of trouble. Mjomba wrote that Adam and Eve found themselves betraying the Prime Mover again and again as a result of being too trustful of themselves, and neglecting things like prayer and mortification; and that it was only after they had indulged themselves and discovered - too late - that temporal joys were indeed ephemeral and passing that they would nudge themselves back into the realization that it was unwise to be too trustful of themselves or to neglect prayer and fasting.

Mjomba wrote that Adam and Eve committed sins all over again even though they had both "accepted" the promised Deliverer in the exact same way Simeon, John the Baptist, Simon Peter, and others would accept Him and had promised full cooperation. According to Mjomba's thesis, they certainly knew that they would be deceiving themselves if they started imagining that they were safe from the Evil One, let alone "saved". And any suggestion that one became "saved" merely by "accepting" the Deliverer however firmly would have been rebuffed by the first couple.

8. The Seminary Brotherhood

Reflecting back on life at St. Augustine's Seminary, Christian Mjomba could not help marvelling at the fact that that was indeed the place to which he had been attracted as a young man, and to which he had even grown endeared. He was surprised that his mental journey not only was transcending time and space, but was also occurring in what appeared to be the twinkling of an eye.

The strange spell, under which he was labouring and which was undoubtedly also responsible for the sudden onslaught of sullenness and gloom, now steered his attention into a slightly different direction. Without electing to do so, Mjomba found himself focusing his attention on the fact that at the time he commenced work on his book, he and his class were at an advanced stage in their preparations for the sub-deaconate and the deaconate, the "major" orders that preceded ordination to the holy priesthood.

Mjomba noted with a faint but discernible smile that, amid all that, he had harbored the rather weird notion that he had made an important discovery pertaining to the phenomenon of insanity. He had succeeded in doing so while working secretly but persistently on the dossier on Innocent Kintu, a fellow seminarian and also tribesman who had been taken ill with a strange ailment. Mjomba actually believed that his discovery was likely to make psychiatry turn a new leaf!

Frowning, Mjomba thought about his earlier years as a junior seminarian and recalled with nostalgia that he had been determined from his earliest days to carefully nurture his vocation to the priesthood, and that he had easily found seminary life fascinating. Later, when the opportunity to contribute to human knowledge came beckoning, he had taken it in stride just as easily. With plenty of time allotted to such things as study and meditation at the senior seminary, enabling him to mature relatively quickly in those favourable surroundings, it did indeed appear as if everything had been mapped out in advance by Providence.

In the junior seminary, Mjomba, the son of simple Welekha peasants, had received what amounted to a classic education as he progressed from Preparatory Class (or Prep as it was called) to Low Figures, High Figures, and onto Grammar, Syntax, Poetry and finally Rhetoric. That education included world history, European literature, Latin and even some Greek. Mjomba particularly enjoyed Julius Caesar's *De Bello Gallico* and, of all things, Ovid. In the senior seminary, as he was introduced, along with his compatriots, to Scholastic Philosophy, Canon Law, Moral and Dogmatic Theology, and Biblical Exegesis amongst others at the senior seminary, the speed with which Mjomba grew in self-actualization had actually known no bounds.

Mjomba had always felt fortunate that his ambition to serve God had put him in line for what amounted to a first class education. He had been particularly happy that the rector at St. Augustine's, to assure his candidates for the priesthood a well-rounded education, on a regular basis invited religious scholars of other schools of thought to address the student body. The visiting scholars included Buddhists, Hindus, Moslems, and even followers of Confucius.

Ever a keen participant in the ensuing discussions, Mjomba had been struck by the profound insights that this dialogue afforded whoever was eager to expand his knowledge. As a result of the exposure to the wider metaphysical realms, he had developed a special interest in the unique and rather extensive collection of materials on world philosophies and religions in the seminary library. The availability of those materials enabled him to pursue his own independent investigation of various theories propagated by the philosophers of the orient and the premises underlying those theories.

But Mjomba had not been entirely happy in certain other respects. Although he kept mum about it, he had gradually began to lament, albeit in silence, the fact that the seminary's own contemplative practices did not incorporate things like Yoga and the techniques of Transcendental Meditation as taught by the great

Maharishi - at least not directly. And while he, like everyone else in the seminary, believed that the writings of thinkers and philosophers of the orient contained many erudite things, it seemed to him, in so far as oriental wisdom went, that non-Christian faiths, Islam for example, had incorporated more of it than had Christianity.

Mjomba was further disappointed that the Church's definition of Christian did not include Moslems, although they accepted much of the Old Testament, including the vast majority of the prophets referred to therein, and even though they revered the Lord Jesus as Messiah and Savior of the world. In any event, since Christ came to save all men, such a narrow definition seemed hopelessly out of sync with the thrust of the message of redemption.

It bothered Mjomba that the Catholic Church went on to count members of many other groups whose doctrines were admittedly outlandish among the world's body of Christians. And even then, he himself wasn't so sure how an "outlandish" doctrine might be defined. He sometimes wondered what Buddhists, Moslems, Hindus and others thought of the Catholic Church's doctrines!

Actually, since all religions were God-given by definition, Mjomba thought the notions of true and false or outlandish religions, and the distinctions made by preachers between different faiths on those grounds, themselves had a ring of untruth, certainly unreality, about them. Mjomba sometimes wondered what things would be like in this former Garden of Eden if everybody woke up one morning to discover that there was actually one single, acknowledged True Religion to which every soul on the earth subscribed without question.

He noted that, by implication, every member of the human race would either be living in Elysium or in the New Jerusalem, and would accordingly not be in need of salvation. Or, as the banished but incorrigible descendants of Adam and Eve, they would all, without a single exception, be living lives that put them beyond the pale of salvation in that imaginary Utopia, as would be evident from the level of interest in the subject of religion. But it would also be a Utopia that also assumed that humans had a nature that was completely different from their present one - the nature of either angels (sinless beings) or of demons (long lost souls)!

The absence of a multiplicity of religions would in effect make all these bickering preachers redundant! Mjomba's conclusion was that it was important that all religions, without exception, were treated as God-given and fully respected by everyone. Actually, with the exception of the few individuals whose practice of religion was truly heroic, all other so-called believers or supposedly God-fearing people, regardless of their religious persuasion, in Mjomba's view worshipped mere personalized images of the Deity they were supposed to worship, and could therefore be said to be idolaters.

The fact that most people's idea of the Supreme Being was so hazy seemed to be proof enough of that. But the many heinous crimes committed through the ages in the name of religion represented, for Mjomba, an even more compelling reason for his conclusion that these people, despite what they said, actually worshipped something other than the Supreme Being, and consequently laid a false claim on being godly people.

Noting that preachers liked to brag about being in the "business of saving souls", Mjomba wrote that by far the vast majority were in that business for the money - period. And they wanted the *status quo* in the Church to continue because it served their purposes quite well. In order to rake in the money faster, they went to great pains to show how their "ministry" was so unique! In the process, they had diversified and tailored the highly marketable product called "Key to Heaven" to suit the whims and desires of every Dick and Harry - as if that were possible!

Mjomba decried the fact that many unwary souls in search of the Truth invariably became ensnared in the schemes of those marketing geniuses. But in their haste to use "Peter's Pence" to enrich themselves, those who "owned" those "ministries" and the preachers whose job was to attract and retain a large following, all forgot something.

According to Mjomba, while all sorts of people had set up ministries to "preach the Word" and had established churches for the purpose of "ministering to their flocks", they all conveniently forgot that the first question they themselves would be asked on exiting this life for the afterlife would be: "You and others in your profession - why did you, if you were genuinely interested in saving souls through preaching the Word - not begin by sitting down, not just with your 'Christian' buddies, but with Hindus, Buddhists, Moslems and others, and agreeing or at least attempting to agree on the one most fundamental thing, namely what that Word was. Did you find that hard to do because it would have inevitably meant sacrificing your money spinning machine or so-called 'ministry' in the process? And you claim that you actually performed so many 'miracles' in my name. Did it not strike you that the very first miracle you needed to *pray* for, especially given your unflinching faith in me according to your own avowals, ought to have been that you - despite your totally wrong motives - might get to know me and also get to understand that the Word or Truth is indivisible? Or did you - and your buddies - look upon this as just another way of making a living? *Diversifying* the Gospel message and *marketing* it to different audiences *using tips you picked up in Biz School*? And now, tell Me - would you go back and do what you did all over again if you were given an opportunity?"

As he worked through his thesis, Mjomba wondered if there was some way of putting it which would jolt the world's religious leaders to some action in that regard and save them face on Judgement Day in the process!

But Mjomba acknowledged that, a dissembling lot, it was not entirely inconceivable that if the Deliverer were to suddenly appear in person in their midst, these selfsame preachers would do everything within their power to keep Him out of the *Church* He Himself founded and over which they claimed to be guardians! Mjomba clarified what he meant by "Church" in that context, namely the Mystical Body of Christ which included the crowds those preachers claimed as their "flock" - yes, their flock, and theirs alone!

Mjomba wrote that this, sadly, was well within the realm of possibilities, particularly given the fact that many Christian "churches" had already decided to have no place in their liturgy for some of the sacraments the Deliverer instituted with such solemnity, among them the Sacrament of the Blessed Eucharist. Mjomba lamented that humans had not stopped at distorting the nature of the Church, herself a sacrament of the Deliverer's action at work in her through the mission of the Holy Ghost, in their perception of it and, after discarding some of the sacraments themselves, could be counted on to try to get rid of His messengers as well as Himself as the end drew near.

Mjomba could not think of a Christian denomination that could claim unequivocally that the Church it represented had always been "a place of prayer for all nations". Perhaps no individual church denomination was meant to be "a place of prayer for all nations" in the same way the temple in Jerusalem had been at the time the Deliverer walked in and over-turned the tables of the merchants who operated from there, Mjomba wrote!

Obviously a believer in the existence of God, Mjomba thought that the most potent argument for His existence related to the Last Judgement. In Mjomba's perception, given the evils humans did to one another, nothing would make sense if there was no Supreme Being who would avenge the miseries suffered by people at the hands of others. Even so, Mjomba had been tempted on more than one occasion to suppose that there not only had to be many gods, but also many heavens to accommodate the many self-proclaimed prophets who were irreconcilable when the world, exactly as in the beginning, finally came to an end with a big bang! It would actually have made a lot of sense, he once told himself, if someone had come forward to point out that an important text, essential to understanding the nature of humans, had for some reason been eliminated from the Book of Genesis in the course of the centuries: "And God said: Let there be many gods - and also many heavens!"

A heaven for the wicked...

As if the attempt to make the all good and all knowing Prime Mover responsible for putting the idea of idolatry in the heads of humans was not atrocious enough, Mjomba, a virtual slave of his own imagination, also concocted the notion of a "hell in heaven"! He even told himself that it wasn't an entirely implausible idea. Given the fact that every generation without exception had had its peculiar crop of self-justified but decidedly sick people who claimed a monopoly on heaven for themselves and their followers, Mjomba thought the notion of a "hell in heaven" made a lot of sense. And that was even before the myriad truly evil characters responsible for the many crimes committed against humanity in the course of human history, and many of whom were even glorified as heroes in history books, were brought into the picture.

Mjomba imagined that these "dissembling" individuals, when they finally departed this world for the next, went to the "heaven of their dreams" all right - a heaven which, in these cases, also had a provision for the hell these folks so richly deserved! When thinking about this particular category of people, the contrasting images which crowded Mjomba's mind ranged from government functionaries and their lackeys who maltreated others under the guise of performing a public service to hypocritical members of religious orders whose deeds of commission and omission caused others severe mental anguish.

A heaven for the wicked? The idea was not really as asinine as it sounded at first. Satan, clever devil that he (or she) was, surely would not leave those who had faithfully done his bidding in this life completely in the lurch in the next. In Mjomba's view, the idea of a heaven for the wicked, albeit one which ultimately was hellish, was a difficult one to dismiss as completely preposterous.

That was not to say it wasn't a frightening thought! It rankled Mjomba to think that the wicked might indeed have a place of refuge where they could find solace of some kind. That in turn raised the possibility, even though remote, that conditions in the hellish heaven just might be tolerable; and, perhaps, even tolerable enough to enable the wicked to gloat with pleasure over their wicked deeds through all eternity! It was like giving them the last laugh.

Mjomba wished that his imagination didn't devise notions of that sort. But he could not stop the grotesque images from invading his mind, and taking note of them at least allowed new ones to take the place of old ones, a circumstance which made it possible for him to avoid being overly engrossed by any individual image.

Even though he did not use it much, Mjomba just loved the expression "devil incarnate" very much, and he believed that many of the characters who would end up in the hellish heaven generally fit the bill pretty well. But especially, he thought, the following classes of people: those unscrupulous and usually also invisible power brokers in government administrations around the world who were primarily responsible for putting in place inequitable policies that violated the rights of those in society not in a position to defend themselves; merchants and the hired guns of greedy corporations who had no scruples whatsoever about using the so-called corporate clout of their clients to blackmail members of the public into parting with their hard earned cash and other possessions; and preachers who went out of their way to hood-wink the gullible members of their congregations by scaring the hell out of them while enriching their coffers.

Having noted that the idea of a "hellish heaven" was indeed plausible, Mjomba had inevitably stopped to consider a different but related idea, namely the idea of a "heavenly hell". Unlike the former idea which was merely plausible, the latter notion seemed a given. As Mjomba imagined it, after enduring what was mostly a hell-on-earth in resignation, good men and women departed this world only to find themselves unexpectedly propelled into a place that defied description - truly a heavenly hell! Wondering, as he often did, about which heaven would be more crowded, Mjomba had little doubt that it was the former, and he sometimes worried that, while he had the free exercise of his will, he could easily find himself consigned to the camp of the devils incarnate on Judgement Day. And that genuine fear prevented him from laughing off the idea of a hellish heaven and its parallel notion of a heavenly hell every time he felt like doing so.

Mjomba dearly wished that he was wrong - that his reading of the situation couldn't possibly be correct! That, after all was said and done, the bad guys received their just punishment, and the good guys their just reward, and the bad guys the punishment they so richly deserved. It would be just dreadful if there was even the remotest possibility of an order in which evil was rewarded. That would be an order in which the Diabolos, not the Prime Mover, effectively called the shots instead of being punished. That was a situation that was plain unacceptable - a contradiction in terms. And if that were the case, it would mean that devilish humans would not get what they deserved upon their departure for the afterlife.

The fact was that evil people themselves had a way of making it appear as if they were the wizened ones and couldn't therefore have it wrong. They had a way of making it appear as if the good guys were the stupid ones and, as such, were wasting the precious time they had on their hands - the time they could be using to fulfil themselves even at the expense of others and become actualized. And then there was the fact that Adam and Eve had demonstrated so early on in the history of humankind that one could do as one pleased, and still thrive in this world. Indeed, if you looked around, you were much more likely to find that it was the bad guys who were enjoying and in control, and that it was the good guys who were being exploited and at the receiving end.

But if it were to happen that it was the bad guys, not the good guys, who would end up as the ultimate winners, it would first of all make a complete mockery of the good old maxim that *charity was capable of concealing a multitude of sins* - the maxim that was supposed to demonstrate that there was some benefit to remaining decent or the good guy. But that adage itself implied, Mjomba noted, that charity or plain decency was a rare commodity, since the saying would otherwise be of no value. Mjomba felt a measure of relief as he noted that the first human beings had been thrown out of the Garden of Eden for acting atrociously. It wouldn't have been right if they had done what they did and just got away scot-free.

Even so, such sentiments seemed right on and logical, Mjomba wasn't sure that he wouldn't get into trouble for suggesting that human beings deserved everything they got for deviating from the path of righteousness. Mjomba could not help shuddering at the thought that his ideas, if expressed by him publicly, would put him at loggerheads with his Church. This was because his Church, in step with other denominations, taught that it alone was the official custodian of revealed Truth. And, here he was, confusing the situation by suggesting that the Diabolos might have a role in determining events that would transpire on the last day.

There were other aspects of Catholic doctrine which also riled the former seminarian. A keen student of Church History, Mjomba was actually scandalized by what he regarded as an impious sense of self-righteousness on which he blamed the desire of many in Christendom in the Middle Ages to see foes excommunicated and barred from activities of the so-called visible Church.

It was his expectation that sometime in the future, perhaps even in his lifetime, his Church would come around and apologize for its role in the break-up of Christendom, among other things! He thought such a development was inevitable for a number of reasons. After Adam and Eve had been cast out from the Garden of Eden after they had sinned, it simply did not make any sense, now that the Redeemer had come as promised, for anybody to claim that the Church was for some people and not for others.

Even though the Messiah condemned the actions of Judas Iscariot, the man who betrayed him to his enemies, in the strongest terms, there was no evidence that even he was excommunicated from the visible Church. But could it be that Judas was in fact excommunicated, but it just happens to be one of the many things that the scriptures, which were not intended to include all revealed truth, skipped?

While Mjomba admired Peter for being such a natural turncoat, eager to demonstrate his loyalty by striking out with his sword and cutting off the ear of Malchus, a servant of Caiaphas, the high priest, ear one moment and emphatically denying that he was one of the Savior's disciples in another, he found a lot to admire in the betrayer.

Here was a man who had, first of all, left all to follow in the foot-steps of the Messiah, volunteered to risk his life by being the one to keep the group's purse, and who was so filled with anguish over his role in the fate of the Savior he not only hastened to return to those who were actually guilty of handing Him over to the Roman imperialists the proceeds of his crime; and who deemed his own life not worth living after failing to persuade them not to proceed as they planned. Mjomba also thought that Judas was very much on the Savior's mind when He prayed to His heavenly Father for the forgiveness of His enemies, affirming that they did not, indeed, know what they were doing.

With regard to the original matter under discussion, Mjomba noted that rifts in matters of doctrine in fact abounded in the early Church, and that they never deteriorated into any excommunications"! But perhaps at a certain point in time "charity", that virtue which covers a multitude of sins, became rarer and rarer among churchmen, making the Reformation inevitable. Talking about charity, Mjomba often wondered how a person like Peter who was so prone to bungling would have fared at the hands of churchmen of a later age!

Given what befell Joan of Arc, it wasn't difficult for Mjomba to imagine what might have been the fate of Peter had he been a contemporary of the Spanish saint. And there would have been less likelihood for a person who had participated in the incarceration and murder of Christians like Saul making a mark as an Apostle of the Gentiles or anything else. With respect to people like Mary Magdalene and her likes, Mjomba wondered if any amount of public penance could have been enough in a different age to persuade anyone that they no longer posed a danger to society.

It did not really surprise Mjomba that, on their arrival in Africa, Christian missionaries had promptly denounced the ancient beliefs of his people as satanic. If they believed in the supernatural and in *Katonda*, *Were*, *Mwenyezi Mungu* or in a Creator who went by some other name, that was automatically witchcraft. Any belief that recognised the after-life was *animism* - and, of course, infinitely worse than the worship by Romans and Greeks of statues, when they were not actually treating the dictators loading over them as divinities. And if demons had been human, it would undoubtedly have been Africa where they would have emerged from.

What surprised Mjomba, above all, was the particularly virulent manner in which Westerners regarded Africa as the source of all bad things. Mjomba also made reference to a later generation of "scholars" who usually hailed from segregated America, and for whom all things African proved just ideal for airing racially biased views. Mjomba wrote that it was especially the latter who seemed bent on tracing weird practices prevailing in "advanced" societies like mass suicides, human sacrifices, and all manner of cults, *et cetera* to Africa. Mjomba wrote that these creative and rather uncanny individuals, following their treks through Africa on foot and on camel, produced best sellers in which their historic "discoveries", suitably embellished with some of the most interesting anecdotes, were laid out.

It was clearly a magnificent way of becoming an instant authority on Africa which people like Dr. Livingstone and others set in motion - a trek through Africa on foot and camel! Mjomba added that with travel made easier with the invention of air planes, it was no wonder that all the deadly diseases that afflicted Europe and America like Malaria (as if there were no Malaria carrying mosquitoes on other continents), the West Nile virus (which was evident from the name given to that virus), the AIDS virus and others had been traced back to Africa.

Mjomba worried that may be the Mad Cow disease discovered in Europe would also eventually be traced back to the "Dark Continent" as Africa was, apparently, still regarded by some folks in Europe and America on the sly. It was, according to him, quite possible that there might be some people who might try, even at that late stage, to re-write history and place the origins of the black plague which ravaged Europe in those olden times in places in Africa that Westerners of that era did not know existed.

Given the extent of the misinformation, the outright ignorance and the deep seated prejudices, Christians in the new world in particular, Mjomba wrote, had reason to be apprehensive about the integrity of the "Church's teachings". It was prudent to be apprehensive because, since the Church's inauguration on the day of Pentecost, it's teachings had been manipulated and exploited for personal ends by all manner of people with all sorts of motives, Mjomba declared. There was the fact that Christians the world over were now permanently burdened with the cost of Christmas trees, a relic from Europe's idolatrous past, to cite just one example. But, according to him, the fact that some of the worst human rights abusers in human history not only had burst in on the world scene equipped with ideologies that were firmly rooted in Christianity and who were themselves Christians appeared to confirm his view that it was critically important to be apprehensive on that score.

While admitting that unity among the Prime Mover's chosen people (by which Mjomba understood everyone whom the Prime Mover had chosen to bring into being) was a major concern even before the Deliverer left Mother Earth to return to His Father on Ascension Day, Mjomba wrote that, in addition to having to contend with divisiveness in their local churches, Christians in the New World had also to deal with divisions that had been originally fomented in the West, and had now become a permanent feature of Christendom. He claimed that the Church in Africa was saddled with the cumulative consequences of Western schisms and heresies - schisms and heresies that might not have arisen in a different cultural and/or social setting.

Noting that the apostles - including Peter who had denied the Deliverer several times when He needed the support of his band of disciples most - were human, Mjomba supposed that the successors to the twelve apostles also were human. That was why they had evidently made mistakes in judgement over time throughout the Church's history. Mjomba wrote that some of those "apostles", from time immemorial, have exuded an aura of self-importance and outright arrogance - as if they were co-judges with the Deliverer, not people who were sent to minister. And when they were not involved in scandal, they acted so self-righteously, you would think that they themselves did not need to be forgiven seven times seven times a day like everyone else.

Others brooked no criticism - as if they too were infallible, not just the Pontiff of Rome when he was speaking *ex cathedra*! Mjomba hastened to add, with emphasis, that the purpose of his analysis was not to lay blame for human errors contributing to disunity in God's Church, but rather to throw additional light on the specific nature of that problem and to trace it back to its source, namely the Evil Genius.

On the question of beliefs being satanic, Mjomba argued in his thesis that, throughout the ages, Africans seemed better informed than, say, the Greeks who used to fabricate idols from stone only to quickly turn around and venerate them! That was a world of a difference from making a hypothesis that spirits survived upon the death of humans, and that they might be lurking in trunks of two hundred year old trees or in the vicinity of graveyards, and acting accordingly!

Mjomba wrote that even though he still considered himself a Christian and a Catholic at that, he did not really see very much difference between the deity worshipped in the West and the Deity his Wazunda ancestors worshipped. May be it all boiled down to labels: Were, the all-knowing, life-giving Wind for whom the people of Zunda-land reserved the greatest respect and honor, versus the Trinity of the Western world for instance!

When the Wazunda went hunting in the forest, planted crops, celebrated a good harvest or the coming of age of their youth with feasting and dancing, or did anything involving two or more members of the community, they did it to the greater glory of the life-giving Wind. Now, that seemed a distinctly more impressive form of worship than the Christian worship which, for the most part, ended at the church door-step. That is what missionaries, in their ignorance no doubt, regarded as diabolic. And they had unfortunately succeeded in persuading everybody, including the Wazunda themselves, that this was in fact the case!

With theology text-books making only negative references to animism, as the religion of his forefathers was now officially labeled, the fact that it was pregnant with many erudite things had been lost sight of. The doctrines of Buddhism, Islam and Hinduism fared distinctly better in this regard, even though they too were regarded by

Westerners as outlandish. The fact that the latter religions one and all still boasted followers whose numbers run into the millions did not seem to matter in the least.

Mjomba had often let his imagination run wild as he pondered these things, and he had at times wondered if Christianity would not one day be completely eclipsed by these other religions as the number of their followers grew and multiplied! And talking about being eclipsed, Mjomba would have vouched that the number of practising Christians in Europe and in America had already been eclipsed by the number of those who professed agnosticism.

But it had been with respect to African customs and traditions that Mjomba had found most fault with his Church. Whereas Christianity in general seemed to operate on the premise that native customary practices in Africa, when not steeped in animism - and "debased" thereby - were good for nothing, Islam, for one, held many of those practices in esteem, its positions on the role of women in society and on polygamy being cases in point.

And then, even though Islam made more rather than less demands on its African converts in other respects than did Christianity, it was a religion that was, surprisingly, well regarded on the African continent. That Christianity continued, despite the odds stacked against it, to draw into its fold the number of followers it did, was certainly something that could be said in its favour on the other hand. But it still remained inexplicable.

Far from quenching Mjomba's thirst for knowledge about the strange world in which he had found himself, these excellent opportunities for discovery apparently only kindled it. This was particularly so with regard to the effect of the new social order on the lives of individuals in his Wazunda tribal society.

9. Unknown disease with no known cure

The changes just then sweeping the region, far from being confined to the religious sphere alone, were having a far reaching impact in the cultural, political, and economic spheres as well. An offspring of a generation whose lives straddled the pre-colonial and post-colonial era himself, Mjomba could not really help being curious about the way people on the continent were adapting to the stupendous changes which seemed to be taking place around them all the time.

Even though the changing social infrastructure seemed to be working to the advantage of the populace at large - at least to the extent that East Africans were being introduced to things like a money economy and modern industrialization, Mjomba had no doubt about the fact some sections of the populace were being adversely affected. There was of course a tiny and powerful elite - the "black Europeans" - for whom the new social order was a boon of untold proportions. It was also pretty obvious which grouping he himself belonged to.

One development which Mjomba found particularly unsettling pertained to "Brain Death", the mysterious disease which was responsible for reducing, first, Andrea Mkicha, a childhood friend, and then Innocent Kintu, a fellow member of the seminary brotherhood at St. Augustine's, to "vegetables". It was the strangest disease ever to strike sub-Saharan Africa. After it struck, in addition to transforming its victims such that he or she could no longer recognize previous acquaintances, it also caused them to completely disregard everything from the need for nourishment to the importance of personal hygiene.

And then this hitherto unknown disease with no known cure targeted the "most promising" folks, which meant the so-called "best and brightest" members of society's tiny elite. Because it was these who also usually scooped up the available scholarships and fellowships to study abroad when they did not take up the few available places at institutions of higher learning in the region, there was a growing suspicion that the dread disease was in fact being "imported" from Europe and America! The fact that the disease's victims were mostly members of well-to-do families who had the most contact with Westerners appeared to confirm that suspicion.

It seemed such a waste that the victims of the disease tended to be individuals who were close to completing advanced studies in their specialization or at the apex of successful academic careers. And as some of those who had gone off to study in Europe and America returned "brain dead" - that was how ordinary Wazunda folks described the strange disease and also how it got its name - young people, in a new and extraordinary development, had begun to shirk overseas study opportunities.

Mjomba had been very much aware of the fact that he himself belonged to the country's emerging elite. But the other and, perhaps even more important fact, that he had grown up surrounded by illiteracy on a monumental scale, had never been lost on him. In spite of it, or perhaps even because of it, apart from his desire to succeed in life, his next most pressing ambition which he had developed along the way was to learn as much as possible about other people, especially those the society he lived in now tended to marginalize.

Mjomba had always suspected that it was this strange combination of his desire to succeed in life on the one hand and his desire to understand the plight of the disadvantaged members of society which had eventually landed him in the seminary. But he could not rule out other motives, like for instance his desire to meet the challenge which seminary life posed, including things like life-long celibacy. He had often wondered if there was any difference between a yearning to prove oneself and striving to learn something for learning's sake.

Talking about yearning for knowledge for its own sake, Mjomba sometimes longed that he had lived at the time of St. Augustine when, so it was said, earning the qualification of Doctor of Philosophy meant you actually knew everything there was to be known about everything that had been discovered! The fact that this eminent "father of the Church" hailed from Hippo, the ancient North African city, made him more than a father of the Church. It automatically made the "Doctor of the Church", as Augustine was also known, Mjomba's mentor as well!

It was, in a way, funny that the phrase "Doctor of Philosophy" also summed up, and rather succinctly for that matter, what the words "traditional medicine-man" conveyed to Mjomba. "PhD" seemed to epitomize everything that a medicine-man in traditional African society was supposed to be. In addition to practising the art of healing, he too was expected to know everything that there was to be known about everything that had been discovered!

Mjomba had often come close to agreeing with those who thought that there was something definitely suspect with Western education, and who accordingly argued that being under the tutelage of the medicine-men was a far better proposition than going off to Europe or America in pursuit of "paper" qualifications.

While he had been aware that those who went to study abroad invariably developed "ivory tower" mentalities as they were called, he was not aware that those who pursued traditional wisdom got into any sort of mental fixations; and certainly none approximating an "ivory tower" mentality! Still, even though Mjomba was concerned at the time about the possibility that Westerners might actually not be as sophisticated and erudite as they looked on the surface, his thoughts in that regard remained just that - thoughts - and did not at all affect his deep seated love of knowledge in the Western sense.

Mjomba did not care if it sometimes appeared as if he was yearning for knowledge for its own sake. Since the very definition of the word "philosophy" implied a love of knowledge for its own sake, it seemed unlikely that he could go wrong on that score.

With respect to the real matter at issue - whether he should don his traditional "toga" and begin an apprenticeship under the direction of the village seers or continue with his Western education in the classics, fate clearly appeared to have determined for him in advance the route to take; and Mjomba thought travelling along that predetermined route spelled lots of fun too.

It could very well be that growing up with one leg in a tradition-bound society and the other in a modern, fast changing environment actually fuelled his thirst for learning. Whatever it was, Mjomba could not help being troubled by the notion that, somehow, too much knowledge occasionally killed the brain!

Mjomba got a premonition of things to come when he was in his third year in the senior seminary. That was when Andrea Mkicha, Mjomba's childhood friend who had gone off to study in America on an 'IIE' scholarship (whatever that meant!), returned prematurely showing symptoms of "brain death". The experience had been shattering to Mkicha's relatives who had expected him to come home loaded with degrees. Mkicha had been one of the first victims to fall prey to the strange malady. The doctors had not detected anything wrong with him physically; but he had continued to act funny, as if he was possessed.

Even though no blood relation of Mkicha's, Mjomba had always considered himself a member of the extended family of his pal; and the news about his old chum's condition had left him thoroughly dejected and disheartened. The fact that his interest in the general subject of mental health had already been building up for sometime mattered very little since the diagnosis of his friend's illness by experts had turned up nothing. What mattered was that the "brain killer" had again proved that it could strike and vanish without a trace.

In point of fact, Mjomba who was already quite concerned that the populace at large was having to own up to the reality of a fast changing social, economic and political environment, now also had a growing interest in the mental well being of those members of his tribe who happened to be well schooled. He had always supposed that it was they who would be at the vanguard of progress in the modern sense and, as such, were the hope of his tradition-bound tribesmen.

And then, while interested in the lot of his countrymen, he also had to contend with the fact that he himself belonged to the group most at risk from "brain death". This was no idol threat from the hitherto unknown disease with no known cure, given the fact that some of his closest buddies had already fallen prey to it! It was, indeed, a combination of all those things that caused any mention of the word "bookish" at this time to send jitters down his spinal cord!

On the other hand, Mjomba's interests had been expanding imperceptibly and on the point of encompassing the general question of how peoples of Africa - and of the rest of the world, for that matter - reconciled their traditional beliefs with foreign ideologies.

Up until then, Christian Mjomba had held the view that the peculiar codes of conduct in force in seminaries, particularly the near monastic regime of life at St. Augustine's, made those institutions unlikely places for breeding characters "on the lunatic fringe".

But that started to change the moment Innocent Kintu, a first year Philosophy student, lapsed into a condition that seemed identical in almost every respect to that of Mkicha and then, lo and behold, failed to come out of it! To his disappointment, some of his fellow seminarians described what overtook Brother Kintu somewhat differently, saying he had simply "gone off the rails". But since those who traditionally "went off the rails" had never been known to get back on, that characterization of the situation had brought Mjomba little comfort.

Up until that point in time, Mjomba had not taken any particular interest in the behaviour of Brother Kintu. But now, he begun quite involuntarily to feel a measure of concern that grew and eventually became comparable to that of a doctor for his/her patient.

He had, in any event, by that time already resolved to devote not just the periods allotted for meditation but the great bulk of his regular study time as well to exploring - and trying in general to grapple with - the subject of psychosis, even though he did not initially know the difference between that and "neurosis". He would actually have readily admitted at that time that he was not in a position to tell the behaviour of someone who was a moron, a nincompoop, or just a dunce from that of a miscreant - or even from that of some individual who just chose to play a role in society which amounted to simple mischief.

However, with *Logica Minor*, *Logica Major*, Psychology, Scriptural Exegesis and, above all, Metaphysics behind him, Mjomba clearly savored the idea that he was initiating a real life case study of a truly mysterious subject. The expression "mysterious disease" would in a way have captured very well whatever Westerners meant or purported to mean by "insanity". In the experience of the Welekha, there was no such a thing as "insanity". And Mjomba did not quite understand why the West did not embrace the position of the Welekha on "insanity"; because, even though they referred to it as a disease, by their own admission, they did not know what it was, with Freud, their foremost scholar on the subject, using another meaningless term to describe it, namely "neurosis"! And the only thing they definitively knew about the different types of neuroses apparently being that it was caused by suppressing some other mysterious thing which they labeled "the libido".

Mjomba found it a very exciting prospect that he, Mjomba, was in effect embarking on research into something that was entirely mysterious - insanity, schizophrenia, lunacy, neurosis, mischief, or whatever label you used to describe the "unknown disease with no known cure"! "Insanity" or "mysterious disease with no known cure" was a subject that Mjomba, fresh from investigating those other abstract subjects, imagined would be extremely fascinating and engaging.

It was thus that the Reverend Mjomba, while seeking answers to questions relating to the psychotic condition of religious types like Brother Kintu, had found himself pursuing questions relating to the phenomenon of insanity as it affected not just the elite in his society but everybody in general almost as a matter of course.

In the meantime, as Mjomba went about these activities, new problems arose. He had, for one, found himself almost constantly nagged by his conscience for ignoring the maxim that obedience was better than virtue! For obvious reasons, he had decided to go about his research quietly, and had avoided letting anyone, his spiritual director included, get wind of it. And for that - for breaking that cardinal rule - his feelings of guilt would haunt him for the remainder of his days at St. Augustine's!

Mjomba was understandably also badgered, during that period, by the fearsome thought that he ran the gauntlet of catching the strange disease and would almost certainly succumb to it unless he succeeded in the research he had started. But these very pursuits, because they were intellectual, likely were enhancing his chances of falling prey to the strange malady! These were irrational fears to be sure; but try as he might to cast them off, he never succeeded in shrugging off the idea that he was on a perilous course.

Racked by these fears on the one hand, and tormented by his conscience on the other, Mjomba sometimes wondered if his efforts in the direction he had chosen to take were of any worth. The two, like a double-edged sword, worked away at him persistently and at times very nearly caused him to lose his nerve.

To make things even worse, and particularly because there was nothing Mjomba would have liked more than a tranquil, recollected state of mind, he had found his mind constantly besieged throughout that time by a train of disquieting thoughts. One numbing thought which had kept recurring suggested that the miseries he endured were, one and all, a well-deserved punishment for allowing himself to capitulate to the wiles of Satan and to personal pride!

Still, none of these things succeeded in deflecting Mjomba from his course. He had continued throughout his ordeals to associate the full attainment of his self-actualization with success in his self-imposed mission, which he likened to redemption. He had likewise refused to be intimidated by the widespread reports that the dread disease, now dubbed the "the disease of the mentally active" by the village folk, had broken its boundaries and no longer appeared to be confined to returning intellectuals from Europe and America. Well, given the evidence, it indeed had begun to affect locally bred intellectual types as well!

Some unscrupulous members of the seminary brotherhood had began suggesting, much to Mjomba's chagrin, that it was something other than insanity which was sweeping the region and the rest of the world. They claimed that these were simply symptoms of a metaphysical condition engendered by the *"Devil's Claw*", a phrase they used to denote possession by Beelzebub!

There were still others who went even further. Taking their cue from the Western characterization of Animism, the traditional religion of people in the region, as a wayward and ungodly enterprise, they declared that the peculiar lapses of the mind which had been observed were also typical cases of possession by ancestral spirits in the service of the Evil One!

It was around this time that Mjomba - of all things - met and fell head-long in love with Jamila. And in a way, he owed it all to Brother Innocent Kintu. With the latter's problem refusing to go away of its own, the seminary authorities had eventually decided to entrust the stricken brother to the care of a Dr. Claus Gringo, a leading psychiatrist at the National Medical Teaching Hospital, or NMTH as it was popularly known.

The campus of the NMTH, the country's only teaching hospital, had changed the western skyline of Dar es Salaam. The beauty of the metropolis to the west had suffered near irrevocable damage as some ten thousand hectares of high ground on the city's western perimeters were systematically turned into a veritable forest of high rises for the university campus. To make things worse the campus, which some locals erroneously considered to be an exact replica of Oxford University, was fenced in - suitably others believed. It looked entirely out of place in the sedate surroundings of the "Heaven of Peace"!

It was not uncommon to hear talk to the effect that the "people on the hill" lived in an "Ivory Tower" and out of touch with reality as a result, adding to the mystique surrounding the NMTH. What was more, the university's residents had demanded - and had, indeed, been allowed to enjoy - something the rest of the populace did not enjoy, something called academic freedom!

The seminary authorities were hopeful that the well-known and undoubtedly brilliant academic, a native of neighboring Uganda, could nudge Brother Kintu back into his usual senses by applying a dose of the wisdom he had acquired at the illustrious Makerere University, and sharpened over the additional period of twelve years or so that Dr. Gringo had spent at Stanford University in America where he specialized in Psychiatric Medicine.

St. Augustine's entire student body had been hopeful likewise, if only because it clearly took longer to become a psychiatrist than to become a priest! Mjomba, for his part, had believed that such an outcome, while unlikely in the normal course of events, came well within the realm of possibilities with himself in the picture. On the day Mjomba met and fell in love with Jamila, he had come to NMHT's Psychiatric Department, which also happened to be Jamila's place of work, to volunteer that critical assistance.

Approximately a year had passed since he had commenced his research on Kintu with the specific objective of resolving the issue regarding the exact nature of the strange malady. And now, on the verge of completing the equally exacting task of documenting details of his "discovery", the Rev. Mjomba was keeping his appointment with Prof. Gringo when he accosted the then Jamila Kivumbi in the latter's office.

The seminarian, who had been brought up to admire women only as God's creatures, had been swept off his feet at the sight of the ravishing Jamila, a quadroon whose maiden name meant "awesome beauty"!

Jamila had been swept off her own feet simultaneously. No sooner had she set her sight on the charming young man in a cleric's garb than she had decided, in her innocence, that the only way of paying adequate tribute to his good looks and charm was to look him straight in the eye and not say quits until his gaze met hers.

It would probably have ended disastrously for both of them had it not for the fact that the Rev. Mjomba was required to retreat behind the confining walls of St. Augustine's Seminary, a good half day's journey away, immediately his consultation with the psychiatrist concluded.

By the time he made his appearance at the National Medical Teaching Hospital's Psychiatric Unit, the wily churchman had taken great pains to learn first hand the personal history of his fellow seminarian. He had been steadfast and as diligent as any one could be in his application of the Thomist Method to the analysis required to unlock the secrets behind the phenomenon of insanity and in the process uncover the real causes of Brother Kintu's psychotic condition. He had left no stone unturned as he delved into Kintu's background in search of clues, working away at it during the school term and his vacations alike.

The seminarian had intended to come for his appointment with the professor armed with a dossier on Brother Kintu. But it just so happened that he had not been able to transcribe his notes into something more legible in time for his trip to Dar es Salaam. He had come armed instead with confidence that he had enough mastery of his pet subject as well as the ability to expound on the subject of insanity to the professor's satisfaction if not awe. And, above all, he was determined to take the lid off the mystery surrounding the plague known throughout the region as "brain death" once and for all!

With unbounded imagination and great tenacity, in addition to documenting Brother Kintu's "psychic roots" - Mjomba's favourite term for describing Kintu's chequered background - in great detail, Mjomba had succeeded in envisioning and portraying the Church as a major player in the downfall of the likes of Brother Innocent Kintu. And he had even gone on to effectively depict the quiet corridors of St. Augustine's Seminary as a potential breeding ground for the mentally deranged! Strangely, he did not feel any scruples for using his inside knowledge of the Catholic Church in making his point.

In the immediate aftermath of his highly successful session with Prof. Gringo, the seminarian had been somewhat surprised to find that the "dossier" contained the ingredients of a first class novel - the sort of novel that would, he had no doubt, set trends in addition to leaving fame as well as fortune to its author! A maverick in a world he believed was largely governed by group-think, Mjomba apparently resolved at that time not to allow himself to be circumscribed by rules of any sort as he went about writing his "best seller".

A non-conformist *par excellence*, he even set down his own rules. He would aim, first and foremost, to produce something good! In the process of doing so, he would not write for any specific audience. In his view, that sort of thing created unnecessary obligations which interfered with people's freedom of expression and which, in the final analysis, imposed unnecessary limits on an individual's fling at creativity!

His novel would, likewise, not be structured. He frowned on the very notion of doing things to form, and would have argued that the very next step in that direction was to do things to form for form's sake.

Mjomba had heard about writers' forums, and believed that the so-called literary conventions had been formulated in those forums for a reason. He in fact had a lingering notion that it was the most unworthy members of this league who were behind those conventions for their own benefit no doubt. And it did not surprise him that the league in question also constituted what was possibly the most exclusive club!

Mjomba frowned upon what he considered unfortunate restrictive rules on how to express oneself. He could not see any purpose for them other than that of protecting the monopoly of a few. He hated to think that other well meaning authors indirectly supported a scheme which infringed on the right of all citizens to free expression in such an obvious manner! He was certainly determined not to allow any of that nonsense to influence his literary venture.

At one time, Mjomba even entertained the somewhat strange idea that his book would be a better work if it had no introduction or conclusion! And he wanted his work to be "original", by which he also meant unedited! He would even have preferred that his book was title-less; although he finally wavered in that respect and allowed that a best seller had to have a title of some kind.

Trying to think of one, an almost endless flood of possible titles for his book had filed through his mind. They included some really strange ones like "The Bombshell", "The Bomb", "On a Shuttle to Whiteman's Heaven", "Discourse with Madmen", "The Thesis, Antithesis and Synthesis", "The Madman", "Psychic Wars", "The Devil's Claw", "Blockbuster", "On the Invisible Trail", "The Vatican Tape", "On the Lunatic Fringe", "The Disease", "Crazy", "Weird

Cure", "Hell in Heaven", "Heaven in Hell", "The Millennium Book", "A Trip to Mjomba-land", "Rap Book", "And the Ancestral Spirits Go Matching On" and, perhaps the strangest of them all, "In Search of the Chigoe"!

Indeed "In Search of the Chigoe" had sounded just right. Mjomba would never forget the advice that his great grandfather, who lived to be a hundred and one years of age and was highly respected by all for his intellectual prowess right up to the time he departed to join the ancestral spirits, used to dispense to young people in the village. "If you allow the chigoe to get embedded in your brain, it will drive you mad the same way it drives cattle mad when it gets lodged in a spot that lay midway between the horns! You start that process when you give chiggers a home in your feet. So root them out at the first available opportunity!" he had admonished.

It was typical of Mjomba that if he became involved in an activity, his involvement became a real obsession, and he usually did not quit until he had endeavoured to fathom each and every angle of the activity or subject. A virtual captive of his own imagination on this occasion as on other similar occasions, Mjomba wasn't about to quit until he had checked out the most unlikely titles as well. One such title, which he regretted not being able to include in his short list, was *The Gospel According to Iscariot*. Even so, it was not before he had tried to think of something that would have justified it's inclusion.

But on one thing, Mjomba adamantly refused to compromise, namely the idea of book reviews. Mjomba derided the very idea. He argued that the writings that together constituted what was now known as the Bible, having been rejected by the major publishers of the day, ended up being self-published and never got the opportunity to be reviewed in any literary journal. But according to Mjomba, reviewing forthcoming book titles was really a cheap sales gimmick designed to promote selected authors' writings regardless of their true literary merit.

Besides, the problem with "marketing", according to Mjomba, was that it appealed, not to the higher faculties, but to man's base instincts. Mjomba claimed that marketing techniques mimicked the highly successful but questionable methods employed by Beelzebub in tempting Adam and Eve and their descendants! He, thus, not only didn't have any intention of seeking reviews for his "Masterpiece", but he was prepared to take any prospective "book reviewer" to task for trying to reduce his masterpiece to something that was cheap and run-of-the-mill.

It must be noted, to Mjomba's credit, that he even considered modifying the plot of his book slightly so that "Father Campbell", his novel's principal character whom he had also cast as Father Rector at the institution that was going to play the role of St. Augustine's Senior Seminary in the book, would preside over a staff of eleven. That would in turn have made for a realistic scenario in which the priests would have been nicknamed by the seminary's student body after the apostles, with the name of the betrayer being reserved for the rector.

With the main spokesperson for Catholicism in the book going by the name of Iscariot, it would have been in order for the fictitious author to entitle his work *The Gospel According to Judas Iscariot*. Mjomba regretted that he did not have the gall to publish a book with such a title. He simply could not predict what people's emotions on seeing such a book on the bookstand might be. It would, of course, be fine with him if that title led them to buy the book. But Mjomba feared that it could just as easily cause them to boycott it.

It always sounded so exciting to be a best selling author. Mjomba thought he just could not wait to savor the joys of being one. But, despite the fact that he himself often dreamed of a great windfall from sales of his book, Mjomba would still have contended that it was intrinsically wrong for anyone to write for money.

These views did not prevent him from interrupting his chores ever so often to imagine long queues of eager buyers lining up to snap up copies of "The Bombshell" from book-shelves in far away places like Paris, London, Los Angeles, Toronto, and even Moscow! Mjomba would certainly have argued that his book, by the very way it was conceived, guaranteed that kind of interest around the globe as well as the associated financial gain; but that these things did not in themselves form what could be characterized as a *raison de tre* for his fling at being an author. That, at any rate, was how he now liked to view himself and his book venture.

In the years which followed his original encounter with Prof. Gringo, the maverick Mjomba had allowed his ideas an almost limitless period to hibernate, moving to complete the expansion of material into a full-fledged historical novel nearly a decade later.

During the intervening period, a lot of things had taken place, most notably Mjomba's "conversion" to Islam and subsequent marriage to the woman of his dreams. Mjomba had at one time discarded his old given name and adopted the name of Ibrahim to emphasize the importance he placed on his new circumstances and the change of his awareness of reality. But he had reverted to using his original given name soon after at the urging of Jamila who confessed to being quite fond of the name Christian.

And while he hardly observed any teachings of his newfound faith, he revelled in the notion that he was a "born again" person, even though not in the Christian Evangelical sense. He had also subsequently attended the elitist Makerere University whence, following in the foot steps of his friend and mentor in the person of Prof. Gringo, he had proceeded to the Leland Stanford, Jr. University in California where he studied Management and Finance.

Already a father of two now, the liberated Mjomba was determined to complete the book before their third child was born. But he was also just as determined to keep the project concealed from Jamila until its completion. Since he could not do any script-writing at home for that reason, he had found it necessary to use the luncheon periods for that purpose, affording himself a sandwich for lunch instead of the usual three course lunch his wife insisted was essential to maintain his health.

Christian Mjomba's thoughts were far from all that - and the book - now as he reflected on his domestic life. He felt he had to admit to a kind of fear which the sight of his pregnant wife had of late begun to arouse in him. He had already become so prone to it that he now recoiled instinctively whenever she came into view. Even so, he had not imagined that his face could be a mask of fear as Jamila's reaction that morning had appeared to suggest.

As he sat there slumped in thought, a tiny part of his brain seemed to twitch, and then without as much as a warning, his spirits started to rise. He was beginning to straighten up in his seat when he felt a twitch in a different part of his brain. It was at that point that, with the shattering speed of lightening accompanied by what sounded like a clap of thunder, the cause of his fear suddenly became obvious.

This was followed by an even stranger thing. Mjomba's mind, acting impulsively, refused to let itself be confronted with the subject. He was loathe to admit that he had not been paying enough attention to his wife's needs even though the size of her tummy indicated that she could have a baby at any time.

It was precisely during the previous week that work on the book had been most demanding. After chronicling all the events which led to his hero's mental collapse, Mjomba had found himself faced with the almost impossible task of reconciling certain obvious formal conclusions with some of the pet theories on the causes of insanity as enunciated by the character in the book personifying himself. These theories, while not so compelling in themselves, were already so interwoven with the rest of the story, any move to discard any one of them threatened to result in a story so diluted as to make it worthless altogether. To retain them intact, on the other hand, seemed to spell inconsistency of such a magnitude, his own credibility as an author would be at stake.

Thoroughly flustered, Mjomba was very nearly driven at one stage to destroy in one stroke of the pen the mannequin representing himself in the person of Moses Kapere - his alter ego in the book. He faulted this facsimile of himself now for being too unwieldy and headstrong, and for preventing him from modifying the roles of his characters to accommodate his pet theories. He also saw this character, whose only distinction consisted of the fact that it was his very own creation, as the biggest threat to the project to which he had devoted so much of his life. He felt that if he had been in a position to do so without bringing irreparable ruin to his project and consequently also to himself, he would have been glad to expunge it from existence and start creating another one all over. It still remained that he had painstakingly created that likeness of himself over a period of many months, and it would in fact break his heart if he went that route.

Mjomba felt helpless and cornered. He felt, on the one hand, that he could not really countenance the thought that his own creation somehow was turning out to be not so terrific after all, and that it had become necessary to consider whether or not it should continue to exist. But he considered it out of question, on the other hand, for him to capitulate to pressure of any kind from any quarter, and certainly not to pressure from a jerk who owed his very existence to him!

That sort of pressure, which seemed calculated to cause Mjomba to circumscribe his freedom of expression, was unacceptable. It was still his intention to see his book gain instant and universal acclaim as an immortal work, and it was completely unthinkable that he could give in to blackmail emanating from any quarter, the mannequin he had created of himself included.

Too vain to concede defeat to his own effigy in that very unusual battle of wits, Mjomba had refused to yield. Suffice it to say that it had only been through some of the most excruciating and exacting of efforts at concentration that he had succeeded in balancing his arguments in favour of Theory "R", the theory he hoped would advance medical science and seal his fate as a celebrated author and thinker.

10. Primrose

After a good deal of soul searching, Mjomba had decided that both Jamila and himself were fairly worried - as indeed they were entitled to be. Following the months and finally weeks of waiting, it had begun to look as if the baby really could come any time!

Mjomba felt slightly unnerved as he recalled that his wife no longer ventured outdoors as often as she used to or might have wished, He shied at the idea that while he himself still went to work as usual, he was visibly weighed down with anxiety for Jamila and the unborn infant without being conscious of it.

The previous evening Mjomba, the less worried of the two no doubt despite his appearance, had reluctantly agreed that he would arrange to take his accumulated leave - thirty or so days in all - without further delay. He had taken leave on the occasion of the birth of Kinte two years earlier. If the circumstances had permitted him to do so when Kunta, now four, was born, he would probably have done the same thing.

On the present occasion, he had yet to observe signs of childbirth and consequently was inclined to maintain a wait-and-see attitude. He would accordingly have preferred to go on his vacation when signs showed that childbirth was imminent. Although he loved his wife dearly, he also regarded his job highly and was not the sort of person to walk away from his desk - and stay away for a whole month at that - lightly!

Mjomba let his mind wander back to the time, four years earlier, when he had sat through his Winter Quarter examinations at Stanford while Jamila was being prepared for the theatre at the nearby Stanford Medical Center. Almost exactly two and a half years before, he had arrived here on a scholarship awarded by the Institute of International Education. He had decided to come along with his spouse of three months at his own expense.

It stood out as the only time he had felt doubts about the wisdom of having Jamila accompany him on the overseas trip. After sitting what later turned out to be among his best exam papers, the youthful scholar from the Third World had jumped on his bicycle and had made it to the maternity ward barely in time to embrace the still blood-stained and slimy little Kunta as he was being transferred to the nursery in a nurse's arms.

Mjomba's mental processes were accustomed to revert to the family's sojourn in America whenever an occasion presented itself. He beamed with pleasure at the thought that Kunta, a United States citizen by birth, would always be an ever-present symbol of the happy days he and Jamila spent in California, as would also be the passport Kunta would carry, with the picture of a wide-eyed eagle on its cover. More so, he had once confided to a friend, than the coveted MBA he had bagged for his academic endeavours!

More than at any time before, Mjomba was nonplussed that the Americans, with all their gadgetry, had failed in their attempt to pin-point his wife's exact due date! It did not surprise him when on their return to Africa, Kinte's expected date of birth as forecast by the doctor at the National Medical Teaching Hospital had also turned out to be wrong.

We've at least leant not to bank too much on doctors' forecasts, thought Mjomba, slightly bemused. They might be fonts of life-saving knowledge, he told himself mentally; but their knowledge had proved deficient when it came to forecasting the birth dates of Kunta and Kinte at any rate. He was in jitters as he wondered what doctors two hundred years from now would think about the latest gadgets in use at the Stanford Medical Center - some of them so top-of-the-line they were, he suspected, unavailable anywhere else outside of Stanford University's boundaries!

Mjomba reflected ruefully that neither his wife nor himself seemed to have learnt from their experiences how to control their anxiety. Just as on the occasion of Kinte's birth, Jamila was registered at both Dr. Mambo's private maternity clinic and the National Medical Teaching Hospital as well for her prenatal care. He vividly recalled that he was the one who had insisted that she receive her prenatal treatment at both places on both occasions. The idea that Jamila had been visiting two hospitals for the same thing now looked decidedly crazy.

Not unlike many of the supposedly moneyed city folk of Dar es Salaam, Mjomba had a bias for the treatment private clinics dispensed, and accordingly preferred them to the Government hospitals in spite of the added cost which went with it.

He made a half-hearted attempt to justify his previous insistence that his wife see the doctors at both places, and he abandoned it almost as soon as he had begun. As if in confirmation of the stupidity of his action, it suddenly dawned on him that Dr. Mambo had given February 26, three days away, as the expected date of delivery while, according to the doctor at the "NMTH", the due date was February 29!

Attired in a close fitting, lilac coloured Kaunda suit and rocking gently in the swivel chair, Mjomba buzzed his secretary. He felt a great deal more up-beat than he had felt at any time since reporting to work that morning.

"Primrose, kindly get me a leave form" he said in a husky voice.

A typical "siren" and still single at twenty-seven, Prim, as she was known among her friends, apparently deemed it permissible whenever she addressed her young but fairly highly educated boss on the intercom to put on her "charm".

And, predictably, there had never been any doubt in her mind regarding the fact that Mjomba took delight in listening to her affected tones. The sharp-witted Primrose, besides, took full advantage of whatever information came her way in her capacity as his confidential secretary to deliver her point home in that regard. Her tendency to do this had increased sharply since her recent discovery that in addition to being a Stanford alumnus, Mjomba had also studied at St. Augustine's Seminary.

Like most informed people in the region, Primrose knew that those who went to St. Augustine's Seminary studied Philosophy and

Theology, abstract subjects that, at least in the view of the majority, did not appear to have ant real relevance to ordinary life and were consequently regarded as esoteric. It was precisely for that reason that St. Augustine's Seminary was held in such high regard by many people, some of whom would remark that it could not possibly be called "Major" for nothing.

Regarding Mjomba's attendance at St. Augustine's Seminary Primrose was certain that if she had not been involved in helping him to prepare his book manuscript for publication, she would not have come by that valuable information. She had a lingering suspicion that it was one aspect of Mjomba's life he didn't really want every Dick and Harry to know about - in the exact same way he did not want any Dick and Harry to know about his literary project. This was despite the fact that St. Augustine's was a well-known, universally respected center of learning. Her own feeling on first learning that Mjomba was an ex-seminarian was that her boss had quit the seminary because he had a special fondness for women. That was what was said by people about ex-seminarians.

Primrose knew that it was an unfair conclusion about people who decided for reasons best known to themselves that they did not have a calling for the Catholic priesthood. But, as a woman, Primrose sometimes thought that as far as stereotypes went, this one was just fine. She even wondered why, in their defense, ex-seminarians did not advance the argument that they adored women very much. As her current date whom she hoped to marry was always saying, women were second only to angels in loveliness as creatures of the Almighty, and she did not understand why he kept repeating it. She loved her date so much she often told herself that she would not have doubted his words even if he had said it just once!

Primrose adored Mjomba openly. But that did not in any way appear to affect the respect she felt for her boss or, indeed, her loyalty to him. The language of material she had typed for him had tended to be of a standard which put the proper appreciation of her boss's work beyond her general capabilities; but she had been content to regard it as her privilege to be able to help in bringing his dream of becoming an illustrious author closer to reality.

While he enjoyed the treat all right, Mjomba had long ago decided that it would serve him best in the long run if he gave the appearance of "tolerating" his secretary's behaviour without either openly approving or disapproving it.

Primrose knew that Mrs. Mjomba was close to delivery, and she decided to use that knowledge to the fullest. "Yeah, maternity leave!' she crooned, her lyrical voice reverberating with mirth. "I will take care of the formalities for the leave. How long - a month…month and a half? That should be enough for you. According to your last pay-stub, you have forty-five days unused, Sir."

For reasons best known to herself, Primrose seemed more inclined to use the formal address when joking around with her boss. And she was usually much more informal when serious business being conducted.

"First of all, I know you would very much like to knight me!" Mjomba retorted in his usual, jocular manner. "But, quite frankly, I am still very keen to give the real thing a shot. There is a slim chance I could get the Knighthood from Her Majesty the Queen herself; and I would therefore appreciate it very much if you would keep 'Sir' in reserve for now!"

Ignoring his secretary's side-splitting laughter at the other end of the intercom, he continued: "But you are otherwise right regarding maternity leave. I only need one month - should be fully recovered in that time. See! We men are different from you women - when it is your turn, we will be talking the standard six month's maternity leave, won't we? You take a little longer to recover..."

His finger still on the buzzer, he added tauntingly: "As a true African, I do not actually believe in the equality of the sexes. And I'm sure you do not disagree with me on that! Isn't it the reason you've never invited me to join the Feminist Movement?" He was referring to the fact that Primrose was the elected head of the union of secretarial staff at the Port Authority.

"You are useless" Primrose chortled amid giggles.

Mjomba was capable of sounding infinitely flattering. And he sounded at his best as he added: "Sweetheart, make my leave effective tomorrow."

With that, he was about to break off the conversation when, her voice as affected as ever, Primrose hissed from her end of the line: "Do not pretend. You are envious!"

"By the way, Chief, you could use my entitlement of four months' maternity leave..." she added with a triumphant giggle.

Even after his phone set had gone dead, the sound of her titter continued to seep into Mjomba's office through the wall separating the two sections of his *office en suite*.

Mjomba was engrossed with his tête-à-tête with his secretary only very briefly after it ended. He typically never allowed himself to be preoccupied with the frequent tête-à-têtes he had with Primrose for any length of time after they ended. He did not do so on this occasion either. But he felt a sting of guilt for allowing himself to enjoy the chat with his secretary. He did not understand why he felt like that. It was something which had never happened before.

Even though there did not appear to be any logic to it, Mjomba just felt that he was being unfair to his beloved Jamila by enjoying these light-hearted moments with Prim. And it was not because Jamila would have disliked the idea of him joking around in that fashion with other women. He knew his spouse too well to suspect her of that sort of thing. He wondered if his feelings of guilt arose from the fact that he was laughing and smiling so soon after fretting over Jamila's condition.

But Mjomba's conscience continued to badger him with the "fact" that he had allowed himself to indulge in that manner. It made him feel that his concern for Jamila moments earlier had not been really genuine. This was even though he was convinced that this was not so. He was, therefore, glad to put the banter he had just indulged in behind him quickly.

Jerking himself to attention, he looked like the typical young-and-upcoming executive as he steered his medium-sized hulk the few inches it had strayed from the flat-topped mahogany desk. But his mind was still wandering, as he turned to survey the contents of his In-Tray; and it took the wail of the siren announcing the twelve o'clock shift at the Docks to bring him to.

11. The Countdown

The whine of the siren was at its highest pitch when the buzzer went off. With a practised movement of the arm, Mjomba picked up the telephone receiver and listened to Primrose's affected, almost lyrical voice.

After announcing that a Mrs. Killian was on the line, his secretary deliberately took time to replace her receiver and was able in the process to catch the words: "*Mama Kunta anaumwa vibaya sana...*" (Translated: "the Mother of Kunta is in labor…).

It was, perhaps, the pay. But the glamour associated with working in the Port Authority's Accounting and Finance Department undoubtedly had something to do with it, as was also the fact that the concentration of people with professional designations in that department was second only to that in the Engineering Department. In any event, over the years, these various factors had led to a conspicuous cluster of top-flight secretaries on the two floors of the Trade Center occupied by Accounting and Finance.

That had in turn assured that communications between the different finance sections, whose heads apparently shared a common passion for top-of-the-line telephone sets, was almost as good as it could be and easily the most efficient compared with inter-office communication in other departments.

Within minutes following Mjomba's conversation with his secretary, telephones in the department and elsewhere were buzzing with the news that the wife of the Deputy Controller Finance, regarded by all the female members of the department's staff without exception as a stunning beauty and a model of comeliness and charm, was in labour!

Mjomba was on his legs when Mrs. Killian, a neighbor, rang off with a click. He felt an irresistible urge to bolt, and was surprised that he remained stationary. His hands were groping about in his pockets for his car's ignition keys at the same time as he was trying to figure out in his mind if there wasn't anything else of importance that he was about to forget in the rush. He had completely forgotten that on his way to the office, as he drove past the Ocean View Motor Garage, he had decided to leave the car there for routine maintenance in view of his leave plans, and that he had been given a lift to the Trade Center in the auto repair shop's courtesy shuttle.

It was then that his eyes alighted on the blue binder which lay next to the In-Tray. In spite of his quickening pulse, Mjomba seemed in absolute control of his reflexes as he snatched it up, and then proceeded to carefully place the pages of his manuscript in the binder. Shoving the binder under his left armpit, he reached for his attaché case and was making a dash for the doorway when he stopped in his tracks. Mjomba's recollection that he had checked the car in at the Ocean View Motor Garage that morning for routine maintenance in view of his leave plans could not have been more timely. Without a prior booking, his Ford Cortina would not normally be ready for collection until at least three in the afternoon!

Christian Mjomba sat himself down heavily and dialled Office Services. Finding the number engaged, he hesitated, then persuaded himself that it might be worth while to give it another try after a couple of seconds. But before he could try the number a second time, he decided that it was crazy of him to expect to get a staff car at that short notice from the "bunch" on the ninth floor!

Unlike the brass of Accounting and Finance who had received their education mostly in elite institutions in the West and were given to swaggering, the Chief of Office Services had received his Management diploma in Communist Russia, and his reticent deportment was often times the object of muted wisecracks by junior Accounting and Finance staff with what appeared to be the tacit approval of the department's senior staff. Even though, because of the enormous power he wielded which was exemplified by the extensive demand for office services throughout the Port Authority, it was rumoured that he had once used the shoe in a Chief Officers' meeting after the manner of a former Chairman of the Union of the Soviet Socialist Republics at the United Nations in New York!

Not surprisingly, over time, Office Services in general had been type-cast in an image that hinted at bungling and mismanagement. Actually, that department's problems stemmed from the fact that the Port Authority's Chief Accountant and Financial Controller, with a deft hand at figures, succeeded expertly year in and year out in getting the lion's share of corporate funds at budget time mostly at the expense of Office Services which, consequently, never managed to haggle for enough to enable it to purchase the automotive and other equipment it needed to do a good job.

And when the amiable Czar of Office Services would lament, in conversations with Accounting and Finance division chiefs at parties thrown in honor of Members of the Board in the aftermath of the Budget sessions, at the paucity of funds in his approved Budget, pointing as he usually did to the double-digit figures the Board authorized for Accounting and Finance which were in stark contrast to the mostly single-digit figures authorized for his department, some of them found enormous pleasure in drawing attention to the fact that it the incumbent of that position was out of town. This was supposed to imply that he shouldered considerably more responsibilities and consequently deserved a bigger budget for that reason!

Barricaded in his office, the Deputy Controller Finance was beside himself. The idea crossed his mind that he would deserve to be damned if he put any reliance on the people of Office Services in an emergency such as this one. He had always had the distinct feeling that they did not work for money. Since they certainly did not work for the sake of it, he often times wondered what it was they had on their minds each morning when they set out from their homes for the Trade Center. And then it suddenly occurred to him that there was probably no need for the rush any way; the earliest due date was, as he recalled, a clear three days off!

Mjomba was more composed now as he stuffed the manila envelope into his brief case. His face was expressionless, nonetheless, as he bade his secretary a hearty farewell and set off from the Trade

Center. It was unusual for a Port Authority official of his standing to be seen heading for the bus stage. Inexplicably, he declined numerous offers of lifts by Port Authority employees who drove up to him and volunteered to drive him to his destination in their personal autos. It was as if he preferred to roast in the Dar es Salaam sun rather than inside those cars, none of which had air-conditioning.

It did not take long for a wobbly "DTC" bus, as residents of the sprawling metropolis referred to buses operated by the government owed Dar es Salaam Transport Corporation, to come chugging along, a cloud of dust trailing it. It was a while since Mjomba had last used public transportation. The lone passenger boarding the DTC bus at that "stage", he was curious about the conditions inside. Hoping to use the opportunity to "practice his psychology", he looked for a back seat from where he could observe the demeanour of the bus's other passengers. Once inside, however, a dock worker who had promptly recognized him jumped up and offered his seat.

Mjomba knew at once that it would be remiss for him to decline the offer. If he had tried to decline the offer, the dock worker would simply have insisted that he take it - that was how respectful Tanzanians were. Even though he would have enjoyed the ride standing, Mjomba thanked the dock worker and eased his frame onto the metal seat.

The combination of being located close to the Equator and also being at Sea Level sometimes caused Dar es Salaam to literally sizzle in the hot sun - exactly like North America during the summer. The only difference was that here, unlike in America, the buses did not have air-conditioning. Imports from the Peoples' Socialist Republic of China which was one the few countries with which Socialist Tanzania enjoyed cordial relations, they were equipped with metal seats as opposed to rubber cushioned seats, perhaps because the former tended to have a longer life. But those metal seats, particularly those which were directly exposed to the sun, could also get pretty hot. With respect to the particular seat that Mjomba was offered, it was the metal used as the back rest which had been directly exposed to the sun's naked rays and which made him feel as though the skin on his back was being peeled off.

Mjomba remained seated because that was the only way he would avoid offending the polite dock worker. At one point, he thought that he wouldn't survive the short ride to the Old Post Office, which was his destination. But he bit his lips and pretended that he was enjoying the ride. In the meantime, anyone could easily have told those passengers who recognized the boss of Accounting and Finance and those who didn't by the way they either showed deference for his presence by relapsing into an awkward silence or ogled at him because he seemed in obvious discomfort.

The journey over the short distance in the squelching heat seemed to take forever, and caused Mjomba to re-live his memories of the rides he had enjoyed in ultra-modern air-conditioned buses on many an occasion in America! Ever since Mjomba enjoyed his very first such ride in the airport bus from JFK International Airport to New York's Central Station when he and Jamila arrived in America, he had become inclined to feel that distances did not seem to matter anymore! Because of this, he would almost certainly have reacted with ambivalence if, for example, he had been asked to trade his low rise apartment in Escondido Village on the Stanford campus for married quarters in the nearby City of Palo Alto, Menlo Park or elsewhere requiring him to commute to the School of Business where he took his classes by public transport.

An even more enjoyable way of getting to school would have been on bicycle. Palo Alto, Menlo Park and the neighboring cities had special bicycle lanes which eliminated all danger from vehicular traffic. Moreover, Mjomba needed the exercise and would have been happy to commute to the "GSB" in that manner. Thinking about the options he had in America, Mjomba had to stifle a giggle when he tried to imagine what would be on the minds of dock workers in Dar es Salaam if they saw him one day cruising to work on a bicycle! They definitely would think he had gone bonkers or something. Only the poorest of the poor exposed themselves to the dangers of riding bicycles here. Just as cars were status symbols differentiating the elite from the rest of the populace, bicycles too were status symbols of sorts demarcating the "have-nots" from those who were affluent or on the road to achieving that status. You could not be affluent and go anywhere on a bicycle!

And if there was one thing about life in America which Mjomba thought was on the down-side, it was that the well-to-do rubbed shoulders with the "ordinary" folks on the "BART" in San Francisco and subway systems in other cities, and even on buses, no body was considered special. Americans did not recognize status symbols, and that took the fun out of life. It took Mjomba a while to get used to the fact that travelling to America had caused him to loose his "elite" status. But he never got used to the idea that he was a member of a "minority" simply because he was black! Any way, how on *earth* could one talk of "whites" or people of European ancestry being in the majority when there were all those Chinese who numbered in the billions! That was unless one was really parochial in one's outlook and was unable to see beyond the borders of one's country - or if one decided that Chinese also were "white" after all and not something else!

Mjomba wasn't surprised that everybody on that bus was staring at him as if his face matched one of those on the FBI's Ten Most Wanted list. As if by coincidence, a privately operated mini-bus sporting a faded poster of the FBI's Ten Most Wanted list just then whizzed past his bus and sped on ahead so it would be first in line to pick up passengers at the next Bus stop. The mini-bus, reeling under its load of passengers, careened so dangerously close to pedestrians crowding the walk-way on the far side of the road as it overtook the DTC vehicle, Mjomba found himself cursing under his breath, and wondering if that offending driver did not qualify to be on the FBI's Ten Most Wanted list!

Disembarking from the DTC at the Old Post Office, Mjomba found himself momentarily caught up in the maddening pace set by ordinary Dar es Salaamites as they went about their business. Whereas everybody talked about the pace of life in Europe and America being fast, it had never really occurred to Mjomba until that time that the pace of life in Dar es Salaam might also be fast. He was ready to concede that he himself had been living in an ivory tower and detached from the ordinary Dar es Salaamites - the real people!

He now realised that Dar es Salaam's impoverished residents had actually set a pace that, in many respects, was even faster than the pace of life in the West. Because there were no queues at bus stops, everybody scrambled to be first on the bus and get a seat. And the way the buses, the mini-buses particularly, were crammed with people, they might have been tins of sardines. Mjomba sympathized with the women and children who were at a distinct disadvantage in obtaining seating.

He thought it was very funny that a virtual stranger had offered him a seat; but then he realised that it was probably because that "polite" individual knew that the gesture was really nothing compared to a favor(s) someone in Mjomba's position could do. Imagining himself in the shoes of the "polite" dock worker, Mjomba agreed that, indeed, one never knew when one might be in need of such a favor.

Mjomba persuaded himself to "get a move on" as a colleague of his liked to say. After disembarking from the DTC bus, the bustle around him had caused him to stop and stare at the concourse of men, women and children as they went about their business.

Ocean View Garage was less than a mile from the Old Post Office. Even though DTC buses bound for a variety of destinations including places with such exotic sounding names as "Mwanyanamala", "Kinondoni" and "Karioko" by-passed it, Mjomba, who was glad to escape the gawking eyes of fellow passengers on the DTC bus from which he had disembarked, opted for a stroll along Ocean Drive.

He was obviously "spoilt" and did not think he could withstand the scotching heat *inside* those crowded buses anymore. The cool breeze blowing inland from the direction of Zanzibar made the walk a much more pleasant experience than the bus ride. But he could not help wondering how Dar es Salaam's poor survived those dreadful conditions. He did not at first understand why the authorities did not make any effort to import air-conditioned buses equipped with upholstered seats rather than hard, metal seats which heated so easily in the scotching sun.

The overflowing number of Dar es Salaamites who packed the existing DTC buses and the few privately owned mini-buses, which had been previously banned under the Government's socialist policies and had only recently been permitted to operate in the city, were certainly enough to keep double that number of DTC buses and mini-buses overloaded most of the time. Mjomba, therefore, initially figured that the Government had everything to gain by importing or itself assembling double that number of buses.

He was also sure that, even though poor, the people would be only too glad to dish out a little more in bus fare for a comfortable seat - if things came to that. The most important thing was that, in a stroke, the quality of life of so many people would be affected for the better. But then, Tanzania was the only African country with free universal primary school education and also free universal health care, which called for the construction and staffing of a vast number of schools and health clinics in a matter of months. Certainly ambitious policies; but Tanzanians, lead by the Oxford educated *Mwalimu* or, as Westerners would have put it, *Professor* Nyerere, appeared quite determined to back them up with action.

It occurred to Mjomba that the inconvenience of the Dar es Salaamites just might be the price that had to be paid to get the rest of the country - in fact the heart of the nation also on its feet and moving! Moreover, in the eyes of the Western world, Tanzania was essentially a rogue state, because of its socialist leanings. Which meant that the people of that country did not have full and free access to the assistance that would normally have been available from institutions like the World Bank and the International Monetary Fund. With the Cold War still raging, that was the cold reality.

As he ambled along the elegant Nkrumah Boulevard past the State House, a demure building that had previously belonged to an Asian trader, and the debonair Aga Khan Hospital close by, the thought kept occurring to him that he ought to have telephoned the garage to confirm that work on his car was proceeding on schedule.

Even though he made it to the garage in forty five minutes, which was just about the same length of time it would have taken him if he had waited and caught the next DTC bus going in that direction, the fact he hadn't phoned prevented him from fully enjoying his stroll.

At the garage, Mjomba's heart sank and he was temporarily paralysed by a lump in his throat on learning that the car had in fact been ready for release to him for some hours, having been attended to in double-quick time in deference to his entreaty early that day. He was agitated for no apparent reason and found himself struggling vainly to refrain from making comparisons between the performance of the garage and performance of Office Services or the city's DTC that day. He did not want to believe that there could be such a stark contrast between the performance of a small, privately managed enterprise and the performance of a whole department of the Port Authority or that of one of the largest corporations in the country!

Before jumping into the driver's seat, Mjomba tossed the envelope containing the manuscript into the front passenger seat, its usual place. He seemed to like having the manuscript in sight as much as possible, as if it was by a process of osmosis that he received the inspiration he needed for developing his dossier on Innocent Kintu into a full fledged, best selling novel!

With his briefcase in its usual place on the back seat, he steered the sedan into Umoja wa Wanawake Way to head home. He could not fail to notice the improved performance brought on by the new tyre-rod ends and the wheel alignment. Mjomba had already driven past the Kanji Sulemani Stores on the final homeward stretch when he remembered the Baby Oil!

He made a U-turn at the Kaunda/Msasani Roads junction and raced back towards the Kanji Sulemani Stores. As he did so, his mind suddenly became besieged with images of the assortment of baby items that he and his wife had been "showered" with by their newfound friends in America on the occasion of Kunta's birth four years earlier.

Although neither Jamila nor himself were white - or perhaps because of it and their distinctive British accent - they had made many friends in the relatively short period they had been in America; and the baby shower, which came as a complete surprise, had turned out to be quite a shower! As he thought about the many items they had had to exchange at the nearby Macy's and the Emporium, a vein in his right cheek-bone began twitching at a rapidly accelerating pace, triggered no doubt by the flood of images.

Mjomba had been dismayed on at least one other occasion - the occasion of Kinte's birth two years before - that baby showers as an institution did not figure in his own tribal customs! He shut his eyes briefly, as if in admission of the immutability of that situation, opening them just in time to avoid a head-on collision with an approaching vehicle. But there was no way he could stop his mind wandering now!

Mjomba again felt a lump rise to his throat as he turned to consider the results of his efforts of the past several days which were intended to make up for what the couple missed by being in Africa instead of America. Armed with a list of baby items prepared by Jamila on the one hand and a purse that was far from adequate on the other, he had done the rounds of shops in the teaming capital, buying an item here and noting the price of another there.

Heralding the seasonal rains, the heat and the accompanying humidity had been unbearable and inhibiting. Then there was the fact that since the socialist revolution, and particularly when the country adopted the "glorious" *Ujamaa* doctrine or African Socialism, most items which had previously flooded the local market had disappeared from the shelves.

And, when they happened to be available, they were so expensive, even for someone of his station, it had stopped being an exaggeration to use terms like "paying through the nose" or "paying dearly" for a commodity. Plagued with that combination of troubles, the results of his mission had been decidedly poor as a consequence.

While a newborn babe, in the view of the Mjombas, could do without such things as pants and coats in the less than friendly weather of the "Heaven of Peace", Baby Oil was considered indispensable - a veritable soothing balm in Dar es Salaam's nigh permanent heat wave. Kanji Sulemani Stores did not have Baby Oil in stock, and the revelation left Mjomba feeling like a dumbbell!

If you missed an item at the Kanji Sulemani Stores for which they were stockists, it was usually a safe bet that the whole town had run out of it. The very idea now made him feel exasperated and steamed up. The previous day, the Asian attendant had shaken her head from side to side and advised her eager customer to "make another try tomorrow". The sight of the same attendant shaking her head from side to side in her accustomed manner caused him to splutter on his way out: "What the heck...shortages! As if it wasn't bad enough paying out a fortune when something happened to be available!"

In spite of his woes, Mjomba made it home in time to take Jamila to hospital. In the general anxiety, everybody there had ignored Kunta and Kinte. They were in the lounge by themselves, their attention riveted to a solitary bag stuffed with baby things, some of them leftovers from Kunta's epoch as a tot.

Mjomba bounded past them into the hallway leading to the master bedroom only to be met by his wife in the narrow passage. Waited on by women-folk from adjoining homes, Jamila had bathed and donned her favourite maternity outfit - a light green pleated blouse worn over a chestnut spotted *Kanga*.

Minutes later, outside the beach bungalow, Jamila hesitated as her husband swung the Ford's doors open. It was common knowledge that few owners of cars with low suspensions in this former British possession could afford to maintain the shock absorbers in anything approximating a good state of repair. Ocean View Motor Garage had only that afternoon attached, for the fifth consecutive time, a note on the Ford's repair bill advising that the shock absorbers needed attention! Jamila seemed to guess as much.

At the behest of Mrs. Killian, the hospital-bound retinue piled into her Volkswagen - Jamila, Mjomba, Kunta, Kinte, Mrs. Killian herself and Priscilla, her-two-year-old daughter. Mrs. Killian, who was expecting - and whose tummy made her look eight rather than five months pregnant - had stopped driving as a precaution and easily prevailed on Mjomba to take the wheel.

They made it to Dr. Mambo's Clinic with considerable aplomb, thanks to the performance the kids put up along the way. His wife's labour pains notwithstanding, Mjomba could not resist the laughter each time one of them pointed to the bulging tummy of either Mrs. Killian or of Jamila and, with childlike simplicity and grief-stricken voice, intoned: "Painful?"

When they had filed out of the *Beetle*, Kunta, ebullient as ever, led the column to the hospital's Reception Desk, followed by Mrs. Killian who had Jamila in tow. Mjomba brought up the rear with Priscilla and Kinte swinging under his arms. As they trooped in, two smiling nurses surrounded Mrs. Killian and began to steer her towards a wheel-chair! Watching the scene from the back of the queue, Mjomba could not help laughing - indeed not even his wife was able not to laugh despite the labor pains.

The place, a favourite haunt for patients with middle-class incomes, was buzzing with activity. Doctors' paths criss-crossed and nurses, bursting with mysterious enthusiasm, darted here and there. As soon as several of their number laid their hands on Jamila, they whisked her away into an Examination Room and out of sight.

About fifteen minutes or so after his abrupt and all too sudden separation from his wife, Mjomba, anxiety written all over his face, busied himself with the children in an effort to hide his own strangely sharp feelings of expectancy. Jamila's regular doctor, an Oxford educated obstetrician of half-Asian and half-Arab heritage, spied him and made a beeline for him.

"Your wife's almost ready now," she whispered in his ear.

"Is it a boy or a girl?" Mjomba asked, excited. He was convinced that he had noticed a reassuring smile flash on her face. It was an oval, Semitic face which struck Mjomba as being very sensual. The facial features of the doctor, a close family friend, had always reminded him of those of Jamila who, like the doctor, boasted a mixed African, Arab and European ancestry.

Jamila's maternal great grandmother was a slave woman her great grandfather, a former slave trader, had added to his harem just before that dreadful institution was outlawed. That was also before the ageing slave trader turned to the lucrative spice trade and settled down in Zanzibar off mainland Tanganyika as Tanzania was then known. Jamila's paternal grandfather on the other hand was a native of the Seychelles islands which lie smack in the middle of the Indian Ocean. Like most native sons of those islands, his family tree included people of combined African, Arab, French, Indian and Chinese descent. It did not, therefore, surprise Mjomba that his wife still retained Semitic features amongst others. For some reason, though, his focus had always been on her Arab ancestry.

Still, a favourite joke of his was that his flame was the incarnation of everything that was desirable in a woman by virtue of her lineage - just like Eve of the Old Testament! But he sometimes also claimed, when it suited him, that his wife's comeliness owed more to the fact that the old slave trader apparently had still got an eye for original beauty and charm when he added Jamila's grandmother to his flock of wives.

Mjomba, who had on one occasion been forced by Jamila to confess that he was a secret admirer of her doctor, thought it a strange coincidence that his wife's paediatrician not only bore a great deal of likeness to her, but also apparently had Arab blood in her. He sometimes wondered whether her descendants were slaves, or slave merchants, or both.

"Jamila is almost ready to start delivering the baby," volunteered Mrs. Killian in explanation. She had over-heard the exchange and had concluded that she stood considerably less chance of being misunderstood by the distracted Mjomba than did the doctor.

The doctor's reassuring smile was still playing on her face and the laughter was restrained as she said: "Next time, make it the hospital a little earlier or it might be in the taxi!"

The doctor's warning caused memories of an incident to which he had been witness about a year or so before to come tumbling back into his brain. He had given a lift to a neighbor at early dawn to Dr.

Mambo's Clinic and was waiting by the clinic's entrance, located not far from where they were, for the neighbor to emerge from the wards when a taxi cab appeared from no where and pulled up next to his battered Ford.

The cab driver had scarcely brought his weather-beaten Peugeot 404 station wagon, with its complement of two female passengers and a worried looking man roughly Mjomba's own age, to a standstill when he leapt out and scrambled for the Reception Desk. But by the time the cabbie emerged from the building with a nursing sister close on his heels, the number of his passengers had grown to four!

It was a painful sight which met Mjomba's eyes when, ambling out of the Ford like someone in a stupor, he stood helplessly by and watched the nursing sister sever the umbilical cord joining mother and babe using what looked like a common pair of scissors right there in the taxi!

Recalling the incident, he found himself re-living the experience all over again, and struggling to contain his sharp feelings of anger at the adult passengers in that vehicle and anxiety for the child which the sight of the naked and crying babe being rushed up the hospital's stairway in a nurse's arms had evoked in him at the time. It suddenly seemed to Mjomba an appropriate time to relate the incident. But the doctor was gone before he could engage her in further dialogue.

Mjomba had a mind to maintain a vigil at the hospital for at least those crucial final hours of the countdown. As the entourage, consisting now of Mrs. Killian, her daughter Priscilla, Kunta, Kinte and himself, headed off towards Msasani Peninsula in the *Beetle* with himself at wheel, Mjomba after due consultations with Mrs. Killian, made a detour allowing him to call on his in-laws to request help for little Kunta and Kinte. Thrilled to learn that another grand-child was on the way, the senior Kivumbis were only too glad to let Fatuma, a seventeen year-old cousin of Jamila's and a favourite with the kids, join the entourage for the rest of its journey.

Later that evening, the seven O'clock news was being announced over the National Broadcasting Service when, leaving the children in the competent hands of Fatuma, Mjomba jumped into the Ford and headed for Dr. Mambo's Clinic, heart pounding.

Jamila and her husband openly dreaded caesarean sections despite the fact that a section probably saved Kunta's life at birth. From what Jamila had been able to piece together later from her fragmentary memory of the events of that afternoon at the Stanford Medical Center, the team of distinguished doctors had initially let her attempt natural delivery.

The baby's head had apparently started to appear when readings on the battery of scientific instruments there by her bedside started to signal danger with regard to the baby's condition. The readings, which only days before had magically established the child's gender, were none-too-encouraging for a little while, a reflection on the unprecedented level of hypertension to which Jamila was an unfortunate prey. That had prompted the doctors to transfer her to the operating table right there and then.

Mjomba had been informed in advance of his wife's confinement at the Medical Center that he not only was free to attend delivery, but could also photograph the proceedings if he so wished. It had predictably taken some persuading to get Jamila to agree to be photographed while giving birth. but, as usual, she had acquiesced to her husband's will and consented to his plan to capture on film the different stages of their child's development starting right from the moment of his birth.

The couple already owned a variant of the famous Polaroid Land camera which Mjomba had bought as a present for his wife at Orley Airport during their stop-over in Paris on their San Francisco bound flight a year earlier. But Mjomba was so consumed by the idea of recording their child's history, he even deemed it worthwhile to invest in a reasonably good movie camera. In that way they would be able in their old age to sit back and view day-long movies featuring their kid, so Mjomba imagined, instead of having to flip through hundreds of still photos! He had accordingly proceeded to the Emporium and procured a Kodak XL 360 camera, and a Kodak

Movie-Deck 435 to go with it, charging the cost against his student Triple 'E' Account.

The knowledge that he could not be permitted inside the operating theatre in the event of his wife's delivery by caesarean section had laid the ground for Mjomba's somewhat irrational aversion for that form of childbirth, an aversion that was reinforced by the fact that medical operations in Africa and elsewhere in the third world were fraught with danger for obvious reasons.

In the course of time, the disappointed Mjomba had gradually lost track of the fact that his examinations schedule had in any case already precluded him from picture taking. And so, his pathological dislike for operations, coupled with his natural dread for blood-letting in general, made a caesarean section the last thing he could wish for his wife.

Jamila, for her part, had a long standing dread for delivery by caesarean section, stemming from an incident that occurred while she was still a child. A woman who was their distant relation had died while giving birth and, although the cause of death had nothing to do with caesarean sections, Jamila's grandmother, discussing the dangers of childbirth in general with other women while the wake was still under way, had said that a woman could not very safely bear a second child if she had had her first through the caesarean method. She had said this within ear-shot of her grand daughter!

Caesarean sections were, of course, virtually unknown during the old lady's time; but her words, which were regarded by her audience as words that were pregnant with wisdom, had left a lasting impression on the young Jamila.

To the couple's immense relief, despite the section Jamila had had for Kunta's birth, Jamila gave birth to Kinte three years later through natural, uncomplicated delivery. Taking place in Socialist Tanzania which was regarded by Westerners as a typical basket case and a banana republic, it came as a bit of a surprise. And one would accordingly have expected Mjomba to rise to the occasion and give the Cuban doctors who were the mainstay of his country's health system some credit. But this had instead provided Mjomba an excuse to shower more praise on the Americans who "had done it again"!

Many of Mjomba's friends, a good number of whom had received their education in the Soviet Union and Communist China, would in any case have sworn that they had it on good authority that if a child was delivered by caesarean section in any hospital in that former British trust territory, the chances of the child's mother subsequently having another baby by natural birth were nil. Bolstered by the popular myths, they would even have happily wagered everything they were worth that such a mother could never live through two more child births!

On the present occasion, the doctors had said that the odds against a caesarean outweighed those against a trouble free natural child-birth. In spite of the assurances, the couple's anxiety had remained boundless. Not even the growing excitement, as the days of Jamila's confinement wore on, had seemed able to affect the gloom which characterized everything they did.

All that notwithstanding, Mjomba's mind, as he sauntered casually into the desolate reception area of Dr. Mambo's Clinic, had somehow already ruled out the prospects for a caesarean section. At that juncture, he merely expected a nurse to emerge from one of the corridors and overwhelm him with the news that his wife had delivered a baby, preferably a girl this time, and that both mother and child were doing fine.

He met with unexpected disappointment, though for a different reason. The nurse who approached, as he stood erect in the center of the hallway, belonged to a new shift; and her gaze told him before she even spoke that he looked very much like an intruder. And it also occurred to him just then that visiting time had in fact expired hours earlier!

The nurse allowed the inevitable smile to form on her face as she confronted him. “Good evening. What can I do for you, Sir?”

Mjomba initially felt like telling the nurse to stop “Sirring” him and to do what he imagined nurses were expected to do first and foremost, namely to empathize with everybody both infirm and able bodied. (You really could never tell if the ones who looked able bodied were not sick in other ways!) Instead, he faltered repeatedly as he struggled to explain himself.

He had hardly concluded when she vanished into a corridor, only to return shortly afterward intoning from the distance: "*Bado ... bado kidogo.*" Even though most spoke English very well, Tanzanians just loved to speak Swahili, their national language.

And one thing which could be said about Swahili was that it was serving as a bridge uniting the vastly diverging peoples of a country the size of Texas and with a population that was twice that of France! And it also seemed to be true that "speaking the national language" was often used as an excuse to engage strangers one would not otherwise be able to approach in conversation. And that was especially so if you had some inkling that they were not particularly fluent in it.

None of this was the case here, however. With just a hint of sympathy in her voice, the nurse added: "Could take another hour!"

"Fine! I will call later" Mjomba said, his manner business-like now. And as he did so, he turned and set out purposelessly down the darkened street.

Mjomba's throat was scorched and he felt badly in need of a drink. But, on a strange impulse, he fought to keep thoughts relating to his own comfort from his head. Summoning all his will power, he tried to restrict the meanderings of his faculties of the intellect and imagination to considerations that strictly pertained to the welfare of Jamila and nothing else! Like a mystic contemplating the sufferings of a divinity, he even attempted putting himself mentally in his wife's position and enduring the labour pains with her! But the result, perhaps predictably, was total confusion.

Mjomba regained control of himself presently however and, turning left into India Street, quickened his steps in the direction of the Solar Clock in the heart of downtown Dar es Salaam. He was hoping, as he approached Independence Avenue, that he could kill time window shopping along the famous tree-lined thoroughfare.

Mjomba found that he was the only one dawdling about on the street. It was then that, bewildered and confused as ever, he considered downing a beer or two at the rooftop Moonlite Bar down the road. The red and blue lights of the establishment cast an enigmatic pall over the street and the surroundings as he approached.

He climbed wearily to the top of the dingy stairway. The bar chatter, a mere distant hum of voices when he began the ascent, was now a thunderous drone that invaded his ears from all sides. Intending to pause only briefly in front of the swing doors before gaining entrance, he took in his breath and readied to brush them aside with his arms. He even allowed himself the indulgence of letting his imagination run ahead of him, so that he now already saw himself occupying a high stool at the bar and a suitably cold, if unlabeled, bottle of Kilimanjaro Beer and a large glass before him. He had filled the glass - in his mind - and was all but feeling the cold beer trickle down his parched throat when he came out of his doldrums.

Regaining his presence in front of the swing doors of the bar, Mjomba could not help wondering why the thought had not crossed his mind earlier than that! How on earth could he possibly be thinking of revelling in booze, and on an empty stomach at that, just as his wife was in labour!

He did not stop to consider the possibility of treating himself to a Fanta or a Coke, both of which were a rarity at drinking places and unlikely to be in stock at the Moonlite any way. Turning away from the hubbub, he made straight for his car in the parking lot of Dr. Mambo's Clinic. He jumped in and, adjusting the reclining angle of the driver's seat, he lowered it to its extremity. He eased himself into it, determined as ever to complete his vigil as planned.

It was forty minutes or so later when, blinking wearily and looking thoroughly flustered, Mjomba once more sauntered into the clinic's reception hall. Several nurses, including the one who had interviewed him earlier, were relaxing on a bench.

They all seemed to stare at him with knowing looks. But it was their colleague who spoke: "Mr. Christian Mjomba?"

Her voice and face were familiar enough and her manner was polite, if cautious.

A casual glance at the girls and, in particular, the speaker and he became convinced that he had been the subject of their chatter shortly, if not immediately, before he made his reappearance. Staring back at them, he imagined their countenances, so prim and un-demeaning now, enveloped in giggles; and he thought: "How pert of them!"

Aloud, Mjomba replied "Yes," and waited for the news he had already sensed would not be forthcoming.

"I'm sorry," the nurse went on after the pause. "But we don't have any news for you yet. In fact, as it is already pretty late... "

"I know, I know" Mjomba cut in. With full anticipation of what she had been about to say, he continued: "Think I will be better off waiting at home."

"Would you like us to telephone you if there is news?" she piped in his general direction. Her tone was rhetorical and she seemed to expect no more than a nod. But Mjomba raised his voice and began thanking her profusely for the idea.

"Oh, we will be glad to do that" the nurse said cheerily, her mates nodding approval the while. Another nurse consulted a chart she took from a shelf and read out Mjomba's residential telephone number inquiringly.

"That's it, that's it" he said with a wan smile.

Before retracing his steps to the car, Mjomba turned to the first nurse and, wringing his hands, said: "I will be most grateful indeed!"

The hands of Jamila's Omega watch which he had borrowed indicated the time as 10:00 O'clock sharp as he started the car's engine to drive away. He half expected to find a message at home instructing him to head back to the clinic on arrival home, but none had been received.

The children were comfortably in bed. Provided with ample warning of her uncle's arrival by the Ford's head lamps, which illuminated the dimly lit living-room as Mjomba was negotiating the last bend in the winding stretch of dirt road leading up to the gates of the bungalow, Fatuma started to lay out his dinner on the table even before the sound of the doorbell, a near perfect facsimile of the purr of a nightingale, tingled overhead.

Mjomba left the dinner untouched for lack of appetite. He took a "cold" shower instead and stepped out of it without noticing that the water, which was hot enough to kill a fly because of exposure to muggy temperatures earlier on in the day, put it in a different class of shower altogether.

After that he selected a seat by the telephone, tuned his Satellite receiver into the Voice of America, and settled back to listen to the African Panorama Show.

As he recalled later, a male announcer on the "show" had given the time as "Thirty minutes past the hour", which Mjomba had interpreted as 11:30 p.m. Then a sprightly female voice had come on the air to announce: "'Tis Request Time!"

Apparently, weariness had overcome him in the moments that followed, sending him into a deep slumber. For beyond that, his mind registered nothing - apart, that is, from the dream.

When the telephone rang, the fifteen minute programme was still continuing. But in that short space of time, he not only had travelled in his dream to far away California and back, but he had also made it to the near-by National Medical Teaching Hospital and back, the places of birth of Kunta and Kinte respectively.

At the Stanford Medical Center off the panoramic High Way One, Mjomba found himself gazing through a glass partition at his day-old son. Freshly circumcised and naked, poor little Kunta had his tiny legs held apart to allow the bulb's heat to dry the wound. And now he whimpered ever so piteously as if to say that no more and no less than the return of his foreskin could persuade him to make a truce with the world!

The only one of African stock among the nursery's occupants on the day in question, Kunta was possessed of a hue that made him appear no different nonetheless from his white and yellow comrades. He was recognizable only by the name plate which was pinned to his crib and by his wonderfully rich crop of hair - Mjomba had it on good authority that African babies typically arrived with lots more hair on their crown than babies of other ethnic groups!.

Closer home at the NMTH where Mjomba was transported in his sleep for the final leg of his phenomenal trip, he had slipped into the nursery disguised as Jamila so he could take a stealthy look at the day old Kinte.

Although the necessity of the disguise was not immediately apparent, his action would be fully justified by what transpired next in the dream.

Mjomba was shocked to discover that two, and in some cases three, infants were being made to share a crib! However, before he could recover from his shock or locate the boy in the crowd of the nursery's wailing in-mates, the plot was discovered.

The guard, a wretched looking old man who had initially pretended to be fast asleep, had in fact been awake and quite alert. But, apparently also a deaf mute, he proved impervious to the intruder's pleas and even offer of a bribe, and proceeded to set off the alarm!

Even before the old guard's emasculated hands had found a proper grip on the mechanism's lever, there was a pealing sound not unlike that of a fire alarm. The sound promptly merged with the telephone's muffled purr as Mjomba, his forehead ringed with beads of sweat, awoke.

If the anxiety precipitated by the neighbor's telephone call that afternoon, and the exhaustion from the subsequent events had dulled the expectant Mjomba's mental faculties, the events of the dream, so nightmarish and livid, had tended to sharpen them. But his wits were still a shade blunted as he stirred to answer the telephone. His bruised nerves were screaming for more relaxation; and it was not until he heard the faintly familiar voice of a girl talking that he completely awoke to reality, which now burst in on him like a clap of thunder.

Even though, when the nurse's voice came crackling through the ear-piece with the news that his wife had just given birth to a baby boy, the Mjombas' third, it all sounded like another dream to the awaking man. Bubbling faster than Mjomba could follow, the nurse said he weighed seven pounds - a giant of a baby, Mjomba thought, considering his mother's size.

The nurse had added: "A beautiful, chocolate coloured little thing with an ample tuft of Negroid hair on his dome!"

As with Kunta and Kinte, the new arrival's hue apparently took after that of their mom, a ravishing bronze beauty herself. The clear tone of Jamila's skin combined with the classic dimensions of her head, body, and legs, and the tantalizing natural grace she exuded to make her a veritable lily in Mjomba's life. But, strangely, it was upon a black and white photograph acquired during their courtship that Mjomba frequently gazed to keep himself reminded of his "lily flower".

To his artistic mind, the abstractness of a black and white portrait of his enchantress, because it left more to the imagination, was more preferable to the brightness of a coloured portrait!

Christian Mjomba fancied the picture of his then smiling bride-to-be so much that he continued to carry the old picture with him everywhere he went inside the covers of a note-book long after they had been wedded.

Standing there shouting excitedly into the telephone, Mjomba scarcely noticed the figure of Fatuma who had been aroused from her sleep by the commotion, and now looked on from the passage-way, her complexion wrapped up in glee.

A strange elation took hold of her when she noticed that his gaze concentrated on a faded but still expressive black and white photograph of her aunt.

Setting down the receiver, Mjomba nearly ran into Fatuma. But he realised almost at once that the Ford's ignition keys were in his trouser pocket, and made an about-turn which prevented a collision but left her dazed all the same. With gestured hand signals and muttered words that fell far short of a comprehensible manner of speech, he attempted, as he backed out of the house, to direct her to lock the door after him. He bolted for the garage door before he could finish.

Outnumbered three to one...

The pains and pangs of childbirth behind her, Jamila was nestled contentedly in the trim hospital bed and sipping tea to quell her rising desire for food when her husband came swaying into the recovery room. Mjomba could see that she was thrilled and utterly mirthful. He flopped down by his wife's bedside and hugged her vigorously.

In reply to his "Hurray!", she plunged into a vivid description of the ordeal she had been through only minutes before - how she had "pushed and pushed" and come close to giving up in her exhaustion! She had scarcely finished when he too began to describe how he had kept vigil, and how he had come close to abandoning it in despair!

When he had finished, Jamila revealed that the child had really started to come as her husband took off in their battered Ford less than an hour earlier! She not only had overheard the conversations in the reception hall, but could tell when he drove off because the Ford's exhaust pipe had a defective muffler.

Their chatter, seemingly endless, did not appear as if it was about to bore them in any way. They continued to vie with one another in recalling anecdotes from the day's huge store of events. Mjomba, bubbling with joy, had all but forgotten about the other hero of the day in the course of the chatter. But now, as the nurse who had broken the good news to him over the telephone appeared in the doorway, a small bundle balanced between her arms, the atmosphere in the room changed visibly.

"Flora, this is Christian, my husband," Jamila said as the nurse walked into the room.

"We've already met" Mjomba interposed as he gingerly took the "bundle" in his arms and stared down at the pink, round face. Still wrapped up in his swaddling clothes, the new-born babe looked like an angel and far from being battle-scarred, despite his gruelling and traumatic entry into the world.

Flora watched on as Mjomba turned to his wife and, eyebrows up-raised, said half in jest: "Love, one more perhaps-not-so-tough job this time for you. Will you choose the name by which this young chap shall be known?"

"Kintu!" The syllables seemed to come automatically from Jamila's lips, and for a long moment seemed to hold Mjomba dumbfounded. The previously garrulous executive made no effort to hide his surprise. And, all this while, his wife was grinning; a taut, waspish grin, as if she were intent on hiding something from him - which she evidently was.

That very week, Jamila had seen her husband do something which had caused her to ponder many things. She had seen him sleep walking, pacing to and fro in his sleep in their master bedroom, like someone deep in thought. She had also noticed that he kept repeating the words "Kunta, Kinte, Kintu... Gunta, Ginte, Gintu" as he did so!

The meanderings of her thoughts, subsequently, as she sought to put what she had heard in some kind of perspective, had initially led her to ROOTS, Alex Haley's best seller which had a prominent place on the mantle above the fire place! But that famed masterpiece had failed to adequately explain the name "Kintu".

The passage of time had completely erased from her memory anything that might have connected "Kintu" with the patient Prof. Gringo had treated and, as far as she knew, subsequently discharged almost a decade before. She would not even have cared to know that Innocent Kintu, who now went by the names of Justice Maramba and who was a celebrated libertine, had taken the advice of Prof. Gringo seriously and had used Theory "R" both to understand his distorted psychological make-up and to correct his flawed view of the world.

Jamila herself had never really shown much interest in the so-called Theory "R", or in the fact that it might have the potential for inducing the cure of mentally deranged persons who felt that the rest of the world, rather than themselves, had got their act wrong! It was doubtful that she would even have cared to know that it was that same Innocent Kintu who was currently her country's Acting Chief Justice - Justice Innocent Maramba - and who was likely to be confirmed in that elevated position, with powers to send people to their deaths, by His Excellency the President!

No interpreter of dreams, Jamila had nonetheless settled on one thing - if the new baby would turn out to be a boy as the ultra-sound scan at the NMTH was suggesting, she would not mind calling him Kintu, Gintu, Gunta or whatever! They all sounded good enough and even an improvement on Haley's "Gunte" anyway - as long it was going to make Mjomba happy. But, having attained her ambition, she now felt either too shy or thought it would be too much of an embarrassment to her idol to explain what had transpired! And even though she was already on first name terms with Flora, she did not consider it proper to bring up such a matter in front of the nurse!

Black as coal and some ten years or so Jamila's junior, Flora was spectacularly formed and quite a stunning beauty herself. She observed the goings-on with what appeared, at first, to be detached concern.

The daughter of a Baptist minister, Flora had been brought up to see only good in people. But now, confronted with what she thought was mischief on an imaginable scale, she found herself empathising with Mjomba and almost hating the woman she had up until now shown so much respect and esteem.

Flora had come to Dr. Mambo's Clinic straight from nursing school. And Mrs. Mjomba, whom she greatly admired above all for her grace, loomed up in her perception as just the right sort of role model for her. It was precisely because of her high expectations of the woman she was already proud to refer to as "My patient" that she now felt such enormous disappointment. She could not bring herself to believe that people of her gender could actually be so impish.

Staring wide eyed at Jamila, Flora was now convinced that under the mask of that awesome beauty lay a nefarious and cruel nature. She had reached that conclusion sorely from surveying the shape of Jamila's mouth at the height of her fleeting stand-off with her handsome hubby. Flora even stopped concealing the fact that she was finding him enormously attractive, and began to gawk idolizingly at the man she did not have any scruples about nagging scarcely an hour before.

Staring straight into Mjomba's eyes, and her comely face a mirror of concern for her newfound idol, Flora now flexed the muscles of her well rounded curves.

When she was sure that her movement had attracted his attention, she took her time to brush aside imaginary dust from her satin-white skirt; and she did not at all seem bothered by the fact that Jamila saw and noted both the eager expression on her face and the mischievous grin accompanying it!

In normal circumstances, nothing would have sounded more familiar to Mjomba than the syllables which formed the name "Kintu". And yet, coming from his wife's mouth at that moment, those syllables sounded so unfamiliar, they might as well have been a different set of syllables altogether! Following a strange law of nature, "Kintu" had taken on a completely different ring in Mjomba's ears.

Mjomba urged himself to calm down and remain that way for a while. This wasn't the first time this kind of thing had happened to him. He was aware that when composing an essay involving ideological conflict, the characters sometimes tended almost naturally to withdraw to the background in the mind of the essayist to allow the ideas attributed to them to get the prominence they deserved. He tried to reassure himself that, perhaps, in this particular instance something was causing the name "Kintu" to pale into something that sounded only remotely familiar to Mjomba to allow a different side to the story to get the prominence it deserved?

Like so many things about which one has only half a recollection, the name continued to defy association with every object his groping mind resurrected. During the minute or so which followed (a minute that looked more like a decade to the embattled Mjomba), "Kintu" remained a little more than a mere sound with no apparent meaning to it.

Or was it that Kintu, the principal character in Mjomba's book, had now assumed a nature all of its own - a nature that perhaps was so complex it had become a puzzle which could elude its own inventor's efforts to solve it! Mjomba smiled at the thought that someone who was responsible for bringing an object into life could in fact end up being rebuffed by his own invention in that fashion! He thought about the innumerable number of times he had painstakingly developed ideas for his "masterpiece" in his mind only to see them slip from his memory and, recede beyond his powers of recall and become lost forever!

Instead of helping Mjomba to nail down the original source of the name Jamila had picked for their son, these thoughts, as they churned through his mind, only caused him to become increasingly depressed. Even though something told him that the obvious solution to his problem was to stop getting mired in thoughts of that kind and to assume a more relaxed stance, he was unable to abandon the subject at that juncture now that he had become so involved with it.

Instead, he now recalled how, at an earlier time, he had been about to lose a battle of wits - or so he then thought - in somewhat similar circumstances between himself and a character he had created for a special role in his "masterpiece" and had to retreat in shame! As he recalled it, he had suddenly found himself at loggerheads on some point with the character in question, and had began recoiling in fear, because the character, which had taken on a life all of its won, refused to take any nonsense or to budge from the position it had taken. That had caused Mjomba to decide that it was better to throw in the towel.

To allay his mounting fears and lay them to rest on that occasion, he had gradually succeeded in persuading himself that it was all a figment of his imagination - probably due to fatigue - and that there was really nothing amiss between himself and the fictional character in the "masterpiece"! To be fair to Mjomba, his day had been a full one, to be sure; and it could well be that the pressures he was under were intense and enough to drive any average person nuts in very much the same way.

"Honey" Mjomba said finally, his mind still swimming in the world of imagery; "If I had been the one searching for a name for the baby and had come across this one, my choice would have been no different!"

As he spoke, Flora, who had been holding her breath and had also been praying that he would come up with a response that was adequate, emptied her lungs of the stale air with an audible hiss. Visibly relieved and relaxed, she turned and faced him without bothering to conceal the fondness with which she now regarded him. She did this just as Jamila's long eyelashes flickered up and down in quick succession as she on her part shed imaginary tears of joy!

Blushing, Mjomba was surprised that Flora had been inching ever closer to the spot where he had retreated while trying to solve the "Kintu" puzzle, and now stood practically facing him with only a foot or so between them!

Even before the nurse advanced that close, Mjomba was already finding it hard to hide the fact that he was feeling awkward, not just because of the silence which had followed his meaningless utterance, but even more so because of Flora's presence and peculiar demeanour.

He told himself that he should become annoyed with the nurse for getting a kick out of making him feel so uncomfortable. Secretly, he felt exhilarated by her chicanery, however, and wondered why.

Flora was clearly envious of her patient, and appeared to be interested in drawing Mjomba's attention away from Jamila as much as possible, and she did not seem to care a hoot how either of them took it.

Mjomba hardly felt relieved when Jamila, her eyes misty and heart-beat racing, rested her hand on his lap and then, her gaze intent on him, said: "Darling, you must find Kintu a middle name so he will be just like his buddies!"

He felt a lump suddenly form in his throat, and breathing became difficult as he tried to think of a name - any well sounding name - only to find himself stuck!

He could not believe what was happening. He, Christian Mjomba, who bragged about one day being able to bequeath to the world a masterpiece that likely would also get into the Guinness's Book of Records as the best selling literary work of all time, and who was so confident about his ability to send shock waves into the scientific community by explaining away madness, could not come up with a middle name for his son? A son, moreover, so beloved he had gladly stayed up all night so he could snuggle and hug him and welcome him into the world as soon as possible after his arrival?

Mjomba stole a quick look at the nurse. A thought - although only a thought - had just occurred to him that it was perhaps her presence which was rendering his vaunted mental faculties suddenly so ineffectual! He looked away swiftly, hoping to thereby prevent Jamila from catching him at it. But it was too late. His wife, who was wide-eyed, not only noticed everything but had obviously been anticipating Mjomba's move. She threw a glance first in his direction and then in the direction of Flora who herself had been on the alert and had not failed to return Mjomba's glance.

At that point in time, Flora reminded Mjomba of his secretary. The nurse's seductive posture as she stood there in front of them was clearly enough evidence, if any evidence was necessary, that the minister's daughter had taken out all the stops in a deliberate attempt to both tease and harass him.

Mjomba shut his eyes and paused to think about Innocent Kintu, the central character of his "masterpiece". As images of the nurse's beguiling manner came flocking back, he came close to concluding that a non-fictional character like Kintu could in fact be considered fictional when contrasted with a character like Flora!

Although sure that the worst was about to happen, miraculously it did not. Jamila, hiding the fact that he had just been a witness to her own hubby's cheating eyes - or something approximating it - behind a mask of blind selfless love, merely edged closer to him so that their cheeks all but touched.

That is not to say this was something Mjomba would have liked to see happen to him. At that particular moment, there was nothing Mjomba would have wanted more than to be many miles away from Jamila!

Severely embarrassed by both women, Mjomba wished that Flora's attitude to him was different or at least cold - just like the attitude she had displayed earlier on that evening when the very tone of her voice seemed hostile. He would have gladly turned to face her now as a way of appeasing his indignant wife.

Mjomba was on the point of despair when an idea that was as strange as it was outlandish suggested itself. Here he was, being treated like oaf by the two women! The conclusion that another woman might have a hand in it, even though remote, was suddenly appealing. And the most likely suspect was Primrose, no doubt, he told himself. After a short while, he was convinced that it had to be his secretary who had set him up!

And with that, Mjomba was soon quite agitated as he tried to figure out exactly how Primrose had gone about letting his wife in on the secret pertaining to the book project. Mjomba was overwhelmed with emotion at the thought that Primrose, while physically distant, could be involved in his miseries. He also began to wonder, even though in a somewhat fuzzy way at this point, what it was Primrose expected to obtain from being a traitor to him in that fashion.

Almost overwhelmed by his feelings of antipathy for women in general at that juncture, Mjomba could not resist putting the rhetorical question to himself. Well, if it was not his secretary who was behind this, who else could it possibly be? How could Jamila otherwise ever have come up with the name Kintu! Mjomba was certain that Jamila had no personal recollection of anything that had occurred during those early days of their courtship relating to the case of Innocent Kintu.

Mjomba felt certain that it was Primrose who had to be the missing link his groping mind had been trying to nail down. At that moment, as he reached the conclusion that Jamila and Primrose had been in secret communication regarding his literary project, the single word he had been attempting to pin down in his mind's inner-most recesses - before he made the mistake of trying to steal a glance at Flora - materialised from out yonder and settled on the edge of his mind.

To Mjomba's weary mind, the naked forty Watt bulb lighting up his wife's recovery room, had it been lighting up his inner sanctum, might as well have been replaced by the sun itself in that fraction of a second as the word "masterpiece" formed in his thought processes!

The unbroken silence persisted for another uneasy second. And then it was promptly shattered as Mjomba announced triumphantly: "He will just be known as Kintu Gunte wa Mjomba - That is what he is going to be called" he said with finality.

Aside and out of ear-shot, he mumbled: "Kintu Gunte wa Mjomba...doesn't sound bad at all - they actually even rhyme! Kintu Gunte wa Mjomba...Kintu Gunte wa Mjomba!"

Jamila's face registered some puzzlement; and, as if in sympathy, the dimples which were playing on Flora's cheeks also vanished.

"OK! Honey," said Mjomba, brightening. "I guess I cannot keep the secret to myself any longer...!"

"Secret! What secret?" Jamila asked methodically. Her quizzical expression was shared by Flora.

"Guess what! 'Tis yourself who led me to it with your very appropriate choice of name for this guy!"

Slowly he added: "Although I now also know very well the tricks you have all been up to, don't you think?"

Then, as nothing appeared to register - nothing at all, he went on: "Over the past nine months, I have been engaged in writing a book...a masterpiece!"

"A book...a masterpiece? You don't say?" Jamila intoned, a look of disbelief in her eyes.

"Yes, and wait - 'Tis going to be quite a book! I have decided to dedicate it to you and the children. It is designed, naturally, to be a best seller...!"

"Best seller!" Jamila echoed, cutting him short.

"Yes, it will top the best seller lists." Mjomba's voice was vibrant and a shade emphatic.

"And...here - just listen to the title: *The Psychic Roots of a Nut!*" he said, his gaze transfixed to a dot in the ceiling.

"'Tis leaden with stuff every literate person just has to know!" he went on. "And although it is about madmen, it will appeal likewise to ordinary folk struggling to stay on the rails - like us here!"

As Jamila and Flora broke out into a laugh, Mjomba continued: "I predict that Kintu, the book's hero, will become an even greater celebrity than Gunte. And I am not talking about our Kintu here. Gunte of ROOTS, Alex Haley's immortal work!"

Jamila recovered from her laughter in time to say, "What is all this nonsense, Christian?"

In response, Mjomba snapped his fingers. "Hey, hold it!" He said, half shouting. "I think I've got the manuscript in the car!"

He scrambled off the side of the bed and, thrusting the little "bundle" he held into Flora's waiting arms, scampered off towards the parking lot. The laughter was mildly restrained when he whizzed back into the room seconds later, flourishing a small blue folder bulging with neatly typed pages.

"Here it is" Mjomba said, breathless. "You see, not many books have been written about nut cases, let alone the mental roots of..."

"Darling" Jamila cut in, an expression of obviously contrived earnestness enveloping her face; "Are you sure you are not going haywire yourself?"

When she saw that he remained unmoved, she feigned an exaggerated appearance of despair and cast an awkward glance in Flora's direction.

"The narrative is fairly adequate as it stands now" Mjomba pursued, when Jamila and Flora stopped giggling. "I still have to find a publisher; but even so I do not expect he will edit away very much..."

"Now you are talking!" Jamila interjected. "First get a publishing house to accept your manuscript for publication, and stop counting the chicks before they are hatched - or is it Flora here whom you are trying to impress?"

The nurse, whose participation in the proceedings, had so far been confined to giggles and diffident eye winks, broke herself-imposed silence: "Your husband has already won me over as his literary fan" she said, her tone subdued. Then, her eyes full upon Mjomba, she continued: "It sounds a very interesting book you are writing; and, though I am no great reader of books, you can already be sure of at least one customer...!"

Following the burst of energy Mjomba had expended dashing to and fro to get the manuscript and his subsequent verbal exchange with Jamila, the sound of Flora's voice made him feel a good deal more relaxed. He took the opportunity afforded by the pause in her address to take in her figure which he suddenly found to be strikingly well proportioned and captivating. He did not wait for his newly found fan to finish.

"Not a bit of it, Flora" he chortled; "I believe I can safely promise you a free autographed copy."

Dragging his gaze away from the large shadowy eyes, he added: "I can't even believe I have finally succeeded in pulling off something so...so ingenious! Until this moment, only my secretary knew I was preoccupied with this project. I gave myself a dead-line to accomplish the task as part of the fun, and all the time I had to keep Mama Kunte here - well, also Mama Kintu Gunte wa Mjomba now - in the dark about what probably is my life's most important single achievement. I cannot recall the number of revisions I made. Actually, especially of late, I have often been scared to turn over a page for fear I would start re-writing some paragraph all over again...!"

In a voice that was devoid of all reticence, Flora cut him short: "Would you mind telling me what *The Psychic Roots of a Nut* is about, Mr. Mjomba?"

Mjomba thought he noticed something intriguing about Flora's manner, particularly her decision to address him as "Mr. Mjomba" as opposed to something else. In any case her dark handsome features now loomed up in his mind as a devastating contrast to his wife's and, funnily, also as a challenge! He was bugged by the fact that she had looked just like any other ordinary plain girl in a nurse's uniform when they first accosted each other just hours before!

With Jamila momentarily preoccupied with Kintu, he allowed himself a quick probing stare at Flora only to be met with a direct electrifying gaze. In that instant, he almost forgot himself. His eyes shut as he realised that he was again the object of Flora's intense, and quite unabashed scrutiny. But, even with the image of the girl shut out, he still found himself only partially in control of his emotions. He felt like a spell was being unleashed on him. In an attempt to conceal the effect all that was having on him, Mjomba backed to the edge of the bed and, clasping his sweating hands together, seated himself down by his wife's side.

As Mjomba was beginning uncertainly to give a condensed version of the material of his forthcoming book, Jamila nudged him in the side with a forefinger to draw his straying attention.

Feeling a good deal steadier after that treatment, Mjomba went on: "Kintu - not our Kintu but the book's hero - is born into a land where animism reigns supreme, and of parents who are among the territory's very first converts to Christianity, Innocent Kintu sets out to observe the precepts he is taught strictly from the very beginning. He is determined to pursue the dictates of his faith to their logical conclusion - never mind that the tenets of the strange new religion are in apparent and fairly outrageous conflict with the traditional beliefs and customs of his people.

"For a time, he succeeds in fulfilling his heart's wish, and is even regarded as his tribe's standard bearer. Then the unexpected occurs - Innocent Kintu is taken ill!

"But just as Kintu, a senior seminarist now and a favoured candidate for the priesthood, is sliding into what members of the seminary faculty suppose is insanity, one Moses Kapere - a fellow seminarian and a tribesman of Kintu's - also finds himself all of a sudden fighting to keep his own scruples and misgivings from driving him off the rails!

"The 'Rod', as Kapere has been nicknamed by his brethren, avoids a crushing depression only to land in a baffling triple dilemma. If his tribesman's brand of Christianity is the right one, then his own practice of religion, which supposedly is liberal and unpretentious in contrast to the blind, almost impulsive spirituality of his brother-in-Christ, is ill founded and sham! But the realization that Brother Innocent and himself could still both be fakes leaves him in a trap.

"Thus, unless and until he resolves the mystery surrounding the brother's behaviour, there may well be little likelihood that he himself will ever fully realize his own identity in the mystifying circumstances of the New World!

"It is this equally strange set of circumstances which prepares the ground for a giant step for science - the discovery by the 'Rod' of Theory "R"! That theory not only solves the mystery of Brother Innocent's malady, but also helps medicine and in particular psychiatry turn a completely new leaf!"

At the end of Mjomba's exposition, all three, oblivious of their individual problems at the start, burst out into a merry laugh. Mjomba's guffaw was a low-pitched, sonorous affair, exaggerated to camouflage the fact that it was all feigned. And it contrasted with the thrill, child-like tantrums of the women, who appeared genuinely impressed by the presentation.

Mjomba stopped "laughing" a little earlier than the others and intoned: "But there is a catch! Moses Kapere, the Rod, is actually me. The true life 'Innocent' is another story altogether...!"

Mjomba waited for the wail of laughter to recede before launching himself into the story from a completely different angle: "The perfect madman who can only exist in the figment of the mind, the Innocent Kintu you will discover between these pages is a completely reinvented character who, I dare say, owes everything to my imagination and ingenuity. A one-faced character, incapable by definition of leading a double life, he still ends up living two lives all the same - and to the full, actually!"

Mjomba was very well aware that there had been a time when the original Innocent Kintu, now Acting Chief Justice Maramba and a respected member of the bench, fitted that description to the letter. The only other person who was aware of that fact was Prof. Gringo, now a Professor Emeritus and also Vice Chancellor of the prestigious

Makerere University. They also both knew how Judge Maramba's cure had come about, namely with the assistance of Theory "R".

But the special bond of friendship that had formed between the three men in the aftermath of the landmark "cure" had foreshadowed everything else, including what they might have jointly reaped materially from it. They had come to an agreement that the reputation and future career of their beloved friend and confidant would be at stake if it were revealed that "His Honor" had at one time suffered from one of the most terrible form of insanity; and Prof. Gringo had immediately moved to alter the medical records of his former patient to make it look as if he had just been misunderstood and that there hadn't been anything wrong with his "patient".

With Maramba's stellar performance at Oxford and Yale from where he had earned advanced law degrees in succession, and his appointment almost immediately upon his return to the plum job on the bench, neither Prof. Gringo nor Mjomba had felt any regrets about their action. And, needless to say, it did not surprise them that things turned out the way they did for their friend. As far as they were concerned, if you borrowed a leaf from the Psychic Roots of Innocent Kintu as Dr. Maramba had done and reorganized your life accordingly especially in the world of academia where success depended entirely on one's ability to think right, the sky would be the only limit in a literal sense.

In return, Dr. Maramba had used his influence with the republic's President, an Oxford alumnus like himself, to get Prof. Gringo where he now was. As for Mjomba, the rumours were already rife that he might become the country's deputy Minister of Finance. It was precisely because of these machinations that Prof. Gringo had made little progress in persuading the scientific community that Theory "R" worked.

A practising psychiatrist still and professor emeritus at Julius Nyerere University, Prof. Gringo now viewed the problem differently. He needed patients who were capable of digesting the theoretical part of Theory "R", and who could then proceed to also use it as a tool for self-therapy, following in Maramba's foot steps, and eventually induce their own cure that way. Experience had taught him that those types of patients were not easy to come by.

The professor sometimes wished that he himself had heard about theory 'R' earlier than he did. As a research fellow at the Hoover Institution during his final year at Stanford, he had been commissioned by the think tank to develop psychological profiles of the new crop of military leaders in Africa, following the waive of coup d'états in the early sixties. He was now of the firm belief that his profiles would have been much more precise if he had had the benefit of Mjomba's discovery.

The professor, who happened to belong to the same clan as that to which the King of Buganda belonged and considered himself a member of royalty for that reason, would have been very delighted if his scope of work had included profiles for the world's so-called democratic leaders as well. A rank conservative, he was inclined to the view that they too were usurpers driven by a yearning to fill the role of royalty, and he would have welcomed an opportunity to probe their mental processes.

He wondered what went on in their minds as they went about their business as heads of state in their respective countries! He tried and failed to understand how politicians in the West could ever justify the actions that had led to the two world wars, for instance! Certainly individuals who could produce and go on to employ weapons of mass destruction of kind that brought death and ruin to the cities of Hiroshima and Nagasaki, and then continue with their lives as if nothing had happened, did not just deserve to have their heads examined, in Mjomba's view they deserved to be confined in a maximum security detention center for the rest of their lives and denied any opportunity to harm their fellow humans in such a senseless fashion ever again.

As far as the professor was concerned, so called democratic leaders, be it in the West or the East, were really no different from the crop of coup leaders whose turn it now was to hit the headlines. In his view, to accede to the lofty places politicians in those "democracies" occupied, they had merely employed a different method, namely popular revolution which went by the more dignified name of the popular ballot. Prof. Gringo knew too well that in the majority of cases, those so-called popular revolutions had initially been supported by the now rather unpopular bullet in any case.

In the opinion of the man of letters, the exercise of territorial rule was a form of reigning. If a common man who was not representing royalty was allowed to reign, there were no grounds to stop any other common man from doing the same by one method or another. The solution seemed obvious to the professor. The business of governing was better left to those who were born to govern!

He had no doubt in his mind that Theory "R" would have been not only helpful but critical in proving his point in all these cases of what he regarded as "usurped power". And, with respect to the wider applicability of the theory, there was in Prof. Gringo's estimation, no question whatsoever concerning its potential with regards the theory's wider applicability.

And when, as happened from time to time, feelings of guilt for not doing everything in his power to popularise the cure and demonstrate to the world that the end was in sight for one of the most pernicious conditions ever to plague man threatened to overwhelm him, he always had what he considered to be a very good ready excuse: He would have to first of all persuade the world that Theory "R" really worked in the judge's case - something he was not at all prepared to do. But he still dreamed of the day when he might be in a position to show conclusively that the theory worked using other cases.

And now that Innocent Kintu, aka Justice Maramba, was on the verge of becoming his adopted country's Chief Justice, Prof. Gringo even felt that he had a duty to the Tanzania people to keep the medical history of the Acting Chief Justice under wraps forever. Prof. Gringo agreed with Mjomba that, before his cure, Justice Maramba fit the description of the "perfect madman". But even though he now considered Kintu one of the most predictable individuals alive, he knew he could not under any circumstances reveal that Justice Maramba had been down that road - the perfect madman, and even less a one-faced character "incapable by definition of leading a double life" as Prof. Gringo always liked to add!

Mjomba had been fully supportive of the professor in this matter from the start. Accordingly, as the two women gasped with laughter over his description of the hero of his book, Mjomba stood back and, inside, enjoyed a laugh of his own, sure that his lie had carried the day.

And he did not wait to give them a break in their laughter either, for he presently added: "Dr. Claus Gringo, Kintu's psychiatrist had an assistant...a quadroon! Flora, do I need to say the rest?"

The fresh burst of laughter petered out only to become thunderous once more as he added: "I'm sure you already recognize it - the old story of the scramble for Africa! It started off as scramble for Africa's wealth; then it became a scramble for our bodies with slavery. The advent of the churches turned it into a scramble for our souls!"

He had hardly finished talking when Jamila, still jittery with laughter, said haltingly: "Flora, I should have warned you not to encourage him in this ... the next thing we are going to hear is that he is offering to be nominated for the Nobel Prize for Literature or something!"

It was Mjomba's turn now to explode with laughter. In the meantime Flora, whose adulation of Mjomba at this point, made her a reluctant party in anything which even remotely threatened to diminish his stature, found herself interjecting: "Medicine! He should go for the Nobel Prize for Medicine."

She saw Jamila react to her suggestion with a start, but continued with a lofty indifference: "Unless you think he is a mad author who has gone out of his way to explain away insanity as a joke!"

The drone of bells, as a distant clock struck mid-night, brought everyone to attention and averted what might have turned out to be an ugly incident, with Jamila apparently inclined to say disparaging things about her husband on the one hand, and Flora all too keen to glorify everything about him on the other.

Mjomba, who had cut his own concocted spasms of laughter short in the meantime, had his mind elsewhere. This being his first real opportunity to demonstrate that the course of the world was about to be changed by the Psychic Roots of a Nut, he was considering recounting what the book was about all over again, although from a completely different angle this time - the same angle he had used when he scribbled his suggested blurb the day before. But before he could barge in with the modified summary of the book, the already ugly mood in the room changed for the worse.

Just then, little Kintu Gunte wa Mjomba fell into a violent temper, and began flaying about with his tiny but tight-fisted hands, in an apparent effort to connect to Flora's head! He tried to kick the sides of his captor, but only caused his unpractised legs to become entangled in the web of swaddling bands enfolding him.

As if determined to exercise his autonomy and personal freedom, he began to scream in his tiny, squeaky voice that was not unlike a kitten's. Finally, defeated, Flora bade the couple good-morning and reluctantly retreated with her charge into the sanctuary of the nursery.

As soon as he was left alone in the room with his wife, the senior Mjomba kissed her on the cheek before dropping the blue folder carefully in her lap.

"Put it away until tomorrow, Honey" he said, turning his own cheek. "You need all your rest as of now - and, besides, my book is really meant to be read in perfect peace by the fireside!"

Jamila fell into a deep slumber almost as soon as Mjomba departed.

Fiend in Flora...

Flora was not expecting to find Mjomba around when she finished putting her charge to bed and returned five minutes or so later. Thinking that Jamila would be delighted to know that her baby was comfortably in bed, especially in view of the maelstrom her husband had generated, the nurse headed for Jamila's room.

Flora's mind was otherwise set on getting back to her associates in the nurses' Common Room as fast as her legs could carry her there. She had no doubt that her experiences during the half hour or so that she had been away contained abundant material to keep her friends on the shift entertained and cheered up until morning. Telling each other yarns from their experiences was an established way of killing time on that dull shift. Stories involving love affairs fascinated the girls the most, and Flora could not wait to carp about how she had come close to "overthrowing a government", the expression they used to refer to any action that caused an existing love relationship to break-up! It was not unusual for the storyteller to stretch the facts of a case if necessary to make the story more interesting. Flora did not feel that it would be necessary to resort to that in this particular case, however.

She could not wait to get back to the Common Room with her hot tale, and she quickened her steps accordingly. One thing she could, however, not entirely erase from her memory, as she closed in on the sick bay where Jamila's room was located, was the way she had conducted herself in front of Jamila and her husband.

But her mind was, even though, not entirely wanting in so far as laying blame was concerned. If there was one thing Flora was ready to swear to, Mjomba was completely to blame for whatever had transpired and, indeed, almost pushed her over the brink! It was undoubtedly all his fault, she told herself!

On her lips as she prepared to announce her arrival to Jamila was the single word "Men"!

"Men!" she was also in fact ready to exclaim as soon as she came within earshot of her waiting pals; "They all are the same."

It was after all Mjomba who, with his singular charm and allure, had encroached on her space there within the precincts of Dr. Mambo's Clinic. Her colleagues could have vouched that it was completely out of character for her to behave as she had done in front of Jamila and her hubby without prodding of some kind. Well, had he not been a good man, she would be thinking of suing just now - for sexual abuse! Lucky for him that she now only proposed to make that curious and somewhat unseemly encounter the main subject of their chatter there within the confines of the Common Room.

The light in Jamila's room was still on. The recent rivalry already apparently forgotten, Flora slowed her pace so she would have more time to be recollected before announcing her arrival. After all she did not have any beef against her genteel patient, she told herself.

She was able to make out Jamila's form from a distance. Slouched against her pillow and clasping the blue folder close to her breast, Jamila appeared to be engrossed in her husband's work. It was only after Flora approached the bed and was about to address her mentor turned rival that she realized that Jamila was asleep. Slumped to one side, Jamila was sound asleep and snoring fitfully. At that moment, a thought as absurd as it was reckless thrust itself into her mind. She could almost hear the fiend in her whisper that this was the time to get even with Jamila and also her chance - perhaps the only one she would ever get - to beat Jamila to it by filching the manuscript from the sleeping woman, withdrawing to a secluded spot, and being the first to peruse the work of the man she had fallen for!

Flora strove to stifle a mischievous smile that had begun to envelope her face. She chastised her inner-self and even closed her eyes as she struggled to avoid giving the wicked proposition any consideration. Flora felt a deep sense of guilt for what struck her as a diabolical idea. She could have sworn that it wasn't her idea at all.

She did not stop to reflect if the "weird" notion sprung from that frail part of her which her own dad used to refer to as the flesh - the part of human nature which, according to what she had been taught, had been irrevocably sullied by concupiscence after the fall of Adam and Eve; or if the wicked scheme was an idea that Beelzebub (whoever he was!), taking advantage of her feeble nature, was attempting to plant in her mind; or if the whole thing was just another side of her good-natured old self and did not merit any further thought for that reason. But, for certain, it was less likely, she thought, to be a case of possession by that cryptic and formless archenemy of humankind who sometimes also went by the name of Mephistopheles

- she could not see any reason why the archenemy would choose her of all people for any wicked scheme he might have in mind!

And, no believer in animism, she would have scorned the suggestion that the spirits of her ancestors had something to do with it. If there was another thing Flora was again ready to swear to, it was that Christian Mjomba, by thrusting himself unannounced into her life, was completely to blame for whatever was going on!

Flora believed in miracles, but could not bring herself to accept that one happened just as she was fretting over the wicked ideas which were descending on her out of no where. But, in a split second, the mischievous ideas were gone, making her start to wonder if her fears were all imaginary! There was no mischievous smile for Flora to suppress, and no urge to snicker either! All the naughty ideas were gone in an instant.

Assuming a businesslike air on what seemed like an impulse, Flora stepped inside the room, smoothed the bedding methodically and, finding a pillow, tucked it carefully under Jamila's head. Then, stepping back, she surveyed the scene one more time before reaching for the light switch. Finally, satisfied that her patient was comfortably asleep, Flora dimmed the lights and slid noiselessly out of Jamila's room into the brilliance of the brightly lit hallway. But she made an about-turn almost instantaneously, and slipped back inside the darkened sick bay.

Then, moving stealthily, Flora just let her feet bear her along noiselessly like a snake gliding over bushy ground. As she approached Jamila's bedside, she resembled a leopard that was about to prance on its prey, and did not once take her eyes off the blue folder which the sleeping Jamila seemed to be hugging as never before. Then gently, very gently, Flora extricated the blue folder from Jamila's clasp. She was surprised at the firm hold which the sleeping woman maintained on the folder, and in the end found that she had to yank it away from Jamila's grip with a certain amount of force.

Clutching her prize close to her own breast now and her heart beating wildly, Flora hastened out of the room. She headed for the administrative wing without stopping once to think. The place was deserted and looked forbidding at that time of night. Her quick steps brought her presently to the Matron's office located in the Maternity Wing's interior.

Once inside, Flora closed the door behind her and switched on the lights. She was already turning the manuscript's pages over even as she skirted the ornate, flat-topped desk used by the Matron. Her face buried in the papers now, she made for the photocopier at the far end of the room almost blindly. She mechanically reached for the "ON" switch on the under side of the apparatus and depressed it without looking.

Flora did not wait and started to extricate the single pink sheet that lay ineptly among the manuscript's pages like a page marker. The "marker" stood out clearly from among the rest of the manuscript's pages which were milky white. On inspection, the "marker" turned out to be the blurb in draft - or so it's two-letter header **"Suggested Blurb"** in bold face proclaimed it to be. Just what she needed, she whispered to herself, before reverting her attention to the copier which remained silent. Setting the blurb and the rest of the manuscript down on the matron's desk while taking care not to throw the neat but loose bundle of papers into disarray, Flora checked to make certain that she had depressed the right button on the copier.

She was clearly relieved to discover that the cause of the machine's failure was the fact that its power cable was unplugged. Snatching up the blurb, she started reading it silently to her self even as she was fumbling with the power cable. She somehow succeeded in getting the cable in its socket on the wall at the first try even though she did it blindly without looking.

Flora was well aware that her presence in the area at that hour would raise eyebrows if discovered. But she also knew that the chances of any one observing her were very slim. Even so, the whine of the machine's compressors as the copier began to warm up sent a chill down her spine. To her ears, the whine of the Xerox copier as it broke the deadening silence sounded like the noise of a garbage truck in gear, and nearly caused her to flee. But she recovered quickly and continued to pore over the blurb.

When Flora snatched the manuscript from Jamila's unrelenting grip, her intention had been to photocopy the approximately two hundred pages or so making it up for her own use and then quietly slip the original manuscript back into Jamila's waiting arms. Although that was still Flora's intention, there were already signs that there was something in the offing that was likely to alter the course of events.

The first thing that had caught Flora's attention when the lights in the Matron's office came on was the pink coloured sheet which had obviously been shoved into the folder at the last minute. It was this sheet which Flora now clasped gingerly between her thumb and pointing finger as she readied the photocopying machine.

The nurse stood there motionless, her eyes glued to the page with the blurb, while the photocopying machine warmed up. She continued to do so even after the erratic drone of the copier gave way to a smooth whirr, signalling that the copier was all ready and set to do its job at the touch of the button. Flora remained transfixed in the same spot as her eyes darted first from one side of the yellow page to the other, and then up and down the page as she perused the text of the blurb several times over.

If Mjomba's smooth talk earlier on had already sold the story of Innocent Kintu to the nurse, the catchy blurb now nailed the deal, if any nailing was necessary. Her scrutiny of the blurb drafted by Mjomba, the man who had proved to be such a fatal attraction before little Kintu Gunte wa Mjomba spoilt everything for her by getting into a sudden fit, convinced her that she had not been entirely out of her senses to fall for him. And all the while, as she gradually absorbed the message contained in the blurb's five odd sentences, she wondered what the rest of the manuscript might have in store!

While perusing the blurb, Flora felt as though Mjomba was verily present; and she decided to prolong that feeling by reading it slowly and several times over. The five odd sentences making up the blurb also sparked in her something else. It was a sudden interest in the book's subject matter!

Her mind, already in turmoil because she knew very well that "overthrowing the government of Jamila" was not a practical proposition for her at this time, and because of her suspicion that Jamila would in any case put up the stiffest fight to keep Mjomba all for herself, began to swarm with images of a cast of immortal characters who were ready to act out Innocent Kintu's story at the word "go". It did not matter that the blurb was as brief as it was. What really mattered was its theme which seemed to be simply loaded - just like a sparkling model of a new line of automobiles!

Flora was already thinking that the story about Innocent Kintu was likely only a smoke screen for an autobiographical work. The blurb itself referred to "the dramatic story of an aspiring author who had seen his friends fall prey, one by one, to a hither-to unheard of brain condition". Flora was convinced that the fictitious author had to be Mjomba himself! For a minute or so she stood there, immobile; like someone who had become paralysed in her tracks and had turned into a statue. She was helpless as more images suggested by the blurb continued to stream through her mind.

Flipping over the pages, she stopped at the "foreword" and buried her head inside once more. The fact that the foreword run into three pages rather than half a page as she had noticed with some of the novels she recalled reading didn't seem to matter to her at all. Then, even though she was just perusing through text, she felt as though she was watching a James Bond movie with Mjomba playing the part of that famous actor. In her mind's eye, she saw Mjomba setting out on his long journey of discovery which easily fit into her idea of a "mission impossible". She believed that after seeing Innocent Kintu fall prey to the hitherto unheard of disease, her idol was fearing for himself and was setting out to gain insight into the disorder - the only way out of his bind.

According to the blurb, the strange disease appeared to single out intellectuals! With a certain amount of temerity, she followed Mjomba's trail as he grappled with the immediate problem faced by his pal and himself, and then as he battled to simultaneously establish himself as a writer of consequence.

The nurse's compassion was bottomless as the "fictitious" author began to show signs that he might himself be going crazy. But her sorrow for him was balanced by the fact that he already believed, at that early stage, that he had stumbled onto a remarkable scientific discovery. But even then, her interest was focused on the inventor rather than on his invention.

Flora's obsession with the fictitious author hit a bump when the blurb went on to declare that all of this transpired as the troubled but handsome essayist, a member of the seminary brotherhood who had been on the verge of taking the perpetual vow of chastity at the time, met and wed a dazzling beauty. There was no doubt in Flora's mind that this dazzling beauty was Jamila.

But, instead of dissuading her from reading further, that part of the foreword whose veracity Mjomba himself had confirmed only minutes earlier, simply propelled her to read on. If anything, she now felt that she had no choice but to finish reading the rest of the manuscript right there and then, at least so she would know the odds against her!

A full three hours later, when the sounds of day break brought her to, Flora would be unable to explain how she had switched off the photocopier, found her way to the matron's desk, and settled down in the matron's cosy chair to finish reading Christian Mjomba's "masterpiece". It was because she did those things completely instinctively.

Once in the Matron's seat, Flora had apparently begun to read the manuscript to herself aloud. Starting with the page of contents, she had eagerly delved into the rest of the material and become so carried away with the story, she had felt just like someone who was watching a motion picture. It was when the "movie" concluded around dawn that she had risen up to leave the "theatre" and had been surprised to discover herself in the matron's office!

12. Mjomba's "Death and Resurrection"

His demeanor looking steely in the glimmer of the streetlights dotting the hospital grounds, Christian Mjomba made for the spot where he had parked the Ford as if drawn there by a magnet. For all practical purposes, his mind was blank and free of all concerns as he steered into *Umoja wa Wanawake* Drive to head home.

It was as he approached the house and was guiding the car into the lock-up garage that something really strange happened. It started with a cock's crow which sounded just like a bugle as it rose from a neighbor's poultry shed which backed up to his garage and shattered the silence. That was immediately followed by the squeaking of a partridge awakening with a stir in nearby bushes, which must have awoken the entire population of bird-life inhabiting trees in the area causing, and which in turn proceeded to serenade him with a majestic cacophony of melodies.

All might have been well had the welcoming not reminded him of the one morning he had arrived home from a night of debauchery. The evening before, a couple of people he barely knew had persuaded him to join them for what they described as a light social evening; and, before he knew it, the group, including himself, had found itself at this place called Hannibal's Cove.

Once the group had settled down to the roast meat and booze, which included exotic cocktails such as Africoco and Red Top, it had proved impossible for Mjomba to tear himself away from the company. Dead drunk and ill with a splitting headache, he had staggered from the joint when it was already daybreak, miraculously guided the Ford home without any incident along the way, only to crash it into his garage door! That had apparently startled the single cock which shared quarters with the chickens in the shed which backed up to his garage, and got it crowing perhaps a little earlier than usual. What then followed was the exact same welcome from the bird realm, triggered no doubt by the rooster's crow. But it had, naturally, been quite a different story when he confronted Jamila in the house. Although all was now long forgotten - and forgiven, that episode of all things was the last thing Mjomba would have wanted to be reminded of on this particular morning as he arrived home from Dr. Mambo's Clinic.

There was no undoing what had come to pass, however. But, even though he did not anticipate a dressing down of any sort on this particular occasion, he was unable to erase from his head the feeling that the serenade might be a bad omen. Inside the house, Mjomba hurried to bed and closed his eyes in an attempt to shut out memories of his fling at wanton living - the only one he recalled ever having! The attempt appeared to succeed as he rolled over and, with a loud snore, fell asleep. But it was also then that he started to dream.

Free from the shackles of his terrestrial existence, Mjomba easily travelled back, in the illusory world of dreams, to Dr. Mambo's Clinic. Even though not something he did often, Mjomba felt very much at home pursuing his adventures in the nether world and gave the impression that he was as practised in matters of that world as anyone else fortunate enough to belong there.

And so, there he was, gliding effortlessly in the hallway through which, utterly exhausted as a result of going non-stop since emerging from his office at the Trade Center early the previous day and in a virtual stupor, he had wearily trudged scarcely a half hour earlier, careful not to trip and find himself sprawling on the floor. He had not been prepared to risk making himself a laughing stock in front of Flora and her work-mates then. But now, the glorious state which came with his new predicament precluded any such misadventure.

Like the good devoted husband he was, Mjomba's thoughts immediately turned to his wife. "You need all your rest as of now" he recalled saying to her not long before. He had not doubted that Jamila, his beloved, would do as behoved a loving wife and take her much needed rest in response to his plea. He only needed to shift his head in her direction from wherever he was to see if she had followed his advice. As he did so, he observed that his belle had, indeed, fallen into a deep slumber. He noticed in an instant that, even as she lay sleeping, Jamila was still clutching the manuscript for his forth-coming best seller with both hands as if reading from it.

The light in her room was still on. Suddenly Mjomba appeared visibly agitated, in spite of the fact that he was living in a cosmic world, as he spied Flora saunter into Jamila's recovery room. He observed with keen interest as the girl, a comely figure of enormous beauty even by cosmic standards, looked over his wife. Apparently satisfied that her patient was comfortably in bed, Flora reached out for the light switch on the table lamp by the bedside.

Mjomba noted that the light in the room dimmed very gradually, in the exact same way the lights in some theatres still did, until the room in which his dear Jamila lay asleep was finally enveloped in near total darkness. But not before something else had transpired.

Even though enjoying an existence on a plane that, for all practical purposes, was hallowed, Mjomba, his exalted state notwithstanding, could not suppress a giggle as he watched the still earth-bound Flora, a wicked grin on her face, do something really funny.

He saw the nurse stoop low over the sleeping Jamila to kiss her on the cheek; but in the same movement, the girl also peeped inside the open covers of the manuscript, which remained in his wife's firm grip and close to her bosom - at least for now. Then, moving gracefully, Flora stepped out of the darkening room and into the brilliance of the brightly-lit hallway. But she had scarcely done that when she suddenly made an about turn. She moved stealthily now and just let her feet bear her along noiselessly as if she were a snake. Inside the darkened room and as she approached Jamila's bedside, she resembled a leopard that was about to pounce on its quarry. Then, gently, very gently, Flora attempted to extricate the manuscript from his wife's grasp. She seemed surprised at the firm hold which the sleeping woman maintained on the blue binder. In the end, Flora found she had to yank the manuscript away forcibly from Jamila's firm grip.

Finally, clutching her prize close to her own breast now, and her heart visibly beating wildly, Flora hastened out of the room. Without stopping to think, she made her gate-away at a quickening pace and, wheeling round a corner, momentarily vanished from Mjomba's view.

It was Mjomba's turn to get on the move now. He spun around and then, gliding along like a seraph himself, sped after her. He easily caught up with the nurse, but decided to follow her at a safe distance instead. He could see that she was heading for the clinic's administrative wing. The place, normally abuzz with activity, was deserted and looked forbidding at that time of the night even to Mjomba. Flora's quick steps brought her presently to the matron's office located in the administrative wing's interior. Once inside, she closed the door behind her.

All Mjomba had to do to gain entrance was to incline his frame slightly to one side, eyeball the part of the door or wall he intended to penetrate and then will himself through it by virtue of being a spiritual or incorporeal being first and foremost, and a corporeal or physical entity only in an ancillary sense. And sure enough, that puissant combination of will power and faith in himself saw him materialise instantaneously on the other side of the door as if he were a spook. Because he wasn't used to doing that sort of thing, Mjomba shut his eyes instinctively as he approached the door and opened them when he realised that he was safely inside.

He got there in time to see Flora switch on the lights. She stared around her, clearly pleased that she was now all alone - or so she thought! With a fleeting glance, she quickly noted the different items in the office, among them the matron's work desk, the Xerox copier, and a book-shelf which held imposing medical tomes.

There appeared to be something spellbinding about the photocopier, because her eyes lingered on it for a while before they moved on to survey the other items in the room. She did not see the ghost of Mjomba perched atop the bookshelf, although her eyes rested briefly on two wooden carvings depicting Masai warriors which were literally framing his face. But she could not help noting that, after the matron's desk, the bookshelf was the most prominent item in the room.

Mjomba watched idly as the girl skirted the matron's ornate, flat-topped mahogany desk while turning over the pages of the manuscript at the same time, and head straight for the copier at the far end of the office almost blindly. He looked astonished and intrigued, observing Flora perform what he regarded as an interesting feat without incident - and then he immediately checked himself. For here he was, relishing the joys of the supra-natural realm, and at the same time indulging in mundane things like the display of emotion. It was in fact the second time he had caught himself displaying his feelings, the first time being the giggle he failed to suppress when he saw Flora plant a kiss on Jamila's cheek.

As he was well aware, the ground rules of his existence in the enchanted realm of pure spirits did not permit one to feel "intrigued" or "fascinated", or anything of that sort. Such states of mind, because they were originally designed to satisfy the lower needs of human beings, could never be agreeable with the lofty nature that people in the dream world enjoyed!

Like the rest of the mystic creatures that dwelt in the fantasy world in which he now found himself, Mjomba had a pretty clear perception of the consequences of violating the mystic cannons of behaviour. Discernment of the precepts that were in force moreover came naturally to the dream world's subjects, and not through studying legal manuals or handbooks as was the case back on Earth. Knowledge of such things came to them through introspection. Awareness of the self automatically triggered a thorough comprehension of the basic rules governing one's mystic environment. There was therefore no excuse for not knowing what one was supposed to know, and certainly no excuse for breaking any mystic cannon of conduct.

Mjomba thus also knew well enough that the penalty for violating a rule, although always commensurate with the gravity of the transgression, tended to be severe at least in human terms. (Talking about seeing things in human terms, Mjomba had no inkling as to how he had come by the undoubtedly canny ability to see things in that dimension!) The reason infractions of the rules attracted severe punishment was because they were always accompanied by full knowledge that they were misdeeds. Additionally, the misdeeds were always done without any coercion whatsoever, be it moral or mystical.

Another point to be noted was the fact that the sinners or transgressors themselves invariably conceded on their own volition that the punishment meted out was well earned. Mjomba understood introspectively that this had something to do with the fact that mystic creatures, because of the manner in which their cognitive faculties worked, never needed reminders that their existence in that realm was entirely gratuitous, a pure favour or gift attributable to the action of His Mystic Majesty which some, somewhat gamely, referred to as the Big Bang.

And so, just as Mjomba was starting to feel fascinated by what he was seeing, he froze in his tracks, as a result of which his boyish face was left wrapped up in a half smile. His near fatal error clearly told on his demeanour, which immediately changed from frivolous to sombre. His quick action had averted retribution from His Mystic Majesty. But even though well pleased with himself for acting promptly and averting calamity, he now desisted from showing it, because that too would be in violation of the rules!

Flora, her face completely buried in his manuscript and obstructed from view, was preparing to switch on the photocopier when the draft blurb, which was typed on the only coloured sheet in the sheath of papers, caught her attention. The pink sheet lay ineptly and shrivelled inside the otherwise neat bundle of papers, and caused her to conclude that it had been shoved into the original batch of papers at the last moment. She reached out mechanically for the power switch on the side of the copier and depressed it without taking her eyes off the blurb.

With Mjomba watching intently, the nurse came to with a start when the copier failed to react. She looked up from the papers for the first time and was clearly relieved to discover that the copier's power cable had been unplugged from its wall socket. But her gaze immediately dipped, and her attention again became focused on the blurb as she reached out with her right arm and plugged the copier's power cord into the wall socket.

Mjomba observed all this from his vantage point atop the matron's bookshelf and did not miss any detail. In his supra-natural state, even though he may not have been able to do things like forecast the future or anticipate each and every act of individuals from studying their habits, he was certainly capable of making out what was on their minds by just observing their actions. And when an individual was reading from a book or from a piece of paper, it was quite easy for Mjomba to scrutinize the same material and to make his own conclusions about it by just observing movements of the reader's eyelids.

Mjomba could therefore tell that Flora was apprehensive that her presence in the area at that hour would raise eyebrows if discovered. He also knew from studying her demeanour her thoughts about the chances of anyone observing her there being very slim. And when the nurse depressed the copier's "ON" button the second time, it did not come as a complete surprise to him when the whine of the machine's compressors, as it sprung to life and begun to warm up, sent a chill down her spine.

Mjomba's own reaction at that stage was completely cool for once - as it was expected to be. He would ordinarily have found it hard to hide the empathy he felt for Flora. He was, however, determined this time not to allow his feelings to ruin things for him, and he succeeded, although not without a struggle, in suppressing them.

Something in his psyche caused him to focus on Flora's thoughts earlier when she snatched the manuscript from Jamila's unrelenting grip. Her intention had been to obtain her own photocopy of each one of its two hundred or so odd pages, and then quietly slip the original manuscript back into Jamila's waiting arms. She, of course, knew nothing at that juncture regarding the blurb.

While the photocopying machine warmed up, Flora, who was also fairly exhausted by the evening's event's, sat herself down at the matron's desk and started reading the proposed blurb for Mjomba's masterpiece. She sat there motionless, her eyes glued to the pink sheet. She continued to do so even after the loud drone of the copier ceased, signalling that it was all ready and set to do her bidding at the touch of a button if she chose to proceed with her plan.

If Mjomba's smooth talk earlier on had already sold the story of Innocent Kintu to Flora, the catchy blurb now nailed the deal, if any nailing was still necessary. And as Flora's eyes darted from the blurb to the first page of the manuscript and then to the second and so on, occasionally reading a paragraph several times over, the smile on her impish face became more and more bemused. It became clear before long that she was unable to interrupt the enjoyment she was deriving from perusing the material for Mjomba's masterpiece for any reason whatsoever.

But while Flora was preoccupied thus and obviously enjoying what she was reading, the opposite appeared to be true for Mjomba. With each sentence she read, Mjomba's demeanour, hitherto so remarkable for the serenity and calm it enthused, began to change, until finally, irate with no one in particular but nonetheless bursting with feelings of anger and disappointment, Mjomba began to flay his arms from side to side like earthlings sometimes did when they were in great distress.

Mjomba could not imagine that the world around him could be so dreamlike and unreal. The material Flora had filched from his wife had turned out, inexplicably, to be so radically different from his original manuscript, it could not even have qualified as apocryphal. As he followed the movement of Flora's eye-lids and translated them into the words she was reading, he noticed that it was not just the story line that was completely uninteresting and dull. The expressions employed to describe scenes in the story were so poorly chosen, they could not possibly have been his! What was more, he wouldn't have liked someone like Flora, whom he wanted to impress, to associate material that was so poorly conceived and written with him. How the phoney material came to be in the same binder in which his manuscript had been was a complete mystery, and he also could not understand how Flora could enjoy reading a piece of work that was so poorly conceived and written.

As the indignant Mjomba stood there swaying from side to side and beating his breast with his fists in exasperation, he saw that his reaction to the unfolding events was going to add to the problem, but he had already made up his mind that he couldn't care less now. The outrage induced by the turn of events had caused him to overlook the fact that, in the mystic domain to which he still belonged, the essences there were not permitted to behave like the lower earthly beings. You allowed yourself to be drawn out of your element in any manner at your peril. But here he was, indulging in subliminal feelings, although he was supposed to be existing well above, and indeed beyond, the influences of things that pampered to temporal appetites or the flesh! But even though he saw his mistake, there was no turning back now. And so, visibly jarred by what he had witnessed, he allowed himself to completely wallow in self-pity.

To add to the confusion, Mjomba now noticed that Flora had proceeded to the copier in what appeared to be a flash. At her touch, the Xerox came alive and begun churning out copies of the phoney work which still sported his name as its author. Observing Flora's strange antics, which he found to be very hurtful and chastening, he literally gagged at the thought that spurious copies of his manuscript might already be in circulation around the globe!

Mjomba was in a virtual daze as he watched the copier churn out a complete set of the "manuscript". It seemed a little far fetched to suppose at that juncture that thieves had somehow succeeded in stealing his life's work, and had replaced it with a substitute that was so substandard; and he decided that it was, indeed, a little far fetched to imagine that there were any thieves at work here. But this was just because the prospect of that happening was something he would not have been able to stomach!

The whole world around him looked decidedly different now and indeed appeared to be sinking. He could not contain himself, and was soon audibly castigating himself for having trusted Flora from the beginning. He had no doubt that she had a major role in whatever had happened to his manuscript, and wished he had stopped her in her tracks or even raised an alarm when he witnessed the theft of his manuscript from Jamila's recovery room.

Flora turned off the copier's power and the apparatus's mechanical life came to an abrupt end, its work done. But this apparently also coincided with the fall of the dreaming Mjomba from mystic grace. He watched helplessly as his ghost plunged from its mysterious and elevated plane of existence to an earthly one in that same fraction of time.

Mjomba had by now already written off any chances of continuing on as a respectable member of the mystic realm, and knew that his banishment from that realm was imminent. He had successfully stood up to His Mystic Majesty by breaking the rules and regulations which governed the mystic realm; but, surprisingly, he now felt relief of sorts. This was even though many questions regarding the whereabouts of his original manuscript remained unanswered. He thought it was nice to be free from those burdensome mystic canons; and for a moment he positively relished the feeling of being autonomous and answerable to no other being. He had no illusions about the fact that he was about to face judgement for his intransigence, but even that did not seem to matter - for now!

Mjomba was still in that ambivalent state of mind when he noticed the change that had started to come over the proceedings. It was in the form of music which caught his ear and gradually grew in volume. Mjomba began to discern the sounds of a chorale being performed by a choir, or what sounded like one, in the background. It took a while before the noise from Flora's activities in the matron's office and the distant sounds of the night were completely drowned out by the recital by what, without a doubt, was one of the most accomplished choirs Mjomba had ever heard.

He recognised the chant as Gregorian even before the voices themselves were completely audible. The chorale's phrases were already quite distinct and Mjomba could make them out even as he was still struggling to trace and locate the source of the music. It was the famous Canticle of Mary which was being sung to an ancient tune - one that had been Mjomba's favourite during his seminary days. He felt an awesome, almost unbearable, feeling of nostalgia well up inside of him as he listened to the cantors intone the first lines of each stanza, followed immediately by a fitting bellow executed by the main body of the choir singing the rest of the stanza in chorus.

Captivated by the beautiful sounds, Mjomba seemed completely oblivious to his impending metamorphosis. He noted the brief pause as members of the disciplined choir took in a breath; and then, in breach of normal practice, he did something seminarians never did. He began to sway to the music!

The fact that Mjomba's movements were almost imperceptible was immaterial. The theological position regarding "sacred" music was that to sing it was to pray twice. And "swaying" to the music, because it was suggestive of sentimentalism, was something that just wasn't done. It was completely anathema. It was actually standard practice for seminarians the world over not to display any kind of emotion when at worship. They didn't even close their eyes when saying their prayers. They just stared in the distance and kept mumbling whatever petitions they were presenting to the Prime Mover.

And, of course, it was not just seminarians who practised those habits which many, particularly the brethren who belonged to the Evangelical confession, found very "strange". It was an established fact which went back to the time when Latin was the Church's official language that Catholics did not have to understand what they were even saying when praying. And that had also popularized the notion that Catholics typically acted as if they were already assured of salvation by the mere fact of being Catholics, and did not feel obligated to put their faith "on show" as appeared to be the case with members of other faiths.

Mjomba, in contravention of those well established and tested traditions, continued swaying to the beat of the chorale when the cantors chanted the next stanza, which began with the words "And His mercy is from age to age, on those who fear Him". Something told him that a choir that was capable of such an accomplished performance had to be hailing from the "New Jerusalem".

It was as the rest of the choir from the New Jerusalem or wherever rejoined with "He puts forth His arm in strength and scatters the proud-hearted" with another fitting bellow that Mjomba became engulfed in the chilling transformation. His feelings of nostalgia were already quite severe as the cantors intoned the next stanza. But they suddenly changed to feelings of extreme dread and then became overwhelming as the cantors' subdued chant was replaced by the roaring refrain from the rest of the choir!

And then, instead of the cantors resuming with "He casts the mighty from their thrones and raises the lowly" as Mjomba expected, it was the entire choir which now pressed on with the chant, yelping out those words in an ever rising crescendo.

Even at that late stage, Mjomba longed for some respite which he was hoping would come with a decrescendo. He was surprised that the choir - that choir which had already impressed him so with its flawless delivery of the Canticle of Mary and which he had already grown to cherish so much - was preparing to press on with yet another crescendo for the very next stanza. He could tell because of the intervening pose that was longer than usual, and by the fact that everyone in the choir was taking advantage of it to take in a really deep breath - or so he imagined. Having sang the *Magnificat* a countless number of times himself during the years he was first a minor and then a major seminarian, Mjomba knew exactly what the words of that next stanza were even before members of the choir from the New Jerusalcm resumed the chant.

The din accompanying the rendition of the expression "He fills the starving with good things, and sends the rich away empty" initially suggested some kind of rally. But instead of one rally, there was wave upon wave of echoing sound, as the individual words making up that expression were sang with slow and carefully measured articulation! The clarity and decisiveness with which they were sung appeared designed to move the haughtiest of the haughty to humble compunction.

And then there came this one final, absolutely colossal and shattering babel as the celestial choir, evidently comprising of thousands upon thousands of souls, uttered the words "And He sends the rich away empty". Those final words of the canticle were sung to a crescendo so powerful that objects on the mantel and on the top-most bookshelf began to plunge to the floor. That was immediately followed by what looked and sounded like a powerful earthquake. The walls of the matron's office began to cave in and to tumble to the ground.

Mjomba did not know what had happened to Flora in the meantime. He was so engrossed in his own uncertain fate, he had neither the time nor, indeed, the liberty to think about the well-being of others. He suspected, in any case, that it was Flora who had set him up after allowing herself to be used as a ruse to lure him into the situation in which he now found himself.

Mjomba knew instinctively at that time that the end was near. He also knew without a doubt that at the gates of paradise where he had found himself - a nirvana where things that were impossible on earth were possible - that sort of finale presaged sentencing by His Mystic Majesty. In his particular case, since he had already fallen from grace, this could only be a prelude to banishment to the bottomless pit.

The odds of escaping damnation - and the fires of hell that accompanied such sentencing - were clearly stacked against him. And, as if to seal his fate, he now recalled in vivid detail the events of the day that he, Mjomba, a cradle Catholic whose baptismal name "Christian" was derived from the name of His Deliverer which meant "the anointed one", had discarded that beautiful name in a pointless effort to endear himself to his Muslim wife and stopped going to church to receive the sacraments!

Mjomba stood convicted because, when he stopped going to church and receiving the sacraments, he turned his back on the Deliverer who was quoted by Luke as saying in no unmistakeable words: "Watch ye, therefore, praying at all times, that you may be accounted worthy to escape all these things that are to come, and to stand before the Son of man." How could he now expect to be on the Prime Mover's guest list for the divine banquet when he hadn't as much as tried to put on what the Apostle of the Gentiles called "the armour of light"!

Just as the Sadducees had the wrong ideas about marriage and were chided by the Deliverer for not understanding either the scriptures or the power of God, Mjomba clearly did not understand reality and had his priorities wrong when he sought to please Jamila at the expense of his eternal life. Now that he had crossed to the other side of the gulf that separated the living from the dead where upon rising from the dead humans were as the angels in heaven who neither wed nor become wedded, there was no question that it would have augured much better for both of them if he, Mjomba, had put his eternal life first.

The sentence that was about to be meted out to him was analogous to death, because that was what losing the fight against His Mystic Majesty in reality amounted to. He had crossed the Prime Mover in a manner that was so inexcusable, he himself had already lost all hope that forgiveness by the Almighty One could ever come his way. He knew, in a word, that his final damnation was at hand!

Mjomba began to experience "death" first hand as he felt what he thought were pieces of rubble from the ceiling falling on him. He went numb, then instantaneously began to feel an overpowering, searing and cruel thirst. He wished in vain for a drop of some liquid - any liquid - to use to soothe his parched throat. But in the midst of all that, there was one thing, Mjomba felt certain, was contributing most to his final demise. It was the pitiless searing that enveloped his entire person. He felt as though his body had been lowered into a pool of boiling oil and was being kept there while it vaporised.

Mjomba recalled the time when, chatting about the unknown in general and about death in particular with Primrose, they had jokingly "promised" each other in a "pact" that whoever died first would return and let the survivor know, in a dream or even in an apparition, what exactly happened when people passed away, and what was on the "other side"! Even though everything that was happening was taking place in a dream, Mjomba not only found himself recalling the "pact" he had made with his secretary, but felt he had a binding obligation to fulfill its terms. But he was now dismayed to discover that a gulf was starting to form between himself and the folks he had left behind, and that even though he would have liked to pay the folks he had left behind a visit for the purpose of informing them about his terrible agony of death and the judgement that was about to get under way, there really was no way to turn back, once one had started out on the one way trip to the next life. He was, accordingly, very sorry that he could not keep his part of the bargain in that matter.

And it was also as he was thinking about his pact with Primrose that he was given to understand that he was dying in mortal sin with no time to go to confession, and was accordingly being denied any chance of expiating his sins in Purgatory. That news was really disappointing because he would have been glad to spend a thousand years in Purgatory rather than continue to endure what he was enduring forever and ever.

As has already been stated, Mjomba had known very well that moody or spirited episodes, whether joyous or saturnine, were incompatible with the contemplation of His Mystic Majesty. One reason for that was that the source of sentimental feelings lay outside of the mystic splendor. But the truth of the matter was that one could not fulfil the grave duty of contemplating the Mystic Being while allowing one's attention to be deflected by evanescent or other emotion arousing objects. Mjomba now hated himself for having allowed himself to fall for the subterfuge which, without a doubt, had been engineered by the mystic essences that had been disgraced for similar reasons before him and wanted company. He felt an overpowering feeling of guilt that was, however, shorn of all remorse.

Well-knowing that he was accursed, Mjomba could not desist from uttering what he expected to be his own last curse as an inhabitant of the mystic habitat. He accordingly devised a plan to utter a general curse - one that would not be directed at any particular individual or object. He no longer felt any concern about the consequences of his actions. Mjomba felt that his impiety would suit the present occasion better if it had a pervasiveness about it rather than if the impiety was narrowly directed. He was already resigned, after all, to the seemingly obvious fact that he was a sinner whose despicable act of sacrilege had now put him beyond the pale of redemption. At this particular stage, he was, indeed, supposed to be incapable of the very act of repentance, and it was only God who knew if his present determination to do the very worst by uttering a curse was likely to bode better or worse for him at his final judgement which he knew was now imminent.

Like the suicidal person who was desperate to cut it all short in one stroke but was lacking the where-with-all or the will to bring about his end, Mjomba opened his mouth - or what remained of it after the battering it had received during the continuing earthquake - in readiness to commit that final act of sin. He seemed sinfully delighted as he got ready to swear the name of His Mystic Majesty in vain.

Before he could formulate the appropriate words for the much-anticipated curse - what he would have liked to call the mother of all curses - the moment he had been waiting for arrived. This was the moment during which he expected to be ushered into the presence of His Mystic Majesty. Mjomba was struck by the fact that the events taking place appeared to be following a designated pattern.

Mjomba was totally resigned to the fact that the time for him to die was finally at hand. He believed, up until that moment, that he was just about as ready for the final separation of his mystic soul from its physical habitat as any one could possibly be. He knew that it was going to be a nerve wrenching experience, but he was ready - or so he thought.

For a fleeting moment, he even felt like a traveler on a homeward stretch. And in that fleeting moment - a mere fraction of a second which he would have liked to see stretch into infinity - everything around him suddenly appeared quaintly familiar as if his journey, which was about to conclude, had begun right there. His composure came close to being shattered in that fraction of a second as it occurred to him that this might in fact be the place where he had first learnt to discern right from wrong and where his conscience had been formed, and that the figure of the Judge, whom he had still to meet in person, might likewise turn out to be a very familiar one, particularly as the Judge also happened to be his Creator!

Indeed, the thought that his recollection of these surroundings dated back to the moment he, Mjomba, was created wasn't very distant from his mind. He imagined that it was also the time when his conscience was formed - as His Mystic Majesty gazed knowingly upon him after willing him out of nothingness and even endowing him with a free will out of His boundless generosity.

Mjomba did not have the slightest doubt in his mind that the period starting from the moment his conscience was formed, giving him a road map for his sojourn on earth, to the time of his homecoming had been solely intended for making preparations for his reunion with His Mystic Majesty. It effectively meant that he was supposed to grow and wax strong, in the intervening period, and bedeck himself with virtues in readiness for his final rendezvous with His Mystic Majesty at the divine banquet. He could, indeed, sense that there was partying and revelry going on somewhere in the vicinity, and had no doubt that it was the divine banquet taking off. The sounds that caught his ear included recitations of psalms and chants in praise of His Mystic Majesty.

Talking about sounds catching the ear - it was plain to Mjomba, as the seconds leading up to his last judgement ticked away, that whereas one could talk about silence here in the afterlife, there really was no such a thing on the other side of the Gulf on "earth". Creatures there just imagined it. The reality was that when humans were born and embarked on the process of adapting to the environment, their eardrums selectively recognized certain noises as "sound" - specifically the noises whose sources they could identify. Humans then typically chose to completely ignore the noises that did not make any sense to them. Those were the noises that the eardrums filtered out - because humans and other creatures refused to recognize them as "sound".

When "sleeping" babies smiled and grinned, they were not really asleep, even though the adults around thought so. They were wide awake and, with their eye-lids barely closed, were busy trying to differentiate between the noises which made sense and which they were going to recognize as sounds, and deciding on which ones they were going to ignore for the rest of their lives in the "realm of the living".

The same was true for people who were "unconscious" or "brain dead". Mesmerized by things of the senses, folks on earth were prone to jump to the conclusion that everything was lost when their dear ones who were "unwell" stopped physical activity. Doctors and others at the bedside of "the dying" were typical. The problem was really not with those who were "unconscious' or "comatose", but with the folks who were supposedly "well" and in good health. Because they were earth-bound and regarded the five senses as indispensable, they mistakenly equated "physical activity" with "well-ness", and clung to the erroneous notion that loved ones who felt "unwell" were "slipping away" and possibly receding into a state of inertness and virtual non-existence the moment they stopped "registering a pulse" or showing other "signs of life" like dilated pupils and the apparent inability to react to pinpricks and things of that nature.

In such situations people, who were unable to discern the patient's ability to use his/her senses, typically started hunkering to disconnect essential life-support systems for the individual who was comatose or supposedly "brain-dead". They were unable to get away from the notion that physical (as opposed to spiritual) activity was indicative of good health and well-being, and were consequently prone to misreading the real "signs of life".

When an individual stopped acting in the way folks around him/her were used to, instead of humbly accepting the fact that there are plenty of things that they know next to nothing about, those stupid fools usually start to place the blame for their inability to make heads or tails of the situation on the poor outgunned and outmanned individual instinctively, and are quick to conclude that the "poor chap" (who is displaying the "puzzling" behaviour) must be developing a mental abnormality of some kind. When a good natured, normally talkative, individual suddenly loses his/her voice, the fruitless attempts of that individual to regain his/her vocal expression will tend to be viewed as a sign that he/she was now deliberately acting funny and in the process of "losing it" or "going off his/her rocker"! That was how really stupid and crazy people were!

An unconscious or comatose person was actually very much awake and conscious. Those who were certified as "brain dead" were in the exact same boat as sleeping infants. They might appear to be oblivious to their surroundings; but they were very much "awake" in point of fact, and much more conscious of the goings-on in the room far more than the distracted doctors and grieving "loved ones" present at their bedside. Even without batting an eye, they usually discerned the intentions of the folks in the vicinity as they prepared to disconnect their life support systems and effectively kill them.

And it was of course quite clear that the driving motive behind the actions of those who were supposedly "alright", but were gearing to cut short their lives, was impatience and frustration. In the end it translated down to an unwillingness to sacrifice more of their comforts and time to continue providing the "palliative" care the patients required to continue living. It was an irony of fate that in the early and final phases of life, when infants and folks on their deathbeds were so close to their Maker and were in fact more alert to their surroundings and spiritually more active than at any other time in their lives, those around them became prone to misconstrue the situation and to regard them as completely inert, unconscious or brain dead, and "unresponsive".

Here, in the "realm of the dead", it was all silence, except for the sounds of praise and adoration that came from the redeemed souls as they exalted in the presence of His Mystic Majesty, and the shouts - or more precisely screams - of desperation and mourning as the damned which arose from the Pit or hell.

One other thing: the "appearance" of creatures here in the afterlife did not even come close to what they looked like back in the realm of the living. If you had tried your best not to hurt anyone while you lived, you looked handsome; and you looked even more so if you had also led an ascetic life. But if you had murdered, stolen or hurt others in some way - and especially if you had combined that with a life of debauchery - you came out looking so evil and so unlike His Mystic Majesty, the last thing you wanted to do was be seen in His presence.

And, instead of belching out sounds of praise and adoration from your guts, the only noises you would be capable of producing would be desperate cries amid what sounded like the gnashing of teeth. Those were the sorts of noises that could not be allowed to disturb the peace and tranquillity that reigned in "heaven"; and hence His Mystic Majesty's decision to banish all those who ended up like that from His sight.

And one thing was absolutely clear to Mjomba, now that he was far removed from the realm of the living: if you were not absolutely perfect - that is, if you were not entirely focused both on the Prime Mover who was the last end of all creatures that were fashioned in the image of the Prime Mover, and were still attached in some way to any "worldly" pleasure or distraction - there was no way you could survive the radiance of His Mystic Majesty! You would even have enough trouble trying to hang around in the glitter of those who had just emerged from Purgatory after finally atoning for sins committed by them over the course of their lifetime.

The litmus test was that if you were afforded the opportunity of a second lifetime back "on earth", you not only would be prepared to have as your preferred bed-fellows those you previously deemed your nemesis or worst enemies the first time around, but would also be prepared to lay down your life for them! And, while at it, should it happen that someone misunderstood you and decided to slap you on the cheek, you perforce would have to ask for his pardon and then turn the other cheek as well.

And you, of course, would also be at pains to ensure that you remained "detached" from all temporal things, including the desire to "save your life" and all the different forms that took! Thus, if you had previously allowed lukewarmness to govern your relations with the Prime Mover, in your second lifetime, you would say Bye Bye to all that and, rather than make a living in an occupation that involved betraying your trust in Him in any manner, knowing that you are weak and your own efforts ineffectual in these matters, you would spend all your time beseeching the Prime Mover for the strength to unhesitatingly opt to die a pauper or even starve to death rather than sin against your Maker.

That, combined with unceasing prayers and contemplation, including attendance at daily Mass and devotions to the saints - and particularly devotions to the Mother of the Deliverer - in addition to selfless service to the poor and a sustained regime of acts of self-immolation and penance should guarantee you a pass on the Church Triumphant Entrance Test and a modest mansion in heaven.

Devotions to the woman whom the evangelist describes as "having the sun itself for her raiment" cannot be overemphasized. For, even though a creature, her glitter in heaven which far exceeds the glitter of all the angels and saints combined, would be particularly punishing for the unworthy. And it so happened that, by the same token, it was through her incessant pleas to her Divine Son and Judge that time served by souls in Purgatory was reduced often by as much as a half and their entry into paradise was speeded up.

Any way - to return to the subject under discussion - your inability or unwillingness to do those things would be proof that you never had any love for your neighbours and avowals by you to the effect that you loved the Prime Mover in your first life were all a bunch of lies!

Mjomba saw more clearly than ever before that it indeed was easier for the proverbial camel to pass through the eye of a needle than for a rich man to negotiate his way through the gates of heaven.

Humans were so dumb, Mjomba reminisced. Some who killed even thought they could cover their tracks by being careful not to leave behind any tell-tale evidence trying them to the ghastly act. Others even made things worse by trying to cloak the fact that they were "partners with the Evil One" in sin behind a facade of piety and self-righteousness. They thought they could hoodwink everybody in the process, including the Prime Mover Himself, by committing murder and other "mortal" sins in that fashion.

They were dumb because the "hypocrites" forgot that any mortal sin - and certainly any act of murder - itself represented by its nature an indelible mark that became etched on the conscience of the sinner, setting the perpetrator apart from "God's chosen"! The act of sinning in itself constituted genetic evidence (for the misdeed) that could not be obliterated without "destroying" the offender - something the Prime Mover had said He would never do and that was, certainly, beyond the power of evil doers themselves.

And that led Mjomba to note one additional thing which, namely, was that some humans who murdered believed, quite mistakenly, that they were despatching their victims to an early miserable end. In reality, their actions resulted in the very opposite - the murderers were despatching those they hated to a blissful afterlife and guaranteeing themselves an ignominious end in the Pit in the company of demons and other murderers.

After electing to do the opposite of what he himself had been expected to do in life, Mjomba now could not bring himself to approach that banquet table (wherever it was) in his present forlorn shape. And he knew that it was far too late now to do anything about it and - even worse - that it was all his fault!

Mjomba even succeeded, in that short space of time, in reflecting on the fact that it was undoubtedly his conscience, coupled with his proximity to the Prime Mover, which caused him to accept his fate, dreadful and awesome though it was, as something he entirely deserved. If he had been in a position to do so now, he would have willingly cut off any offending limb in addition to punishing himself in all sorts of ways to atone for his sins. But it was too late now. He understood that he could only steel himself for the ultimate punishment which would consist in knowing that for all eternity he was not going to have fiends for company and would not be able to see his Creator face to face! The pain from knowing that he had allowed himself to sink so low and to identify with the fiends and others who were enemies of everything that was noble and wholesome in the period he had been a member of the Pilgrim Church was already quite intolerable.

It struck Mjomba that if he had neglected to acknowledge his Creator in the way he had been expected to during his sojourn in the mystic realm, it was highly unlikely that he had accorded his fellow humans the attention, respect and love they were entitled to. He thought of the turmoil in which much of the "world" was usually gripped practically all the time and which made the lives of innumerable souls absolutely miserable, and shuddered at the thought that most of the human suffering was avoidable because the wars and other causes of human misery were the work of humans who acted irrationally and were selfish and despicable like himself.

Even with the devil and his lieutenants swarming the mystic realm at any given time and making all sorts of wicked suggestions, it was very clear and unequivocal that those humans who were responsible for the sufferings of others, because they were endowed with the faculties of reason and free will, could not escape "judgement". They couldn't even plead incapacity because there was no such a thing as insanity in the afterlife! The fools had doomed themselves - period. Mjomba, who was already grieving the fact that he had squandered his own blessings as a member of the Pilgrim Church in the mystic realm, didn't feel that he himself deserved any pity and found that he wasn't feeling any pity for them either

Mjomba entered into the final throes of his death. He could not help noticing, as he did so, that they coincided with the fact that his soul, which normally informed his body, was now finding the conditions of that "habitat" increasingly incapable of sustaining it for any further length of time. Mjomba was astounded by the fact that his "preparedness" added up to naught virtually!

He knew it wasn't just a coincidence that he was finding himself overwhelmed, as he entered that phase, by a numbing feeling that effectively shut out all pain, physical and mental. But then, contrary to what he had been expecting, his "vision", hitherto blurry and pretty much a drag by reason of having to constantly touch base with his cognitive faculties, suddenly became transformed into a sharp stinging activity that appeared to draw on some kind of prescience or divination that emanated from his inner core. First of all, he had never suspected before that he had any capacity for prescience or divination, let alone to that degree! And secondly, it had never dawned on him that there was anything to such things as "prescience", "clairvoyance" or "psychic powers". He always imagined that these were catchwords that individuals claiming to be in touch with the occult employed to hoodwink their unsuspecting clients.

These developments, which were entirely unforeseen, had the effect of both disarming Mjomba and making his responses to events from then on "typical" of persons in their death throes. He reflected on the conventional depictions of individuals in their demise which used terms such as "painful", "silent" and "painless" to describe the phenomenon of dying. He would have vouched, with the sharp presence of mind which he now commanded, that the media types and all the other so-called experts who pontificated on matters of death back on the other side of the "gulf" were way off the mark.

If his experience up until that moment were anything to go by, no amount of pain, physical or otherwise, could be compared to the distress faced by a solitary soul that was awaiting judgement - and especially that soul which knew well enough that instead of coming out of it shining, it faced the inevitable, thoroughly merited, reproach by His Mystic Majesty for having had the audacity to suggest that the "Master" was the type who reaped what He did not sow, and then gone on to "bury" the talents that the Master had entrusted to him for safe-keeping! It weighed heavily on Mjomba to think that he had dissipated, not a few, but an untold number of opportunities to bloom in sanctifying grace, and thus fortified, proceed to shape up in mystic blessedness and in the likeness his soul bore to his Mystic Majesty!

And here he now was, awaiting the damning sentence and denunciation by His Mystic Majesty. It was the kind of denunciation that unrepentant sinners, aware that they fully deserved it, pined for. But it was one they dreaded at one and the same time and would have wished to avoid at all costs because of the indescribable mental agony accompanying it! Being spiritual essences, that agony dwarfed any physical pain that humans could endure without passing out!

Not surprisingly, the suffering and agony that Mjomba himself had felt as the bricks from the walls of the matron's office plummeted on top of him reducing him to granules amounted in retrospect to a painless scratch compared with the grief with which he was smitten as his now certain encounter with His Mystic Majesty approached and, along with it, the looming prospect of being banished forever from His majestic presence for what he now saw as the vile life he had led.

If it had been possible to choose between living a thousand distressingly drab lives which entailed dying a thousand excruciatingly painful deaths, and standing there contemplating the mirrored image of his unworthy self as he awaited his final judgement, with hind sight he unhesitatingly would have chosen the former.

It was clearly too late to do anything about his fate now. Like the rich man, in the bible story, who would have loved to sneak back to earth to alert his kinsmen about their eventual fate if they did not mend their ways, Mjomba wished for the impossible as he pondered his impending damnation. He would have loved to be allowed just a few moments during which he would slip back into the realm he had just left so he could at least warn Jamila and, perhaps Primrose and even Flora, as well as Prof. Gringo, his good friend and mentor, about what lay beyond the grave.

And he, of course, would not forget his former schoolmate who now sat on the Bench and routinely sent others to their death because they were supposedly "criminals". Mjomba vowed that if he were given an opportunity, he would successfully persuade Justice Maramba to use his powers as the nation's chief justice not just to stay all executions in the country and pardon everyone on death row, but also to arrange to send home all the folks who were now incarcerated in jails with no more than a warning that they conduct themselves lawfully, making sure that they did not allow themselves to be brought before any court ever again. A recital of his experiences "on the other side of the gulf" to an assembly of the ex-convicts would, Mjomba felt certain, convince them to stay out of trouble with the law.

Talking about death row and the so-called capital "punishment", it was obvious to Mjomba, now that he was minutes - or rather moments - away from his judgement, that taking away the life of a human, or killing under any pretext, was so totally wrong. He could not believe that the current, supposedly enlightened, generation of humans back on earth not only still had "death chambers" and things of that sort, but frequently pursued scorched earth policies to "liquidate" enemies.

Or was it perhaps this tendency on his part and that of other humans, when rationalizing about any thing, to seek to establish "the logical conclusion" to arguments. That, after all, was something no one, including the most illogical, could ever really "wish away" as Mjomba put it. It was a fact of life that those who killed did so to inflict hurt. Since it would be illogical to knowingly seek to dispatch your enemy to heaven by visiting upon him/her death prematurely, you would not do it. One logical conclusion, therefore, was that people killed enemies with the intention of dispatching them to hell!

Now, that was the very opposite of what humans were commanded to do, namely love one another. You could not possibly love someone and be praying at the same time that the object of your love should disappear in hell! And you, of course, could not get a better example of a mortal sin than desiring, not just to cut short the life of another human, but to do so with the specific aim of causing that human, who was created in the image of the Prime Mover just like yourself, to forfeit heaven. That was a very pathetic situation in which humans, already under the death sentence because of their rebellion against the Prime Mover, self-righteously turned on fellow humans and put them to death on what was really a pretext!

Mjomba quipped that it was not all that rare to find that the "death sentence" hanging over the heads of members of the bench as a result of being the poor and forsaken children of Adam and Eve being carried out long before the "death sentences" passed by those self-same justices on so-called convicts were carried out.

Given his own situation which was already hopeless, Mjomba did not wish to make it worse by appearing to be doing the very thing he was condemning, namely passing his own "capital sentence" on those capital punishment advocates back on earth, including his dear friend Justice Maramba, by emphasizing that their refusal to forgive their enemies effectively made them unworthy of forgiveness.

And so, instead of making his argument compelling by pursuing it to its logical conclusion, and showing that capital punishment advocates were themselves in the same if not worst situation as the "criminals" they were so quick to condemn, he tampered it by supposing that when the time came for these "stupid fools" to themselves die, the prospect of giving up their own ghosts (which would be in the exact same manner as their victims had done before them) *most likely* caused these folks to wake up to the reality of their situation, and to regret their error - just before it became their turn to confront the Judge. As if to mitigate the sentence he was facing, Mjomba allowed himself to regret aloud that he unfortunately could not do more than that for the earthlings who were bent on revenge.

Knowing that the professor was a person of great means, Mjomba would have particularly welcomed the opportunity to try and convince the man of letters to give it all away to the poor.

Recalling that the Deliverer had urged the rich man who came to him seeking advice to sell all his possession all and give the proceeds, not to Judas Iscariot, his purse bearer or treasurer, but to the poor, Mjomba made a point of reminding himself that, if he were to get the opportunity to return to earth, he would caution his friend, after he got rid of his rental properties and especially his considerable interests in corporations, to distribute the money to the homeless in Calcutta, Nairobi, New York, and other places like that directly and not to churches or so-called charities that were likely to use most of it on "staff salaries" and "bonuses" and other things like that.

It seemed patently absurd for anyone in the mystic realm - the realm in which creatures that had been cast in the image of the Prime Mover at creation spent were "on trial" before going to their reward in their after life, to be acquisitive or possessive. He, indeed, could not recall any instance in which anybody gave a thought to keeping cash handy so that the individual in question could take it along to heaven or hell when one died! Reflecting on his own past, Mjomba thought he himself must have been stark mad to aspire to riches and fame the way he used to! Suffice it to say that he would now have welcomed the opportunity to travel back to the earth and confront Prof. Gringo with these obvious facts.

Mjomba also would, if he were allowed to cross the Gulf and return to earth, approach the Holy Father with one simple request: he would ask that he, Mjomba, be allowed to lead an army of Capuchin monks to Hollywood. Their objective would be to persuade the people there to use "show biz" so-called to heighten general awareness for the fact that the human body was the temple of the Prime Mover and the dwelling of the Word through Whom the universe came into being; that it was subsequently the Spirit of the God the Father, and not humans who had ownership over the human body; and that immorality was consequently self-defeating. Mjomba was quite confident that the world's capital of showbiz, hosting a delegation that was lead by someone who had come back from the dead, would be persuaded to change its ways.

Mjomba would, likewise, seek the pope's permission to head a delegation of Carmelite nuns to the capitals of the world in order to dissuade governments from starting wars. That mission would be even more important than the mission to convert Hollywood, because while His Mystic majesty found immorality despicable and repulsive, He did not easily forgive the sin of starting a war in which people went out and killed each other, regardless of the way it was justified, because He created humans to live as family and love one another!

Still, Mjomba had this gnawing feeling that his message, like the divine messages transmitted to earthlings through prophets, would also go unheeded; and, in any case, the chances of his being allowed to be such a messenger, given the vile life he himself had led, were pretty slim. Still, he hankered, vainly as it would turn out, for the chance to just give it a try - to go through the motions. And should the kindred and friends whose hearts he would be trying to change turn on him and cause him to suffer martyrdom like the prophets did, he would appreciate that even more.

These thoughts made Mjomba envious of martyrs and others whose upright lives, empathy for the down-trodden and the helpless, and determination to do what was right according to their consciences caused them to suffer in silence for the cause of justice. He regretted that he could not manage a laugh now. But reflecting back on the fact that he himself used to regard individuals with those kinds of ideas as damn fools, he sincerely wished he could open his mouth and laugh lustily at himself for ever having entertained thoughts like those and, alas, making such a damn fool of himself in the process.

Mjomba was still fully conscious and alert, the excruciating mental and physical pain plaguing him notwithstanding; and he could sense it when the scales finally fell from his eyes. They were the scales that had continued to provide a shield of sorts from the radiance of His Mystic Majesty. He could tell that this also signalled the final separation of his mystic soul from his earth bound body. He, of course, also knew that this unique event was touched off by the failure of his heart, that extra-ordinary organ which had served both as the seat of love and also as the wellspring from which had flowed an unending stream of life-giving "plasma" from the moment he had graduated in his mother's womb to a hatched egg, or foetus, from one that hadn't been!

At that particular point in time and in the situation in which he had found himself, Mjomba would not have cared less as to which of those two milestones - his first heart beat or the final rapture as he went into cardiac arrest and died - deserved more attention. All he was really concerned about was that the great moment for his rendezvous with His Mystic Majesty was at hand and, for all practical purposes, had sneaked in on him like a thief in the night.

Mjomba kept repeating to himself that he should have known better than to trade in his birthright to eternal glory in the presence of His Mystic Majesty for terrestrial happiness. But he was still reeling from his realization that he was now doomed and "lost" in the true sense of that word when, with a quiver, his cardiovascular organ, throbbed its last and final time, and then he immediately begun returning, along with whatever remained of his physical frame, to the dust from which they had originally been fashioned in the first place. His breast, already battered by the bricks and mortar and nearly unrecognizable, heaved, allowing him to hear and witness that definitively final and distinctive heartbeat for himself.

Mjomba imagined that this was the routine which applied in each and every instance of demise among humans. He was amazed that the unspeakable agony that had characterized his wait subsided just enough to allow him to focus on those climactic events. While listening to his last heartbeat, Mjomba had also steeled himself for the separation of his soul from the body. Intent on hearing the last heartbeat and on getting a feel for that final rapture as well, he had been comfortable dividing his attention in that fashion. But there was no doubt that he had expected to find the latter more entrancing. For, even though he had envisioned it coming on the heels of his heart stoppage, the pain he felt had caused him to begin anticipating the separation well before it was due - at least two or, may be, even three heartbeats earlier.

Even though he knew that he was headed for damnation, Mjomba could not help taking in the sight of his spiritual self as he floated across the gulf that separated the realm of the living from that of the departed. It was as if his soul had been reduced to an icon in one directory of a personal computer where it did no longer belonged, and was being imported into a completely different directory where it now belonged using an invisible mouse. Mjomba could almost trace the path of his soul as it was "physically" dragged there and then released into an empty niche in the new directory where it now belonged with a single, expert click of the mouse.

Yes, expert click of the mouse. It was pretty clear to Mjomba by now that, in the mystic realm, everything was done "expertly". Mystic creatures did not fumble. And certainly, of course, not His Mystic Majesty! Mjomba had not failed to notice that the fellow guarding the entrance to heaven (through which the just went in single file after being commended by the His Mystic Majesty for their faithfulness to Him and for passing the Church Triumphant Entrance Test with flying colors) was St. Peter. He was easily recognizable by his bold head, which was partly concealed by a white skull cap or mitre, and his tall walking cane, undoubtedly one of many he had used to lean on as he went from place to place in what was then known as Asia Minor preaching the Gospel of the Deliverer.

It was a mystery to Mjomba how the rugged hiking staff and the skull cap had found their way into the mystic realm just as his own presence there in the mystic realm was a total mystery. But it was no mystery that Peter, who had "fumbled" so many times as an earthling (particularly in the period before the Paraclete came down from heaven as promised and buffed up his faith) now radiated anything but faithlessness, uncertainty or an inclination to "bumble". Now a living symbol of faith in the mystic realm, Peter, the first Bishop of Rome who had the power to "excommunicate" but thought the better of using it, more than any one else there, was a picture of calm, preciseness, and of course "expertness".

(It was revealed to Mjomba while he was up there in the mystic realm that excommunicating someone was analogous to killing in self-defense; and that while Peter could have excommunicated "dissidents" in the early Church, particularly those who were insistent that only Jews could be Christians, he chose instead to embark on an all out crusade to educate and enlighten people both in Palestine, Asia Minor, and in Italy - or Italia as it was then know - about the truth. Not one to be stopped by anything when the truth was at stake, Peter even took writing lessons from Luke and one Josephus so he too could communicate by means of epistles like John and Paul were doing.)

Everything that took place around the man who had also been known as "the Rock" was done very efficiently; and there was absolutely no possibility of some unworthy soul sneaking past him into heaven. Even if some sinful earthling, arriving here without enough *spiritual* possessions to merit a place in heaven, were still bent on trying to bribe his/her way past St. Peter into heaven, that option was effectively closed. Firstly, *spiritual* possessions just did not lend themselves to that sort of thing. Secondly, souls arrived here for their judgement without any *material* possessions (and you could not *bribe* with nothing). And, thirdly, there was just that one "Gate of Heaven", and no other.

It struck Mjomba as something of great moment to live to see his own soul take on the shape of a kite, to follow its flight as it floated gradually and unhindered over the gulf separating the realm of the living from that of the dead, and to observe it landing gently in its allocated spot on the other side of the Gulf within sight of the Gate of Heaven. Mjomba was beginning to think that there actually might be nothing more to it than that. But he soon realized in that timeless second that things were otherwise.

It at first sounded as though it was Mjomba's last heartbeat that was being amplified in an inexplicable fashion and was coming across as a loud "twang". Mjomba realised, too late, that the "twang" was accompanied by what felt like a brick landing on his head. It was all the more terrifying because he knew that he did not have a body. But he still made up his mind that it was do or die, as he "scrambled" to avoid additional "blows" he imagined were now going to follow fast and furious, and rain down on him. Or perhaps it was his fearfulness that had transformed his last heartbeat into what now came across as blows to his "body".

Mjomba assumed that it was because he was a hardened sinner that he failed to realize what the blows signified until almost the very end. As it turned out, for every mortal sin he had committed, he received a blow to the head. The blows for the venial sins he had committed were administered to other less vital parts of his body. The blows to the head were obviously intended to be mortal blows just as the vices they were intended to avenge were deadly vices. Even though the blows representing his lesser sins were not as deadly in their force as they landed on various parts of his body, they were unbearable all the same.

Mjomba thought that the whole spectrum of physical pain that humans anywhere ever endured was represented in the variety of pain he was enduring. The pain inflicted differed according to the size and shape of the "brick", and he could tell from the way they landed that they seemed to come in all sorts of shapes and sizes, and also from the speed at which they hurtled to his body from wherever they came from. He was made to understand that the pain from the blows he received for venial sins were tampered somewhat by any good turns he had done to anyone during his sojourn on earth. But, to the extent that he had been either vengeful or unforgiving to others, to that extent any relief he would otherwise have received was denied.

The relief he received notwithstanding, Mjomba had no doubt that he should have died from any single one of those blows - and he would have preferred to die rather than continue to endure the blows the bricks were inflicting on him. Because they were bricks and not living things, he could not really implore them to finish him off quickly - even if that had been possible - or to spare him. Even though he knew that much, the pain made him delirious and incapable of thinking straight, and he soon found himself mumbling things to that effect all the same. It was all to no avail because, to all intents and purposes, he had already kicked the bucket!

He decided that there was no point in trying to make out at that juncture if what was happening pertained to the heartbeat or if it was directly related to his transition from the realm of the living to that of the departed. Even though in turmoil, he urged himself to just be content with acknowledging that whatever it was, it was utterly phenomenal! The sheer terror it was inspiring in him made it so. And since there was now no stopping what had been decreed to transpire as of that moment, Mjomba resigned himself to his fate, even though his survival instinct, which was now entirely out of control, continued to battle on.

Then for an instant, but a very brief instant indeed, it appeared to Mjomba as if there might not be anything at all to all that had transpired from the time he had found himself in the mystic realm as he sprang into action and pursued the nurse in his eagerness to see the fate of the manuscript she had filched from Jamila's recovery room up until that moment. He was beginning to think that it might all thankfully be a dream - and that included what was looking more and more like his certain damnation - when, lo and behold, all hell broke loose! And this was the real, not figurative, hell.

It began with a shattering sound not unlike that of a mammoth herd comprising hundreds of thousands of wild buffalo approaching at a gallop. It was a sound that was utterly unfathomable, and the same applied to the sight that met Mjomba's gaze when he plucked the gaze to look. Mjomba had less than a split second to grasp what was afoot, namely that an army of demons headed by none other than Lucifer himself was charging him, and that those diabolical creatures were about to sweep him away and into the infernal pit with them. This was evidently what the Gospels meant by "perdition" and, as Mjomba quickly sensed, it wasn't going to pleasant at all.

The creature that was at the head of the forces of evil that were descending on him was hideous and loathsome in the extreme, not to mention menacing. It was clear that Mjomba had been courting danger in a most reckless manner when he engaged the services of the devil in the production of his thesis, and let the evil one be his virtual advisor. The devil's involvement with his book project could not possibly bode well for anyone who picked it up to read, Mjomba now admitted; and he resolved that, beginning that moment, the purpose for pursuing Flora into the mystic realm was going to be to stop the manuscript from falling into the hands of any human of good will. And he noted, in that regard, that Flora, even though her own intention wasn't above board, was inadvertently helping to assure the salvation of the soul of his own beloved Jamila by her act of theft.

Seeing that it was of the utmost importance now more than ever before to try and stop Flora from disseminating the contents of his manuscript, Mjomba attempted to get up and resume his pursuit of the girl only to discover that he couldn't muster the strength to even as much as stand upright. It was so frustrating not to be able to get up and speed after the girl when so much was at stake. Mjomba attributed his inability to do so to the approaching Enemy, the church's official name for Beelzebub, and one Mjomba agreed was appropriate and right on.

Mjomba realized that it was the intention of the nondescript creatures that were charging at him to not only crush him and then bury him in the hell where they themselves belonged, but to do to him something that was even worse. Fashioned in the image of His Mystic Majesty, by virtue of which he could invoke the assistance of the Almighty One and Prime Mover if he chose to if he ever found himself in the midst of adversity, Mjomba's condition as a damned soul was not going to permit him ever to say the Our Father or to even as much as wish to be shielded by His Mystic Majesty against the invectives of his enemies.

Even though Mjomba had crossed His Mystic Majesty almost as soon as he had stepped into the mystic realm, and had seemed prepared to accept the consequences for his indiscretions, that (he now realized) was vastly different from being damned in the same way Satan and the host of demons that had opted to do his bidding had been damned and cast into hell. That was not at all what Mjomba had in mind when he decided to cross His Mystic Majesty. And it wasn't what he had in mind when he decided to use the Evil One as his mouthpiece for expounding on the Church's doctrines either. When he fell for the temptation to get a helping hand from Old Scratch so that he might be able to turn in a winning thesis, he had been thinking of Lucifer the Archangel, who with Michael the Archangel had ministered to the Prime Mover before Lucifer chose to go his own ways.

Mjomba's reaction to his now impending damnation was instinctive. Totally mollified, Mjomba found himself doing something he had been use to doing often during his years in Minor and Major Seminary, but hadn't done in a long time. He found himself reciting the Aspirations to the Holy family; and he recited them slowly and deliberately, almost as if determined to defy Satan and the army of totally enraged demons that was bearing down upon him: "*Jesus, Mary and Joseph, I give you my heart and my soul. Jesus, Mary and Joseph, assist me in my last agony. Jesus, Mary and Joseph, may I breathe forth my soul in peace with you…*"

And as he prayed, the advance of the demons that had appeared unstoppable started to show signs that it might slow down just enough to enable him to complete the invocation. And that was when the pain from being buffeted by the falling bricks and debris from the earthquake became completely unbearable.

Mjomba, who believed that he had already breathed his last and was well on his way to join his ancestors, had concluded that the bedlam and chaos that reigned all around was evidence that he had died in the state of mortal sin, and probably had been adjudged as even unworthy to be ushered into the presence of His Mystic Majesty. He even acknowledged that the supreme self-confidence, cheek and bravado that somehow had taken control of him in the moments leading to his death had dissolved so that he now couldn't hurt a fly even if he wanted to! He had no doubt that the prophetic words of the Canticle of Mary to the effect that His Mystic Majesty scatters the proud in their conceit were still fresh in his mind. And, Yes - Mjomba now finally also admitted that there was do doubt whatsoever that when His Mystic Majesty showed the strength of His arm, that was all there was to it. There was no creature whatsoever that could gainsay or challenge the outcome, and that included the Ruler of the Underworld!

In a complete reversal of his attitude, Mjomba now wished that he had hearkened to his professors who were for the most part set against his dilly-dallying with Old Scratch, and to people like St. Francis De Sales who advised that it should be the principal business of humans "'to conquer themselves and, from day to day, to go on increasing in strength and perfection", and Catherine of Siena who wrote: "Our captain on this battlefield is Christ Jesus. We have discovered what we have to do. Christ has bound our enemies for us and weakened them that they cannot overcome us unless we so choose to let them. So we must fight courageously and mark ourselves with the sign of the most Holy Cross."

He now realized, too late, that they were all echoing the Deliverer Himself who told His disciples in Luke 21:36: "Watch ye, therefore, praying at all times, that you may be accounted worthy to escape all these things that are to come, and to stand before the Son of man." And Mjomba finally also admitted, again too late, that he had failed to pay heed to the Deliverer's admonition that it was easier for a camel to pass through the eye of a needle, than for a rich man to enter into the kingdom of God.

Before he died, Mjomba, as a member of the seminary brotherhood, had had far more exposure to the doctrines of the Church than most other folks, had been fully aware of these things. He regretted that he had not made it a habit while he lived to invoke the names of the Deliverer, His virgin mother, and the Deliverer's foster father at least mentally everyday; and he definitely should have been in the habit of reading selections from folks like St. John Chrysostom and St. Ignatius Loyola who all emphasized the importance of constant prayer and meditation. But Mjomba readily conceded as he strained to withstand the relentless assault by the elements on his person, that this was now not the time to dwell on those things.

Mjomba was quick to note that the severe "blows" raining down on him were accompanied by what he could only describe as bedlam of a really massive order. It was as if all the lost souls were gathered in one giant pit and that, even though they were damned and written off, after a break or pause had succeeded in mustering fresh energy and were resuming their dejected, yet bawdy, howl of eternal despair from their location at the bottom of the cavernous - and needless to add also hellish - sink hole which was now their home. As before, the tremendous roar also caused him to experience a searing sensation - as if he still had his body with him and it was again being doused with sulphuric acid or some other such flaming liquid.

It was then that the strangest thing of all occurred. The imaginary blows to his body stopped as suddenly as they had began. That was, however, followed by a silence so numbing and ominous, Mjomba immediately began to wish that the pandemonium had not stopped. It was this unexpected, totally awesome, deathly calm - a deafening stillness - which now finally jolted him out of his slumber. Mjomba lunged out of bed, his face a twisted mask that spoke volumes about the mystifying experience he had been through as he lay dreaming on his coach.

Even after he had awakened, Mjomba apparently still imagined that he was in the strange mystic world, and not far from the abominable pit and its accursed population. He was now awake, but the sounds of the accursed spirits, as they shouted and screamed curses to His Mystic Majesty in their loathsome place of abode, broke through the stillness and started ringing in his ears all over again almost as if they were real. To counter them, Mjomba opened his own mouth and began screaming out aloud for all he was worth. The result was some sort of primal scream the like of which only a few living creatures could parody. It was a howl that would even have caused a charging buffalo to halt its tracks. That howl did more than that to Fatuma who had been in the process of laying the table for breakfast and, terrified by Mjomba's shouts, had just dropped a tray loaded with various items she had hoped would make a nice breakfast for him smack on top of his head by accident.

Mjomba continued to holler: "Hooo! Hooo! Hooo! The world is coming to an end..."

As he did so, the terrified Fatuma barged out of the room and rushed the phone, with Mjomba now hard on her heels. It appeared as if he wanted her out of his bedroom as soon as possible and at any cost.

"Oh! What are you also doing here?" he roared as he took after her. He was, for all practical purposes, still living in his dream. Meanwhile, during her flight, Fatuma dropped the empty tray in Mjomba's path hoping that it would slow him just enough to allow her to punch the numbers "911" into the dial.

"Oh! The devil…the demons…the demons! So, so many of them! What is that?" Mjomba was roaring even as he missed his step and landed head first on the hard cement floor.

For her part, Fatuma was convinced that her uncle had gone bananas and was trying to kill her. When she got to the children's bedroom, she headed straight for the cute little telephone set on the dressing table.

"Oh, I'm sorry, Fatuma. I was dreaming...!" Mjomba gasped as he finally caught up with her. Panting and still quite distracted, he made a bee-line for Ali's bedroom chair and slumped into it. He had apparently come to when he stumbled and fell. Fatuma, who had already picked up the phone and was trying frantically to punch in the emergency number, stood there paralysed

"Uncle, are you alright? It was my fault. I'm sure I hurt you!" she mumbled apologetically. A short while earlier, she had actually been praying that he would trip and hurt himself so badly he would have no choice but to abandon his pursuit. But, seeing him dishevelled and in a sorry state, she now felt that she was partly responsible for his plight, and blamed herself for over-reacting. She could see that he was still frightened, but did not quite understand why.

"Where are the children?" Mjomba asked, noting that their beds were empty.

"In the basement, watching TV," Fatuma replied.

"Oh, yes of course," he rejoined, remembering that Musa and Ali always got out of bed very early and headed to the basement to enjoy their favourite cartoons.

Although still reeling from the terrifying experience of being pursued by her uncle, Fatuma managed a big broad smile that Mjomba found very comforting.

A stubborn piece of bacon and the yoke from the fried eggs she had prepared for him still dangled from his greying hair. Otherwise, nothing of his breakfast which she had carefully arranged on the tray and was in the process of delivering to him in his bed - the pot of hot black coffee, the cup and its saucer, a large slice of pawpaw, etc. - had survived.

Fatuma's enthusiasm evaporated as she recounted how she had accidentally splashed the coffee over her uncle's face as she was leaning forward to check if he really was talking in his sleep or was awake and addressing her. And she now confessed that she had not been prepared for his reaction and, in particular, his resonating screams. Mjomba fought to suppress laughter, and Fatuma herself could not help sniggering as she remarked that he had really terrified her when he lunged from his bed and started after her. Although the thought that the lovely china she had carefully laid out on the tray shortly before the misadventure lay in fragments either on the bed or on the floor of the master bedroom had a dampening effect on her exuberance at this time, that would not be the case that evening when she would relate the incident to Jamila.

"I wasn't sure if you were asleep, and was checking when..."

Mjomba stopped her with a wave of his hand, upon which they both exploded in laughter.

None of them had noticed Ali and Musa who were smiling at them from the hallway. Still clad in their sleeping gowns, they had overheard the pandemonium and had dashed upstairs to find out what the heck was going on. Ali and Musa had found Fatuma wonderful and they, accordingly, had not really missed their mom. But the thought on their minds, as they were scurrying upstairs, had been that their mom was back with the baby! They were evidently disappointed that nothing really exciting had happened to justify the bedlam that had sent them charging upstairs. And now, as they turned to head back to the basement and the world of cartoons, they did not hide their obvious disappointment.

Fatuma must have read their minds, and was starting after them when Mjomba reached out and grabbed her hand to stop her exit.

"I'm sorry for all this," he murmured. "Don't worry about my room. I'll clean up."

"No, it's all my fault. I want to make sure Ali and Musa are OK, and I will be right back."

Fatuma decided on the spur of the moment that the kids were fine. It would not have done any good reminding them of the unexplained commotion upstairs, which would be the case if she turned up in the basement at that time. She, accordingly, headed instead for the kitchen where she picked up a mop and a towel.

The circumstances in which she had aborted her earlier mission to deliver breakfast to her uncle had left her feeling that she had turned her aunt's elegant bedroom into one which was topsy-turvy and an utter wreck. She, accordingly, couldn't wait to get there and clean up. When she did, she was somewhat surprised that it wasn't in such a terrible mess after all. But she was still glad that Mjomba was there to help her tidy the place up. When she had packed up the cleaning items to return to the kitchen to continue with her early morning chores, she noticed that Mjomba was retrieving some writing materials from a drawer.

With pen and paper in hand, Mjomba, who was feeling as if he had not had an ounce of sleep, slipped into his bed with the intention of jotting down details of his nightmarish dream before they evaporated. Very much to his amazement, he found that the only thing he could recall was the fact that he was on his deathbed - yes, his deathbed - and bound for hell! He, Mjomba, on a deathbed bound for hell? It was unbelievable!

He had a faint recollection about being ushered into the presence of a stately, and rather awesome Being with the unlikely title of His Mystic Majesty, and also about Purgatory and the reason why it wasn't among the stops he had been scheduled to make en route to his afterlife. But when he endeavoured to commit to writing his fragmentary recollection of these things, his recollection of them faded as soon as he began scribbling on his writing pad.

Mjomba's memory of the gates of hell, which came in fits and starts but was still petrifying all the same, was even more elusive. After about twenty minutes of that game of hide and seek, Mjomba stared at the pad and was shocked to see that he had filled an entire sheet with incomplete words and otherwise meaningless phrases that he had scrawled on the pad in a fruitless attempt to reduce his feelings to written expressions.

Fifteen minutes later, Mjomba was still smarting from the fact that he was having a serious lapse of memory at precisely the time he needed it most to record what he saw as an incredible and extremely absorbing story when Fatuma cautiously walked in with a tray loaded with freshly made coffee, and egg and bacon on toast.

When Mjomba saw her, the dream's very subject matter vanished from his mind. He was animated as he flung the pad and the pen into a corner and did not seem concerned about the effect of that obviously irrational action on the girl.

Fatuma's instinct was to hand over the breakfast tray to her uncle, and then proceed to retrieve the items he had so carelessly tossed on the floor with the intention of placing them neatly on one of the bedside tables or on the dresser. But, remembering what had occurred earlier that morning, she decided to take the cue from his action and to retreat from the master bedroom as quickly as possible - after making sure that the tray was in his firm grip.

Perhaps it was his disappointment with himself for being unable to remember details of his nightmarish dream. Or may be it was the fact that he was genuinely starving and the aroma of the coffee was inviting. Whatever it was, it caused Mjomba to reach out eagerly for the tray and to belatedly set about enjoying his breakfast. He took a big bite into the toast with its load of scrambled eggs and bacon, sipped coffee from the slender, hand engraved china, and then sank back into the cushion and closed his eyes to enjoy what he considered to be the fruit of his sweat.

13. The "Masterpiece"

Jamila felt well enough to go home the next day. There was, moreover, nothing she wished for so much as to be reunited with her family and be able to share her joy with her neighbors, relatives and friends in the snug comfort of her home. She was therefore heavily disappointed when Dr. Mambo, doing the rounds himself at dawn, insisted on detaining her for at least another twelve hours in a different and also more comfortable room. Dr. Mambo had no reason to doubt that Jamila's personal physician would not concur with his decision to keep her there a little while longer - "just to be sure" as he was wont to say to his own patients.

Jamila, who still clung to the idea she had got from her great grandmother many years earlier that hospitals were places where people went to die, thought that Dr. Mambo had to be kidding when he uses the same phrase to her. Since there was nothing wrong with her baby either, she really wanted out of there as soon as possible.

In the wake of Dr. Mambo's departure, she was disconsolate - and all the more so for want of something active to do. As always happened at such times, she felt irritable. And, rather strangely, it was her husband, not her condition or Dr. Mambo, who loomed up in her mind as the apparent cause of her misery! She ate her breakfast, consisting of a slice of pawpaw, scrambled eggs on toast, bacon and tea, in sullen silence. Even though she had a dislike for Flora, she began to wish that the girl, whom she now merely saw as chatty and fun to have close by, were around to help her focus her mind on anything but Mjomba whom she literally hated now. And even as she was being transferred to her new room and a different bed with fresh linen not long afterward, her charm and good looks were overshadowed by her moroseness.

About an hour later, she was all but resigned to her gloom when the blue folder on the stool by her bedside caught her gaze. The ordeal of the previous day and everything else that had happened, including her husband's late night visit - and the manuscript - had gone out of her mind, wiped out by her uninterrupted five hour slumber and the morning's events. But now, everything came tumbling back.

The Psychic Roots of a Nut! The idea of her husband writing a book now, all of a sudden, seemed so plausible! Yes, for all the bustle and activity that characterised his everyday schedule - for all his inexhaustible fountain of love for her - Mjomba was, she clearly realised now, the "thinking" type of a man! That was the impression he had given her years before when their paths first crossed, and it now seemed to find confirmation in his fling at being an author!

For some reason, Jamila's memory of that first meeting remained amazingly fresh, almost as if it all had taken place months rather than years before - eight years to be exact! She still could have told, even after all those years, the exact type of attire he wore, including the colour and shape of his shoes. The picture of him in his majestic apparel of a travelling clergyman had stuck fast in her imagination, seemingly not to be erased by even the passage of time.

Although she had been brought up in the Moslem tradition as befitted the daughter of an Al Hajj, the ascendancy of Christianity in the region and the growing impact of foreign cultural influences on the land had caused her adherence to the Moslem faith to gradually wear off.

She had been prepared to become a Christian for his sake and as a prelude to exchanging their marriage vows. She had been pleasantly surprised to find him keen to embrace Islam. But the adoption of Islam by the former Reverend Christian Mjomba had meant little in practice, apart from his subsequent change of name from Christian to Ibrahim and the fact that he stopped going to church.

Secretly she had been happy that Ibrahim, or "Ib" as she sometimes called him for short, continued to collect and read scholarly works on Christianity in general and Catholicism in particular, and generally kept away from religious gatherings of Christians and Moslems alike.

Jamila had always felt a little shy about extolling her husband's intellectual endowments. But there had perpetually lain at the back of her mind, nonetheless, the thought that he was potentially if not actually a genius. If he were writing a book, she now reflected, he would of course use the opportunity to delve into the most obscure subject of them all - namely insanity! Indeed she could not think of a better sounding title for a book dedicated to her self and her children than that which her husband, staring fixedly at an imaginary point in the ceiling of her recovery room, had announced. *The Psychic Roots of a Nut*!

She suddenly felt that she had to read the manuscript and hopefully finish doing so before facing Ib later that day. All signs of dejection were gone as Jamila settled back between the fresh linen and began leafing through the leaves of Mjomba's "masterpiece".

She found the material, which was split into four main sections and numerous sub-sections, gripping from the very first. In a clear departure from the usual manner in which novels were written, her husband had employed the present tense throughout to put his message across. Kintu's psychological development comprised the first and second parts of the "novel", and they were replete with interesting twists and turns.

There was some similarity between *The Psychic Roots of Innocent Kintu* and Alex Haley's *Roots*. In contrast to Alex Haley's famous work that sought to establish the ancestral roots of Gunte, her husband's study went all out to establish the mental roots of Kintu, his unsung hero. It was a formidable task which, she nonetheless finally admitted, he had acquitted himself of most admirably.

The third section, in contrast to the first two, was abstract and full of philosophical erudition. As if that were not enough, the rhetoric in that part of the "masterpiece" was at times so thick, she could hardly see the wood for the trees as they say. But it contained the biggest stock of surprises - she, Jamila, indeed featured in it!

In the fourth and also final section, her husband simply went crazy as he cast her former boss in the role of someone who was harassed by the ancestral spirits. Although she would have wanted to wipe all memories of Flora from her mind, she could not help recalling Flora's last words the previous night - words that had implied that her husband was not a mad author.

The Psychic Roots of a Nut certainly did not suggest that its author was the kind who would vanish in the main stream. She mused that he was destined to be either a best seller or a worst seller, but not one belonging to the run-of-the-mill. But she was, of course, more inclined to the view that it was just a matter of time - as a matter of fact weeks if not days - before he became a celebrity. At one point, her face aglow with excitement, Jamila peered at an invisible dot in the ceiling and wondered how she would make out as the spouse of a famous author.

Quite early on as she devoured the paragraphs, then pages and eventually sections of her husband's work, something rather uncharacteristic of novels begun to unveil, and to suggest that this was the most unusual one she had ever read and probably would ever read.

Although the characters in the first and second parts of the book were mute and spoke not a word, her husband had somehow succeeded in ascribing to them thoughts in a way which stripped all mystery from their actions. Although she had heard before this the truism popularized by Darwin that actions spoke louder than words, she had never imagined that it could all be so true!

Then, the "novel" aimed surely enough at explaining the unexplainable - insanity! But could Ibrahim Mjomba, the man she had known as her husband for a full six years now, really unravel the mysterious subject as she had earlier been inclined to think? She remembered how incredulous she had felt eight years before when Ib and Professor Claus Gringo were in consultation with herself in attendance, and had begun to discuss precisely that same subject. She did not recall anything beyond that because, after concluding shortly thereafter that the man in the attire of a travelling cleric was the handsomest person she had ever seen, she had immediately lost all interest in the substance of their discussion from there on. Little did she suspect at the time that she would be faced with the same question at a later date and that she would have to answer it one way or another.

Jamila's incredulity in turn gave rise to suspicions that, apart from the section of the manuscript in which she herself featured, the accounts she was perusing were possibly entirely fictitious in character! And, as she delved deeper and deeper into the material, she gradually began to realize that it was indeed a question she had to answer one way or another before the day was out - and on the basis of the account before her rather than her wifely feelings for Ib.

As the morning wore on, Jamila begun discovering to her amazement, as she delved further into the material, that the more she doubted her husband's ability to explain the unexplainable, the more the material impressed her with its realism and logic! It seemed as if her husband's work was designed to arouse scepticism in the reader - in the same way a good story caused anticipation to build up in the mind of a reader - only to turn around and use the scepticism to take the reader a few more steps towards the book's climactic point.

The biblical clarity of the first two sections of the "novel" caused her lurking suspicion that the work might have been intended as some sort of joke by her husband to remain at bay. But, as Jamila finally turned to the book's final section in which she herself was featured, the pieces of the puzzle began to fall in place all at once.

Nudging herself into a comfortable seating position on the bed as her wandering eyes picked her name from a page, she quickly became engrossed with her part in the book at the same time. Memories of the events of that morning, almost a decade earlier, when Professor Gringo, her boss, and the brash young cleric were locked in an abstract discussion revolving around one of the professor's patients, came tumbling back into her mind. She easily recalled how their voluble chatter had aroused in her a strange curiosity, causing her at one point to abandon her post at the secretarial desk so that she could indulge in eavesdropping.

Observing the performance of the young "padre" through the keyhole had suddenly evoked in her the most unimaginable, altogether wanton, feelings of lust. Bewildered, she had slunk back to her workstation and attempted in vain to banish memories of the experience from her mind by banging away at her electric typewriter.

Jamila was light-hearted and curiously happy as she came to the concluding pages of the "masterpiece". Turning over the last leaf, she kidded herself that, for all its rhetoric and abstruseness, the final section was the best by far. And it all seemed so much evidence, if indeed she needed any more, of Ib's complicated nature; and she found her husband all the more worthy of her admiration.

While the former Jamila Kivumbi's mind was preoccupied with the sagacious material in the closing pages of her husband's work, not many blocks away events, which might have come straight from a James Hadley Chase thriller, were unfolding with Ibrahim Mjomba at their center!

The "Clown"...

The needle of the Ford Cortina's speedometer seemed to be jammed at the 40 kilometre mark as the battered car roared along past the new Post Office and approached the Askari Monument in downtown Dar es Salaam. The din caused by the absence of the silencer was now supplemented by a rattling sound not unlike the clatter produced by a quartet of belled cows moving at a canter.

In his final bid to get baby oil following a tip-off volunteered by a neighbor's domestic worker, Mjomba had spent most of the morning searching for a backyard store on the southern outskirts of the city. He had had to motor over roads which, while listed on the map as major thoroughfares, had turned out to be rough tracks filled with potholes big enough in a few instances to conceal a four year-old - and which, he discovered to his horror, they often did.

Mjomba's inability to skirt all the pot-holes in his path had proved rather telling on the Ford Cortina's low-lying suspension. His sympathy for the machine, as its under-carriage again and again scraped the road surface, had in time given way to gloomy resignation.

The auto must have shed the rubber bushes as he approached the shack where the baby oil was sold. Mjomba, who intended to purchase all the stock of baby oil on hand, learnt to his surprise that it was actually one of the store's slowest moving items in that store's wares. Unmoved by that information, he had proceeded all the same to snap up the store's remaining stock of baby oil - a measly five cartons, in his eyes, each of which contained no less than a dozen bottles of the imported product.

As he set off on the journey down-town, which also felt like a journey back to civilization, the lower ends of the vehicle's rear shock absorbers, no longer insulated from their metal housing, had started beating out their strange new rhythm with a mercilessness which caused him to soon forget his newly acquired taste of sweet success. The taste, derived from his knowledge that nothing on the list of baby items that Jamila had given him a couple of days earlier remained to be bought, had turned to instant bitterness as Mjomba tried to imagine what it would cost him to get the car fixed.

Even though he enjoyed driving autos, he didn't have a clue about how they operated - he considered that to be the job of vehicle mechanics. And he believed that the more shattering the noise an auto produced when one or more of it's parts begun malfunctioning, the more expensive it would be to fix the problem causing the noise! In some ways he was right because some auto repair garages used all sorts of excuses to inflate the repair bill including billing for imaginary defects; and that was not taking into account the likelihood of the establishment's underpaid employees, operating on their own, making off with some of the vehicle's working parts.

Mjomba had listened in confusion to the violent and, as it turned out, non-stop clanking noise originating from the auto's rear; and, after deciding that he had enough problems and could not risk being stranded in an unfamiliar part of the sprawling city, he had fought the temptation to stop the vehicle and seek out the cause of the noise and assess the extent of the damage to his beloved Ford Cortina with a stubborn determination. He, however, had not failed to notice the strange fact that the medley of jangling sounds increased in their intensity as the speed of the auto decreased - and vice versa!

The city sounds in the vicinity of the Askari Monument were drowned out completely by the noise as the Ford Cortina slowed down behind a queue of cars. One and all, the milling crowds stopped to stare. Disappointment became registered on the faces of the majority of onlookers as the source of the din turned out to be a slow moving, if somewhat battered, family sedan and not a fire engine in full throttle. Mjomba, his form rigid in the driver's seat, seemed unconcerned by all the attention.

Next to him on the front seat was a gigantic bouquet of flowers neatly wrapped up in gift paper. In the back seat, Fatuma struggled to keep Kunta and Kinte in check. An unusually joyous and expectant atmosphere prevailed, and it received a periodic boost from Mjomba's ingratiating backward glances which revealed a broad smile.

Every time he looked back over his shoulder, the children ogled at the image of a crested crane emblazoned just below the knot of the blue-grey tie.

If Ali and Musa had seen their dad in a tie before, they evidently no longer had any recollection of it. Unlike the climate inland, the weather conditions in Dar es Salaam were typical of those that prevailed along Africa's coastline and included a dose of humidity that could be quite inhibiting. This was a function of being on or near the Equator and at sea level all at once. Consequently, in Dar es Salaam's year-round sweltering heat, only magistrates and advocates donned ties; and Mjomba, like all other right thinking city folk, had never had any reason to go against that sensible tradition.

Indeed, apart from an odd collection of ties and western suits that were leftovers from his grad-school days in America, his wardrobe consisted mostly of "Kaunda" suits complete with matching scarves, fancy Afro shirts and jeans.

Mjomba looked manifestly like some old-time clown with the noose-like object around his neck. The picture of a bird just below the knot now made him look all the more clownish, the fact that it constituted the emblem of his Alma Mater notwithstanding. Fatuma blushed many times, even Mjomba himself choked repeatedly with laughter seeing Ali and Musa bursting with infectious joy

As he turned into the driveway of Dr. Mambo's Clinic, the thought crossed his mind that the drive from their bungalow to the Clinic, normally a twenty-five minute drive, had been accomplished in something like the twinkling of an eye. It was not that his mind had been preoccupied with anything in particular. On the contrary, it had in fact been as close to the proverbial *tabula rasa* as it possibly could have been without actually being a "smoothed tablet".

He had made a desperate, woefully futile effort to get his mind attuned to the clangour produced by the Ford Cortina as he set out from home that afternoon, but had decided that he wouldn't allow anything whatsoever to disturb his hard earned peace of mind at least for the rest of that afternoon - except for the attention he was receiving from Ali and Musa, that is. With his reason relieved of its usual guiding role, his automatic reflexes had taken over charge; and so he came to, now a full twenty-five minutes later, to find himself guiding the ageing auto into the crowded parking lot instinctively!

To all appearances, Mjomba's mind was far away as he snatched up the flowers and banged the car's door behind him. He strode along, head held high and the bouquet, which he gripped with both hands abreast of him, looking very much like a fixed bayonet in a soldier's arms. Perhaps because he knew he could trust Fatuma to take care of Ali and Musa as the party headed for the wards, Mjomba matched on oblivious, for all practical purposes, to the fact that he had been travelling in their company.

He suddenly had the sensation of walking into someone! The next moment he was nagged by an overwhelming sense of being off balance, and he instinctively shut his eyes to prevent them from being poked by whatever he was walking into. He tried to bring himself to a halt as best he could while still clutching onto the flowers, but instead felt his legs tripping each other. He was all but resigned to the fact that there was going to be an ensuing thud and all that it would entail when he became conscious of something very strange. He was enveloped in, of all things, the fragrance of a perfume, the scent from which was simply stunning!

Mjomba was still expecting to hit the pavement and was wondering if he would break any bones during the fall when he felt someone seize and steady him. He simultaneously heard the words "Oh, excuse me!", or something to that effect. They were spoken in the barest whisper and came from a female voice that sounded faintly familiar! He heard them at the same time as he was feeling the provocatively soft touch of fingertips he imagined were suitably long and slender about his loins.

Flora's hands were still flaying about for support when Mjomba opened his eyes. In the same split second, he flung the flowers out of the way to one side and then shot out his right hand, just in time to stop the nurse from striking the paved ground.

After clambering out of the auto, Ali and Musa had merely skirted the colliding pair and raced on, unconcerned, towards the Reception in their haste to rejoin their mom. Fatuma, trailing behind them, had stopped in her tracks and stared with open mouth as the nurse's white uniform blew up a cloud of dust. She had scarcely closed her mouth when, certain that the nurse who had walked into her uncle from no where was going to end up sprawled on the floor, she clutched her chin and braced for worst - almost as if she were the one who was plummeting to the ground.

But even before she could finish sighing with relief that an awkward situation had been averted by her uncle's quick action, she found herself watching with her heart literally in her mouth as Mjomba and the nurse first exchanged glances which indicated that they knew each other, and then broke out into a merry laugh!

All three were jolted to attention by shouts that emanated from a nearby hallway and filled the air. Two plaintive voices were screaming: "*Mama! Mtoto, Mama, Mtoto...!*"

Mjomba, Flora and Fatuma were drawn to Jamila's room as if by a magnet. Jamila and little Kunta were being mobbed by Ali and Musa when Mjomba, clutching the bouquet of flowers which had somehow survived the collision and was undamaged, stepped inside the box-like recovery room. Flora and Fatuma, their faces all giggles, closed in around the berth. Jamila took in the bouquet of flowers and the Stanford tie in a glance, and tried to conceal her obvious pleasure at seeing the room filled with all the smiling faces.

For a moment, Kunta's well-being seemed in jeopardy as Jamila left Ali and Musa who were still mobbing Kunta to their own devices to give Mjomba his due attention. Luckily for Kunta, Flora did not waste any time taking over control of the situation and installing herself as overseer of Kunta's first encounter with his astute if over-eager siblings. Unlike Flora, who couldn't resist stealing a glance, Fatuma, standing at a respectable distance near a window, turned to admire a nearby rose bush as husband and wife embraced and their lips sought out each other. Almost immediately afterward, Jamila's lips were heard making tiny little noises and giving the impression that she was struggling to free herself from Mjomba's grip! She suddenly did, but just long enough to enable her to hiss: "Oh, I love you...and *The Psychic Roots of a Nut* - it is the best novel I've ever read! But it has the wrong title. Darling, promise that you will change it to *The Masterpiece*!"

Jamila's gleaming eyes looked like a pair of diamonds as they sought out the blue folder that now lay on the night stand. They seemed to derive similar satisfaction from lingering over the folder to that which their owner was deriving from the man's embrace.